The
Dr. Thorndyke Short Story Omnibus

by

R. Austin Freeman

First published as:
'The Famous Cases of Dr. Thorndyke'

Published in the USA as
'The Dr. Thorndyke Omnibus'

"The Discovery"
(THE BLUE SEQUIN)

Contents

The Singing Bone

Original Preface to "The Singing Bone"

The peculiar construction of the first four stories in the present collection will probably strike both reader and critic and seem to call for some explanation, which I accordingly proceed to supply.

In the conventional "detective story" the interest is made to focus on the question, "Who did it?" The identity of the criminal is a secret that is jealously guarded up to the very end of the book, and its disclosure forms the final climax.

This I have always regarded as somewhat of a mistake. In real life, the identity of the criminal is a question of supreme importance for practical reasons; but in fiction, where no such reasons exist, I conceive the interest of the reader to be engaged chiefly by the demonstration of unexpected consequences of simple actions, of unsuspected causal connections, and by the evolution of an ordered train of evidence from a mass of facts apparently incoherent and unrelated. The reader's curiosity is concerned not so much with the question "Who did it?" as with the question "How was the discovery achieved?" That is to say, the ingenious reader is interested more in the intermediate action than in the ultimate result.

The offer by a popular author of a prize to the reader who should identify the criminal in a certain "detective story," exhibiting as it did the opposite view, suggested to me an interesting question.

Would it be possible to write a detective story in which from the outset the reader was taken entirely into the author's confidence, was made an actual witness of the crime and furnished with every fact that could possibly be used in its detection? Would there be any story left when the reader had all the facts? I believed that there would; and as an experiment to test the justice of my belief, I wrote "The Case of

Oscar Brodski." Here the usual conditions are reversed; the reader knows everything, the detective knows nothing, and the interest focuses on the unexpected significance of trivial circumstances.

By excellent judges on both sides of the Atlantic--including the editor of 'Pearson's Magazine'--this story was so far approved of that I was invited to produce others of the same type.

Three more were written and are here included together with one of the more orthodox character-, so that the reader can judge of the respective merits of the two methods of narration.

Nautical readers will observe that I have taken the liberty (for obvious reasons connected with the law of libel) of planting a screw-pile lighthouse on the Girdler Sand in place of the light-vessel. I mention the matter to forestall criticism and save readers the trouble of writing to point out the error.

R. A. F., Gravesend

The Case of Oscar Brodski

Part I. The Mechanism of Crime

A surprising amount of nonsense has been talked about conscience. On the one hand remorse (or the "again-bite," as certain scholars of ultra-Teutonic leanings would prefer to call it); on the other hand "an easy conscience": these have been accepted as the determining factors of happiness or the reverse.

Of course there is an element of truth in the "easy conscience" view, but it begs the whole question. A particularly hardy conscience may be quite easy under the most unfavourable conditions--conditions in which the more feeble conscience might be severely afflicted with the "again-bite." d, then, it seems to be the fact that some fortunate persons have no conscience at all; a negative gift that raises them above the mental vicissitudes of the common herd of humanity.

Now, Silas Hickler was a case in point. No one, looking into his cheerful, round face, beaming with benevolence and wreathed in perpetual smiles, would have imagined him to be a criminal. Least of all, his worthy, high-church housekeeper, who was a witness to his unvarying amiability, who constantly heard him carolling light-heartedly about the house and noted his appreciative zest at meal-times.

Yet it is a fact that Silas earned his modest, though comfortable, income by the gentle art of burglary. A precarious trade and risky withal, yet not so very hazardous if pursued with judgment and moderation. And Silas was eminently a man of judgment. He worked invariably alone. He kept his own counsel. No confederate had he to turn King's Evidence at a pinch; no one he knew would bounce off in a fit of temper to Scotland Yard. Nor was he greedy and thriftless, as most criminals are. His "scoops" were few and far between, carefully planned, secretly executed, and the proceeds judiciously invested in "weekly property."

In early life Silas had been connected with the diamond industry, and he still did a little rather irregular dealing. In the trade he was suspected of transactions with I.D.B.'s, and one or two indiscreet dealers had gone so far as to whisper the ominous word "fence." But Silas smiled a benevolent smile and went his way. He knew what he knew, and his clients in Amsterdam were not inquisitive.

Such was Silas Hickler. As he strolled round his garden in the dusk of an October evening, he seemed the very type of modest, middle-class prosperity. He was dressed in the travelling suit that he wore on his little continental trips; his bag was packed and stood in readiness on the sitting-room sofa. A parcel of diamonds (purchased honestly, though without impertinent questions, at Southampton) was in the inside pocket of his waistcoat, and another more valuable parcel was stowed in a cavity in the heel of his right boot. In an hour and a half it would be time for him to set out to catch the boat train at the junction; meanwhile there was nothing to do but to stroll round the fading garden and consider how he should invest the proceeds of the impending deal. His housekeeper had gone over to Welham for the week's shopping, and would probably not be back until eleven o'clock. He was alone in the premises and just a trifle dull.

He was about to turn into the house when his ear caught the sound of footsteps on the unmade road that passed the end of the garden. He paused and listened. There was no other dwelling near, and the road led nowhere, fading away into the waste land beyond the house. Could this be a visitor? It seemed unlikely, for visitors were few at Silas Hickler's house. Meanwhile the footsteps continued to approach, ringing out with increasing loudness on the hard, stony path.

Silas strolled down to the gate, and, leaning on it, looked out with some curiosity. Presently a glow of light showed him the face of a man, apparently lighting his pipe; then a dim figure detached itself from the enveloping gloom, advanced towards him and halted opposite the garden. The stranger removed a cigarette from his mouth and, blowing out a cloud of smoke, asked -

"Can you tell me if this road will take me to Badsham Junction?"

"No," replied Hickler, "but there is a footpath farther on that leads to the station."

"Footpath!" growled the stranger. "I've had enough of footpaths. I came down from town to Catley intending to walk across to the junction. I started along the road, and then some fool directed me to a short cut, with the result that I have been blundering about in the dark for the last half-hour. My sight isn't very good, you know," he added.

"What train do you want to catch?" asked Hickler.

"Seven fifty-eight," was the reply.

"I am going to catch that train myself," said Silas, "but I shan't be starting for another hour. The station is only three-quarters of a mile from here. If you like to come in and take a rest, we can walk down together and then you'll be sure of not missing your way."

"It's very good of you," said the stranger, peering, with spectacled eyes, at the dark house, "but--I think -?"

"Might as well wait here as at the station," said Silas in his genial way, holding the gate open, and the stranger, after a momentary hesitation, entered and, flinging away his cigarette, followed him to the door of the cottage.

The sitting-room was in darkness, save for the dull glow of the expiring fire, but, entering before his guest, Silas applied a match to the lamp that hung from the ceiling. As the flame leaped up, flooding the little interior with light, the two men regarded one another with mutual curiosity.

"Brodski, by Jingo!" was Hickler's silent commentary, as he looked at his guest. "Doesn't know me, evidently--wouldn't, of course, after all these years and with his bad eyesight. Take a seat, sir," he added aloud. "Will you join me in a little refreshment to while away the time?"

Brodski murmured an indistinct acceptance, and, as his host turned to open a cupboard, he deposited his hat (a hard, grey felt) on a chair in a corner, placed his bag on the edge of the table, resting his umbrella against it, and sat down in a small arm-chair.

"Have a biscuit?" said Hickler, as he placed a whisky-bottle on the table together with a couple of his best star-pattern tumblers and a siphon.

"Thanks, I think I will," said Brodski. "The railway journey and all this confounded tramping about, you know -?"

"Yes," agreed Silas. "Doesn't do to start with an empty stomach. Hope you don't mind oat-cakes; I see they're the only biscuits I have."

Brodski hastened to assure him that oat-cakes were his special and peculiar fancy, and in confirmation, having mixed himself a stiff jorum, he fell to upon the biscuits with evident gusto.

Brodski was a deliberate feeder, and at present appeared to be somewhat sharp set. His measured munching being unfavourable to conversation, most of the talking fell to Silas; and, for once, that genial transgressor found the task embarrassing. The natural thing would have been to discuss his guest's destination and perhaps the object of his journey; but this was precisely what Hickler avoided doing. For he knew both, and instinct told him to keep his knowledge to himself.

Brodski was a diamond merchant of considerable reputation, and in a large way of business. He bought stones principally in the rough, and of these he was a most excellent judge. His fancy was for stones of somewhat unusual size and value, and it was well known to be his custom, when he had accumulated a sufficient stock, to carry them himself to Amsterdam and supervise the cutting of the rough stones. Of this Hickler was aware, and he had no doubt that Brodski was now starting on one of his periodical excursions; that somewhere in the recesses of his rather shabby clothing was concealed a paper packet possibly worth several thousand pounds.

Brodski sat by the table munching monotonously and talking little. Hickler sat opposite him, talking nervously and rather wildly at times, and watching his guest with a growing fascination. Precious stones, and especially diamonds, were Hickler's specialty. "Hard stuff"--silver plate--he avoided entirely; gold, excepting in the form of specie, he seldom touched; but stones, of which he could carry off a whole consignment in the heel of his boot and dispose of with absolute safety, formed the staple of his industry. And here was a man sitting opposite him with a parcel in his pocket containing the equivalent of a dozen of his most successful "scoops"; stones worth perhaps -? Here he pulled himself up short and began to talk rapidly, though without much coherence. For, even as he talked, other Words, formed subconsciously, seemed to insinuate themselves into the interstices of the sentences, and to carry on a parallel train of thought.

"Gets chilly in the evenings now, doesn't it?" said Hickler.

"It does indeed," Brodski agreed, and then resumed his slow munching, breathing audibly through his nose.

"Five thousand at least," the subconscious train of thought resumed; "probably six or seven, perhaps ten." Silas fidgeted in his chair and endeavoured to concentrate his ideas on some topic of interest. He was growing disagreeably conscious of a new and unfamiliar state of mind.

"Do you take any interest in gardening?", he asked. Next to diamonds and weekly "property," his besetting weakness was fuchsias.

Brodski chuckled sourly. "Hatton Garden is the nearest approach -?" He broke off suddenly, and then added, "I am a Londoner, you know."

The abrupt break in the sentence was not unnoticed by Silas, nor had he any difficulty in interpreting it. A man who carries untold wealth upon his person must needs be wary in his speech.

"Yes," he answered absently, "it's hardly a Londoner's hobby." And then, half consciously, he began a rapid calculation. Put it at five thousand pounds. What would that represent in weekly property? His last set of houses had cost two hundred and fifty pounds apiece, and he had let them at ten shillings and sixpence a week. At that rate, five thousand pounds represented twenty houses at ten and sixpence a week--say ten pounds a week--one pound eight shillings a day--five hundred and twenty pounds a year--for life. It was a competency. Added to what he already had, it was wealth. With that income he could fling the tools of his trade into the river and live out the remainder of his life in comfort and security.

He glanced furtively at his guest across the table, and then looked away quickly as he felt stirring within him an impulse the nature of which he could not mistake. This must be put an end to. Crimes against the person he had always looked upon as sheer insanity. There was, it is true, that little affair of the Weybridge policeman, but that was unforeseen and unavoidable, and it was the constable's doing after all. And there was the old housekeeper at Epsom, too, but, of course, if the old idiot would shriek in that insane fashion--well, it was an accident, very regrettable, to be sure, and no one could be more sorry for the mishap than himself. "But deliberate homicide!--robbery from the person! It was the act of a stark lunatic.

Of course, if he had happened to be that sort of person, here was the opportunity of a lifetime. The immense booty, the empty house, the solitary neighbourhood, away from the main road and from other habitations; the time, the darkness--but, of course, there was the body to be thought of; that was always the difficulty. What to do with the body? Here he caught the shriek of the up express, rounding the curve in the line that ran past the waste land at the back of the house. The sound started a new train of thought, and, as he followed it out, his eyes fixed themselves on the unconscious and taciturn Brodski, as he sat thoughtfully sipping his whisky. At length, averting his gaze with an effort, he rose suddenly from his chair and turned to look at the clock on the mantelpiece, spreading out his hands before the dying fire. A tumult of strange sensations warned him to leave the house. He shivered slightly, though he was rather hot than chilly, and, turning his head, looked at the door.

"Seems to be a confounded draught," he said, with another slight shiver; "did I shut the door properly, I wonder?" He strode across the room and, opening the door wide, looked out into the dark garden. A desire, sudden and urgent, had come over him to get out into the open air, to be on the road and have done with this madness that was knocking at the door of his brain.

"I wonder if it is worth while to start yet," he said, with a yearning glance at the murky, starless sky.

Brodski roused himself and looked round. "Is your clock right?" he asked.

Silas reluctantly admitted that it was.

"How long will it take us to walk to the station?" inquired Brodski.

"Oh, about twenty-five minutes to half-an-hour," replied Silas, unconsciously exaggerating the distance.

"Well," said Brodski, "we've got more than an hour yet, and it's more comfortable here than hanging about the station. I don't see the use of starting before we need."

"No; of course not," Silas agreed. A wave of strange emotion, half-regretful, half-triumphant, surged through his brain. For some moments he remained standing on the threshold, looking out dreamily into the night. Then he softly closed the door; and, seemingly without the exercise of his volition, the key turned noiselessly in the lock.

He returned to his chair and tried to open a conversation with the taciturn Brodski, but the words came faltering and disjointed. He felt his face growing hot, his brain full and intense, and there was a faint, high-pitched singing in his ears. He was conscious of watching his guest with a new and fearful interest, and, by sheer force of will, turned away his eyes; only to find them a moment later involuntarily returning to fix the unconscious man with yet more horrible intensity. And ever through his mind walked, like a dreadful procession, the thoughts of what that other man--the man of blood and violence--would do in these circumstances. Detail by detail the hideous synthesis fitted together the parts of the imagined crime, and arranged them in due sequence until they formed a succession of events, rational, connected and coherent.

He rose uneasily from his chair, with his eyes still riveted upon his guest. He could not sit any longer opposite that man with his hidden store of precious gems. The impulse that he recognized with fear and wonder was growing more ungovernable from moment to moment. If he stayed it would presently overpower him, and then? He shrank with horror from the dreadful thought, but his fingers itched to handle the diamonds. For Silas was, after all, a criminal by nature and habit. He was a beast of prey. His livelihood had never been earned; it had been taken by stealth or, if necessary, by force. His instincts were predacious, and the proximity of unguarded valuables suggested to him, as a logical consequence, their abstraction or seizure. His unwillingness to let these diamonds go away beyond his reach was fast becoming overwhelming.

But he would make one more effort to escape. He would keep out of Brodski's actual presence until the moment for starting came.

"If you'll excuse me," he said, "I will go and put on a thicker pair of boots. After all this dry weather we may get a change, and damp feet are very uncomfortable when you are travelling."

"Yes; dangerous too," agreed Brodski.

Silas walked through into the adjoining kitchen, where, by the light of the little lamp that was burning there, he had seen his stout, country boots placed, cleaned and in readiness, and sat down upon a chair to make the change. He did not, of course, intend to wear the country boots, for the diamonds were concealed in those he had on. But he would make the change and then alter his mind; it would all help to pass the time. He took a deep breath. It was a relief, at any rate, to be out of that room. Perhaps if he stayed away, the temptation would pass. Brodski would go on his way--he wished that he was going alone--and the danger would be over--at least--and the opportunity would have gone--the diamonds -?

He looked up as he slowly unlaced his boot. From where he sat he could see Brodski sitting by the table with his back towards the kitchen door. He had finished eating, now, and was composedly rolling a cigarette. Silas breathed heavily, and, slipping off his boot, sat for a while motionless, gazing steadily at the other man's back. Then he unlaced the other boot, still staring abstractedly at his unconscious guest, drew it off, and laid it very quietly on the floor.

Brodski calmly finished rolling his cigarette, licked the paper, put away his pouch, and, having dusted the crumbs of tobacco from his knees, began to search his pockets for a match. Suddenly, yielding to an uncontrollable impulse, Silas stood up and began stealthily to creep along the passage to the sitting-room. Not a sound came from his stockinged feet. Silently as a cat he stole forward, breathing softly with parted lips, until he stood at the threshold of the room. His face flushed duskily, his eyes, wide and staring, glittered in the lamplight, and the racing blood hummed in his ears.

Brodski struck a match--Silas noted that it was a wooden vesta--lighted his cigarette, blew out the match and flung it into the fender. Then he replaced the box in his pocket and commenced to smoke.

Slowly and without a sound Silas crept forward into the room, step by step, with catlike stealthiness, until he stood close behind Brodski's chair--so close that he had to turn his head that his breath might not stir the hair upon the other man's head. So, for half-a-minute, he stood motionless, like a symbolical statue of Murder, glaring down with horrible, glittering eyes upon the unconscious diamond merchant, while his quick breath passed without a sound through his open mouth and his fingers writhed slowly like the tentacles of a giant hydra. And then, as noiselessly as ever, he backed away to the door, turned quickly and walked back into the kitchen.

He drew a deep breath. It had been a near thing. Brodski's life had hung upon a thread For it had been so easy. Indeed, if he had happened, as he stood behind the man's chair, to have a weapon--a hammer, for instance, or even a stone?

He glanced round the kitchen and his eyes lighted on a bar that had been left by the workmen who had put up the new greenhouse. It was an odd piece cut off from a square, wrought-iron stanchion, and was about a foot long and perhaps three-quarters of an inch thick. Now, if he had had that in his hand a minute ago -

He picked the bar up, balanced it in his hand and swung it round his head. A formidable weapon this: silent, too. And it fitted the plan that had passed through his brain. Bah! He had better put the thing down.

But he did not. He stepped over to the door and looked again at Brodski, sitting, as before, meditatively smoking, with his back towards the kitchen.

Suddenly a change came over Silas. His face flushed, the veins of his neck stood out and a sullen scowl settled on his face. He drew out his watch, glanced at it earnestly and replaced it. Then he strode swiftly but silently along the passage into the sitting-room.

A pace away from his victim's chair he halted and took deliberate aim. The bar swung aloft, but not without some faint rustle of movement, for Brodski looked round quickly even as the iron whistled through the air. The movement disturbed the murderer's aim, and the bar glanced off his victim's head, making only a trifling wound. Brodski sprang up with a tremulous, bleating cry, and clutched his assailant's arms with the tenacity of mortal terror.

Then began a terrible struggle, as the two men, locked in a deadly embrace, swayed to and fro and trampled backwards and forwards. The chair was overturned, an empty glass swept from the table and, with Brodski's spectacles, crushed beneath stamping feet. And thrice that dreadful, pitiful, bleating cry rang out into the night, filling Silas, despite his murderous frenzy, with terror lest some chance wayfarer should hear it. Gathering his great strength for a final effort, he forced his victim backwards onto the table and, snatching up a corner of the tablecloth, thrust it into his face and crammed it into his mouth as it opened to utter another shriek. And thus they remained for a full two minutes, almost motionless, like some dreadful group of tragic allegory. Then, when the last faint twitchings had died away, Silas relaxed his grasp and let the limp body slip softly onto the floor.

It was over. For good or for evil, the thing was done. Silas stood up, breathing heavily, and, as he wiped the sweat from his face, he looked at the clock. The hands stood at one minute to seven. The whole thing had taken a little over three minutes. He had nearly an hour in which to finish his task The goods train that entered into his scheme came by at twenty minutes past, and it was only three hundred yards to the line. Still, he must not waste time. He was now quite composed, and only disturbed by the thought that Brodski's cries might have been heard. If no one had heard them it was all plain sailing.

He stooped, and, gently disengaging the table-cloth from the dead man's teeth, began a careful search of his pockets. He was not long finding what he sought, and, as he pinched the paper packet and felt the little hard bodies grating on one another inside, his faint regrets for what had happened were swallowed up in self-congratulations.

He now set about his task with business-like briskness and an attentive eye on the clock. A few large drops of blood had fallen on the table-cloth, and there was a small bloody smear on the carpet by the dead man's head. Silas fetched from the kitchen some water, a nail-brush and a dry cloth, and, having washed out the stains from the table-cover--not forgetting the deal table-top underneath--and cleaned away the smear from the carpet and rubbed the damp places dry, he slipped a sheet of paper under the head of the corpse to prevent further contamination. Then he set the tablecloth straight, stood the chair upright, laid the broken spectacles on the table and picked up the cigarette, which had been trodden flat in the struggle, and flung it under the grate. Then there was the broken glass, which he swept up into a dust-pan. Part of it was the remains of the shattered tumbler, and the rest the fragments of the broken spectacles. He turned it out onto a sheet of paper and looked it over carefully, picking out the larger recognizable pieces of the spectacle-glasses and putting them aside on a separate slip of paper, together with a sprinkling of the minute fragments. The remainder he shot back into the dust-pan and, having hurriedly put on his boots, carried it out to the rubbish-heap at the back of the house.

It was now time to start. Hastily cutting off a length of string from his string-box--for Silas was an orderly man and despised the oddments of string with which many people make shift--he tied it to the dead man's bag and umbrella and slung them from his shoulder. Then he folded up the paper of broken glass, and, slipping it and the spectacles into his pocket, picked up the body and threw it over his shoulder. Brodski was a small, spare man, weighing not more than nine stone; not a very formidable burden for a big, athletic man like Silas.

The night was intensely dark, and, when Silas looked out of the back gate over the waste land that stretched from his house to the railway, he could hardly see twenty yards ahead. After listening cautiously and hearing no sound, he went out, shut the gate softly behind him and set forth at a good pace, though carefully, over the broken ground. His progress was not as silent as he could have wished for, though.

The scanty turf that covered the gravelly land was thick enough to deaden his footfalls, the swinging bag and umbrella made an irritating noise; indeed, his movements were more hampered by them than by the weightier burden.

The distance to the line was about three hundred yards. Ordinarily he would have walked it in from three to four minutes, but now, going cautiously with his burden and stopping now and again to listen, it took him just six minutes to reach the three-bar fence that separated the waste land from the railway. Arrived here he halted for a moment and once more listened attentively, peering into the darkness on all sides. Not a living creature was to be seen or heard in this desolate spot, but far away, the shriek of an engine's whistle warned him to hasten.

Lifting the corpse easily over the fence, he carried it a few yards farther to a point where the line curved sharply.

Here he laid it face downwards, with the neck over the near rail. Drawing out his pocket-knife, he cut through the knot that fastened the umbrella to the string and also secured the bag; and when he had flung the bag and umbrella on the track beside the body, he carefully pocketed the string, excepting the little loop that had fallen to the ground when the knot was cut.

The quick snort and clanking rumble of an approaching goods train began now to be clearly audible. Rapidly, Silas; drew from his pockets the battered spectacles and the packet of broken glass. The former he threw down by the dead man's head, and then, emptying the packet into his hand, sprinkled the fragments of glass around the spectacles.

He was none too soon. Already the quick, laboured puffing of the engine sounded close at hand. His impulse was to stay and watch; to witness the final catastrophe that should convert the murder into an accident or suicide. But it was hardly safe: it would be better that he should not be near lest he should not be able to get away without being seen. Hastily he climbed back over the fence and strode away across the rough fields, while the train came snorting and clattering towards the curve.

He had nearly reached his back gate when a sound from the line brought him to a sudden halt; it was a prolonged whistle accompanied by the groan of brakes and the loud clank of colliding trucks. The snorting of the engine had ceased and was replaced by the penetrating hiss of escaping steam.

The train had stopped!

For one brief moment Silas stood with bated breath and mouth agape like one petrified; then he strode forward quickly to the gate, and, letting himself in, silently slid the bolt. He was undeniably alarmed. What could have happened on the line? It was practically certain that the body had been seen; but what was happening now? and would they come to the house? He entered the kitchen, and having paused again to listen--for somebody might come and knock at the door at any moment--he walked through the sitting-room and looked round. All seemed in order there. There was the bar, though, lying where he had dropped it in the scuffle. He picked it up and held it under the lamp. There was no blood on it; only one or two hairs. Somewhat absently he wiped it with the table-cover, and then, running out through the kitchen into the back garden, dropped it over the wall into a bed of nettles. Not that there was anything incriminating in the bar, but, since he had used it as a weapon, it had somehow acquired a sinister aspect to his eye.

He now felt that it would be well to start for the station at once. It was not time yet, for it was barely twenty-five minutes past seven; but he did not wish to be found in the house if any one should come. His soft hat was on the sofa with his bag, to which his umbrella was strapped. He put on the hat, caught up the bag and stepped over to the door; then he came back to turn down the lamp. And it was at this moment, when he stood with his hand raised to the burner, that his eyes, travelling by chance into the dim corner of the room, lighted on

Brodski's grey felt hat, reposing on the chair where the dead man had placed it when he entered the house.

Silas stood for a few moments as if petrified, with the chilly sweat of mortal fear standing in beads upon his forehead. Another instant and he would have turned the lamp down and gone on his way; and then -? He strode over to the chair, snatched up the hat and looked inside it. Yes, there was the name, "Oscar Brodski," written plainly on the lining. If he had gone away, leaving it to be discovered, he would have been lost; indeed, even now, if a search-party should come to the house, it was enough to send him to the gallows.

His limbs shook with horror at the thought, but in spite of his panic he did not lose his self-possession. Darting through into the kitchen, he grabbed up a handful of the dry brush-wood that was kept for lighting fires and carried it to the sitting-room grate where he thrust it on the extinct, but still hot, embers, and crumpling up the paper that he had placed under Brodski's head--on which paper he now noticed, for the first time, a minute bloody smear--he poked it in under the wood, and striking a wax match, set light to it. As the wood flared up, he hacked at the hat with his pocket knife and threw the ragged strips into the blaze.

And all the while his heart was thumping and his hands a-tremble with the dread of discovery. The fragments of felt were far from inflammable, tending rather to fuse into cindery masses that smoked and smouldered than to burn away into actual ash. Moreover, to his dismay, they emitted a powerful resinous stench mixed with the odour of burning hair, so that he had to open the kitchen window (since he dared not unlock the front door) to disperse the reek. And still, as he fed the fire with small cut fragments, he strained his ears to catch, above the crackling of the wood, the sound of the dreaded footsteps, the knock on the door that should be as the summons of Fate.

The time, too, was speeding on. Twenty-one minutes to eight! In a few minutes more he must set out or he would miss the train. He dropped the dismembered hat-brim on the blazing wood and ran upstairs to open a window, since he must close that in the kitchen before he left. When he came back, the brim had already curled up into a black, clinkery mass that bubbled and hissed as the fat, pungent smoke rose from it sluggishly to the chimney.

Nineteen minutes to eight! It was time to start. He took up the poker and carefully beat the cinders into small particles, stirring them into the glowing embers of the wood and coal. There was nothing unusual in the appearance of the grate. It was his constant custom to burn letters and other discarded articles in the sitting-room fire: his housekeeper would notice nothing out of the common. Indeed, the cinders would probably be reduced to ashes before she returned. He had been careful to notice that there were no metallic fittings of any kind in the hat, which might have escaped burning.

Once more he picked up his bag, took a last look round, turned down the lamp and, unlocking the door, held it open for a few moments. Then he went out, locked the door, pocketed the key (of which his housekeeper had a duplicate) and set off at a brisk pace for the station.

He arrived in good time after all, and, having taken his ticket, strolled through onto the platform. The train was not yet signalled, but there seemed to be an unusual stir in the place. The passengers were collected in a group at one end of the platform, and were all looking in one direction down the line; and, even as he walked towards them, with a certain tremulous, nauseating curiosity, two men emerged from the darkness and ascended the slope to the platform, carrying a stretcher covered with a tarpaulin. The passengers parted to let the bearers pass, turning fascinated eyes upon the shape that showed faintly through the rough pall; and, when the stretcher had been borne into the lamp-room, they fixed their attention upon a porter who followed carrying a hand-bag and an umbrella.

Suddenly one of the passengers started forward with an exclamation.

"Is that his umbrella?" he demanded.

"Yes, sir," answered the porter, stopping and holding it out for the speaker's inspection.

"My God!" ejaculated the passenger; then, turning sharply to a tall man who stood close by, he said excitedly: "That's Brodski's umbrella. I could swear to it. You remember Brodski?" The tall man nodded, and the passenger, turning once more to the porter, said: "I identify that umbrella. It belongs to a gentleman named Brodski. If you look in his hat you will see his name written in it. He always writes his name in his hat."

"We haven't found his hat yet," said the porter; "but here is the station-master coming up the line." He awaited the arrival of his superior and then announced: "This gentleman, sir, has identified the umbrella."

"Oh," said the station-master, "you recognize the umbrella, sir, do you? Then perhaps you would step into the lamp-room and see if you can identify the body."

"Is it--is he--very much injured?" the passenger asked tremulously.

"Well, yes," was the reply. "You see, the engine and six of the trucks went over him before they could stop the train. Took his head clean off, in fact."

"Shocking! shocking!" gasped the passenger. "I think, if you don't mind-- I'd--I'd rather not. You don't think it's necessary, doctor, do you?"

"Yes, I do," replied the tall man. "Early identification may be of the first importance."

"Then I suppose I must," said the passenger.

Very reluctantly he allowed himself to be conducted by the station-master to the lamp-room, as the clang of the bell announced the approaching train. Silas Hickler followed and took his stand with the expectant crowd outside the closed door. In a few moments the passenger burst out, pale and awe-stricken, and rushed up to his tall friend. "It is!" he exclaimed breathlessly. "It's Brodski! Poor old Brodski! Horrible! horrible! He was to have met me here and come on with me to Amsterdam."

"Had he any--merchandize about him?" the tall man asked; and Silas strained his ears to catch the reply.

"He had some stones, no doubt, but I don't know what.

His clerk will know, of course. By the way, doctor, could you watch the case for me? Just to be sure it was really an accident or--you know what. We were old friends, you know, fellow townsmen, too; we were both born in Warsaw. I'd like you to give an eye to the case."

"Very well," said the other. "I will satisfy myself that--there is nothing more than appears, and let you have a report. Will that do?"

"Thank you. It's excessively good of you, doctor. Ah! here comes the train. I hope it won't inconvenience you to stay and see to this matter."

"Not in the least," replied the doctor. "We are not due at Warmington until to-morrow afternoon, and I expect we can find out all that is necessary to know before that."

Silas looked long and curiously at the tall, imposing man who was, as it were, taking his seat at the chessboard, to play against him for his life. A formidable antagonist he looked, with his keen, thoughtful face, so resolute and calm. As Silas stepped into his carriage he thought with deep discomfort of Brodski's hat, and hoped that he had made no other oversight.

Part II. The Mechanism Of Detection

(Related by Christopher Jervis, M.D.)

I he singular circumstances that attended the death of Mr. Oscar Brodski, the well-known diamond merchant of Hatton Garden, illustrated very forcibly the importance of one or two points in medico-legal practice which Thorndyke was accustomed to insist were not sufficiently appreciated. What those points were, I shall leave my friend and teacher to state at the proper place; and meanwhile, as the case is in the highest degree instructive, I shall record the incidents in the order of their occurrence.

The dusk of an October evening was closing in as Thorndyke and I, the sole occupants of a smoking compartment, found ourselves approaching the little station of Ludham; and, as the train slowed down, we peered out at the knot of country, people who were waiting on the platform. Suddenly Thorndyke exclaimed in a tone of surprise: "Why, that is surely Boscovitch!" and almost at the same moment a brisk, excitable little man darted at the door of our compartment and literally tumbled in.

"I hope I don't intrude on this learned conclave," he said, shaking hands genially and banging his Gladstone with impulsive violence into the rack; "but I saw your faces at the window, and naturally jumped at the chance of such pleasant companionship."

"You are very flattering," said Thorndyke; "so flattering that you leave us nothing to say. But what in the name of fortune are you doing at-- what's the name of the place--Ludham?"

"My brother has a little place a mile or so from here, and I have been spending a couple of days with him," Mr. Boscovitch explained. "I shall change at Badsham Junction and catch the boat train for Amsterdam. But whither are you two bound? I see you have your mysterious little green box up on the hat-rack, so I infer that you are on some romantic quest, eh? Going to unravel some dark and intricate crime?"

"No," replied Thorndyke. "We are bound for Warmington on a quite prosaic errand. I am instructed to watch the proceedings at an inquest there to-morrow on behalf of the Griffin Life Insurance Office, and we are travelling down to-night as it is rather a cross-country journey."

"But why the box of magic?" asked Boscovitch, glancing up at the hat-rack.

"I never go away from home without it," answered Thorndyke. "One never knows what may turn up; the trouble of carrying it is small when set off against the comfort of having appliances at hand in an emergency."

Boscovitch continued to stare up at the little square case covered with Willesden canvas. Presently he remarked: "I often used to wonder what you had in it when you were down at Chelmsford in connection with that bank murder--what an amazing case that was, by the way, and didn't your methods of research astonish the police!" As he still looked up wistfully at the case, Thorndyke good-naturedly lifted it down and unlocked it. As a matter of fact he was rather proud of his "portable laboratory," and certainly it was a triumph of condensation, for, small as it was--only a foot square by four inches deep--it contained a fairly complete outfit for a preliminary investigation.

"Wonderful!" exclaimed Boscovitch, when the case lay open before him, displaying its rows of little re-agent bottles, tiny test-tubes, diminutive spirit-lamp, dwarf microscope and assorted instruments on the same Lilliputian scale; "it's like a doll's house--everything looks as if it was seen through the wrong end of a telescope. But are these tiny things really efficient? That microscope now -?"

"Perfectly efficient at low and moderate magnifications," said Thorndyke. "It looks like a toy, but it isn't one; the lenses are the best that can be had. Of course a full-sized instrument would be infinitely more convenient--but I shouldn't have it with me, and should have to make shift with a pocket-lens. And so with the rest of the under-sized appliances; they are the alternative to no appliances."

Boscovitch pored over the case and its contents, fingering the instruments delicately and asking questions innumerable about their uses; indeed, his curiosity was but half appeased when, half-an-hour later, the train began to slow down.

"By Jove!" he exclaimed, starting up and seizing his bag, "here we are at the junction already. You change here too, don't you?"

"Yes," replied Thorndyke. "We take the branch train on to Warmington."

As we stepped out onto the platform, we became aware that something unusual was happening or had happened. All the passengers and most of the porters and supernumeraries were gathered at one end of the station, and all were looking intently into the darkness down the line.

"Anything wrong?" asked Mr. Boscovitch, addressing the station-inspector.

"Yes, sir," the official replied; "a man has been run over by the goods train about a mile down the line. The station-master has gone down with a stretcher to bring him in, and I expect that is his lantern that you see coming this way."

As we stood watching the dancing light grow momentarily brighter, flashing fitful reflections from the burnished rails, a man came out of the booking-office and joined the group of onlookers. He attracted my attention, as I afterwards remembered, for two reasons: in the first place his round, jolly face was excessively pale and bore a strained and wild expression, and, in the second, though he stared into the darkness with eager curiosity he asked no questions.

The swinging lantern continued to approach, and then suddenly two men came into sight bearing a stretcher covered with a tarpaulin, through which the shape of a human figure was dimly discernible. They ascended the slope to the platform, and proceeded with their burden to the lamp-room, when the inquisitive gaze of the passengers was transferred to a porter who followed carrying a handbag and umbrella and to the station-master who brought up the rear with his lantern.

As the porter passed, Mr. Boscovitch started forward with sudden excitement.

"Is that his umbrella?" he asked.

"Yes, sir," answered the porter, stopping and holding it out for the speaker's inspection.

"My God!" ejaculated Boscovitch; then, turning sharply to Thorndyke, he exclaimed: "That's Brodski's umbrella. I could swear to it. You remember Brodski?"

Thorndyke nodded, and Boscovitch, turning once more to the porter, said: "I identify that umbrella. It belongs to a gentleman named Brodski. If you look in his hat, you will see his name written in it. He always writes his name in his hat."

"We haven't found his hat yet," said the porter; "but here is the station-master." He turned to his superior and announced: "This gentleman, sir, has identified the umbrella."

"Oh," said the station-master, "you recognize the umbrella, sir, do you? Then perhaps you would step into the lamp-room and see if you can identify the body."

Mr. Boscovitch recoiled with a look of alarm. "Is it? is he--very much injured?" he asked nervously.

"Well, yes," was the reply. "You see, the engine and six of the trucks went over him before they could stop the train. Took his head clean off, in fact."

"Shocking! shocking!" gasped Boscovitch. "I think? if you don't mind-- I'd--I'd rather not. You don't think it necessary, doctor, do you?"

"Yes, I do," replied Thorndyke. "Early identification may be of the first importance."

"Then I suppose I must," said Boscovitch; and, with extreme reluctance, he followed the station-master to the lamp-room, as the loud ringing of the bell announced the approach of the boat train. His inspection must have been of the briefest, for, in a few moments, he burst out, pale and awe-stricken, and rushed up to Thorndyke.

"It is!" he exclaimed breathlessly. "It's Brodski! Poor" old Brodski! Horrible! horrible! He was to have met me here and come on with me to Amsterdam."

"Had he any--merchandize about him?" Thorndyke asked; and, as he spoke, the stranger whom I had previously noticed edged up closer as if to catch the reply.

"He had some stones, no doubt," answered Boscovitch, "but I don't know what they were. His clerk will know, of course. By the way, doctor, could you watch the case for me? Just to be sure it was really an accident or-- you know what. We were old friends, you know, fellow townsmen, too; we were both born in Warsaw. I'd like you to give an eye to the case."

"Very well," said Thorndyke. "I will satisfy myself that there is nothing more than appears, and let you have a report. Will that do?"

"Thank you," said Boscovitch. "It's excessively good of you, doctor. Ah, here comes the train. I hope it won't inconvenience you to stay and see to the matter."

"Not in the least," replied Thorndyke. "We are not due at Warmington until to-morrow afternoon, and I expect we can find out all that is necessary to know and still keep our appointment."

As Thorndyke spoke, the stranger, who had kept close to us with the evident purpose of hearing what was said, bestowed on him a very curious and attentive look; and it was only when the train had actually come to rest by the platform that he hurried away to find a compartment.

No sooner had the train left the station than Thorndyke sought out the station-master and informed him of the instructions that he had received from Boscovitch. "Of course," he added, in conclusion, "we must not move in the matter until the police arrive. I suppose they have been informed?"

"Yes," replied the station-master; "I sent a message at once to the Chief Constable, and I expect him or an inspector at any moment. In fact, I think I will slip out to the approach and see if he is coming." He evidently wished to have a word in private with the police officer before committing himself to any statement.

As the official departed, Thorndyke and I began to pace the now empty platform, and my friend, as was his wont, when entering on a new inquiry, meditatively reviewed the features of the problem.

"In a case of this kind," he remarked, "we have to decide on one of three possible explanations: accident, suicide or homicide; and our decision will be determined by inferences from three sets of facts: first, the general facts of the case; second, the special data obtained by examination of the body, and, third, the special data obtained by examining the spot on which the body was found. Now the only general facts at present in our possession are that the deceased was a diamond merchant making a journey for a specific purpose and probably having on his person property of small bulk and great value. These facts are somewhat against the hypothesis of suicide and somewhat favourable to that of homicide. Facts relevant to the question of accident would be the existence or otherwise of a level crossing, a road or path leading to the line, an enclosing fence with or without a gate, and any other facts rendering probable or otherwise the accidental presence of the deceased at the spot where the body was found. As we do not possess these facts, it is desirable that we extend our knowledge."

"Why not put a few discreet questions to the porter who brought in the bag and umbrella?" I suggested. "He is at this moment in earnest conversation with the ticket collector and would, no doubt, be glad of a new listener."

"An excellent suggestion, Jervis," answered Thorndyke. "Let us see what he has to tell us." We approached the porter and found him, as I had anticipated, bursting to unburden himself of the tragic story.

"The way the thing happened, sir, was this," he said, in answer to Thorndyke's question: "There's a sharpish bend in the road just at that place, and the goods train was just rounding the curve when the driver suddenly caught sight of something lying across the rails. As the engine turned, the head-lights shone on it and then he saw it was a man. He shut off steam at once, blew his whistle, and put the brakes down hard, but, as you know, sir, a goods train takes some stopping; before they could bring her up, the engine and half-a-dozen trucks had gone over the poor beggar."

"Could the driver see how the man was lying?" Thorndyke asked.

"Yes, he could see him quite plain, because the headlights were full on him. He was lying on his face with his neck over the near rail on the down side. His head was in the four-foot and his body by the side of the track. It looked as if he had laid himself out a-purpose."

"Is there a level crossing thereabouts?" asked Thorndyke.

"No, sir. No crossing, no road, no path, no nothing," said the porter, ruthlessly sacrificing grammar to emphasis. "He must have come across the fields and climbed over the fence to get onto the permanent way. Deliberate suicide is what it looks like."

"How did you learn all this?" Thorndyke inquired.

"Why, the driver, you see, sir, when him and his mate had lifted the body off the track, went on to the next signal-box and sent in his report by telegram. The station-master told me all about it as we walked down the line."

Thorndyke thanked the man for his information, and, as we strolled back towards the lamp-room, discussed the bearing of these new facts.

"Our friend is unquestionably right in one respect," he said; "this was not an accident. The man might, if he were near-sighted, deaf or stupid, have climbed over the fence and got knocked down by the train. But his position, lying across the rails, can only be explained by one of two hypotheses: either it was, as the porter says, deliberate suicide, or else the man was already dead or insensible. We must leave it at that until we have seen the body, that is, if the police will allow us to see it. But here comes the station-master and an officer with him. Let us hear what they have to say."

The two officials had evidently made up their minds to decline any outside assistance. The divisional surgeon would make the necessary examination, and information could be obtained through the usual channels. The production of Thorndyke's card, however, somewhat altered the situation. The police inspector hummed and hawed irresolutely, with the card in his hand, but finally agreed to allow us to view the body, and we entered the lamp-room together, the station-master leading the way to turn up the gas.

The stretcher stood on the floor by one wall, its grim burden still hidden by the tarpaulin, and the hand-bag and umbrella lay on a large box, together with the battered frame of a pair of spectacles from which the glasses had fallen out.

"Were these spectacles found by the body?" Thorndyke inquired.

"Yes," replied the station-master. "They were close to the head and the glass was scattered about on the ballast."

Thorndyke made a note in his pocket-book, and then, as the inspector removed the tarpaulin, he glanced down on the corpse, lying limply on the stretcher and looking grotesquely horrible with its displaced head and distorted limbs. For fully a minute he remained silently stooping over the uncanny object, on which the inspector was now throwing the light of a large lantern; then he stood up and said quietly to me: "I think we can eliminate two out of the three hypotheses."

The inspector looked at him quickly, and was about to ask a question, when his attention was diverted by the travelling-case which Thorndyke had laid on a shelf and now opened to abstract a couple of pairs of dissecting forceps.

"We've no authority to make a post mortem, you know," said the inspector.

"No, of course not," said Thorndyke. "I am merely going to look into the mouth." With one pair of forceps he turned back the lip and, having scrutinized its inner surface, closely examined the teeth.

"May I trouble you for your lens, Jervis?" he said; and, as I handed him my doublet ready opened, the inspector brought the lantern close to the dead face and leaned forward eagerly. In his usual systematic fashion, Thorndyke slowly passed the lens along the whole range of sharp, uneven teeth, and then, bringing it back to the centre, examined with more minuteness the upper incisors. At length, very delicately, he picked out with his forceps some minute object from between two of the upper front teeth and held it in the focus of the lens. Anticipating his next move, I took a labelled microscope-slide from the case and handed it to him together with a dissecting needle, and, as he transferred the object to the slide and spread it out with the needle, I set up the little microscope on the shelf.

"A drop of Farrant and a cover-glass, please, Jervis," said Thorndyke.

I handed him the bottle, and, when he had let a drop of the mounting fluid fall gently on the object and put on the cover-slip, he placed the slide on the stage of the microscope and examined it attentively.

Happening to glance at the inspector, I observed on his countenance a faint grin, which he politely strove to suppress when he caught my eye.

"I was thinking, sir," he said apologetically, "that it's a bit off the track to be finding out what he had for dinner. He didn't die of unwholesome feeding."

Thorndyke looked up with a smile. "It doesn't do, inspector, to assume that anything is off the track in an inquiry of this kind. Every fact must have some significance, you know."

"I don't see any significance in the diet of a man who has had his head cut off," the inspector rejoined defiantly.

"Don't you?" said Thorndyke. "Is there no interest attaching to the last meal of a man who has met a violent death? These crumbs, for instance, that are scattered over the dead man's waistcoat. Can we learn nothing from them?"

"I don't see what you can learn," was the dogged rejoinder.

Thorndyke picked off the crumbs, one by one, with his forceps, and having deposited them on a slide, inspected them, first with the lens and then through the microscope.

"I learn," said he, "that shortly before his death, the deceased partook of some kind of whole-meal biscuits, apparently composed partly of oatmeal."

"I call that nothing," said the inspector. "The question that we have got to settle is not what refreshments had the deceased been taking, but what was the cause of his death: did he commit suicide? was he killed by accident? or was there any foul play?"

"I beg your pardon," said Thorndyke, "the questions that remain to be settled are, who killed the deceased and with what motive? The others are already answered as far as I am, concerned."

The inspector stared in sheer amazement not unmixed with incredulity.

"You haven't been long coming to a conclusion, sir," he said.

"No, it was a pretty obvious case of murder," said Thorndyke. "As to the motive, the deceased was a diamond merchant and is believed to have had a quantity of stones about his person. I should suggest that you search the body."

The inspector gave vent to an exclamation of disgust. "I see," he said. "It was just a guess on your part. The dead man was a diamond merchant and had valuable property about him; therefore he was murdered." He drew himself up, and, regarding Thorndyke with stern reproach, added: "But you must understand, sir, that this is a judicial inquiry, not a prize competition in a penny paper. And, as to searching the body, why, that is what I principally came for." He ostentatiously turned his back on us and proceeded systematically to turn out the dead man's pockets, laying the articles, as he removed them, on the box by the side of the hand-bag and umbrella.

While he was thus occupied, Thorndyke looked over the body generally, paying special attention to the soles of the boots, which, to the inspector's undissembled amusement, he very thoroughly examined with the lens.

"I should have thought, sir, that his feet were large enough to be seen with the naked eye," was his comment; "but perhaps," he added, with a sly glance at the station-master, "you're a little near-sighted."

Thorndyke chuckled good-humouredly, and, while the officer continued his search, he looked over the articles that had already been laid on the box. The purse and pocket-book he naturally left for the inspector to open, but the reading-glasses, pocket-knife and card-case and other small pocket articles were subjected to a searching scrutiny. The inspector watched him out of the corner of his eye with furtive amusement; saw him hold up the glasses to the light to estimate their refractive power, peer into the tobacco pouch, open the cigarette book and examine the watermark of the paper, and even inspect the contents of the silver match-box.

"What might you have expected to find in his tobacco pouch?" the officer asked, laying down a bunch of keys from the dead man's pocket.

"Tobacco," Thorndyke replied stolidly; "but I did not expect to find fine-cut Latakia. I don't remember ever having seen pure Latakia smoked in cigarettes." "You do take an interest in things, sir," said the inspector, with a side glance at the stolid station-master.

"I do," Thorndyke agreed; "and I note that there are no diamonds among this collection."

"No, and we don't know that he had any about him; but there's a gold watch and chain, a diamond scarf-pin, and a purse containing"--he opened it and tipped out its contents into his hand--"twelve pounds in gold. That doesn't look much like robbery, does it? What do you say to the murder theory now?"

"My opinion is unchanged," said Thorndyke, "and I should like to examine the spot where the body was found. Has the engine been inspected?" he added, addressing the station-master.

"I telegraphed to Bradfield to have it examined," the official answered. "The report has probably come in by now. I'd better see before we start down the line."

We emerged from the lamp-room and, at the door, found the station-inspector waiting with a telegram. He handed it to the station-master, who read it aloud.

"THE ENGINE HAS BEEN CAREFULLY EXAMINED BY ME. I FIND SMALL SMEAR OF BLOOD ON NEAR LEADING WHEEL AND SMALLER ONE ON NEXT WHEEL FOLLOWING. NO OTHER MARKS." He glanced questioningly at Thorndyke, who nodded and remarked: "It will be interesting to see if the line tells the same tale."

The station-master looked puzzled and was apparently about to ask for an explanation; but the inspector, who had carefully pocketed the dead man's property, was impatient to start and, accordingly, when Thorndyke had repacked his case and had, at his own request, been furnished with a lantern, we set off down the permanent way, Thorndyke carrying the light and I the indispensable green case.

"I am a little in the dark about this affair," I said, when we had allowed the two officials to draw ahead out of earshot; "you came to a conclusion remarkably quickly. What was it that so immediately determined the opinion of murder as against suicide?"

"It was a small matter but very conclusive," replied Thorndyke. "You noticed a small scalp-wound above the left temple? It was a glancing wound, and might easily have been made by the engine. But the wound had bled; and it had bled for an appreciable time. There were two streams of blood from it, and in both the blood was firmly clotted and partially dried. But the man had been decapitated; and this wound, if inflicted by the engine, must have been made after the decapitation, since it was on the side most distant from the engine as it approached. Now, a decapitated head does not bleed. Therefore, this wound was inflicted before the decapitation.

"But not only had the wound bled: the blood had trickled down in two streams at right angles to one another. First, in the order of time as shown by the appearance of the stream, it had trickled down the side of the face and dropped on the collar. The second stream ran from the wound to the back of the head. Now, you know, Jervis, there are no exceptions to the law of gravity. If the blood ran down the face towards the chin, the face must have been upright at the time; and if the blood trickled from the front to the back of the head, the head must have been horizontal and face upwards. But the man when he was seen by the engine-driver, was lying face downwards. The only possible inference is that when the wound was inflicted, the man was in the upright position-- standing or sitting; and that subsequently, and while he was still alive, he lay on his back for a sufficiently long time for the blood to have trickled to the back of his head."

"I see. I was a duffer not to have reasoned this out for myself," I remarked contritely.

"Quick observation and rapid inference come by practice," replied Thorndyke. "What did you notice about the face?"

"I thought there was a strong suggestion of asphyxia."

"Undoubtedly," said Thorndyke. "It was the face of a suffocated man. You must have noticed, too, that the tongue was very distinctly swollen and that on the inside of the upper lip were deep indentations made by the teeth, as well as one or two slight wounds, obviously caused by heavy pressure on the mouth. And now observe how completely these facts and inferences agree with those from the scalp wound. If we knew that the deceased had received a blow on the head, had struggled with his assailant and been finally borne down and suffocated, we should look for precisely those signs which we have found."

"By the way, what was it that you found wedged between the teeth? I did not get a chance to look through the microscope."

"Ah!" said Thorndyke, "there we not only get confirmation, but we carry our inferences a stage further. The object was a little tuft of some textile fabric. Under the microscope I found it to consist of several different fibres, differently dyed. The bulk of it consisted of wool fibres dyed crimson, but there were also cotton fibres dyed blue and a few which looked like jute, dyed yellow. It was obviously a parti-coloured fabric and might have been part of a woman's dress, though the presence of the jute is much more suggestive of a curtain or rug of inferior quality."

"And its importance?"

"Is that, if it is not part of an article of clothing, then it must have come from an article of furniture, and furniture suggests a habitation."

"That doesn't seem very conclusive," I objected.

"It is not; but it is valuable corroboration."

"Of what?"

"Of the suggestion offered by the soles of the dead man's boots. I examined them most minutely and could find no trace of sand, gravel or earth, in spite of the fact that he must have crossed fields and rough land to reach the place where he was found. What I did find was fine tobacco ash, a charred mark as if a cigar or cigarette had been trodden on, several crumbs of biscuit, and, on a projecting brad, some coloured fibres, apparently from a carpet. The manifest suggestion is that the man was killed in a house with a carpeted floor, and carried from thence to the railway."

I was silent for some moments. Well as I knew Thorndyke, I was completely taken by surprise; a sensation, indeed, that I experienced anew every time that I accompanied him on one of his investigations. His marvellous power of co-ordinating apparently insignificant facts, of arranging them into an ordered sequence and making them tell a coherent story, was a phenomenon that I never got used to; every exhibition of it astonished me afresh.

"If your inferences are correct," I said, "the problem is practically solved. There must be abundant traces inside the house. The only question is, which house is it?"

"Quite so," replied Thorndyke; "that is the question, and a very difficult question it is. A glance at that interior would doubtless clear up the whole mystery. But how are we to get that glance? We cannot enter houses speculatively to see if they present traces of a murder. At present, our clue breaks off abruptly. The other end of it is in some unknown house, and, if we cannot join up the two ends, our problem remains unsolved. For the question is, you remember, Who killed Oscar Brodski?"

"Then what do you propose to do?" I asked.

"The next stage of the inquiry is to connect some particular house with this crime. To that end, I can only gather up all available facts and consider each in all its possible bearings. If I cannot establish any such connection, then the inquiry will have failed and we shall have to make a fresh start--say, at Amsterdam, if it turns out that Brodski really had diamonds on his person, as I have no doubt he had."

Here our conversation was interrupted by our arrival at the spot where the body had been found. The station-master had halted, and he and the inspector were now examining the near rail by the light of their lanterns

"There's remarkably little blood about," said the former. "I've seen a good many accidents of this kind and there has always been a lot of blood, both on the engine and on the road. It's very curious."

Thorndyke glanced at the rail with but slight attention: that question had ceased to interest him. But the light of his lantern flashed onto the ground at the side of the track--a loose, gravelly soil mixed with fragments of chalk--and from thence to the soles of the inspector's boots, which were displayed as he knelt by the rail.

"You observe, Jervis?" he said in a low voice, and I nodded. The inspector's boot-soles were covered with adherent particles of gravel and conspicuously marked by the chalk on which he had trodden.

"You haven't found the hat, I suppose?" Thorndyke asked, stooping to pick up a short piece of string that lay on the ground at the side of the track.

"No," replied the inspector, "but it can't be far off. You seem to have found another clue, sir," he added, with a grin, glancing at the piece of string.

"Who knows," said Thorndyke. "A short end of white twine with a green strand in it. It may tell us something later. At any rate we'll keep it," and, taking from his pocket a small tin box containing, among other things, a number of seed envelopes, he slipped the string into one of the latter and scribbled a note in pencil on the outside. The inspector watched his proceedings with an indulgent smile, and then returned to his examination of the track, in which Thorndyke now joined.

"I suppose the poor chap was near-sighted," the officer remarked, indicating the remains of the shattered spectacles; "that might account for his having strayed onto the line."

"Possibly," said Thorndyke. He had already noticed the fragments scattered over a sleeper and the adjacent ballast, and now once more produced his "collecting-box," from which he took another seed envelope. "Would you hand me a pair of forceps, Jervis," he said; "and perhaps you wouldn't mind taking a pair yourself and helping me to gather up these fragments."

As I complied, the inspector looked up curiously.

"There isn't any doubt that these spectacles belonged to the deceased, is there?" he asked. "He certainly wore spectacles, for I saw the mark on his nose."

"Still, there is no harm in verifying the fact," said Thorndyke, and he added to me in a lower tone, "Pick up every particle you can find, Jervis. It may be most important."

"I don't quite see how," I said, groping amongst the shingle by the light of the lantern in search of the tiny splinters of glass.

"Don't you?" returned Thorndyke. "Well, look at these fragments; some of them are a fair size, but many of these on the sleeper are mere grains. And consider their number. Obviously, the condition of the glass does not agree with the circumstances in which we find it. These are thick concave spectacle-lenses broken into a great number of minute fragments. Now how were they broken? Not merely by falling, evidently: such a lens, when it is dropped, breaks into a small number of large pieces. Nor were they broken by the wheel passing over them, for they would then have been reduced to fine powder, and that powder would have been visible on the rail, which it is not. The spectacle-frames, you may remember, presented the same incongruity: they were battered and damaged more than they would have been by falling, but not nearly so much as they would have been if the wheel had passed over them."

"What do you suggest, then?" I asked.

"The appearances suggest that the spectacles had been trodden on. But, if the body was carried here the probability is that the spectacles were carried here too, and that they were then already broken; for it is more likely that they were trodden on during the struggle than that the murderer trod on them after bringing them here. Hence the importance of picking up every fragment."

"But why?" I inquired, rather foolishly, I must admit.

"Because, if, when we have picked up every fragment that we can find, there still remains missing a larger portion of the lenses than we could reasonably expect, that would tend to support our hypothesis and we might find the missing remainder elsewhere. If, on the other hand, we find as much of the lenses as we could expect to find, we must conclude that they were broken on this spot."

While we were conducting our search, the two officials were circling around with their lanterns in quest of the missing hat; and, when we had at length picked up the last fragment, and a careful search, even aided by a lens, failed to reveal any other, we could see their lanterns moving, like will-o'-the-wisps, some distance down the line.

"We may as well see what we have got before our friends come back," said Thorndyke, glancing at the twinkling lights. "Lay the case down on the grass by the fence; it will serve for a table."

I did so, and Thorndyke, taking a letter from his pocket, opened it, spread it out flat on the case, securing it with a couple of heavy stones, although the night was quite calm. Then he tipped the contents of the seed envelope out on the paper, and carefully spreading out the pieces of glass, looked at them for some moments in silence. And, as he looked, there stole over his face a very curious expression; with sudden eagerness he began picking out the large fragments and laying them on two visiting-cards which he had taken from his card-case. Rapidly and with wonderful deftness he fitted the pieces together, and, as the reconstituted lenses began gradually to take shape on their cards I looked on with growing excitement, for something in my colleague's manner told me that we were on the verge of a discovery.

At length the two ovals of glass lay on their respective cards, complete save for one or two small gaps; and the little heap that remained consisted of fragments so minute as to render further reconstruction impossible. Then Thorndyke leaned back and laughed softly.

"This is certainly an unlooked-for result," said he.

"What is?" I asked.

"Don't you see, my dear fellow? There's too much glass. We have almost completely built up the broken lenses, and the fragments that are left over are considerably more than are required to fill up the gaps."

I looked at the little heap of small fragments and saw at once that it was as he had said. There was a surplus of small pieces.

"This is very extraordinary," I said. "What do you think can be the explanation?"

"The fragments will probably tell us," he replied, "if we ask them intelligently."

He lifted the paper and the two cards carefully onto the ground, and, opening the case, took out the little microscope, to which he fitted the lowest-power objective and eye-piece--having a combined magnification of only ten diameters. Then he transferred the minute fragments of glass to a slide, and, having arranged the lantern as a microscope-lamp, commenced his examination.

"Ha!" he exclaimed presently. "The plot thickens. There is too much glass and yet too little; that is to say, there are only one or two fragments here that belong to the spectacles; not nearly enough to complete the building up of the lenses. The remainder consists of a soft, uneven, moulded glass, easily distinguished from the clear, hard optical glass. These foreign fragments are all curved, as if they had formed part of a cylinder, and are, I should say, portions of a wine-glass or tumbler." He moved the slide once or twice, and then continued: "We are in luck, Jervis. Here is a fragment with two little diverging lines etched on it, evidently the points of an eight-rayed star--and here is another with three points--the ends of three rays. This enables us to reconstruct the vessel perfectly. It was a clear, thin glass--probably a tumbler-- decorated with scattered stars; I dare say you know the pattern. Sometimes there is an ornamented band in addition, but generally the stars form the only decoration. Have a look at the specimen."

I had just applied my eye to the microscope when the station-master and the inspector came up. Our appearance, seated on the ground with the microscope between us, was too much for the police officer's gravity, and he laughed long and joyously.

"You must excuse me, gentlemen," he said apologetically, "but really, you know, to an old hand, like myself, it does look a little--well--you understand--I dare say a microscope is a very interesting and amusing thing, but it doesn't get you much forwarder in a case like this, does it?"

"Perhaps not," replied Thorndyke. "By the way, where did you find the hat, after all?"

"We haven't found it," the inspector replied.

"Then we must help you to continue the search," said Thorndyke. "If you will wait a few moments, we will come with you." He poured a few drops of xylol balsam on the cards to fix the reconstituted lenses to their supports and then, packing them and the microscope in the case, announced that he was ready to start.

"Is there any village or hamlet near?" he asked the station-master.

"None nearer than Corfield. That is about half-a-mile from here."

"And where is the nearest road?"

"There is a half-made road that runs past a house about three hundred yards from here. It belonged to a building estate that was never built. There is a footpath from it to the station."

"Are there any other houses near?"

"No. That is the only house for half-a-mile round, and there is no other road near here."

"Then the probability is that Brodski approached the railway from that direction, as he was found on that side of the permanent way."

The inspector agreeing with this view, we all set off slowly towards the house, piloted by the station-master and searching the ground as we went. The waste land over which we passed was covered with patches of docks and nettles, through each of which the inspector kicked his way, searching with feet and lantern for the missing hat. A walk of three hundred yards brought us to a low wall enclosing a garden, beyond which we could see a small house; and here we halted while the inspector waded into a large bed of nettles beside the wall and kicked vigorously. Suddenly there came a clinking sound mingled with objurgations, and the inspector hopped out holding one foot and soliloquizing profanely.

"I wonder what sort of a fool put a thing like that into a bed of nettles!" he exclaimed, stroking the injured foot. Thorndyke picked the object up and held it in the light of the lantern, displaying a piece of three-quarter inch rolled iron bar about a foot long. "It doesn't seem to have been there very long," he observed, examining it closely, "there is hardly any rust on it."

"It has been there long enough for me," growled the inspector, "and I'd like to bang it on the head of the blighter that put it there."

Callously indifferent to the inspector's sufferings, Thorndyke continued calmly to examine the bar. At length, resting his lantern on the wall, he produced his pocket-lens, with which he resumed his investigation, a proceeding that so exasperated the inspector that that afflicted official limped off in dudgeon, followed by the station-master, and we heard him, presently, rapping at the front door of the house.

"Give me a slide, Jervis, with a drop of Farrant on it," said Thorndyke. "There are some fibres sticking to this bar."

I prepared the slide, and, having handed it to him together with a cover-glass, a pair of forceps and a needle, set up the microscope on the wall.

"I'm sorry for the inspector," Thorndyke remarked, with his eye applied to the little instrument, "but that was a lucky kick for us. Just take a look at the specimen."

I did so, and, having moved the slide about until I had seen the whole of the object, I gave my opinion. "Red wool fibres, blue cotton fibres and some yellow vegetable fibres that look like jute."

"Yes," said Thorndyke; "the same combination of fibres as that which we found on the dead man's teeth and probably from the same source. This bar has probably been wiped on that very curtain or rug with which poor Brodski was stifled. We will place it on the wall for future reference, and meanwhile, by hook or by crook, we must get into that house. This is much too plain a hint to be disregarded."

Hastily repacking the case, we hurried to the front of the house, where we found the two officials looking rather vaguely up the unmade road.

"There's a light in the house," said the inspector, "but there's no one at home. I have knocked a dozen times and got no answer. And I don't see what we are hanging about here for at all. The hat is probably close to where the body was found, and we shall find it in the morning."

Thorndyke made no reply, but, entering the garden, stepped up the path, and having knocked gently at the door, stooped and listened attentively at the key-hole.

"I tell you there's no one in the house, sir," said the inspector irritably; and, as Thorndyke continued to listen, he walked away, muttering angrily. As soon as he was gone, Thorndyke flashed his lantern over the door, the threshold, the path and the small flower-beds; and, from one of the latter, I presently saw him stoop and pick something up.

"Here is a highly instructive object, Jervis," he said, coming out to the gate, and displaying a cigarette of which only half-an-inch had been smoked.

"How instructive?" I asked. "What do you learn from it?"

"Many things," he replied. "It has been lit and thrown away unsmoked; that indicates a sudden change of purpose. It was thrown away at the entrance to the house, almost certainly by some one entering it. That person was probably a stranger, or he would have taken it in with him. But he had not expected to enter the house, or he would not have lit it. These are the general suggestions; now as to the particular ones. The paper of the cigarette is of the kind known as the 'Zig-Zag' brand; the very conspicuous water-mark is quite easy to see. Now Brodski's cigarette book was a 'Zig-Zag' book--so called from the way in which the papers pull out. But let us see what the tobacco is like." With a pin from his coat, he hooked out from the unburned end a wisp of dark, dirty brown tobacco, which he held out for my inspection.

"Fine-cut Latakia," I pronounced, without hesitation.

"Very well," said Thorndyke. "Here is a cigarette made of an unusual tobacco similar to that in Brodski's pouch and wrapped in an unusual paper similar to those in Brodski's cigarette book. With due regard to the fourth rule of the syllogism, I suggest that this cigarette was made by Oscar Brodski. But, nevertheless, we will look for corroborative detail."

"What is that?" I asked.

"You may have noticed that Brodski's match-box contained round wooden vestas--which are also rather unusual. As he must have lighted the cigarette within a few steps of the gate, we ought to be able to find the match with which he lighted it. Let us try up the road in the direction from which he would probably have approached."

We walked very slowly up the road, searching the ground with the lantern, and we had hardly gone a dozen paces when I espied a match lying on the rough path and eagerly picked it up. It was a round wooden vesta.

Thorndyke examined it with interest and having deposited it, with the cigarette, in his "collecting-box," turned to retrace his steps. "There is now, Jervis, no reasonable doubt that Brodski was murdered in that house. We have succeeded in connecting that house with the crime, and now we have got to force an entrance and join up the other clues." We walked quickly back to the rear of the premises, where we found the inspector conversing disconsolately with the station-master.

"I think, sir," said the former, "we had better go back now; in fact, I don't see what we came here for, but--here! I say, sir, you mustn't do that!" For Thorndyke, without a word of warning, had sprung up lightly and thrown one of his long legs over the wall.

"I can't allow you to enter private premises, sir," continued the inspector; but Thorndyke quietly dropped down on the inside and turned to face the officer over the wall.

"Now, listen to me, inspector," said he. "I have good reasons for believing that the dead man, Brodski, has been in this house, in fact, I am prepared to swear an information to that effect. But time is precious; we must follow the scent while it is hot. And I am not proposing to break into the house off-hand. I merely wish to examine the dust-bin."

"The dust-bin!" gasped the inspector. "Well, you really are a most extraordinary gentleman! What do you expect to find in the dust-bin?"

"I am looking for a broken tumbler or wine-glass. It is a thin glass vessel decorated with a pattern of small, eight-pointed stars. It may be in the dust-bin or it may be inside the house."

The inspector hesitated, but Thorndyke's confident manner had evidently impressed him.

"We can soon see what is in the dust-bin," he said, "though what in creation a broken tumbler has to do with the case is more than I can understand. However, here goes." He sprang up onto the wall, and, as he dropped down into the garden, the station-master and I followed.

Thorndyke lingered a few moments by the gate examining the ground, while the two officials hurried up the path. Finding nothing of interest, however, he walked towards the house, looking keenly about him as he went; but we were hardly half-way up the path when we heard the voice of the inspector calling excitedly.

"Here you are, sir, this way," he sang out, and, as we hurried forward, we suddenly came on the two officials standing over a small rubbish-heap and looking the picture of astonishment. The glare of their lanterns illuminated the heap, and showed us the scattered fragments of a thin glass, star-pattern tumbler.

"I can't imagine how you guessed it was here, sir," said the inspector, with a new-born respect in his tone, "nor what you're going to do with it now you have found it."

"It is merely another link in the chain of evidence," said Thorndyke, taking a pair of forceps from the case and stooping over the heap. "Perhaps we shall find something else." He picked up several small fragments of glass, looked at them closely and dropped them again. Suddenly his eye caught a small splinter at the base of the heap. Seizing it with the forceps, he held it close to his eye in the strong lamplight, and, taking out his lens, examined it with minute attention. "Yes," he said at length, "this is what I was looking for. Let me have those two cards, Jervis."

I produced the two visiting-cards with the reconstructed lenses stuck to them, and, laying them on the lid of the case, threw the light of the lantern on them. Thorndyke looked at them intently for some time, and from them to the fragment that he held. Then, turning to the inspector, he said: "You saw me pick up this splinter of glass?"

"Yes, sir," replied the officer.

"And you saw where we found these spectacle-glasses and know whose they were?"

"Yes, sir. They are the dead man's spectacles, and you found them where the body had been."

"Very well," said Thorndyke; "now observe;" and, as the two officials craned forward with parted lips, he laid the little splinter in a gap in one of the lenses and then gave it a gentle push forward, when it occupied the gap perfectly, joining edge to edge with the adjacent fragments and rendering that portion of the lens complete.

"My God!" exclaimed the inspector. "How on earth did you know?"

"I must explain that later," said Thorndyke. "Meanwhile we had better have a look inside the house. I expect to find there a cigarette--or possibly a cigar--which has been trodden on, some whole-meal biscuits, possibly a wooden vesta, and perhaps even the missing hat."

At the mention of the hat, the inspector stepped eagerly to the back door, but, finding it bolted, he tried the window. This also was securely fastened and, on Thorndyke's advice, we went round to the front door.

"This door is locked too," said the inspector. "I'm afraid we shall have to break in. It's a nuisance, though."

"Have a look at the window," suggested Thorndyke.

The officer did so, struggling vainly to undo the patent catch with his pocket-knife.

"It's no go," he said, coming back to the door. "We shall have to -?" He broke off with an astonished stare, for the door stood open and Thorndyke was putting something in his pocket.

"Your friend doesn't waste much time--even in picking a lock," he remarked to me, as we followed Thorndyke into the house; but his reflections were soon merged in a new surprise. Thorndyke had preceded us into a small sitting-room dimly lighted by a hanging lamp turned down low.

As we entered he turned up the light and glanced about the room. A whisky-bottle was on the table, with a siphon, a tumbler and a biscuit-box. Pointing to the latter, Thorndyke said to the inspector: "See what is in that box."

The inspector raised the lid and peeped in, the station-master peered over his shoulder, and then both stared at Thorndyke.

"How in the name of goodness did you know that there were whole-meal biscuits in the house, sir?" exclaimed the station-master.

"You'd be disappointed if I told you," replied Thorndyke. "But look at this." He pointed to the hearth, where lay a flattened, half-smoked cigarette and a round wooden vesta. The inspector gazed at these objects in silent wonder, while, as to the station-master, he continued to stare at Thorndyke with what I can only describe as superstitious awe.

"You have the dead man's property with you, I believe?" said my colleague.

"Yes," replied the inspector; "I put the things in my pocket for safety."

"Then," said Thorndyke, picking up the flattened cigarette, "let us have a look at his tobacco-pouch."

As the officer produced and opened the pouch, Thorndyke neatly cut open the cigarette with his sharp pocket-knife. "Now," said he, "what kind of tobacco is in the pouch?"

The inspector took out a pinch, looked at it and smelt it distastefully. "It's one of those stinking tobaccos," he said, "that they put in mixtures--Latakia, I think."

"And what is this?" asked Thorndyke, pointing to the open cigarette.

"Same stuff, undoubtedly," replied the inspector.

"And now let us see his cigarette papers," said Thorndyke.

The little book, or rather packet--for it consisted of separated papers--was produced from the officer's pocket and a sample paper abstracted. Thorndyke laid the half-burnt paper beside it, and the inspector, having examined the two, held them up to the light.

"There isn't much chance of mistaking that 'Zig-Zag' watermark," he said. "This cigarette was made by the deceased; there can't be the shadow of a doubt."

"One more point," said Thorndyke, laying the burnt wooden vesta on the table. "You have his match-box?"

The inspector brought forth the little silver casket, opened it and compared the wooden vestas that it contained with the burnt end. Then he shut the box with a snap.

"You've proved it up to the hilt," said he. "If we could only find the hat, we should have a complete case."

"I'm not sure that we haven't found the hat," said Thorndyke. "You notice that something besides coal has been burned in the grate."

The inspector ran eagerly to the fire-place and began with feverish hands, to pick out the remains of the extinct fire. "The cinders are still warm," he said, "and they are certainly not all coal cinders. There has been wood burned here on top of the coal, and these little black lumps are neither coal nor wood. They may quite possibly be the remains of a burnt hat, but, lord! who can tell? You can put together the pieces of broken spectacle-glasses, but you can't build up a hat out of a few cinders." He held out a handful of little, black, spongy cinders and looked ruefully at Thorndyke, who took them from him and laid them out on a sheet of paper.

"We can't reconstitute the hat, certainly," my friend agreed, "but we may be able to ascertain the origin of these remains. They may not be cinders of a hat, after all." He lit a wax match and, taking up one of the charred fragments, applied the flame to it. The cindery mass fused at once with a crackling, seething sound, emitting a dense smoke, and instantly the air became charged with a pungent, resinous odour mingled with the smell of burning animal matter.

"Smells like varnish," the station-master remarked.

"Yes. Shellac," said Thorndyke; "so the first test gives a positive result. The next test will take more time."

He opened the green case and took from it a little flask, fitted for Marsh's arsenic test, with a safety funnel and escape tube, a small folding tripod, a spirit lamp and a disc of asbestos to serve as a sand-bath. Dropping into the flask several of the cindery masses, selected after careful inspection, he filled it up with alcohol and placed it on the disc, which he rested on the tripod. Then he lighted the spirit lamp underneath and sat down to wait for the alcohol to boil.

"There is one little point that we may as well settle," he said presently, as the bubbles began to rise in the flask. "Give me a slide with a drop of Farrant on it, Jervis."

I prepared the slide while Thorndyke, with a pair of forceps, picked out a tiny wisp from the table-cloth. "I fancy we have seen this fabric before," he remarked, as he laid the little pinch of fluff in the mounting fluid and slipped the slide onto the stage of the microscope. "Yes," he continued, looking into the eye-piece, "here are our old acquaintances, the red wool fibres, the blue cotton and the yellow jute. We must label this at once or we may confuse it with the other specimens."

"Have you any idea how the deceased met his death?" the inspector asked.

"Yes," replied Thorndyke. "I take it that the murderer enticed him into this room and gave him some refreshments. The murderer sat in the chair in which you are sitting, Brodski sat in that small arm-chair. Then I imagine the murderer attacked him with that iron bar that you found among the nettles, failed to kill him at the first stroke, struggled with him and finally suffocated him with the table-cloth. By the way, there is just one more point. You recognize this piece of string?" He took from his "collecting-box" the little end of twine that had been picked up by the line. The inspector nodded. "Look behind you, you will see where it came from."

The officer turned sharply and his eye lighted on a string-box on the mantelpiece. He lifted it down, and Thorndyke drew out from it a length of white twine with one green strand, which he compared with the piece in his hand. "The green strand in it makes the identification fairly certain," he said. "Of course the string was used to secure the umbrella and hand-bag. He could not have carried them in his hand, encumbered as he was with the corpse. But I expect our other specimen is ready now." He lifted the flask off the tripod, and, giving it a vigorous shake, examined the contents through his lens. The alcohol had now become dark-brown in colour, and was noticeably thicker and more syrupy in consistence.

"I think we have enough here for a rough test," said he, selecting a pipette and a slide from the case. He dipped the former into the flask and, having sucked up a few drops of the alcohol from the bottom, held the pipette over the slide on which he allowed the contained fluid to drop.

Laying a cover-glass on the little pool of alcohol, he put the slide on the microscope stage and examined it attentively, while we watched him in expectant silence.

At length he looked up, and, addressing the inspector, asked: "Do you know what felt hats are made of?"

"I can't say that I do, sir," replied the officer.

"Well, the better quality hats are made of rabbits' and hares' wool--the soft under-fur, you know--cemented together with shellac. Now there is very little doubt that these cinders contain shellac, and with the microscope I find a number of small hairs of a rabbit. I have, therefore, little hesitation in saying that these cinders are the remains of a hard felt hat; and, as the hairs do not appear to be dyed, I should say it was a grey hat."

At this moment our conclave was interrupted by hurried footsteps on the garden path and, as we turned with one accord, an elderly woman burst into the room.

She stood for a moment in mute astonishment, and then, looking from one to the other, demanded: "Who are you? and what are you doing here?"

The inspector rose. "I am a police officer, madam," said he. "I can't give you any further information just now, but, if you will excuse me asking, who are you?"

"I am Mr. Hickler's housekeeper," she replied.

"And Mr. Hickler; are you expecting him home shortly?"

"No, I am not," was the curt reply. "Mr. Hickler is away from home just now. He left this evening by the boat train."

"For Amsterdam?" asked Thorndyke.

"I believe so, though I don't see what business it is of yours," the housekeeper answered.

"I thought he might, perhaps, be a diamond broker or merchant," said Thorndyke. "A good many of them travel by that train."

"So he is," said the woman, "at least, he has something to do with diamonds."

"Ah. Well, we must be going, Jervis," said Thorndyke, "we have finished here, and we have to find an hotel or inn. Can I have a word with you, inspector?"

The officer, now entirely humble and reverent, followed us out into the garden to receive Thorndyke's parting advice.

"You had better take possession of the house at once, and get rid of the housekeeper. Nothing must be removed. Preserve those cinders and see that the rubbish-heap is not disturbed, and, above all, don't have the room swept. An officer will be sent to relieve you."

With a friendly "good-night" we went on our way, guided by the station-master; and here our connection with the case came to an end. Hickler (whose Christian name turned out to be Silas) was, it is true, arrested as he stepped ashore from the steamer, and a packet of diamonds, subsequently identified as the property of Oscar Brodski, found upon his person. But he was never brought to trial, for on the return voyage he contrived to elude his guards for an instant as the ship was approaching the English coast, and it was not until three days later, when a hand-cuffed body was cast up on the lonely shore by Orfordness, that the authorities knew the fate of Silas Hickler.

"An appropriate and dramatic end to a singular and yet typical case," said Thorndyke, as he put down the newspaper. "I hope it has enlarged your knowledge, Jervis, and enabled you to form one or two useful corollaries."

"I prefer to hear you sing the medico-legal doxology," I answered, turning upon him like the proverbial worm and grinning derisively (which the worm does not).

"I know you do," he retorted, with mock gravity, "and I lament your lack of mental initiative. However, the points that this case illustrates are these: First, the danger of delay; the vital importance of instant action before that frail and fleeting thing that we call a clue has time to evaporate. A delay of a few hours would have left us with hardly a single datum. Second, the necessity of pursuing the most trivial clue to an absolute finish, as illustrated by the spectacles. Third, the urgent need of a trained scientist to aid the police; and, last," he concluded, with a smile, "we learn never to go abroad without the invaluable green case."

A Case of Premeditation

Part I. The Elimination of Mr. Pratt

The wine merchant who should supply a consignment of petit vin to a customer who had ordered, and paid for, a vintage wine, would render himself subject to unambiguous comment. Nay! more; he would be liable to certain legal penalties. And yet his conduct would be morally indistinguishable from that of the railway company which, having accepted a first-class fare, inflicts upon the passenger that kind of company which he has paid to avoid. But the corporate conscience, as Herbert Spencer was wont to explain, is an altogether inferior product to that of the individual.

Such were the reflections of Mr. Rufus Pembury when, as the train was about to move out of Maidstone (West) station, a coarse and burly man (clearly a denizen of the third-class) was ushered into his compartment by the guard. He had paid the higher fare, not for cushioned seats, but for seclusion or, at least, select companionship. The man's entry had deprived him of both, and he resented it.

But if the presence of this stranger involved a breach of contract, his conduct was a positive affront--an indignity; for, no sooner had the train started than he fixed upon Mr. Pembury a gaze of impertinent intensity, and continued thereafter to regard him with a stare as steady and unwinking as that of a Polynesian idol.

It was offensive to a degree, and highly disconcerting withal. Mr. Pembury fidgeted in his seat with increasing discomfort and rising temper. He looked into his pocket-book, read one or two letters and sorted a collection of visiting-cards. He even thought of opening his umbrella. Finally, his patience exhausted and his wrath mounting to boiling-point, he turned to the stranger with frosty remonstrance.

"I imagine, sir, that you will have no difficulty in recognizing me, should we ever meet again--which God forbid."

"I should recognize you among ten thousand," was the reply, so unexpected as to leave Mr. Pembury speechless.

"You see," the stranger continued impressively, "I've got the gift of faces. I never forget."

"That must be a great consolation," said Pembury.

"It's very useful to me," said the stranger, "at least, it used to be, when I was a warder at Portland--you remember me, I dare say: my name is Pratt. I was assistant-warder in your time. God-forsaken hole, Portland, and mighty glad I was when they used to send me up to town on reckernizing duty. Holloway was the house of detention then, you remember; that was before they moved to Brixton."

Pratt paused in his reminiscences, and Pembury, pale and gasping with astonishment, pulled himself together.

"I think," said he, "you must be mistaking me for some one else."

"I don't," replied Pratt. "You're Francis Dobbs, that's who you are. Slipped away from Portland one evening about twelve years ago. Clothes washed up on the Bill next day. No trace of fugitive. As neat a mizzle as ever I heard of. But there are a couple of photographs and a set of fingerprints at the Habitual Criminals Register. P'r'aps you'd like to come and see 'em?"

"Why should I go to the Habitual Criminals Register?" Pembury demanded faintly.

"Ah! Exactly. Why should you? When you are a man of means, and a little judiciously invested capital would render it unnecessary?"

Pembury looked out of the window, and for a minute or more preserved a stony silence. At length he turned suddenly to Pratt. "How much?" he asked.

"I shouldn't think a couple of hundred a year would hurt you," was the calm reply.

Pembury reflected awhile. "What makes you think I am a man of means?" he asked presently.

Pratt smiled grimly. "Bless you, Mr. Pembury," said he, "I know all about you. Why, for the last six months I have been living within half-a-mile of your house."

"The devil you have!"

"Yes. When I retired from the service, General O'Gorman engaged me as a sort of steward or caretaker of his little place at Baysford--he's very seldom there himself--and the very day after I came down, I met you and spotted you, but, naturally, I kept out of sight myself. Thought I'd find out whether you were good for anything before I spoke, so I've been keeping my ears open and I find you are good for a couple of hundred."

There was an interval of silence, and then the ex-warder resumed--"That's what comes of having a memory for faces. Now there's Jack Ellis, on the other hand; he must have had you under his nose for a couple of years, and yet he's never twigged--he never will either," added Pratt, already regretting the confidence into which his vanity had led him.

"Who is Jack Ellis?" Pembury demanded sharply.

"Why, he's a sort of supernumerary at the Baysford Police Station; does odd jobs; rural detective, helps in the office and that sort of thing. He was in the Civil Guard at Portland, in your time, but he got his left forefinger chopped off, so they pensioned him, and, as he was a Baysford man, he got this billet. But he'll never reckernize you, don't you fear."

"Unless you direct his attention to me," suggested Pembury.

"There's no fear of that," laughed Pratt. "You can trust me to sit quiet on my own nest-egg. Besides, we're not very friendly. He came nosing round our place after the parlour maid--him a married man, mark you! But I soon boosted him out, I can tell you; and Jack Ellis don't like me now."

"I see," said Pembury reflectively; then, after a pause, he asked: "Who is this General O'Gorman? I seem to know the name."

"I expect you do," said Pratt. "He was governor of Dartmoor when I was there--that was my last billet--and, let me tell you, if he'd been at Portland in your time, you'd never have got away."

"How is that?"

"Why, you see, the general is a great man on bloodhounds. He kept a pack at Dartmoor and, you bet, those lags knew it. There were no attempted escapes in those days. They wouldn't have had a chance."

"He has the pack still, hasn't he?" asked Pembury.

"Rather. Spends any amount of time on training 'em, too. He's always hoping there'll be a burglary or a murder in the neighbourhood so as he can try 'em, but he's never got a chance yet. P'r'aps the crooks have heard about 'em. But, to come back to our little arrangement: what do you say to a couple of hundred, paid quarterly, if you like?"

"I can't settle the matter off-hand," said Pembury. "You must give me time to think it over."

"Very well," said Pratt. "I shall be back at Baysford tomorrow evening. That will give you a clear day to think it over. Shall I look in at your place to-morrow night?"

"No," replied Pembury; "you'd better not be seen at my house, nor I at yours. If I meet you at some quiet spot, where we shan't be seen, we can settle our business without any one knowing that we have met. It won't take long, and we can't be too careful."

"That's true," agreed Pratt. "Well, I'll tell you what. There's an avenue leading up to our house; you know it, I expect. There's no lodge, and the gates are always ajar, excepting at night. Now I shall be down by the six-thirty at Baysford. Our place is a quarter of an hour from the station. Say you meet me in the avenue at a quarter to seven."

"That will suit me," said Pembury; "that is, if you are sure the bloodhounds won't be straying about the grounds."

"Lord bless you, no!" laughed Pratt. "D'you suppose the general lets his precious hounds stray about for any casual crook to feed with poisoned sausage? No, they're locked up safe in the kennels at the back of the house. Hallo! This'll be Swanley, I expect. I'll change into a smoker here and leave you time to turn the matter over in your mind. So long. To-morrow evening in the avenue at a quarter to seven. And, I say, Mr. Pembury, you might as well bring the first instalment with you--fifty, in small notes or gold."

"Very well," said Mr. Pembury. He spoke coldly enough, but there was a flush on his cheeks and an angry light in his eyes, which, perhaps, the ex-warder noticed; for when he had stepped out and shut the door, he thrust his head in at the window and said threateningly -

"One more word, Mr. Pembury-Dobbs: no hanky-panky, you know. I'm an old hand and pretty fly, I am. So don't you try any chickery-pokery on me. That's all." He withdrew his head and disappeared, leaving Pembury to his reflections.

The nature of those reflections, if some telepathist? transferring his attention for the moment from hidden courtyards or missing thimbles to more practical matters--could have conveyed them into the mind of Mr. Pratt, would have caused that quondam official some surprise and, perhaps, a little disquiet. For long experience of the criminal, as he appears when in durance, had produced some rather misleading ideas as to his behaviour when at large. In fact, the ex-warder had considerably under-estimated the ex-convict.

Rufus Pembury, to give his real name--for Dobbs was literally a nom de guerre--was a man of strong character and intelligence. So much so that, having tried the criminal career and found it not worth pursuing, he had definitely abandoned it. When the cattle-boat that picked him up off Portland Bill had landed him at an American port, he brought his entire ability and energy to bear on legitimate commercial pursuits, and with such success that, at the end of ten years, he was able to return to England with a moderate competence. Then he had taken a modest house near the little town of Baysford, where he had lived quietly on his savings for the last two years, holding aloof without much difficulty from the rather exclusive local society; and here he might have lived out the rest of his life in peace but for the unlucky chance that brought the man Pratt into the neighbourhood. With the arrival of Pratt his security was utterly destroyed.

There is something eminently unsatisfactory about a blackmailer. No arrangement with him has any permanent validity. No undertaking that he gives is binding. The thing which he has sold remains in his possession to sell over again. He pockets the price of emancipation, but retains the key of the fetters. In short, the blackmailer is a totally impossible person.

Such were the considerations that had passed through the mind of Rufus Pembury, even while Pratt was making his proposals; and those proposals he had never for an instant entertained. The ex-warder's advice to him to "turn the matter over in his mind" was unnecessary. For his mind was already made up. His decision was arrived at in the very moment when Pratt had disclosed his identity. The conclusion was self-evident. Before Pratt appeared he was living in peace and security. While Pratt remained, his liberty was precarious from moment to moment. If Pratt should disappear, his peace and security would return. Therefore Pratt must be eliminated.

It was a logical consequence.

The profound meditations, therefore, in which Pembury remained immersed for the remainder of the journey, had nothing whatever to do with the quarterly allowance; they were concerned exclusively with the elimination of ex-warder Pratt.

Now Rufus Pembury was not a ferocious man. He was not even cruel. But he was gifted with a certain magnanimous cynicism which ignored the trivialities of sentiment and regarded only the main issues. If a wasp hummed over his tea-cup, he would crush that wasp; but not with his bare hand. The wasp carried the means of aggression. That was the wasp's look-out. His concern was to avoid being stung.

So it was with Pratt. The man had elected, for his own profit, to threaten Pembury's liberty. Very well. He had done it at his own risk. That risk was no concern of Pembury's. His concern was his own safety.

When Pembury alighted at Charing Cross, he directed his steps (after having watched" Pratt's departure from the station) to Buckingham Street, Strand, where he entered a quiet private hotel. He was apparently expected, for the manageress greeted him by his name as she handed him his key.

"Are you staying in town, Mr. Pembury?" she asked.

"No," was the reply. "I go back to-morrow morning, but I may be coming up again shortly. By the way, you used to have an encyclopaedia in one of the rooms. Could I see it for a moment?"

"It is in the drawing-room," said the manageress. "Shall I show you--but you know the way, don't you?"

Certainly Mr. Pembury knew the way. It was on the first floor; a pleasant old-world room looking on the quiet old street; and on a shelf, amidst a collection of novels, stood the sedate volumes of Chambers's Encyclopaedia.

That a gentleman from the country should desire to look up the subject of "hounds" would not, to a casual observer, have seemed unnatural. But when from hounds the student proceeded to the article on blood, and thence to one devoted to perfumes, the observer might reasonably have felt some surprise; and this surprise might have been augmented if he had followed Mr. Pembury's subsequent proceedings, and specially if he had considered them as the actions of a man whose immediate aim was the removal of a superfluous unit of the population.

Having deposited his bag and umbrella in his room, Pembury set forth from the hotel as one with a definite purpose; and his footsteps led, in the first place, to an umbrella shop on the Strand, where he selected a thick rattan cane. There was nothing remarkable in this, perhaps; but the cane was of an uncomely thickness and the salesman protested. "I like a thick cane," said Pembury.

"Yes, sir; but for a gentleman of your height" (Pembury was a small, slightly-built man) "I would venture to suggest -?"

"I like a thick cane," repeated Pembury. "Cut it down to the proper length and don't rivet the ferrule on. I'll cement it on when I get home."

His next investment would have seemed more to the purpose, though suggestive of unexpected crudity of method. It was a large Norwegian knife. But not content with this he went on forthwith to a second cutler's and purchased a second knife, the exact duplicate of the first. Now, for what purpose could he want two identically similar knives? And why not have bought them both at the same shop? It was highly mysterious.

Shopping appeared to be a positive mania with Rufus Pembury. In the course of the next half-hour he acquired a cheap hand-bag, an artist's black-japanned brush-case, a; three-cornered file, a stick of elastic glue and a pair of iron crucible-tongs. Still insatiable, he repaired to an old-fashioned chemist's shop in a by-street, where he further enriched himself with a packet of absorbent cotton-wool and an ounce of permanganate of potash; and, as the chemist wrapped up these articles, with the occult and necromantic air peculiar to chemists, Pembury watched him impassively.

"I suppose you don't keep musk?" he asked carelessly.

The chemist paused in the act of heating a stick of sealing-wax, and appeared as if about to mutter an incantation. But he merely replied: "No, sir. Not the solid musk; it's so very costly. But I have the essence."

"That isn't as strong as the pure stuff, I suppose?"

"No," replied the chemist, with a cryptic smile, "not so strong, but strong enough. These animal perfumes are so very penetrating, you know; and so lasting. Why, I venture to say that if you were to sprinkle a table-spoonful of the essence in the middle of St. Paul's, the place would smell of it six months hence."

"You don't say so!" said Pembury. "Well, that ought to be enough for anybody. I'll take a small quantity, please, and, for goodness' sake, see that there isn't any on the outside of the bottle. The stuff isn't for myself, and I don't want to go about smelling like a civet cat."

"Naturally you don't, sir," agreed the chemist. He then produced an ounce bottle, a small glass funnel and a stoppered bottle labelled "Ess. Moschi," with which he proceeded to perform a few trifling feats of legerdemain.

"There, sir," said he, when he had finished the performance, "there is not a drop on the outside of the bottle, and, if I fit it with a rubber cork, you will be quite secure."

Pembury's dislike of musk appeared to be excessive, for, when the chemist had retired into a secret cubicle as if to hold converse with some familiar spirit (but actually to change half-a-crown), he took the brush-case from his bag, pulled off its lid, and then, with the crucible-tongs, daintily lifted the bottle off the counter, slid it softly into the brush-case, and, replacing the lid, returned the case and tongs to the bag. The other two packets he took from the counter and dropped into his pocket, and, when the presiding wizard, having miraculously transformed a single half-crown into four pennies, handed him the product, he left the shop and walked thoughtfully back towards the Strand. Suddenly a new idea seemed to strike him. He halted, considered for a few moments and then strode away northward to make the oddest of all his purchases.

The transaction took place in a shop in the Seven Dials, whose strange stock-in-trade ranged the whole zoological gamut, from water-snails to Angora cats. Pembury looked at a cage of guinea-pigs in the window and entered the shop.

"Do you happen to have a dead guinea-pig?" he asked.

"No; mine are all alive," replied the man, adding, with a sinister grin: "But they're not immortal, you know."

Pembury looked at the man distastefully. There is an appreciable difference between a guinea-pig and a blackmailer. "Any small mammal would do," he said.

"There's a dead rat in that cage, if he's any good," said the man. "Died this morning, so he's quite fresh."

"I'll take the rat," said Pembury; "he'll do quite well."

The little corpse was accordingly made into a parcel and deposited in the bag, and Pembury, having tendered a complimentary fee, made his way back to the hotel.

After a modest lunch he went forth and spent the remainder of the day transacting the business which had originally brought him to town. He dined at a restaurant and did not return to his hotel until ten o'clock, when he took his key, and tucking under his arm a parcel that he had brought in with him, retired for the night. But before undressing--and after locking his door--he did a very strange and unaccountable thing. Having pulled off the loose ferrule from his newly-purchased cane, he bored a hole in the bottom of it with the spike end of the file. Then, using the latter as a broach, he enlarged the hole until only a narrow rim of the bottom was left. He next rolled up a small ball of cottonwool and pushed it into the ferrule; and having smeared the end of the cane with elastic glue, he replaced the ferrule, warming it over the gas to make the gluc stick.

When he had finished with the cane, he turned his attention to one of the Norwegian knives. First, he carefully removed with the file most of the bright, yellow varnish from the wooden case or handle.

Then he opened the knife, and, cutting the string of the parcel that he had brought in, took from it the dead rat which he had bought at the zoologist's. Laying the animal on a sheet of paper, he cut off its head, and, holding it up by the tail, allowed the blood that oozed from the neck to drop on the knife, spreading it over both sides of the blade and handle with his finger.

Then he laid the knife on the paper and softly opened the window. From the darkness below came the voice of a cat, apparently perfecting itself in the execution of chromatic scales; and in that direction Pembury flung the body and head of the rat, and closed the window. Finally, having washed his hands and stuffed the paper from the parcel into the fire-place, he went to bed.

But his proceedings in the morning were equally mysterious. Having breakfasted betimes, he returned to his bedroom and locked himself in. Then he tied his new cane, handle downwards, to the leg of the dressing-table. Next, with the crucible-tongs, he drew the little bottle of musk from the brush-case, and, having assured himself, by sniffing at it, that the exterior was really free from odour, he withdrew the rubber cork. Then, slowly and with infinite care, he poured a few drops-- perhaps half-a-teaspoonful--of the essence on the cotton-wool that bulged through the hole in the ferrule, watching the absorbent material narrowly as it soaked up the liquid. When it was saturated he proceeded to treat the knife in the same fashion, letting fall a drop of the essence on the wooden handle--which soaked it up readily. This done, he slid up the window and looked out. Immediately below was a tiny yard in which grew, or rather survived, a couple of faded laurel bushes. The body of the rat was nowhere to be seen; it had apparently been spirited away in the night. Holding out the bottle, which he still held, he dropped it into the bushes, flinging the rubber cork after it.

His next proceeding was to take a tube of vaseline from his dressing-bag and squeeze a small quantity onto his fingers. With this he thoroughly smeared the shoulder of the brush-case and the inside of the lid, so as to ensure an air-tight joint. Having wiped his fingers, he picked the knife up with the crucible-tongs, and, dropping it into the brush-case, immediately pushed on the lid. Then he heated the tips of the tongs in the gas flame to destroy the scent, packed the tongs and brush-case in the bag, untied the cane--carefully avoiding contact with the ferrule-- and, taking up the two bags, went out, holding the cane by its middle.

There was no difficulty in finding an empty compartment, for first-class passengers were few at that time in the morning. Pembury waited on the platform until the guard's whistle sounded, when he stepped into the compartment, shut the door and laid the cane on the seat with its ferrule projecting out of the off-side window, in which position it remained until the train drew up in Baysford station.

Pembury left his dressing-bag at the cloak-room, and, still grasping the cane by its middle, he sallied forth. The town of Baysford lay some half-a-mile to the east of the station; his own house was a mile along the road to the west; and half-way between his house and the station was the residence of General O'Gorman. He knew the place well. Originally a farmhouse, it stood on the edge of a great expanse of flat meadows and communicated with the road by an avenue, nearly three hundred yards long, of ancient trees. The avenue was shut off from the road by a pair of iron gates, but these were merely ornamental, for the place was unenclosed and accessible from the surrounding meadows--indeed, an indistinct footpath crossed the meadows and intersected the avenue about half-way up.

On this occasion Pembury, whose objective was the avenue, elected to approach it by the latter route; and at each stile or fence that he surmounted, he paused to survey the country. Presently the avenue arose before him, lying athwart the narrow track, and, as he entered it between two of the trees, he halted and looked about him.

He stood listening for a while. Beyond the faint rustle of leaves no sound was to be heard. Evidently there was no one about, and, as Pratt was at large, it was probable that the general was absent.

And now Pembury began to examine the adjacent trees with more than a casual interest. The two between which he had entered were respectively an elm and a great pollard oak, the latter being an immense tree whose huge, warty bole divided about seven feet from the ground into three limbs, each as large as a fair-sized tree, of which the largest swept outward in a great curve half-way across the avenue. On this patriarch Pembury bestowed especial attention, walking completely round it and finally laying down his bag and cane (the latter resting on the bag with the ferrule off the ground) that he might climb up, by the aid of the warty outgrowths, to examine the crown; and he had just stepped up into the space between the three limbs, when the creaking of the iron gates was followed by a quick step in the avenue. Hastily he let himself down from the tree, and, gathering up his possessions, stood close behind the great bole.

"Just as well not to be seen," was his reflection, as he hugged the tree closely and waited, peering cautiously round the trunk. Soon a streak of moving shadow heralded the stranger's approach, and he moved round to keep the trunk between himself and the intruder. On the footsteps came, until the stranger was abreast of the tree; and when he had passed Pembury peeped round at the retreating figure. It was only the postman, but then the man knew him, and he was glad he had kept out of sight.

Apparently the oak did not meet his requirements, for he stepped out and looked up and down the avenue. Then, beyond the elm, he caught sight of an ancient pollard hornbeam--a strange, fantastic tree whose trunk widened out trumpet-like above into a broad crown, from the edge of which multitudinous branches uprose like the limbs of some weird hamadryad.

That tree he approved at a glance, but he lingered behind the oak until the postman, returning with brisk step and cheerful whistle, passed down the avenue and left him once more in solitude. Then he moved on with a resolute air to the hornbeam.

The crown of the trunk was barely six feet from the ground. He could reach it easily, as he found on trying. Standing the cane against the tree--ferrule downwards, this time--he took the brush-case from the bag, pulled off the lid, and, with the crucible-tongs, lifted out the knife and laid it on the crown of the tree, just out of sight, leaving the tongs? also invisible--still grasping the knife. He was about to replace the brush-case in the bag, when he appeared-to alter his mind. Sniffing at it, and finding it reeking with the sickly perfume, he pushed the lid on again and threw the case up into the tree, where he heard it roll down into the central hollow of the crown. Then he closed the bag, and, taking the cane by its handle, moved slowly away in the direction whence he had come, passing out of the avenue between the elm and the oak.

His mode of progress was certainly peculiar. He walked with excessive slowness, trailing the cane along the ground, and every few paces he would stop and press the ferrule firmly against the earth, so that, to any one who should have observed him, he would have appeared to be wrapped in an absorbing reverie.

Thus he moved on across the fields, not, however, returning to the high road, but crossing another stretch of fields until he emerged into a narrow lane that led out into the High Street. Immediately opposite to the lane was the police station, distinguished from the adjacent cottages only by its lamp, its open door and the notices pasted up outside. Straight across the road Pembury walked, still trailing the cane, and halted at the station door to read the notices, resting his cane on the doorstep as he did so. Through the open doorway he could see a man writing at a desk. The man's back was towards him, but, presently, a movement brought his left hand into view, and Pembury noted that the forefinger was missing. This, then, was Jack Ellis, late of the Civil Guard at Portland.

Even while he was looking the man turned his head, and Pembury recognized him at once. He had frequently met him on the road between Baysford and the adjoining village of Thorpe, and always at the same time. Apparently Ellis paid a daily visit to Thorpe--perhaps to receive a report from the rural constable--and he started between three and four and returned between seven and a quarter past.

Pembury looked at his watch. It was a quarter past three. He moved away thoughtfully (holding his cane, now, by the middle), and began to walk slowly in the direction of Thorpe--westward.

For a while he was deeply meditative, and his face wore a puzzled frown. Then, suddenly, his face cleared and he strode forward at a brisker pace. Presently he passed through a gap in the hedge, and, walking in a field parallel with the road, took out his purse--a small pigskin pouch.

Having frugally emptied it of its contents, excepting a few shillings, he thrust the ferrule of his cane into the small compartment ordinarily reserved for gold or notes.

And thus he continued to walk on slowly, carrying the cane by the middle and the purse jammed on the end.

At length he reached a sharp double curve in the road whence he could see back for a considerable distance; and here opposite a small opening, he sat down to wait. The hedge screened him effectually from the gaze of passers-by--though these were few enough--without interfering with his view.

A quarter of an hour passed. He began to be uneasy. Had he been mistaken? Were Ellis's visits only occasional instead of daily, as he had thought? That would be tiresome though not actually disastrous. But at this point in his reflections a figure came into view, advancing along the road with a steady swing. He recognized the figure. It was Ellis.

But there was another figure advancing from the opposite direction: a labourer, apparently. He prepared to shift his ground, but another glance showed him that the labourer would pass first. He waited. The labourer came on and, at length, passed the opening, and, as he did so, Ellis disappeared for a moment in a bend of the road. Instantly Pembury passed his cane through the opening in the hedge, shook off the purse and pushed it into the middle of the foot-way. Then he crept forward, behind the hedge, towards the approaching official, and again sat down to wait. On came the steady tramp of the unconscious Ellis, and, as it passed, Pembury drew aside an obstructing branch and peered out at the retreating figure. The question now was, would Ellis see the purse? It was not a very conspicuous object.

The footsteps stopped abruptly. Looking out, Pembury saw the police official stoop, pick up the purse, examine its contents and finally stow it in his trousers pocket. Pembury heaved a sigh of relief; and, as the dwindling figure passed out of sight round a curve in the road, he rose, stretched himself and strode away briskly.

Near the gap was a group of ricks, and, as he passed them, a fresh idea suggested itself. Looking round quickly he passed to the farther side of one and, thrusting his cane deeply into it, pushed it home with a piece of stick that he picked up near the rick, until the handle was lost among the straw. The bag was now all that was left, and it was empty--for his other purchases were in the dressing-bag, which, by the way, he must fetch from the station. He opened it and smelt the interior, but, though he could detect no odour, he resolved to be rid of it if possible.

As he emerged from the gap a wagon jogged slowly past. It was piled high with sacks, and the tail-board Was down. Stepping into the road, he quickly overtook the wagon, and, having glanced round, laid the bag lightly on the tail-board. Then he set off for the station.

On arriving home he went straight up to his bedroom, and, ringing for his housekeeper, ordered a substantial meal. Then he took off his clothes and deposited them, even to his shirt, socks and necktie, in a trunk, wherein his summer clothing was stored with a plentiful sprinkling of naphthol to preserve it from the moth. Taking the packet of permanganate of potash from his dressing-bag, he passed into the adjoining bathroom, and, tipping the crystals into the bath, turned on the water. Soon the bath was filled with a pink solution of the salt, and into this he plunged, immersing his entire body and thoroughly soaking his hair. Then he emptied the bath and rinsed himself in clear water, and, having dried himself, returned to the bedroom and dressed himself in fresh clothing. Finally he took a hearty meal, and then lay down on the sofa to rest until it should be time to start for the rendezvous.

Half-past six found him lurking in the shadow by the station-approach, within sight of the solitary lamp. He heard the train come in, saw the stream of passengers emerge, and noted one figure detach itself from the throng and turn on to the Thorpe road. It was Pratt, as the lamplight showed him; Pratt, striding forward to the meeting-place with an air of jaunty satisfaction and an uncommonly creaky pair of boots.

Pembury followed him at a safe distance, and rather by sound than sight, until he was well past the stile at the entrance to the footpath. Evidently he was going on to the gates. Then Pembury vaulted over the stile and strode away swiftly across the dark meadows.

When he plunged into the deep gloom of the avenue, his first act was to grope his way to the hornbeam and slip his hand up onto the crown and satisfy himself that the tongs were as he had left them. Reassured by the touch of his fingers on the iron loops, he turned and walked slowly down the avenue. The duplicate knife--ready opened--was in his left inside breast-pocket, and he fingered its handle as he walked.

Presently the iron gate squeaked mournfully, and then the rhythmical creak of a pair of boots was audible, coming up the avenue. Pembury walked forward slowly until a darker smear emerged from the surrounding gloom, when he called out -

"Is that you, Pratt?"

"That's me," was the cheerful, if ungrammatical response, and, as he drew nearer, the ex-warder asked: "Have you brought the rhino, old man?"

The insolent familiarity of the man's tone was agreeable to Pembury: it strengthened his nerve and hardened his heart. "Of course," he replied; "but we must have a definite understanding, you know."

"Look here," said Pratt, "I've got no time for jaw. The General will be here presently; he's riding over from Bingfield with a friend. You hand over the dibs and we'll talk some other time."

"That is all very well," said Pembury, "but you must understand -?" He paused abruptly and stood still. They were now close to the hornbeam, and, as he stood, he stared up into the dark mass of foliage.

"What's the matter?" demanded Pratt. "What are you staring at?" He, too, had halted and stood gazing intently into the darkness.

Then, in an instant, Pembury whipped out the knife and drove it, with all his strength, into the broad back of the ex-warder, below the left shoulder-blade.

With a hideous yell Pratt turned and grappled with his assailant. A powerful man and a competent wrestler, too, he was far more than a match for Pembury unarmed, and, in a moment, he had him by the throat. But Pembury clung to him tightly, and, as they trampled to and fro and round and round, he stabbed again and again with the viciousness of a scorpion, while Pratt's cries grew more gurgling and husky. Then they fell heavily to the ground, Pembury underneath. But the struggle was over. With a last bubbling groan, Pratt relaxed his hold and in a moment grew limp and inert. Pembury pushed him off and rose, trembling and breathing heavily.

But he wasted no time. There had been more noise than he had bargained for. Quickly stepping up to the hornbeam, he reached up for the tongs. His fingers slid into the looped handles; the tongs grasped the knife, and he lifted it out from its hiding-place and carried it to where the corpse lay, depositing it on the ground a few feet from the body. Then he went back to the tree and carefully pushed the tongs over into the hollow of the crown.

At this moment a woman's voice sounded shrilly from the top of the avenue.

"Is that you, Mr. Pratt?" it called.

Pembury started and then stepped back quickly, on tiptoe, to the body. For there was the duplicate knife. He must take that away at all costs.

The corpse was lying on its back. The knife was underneath it, driven in to the very haft. He had to use both hands to lift the body, and even then he had some difficulty in disengaging the weapon. And, meanwhile, the voice, repeating its question, drew nearer.

At length he succeeded in drawing out the knife and thrust it into his breast-pocket. The corpse fell back, and he stood up gasping.

"Mr. Pratt! Are you there?" The nearness of the voice startled Pembury, and, turning sharply, he saw a light twinkling between the trees. And then the gates creaked loudly and he heard the crunch of a horse's hoofs on the gravel.

He stood for an instant bewildered--utterly taken by surprise. He had not reckoned on a horse. His intended flight across the meadows towards Thorpe was now impracticable. If he were overtaken he was lost, for he knew there was blood on his clothes and his hands were wet and slippery-- to say nothing of the knife in his pocket.

But his confusion lasted only for an instant. He remembered the oak tree; and, turning out of the avenue, he ran to it, and, touching it as little as he could with his bloody hands, climbed quickly up into the crown. The great horizontal limb was nearly three feet in diameter, and, as he lay out on it, gathering his coat closely round him, he was quite invisible from below.

He had hardly settled himself when the light which he had seen came into full view, revealing a woman advancing with a stable lantern in her hand. And, almost at the same moment, a streak of brighter light burst from the opposite direction. The horseman was accompanied by a man on a bicycle.

The two men came on apace, and the horseman, sighting the woman, called out: "Anything the matter, Mrs. Parton?" But, at that moment, the light of the bicycle lamp fell full on the prostrate corpse. The two men uttered a simultaneous cry of horror; the woman shrieked aloud: and then the horseman sprang from the saddle and ran forward to the body.

"Why," he exclaimed, stooping over it, "it's Pratt;" and, as the cyclist came up and the glare of his lamp shone on a great pool of blood, he added: "There's been foul play here, Hanford."

Hanford flashed his lamp around the body, lighting up the ground for several yards.

"What is that behind you, O'Gorman?" he said suddenly; "isn't it a knife?" He was moving quickly towards it when O'Gorman held up his hand.

"Don't touch it!" he exclaimed. "We'll put the hounds onto it. They'll soon track the scoundrel, whoever he is. By God! Hanford, this fellow has fairly delivered himself into our hands." He stood for a few moments looking down at the knife with something uncommonly like exultation, and then, turning quickly to his friend, said: "Look here, Hanford; you ride off to the police station as hard as you can pelt. It is only three-quarters of a mile; you'll do it in five minutes. Send or bring an officer and I'll scour the meadows meanwhile. If I haven't got the scoundrel when you come back, we'll put the hounds onto this knife and run the beggar down."

"Right," replied Hanford, and without another word he wheeled his machine about, mounted and rode away into the darkness.

"Mrs. Parton," said O'Gorman, "watch that knife. See that nobody touches it while I go and examine the meadows."

"Is Mr. Pratt dead, sir?" whimpered Mrs. Parton.

"Gad! I hadn't thought of that," said the general. "You'd better have a look at him; but mind! nobody is to touch that knife or they will confuse the scent."

He scrambled into the saddle and galloped away across the meadows in the direction of Thorpe; and, as Pembury listened to the diminuendo of the horse's hoofs, he was glad that he had not attempted to escape; for that was the direction in which he had meant to go, and he would surely have been overtaken.

As soon as the general was gone, Mrs. Parton, with many a terror-stricken glance over her shoulder, approached the corpse and held the lantern close to the dead face. Suddenly she stood up, trembling violently, for footsteps were audible coming down the avenue. A familiar voice reassured her.

"Is anything wrong, Mrs. Parton?" The question proceeded from one of the maids who had come in search of the elder woman, escorted by a young man, and the pair now came out into the circle of light.

"Good God!" ejaculated the man. "Who's that?"

"It's Mr. Pratt," replied Mrs. Parton. "He's been murdered."

The girl screamed, and then the two domestics approached on tiptoe, staring at the corpse with the fascination of horror.

"Don't touch that knife," said Mrs. Parton, for the man was about to pick it up. "The general's going to put the bloodhounds onto it."

"Is the general here, then?" asked the man; and, as he spoke, the drumming of hoofs, growing momentarily louder, answered him from the meadow.

O'Gorman reined in his horse as he perceived the group of servants gathered about the corpse. "Is he dead, Mrs. Parton?" he asked.

"I am afraid so, sir," was the reply.

"Ha! Somebody ought to go for the doctor; but not you, Bailey. I want you to get the hounds ready and wait with them at the top of the avenue until I call you."

He was off again into the Baysford meadows, and Bailey hurried away, leaving the two women staring at the body and talking in whispers.

Pembury's position was cramped and uncomfortable. He dared not move, hardly dared to breathe, for the women below him were not a dozen yards away; and it was with mingled feelings of relief and apprehension that he presently saw from his elevated station a group of lights approaching rapidly along the road from Baysford. Presently they were hidden by the trees, and then, after a brief interval, the whirr of wheels sounded on the drive and streaks of light on the tree-trunks announced the new arrivals. There were three bicycles, ridden respectively by Mr. Hanford, a police inspector and a sergeant; and, as they drew up, the general came thundering back into the avenue.

"Is Ellis with you?" he asked, as he pulled up.

"No, sir," was the reply. "He hadn't come in from Thorpe when we left. He's rather late to-night."

"Have you sent for a doctor?"

"Yes, sir, I've sent for Dr. Hills," said the inspector, resting his bicycle against the oak. Pembury could smell the reek of the lamp as he crouched. "Is Pratt dead?"

"Seems to be," replied O'Gorman, "but we'd better leave that to the doctor. There's the murderer's knife. Nobody has touched it. I'm going to fetch the bloodhounds now."

"Ah! that's the thing," said the inspector. "The man can't be far away." He rubbed his hands with a satisfied air as O'Gorman cantered away up the avenue.

In less than a minute there came out from the darkness the deep baying of a hound followed by quick footsteps on the gravel. Then into the circle of light emerged three sinister shapes, loose-limbed and gaunt, and two men advancing at a shambling trot.

"Here, inspector," shouted the general, "you take one; I can't hold 'em both."

The inspector ran forward and seized one of the leashes, and the general led his hound up to the knife, as it lay on the ground. Pembury, peering cautiously round the bough, watched the great brute with almost impersonal curiosity; noted its high poll, its wrinkled forehead and melancholy face as it stooped to snuff suspiciously at the prostrate knife.

For some moments the hound stood motionless, sniffing at the knife; then it turned away and walked to and fro with its muzzle to the ground. Suddenly it lifted its head, bayed loudly, lowered its muzzle and started forward between the oak and the elm, dragging the general after it at a run.

The inspector next brought his hound to the knife, and was soon bounding away to the tug of the leash in the general's wake.

"They don't make no mistakes, they don't," said Bailey, addressing the gratified sergeant, as he brought forward the third hound; "you'll see--?" But his remark was cut short by a violent jerk of the leash, and the next moment he was flying after the others, followed by Mr. Hanford.

The sergeant daintily picked the knife up by its ring, wrapped it in his handkerchief and bestowed it in his pocket. Then he ran off after the hounds.

Pembury smiled grimly. His scheme was working out admirably in spite of the unforeseen difficulties. If those confounded women would only go away, he could come down and take himself off while the course was clear. He listened to the baying of the hounds, gradually growing fainter in the increasing distance, and cursed the dilatoriness of the doctor. Confound the fellow! Didn't he realize that this was a case of life or death?

Suddenly his ear caught the tinkle of a bicycle bell; a fresh light appeared coming up the avenue and then a bicycle swept up swiftly to the scene of the tragedy, and a small elderly man jumped down by the side of the body. Giving his machine to Mrs. Parton, he stooped over the dead man, felt the wrist, pushed back an eyelid, held a match to the eye and then rose. "This is a shocking affair, Mrs. Parton," said he. "The poor fellow is quite dead. You had better help me to carry him to the house. If you two take the feet I will take the shoulders."

Pembury watched them raise the body and stagger away with it up the avenue. He heard their shuffling steps die away and the door of the house shut. And still he listened. From far away in the meadows came, at intervals, the baying of the hounds. Other sounds there was none. Presently the doctor would come back for his bicycle, but, for the moment, the coast was clear. Pembury rose stiffly. His hands had stuck to the tree where they had pressed against it, and they were still sticky and damp. Quickly he let himself down to the ground, listened again for a moment, and then, making a small circuit to avoid the lamplight, softly crossed the avenue and stole away across the Thorpe meadows.

The night was intensely dark, and not a soul was stirring in the meadows. He strode forward quickly, peering into the darkness and stopping now and again to listen; but no sound came to his ears, save the now faint baying of the distant hounds. Not far from his house, he remembered, was a deep ditch spanned by a wooden bridge, and towards this he now made his way; for he knew that his appearance was such as to convict him at a glance. Arrived at the ditch, he stooped to wash his hands and wrists; and, as he bent forward, the knife fell from his breast-pocket into the shallow water at the margin. He groped for it, and, having found it, drove it deep into the mud as far out as he could reach. Then he wiped his hands on some water-weed, crossed the bridge and started homewards.

He approached his house from the rear, satisfied himself that his housekeeper was in the kitchen, and, letting himself in very quietly with his key, went quickly up to his bedroom. Here he washed thoroughly--in the bath, so that he could get rid of the discoloured water--changed his clothes and packed those that he took off in a portmanteau.

By the time he had done this the gong sounded for supper. As he took his seat at the table, spruce and fresh in appearance, quietly cheerful in manner, he addressed his housekeeper. "I wasn't able to finish my business in London," he said. "I shall have to go up again tomorrow."

"Shall you come home the same day?" asked the housekeeper.

"Perhaps," was the reply, "and perhaps not. It will depend on circumstances."

He did not say what the circumstances might be, nor did the housekeeper ask. Mr. Pembury was not addicted to confidences. He was an eminently discreet man: and discreet men say little.

Part II. Rival Sleuth-Hounds

(Related by Christopher Jervis, M.D.)

The half-hour that follows breakfast, when the fire has, so to speak, got into its stride, and the morning pipe throws up its clouds of incense, is, perhaps, the most agreeable in the whole day. Especially so when a sombre sky, brooding over the town, hints at streets pervaded by the chilly morning air, and hoots from protesting tugs upon the river tell of lingering mists, the legacy of the lately-vanished night.

The autumn morning was raw: the fire burned jovially. I thrust my slippered feet towards the blaze and meditated, on nothing in particular, with cat-like enjoyment. Presently a disapproving grunt from Thorndyke attracted my attention, and I looked round lazily. He was extracting, with a pair of office shears, the readable portions of the morning paper, and had paused with a small cutting between his finger and thumb. "Bloodhounds again," said he. "We shall be hearing presently of the revival of the ordeal by fire."

"And a deuced comfortable ordeal, too, on a morning like this," I said, stroking my legs ecstatically. "What is the case?"

He was about to reply when a sharp rat-tat from the little brass knocker announced a disturber of our peace. Thorndyke stepped over to the door and admitted a police inspector in uniform, and I stood up, and, presenting my dorsal aspect to the fire, prepared to combine bodily comfort with attention to business.

"I believe I am speaking to Dr. Thorndyke," said the officer, and, as Thorndyke nodded, he went on: "My name, sir, is Fox, Inspector Fox of the Baysford Police. Perhaps you've seen the morning paper?"

Thorndyke held up the cutting, and, placing a chair by the fire, asked the inspector if he had breakfasted.

"Thank you, sir, I have," replied Inspector Fox. "I came up to town by the late train last night so as to be here early, and stayed at an hotel. You see, from the paper, that we have had to arrest one of our own men. That's rather awkward, you know, sir."

"Very," agreed Thorndyke.

"Yes; it's bad for the force and bad for the public too. But we had to do it. There was no way out that we could see. Still, we should like the accused to have every chance, both for our sake and his own, so the chief constable thought he'd like to have your opinion on the case, and he thought that, perhaps, you might be willing to act for the defence."

"Let us have the particulars," said Thorndyke, taking a writing-pad from a drawer and dropping into his armchair. "Begin at the beginning," he added, "and tell us all you know."

"Well," said the inspector, after a preliminary cough, "to begin with the murdered man: his name is Pratt. He was a retired prison warder, and was employed as steward by General O'Gorman, who is a retired prison governor--you may have heard of him in connection with his pack of bloodhounds. Well, Pratt came down from London yesterday evening by a train arriving at Baysford at six-thirty. He was seen by the guard, the ticket collector and the outside porter. The porter saw him leave the station at six-thirty-seven. General O'Gorman's house is about half-a-mile from the station. At five minutes to seven the general and a gentleman named Hanford and the general's housekeeper, a Mrs. Parton, found Pratt lying dead in the avenue that leads up to the house. He had apparently been stabbed, for there was a lot of blood about, and a knife--a Norwegian knife--was lying on the ground near the body. Mrs. Parton had thought she heard some one in the avenue calling out for help, and, as Pratt was just due, she came out with a lantern. She met the general and Mr. Hanford, and all three seem to have caught sight of the body at the same moment. Mr. Hanford cycled down to us, at once, with the news; we sent for a doctor, and I went back with Mr. Hanford and took a sergeant with me. We arrived at twelve minutes past seven, and then the general, who had galloped his horse over the meadows each side of the avenue without having seen anybody, fetched out his bloodhounds and led them up to the knife. All three hounds took up the scent at once--I held the leash of one of them--and they took us across the meadows without a pause or a falter, over stiles and fences, along a lane, out into the town, and then, one after the other, they crossed the road in a bee-line to the police station, bolted in at the door, which stood open, and made straight for the desk, where a supernumerary officer, named Ellis, was writing. They made a rare to-do, struggling to get at him, and it was as much as we could manage to hold them back. As for Ellis, he turned as pale as a ghost."

"Was any one else in the room?" asked Thorndyke.

"Oh, yes. There were two constables and a messenger. We led the hounds up to them, but the brutes wouldn't take any notice of them. They wanted Ellis."

"And what did you do?"

"Why, we arrested Ellis, of course. Couldn't do anything else-- especially with the general there."

"What had the general to do with it?" asked Thorndyke.

"He's a J.P. and a late governor of Dartmoor, and it was his hounds that had run the man down. But we must have arrested Ellis in any case."

"Is there anything against the accused man?"

"Yes, there is. He and Pratt were on distinctly unfriendly terms. They were old comrades, for Ellis was in the Civil Guard at Portland when Pratt was warder there--he was pensioned off from the service because he got his left forefinger chopped off--but lately they had had some unpleasantness about a woman, a parlour maid of the general's. It seems that Ellis, who is a married man, paid the girl too much attention--or Pratt thought he did--and Pratt warned Ellis off the premises. Since then they had not been on speaking terms."

"And what sort of a man is Ellis?"

"A remarkably decent fellow he always seemed; quiet, steady, good-natured; I should have said he wouldn't have hurt a fly. We all liked him--better than we liked Pratt, in fact; poor Pratt was what you'd call an old soldier--sly, you know, sir--and a bit of a sneak."

"You searched and examined Ellis, of course?"

"Yes. There was nothing suspicious about him except that he had two purses. But he says he picked up one of them? a small, pigskin pouch--on the footpath of the Thorpe road yesterday afternoon; and there's no reason to disbelieve him. At any rate, the purse was not Pratt's."

Thorndyke made a note on his pad, and then asked: "There were no blood-stains or marks on his clothing?"

"No. His clothing was not marked or disarranged in any way."

"Any cuts, scratches or bruises on his person?"

"None whatever," replied the inspector.

"At what time did you arrest Ellis?"

"Half-past seven exactly."

"Have you ascertained what his movements were? Had he been near the scene of the murder?"

"Yes; he had been to Thorpe and would pass the gates of the avenue on his way back. And he was later than usual in returning, though not later than he has often been before."

"And now, as to the murdered man: has the body been examined?"

"Yes; I had Dr. Hills's report before I left. There were no less than seven deep knife-wounds, all on the left side of the back. There was a great deal of blood on the ground, and Dr. Hills thinks Pratt must have bled to death in a minute or two."

"Do the wounds correspond with the knife that was found?"

"I asked the doctor that, and he said 'Yes,' though he wasn't going to swear to any particular knife. However, that point isn't of much importance. The knife was covered with blood, and it was found close to the body."

"What has been done with it, by the way?" asked Thorndyke.

"The sergeant who was with me picked it up and rolled it in his handkerchief to carry in his pocket. I took it from him, just as it was, and locked it in a dispatch-box."

"Has the knife been recognized as Ellis's property?"

"No, sir, it has not."

"Were there any recognizable footprints or marks of a struggle?" Thorndyke asked.

The inspector grinned sheepishly. "I haven't examined the spot, of course, sir," said he, "but, after the general's horse and the bloodhounds and the general on foot and me and the gardener and the sergeant and Mr. Hanford had been over it twice, going and returning, why, you see, sir -?"

"Exactly, exactly," said Thorndyke. "Well, inspector, I shall be pleased to act for the defence; it seems to me that the case against Ellis is in some respects rather inconclusive."

The inspector was frankly amazed. "It certainly hadn't struck me in that light, sir," he said.

"No? Well, that is my view; and I think the best plan will be for me to come down with you and investigate matters on the spot."

The inspector assented cheerfully, and, when we had provided him with a newspaper, we withdrew to the laboratory to consult time-tables and prepare for the expedition.

"You are coming, I suppose, Jervis?" said Thorndyke.

"If I shall be of any use," I replied.

"Of course you will," said he. "Two heads are better than one, and, by the look of things, I should say that ours will be the only ones with any sense in them. We will take the research case, of course, and we may as well have a camera with us. I see there is a train from Charing Cross in twenty minutes."

For the first half-hour of the journey Thorndyke sat in his corner, alternately conning over his notes and gazing with thoughtful eyes out of the window. I could see that the case pleased him, and was careful not to break in upon his train of thought. Presently, however, he put away his notes and began to fill his pipe with a more companionable air, and then the inspector, who had been wriggling with impatience, opened fire.

"So you think, sir, that you see a way out for Ellis?"

"I think there is a case for the defence," replied Thorndyke. "In fact, I call the evidence against him rather flimsy."

The inspector gasped. "But the knife, sir? What about the knife?"

"Well," said Thorndyke, "what about the knife? Whose knife was it? You don't know. It was covered with blood. Whose blood? You don't know. Let us assume, for the sake of argument, that it was the murderer's knife. Then the blood on it was Pratt's blood. But if it was Pratt's blood, when the hounds had smelt it they should have led you to Pratt's body, for blood gives a very strong scent. But they did not. They ignored the body. The inference seems to be that the blood on the knife was not Pratt's blood."

The inspector took off his cap and gently scratched the back of his head. "You're perfectly right, sir," he said. "I'd never thought of that. None of us had."

"Then," pursued Thorndyke, "let us assume that the knife was Pratt's. If so, it would seem to have been used in self-defence. But this was a Norwegian knife, a clumsy tool--not a weapon at all--which takes an appreciable time to open and requires the use of two free hands. Now, had Pratt both hands free? Certainly not after the attack had commenced. There were seven wounds, all on the left side of the back; which indicates that he held the murderer locked in his arms and that the murderer's arms were around him. Also, incidentally, that the murderer is right-handed. But, still, let us assume that the knife was Pratt's. Then the blood on it was that of the murderer. Then the murderer must have been wounded. But Ellis was not wounded. Then Ellis is not the murderer. The knife doesn't help us at all."

The inspector puffed out his cheeks and blew softly. "This is getting out of my depth," he said. "Still, sir, you can't get over the bloodhounds. They tell us distinctly that the knife is Ellis's knife and I don't see any answer to that."

"There is no answer because there has been no statement. The bloodhounds have told you nothing. You have drawn certain inferences from their actions, but those inferences may be totally wrong and they are certainly not evidence."

"You don't seem to have much opinion of bloodhounds," the inspector remarked.

"As agents for the detection of crime," replied Thorndyke, "I regard them as useless. You cannot put a bloodhound in the witness-box. You can get no intelligible statement from it. If it possesses any knowledge, it has no means of communicating it. The fact is," he continued, "that the entire system of using bloodhounds for criminal detection is based on a fallacy. In the American plantations these animals were used with great success for tracking runaway slaves. But the slave was a known individual. All that was required was to ascertain his whereabouts. That is not the problem that is presented in the detection of a crime. The detective is not concerned in establishing the whereabouts of a known individual, but in discovering the identity of an unknown individual. And for this purpose bloodhounds are useless. They may discover such identity, but they cannot communicate their knowledge. If the criminal is unknown, they cannot identify him: if he is known, the police have no need of the bloodhound.

"To return to our present case," Thorndyke resumed, after a pause; "we have employed certain agents--the hounds--with whom we are not en rapport, as the spiritualists would say; and we have no 'medium.' The hound possesses a special sense--the olfactory--which in man is quite rudimentary. He thinks, so to speak, in terms of smell, and his thoughts are untranslatable to beings in whom the sense of smell is undeveloped. We have presented to the hound a knife, and he discovers in it certain odorous properties; he discovers similar or related odorous properties in a tract of land and a human individual--Ellis. We cannot verify his discoveries or ascertain their nature. What remains? All that we can say is that there appears to exist some odorous relation between the knife and the man Ellis. But until we can ascertain the nature of that relation, we cannot estimate its evidential value or bearing. All the other 'evidence' is the product of your imagination and that of the general. There is, at present, no case against Ellis."

"He must have been pretty close to the place when the murder happened," said the inspector.

"So. probably, were many other people," answered Thorndyke; "but had he time to wash and change? Because he would have needed it."

"I suppose he would," the inspector agreed dubiously.

"Undoubtedly. There were seven wounds which would have taken some time to inflict. Now we can't suppose that Pratt stood passively while the other man stabbed him? indeed, as I have said, the position of the wounds shows that he did not. There was a struggle.

The two men were locked together. One of the murderer's hands was against Pratt's back; probably both hands were, one clasping and the other stabbing. There must have been blood on one hand and probably on both. But you say there was no blood on Ellis, and there doesn't seem to have been time or opportunity for him to wash."

"Well, it's a mysterious affair," said the inspector; "but I don't see how you are going to get over the bloodhounds."

Thorndyke shrugged his shoulders impatiently. "The bloodhounds are an obsession," he said. "The whole problem really centres around the knife. The questions are, Whose knife was it? and what was the connection between it and Ellis? There is a problem, Jervis," he continued, turning to me, "that I submit for your consideration. Some of the possible solutions are exceedingly curious."

As we set out from Baysford station, Thorndyke looked at his watch and noted the time. "You will take us the way that Pratt went," he said.

"As to that," said the inspector, "he may have gone by the road or by the footpath; but there's very little difference in the distance."

Turning away from Baysford, we walked along the road westward, towards the village of Thorpe, and presently passed on our right a stile at the entrance to a footpath.

"That path," said the inspector, "crosses the avenue about half-way up. But we'd better keep to the road." A quarter of a mile further on we came to a pair of rusty iron gates one of which stood open, and, entering, we found ourselves in a broad drive bordered by two rows of trees, between the trunks of which a long stretch of pasture meadows could be seen on either hand. It was a fine avenue, and, late in the year as it was, the yellowing foliage clustered thickly overhead.

When we had walked about a hundred and fifty yards from the gates, the inspector halted.

"This is the place," he said; and Thorndyke again noted the time.

"Nine minutes exactly," said he. "Then Pratt arrived here about fourteen minutes to seven, and his body was found at five minutes to seven--nine minutes after his arrival. The murderer couldn't have been far away then."

"No, it was a pretty fresh scent," replied the inspector. "You'd like to see the body first, I think you said, sir?"

"Yes; and the knife, if you please."

"I shall have to send down to the station for that. It's locked up in the office."

He entered the house, and, having dispatched a messenger to the police station, came out and conducted us to the outbuilding where the corpse had been deposited. Thorndyke made a rapid examination of the wounds and the holes in the clothing, neither of which presented anything particularly suggestive. The weapon used had evidently been a thick-backed, single-edged knife similar to the one described, and the discolouration around the wounds indicated that the weapon had a definite shoulder like that of a Norwegian knife, and that it had been driven in with savage violence.

"Do you find anything that throws any light on the case?" the inspector asked, when the examination was concluded.

"That is impossible to say until we have seen the knife," replied Thorndyke; "but while we are waiting for it, we may as well go and look at the scene of the tragedy. These are Pratt's boots, I think?" He lifted a pair of stout laced boots from the table and turned them up to inspect the soles.

"Yes, those are his boots," replied Fox, "and pretty easy they'd have been to track, if the case had been the other way about. Those Blakey's protectors are as good as a trademark."

"We'll take them, at any rate," said Thorndyke; and, the inspector having taken the boots from him, we went out and retraced our steps down the avenue.

The place where the murder had occurred was easily identified by a large dark stain on the gravel at one side of the drive, half-way between two trees--an ancient pollard hornbeam and an elm. Next to the elm was a pollard oak with a squat, warty bole about seven feet high, and three enormous limbs, of which one slanted half-way across the avenue; and between these two trees the ground was covered with the tracks of men and hounds superimposed upon the hoof-prints of a horse.

"Where was the knife found?" Thorndyke asked.

The inspector indicated a spot near the middle of the drive, almost opposite the hornbeam and Thorndyke, picking up a large stone, laid it on the spot. Then he surveyed the scene thoughtfully, looking up and down the drive and at the trees that bordered it, and, finally, walked slowly to the space between the elm and the oak, scanning the ground as he went. "There is no dearth of footprints," he remarked grimly, as he looked down at the trampled earth.

"No, but the question is, whose are they?" said the inspector.

"Yes, that is the question," agreed Thorndyke; "and we will begin the solution by identifying those of Pratt."

"I don't see how that will help us," said the inspector. "We know he was here."

Thorndyke looked at him in surprise, and I must confess that the foolish remark astonished me too, accustomed as I was to the quick-witted officers from Scotland Yard.

"The hue and cry procession," remarked Thorndyke, "seems to have passed out between the elm and the oak; elsewhere the ground seems pretty clear." He walked round the elm, still looking earnestly at the ground, and presently continued: "Now here, in the soft earth bordering the turf, are the prints of a pair of smallish feet wearing pointed boots; a rather short man, evidently, by the size of foot and length of stride, and he doesn't seem to have belonged to the procession. But I don't see any of Pratt's; he doesn't seem to have come off the hard gravel." He continued to walk slowly towards the hornbeam with his eyes fixed on the ground. Suddenly he halted and stooped with an eager look at the earth; and, as Fox and I approached, he stood up and pointed. "Pratt's footprints-- faint and fragmentary, but unmistakable. And now, inspector, you see their importance. They furnish the time factor in respect of the other footprints. Look at this one and then look at that." He pointed from one to another of the faint impressions of the dead man's foot.

"You mean that there are signs of a struggle?" said Fox.

"I mean more than that," replied Thorndyke. "Here is one of Pratt's footprints treading into the print of a small, pointed foot; and there at the edge of the gravel is another of Pratt's nearly obliterated by the tread of a pointed foot. Obviously the first pointed footprint was made before Pratt's, and the second one after his; and the necessary inference is that the owner of the pointed foot was here at the same time as Pratt."

"Then he must have been the murderer!" exclaimed Fox.

"Presumably," answered Thorndyke; "but let us see whither he went. You notice, in the first place, that the man stood close to this tree"--he indicated the hornbeam--"and that he went towards the elm. Let us follow him. He passes the elm, you see, and you will observe that these tracks form a regular series leading from the hornbeam and not mixed up with the marks of the struggle. They were, therefore, probably made after the murder had been perpetrated. You will also notice that they pass along the backs of the trees--outside the avenue, that is; what does that suggest to you?"

"It suggests to me," I said, when the inspector had shaken his head hopelessly, "that there was possibly some one in the avenue when the man was stealing off."

"Precisely," said Thorndyke. "The body was found not more than nine minutes after Pratt arrived here. But the murder must have taken some time. Then the housekeeper thought she heard some one calling and came out with a lantern, and, at the same time, the general and Mr. Hanford came up the drive. The suggestion is that the man sneaked along outside the trees to avoid being seen. However, let us follow the tracks. They pass the elm and they pass on behind the next tree; but wait! There is something odd here." He passed behind the great pollard oak and looked down at the soft earth by its roots. "Here is a pair of impressions much deeper than the rest, and they are not a part of the track since their toes point towards the tree. What do you make of that?" Without waiting for an answer he began closely to scan the bole of the tree and especially a large, warty protuberance about three feet from the ground. On the bark above this was a vertical mark, as if something had scraped down the tree, and from the wart itself a dead twig had been newly broken off and lay upon the ground. Pointing to these marks Thorndyke set his foot on the protuberance, and, springing up, brought his eye above the level of the crown, whence the great boughs branched off.

"Ah!" he exclaimed. "Here is something much more definite." With the aid of another projection, he scrambled up into the crown of the tree, and, having glanced quickly round, beckoned to us. I stepped up on the projecting lump and, as my eyes rose above the crown, I perceived the brown, shiny impression of a hand on the edge.

Climbing into the crown, I was quickly followed by the inspector, and we both stood up by Thorndyke between the three boughs. From where we stood we looked on the upper side of the great limb that swept out across the avenue; and there on its lichen-covered surface, we saw the imprints in reddish-brown of a pair of open hands.

"You notice," said Thorndyke, leaning out upon the bough, "that he is a short man; I cannot conveniently place my hands so low. You also note that he has both forefingers intact, and so is certainly not Ellis."

"If you mean to say, sir, that these marks were made by the murderer," said Fox, "I say it's impossible. Why, that would mean that he was here looking down at us when we were searching for him with the hounds. The presence of the hounds proves that this man could not have been the murderer."

"On the contrary," said Thorndyke, "the presence of this man with bloody hands confirms the other evidence, which all indicates that the hounds were never on the murderer's trail at all. Come now, inspector, I put it to you: Here is a murdered man; the murderer has almost certainly blood upon his hands; and here is a man with bloody hands, lurking in a tree within a few feet of the corpse and within a few minutes of its discovery (as is shown by the footprints); what are the reasonable probabilities?"

"But you are forgetting the bloodhounds, sir, and the murderer's knife," urged the inspector.

"Tut, tut, man!" exclaimed Thorndyke; "those bloodhounds are a positive obsession. But I see a sergeant coming up the drive, with the knife, I hope. Perhaps that will solve the riddle for us."

The sergeant, who carried a small dispatch-box, halted opposite the tree in some surprise while we descended, when he came forward with a military salute and handed the box to the inspector, who forthwith unlocked it, and, opening the lid, displayed an object wrapped in a pocket-handkerchief.

"There is the knife, sir," said he, "just as I received it. The handkerchief is the sergeant's."

Thorndyke unrolled the handkerchief and took from it a large-sized Norwegian knife, which he looked at critically and then handed to me. While I was inspecting the blade, he shook out the handkerchief and, having looked it over on both sides, turned to the sergeant.

"At what time did you pick up this knife?" he asked.

"About seven-fifteen, sir; directly after the hounds had started. I was careful to pick it up by the ring, and I wrapped it in the handkerchief at once."

"Seven-fifteen," said Thorndyke. "Less than half-an-hour after the murder. That is very singular. Do you observe the state of this handkerchief? There is not a mark on it. Not a trace of any bloodstain; which proves that when the knife was picked up, the blood on it was already dry. But things dry slowly, if they dry at all, in the saturated air of an autumn evening. The appearances seem to suggest that the blood on the knife was dry when it was thrown down. By the way, sergeant, what do you scent your handkerchief with?"

"Scent, sir!" exclaimed the astonished officer in indignant accents; "me scent my handkerchief! No, sir, certainly not. Never used scent in my life, sir."

Thorndyke held out the handkerchief, and the sergeant sniffed at it incredulously. "It certainly does seem to smell of scent," he admitted, "but it must be the knife." The same idea having occurred to me, I applied the handle of the knife to my nose and instantly detected the sickly-sweet odour of musk.

"The question is," said the inspector, when the two articles had been tested by us all, "was it the knife that scented the Handkerchief or the handkerchief that scented the knife?"

"You heard what the sergeant said," replied Thorndyke. "There was no scent on the handkerchief when the knife was wrapped in it. Do you know, inspector, this scent seems to me to offer a very curious suggestion. Consider the facts of the case: the distinct trail leading straight to Ellis, who is, nevertheless, found to be without a scratch or a spot of blood; the inconsistencies in the case that I pointed out in the train, and now this knife, apparently dropped with dried blood on it and scented with musk. To me it suggests a carefully-planned, coolly-premeditated crime. The murderer knew about the general's bloodhounds and made use of them as a blind. He planted this knife, smeared with blood and tainted with musk, to furnish a scent. No doubt some object, also scented with musk, would be drawn over the ground to give the trail. It is only a suggestion, of course, but it is worth considering."

"But, sir," the inspector objected eagerly, "if the murderer had handled the knife, it would have scented him too."

"Exactly; so, as we are assuming that the man is not a fool, we may assume that he did not handle it. He will have left it here in readiness, hidden in some place whence he could knock it down, say, with a stick, without touching it."

"Perhaps in this very tree, sir," suggested the sergeant, pointing to the oak.

"No," said Thorndyke, "he would hardly have hidden in the tree where the knife had been. The hounds might have scented the place instead of following the trail at once. The most likely hiding-place for the knife is the one nearest the spot where it was found." He walked over to the stone that marked the spot, and looking round, continued: "You see, that hornbeam is much the nearest, and its flat crown would be very convenient for the purpose--easily reached even by a short man, as he appears to be. Let us see if there are any traces of it. Perhaps you will give me a 'back up', sergeant, as we haven't a ladder."

The sergeant assented with a faint grin, and stooping beside the tree in an attitude suggesting the game of leapfrog, placed his hands firmly on his knees. Grasping a stout branch, Thorndyke swung himself up on the sergeant's broad back, whence he looked down into the crown of the tree. Then, parting the branches, he stepped onto the ledge and disappeared into the central hollow.

When he re-appeared he held in his hands two very singular objects: a pair of iron crucible-tongs and an artist's brush-case of black-japanned tin. The former article he handed down to me, but the brush-case he held carefully by its wire handle as he dropped to the ground.

"The significance of these things is, I think, obvious," he said. "The tongs were used to handle the knife with and the case to carry it in, so that it should not scent his clothes or bag. It was very carefully planned."

"If that is so," said the inspector, "the inside of the case ought to smell of musk."

"No doubt," said Thorndyke; "but before we open it, there is a rather important matter to be attended to. Will you give me the Vitogen powder, Jervis?"

I opened the canvas-covered "research case" and took from it an object like a diminutive pepper-caster--an iodo-form dredger in fact--and handed it to him. Grasping the brush-case by its wire handle, he sprinkled the pale yellow powder from the dredger freely all round the pull-off lid, tapping the top with his knuckles to make the fine particles spread. Then he blew off the superfluous powder, and the two police officers gave a simultaneous gasp of joy; for now, on the black background, there stood out plainly a number of finger-prints, so clear and distinct that the ridge-pattern could be made out with perfect ease.

"These will probably be his right hand," said Thorndyke. "Now for the left." He treated the body of the case in the same way, and, when he had blown off the powder, the entire surface was spotted with yellow, oval impressions. "Now, Jervis," said he, "if you will put on a glove and pull off the lid, we can test the inside."

There was no difficulty in getting the lid off, for the shoulder of the case had been smeared with vaseline--apparently to produce an airtight joint--and, as it separated with a hollow sound, a faint, musky odour exhaled from its interior.

"The remainder of the inquiry," said Thorndyke, when I pushed the lid on again, "will be best conducted at the police station, where, also, we can photograph these fingerprints."

"The shortest way will be across the meadows," said Fox; "the way the hounds went."

By this route we accordingly travelled, Thorndyke carrying the brush-case tenderly by its handle.

"I don't quite see where Ellis comes in in this job," said the inspector, as we walked along, "if the fellow had a grudge against Pratt. They weren't chums."

"I think I do," said Thorndyke. "You say that both men were prison officers at Portland at the same time. Now doesn't it seem likely that this is the work of some old convict who had been identified--and perhaps blackmailed--by Pratt, and possibly by Ellis too? That is where the value of the finger-prints comes in. If he is an old 'lag' his prints will be at Scotland Yard. Otherwise they are not of much value as a clue."

"That's true, sir," said the inspector. "I suppose you want to see Ellis."

"I want to see that purse that you spoke of, first," replied Thorndyke. "That is probably the other end of the clue."

As soon as we arrived at the station, the inspector unlocked a safe and brought out a parcel. "These are Ellis's things," said he, as he unfastened it, "and that is the purse."

He handed Thorndyke a small pigskin pouch, which my colleague opened, and having smelt the inside, passed to me. The odour of musk was plainly perceptible, especially in the small compartment at the back.

"It has probably tainted the other contents of the parcel," said Thorndyke, sniffing at each article in turn, "but my sense of smell is not keen enough to detect any scent. They all seem odourless to me, whereas the purse smells quite distinctly. Shall we have Ellis in now?"

The sergeant took a key from a locked drawer and departed for the cells, whence he presently re-appeared accompanied by the prisoner--a stout, burly man, in the last stage of dejection.

"Come, cheer up, Ellis," said the inspector. "Here's Dr. Thorndyke come down to help us and he wants to ask you one or two questions."

Ellis looked piteously at Thorndyke, and exclaimed: "I know nothing whatever about this affair, sir, I swear to God I don't."

"I never supposed you did," said Thorndyke. "But there are one or two things that I want you to tell me. To begin with, that purse: where did you find it?"

"On the Thorpe road, sir. It was lying in the middle of the footway."

"Had any one else passed the spot lately? Did you meet or pass any one?"

"Yes, sir, I met a labourer about a minute before I saw the purse. I can't imagine why he didn't see it."

"Probably because it wasn't there," said Thorndyke. "Is there a hedge there?"

"Yes, sir; a hedge on a low bank."

"Ha! Well, now, tell me: is there any one about here whom you knew when you and Pratt were together at Portland? Any old lag--to put it bluntly--whom you and Pratt have been putting the screw on."

"No, sir, I swear there isn't. But I wouldn't answer for Pratt. He had a rare memory for faces."

Thorndyke reflected. "Were there any escapes from Portland in your time?" he asked.

"Only one--a man named Dobbs. He made off to the sea in a sudden fog and he was supposed to be drowned. His clothes washed up on the Bill, but not his body. At any rate, he was never heard of again."

"Thank you, Ellis. Do you mind my taking your fingerprints?"

"Certainly not, sir," was the almost eager reply; and the office inking-pad being requisitioned, a rough set of finger-prints was produced; and when Thorndyke had compared them with those on the brush-case and found no resemblance, Ellis returned to his cell in quite buoyant spirits.

Having made several photographs of the strange fingerprints, we returned to town that evening, taking the negatives with us; and while we waited for our train, Thorndyke gave a few parting injunctions to the inspector. "Remember," he said, "that the man must have washed his hands before he could appear in public. Search the banks of every pond, ditch and stream in the neighbourhood for footprints like those in the avenue; and, if you find any, search the bottom of the water thoroughly, for he is quite likely to have dropped the knife into the mud."

The photographs, which we handed in at Scotland Yard that same night, enabled the experts to identify the fingerprints as those of Francis Dobbs, an escaped convict. The two photographs--profile and full-face-- which were attached to his record, were sent down to Baysford with a description of the man, and were, in due course, identified with a somewhat mysterious individual, who passed by the name of Rufus Pembury and who had lived in the neighbourhood as a private gentleman for some two years. But Rufus Pembury was not to be found either at his genteel house or elsewhere. All that was known was, that on the day after the murder, he had converted his entire "personality" into "bearer securities," and then vanished from mortal ken. Nor has he ever been heard of to this day.

"And, between ourselves," said Thorndyke, when we were discussing the case some time after, "he deserved to escape. It was clearly a case of blackmail, and to kill a blackmailer--when you have no other defence against him--is hardly murder. As to Ellis, he could never have been convicted, and Dobbs, or Pembury, must have known it. But he would have been committed to the Assizes, and that would have given time for all traces to disappear. No, Dobbs was a man of courage, ingenuity and resource; and, above all, he knocked the bottom out of the great bloodhound superstition."

The Echo of a Mutiny

Part I. Death on the Girdler

Popular belief ascribes to infants and the lower animals certain occult powers of divining character denied to the reasoning faculties of the human adult; and is apt to accept their judgment as finally overriding the pronouncements of mere experience.

Whether this belief rests upon any foundation other than the universal love of paradox it is unnecessary to inquire. It is very generally entertained, especially by ladies of a certain social status; and by Mrs. Thomas Solly it was loyally maintained as an article of faith.

"Yes," she moralized, "it's surprisin' how they know, the little children and the dumb animals. But they do. There's no deceivin' them. They can tell the gold from the dross in a moment, they can, and they reads the human heart like a book. Wonderful, I call it. I suppose it's instinct."

Having delivered herself of this priceless gem of philosophic thought, she thrust her arms elbow-deep into the foaming wash-tub and glanced admiringly at her lodger as he sat in the doorway, supporting on one knee an obese infant of eighteen months and on the other a fine tabby cat.

James Brown was an elderly seafaring man, small and slight in build and in manner suave, insinuating and perhaps a trifle sly. But he had all the sailor's love of children and animals, and the sailor's knack of making himself acceptable to them, for, as he sat with an empty pipe wobbling in the grasp of his toothless gums, the baby beamed with humid smiles, and the cat, rolled into a fluffy ball and purring like a stocking-loom, worked its fingers ecstatically as if it were trying on a new pair of gloves.

"It must be mortal lonely out at the lighthouse," Mrs. Solly resumed. "Only three men and never a neighbour to speak to; and, Lord! what a muddle they must be in with no woman to look after them and keep 'em tidy. But you won't be overworked, Mr. Brown, in these long days; daylight till past nine o'clock. I don't know what you'll do to pass the time."

"Oh, I shall find plenty to do, I expect," said Brown, "what with cleanin' the lamps and glasses and paintin' up the ironwork. And that reminds me," he added, looking round at the clock, "that time's getting on. High water at half-past ten, and here it's gone eight o'clock."

Mrs. Solly, acting on the hint, began rapidly to fish out the washed garments and wring them out into the form of short ropes. Then, having dried her hands on her apron, she relieved Brown of the protesting baby.

"Your room will be ready for you, Mr. Brown," said she, "when your turn comes for a spell ashore; and main glad me and Tom will be to see you back."

"Thank you, Mrs. Solly, ma'am," answered Brown, tenderly placing the cat on the floor; "you won't be more glad than what I will." He shook hands warmly with his landlady, kissed the baby, chucked the cat under the chin, and, picking up his little chest by its becket, swung it onto his shoulder and strode out of the cottage.

His way lay across the marshes, and, like the ships in the offing, he shaped his course by the twin towers of Reculver that stood up grotesquely on the rim of the land; and as he trod the springy turf, Tom Solly's fleecy charges looked up at him with vacant stares and valedictory bleatings. Once, at a dyke-gate, he paused to look back at the fair Kentish landscape: at the grey tower of St. Nicholas-at-Wade peeping above the trees and the faraway mill at Sarre, whirling slowly in the summer breeze; and, above all, at the solitary cottage where, for a brief spell in his stormy life, he had known the homely joys of domesticity and peace. Well, that was over for the present, and the lighthouse loomed ahead. With a half-sigh he passed through the gate and walked on towards Reculver.

Outside the whitewashed cottages with their official black chimneys a petty-officer of the coast-guard was adjusting the halyards of the flagstaff. He looked round as Brown approached, and hailed him cheerily.

"Here you are, then," said he, "all figged out in your new togs, too. But we're in a bit of a difficulty, d'ye see. We've got to pull up to Whitstable this morning, so I can't send a man out with you and I can't spare a boat."

"Have I got to swim out, then?" asked Brown.

The coast-guard grinned. "Not in them new clothes, mate," he answered. "No, but there's old Willett's boat; he isn't using her to-day; he's going over to Minster to see his daughter, and he'll let us have the loan of the boat. But there's no one to go with you, and I'm responsible to Willett."

"Well, what about it?" asked Brown, with the deep-sea sailor's (usually misplaced) confidence in his power to handle a sailing-boat. "D'ye think I can't manage a tub of a boat? Me what's used the sea since I was a kid of ten?"

"Yes," said the coast-guard; "but who's to bring her back?"

"Why, the man that I'm going to relieve," answered Brown. "He don't want to swim no more than what I do."

The coast-guard reflected with his telescope pointed at a passing barge. "Well, I suppose it'll be all right," he concluded; "but it's a pity they couldn't send the tender round. However, if you undertake to send the boat back, we'll get her afloat. It's time you were off."

He strolled away to the back of the cottages, whence he presently returned with two of his mates, and the four men proceeded along the shore to where Willett's boat lay just above high-water mark.

The Emily was a beamy craft of the type locally known as a "half-share skiff," solidly built of oak, with varnished planking and fitted with main and mizzen lugs. She was a good handful for four men, and, as she slid over the soft chalk rocks with a hollow rumble, the coast-guards debated the advisability of lifting out the bags of shingle with which she was ballasted. However, she was at length dragged down, ballast and all, to the water's edge, and then, while Brown stepped the mainmast, the petty-officer gave him his directions. "What you've got to do," said he, "is to make use of the flood-tide.

Keep her nose nor'-east, and with this trickle of nor'-westerly breeze you ought to make the light-house in one board. Anyhow don't let her get east of the lighthouse, or, when the ebb sets in, you'll be in a fix."

To these admonitions Brown listened with jaunty indifference as he hoisted the sails and watched the incoming tide creep over the level shore. Then the boat lifted on the gentle swell. Putting out an oar, he gave a vigorous shove off that sent the boat, with a final scrape, clear of the beach, and then, having dropped the rudder onto its pintles, he seated himself and calmly belayed the main-sheet.

"There he goes," growled the coast-guard; "makin' fast his sheet. They will do it" (he invariably did it himself), "and that's how accidents happen. I hope old Willett'll see his boat back all right."

He stood for some time watching the dwindling boat as it sidled across the smooth water; then he turned and followed his mates towards the station.

Out on the south-western edge of the Girdler Sand, just inside the two-fathom line, the spindle-shanked lighthouse stood a-straddle on its long screw-piles like some uncouth red-bodied wading bird. It was now nearly half flood tide. The highest shoals were long since covered, and the lighthouse rose above the smooth sea as solitary as a slaver becalmed in the "middle passage."

On the gallery outside the lantern were two men, the entire staff of the building, of whom one sat huddled in a chair with his left leg propped up with pillows on another, while his companion rested a telescope on the rail and peered at the faint grey line of the distant land and the two tiny points that marked the twin spires of Reculver.

"I don't see any signs of the boat, Harry," said he.

The other man groaned. "I shall lose the tide," he complained, "and then there's another day gone."

"They can pull you down to Birchington and put you in the train," said the first man.

"I don't want no trains," growled the invalid. "The boat'll be bad enough. I suppose there's nothing coming our way, Tom?"

Tom turned his face eastward and shaded his eyes. "There's a brig coming across the tide from the north," he said. "Looks like a collier." He pointed his telescope at the approaching vessel, and added: "She's got two new cloths in her upper fore top-sail, one on each leech."

The other man sat up eagerly. "What's her trysail like, Tom?" he asked.

"Can't see it," replied Tom. "Yes, I can, now: it's tanned. Why, that'll be the old Utopia, Harry; she's the only brig I know that's got a tanned trysail."

"Look here, Tom," exclaimed the other, "If that's the Utopia, she's going to my home and I'm going aboard of her. Captain Mockett'll give me a passage, I know."

"You oughtn't to go until you're relieved, you know, Barnett," said Tom doubtfully; "it's against regulations to leave your station."

"Regulations be blowed!" exclaimed Barnett. "My leg's more to me than the regulations. I don't want to be a cripple all my life. Besides, I'm no good here, and this new chap, Brown, will be coming out presently. You run up the signal, Tom, like a good comrade, and hail the brig."

"Well, it's your look-out," said Tom, "and I don't mind saying that if I was in your place I should cut off home and see a doctor, if I got the chance." He sauntered off to the flag-locker, and, selecting the two code-flags, deliberately toggled them onto the halyards. Then, as the brig swept up within range, he hoisted the little balls of bunting to the flagstaff-head and jerked the halyards, when the two flags blew out making the signal "Need assistance."

Promptly a coal-soiled answering pennant soared to the brig's main-truck; less promptly the collier went about, and, turning her nose down stream, slowly drifted stern-forwards towards the lighthouse. Then a boat slid out through her gangway, and a couple of men plied the oars vigorously.

"Lighthouse ahoy!" roared one of them, as the boat came within hail. "What's amiss?"

"Harry Barnett has broke his leg," shouted the lighthouse keeper, "and he wants to know if Captain Mockett will give him a passage to Whitstable."

The boat turned back to the brig, and after a brief and bellowed consultation, once more pulled towards the lighthouse.

"Skipper says yus," roared the sailor, when he was within ear-shot, "and he says look alive, 'cause he don't want to miss his tide."

The injured man heaved a sigh of relief. "That's good news," said he, "though, how the blazes I'm going to get down the ladder is more than I can tell. What do you say, Jeffreys?"

"I say you'd better let me lower you with the tackle," replied Jeffreys. "You can sit in the bight of a rope and I'll give you a line to steady yourself with."

"Ah, that'll do, Tom," said Barnett; "but, for the Lord's sake, pay out the fall-rope gently."

The arrangements were made so quickly that by the time the boat was fast alongside everything was in readiness, and a minute later the injured man, dangling like a gigantic spider from the end of the tackle, slowly descended, cursing volubly to the accompaniment of the creaking of the blocks. His chest and kit-bag followed, and, as soon as these were unhooked from the tackle, the boat pulled off to the brig, which was now slowly creeping stern-foremost past the lighthouse. The sick man was hoisted up the side, his chest handed up after him, and then the brig was put on her course due south across the Kentish Flats.

Jeffreys stood on the gallery watching the receding vessel and listening to the voices of her crew as they grew small and weak in the increasing distance. Now that his gruff companion was gone, a strange loneliness had fallen on the lighthouse. The last of the homeward-bound ships had long since passed up the Princes Channel and left the calm sea desolate and blank. The distant buoys, showing as tiny black dots on the glassy surface, and the spindly shapes of the beacons which stood up from invisible shoals, but emphasized the solitude of the empty sea, and the tolling of the bell buoy on the Shivering Sand, stealing faintly down the wind, sounded weird and mournful. The day's work was already done. The lenses were polished, the lamps had been trimmed, and the little motor that worked the foghorn had been cleaned and oiled. There were several odd jobs, it is true, waiting to be done, as there always are in a lighthouse; but, just now, Jeffreys was not in a working humour. A new comrade was coming into his life to-day, a stranger with whom he was to be shut up alone, night! and day, for a month on end, and whose temper and tastes and habits might mean for him pleasant companionship or jangling and discord without end. Who was this man Brown? What had he been? and what was he like? These were the questions that passed, naturally enough, through the lighthouse keeper's mind and distracted him from his usual thoughts and occupations.

Presently a speck on the landward horizon caught his eye. He snatched up the telescope eagerly to inspect it. Yes, it was a boat; but not the coast-guard's cutter, for which he was looking. Evidently a fisherman's boat and with only one man in it. He laid down the telescope with a sigh of disappointment, and, filling his pipe, leaned on the rail with a dreamy eye bent on the faint grey line of the land.

Three long years had he spent in this dreary solitude, so repugnant to his active, restless nature: three blank, interminable years, with nothing to look back on but the endless succession of summer calms, stormy nights and the chilly fogs of winter, when the unseen steamers hooted from the void and the fog-horn bellowed its hoarse warning.

Why had he come to this God-forsaken spot? and why did he stay, when the wide world called to him? And then memory painted him a picture on which his mind's eye had often looked before and which once again arose before him, shutting out the vision of the calm sea and the distant land. It was a brightly-coloured picture. It showed a cloudless sky brooding over the deep blue tropic sea: and in the middle of the picture, see-sawing gently on the quiet swell, a white-painted barque.

Her sails were clewed up untidily, her swinging yards jerked at the slack braces and her untended wheel revolved to and fro to the oscillations of the rudder.

She was not a derelict, for more than a dozen men were on her deck; but the men were all drunk and mostly asleep, and there was never an officer among them.

Then he saw the interior of one of her cabins. The chart-rack, the tell-tale compass and the chronometers marked it as the captain's cabin. In it were four men, and two of them lay dead on the deck. Of the other two, one was a small, cunning-faced man, who was, at the moment, kneeling beside one of the corpses to wipe a knife upon its coat. The fourth man was himself.

Again, he saw the two murderers stealing off in a quarter-boat, as the barque with her drunken crew drifted towards the spouting surf of a river-bar. He saw the ship melt away in the surf like an icicle in the sunshine; and, later, two shipwrecked mariners, picked up in an open boat and set ashore at an American port.

That was why he was here. Because he was a murderer. The other scoundrel, Amos Todd, had turned Queen's Evidence and denounced him, and he had barely managed to escape. Since then he had hidden himself from the great world, and here he must continue to hide, not from the law--for his person was unknown now that his shipmates were dead--but from the partner of his crime. It was the fear of Todd that had changed him from Jeffrey Rorke to Tom Jeffreys and had sent him to the Girdler, a prisoner for life. Todd might die--might even now be dead--but he would never hear of it: would never hear the news of his release.

He roused himself and once more pointed his telescope at the distant boat. She was considerably nearer now and seemed to be heading out towards the lighthouse. Perhaps the man in her was bringing a message; at any rate, there was no sign of the coast-guard's cutter.

He went in, and, betaking himself to the kitchen, busied himself with a few simple preparations for dinner. But there was nothing to cook, for there remained the cold meat from yesterday's cooking, which he would make sufficient, with some biscuit in place of potatoes. He felt restless and unstrung; the solitude irked him, and the everlasting wash of the water among the piles jarred on his nerves.

When he went out again into the gallery the ebb-tide had set in strongly and the boat was little more than a mile distant; and now, through the glass, he could see that the man in her wore the uniform cap of the Trinity House. Then the man must be his future comrade, Brown; but this was very extraordinary. What were they to do with the boat? There was no one to take her back.

The breeze was dying away. As he watched the boat, he saw the man lower the sail and take to his oars; and something of hurry in the way the man pulled over the gathering tide, caused Jeffreys to look round the horizon. And then, for the first time, he noticed a bank of fog creeping up from the east and already so near that the beacon on the East Girdler had faded out of sight. He hastened in to start the little motor that compressed the air for the fog-horn and waited awhile to see that the mechanism was running properly. Then, as the deck vibrated to the roar of the horn, he went out once more into the gallery.

The fog was now all round the lighthouse and the boat was hidden from view. He listened intently. The enclosing wall of vapour seemed to have shut out sound as well as vision. At intervals the horn bellowed its note of warning, and then all was still save the murmur of the water among the piles below, and, infinitely faint and far away, the mournful tolling of the bell on the Shivering Sand.

At length there came to his ear the muffled sound of oars working in the holes; then, at the very edge of the circle of grey water that was visible, the boat appeared through the fog, pale and spectral, with a shadowy figure pulling furiously. The horn emitted a hoarse growl; the man looked round, perceived the lighthouse and altered his course towards it.

Jeffreys descended the iron stairway, and, walking along the lower gallery, stood at the head of the ladder earnestly watching the approaching stranger. Already he was tired of being alone. The yearning for human companionship had been growing ever since Barnett left. But what sort of comrade was this stranger who was coming into his life? And coming to occupy so dominant a place in it.

The boat swept down swiftly athwart the hurrying tide. Nearer it came and yet nearer: and still Jeffreys could catch no glimpse of his new comrade's face. At length it came fairly alongside and bumped against the fender-posts; the stranger whisked in an oar and grabbed a rung of the ladder, and Jeffreys dropped a coil of rope into the boat. And still the man's face was hidden.

Jeffreys leaned out over the ladder and watched him anxiously, as he made fast the rope, unhooked the sail from the traveller and unstepped the mast. When he had set all in order, the stranger picked up a small chest, and, swinging it over his shoulder, stepped onto the ladder. Slowly, by reason of his encumbrance, he mounted, rung by rung, with never an upward glance, and Jeffreys gazed down at the top of his head with growing curiosity. At last he reached the top of the ladder and Jeffreys stooped to lend him a hand. Then, for the first time, he looked up, and Jeffreys started back with a blanched face.

"God Almighty!" he gasped. "It's Amos Todd!"

As the newcomer stepped on the gallery, the fog-horn emitted a roar like that of some hungry monster. Jeffreys turned abruptly without a word, and walked to the stairs, followed by Todd, and the two men ascended with never a sound but the hollow clank of their footsteps on the iron plates. Silently Jeffreys stalked into the living-room and, as his companion followed, he turned and motioned to the latter to set down his chest.

"You ain't much of a talker, mate," said Todd, looking round the room in some surprise; "ain't you going to say 'good-morning'? We're going to be good comrades, I hope. I'm Jim Brown, the new hand, I am; what might your name be?"

Jeffreys turned on him suddenly and led him to the window. "Look at me carefully, Amos Todd," he said sternly, "and then ask yourself what my name is."

At the sound of his voice Todd looked up with a start and turned pale as death. "It can't be," he whispered, "it can't be Jeff Rorke!"

The other man laughed harshly, and leaning forward, said in a low voice: "Hast thou found me, O mine enemy!"

"Don't say that!" exclaimed Todd. "Don't call me your enemy, Jeff. Lord knows but I'm glad to see you, though I'd never have known you without your beard and with that grey hair. I've been to blame, Jeff, and I know it; but it ain't no use raking up old grudges. Let bygones be bygones, Jeff, and let us be pals as we used to be." He wiped his face with his handkerchief and watched his companion apprehensively.

"Sit down," said Rorke, pointing to a shabby rep-covered arm-chair; "sit down and tell me what you've done with all that money. You've blued it all, I suppose, or you wouldn't be here."

"Robbed, Jeff," answered Todd; "robbed of every penny. Ah! that was an unfortunate affair, that job on board the old Sea-flower. But it's over and done with and we'd best forget it. They're all dead but us, Jeff, so we're safe enough so long as we keep our mouths shut; all at the bottom of the sea--and the best place for 'em too."

"Yes," Rorke replied fiercely, "that's the best place for your shipmates when they know too much; at the bottom of the sea or swinging at the end of a rope." He paced up and down the little room with rapid strides, and each time that he approached Todd's chair the latter shrank back with an expression of alarm.

"Don't sit there staring at me," said Rorke. "Why don't you smoke or do something?"

Todd hastily produced a pipe from his pocket, and having filled it from a moleskin pouch, stuck it in his mouth while he searched for a match. Apparently he carried his matches loose in his pocket, for he presently brought one forth--a red-headed match, which, when he struck it on the wall, lighted with a pale-blue flame. He applied it to his pipe, sucking in his cheeks while he kept his eyes fixed on his companion. Rorke, meanwhile, halted in his walk to cut some shavings from a cake of hard tobacco with a large clasp-knife; and, as he stood, he gazed with frowning abstraction at Todd.

"This pipe's stopped," said the latter, sucking ineffectually at the mouthpiece. "Have you got such a thing as a piece of wire, Jeff?"

"No, I haven't," replied Rorke; "not up here. I'll get a bit from the store presently. Here, take this pipe till you can clean your own: I've got another in the rack there." The sailor's natural hospitality overcoming for the moment his animosity, he thrust the pipe that he had just filled towards Todd, who took it with a mumbled "Thank you" and an anxious eye on the open knife. On the wall beside the chair was a roughly-carved pipe-rack containing: several pipes, one of which Rorke lifted out; and, as he leaned over the chair to reach it, Todd's face went several shades paler.

"Well, Jeff," he said, after a pause, while Rorke cut a fresh "fill" of tobacco, "are we going to be pals same as what we used to be?"

Rorke's animosity lighted up afresh. "Am I going to be pals with the man that tried to swear away my life?" he said sternly; and after a pause he added: "That wants thinking about, that does; and meantime I must go and look at the engine."

When Rorke had gone the new hand sat, with the two pipes in his hands, reflecting deeply. Abstractedly he stuck the fresh pipe into his mouth, and, dropping the stopped one into the rack, felt for a match. Still with an air of abstraction he lit the pipe, and having smoked for a minute or two, rose from the chair and began softly to creep across the room, looking about him and listening intently. At the door he paused to look out into the fog, and then, having again listened attentively, he stepped on tip-toe out onto the gallery and along towards the stairway. Of a sudden the voice of Rorke brought him up with a start.

"Hallo, Todd! where are you off to?"

"I'm just going down to make the boat secure," was the reply.

"Never you mind about the boat," said Rorke. "I'll see to her."

"Right-o, Jeff," said Todd, still edging towards the stairway. "But, I say, mate, where's the other man--the man that I'm to relieve?"

"There ain't any other man," replied Rorke; "he went off aboard a collier."

Todd's face suddenly became grey and haggard. "Then there's no one here but us two!" he gasped; and then, with an effort to conceal his fear, he asked: "But who's going to take the boat back?"

"We'll see about that presently," replied Rorke; "you get along in and unpack your chest."

He came out on the gallery as he spoke, with a lowering frown on his face. Todd cast a terrified glance at him, and then turned and ran for his life towards the stairway.

"Come back!" roared Rorke, springing forward along the gallery; but Todd's feet were already clattering down the iron steps. By the time Rorke reached the head of the stairs, the fugitive was near the bottom; but here, in his haste, he stumbled, barely saving himself by the handrail, and when he recovered his balance Rorke was upon him. Todd darted to the head of the ladder, but, as he grasped the stanchion, his pursuer seized him by the collar. In a moment he had turned with his hand under his coat. There was a quick blow, a loud curse from Rorke, an answering yell from Todd, and a knife fell spinning through the air and dropped into the fore-peak of the boat below.

"You murderous little devil!" said Rorke in an ominously quiet voice, with his bleeding hand gripping his captive by the throat. "Handy with your knife as ever, eh? So you were off to give information, were you?"

"No, I wasn't Jeff," replied Todd in a choking voice; "I wasn't, s'elp me, God. Let go, Jeff. I didn't mean no harm. I was only--" With a sudden wrench he freed one hand and struck out frantically at his captor's face. But Rorke warded off the blow, and, grasping the other wrist, gave a violent push and let go. Todd staggered backward a few paces along the staging, bringing up at the extreme edge; and here, for a sensible time, he stood with wide-open mouth and starting eye-balls, swaying and clutching wildly at the air. Then, with a shrill scream, he toppled backwards and fell, striking a pile in his descent and rebounding into the water.

In spite of the audible thump of his head on the pile, he was not stunned, for when he rose to the surface, he struck out vigorously, uttering short, stifled cries for help. Rorke watched him with set teeth and quickened breath, but made no move. Smaller and still smaller grew the head with its little circle of ripples, swept away on the swift ebb-tide, and fainter the bubbling cries that came across the smooth water. At length as the small black spot began to fade in the fog, the drowning man, with a final effort, raised his head clear of the surface and sent a last, despairing shriek towards the lighthouse. The fog-horn sent back an answering bellow; the head sank below the surface and was seen no more; and in the dreadful stillness that settled down upon the sea there sounded faint and far away the muffled tolling of a bell.

Rorke stood for some minutes immovable, wrapped in thought. Presently the distant hoot of a steamer's whistle aroused him. The ebb-tide shipping was beginning to come down and the fog might lift at any moment; and there was the boat still alongside. She must be disposed of at once. No one had seen her arrive and no one must see her made fast to the lighthouse. Once get rid of the boat and all traces of Todd's visit would be destroyed. He ran down the ladder and stepped into the boat. It was simple. She was heavily ballasted, and would go down if she filled.

He shifted some of the bags of shingle, and, lifting the bottom boards, pulled out the plug. Instantly a large jet of water spouted up into the bottom. Rorke looked at it critically, and, deciding that it would fill her in a few minutes, replaced the bottom boards; and having secured the mast and sail with a few turns of the sheet round a thwart, to prevent them from floating away, he cast off the mooring-rope and stepped on the ladder.

As the released boat began to move away on the tide, he ran up and mounted to the upper gallery to watch her disappearance. Suddenly he remembered Todd's chest. It was still in the room below. With a hurried glance around into the fog, he ran down to the room, and snatching up the chest, carried it out on the lower gallery. After another nervous glance around to assure himself that no craft was in sight, he heaved the chest over the handrail, and, when it fell with a loud splash into the sea, he waited to watch it float away after its owner and the sunken boat. But it never rose; and presently he returned to the upper gallery.

The fog was thinning perceptibly now, and the boat remained plainly visible as she drifted away. But she sank more slowly than he had expected, and presently as she drifted farther away, he fetched the telescope and peered at her with growing anxiety. It would be unfortunate if any one saw her; if she should be picked up here, with her plug out, it would be disastrous.

He was beginning to be really alarmed. Through the glass he could see that the boat was now rolling in a sluggish, water-logged fashion, but she still showed some inches of free-board, and the fog was thinning every moment.

Presently the blast of a steamer's whistle sounded close at hand. He looked round hurriedly and, seeing nothing, again pointed the telescope eagerly at the dwindling boat. Suddenly he gave a gasp of relief. The boat had rolled gunwale under; had staggered back for a moment and then rolled again, slowly, finally, with the water pouring in over the submerged gunwale.

In a few more seconds she had vanished. Rorke lowered the telescope and took a deep breath. Now he was safe. The boat had sunk unseen. But he was better than safe: he was free. His evil spirit, the standing menace of his life, was gone, and the wide world, the world of life, of action, of pleasure, called to him.

In a few minutes the fog lifted. The sun shone brightly on the red-funnelled cattle-boat whose whistle had startled him just now, the summer blue came back to sky and sea, and the land peeped once more over the edge of the horizon.

He went in, whistling cheerfully, and stopped the motor; returned to coil away the rope that he had thrown to Todd; and, when he had hoisted a signal for assistance, he went in once more to eat his solitary meal in peace and gladness.

Part II. "The Singing Bone"

(Related by Christopher Jervis, M.D.)

In every kind of scientific work a certain amount of manual labour naturally appertains, labour that cannot be performed by the scientist himself, since art is long but life is short. A chemical analysis involves a laborious "clean up" of apparatus and laboratory, for which the chemist has no time; the preparation of a skeleton--the maceration, bleaching, "assembling," and riveting together of bones--must be carried out by some one whose time is not too precious. And so with other scientific activities. Behind the man of science with his outfit of knowledge is the indispensable mechanic with his outfit of manual skill.

Thorndyke's laboratory assistant, Polton, was a fine example of the latter type, deft, resourceful, ingenious and untiring. He was somewhat of an inventive genius, too; and it was one of his inventions that connected us with the singular case that I am about to record.

Though by trade a watchmaker, Polton was, by choice, an optician. Optical apparatus was the passion of his life; and when, one day, he produced for our inspection an improved prism for increasing the efficiency of gas-buoys, Thorndyke at once brought the invention to the notice of a friend at the Trinity House.

As a consequence, we three--Thorndyke, Polton and I--found ourselves early on a fine July morning making our way down Middle Temple Lane bound for the Temple Pier. A small oil-launch lay alongside the pontoon, and, as we made our appearance, a red-faced, white-whiskered gentleman stood up in the cockpit.

"Here's a delightful morning, doctor," he sang out in a fine, brassy, resonant, sea-faring voice; "sort of day for a trip to the lower river, hey? Hallo, Polton! Coming down to take the bread out of our mouths, are you? Ha, ha!" The cheery laugh rang out over the river and mingled with the throb of the engine as the launch moved off from the pier.

Captain Grumpass was one of the Elder Brethren of the Trinity House. Formerly a client of Thorndyke's he had subsided, as Thorndyke's clients were apt to do, into the position of a personal friend, and his hearty regard included our invaluable assistant.

"Nice state of things," continued the captain, with a chuckle, "when a body of nautical experts have got to be taught their business by a parcel of lawyers or doctors, what? I suppose trade's slack and 'Satan findeth mischief still,' hey, Polton?"

"There isn't much doing on the civil side, sir," replied Polton, with a quaint, crinkly smile, "but the criminals are still going strong."

"Ha! mystery department still flourishing, what? And, by Jove! talking of mysteries, doctor, our people have got a queer problem to work out; something quite in your line--quite. Yes, and, by the Lord Moses, since I've got you here, why shouldn't I suck your brains?"

"Exactly," said Thorndyke. "Why shouldn't you?"

"Well, then, I will," said the captain, "so here goes. All hands to the pump!" He lit a cigar, and, after a few preliminary puffs, began: "The mystery, shortly stated, is this: one of our lighthousemen has disappeared--vanished off the face of the earth and left no trace. He may have bolted, he may have been drowned accidentally or he may have been murdered. But I'd rather give you the particulars in order. At the end of last week a barge brought into Ramsgate a letter from the screw-pile lighthouse on the Girdler. There are only two men there, and it seems that one of them, a man named Barnett, had broken his leg, and he asked that the tender should be sent to bring him ashore. Well, it happened that the local tender, the Warden, was up on the slip in Ramsgate Harbour, having a scrape down, and wouldn't be available for a day or two, so, as the case was urgent, the officer at Ramsgate sent a letter to the lighthouse by one of the pleasure steamers saying that the man should be relieved by boat on the following morning, which was Saturday. He also wrote to a new hand who had just been taken on, a man named James Brown, who was lodging near Reculver, waiting his turn, telling him to go out on Saturday morning in the coast-guard's boat; and he sent a third letter to the coast-guard at Reculver asking him to take Brown out to the lighthouse and bring Barnett ashore. Well, between them, they made a fine muddle of it. The coast-guard couldn't spare either a boat or a man, so they borrowed a fisherman's boat, and in this the man Brown started off alone, like an idiot, on the chance that Barnett would be able to sail the boat back in spite of his broken leg.

"Meanwhile Barnett, who is a Whitstable man, had signalled a collier bound for his native town, and got taken off; so that the other keeper, Thomas Jeffreys, was left alone until Brown should turn up.

"But Brown never did turn up. The coast-guard helped him to put off and saw him well out to sea, and the keeper, Jeffreys, saw a sailing-boat with one man in her making for the lighthouse. Then a bank of fog came up and hit the boat, and when the fog cleared she was nowhere to be seen. Man and boat had vanished and left no sign."

"He may have been run down," Thorndyke suggested.

"He may," agreed the captain, "but no accident has been reported. The coast-guards think he may have capsized in a squall--they saw him make the sheet fast. But there weren't any squalls; the weather was quite calm."

"Was he all right and well when he put off?" inquired Thorndyke.

"Yes," replied the captain, "the coast-guards' report is highly circumstantial; in fact, it's full of silly details that have no bearing on anything. This is what they say." He pulled out an official letter and read: "'When last seen, the missing man was seated in the boat's stern to windward of the helm. He had belayed the sheet. He was holding a pipe and tobacco-pouch in his hands and steering with his elbow. He was filling the pipe from the tobacco-pouch.' There! 'He was holding the pipe in his hand,' mark you! not with his toes; and he was filling it from a tobacco-pouch, whereas you'd have expected him to fill it from a coalscuttle or a feeding-bottle. Bah!" The captain rammed the letter back in his pocket and puffed scornfully at his cigar.

"You are hardly fair to the coast-guard," said Thorndyke, laughing at the captain's vehemence. "The duty of a witness is to give all the facts, not a judicious selection."

"But, my dear sir," said Captain Grumpass, "what the deuce can it matter what the poor devil filled his pipe from?"

"Who can say?" answered Thorndyke. "It may turn out to be a highly material fact. One never knows beforehand. The value of a particular fact depends on its relation to the rest of the evidence."

"I suppose it does," grunted the captain; and he continued to smoke in reflective silence until we opened Black-wall Point, when he suddenly stood up.

"There's a steam trawler alongside our wharf," he announced. "Now what the deuce can she be doing there?" He scanned the little steamer attentively, and continued:

"They seem to be landing something, too. Just pass me those glasses, Polton. Why, hang me! it's a dead body! But why on earth are they landing it on our wharf? They must have known you were coming, doctor."

As the launch swept alongside the wharf, the captain sprang up lightly and approached the group gathered round the body. "What's this?" he asked. "Why have they brought this thing here?"

The master of the trawler, who had superintended the landing, proceeded to explain.

"It's one of your men, sir," said he. "We saw the body lying on the edge of the South Shingles Sand, close to the beacon, as we passed at low water, so we put off the boat and fetched it aboard. As there was nothing to identify the man by, I had a look in his pockets and found this letter."

He handed the captain an official envelope addressed to: "Mr. J. Brown, co Mr. Solly, Shepherd, Reculver, Kent."

"Why, this is the man we were speaking about, doctor," exclaimed Captain Grumpass. "What a very singular coincidence. But what are we to do with the body?"

"You will have to write to the coroner," replied Thorndyke. "By the way, did you turn out all the pockets?" he asked, turning to the skipper of the trawler.

"No, sir," was the reply. "I found the letter in the first pocket that I felt in, so I didn't examine any of the others. Is there anything more that you want to know, sir?"

"Nothing but your name and address, for the coroner," replied Thorndyke, and the skipper, having given this information and expressed the hope that the coroner would not keep him "hanging about," returned to his vessel and pursued his way to Billingsgate.

"I wonder if you would mind having a look at the body of this poor devil, while Polton is showing us his contraptions," said Captain Grumpass.

"I can't do much without a coroner's order," replied Thorndyke; "but if it will give you any satisfaction, Jervis and I will make a preliminary inspection with pleasure."

"I should be glad if you would," said the captain. "We should like to know that the poor beggar met his end fairly."

The body was accordingly moved to a shed, and, as Polton was led away, carrying the black bag that contained his precious model, we entered the shed and commenced our investigation.

The deceased was a small, elderly man, decently dressed in a somewhat nautical fashion. He appeared to have been dead only two or three days, and the body, unlike the majority of sea-borne corpses, was uninjured by fish or crabs. There were no fractured bones or other gross injuries, and no wounds, excepting a rugged tear in the scalp at the back of the head.

"The general appearance of the body," said Thorndyke, when he had noted these particulars, "suggests death by drowning, though, of course, we can't give a definite opinion until a post mortem has been made."

"You don't attach any significance to that scalp-wound, then?" I asked.

"As a cause of death? No. It was obviously inflicted during life, but it seems to have been an oblique blow that spent its force on the scalp, leaving the skull uninjured. But it is very significant in another way."

"In what way?" I asked.

Thorndyke took out his pocket-case and extracted a pair of forceps. "Consider the circumstances," said he. "This man put off from the shore to go to the lighthouse, but never arrived there. The question is, where did he arrive?" As he spoke he stooped over the corpse and turned back the hair round the wound with the beak of the forceps. "Look at those white objects among the hair, Jervis, and inside the wound. They tell us something, I think."

I examined, through my lens, the chalky fragments to which he pointed. "These seem to be bits of shells and the tubes of some marine worm," I said.

"Yes," he answered; "the broken shells are evidently those of the acorn barnacle, and the other fragments are mostly pieces of the tubes of the common serpula. The inference that these objects suggest is an important one. It is that this wound was produced by some body encrusted by acorn barnacles and serpula; that is to say, by a body that is periodically submerged. Now, what can that body be, and how can the deceased have knocked his head against it?"

"It might be the stem of a ship that ran him down," I suggested.

"I don't think you would find many serpulae on the stem of a ship," said Thorndyke. "The combination rather suggests some stationary object between tidemarks, such as a beacon. But one doesn't see how a man could knock his head against a beacon, while, on the other hand, there are no other stationary objects out in the estuary to knock against except buoys, and a buoy presents a flat surface that could hardly have produced this wound. By the way, we may as well see what there is in his pockets, though it is not likely that robbery had anything to do with his death."

"No," I agreed, "and I see his watch is in his pocket; quite a good silver one," I added, taking it out. "It has stopped at 12.13."

"That may be important," said Thorndyke, making a note of the fact; "but we had better examine the pockets one at a time, and put the things back when we have looked at them."

The first pocket that we turned out was the left hip-pocket of the monkey jacket. This was apparently the one that the skipper had rifled, for we found in it two letters, both bearing the crest of the Trinity House. These, of course, we returned without reading, and then passed on to the right pocket. The contents of this were common-place enough, consisting of a briar pipe, a moleskin pouch and a number of loose matches.

"Rather a casual proceeding, this," I remarked, "to carry matches loose in the pocket, and a pipe with them, too."

"Yes," agreed Thorndyke; "especially with these very inflammable matches. You notice that the sticks had been coated at the upper end with sulphur before the red phosphorous heads were put on. They would light with a touch, and would be very difficult to extinguish; which, no doubt, is the reason that this type of match is so popular among seamen, who have to light their pipes in all sorts of weather." As he spoke he picked up the pipe and looked at it reflectively, turning it over in his hand and peering into the bowl.

Suddenly he glanced from the pipe to the dead man's face and then, with the forceps, turned back the lips to look into the mouth.

"Let us see what tobacco he smokes," said he.

I opened the sodden pouch and displayed a mass of dark, fine-cut tobacco. "It looks like shag," I said.

"Yes, it is shag," he replied; "and now we will see what is in the pipe. It has been only half-smoked out." He dug out the "dottle" with his pocket-knife onto a sheet of paper, and we both inspected it. Clearly it was not shag, for it consisted of coarsely-cut shreds and was nearly black.

"Shavings from a cake of 'hard,'" was my verdict, and Thorndyke agreed as he shot the fragments back into the pipe.

The other pockets yielded nothing of interest, except a pocket-knife, which Thorndyke opened and examined closely. There was not much money, though as much as one would expect, and enough to exclude the idea of robbery.

"Is there a sheath-knife on that strap?" Thorndyke asked, pointing to a narrow leather belt. I turned back the jacket and looked.

"There is a sheath," I said, "but no knife. It must have dropped out."

"That is rather odd," said Thorndyke. "A sailor's sheath-knife takes a deal of shaking out as a rule. It is intended to be used in working on the rigging when the man is aloft, so that he can get it out with one hand while he is holding on with the other. It has to be and usually is very secure, for the sheath holds half the handle as well as the blade. What makes one notice the matter in this case is that the man, as you see, carried a pocket-knife; and, as this would serve all the ordinary purposes of a knife, it seems to suggest that the sheath-knife was carried for defensive purposes: as a weapon, in fact. However, we can't get much further in the case without a post mortem, and here comes the captain."

Captain Grumpass entered the shed and looked down commiseratingly at the dead seaman.

"Is there anything, doctor, that throws any light on the man's disappearance?" he asked.

"There are one or two curious features in the case," Thorndyke replied; "but, oddly enough, the only really important point arises out of that statement of the coastguard's, concerning which you were so scornful."

"You don't say so!" exclaimed the captain.

"Yes," said Thorndyke; "the coast-guard states that when last seen deceased was filling his pipe from his tobacco-pouch. Now his pouch contains shag; but the pipe in his pocket contains hard cut."

"Is there no cake tobacco in any of the pockets?"

"Not a fragment. Of course, it is possible that he might have had a piece and used it up to fill the pipe; but there is no trace of any on the blade of his pocket-knife, and you know how this juicy black cake stains a knife-blade. His sheath-knife is missing, but he would hardly have used that to shred tobacco when he had a pocket-knife."

"No," assented the captain; "but are you sure he hadn't a second pipe?"

"There was only one pipe," replied Thorndyke, "and that was not his own."

"Not his own!" exclaimed the captain, halting by a huge, chequered buoy, to stare at my colleague. "How do you know it was not his own?"

"By the appearance of the vulcanite mouthpiece," said Thorndyke. "It showed deep tooth-marks; in fact, it was nearly bitten through. Now a man who bites through his pipe usually presents certain definite physical peculiarities, among which is, necessarily, a fairly good set of teeth. But the dead man had not a tooth in his head."

The captain cogitated a while, and then remarked: "I don't quite see the bearing of this."

"Don't you?" said Thorndyke. "It seems to me highly suggestive. Here is a man who, when last seen, was filling his pipe with a particular kind of tobacco. He is picked up dead, and his pipe contains a totally different kind of tobacco. Where did that tobacco come from? The obvious suggestion is that he had met some one."

"Yes, it does look like it," agreed the captain.

"Then," continued Thorndyke, "there is the fact that his sheath-knife is missing. That may mean nothing, but we have to bear it in mind. And there is another curious circumstance: there is a wound on the back of the head caused by a heavy bump against some body that was covered with acorn barnacles and marine worms. Now there are no piers or stages out in the open estuary. The question is, what could he have struck?"

"Oh, there is nothing in that," said the captain. "When a body has been washing about in a tide-way for close on three days--"

"But this is not a question of a body," Thorndyke interrupted. "The wound was made during life."

"The deuce it was!" exclaimed the captain. "Well, all I can suggest is that he must have fouled one of the beacons in the fog, stove in his boat and bumped his head, though, I must admit, that's rather a lame explanation." He stood for a minute gazing at his toes with a cogitative frown and then looked up at Thorndyke.

"I have an idea," he said. "From what you say, this matter wants looking into pretty carefully. Now, I am going down on the tender to-day to make inquiries on the spot. What do you say to coming with me as adviser--as a matter of business, of course--you and Dr. Jervis? I shall start about eleven; we shall be at the lighthouse by three o'clock, and you can get back to town to-night, if you want to. What do you say?"

"There's nothing to hinder us," I put in eagerly, for even at Bugsby's Hole the river looked very alluring on this summer morning.

"Very well," said Thorndyke, "we will come. Jervis is evidently hankering for a sea-trip, and so am I, for that matter."

"It's a business engagement, you know," the captain stipulated.

"Nothing of the kind," said Thorndyke; "it's unmitigated pleasure; the pleasure of the voyage and your high well-born society."

"I didn't mean that," grumbled the captain, "but, if you are coming as guests, send your man for your nightgear and let us bring you back to-morrow evening."

"We won't disturb Polton," said my colleague; "we can take the train from Blackwall and fetch our things ourselves. Eleven o'clock, you said?"

"Thereabouts," said Captain Grumpass; "but don't put yourselves out."

The means of communication in London have reached an almost undesirable state of perfection. With the aid of the snorting train and the tinkling, two-wheeled "gondola," we crossed and re-crossed the town with such celerity that it was barely eleven when we re-appeared on Trinity Wharf with a joint Gladstone and Thorndyke's little green case.

The tender had hauled out of Bow Creek, and now lay alongside the wharf with a great striped can buoy dangling from her derrick, and Captain Grumpass stood at the gangway, his jolly, red face beaming with pleasure. The buoy was safely stowed forward, the derrick hauled up to the mast, the loose shrouds rehooked to the screw-lanyards, and the steamer, with four jubilant hoots, swung round and shoved her sharp nose against the incoming tide.

For near upon four hours the ever-widening stream of the "London River" unfolded its moving panorama. The smoke and smell of Woolwich Reach gave place to lucid air made soft by the summer haze; the grey huddle of factories fell away and green levels of cattle-spotted marsh stretched away to the high land bordering the river valley. Venerable training ships displayed their chequered hulls by the wooded shore, and whispered of the days of oak and hemp, when the tall three-decker, comely and majestic, with her soaring heights of canvas, like towers of ivory, had not yet given place to the mud-coloured saucepans that fly the white ensign now-a-days and devour the substance of the British taxpayer: when a sailor was a sailor and not a mere seafaring mechanic. Sturdily breasting the flood tide, the tender threaded her way through the endless procession of shipping; barges, billy-boys, schooners, brigs; lumpish Black-seamen, blue-funnelled China tramps, rickety Baltic barques with twirling windmills, gigantic liners, staggering under a mountain of top-hamper. Erith, Purfleet, Greenhithe, Grays greeted us and passed astern. The chimneys of Northfleet, the clustering roofs of Gravesend, the populous anchorage and the lurking batteries, were left behind, and, as we swung out of the Lower Hope, the wide expanse of sea reach spread out before us like a great sheet of blue-shot satin.

About half-past twelve the ebb overtook us and helped us on our way, as we could see by the speed with which the distant land slid past, and the freshening of the air as we passed through it.

But sky and sea were hushed in a summer calm. Balls of fleecy cloud hung aloft, motionless in the soft blue; the barges drifted on the tide with drooping sails, and a big, striped bell buoy--surmounted by a staff and cage and labelled, "Shivering Sand"--sat dreaming in the sun above its motionless reflection, to rouse for a moment as it met our wash, nod its cage drowsily, utter a solemn ding-dong, and fall asleep again.

It was shortly after passing the buoy that the gaunt shape of a screw-pile lighthouse began to loom up ahead, its dull-red paint turned to vermilion by the early afternoon sun. As we drew nearer, the name Girdler, painted in huge, white letters, became visible, and two men could be seen in the gallery around the lantern, inspecting us through a telescope.

"Shall you be long at the lighthouse, sir?" the master of the tender inquired of Captain Grumpass; "because we're going down, to the North-East Pan Sand to fix this new buoy and take up the old one."

"Then you'd better put us off at the lighthouse and come back for us when you've finished the job," was the reply. "I don't know how long we shall be."

The tender was brought to, a boat lowered, and a couple of hands pulled us across the intervening space of water.

"It will be a dirty climb for you in your shore-going clothes," the captain remarked--he was as spruce as a new pin himself, "but the stuff will all wipe off." We looked up at the skeleton shape. The falling tide had exposed some fifteen feet of the piles, and piles and ladder alike were swathed in sea-grass and encrusted with barnacles and worm-tubes. But we were not such town-sparrows as the captain seemed to think, for we both followed his lead without difficulty up the slippery ladder, Thorndyke clinging tenaciously to his little green case, from which he refused to be separated even for an instant.

"These gentlemen and I," said the captain, as we stepped on the stage at the head of the ladder, "have come to make inquiries about the missing man, James Brown. Which of you is Jeffreys?"

"I am, sir," replied a tall, powerful, square-jawed, beetle-browed man, whose left hand was tied up in a rough bandage.

"What have you been doing to your hand?" asked the captain.

"I cut it while I was peeling some potatoes," was the reply. "It isn't much of a cut, sir."

"Well, Jeffreys," said the captain, "Brown's body has been picked up and I want particulars for the inquest. You'll be summoned as a witness, I suppose, so come in and tell us all you know."

We entered the living-room and seated ourselves at the table. The captain opened a massive pocket-book, while Thorndyke, in his attentive, inquisitive fashion, looked about the odd, cabin-like room as if making a mental inventory of its contents.

Jeffreys' statement added nothing to what we already knew. He had seen a boat with one man in it making for the lighthouse. Then the fog had drifted up and he had lost sight of the boat. He started the fog-horn and kept a bright look-out, but the boat never arrived. And that was all he knew. He supposed that the man must have missed the lighthouse and been carried away on the ebb-tide, which was running strongly at the time.

"What time was it when you last saw the boat?" Thorndyke asked.

"About half-past eleven," replied Jeffreys.

"What was the man like?" asked the captain.

"I don't know, sir; he was rowing, and his back was towards me."

"Had he any kit-bag or chest with him?" asked Thorndyke.

"He'd got his chest with him," said Jeffreys.

"What sort of chest was it?" inquired Thorndyke.

"A small chest, painted green, with rope beckets."

"Was it corded?"

"It had a single cord round, to hold the lid down."

"Where was it stowed?"

"In the stern-sheets, sir."

"How far off was the boat when you last saw it?"

"About half-a-mile."

"Half-a-mile!" exclaimed the captain. "Why, how the deuce could you see that chest half-a-mile away?"

The man reddened and cast a look of angry suspicion at Thorndyke. "I was watching the boat through the glass, sir," he replied sulkily.

"I see," said Captain Grumpass. "Well, that will do, Jeffreys. We shall have to arrange for you to attend the inquest. Tell Smith I want to see him."

The examination concluded, Thorndyke and I moved our chairs to the window, which looked out over the sea to the east. But it was not the sea or the passing ships that engaged my colleague's attention. On the wall, beside the window, hung a rudely-carved pipe-rack containing five pipes. Thorndyke had noted it when we entered the room, and now, as we talked, I observed him regarding it from time to time with speculative interest.

"You men seem to be inveterate smokers," he remarked to the keeper, Smith, when the captain had concluded the arrangements for the "shift."

"Well, we do like our bit of 'baccy, sir, and that's a fact," answered Smith. "You see, sir," he continued, "it's a lonely life, and tobacco's cheap out here."

"How is that?" asked Thorndyke.

"Why, we get it given to us. The small craft from foreign, especially the Dutchmen, generally heave us a cake or two when they pass close. We're not ashore, you see, so there's no duty to pay."

"So you don't trouble the tobacconists much? Don't go in for cut tobacco?"

"No, sir; we'd have to buy it, and then the cut stuff wouldn't keep. No, it's hard-tack to eat out here and hard tobacco to smoke."

"I see you've got a pipe-rack, too, quite a stylish affair."

"Yes," said Smith, "I made it in my off-time. Keeps the place tidy and looks more ship-shape than letting the pipes lay about anywhere."

"Some one seems to have neglected his pipe," said Thorndyke, pointing to one at the end of the rack which was coated with green mildew.

"Yes; that's Parsons, my mate. He must have left it when he went off near a month ago. Pipes do go mouldy in the damp air out here."

"How soon does a pipe go mouldy if it is left untouched?" Thorndyke asked.

"It's according to the weather," said Smith. "When it's warm and damp they'll begin to go in about a week. Now here's Barnett's pipe that he's left behind--the man that broke his leg, you know, sir--it's just beginning to spot a little. He couldn't have used it for a day or two before he went."

"And are all these other pipes yours?"

"No, sir. This here one is mine. The end one is Jeffreys', and I suppose the middle one is his too, but I don't know it."

"You're a demon for pipes, doctor," said the captain, strolling up at this moment; "you seem to make a special study of them."

"'The proper study of mankind is man,'" replied Thorndyke, as the keeper retired, "and 'man' includes those objects on which his personality is impressed. Now a pipe is a very personal thing. Look at that row in the rack. Each has its own physiognomy which, in a measure, reflects the peculiarities of the owner. There is Jeffreys' pipe at the end, for instance. The mouth-piece is nearly bitten through, the bowl scraped to a shell and scored inside and the brim battered and chipped. The whole thing speaks of rude strength and rough handling. He chews the stem as he smokes, he scrapes the bowl violently, and he bangs the ashes out with unnecessary force. And the man fits the pipe exactly: powerful, square-jawed and, I should say, violent on occasion."

"Yes, he looks a tough customer, does Jeffreys," agreed the captain.

"Then," continued Thorndyke, "there is Smith's pipe, next to it; 'coked' up until the cavity is nearly filled and burnt all round the edge; a talker's pipe, constantly going out and being relit. But the one that interests me most is the middle one."

"Didn't Smith say that was Jeffreys' too?" I said.

"Yes," replied Thorndyke, "but he must be mistaken. It is the very opposite of Jeffreys' pipe in every respect. To begin with, although it is an old pipe, there is not a sign of any tooth-mark on the mouth-piece. It is the only one in the rack that is quite unmarked. Then the brim is quite uninjured: it has been handled gently, and the silver band is jet-black, whereas the band on Jeffreys' pipe is quite bright."

"I hadn't noticed that it had a band," said the captain. "What has made it so black?"

Thorndyke lifted the pipe out of the rack and looked at it closely. "Silver sulphide," said he, "the sulphur no doubt derived from something carried in the pocket."

"I see," said Captain Grumpass, smothering a yawn and gazing out of the window at the distant tender. "Incidentally it's full of tobacco. What moral do you draw from that?"

Thorndyke turned the pipe over and looked closely at the mouth-piece. "The moral is," he replied, "that you should see that your pipe is clear before you fill it." He pointed to the mouth-piece, the bore of which was completely stopped up with fine fluff.

"An excellent moral too," said the captain, rising with another yawn. "If you'll excuse me a minute I'll just go and see what the tender is up to. She seems to be crossing to the East Girdler." He reached the telescope down from its brackets and went out onto the gallery.

As the captain retreated, Thorndyke opened his pocket-knife, and, sticking the blade into the bowl of the pipe, turned the tobacco out into his hand.

"Shag, by Jove!" I exclaimed.

"Yes," he answered, poking it back into the bowl. "Didn't you expect it to be shag?"

"I don't know that I expected anything," I admitted. "The silver band was occupying my attention."

"Yes, that is an interesting point," said Thorndyke, "but let us see what the obstruction consists of." He opened the green case, and, taking out a dissecting needle, neatly extracted a little ball of fluff from the bore of the pipe. Laying this on a glass slide, he teased it out in a drop of glycerine and put on a cover-glass while I set up the microscope.

"Better put the pipe back in the rack," he said, as he laid the slide on the stage of the instrument. I did so and then turned, with no little excitement, to watch him as he examined the specimen. After a brief inspection he rose and waved his hand towards the microscope.

"Take a look at it, Jervis," he said.

I applied my eye to the instrument, and, moving the slide about, identified the constituents of the little mass of fluff. The ubiquitous cotton fibre was, of course, in evidence, and a few fibres of wool, but the most remarkable objects were two or three hairs--very minute hairs of a definite zigzag shape and having a flat expansion near the free end like the blade of a paddle.

"These are the hairs of some small animal," I said; "not a mouse or rat or any rodent, I should say. Some small insectivorous animal, I fancy. Yes! Of course! They are the hairs of a mole." I stood up, and, as the importance of the discovery flashed on me, I looked at my colleague in silence.

"Yes," he said, "they are unmistakable; and they furnish the keystone of the argument."

"You think that this is really the dead man's pipe, then?" I said.

"According to the law of multiple evidence," he replied, "it is practically a certainty. Consider the facts in sequence. Since there is no sign of mildew on it, this pipe can have been here only a short time, and must belong either to Barnett, Smith, Jeffreys or Brown. It is an old pipe, but it has no tooth-marks on it. Therefore it has been used by a man who has no teeth. But Barnett, Smith and Jeffreys all have teeth and mark their pipes, whereas Brown has no teeth. The tobacco in it is shag. But these three men do not smoke shag, whereas Brown had shag in his pouch. The silver band is encrusted with sulphide; and Brown carried sulphur-tipped matches loose in his pocket with his pipe. We find hairs of a mole in the bore of the pipe; and Brown carried a moleskin pouch in the pocket in which he appears to have carried his pipe. Finally, Brown's pocket contained a pipe which was obviously not his and which closely resembled that of Jeffreys; it contained tobacco similar to that which Jeffreys smokes and different from that in Brown's pouch. It appears to me quite conclusive, especially when we add to this evidence the other items that are in our possession."

"What items are they?" I asked.

"First there is the fact that the dead man had knocked his head heavily against some periodically submerged body covered with acorn barnacles and serpulae. Now the piles of this lighthouse answer to the description exactly, and there are no other bodies in the neighbourhood that do: for even the beacons are too large to have produced that kind of wound. Then the dead man's sheath-knife is missing, and Jeffreys has a knife-wound on his hand. You must admit that the circumstantial evidence is overwhelming."

At this moment the captain bustled into the room with the telescope in his hand. "The tender is coming up towing a strange boat," he said. "I expect it's the missing one, and, if it is, we may learn something. You'd better pack up your traps and get ready to go on board."

We packed the green case and went out into the gallery, where the two keepers were watching the approaching tender; Smith frankly curious and interested, Jeffreys restless, fidgety and noticeably pale. As the steamer came opposite the lighthouse, three men dropped into the boat and pulled across, and one of them--the mate of the tender--came climbing up the ladder.

"Is that the missing boat?" the captain sang out.

"Yes, sir," answered the officer, stepping onto the staging and wiping his hands on the reverse aspect of his trousers, "we saw her lying on the dry patch of the East Girdler. There's been some hanky-panky in this job, sir."

"Foul play, you think, hey?"

"Not a doubt of it, sir. The plug was out and lying loose in the bottom, and we found a sheath-knife sticking into the kelson forward among the coils of the painter. It was stuck in hard as if it had dropped from a height."

"That's odd," said the captain. "As to the plug, it might have got out by accident."

"But it hadn't sir," said the mate. "The ballast-bags had been shifted along to get the bottom boards up. Besides, sir, a seaman wouldn't let the boat fill; he'd have put the plug back and baled out."

"That's true," replied Captain Grumpass; "and certainly the presence of the knife looks fishy. But where the deuce could it have dropped from, out in the open sea? Knives don't drop from the clouds--fortunately. What do you say, doctor?"

"I should say that it is Brown's own knife, and that it probably fell from this staging."

Jeffreys turned swiftly, crimson with wrath. "What d'ye mean?" he demanded. "Haven't I said that the boat never came here?"

"You have," replied Thorndyke; "but if that is so, how do you explain the fact that your pipe was found in the dead man's pocket and that the dead man's pipe is at this moment in your pipe-rack?"

The crimson flush on Jeffreys' face faded as quickly as it had come. "I don't know what you're talking about," he faltered.

"I'll tell you," said Thorndyke. "I will relate what happened and you shall check my statements. Brown brought his boat alongside and came up into the living-room, bringing his chest with him. He filled his pipe and tried to light it, but it was stopped and wouldn't draw. Then you lent him a pipe of yours and filled it for him. Soon afterwards you came out on this staging and quarrelled. Brown defended himself with his knife, which dropped from his hand into the boat. You pushed him off the staging and he fell, knocking his head on one of the piles. Then you took the plug out of the boat and sent her adrift to sink, and you flung the chest into the sea. This happened about ten minutes past twelve. Am I right?"

Jeffreys stood staring at Thorndyke, the picture of amazement and consternation; but he uttered no word in reply. "Am I right?" Thorndyke repeated. "Strike me blind!" muttered Jeffreys. "Was you here, then? You talk as if you had been. Anyhow," he continued, recovering somewhat, "you seem to know all about it. But you're wrong about one thing. There was no quarrel. This chap, Brown, didn't take to me and he didn't mean to stay out here. He was going to put off and go ashore again and I wouldn't let him. Then he hit out at me with his knife and I knocked it out of his hand and he staggered backwards and went overboard."

"And did you try to pick him up?" asked the captain.

"How could I," demanded Jeffreys, "with the tide racing down and me alone on the station? I'd never have got back."

"But what about the boat, Jeffreys? Why did you scuttle her?"

"The fact is," replied Jeffreys, "I got in a funk, and I thought the simplest plan was to send her to the cellar and know nothing about it. But I never shoved him over. It was an accident, sir; I swear it!"

"Well, that sounds a reasonable explanation," said the captain. "What do you say, doctor?"

"Perfectly reasonable," replied Thorndyke, "and, as to its truth, that is no affair of ours."

"No. But I shall have to take you off, Jeffreys, and hand you over to the police. You understand that?"

"Yes, sir, I understand," answered Jeffreys.

"That was a queer case, that affair on the Girdler," remarked Captain Grumpass, when he was spending an evening with us some six months later. "A pretty easy let off for Jeffreys, too--eighteen months, wasn't it?"

"Yes, it was a very queer case indeed," said Thorndyke. "There was something behind that 'accident,' I should say. Those men had probably met before."

"So I thought," agreed the captain. "But the queerest part of it to me was the way you nosed it all out. I've had a deep respect for briar pipes since then. It was a remarkable case," he continued. "The way in which you made that pipe tell the story of the murder seems to me like sheer enchantment."

"Yes," said I, "it spoke like the magic pipe--only that wasn't a tobacco-pipe--in the German folk-story of the 'Singing Bone.' Do you remember it? A peasant found the bone of a murdered man and fashioned it into a pipe. But when he tried to play on it, it burst into a song of its own -

'My brother slew me and buried my bones

Beneath the sand and under the stones.' "

"A pretty story," said Thorndyke, "and one with an excellent moral. The inanimate things around us have each of them a song to sing to us if we are but ready with attentive ears."

A Wastrel's Romance

Part I. The Spinsters' Guest

The lingering summer twilight was fast merging into night as a solitary cyclist, whose evening-dress suit was thinly disguised by an overcoat, rode slowly along a pleasant country road. From time to time he had been overtaken and passed by a carriage, a car or a closed cab from the adjacent town, and from the festive garb of the occupants he had made shrewd guesses at their destination. His own objective was a large house, standing in somewhat extensive grounds just off the road, and the peculiar circumstances that surrounded his visit to it caused him to ride more and more slowly as he approached his goal.

Willowdale--such was the name of the house--was, tonight, witnessing a temporary revival of its past glories. For many months it had been empty and a notice-board by the gate-keeper's lodge had silently announced its forlorn state; but to-night, its rooms, their bare walls clothed in flags and draperies, their floors waxed or carpeted, would once more echo the sound of music and cheerful voices and vibrate to the tread of many feet. For on this night the spinsters of Raynesford were giving a dance; and chief amongst the spinsters was Miss Halliwell, the owner of Willowdale.

It was a great occasion. The house was large and imposing; the spinsters were many and their purses were long. The guests were numerous and distinguished, and included no less a person than Mrs. Jehu B. Chater. This was the crowning triumph of the function, for the beautiful American widow was the lion (or should we say lioness?) of the season. Her wealth was, if not beyond the dreams of avarice, at least beyond the powers of common British arithmetic, and her diamonds were, at once, the glory and the terror of her hostesses.

All these attractions notwithstanding, the cyclist approached the vicinity of Willowdale with a slowness almost hinting at reluctance; and when, at length, a curve of the road brought the gates into view, he dismounted and halted irresolutely. He was about to do a rather risky thing, and, though by no means a man of weak nerve, he hesitated to make the plunge.

The fact is, he had not been invited.

Why, then, was he going? And how was he to gain admittance? To which questions the answer involves a painful explanation.

Augustus Bailey lived by his wits. That is the common phrase, and a stupid phrase it is. For do we not all live by our wits, if we have any? And does it need any specially brilliant wits to be a common rogue? However, such as his wits were, Augustus Bailey lived by them, and he had not hitherto made a fortune.

The present venture arose out of a conversation overheard at a restaurant table and an invitation-card carelessly laid down and adroitly covered with the menu. Augustus had accepted the invitation that he had not received (on a sheet of Hotel Cecil notepaper that he had among his collection of stationery) in the name of Geoffrey Harrington-Baillie; and the question that exercised his mind at the moment was, would he or would he not be spotted? He had trusted to the number of guests and the probable inexperience of the hostesses. He knew that the cards need not be shown, though there was the awkward ceremony of announcement.

But perhaps it wouldn't get as far as that. Probably not, if his acceptance had been detected as emanating from an uninvited stranger.

He walked slowly towards the gates with growing discomfort. Added to his nervousness as to the present were certain twinges of reminiscence. He had once held a commission in a line regiment--not for long, indeed; his "wits" had been too much for his brother officers--but there had been a time when he would have come to such a gathering as this an invited guest. Now, a common thief, he was sneaking in under a false name, with a fair prospect of being ignominiously thrown out by the servants.

As he stood hesitating, the sound of hoofs on the road was followed by the aggressive bellow of a motor-horn. The modest twinkle of carriage lamps appeared round the curve and then the glare of acetylene headlights. A man came out of the lodge and drew open the gates; and Mr. Bailey, taking his courage in both hands, boldly trundled his machine up the drive.

Half-way up--it was quite a steep incline--the car whizzed by; a large Napier filled with a bevy of young men who economized space by sitting on the backs of the seats and on one another's knees. Bailey looked at them and decided that this was his chance, and, pushing forward, he saw his bicycle safely bestowed in the empty coach-house and then hurried on to the cloak-room. The young men had arrived there before him and, as he entered, were gaily peeling off their overcoats and flinging them down on a table. Bailey followed their example, and, in his eagerness to enter the reception-room with the crowd, let his attention wander from the business of the moment, and, as he pocketed the ticket and hurried away, he failed to notice that the bewildered attendant had put his hat with another man's coat and affixed his duplicate to them both.

"Major Podbury, Captain Barker-Jones, Captain Sparker, Mr. Watson, Mr. Goldsmith, Mr. Smart, Mr. Harrington-Baillie!"

As Augustus swaggered up the room, hugging the party of officers and quaking inwardly, he was conscious that his hostesses glanced from one man to another with more than common interest.

But at that moment the footman's voice rang out, sonorous and clear--

"Mrs. Chater, Colonel Grumpier!" and, as all eyes were turned towards the new arrivals, Augustus made his bow and passed into the throng. His little game of bluff had "come off," after all.

He withdrew modestly into the more crowded portion of the room, and there took up a position where he would be shielded from the gaze of his hostesses. Presently, he reflected, they would forget him, if they had really thought about him at all, and then he would see what could be done in the way of business. He was still rather shaky, and wondered how soon it would be decent to steady his nerves with a "refresher." Meanwhile he kept a sharp look-out over the shoulders of neighbouring guests, until a movement in the crowd of guests disclosed Mrs. Chater shaking hands with the presiding spinster. Then Augustus got a most uncommon surprise.

He knew her at the first glance. He had a good memory for faces, and Mrs. Chater's face was-one to remember. Well did he recall the frank and lovely American girl with whom he had danced at the regimental ball years ago. That was in the old days when he was a subaltern, and before that little affair of the pricked court-cards that brought his military career to an end. They had taken a mutual liking, he remembered, that sweet-faced Yankee maid and he; had danced many dances and had sat out others, to talk mystical nonsense which, in their innocence, they had believed to be philosophy. He had never seen her since. She had come into his life and gone out of it again, and he had forgotten her name, if he had ever known it. But here she was, middle-aged now, it was true, but still beautiful and a great personage withal. And, ye gods! what diamonds! And here was he, too, a common rogue, lurking in the crowd that he might, perchance, snatch a pendant or "pinch" a loose brooch.

Perhaps she might recognize him. Why not? He had recognized her. But that would never do. And thus reflecting, Mr. Bailey slipped out to stroll on the lawn and smoke a cigarette. Another man, somewhat older than himself, was pacing to and fro thoughtfully, glancing from time to time through the open windows into the brilliantly-lighted rooms. When they had passed once or twice, the stranger halted and addressed him.

"This is the best place on a night like this," he remarked; "it's getting hot inside already. But perhaps you're keen on dancing."

"Not so keen as I used to be," replied Bailey; and then, observing the hungry look that the other man was bestowing on his cigarette, he produced his case and offered it.

"Thanks awfully!" exclaimed the stranger, pouncing with avidity on the open case. "Good Samaritan, by Jove. Left my case in my overcoat. Hadn't the cheek to ask, though I was starving for a smoke." He inhaled luxuriously, and, blowing out a cloud of smoke, resumed: "These chits seem to be running the show pretty well, h'm? Wouldn't take it for an empty house to look at it, would you?"

"I have hardly seen it," said Bailey; "only just come, you know."

"We'll have a look round, if you like," said the genial stranger, "when we've finished our smoke, that is. Have a drink too; may cool us a bit. Know many people here?"

"Not a soul," replied Bailey. "My, hostess doesn't seem to have turned up."

"Well, that's easily remedied," said the stranger. "My daughter's one of the spinsters--Granby, my name; when we've had a drink, I'll make her find you a partner--that is, if you care for the light fantastic."

"I should like a dance or two," said Bailey, "though I'm getting a bit past it now, I suppose. Still, it doesn't do to chuck up the sponge prematurely."

"Certainly not," Granby agreed jovially; "a man's as young as he feels. Well, come and have a drink and then we'll hunt up my little girl." The two men flung away the stumps of their cigarettes and headed for the refreshments.

The spinsters' champagne was light, but it was well enough if taken in sufficient quantity; a point to which Augustus? and Granby too--paid judicious attention; and when he had supplemented the wine with a few sandwiches, Mr. Bailey felt in notably better spirits. For, to tell the truth, his diet, of late, had been somewhat meagre. Miss Granby, when found, proved to be a blonde and guileless "flapper" of some seventeen summers, childishly eager to play her part of hostess with due dignity; and presently Bailey found himself gyrating through the eddying crowd in company with a comely matron of thirty or thereabouts.

The sensations that this novel experience aroused rather took him by surprise. For years past he had been living a precarious life of mean and sordid shifts that oscillated between mere shabby trickery and downright crime; now conducting a paltry swindle just inside the pale of the law, and now, when hard pressed, descending to actual theft; consorting with shady characters, swindlers and knaves and scurvy rogues like himself; gambling, borrowing, cadging and, if need be, stealing, and always slinking abroad with an apprehensive eye upon "the man in blue."

And now, amidst the half-forgotten surroundings, once so familiar; the gaily-decorated rooms, the rhythmic music, the twinkle of jewels, the murmur of gliding feet and the rustle of costly gowns, the moving vision of honest gentlemen and fair ladies; the shameful years seemed to drop away and leave him to take up the thread of his life where it had snapped so disastrously. After all, these were his own people. The seedy knaves in whose steps he had walked of late were but aliens met by the way.

He surrendered his partner, in due course, with regret--which was mutual--to an inarticulate subaltern, and was meditating another pilgrimage to the refreshment-room, when he felt a light touch upon his arm. He turned swiftly. A touch on the arm meant more to him than to some men. But it was no wooden-faced plain-clothes man that he confronted; it was only a lady. In short, it was Mrs. Chater, smiling nervously and a little abashed by her own boldness.

"I expect you've forgotten me," she began apologetically, but Augustus interrupted her with an eager disclaimer.

"Of course I haven't," he said; "though I have forgotten your name, but I remember that Portsmouth dance as well as if it were yesterday; at least one incident in it--the only one that was worth remembering. I've often hoped that I might meet you again, and now, at last, it has happened."

"It's nice of you to remember," she rejoined. "I've often and often thought of that evening and all the wonderful things that we talked about. You were a nice boy then; I wonder what you are like now. What a long time ago it is!"

"Yes," Augustus agreed gravely, "it is a long time. I know it myself; but when I look at you, it seems as if it could only have been last season."

"Oh, fie!" she exclaimed. "You are not simple as you used to be. You didn't flatter then; but perhaps there wasn't the need." She spoke with gentle reproach, but her pretty face flushed with pleasure nevertheless, and there was a certain wistfulness in the tone of her concluding sentence.

"I wasn't flattering," Augustus replied, quite sincerely; "I knew you directly you entered the room and marvelled that Time had been so gentle with you. He hasn't been as kind to me."

"No. You have gotten a few grey hairs, I see, but after all, what are grey hairs to a man? Just the badges of rank, like the crown on your collar or the lace on your cuffs, to mark the steps of your promotion-- for I guess you'll be a colonel by now."

"No," Augustus answered quickly, with a faint flush, "I left the army some years ago."

"My! what a pity!" exclaimed Mrs. Chater. "You must tell me all about it--but not now. My partner will be looking for me. We will sit out a dance and have a real gossip. But I've forgotten your name--never could recall it, in fact, though that didn't prevent me from remembering you; but, as our dear W. S. remarks, 'What's in a name--' "

"Ah, indeed," said Mr. Harrington-Baillie; and apropos of that sentiment, he added: "Mine is Rowland--Captain Rowland. You may remember it now."

Mrs. Chater did not, however, and said so. "Will number six do?" she asked, opening her programme; and, when Augustus had assented, she entered his provisional name, remarking complacently: "We'll sit out and have a right-down good talk, and you shall tell me all about yourself and if you still think the same about free-will and personal responsibility. You had very lofty ideals, I remember, in those days, and I hope you have still. But one's ideals get rubbed down rather faint in the friction of life. Don't you think so?"

"Yes, I am afraid you're right," Augustus assented gloomily. "The wear and tear of life soon fetches the gilt off the gingerbread. Middle age is apt to find us a bit patchy, not to say naked."

"Oh, don't be pessimistic," said Mrs. Chater; "that is the attitude of the disappointed idealist, and I am sure you have no reason, really, to be disappointed in yourself. But I must run away now. Think over all the things you have to tell me, and don't forget that it is number six." With a bright smile and a friendly nod she sailed away, a vision of glittering splendour, compared with which Solomon in all his glory was a mere matter of commonplace bullion.

The interview, evidently friendly and familiar, between the unknown guest and the famous American widow had by no means passed unnoticed; and in other circumstances, Bailey might have endeavoured to profit by the reflected glory that enveloped him. But he was not in search of notoriety; and the same evasive instinct that had led him to sink Mr. Harrington-Baillie in Captain Rowland, now advised him to withdraw his dual personality from the vulgar gaze. He had come here on very definite business. For the hundredth time he was "stony-broke," and it was the hope of picking up some "unconsidered trifles" that had brought him. But, somehow, the atmosphere of the place had proved unfavourable. Either opportunities were lacking or he failed to seize them. In any case, the game pocket that formed an unconventional feature of his dress-coat was still empty, and it looked as if a pleasant evening and a good supper were all that he was likely to get. Nevertheless, be his conduct never so blameless, the fact remained that he was an uninvited guest, liable at any moment to be ejected as an impostor, and his recognition by the widow had not rendered this possibility any the more remote.

He strayed out onto the lawn, whence the grounds fell away on all sides. But there were other guests there, cooling themselves after the last dance, and the light from the rooms streamed through the windows, illuminating their figures, and among them, that of the too-companionable Granby. Augustus quickly drew away from the lighted area, and, chancing upon a narrow path, strolled away along it in the direction of a copse or shrubbery that he saw ahead. Presently he came to an ivy-covered arch, lighted by one or two fairy lamps, and, passing through this, he entered a winding path, bordered by trees and shrubs and but faintly lighted by an occasional coloured lamp suspended from a branch.

Already he was quite clear of the crowd; indeed, the deserted condition of the pleasant retreat rather surprised him, until he reflected that to couples desiring seclusion there were whole ranges of untenanted rooms and galleries available in the empty house.

The path sloped gently downwards for some distance; then came a long flight of rustic steps and, at the bottom, a seat between two trees. In front of the seat the path extended in a straight line, forming a narrow terrace; on the right the ground sloped up steeply towards the lawn; on the left it fell away still more steeply towards the encompassing wall of the grounds; and on both sides it was covered with trees and shrubs.

Bailey sat down on the seat to think over the account of himself that he should present to Mrs. Chater. It was a comfortable seat, built into the trunk of an elm, which formed one end and part of the back. He leaned against the tree, and, taking out his silver case, selected a cigarette. But it remained unlighted between his fingers as he sat and meditated upon his unsatisfactory past and the melancholy tale of what might have been. Fresh from the atmosphere of refined opulence that pervaded the dancing-rooms, the throng of well-groomed men and dainty women, his mind travelled back to his sordid little flat in Bermondsey, encompassed by poverty and squalor, jostled by lofty factories, grimy with the smoke of the river and the reek from the great chimneys. It was a hideous contrast. Verily the way of the transgressor was not strewn with flowers.

At that point in his meditations he caught the sound of voices and footsteps on the path above and rose to walk on along the path. He did not wish to be seen wandering alone in the shrubbery. But now a woman's laugh sounded from somewhere down the path. There were people approaching that way too. He put the cigarette back in the case and stepped round behind the seat, intending to retreat in that direction, but here the path ended, and beyond was nothing but a rugged slope down to the wall thickly covered with bushes. And while he was hesitating, the sound of feet descending the steps and the rustle of a woman's dress left him to choose between staying where he was or coming out to confront the new-comers. He chose the former, drawing up close behind the tree to wait until they should have passed on.

But they were not going to pass on. One of them--a woman--sat down on the seat, and then a familiar voice smote on his ear.

"I guess I'll rest here quietly for a while; this tooth of mine is aching terribly; and, see here, I want you to go and fetch me something. Take this ticket to the cloak-room and tell the woman to give you my little velvet bag. You'll find in it a bottle of chloroform and a packet of cotton-wool."

"But I can't leave you here all alone, Mrs. Chater," her partner expostulated.

"I'm not hankering for society just now," said Mrs. Chater. "I want that chloroform. Just you hustle off and fetch it, like a good boy. Here's the ticket."

The young officer's footsteps retreated rapidly, and the voices of the couple advancing along the path grew louder. Bailey, cursing the chance that had placed him in his ridiculous and uncomfortable position, heard them approach and pass on up the steps; and then all was silent, save for an occasional moan from Mrs. Chater and the measured creaking of the seat as she rocked uneasily to and fro. But the young man was uncommonly prompt in the discharge of his mission, and in a very few minutes Bailey heard him approaching at a run along the path above and then bounding down the steps.

"Now I call that real good of you," said the widow gratefully. "You must have run like the wind. Cut the string of the packet and then leave me to wrestle with this tooth."

"But I can't leave you here all--"

"Yes, you can," interrupted Mrs. Chater. "There won't be any one about-- the next dance is a waltz. Besides, you must go and find your partners."

"Well, if you'd really rather be alone," the subaltern began; but Mrs. Chater interrupted him.

"Of course I would, when I'm fixing up my teeth. Now go along, and a thousand thanks for your kindness."

With mumbled protestations the young officer slowly retired, and Bailey heard his reluctant feet ascending the steps. Then a deep silence fell on the place in which the rustle of paper and the squeak of a withdrawn cork seemed loud and palpable. Bailey had turned with his face towards the tree, against which he leaned with his lips parted scarcely daring to breathe. He cursed himself again and again for having thus entrapped himself for no tangible reason, and longed to get away. But there was no escape now without betraying himself. He must wait for the woman to go.

Suddenly, beyond the edge of the tree, a hand appeared holding an open packet of cotton-wool. It laid the wool down on the seat, and, pinching off a fragment, rolled it into a tiny ball. The fingers of the hand were encircled by rings, its wrist enclosed by a broad bracelet; and from rings and bracelet the light of the solitary fairy-lamp, that hung from a branch of the tree, was reflected in prismatic sparks. The hand was withdrawn and Bailey stared dreamily at the square pad of cotton-wool. Then the hand came again into view. This time it held a small phial which it laid softly on the seat, setting the cork beside it. And again the light flashed in many-coloured scintillations from the encrusting gems.

Bailey's knees began to tremble, and a chilly moisture broke out upon his forehead.

The hand drew back, but, as it vanished, Bailey moved his head silently until his face emerged from behind the tree. The woman was leaning back, her head resting against the trunk only a few inches away from his face. The great stones of the tiara flashed in his very eyes. Over her shoulder, he could even see the gorgeous pendant, rising and falling on her bosom with ever-changing fires; and both her raised hands were a mass of glitter and sparkle, only the deeper and richer for the subdued light.

His heart throbbed with palpable blows that drummed aloud in his ears. The sweat trickled clammily down his face, and he clenched his teeth to keep them from chattering. An agony of horror--of deadly fear--was creeping over him? a terror of the dreadful impulse that was stealing away his reason and his will.

The silence was profound. The woman's soft breathing, the creak of her bodice, were plainly--grossly--audible; and he checked his own breath until he seemed on the verge of suffocation.

Of a sudden through the night air was borne faintly the dreamy music of a waltz. The dance had begun. The distant sound but deepened the sense of solitude in this deserted spot.

Bailey listened intently. He yearned to escape from the invisible force that seemed to be clutching at his wrists, and dragging him forward inexorably to his doom.

He gazed down at the woman with a horrid fascination. He struggled to draw back out of sight--and struggled in vain.

Then, at last, with a horrible, stealthy deliberation, a clammy, shaking hand crept forward towards the seat. Without a sound it grasped the wool, and noiselessly, slowly drew back. Again it stole forth. The fingers twined snakily around the phial, lifted it from the seat and carried it back into the shadow.

After a few seconds it reappeared and softly replaced the bottle--now half empty. There was a brief pause. The measured cadences of the waltz stole softly through the quiet night and seemed to keep time with the woman's breathing. Other sound there was none. The place was wrapped in the silence of the grave.

Suddenly, from the hiding-place, Bailey leaned forward over the back of the seat. The pad of cotton-wool was in his hand.

The woman was now leaning back as if dozing, and her hands rested in her lap. There was a swift movement. The pad was pressed against her face and her head dragged back against the chest of the invisible assailant. A smothered gasp burst from her hidden lips as her hands flew up to clutch at the murderous arm; and then came a frightful struggle, made even more frightful by the gay and costly trappings of the writhing victim. And still there was hardly a sound; only muffled gasps, the rustle of silk, the creaking of the seat, the clink of the falling bottle and, afar off, with dreadful irony, the dreamy murmur of the waltz.

The struggle was but brief. Quite suddenly the jewelled hands dropped, the head lay resistless on the crumpled shirt-front, and the body, now limp and inert, began to slip forward off the seat. Bailey, still grasping the passive head, climbed over the back of the seat and, as the woman slid gently to the ground, he drew away the pad and stooped over her. The struggle was over now; the mad fury of the moment was passing swiftly into the chill of mortal fear.

He stared with incredulous horror into the swollen face, but now so comely, the sightless eyes that but a little while since had smiled into his with such kindly recognition.

He had done this! He, the sneaking wastrel, discarded of all the world, to whom this sweet woman had held out the hand of friendship. She had cherished his memory, when to all others he was sunk deep under the waters of oblivion. And he had killed her--for to his ear no breath of life seemed to issue from those purple lips.

A sudden hideous compunction for this irrevocable thing that he had done surged through him, and he stood up clutching at his damp hair with a hoarse cry that was like the cry of the damned.

The jewels passed straightaway out of his consciousness. Everything was forgotten now but the horror of this unspeakable thing that he had done. Remorse incurable and haunting fear were all that were left to him.

The sound of voices far away along the path aroused him, and the vague horror that possessed him materialized into abject bodily fear. He lifted the limp body to the edge of the path and let it slip down the steep declivity among the bushes. A soft, shuddering sigh came from the parted lips as the body turned over, and he paused a moment to listen. But there was no other sound of life. Doubtless that sigh was only the result of the passive movement.

Again he stood for an instant as one in a dream, gazing at the huddled shape half hidden by the bushes, before he climbed back to the path; and even then he looked back once more, but now she was hidden from sight. And, as the voices drew nearer, he turned, and ran up the rustic steps.

As he came out on the edge of the lawn the music ceased, and, almost immediately, a stream of people issued from the house. Shaken as he was, Bailey yet had wits enough left to know that his clothes and hair were disordered and that his appearance must be wild.

Accordingly he avoided the dancers, and, keeping to the margin of the lawn, made his way to the cloak-room by the least frequented route. If he had dared, he would have called in at the refreshment-room, for he was deadly faint and his limbs shook as he walked. But a haunting fear pursued him and, indeed, grew from moment to moment. He found himself already listening for the rumour of the inevitable discovery.

He staggered into the cloak-room, and, flinging his ticket down on the table, dragged out his watch. The attendant looked at him curiously and, pausing with the ticket in his hand, asked sympathetically: "Not feeling very well, sir?"

"No," said Bailey. "So beastly hot in there."

"You ought to have a glass of champagne, sir, before you start," said the man.

"No time," replied Bailey, holding out a shaky hand for his coat. "Shall lose my train if I'm not sharp."

At this hint the attendant reached down the coat and hat, holding up the former for its owner to slip his arms into the sleeves. But Bailey snatched it from him, and, flinging it over his arm, put on his hat and hurried away to the coachhouse. Here, again, the attendant stared at him in astonishment, which was not lessened when Bailey, declining his offer to help him on with his coat, bundled the latter under his arm, clicked the lever of the "variable" on to the ninety gear, sprang onto the machine and whirled away down the steep drive, a grotesque vision of flying coat-tails.

"You haven't lit your lamp, sir," roared the attendant; but Bailey's ears were deaf to all save the clamour of the expected pursuit.

Fortunately the drive entered the road obliquely, or Bailey must have been flung into the opposite hedge. As it was, the machine, rushing down the slope, flew out into the road with terrific velocity; nor did its speed diminish then, for its rider, impelled by mortal terror, trod the pedals with the fury of a madman. And still, as the machine whizzed along the dark and silent road, his ears were strained to catch the clatter of hoofs or the throb of a motor from behind.

He knew the country well, in fact, as a precaution, he had cycled over the district only the day before; and he was ready, at any suspicious sound, to slip down any of the lanes or byways, secure of finding his way. But still he sped on, and still no sound from the rear came to tell him of the dread discovery.

When he had ridden about three miles, he came to the foot of a steep hill. Here he had to dismount and push his machine up the incline, which he did at such speed that he arrived at the top quite breathless. Before mounting again he determined to put on his coat, for his appearance was calculated to attract attention, if nothing more. It was only half-past eleven, and presently he would pass through the streets of a small town. Also he would light his lamp. It would be fatal to be stopped by a patrol or rural constable.

Having lit his lamp and hastily put on his coat he once more listened intently, looking back over the country that was darkly visible from the summit of the hill. No moving lights were to be seen, no ringing hoofs or throbbing engines to be heard, and, turning to mount, he instinctively felt in his overcoat pocket for his gloves.

A pair of gloves came out in his hand, but he was instantly conscious that they were not his. A silk muffler was there also; a white one. But his muffler was black.

With a sudden shock of terror he thrust his hand into the ticket-pocket, where he had put his latch-key. There was no key there; only an amber cigar-holder, which he had never seen before. He stood for a few moments in utter consternation. He had taken the wrong coat. Then he had left his own coat behind. A cold sweat of fear broke out afresh on his face as he realized this. His Yale latch-key was in its pocket; not that that mattered very much. He had a duplicate at home, and, as to getting in, well, he knew his own outside door and his tool-bag contained one or two trifles not usually found in cyclists' tool-bags. The question was whether that coat contained anything that could disclose his identity. And then suddenly he remembered, with a gasp of relief, that he had carefully turned the pockets out before starting.

No; once let him attain the sanctuary of his grimy little flat, wedged in as it was between the great factories by the river-side, and he would be safe: safe from everything but the horror of himself, and the haunting vision of a jewelled figure huddled up in a silken heap beneath the bushes.

With a last look round he mounted his machine, and, driving it over the brow of the hill, swept away into the darkness.

Part II. Munera Pulveris

(Related by Christopher Jervis, M.D.)

It is one of the drawbacks of medicine as a profession that one is never rid of one's responsibilities. The merchant, the lawyer, the civil servant, each at the appointed time locks up his desk, puts on his hat and goes forth a free man with an interval of uninterrupted leisure before him. Not so the doctor. Whether at work or at play, awake or asleep, he is the servant of humanity, at the instant disposal of friend or stranger alike whose need may make the necessary claim.

When I agreed to accompany my wife to the spinsters' dance at Raynesford, I imagined that, for that evening, at least, I was definitely off duty; and in that belief I continued until the conclusion of the eighth dance. To be quite truthful, I was not sorry when the delusion was shattered. My last partner was a young lady of a slanginess of speech that verged on the inarticulate. Now it is not easy to exchange ideas in "pidgin" English; and the conversation of a person to whom all things are either "ripping" or "rotten" is apt to lack subtlety. In fact, I was frankly bored; and, reflecting on the utility of the humble sandwich as an aid to conversation, I was about to entice my partner to the refreshment-room when I felt some one pluck at my sleeve. I turned quickly and looked into the anxious and rather frightened face of my wife.

"Miss Halliwell is looking for you," she said. "A lady has been taken ill. Will you come and see what is the matter?" She took my arm and, when I had made my apologies to my partner, she hurried me on to the lawn.

"It's a mysterious affair," my wife continued. "The sick lady is a Mrs. Chater, a very wealthy American widow. Edith Halliwell and Major Podbury found her lying in the shrubbery all alone and unable to give any account of herself. Poor Edith is dreadfully upset. She doesn't know what to think."

"What do you mean?" I began; but at this moment Miss Halliwell, who was waiting by an ivy-covered rustic arch, espied us and ran forward.

"Oh, do hurry, please, Dr. Jervis," she exclaimed; "such a shocking thing has happened. Has Juliet told you?" Without waiting for an answer, she darted through the arch and preceded us along a narrow path at the curious, flat-footed, shambling trot common to most adult women. Presently we descended a flight of rustic steps which brought us to a seat, from whence extended a straight path cut like a miniature terrace on a steep slope, with a high bank rising to the right and declivity falling away to the left. Down in the hollow, his head and shoulders appearing above the bushes, was a man holding in his hand a fairy-lamp that he had apparently taken down from a tree. I climbed down to him, and, as I came round the bushes, I perceived a richly-dressed woman lying huddled on the ground. She was not completely insensible, for she moved slightly at my approach, muttering a few words in thick, indistinct accents. I took the lamp from the man, whom I assumed to be Major Podbury, and, as he delivered it to me with a significant glance and a faint lift of the eyebrows, I understood Miss Halliwell's agitation. Indeed--for one horrible moment I thought that she was right--that the prostrate woman was intoxicated. But when I approached nearer, the flickering light of the lamp made visible a square reddened patch on her face, like the impression of a mustard plaster, covering the nose and mouth; and then I scented mischief of a more serious kind.

"We had better carry her up to the seat," I said, handing the lamp to Miss Halliwell. "Then we can consider moving her to the house." The major and I lifted the helpless woman and, having climbed cautiously up to the path, laid her on the seat.

"What is it, Dr. Jervis?" Miss Halliwell whispered.

"I can't say at the moment," I replied; "but it's not what you feared."

"Thank God for that!" was her fervent rejoinder. "It would have been a shocking scandal."

I took the dim lamp and once more bent over the half-conscious woman.

Her appearance puzzled me not a little. She looked like a person recovering from an anaesthetic, but the square red patch on her face, recalling, as it did, the Burke murders, rather suggested suffocation. As I was thus reflecting, the light of the lamp fell on a white object lying on the ground behind the seat, and holding the lamp forward, I saw that it was a square pad of cotton-wool. The coincidence of its shape and size with that of the red patch on the woman's face instantly struck me, and I stooped down to pick it up;

and then I saw, lying under the seat, a small bottle. This also I picked up and held in the lamplight. It was a one-ounce phial, quite empty, and was labelled "Methylated Chloroform." Here seemed to be a complete explanation of the thick utterance and drunken aspect; but it was an explanation that required, in its turn, to be explained. Obviously no robbery had been committed, for the woman literally glittered with diamonds. Equally obviously she had not administered the chloroform to herself.

There was nothing for it but to carry her indoors and await her further recovery, so, with the major's help, we conveyed her through the shrubbery and kitchen garden to a side door, and deposited her on a sofa in a half-furnished room.

Here, under the influence of water dabbed on her face and the plentiful use of smelling salts', she quickly revived, and was soon able to give an intelligible account of herself.

The chloroform and cotton-wool were her own. She had used them for an aching tooth; and she was sitting alone on the seat with the bottle and the wool beside her when the incomprehensible thing had happened. Without a moment's warning a hand had come from behind her and pressed the pad of wool over her nose and mouth. The wool was saturated with chloroform, and she had lost consciousness almost immediately.

"You didn't see the person, then?" I asked.

"No, but I know he was in evening dress, because I felt my head against his shirt-front."

"Then," said I, "he is either here still or he has been to the cloak-room. He couldn't have left the place without an overcoat."

"No, by Jove!" exclaimed the major; "that's true. I'll go and make inquiries." He strode away all agog, and I, having satisfied myself that Mrs. Chater could be left safely, followed him almost immediately.

I made my way straight to the cloak-room, and here I found the major and one or two of his brother officers putting on their coats in a flutter of gleeful excitement.

"He's gone," said Podbury, struggling frantically into his overcoat; "went off nearly an hour ago on a bicycle. Seemed in a deuce of a stew, the attendant says, and no wonder. We're goin' after him in our car. Care to join the hunt?"

"No, thanks. I must stay with the patient. But how do you know you're after the right man?"

"Isn't any other. Only one Johnnie's left. Besides--here, confound it! you've given me the wrong coat!" He tore off the garment and handed it back to the attendant, who regarded it with an expression of dismay.

"Are you sure, sir?" he asked.

"Perfectly," said the major. "Come, hurry up, my man."

"I'm afraid, sir," said the attendant, "that the gentleman who has gone has taken your coat. They were on the same peg, I know. I am very sorry, sir."

The major was speechless with wrath. What the devil was the good of being sorry; and how the deuce was he to get his coat back -

"But," I interposed, "if the stranger has got your coat, then this coat must be his."

"I know," said Podbury; "but I don't want his beastly coat."

"No," I replied, "but it may be useful for identification."

This appeared to afford the bereaved officer little consolation, but as the car was now ready, he bustled away, and I, having directed the man to put the coat away in a safe place, went back to my patient.

Mrs. Chater was by now fairly recovered, and had developed a highly vindictive interest in her late assailant. She even went so far as to regret that he had not taken at least some of her diamonds, so that robbery might have been added to the charge of attempted murder, and expressed the earnest hope that the officers would not be foolishly gentle in their treatment of him when they caught him.

"By the way, Dr. Jervis," said Miss Halliwell, "I think I ought to mention a rather curious thing that happened in connection with this dance. We received an acceptance from a Mr. Harrington-Baillie, who wrote from the Hotel Cecil. Now I am certain that no such name was proposed by any of the spinsters."

"But didn't you ask them?" I inquired.

"Well, the fact is," she replied, "that one of them, Miss Waters, had to go abroad suddenly, and we had not got her address;

and as it was possible that she might have invited him, I did not like to move in the matter. I am very sorry I didn't now. We may have let in a regular criminal? though why he should have wanted to murder Mrs. Chater I cannot imagine."

It was certainly a mysterious affair, and the mystery was in no wise dispelled by the return of the search party an hour later. It seemed that the bicycle had been tracked for a couple of miles towards London, but then, at the cross-roads, the tracks had become hopelessly mixed with the impressions of other machines and the officers, after cruising about vaguely for a while, had given up the hunt and returned.

"You see, Mrs. Chater," Major Podbury explained apologetically, "the fellow must have had a good hour's start, and that would have brought him pretty close to London."

"Do you mean to tell me," exclaimed Mrs. Chater, regarding the major with hardly-concealed contempt, "that that villain has got off scot-free?"

"Looks rather like it," replied Podbury, "but if I were you I should get the man's description from the attendants who saw him and go up to Scotland Yard to-morrow. They may know the Johnny there, and they may even recognize the coat if you take it with you."

"That doesn't seem very likely," said Mrs. Chater, and it certainly did not; but since no better plan could be suggested the lady decided to adopt it; and I supposed that I had heard the last of the matter.

In this, however, I was mistaken. On the following day, just before noon, as I was drowsily considering the points in a brief dealing with a question of survivorship, while Thorndyke drafted his weekly lecture, a smart rat-tat at the door of our chambers announced a visitor. I rose wearily--I had had only four hours' sleep--and opened the door, whereupon there sailed into the room no less a person than Mrs. Chater, followed by Superintendent Miller, with a grin on his face and a brown-paper parcel under his arm.

The lady was not in the best of tempers, though wonderfully lively and alert considering the severe shock that she had suffered so recently, and her disapproval of Miller was frankly obvious.

"Dr. Jervis has probably told you about the attempt to murder me last night," she said, when I had introduced her to my colleague. "Well, now, will you believe it? I have been to the police, I have given them a description of the murderous villain, and I have even shown them the very coat that he wore, and they tell me that nothing can be done. That, in short, this scoundrel must be allowed to go his way free and unmolested."

"You will observe, doctor," said Miller, "that this lady has given us a description that would apply to fifty per cent, of the middle-class men of the United Kingdom, and has shown us a coat without a single identifying mark of any kind on it, and expects us to lay our hands on the owner without a solitary clue to guide us. Now we are not sorcerers at the Yard; we're only policemen. So I have taken the liberty of referring Mrs. Chater to you." He grinned maliciously and laid the parcel on the table.

"And what do you want me to do?" Thorndyke asked quietly.

"Why sir," said Miller, "there is a coat. In the pockets were a pair of gloves, a muffler, a box of matches, a tram-ticket and a Yale key. Mrs. Chater would like to know whose coat it is." He untied the parcel with his eye cocked at our rather disconcerted client, and Thorndyke watched him with a faint smile.

"This is very kind of you, Miller," said he, "but I think a clairvoyant would be more to your purpose."

The superintendent instantly dropped his facetious manner.

"Seriously, sir," he said, "I should be glad if you would take a look at the coat. We have absolutely nothing to go on, and yet we don't want to give up the case. I have gone through it most thoroughly and can't find any clue to guide us. Now I know that nothing escapes you, and perhaps you might notice something that I have overlooked; something that would give us a hint where to start on, our inquiry. Couldn't you turn the microscope on it, for instance?" he added, with a deprecating smile.

Thorndyke reflected, with an inquisitive eye on the coat. I saw that the problem was not without its attractions to him; and when the lady seconded Miller's request with persuasive eagerness, the inevitable consequence followed.

"Very well," he said. "Leave the coat with me for an hour or so and I will look it over. I am afraid there is not the remotest chance of our learning anything from it, but even so, the examination will have done no harm. Come back at two o'clock; I shall be ready to report my failure by then."

He bowed our visitors out and, returning to the table, looked down with a quizzical smile on the coat and the large official envelope containing articles from the pockets.

"And what does my learned brother suggest?" he asked, looking up at me.

"I should look at the tram-ticket first," I replied, "and then--well, Miller's suggestion wasn't such a bad one; to explore the surface with the microscope."

"I think we will take the latter measure first," said he. "The tram-ticket might create a misleading bias. A man may take a tram anywhere, whereas the indoor dust on a man's coat appertains mostly to a definite locality."

"Yes," I replied; "but the information that it yields is excessively vague."

"That is true," he agreed, taking up the coat and envelope to carry them to the laboratory, "and yet, you know, Jervis, as I have often pointed out, the evidential value of dust is apt to be under-estimated. The naked-eye appearances? which are the normal appearances--are misleading. Gather the dust, say, from a table-top, and what have you? A fine powder of a characterless grey, just like any other dust from any other table-top. But, under the microscope, this grey powder is resolved into recognizable fragments of definite substances, which fragments may often be traced with certainty to the masses from which they have been detached. But you know all this as well as I do."

"I quite appreciate the value of dust as evidence in certain circumstances," I replied, "but surely the information that could be gathered from dust on the coat of an unknown man must be too general to be of any use in tracing the owner."

"I am afraid you are right," said Thorndyke, laying the coat on the laboratory bench; "but we shall soon see, if Polton will let us have his patent dust-extractor."

The little apparatus to which my colleague referred was the invention of our ingenious laboratory assistant, and resembled in principle the "vacuum cleaners" used for restoring carpets. It had, however, one special feature: the receiver was made to admit a microscope-slide, and on this the dust-laden air was delivered from a jet.

The "extractor" having been clamped to the bench by its proud inventor, and a wetted slide introduced into the receiver, Thorndyke applied the nozzle of the instrument to the collar of the coat while Polton worked the pump. The slide was then removed and, another having been substituted, the nozzle was applied to the right sleeve near the shoulder, and the exhauster again worked by Polton. By repeating this process, half-a-dozen slides were obtained charged with dust from different parts of the garment, and then, setting up our respective microscopes, we proceeded to examine the samples.

A very brief inspection showed me that this dust contained matter not usually met with--at any rate, in appreciable quantities. There were, of course, the usual fragments of wool, cotton and other fibres derived from clothing and furniture, particles of straw, husk, hair, various mineral particles and, in fact, the ordinary constituents of dust from clothing. But, in addition to these, and in much greater quantity, were a number of other bodies, mostly of vegetable origin and presenting well-defined characters in considerable variety, and especially abundant were various starch granules.

I glanced at Thorndyke and observed he was already busy with a pencil and a slip of paper, apparently making a list of the objects visible in the field of the microscope. I hastened to follow his example, and for a time we worked on in silence. At length my colleague leaned back in his chair and read over his list.

"This is a highly interesting collection, Jervis," he remarked. "What do you find on your slides out of the ordinary?"

"I have quite a little museum here," I replied, referring to my list. "There is, of course, chalk from the road at Raynesford. In addition to this I find various starches, principally wheat and rice, especially rice, fragments of the cortices of several seeds, several different stone-cells, some yellow masses that look like turmeric, black pepper resin-cells, one 'port wine' pimento cell, and one or two particles of graphite."

"Graphite!" exclaimed Thorndyke. "I have found no graphite, but I have found traces of cocoa--spiral vessels and starch grains--and of hops-- one fragment of leaf and several lupulin glands. May I see the graphite?"

I passed him the slide and he examined it with keen interest. "Yes," he said, "this is undoubtedly graphite, and no less than six particles of it. We had better go over the coat systematically. You see the importance of this?"

"I see that this is evidently factory dust and that it may fix a locality, but I don't see that it will carry us any farther."

"Don't forget that we have a touchstone," said he; and, as I raised my eyebrows inquiringly, he added, "The Yale latchkey. If we can narrow the locality down sufficiently, Miller can make a tour of the front doors."

"But can we?" I asked incredulously. "I doubt it."

"We can try," answered Thorndyke. "Evidently some of the substances are distributed over the entire coat, inside and out, while others, such as the graphite, are present only on certain parts. We must locate those parts exactly and then consider what this special distribution means." He rapidly sketched out on a sheet of paper a rough diagram of the coat, marking each part with a distinctive letter, and then, taking a number of labelled slides, he wrote a single letter on each. The samples of dust taken on the slides could thus be easily referred to the exact spots whence they had been obtained.

Once more we set to work with the microscope, making, now and again, an addition to our lists of discoveries, and, at the end of nearly an hour's strenuous search, every slide had been examined and the lists compared.

"The net result of the examination," said Thorndyke, "is this. The entire coat, inside and out, is evenly powdered with the following substances: Rice-starch in abundance, wheat-starch in less abundance, and smaller quantities of the starches of ginger, pimento and cinnamon; bast fibre of cinnamon, various seed cortices, stone-cells of pimento, cinnamon, cassia and black pepper, with other fragments of similar origin, such as resin-cells and ginger pigment--not turmeric. In addition there are, on the right shoulder and sleeve, traces of cocoa and hops, and on the back below the shoulders a few fragments of graphite. Those are the data; and now, what are the inferences? Remember this is not mere surface dust, but the accumulation of months, beaten into the cloth by repeated brushing-- dust that nothing but a vacuum apparatus could extract."

"Evidently," I said, "the particles that are all over the coat represent dust that is floating in the air of the place where the coat habitually hangs. The graphite has obviously been picked up from a seat and the cocoa and hops from some factories that the man passes frequently, though I don't see why they are on the right side only."

"That is a question of time," said Thorndyke, "and incidentally throws some light on our friend's habits. Going from home, he passes the factories on his right; returning home, he passes them on his left, but they have then stopped work. However, the first group of substances is the more important as they indicate the locality of his dwelling--for he is clearly not a workman or factory employee. Now rice-starch, wheat-starch and a group of substances collectively designated 'spices' suggest a rice-mill, a flour-mill and a spice factory. Polton, may I trouble you for the Post Office Directory?"

He turned over the leaves of the "Trades" section and resumed: "I see there are four rice-mills in London, of which the largest is Carbutt's at Dockhead. Let us look at the spice-factories." He again turned over the leaves and read down the list of names. "There are six spice-grinders in London," said he. "One of them, Thomas Williams & Co., is at Dockhead. None of the others is near any rice-mill. The next question is as to the flour-mill. Let us see. Here are the names of several flour millers, but none of them is near either a rice-mill or a spice-grinder, with one exception: Seth Taylor's, St. Saviour's Flour Mills, Dockhead."

"This is really becoming interesting," said I.

"It has become interesting," Thorndyke retorted. "You observe that at Dockhead we find the peculiar combination of factories necessary to produce the composite dust in which this coat has hung; and the directory shows us that this particular combination exists nowhere else in London. Then the graphite, the cocoa and the hops tend to confirm the other suggestions. They all appertain to industries of the locality. The trams which pass Dockhead, also, to my knowledge, pass at no great distance from the black-lead works of Pearce Duff & Co. in Rouel Road, and will probably collect a few particles of black-lead on the seats in certain states of the wind. I see, too, that there is a cocoa factory--Payne's-- in Goat Street, Horsleydown, which lies to the right of the tram line going west, and I have noticed several hop warehouses on the right side of Southwark Street, going west. But these are mere suggestions; the really important data are the rice and flour mills and the spice-grinders, which seem to point unmistakably to Dockhead."

"Are there any private houses at Dockhead?" I asked.

"We must look up the 'Street' list," he replied. "The Yale latch-key rather suggests a flat, and a flat with a single occupant, and the probable habits of our absent friend offer a similar suggestion." He ran his eye down the list and presently turned to me with his finger on the page.

"If the facts that we have elicited--the singular series of agreements with the required conditions--are only a string of coincidences, here is another. On the south side of Dockhead, actually next door to the spice-grinders and opposite to Carbutt's rice-mills, is a block of workmen's flats, Hanover Buildings. They fulfil the conditions exactly. A coat hung in a room in those flats, with the windows open (as they would probably be at this time of year), would be exposed to the air containing a composite dust of precisely the character of that which we have found. Of course, the same conditions obtain in other dwellings in this part of Dockhead, but the probability is in favour of the buildings. And that is all that we can say. It is no certainty. There may be some radical fallacy in our reasoning. But, on the face of it, the chances are a thousand to one that the door that that key will open is in some part of Dockhead, and most probably in Hanover Buildings. We must leave the verification to Miller."

"Wouldn't it be as well to look at the tram-ticket?" I asked.

"Dear me!" he exclaimed. "I had forgotten the ticket. Yes, by all means." He opened the envelope and, turning its contents out on the bench, picked up the dingy slip of paper. After a glance at it he handed it to me. It was punched for the journey from Tooley Street to Dockhead.

"Another coincidence," he remarked; "and by yet another, I think I hear Miller knocking at our door."

It was the superintendent, and, as we let him into the room, the hum of a motor-car entering from Tudor Street announced the arrival of Mrs. Chater. We waited for her at the open door, and, as she entered, she held out her hands impulsively.

"Say, now, Dr. Thorndyke," she exclaimed, "have you gotten something to tell us?"

"I have a suggestion to make," replied Thorndyke. "I think that if the superintendent will take this key to Hanover Buildings, Dockhead, Bermondsey, he may possibly find a door that it will fit."

"The deuce!" exclaimed Miller. "I beg your pardon, madam; but I thought I had gone through that coat pretty completely. What was it that I had overlooked, sir? Was there a letter hidden in it, after all?"

"You overlooked the dust on it, Miller; that is all," said Thorndyke.

"Dust!" exclaimed the detective, staring round-eyed at my colleague. Then he chuckled softly. "Well," said he, "as I said before, I'm not a sorcerer; I'm only a policeman." He picked up the key and asked: "Are you coming to see the end of it, sir?"

"Of course he is coming," said Mrs. Chater, "and Dr. Jervis too, to identify the man. Now that we have gotten the villain we must leave him no loophole for escape."

Thorndyke smiled dryly. "We will come if you wish it, Mrs. Chater," he said, "but you mustn't look upon our quest as a certainty. We may have made an entire miscalculation, and I am, in fact, rather curious to see if the result works out correctly. But even if we run the man to earth, I don't see that you have much evidence against him. The most that you can prove is that he was at the house and that he left hurriedly."

Mrs. Chater regarded my colleague for a moment in scornful silence, and then, gathering up her skirts, stalked out of the room. If there is one thing that the average woman detests more than another, it is an entirely reasonable man.

The big car whirled us rapidly over Blackfriars Bridge into the region of the Borough, whence we presently turned down Tooley Street towards Bermondsey.

As soon as Dockhead came into view, the detective, Thorndyke and I, alighted and proceeded on foot, leaving our client, who was now closely veiled, to follow at a little distance in the car. Opposite the head of St. Saviour's Dock, Thorndyke halted and, looking over the wall, drew my attention to the snowy powder that had lodged on every projection on the backs of the tall buildings and on the decks of the barges that were loading with the flour and ground rice. Then, crossing the road, he pointed to the wooden lantern above the roof of the spice works, the louvres of which were covered with greyish-buff dust.

"Thus," he moralized, "does commerce subserve the ends of justice--at least, we hope it does," he added quickly, as Miller disappeared into the semi-basement of the buildings.

We met the detective returning from his quest as we entered the building.

"No go there," was his report. "We'll try the next floor."

This was the ground-floor, or it might be considered the first floor. At any rate, it yielded nothing of interest, and, after a glance at the doors that opened on the landing, he strode briskly up the stone stairs. The next floor was equally unrewarding, for our eager inspection disclosed nothing but the gaping keyhole associated with the common type of night-latch.

"What name was you wanting?" inquired a dusty knight of industry who emerged from one of the flats.

"Muggs," replied Miller, with admirable promptness.

"Don't know 'im," said the workman. "I expect it's farther up."

Farther up we accordingly went, but still from each door the artless grin of the invariable keyhole saluted us with depressing monotony. I began to grow uneasy, and when the fourth floor had been explored with no better result, my anxiety became acute. A mare's nest may be an interesting curiosity, but it brings no kudos to its discoverer.

"I suppose you haven't made any mistake, sir?" said Miller, stopping to wipe his brow.

"It's quite likely that I have," replied Thorndyke, with unmoved composure. "I only proposed this search as a tentative proceeding, you know."

The superintendent grunted. He was accustomed--as was I too, for that matter--to regard Thorndyke's "tentative suggestions" as equal to another man's certainties.

"It will be an awful suck-in for Mrs. Chater if we don't find him after all," he growled as we climbed up the last flight. "She's counted her chickens to a feather." He paused at the head of the stairs and stood for a few moments looking round the landing. Suddenly he turned eagerly, and, laying his hand on Thorndyke's arm, pointed to a door in the farthest corner.

"Yale lock!" he whispered impressively.

We followed him silently as he stole on tip-toe across the landing, and watched him as he stood for an instant with the key in his land looking gloatingly at the brass disc. We saw him softly apply the nose of the fluted key-blade to the crooked slit in the cylinder, and, as we watched, it slid noiselessly up to the shoulder. The detective looked round with a grin of triumph, and, silently withdrawing the key, stepped back to us.

"You've run him to earth, sir," he whispered, "but I don't think Mr. Fox is at home. He can't have got back yet."

"Why not?" asked Thorndyke.

Miller waved his hand towards the door. "Nothing has been disturbed," he replied. "There's not a mark on the paint. Now he hadn't got the key, and you can't pick a Yale lock. He'd have had to break in, and he hasn't broken in."

Thorndyke stepped up to the door and softly pushed in the flap of the letter-slit, through which he looked into the flat.

"There's no letter-box," said he. "My dear Miller, I would undertake to open that door in five minutes with a foot of wire and a bit of resined string."

Miller shook his head and grinned once more. "I am glad you're not on the lay, sir; you'd be one too many for us. Shall we signal to the lady?"

I went out onto the gallery and looked down at the waiting car., Mrs. Chater was staring intently up at the building, and the little crowd that the car had collected stared alternately at the lady and at the object of her regard. I wiped my face with my handkerchief--the signal agreed upon--and she instantly sprang out of the car, and in an incredibly short time she appeared on the landing, purple and gasping, but with the fire of battle flashing from her eyes.

"We've found his flat, madam," said Miller, "and we're going to enter. You're not intending to offer any violence, I hope," he added, noting with some uneasiness the lady's ferocious expression.

"Of course I'm not," replied Mrs. Chater. "In the States ladies don't have to avenge insults themselves. If you were American men you'd hang the ruffian from his own bedpost."

"We're riot American men, madam," said the superintendent stiffly. "We are law-abiding Englishmen, and, moreover, we are all officers of the law. These gentlemen are barristers and I am a police officer."

With this preliminary caution, he once more inserted the key, and as he turned it and pushed the door open, we all followed him into the sitting-room.

"I told you so, sir," said Miller, softly shutting the door; "he hasn't come back yet."

Apparently he was right. At any rate, there was no one in the flat, and we proceeded unopposed on our tour of inspection. It was a miserable spectacle, and, as we wandered from one squalid room to another, a feeling of pity for the starving wretch into whose lair we were intruding stole over me and began almost to mitigate the hideousness of his crime. On all sides poverty--utter, grinding poverty--stared us in the face. It looked at us hollow-eyed in the wretched sitting-room, with its bare floor, its solitary chair and tiny deal table; its unfurnished walls and windows destitute of blind or curtain. A piece of Dutch cheese-rind on the table, scraped to the thinness of paper, whispered of starvation; and famine lurked in the gaping cupboard, in the empty bread-tin, in the tea-caddy with its pinch of dust at the bottom, in the jam-jar, wiped clean, as a few crumbs testified, with a crust of bread. There was not enough food in the place to furnish a meal for a healthy mouse.

The bedroom told the same tale, but with a curious variation. A miserable truckle-bed with a straw mattress and a cheap jute rug for bed-clothes, an orange-case, stood on end, for a dressing-table, and another, bearing a tin washing-bowl, formed the wretched furniture. But the suit that hung from a couple of nails was well-cut and even fashionable, though shabby; and another suit lay on the floor, neatly folded and covered with a newspaper; and, most incongruous of all, a silver cigarette-case reposed on the dressing-table.

"Why on earth does this fellow starve," I exclaimed, "when he has a silver case to pawn?"

"Wouldn't do," said Miller. "A man doesn't pawn the implements of his trade."

Mrs. Chater, who had been staring about her with the mute amazement of a wealthy woman confronted, for the first time, with abject poverty, turned suddenly to the superintendent. “This can’t be the man!” she exclaimed. “You have made some mistake. This poor creature could never have made his way into a house like Willowdale.”

Thorndyke lifted the newspaper. Beneath it was a dress suit with the shirt, collar and tie all carefully smoothed out and folded. Thorndyke unfolded the shirt and pointed to the curiously crumpled front. Suddenly he brought it close to his eye and then, from the sham diamond stud, he drew a single hair--a woman’s hair.

“That is rather significant,” said he, holding it up between his finger and thumb; and Mrs. Chater evidently thought so too, for the pity and compunction suddenly faded from her face, and once more her eyes flashed with vindictive fire.

“I wish he would come,” she exclaimed viciously. “Prison won’t be much hardship to him after this”, but I want to see him in the dock all the same.”

“No,” the detective agreed, “it won’t hurt him much to swap this for Portland. Listen!”

A key was being inserted into the outer door, and as we all stood like statues, a man entered and closed the door after him. He passed the door of the bedroom without seeing us, and with the dragging steps of a weary, dispirited man. Almost immediately we heard him go to the kitchen and draw water into some vessel. Then he went back to the sitting-room.

“Come along,” said Miller, stepping silently towards the door. We followed closely, and as he threw the door open, we looked in over his shoulder.

The man had seated himself at the table, on which now lay a hunk of household bread resting on the paper in which he had brought it, and a tumbler of water. He half rose as the door opened, and as if petrified remained staring at Miller with a dreadful expression of terror upon his livid face.

At this moment I felt a hand on my arm, and Mrs. Chater brusquely pushed past me into the room. But at the threshold she stopped short; and a singular change crept over the man’s ghastly face, a change so remarkable that I looked involuntarily from him to our client. She had turned, in a moment, deadly pale, and her face had frozen into an expression of incredulous horror.

The dramatic silence was broken by the matter-of-fact voice of the detective.

"I am a police officer," said he, "and I arrest you for -?"

A peal of hysterical laughter from Mrs. Chater interrupted him, and he looked at her in astonishment. "Stop, stop!" she cried in a shaky voice. "I guess we've made a ridiculous mistake. This isn't the man. This gentleman is Captain Rowland, an old friend of mine."

"I'm sorry he's a friend of yours," said Miller, "because I shall have to ask you to appear against him."

"You can ask what you please," replied Mrs. Chater. "I tell you he's not the man."

The superintendent rubbed his nose and looked hungrily at his quarry. "Do I understand, madam," he asked stiffly, "that you refuse to prosecute?"

"Prosecute!" she exclaimed. "Prosecute my friends for offences that I know they have not committed? Certainly I refuse."

The superintendent looked at Thorndyke, but my colleague's countenance had congealed into a state of absolute immobility and was as devoid of expression as the face of a Dutch clock.

"Very well," said Miller, looking sourly at his watch. "Then we have had our trouble for nothing. I wish you good afternoon, madam."

"I am sorry I troubled you, now," said Mrs. Chater.

"I am sorry you did," was the curt reply; and the superintendent, flinging the key on the table, stalked out of the room.

As the outer door slammed the man sat down with an air of bewilderment; and then, suddenly flinging his arms on the table, he dropped his head on them and burst into a passion of sobbing.

It was very embarrassing. With one accord Thorndyke and I turned to go, but Mrs. Chater motioned us to stay. Stepping over to the man, she touched him lightly on the arm.

"Why did you do it?" she asked in a tone of gentle reproach.

The man sat up and flung out one arm in an eloquent gesture that comprehended the miserable room and the yawning cupboard.

"It was the temptation of a moment," he said. "I was penniless, and those accursed diamonds were thrust in my face; they were mine for the taking. I was mad, I suppose."

"But why didn't you take them?" she said. "Why didn't you?"

"I don't know. The madness passed; and then--when I saw you lying there--? Oh, God! Why don't you give me up to the police?" He laid his head down and sobbed afresh.

Mrs. Chater bent over him with tears standing in her pretty grey eyes. "But tell me," she said, "why didn't you take the diamonds? You could if you'd liked, I suppose?"

"What good were they to me?" he demanded passionately. "What did any thing matter to me? I thought you were dead."

"Well, I'm not, you see," she said, with a rather tearful smile; "I'm just as well as an old woman like me can expect to be. And I want your address, so that I can write and give you some good advice."

The man sat up and produced a shabby cardcase from his pocket, and, as he took out a number of cards and spread them out like the "hand" of a whist player, I caught a twinkle in Thorndyke's eye.

"My name is Augustus Bailey," said the man. He selected the appropriate card, and, having scribbled his address on it with a stump of lead pencil, relapsed into his former position.

"Thank you," said Mrs. Chater, lingering for a moment by the table. "Now we'll go. Good-bye, Mr. Bailey. I shall write to-morrow, and you must attend seriously to the advice of an old friend."

I held open the door for her to pass out and looked back before I turned to follow. Bailey still sat sobbing quietly, with his hand resting on his arms; and a little pile of gold stood on the corner of the table.

"I expect, doctor," said Mrs. Chater, as Thorndyke handed her into the car, "you've written me down a sentimental fool."

Thorndyke looked at her with an unwonted softening of his rather severe face and answered quietly, "It is written: Blessed are the Merciful."

The Old Lag

Part I. The Changed Immutable

Among the minor and purely physical pleasures of life, I am disposed to rank very highly that feeling of bodily comfort that one experiences on passing from the outer darkness of a wet winter's night to a cheerful interior made glad by mellow lamplight and blazing hearth. And so I thought when, on a dreary November night, I let myself into our chambers in the Temple and found my friend smoking his pipe in slippered ease, by a roaring fire, and facing an empty arm-chair evidently placed in readiness for me.

As I shed my damp overcoat, I glanced inquisitively at my colleague, for he held in his hand an open letter, and I seemed to perceive in his aspect something meditative and self-communing--something, in short, suggestive of a new case.

"I was just considering," he said, in answer to my inquiring look, "whether I am about to become an accessory after the fact. Read that and give me your opinion."

He handed me the letter, which I read aloud.

"dear sir,--I am in great danger and distress. A warrant has been issued for my arrest on a charge of which I am entirely innocent. Can I come and see you, and will you let me leave in safety? The bearer will wait for a reply."

"I said 'Yes,' of course; there was nothing else to do," said Thorndyke. "But if I let him go, as I have promised to do, I shall be virtually conniving at his escape."

"Yes, you are taking a risk," I answered. "When is he coming?"

"He was due five minutes ago--and I rather think--yes, here he is."

A stealthy tread on the landing was followed by a soft tapping on the outer door.

Thorndyke rose and, flinging open the inner door, unfastened the massive "oak."

"Dr. Thorndyke?" inquired a breathless, quavering voice.

"Yes, come in. You sent me a letter by hand?"

"I did, sir," was the reply; and the speaker entered, but at the sight of me he stopped short.

"This is my colleague, Dr. Jervis," Thorndyke explained. "You need have no -?"

"Oh, I remember him," our visitor interrupted in a tone of relief. "I have seen you both before, you know, and you have seen me too--though I don't suppose you recognize me," he added, with: a sickly smile.

"Frank Belfield?" asked Thorndyke, smiling also.

Our visitor's jaw fell and he gazed at my colleague in sudden dismay.

"And I may remark," pursued Thorndyke, "that for a man in your perilous position, you are running most unnecessary risks. That wig, that false beard and those spectacles--through which you obviously cannot see--are enough to bring the entire police force at your heels. It is not wise for a man who is wanted by the police to make up as though he had just escaped from a comic opera."

Mr. Belfield seated himself with a groan, and, taking off his spectacles, stared stupidly from one of us to the other.

"And now tell us about your little affair," said Thorndyke. "You say that you are innocent?"

"I swear it, doctor," replied Belfield; adding, with great earnestness, "And you may take it from me, sir, that if I was not, I shouldn't be here. It was you that convicted me last time, when I thought myself quite safe, so I know your ways too well to try to gammon you."

"If you are innocent," rejoined Thorndyke, "I will do what I can for you; and if you are not--well, you would have been wiser to stay away."

"I know that well enough," said Belfield, "and I am only afraid that you won't believe what I am going to tell you."

"I shall keep an open mind, at any rate," replied Thorndyke.

"If you only will," groaned Belfield, "I shall have a look in, in spite of them all. You know, sir, that I have been on the crook, but I have paid in full. That job when you tripped me up was the last of it--it was, sir, so help me. It was a woman that changed me--the best and truest woman on God's earth. She said she would marry me when I came out if I promised her to go straight and live an honest life. And she kept her promise--and I have kept mine. She found me work as clerk in a warehouse and I have stuck to it ever since, earning fair wages and building up a good character as an honest, industrious man. I thought all was going well, and that I was settled for life, when only this very morning the whole thing comes tumbling about my ears like a house of cards."

"What happened this morning, then?" asked Thorndyke.

"Why, I was on my way to work when, as I passed the police station, I noticed a bill with the heading 'Wanted' and a photograph. I stopped for a moment to look at it, and you may imagine my feelings when I recognized my own portrait--taken at Holloway--and read my own name and description. I did not stop to read the bill through, but ran back home and told my wife, and she ran down to the station and read the bill carefully. Good God, sir! What do you think I am wanted for?" He paused for a moment, and then replied in breathless tones to his own question: "The Camber-well murder!"

Thorndyke gave a low whistle.

"My wife knows I didn't do it," continued Belfield, "because I was at home all the evening and night; but what use is a man's wife to prove an alibi?"

"Not much, I fear," Thorndyke admitted; "and you have no other witness?"

"Not a soul. We were alone all the evening."

"However," said Thorndyke, "if you are innocent--as I am assuming--the evidence against you must be entirely circumstantial and your alibi may be quite sufficient. Have you any idea of the grounds of suspicion against you?"

"Not the faintest. The papers said that the police had an excellent clue, but they did not say what it was. Probably some one has given false information for the -?"

A sharp rapping at the outer door cut short the explanation, and our visitor rose, trembling and aghast, with beads of sweat standing upon his livid face.

"You had better go into the office, Belfield, while we see who it is," said Thorndyke. "The key is on the inside."

The fugitive wanted no second bidding, but hurried into the empty apartment, and, as the door closed, we heard the key turn in the lock.

As Thorndyke threw open the outer door, he cast a meaning glance at me over his shoulder which I understood when the newcomer entered the room; for it was none other than Superintendent Miller of Scotland Yard.

"I have just dropped in," said the superintendent, in his brisk, cheerful way, "to ask you to do me a favour. Good-evening, Dr. Jervis. I hear you are reading for the bar; learned counsel soon, sir, hey? Medico-legal expert. Dr. Thorndyke's mantle going to fall on you, sir?"

"I hope Dr. Thorndyke's mantle will continue to drape his own majestic form for many a long year yet," I answered; "though he is good enough to spare me a corner--but what on earth have you got there?" For during this dialogue the superintendent had been deftly unfastening a brown-paper parcel, from which he now drew a linen shirt, once white, but now of an unsavoury grey.

"I want to know what this is," said Miller, exhibiting a brownish-red stain on one sleeve. "Just look at that, sir, and tell me if it is blood, and, if so, is it human blood?"

"Really, Miller," said Thorndyke, with a smile, "you flatter me; but I am not like the wise woman of Bagdad who could tell you how many stairs the patient had tumbled down by merely looking at his tongue. I must examine this very thoroughly. When do you want to know?"

"I should like to know to-night," replied the detective.

"Can I cut a piece out to put under the microscope?"

"I would rather you did not," was the reply.

"Very well; you shall have the information in about an hour."

"It's very good of you, doctor," said the detective; and he was taking up his hat preparatory to departing, when Thorndyke said suddenly--"By the way, there is a little matter that I was going to speak to you about. It refers to this Camberwell murder case. I understand you have a clue to the identity of the murderer?"

"Clue!" exclaimed the superintendent contemptuously. "We have spotted our man all right, if we could only lay hands on him; but he has given us the slip for the moment."

"Who is the man?" asked Thorndyke.

The detective looked doubtfully at Thorndyke for some seconds and then said, with evident reluctance: "I suppose there is no harm in telling you--especially as you probably know already"--this with a sly grin; "it's an old crook named Belfield."

"And what is the evidence against him?"

Again the superintendent looked doubtful and again relented.

"Why, the case is as clear as--as cold Scotch," he said (here Thorndyke in illustration of this figure of speech produced a decanter, a syphon and a tumbler, which he pushed towards the officer). "You see, sir, the silly fool went and stuck his sweaty hand on the window; and there we found the marks--four fingers and a thumb, as beautiful prints as you could wish to see. Of course we cut out the piece of glass and took it up to the Finger-print Department; they turned up their files and out came Mr. Belfield's record, with his finger-prints and photograph all complete."

"And the finger-prints on the window-pane were identical with those on the prison form?"

"Identical."

"H'm!" Thorndyke reflected for a while, and the superintendent watched him foxily over the edge of his tumbler.

"I guess you are retained to defend Belfield," the latter observed presently.

"To look into the case generally," replied Thorndyke.

"And I expect you know where the beggar is hiding," continued the detective.

"Belfield's address has not yet been communicated to me," said Thorndyke. "I am merely to investigate the case--and there is no reason, Miller, why you and I should be at cross purposes. We are both working at the case; you want to get a conviction and you want to convict the right man."

"That's so--and Belfield's the right man--but what do you want of us, doctor?"

"I should like to see the piece of glass with the finger-prints on it, and the prison form, and take a photograph of each. And I should like to examine the room in which the murder took place--you have it locked up, I suppose?"

"Yes, we have the keys. Well, it's all rather irregular, letting you see the things. Still, you've always played the game fairly with us, so we might stretch a point. Yes, I will. I'll come back in an hour for your report and bring the glass and the form. I can't let them go out of my custody, you know. I'll be off now--no, thank you, not another drop."

The superintendent caught up his hat and strode away, the personification of mental alertness and bodily vigour.

No sooner had the door closed behind him than Thorndyke's stolid calm changed instantaneously into feverish energy. Darting to the electric bell that rang into the laboratories above, he pressed the button while he gave me my directions.

"Have a look at that blood-stain, Jervis, while I am finishing with Belfield. Don't wet it; scrape it into a drop of warm normal saline solution."

I hastened to reach down the microscope and set out on the table the necessary apparatus and reagents, and, as I was thus occupied, a latch-key turned in the outer door and our invaluable helpmate, Polton, entered the room in his habitual silent, unobtrusive fashion.

"Let me have the finger-print apparatus, please, Polton," said Thorndyke; "and have the copying camera ready by nine o'clock. I am expecting Mr. Miller with some documents."

As his laboratory assistant departed, Thorndyke rapped at the office door.

"It's all clear, Belfield," he called; "you can come out."

The key turned and the prisoner emerged, looking ludicrously woebegone in his ridiculous wig and beard.

"I am going to take your finger-prints, to compare with some that the police found on the window."

"Finger-prints!" exclaimed Belfield, in a tone of dismay. "They don't say they're my finger-prints, do they, sir?"

"They do indeed," replied Thorndyke, eyeing the man narrowly. "They have compared them with those taken when you were at Holloway, and they say that they are identical."

"Good God!" murmured Belfield, collapsing into a chair, faint and trembling. "They must have made some awful mistake. But are mistakes possible with finger-prints?"

"Now look here, Belfield," said Thorndyke. "Were you in that house that night, or were you not? It is of no use for you to tell me any lies."

"I was not there, sir; I swear to God I was not."

"Then they cannot be your finger-prints, that is obvious." Here he stepped to the door to intercept Polton, from whom he received a substantial box, which he brought in and placed on the table.

"Tell me all you know about this case," he continued, as he set out the contents of the box on the table.

"I know nothing about it whatever," replied Belfield; "nothing, at least, except -?"

"Except what?" demanded Thorndyke, looking up sharply as he squeezed a drop from a tube of finger-print ink onto a smooth copper plate.

"Except that the murdered man, Caldwell, was a retired fence."

"A fence, was he?" said Thorndyke in a tone of interest.

"Yes; and I suspect he was a 'nark' too. He knew more than was wholesome for a good many."

"Did he know anything about you?"

"Yes; but nothing that the police don't know."

With a small roller Thorndyke spread the ink upon the plate into a thin film. Then he laid on the edge of the table a smooth white card and, taking Belfield's right hand, pressed the forefinger firmly but quickly, first on the inked plate and then on the card, leaving on the latter a clear print of the finger-tip. This process he repeated with the other fingers and thumb, and then took several additional prints of each.

"That was a nasty injury to your forefinger, Belfield," said Thorndyke, holding the finger to the light and examining the tip carefully. "How did you do it?"

"Stuck a tin-opener into it--a dirty one, too. It was bad for weeks; in fact, Dr. Sampson thought at one time that he would have to amputate the finger."

"How long ago was that?"

"Oh, nearly a year ago, sir."

Thorndyke wrote the date of the injury by the side of the finger-print and then, having rolled up the inking plate afresh, laid on the table several larger cards. "I am now going to take the prints of the four fingers and the thumb all at once," he said.

"They only took the four fingers at once at the prison," said Belfield. "They took the thumb separately."

"I know," replied Thorndyke; "but I am going to take the impression just as it would appear on the window glass."

He took several impressions thus, and then, having looked at his watch, he began to repack the apparatus in its box. While doing this, he glanced, from time to time, in meditative fashion, at the suspected man who sat, the living picture of misery and terror, wiping the greasy ink from his trembling fingers with his handkerchief.

"Belfield," he said at length, "you have sworn to me that you are an innocent man and are trying to live an honest life. I believe you; but in a few minutes I shall know for certain."

"Thank God for that, sir," exclaimed Belfield, brightening up wonderfully.

"And now," said Thorndyke, "you had better go back into the office, for I am expecting Superintendent Miller, and he may be here at any moment."

Belfield hastily slunk back into the office, locking the door after him, and Thorndyke, having returned the box to the laboratory and deposited the cards bearing the finger-prints in a drawer, came round to inspect my work. I had managed to detach a tiny fragment of dried clot from the blood-stained garment, and this, in a drop of normal saline solution, I now had under the microscope.

"What do you make out, Jervis?" my colleague asked.

"Oval corpuscles with distinct nuclei," I answered.

"Ah," said Thorndyke, "that will be good hearing for some poor devil. Have you measured them?"

"Yes. Long diameter one twenty-one hundredth of an inch; short diameter about one thirty-four hundredth of an inch."

Thorndyke reached down an indexed note-book from a shelf of reference volumes and consulted a table of histological measurements.

"That would seem to be the blood of a pheasant, then, or it might, more probably, be that of a common fowl." He applied his eye to the microscope and, fitting in the eyepiece micrometer, verified my measurements. He was thus employed when a sharp tap was heard on the outer door, and rising to open it he admitted the superintendent.

"I see you are at work on my little problem, doctor," said the latter, glancing at the microscope. "What do you make of that stain?"

"It is the blood of a bird--probably a pheasant, or perhaps a common fowl."

The superintendent slapped his thigh. "Well, I'm hanged!" he exclaimed. "You're a regular wizard, doctor, that's what you are. The fellow said he got that stain through handling a wounded pheasant and here are you able to tell us yes or no without a hint from us to help you. Well, you've done my little job for me, sir, and I'm much obliged to you; now I'll carry out my part of the bargain." He opened a hand-bag and drew forth a wooden frame and a blue foolscap envelope and laid them with extreme care on the table.

"There you are, sir," said he, pointing to the frame; "you will find Mr. Belfield's trade-mark very neatly executed, and in the envelope is the finger-print sheet for comparison."

Thorndyke took up the frame and examined it. It enclosed two sheets of glass, one being the portion of the window-pane and the other a cover-glass to protect the fingerprints. Laying a sheet of white paper on the table, where the light was strongest, Thorndyke held the frame over it and gazed at the glass in silence, but with that faint lighting up of his impassive face which I knew so well and which meant so much to me. I walked round, and looking over his shoulder saw upon the glass the beautifully distinct imprints of four fingers and a thumb--the finger-tips, in fact, of an open hand.

After regarding the frame attentively for some time, Thorndyke produced from his pocket a little wash-leather bag, from which he extracted a powerful doublet lens, and with the aid of this he again explored the finger-prints, dwelling especially upon the print of the forefinger.

"I don't think you will find much amiss with those finger-prints, doctor," said the superintendent, "they are as clear as if he made them on purpose."

"They are indeed," replied Thorndyke, with an inscrutable smile, "exactly as if he had made them on purpose. And how beautifully clean the glass is--as if he had polished it before making the impression."

The superintendent glanced at Thorndyke with quick suspicion; but the smile had faded and given place to a wooden immobility from which nothing could be gleaned.

When he had examined the glass exhaustively, Thorndyke drew the finger-print form from its envelope and scanned it quickly, glancing repeatedly from the paper to the glass and from the glass to the paper. At length he laid them both on the table, and turning to the detective looked him steadily in the face.

"I think, Miller," said he, "that I can give you a hint."

"Indeed, sir? And what might that be?"

"It is this: you are after the wrong man."

The superintendent snorted--not a loud snort, for that would have been rude, and no officer could be more polite than

Superintendent Miller. But it conveyed a protest which he speedily followed up in words.

"You don't mean to say that the prints on that glass are not the finger-prints of Frank Belfield?"

"I say that those prints were not made by Frank Belfield," Thorndyke replied firmly.

"Do you admit, sir, that the finger-prints on the official form were made by him?"

"I have no doubt that they were."

"Well, sir, Mr. Singleton, of the Finger-print Department, has compared the prints on the glass with those on the form and he says they are identical; and I have examined them and I say they are identical."

"Exactly," said Thorndyke; "and I have examined them and I say they are identical--and that therefore those on the glass cannot have been made by Belfield."

The superintendent snorted again--somewhat louder this time--and gazed at Thorndyke with wrinkled brows.

"You are not pulling my leg, I suppose, sir?" he asked, a little sourly.

"I should as soon think of tickling a porcupine," Thorndyke answered, with a suave smile.

"Well," rejoined the bewildered detective, "if I didn't know you, sir, I should say you were talking confounded nonsense. Perhaps you wouldn't mind explaining what you mean."

"Supposing," said Thorndyke, "I make it clear to you that those prints on the window-pane were not made by Belfield. Would you still execute the warrant?"

"What do you think?" exclaimed Miller. "Do you suppose we should go into court to have you come and knock the bottom out of our case, like you did in that Hornby affair? By the way, that was a finger-print case too, now I come to think of it," and the superintendent suddenly became thoughtful.

"You have often complained," pursued Thorndyke, "that I have withheld information from you and sprung unexpected evidence on you at the trial. Now I am going to take you into my confidence, and when I have proved to you that this clue of yours is a false one, I shall expect you to let this poor devil Belfield go his way in peace."

The superintendent grunted--a form of utterance that committed him to nothing.

"These prints," continued Thorndyke, taking up the frame once more, "present several features of interest, one of which, at least, ought not to have escaped you and Mr. Singleton, as it seems to have done. Just look at that thumb."

The superintendent did so, and then pored over the official paper.

"Well," he said, "I don't see anything the matter with it. It's exactly like the print on the paper."

"Of course it is," rejoined Thorndyke, "and that is just the point. It ought not to be. The print of the thumb on the paper was taken separately from the fingers. And why? Because it was impossible to take it at the same time. The thumb is in a different plane from the fingers; when the hand is laid flat on any surface--as this window-pane, for instance-- the palmar surfaces of the fingers touch it, whereas it is the side of the thumb which comes in contact and not the palmar surface. But in this"--he tapped the framed glass with his finger--the prints show the palmar surfaces of all the five digits in contact at once, which is an impossibility. Just try to put your own thumb in that position and you will see that it is so."

The detective spread out his hand on the table and immediately perceived the truth of my colleague's statement.

"And what does that prove?" he asked.

"It proves that the thumb-print on the window-pane was not made at the same time as the finger-prints--that it was added separately; and that fact seems to prove that the prints were not made accidentally, but--as you ingeniously suggested just now--were put there for a purpose."

"I don't quite see the drift of all this," said the superintendent, rubbing the back of his head perplexedly; "and you said a while back that the prints on the glass can't be Belfield's because they are identical with the prints on the form. Now that seems to me sheer nonsense, if you will excuse my saying so."

"And yet," replied Thorndyke, "it is the actual fact. Listen: these prints"--here he took up the official sheet--"were taken at Holloway six years ago. These"--pointing to the framed glass--"were made within the present week. The one is, as regards the ridge-pattern, a perfect duplicate of the other. Is that not so?"

"That is so, doctor," agreed the superintendent.

"Very well. Now suppose I were to tell you that within the last twelve months something had happened to Belfield that made an appreciable change in the ridge-pattern on one of his fingers?"

"But is such a thing possible?"

"It is not only possible but it has happened. I will show you."

He brought forth from the drawer the cards on which Belfield had made his finger-prints, and laid them before the detective.

"Observe the prints of the forefinger," he said, indicating them; "there are a dozen, in all, and you will notice in each a white line crossing the ridges and dividing them. That line is caused by a scar, which has destroyed a portion of the ridges, and is now an integral part of Belfield's finger-print.

And since no such blank line is to be seen in this print on the glass-- in which the ridges appear perfect, as they were before the injury--it follows that that print could not have been made by Belfield's finger."

"There is no doubt about the injury, I suppose?"

"None whatever. There is the scar to prove it, and I can produce the surgeon who attended Belfield at the time."

The officer rubbed his head harder than before, and regarded Thorndyke with puckered brows.

"This is a teaser," he growled, "it is indeed. What you say, sir, seems perfectly sound, and yet--there are those finger-prints on the window-glass. Now you can't get fingerprints without fingers, can you?"

"Undoubtedly you can," said Thorndyke.

"I should want to see that done before I could believe even you, sir," said Miller.

"You shall see it done now," was the calm rejoinder. "You have evidently forgotten the Hornby case--the case of the Red Thumb-mark, as the newspapers called it."

"I only heard part of it," replied Miller, "and I didn't really follow the evidence in that."

"Well, I will show you a relic of that case," said Thorndyke. He unlocked a cabinet and took from one of the shelves a small box labelled "Hornby," which, being opened, was seen to contain a folded paper, a little red-covered oblong book and what looked like a large boxwood pawn.

"This little book," Thorndyke continued, "is a 'thumbograph'--a sort of finger-print album--I dare say you know the kind of thing."

The superintendent nodded contemptuously at the little volume.

"Now while Dr. Jervis is finding us the print we want, I will run up to the laboratory for an inked slab."

He handed me the little book and, as he left the room, I began to turn over the leaves--not without emotion, for it was this very "thumbograph" that first introduced me to my wife, as is related elsewhere--glancing at the various prints above the familiar names and marvelling afresh at the endless variations of pattern that they displayed. At length I came upon two thumb-prints of which one--the left--was marked by a longitudinal white line--evidently the trace of a scar; and underneath them was written the signature "Reuben Hornby."

At this moment Thorndyke re-entered the room carrying the inked slab, which he laid on the table, and seating himself between the superintendent and me, addressed the former.

"Now, Miller, here are two thumb-prints made by a gentleman named Reuben Hornby. Just glance at the left one; it is a highly characteristic print."

"Yes," agreed Miller, "one could swear to that from memory, I should think."

"Then look at this." Thorndyke took the paper from the box and, unfolding it, handed it to the detective. It bore a pencilled inscription, and on it were two blood-smears and a very distinct thumb-print in blood. "What do you say to that thumb-print?"

"Why," answered Miller, "it's this one, of course; Reuben Hornby's left thumb."

"Wrong, my friend," said Thorndyke. "It was made by an ingenious gentleman named Walter Hornby (whom you followed from the Old Bailey and lost on Ludgate Hill); but not with his thumb."

"How, then?" demanded the superintendent incredulously.

"In this way." Thorndyke took the boxwood "pawn" from its receptacle and pressed its flat base onto the inked slab; then lifted it and pressed it onto the back of a visiting-card, and again raised it; and now the card was marked by a very distinct thumb-print.

"My God!" exclaimed the detective, picking up the card and viewing it with a stare of dismay, "this is the very devil, sir. This fairly knocks the bottom out of finger-print identification. May I ask, sir, how you made that stamp--for I suppose you did make it?"

"Yes, we made it here, and the process we used was practically that used by photo-engravers in making line blocks; that is to say, we photographed one of Mr. Hornby's thumb-prints, printed it on a plate of chrome-gelatine, developed the plate with hot water and this"--here he touched the embossed surface of the stamp--"is what remained. But we could have done it in various other ways; for instance, with common transfer paper and lithographic stone; indeed, I assure you, Miller, that there is nothing easier to forge than a finger-print, and it can be done with such perfection that the forger himself cannot tell his own forgery from a genuine original, even when they are placed side by side."

"Well, I'm hanged," grunted the superintendent, "you've fairly knocked me, this time, doctor." He rose gloomily and prepared to depart. "I suppose," he added, "your interest in this case has lapsed, now Belfield's out of it?"

"Professionally, yes; but I am disposed to finish the case for my own satisfaction. I am quite curious as to who our too-ingenious friend may be."

Miller's face brightened. "We shall give you every facility, you know-- and that reminds me that Singleton gave me these two photographs for you, one of the official paper and one of the prints on the glass. Is there anything more that we can do for you?"

"I should like to have a look at the room in which the murder took place."

"You shall, doctor; to-morrow, if you like; I'll meet you there in the morning at ten, if that will do."

It would do excellently, Thorndyke assured him, and with this the superintendent took his departure in renewed spirits.

We had only just closed the door when there came a hurried and urgent tapping upon it, whereupon I once more threw it open, and a quietly-dressed woman in a thick veil, who was standing on the threshold, stepped quickly past me into the room.

"Where is my husband?" she demanded, as I closed the door; and then, catching sight of Thorndyke, she strode up to him with a threatening air and a terrified but angry face.

"What have you done with my husband, sir?" she repeated. "Have you betrayed him, after giving your word? I met a man who looked like a police officer on the stairs."

"Your husband, Mrs. Belfield, is here and quite safe," replied Thorndyke. "He has locked himself in that room," indicating the office.

Mrs. Belfield darted across and .rapped smartly at the door. "Are you there, Frank?" she called.

In immediate response the key turned, the door opened and Belfield emerged looking very pale and worn.

"You have kept me a long time in there, sir," he said.

"It took me a long time to prove to Superintendent Miller that he was after the wrong man. But I succeeded, and now, Belfield, you are free. The charge against you is withdrawn."

Belfield stood for a while as one stupefied, while his wife, after a moment of silent amazement, flung her arms round his neck and burst into tears. "But how did you know I was innocent, sir?" demanded the bewildered Belfield.

"Ah! how did I? Every man to his trade, you know. Well, I congratulate you, and now go home and have a square meal and get a good night's rest."

He shook hands with his clients--vainly endeavouring to prevent Mrs. Belfield from kissing his hand--and stood at the open door listening until the sound of their retreating footsteps died away.

"A noble little woman, Jervis," said he, as he closed the door. "In another moment she would have scratched my face--and I mean to find out the scoundrel who tried to wreck her happiness."

Part II. The Ship of the Desert

The case which I am now about to describe has always appeared to me a singularly instructive one, as illustrating the value and importance of that fundamental rule in the carrying out of investigations which Thorndyke had laid down so emphatically--the rule that all facts, in any way relating to a case, should be collected impartially and without reference to any theory, and each fact, no matter how trivial or apparently irrelevant, carefully studied. But I must not anticipate the remarks of my learned and talented friend on this subject which I have to chronicle anon; rather let me proceed to the case itself.

I had slept at our chambers in King's Bench Walk--as I commonly did two or three nights a week--and on coming down to the sitting-room, found Thorndyke's man, Polton, putting the last touches to the breakfast-table, while Thorndyke himself was poring over two photographs of fingerprints, of which he seemed to be taking elaborate measurements with a pair of hair-dividers. He greeted me with his quiet, genial smile and, laying down the dividers, took his seat at the breakfast-table.

"You are coming with me this morning, I suppose," said he; "the Camberwell murder case, you know."

"Of course I am if you will have me, but I know practically nothing of the case. Could you give me an outline of the facts that are known?"

Thorndyke looked at me solemnly, but with a mischievous twinkle. "This," he said, "is the old story of the fox and the crow; you 'bid me discourse,' and while I 'enchant thine ear,' you claw to windward with the broiled ham. A deep-laid plot, my learned brother."

"And such," I exclaimed, "is the result of contact with the criminal classes!"

"I am sorry that you regard yourself in that light," he retorted, with a malicious smile. "However, with regard to this case. The facts are briefly these: The murdered man, Caldwell, who seems to have been formerly a receiver of stolen goods and probably a police spy as well, lived a solitary life in a small house with only an elderly woman to attend him.

"A week ago this woman went to visit a married daughter and stayed the night with her, leaving Caldwell alone in the house. When she returned on the following morning she found her master lying dead on the floor of his office, or study, in a small pool of blood.

"The police surgeon found that he had been dead about twelve hours. He had been killed by a single blow, struck from behind, with some heavy implement, and a jemmy which lay on the floor beside him fitted the wound exactly. The deceased wore a dressing-gown and no collar, and a bedroom candlestick lay upside down on the floor, although gas was laid on in the room; and as the window of the office appears to have been forced with the jemmy that was found, and there were distinct footprints on the flower-bed outside the window, the police think that the deceased was undressing to go to bed when he was disturbed by the noise of the opening window; that he went down to the office and, as he entered, was struck down by the burglar who was lurking behind the door. On the window-glass the police found the greasy impression of an open right hand, and, as you know, the finger-prints were identified by the experts as those of an old convict named Belfield. As you also know, I proved that those finger-prints were, in reality, forgeries, executed with rubber or gelatine stamps. That is an outline of the case."

The close of this recital brought our meal to an end, and we prepared for our visit to the scene of the crime. Thorndyke slipped into his pocket his queer outfit--somewhat like that of a field geologist--locked up the photographs, and we set forth by way of the Embankment.

"The police have no clue, I suppose, to the identity of the murderer, now that the finger-prints have failed?" I asked, as we strode along together.

"I expect not," he replied, "though they might have if they examined their material. I made out a rather interesting point this morning, which is this: the man who made those sham finger-prints used two stamps, one for the thumb and the other for the four fingers;

and the original from which those stamps were made was the official finger-print form."

"How did you discover that?" I inquired.

"It was very simple. You remember that Mr. Singleton of the Finger-print Department sent me, by Superintendent Miller, two photographs, one of the prints on the window and one of the official form with Belfield's finger-prints on it. Well, I have compared them and made the most minute measurements of each, and they are obviously duplicates. Not only are all the little imperfections on the form--due to defective inking-- reproduced faithfully on the window-pane, but the relative positions of the four fingers on both cases agree to the hundredth of an inch. Of course the thumb stamp was made by taking an oval out of the rolled impression on the form."

"Then do you suggest that this murder was committed by some one connected with the Finger-print Department at Scotland Yard?"

"Hardly. But some one has had access to the forms. There has been leakage somewhere."

When we arrived at the little detached house in which the murdered man had lived, the door was opened by an elderly woman, and our friend, Superintendent Miller, greeted us in the hall.

"We are all ready for you, doctor," said he. "Of course, the things have all been gone over once, but we are turning them out more thoroughly now." He led the way into the small, barely-furnished office in which the tragedy had occurred. A dark stain on the carpet and a square hole in one of the window-panes furnished memorials of the crime, which were supplemented by an odd assortment of objects laid out on the newspaper-covered table. These included silver teaspoons, watches, various articles of jewellery, from which the stones had been removed-- none of them of any considerable value--and a roughly-made jemmy.

"I don't know why Caldwell should have kept all these odds and ends," said the detective superintendent. "There is stuff here, that I can identify, from six different burglaries--and not a conviction among the six."

Thorndyke looked over the collection with languid interest; he was evidently disappointed at finding the room so completely turned out.

"Have you any idea what has been taken?" he asked.

"Not the least. We don't even know if the safe was opened. The keys were on the writing-table, so I suppose he went through everything, though I don't see why he left these things if he did. We found them all in the safe."

"Have you powdered the jemmy?"

The superintendent turned very red. "Yes," he growled, "but some half-dozen blithering idiots had handled the thing before I saw it--been trying it on the window, the blighters--so, of course, it showed nothing but the marks of their beastly paws."

"The window had not really been forced, I suppose?" said Thorndyke.

"No," replied Miller, with a glance of surprise at my colleague, "that was a plant; so were the footprints. He must have put on a pair of Caldwell's boots and gone out and made them--unless Caldwell made them himself, which isn't likely."

"Have you found any letter or telegram?"

"A letter making an appointment for nine o'clock on the night of the murder. No signature or address, and the handwriting evidently disguised."

"Is there anything that furnishes any sort of clue?"

"Yes, sir, there is. There's this, which we found in the safe." He produced a small parcel which he proceeded to unfasten, looking somewhat queerly at Thorndyke the while. It contained various odds and ends of jewellery, and a smaller parcel formed of a pocket-handkerchief tied with tape. This the detective also unfastened, revealing half-a-dozen silver teaspoons, all engraved with the same crest, two salt-cellars and a gold locket bearing a monogram. There was also a half-sheet of note-paper on which was written, in a manifestly disguised hand: "There are the goods I told you about.? F. B." But what riveted Thorndyke's attention and mine was the handkerchief itself (which was not a very clean one and was sullied by one or two small blood-stains), for it was marked in one corner with the name "F. Belfield," legibly printed in marking-ink with a rubber stamp.

Thorndyke and the superintendent looked at one another and both smiled.

"I know what you are thinking, sir," said the latter.

"I am sure you do," was the reply, "and it is useless to pretend that you don't agree with me."

"Well, sir," said Miller doggedly, "if that handkerchief has been put there as a plant, it's Belfield's business to prove it. You see, doctor," he added persuasively, "it isn't this job only that's affected. Those spoons, those salt-cellars and that locket are part of the proceeds of the Winchmore Hill burglary, and we want the gentleman who did that crack--we want him very badly."

"No doubt you do," replied Thorndyke, "but this handkerchief won't help you. A sharp counsel--Mr. Anstey, for instance--would demolish it in five minutes. I assure you, Miller, that handkerchief has no evidential value whatever, whereas it might prove an invaluable instrument of research. The best thing you can do is to hand it over to me and let me see what I can learn from it."

The superintendent was obviously dissatisfied, but he eventually agreed, with manifest reluctance, to Thorndyke's suggestion.

"Very well, doctor," he said; "you shall have it for a day or two. Do you want the spoons and things as well?"

"No. Only the handkerchief and the paper that was in it."

The two articles were accordingly handed to him and deposited in a tin box which he usually carried in his pocket, and, after a few more words with the disconsolate detective, we took our departure.

"A very disappointing morning," was Thorndyke's comment as we walked away. "Of course the room ought to have been examined by an expert before anything was moved."

"Have you picked up anything in the way of information?" I asked.

"Very little excepting confirmation of my original theory. You see, this man Caldwell was a receiver and evidently a police spy. He gave useful information to the police, and they, in return, refrained from inconvenient inquiries. But a spy, or 'nark,' is nearly always a blackmailer too, and the probabilities in this case are that some crook, on whom Caldwell was putting the screw rather too tightly, made an appointment for a meeting when the house was empty, and just knocked Caldwell on the head. The crime was evidently planned beforehand, and the murderer came prepared to kill several birds with one stone. Thus he brought with him the stamps to make the sham finger-prints on the window, and I have no doubt that he also brought this handkerchief and the various oddments of plate and jewellery from those burglaries that Miller is so keen about, and planted them in the safe. You noticed, I suppose, that none of the things were of any value, but all were capable of easy identification?"

"Yes, I noticed that. His object, evidently, was to put those burglaries as well as the murder onto poor Belfield."

"Exactly. And you see what Miller's attitude is; Belfield is the bird in the hand, whereas the other man--if there is another--is still in the bush; so Belfield is to be followed up and a conviction obtained if possible. If he is innocent, that is his affair, and it is for him to prove it."

"And what shall you do next?" I asked.

"I shall telegraph to Belfield to come and see us this evening. He may be able to tell us something about this handkerchief that, with the clue we already have, may put us on the right track. What time is your consultation?"

"Twelve-thirty--and here comes my 'bus. I shall be in to lunch." I sprang onto the footboard, and as I took my seat on the roof and looked back at my friend striding along with an easy swing, I knew that he was deep in thought, though automatically attentive to all that was happening. My consultation--it was a lunacy case of some importance-- was over in time to allow of my return to our chambers punctually at the luncheon hour; and as I entered, I was at once struck by something new in Thorndyke's manner--a certain elation and gaiety which I had learned to associate with a point scored successfully in some intricate and puzzling case. He made no confidences, however, and seemed, in fact, inclined to put away, for a time, all his professional cares and business.

"Shall we have an afternoon off, Jervis?" he said gaily. "It is a fine day and work is slack just now. What say you to the Zoo? They have a splendid chimpanzee and several specimens of that remarkable fish *Periophthalmos Kolreuteri*. Shall we go?"

"By all means," I replied; "and we will mount the elephant, if you like, and throw buns to the grizzly bear and generally renew our youth like the eagle."

But when, an hour later, we found ourselves in the gardens, I began to suspect my friend of some ulterior purpose in this holiday jaunt; for it was not the chimpanzee or even the wonderful fish that attracted his attention. On the contrary, he hung about the vicinity of the lamas and camels in a way that I could not fail to notice; and even there it appeared to be the sheds and houses rather than the animals themselves that interested him.

"Behold, Jervis," he said presently, as a saddled camel of seedy aspect was led towards its house, "behold the ship of the desert, with raised saloon-deck amidships, fitted internally with watertight compartments and displaying the effects of rheumatoid arthritis in his starboard hip-joint. Let us go and examine him before he hauls into dock." We took a cross-path to intercept the camel on its way to its residence, and Thorndyke moralized as we went.

"It is interesting," he remarked, "to note the way in which these specialized animals, such as the horse, the reindeer and the camel, have been appropriated by man, and their special character made to subserve human needs. Think, for instance, of the part the camel has played in history, in ancient commerce--and modern too, for that matter--and in the diffusion of culture; and of the role he has enacted in war and conquest from the Egyptian campaign of Cambyses down to that of Kitchener. Yes, the camel is a very remarkable animal, though it must be admitted that this particular specimen is a scurvy-looking beast."

The camel seemed to be sensible of these disparaging remarks, for as it approached it saluted Thorndyke with a supercilious grin and then turned away its head.

"Your charge is not as young as he used to be," Thorndyke observed to the man who was leading the animal.

"No, sir, he isn't; he's getting old, and that's the fact. He shows it too."

"I suppose," said Thorndyke, strolling towards the house by the man's side, "these beasts require a deal of attention?"

"You're right, sir; and nasty-tempered brutes they are."

"So I have heard; but they are interesting creatures, the camels and lamas. Do you happen to know if complete sets of photographs of them are to be had here?"

"You can get a good many at the lodge, sir," the man replied, "but not all, I think. If you want a complete set, there's one of our men in the camel-house that could let you have them; he takes the photos himself, and very clever he is at it, too. But he isn't here just now."

"Perhaps you could give me his name so that I could write to him," said Thorndyke.

"Yes, sir. His name is Woodthorpe--Joseph Woodthorpe. He'll do anything for you to order. Thank you, sir; good-afternoon, sir;" and pocketing an unexpected tip, the man led his charge towards its lair.

Thorndyke's absorbing interest in the camels seemed now suddenly to become extinct, and he suffered me to lead him to any part of the gardens that attracted me, showing an imperial interest in all the inmates from the insects to the elephants, and enjoying his holiday--if it was one-- with the gaiety and high spirits of a schoolboy. Yet he never let slip a chance of picking up a stray hair or feather, but gathered up each with care, wrapped it in its separate paper, on which was written its description, and deposited it in his tin collecting-box.

"You never know," he remarked, as we turned away from the ostrich enclosure, "when a specimen for comparison may be of vital importance. Here, for instance, is a small feather of a cassowary, and here the hair of a wapiti deer; now the recognition of either of those might, in certain circumstances, lead to the detection of a criminal or save the life of an innocent man. The thing has happened repeatedly, and may happen again to-morrow."

"You must have an enormous collection of hairs in your cabinet," I remarked, as we walked home.

"I have," he replied, "probably the largest in the world. And as to other microscopical objects of medico-legal interest, such as dust and mud from different localities and from special industries and manufactures, fibres, food-products and drugs, my collection is certainly unique."

"And you have found your collection useful in your work?" I asked.

"Constantly. Over and over again I have obtained, by reference to my specimens, the most unexpected evidence, and the longer I practise, the more I become convinced that the microscope is the sheet-anchor of the medical jurist."

"By the way," I said, "you spoke of sending a telegram to Belfield. Did you send it?"

"Yes. I asked him to come to see me to-night at half-past eight, and, if possible, bring his wife with him. I want to get to the bottom of that handkerchief mystery."

"But do you think he will tell you the truth about it?"

"That is impossible to judge; he will be a fool if he does not. But I think he will; he has a godly fear of me and my methods."

As soon as our dinner was finished and cleared away, Thorndyke produced the "collecting-box" from his pocket, and began to sort out the day's "catch," giving explicit directions to Polton for the disposal of each specimen. The hairs and small feathers were to be mounted as microscopic objects, while the larger feathers were to be placed, each in its separate labelled envelope, in its appropriate box. While these directions were being given, I stood by the window absently gazing out as I listened, gathering many a useful hint in the technique of preparation and preservation, and filled with admiration alike at my colleague's exhaustive knowledge of practical detail and the perfect manner in which he had trained his assistant. Suddenly I started, for a well-known figure was crossing from Crown Office Row and evidently bearing down on our chambers.

"My word, Thorndyke," I exclaimed, "here's a pretty mess!"

"What is the matter?" he asked, looking up anxiously.

"Superintendent Miller heading straight for our doorway. And it is now twenty minutes past eight."

Thorndyke laughed. "It will be a quaint position," he remarked, "and somewhat of a shock for Belfield. But it really doesn't matter; in fact, I think, on the whole, I am rather pleased that he should have come."

The superintendent's brisk knock was heard a few moments later, and when he was admitted by Polton, he entered and looked round the room a little, sheepishly.

"I am ashamed to come worrying you like this, sir," he began apologetically.

"Not at all," replied Thorndyke, serenely slipping the cassowary's feather into an envelope, and writing the name, date and locality on the outside. "I am your servant in this case, you know. Polton, whisky and soda for the superintendent."

"You see, sir," continued Miller, "our people are beginning to fuss about this case, and they don't approve of my having handed that handkerchief and the paper over to you as they will have to be put in evidence."

"I thought they might object," remarked Thorndyke.

"So did I, sir; and they do. And, in short, they say that I have got to get them back at once. I hope it won't put you out, sir."

"Not in the least," said Thorndyke. "I have asked Belfield to come here to-night--I expect him in a few minutes--and when I have heard what he has to say I shall have no further use for the handkerchief."

"You're not going to show it to him!" exclaimed the detective, aghast.

"Certainly I am."

"You mustn't do that, sir. I can't sanction it; I can't indeed."

"Now, look you here, Miller," said Thorndyke, shaking his forefinger at the officer; "I am working for you in this case, as I have told you. Leave the matter in my hands. Don't raise silly objections; and when you leave here tonight you will take with you not only the handkerchief and the paper, but probably also the name and address of the man who committed this murder and those various burglaries that you are so keen about."

"Is that really so, sir?" exclaimed the astonished detective. "Well, you haven't let the grass grow under your feet. Ah!" as a gentle rap at the door was heard, "here's Belfield, I suppose."

It was Belfield--accompanied by his wife--and mightily disturbed they were when their eyes lighted on our visitor.

"You needn't be afraid of me, Belfield," said Miller, with ferocious geniality; "I am not here after you." Which was not literally true, though it served to reassure the affrighted ex-convict.

"The superintendent dropped in by chance," said Thorndyke; "but it is just as well that he should hear what passes. I want you to look at this handkerchief and tell me if it is yours. Don't be afraid, but just tell us the simple truth."

He took the handkerchief out of a drawer and spread it on the table; and I now observed that a small square had been cut out of one of the bloodstains.

Belfield took the handkerchief in his trembling hands, and as his eye fell on the stamped name in the corner he turned deadly pale.

"It looks like mine," he said huskily. "What do you say, Liz?" he added, passing it to his wife.

Mrs. Belfield examined first the name and then the hem. "It's yours, right enough, Frank," said she. "It's the one that got changed in the wash. You see, sir," she continued, addressing Thorndyke, "I bought him half-a-dozen new ones about six months ago, and I got a rubber stamp made and marked them all. Well, one day when I was looking over his things I noticed that one of his handkerchiefs had got no mark on it. I spoke to the laundress about it, but she couldn't explain it, so as the right one never came back, I marked the one that we got in exchange."

"How long ago was that?" asked Thorndyke.

"About two months ago I noticed it."

"And you know nothing more about it."

"Nothing whatever, sir. Nor you, Frank, do you?"

Her husband shook his head gloomily, and Thorndyke replaced the handkerchief in the drawer.

"And now," said he, "I am going to ask you a question on another subject. When you were at Holloway there was a warder--or assistant warder-- there, named Woodthorpe. Do you remember him?"

"Yes, sir, very well indeed; in fact, it was him that -?"

"I know," interrupted Thorndyke. "Have you seen him since you left Holloway?"

"Yes, sir, once. It was last Easter Monday. I met him at the Zoo; he is a keeper there now in the camel-house" (here a sudden light dawned upon me and I chuckled aloud, to Belfield's great astonishment). "He gave my little boy a ride on one of the camels and made himself very pleasant."

"Do you remember anything else happening?" Thorndyke inquired.

"Yes, sir. The camel had a little accident; he kicked out--he was an ill-tempered beast--and his leg hit a post; there happened to be a nail sticking out from that post, and it tore up a little flap of skin. Then Woodthorpe got out his handkerchief to tie up the wound, but as it was none of the cleanest, I said to him: 'Don't use that, Woodthorpe; have mine,' which was quite a clean one. So he took it and bound up the camel's leg, and he said to me: 'I'll have it washed and send it to you if you give me your address.' But I told him there was no need for that; I should be passing the camel-house on my way out and I would look in for the handkerchief. And I did: I looked in about an hour later, and Woodthorpe gave me my handkerchief, folded up but not washed."

"Did you examine it to see if it was yours?" asked Thorndyke.

"No, sir. I just slipped it in my pocket as it was."

"And what became of it afterwards?"

"When I got home I dropped it into the dirty-linen basket."

"Is that all you know about it?"

"Yes, sir; that is all I know."

"Very well, Belfield, that will do. Now you have no reason to be uneasy. You will soon know all about the Camberwell murder--that is, if you read the papers."

The ex-convict and his wife were obviously relieved by this assurance and departed in quite good spirits. When they were gone, Thorndyke produced the handkerchief and the half-sheet of paper and handed them to the superintendent, remarking--"This is highly satisfactory, Miller; the whole case seems to join up very neatly indeed. Two months ago the wife first noticed the substituted handkerchief, and last Easter Monday--a little over two months ago--this very significant incident took place in the Zoological Gardens."

"That is all very well, sir," objected the superintendent, "but we've only their word for it, you know."

"Not so," replied Thorndyke. "We have excellent corroborative evidence. You noticed that I had cut a small piece out of the blood-stained portion of the handkerchief?"

"Yes; and I was sorry you had done it. Our people won't like that."

"Well, here it is, and we will ask Dr. Jervis to give us his opinion of it."

From the drawer in which the handkerchief had been hidden he brought forth a microscope slide, and setting the microscope on the table, laid the slide on the stage.

"Now, Jervis," he said, "tell us what you see there."

I examined the edge of the little square of fabric (which had been mounted in a fluid reagent) with a high-power objective, and was, for a time, a little puzzled by the appearance of the blood that adhered to it.

"It looks like bird's blood," I said presently, with some hesitation, "but yet I can make out no nuclei." I looked again, and then, suddenly, "By Jove!" I exclaimed, "I have it; of course! It's the blood of a camel!"

"Is that so, doctor?" demanded the detective, leaning forward in his excitement.

"That is so," replied Thorndyke. "I discovered it after I came home this morning. You see," he explained, "it is quite unmistakable. The rule is that the blood corpuscles of mammals are circular; the one exception is the camel family, in which the corpuscles are elliptical."

"Why," exclaimed Miller, "that seems to connect Woodthorpe with this Camberwell job."

"It connects him with it very conclusively," said Thorndyke. "You are forgetting the finger-prints."

The detective looked puzzled. "What about them?" he asked.

"They were made with stamps--two stamps, as a matter of fact--and those stamps were made by photographic process from the official finger-print form. I can prove that beyond all doubt."

"Well, suppose they were. What then?"

Thorndyke opened a drawer and took out a photograph, which he handed to Miller. "Here," he said, "is the photograph of the official finger-print form which you were kind enough to bring me. What does it say at the bottom there?" and he pointed with his finger.

The superintendent read aloud: "Impressions taken by Joseph Woodthorpe. Rank, Warder; Prison, Holloway." He stared at the photograph for a moment, and then exclaimed--"Well, I'm hanged! You have worked this out neatly, doctor! and so quick too. We'll have Mr. Woodthorpe under lock and key the first thing to-morrow morning. But how did he do it, do you think?"

"He might have taken duplicate finger-prints and kept one form; the prisoners would not know there was anything wrong; but he did not in this case. He must have contrived to take a photograph of the form before sending it in--it would take a skilful photographer only a minute or two with a suitable hand-camera placed on a table at the proper distance from the wall; and I have ascertained that he is a skilful photographer. You will probably find the apparatus, and the stamps too, when you search his rooms."

"Well, well. You do give us some surprises, doctor. But I must be off now to see about this warrant. Good-night, sir, and many thanks for your help."

When the superintendent had gone we sat for a while looking at one another in silence. At length Thorndyke spoke. "Here is a case, Jervis," he said, "which, simple as it is, teaches a most invaluable lesson--a lesson which you should take well to heart. It is this: The evidential value of any fact is an unknown quantity until the fact has been examined. That seems a self-evident truth, but like many other self-evident truths, it is constantly overlooked in practice. Take this present case. When I left Caldwell's house this morning the facts in my possession were these: (1) The man who murdered Caldwell was directly or indirectly connected with the Finger-print Department. (2) He was almost certainly a skilled photographer. (3) He probably committed the Winchmore Hill and the other burglaries. (4) He was known to Caldwell, had had professional dealings with him and was probably being blackmailed. This was all; a very vague clue, as you see.

"There was the handkerchief, planted, as I had no doubt; but could not prove; the name stamped on it was Belfield's, but any one can get a rubber stamp made. Then it was stained with blood, as handkerchiefs often are; that blood might or might not be human blood; it did not seem to matter a straw whether it was or not.

Nevertheless, I said to myself: If it is human, or at least mammalian blood, that is a fact; and if it is not human blood, that is also a fact. I will have that fact, and then I shall know what its value is. I examined the stain when I reached home, and behold! it was camel's blood; and immediately this insignificant fact swelled up into evidence of primary importance. The rest was obvious. I had seen Woodthorpe's name on the form, and I knew several other officials. My business was to visit all places in London where there were camels, to get the names of all persons connected with them and to ascertain if any among them was a photographer. Naturally I went first to the Zoo, and at the very first cast hooked Joseph Woodthorpe. Wherefore I say again: Never call any fact irrelevant until you have examined it."

The remarkable evidence given above was not heard at the trial, nor did Thorndyke's name appear among the witnesses; for when the police searched Woodthorpe's rooms, so many incriminating articles were found (including a pair of fingerprint stamps which exactly answered to Thorndyke's description of them, and a number of photographs of finger-print forms) that his guilt was put beyond all doubt; and society was shortly after relieved of a very undesirable member.

The Great Portrait Mystery

The Missing Mortgagee

Part I

Early in the afternoon of a warm, humid November day, Thomas Elton sauntered dejectedly along the Margate esplanade, casting an eye now on the slate-coloured sea with its pall of slate-coloured sky, and now on the harbour, where the ebb tide was just beginning to expose the mud. It was a dreary prospect, and Elton varied it by observing the few fishermen and fewer promenaders who walked foot to foot with their distorted reflections in the wet pavement; and thus it was that his eye fell on a smartly- dressed man who had just stepped into a shelter to light a cigar.

A contemporary joker has classified the Scotsmen who abound in South Africa into two groups: those, namely, who hail from Scotland, and those who hail from Palestine. Now, something in the aspect of the broad back that was presented to his view, in that of the curly, black hair and the exuberant raiment, suggested to Elton a Scotsman of the latter type. In fact, there was a suspicion of disagreeable familiarity in the figure which caused him to watch it and slacken his pace. The man backed out of the shelter, diffusing azure clouds, and, drawing an envelope from his pocket, read something that was written on it. Then he turned quickly-- and so did Elton, but not quickly enough. For he was a solitary figure on that bald and empty expanse, and the other had seen him at the first glance. Elton walked away slowly, but he had not gone a dozen paces when he felt the anticipated slap on the shoulder and heard the too well-remembered voice.

"Blow me, if I don't believe you were trying to cut me, Tom," it said.

Elton looked round with ill-assumed surprise. “Hallo, Gordon! Who the deuce would have thought of seeing you here?”

Gordon laughed thickly. “Not you, apparently; and you don’t look as pleased as you might now you have seen me. Whereas I’m delighted to see you, and especially to see that things are going so well with you.”

“What do you mean?” asked Elton.

“Taking your winter holiday by the sea, like a blooming duke.”

“I’m not taking a holiday,” said Elton. “I was so worn out that I had to have some sort of change; but I’ve brought my work down with me, and I put in a full seven hours every day.”

“That’s right,” said Gordon. “‘Consider the ant.’ Nothing like steady industry! I’ve brought my work down with me too; a little slip of paper with a stamp on it. You know the article, Tom.”

“I know. But it isn’t due till to-morrow, is it?”

“Isn’t it, by gum! It’s due this very day, the twentieth of the month. That’s why I’m here. Knowing your little weakness in the matter of dates, and having a small item to collect in Canterbury, I thought I’d just come on, and save you the useless expense that results from forgetfulness.”

Elton understood the hint, and his face grew rigid.

“I can’t do it, Gordon; I can’t really. Haven’t got it, and shan’t have it until I’m paid for the batch of drawings that I’m working on now.”

“Oh, but what a pity!” exclaimed Gordon, taking the cigar from his thick, pouting lips to utter the exclamation. “Here you are, blueing your capital on seaside jaunts and reducing your income at a stroke by a clear four pounds a year.”

“How do you make that out?” demanded Elton.

“Tut, tut,” protested Gordon, “what an unbusinesslike chap you are! Here’s a little matter of twenty pounds quarter’s interest. If it’s paid now, it’s twenty. If it isn’t, it goes on to the principal and there’s another four pounds a year to be paid. Why don’t you try to be more economical, dear boy?”

Elton looked askance at the vampire by his side; at the plump blue-shaven cheeks, the thick black eyebrows, the drooping nose, and the full, red lips that embraced the cigar, and though he was a mild tempered man he felt that he could have battered that sensual, complacent face out of all human likeness, with something uncommonly like enjoyment. But of these thoughts nothing appeared in his reply, for a man cannot afford to say all he would wish to a creditor who could ruin him with a word.

"You mustn't be too hard on me, Gordon," said he. "Give me a little time. I'm doing all I can, you know. I earn every penny that I am able, and I have kept my insurance paid up regularly. I shall be paid for this work in a week or two and then we can settle up."

Gordon made no immediate reply, and the two men walked slowly eastward, a curiously ill-assorted pair: the one prosperous, jaunty, overdressed; the other pale and dejected, and, with his well-brushed but napless clothes, his patched boots and shiny-brimmed hat, the very type of decent, struggling poverty.

They had just passed the pier, and were coming to the base of the jetty, when Gordon next spoke.

"Can't we get off this beastly wet pavement?" he asked, looking down at his dainty and highly-polished boots. "What's it like down on the sands?"

"Oh, it's very good walking," said Elton, "between here and Foreness, and probably drier than the pavement."

"Then," said Gordon, "I vote we go down"; and accordingly they descended the sloping way beyond the jetty. The stretch of sand left by the retiring tide was as smooth and firm as a sheet of asphalt, and far more pleasant to walk upon.

"We seem to have the place all to ourselves," remarked Gordon, "with the exception of some half- dozen dukes like yourself."

As he spoke, he cast a cunning black eye furtively at the dejected man by his side, considering how much further squeezing was possible, and what would be the probable product of a further squeeze; but he quickly averted his gaze as Elton turned on him a look eloquent of contempt and dislike. There was another pause, for Elton made no reply to the last observation; then Gordon changed over from one arm to the other the heavy fur overcoat that he was carrying. "Needn't have brought this beastly thing," he remarked, "if I'd known it was going to be so warm."

"Shall I carry it for you a little way?" asked the naturally polite Elton.

"If you would, dear boy," replied Gordon. "It's difficult to manage an overcoat, an umbrella and cigar all at once."

He handed over the coat with a sigh of relief, and having straightened himself and expanded his chest, remarked: "I suppose you're beginning to do quite well now, Tom?"

Elton shook his head gloomily. "No," he answered, "it's the same old grind."

"But surely they're beginning to recognise your talents by this time," said Gordon, with the persuasive air of a counsel.

"That's just the trouble," said Elton. "You see, I haven't any, and they recognised the fact long ago. I'm just a journeyman, and journeyman's work is what I get given to me."

"You mean to say that the editors don't appreciate talent when they see it."

"I don't know about that," said Elton, "but they're most infernally appreciative of the lack of it."

Gordon blew out a great cloud of smoke, and raised his eyebrows reflectively. "Do you think," he said after a brief pause, "you give 'em a fair chance? I've seen some of your stuff. It's blooming prim, you know. Why don't you try something more lively? More skittish, you know, old chap; something with legs, you know, and high shoes. See what I mean, old chap? High with good full calves and not too fat in the ankle. That ought to fetch 'em; don't you think so?"

Elton scowled. "You're thinking of the drawings in 'Hold Me Up,'" he said scornfully, "but you're mistaken. Any fool can draw a champagne bottle upside down with a French shoe at the end of it."

"No doubt, dear boy," said Gordon, "but I expect that sort of fool knows what pays."

"A good many fools seem to know that much," retorted Elton; and then he was sorry he had spoken, for Gordon was not really an amiable man, and the expression of his face suggested that he had read a personal application into the rejoinder. So, once more, the two men walked on in silence.

Presently their footsteps led them to the margin of the weed-covered rocks, and here, from under a high heap of bladder-wrack, a large green shorecrab rushed out and menaced them with uplifted claws. Gordon stopped and stared at the creature with Cockney surprise, prodding it with his umbrella, and speculating aloud as to whether it was good to eat. The crab, as if alarmed at the suggestion, suddenly darted away and began to scuttle over the green-clad rocks, finally plunging into a large, deep pool. Gordon pursued it, hobbling awkwardly over the slippery rocks, until he came to the edge of the pool, over which he stooped, raking inquisitively among the weedy fringe with his umbrella. He was so much interested in his quarry that he failed to allow for the slippery surface on which he stood. The result was disastrous. Of a sudden, one foot began to slide forward, and when he tried to recover his balance, was instantly followed by the other. For a moment he struggled frantically to regain his footing, executing a sort of splashing, stamping dance on the margin. Then, the circling sea birds were startled by a yell of terror, an ivory-handled umbrella flew across the rocks, and Mr. Solomon Gordon took a complete header into the deepest part of the pool. What the crab thought of it history does not relate. What Mr. Gordon thought of it is unsuitable for publication; but, as he rose, like an extremely up-to-date merman, he expressed his sentiments with a wealth of adjectives that brought Elton in the verge of hysteria.

"It's a good job you brought your overcoat, after all," Elton remarked for the sake of saying something, and thereby avoiding the risk of exploding into undeniable laughter. The Hebrew made no reply--at least, no reply that lends itself to verbatim report--but staggered towards the hospitable overcoat, holding out his dripping arms. Having inducted him into the garment and buttoned him up, Elton hurried off to recover the umbrella (and, incidentally, to indulge himself in a broad grin), and, having secured it, angled with it for the smart billycock which was floating across the pool.

It was surprising what a change the last minute or two had wrought. The positions of the two men were now quite reversed. Despite his shabby clothing, Elton seemed to walk quite jauntily as compared with his shuddering companion who trotted by his side with short miserable steps, shrinking into the uttermost depths of his enveloping coat, like an alarmed winkle into its shell, puffing out his cheeks and anathematising the Universe in general as well as his chattering teeth would let him.

For some time they hurried along towards the slope by the jetty without exchanging any further remarks; then suddenly, Elton asked: "What are you going to do, Gordon? You can't travel like that."

"Can't you lend me a change?" asked Gordon. Elton reflected. He had another suit, his best suit, which he had been careful to preserve in good condition for use on those occasions when a decent appearance was indispensable. He looked askance at the man by his side and something told him that the treasured suit would probably receive less careful treatment than it was accustomed to. Still the man couldn't be allowed to go about in wet clothes.

"I've got a spare suit," he said. "It isn't quite up to your style, and may not be much of a fit, but I daresay you'll be able to put up with it for an hour or two."

"It'll be dry anyhow," mumbled Gordon, "so we won't trouble about the style. How far is it to your rooms?"

The plural number was superfluous. Elton's room was in a little ancient flint house at the bottom of a narrow close in the old quarter of the town. You reached it without any formal preliminaries of bell or knocker by simply letting yourself in by a street door, crossing a tiny room, opening the door of what looked like a narrow cupboard, and squeezing up a diminutive flight of stairs, which was unexpectedly exposed to view. By following this procedure, the two men reached a small bed-sitting-room; that is to say, it was a bed room, but by sitting down on the bed, you converted it into a sitting-room.

Gordon puffed out his cheeks and looked round distastefully.

"You might just ring for some hot water, old chappie," he said.

Elton laughed aloud. "Ring!" he exclaimed. "Ring what? Your clothes are the only things that are likely to get wrung."

"Well, then, sing out for the servant," said Gordon.

Elton laughed again. "My dear fellow," said he, "we don't go in for servants. There is only my land lady and she never comes up here. She's too fat to get up the stairs, and besides, she's got a game leg. I look after my room myself. You'll be all right if you have a good rub down."

Gordon groaned, and emerged reluctantly from the depths of his overcoat, while Elton brought forth from the chest of drawers the promised suit and the necessary undergarments. One of these latter Gordon held up with a sour smile, as he regarded it with extreme disfavour.

"I shouldn't think," said he, "you need have been at the trouble of marking them so plainly. No one's likely to want to run away with them."

The undergarments certainly contrasted very unfavourably with the delicate garments which he was peeling off, excepting in one respect; they were dry; and that had to console him for the ignominious change.

The clothes fitted quite fairly, notwithstanding the difference between the figures of the two men; for while Gordon was a slender man grown fat, Elton was a broad man grown thin; which, in a way, averaged their superficial area.

Elton watched the process of investment and noted the caution with which Gordon smuggled the various articles from his own pockets into those of the borrowed garments without exposing them to view; heard the jingle of money; saw the sumptuous gold watch and massive chain transplanted and noted with interest the large leather wallet that came forth from the breast pocket of the wet coat. He got a better view of this from the fact that Gordon himself examined it narrowly, and even opened it to inspect its contents.

"Lucky that wasn't an ordinary pocketbook." he remarked. "If it had been, your receipt would have got wet, and so would one or two other little articles that wouldn't have been improved by salt water. And, talking of the receipt, Tom, shall I hand it over now?"

"You can if you like," said Elton; "but as I told you, I haven't got the money"; on which Gordon muttered: "Pity, pity," and thrust the wallet into his, or rather, Elton's breast pocket.

A few minutes later, the two men came out together into the gathering darkness, and as they walked slowly up the close, Elton asked: "Are you going up to town to-night, Gordon?"

"How can I?" was the reply. "I can't go without my clothes. No, I shall run over to Broadstairs. A client of mine keeps a boarding-house there. He'll have to put me up for the night, and if you can get my clothes cleaned and dried I can come over for them to-morrow."

These arrangements having been settled, the two men adjourned, at Gordon's suggestion, for tea at one of the restaurants on the Front; and after that, again at Gordon's suggestion, they set forth together along the cliff path that leads to Broadstairs by way of Kingsgate.

"You may as well walk with me into Broadstairs," said Gordon; "I'll stand you the fare back by rail"; and to this Elton had agreed, not because he was desirous of the other man's company, but because he still had some lingering hopes of being able to adjust the little difficulty respecting the instalment.

He did not, however, open the subject at once. Profoundly as he loathed and despised the human spider whom necessity made his associate for the moment, he exerted himself to keep up a current of amusing conversation. It was not easy; for Gordon, like most men whose attention is focussed on the mere acquirement of money, looked with a dull eye on the ordinary interests of life. His tastes in art he had already hinted at, and his other tastes lay much in the same direction. Money first, for its own sake, and then those coarser and more primitive gratifications that it was capable of purchasing. This was the horizon that bounded Mr. Solomon Gordon's field of vision.

Nevertheless, they were well on their way before Elton alluded to the subject that was uppermost in both their minds.

"Look here, Gordon," he said at length, "can't you manage to give me a bit more time to pay up this instalment? It doesn't seem quite fair to keep sending up the principal like this."

"Well, dear boy," replied Gordon, "it's your own fault, you know. If you would only bear the dates in mind, it wouldn't happen."

"But," pleaded Elton, "just consider what I'm paying you. I originally borrowed fifty pounds from you, and I'm now paying you eighty pounds a year in addition to the insurance premium. That's close on a hundred a year; just about half that I manage to earn by slaving like a nigger. If you stick it up any farther you won't leave me enough to keep body and soul together; which really means that I shan't be able to pay you at all."

There was a brief pause; then Gordon said dryly: "You talk about not paying, dear boy, as if you had forgotten about that promissory note."

Elton set his teeth. His temper was rising rapidly. But he restrained himself.

"I should have a pretty poor memory if I had," he replied, "considering the number of reminders you've given me."

"You've needed them, Tom," said the other. "I've never met a slacker man in keeping to his engagements."

At this Elton lost his temper completely.

"That's a damned lie!" he exclaimed, "and you know it, you infernal, dirty, blood-sucking parasite "

Gordon stopped dead.

"Look here, my friend," said he; "none of that. If I've any of your damned sauce, I'll give you a sound good hammering."

"The deuce you will!" said Elton, whose fingers were itching, not for the first time, to take some recompense for all that he had suffered from the insatiable usurer. "Nothing's preventing you now, you know, but I fancy cent. per cent. is more in your line than fighting."

"Give me any more sauce and you'll see," said Gordon.

"Very well," was the quiet rejoinder. "I have great pleasure in informing you that you are a human maw-worm. How does that suit you?"

For reply, Gordon threw down his overcoat and umbrella on the grass at the side of the path, and deliberately slapped Elton on the cheek.

The reply followed instantly in the form of a smart left-hander, which took effect on the bridge of the Hebrew's rather prominent nose. Thus the battle was fairly started, and it proceeded with all the fury of accumulated hatred on the one side and sharp physical pain on the other. What little science there was appertamed to Elton, in spite of which, however, he had to give way to his heavier, better nourished and more excitable opponent. Regardless of the punishment he received, the infuriated Jew rushed at him and, by sheer weight of onslaught, drove him backward across the little green.

Suddenly, Elton, who knew the place by daylight, called out in alarm.

"Look out, Gordon! Get back, you fool!"

But Gordon, blind with fury, and taking this as attempt to escape, only pressed him harder. Elton's pugnacity died out instantly in mortal terror. He shouted out another warning and as Gordon still pressed him, battering furiously, he did the only thing that was possible: he dropped to the ground. And then, in the twinkling of an eye came the catastrophe. Borne forward by his own momentum, Gordon stumbled over Elton's prostrate body, staggered forward a few paces, and fell. Elton heard a muffled groan that faded quickly, and mingled with the sound of falling earth and stones. He sprang to his feet and looked round and saw that he was alone.

For some moments he was dazed by the suddenness of the awful thing that had happened. He crept timorously towards the unseen edge of the cliff, and listened.

There was no sound save the distant surge of the breakers, and the scream of an invisible sea-bird. It was useless to try to look over. Near as he was, he could not, even now, distinguish the edge of the cliff from the dark beach below. Suddenly he bethought him of a narrow cutting that led down from the cliff to the shore. Quickly crossing the green, and mechanically stooping to pick up Gordon's overcoat and umbrella, he made his way to the head of the cutting and ran down the rough chalk roadway. At the bottom he turned to the right and, striding hurriedly over the smooth sand, peered into the darkness at the foot of the cliff.

Soon there loomed up against the murky sky the shadowy form of the little headland on which he and Gordon had stood; and, almost at the same moment, there grew out of the darkness of the beach a darker spot amidst a constellation of smaller spots of white. As he drew nearer the dark spot took shape; a horrid shape with sprawling limbs and a head strangely awry. He stepped forward, trembling, and spoke the name that the thing had borne. He grasped the flabby hand, and laid his fingers on the wrist; but it only told him the same tale as did that strangely misplaced head. The body lay face downwards, and he had not the courage to turn it over; but that his enemy was dead he had not the faintest doubt. He stood up amidst the litter of fallen chalk and earth and looked down at the horrible, motionless thing, wondering numbly and vaguely what he should do. Should he go and seek assistance? The answer to that came in another question. How came that body to be lying on the beach? And what answer should he give to the inevitable questions? And swiftly there grew up in his mind, born of the horror of the thing that was, a yet greater horror of the thing that might be.

A minute later, a panic-stricken man stole with stealthy swiftness up the narrow cutting and set forth towards Margate, stopping anon to listen, and stealing away off the path into the darkness, to enter the town by the inland road.

Little sleep was there that night for Elton in his room in the old flint house. The dead man's clothes, which greeted him on his arrival, hanging limply on the towel-horse where he had left them, haunted him through the night. In the darkness, the sour smell of damp cloth assailed him with an endless reminder of their presence, and after each brief doze, he would start up in alarm and hastily light his candle; only to throw its flickering light on those dank, drowned-looking vestments. His thoughts, half-controlled, as night thoughts are, flitted erratically from the unhappy past to the unstable present, and thence to the incalculable future. Once he lighted the candle specially to look at his watch to see if the tide had yet crept up to that solitary figure on the beach; nor could he rest again until the time of high water was well past. And all through these wanderings of his thoughts there came, recurring like a horrible refrain, the question what would happen when the body was found? Could he be connected with it and, if so, would he be charged with murder? At last he fell asleep and slumbered on until the landlady thumped at the staircase door to announce that she had brought his breakfast.

As soon as he was dressed he went out. Not, how ever, until he had stuffed Gordon's still damp clothes and boots, the cumbrous overcoat and the smart billy-cock hat into his trunk, and put the umbrella into the darkest corner of the cupboard. Not that anyone ever came up to the room, but that, already, he was possessed with the uneasy secretiveness of the criminal. He went straight down to the beach; with what purpose he could hardly have said, but an irresistible impulse drove him thither to see if it was there. He went down by the jetty and struck out eastward over the smooth sand, looking about him with dreadful expectation for some small crowd or hurrying messenger. From the foot of the cliffs, over the rocks to the distant line of breakers, his eye roved with eager dread, and still he hurried eastward, always drawing nearer to the place that he feared to look on. As he left the town behind, so he left behind the one or two idlers on the beach, and when he turned Foreness Point he lost sight of the last of them and went forward alone. It was less than half an hour later that the fatal head land opened out beyond Whiteness.

Not a soul had he met along that solitary beach, and though, once or twice, he had started at the sight of some mass of drift wood or heap of seaweed, the dreadful thing that he was seeking had not yet appeared. He passed the opening of the cutting and approached the headland, breathing fast and looking about him fearfully. Already he could see the larger lumps of chalk that had fallen, and looking up, he saw a clean, white patch at the summit of the cliff. But still there was no sign of the corpse. He walked on more slowly now, considering whether it could have drifted out to sea, or whether he should find it in the next bay. And then, rounding the head land, he came in sight of a black hole at the cliff foot, the entrance to a deep cave. He approached yet more slowly, sweeping his eye round the little bay, and looking apprehensively at the cavity before him. Suppose the thing should have washed in there. It was quite possible. Many things did wash into that cave, for he had once visited it and had been astonished at the quantity of seaweed and jetsam that had accumulated within it. But it was an uncomfortable thought. It would be doubly horrible to meet the awful thing in the dim twilight of the cavern. And yet, the black archway seemed to draw him on, step by step, until he stood at the portal and looked in. It was an eerie place, chilly and damp, the clammy walls and roof stained green and purple and black with encrusting lichens. At one time, Elton had been told, it used to be haunted by smugglers, and then communicated with an underground passage; and the old smuggler's look-out still remained; a narrow tunnel, high up the cliff, looking out into Kingsgate Bay; and even some vestiges of the rude steps that led up to the look-out platform could still be traced, and were not impossible to climb. Indeed, Elton had, at his last visit, climbed to the platform and looked out through the spy-hole. He recalled the circumstance now, as he stood, peering nervously into the darkness, and straining his eyes to see what jetsam the ocean had brought since then.

At first he could see nothing but the smooth sand near the opening; then, as his eyes grew more accustomed to the gloom, he could make out the great heap of seaweed on the floor of the cave.

Insensibly, he crept in, with his eyes riveted on the weedy mass and, as he left the daylight behind him, so did the twilight of the cave grow clearer. His feet left the firm sand and trod the springy mass of weed, and in the silence of the cave he could now hear plainly the rain-like patter of the leaping sand-hoppers. He stopped for a moment to listen to the unfamiliar sound, and still the gloom of the cave grew lighter to his more accustomed eyes.

And then, in an instant, he saw it. From a heap of weed, a few paces ahead, projected a boot; his own boot; he recognised the patch on the sole; and at the sight, his heart seemed to stand still. Though he had somehow expected to find it here, its presence seemed to strike him with a greater shock of horror from that very circumstance.

He was standing stock still, gazing with fearful fascination at the boot and the swelling mound of weed, when, suddenly, there struck upon his ear the voice of a woman, singing.

He started violently. His first impulse was to run out of the cave. But a moment's reflection told him what madness this would be. And then the voice drew nearer, and there broke out the high, rippling laughter of a child. Elton looked in terror at the bright opening of the cavern's mouth, expecting every moment to see it frame a group of figures. If that happened, he was lost, for he would have been seen actually with the body. Suddenly he bethought him of the spy-hole and the platform, both of which were invisible from the entrance; and turning, he ran quickly over the sodden weed till he came to the remains of the steps. Climbing hurriedly up these, he reached the platform, which was enclosed in a large niche, just as the reverberating sound of voices told him that the strangers were within the mouth of the cave. He strained his ears to catch what they were saying and to make out if they were entering farther. It was a child's voice that he had first heard, and very weird were the hollow echoes of the thin treble that were flung back from the rugged walls. But he could not hear what the child had said. The woman's voice, however, was quite distinct, and the words seemed significant in more senses than one.

"No, dear," it said, "you had better not go in. It's cold and damp. Come out into the sunshine."

Elton breathed more freely. But the woman was more right than she knew. It was cold and damp, that thing under the black tangle of weed. Better far to be out in the sunshine. He himself was already longing to escape from the chill and gloom, of the cavern. But he could not escape yet. Innocent as he actually was, his position was that of a murderer. He must wait until the coast was clear, and then steal out, to hurry away unobserved.

He crept up cautiously to the short tunnel and peered out through the opening across the bay. And then his heart sank. Below him, on the sunny beach, a small party of visitors had established themselves just within view of the mouth of the cave; and even as he looked, a man approached from the wooden stairway down the cliff, carrying a couple of deck chairs. So, for the present his escape was hopelessly cut off.

He went back to the platform and sat down to wait for his release; and, as he sat, his thoughts went back once more to the thing that lay under the weed. How long would it lie there undiscovered? And what would happen when it was found? What was there to connect him with it? Of course, there was his name on the clothing, but there was nothing incriminating in that, if he had only had the courage to give information at once. But it was too late to think of that now. Besides, it suddenly flashed upon him, there was the receipt in the wallet. That receipt mentioned him by name and referred to a loan. Obviously, its suggestion was most sinister, coupled with his silence. It was a deadly item of evidence against him. But no sooner had he realised the appalling significance of this document than he also realised that it was still within his reach. Why should he leave it there to be brought in evidence--in false evidence, too-- against him?

Slowly he rose and, creeping down the tunnel, once more looked out. The people were sitting quietly in their chairs, the man was reading, and the child was digging in the sand. Elton looked across the bay to make sure that no other person was approaching, and then, hastily climbing down the steps, walked across the great bed of weed, driving an army of sand-hoppers before him. He shuddered at the thought of what he was going to do, and the clammy chill of the cave seemed to settle on him in a cold sweat.

He came to the little mound from which the boot projected, and began, shudderingly and with faltering hand, to lift the slimy, tangled weed. As he drew aside the first bunch, be gave a gasp of horror and quickly replaced it. The body was lying on its back, and, as he lifted the weed he had uncovered--not the face, for the thing had no face. It had struck either the cliff or a stone upon the beach and--but there is no need to go into particulars: it had no face. When he had recovered a little, Elton groped shudderingly among the weed until he found the breast-pocket from which he quickly drew out the wallet, now clammy, sodden and loathsome. He was rising with it in his hand when an apparition, seen through the opening of the cave, arrested his movement as if he had been suddenly turned into stone. A man, apparently a fisherman or sailor, was sauntering past some thirty yards from the mouth of the cave, and at his heels trotted a mongrel dog. The dog stopped, and, lifting his nose, seemed to sniff the air; and then he began to walk slowly and suspiciously towards the cave. The man sauntered on and soon passed out of view; but the dog still came on towards the cave, stopping now and again with upraised nose.

The catastrophe seemed inevitable. But just at that moment the man's voice rose, loud and angry, evidently calling the dog. The animal hesitated, looking wistfully from his master to the cave; but when the summons was repeated, he turned reluctantly and trotted away.

Elton stood up and took a deep breath. The chilly sweat was running clown his face, his heart was thumping and his knees trembled, so that he could hardly get back to the platform. What hideous peril had he escaped and how narrowly! For there he had stood; and had the man entered, he would have been caught in the very act of stealing the incriminating document from the body. For that matter, he was little better off now, with the dead man's property on his person, and he resolved instantly to take out and destroy the receipt and put back the wallet. But this was easier thought of than done. The receipt was soaked with sea water, and refused utterly to light when he applied a match to it. In the end, he tore it up into little fragments and deliberately swallowed them, one by one.

But to restore the wallet was more than he was equal to just now. He would wait until the people had gone home to lunch, and then he would thrust it under the weed as he ran past. So he sat down again and once more took up the endless thread of his thoughts.

The receipt was gone now, and with it the immediate suggestion of motive. There remained only the clothes with their too legible markings. They certainly connected him with the body, but they offered no proof of his presence at the catastrophe. And then, suddenly, another most startling idea occurred to him. Who could identify the body--the body that had no face? There was the wallet, it was true, but he could take that away with him, and there was a ring on the finger and some articles in the pockets which might be identified. But--a voice seemed to whisper to him--these things were removable, too. And if he removed them, what then? Why, then, the body was that of Thomas Elton, a friendless, poverty-stricken artist, about whom no one would trouble to ask any questions.

He pondered on this new situation profoundly. It offered him a choice of alternatives. Either he might choose the imminent risk of being hanged for a murder that he had not committed, or he might surrender his identity for ever and move away to a new environment.

He smiled faintly. His identity! What might that be worth to barter against his life? Only yesterday he would gladly have surrendered it as the bare price of emancipation from the vampire who had fastened on to him.

He thrust the wallet into his pocket and buttoned his coat. Thomas Elton was dead; and that other man, as yet unnamed, should go forth, as the woman had said, into the sunshine.

Part II

(Related by Christopher Jervis, M.D.)

From various causes, the insurance business that passed through Thorndyke's hands had, of late, considerably increased. The number of societies which regularly employed him had grown larger, and, since the remarkable case of Percival Bland, the "Griffin" had made it a routine practice to send all inquest cases to us for report.

It was in reference to one of these latter that Mr. Stalker, a senior member of the staff of that office, called on us one afternoon in December; and when he had laid his bag on the table and settled himself comfortably before the fire, he opened the business without preamble.

"I've brought you another inquest case," said he; "a rather queer one, quite interesting from your point of view. As far as we can see, it has no particular interest for us excepting that it does rather look as if our examining medical officer had been a little casual."

"What is the special interest of the case from our point of view?" asked Thorndyke.

"I'll just give you a sketch of it," said Stalker, "and I think you will agree that it's a case after your own heart.

"On the 24th of last month, some men who were collecting seaweed, to use as manure, discovered in a cave at Kingsgate, in the Isle of Thanet, the body of a man, lying under a mass of accumulated weed. As the tide was rising, they put the body into their cart and conveyed it to Margate, where, of course, an inquest was held, and the following facts were elicited. The body was that of a man named Thomas Elton. It was identified by the name-marks on the clothing, by the visiting-cards and a couple of letters which were found in the pockets. From the address on the letters it was seen that Elton had been staying in Margate, and on inquiry at that address, it was learnt from the old woman who let the lodgings, that he had been missing about four days. The landlady was taken to the mortuary, and at once identified the body as that of her lodger. It remained only to decide how the body came into the cave; and this did not seem to present much difficulty; for the neck had been broken by a tremendous blow, which had practically destroyed the face, and there were distinct evidences of a breaking away of a portion of the top of the cliff, only a few yards from the position of the cave. There was apparently no doubt that Elton had fallen sheer from the top of the overhanging cliff on to the beach. Now, one would suppose with the evidence of this fall of about a hundred and fifty feet, the smashed face and broken neck, there was not much room for doubt as to the cause of death. I think you will agree with me, Dr. Jervis?"

Certainly," I replied; "it must be admitted that a broken neck is a condition that tends to shorten life."

"Quite so," agreed Stalker; "but our friend, the local coroner, is a gentleman who takes nothing for granted--a very Thomas Didymus, who apparently agrees with Dr. Thorndyke that if there is no post mortem, there is no inquest. So he ordered a post mortem, which would have appeared to me an absurdly unnecessary proceeding, and I think that even you will agree with me, Dr. Thorndyke."

But Thorndyke shook his head.

"Not at all," said he. "It might, for instance, be much more easy to push a drugged or poisoned man over a cliff than to put over the same man in his normal state. The appearance of violent accident is an excellent mask for the less obvious forms of murder."

"That's perfectly true," said Stalker; "and I suppose that is what the coroner thought. At any rate, he had the post-mortem made, and the result was most curious; for it was found, on opening the body, that the deceased had suffered from a smallish thoracic aneurism, which had burst. Now, as the aneurism must obviously have burst during life, it leaves the cause of death--so I understand--uncertain; at any rate, the medical witness was unable to say whether the deceased fell over the cliff in consequence of the bursting of the aneurism or burst the aneurism in consequence of falling over the cliff. Of course, it doesn't matter to us which way the thing happened; the only question which interests us is, whether a comparatively recently insured man ought to have had an aneurism at all."

"Have you paid the claim?" asked Thorndyke.

"No, certainly not. We never pay a claim until we have had your report. But, as a matter of fact, there is another circumstance that is causing delay. It seems that Elton had mortgaged his policy to a money lender, named Gordon, and it is by him that the claim has been made, or rather, by a clerk of his, named Hyams. Now, we have had a good many dealings with this man Gordon, and hitherto be has always acted in person; and as he is a somewhat slippery gentleman we have thought it desirable to have the claim actually signed by him. And that is the difficulty. For it seems that Mr. Gordon is abroad, and his whereabouts unknown to Hyams; so, as we certainly couldn't take Hyams's receipt for payment, the matter is in abeyance until Hyams can communicate with his principal. And now, I must be running away. I have brought you, as you will see, all the papers, including the policy and the mortgage deed."

As soon as he was gone, Thorndyke gathered up the bundle of papers and sorted them out in what be apparently considered the order of their importance. First be glanced quickly through the proposal form, and then took up the copy of the coroner's depositions.

"The medical evidence," be remarked, "is very full and complete. Both the coroner and the doctor seem to know their business."

Seeing that the man apparently fell over a cliff," said I, "the medical evidence would not seem to be of first importance. It would seem to be more to the point to ascertain how he came to fall over."

"That's quite true," replied Thorndyke; "and yet, this report contains some rather curious matter. The deceased had an aneurism of the arch; that was probably rather recent. But he also had some slight, old-standing aortic disease, with full compensatory hypertrophy. He also had a nearly complete set of false teeth. Now, doesn't it strike you, Jervis, as rather odd that a man who was passed only five years ago as a first-class life, should, in that short interval, have become actually uninsurable?"

'Yes, it certainly does look," said I, " as if the fellow had had rather bad luck. What does the proposal form say?"

I took the document up and ran my eyes over it. On Thorndyke's advice, medical examiners for the "Griffin" were instructed to make a somewhat fuller report than is usual in some companies. In this case, the ordinary answers to questions set forth that the heart was perfectly healthy and the teeth rather exceptionally good, and then, in the summary at the end, the examiner remarked: "the proposer seems to be a completely sound and healthy man; he presents no physical defects whatever, with the exception of a bony ankylosis of the first joint of the third finger of the left hand, which he states to have been due to an injury."

Thorndyke looked up quickly. "Which finger, did you say?" he asked.

"The third finger of the left hand," I replied.

Thorndyke looked thoughtfully at the paper that he was reading. "It's very singular," said he, "for I see that the Margate doctor states that the deceased wore a signet ring on the third finger of the left hand. Now, of course, you couldn't get a ring on to a finger with bony ankylosis of the joint."

"He must have mistaken the finger," said I, "or else the insurance examiner did."

"That is quite possible," Thorndyke replied; "but, doesn't it strike you as very singular that, whereas the insurance examiner mentions the ankylosis, which was of no importance from an insurance point of view, the very careful man who made the post-mortem should not have mentioned it, though, owing to the unrecognisable condition of the face, it was of vital importance for the purpose of identification?"

I admitted that it was very singular indeed, and we then resumed our study of the respective papers. But presently I noticed that Thorndyke had laid the report upon his knee, and was gazing speculatively into the fire.

I gather," said I, "that my learned friend finds some matter of interest in this case."

For reply, he handed me the bundle of papers, recommending me to look through them.

"Thank you," said I, rejecting them firmly, "but I think I can trust you to have picked out all the plums."

Thorndyke smiled indulgently. "They're not plums, Jervis," said he; "they're only currants, but they make quite a substantial little heap."

I disposed myself in a receptive attitude (somewhat after the fashion of the juvenile pelican) and he continued: "If we take the small and unimpressive items and add them together, you will see that a quite considerable sum of discrepancy results, thus:

"In 1903, Thomas Elton, aged thirty-one, had a set of sound teeth. In 1908, at the age of thirty-six, he was more than half toothless. Again, at the age of thirty-one, his heart was perfectly healthy. At the age of thirty-six, he had old aortic disease, with fully established compensation, and an aneurism that was possibly due to it. When he was examined he had a noticeable incurable malformation; no such malformation is mentioned in connection with the body.

"He appears to have fallen over a cliff; and he had also burst an aneurism. Now, the bursting of the aneurism must obviously have occurred during life; but it would occasion practically instantaneous death. Therefore, if the fall was accidental, the rupture must have occurred either as he stood at the edge of the cliff, as he was in the act of falling, or on striking the beach.

"At the place where he apparently fell, the footpath is some thirty yards distant from the edge of the cliff.

"It is not known how he came to that spot, or whether he was alone at the time.

"Someone is claiming five hundred pounds as the immediate result of his death.

"There, you see, Jervis, are seven propositions, none of them extremely striking, but rather suggestive when taken together."

"You seem," said I, "to suggest a doubt as to the identity of the body."

"I do," he replied. "The identity was not clearly established."

"You don't think the clothing and the visiting-cards conclusive."

"They're not parts of the body," he replied. "Of course, substitution is highly improbable. But it is not impossible."

"And the old woman--" I suggested, but he interrupted me.

"My dear Jervis," he exclaimed; "I'm surprised at you. How many times has it happened within our knowledge that women have identified the bodies of total strangers as those of their husbands, fathers or brothers? The thing happens almost every year. As to this old woman, she saw a body with an unrecognisable face, dressed in the clothes of her missing lodger. Of course, it was the clothes that she identified."

"I suppose it was," I agreed; and then I said: "You seem to suggest the possibility of foul play."

"Well," he replied, "if you consider those seven points, you will agree with me that they present a cumulative discrepancy which it is impossible to ignore. The whole significance of the case turns on the question of identity; for, if this was not the body of Thomas Elton, it would appear to have been deliberately prepared to counterfeit that body. And such deliberate preparation would manifestly imply an attempt to conceal the identity of some other body.

"Then," he continued, after a pause, "there is this deed. It looks quite regular and is correctly stamped, but it seems to me that the surface of the paper is slightly altered in one or two places and if one holds the document up to the light, the paper looks a little more transparent in those places." He examined the document for a few seconds with his pocket lens, and then passing lens and document to me, said: "Have a look at it, Jervis, and tell me what you think."

I scrutinised the paper closely, taking it over to the window to get a better light; and to me, also, the paper appeared to be changed in certain places.

"Are we agreed as to the position of the altered places?" Thorndyke asked when I announced the fact.

"I only see three patches," I answered. "Two correspond to the name, Thomas Elton, and the third to one of the figures in the policy number."

"Exactly," said Thorndyke, "and the significance is obvious. If the paper has really been altered, it means that some other name has been erased and Elton's substituted; by which arrangement, of course, the correctly dated stamp would be secured. And this--the alteration of an old document--is the only form of forgery that is possible with a dated, impressed stamp."

"Wouldn't it be rather a stroke of luck," I asked, "for a forger to happen to have in his possession a document needing only these two alterations?"

"I see nothing remarkable in it," Thorndyke replied. "A moneylender would have a number of documents of this kind in hand, and you observe that be was not bound down to any particular date. Any date within a year or so of the issue of the policy would answer his purpose. This document is, in fact, dated, as you see, about six months after the issue of the policy."

"I suppose," said I, "that you will draw Stalker's attention to this matter."

"He will have to be informed, of course," Thorndyke replied; "but I think it would be interesting in the first place to call on Mr. Hyams. You will have noticed that there are some rather mysterious features in this case, and Mr. Hyams's conduct, especially if this document should turn out to be really a forgery, suggests that he may have some special information on the subject." He glanced at his watch and, after a few moments' reflection, added: "I don't see why we shouldn't make our little ceremonial call at once. But it will be a delicate business, for we have mighty little to go upon. Are you coming with me?"

If I had had any doubts, Thorndyke's last remark disposed of them; for the interview promised to be quite a sporting event. Mr. Hyams was presumably not quite newly-hatched, and Thorndyke, who utterly despised bluff of any kind, and whose exact mind refused either to act or speak one hair's breadth beyond his knowledge, was admittedly in somewhat of a fog. The meeting promised to be really entertaining.

Mr. Hyams was “discovered,” as the playwrights have it, in a small office at the top of a high building in Queen Victoria Street. He was a small gentleman, of sallow and greasy aspect, with heavy eyebrows and a still heavier nose.

“Are you Mr. Gordon?” Thorndyke suavely inquired as we entered.

Mr. Hyams seemed to experience a momentary doubt on the subject, but finally decided that he was not. “But perhaps,” he added brightly, “I can do your business for you as well.”

“I daresay you can,” Thorndyke agreed significantly; on which we were conducted into an inner den, where I noticed Thorndyke’s eye rest for an instant on a large iron safe.

“Now,” said Mr. Hyams, shutting the door ostentatiously, “what can I do for you?”

“I want you,” Thorndyke replied, “to answer one or two questions with reference to the claim made by you on the’ Griffin’ Office in respect of Thomas Elton.”

Mr. Hyams’s manner underwent a sudden change. He began rapidly to turn over papers, and opened and shut the drawers of his desk, with an air of restless preoccupation.

“Did the ‘Griffin’ people send you here?” he demanded brusquely.

“They did not specially instruct me to call on you,” replied Thorndyke.

“Then,” said Hyams bouncing out of his chair, “I can’t let you occupy my time. I’m not here to answer conundrums from Torn, Dick or Harry.”

Thorndyke rose from his chair. “Then I am to understand,” he said, with unruffled suavity, “that you would prefer me to communicate with the Directors, and leave them to take any necessary action.”

This gave Mr. Hyams pause. “What action do you refer to?” he asked. “And, who are you?”

Thorndyke produced a card and laid it on the table. Mr. Hyams had apparently seen the name before, for he suddenly grew rather pale and very serious.

"What is the nature of the questions that you wished to ask?" he inquired.

"They refer to this claim," replied Thorndyke. "The first question is, where is Mr. Gordon?"

"I don't know," said Hyams.

"Where do you think he is?" asked Thorndyke.

"I don't think at all," replied Hyams, turning a shade paler and looking everywhere but at Thorndyke.

"Very well," said the latter, "then the next question is, are you satisfied that this claim is really payable?"

"I shouldn't have made it if I hadn't been," replied Hyams.

"Quite so," said Thorndyke; "and the third question is, are you satisfied that the mortgage deed was executed as it purports to have been?"

"I can't say anything about that," replied Hyams, who was growing every moment paler and more fidgety, "it was done before my time."

"Thank you," said Thorndyke. "You will, of course, understand why I am making these inquiries."

"I don't," said Hyams.

"Then," said Thorndyke, "perhaps I had better explain. We are dealing, you observe, Mr. Hyams, with the case of a man who has met with a violent death under somewhat mysterious circumstances. We are dealing, also, with another man who has disappeared, leaving his affairs to take care of themselves; and with a claim, put forward by a third party, on behalf of the one man in respect of the other. When I say that the dead man has been imperfectly identified, and that the document supporting the claim presents certain peculiarities, you will see that the matter calls for further inquiry."

There was an appreciable interval of silence. Mr. Hyams had turned a tallowy white, and looked furtively about the room, as if anxious to avoid the stony gaze that my colleague had fixed on him.

"Can you give us no assistance?" Thorndyke inquired, at length.

Mr. Hyams chewed a pen-holder ravenously, as he considered the question. At length, he burst out in an agitated voice: "Look here, sir, if I tell you what I know, will you treat the information as confidential?

"I can't agree to that, Mr. Hyams," replied Thorndyke. "It might amount to compounding a felony. But you will be wiser to tell me what you know. The document is a side-issue, which my clients may never raise, and my own concern is with the death of this man."

Hyams looked distinctly relieved. "If that's so," said he, "I'll tell you all I know, which is precious little, and which just amounts to this: Two days after Elton was killed, someone came to this office in my absence and opened the safe. I discovered the fact the next morning. Someone had been to the safe and rummaged over all the papers. It wasn't Gordon, because he knew where to find everything; and it wasn't an ordinary thief, because no cash or valuables had been taken. In fact, the only thing that I missed was a promissory note, drawn by Elton."

"You didn't miss a mortgage deed?" suggested Thorndyke, and Hyams, having snatched a little further refreshment from the pen-holder, said he did not.

"And the policy," suggested Thorndyke, "was apparently not taken?"

"No," replied Hyams "but it was looked for. Three bundles of policies had been untied, but this one happened to be in a drawer of my desk and I had the only key."

"And what do you infer from this visit?" Thorndyke asked.

"Well," replied Hyams, "the safe was opened with keys, and they were Gordon's keys--or at any rate, they weren't mine--and the person who opened it wasn't Gordon; and the things that were taken--at least the thing, I mean--chiefly concerned Elton. Naturally I smelt a rat; and when I read of the finding of the body, I smelt a fox."

"And have you formed any opinion about the body that was found?"

"Yes, I have," he replied. "My opinion is that it was Gordon's body: that Gordon had been putting the screw on Elton, and Elton had just pitched him over the cliff and gone down and changed clothes with the body. Of course, that's only my opinion. I may be wrong; but I don't think I am."

As a matter of fact, Mr. Hyams was not wrong. An exhumation, consequent on Thorndyke's challenge of the identity of the deceased, showed that the body was that of Solomon Gordon. A hundred pounds reward was offered for information as to Elton's whereabouts. But no one ever earned it. A letter, bearing the post mark of Marseilles, and addressed by the missing man to Thorndyke, gave a plausible account of Gordon's death; which was represented as having occurred accidentally at the moment when Gordon chanced to be wearing a suit of Elton's clothes.

Of course, this account may have been correct, or again, it may have been false; but whether it was true or false, Elton, from that moment, vanished from our ken and has never since been heard of.

Percival Bland's Proxy

Part I

Mr. Percival Bland was a somewhat uncommon type of criminal. In the first place he really had an appreciable amount of common-sense. If he had only had a little more, he would not have been a criminal at all. As it was, he had just sufficient judgment to perceive that the consequences of unlawful acts accumulate as the acts are repeated; to realise that the criminal's position must, at length, become untenable; and to take what he considered fair precautions against the inevitable catastrophe.

But in spite of these estimable traits of character and the precautions aforesaid, Mr. Bland found himself in rather a tight place and with a prospect of increasing tightness. The causes of this uncomfortable tension do not concern us, and may be dismissed with the remark, that, if one perseveringly distributes flash Bank of England notes among the money-changers of the Continent, there will come a day of reckoning when those notes are tendered to the exceedingly knowing old lady who lives in Threadneedle Street.

Mr. Bland considered uneasily the approaching storm-cloud as he raked over the "miscellaneous property" in the Sale-rooms of Messrs. Plimpton. He was a confirmed frequenter of auctions, as was not unnatural, for the criminal is essentially a gambler. And criminal and gambler have one quality in common: each hopes to get something of value without paying the market price for it.

So Percival turned over the dusty oddments and his own difficulties at one and the same time. The vital questions were: When would the storm burst? And would it pass by the harbour of refuge that he bad been at such pains to construct? Let us inspect that harbour of refuge.

A quiet flat in the pleasant neighbourhood of Battersea bore a name-plate inscribed, Mr. Robert Lindsay; and the tenant was known to the porter and the char woman who attended to the flat, as a fair-haired gentle man who was engaged in the book trade as a travelling agent, and was consequently a good deal away from home. Now Mr. Robert Lindsay bore a distinct resemblance to Percival Bland; which was not surprising seeing that they were first cousins (or, at any rate, they said they were; and we may presume that they knew). But they were not very much alike. Mr. Lindsay had flaxen, or rather sandy, hair; Mr. Bland's hair was black. Mr. Bland had a mole under his left eye; Mr. Lindsay had no mole under his eye-- but carried one in a small box in his waistcoat pocket.

At somewhat rare intervals the Cousins called on one another; but they had the very worst of luck, for neither of them ever seemed to find the other at home. And what was even more odd was that whenever Mr. Bland spent an evening at home in his lodgings over the oil shop in Bloomsbury, Mr. Lindsay's flat was empty; and as sure as Mr. Lindsay was at home in his flat so surely were Mr. Bland's lodgings vacant for the time being. It was a queer coincidence, if anyone had noticed it; but nobody ever did.

However, if Percival saw little of his cousin, it was not a case of "out of sight, out of mind." On the contrary; so great was his solicitude for the latter's welfare that he not only had made a will constituting him his executor and sole legatee, but he had actually insured his life for no less a sum than three thousand pounds; and this will, together with the insurance policy, investment securities and other necessary documents, he had placed in the custody of a highly respectable solicitor. All of which did him great credit. It isn't every man who is willing to take so much trouble for a mere cousin.

Mr. Bland continued his perambulations, pawing over the miscellaneous raffle from sheer force of habit, reflecting on the coming crisis in his own affairs, and on the provisions that he had made for his cousin Robert. As for the latter, they were excellent as far as they went, but they lacked definiteness and perfect completeness. There was the contingency of a "stretch," for instance; say fourteen years' penal servitude. The insurance policy did not cover that. And, meanwhile, what was to become of the estimable Robert?

He had bruised his thumb somewhat severely in a screw-cutting lathe, and had abstractedly turned the handle of a bird-organ until politely requested by an attendant to desist, when he came upon a series of boxes containing, according to the catalogue, "a collection of surgical instruments the property of a lately deceased practitioner." To judge by the appearance of the instruments, the practitioner must have commenced practice in his early youth and died at a very advanced age. They were an uncouth set of tools, of no value whatever excepting as testimonials to the amazing tenacity of life of our ancestors; but Percival fingered them over according to his wont, working the handle of a complicated brass syringe and ejecting a drop of greenish fluid on to the shirt of a dressy Hebrew (who requested him to "point the dam' thing at thomeone elth nectht time"), opening musty leather cases, clicking off spring scarifiers and feeling the edges of strange, crooked, knives. Then he came upon a largish black box, which, when he raised the lid, breathed out an ancient and fish-like aroma and exhibited a collection of bones, yellow, greasy and spotted in places with mildew. The catalogue described them as" a complete set of human osteology" but they were not an ordinary "student's set," for the bones of the hands and feet, instead of being strung together on cat-gut, were united by their original ligaments and were of an unsavoury brown colour.

"I thay, misther," expostulat the Hebrew, "shut that bocth. Thmellth like a blooming inquetht."

But the contents of the black box seemed to have a fascination for Percival. He looked in at those greasy remnants of mortality, at the brown and mouldy hands and feet and the skull that peeped forth eerily from the folds of a flannel wrapping; and they breathed out something more than that stale and musty odour. A suggestion--vague and general at first, but rapidly crystallising into distinct shape--seemed to steal out of the black box into his consciousness; a suggestion that somehow seemed to connect itself with his estimable cousin Robert.

For upwards of a minute he stood motionless, as one immersed in reverie, the lid poised in his hand and a dreamy eye fixed on the half skull. A stir in the room roused him. The sale was about to begin. The members of the knock-out and other habitués seated themselves on benches around a long, baize table; the attendants took possession of the first lots and opened their catalogues as if about to sing an introductory chorus; and a gentleman with a waxed moustache and a striking resemblance to his late Majesty, the third Napoleon, having ascended to the rostrum bespoke the attention of the assembly by a premonitory tap with his hammer.

How odd are some of the effects of a guilty conscience! With what absurd self-consciousness do we read into the minds of others our own undeclared intentions, when those intentions are unlawful! Had Percival Bland wanted a set of human bones for any legitimate purpose--such as anatomical study--he would have bought it openly and unembarrassed. Now, he found himself earnestly debating whether he should not bid for some of the surgical instruments, just for the sake of appearances; and there being little time in which to make up his mind--for the deceased practitioner's effects came first in the catalogue--he was already the richer by a set of cupping- glasses, a tooth-key, and an instrument of unknown use and diabolical aspect, before the fateful lot was called.

At length the black box was laid on the table, an object of obscene mirth to the knockers-out, and the auctioneer read the entry: "Lot seventeen; a complete set of human osteology. A very useful and valuable set of specimens, gentlemen."

He looked round at the assembly majestically, oblivious of sundry inquiries as to the identity of the deceased and the verdict of the coroner's jury, and finally suggested five shillings.

"Six," said Percival.

An attendant held the box open, and, chanting the mystic word "Loddlemen!" (which, being interpreted, meant " Lot, gentlemen "), thrust it under the rather bulbous nose of the smart Hebrew; who remarked that "they 'ummed a bit too much to thoot him " and pushed it away.

"Going at six shillings," said the auctioneer, reproachfully; and as nobody contradicted him, he smote the rostrum with his hammer and the box was delivered into the hands of Percival on the payment of that modest sum.

Having crammed the cupping-glasses, the tooth-key and the unknown instrument into the box, Percival obtained from one of the attendants a length of cord, with which he secured the lid. Then he carried his treasure out into the street, and, chartering a four- wheeler, directed the driver to proceed to Charing Cross Station. At the station he booked the box in the cloak (in the name of Simpson) and left it for a couple of hours; at the expiration of which he returned, and, employing a different porters had it conveyed to a hansom, in which it was borne to his lodgings over the oil-shop in Bloomsbury. There he, himself, carried it, unobserved, up the stairs, and, depositing it in a large cupboard, locked the door and pocketed the key.

And thus was the curtain rung down on the first act. The second act opened only a couple of days later, the office of call-boy--to pursue the metaphor to the bitter end--being discharged by a Belgian police official who emerged from the main entrance to the Bank of England. What should have led Percival Bland into so unsafe a neighbourhood it is difficult to imagine, unless it was that strange fascination that seems so frequently to lure the criminal to places associated with his crime. But there he was within a dozen paces of the entrance when the officer came forth, and mutual recognition was instant. Almost equally instantaneous was the self-possessed Percival's decision to cross the road.

It is not a nice road to cross. The old horse would condescend to shout a warning to the indiscreet wayfarer. Not so the modern chauffeur, who looks stonily before him and leaves you to get out of the way of Juggernaut. He knows his "exonerating" coroner's jury. At the moment, however, the procession of Juggernauts was at rest; but Percival had seen the presiding policeman turn to move away and he darted across the fronts of the vehicles even as they started. The foreign officer followed. But in that moment the whole procession had got in motion. A motor omnibus thundered past in front of him; another was bearing down on him relentlessly. He hesitated, and sprang back; and then a taxi-cab, darting out from behind, butted him heavily, sending him sprawling in the road, whence he scrambled as best he could back on to the pavement.

Percival, meanwhile, had swung himself lightly on to the footboard of the first omnibus just as it was gathering speed. A few seconds saw him safely across at the Mansion House, and in a few more, he was whirling down Queen Victoria Street. The danger was practically over, though he took the precaution to alight at St. Paul's, and, crossing to Newgate Street, board another west-bound omnibus.

That night he sat in his lodgings turning over his late experience. It had been a narrow shave. That sort of thing mustn't happen again. In fact, seeing that the law was undoubtedly about to be set in motion, it was high time that certain little plans of his should be set in motion, too. Only, there was a difficulty; a serious difficulty.

And as Percival thought round and round that difficulty his brows wrinkled and he hummed a soft refrain.

"Then is the time for disappearing,

Take a header--down you go--"

A tap at the door cut his song short. It was his landlady, Mrs. Brattle; a civil woman, and particularly civil just now. For she had a little request to make.

"It was about Christmas Night, Mr. Bland," said Mrs. Brattle. "My husband and me thought of spending the evening with his brother at Hornsey, and we were going to let the maid go home to her mother's for the night, if it wouldn't put you out."

"Wouldn't put me out in the least, Mrs. Brattle," said Percival.

"You needn't sit up for us, you see," pursued Mrs. Brattle, "if you just leave the side door unbolted. We shan't be home before two or three; but we'll come in quiet not to disturb you."

"You won't disturb me," Percival replied with a genial laugh. "I'm a sober man in general but 'Christmas comes but once a year'. When once I'm tucked up in bed, I shall take a bit of waking on Christmas Night."

Mrs. Brattle smiled indulgently. "And you won't feel lonely, all alone in the house?"

"Lonely!" exclaimed Percival. "Lonely! With a roaring fire, a jolly book, a box of good cigars and a bottle of sound port--ah, and a second bottle if need be. Not I."

Mrs. Brattle shook her head. "Ah," said she, "you bachelors! Well, well. It's a good thing to be independent," and with this profound reflection she smiled herself out of the room and descended the stairs.

As her footsteps died away Percival sprang from his chair and began excitedly to pace the room. His eyes sparkled and his face was wreathed with smiles. Presently he halted before the fireplace and, gazing into the embers, laughed aloud.

"Damn funny!" said he. "Deuced rich! Neat! Very neat! Ha! Ha!" And here he resumed his interrupted song: "When the sky above is clearing, When the sky above is clearing, Bob up serenely, bob up serenely, Bob up serenely from below!"

Which may be regarded as closing the first scene, of the second act.

During the few days that intervened before Christmas Percival went abroad but little; and yet be was a busy man. He did a little surreptitious shopping, venturing out as far as Charing Cross Road; and his purchases were decidedly miscellaneous. A porridge saucepan, a second-hand copy of "Gray's Anatomy," a rabbit skin, a large supply of glue and upwards of ten pounds of shin of beef seems a rather odd assortment; and it was a mercy that the weather was frosty, for otherwise Percival's bedroom, in which these delicacies were deposited under lock and key, would have yielded odorous traces of its wealth.

But it was in the long evenings that his industry was most conspicuous; and then it was that the big cupboard with the excellent lever lock, which he himself had fixed on, began to fill up with the fruits of his labours. In those evenings the porridge saucepan would simmer on the hob with a rich lading of good Scotch glue, the black box of the deceased practitioner would be hauled forth from its hiding-place, and the well-thumbed "Gray" laid open on the table.

It was an arduous business though; a stiffer task than he had bargained for. The right and left bones were so confoundedly alike, and the bones that joined were so difficult to fit together. However, the plates in "Gray" were large and very clear, so it was only a question of taking enough trouble.

His method of work was simple and practical. Having fished a bone out of the box, he would compare it with the illustrations in the book until he had identified it beyond all doubt, when he would tie on it a paper label with its name and side--right or left. Then he would search for the adjoining bone, and, having fitted the two together, would secure them with a good daub of glue and lay them in the fender to dry. It was a crude and horrible method of articulation that would have made a museum curator shudder. But it seemed to answer Percival's purpose--whatever that may have been--for gradually the loose "items" came together into recognisable members such as arms and legs, the vertebra--which were, fortunately, strung in their order on a thick cord--were joined up into a solid backbone, and even the ribs, which were the toughest job of all, fixed on in some semblance of a thorax. It was a wretched performance. The bones were plastered with gouts of glue and yet would have broken apart at a touch. But, as we have said, Percival seemed satisfied, and as he was the only person concerned, there was no more to be said.

In due course, Christmas Day arrived. Percival dined with the Brattles at two, dozed after dinner, woke up for tea, and then, as Mrs. Brattle, in purple and fine raiment, came in to remove the tea-tray, he spread out on the table the materials for the night's carouse. A quarter of an hour later, the side slammed, and, peering out of the window, he saw the shopkeeper and his wife hurrying away up the gas-lit street towards the nearest omnibus route.

Then Mr. Percival Bland began his evening's entertainment; and a most remark entertainment it was, even for a solitary bachelor, left alone in a house on Christmas Night. First, he took off his clothing and dressed himself in a fresh suit. Then, from the cupboard he brought forth the reconstituted "set of osteology" and, laying the various members on the table, returned to the bedroom, whence he presently reappeared with a large, savoury parcel which he had disinterred from a trunk. The parcel being opened revealed his accumulated purchases in the matter of shin of beef.

With a large knife, providently sharpened before hand, he cut the beef into large, thin slices which he proceed to wrap around the various bones that formed the "complete set"; whereby their nakedness was certainly mitigated though their attractiveness was by no means increased. Having thus "clothed the dry bones," he gathered up the scraps of offal that were left, to be placed presently inside the trunk. It was an extraordinary proceeding, but the next was more extraordinary still.

Taking up the newly clothed members one by one, he began very carefully to insinuate them into the garments that he had recently shed. It was a ticklish business, for the glued joints were as brittle as glass. Very cautiously the legs were separately inducted, first into underclothing and then into trousers, the skeleton feet were fitted with the cast-off socks and delicately persuaded into the boots. The arms, in like manner, were gingerly pressed into their various sleeves and through the arm-holes of the waistcoat; and then came the most difficult task of all--to fit the garments on the trunk. For the skull and ribs, secured to the back-bone with mere spots of glue, were ready to drop off at a shake; and yet the garments had to be drawn over them with the arms enclosed in the sleeves. But Percival managed it at last by resting his "restoration" in the big, padded arm-chair and easing the garments on inch by inch.

It now remained only to give the finishing touch; which was done by cutting the rabbit-skin to the requisite shape and affixing it to the skull with a thin coat of stiff glue; and when the skull had thus been finished with a sort of crude, makeshift wig, its appearance was so appalling as even to disturb the nerves of the matter-of-fact Percival. However, this was no occasion for cherishing sentiment. A skull in an extemporised wig or false scalp might be, and in fact was, a highly unpleasant object; but so was a Belgian police officer.

Having finished the "restoration," Percival fetched the water-jug from his bedroom, and, descending to the shop, the door of which had been left unlocked, tried the taps of the various drums and barrels until he came to the one which contained methylated spirit; and from this he filled his jug and returned to the bedroom. Pouring the spirit out into the basin, he tucked a towel round his neck and filling his sponge with spirit proceeded very vigorously to wash his hair and eyebrows; and as, by degrees, the spirit in the basin grew dark and turbid, so did his hair and eyebrows grow lighter in colour until, after a final energetic rub with a towel, they had acquired a golden or sandy hue indistinguishable from that of the hair of his cousin Robert. Even the mole under his eye was susceptible to the changing conditions, for when he had wetted it thoroughly with spirit, he was able, with the blade of a penknife to peel it off as neatly as if it had been stuck on with spirit-gum. Having done which, he deposited it in a tiny box which he carried in his waistcoat pocket.

The proceedings which followed were unmistakable as to their object. First he carried the basin of spirit through into the sitting-room and deliberately poured its contents on to the floor by the arm-chair. Then, having returned the basin to the bedroom, he again went down to the shop, where he selected a couple of galvanised buckets from the stock, filled them with paraffin oil from one of the great drums and carried them upstairs. The oil from one bucket he poured over the armchair and its repulsive occupant; the other bucket he simply emptied on the carpet, and then went down to the shop for a fresh supply.

When this proceeding had been repeated once or twice the entire floor and all the furniture were saturated, and such a reek of paraffin filled the air of the room that Percival thought it wise to turn out the gas. Returning to the shop, be poured a bucketful of oil over the stack of bundles of firewood, another over the counter and floor and a third over the loose articles on the walls and hanging from the ceiling. Looking up at the latter be now perceived a number of greasy patches where the oil had soaked through from the floor above, and some of these were beginning to drip on to the shop floor.

He now made his final preparations. Taking a bundle of "Wheel" firelighters, he made a small pile against the stack of firewood. In the midst of the firelighters he placed a ball of string saturated in paraffin; and in the central hole of the ball he stuck a half-dozen diminutive Christmas candles. This mine was now ready. Providing himself with a stock of firelighters, a few balls of paraffined string and a dozen or so of the little candles, he went upstairs to the sitting-room, which was immediately above the shop. Here, by the glow of the fire, he built up one or two piles of firelighters around and partly under the arm-chair, placed the balls of string on the piles and stuck two or three bundles in each ball. Everything was now ready. Stepping into the bedroom, he took from the cupboard a spare overcoat, a new hat and a new umbrella--for he must leave his old hats, coat and umbrella in the hall. He put on the coat and hat, and, with the umbrella in his hand, returned to the sitting-room.

Opposite the arm-chair he stood awhile, irresolute, and a pang of horror shot through him. It was a terrible thing that he was going to do; a thing the consequences of which no one could foresee. He glanced furtively at the awful shape that sat huddled in the chair, its horrible head all awry and its rigid limbs sprawling in hideous grotesque deformity. It was but a dummy, a mere scarecrow; but yet, in the dim firelight, the grisly face under that horrid wig seemed to leer intelligently, to watch him with secret malice out of its shadowy eye-sockets, until he looked away with clammy skin and a shiver of half-superstitious terror.

But this would never do. The evening had run out, consumed by these engrossing labours; it was nearly eleven o'clock, and high time for him to be gone. For if the Brattles should return prematurely he was lost. Pulling himself together with an effort, he struck a match and lit the little candles one after the other. In a quarter of an hour or so, they would have burned down to the balls of string, and then--He walked quickly out of the room; but, at the door, he paused for a moment to look back at the ghastly figure, seated rigidly in the chair with the lighted candles at its feet, like some foul fiend appeased by votive fires. The unsteady flames threw flickering shadows on its face that made it seem to mow and gibber and grin in mockery of all his care and caution. So he turned and tremblingly ran down the stairs--opening the staircase window as he went. Running into the shop, he lit the candles there and ran out again, shutting the door after him.

Secretly and guiltily he crept down the hall, and opening the door a few inches peered out. A blast of icy wind poured in with a light powdering of dry snow. He opened his umbrella, flung open the door, looked up and down the empty street, stepped out, closed the door softly and strode away over the whitening pavement.

Part II

(Related by Christopher Jervis, M.D.)

It was one of the axioms of medico-legal practice laid down by my colleague, John Thorndyke, that the investigator should be constantly on his guard against the effect of suggestion. Not only must all prejudices and preconceptions be avoided, but when information is received from outside, the actual, undeniable facts must be carefully sifted from the inferences which usually accompany them. Of the necessity for this precaution our insurance practice furnished an excellent instance in the case of the fire at Mr. Brattle's oil-shop.

The case was brought to our notice by Mr. Stalker of the "Griffin" Fire and Life Insurance Society a few days after Christmas. He dropped in, ostensibly to wish us a Happy New Year, but a discreet pause in the conversation on Thorndyke's part elicited a further purpose.

"Did you see the account of that fire in Bloomsbury?" Mr. Stalker asked.

"The oil-shop? Yes. But I didn't note any details, excepting that a man was apparently burnt to death and that the affair happened on the twenty-fifth of December."

"Yes, I know," said Mr. Stalker. "It seems uncharitable, but one can't help looking a little askance at these quarter-day fires. And the date isn't the only doubtful feature in this one; the Divisional Officer of the Fire Brigade, who has looked over the ruins, tells me that there are some appearances suggesting that the fire broke out in two different places--the shop and the first-floor room over it. Mind you, he doesn't say that it actually did. The place is so thoroughly gutted that very little is to be learned from it; but that is his impression; and it occurred to me that if you were to take a look at the ruins, your radiographic eye might detect something that he had overlooked."

"It isn't very likely," said Thorndyke. "Every man to his trade. The Divisional Officer looks at a burnt house with an expert eye, which I do not. My evidence would not carry much weight if you were contesting the claim."

"Perhaps not," replied Mr. Stalker, "and we are not anxious to contest the claim unless there is manifest fraud. Arson is a serious matter."

"It is wilful murder in this case," remarked Thorndyke.

"I know," said Stalker. "And that reminds me that the man who was burnt happens to have been insured in our office, too. So we stand a double loss."

"How much?" asked Thorndyke.

"The dead man, Percival Bland, had insured his life for three thousand pounds."

Thorndyke became thoughtful. The last statement had apparently made more impression on him than the former ones.

"If you want me to look into the case for you," said he, "you had better let me have all the papers connected with it, including the proposal forms."

Mr. Stalker smiled. "I thought you would say that--I know you of old, you see--so I slipped the papers in my pocket before coming here."

He laid the documents on the table and asked: "Is there anything that you want to know about the case?"

"Yes," replied Thorndyke. "I want to know all that you can tell me."

"Which is mighty little," said Stalker; "but such as it is, you shall have it.

"The oil-shop man's name is Brattle and the dead man, Bland, was his lodger. Bland appears to have been a perfectly steady, sober man in general; but it seems that he had announced his intention of spending a jovial Christmas Night and giving himself a little extra indulgence. He was last seen by Mrs. Brattle at about half-past six, sitting by a blazing fire, with a couple of unopened bottles of port on the table and a box of cigars. He had a book in his hand and two or three newspapers lay on the floor by his chair. Shortly after this, Mr. and Mrs. Brattle went out on a visit to Hornsey, leaving him alone in the house."

"Was there no servant?" asked Thorndyke.

"The servant had the day and night off duty to go to her mother's. That, by the way, looks a trifle fishy. However, to return to the Brattles; they spent the evening at Hornsey and did not get home until past three in the morning, by which time their house was a heap of smoking ruins. Mrs. Brattle's idea is that Bland must have drunk himself sleepy, and dropped one of the newspapers into the fender, where a chance cinder may have started the blaze. Which may or may not be the true explanation. Of course, an habitually sober man can get pretty mimsey on two bottles of port."

"What time did the fire break out?" asked Thorndyke.

"It was noticed about half-past eleven that flames were issuing from one of the chimneys, and the alarm was given at once. The first engine arrived ten minutes later, but, by that time, the place was roaring like a furnace. Then the water-plugs were found to be frozen hard, which caused some delay; in fact, before the engines were able to get to work the roof had fallen in, and the place was a mere shell. You know what an oil-shop is, when once it gets a fair start."

"And Mr. Bland's body was found in the ruins, I suppose?"

"Body!" exclaimed Mr. Stalker; "there wasn't much body! Just a few charred bones, which they dug out of the ashes next day."

"And the question of identity?"

"We shall leave that to the coroner. But there really isn't any question. To begin with, there was no one else in the house; and then the remains were found mixed up with the springs and castors of the chair that Bland was sitting in when he was last seen. Moreover, there were found, with the bones, a pocket knife, a bunch of keys and a set of steel waistcoat buttons, all identified by Mrs. Brattle as belonging to

Bland. She noticed the cut steel buttons on his waistcoat when she wished him 'good-night.'"

"By the way," said Thorndyke, "was Bland reading by the light of an oil lamp?"

"No," replied Stalker. "There was a two-branch gasalier with a porcelain shade to one burner, and he had that burner alight when Mrs. Brattle left."

Thorndyke reflectively picked up the proposal form, and, having glanced through it, remarked: "I see that Bland is described as unmarried. Do you know why he insured his life for this large amount?"

"No; we assumed that it was probably in connection with some loan that he had raised. I learn from the solicitor who notified us of the death, that the whole of Bland's property is left to a cousin--a Mr. Lindsay, I think. So the probability is that this cousin had lent him money. But it is not the life claim that is interesting us. We must pay that in any case. It is the fire claim that we want you to look into."

"Very well," said Thorndyke; "I will go round presently and look over the ruins, and see if I can detect any substantial evidence of fraud."

"If you would," said Mr. Stalker, rising to take his departures "we should be very much obliged. Not that we shall probably contest the claim in any case."

When he had gone, my colleague and I glanced through the papers, and I ventured to remark: "It seems to me that Stalker doesn't quite appreciate the possibilities of this case."

"No," Thorndyke agreed. "But, of course, it is an insurance company's business to pay, and not to boggle at anything short of glaring fraud. And we specialists too," he added with a smile, "must beware of seeing too much. I suppose that, to a rhinologist, there is hardly such a thing as a healthy nose--unless it is his own--and the uric acid specialist is very apt to find the firmament studded with dumb-bell crystals. We mustn't forget that normal cases do exist, after all."

That is true," said I; "but, on the other hand, the rhinologist's business is with the unhealthy nose, and our concern is with abnormal cases."

Thorndyke laughed. "'A Daniel come to judgement,'" said he. "But my learned friend is quite right. Our function is to pick holes. So let us pocket the documents and wend Bloomsbury way. We can talk the case over as we go."

We walked at an easy pace, for there was no hurry, and a little preliminary thought was useful. After a while, as Thorndyke made no remark, I reopened the subject.

"How does the case present itself to you?" I asked.

"Much as it does to you, I expect," he replied. "The circumstances invite inquiry, and I do not find myself connecting them with the shopkeeper. It is true that the fire occurred on quarter-day; but there is nothing to show that the insurance will do more than cover the loss of stock, chattels and the profits of trade. The other circumstances are much more suggestive. Here is a house burned down and a man killed. That man was insured for three thousand pounds, and, consequently, some person stands to gain by his death to that amount. The whole set of circumstances is highly favourable to the idea of homicide. The man was alone in the house when he died; and the total destruction of both the body and its surroundings seems to render investigation impossible. The cause of death can only be inferred; it cannot be proved; and the most glaring evidence of a crime will have vanished utterly. I think that there is a quite strong prima facie suggestion of murder. Under the known conditions, the perpetration of a murder would have been easy, it would have been safe from detection, and there is an adequate motive.

"On the other hand, suicide is not impossible. The man might have set fire to the house and then killed himself by poison or otherwise. But it is intrinsically less probable that a man should kill him self for another person's benefit than that he should kill another man for his own benefit.

"Finally, there is the possibility that the fire and the man's death were the result of accident; against which is the' official opinion that the fire started in two places. If this opinion is correct, it establishes, in my opinion, a strong presumption of murder against some person who may have obtained access to the house."

This point in the discussion brought us to the ruined house, which stood at the corner of two small streets. One of the firemen in charge admitted us, when we had shown our credentials, through a temporary door and down a ladder into the basement, where we found a number of men treading gingerly, ankle deep in white ash, among a litter of charred wood-work, fused glass, warped and broken china, and more or less recognisable metal objects.

"The coroner and the jury," the fireman explained; "come to view the scene of the disaster." He introduced us to the former, who bowed stiffly and continued his investigations.

"These," said the other fireman, "are the springs of the chair that the deceased was sitting in. We found the body--or rather the bones--lying among them under a heap of hot ashes; and we found the buttons of his clothes and the things from his pockets among the ashes, too. You'll see them in the mortuary with the remains."

"It must have been a terrific blaze," one of the jurymen remarked. "Just look at this, sir," and he handed to Thorndyke what looked like part of a gas-fitting, of which the greater part was melted into shapeless lumps and the remainder encrusted into fused porcelain.

"That," said the fireman, "was the gasalier of the first-floor room, where Mr. Bland was sitting. Ah! you won't turn that tap, sir; nobody'll ever turn that tap again."

Thorndyke held the twisted mass of brass towards me in silence, and, glancing up the blackened walls, remarked: "I think we shall have to come here again with the Divisional Officer, but meanwhile, we had better see the remains of the body. It is just possible that we may learn something from them."

He applied to the coroner for the necessary authority to make the inspection, and, having obtained a rather ungracious and grudging permission to examine the remains when the jury had "viewed" them, began to ascend the ladder.

"Our friend would have liked to refuse permission," he remarked when we had emerged into the street, "but he knew that I could and should have insisted."

So I gathered from his manner," said I. "But what is he doing here? This isn't his district."

"No; he is acting for Bettsford, who is laid up just now; and a very poor substitute he is. A non-medical coroner is an absurdity in any case, and a coroner who is hostile to the medical profession is a public scandal. By the way, that gas-tap offers a curious problem. You noticed that it was turned off?"

"Yes."

"And consequently that the deceased was sitting in the dark when the fire broke out. I don't see the bearing of the fact, but it is certainly rather odd. Here is the mortuary. We had better wait and let the jury go in first."

We had not long to wait. In a couple of minutes or so the "twelve good men and true" made their appearance with a small attendant crowd of ragamuffins. We let them enter first, and then we followed. The mortuary was a good-sized room, well lighted by a glass roof, and having at its centre a long table on which lay the shell containing the remains. There was also a sheet of paper on which had been laid out a set of blackened steel waistcoat buttons, a bunch of keys, a steel-handled pocket-knife, a steel-cased watch on a partly-fused rolled-gold chain, and a pocket corkscrew. The coroner drew the attention of the jury to these objects, and then took possession of them, that they might be identified by witnesses. And meanwhile the jurymen gathered round the shell and stared shudderingly at its gruesome contents.

"I am sorry, gentlemen," said the coroner, "to have to subject you to this painful ordeal. But duty is duty. We must hope, as I think we may, that this poor creature met a painless if in some respects a rather terrible death."

At this point, Thorndyke, who had drawn near to the table, cast a long and steady glance down into the shell; and immediately his ordinarily rather impassive face seemed to congeal; all expression faded from it, leaving it as immovable and uncommunicative as the granite face of an Egyptian statue. I knew the symptom of old and began to speculate on its present significance.

"Are you taking any medical evidence?" he asked.

"Medical evidence!" the coroner repeated, scornfully. "Certainly not, sir! I do not waste the public money by employing so-called experts to tell the jury what each of them can see quite plainly for himself. I imagine," he added, turning to the foreman, "that you will not require a learned doctor to explain to you how that poor fellow mortal met his death?"

And the foreman, glancing askance at the skull, replied, with a pallid and sickly smile, that "he thought not."

"Do you, sir," the coroner continued, with a dramatic wave of the hand towards the plain coffin, "suppose that we shall find any difficulty in determining how that man came by his death?"

"I imagine," replied Thorndyke, without moving a muscle, or, indeed, appearing to have any muscles to move, "I imagine you will find no difficulty what ever."

"So do I," said the coroner.

"Then," retorted Thorndyke, with a faint, inscrutable smile, "we are, for once, in complete agreement."

As the coroner and jury retired, leaving my colleague and me alone in the mortuary, Thorndyke remarked: "I suppose this kind of farce will be repeated periodically so long as these highly technical medical inquiries continue to be conducted by lay persons."

I made no reply, for I had taken a long look into the shell, and was lost in astonishment.

"But my dear Thorndyke!" I exclaimed; "what on earth does it mean? Are we to suppose that a woman can have palmed herself off as a man on the examining medical officer of a London Life Assurance Society?"

Thorndyke shook his head. "I think not," said he. "Our friend, Mr. Bland, may conceivably have been a woman in disguise, but he certainly was not a negress."

"A negress!" I gasped. "By Jove! So it is! I hadn't looked at the skull. But that only makes the mystery more mysterious. Because, you remember, the body was certainly dressed in Bland's clothes."

"Yes, there seems to be no doubt about that. And you may have noticed, as I did," Thorndyke continued dryly, "the remarkably fire-proof character of the waistcoat buttons, watch-case, knife-handle, and other identifiable objects."

"But what a horrible affair!" I exclaimed. "The brute must have gone out and enticed some poor devil of a negress into the house, have murdered her in cold blood and then deliberately dressed the corpse in his own clothes! It is perfectly frightful!"

Again Thorndyke shook his head. "It wasn't as bad as that, Jervis," said he, "though I must confess that I feel strongly tempted to let your hypothesis stand. It would be quite amusing to put Mr. Bland on trial for the murder of an unknown negress, and let him explain the facts himself. But our reputation is at stake. Look at the bones again and a little more critically. You very probably looked for the sex first; then you looked for racial characters. Now carry your investigations a step farther."

"There is the stature," said I. "But that is of no importance, as these are not Bland's bones. The only other point that I notice is that the fire seems to have acted very unequally on the different parts of the body."

"Yes," agreed Thorndyke, "and that is the point. Some parts are more burnt than others; and the parts which are burnt most are the wrong parts. Look at the back-bone, for instance. The vertebrae are as white as chalk. They are mere masses of bone ash. But, of all parts of the skeleton, there is none so completely protected from fire as the back-bone, with the great dorsal muscles behind, and the whole mass of the viscera in front. Then look at the skull. Its appearance is quite inconsistent with the suggested facts. The bones of the face are bare and calcined and the orbits contain not a trace of the eyes or other structures; and yet there is a charred mass of what may or may not be scalp adhering to the crown. But the scalp, as the most exposed and the thinnest covering, would be the first to be destroyed, while the last to be consumed would be the structures about the jaws and the base, of which, you see, not a vestige is left."

Here he lifted the skull carefully from the shell, and, peering in through the great foramen at the base, handed it to me.

"Look in," he said, "through the Foramen Magnum--you will see better if you hold the orbits towards the skylight--and notice an even more extreme inconsistency with the supposed conditions. The brain and membranes have vanished without leaving a trace. The inside of the skull is as clean as if it had been macerated. But this is impossible. The brain is not only protected from the fire; it is also protected from contact with the air. But without access of oxygen, although it might become carbonised, it could not be consumed. No, Jervis; it won't do."

I replaced the skull in the coffin and looked at him in surprise. "What is it that you are suggesting?" I asked.

"I suggest that this was not a body at all, but merely a dry skeleton."

"But," I objected, "what about those masses of what looks like charred muscle adhering to the bones?"

"Yes," he replied, "I have been noticing them. They do, as you say, look like masses of charred muscle. But they are quite shapeless and structureless; I cannot identify a single muscle or muscular group; and there is not a vestige of any of the tendons. Moreover, the distribution is false. For instance, will you tell me what muscle you think that is?"

He pointed to a thick, charred mass on the inner surface of the left tibia or shin-bone. "Now this portion of the bone--as many a hockey-player has had reason to realise--has no muscular covering at all. It lies immediately under the skin."

"I think you are right, Thorndyke," said I. "That lump of muscle in the wrong place gives the whole fraud away. But it was really a rather smart dodge. This fellow Bland must be an ingenious rascal."

"Yes," agreed Thorndyke; "but an unscrupulous villain too. He might have burned down half the street and killed a score of people. He'll have to pay the piper for this little frolic."

"What shall you do now? Are you going to notify the coroner?"

"No; that is not my business. I think we will verify our conclusions and then inform our clients and the police. We must measure the skull as well as we can without callipers, but it is, fortunately, quite typical. The short, broad, flat nasal bones, with the 'Simian groove,' and those large, strong teeth, worn flat by hard and gritty food, are highly characteristic." He once more lifted out the skull, and, with a spring tape, made a few measurements, while I noted the lengths of the principal long bones and the width across the hips.

"I make the cranial-nasal index 55 said he, as he replaced the skull, "and the cranial index about 72, which are quite representative numbers; and, as I see that your notes show the usual disproportionate length of arm and the characteristic curve of the tibia, we may be satisfied. But it is fortunate that the specimen is so typical. To the experienced eye, racial types have a physiognomy which is unmistakable on mere inspection. But you cannot transfer the experienced eye. You can only express personal conviction and back it up with measurements.

"And now we will go and look in on Stalker, and inform him that his office has saved three thousand pounds by employing us. After which it will be West ward Ho! for Scotland Yard, to prepare an unpleasant little surprise for Mr. Percival Bland."

There was joy among the journalists on the following day. Each of the morning papers devoted an entire column to an unusually detailed account of the inquest on the late Percival Bland--who, it appeared, met his death by misadventure--and a verbatim report of the coroner's eloquent remarks on the danger of solitary, fireside tippling, and the stupefying effects of port wine. An adjacent column contained an equally detailed account of the appearance of the deceased at Bow Street Police Court to answer complicated charges of arson, fraud and forgery; while a third collated the two accounts with gleeful commentaries.

Mr. Percival Bland, alias Robert Lindsay, now resides on the breezy uplands of Dartmoor, where, in his abundant leisure, he, no doubt, regrets his misdirected ingenuity. But he has not laboured in vain. To the Lord Chancellor he has furnished an admirable illustration of the danger of appointing lay coroners; and to me an unforgettable warning against the effects of suggestion.

John Thorndyke's Cases

Original Preface to 'John Thorndyke's Cases'

The stories in this collection, inasmuch as they constitute a somewhat new departure in this class of literature, require a few words of introduction. The primary function of all fiction is to furnish entertainment to the reader, and this fact has not been lost sight of. But the interest of so-called 'detective' fiction is, I believe, greatly enhanced by a careful adherence to the probable, and a strict avoidance of physical impossibilities; and, in accordance with this belief, I have been scrupulous in confining myself to authentic facts and practicable methods. The stories have, for the most part, a medico-legal motive, and the methods of solution described in them are similar to those employed in actual practice by medical jurists. The stories illustrate, in fact, the application to the detection of crime of the ordinary methods of scientific research. I may add that the experiments described have in all cases been performed by me, and that the micro-photographs are, of course, from the actual specimens.

I take this opportunity of thanking those of my friends who have in various ways assisted me, and especially the friend to whom I have dedicated this book; by whom I have been relieved of the very considerable labour of making the micro-photographs, and greatly assisted in procuring and preparing specimens. I must also thank Messrs. Pearson for kindly allowing me the use of Mr. H. M. Brock's admirable and sympathetic drawings, and the artist himself for the care with which he has maintained strict fidelity to the text.

R. A. F. Gravesend
September 21, 1909.

The Man with the Nailed Shoes

There are, I suppose, few places even on the East Coast of England more lonely and remote than the village of Little Sundersley and the country that surrounds it. Far from any railway, and some miles distant from any considerable town, it remains an outpost of civilization, in which primitive manners and customs and old-world tradition linger on into an age that has elsewhere forgotten them. In the summer, it is true, a small contingent of visitors, adventurous in spirit, though mostly of sedate and solitary habits, make their appearance to swell its meagre population, and impart to the wide stretches of smooth sand that fringe its shores a fleeting air of life and sober gaiety; but in late September--the season of the year in which I made its acquaintance--its pasture-lands lie desolate, the rugged paths along the cliffs are seldom trodden by human foot, and the sands are a desert waste on which, for days together, no footprint appears save that left by some passing sea-bird.

I had been assured by my medical agent, Mr. Turcival, that I should find the practice of which I was now taking charge 'an exceedingly soft billet, and suitable for a studious man;' and certainly he had not misled me, for the patients were, in fact, so few that I was quite concerned for my principal, and rather dull for want of work. Hence, when my friend John Thorndyke, the well-known medico-legal expert, proposed to come down and stay with me for a weekend and perhaps a few days beyond, I hailed the proposal with delight, and welcomed him with open arms.

"You certainly don't seem to be overworked, Jervis," he remarked, as we turned out of the gate after tea, on the day of his arrival, for a stroll on the shore. "Is this a new practice, or an old one in a state of senile decay?"

"Why, the fact is," I answered, "there is virtually no practice. Cooper-- my principal--has been here about six years, and as he has private means he has never made any serious effort to build one up; and the other man, Dr. Burrows, being uncommonly keen, and the people very conservative, Cooper has never really got his foot in. However, it doesn't seem to trouble him."

"Well, if he is satisfied, I suppose you are," said Thorndyke, with a smile. "You are getting a seaside holiday, and being paid for it. But I didn't know you were as near to the sea as this."

We were entering, as he spoke, an artificial gap-way cut through the low cliff, forming a steep cart-track down to the shore. It was locally known as Sundersley Gap, and was used principally, when used at all, by the farmers' carts which came down to gather seaweed after a gale.

"What a magnificent stretch of sand!" continued Thorndyke, as we reached the bottom, and stood looking out seaward across the deserted beach. "There is something very majestic and solemn in a great expanse of sandy shore when the tide is out, and I know of nothing which is capable of conveying the impression of solitude so completely. The smooth, unbroken surface not only displays itself untenanted for the moment, but it offers convincing testimony that it has lain thus undisturbed through a considerable lapse of time. Here, for instance, we have clear evidence that for several days only two pairs of feet besides our own have trodden this gap."

"How do you arrive at the 'several days'?" I asked.

"In the simplest manner possible," he replied. "The moon is now in the third quarter, and the tides are consequently neap-tides. You can see quite plainly the two lines of seaweed and jetsam which indicate the high-water marks of the spring-tides and the neap-tides respectively. The strip of comparatively dry sand between them, over which the water has not risen for several days, is, as you see, marked by only two sets of footprints, and those footprints will not be completely obliterated by the sea until the next spring-tide--nearly a week from to-day."

"Yes, I see now, and the thing appears obvious enough when one has heard the explanation. But it is really rather odd that no one should have passed through this gap for days, and then that four persons should have come here within quite a short interval of one another."

"What makes you think they have done so?" Thorndyke asked.

"Well," I replied, "both of these sets of footprints appear to be quite fresh, and to have been made about the same time."

"Not at the same time, Jervis," rejoined Thorndyke. "There is certainly an interval of several hours between them, though precisely how many hours we cannot judge, since there has been so little wind lately to disturb them; but the fisherman unquestionably passed here not more than three hours ago, and I should say probably within an hour; whereas the other man--who seems to have come up from a boat to fetch something of considerable weight--returned through the gap certainly not less, and probably more, than four hours ago."

I gazed at my friend in blank astonishment, for these events befell in the days before I had joined him as his assistant, and his special knowledge and powers of inference were not then fully appreciated by me.

"It is clear, Thorndyke," I said, "that footprints have a very different meaning to you from what they have for me. I don't see in the least how you have reached any of these conclusions."

"I suppose not," was the reply; "but, you see, special knowledge of this kind is the stock-in-trade of the medical jurist, and has to be acquired by special study, though the present example is one of the greatest simplicity. But let us consider it point by point; and first we will take this set of footprints which I have inferred to be a fisherman's. Note their enormous size. They should be the footprints of a giant. But the length of the stride shows that they were made by a rather short man. Then observe the massiveness of the soles, and the fact that there are no nails in them. Note also the peculiar clumsy tread--the deep toe and heel marks, as if the walker had wooden legs, or fixed ankles and knees. From that character we can safely infer high boots of thick, rigid leather, so that we can diagnose high boots, massive and stiff, with nailless soles, and many sizes too large for the wearer. But the only boot that answers this description is the fisherman's thigh-boot--made of enormous size to enable him to wear in the winter two or three pairs of thick knitted stockings, one over the other. Now look at the other footprints; there is a double track, you see, one set coming from the sea and one going towards it. As the man (who was bow-legged and turned his toes in) has trodden in his own footprints, it is obvious that he came from the sea, and returned to it. But observe the difference in the two sets of prints; the returning ones are much deeper than the others, and the stride much shorter. Evidently he was carrying something when he returned, and that something was very heavy. Moreover, we can see, by the greater depth of the toe impressions, that he was stooping forward as he walked, and so probably carried the weight on his back. Is that quite clear?"

"Perfectly," I replied. "But how do you arrive at the interval of time between the visits of the two men?"

"That also is quite simple. The tide is now about halfway out; it is thus about three hours since high water. Now, the fisherman walked just about the neap-tide, high-water mark, sometimes above it and sometimes below. But none of his footprints have been obliterated; therefore he passed after high water--that is, less than three hours ago; and since his footprints are all equally distinct, he could not have passed when the sand was very wet. Therefore he probably passed less than an hour ago. The other man's footprints, on the other hand, reach only to the neap-tide, high-water mark, where they end abruptly. The sea has washed over the remainder of the tracks and obliterated them. Therefore he passed not less than three hours and not more than four days ago-- probably within twenty-four hours."

As Thorndyke concluded his demonstration the sound of voices was borne to us from above, mingled with the tramping of feet, and immediately afterwards a very singular party appeared at the head of the gap descending towards the shore. First came a short burly fisherman clad in oilskins and sou'-wester, clumping along awkwardly in his great sea-boots, then the local police-sergeant in company with my professional rival Dr. Burrows, while the rear of the procession was brought up by two constables carrying a stretcher. As he reached the bottom of the gap the fisherman, who was evidently acting as guide, turned along the shore, retracing his own tracks, and the procession followed in his wake.

"A surgeon, a stretcher, two constables, and a police-sergeant," observed Thorndyke. "What does that suggest to your mind, Jervis?"

"A fall from the cliff," I replied, "or a body washed up on the shore."

"Probably," he rejoined; "but we may as well walk in that direction."

We turned to follow the retreating procession, and as we strode along the smooth surface left by the retiring tide Thorndyke resumed: "The subject of footprints has always interested me deeply for two reasons. First, the evidence furnished by footprints is constantly being brought forward, and is often of cardinal importance; and, secondly, the whole subject is capable of really systematic and scientific treatment. In the main the data are anatomical, but age, sex, occupation, health, and disease all give their various indications. Clearly, for instance, the footprints of an old man will differ from those of a young man of the same height, and I need not point out to you that those of a person suffering from *locomotor ataxia* or *paralysis agitans* would be quite unmistakable."

"Yes, I see that plainly enough," I said.

"Here, now," he continued, "is a case in point." He halted to point with his stick at a row of footprints that appeared suddenly above high-water mark, and having proceeded a short distance, crossed the line again, and vanished where the waves had washed over them. They were easily distinguished from any of the others by the clear impressions of circular rubber heels.

"Do you see anything remarkable about them?" he asked.

"I notice that they are considerably deeper than our own," I answered.

"Yes, and the boots are about the same size as ours, whereas the stride is considerably shorter--quite a short stride, in fact. Now there is a pretty constant ratio between the length of the foot and the length of the leg, between the length of leg and the height of the person, and between the stature and the length of stride. A long foot means a long leg, a tall man, and a long stride. But here we have a long foot and a short stride. What do you make of that?" He laid down his stick--a smooth partridge cane, one side of which was marked by small lines into inches and feet--beside the footprints to demonstrate the discrepancy.

"The depth of the footprints shows that he was a much heavier man than either of us," I suggested; "perhaps he was unusually fat."

"Yes," said Thorndyke, "that seems to be the explanation. The carrying of a dead weight shortens the stride, and fat is practically a dead weight. The conclusion is that he was about five feet ten inches high, and excessively fat." He picked up his cane, and we resumed our walk, keeping an eye on the procession ahead until it had disappeared round a curve in the coast-line, when we mended our pace somewhat. Presently we reached a small headland, and, turning the shoulder of cliff, came full upon the party which had preceded us. The men had halted in a narrow bay, and now stood looking down at a prostrate figure beside which the surgeon was kneeling.

"We were wrong, you see," observed Thorndyke. "He has not fallen over the cliff, nor has he been washed up by the sea. He is lying above high-water mark, and those footprints that we have been examining appear to be his."

As we approached, the sergeant turned and held up his hand.

"I'll ask you not to walk round the body just now, gentlemen," he said. "There seems to have been foul play here, and I want to be clear about the tracks before anyone crosses them."

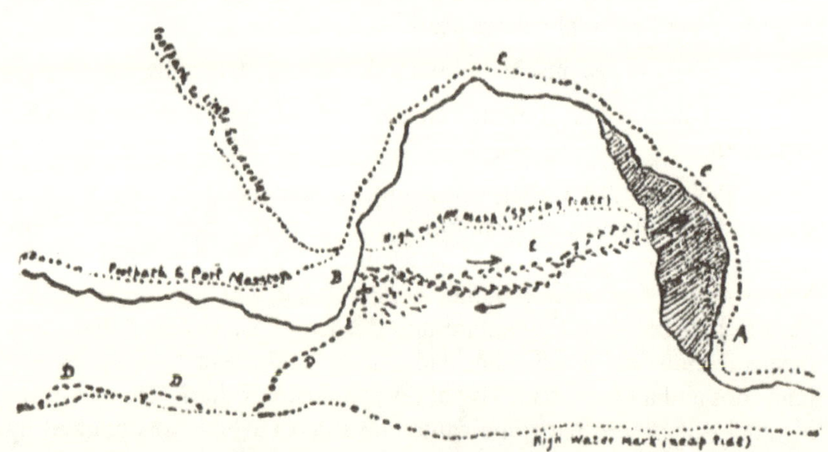

PLAN OF ST. BRIDGET'S BAY. + Position of body. D D D, Tracks of Hearn's shoes. A, Top of Shepherd's Path. E, Tracks of the nailed shoes. B, Overhanging cliff. F, Shepherd's Path ascending shelving cliff. C, Footpath along edge of cliff.

Acknowledging this caution, we advanced to where the constables were standing, and looked down with some curiosity at the dead man. He was a tall, frail-looking man, thin to the point of emaciation, and appeared to be about thirty-five years of age. He lay in an easy posture, with half-closed eyes and a placid expression that contrasted strangely enough with the tragic circumstances of his death.

"It is a clear case of murder," said Dr. Burrows, dusting the sand from his knees as he stood up. "There is a deep knife-wound above the heart, which must have caused death almost instantaneously."

"How long should you say he has been dead, Doctor?" asked the sergeant.

"Twelve hours at least," was the reply. "He is quite cold and stiff."

"Twelve hours, eh?" repeated the officer. "That would bring it to about six o'clock this morning."

"I won't commit myself to a definite time," said Dr. Burrows hastily. "I only say not less than twelve hours. It might have been considerably more."

"Ah!" said the sergeant. "Well, he made a pretty good fight for his life, to all appearances." He nodded at the sand, which for some feet around the body bore the deeply indented marks of feet, as though a furious struggle had taken place. "It's a mighty queer affair," pursued the sergeant, addressing Dr. Burrows. "There seems to have been only one man in it--there is only one set of footprints besides those of the deceased--and we've got to find out who he is; and I reckon there won't be much trouble about that, seeing the kind of trade-marks he has left behind him."

"No," agreed the surgeon; "there ought not to be much trouble in identifying those boots. He would seem to be a labourer, judging by the hob-nails."

"No, sir; not a labourer," dissented the sergeant. "The foot is too small, for one thing; and then the nails are not regular hob-nails. They're a good deal smaller; and a labourer's boots would have the nails all round the edges, and there would be iron tips on the heels, and probably on the toes too. Now these have got no tips, and the nails are arranged in a pattern on the soles and heels. They are probably shooting-boots or sporting shoes of some kind." He strode to and fro with his notebook in his hand, writing down hasty memoranda, and stooping to scrutinize the impressions in the sand. The surgeon also busied himself in noting down the facts concerning which he would have to give evidence, while Thorndyke regarded in silence and with an air of intense preoccupation the footprints around the body which remained to testify to the circumstances of the crime.

"It is pretty clear, up to a certain point," the sergeant observed, as he concluded his investigations, "how the affair happened, and it is pretty clear, too, that the murder was premeditated. You see, Doctor, the deceased gentleman, Mr. Hearn, was apparently walking home from Port Marston; we saw his footprints along the shore--those rubber heels make them easy to identify--and he didn't go down Sundersley Gap. He probably meant to climb up the cliff by that little track that you see there, which the people about here call the Shepherd's Path. Now the murderer must have known that he was coming, and waited upon the cliff to keep a lookout. When he saw Mr. Hearn enter the bay, he came down the path and attacked him, and, after a tough struggle, succeeded in stabbing him. Then he turned and went back up the path. You can see the double track between the path and the place where the struggle took place, and the footprints going to the path are on top of those coming from it."

"If you follow the tracks," said Dr. Burrows, "you ought to be able to see where the murderer went to."

"I'm afraid not," replied the sergeant. "There are no marks on the path itself--the rock is too hard, and so is the ground above, I fear. But I'll go over it carefully all the same."

The investigations being so far concluded, the body was lifted on to the stretcher, and the cortege, consisting of the bearers, the Doctor, and the fisherman, moved off towards the Gap, while the sergeant, having civilly wished us "Good-evening," scrambled up the Shepherd's Path, and vanished above.

"A very smart officer that," said Thorndyke. "I should like to know what he wrote in his notebook."

"His account of the circumstances of the murder seemed a very reasonable one," I said.

"Very. He noted the plain and essential facts, and drew the natural conclusions from them. But there are some very singular features in this case; so singular that I am disposed to make a few notes for my own information."

He stooped over the place where the body had lain, and having narrowly examined the sand there and in the place where the dead man's feet had rested, drew out his notebook and made a memorandum. He next made a rapid sketch-plan of the bay, marking the position of the body and the various impressions in the sand, and then, following the double track leading from and to the Shepherd's Path, scrutinized the footprints with the deepest attention, making copious notes and sketches in his book.

"We may as well go up by the Shepherd's Path," said Thorndyke. "I think we are equal to the climb, and there may be visible traces of the murderer after all. The rock is only a sandstone, and not a very hard one either."

We approached the foot of the little rugged track which zigzagged up the face of the cliff, and, stooping down among the stiff, dry herbage, examined the surface. Here, at the bottom of the path, where the rock was softened by the weather, there were several distinct impressions on the crumbling surface of the murderer's nailed boots, though they were somewhat confused by the tracks of the sergeant, whose boots were heavily nailed. But as we ascended the marks became rather less distinct, and at quite a short distance from the foot of the cliff we lost them altogether, though we had no difficulty in following the more recent traces of the sergeant's passage up the path.

When we reached the top of the cliff we paused to scan the path that ran along its edge, but here, too, although the sergeant's heavy boots had left quite visible impressions on the ground, there were no signs of any other feet. At a little distance the sagacious officer himself was pursuing his investigations, walking backwards and forwards with his body bent double, and his eyes fixed on the ground.

"Not a trace of him anywhere," said he, straightening himself up as we approached. "I was afraid there wouldn't be after all this dry weather. I shall have to try a different tack. This is a small place, and if those boots belong to anyone living here they'll be sure to be known."

"The deceased gentleman--Mr. Hearn, I think you called him," said Thorndyke as we turned towards the village--"is he a native of the locality?"

"Oh no, sir," replied the officer. "He is almost a stranger. He has only been here about three weeks; but, you know, in a little place like this a man soon gets to be known--and his business, too, for that matter," he added, with a smile.

"What was his business, then?" asked Thorndyke.

"Pleasure, I believe. He was down here for a holiday, though it's a good way past the season; but, then, he had a friend living here, and that makes a difference. Mr. Draper up at the Poplars was an old friend of his, I understand. I am going to call on him now."

We walked on along the footpath that led towards the village, but had only proceeded two or three hundred yards when a loud hail drew our attention to a man running across a field towards us from the direction of the cliff.

"Why, here is Mr. Draper himself," exclaimed the sergeant, stopping short and waving his hand. "I expect he has heard the news already."

Thorndyke and I also halted, and with some curiosity watched the approach of this new party to the tragedy. As the stranger drew near we saw that he was a tall, athletic-looking man of about forty, dressed in a Norfolk knickerbocker suit, and having the appearance of an ordinary country gentleman, excepting that he carried in his hand, in place of a walking-stick, the staff of a butterfly-net, the folding ring and bag of which partly projected from his pocket.

"Is it true, Sergeant?" he exclaimed as he came up to us, panting from his exertions. "About Mr. Hearn, I mean. There is a rumour that he has been found dead on the beach."

"It's quite true, sir, I am sorry to say; and, what is worse, he has been murdered."

"My God! you don't say so!"

He turned towards us a face that must ordinarily have been jovial enough, but was now white and scared and, after a brief pause, he exclaimed:

"Murdered! Good God! Poor old Hearn! How did it happen, Sergeant? and when? and is there any clue to the murderer?"

"We can't say for certain when it happened," replied the sergeant, "and as to the question of clues, I was just coming up to call on you."

"On me!" exclaimed Draper, with a startled glance at the officer. "What for?"

"Well, we should like to know something about Mr. Hearn--who he was, and whether he had any enemies, and so forth; anything, in fact, that would give as a hint where to look for the murderer. And you are the only person in the place who knew him at all intimately."

Mr Draper's pallid face turned a shade paler, and he glanced about him with an obviously embarrassed air.

"I'm afraid." he began in a hesitating manner, "I'm afraid I shan't be able to help you much. I didn't know much about his affairs. You see he was--well--only a casual acquaintance--"

"Well," interrupted the sergeant, "you can tell us who and what he was, and where he lived, and so forth. We'll find out the rest if you give us the start."

"I see," said Draper. "Yes, I expect you will." His eyes glanced restlessly to and fro, and he added presently: "You must come up to-morrow, and have a talk with me about him, and I'll see what I can remember."

"I'd rather come this evening," said the sergeant firmly.

"Not this evening," pleaded Draper. "I'm feeling rather--this affair, you know, has upset me. I couldn't give proper attention--"

His sentence petered out into a hesitating mumble, and the officer looked at him in evident surprise at his nervous, embarrassed manner. His own attitude, however, was perfectly firm, though polite.

"I don't like pressing you, sir," said he, "but time is precious--we'll have to go single file here; this pond is a public nuisance. They ought to bank it up at this end. After you, sir."

The pond to which the sergeant alluded had evidently extended at one time right across the path, but now, thanks to the dry weather, a narrow isthmus of half-dried mud traversed the morass, and along this Mr. Draper proceeded to pick his way. The sergeant was about to follow, when suddenly he stopped short with his eyes riveted upon the muddy track. A single glance showed me the cause of his surprise, for on the stiff, putty-like surface, standing out with the sharp distinctness of a wax mould, were the fresh footprints of the man who had just passed, each footprint displaying on its sole the impression of stud-nails arranged in a diamond-shaped pattern, and on its heel a group of similar nails arranged in a cross.

The sergeant hesitated for only a moment, in which he turned a quick startled glance upon us; then he followed, walking gingerly along the edge of the path as if to avoid treading in his predecessor's footprints. Instinctively we did the same, following closely, and anxiously awaiting the next development of the tragedy. For a minute or two we all proceeded in silence, the sergeant being evidently at a loss how to act, and Mr. Draper busy with his own thoughts. At length the former spoke.

"You think, Mr. Draper, you would rather that I looked in on you to-morrow about this affair?"

"Much rather, if you wouldn't mind," was the eager reply.

"Then, in that case," said the sergeant, looking at his watch, "as I've got a good deal to see to this evening, I'll leave you here, and make my way to the station."

With a farewell flourish of his hand he climbed over a stile, and when, a few moments later, I caught a glimpse of him through an opening in the hedge, he was running across the meadow like a hare.

The departure of the police-officer was apparently a great relief to Mr. Draper, who at once fell back and began to talk with us.

"You are Dr. Jervis, I think," said he. "I saw you coming out of Dr. Cooper's house yesterday. We know everything that is happening in the village, you see." He laughed nervously, and added: "But I don't know your friend."

I introduced Thorndyke, at the mention of whose name our new acquaintance knitted his brows, and glanced inquisitively at my friend.

"Thorndyke," he repeated; "the name seems familiar to me. Are you in the Law, sir?"

Thorndyke admitted the impeachment, and our companion, having again bestowed on him a look full of curiosity, continued: "This horrible affair will interest you, no doubt, from a professional point of view. You were present when my poor friend's body was found, I think?"

"No," replied Thorndyke; "we came up afterwards, when they were removing it."

Our companion then proceeded to question as about the murder, but received from Thorndyke only the most general and ambiguous replies. Nor was there time to go into the matter at length, for the footpath presently emerged on to the road close to Mr. Draper's house.

"You will excuse my not asking you in to-night," said he, "but you will understand that I am not in much form for visitors just now."

We assured him that we fully understood, and, having wished him "Good-evening," pursued our way towards the village.

"The sergeant is off to get a warrant, I suppose," I observed.

"Yes; and mighty anxious lest his man should be off before he can execute it. But he is fishing in deeper waters than he thinks, Jervis. This is a very singular and complicated case; one of the strangest, in fact, that I have ever met. I shall follow its development with deep interest."

"The sergeant seems pretty cocksure, all the same," I said.

"He is not to blame for that," replied Thorndyke. "He is acting on the obvious appearances, which is the proper thing to do in the first place. Perhaps his notebook contains more than I think it does. But we shall see."

When we entered the village I stopped to settle some business with the chemist, who acted as Dr. Cooper's dispenser, suggesting to Thorndyke that he should walk on to the house; but when I emerged from the shop some ten minutes later he was waiting outside, with a smallish brown-paper parcel under each arm. Of one of these parcels I insisted on relieving him, in spite of his protests, but when he at length handed it to me its weight completely took me by surprise.

"I should have let them send this home on a barrow," I remarked.

"So I should have done," he replied, "only I did not wish to draw attention to my purchase, or give my address."

Accepting this hint I refrained from making any inquiries as to the nature of the contents (although I must confess to considerable curiosity on the subject), and on arriving home I assisted him to deposit the two mysterious parcels in his room.

When I came downstairs a disagreeable surprise awaited me. Hitherto the long evenings had been spent by me in solitary and undisturbed enjoyment of Dr. Cooper's excellent library, but to-night a perverse fate decreed that I must wander abroad, because, forsooth, a preposterous farmer, who resided in a hamlet five miles distant, had chosen the evening of my guest's arrival to dislocate his bucolic elbow. I half hoped that Thorndyke would offer to accompany me, but he made no such suggestion, and in fact seemed by no means afflicted at the prospect of my absence.

"I have plenty to occupy me while you are away," he said cheerfully; and with this assurance to comfort me I mounted my bicycle and rode off somewhat sulkily along the dark road.

My visit occupied in all a trifle under two hours, and when I reached home, ravenously hungry and heated by my ride, half-past nine had struck, and the village had begun to settle down for the night.

"Sergeant Payne is a-waiting in the surgery, sir," the housemaid announced as I entered the hall.

"Confound Sergeant Payne!" I exclaimed. "Is Dr. Thorndyke with him?"

"No, sir," replied the grinning damsel. "Dr. Thorndyke is hout."

"Hout!" I repeated (my surprise leading to unintentional mimicry).

"Yes, sir. He went hout soon after you, sir, on his bicycle. He had a basket strapped on to it--leastways a hamper--and he borrowed a basin and a kitchen-spoon from the cook."

I stared at the girl in astonishment. The ways of John Thorndyke were, indeed, beyond all understanding.

"Well, let me have some dinner or supper at once," I said, "and I will see what the sergeant wants."

The officer rose as I entered the surgery, and, laying his helmet on the table, approached me with an air of secrecy and importance.

"Well, sir," said he, "the fat's in the fire. I've arrested Mr. Draper, and I've got him locked up in the court-house. But I wish it had been someone else."

"So does he, I expect," I remarked.

"You see, sir," continued the sergeant, "we all like Mr. Draper. He's been among us a matter of seven years, and he's like one of ourselves. However, what I've come about is this; it seems the gentleman who was with you this evening is Dr. Thorndyke, the great expert. Now Mr. Draper seems to have heard about him, as most of us have, and he is very anxious for him to take up the defence. Do you think he would consent?"

"I expect so," I answered, remembering Thorndyke's keen interest in the case; "but I will ask him when he comes in."

"Thank you, sir," said the sergeant. "And perhaps you wouldn't mind stepping round to the court-house presently yourself. He looks uncommon queer, does Mr. Draper, and no wonder, so I'd like you to take a look at him, and if you could bring Dr. Thorndyke with you, he'd like it, and so should I, for, I assure you, sir, that although a conviction would mean a step up the ladder for me, I'd be glad enough to find that I'd made a mistake."

I was just showing my visitor out when a bicycle swept in through the open gate, and Thorndyke dismounted at the door, revealing a square hamper--evidently abstracted from the surgery--strapped on to a carrier at the back. I conveyed the sergeant's request to him at once, and asked if he was willing to take up the case.

"As to taking up the defence," he replied, "I will consider the matter; but in any case I will come up and see the prisoner."

With this the sergeant departed, and Thorndyke, having unstrapped the hamper with as much care as if it contained a collection of priceless porcelain, bore it tenderly up to his bedroom; whence he appeared, after a considerable interval, smilingly apologetic for the delay.

"I thought you were dressing for dinner," I grumbled as he took his seat at the table.

"No," he replied. "I have been considering this murder. Really it is a most singular case, and promises to be uncommonly complicated, too."

"Then I assume that you will undertake the defence?"

"I shall if Draper gives a reasonably straightforward account of himself."

It appeared that this condition was likely to be fulfilled, for when we arrived at the court-house (where the prisoner was accommodated in a spare office, under rather free-and-easy conditions considering the nature of the charge) we found Mr. Draper in an eminently communicative frame of mind.

"I want you, Dr. Thorndyke, to undertake my defence in this terrible affair, because I feel confident that you will be able to clear me. And I promise you that there shall be no reservation or concealment on my part of anything that you ought to know."

"Very well," said Thorndyke. "By the way, I see you have changed your shoes."

"Yes, the sergeant took possession of those I was wearing. He said something about comparing them with some footprints, but there can't be any footprints like those shoes here in Sundersley. The nails are fixed in the soles in quite a peculiar pattern. I had them made in Edinburgh."

"Have you more than one pair?"

"No. I have no other nailed boots."

"That is important," said Thorndyke. "And now I judge that you have something to tell us that bears on this crime. Am I right?"

"Yes. There is something that I am afraid it is necessary for you to know, although it is very painful to me to revive memories of my past that I had hoped were buried for ever. But perhaps, after all, it may not be necessary for these confidences to be revealed to anyone but yourself."

"I hope not," said Thorndyke; "and if it is not necessary you may rely upon me not to allow any of your secrets to leak out. But you are wise to tell me everything that may in any way bear upon the case."

At this juncture, seeing that confidential matters were about to be discussed, I rose and prepared to withdraw; but Draper waved me back into my chair.

"You need not go away, Dr. Jervis," he said. "It is through you that I have the benefit of Dr. Thorndyke's help, and I know that you doctors can be trusted to keep your own counsel and your clients' secrets. And now for some confessions of mine. In the first place, it is my painful duty to tell you that I am a discharged convict--an 'old lag,' as the cant phrase has it."

He coloured a dusky red as he made this statement, and glanced furtively at Thorndyke to observe its effect. But he might as well have looked at a wooden figure-head or a stone mask as at my friend's immovable visage; and when his communication had been acknowledged by a slight nod, he proceeded:

"The history of my wrong-doing is the history of hundreds of others. I was a clerk in a bank, and getting on as well as I could expect in that not very progressive avocation, when I had the misfortune to make four very undesirable acquaintances. They were all young men, though rather older than myself, and were close friends, forming a sort of little community or club. They were not what is usually described as 'fast.' They were quite sober and decently-behaved young follows, but they were very decidedly addicted to gambling in a small way, and they soon infected me. Before long I was the keenest gambler of them all. Cards, billiards, pool, and various forms of betting began to be the chief pleasures of my life, and not only was the bulk of my scanty salary often consumed in the inevitable losses, but presently I found myself considerably in debt, without any visible means of discharging my liabilities. It is true that my four friends were my chief--in fact, almost my only--creditors, but still, the debts existed, and had to be paid.

"Now these four friends of mine--named respectively Leach, Pitford, Hearn, and Jezzard--were uncommonly clever men, though the full extent of their cleverness was not appreciated by me until too late. And I, too, was clever in my way, and a most undesirable way it was, for I possessed the fatal gift of imitating handwriting and signatures with the most remarkable accuracy. So perfect were my copies that the writers themselves were frequently unable to distinguish their own signatures from my imitations, and many a time was my skill invoked by some of my companions to play off practical jokes upon the others. But these jests were strictly confined to our own little set, for my four friends were most careful and anxious that my dangerous accomplishment should not become known to outsiders.

"And now follows the consequence which you have no doubt foreseen. My debts, though small, were accumulating, and I saw no prospect of being able to pay them. Then, one night, Jezzard made a proposition. We had been playing bridge at his rooms, and once more my ill luck had caused me to increase my debt. I scribbled out an IOU, and pushed it across the table to Jezzard, who picked it up with a very wry face, and pocketed it.

"'Look here, Ted,' he said presently, 'this paper is all very well, but, you know, I can't pay my debts with it. My creditors demand hard cash.'

"'I'm very sorry,' I replied, 'but I can't help it.'

"'Yes, you can,' said he, 'and I'll tell you how.' He then propounded a scheme which I at first rejected with indignation, but which, when the others backed him up, I at last allowed myself to be talked into, and actually put into execution. I contrived, by taking advantage of the carelessness of some of my superiors at the bank, to get possession of some blank cheque forms, which I filled up with small amounts--not more than two or three pounds--and signed with careful imitations of the signatures of some of our clients. Jezzard got some stamps made for stamping on the account numbers, and when this had been done I handed over to him the whole collection of forged cheques in settlement of my debts to all of my four companions.

"The cheques were duly presented--by whom I do not know; and although, to my dismay, the modest sums for which I had drawn them had been skilfully altered into quite considerable amounts, they were all paid without demur excepting one. That one, which had been altered from three pounds to thirty-nine, was drawn upon an account which was already slightly overdrawn. The cashier became suspicious; the cheque was impounded, and the client communicated with. Then, of course, the mine exploded. Not only was this particular forgery detected, but inquiries were set afoot which soon brought to light the others. Presently circumstances, which I need not describe, threw some suspicion on me. I at once lost my nerve, and finally made a full confession.

"The inevitable prosecution followed. It was not conducted vindictively. Still, I had actually committed the forgeries, and though I endeavoured to cast a part of the blame on to the shoulders of my treacherous confederates, I did not succeed. Jezzard, it is true, was arrested, but was discharged for lack of evidence, and, consequently, the whole burden of the forgery fell upon me. The jury, of course, convicted me, and I was sentenced to seven years' penal servitude.

"During the time that I was in prison an uncle of mine died in Canada, and by the provisions of his will I inherited the whole of his very considerable property, so that when the time arrived for my release, I came out of prison, not only free, but comparatively rich. I at once dropped my own name, and, assuming that of Alfred Draper, began to look about for some quiet spot in which I might spend the rest of my days in peace, and with little chance of my identity being discovered. Such a place I found in Sundersley, and here I have lived for the last seven years, liked and respected, I think, by my neighbours, who have little suspected that they were harbouring in their midst a convicted felon.

"All this time I had neither seen nor heard anything of my four confederates, and I hoped and believed that they had passed completely out of my life. But they had not. Only a month ago I met them once more, to my sorrow, and from the day of that meeting all the peace and security of my quiet existence at Sundersley have vanished. Like evil spirits they have stolen into my life, changing my happiness into bitter misery, filling my days with dark forebodings and my nights with terror."

Here Mr. Draper paused, and seemed to sink into a gloomy reverie.

"Under what circumstances did you meet these men?" Thorndyke asked.

"Ah!" exclaimed Draper, arousing with sudden excitement, "the circumstances were very singular and suspicious. I had gone over to Eastwich for the day to do some shopping. About eleven o'clock in the forenoon I was making some purchases in a shop when I noticed two men looking in the window, or rather pretending to do so, whilst they conversed earnestly. They were smartly dressed, in a horsy fashion, and looked like well-to-do farmers, as they might very naturally have been since it was market-day. But it seemed to me that their faces were familiar to me. I looked at them more attentively, and then it suddenly dawned upon me, most unpleasantly, that they resembled Leach and Jezzard. And yet they were not quite like. The resemblance was there, but the differences were greater than the lapse of time would account for. Moreover, the man who resembled Jezzard had a rather large mole on the left cheek just under the eye, while the other man had an eyeglass stuck in one eye, and wore a waxed moustache, whereas Leach had always been clean-shaven, and had never used an eyeglass.

"As I was speculating upon the resemblance they looked up, and caught my intent and inquisitive eye, whereupon they moved away from the window; and when, having completed my purchases, I came out into the street, they were nowhere to be seen.

"That evening, as I was walking by the river outside the town before returning to the station, I overtook a yacht which was being towed down-stream. Three men were walking ahead on the bank with a long tow-line, and one man stood in the cockpit steering. As I approached, and was reading the name Otter on the stern, the man at the helm looked round, and with a start of surprise I recognized my old acquaintance Hearn. The recognition, however, was not mutual, for I had grown a beard in the interval, and I passed on without appearing to notice him; but when I overtook the other three men, and recognized, as I had feared, the other three members of the gang, I must have looked rather hard at Jezzard, for he suddenly halted, and exclaimed: 'Why, it's our old friend Ted! Our long-lost and lamented brother!' He held out his hand with effusive cordiality, and began to make inquiries as to my welfare; but I cut him short with the remark that I was not proposing to renew the acquaintance, and, turning off on to a footpath that led away from the river, strode off without looking back.

"Naturally this meeting exercised my mind a good deal, and when I thought of the two men whom I had seen in the town, I could hardly believe that their likeness to my quondam friends was a mere coincidence. And yet when I had met Leach and Jezzard by the river, I had found them little altered, and had particularly noticed that Jezzard had no mole on his face, and that Leach was clean-shaven as of old.

"But a day or two later all my doubts were resolved by a paragraph in the local paper. It appeared that on the day of my visit to Eastwich a number of forged cheques had been cashed at the three banks. They had been presented by three well-dressed, horsy-looking men who looked like well-to-do farmers. One of them had a mole on the left cheek, another was distinguished by a waxed moustache and a single eyeglass, while the description of the third I did not recognize. None of the cheques had been drawn for large amounts, though the total sum obtained by the forgers was nearly four hundred pounds; but the most interesting point was that the cheque-forms had been manufactured by photographic process, and the water-mark skilfully, though not quite perfectly, imitated. Evidently the swindlers were clever and careful men, and willing to take a good deal of trouble for the sake of security, and the result of their precautions was that the police could make no guess as to their identity.

"The very next day, happening to walk over to Port Marston, I came upon the Otter lying moored alongside the quay in the harbour. As soon as I recognized the yacht, I turned quickly and walked away, but a minute later I ran into Leach and Jezzard, who were returning to their craft. Jezzard greeted me with an air of surprise. 'What! Still hanging about here, Ted--' he exclaimed. 'That is not discreet of you, dear boy. I should earnestly advise you to clear out.'

"'What do you mean--' I asked.

"'Tut, tut!' said he. 'We read the papers like other people, and we know now what business took you to Eastwich. But it's foolish of you to hang about the neighbourhood where you might be spotted at any moment.'

"The implied accusation took me aback so completely that I stood staring at him in speechless astonishment, and at that unlucky moment a tradesman, from whom I had ordered some house-linen, passed along the quay. Seeing me, he stopped and touched his hat.

"'Beg pardon, Mr. Draper,' said he, 'but I shall be sending my cart up to Sundersley to-morrow morning if that will do for you.'

"I said that it would, and as the man turned away, Jezzard's face broke out into a cunning smile.

"So you are Mr. Draper, of Sundersley, now, are you--' said he. 'Well, I hope you won't be too proud to come and look in on your old friends. We shall be staying here for some time.'

"That same night Hearn made his appearance at my house. He had come as an emissary from the gang, to ask me to do some work for them--to execute some forgeries, in fact. Of course I refused, and pretty bluntly, too, whereupon Hearn began to throw out vague hints as to what might happen if I made enemies of the gang, and to utter veiled, but quite intelligible, threats. You will say that I was an idiot not to send him packing, and threaten to hand over the whole gang to the police; but I was never a man of strong nerve, and I don't mind admitting that I was mortally afraid of that cunning devil, Jezzard.

"The next thing that happened was that Hearn came and took lodgings in Sundersley, and, in spite of my efforts to avoid him, he haunted me continually. The yacht, too, had evidently settled down for some time at a berth in the harbour, for I heard that a local smack-boy had been engaged as a deck-hand; and I frequently encountered Jezzard and the other members of the gang, who all professed to believe that I had committed the Eastwich forgeries. One day I was foolish enough to allow myself to be lured on to the yacht for a few minutes, and when I would have gone ashore, I found that the shore ropes had been cast off, and that the vessel was already moving out of the harbour. At first I was furious, but the three scoundrels were so jovial and good-natured, and so delighted with the joke of taking me for a sail against my will, that I presently cooled down, and having changed into a pair of rubber-soled shoes (so that I should not make dents in the smooth deck with my hobnails), bore a hand at sailing the yacht, and spent quite a pleasant day.

"From that time I found myself gradually drifting back into a state of intimacy with these agreeable scoundrels, and daily becoming more and more afraid of them. In a moment of imbecility I mentioned what I had seen from the shop-window at Eastwich, and, though they passed the matter off with a joke, I could see that they were mightily disturbed by it. Their efforts to induce me to join them were redoubled, and Hearn took to calling almost daily at my house--usually with documents and signatures which he tried to persuade me to copy.

"A few evenings ago he made a new and startling proposition. We were walking in my garden, and he had been urging me once more to rejoin the gang--unsuccessfully, I need not say. Presently he sat down on a seat against a yew-hedge at the bottom of the garden, and, after an interval of silence, said suddenly:

"'Then you absolutely refuse to go in with us--'

"'Of course I do,' I replied. 'Why should I mix myself up with a gang of crooks when I have ample means and a decent position--'

"'Of course,' he agreed, 'you'd be a fool if you did. But, you see, you know all about this Eastwich job, to say nothing of our other little exploits, and you gave us away once before. Consequently, you can take it from me that, now Jezzard has run you to earth, he won't leave you in peace until you have given us some kind of a hold on you. You know too much, you see, and as long as you have a clean sheet you are a standing menace to us. That is the position. You know it, and

Jezzard knows it, and he is a desperate man, and as cunning as the devil.'

"'I know that,' I said gloomily.

"'Very well,' continued Hearn. 'Now I'm going to make you an offer. Promise me a small annuity--you can easily afford it--or pay me a substantial sum down, and I will set you free for ever from Jezzard and the others.'

"'How will you do that--' I asked.

"'Very simply,' he replied. 'I am sick of them all, and sick of this risky, uncertain mode of life. Now I am ready to clean off my own slate and set you free at the same time; but I must have some means of livelihood in view.'

"'You mean that you will turn King's evidence--' I asked.

"'Yes, if you will pay me a couple of hundred a year, or, say, two thousand down on the conviction of the gang.'

"I was so taken aback that for some time I made no reply, and as I sat considering this amazing proposition, the silence was suddenly broken by a suppressed sneeze from the other side of the hedge.

"Hearn and I started to our feet. Immediately hurried footsteps were heard in the lane outside the hedge. We raced up the garden to the gate and out through a side alley, but when we reached the lane there was not a soul in sight. We made a brief and fruitless search in the immediate neighbourhood, and then turned back to the house. Hearn was deathly pale and very agitated, and I must confess that I was a good deal upset by the incident.

"'This is devilish awkward,' said Hearn. "'It is rather,' I admitted; 'but I expect it was only some inquisitive yokel.'

"'I don't feel so sure of that,' said he. 'At any rate, we were stark lunatics to sit up against a hedge to talk secrets.'

"He paced the garden with me for some time in gloomy silence, and presently, after a brief request that I would think over his proposal, took himself off.

"I did not see him again until I met him last night on the yacht. Pitford called on me in the morning, and invited me to come and dine with them. I at first declined, for my housekeeper was going to spend the evening with her sister at Eastwich, and stay there for the night, and I did not much like leaving the house empty. However, I agreed eventually, stipulating that I should be allowed to come home early, and I accordingly went. Hearn and Pitford were waiting in the boat by the steps--for the yacht had been moved out to a buoy--and we went on board and spent a very pleasant and lively evening. Pitford put me ashore at ten o'clock, and I walked straight home, and went to bed. Hearn would have come with me, but the others insisted on his remaining, saying that they had some matters of business to discuss."

"Which way did you walk home?" asked Thorndyke.

"I came through the town, and along the main road."

"And that is all you know about this affair?"

"Absolutely all," replied Draper. "I have now admitted you to secrets of my past life that I had hoped never to have to reveal to any human creature, and I still have some faint hope that it may not be necessary for you to divulge what I have told you."

"Your secrets shall not be revealed unless it is absolutely indispensable that they should be," said Thorndyke; "but you are placing your life in my hands, and you must leave me perfectly free to act as I think best."

With this he gathered his notes together, and we took our departure.

"A very singular history, this, Jervis," he said, when, having wished the sergeant "Good-night," we stepped out on to the dark road. "What do you think of it?"

"I hardly know what to think," I answered, "but, on the whole, it seems rather against Draper than otherwise. He admits that he is an old criminal, and it appears that he was being persecuted and blackmailed by the man Hearn. It is true that he represents Jezzard as being the leading spirit and prime mover in the persecution, but we have only his word for that. Hearn was in lodgings near him, and was undoubtedly taking the most active part in the business, and it is quite possible, and indeed probable, that Hearn was the actual *deus ex machina*."

Thorndyke nodded. "Yes," he said, "that is certainly the line the prosecution will take if we allow the story to become known. Ha! what is this? We are going to have some rain."

"Yes, and wind too. We are in for an autumn gale, I think."

"And that," said Thorndyke, "may turn out to be an important factor in our case."

"How can the weather affect your case?" I asked in some surprise. But, as the rain suddenly descended in a pelting shower, my companion broke into a run, leaving my question unanswered.

On the following morning, which was fair and sunny after the stormy night, Dr. Burrows called for my friend. He was on his way to the extemporized mortuary to make the post-mortem examination of the murdered man's body. Thorndyke, having notified the coroner that he was watching the case on behalf of the accused, had been authorized to be present at the autopsy; but the authorization did not include me, and, as Dr. Burrows did not issue any invitation, I was not able to be present. I met them, however, as they were returning, and it seemed to me that Dr. Burrows appeared a little huffy.

"Your friend," said he, in a rather injured tone, "is really the most outrageous stickler for forms and ceremonies that I have ever met."

Thorndyke looked at him with an amused twinkle, and chuckled indulgently.

"Here was a body," Dr. Burrows continued irritably, "found under circumstances clearly indicative of murder, and bearing a knife-wound that nearly divided the arch of the aorta; in spite of which, I assure you that Dr. Thorndyke insisted on weighing the body, and examining every organ--lungs, liver, stomach, and brain--yes, actually the brain!--as if there had been no clue whatever to the cause of death. And then, as a climax, he insisted on sending the contents of the stomach in a jar, sealed with our respective seals, in charge of a special messenger, to Professor Copland, for analysis and report. I thought he was going to demand an examination for the tubercle bacillus, but he didn't; which," concluded Dr. Burrows, suddenly becoming sourly facetious, "was an oversight, for, after all, the fellow may have died of consumption."

Thorndyke chuckled again, and I murmured that the precautions appeared to have been somewhat excessive.

"Not at all," was the smiling response. "You are losing sight of our function. We are the expert and impartial umpires, and it is our business to ascertain, with scientific accuracy, the cause of death. The prima facie appearances in this case suggest that the deceased was murdered by Draper, and that is the hypothesis advanced. But that is no concern of ours. It is not our function to confirm an hypothesis suggested by outside circumstances, but rather, on the contrary, to make certain that no other explanation is possible. And that is my invariable practice. No matter how glaringly obvious the appearances may be, I refuse to take anything for granted."

Dr. Burrows received this statement with a grunt of dissent, but the arrival of his dogcart put a stop to further discussion.

Thorndyke was not subpoenaed for the inquest. Dr. Burrows and the sergeant having been present immediately after the finding of the body, his evidence was not considered necessary, and, moreover, he was known to be watching the case in the interests of the accused. Like myself, therefore, he was present as a spectator, but as a highly interested one, for he took very complete shorthand notes of the whole of the evidence and the coroner's comments.

I shall not describe the proceedings in detail. The jury, having been taken to view the body, trooped into the room on tiptoe, looking pale and awe-stricken, and took their seats; and thereafter, from time to time, directed glances of furtive curiosity at Draper as he stood, pallid and haggard, confronting the court, with a burly rural constable on either side.

The medical evidence was taken first. Dr. Burrows, having been sworn, began, with sarcastic emphasis, to describe the condition of the lungs and liver, until he was interrupted by the coroner.

"Is all this necessary?" the latter inquired. "I mean, is it material to the subject of the inquiry?"

"I should say not," replied Dr. Burrows. "It appears to me to be quite irrelevant, but Dr. Thorndyke, who is watching the case for the defence, thought it necessary."

"I think," said the coroner, "you had better give us only the facts that are material. The jury want you to tell them what you consider to have been the cause of death. They don't want a lecture on pathology."

"The cause of death," said Dr. Burrows, "was a penetrating wound of the chest, apparently inflicted with a large knife. The weapon entered between the second and third ribs on the left side close to the sternum or breast-bone. It wounded the left lung, and partially divided both the pulmonary artery and the aorta--the two principal arteries of the body."

"Was this injury alone sufficient to cause death?" the coroner asked.

"Yes," was the reply; "and death from injury to these great vessels would be practically instantaneous."

"Could the injury have been self-inflicted?"

"So far as the position and nature of the wound are concerned," replied the witness, "self-infliction would be quite possible. But since death would follow in a few seconds at the most, the weapon would be found either in the wound, or grasped in the hand, or, at least, quite close to the body. But in this case no weapon was found at all, and the wound must therefore certainly have been homicidal."

"Did you see the body before it was moved?"

"Yes. It was lying on its back, with the arms extended and the legs nearly straight; and the sand in the neighbourhood of the body was trampled as if a furious struggle had taken place."

"Did you notice anything remarkable about the footprints in the sand?"

"I did," replied Dr. Burrows. "They were the footprints of two persons only. One of these was evidently the deceased, whose footmarks could be easily identified by the circular rubber heels. The other footprints were those of a person--apparently a man--who wore shoes, or boots, the soles of which were studded with nails; and these nails were arranged in a very peculiar and unusual manner, for those on the soles formed a lozenge or diamond shape, and those on the heel were set out in the form of a cross."

"Have you ever seen shoes or boots with the nails arranged in this manner?"

"Yes. I have seen a pair of shoes which I am informed belong to the accused; the nails in them are arranged as I have described."

"Would you say that the footprints of which you have spoken were made by those shoes?"

"No; I could not say that. I can only say that, to the best of my belief, the pattern on the shoes is similar to that in the footprints."

This was the sum of Dr. Burrows' evidence, and to all of it Thorndyke listened with an immovable countenance, though with the closest attention. Equally attentive was the accused man, though not equally impassive; indeed, so great was his agitation that presently one of the constables asked permission to get him a chair.

The next witness was Arthur Jezzard. He testified that he had viewed the body, and identified it as that of Charles Hearn; that he had been acquainted with deceased for some years, but knew practically nothing of his affairs. At the time of his death deceased was lodging in the village.

"Why did he leave the yacht?" the coroner inquired. "Was there any kind of disagreement!"

"Not in the least," replied Jezzard. "He grew tired of the confinement of the yacht, and came to live ashore for a change. But we were the best of friends, and he intended to come with us when we sailed."

"When did you see him last?"

"On the night before the body was found--that is, last Monday. He had been dining on the yacht, and we put him ashore about midnight. He said as we were rowing him ashore that he intended to walk home along the sands us the tide was out. He went up the stone steps by the watch-house, and turned at the top to wish us good-night. That was the last time I saw him alive."

"Do you know anything of the relations between the accused and the deceased?" the coroner asked.

"Very little," replied Jezzard. "Mr. Draper was introduced to us by the deceased about a month ago. I believe they had been acquainted some years, and they appeared to be on excellent terms. There was no indication of any quarrel or disagreement between them."

"What time did the accused leave the yacht on the night of the murder?"

"About ten o'clock. He said that he wanted to get home early, as his housekeeper was away and he did not like the house to be left with no one in it."

This was the whole of Jezzard's evidence, and was confirmed by that of Leach and Pitford. Then, when the fisherman had deposed to the discovery of the body, the sergeant was called, and stepped forward, grasping a carpet-bag, and looking as uncomfortable as if he had been the accused instead of a witness. He described the circumstances under which he saw the body, giving the exact time and place with official precision.

"You have heard Dr. Burrows' description of the footprints?" the coroner inquired.

"Yes. There were two sets. One set were evidently made by deceased. They showed that he entered St. Bridget's Bay from the direction of Port Marston. He had been walking along the shore just about high-water mark, sometimes above and sometimes below. Where he had walked below high-water mark the footprints had of course been washed away by the sea."

"How far back did you trace the footprints of deceased?"

"About two-thirds of the way to Sundersley Gap. Then they disappeared below high-water mark. Later in the evening I walked from the Gap into Port Marston, but could not find any further traces of deceased. He must have walked between the tide-marks all the way from Port Marston to beyond Sundersley. When these footprints entered St. Bridget's Bay they became mixed up with the footprints of another man, and the shore was trampled for a space of a dozen yards as if a furious struggle had taken place. The strange man's tracks came down from the Shepherd's Path, and went up it again; but, owing to the hardness of the ground from the dry weather, the tracks disappeared a short distance up the path, and I could not find them again."

"What were these strange footprints like?" inquired the coroner.

"They were very peculiar," replied the sergeant. "They were made by shoes armed with smallish hob-nails, which were arranged in a diamond-shaped pattern on the holes and in a cross on the heels. I measured the footprints carefully, and made a drawing of each foot at the time." Here the sergeant produced a long notebook of funereal aspect, and, having opened it at a marked place, handed it to the coroner, who examined it attentively, and then passed it on to the jury. From the jury it was presently transferred to Thorndyke, and, looking over his shoulder, I saw a very workmanlike sketch of a pair of footprints with the principal dimensions inserted.

Thorndyke surveyed the drawing critically, jotted down a few brief notes, and returned the sergeant's notebook to the coroner, who, as he took it, turned once more to the officer.

"Have you any clue, sergeant, to the person who made these footprints?" he asked.

By way of reply the sergeant opened his carpet-bag, and, extracting therefrom a pair of smart but stoutly made shoes, laid them on the table.

"Those shoes," he said, "are the property of the accused; he was wearing them when I arrested him. They appear to correspond exactly to the footprints of the murderer. The measurements are the same, and the nails with which they are studded are arranged in a similar pattern."

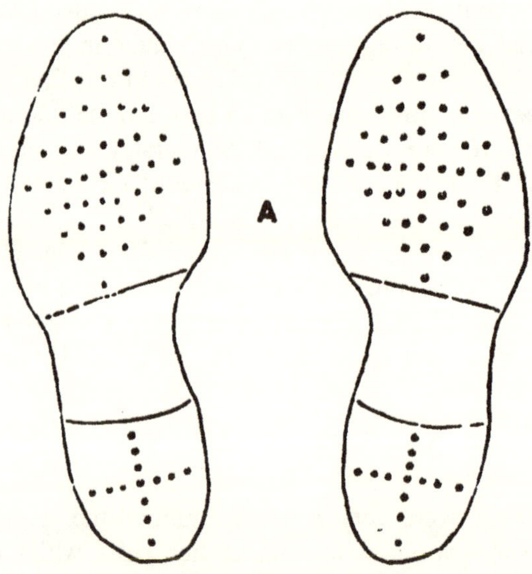

THE SERGEANT'S SKETCH

Extreme length, 11¾ inches.

Width at A, 4½ inches.

Length of heel, 3¼ inches

Width of heel at cross, 3 inches.

"Would you swear that the footprints were made with these shoes?" asked the coroner.

"No, sir, I would not," was the decided answer. "I would only swear to the similarity of size and pattern."

"Had you ever seen these shoes before you made the drawing?"

"No, sir," replied the sergeant; and he then related the incident of the footprints in the soft earth by the pond which led him to make the arrest.

The coroner gazed reflectively at the shoes which he held in his hand, and from them to the drawing; then, passing them to the foreman of the jury, he remarked:

"Well, gentlemen, it is not for me to tell you whether these shoes answer to the description given by Dr. Burrows and the sergeant, or whether they resemble the drawing which, as you have heard, was made by the officer on the spot and before he had seen the shoes; that is a matter for you to decide. Meanwhile, there is another question that we must consider." He turned to the sergeant and asked: "Have you made any inquiries as to the movements of the accused on the night of the murder?"

"I have," replied the sergeant, "and I find that, on that night, the accused was alone in the house, his housekeeper having gone over to Eastwich. Two men saw him in the town about ten o'clock, apparently walking in the direction of Sundersley."

This concluded the sergeant's evidence, and when one or two more witnesses had been examined without eliciting any fresh facts, the coroner briefly recapitulated the evidence, and requested the jury to consider their verdict. Thereupon a solemn hush fell upon the court, broken only by the whispers of the jurymen, as they consulted together; and the spectators gazed in awed expectancy from the accused to the whispering jury. I glanced at Draper, sitting huddled in his chair, his clammy face as pale as that of the corpse in the mortuary hard by, his hands tremulous and restless; and, scoundrel as I believed him to be, I could not but pity the abject misery that was written large all over him, from his damp hair to his incessantly shifting feet.

The jury took but a short time to consider their verdict. At the end of five minutes the foreman announced that they were agreed, and, in answer to the coroner's formal inquiry, stood up and replied:

"We find that the deceased met his death by being stabbed in the chest by the accused man, Alfred Draper."

"That is a verdict of wilful murder," said the coroner, and he entered it accordingly in his notes. The Court now rose. The spectators reluctantly trooped out, the jurymen stood up and stretched themselves, and the two constables, under the guidance of the sergeant, carried the wretched Draper in a fainting condition to a closed fly that was waiting outside.

"I was not greatly impressed by the activity of the defence," I remarked maliciously as we walked home.

Thorndyke smiled. "You surely did not expect me to cast my pearls of forensic learning before a coroner's jury," said he.

"I expected that you would have something to say on behalf of your client," I replied. "As it was, his accusers had it all their own way."

"And why not?" he asked. "Of what concern to us is the verdict of the coroner's jury?"

"It would have seemed more decent to make some sort of defence," I replied.

"My dear Jervis," he rejoined, "you do not seem to appreciate the great virtue of what Lord Beaconsfield so felicitously called 'a policy of masterly inactivity'; and yet that is one of the great lessons that a medical training impresses on the student."

"That may be so," said I. "But the result, up to the present, of your masterly policy is that a verdict of wilful murder stands against your client, and I don't see what other verdict the jury could have found."

"Neither do I," said Thorndyke.

I had written to my principal, Dr. Cooper, describing the stirring events that were taking place in the village, and had received a reply from him instructing me to place the house at Thorndyke's disposal, and to give him every facility for his work. In accordance with which edict my colleague took possession of a well-lighted, disused stable-loft, and announced his intention of moving his things into it. Now, as these "things" included the mysterious contents of the hamper that the housemaid had seen, I was possessed with a consuming desire to be present at the "flitting," and I do not mind confessing that I purposely lurked about the stairs in the hopes of thus picking up a few crumbs of information.

But Thorndyke was one too many for me. A misbegotten infant in the village having been seized with inopportune convulsions, I was compelled, most reluctantly, to hasten to its relief; and I returned only in time to find Thorndyke in the act of locking the door of the loft.

"A nice light, roomy place to work in," he remarked, as he descended the steps, slipping the key into his pocket.

"Yes," I replied, and added boldly: "What do you intend to do up there?"

"Work up the case for the defence," he replied, "and, as I have now heard all that the prosecution have to say, I shall be able to forge ahead."

This was vague enough, but I consoled myself with the reflection that in a very few days I should, in common with the rest of the world, be in possession of the results of his mysterious proceedings. For, in view of the approaching assizes, preparations were being made to push the case through the magistrate's court as quickly as possible in order to obtain a committal in time for the ensuing sessions. Draper had, of course, been already charged before a justice of the peace and evidence of arrest taken, and it was expected that the adjourned hearing would commence before the local magistrates on the fifth day after the inquest.

The events of these five days kept me in a positive ferment of curiosity. In the first place an inspector of the Criminal Investigation Department came down and browsed about the place in company with the sergeant. Then Mr. Bashfield, who was to conduct the prosecution, came and took up his abode at the "Cat and Chicken." But the most surprising visitor was Thorndyke's laboratory assistant, Polton, who appeared one evening with a large trunk and a sailor's hammock, and announced that he was going to take up his quarters in the loft.

As to Thorndyke himself, his proceedings were beyond speculation. From time to time he made mysterious appearances at the windows of the loft, usually arrayed in what looked suspiciously like a nightshirt. Sometimes I would see him holding a negative up to the light, at others manipulating a photographic printing-frame; and once I observed him with a paintbrush and a large gallipot; on which I turned away in despair, and nearly collided with the inspector.

"Dr. Thorndyke is staying with you, I hear," said the latter, gazing earnestly at my colleague's back, which was presented for his inspection at the window.

"Yes," I answered. "Those are his temporary premises."

"That is where he does his bedevilments, I suppose?" the officer suggested.

"He conducts his experiments there," I corrected haughtily.

"That's what I mean," said the inspector; and, as Thorndyke at this moment turned and opened the window, our visitor began to ascend the steps.

"I've just called to ask if I could have a few words with you, Doctor," said the inspector, as he reached the door.

"Certainly," Thorndyke replied blandly. "If you will go down and wait with Dr. Jervis, I will be with you in five minutes."

The officer came down the steps grinning, and I thought I heard him murmur "Sold!" But this may have been an illusion. However, Thorndyke presently emerged, and he and the officer strode away into the shrubbery. What the inspector's business was, or whether he had any business at all, I never learned; but the incident seemed to throw some light on the presence of Polton and the sailor's hammock. And this reference to Polton reminds me of a very singular change that took place about this time in the habits of this usually staid and sedate little man; who, abandoning the somewhat clerical style of dress that he ordinarily affected, broke out into a semi-nautical costume, in which he would sally forth every morning in the direction of Port Marston. And there, on more than one occasion, I saw him leaning against a post by the harbour, or lounging outside a waterside tavern in earnest and amicable conversation with sundry nautical characters.

On the afternoon of the day before the opening of the proceedings we had two new visitors. One of them, a grey-haired spectacled man, was a stranger to me, and for some reason I failed to recall his name, Copland, though I was sure I had heard it before. The other was Anstey, the barrister who usually worked with Thorndyke in cases that went into Court. I saw very little of either of them, however, for they retired almost immediately to the loft, where, with short intervals for meals, they remained for the rest of the day, and, I believe, far into the night. Thorndyke requested me not to mention the names of his visitors to anyone, and at the same time apologized for the secrecy of his proceedings.

"But you are a doctor, Jervis," he concluded, "and you know what professional confidences are; and you will understand how greatly it is in our favour that we know exactly what the prosecution can do, while they are absolutely in the dark as to our line of defence."

I assured him that I fully understood his position, and with this assurance he retired, evidently relieved, to the council chamber.

The proceedings, which opened on the following day, and at which I was present throughout, need not be described in detail. The evidence for the prosecution was, of course, mainly a repetition of that given at the inquest. Mr. Bashfield's opening statement, however, I shall give at length, inasmuch as it summarized very clearly the whole of the case against the prisoner.

"The case that is now before the Court," said the counsel, "involves a charge of wilful murder against the prisoner Alfred Draper, and the facts, in so far as they are known, are briefly these: On the night of Monday, the 27th of September, the deceased, Charles Hearn, dined with some friends on board the yacht Otter. About midnight he came ashore, and proceeded to walk towards Sundersley along the beach. As he entered St. Bridget's Bay, a man, who appears to have been lying in wait, and who came down the Shepherd's Path, met him, and a deadly struggle seems to have taken place. The deceased received a wound of a kind calculated to cause almost instantaneous death, and apparently fell down dead.

"And now, what was the motive of this terrible crime? It was not robbery, for nothing appears to have been taken from the corpse. Money and valuables were found, as far as is known, intact. Nor, clearly, was it a case of a casual affray. We are, consequently, driven to the conclusion that the motive was a personal one, a motive of interest or revenge, and with this view the time, the place, and the evident deliberateness of the murder are in full agreement.

"So much for the motive. The next question is, Who was the perpetrator of this shocking crime? And the answer to that question is given in a very singular and dramatic circumstance, a circumstance that illustrates once more the amazing lack of precaution shown by persons who commit such crimes. The murderer was wearing a very remarkable pair of shoes, and those shoes left very remarkable footprints in the smooth sand, and those footprints were seen and examined by a very acute and painstaking police-officer, Sergeant Payne, whose evidence you will hear presently. The sergeant not only examined the footprints, he made careful drawings of them on the spot--on the spot, mind you, not from memory--and he made very exact measurements of them, which he duly noted down. And from those drawings and those measurements, those tell-tale shoes have been identified, and are here for your inspection.

"And now, who is the owner of those very singular, those almost unique shoes? I have said that the motive of this murder must have been a personal one, and, behold! the owner of those shoes happens to be the one person in the whole of this district who could have had a motive for compassing the murdered man's death. Those shoes belong to, and were taken from the foot of, the prisoner, Alfred Draper, and the prisoner, Alfred Draper, is the only person living in this neighbourhood who was acquainted with the deceased.

"It has been stated in evidence at the inquest that the relations of these two men, the prisoner and the deceased, were entirely friendly; but I shall prove to you that they were not so friendly as has been supposed. I shall prove to you, by the evidence of the prisoner's housekeeper, that the deceased was often an unwelcome visitor at the house, that the prisoner often denied himself when he was really at home and disengaged, and, in short, that he appeared constantly to shun and avoid the deceased.

"One more question and I have finished. Where was the prisoner on the night of the murder? The answer is that he was in a house little more than half a mile from the scene of the crime. And who was with him in that house? Who was there to observe and testify to his going forth and his coming home? No one. He was alone in the house. On that night, of all nights, he was alone. Not a soul was there to rouse at the creak of a door or the tread of a shoe--to tell as whether he slept or whether he stole forth in the dead of the night.

"Such are the facts of this case. I believe that they are not disputed, and I assert that, taken together, they are susceptible of only one explanation, which is that the prisoner, Alfred Draper, is the man who murdered the deceased, Charles Hearn."

Immediately on the conclusion of this address, the witnesses were called, and the evidence given was identical with that at the inquest. The only new witness for the prosecution was Draper's housekeeper, and her evidence fully bore out Mr. Bashfield's statement. The sergeant's account of the footprints was listened to with breathless interest, and at its conclusion the presiding magistrate--a retired solicitor, once well known in criminal practice--put a question which interested me as showing how clearly Thorndyke had foreseen the course of events, recalling, as it did, his remark on the night when we were caught in the rain.

"Did you," the magistrate asked, "take these shoes down to the beach and compare them with the actual footprints?"

"I obtained the shoes at night," replied the sergeant, "and I took them down to the shore at daybreak the next morning. But, unfortunately, there had been a storm in the night, and the footprints were almost obliterated by the wind and rain."

When the sergeant had stepped down, Mr. Bashfield announced that that was the case for the prosecution. He then resumed his seat, turning an inquisitive eye on Anstey and Thorndyke.

The former immediately rose and opened the case for the defence with a brief statement.

"The learned counsel for the prosecution," said he, "has told us that the facts now in the possession of the Court admit of but one explanation-- that of the guilt of the accused. That may or may not be; but I shall now proceed to lay before the Court certain fresh facts--facts, I may say, of the most singular and startling character, which will, I think, lead to a very different conclusion. I shall say no more, but call the witnesses forthwith, and let the evidence speak for itself."

The first witness for the defence was Thorndyke; and as he entered the box I observed Polton take up a position close behind him with a large wicker trunk. Having been sworn, and requested by Anstey to tell the Court what he knew about the case, he commenced without preamble:

"About half-past four in the afternoon of the 28th of September I walked down Sundersley Gap with Dr. Jervis. Our attention was attracted by certain footprints in the sand, particularly those of a man who had landed from a boat, had walked up the Gap, and presently returned, apparently to the boat.

"As we were standing there Sergeant Payne and Dr. Burrows passed down the Gap with two constables carrying a stretcher. We followed at a distance, and as we walked along the shore we encountered another set of footprints--those which the sergeant has described as the footprints of the deceased. We examined these carefully, and endeavoured to frame a description of the person by whom they had been made."

"And did your description agree with the characters of the deceased?" the magistrate asked.

"Not in the least," replied Thorndyke, whereupon the magistrate, the inspector, and Mr. Bashfield laughed long and heartily.

"When we turned into St. Bridget's Bay, I saw the body of deceased lying on the sand close to the cliff. The sand all round was covered with footprints, as if a prolonged, fierce struggle had taken place. There were two sets of footprints, one set being apparently those of the deceased and the other those of a man with nailed shoes of a very peculiar and conspicuous pattern. The incredible folly that the wearing of such shoes indicated caused me to look more closely at the footprints, and then I made the surprising discovery that there had in reality been no struggle; that, in fact, the two sets of footprints had been made at different times."

"At different times!" the magistrate exclaimed in astonishment.

"Yes. The interval between them may have been one of hours or one only of seconds, but the undoubted fact is that the two sets of footprints were made, not simultaneously, but in succession."

"But how did you arrive at that fact?" the magistrate asked.

"It was very obvious when one looked," said Thorndyke. "The marks of the deceased man's shoes showed that he repeatedly trod in his own footprints; but never in a single instance did he tread in the footprints of the other man, although they covered the same area. The man with the nailed shoes, on the contrary, not only trod in his own footprints, but with equal frequency in those of the deceased. Moreover, when the body was removed, I observed that the footprints in the sand on which it was lying were exclusively those of the deceased. There was not a sign of any nail-marked footprint under the corpse, although there were many close around it. It was evident, therefore, that the footprints of the deceased were made first and those of the nailed shoes afterwards."

As Thorndyke paused the magistrate rubbed his nose thoughtfully, and the inspector gazed at the witness with a puzzled frown.

"The singularity of this fact," my colleague resumed, "made me look at the footprints yet more critically, and then I made another discovery. There was a double track of the nailed shoes, leading apparently from and back to the Shepherd's Path. But on examining these tracks more closely, I was astonished to find that the man who had made them had been walking backwards; that, in fact, he had walked backwards from the body to the Shepherd's Path, had ascended it for a short distance, had turned round, and returned, still walking backwards, to the face of the cliff near the corpse, and there the tracks vanished altogether. On the sand at this spot were some small, inconspicuous marks which might have been made by the end of a rope, and there were also a few small fragments which had fallen from the cliff above. Observing these, I examined the surface of the cliff, and at one spot, about six feet above the beach, I found a freshly rubbed spot on which were parallel scratches such as might have been made by the nailed sole of a boot. I then ascended the Shepherd's Path, and examined the cliff from above, and here I found on the extreme edge a rather deep indentation, such as would be made by a taut rope, and, on lying down and looking over, I could see, some five feet from the top, another rubbed spot with very distinct parallel scratches."

"You appear to infer," said the chairman, "that this man performed these astonishing evolutions and was then hauled up the cliff?"

"That is what the appearances suggested," replied Thorndyke.

The chairman pursed up his lips, raised his eyebrows, and glanced doubtfully at his brother magistrates. Then, with a resigned air, he bowed to the witness to indicate that he was listening.

"That same night," Thorndyke resumed, "I cycled down to the shore, through the Gap, with a supply of plaster of Paris, and proceeded to take plaster moulds of the more important of the footprints." (Here the magistrates, the inspector, and Mr. Bashfield with one accord sat up at attention; Sergeant Payne swore quite audibly; and I experienced a sudden illumination respecting a certain basin and kitchen spoon which had so puzzled me on the night of Thorndyke's arrival.) "As I thought that liquid plaster might confuse or even obliterate the prints in sand, I filled up the respective footprints with dry plaster, pressed it down lightly, and then cautiously poured water on to it. The moulds, which are excellent impressions, of course show the appearance of the boots which made the footprints, and from these moulds I have prepared casts which reproduce the footprints themselves.

"The first mould that I made was that of one of the tracks from the boat up to the Gap, and of this I shall speak presently. I next made a mould of one of the footprints which have been described as those of the deceased."

"Have been described!" exclaimed the chairman. "The deceased was certainly there, and there were no other footprints, so, if they were not his, he must have flown to where he was found."

"I will call them the footprints of the deceased," replied Thorndyke imperturbably. "I took a mould of one of them, and with it, on the same mould, one of my own footprints. Here is the mould, and here is a cast from it." (He turned and took them from the triumphant Polton, who had tenderly lifted them out of the trunk in readiness.) "On looking at the cast, it will be seen that the appearances are not such as would be expected. The deceased was five feet nine inches high, but was very thin and light, weighing only nine stone six pounds, as I ascertained by weighing the body, whereas I am five feet eleven and weigh nearly thirteen stone. But yet the footprint of the deceased is nearly twice as deep as mine--that is to say, the lighter man has sunk into the sand nearly twice as deeply as the heavier man."

The magistrates were now deeply attentive. They were no longer simply listening to the despised utterances of a mere scientific expert. The cast lay before them with the two footprints side by side; the evidence appealed to their own senses and was proportionately convincing.

"This is very singular," said the chairman; "but perhaps you can explain the discrepancy?"

"I think I can," replied Thorndyke; "but I should prefer to place all the facts before you first."

"Undoubtedly that would be better," the chairman agreed. "Pray proceed."

"There was another remarkable peculiarity about these footprints," Thorndyke continued, "and that was their distance apart--the length of the stride, in fact. I measured the steps carefully from heel to heel, and found them only nineteen and a half inches. But a man of Hearn's height would have an ordinary stride of about thirty-six inches--more if he was walking fast. Walking with a stride of nineteen and a half inches he would look as if his legs were tied together.

"I next proceeded to the Bay, and took two moulds from the footprints of the man with the nailed shoes, a right and a left. Here is a cast from the mould, and it shows very clearly that the man was walking backwards."

"How does it show that?" asked the magistrate.

"There are several distinctive points. For instance, the absence of the usual 'kick off' at the toe, the slight drag behind the heel, showing the direction in which the foot was lifted, and the undisturbed impression of the sole."

"You have spoken of moulds and casts. What is the difference between them?"

"A mould is a direct, and therefore reversed, impression. A cast is the impression of a mould, and therefore a facsimile of the object. If I pour liquid plaster on a coin, when it sets I have a mould, a sunk impression, of the coin. If I pour melted wax into the mould I obtain a cast, a facsimile of the coin. A footprint is a mould of the foot. A mould of the footprint is a cast of the foot, and a cast from the mould reproduces the footprint."

"Thank you," said the magistrate. "Then your moulds from these two footprints are really facsimiles of the murderer's shoes, and can be compared with these shoes which have been put in evidence?"

"Yes, and when we compare them they demonstrate a very important fact."

"What is that?"

"It is that the prisoner's shoes were not the shoes that made those footprints." A buzz of astonishment ran through the court, but Thorndyke continued stolidly: "The prisoner's shoes were not in my possession, so I went on to Barker's pond, on the clay margin of which I had seen footprints actually made by the prisoner. I took moulds of those footprints, and compared them with these from the sand. There are several important differences, which you will see if you compare them. To facilitate the comparison I have made transparent photographs of both sets of moulds to the same scale. Now, if we put the photograph of the mould of the prisoner's right shoe over that of the murderer's right shoe, and hold the two superposed photographs up to the light, we cannot make the two pictures coincide. They are exactly of the same length, but the shoes are of different shape. Moreover, if we put one of the nails in one photograph over the corresponding nail in the other photograph, we cannot make the rest of the nails coincide. But the most conclusive fact of all--from which there is no possible escape--is that the number of nails in the two shoes is not the same. In the sole of the prisoner's right shoe there are forty nails; in that of the murderer there are forty-one. The murderer has one nail too many."

There was a deathly silence in the court as the magistrates and Mr. Bashfield pored over the moulds and the prisoner's shoes, and examined the photographs against the light. Then the chairman asked: "Are these all the facts, or have you something more to tell us?" He was evidently anxious to get the key to this riddle.

"There is more evidence, your Worship," said Anstey. "The witness examined the body of deceased." Then, turning to Thorndyke, he asked:

"You were present at the post-mortem examination?"

"I was."

"Did you form any opinion as to the cause of death?"

"Yes. I came to the conclusion that death was occasioned by an overdose of morphia."

A universal gasp of amazement greeted this statement. Then the presiding magistrate protested breathlessly:

"But there was a wound, which we have been told was capable of causing instantaneous death. Was that not the case?"

"There was undoubtedly such a wound," replied Thorndyke. "But when that wound was inflicted the deceased had already been dead from a quarter to half an hour."

"This is incredible!" exclaimed the magistrate. "But, no doubt, you can give us your reasons for this amazing conclusion?"

"My opinion," said Thorndyke, "was based on several facts. In the first place, a wound inflicted on a living body gapes rather widely, owing to the retraction of the living skin. The skin of a dead body does not retract, and the wound, consequently, does not gape. This wound gaped very slightly, showing that death was recent, I should say, within half an hour. Then a wound on the living body becomes filled with blood, and blood is shed freely on the clothing. But the wound on the deceased contained only a little blood-clot. There was hardly any blood on the clothing, and I had already noticed that there was none on the sand where the body had lain."

"And you consider this quite conclusive?" the magistrate asked doubtfully.

"I do," answered Thorndyke. "But there was other evidence which was beyond all question. The weapon had partially divided both the aorta and the pulmonary artery--the main arteries of the body. Now, during life, these great vessels are full of blood at a high internal pressure, whereas after death they become almost empty. It follows that, if this wound had been inflicted during life, the cavity in which those vessels lie would have become filled with blood. As a matter of fact, it contained practically no blood, only the merest oozing from some small veins, so that it is certain that the wound was inflicted after death. The presence and nature of the poison I ascertained by analyzing certain secretions from the body, and the analysis enabled me to judge that the quantity of the poison was large; but the contents of the stomach were sent to Professor Copland for more exact examination."

"Is the result of Professor Copland's analysis known?" the magistrate asked Anstey.

"The professor is here, your Worship," replied Anstey, "and is prepared to swear to having obtained over one grain of morphia from the contents of the stomach; and as this, which is in itself a poisonous dose, is only the unabsorbed residue of what was actually swallowed, the total quantity taken must have been very large indeed."

"Thank you," said the magistrate. "And now, Dr. Thorndyke, if you have given us all the facts, perhaps you will tell us what conclusions you have drawn from them."

"The facts which I have stated," said Thorndyke, "appear to me to indicate the following sequence of events. The deceased died about midnight on September 27, from the effects of a poisonous dose of morphia, how or by whom administered I offer no opinion. I think that his body was conveyed in a boat to Sundersley Gap. The boat probably contained three men, of whom one remained in charge of it, one walked up the Gap and along the cliff towards St. Bridget's Bay, and the third, having put on the shoes of the deceased, carried the body along the shore to the Bay. This would account for the great depth and short stride of the tracks that have been spoken of as those of the deceased. Having reached the Bay, I believe that this man laid the corpse down on his tracks, and then trampled the sand in the neighbourhood. He next took off deceased's shoes and put them on the corpse; then he put on a pair of boots or shoes which he had been carrying--perhaps hung round his neck-- and which had been prepared with nails to imitate Draper's shoes. In these shoes he again trampled over the area near the corpse. Then he walked backwards to the Shepherd's Path, and from it again, still backwards, to the face of the cliff. Here his accomplice had lowered a rope, by which he climbed up to the top. At the top he took off the nailed shoes, and the two men walked back to the Gap, where the man who had carried the rope took his confederate on his back, and carried him down to the boat to avoid leaving the tracks of stockinged feet. The tracks that I saw at the Gap certainly indicated that the man was carrying something very heavy when he returned to the boat."

"But why should the man have climbed a rope up the cliff when he could have walked up the Shepherd's Path?" the magistrate asked.

"Because," replied Thorndyke, "there would then have been a set of tracks leading out of the Bay without a corresponding set leading into it; and this would have instantly suggested to a smart police-officer--such as Sergeant Payne--a landing from a boat."

"Your explanation is highly ingenious," said the magistrate, "and appears to cover all the very remarkable facts. Have you anything more to tell us?"

"No, your Worship," was the reply, "excepting" (here he took from Polton the last pair of moulds and passed them up to the magistrate) "that you will probably find these moulds of importance presently."

As Thorndyke stepped from the box--for there was no cross-examination-- the magistrates scrutinized the moulds with an air of perplexity; but they were too discreet to make any remark.

When the evidence of Professor Copland (which showed that an unquestionably lethal dose of morphia must have been swallowed) had been taken, the clerk called out the--to me--unfamiliar name of Jacob Gummer. Thereupon an enormous pair of brown dreadnought trousers, from the upper end of which a smack-boy's head and shoulders protruded, walked into the witness-box.

Jacob admitted at the outset that he was a smack-master's apprentice, and that he bad been "hired out" by his master to one Mr. Jezzard as deck-hand and cabin-boy of the yacht Otter.

"Now, Gummer," said Anstey, "do you remember the prisoner coming on board the yacht?"

"Yes. He has been on board twice. The first time was about a month ago. He went for a sail with us then. The second time was on the night when Mr. Hearn was murdered."

"Do you remember what sort of boots the prisoner was wearing the first time he came?"

"Yes. They were shoes with a lot of nails in the soles. I remember them because Mr. Jezzard made him take them off and put on a canvas pair."

"What was done with the nailed shoes?"

"Mr. Jezzard took 'em below to the cabin."

"And did Mr. Jezzard come up on deck again directly?"

"No. He stayed down in the cabin about ten minutes."

"Do you remember a parcel being delivered on board from a London boot-maker?"

"Yes. The postman brought it about four or five days after Mr. Draper had been on board. It was labelled 'Walker Bros., Boot and Shoe Makers, London.' Mr. Jezzard took a pair of shoes from it, for I saw them on the locker in the cabin the same day."

"Did you ever see him wear them?"

"No. I never see 'em again."

"Have you ever heard sounds of hammering on the yacht?"

"Yes. The night after the parcel came I was on the quay alongside, and I heard someone a-hammering in the cabin."

"What did the hammering sound like?"

"It sounded like a cobbler a-hammering in nails."

"Have you over seen any boot-nails on the yacht?"

"Yes. When I was a-clearin' up the cabin the next mornin', I found a hobnail on the floor in a corner by the locker."

"Were you on board on the night when Mr. Hearn died?" "Yes. I'd been ashore, but I came aboard about half-past nine."

"Did you see Mr. Hearn go ashore?"

"I see him leave the yacht. I had turned into my bunk and gone to sleep, when Mr. Jezzard calls down to me: 'We're putting Mr. Hearn ashore,' says he; 'and then,' he says, 'we're a-going for an hour's fishing. You needn't sit up,' he says, and with that he shuts the scuttle. Then I got up and slid back the scuttle and put my head out, and I see Mr. Jezzard and Mr. Leach a-helpin' Mr. Hearn acrost the deck. Mr. Hearn he looked as if he was drunk. They got him into the boat--and a rare job they had-- and Mr. Pitford, what was in the boat already, he pushed off. And then I popped my head in again, 'cause I didn't want them to see me."

"Did they row to the steps?"

"No. I put my head out again when they were gone, and I heard 'em row round the yacht, and then pull out towards the mouth of the harbour. I couldn't see the boat, 'cause it was a very dark night."

"Very well. Now I am going to ask you about another matter. Do you know anyone of the name of Polton?"

"Yes," replied Gummer, turning a dusky red. "I've just found out his real name. I thought he was called Simmons."

"Tell us what you know about him," said Anstey, with a mischievous smile.

"Well," said the boy, with a ferocious scowl at the bland and smiling Polton, "one day he come down to the yacht when the gentlemen had gone ashore. I believe he'd seen 'em go. And he offers me ten shillin' to let him see all the boots and shoes we'd got on board. I didn't see no harm, so I turns out the whole lot in the cabin for him to look at. While he was lookin' at 'em he asks me to fetch a pair of mine from the fo'c'sle, so I fetches 'em. When I come back he was pitchin' the boots and shoes back into the locker. Then, presently, he nips off, and when he was gone I looked over the shoes, and then I found there was a pair missing. They was an old pair of Mr. Jezzard's, and what made him nick 'em is more than I can understand."

"Would you know those shoes if you saw them!"

"Yes, I should," replied the lad.

"Are these the pair?" Anstey handed the boy a pair of dilapidated canvas shoes, which he seized eagerly.

"Yes, these is the ones what he stole!" he exclaimed.

Anstey took them back from the boy's reluctant hands, and passed them up to the magistrate's desk. "I think," said he, "that if your Worship will compare these shoes with the last pair of moulds, you will have no doubt that these are the shoes which made the footprints from the sea to Sundersley Gap and back again."

The magistrates together compared the shoes and the moulds amidst a breathless silence. At length the chairman laid them down on the desk.

"It is impossible to doubt it," said he. "The broken heel and the tear in the rubber sole, with the remains of the chequered pattern, make the identity practically certain."

As the chairman made this statement I involuntarily glanced round to the place where Jezzard was sitting. But he was not there; neither he, nor Pitford, nor Leach. Taking advantage of the preoccupation of the Court, they had quietly slipped out of the door. But I was not the only person who had noted their absence. The inspector and the sergeant were already in earnest consultation, and a minute later they, too, hurriedly departed.

The proceedings now speedily came to an end. After a brief discussion with his brother-magistrates, the chairman addressed the Court.

"The remarkable and I may say startling evidence, which has been heard in this court to-day, if it has not fixed the guilt of this crime on any individual, has, at any rate, made it clear to our satisfaction that the prisoner is not the guilty person, and he is accordingly discharged. Mr. Draper, I have great pleasure in informing you that you are at liberty to leave the court, and that you do so entirely clear of all suspicion; and I congratulate you very heartily on the skill and ingenuity of your legal advisers, but for which the decision of the Court would, I am afraid, have been very different."

That evening, lawyers, witnesses, and the jubilant and grateful client gathered round a truly festive board to dine, and fight over again the battle of the day. But we were scarcely halfway through our meal when, to the indignation of the servants, Sergeant Payne burst breathlessly into the room.

"They've gone, sir!" he exclaimed, addressing Thorndyke. "They've given us the slip for good."

"Why, how can that be?" asked Thorndyke.

"They're dead, sir! All three of them!"

"Dead!" we all exclaimed.

"Yes. They made a burst for the yacht when they left the court, and they got on board and put out to sea at once, hoping, no doubt, to get clear as the light was just failing. But they were in such a hurry that they did not see a steam trawler that was entering, and was hidden by the pier. Then, just at the entrance, as the yacht was creeping out, the trawler hit her amidships, and fairly cut her in two. The three men were in the water in an instant, and were swept away in the eddy behind the north pier; and before any boat could put out to them they had all gone under. Jezzard's body came up on the beach just as I was coming away."

We were all silent and a little awed, but if any of us felt regret at the catastrophe, it was at the thought that three such cold-blooded villains should have made so easy an exit; and to one of us, at least, the news came as a blessed relief.

The Stranger's Latchkey

The contrariety of human nature is a subject that has given a surprising amount of occupation to makers of proverbs and to those moral philosophers who make it their province to discover and expound the glaringly obvious; and especially have they been concerned to enlarge upon that form of perverseness which engenders dislike of things offered under compulsion, and arouses desire of them as soon as their attainment becomes difficult or impossible. They assure us that a man who has had a given thing within his reach and put it by, will, as soon as it is beyond his reach, find it the one thing necessary and desirable; even as the domestic cat which has turned disdainfully from the preferred saucer, may presently be seen with her head jammed hard in the milk-jug, or, secretly and with horrible relish, slaking her thirst at the scullery sink.

To this peculiarity of the human mind was due, no doubt, the fact that no sooner had I abandoned the clinical side of my profession in favour of the legal, and taken up my abode in the chambers of my friend Thorndyke, the famous medico-legal expert, to act as his assistant or junior, than my former mode of life--that of a locum tenens, or minder of other men's practices--which had, when I was following it, seemed intolerably irksome, now appeared to possess many desirable features; and I found myself occasionally hankering to sit once more by the bedside, to puzzle out the perplexing train of symptoms, and to wield that power--the greatest, after all, possessed by man--the power to banish suffering and ward off the approach of death itself.

Hence it was that on a certain morning of the long vacation I found myself installed at The Larches, Burling, in full charge of the practice of my old friend Dr. Hanshaw, who was taking a fishing holiday in Norway. I was not left desolate, however, for Mrs. Hanshaw remained at her post, and the roomy, old-fashioned house accommodated three visitors in addition. One of these was Dr. Hanshaw's sister, a Mrs. Haldean, the widow of a wealthy Manchester cotton factor; the second was her niece by marriage, Miss Lucy Haldean, a very handsome and charming girl of twenty-three; while the third was no less a person than Master Fred, the only child of Mrs. Haldean, and a strapping boy of six.

"It is quite like old times--and very pleasant old times, too--to see you sitting at our breakfast-table, Dr. Jervis." With these gracious words and a friendly smile, Mrs. Hanshaw handed me my tea-cup.

I bowed. "The highest pleasure of the altruist," I replied, "is in contemplating the good fortune of others."

Mrs. Haldean laughed. "Thank you," she said. "You are quite unchanged, I perceive. Still as suave and as--shall I say oleaginous?"

"No, please don't!" I exclaimed in a tone of alarm.

"Then I won't. But what does Dr. Thorndyke say to this backsliding on your part? How does he regard this relapse from medical jurisprudence to common general practice?"

"Thorndyke," said I, "is unmoved by any catastrophe; and he not only regards the 'Decline and Fall-off of the Medical Jurist' with philosophic calm, but he even favours the relapse, as you call it. He thinks it may be useful to me to study the application of medico-legal methods to general practice."

"That sounds rather unpleasant--for the patients, I mean," remarked Miss Haldean.

"Very," agreed her aunt. "Most cold-blooded. What sort of man is Dr. Thorndyke? I feel quite curious about him. Is he at all human, for instance?"

"He is entirely human," I replied; "the accepted tests of humanity being, as I understand, the habitual adoption of the erect posture in locomotion, and the relative position of the end of the thumb--"

"I don't mean that," interrupted Mrs. Haldean. "I mean human in things that matter."

"I think those things matter," I rejoined. "Consider, Mrs. Haldean, what would happen if my learned colleague were to be seen in wig and gown, walking towards the Law Courts in any posture other than the erect. It would be a public scandal."

"Don't talk to him, Mabel," said Mrs. Hanshaw; "he is incorrigible. What are you doing with yourself this morning, Lucy?"

Miss Haldean (who had hastily set down her cup to laugh at my imaginary picture of Dr. Thorndyke in the character of a quadruped) considered a moment.

"I think I shall sketch that group of birches at the edge of Bradham Wood," she said.

"Then, in that case," said I, "I can carry your traps for you, for I have to see a patient in Bradham."

"He is making the most of his time," remarked Mrs. Haldean maliciously to my hostess. "He knows that when Mr. Winter arrives he will retire into the extreme background."

Douglas Winter, whose arrival was expected in the course of the week, was Miss Haldean's fiancé. Their engagement had been somewhat protracted, and was likely to be more so, unless one of them received some unexpected accession of means; for Douglas was a subaltern in the Royal Engineers, living, with great difficulty, on his pay, while Lucy Haldean subsisted on an almost invisible allowance left her by an uncle.

I was about to reply to Mrs. Haldean when a patient was announced, and, as I had finished my breakfast, I made my excuses and left the table.

Half an hour later, when I started along the road to the village of Bradham, I had two companions. Master Freddy had joined the party, and he disputed with me the privilege of carrying the "traps," with the result that a compromise was effected, by which he carried the camp-stool, leaving me in possession of the easel, the bag, and a large bound sketching-block.

"Where are you going to work this morning?" I asked, when we had trudged on some distance.

"Just off the road to the left there, at the edge of the wood. Not very far from the house of the mysterious stranger." She glanced at me mischievously as she made this reply, and chuckled with delight when I rose at the bait.

"What house do you mean?" I inquired.

"Ha!" she exclaimed, "the investigator of mysteries is aroused. He saith, 'Ha! ha!' amidst the trumpets; he smelleth the battle afar off."

"Explain instantly," I commanded, "or I drop your sketch-block into the very next puddle."

"You terrify me," said she. "But I will explain, only there isn't any mystery except to the bucolic mind. The house is called Lavender Cottage, and it stands alone in the fields behind the wood. A fortnight ago it was let furnished to a stranger named Whitelock, who has taken it for the purpose of studying the botany of the district; and the only really mysterious thing about him is that no one has seen him. All arrangements with the house-agent were made by letter, and, as far as I can make out, none of the local tradespeople supply him, so he must get his things from a distance--even his bread, which really is rather odd. Now say I am an inquisitive, gossiping country bumpkin."

"I was going to," I answered, "but it is no use now."

She relieved me of her sketching appliances with pretended indignation, and crossed into the meadow, leaving me to pursue my way alone; and when I presently looked back, she was setting up her easel and stool, gravely assisted by Freddy.

My "round," though not a long one, took up more time than I had anticipated, and it was already past the luncheon hour when I passed the place where I had left Miss Haldean. She was gone, as I had expected, and I hurried homewards, anxious to be as nearly punctual as possible. When I entered the dining-room, I found Mrs. Haldean and our hostess seated at the table, and both looked up at me expectantly.

"Have you seen Lucy?" the former inquired.

"No," I answered. "Hasn't she come back? I expected to find her here. She had left the wood when I passed just now."

Mrs. Haldean knitted her brows anxiously. "It is very strange," she said, "and very thoughtless of her. Freddy will be famished."

I hurried over my lunch, for two fresh messages had come in from outlying hamlets, effectually dispelling my visions of a quiet afternoon; and as the minutes passed without bringing any signs of the absentees, Mrs. Haldean became more and more restless and anxious. At length her suspense became unbearable; she rose suddenly, announcing her intention of cycling up the road to look for the defaulters, but as she was moving towards the door, it burst open, and Lucy Haldean staggered into the room.

Her appearance filled us with alarm. She was deadly pale, breathless, and wild-eyed; her dress was draggled and torn, and she trembled from head to foot.

"Good God, Lucy!" gasped Mrs. Haldean. "What has happened? And where is Freddy?" she added in a sterner tone.

"He is lost!" replied Miss Haldean in a faint voice, and with a catch in her breath. "He strayed away while I was painting. I have searched the wood through, and called to him, and looked in all the meadows. Oh! where can he have gone?" Her sketching "kit," with which she was loaded, slipped from her grasp and rattled on to the floor, and she buried her face in her hands and sobbed hysterically.

"And you have dared to come back without him?" exclaimed Mrs. Haldean.

"I was getting exhausted. I came back for help," was the faint reply.

"Of course she was exhausted," said Mrs. Hanshaw. "Come, Lucy: come, Mabel; don't make mountains out of molehills. The little man is safe enough. We shall find him presently, or he will come home by himself. Come and have some food, Lucy."

Miss Haldean shook her head. "I can't, Mrs. Hanshaw--really I can't," she said; and, seeing that she was in a state of utter exhaustion, I poured out a glass of wine and made her drink it.

Mrs. Haldean darted from the room, and returned immediately, putting on her hat. "You have got to come with me and show me whore you lost him," she said.

"She can't do that, you know," I said rather brusquely. "She will have to lie down for the present. But I know the place, and will cycle up with you."

"Very well," replied Mrs. Haldean, "that will do. What time was it," she asked, turning to her niece, "when you lost the child? and which way--"

She paused abruptly, and I looked at her in surprise. She had suddenly turned ashen and ghastly; her face had set like a mask of stone, with parted lips and staring eyes that were fixed in horror on her niece.

There was a deathly silence for a few seconds. Then, in a terrible voice, she demanded: "What is that on your dress, Lucy?" And, after a pause, her voice rose into a shriek. "What have you done to my boy?"

I glanced in astonishment at the dazed and terrified girl, and then I saw what her aunt had seen--a good-sized blood-stain halfway down the front of her skirt, and another smaller one on her right sleeve. The girl herself looked down at the sinister patch of red and then up at her aunt. "It looks like--like blood," she stammered. "Yes, it is--I think--of course it is. He struck his nose--and it bled--"

"Come," interrupted Mrs. Haldean, "let us go," and she rushed from the room, leaving me to follow.

I lifted Miss Haldean, who was half fainting with fatigue and agitation, on to the sofa, and, whispering a few words of encouragement into her ear, turned to Mrs. Hanshaw.

"I can't stay with Mrs. Haldean," I said. "There are two visits to be made at Rebworth. Will you send the dogcart up the road with somebody to take my place?"

"Yes," she answered. "I will send Giles, or come myself if Lucy is fit to be left."

I ran to the stables for my bicycle, and as I pedalled out into the road I could see Mrs. Haldean already far ahead, driving her machine at frantic speed. I followed at a rapid pace, but it was not until we approached the commencement of the wood, when she slowed down somewhat, that I overtook her.

"This is the place," I said, as we reached the spot where I had parted from Miss Haldean. We dismounted and wheeled our bicycles through the gate, and laying them down beside the hedge, crossed the meadow and entered the wood.

It was a terrible experience, and one that I shall never forget--the white-faced, distracted woman, tramping in her flimsy house-shoes over the rough ground, bursting through the bushes, regardless of the thorny branches that dragged at skin and hair and dainty clothing, and sending forth from time to time a tremulous cry, so dreadfully pathetic in its mingling of terror and coaxing softness, that a lump rose in my throat, and I could barely keep my self-control.

"Freddy! Freddy-boy! Mummy's here, darling!" The wailing cry sounded through the leafy solitude; but no answer came save the whirr of wings or the chatter of startled birds. But even more shocking than that terrible cry--more disturbing and eloquent with dreadful suggestion--was the way in which she peered, furtively, but with fearful expectation, among the roots of the bushes, or halted to gaze upon every molehill and hummock, every depression or disturbance of the ground.

So we stumbled on for a while, with never a word spoken, until we came to a beaten track or footpath leading across the wood. Here I paused to examine the footprints, of which several were visible in the soft earth, though none seemed very recent; but, proceeding a little way down the track, I perceived, crossing it, a set of fresh imprints, which I recognized at once as Miss Haldean's. She was wearing, as I knew, a pair of brown golf-boots, with rubber pads in the leather soles, and the prints made by them were unmistakable.

"Miss Haldean crossed the path here," I said, pointing to the footprints.

"Don't speak of her before me!" exclaimed Mrs. Haldean; but she gazed eagerly at the footprints, nevertheless, and immediately plunged into the wood to follow the tracks.

"You are very unjust to your niece, Mrs. Haldean," I ventured to protest.

She halted, and faced me with an angry frown.

"You don't understand!" she exclaimed. "You don't know, perhaps, that if my poor child is really dead, Lucy Haldean will be a rich woman, and may marry to-morrow if she chooses?"

"I did not know that," I answered, "but if I had, I should have said the same."

"Of course you would," she retorted bitterly. "A pretty face can muddle any man's judgment."

She turned away abruptly to resume her pursuit, and I followed in silence. The trail which we were following zigzagged through the thickest part of the wood, but its devious windings eventually brought us out on to an open space on the farther side. Here we at once perceived traces of another kind. A litter of dirty rags, pieces of paper, scraps of stale bread, bones and feathers, with hoof-marks, wheel ruts, and the ashes of a large wood fire, pointed clearly to a gipsy encampment recently broken up. I laid my hand on the heap of ashes, and found it still warm, and on scattering it with my foot a layer of glowing cinders appeared at the bottom.

"These people have only been gone an hour or two," I said. "It would be well to have them followed without delay."

A gleam of hope shone on the drawn, white face as the bereaved mother caught eagerly at my suggestion.

"Yes," she exclaimed breathlessly; "she may have bribed them to take him away. Let us see which way they went."

We followed the wheel tracks down to the road, and found that they turned towards London. At the same time I perceived the dogcart in the distance, with Mrs. Hanshaw standing beside it; and, as the coachman observed me, he whipped up his horse and approached.

"I shall have to go," I said, "but Mrs. Hanshaw will help you to continue the search."

"And you will make inquiries about the gipsies, won't you?" she said.

I promised to do so, and as the dogcart now came up, I climbed to the seat, and drove off briskly up the London Road.

The extent of a country doctor's round is always an unknown quantity. On the present occasion I picked up three additional patients, and as one of them was a case of incipient pleurisy, which required to have the chest strapped, and another was a neglected dislocation of the shoulder, a great deal of time was taken up. Moreover, the gipsies, whom I ran to earth on Rebworth Common, delayed me considerably, though I had to leave the rural constable to carry out the actual search, and, as a result, the clock of Burling Church was striking six as I drove through the village on my way home.

I got down at the front gate, leaving the coachman to take the dogcart round, and walked up the drive; and my astonishment may be imagined when, on turning the corner, I came suddenly upon the inspector of the local police in earnest conversation with no less a person than John Thorndyke.

"What on earth has brought you here?" I exclaimed, my surprise getting the better of my manners.

"The ultimate motive-force," he replied, "was an impulsive lady named Mrs. Haldean. She telegraphed for me--in your name."

"She oughtn't to have done that," I said.

"Perhaps not. But the ethics of an agitated woman are not worth discussing, and she has done something much worse--she has applied to the local J.P. (a retired Major-General), and our gallant and unlearned friend has issued a warrant for the arrest of Lucy Haldean on the charge of murder."

"But there has been no murder!" I exclaimed.

"That," said Thorndyke, "is a legal subtlety that he does not appreciate. He has learned his law in the orderly-room, where the qualifications to practise are an irritable temper and a loud voice. However, the practical point is, inspector, that the warrant is irregular. You can't arrest people for hypothetical crimes."

The officer drew a deep breath of relief. He knew all about the irregularity, and now joyfully took refuge behind Thorndyke's great reputation.

When he had departed--with a brief note from my colleague to the General--Thorndyke slipped his arm through mine, and we strolled towards the house.

"This is a grim business, Jervis," said he. "That boy has got to be found for everybody's sake. Can you come with me when you have had some food?"

"Of course I can. I have been saving myself all the afternoon with a view to continuing the search."

"Good," said Thorndyke. "Then come in and feed."

A nondescript meal, half tea and half dinner, was already prepared, and Mrs. Hanshaw, grave but self-possessed, presided at the table.

"Mabel is still out with Giles, searching for the boy," she said. "You have heard what she has done!"

I nodded.

"It was dreadful of her," continued Mrs. Hanshaw, "but she is half mad, poor thing. You might run up and say a few kind words to poor Lucy while I make the tea."

I went up at once and knocked at Miss Haldean's door, and, being bidden to enter, found her lying on the sofa, red-eyed and pale, the very ghost of the merry, laughing girl who had gone out with me in the morning. I drew up a chair, and sat down by her side, and as I took the hand she held out to me, she said:

"It is good of you to come and see a miserable wretch like me. And Jane has been so sweet to me, Dr. Jervis; but Aunt Mabel thinks I have killed Freddy--you know she does--and it was really my fault that he was lost. I shall never forgive myself!"

She burst into a passion of sobbing, and I proceeded to chide her gently.

"You are a silly little woman," I said, "to take this nonsense to heart as you are doing. Your aunt is not responsible just now, as you must know; but when we bring the boy home she shall make you a handsome apology. I will see to that."

She pressed my hand gratefully, and as the bell now rang for tea, I bade her have courage and went downstairs.

"You need not trouble about the practice," said Mrs. Hanshaw, as I concluded my lightning repast, and Thorndyke went off to get our bicycles. "Dr. Symons has heard of our trouble, and has called to say that he will take anything that turns up; so we shall expect you when we see you."

"How do you like Thorndyke?" I asked.

"He is quite charming," she replied enthusiastically; "so tactful and kind, and so handsome, too. You didn't tell us that. But here he is. Good-bye, and good luck."

She pressed my hand, and I went out into the drive, where Thorndyke and the coachman were standing with three bicycles.

"I see you have brought your outfit," I said as we turned into the road; for Thorndyke's machine bore a large canvas-covered case strapped on to a strong bracket.

"Yes; there are many things that we may want on a quest of this kind. How did you find Miss Haldean?"

"Very miserable, poor girl. By the way, have you heard anything about her pecuniary interest in the child's death?"

"Yes," said Thorndyke. "It appears that the late Mr. Haldean used up all his brains on his business, and had none left for the making of his will--as often happens. He left almost the whole of his property--about eighty thousand pounds--to his son, the widow to have a life-interest in it. He also left to his late brother's daughter, Lucy, fifty pounds a year, and to his surviving brother Percy, who seems to have been a good-for-nothing, a hundred a year for life. But--and here is the utter folly of the thing--if the son should die, the property was to be equally divided between the brother and the niece, with the exception of five hundred a year for life to the widow. It was an insane arrangement."

"Quite," I agreed, "and a very dangerous one for Lucy Haldean, as things are at present."

"Very; especially if anything should have happened to the child."

"What are you going to do now?" I inquired, seeing that Thorndyke rode on as if with a definite purpose.

"There is a footpath through the wood," he replied. "I want to examine that. And there is a house behind the wood which I should like to see."

"The house of the mysterious stranger," I suggested.

"Precisely. Mysterious and solitary strangers invite inquiry."

We drew up at the entrance to the footpath, leaving Willett the coachman in charge of the three machines, and proceeded up the narrow track. As we went, Thorndyke looked back at the prints of our feet, and nodded approvingly.

"This soft loam," he remarked, "yields beautifully clear impressions, and yesterday's rain has made it perfect."

We had not gone far when we perceived a set of footprints which I recognized, as did Thorndyke also, for he remarked: "Miss Haldean-- running, and alone." Presently we met them again, crossing in the opposite direction, together with the prints of small shoes with very high heels. "Mrs. Haldean on the track of her niece," was Thorndyke's comment; and a minute later we encountered them both again, accompanied by my own footprints.

"The boy does not seem to have crossed the path at all," I remarked as we walked on, keeping off the track itself to avoid confusing the footprints.

"We shall know when we have examined the whole length," replied Thorndyke, plodding on with his eyes on the ground. "Ha! here is something new," he added, stopping short and stooping down eagerly--"a man with a thick stick--a smallish man, rather lame. Notice the difference between the two feet, and the peculiar way in which he uses his stick. Yes, Jervis, there is a great deal to interest us in these footprints. Do you notice anything very suggestive about them?"

"Nothing but what you have mentioned," I replied. "What do you mean?"

"Well, first there is the very singular character of the prints themselves, which we will consider presently. You observe that this man came down the path, and at this point turned off into the wood; then he returned from the wood and went up the path again. The imposition of the prints makes that clear. But now look at the two sets of prints, and compare them. Do you notice any difference?"

"The returning footprints seem more distinct--better impressions."

"Yes; they are noticeably deeper. But there is something else." He produced a spring tape from his pocket, and took half a dozen measurements. "You see," he said, "the first set of footprints have a stride of twenty-one inches from heel to heel--a short stride; but he is a smallish man, and lame; the returning ones have a stride of only nineteen and a half inches; hence the returning footprints are deeper than the others, and the steps are shorter. What do you make of that?"

"It would suggest that he was carrying a burden when he returned," I replied.

"Yes; and a heavy one, to make that difference in the depth. I think I will get you to go and fetch Willett and the bicycles."

I strode off down the path to the entrance, and, taking possession of Thorndyke's machine, with its precious case of instruments, bade Willett follow with the other two.

When I returned, my colleague was standing with his hands behind him, gazing with intense preoccupation at the footprints. He looked up sharply as we approached, and called out to us to keep off the path if possible.

"Stay here with the machines, Willett," said he. "You and I, Jervis, must go and see where our friend went to when he left the path, and what was the burden that he picked up."

We struck off into the wood, where last year's dead leaves made the footprints almost indistinguishable, and followed the faint double track for a long distance between the dense clumps of bushes. Suddenly my eye caught, beside the double trail, a third row of tracks, smaller in size and closer together. Thorndyke had seen them, too, and already his measuring-tape was in his hand.

"Eleven and a half inches to the stride," said he. "That will be the boy, Jervis. But the light is getting weak. We must press on quickly, or we shall lose it."

Some fifty yards farther on, the man's tracks ceased abruptly, but the small ones continued alone; and we followed them as rapidly as we could in the fading light.

"There can be no reasonable doubt that these are the child's tracks," said Thorndyke; "but I should like to find a definite footprint to make the identification absolutely certain."

A few seconds later he halted with an exclamation, and stooped on one knee. A little heap of fresh earth from the surface-burrow of a mole had been thrown up over the dead leaves; and fairly planted on it was the clean and sharp impression of a diminutive foot, with a rubber heel showing a central star. Thorndyke drew from his pocket a tiny shoe, and pressed it on the soft earth beside the footprint; and when he raised it the second impression was identical with the first.

"The boy had two pairs of shoes exactly alike," he said, "so I borrowed one of the duplicate pair."

He turned, and began to retrace his steps rapidly, following our own fresh tracks, and stopping only once to point out the place where the unknown man had picked the child up. When we regained the path we proceeded without delay until we emerged from the wood within a hundred yards of the cottage.

"I see Mrs. Haldean has been here with Giles," remarked Thorndyke, as he pushed open the garden-gate. "I wonder if they saw anybody."

He advanced to the door, and having first rapped with his knuckles and then kicked at it vigorously, tried the handle.

"Locked," he observed, "but I see the key is in the lock, so we can get in if we want to. Let us try the back."

The back door was locked, too, but the key had been removed.

"He came out this way, evidently," said Thorndyke. "though he went in at the front, as I suppose you noticed. Let us see where he went."

The back garden was a small, fenced patch of ground, with an earth path leading down to the back gate. A little way beyond the gate was a small barn or outhouse.

"We are in luck," Thorndyke remarked, with a glance at the path. "Yesterday's rain has cleared away all old footprints, and prepared the surface for new ones. You see there are three sets of excellent impressions--two leading away from the house, and one set towards it. Now, you notice that both of the sets leading from the house are characterized by deep impressions and short steps, while the set leading to the house has lighter impressions and longer steps. The obvious inference is that he went down the path with a heavy burden, came back empty-handed, and went down again--and finally--with another heavy burden. You observe, too, that he walked with his stick on each occasion."

By this time we had reached the bottom of the garden. Opening the gate, we followed the tracks towards the outhouse, which stood beside a cart-track; but as we came round the corner we both stopped short and looked at one another. On the soft earth were the very distinct impressions of the tyres of a motor-car leading from the wide door of the outhouse. Finding that the door was unfastened, Thorndyke opened it, and looked in, to satisfy himself that the place was empty. Then he fell to studying the tracks.

"The course of events is pretty plain," he observed. "First the fellow brought down his luggage, started the engine, and got the car out--you can see where it stood, both by the little pool of oil, and by the widening and blurring of the wheel-tracks from the vibration of the free engine; then he went back and fetched the boy--carried him pick-a-back, I should say, judging by the depth of the toe-marks in the last set of footprints. That was a tactical mistake. He should have taken the boy straight into the shed."

He pointed as he spoke to one of the footprints beside the wheel-tracks, from the toe of which projected a small segment of the print of a little rubber heel.

We now made our way back to the house, where we found Willett pensively rapping at the front door with a cycle-spanner. Thorndyke took a last glance, with his hand in his pocket, at an open window above, and then, to the coachman's intense delight, brought forth what looked uncommonly like a small bunch of skeleton keys. One of these he inserted into the keyhole, and as he gave it a turn, the lock clicked, and the door stood open.

The little sitting-room, which we now entered, was furnished with the barest necessaries. Its centre was occupied by an oilcloth-covered table, on which I observed with surprise a dismembered "Bee" clock (the works of which had been taken apart with a tin-opener that lay beside them) and a box-wood bird-call. At these objects Thorndyke glanced and nodded, as though they fitted into some theory that he had formed; examined carefully the oilcloth around the litter of wheels and pinions, and then proceeded on a tour of inspection round the room, peering inquisitively into the kitchen and store-cupboard.

"Nothing very distinctive or personal here," he remarked. "Let us go upstairs."

There were three bedrooms on the upper floor, of which two were evidently disused, though the windows were wide open. The third bedroom showed manifest traces of occupation, though it was as bare as the others, for the water still stood in the wash-hand basin, and the bed was unmade. To the latter Thorndyke advanced, and, having turned back the bedclothes, examined the interior attentively, especially at the foot and the pillow. The latter was soiled--not to say grimy--though the rest of the bed-linen was quite clean.

"Hair-dye," remarked Thorndyke, noting my glance at it; then he turned and looked out of the open window. "Can you see the place where Miss Haldean was sitting to sketch?" he asked.

"Yes," I replied; "there is the place well in view, and you can see right up the road. I had no idea this house stood so high. From the three upper windows you can see all over the country excepting through the wood."

"Yes," Thorndyke rejoined, "and he has probably been in the habit of keeping watch up here with a telescope or a pair of field-glasses. Well, there is not much of interest in this room. He kept his effects in a cabin trunk which stood there under the window. He shaved this morning. He has a white beard, to judge by the stubble on the shaving-paper, and that is all. Wait, though. There is a key hanging on that nail. He must have overlooked that, for it evidently does not belong to this house. It is an ordinary town latchkey."

He took the key down, and having laid a sheet of notepaper, from his pocket, on the dressing-table, produced a pin, with which he began carefully to probe the interior of the key-barrel. Presently there came forth, with much coaxing, a large ball of grey fluff, which Thorndyke folded up in the paper with infinite care.

"I suppose we mustn't take away the key," he said, "but I think we will take a wax mould of it."

He hurried downstairs, and, unstrapping the case from his bicycle, brought it in and placed it on the table. As it was now getting dark, he detached the powerful acetylene lamp from his machine, and, having lighted it, proceeded to open the mysterious case. First he took from it a small insufflator, or powder-blower, with which he blew a cloud of light yellow powder over the table around the remains of the clock. The powder settled on the table in an even coating, but when he blew at it smartly with his breath, it cleared off, leaving, however, a number of smeary impressions which stood out in strong yellow against the black oilcloth. To one of these impressions he pointed significantly. It was the print of a child's hand.

He next produced a small, portable microscope and some glass slides and cover-slips, and having opened the paper and tipped the ball of fluff from the key-barrel on to a slide, set to work with a pair of mounted needles to tease it out into its component parts. Then he turned the light of the lamp on to the microscope mirror and proceeded to examine the specimen.

"A curious and instructive assortment this, Jervis," he remarked, with his eye at the microscope: "woollen fibres--no cotton or linen; he is careful of his health to have woollen pockets--and two hairs; very curious ones, too. Just look at them, and observe the root bulbs."

I applied my eye to the microscope, and saw, among other things, two hairs--originally white, but encrusted with a black, opaque, glistening stain. The root bulbs, I noticed, were shrivelled and atrophied.

"But how on earth," I exclaimed, "did the hairs get into his pocket?"

"I think the hairs themselves answer that question," he replied, "when considered with the other curios. The stain is obviously lead sulphide; but what else do you see?"

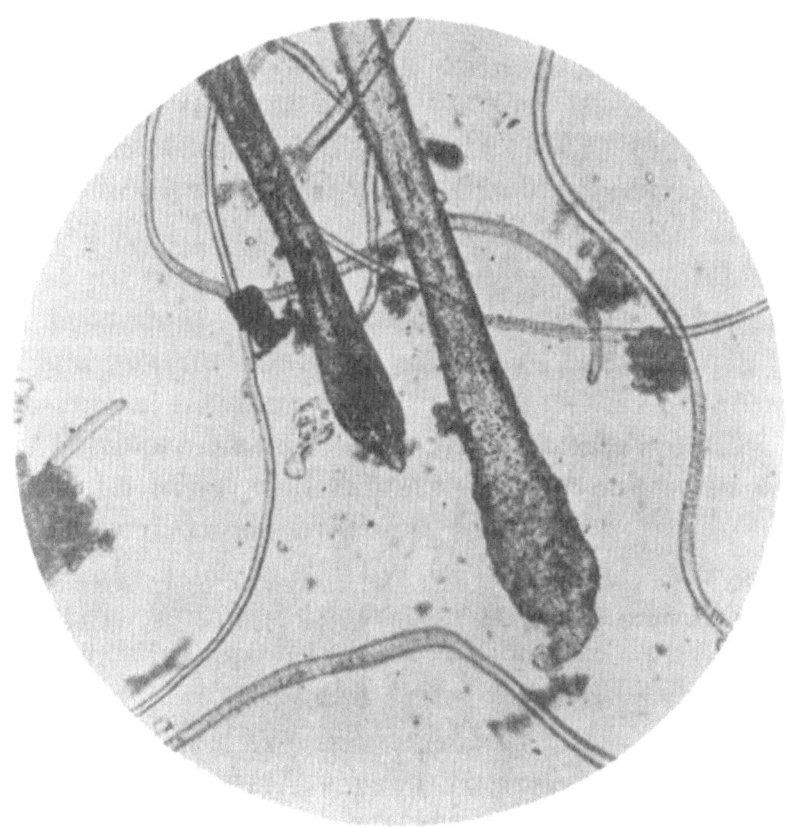

FLUFF FROM KEY-BARREL, MAGNIFIED 77 DIAMETERS.

"I see some particles of metal--a white metal apparently--and a number of fragments of woody fibre and starch granules, but I don't recognize the starch. It is not wheat-starch, nor rice, nor potato. Do you make out what it is?"

Thorndyke chuckled. "Experientia does it," said he. "You will have, Jervis, to study the minute properties of dust and dirt. Their evidential value is immense. Let us have another look at that starch; it is all alike, I suppose."

It was; and Thorndyke had just ascertained the fact when the door burst open and Mrs. Haldean entered the room, followed by Mrs. Hanshaw and the police inspector. The former lady regarded my colleague with a glance of extreme disfavour.

"We heard that you had come here, sir," said she, "and we supposed you were engaged in searching for my poor child. But it seems we were mistaken, since we find you here amusing yourselves fiddling with these nonsensical instruments."

"Perhaps, Mabel," said Mrs. Hanshaw stiffly, "it would be wiser, and infinitely more polite, to ask if Dr. Thorndyke has any news for us."

"That is undoubtedly so, madam," agreed the inspector, who had apparently suffered also from Mrs. Haldean's impulsiveness.

"Then perhaps," the latter lady suggested, "you will inform us if you have discovered anything."

"I will tell you." replied Thorndyke, "all that we know. The child was abducted by the man who occupied this house, and who appears to have watched him from an upper window, probably through a glass. This man lured the child into the wood by blowing this bird-call; he met him in the wood, and induced him--by some promises, no doubt--to come with him. He picked the child up and carried him--on his back, I think--up to the house, and brought him in through the front door, which he locked after him. He gave the boy this clock and the bird-call to amuse him while he went upstairs and packed his trunk. He took the trunk out through the back door and down the garden to the shed there, in which he had a motor-car. He got the car out and came back for the boy, whom he carried down to the car, locking the back door after him. Then he drove away."

"You know he has gone," cried Mrs. Haldean, "and yet you stay here playing with these ridiculous toys. Why are you not following him?"

"We have just finished ascertaining the facts," Thorndyke replied calmly, "and should by now be on the road if you had not come."

Here the inspector interposed anxiously. "Of course, sir, you can't give any description of the man. You have no clue to his identity, I suppose?"

"We have only his footprints," Thorndyke answered, "and this fluff which I raked out of the barrel of his latchkey, and have just been examining. From these data I conclude that he is a rather short and thin man, and somewhat lame. He walks with the aid of a thick stick, which has a knob, not a crook, at the top, and which he carries in his left hand. I think that his left leg has been amputated above the knee, and that he wears an artificial limb. He is elderly, he shaves his beard, has white hair dyed a greyish black, is partly bald, and probably combs a wisp of hair over the bald place; he takes snuff, and carries a leaden comb in his pocket."

As Thorndyke's description proceeded, the inspector's mouth gradually opened wider and wider, until he appeared the very type and symbol of astonishment. But its effect on Mrs. Haldean was much more remarkable. Rising from her chair, she leaned on the table and stared at Thorndyke with an expression of awe--even of terror; and as he finished she sank back into her chair, with her hands clasped, and turned to Mrs. Hanshaw.

"Jane!" she gasped, "it is Percy--my brother-in-law! He has described him exactly, even to his stick and his pocket-comb. But I thought he was in Chicago."

"If that is so," said Thorndyke, hastily repacking his case, "we had better start at once."

"We have the dogcart in the road," said Mrs. Hanshaw.

"Thank you," replied Thorndyke. "We will ride on our bicycles, and the inspector can borrow Willett's. We go out at the back by the cart-track, which joins the road farther on."

"Then we will follow in the dogcart," said Mrs. Haldean. "Come, Jane."

The two ladies departed down the path, while we made ready our bicycles and lit our lamps.

"With your permission, inspector," said Thorndyke, "we will take the key with us."

"It's hardly legal, sir," objected the officer. "We have no authority."

"It is quite illegal," answered Thorndyke; "but it is necessary; and necessity--like your military J.P.--knows no law."

The inspector grinned and went out, regarding me with a quivering eyelid as Thorndyke locked the door with his skeleton key. As we turned into the road, I saw the light of the dogcart behind us, and we pushed forward at a swift pace, picking up the trail easily on the soft, moist road.

"What beats me," said the inspector confidentially, as we rode along, "is how he knew the man was bald. Was it the footprints or the latchkey? And that comb, too, that was a regular knock-out."

These points were, by now, pretty clear to me. I had seen the hairs with their atrophied bulbs--such as one finds at the margin of a bald patch; and the comb was used, evidently, for the double purpose of keeping the bald patch covered and blackening the sulphur-charged hair. But the knobbed stick and the artificial limb puzzled me so completely that I presently overtook Thorndyke to demand an explanation.

"The stick," said he, "is perfectly simple. The ferrule of a knobbed stick wears evenly all round; that of a crooked stick wears on one side-- the side opposite the crook. The impressions showed that the ferrule of this one was evenly convex; therefore it had no crook. The other matter is more complicated. To begin with, an artificial foot makes a very characteristic impression, owing to its purely passive elasticity, as I will show you to-morrow. But an artificial leg fitted below the knee is quite secure, whereas one fitted above the knee--that is, with an artificial knee-joint worked by a spring--is much less reliable. Now, this man had an artificial foot, and he evidently distrusted his knee-joint, as is shown by his steadying it with his stick on the same side. If he had merely had a weak leg, he would have used the stick with his right hand--with the natural swing of the arm, in fact--unless he had been very lame, which he evidently was not. Still, it was only a question of probability, though the probability was very great. Of course, you understand that those particles of woody fibre and starch granules were disintegrated snuff-grains."

This explanation, like the others, was quite simple when one had heard it, though it gave me material for much thought as we pedalled on along the dark road, with Thorndyke's light flickering in front, and the dogcart pattering in our wake. But there was ample time for reflection; for our pace rather precluded conversation, and we rode on, mile after mile, until my legs ached with fatigue. On and on we went through village after village, now losing the trail in some frequented street, but picking it up again unfailingly as we emerged on to the country road, until at last, in the paved High Street of the little town of Horsefield, we lost it for good. We rode on through the town out on to the country road; but although there were several tracks of motors, Thorndyke shook his head at them all. "I have been studying those tyres until I know them by heart," he said. "No; either he is in the town, or he has left it by a side road."

There was nothing for it but to put up the horse and the machines at the hotel, while we walked round to reconnoitre; and this we did, tramping up one street and down another, with eyes bent on the ground, fruitlessly searching for a trace of the missing car.

Suddenly, at the door of a blacksmith's shop, Thorndyke halted. The shop had been kept open late for the shoeing of a carriage horse, which was just being led away, and the smith had come to the door for a breath of air. Thorndyke accosted him genially.

"Good-evening. You are just the man I wanted to see. I have mislaid the address of a friend of mine, who, I think, called on you this afternoon-- a lame gentleman who walks with a stick. I expect he wanted you to pick a lock or make him a key."

"Oh, I remember him!" said the man. "Yes, he had lost his latchkey, and wanted the lock picked before he could get into his house. Had to leave his motor-car outside while he came here. But I took some keys round with me, and fitted one to his latch."

He then directed us to a house at the end of a street close by, and, having thanked him, we went off in high spirits.

"How did you know he had been there?" I asked.

"I didn't; but there was the mark of a stick and part of a left foot on the soft earth inside the doorway, and the thing was inherently probable, so I risked a false shot."

The house stood alone at the far end of a straggling street, and was enclosed by a high wall, in which, on the side facing the street, was a door and a wide carriage-gate. Advancing to the former, Thorndyke took from his pocket the purloined key, and tried it in the lock. It fitted perfectly, and when he had turned it and pushed open the door, we entered a small courtyard. Crossing this, we came to the front door of the house, the latch of which fortunately fitted the same key; and this having been opened by Thorndyke, we trooped into the hall. Immediately we heard the sound of an opening door above, and a reedy, nasal voice sang out:

"Hello, there! Who's that below?"

The voice was followed by the appearance of a head projecting over the baluster rail.

"You are Mr. Percy Haldean, I think," said the inspector. At the mention of this name, the head was withdrawn, and a quick tread was heard, accompanied by the tapping of a stick on the floor. We started to ascend the stairs, the inspector leading, as the authorized official; but we had only gone up a few steps, when a fierce, wiry little man danced out on to the landing, with a thick stick in one hand and a very large revolver in the other.

"Move another step, either of you," he shouted, pointing the weapon at the inspector, "and I let fly; and mind you, when I shoot I hit."

He looked as if he meant it, and we accordingly halted with remarkable suddenness, while the inspector proceeded to parley.

"Now, what's the good of this, Mr. Haldean?" said he. "The game's up, and you know it."

"You clear out of my house, and clear out sharp," was the inhospitable rejoinder, "or you'll give me the trouble of burying you in the garden."

I looked round to consult with Thorndyke, when, to my amazement, I found that he had vanished--apparently through the open hall-door. I was admiring his discretion when the inspector endeavoured to reopen negotiations, but was cut short abruptly.

"I am going to count fifty," said Mr. Haldean, "and if you aren't gone then, I shall shoot."

He began to count deliberately, and the inspector looked round at me in complete bewilderment. The flight of stairs was a long one, and well lighted by gas, so that to rush it was an impossibility. Suddenly my heart gave a bound and I held my breath, for out of an open door behind our quarry, a figure emerged slowly and noiselessly on to the landing. It was Thorndyke, shoeless, and in his shirt-sleeves.

Slowly and with cat-like stealthiness, he crept across the landing until he was within a yard of the unconscious fugitive, and still the nasal voice droned on, monotonously counting out the allotted seconds.

"Forty-one, forty-two, forty-three--"

There was a lightning-like movement--a shout--a flash--a bang--a shower of falling plaster, and then the revolver came clattering down the stairs. The inspector and I rushed up, and in a moment the sharp click of the handcuffs told Mr. Percy Haldean that the game was really up.

Five minutes later Freddy-boy, half asleep, but wholly cheerful, was borne on Thorndyke's shoulders into the private sitting-room of the Black Horse Hotel. A shriek of joy saluted his entrance, and a shower of maternal kisses brought him to the verge of suffocation. Finally, the impulsive Mrs. Haldean, turning suddenly to Thorndyke, seized both his hands, and for a moment I hoped that she was going to kiss him, too. But he was spared, and I have not yet recovered from the disappointment.

The Anthropologist at Large

Thorndyke was not a newspaper reader. He viewed with extreme disfavour all scrappy and miscellaneous forms of literature, which, by presenting a disorderly series of unrelated items of information, tended, as he considered, to destroy the habit of consecutive mental effort.

"It is most important," he once remarked to me, "habitually to pursue a definite train of thought, and to pursue it to a finish, instead of flitting indolently from one uncompleted topic to another, as the newspaper reader is so apt to do. Still, there is no harm in a daily paper--so long as you don't read it."

Accordingly, he patronized a morning paper, and his method of dealing with it was characteristic. The paper was laid on the table after breakfast, together with a blue pencil and a pair of office shears. A preliminary glance through the sheets enabled him to mark with the pencil those paragraphs that were to be read, and these were presently cut out and looked through, after which they were either thrown away or set aside to be pasted in an indexed book.

The whole proceeding occupied, on an average, a quarter of an hour.

On the morning of which I am now speaking he was thus engaged. The pencil had done its work, and the snick of the shears announced the final stage. Presently he paused with a newly-excised cutting between his fingers, and, after glancing at it for a moment, he handed it to me.

"Another art robbery," he remarked. "Mysterious affairs, these--as to motive, I mean. You can't melt down a picture or an ivory carving, and you can't put them on the market as they stand. The very qualities that give them their value make them totally unnegotiable."

"Yet I suppose," said I, "the really inveterate collector--the pottery or stamp maniac, for instance--will buy these contraband goods even though he dare not show them."

"Probably. No doubt the *cupiditas habendi*, the mere desire to possess, is the motive force rather than any intelligent purpose--"

The discussion was at this point interrupted by a knock at the door, and a moment later my colleague admitted two gentlemen. One of these I recognized as a Mr. Marchmont, a solicitor, for whom we had occasionally acted; the other was a stranger--a typical Hebrew of the blonde type-- good-looking, faultlessly dressed, carrying a bandbox, and obviously in a state of the most extreme agitation.

"Good-morning to you, gentlemen," said Mr. Marchmont, shaking hands cordially. "I have brought a client of mine to see you, and when I tell you that his name is Solomon Loewe, it will be unnecessary for me to say what our business is."

"Oddly enough," replied Thorndyke, "we were, at the very moment when you knocked, discussing the bearings of his case."

"It is a horrible affair!" burst in Mr. Loewe. "I am distracted! I am ruined! I am in despair!"

He banged the bandbox down on the table, and flinging himself into a chair, buried his face in his hands.

"Come, come," remonstrated Marchmont, "we must be brave, we must be composed. Tell Dr. Thorndyke your story, and let us hear what he thinks of it."

He leaned back in his chair, and looked at his client with that air of patient fortitude that comes to us all so easily when we contemplate the misfortunes of other people.

"You must help us, sir," exclaimed Loewe, starting up again--"you must, indeed, or I shall go mad. But I shall tell you what has happened, and then you must act at once. Spare no effort and no expense. Money is no object--at least, not in reason," he added, with native caution. He sat down once more, and in perfect English, though with a slight German accent, proceeded volubly: "My brother Isaac is probably known to you by name."

Thorndyke nodded.

"He is a great collector, and to some extent a dealer--that is to say, he makes his hobby a profitable hobby."

"What does he collect?" asked Thorndyke.

"Everything," replied our visitor, flinging his hands apart with a comprehensive gesture--"everything that is precious and beautiful--pictures, ivories, jewels, watches, objects of art and vertu-- everything. He is a Jew, and he has that passion for things that are rich and costly that has distinguished our race from the time of my namesake Solomon onwards. His house in Howard Street, Piccadilly, is at once a museum and an art gallery. The rooms are filled with cases of gems, of antique jewellery, of coins and historic relics--some of priceless value--and the walls are covered with paintings, every one of which is a masterpiece. There is a fine collection of ancient weapons and armour, both European and Oriental; rare books, manuscripts, papyri, and valuable antiquities from Egypt, Assyria, Cyprus, and elsewhere. You see, his taste is quite catholic, and his knowledge of rare and curious things is probably greater than that of any other living man. He is never mistaken. No forgery deceives him, and hence the great prices that he obtains; for a work of art purchased from Isaac Loewe is a work certified as genuine beyond all cavil."

He paused to mop his face with a silk handkerchief, and then, with the same plaintive volubility, continued:

"My brother is unmarried. He lives for his collection, and he lives with it. The house is not a very large one, and the collection takes up most of it; but he keeps a suite of rooms for his own occupation, and has two servants--a man and wife--to look after him. The man, who is a retired police sergeant, acts as caretaker and watchman; the woman as housekeeper and cook, if required, but my brother lives largely at his club. And now I come to this present catastrophe."

He ran his fingers through his hair, took a deep breath, and continued:

"Yesterday morning Isaac started for Florence by way of Paris, but his route was not certain, and he intended to break his journey at various points as circumstances determined. Before leaving, he put his collection in my charge, and it was arranged that I should occupy his rooms in his absence. Accordingly, I sent my things round and took possession.

"Now, Dr. Thorndyke, I am closely connected with the drama, and it is my custom to spend my evenings at my club, of which most of the members are actors. Consequently, I am rather late in my habits;

but last night I was earlier than usual in leaving my club, for I started for my brother's house before half-past twelve. I felt, as you may suppose, the responsibility of the great charge I had undertaken; and you may, therefore, imagine my horror, my consternation, my despair, when, on letting myself in with my latchkey, I found a police-inspector, a sergeant, and a constable in the hall. There had been a robbery, sir, in my brief absence, and the account that the inspector gave of the affair was briefly this:

"While taking the round of his district, he had noticed an empty hansom proceeding in leisurely fashion along Howard Street. There was nothing remarkable in this, but when, about ten minutes later, he was returning, and met a hansom, which he believed to be the same, proceeding along the same street in the same direction, and at the same easy pace, the circumstance struck him as odd, and he made a note of the number of the cab in his pocket-book. It was 72,863, and the time was 11.35.

"At 11.45 a constable coming up Howard Street noticed a hansom standing opposite the door of my brother's house, and, while he was looking at it, a man came out of the house carrying something, which he put in the cab. On this the constable quickened his pace, and when the man returned to the house and reappeared carrying what looked like a portmanteau, and closing the door softly behind him, the policeman's suspicions were aroused, and he hurried forward, hailing the cabman to stop.

"The man put his burden into the cab, and sprang in himself. The cabman lashed his horse, which started off at a gallop, and the policeman broke into a run, blowing his whistle and flashing his lantern on to the cab. He followed it round the two turnings into Albemarle Street, and was just in time to see it turn into Piccadilly, where, of course, it was lost. However, he managed to note the number of the cab, which was 72,863, and he describes the man as short and thick-set, and thinks he was not wearing any hat.

"As he was returning, he met the inspector and the sergeant, who had heard the whistle, and on his report the three officers hurried to the house, where they knocked and rang for some minutes without any result. Being now more than suspicious, they went to the back of the house, through the mews, where, with great difficulty, they managed to force a window and effect an entrance into the house.

"Here their suspicions were soon changed to certainty, for, on reaching the first-floor, they heard strange muffled groans proceeding from one of the rooms, the door of which was locked, though the key had not been removed. They opened the door, and found the caretaker and his wife sitting on the floor, with their backs against the wall. Both were bound hand and foot, and the head of each was enveloped in a green-baize bag; and when the bags were taken off, each was found to be lightly but effectively gagged.

"Each told the same story. The caretaker, fancying he heard a noise, armed himself with a truncheon, and came downstairs to the first-floor, where he found the door of one of the rooms open, and a light burning inside. He stepped on tiptoe to the open door, and was peering in, when he was seized from behind, half suffocated by a pad held over his mouth, pinioned, gagged, and blindfolded with the bag.

"His assailant--whom he never saw--was amazingly strong and skilful, and handled him with perfect ease, although he--the caretaker--is a powerful man, and a good boxer and wrestler. The same thing happened to the wife, who had come down to look for her husband. She walked into the same trap, and was gagged, pinioned, and blindfolded without ever having soon the robber. So the only description that we have of this villain is that furnished by the constable."

"And the caretaker had no chance of using his truncheon?" said Thorndyke.

"Well, he got in one backhanded blow over his right shoulder, which he thinks caught the burglar in the face; but the fellow caught him by the elbow, and gave his arm such a twist that he dropped the truncheon on the floor."

"Is the robbery a very extensive one?"

"Ah!" exclaimed Mr. Loewe, "that is just what we cannot say. But I fear it is. It seems that my brother had quite recently drawn out of his bank four thousand pounds in notes and gold. These little transactions are often carried out in cash rather than by cheque"--here I caught a twinkle in Thorndyke's eve--"and the caretaker says that a few days ago Isaac brought home several parcels, which were put away temporarily in a strong cupboard. He seemed to be very pleased with his new acquisitions, and gave the caretaker to understand that they were of extraordinary rarity and value.

"Now, this cupboard has been cleared out. Not a vestige is left in it but the wrappings of the parcels, so, although nothing else has been touched, it is pretty clear that goods to the value of four thousand pounds have been taken; but when we consider what an excellent buyer my brother is, it becomes highly probable that the actual value of those things is two or three times that amount, or even more. It is a dreadful, dreadful business, and Isaac will hold me responsible for it all."

"Is there no further clue?" asked Thorndyke. "What about the cab, for instance?"

"Oh, the cab," groaned Loewe--"that clue failed. The police must have mistaken the number. They telephoned immediately to all the police stations, and a watch was set, with the result that number 72,863 was stopped as it was going home for the night. But it then turned out that the cab had not been off the rank since eleven o'clock, and the driver had been in the shelter all the time with several other men. But there is a clue; I have it here."

Mr. Loewe's face brightened for once as he reached out for the bandbox.

"The houses in Howard Street," he explained, as he untied the fastening, "have small balconies to the first-floor windows at the back. Now, the thief entered by one of these windows, having climbed up a rain-water pipe to the balcony. It was a gusty night, as you will remember, and this morning, as I was leaving the house, the butler next door called to me and gave me this; he had found it lying in the balcony of his house."

He opened the bandbox with a flourish, and brought forth a rather shabby billycock hat.

"I understand," said he, "that by examining a hat it is possible to deduce from it, not only the bodily characteristics of the wearer, but also his mental and moral qualities, his state of health, his pecuniary position, his past history, and even his domestic relations and the peculiarities of his place of abode. Am I right in this supposition?"

The ghost of a smile flitted across Thorndyke's face as he laid the hat upon the remains of the newspaper. "We must not expect too much," he observed. "Hats, as you know, have a way of changing owners. Your own hat, for instance" (a very spruce, hard felt), "is a new one, I think."

"Got it last week," said Mr. Loewe.

"Exactly. It is an expensive hat, by Lincoln and Bennett, and I see you have judiciously written your name in indelible marking-ink on the lining. Now, a new hat suggests a discarded predecessor. What do you do with your old hats?"

"My man has them, but they don't fit him. I suppose he sells them or gives them away."

"Very well. Now, a good hat like yours has a long life, and remains serviceable long after it has become shabby; and the probability is that many of your hats pass from owner to owner; from you to the shabby-genteel, and from them to the shabby ungenteel. And it is a fair assumption that there are, at this moment, an appreciable number of tramps and casuals wearing hats by Lincoln and Bennett, marked in indelible ink with the name S. Loewe; and anyone who should examine those hats, as you suggest, might draw some very misleading deductions as to the personal habits of S. Loewe."

Mr. Marchmont chuckled audibly, and then, remembering the gravity of the occasion, suddenly became portentously solemn.

"So you think that the hat is of no use, after all?" said Mr. Loewe, in a tone of deep disappointment.

"I won't say that," replied Thorndyke. "We may learn something from it. Leave it with me, at any rate; but you must let the police know that I have it. They will want to see it, of course."

"And you will try to get those things, won't you?" pleaded Loewe.

"I will think over the case. But you understand, or Mr. Marchmont does, that this is hardly in my province. I am a medical jurist, and this is not a medico-legal case."

"Just what I told him," said Marchmont. "But you will do me a great kindness if you will look into the matter. Make it a medico-legal case," he added persuasively.

Thorndyke repeated his promise, and the two men took their departure.

For some time after they had left, my colleague remained silent, regarding the hat with a quizzical smile. "It is like a game of forfeits," he remarked at length, "and we have to find the owner of 'this very pretty thing.'" He lifted it with a pair of forceps into a better light, and began to look at it more closely.

"Perhaps," said he, "we have done Mr. Loewe an injustice, after all. This is certainly a very remarkable hat."

"It is as round as a basin," I exclaimed. "Why, the fellow's head must have been turned in a lathe!"

Thorndyke laughed. "The point," said he, "is this. This is a hard hat, and so must have fitted fairly, or it could not have been worn; and it was a cheap hat, and so was not made to measure. But a man with a head that shape has got to come to a clear understanding with his hat. No ordinary hat would go on at all.

"Now, you see what he has done--no doubt on the advice of some friendly hatter. He has bought a hat of a suitable size, and he has made it hot-- probably steamed it. Then he has jammed it, while still hot and soft, on to his head, and allowed it to cool and set before removing it. That is evident from the distortion of the brim. The important corollary is, that this hat fits his head exactly--is, in fact, a perfect mould of it; and this fact, together with the cheap quality of the hat, furnishes the further corollary that it has probably only had a single owner.

"And now let us turn it over and look at the outside. You notice at once the absence of old dust. Allowing for the circumstance that it had been out all night, it is decidedly clean. Its owner has been in the habit of brushing it, and is therefore presumably a decent, orderly man. But if you look at it in a good light, you see a kind of bloom on the felt, and through this lens you can make out particles of a fine white powder which has worked into the surface."

He handed me his lens, through which I could distinctly see the particles to which he referred.

"Then," he continued, "under the curl of the brim and in the folds of the hatband, where the brush has not been able to reach it, the powder has collected quite thickly, and we can see that it is a very fine powder, and very white, like flour. What do you make of that?"

"I should say that it is connected with some industry. He may be engaged in some factory or works, or, at any rate, may live near a factory, and have to pass it frequently."

"Yes; and I think we can distinguish between the two possibilities. For, if he only passes the factory, the dust will be on the outside of the hat only; the inside will be protected by his head. But if he is engaged in the works, the dust will be inside, too, as the hat will hang on a peg in the dust-laden atmosphere, and his head will also be powdered, and so convey the dust to the inside."

He turned the hat over once more, and as I brought the powerful lens to bear upon the dark lining, I could clearly distinguish a number of white particles in the interstices of the fabric.

"The powder is on the inside, too," I said.

He took the lens from me, and, having verified my statement, proceeded with the examination. "You notice," he said, "that the leather head-lining is stained with grease, and this staining is more pronounced at the sides and back. His hair, therefore, is naturally greasy, or he greases it artificially; for if the staining were caused by perspiration, it would be most marked opposite the forehead."

He peered anxiously into the interior of the hat, and eventually turned down the head-lining; and immediately there broke out upon his face a gleam of satisfaction.

"Ha!" he exclaimed. "This is a stroke of luck. I was afraid our neat and orderly friend had defeated us with his brush. Pass me the small dissecting forceps, Jervis."

I handed him the instrument, and he proceeded to pick out daintily from the space behind the head-lining some half a dozen short pieces of hair, which he laid, with infinite tenderness, on a sheet of white paper.

"There are several more on the other side," I said, pointing them out to him.

"Yes, but we must leave some for the police," he answered, with a smile. "They must have the same chance as ourselves, you know."

"But surely," I said, as I bent down over the paper, "these are pieces of horsehair!"

"I think not," he replied; "but the microscope will show. At any rate, this is the kind of hair I should expect to find with a head of that shape."

"Well, it is extraordinarily coarse," said I, "and two of the hairs are nearly white."

"Yes; black hairs beginning to turn grey. And now, as our preliminary survey has given such encouraging results, we will proceed to more exact methods; and we must waste no time, for we shall have the police here presently to rob us of our treasure."

He folded up carefully the paper containing the hairs, and taking the hat in both hands, as though it were some sacred vessel, ascended with me to the laboratory on the next floor.

"Now, Polton," he said to his laboratory assistant, "we have here a specimen for examination, and time is precious. First of all, we want your patent dust-extractor."

The little man bustled to a cupboard and brought forth a singular appliance, of his own manufacture, somewhat like a miniature vacuum cleaner. It had been made from a bicycle foot-pump, by reversing the piston-valve, and was fitted with a glass nozzle and a small detachable glass receiver for collecting the dust, at the end of a flexible metal tube.

"We will sample the dust from the outside first," said Thorndyke, laying the hat upon the work-bench. "Are you ready, Polton?"

The assistant slipped his foot into the stirrup of the pump and worked the handle vigorously, while Thorndyke drew the glass nozzle slowly along the hat-brim under the curled edge. And as the nozzle passed along, the white coating vanished as if by magic, leaving the felt absolutely clean and black, and simultaneously the glass receiver became clouded over with a white deposit.

"We will leave the other side for the police," said Thorndyke, and as Polton ceased pumping he detached the receiver, and laid it on a sheet of paper, on which he wrote in pencil, "Outside," and covered it with a small bell-glass. A fresh receiver having been fitted on, the nozzle was now drawn over the silk lining of the hat, and then through the space behind the leather head-lining on one side; and now the dust that collected in the receiver was much of the usual grey colour and fluffy texture, and included two more hairs.

"And now," said Thorndyke, when the second receiver had been detached and set aside, "we want a mould of the inside of the hat, and we must make it by the quickest method; there is no time to make a paper mould. It is a most astonishing head," he added, reaching down from a nail a pair of large callipers, which he applied to the inside of the hat; "six inches and nine-tenths long by six and six-tenths broad, which gives us"--he made a rapid calculation on a scrap of paper--"the extraordinarily high cephalic index of 95.6."

Polton now took possession of the hat, and, having stuck a band of wet tissue-paper round the inside, mixed a small bowl of plaster-of-Paris, and very dexterously ran a stream of the thick liquid on to the tissue-paper, where it quickly solidified. A second and third application resulted in a broad ring of solid plaster an inch thick, forming a perfect mould of the inside of the hat, and in a few minutes the slight contraction of the plaster in setting rendered the mould sufficiently loose to allow of its being slipped out on to a board to dry.

We were none too soon, for even as Polton was removing the mould, the electric bell, which I had switched on to the laboratory, announced a visitor, and when I went down I found a police-sergeant waiting with a note from Superintendent Miller, requesting the immediate transfer of the hat.

"The next thing to be done," said Thorndyke, when the sergeant had departed with the bandbox, "is to measure the thickness of the hairs, and make a transverse section of one, and examine the dust. The section we will leave to Polton--as time is an object, Polton you had better imbed the hair in thick gum and freeze it hard on the microtome, and be very careful to cut the section at right angles to the length of the hair--meanwhile, we will get to work with the microscope."

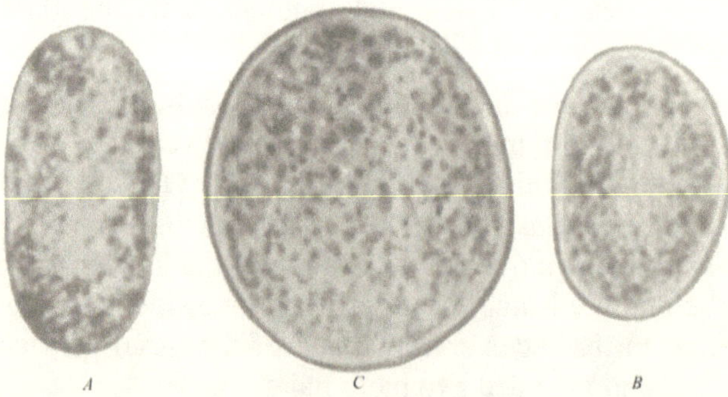

TRANSVERSE SECTIONS OF HUMAN HAIR: A, OF A NEGRO; B, OF AN ENGLISHMAN; C, OF THE BURGLAR. ALL MAGNIFIED 600 DIAMETERS.

The hairs proved on measurement to have the surprisingly large diameter of one one-hundred-and-thirty-fifth of an inch--fully double that of ordinary hairs, although they were unquestionably human. As to the white dust, it presented a problem that even Thorndyke was unable to solve. The application of reagents showed it to be carbonate of lime, but its source for a time remained a mystery.

"The larger particles," said Thorndyke, with his eye applied to the microscope, "appear to be transparent, crystalline, and distinctly laminated in structure. It is not chalk, it is not whiting, it is not any kind of cement. What can it be?"

"Could it be any kind of shell?" I suggested. "For instance--"

"Of course!" he exclaimed, starting up; "you have hit it, Jervis, as you always do. It must be mother-of-pearl. Polton, give me a pearl shirt-button out of your oddments box."

The button was duly produced by the thrifty Polton, dropped into an agate mortar, and speedily reduced to powder, a tiny pinch of which Thorndyke placed under the microscope.

"This powder," said he, "is, naturally, much coarser than our specimen, but the identity of character is unmistakable. Jervis, you are a treasure. Just look at it."

I glanced down the microscope, and then pulled out my watch. "Yes," I said, "there is no doubt about it, I think; but I must be off. Anstey urged me to be in court by 11.30 at the latest."

With infinite reluctance I collected my notes and papers and departed, leaving Thorndyke diligently copying addresses out of the Post Office Directory.

My business at the court detained me the whole of the day, and it was near upon dinner-time when I reached our chambers. Thorndyke had not yet come in, but he arrived half an hour later, tired and hungry, and not very communicative.

"What have I done?" he repeated, in answer to my inquiries. "I have walked miles of dirty pavement, and I have visited every pearl-shell cutter's in London, with one exception, and I have not found what I was looking for. The one mother-of-pearl factory that remains, however, is the most likely, and I propose to look in there to-morrow morning. Meanwhile, we have completed our data, with Polton's assistance. Here is a tracing of our friend's skull taken from the mould;

you see it is an extreme type of brachycephalic skull, and markedly unsymmetrical. Here is a transverse section of his hair, which is quite circular--unlike yours or mine, which would be oval. We have the mother-of-pearl dust from the outside of the hat, and from the inside similar dust mixed with various fibres and a few granules of rice starch. Those are our data."

"Supposing the hat should not be that of the burglar after all?" I suggested.

"That would be annoying. But I think it is his, and I think I can guess at the nature of the art treasures that were stolen."

"And you don't intend to enlighten me?"

"My dear fellow," he replied, "you have all the data. Enlighten yourself by the exercise of your own brilliant faculties. Don't give way to mental indolence."

I endeavoured, from the facts in my possession, to construct the personality of the mysterious burglar, and failed utterly; nor was I more successful in my endeavour to guess at the nature of the stolen property; and it was not until the following morning, when we had set out on our quest and were approaching Limehouse, that Thorndyke would revert to the subject.

"We are now," he said, "going to the factory of Badcomb and Martin, shell importers and cutters, in the West India Dock Road. If I don't find my man there, I shall hand the facts over to the police, and waste no more time over the case."

"What is your man like?" I asked.

"I am looking for an elderly Japanese, wearing a new hat or, more probably, a cap, and having a bruise on his right cheek or temple. I am also looking for a cab-yard; but here we are at the works, and as it is now close on the dinner-hour, we will wait and see the hands come out before making any inquiries."

We walked slowly past the tall, blank-faced building, and were just turning to re-pass it when a steam whistle sounded, a wicket opened in the main gate, and a stream of workmen--each powdered with white, like a miller--emerged into the street. We halted to watch the men as they came out, one by one, through the wicket, and turned to the right or left towards their homes or some adjacent coffee-shop; but none of them answered to the description that my friend had given.

The outcoming stream grew thinner, and at length ceased; the wicket was shut with a bang, and once more Thorndyke's quest appeared to have failed.

"Is that all of them, I wonder?" he said, with a shade of disappointment in his tone; but even as he spoke the wicket opened again, and a leg protruded. The leg was followed by a back and a curious globular head, covered with iron-grey hair, and surmounted by a cloth cap, the whole appertaining to a short, very thick-set man, who remained thus, evidently talking to someone inside.

Suddenly he turned his head to look across the street; and immediately I recognized, by the pallid yellow complexion and narrow eye-slits, the physiognomy of a typical Japanese. The man remained talking for nearly another minute; then, drawing out his other leg, he turned towards us; and now I perceived that the right side of his face, over the prominent cheekbone, was discoloured as though by a severe bruise.

"Ha!" said Thorndyke, turning round sharply as the man approached, "either this is our man or it is an incredible coincidence." He walked away at a moderate pace, allowing the Japanese to overtake us slowly, and when the man had at length passed us, he increased his speed somewhat, so as to maintain the distance.

Our friend stepped along briskly, and presently turned up a side street, whither we followed at a respectful distance, Thorndyke holding open his pocket-book, and appearing to engage me in an earnest discussion, but keeping a sharp eye on his quarry.

"There he goes!" said my colleague, as the man suddenly disappeared-- "the house with the green window-sashes. That will be number thirteen."

It was; and, having verified the fact, we passed on, and took the next turning that would lead us back to the main road.

Some twenty minutes later, as we were strolling past the door of a coffee-shop, a man came out, and began to fill his pipe with an air of leisurely satisfaction. His hat and clothes were powdered with white like those of the workmen whom we had seen come out of the factory. Thorndyke accosted him.

"Is that a flour-mill up the road there?"

"No, sir; pearl-shell. I work there myself."

"Pearl-shell, eh?" said Thorndyke. "I suppose that will be an industry that will tend to attract the aliens. Do you find it so?"

"No, sir; not at all. The work's too hard. We've only got one foreigner in the place, and he ain't an alien--he's a Jap."

"A Jap!" exclaimed Thorndyke. "Really. Now, I wonder if that would chance to be our old friend Kotei--you remember Kotei?" he added, turning to me.

"No, sir; this man's name is Futashima. There was another Jap in the works, a chap named Itu, a pal of Futashima's, but he's left."

"Ah! I don't know either of them. By the way, usen't there to be a cab-yard just about here?"

"There's a yard up Rankin Street where they keep vans and one or two cabs. That chap Itu works there now. Taken to horseflesh. Drives a van sometimes. Queer start for a Jap."

"Very." Thorndyke thanked the man for his information, and we sauntered on towards Rankin Street. The yard was at this time nearly deserted, being occupied only by an ancient and crazy four-wheeler and a very shabby hansom.

"Curious old houses, these that back on to the yard," said Thorndyke, strolling into the enclosure. "That timber gable, now," pointing to a house, from a window of which a man was watching us suspiciously, "is quite an interesting survival."

"What's your business, mister?" demanded the man in a gruff tone.

"We are just having a look at these quaint old houses," replied Thorndyke, edging towards the back of the hansom, and opening his pocket-book, as though to make a sketch.

"Well, you can see 'em from outside," said the man.

"So we can," said Thorndyke suavely, "but not so well, you know."

At this moment the pocket-book slipped from his hand and fell, scattering a number of loose papers about the ground under the hansom, and our friend at the window laughed joyously.

"No hurry," murmured Thorndyke, as I stooped to help him to gather up the papers--which he did in the most surprisingly slow and clumsy manner. "It is fortunate that the ground is dry." He stood up with the rescued papers in his hand, and, having scribbled down a brief note, slipped the book in his pocket.

"Now you'd better mizzle," observed the man at the window.

"Thank you," replied Thorndyke, "I think we had;" and, with a pleasant nod at the custodian, he proceeded to adopt the hospitable suggestion.

"Mr. Marchmont has been here, sir, with Inspector Badger and another gentleman," said Polton, as we entered our chambers. "They said they would call again about five."

"Then," replied Thorndyke, "as it is now a quarter to five, there is just time for us to have a wash while you get the tea ready. The particles that float in the atmosphere of Limehouse are not all mother-of-pearl."

Our visitors arrived punctually, the third gentleman being, as we had supposed, Mr. Solomon Loewe. Inspector Badger I had not seen before, and he now impressed me as showing a tendency to invert the significance of his own name by endeavouring to "draw" Thorndyke; in which, however, he was not brilliantly successful.

"I hope you are not going to disappoint Mr. Loewe, sir," he commenced facetiously. "You have had a good look at that hat--we saw your marks on it--and he expects that you will be able to point us out the man, name and address all complete." He grinned patronizingly at our unfortunate client, who was looking even more haggard and worn than he had been on the previous morning.

"Have you--have you made any--discovery?" Mr Loewe asked with pathetic eagerness.

"We examined the hat very carefully, and I think we have established a few facts of some interest."

"Did your examination of the hat furnish any information as to the nature of the stolen property, sir?" inquired the humorous inspector.

Thorndyke turned to the officer with a face as expressionless as a wooden mask.

"We thought it possible," said he, "that it might consist of works of Japanese art, such as netsukes, paintings, and such like."

Mr. Loewe uttered an exclamation of delighted astonishment, and the facetiousness faded rather suddenly from the inspector's countenance.

"I don't know how you can have found out," said he. "We have only known it half an hour ourselves, and the wire came direct from Florence to Scotland Yard."

"Perhaps you can describe the thief to us," said Mr. Loewe, in the same eager tone.

"I dare say the inspector can do that," replied Thorndyke.

"Yes, I think so," replied the officer. "He is a short strong man, with a dark complexion and hair turning grey. He has a very round head, and he is probably a workman engaged at some whiting or cement works. That is all we know; if you can tell us any more, sir, we shall be very glad to hear it."

"I can only offer a few suggestions," said Thorndyke, "but perhaps you may find them useful. For instance, at 13, Birket Street, Limehouse, there is living a Japanese gentleman named Futashima, who works at Badcomb and Martin's mother-of-pearl factory. I think that if you were to call on him, and let him try on the hat that you have, it would probably fit him."

The inspector scribbled ravenously in his notebook, and Mr. Marchmont-- an old admirer of Thorndyke's--leaned back in his chair, chuckling softly and rubbing his hands.

"Then," continued my colleague, "there is in Rankin Street, Limehouse, a cab-yard, where another Japanese gentleman named Itu is employed. You might find out where Itu was the night before last; and if you should chance to see a hansom cab there--number 22,481--have a good look at it. In the frame of the number-plate you will find six small holes. Those holes may have held brads, and the brads may have held a false number card. At any rate, you might ascertain where that cab was at 11.30 the night before last. That is all I have to suggest."

Mr. Loewe leaped from his chair. "Let us go--now--at once--there is no time to be lost. A thousand thanks to you, doctor--a thousand million thanks. Come!"

He seized the inspector by the arm and forcibly dragged him towards the door, and a few moments later we heard the footsteps of our visitors clattering down the stairs.

"It was not worth while to enter into explanations with them," said Thorndyke, as the footsteps died away--"nor perhaps with you?"

"On the contrary," I replied, "I am waiting to be fully enlightened."

"Well, then, my inferences in this case were perfectly simple ones, drawn from well-known anthropological facts. The human race, as you know, is roughly divided into three groups--the black, the white, and the yellow races. But apart from the variable quality of colour, these races have certain fixed characteristics associated especially with the shape of the skull, of the eye-sockets, and the hair.

"Thus in the black races the skull is long and narrow, the eye-sockets are long and narrow, and the hair is flat and ribbon-like, and usually coiled up like a watch-spring. In the white races the skull is oval, the eye-sockets are oval, and the hair is slightly flattened or oval in section, and tends to be wavy; while in the yellow or Mongol races, the skull is short and round, the eye-sockets are short and round, and the hair is straight and circular in section. So that we have, in the black races, long skull, long orbits, flat hair; in the white races, oval skull, oval orbits, oval hair; and in the yellow races, round skull, round orbits, round hair.

"Now, in this case we had to deal with a very short round skull. But you cannot argue from races to individuals; there are many short-skulled Englishmen. But when I found, associated with that skull, hairs which were circular in section, it became practically certain that the individual was a Mongol of some kind. The mother-of-pearl dust and the granules of rice starch from the inside of the hat favoured this view, for the pearl-shell industry is specially connected with China and Japan, while starch granules from the hat of an Englishman would probably be wheat starch.

"Then as to the hair: it was, as I mentioned to you, circular in section, and of very large diameter. Now, I have examined many thousands of hairs, and the thickest that I have ever seen came from the heads of Japanese; but the hairs from this hat were as thick as any of them. But the hypothesis that the burglar was a Japanese received confirmation in various ways. Thus, he was short, though strong and active, and the Japanese are the shortest of the Mongol races, and very strong and active.

"Then his remarkable skill in handling the powerful caretaker--a retired police-sergeant--suggested the Japanese art of ju-jitsu, while the nature of the robbery was consistent with the value set by the Japanese on works of art. Finally, the fact that only a particular collection was taken, suggested a special, and probably national, character in the things stolen, while their portability--you will remember that goods of the value of from eight to twelve thousand pounds were taken away in two hand-packages--was much more consistent with Japanese than Chinese works, of which the latter tend rather to be bulky and ponderous. Still, it was nothing but a bare hypothesis until we had seen Futashima--and, indeed, is no more now. I may, after all, be entirely mistaken."

He was not, however; and at this moment there reposes in my drawing-room an ancient netsuke, which came as a thank-offering from Mr. Isaac Loewe on the recovery of the booty from a back room in No. 13, Birket Street, Limehouse. The treasure, of course, was given in the first place to Thorndyke, but transferred by him to my wife on the pretence that but for my suggestion of shell-dust the robber would never have been traced. Which is, on the face of it, preposterous.

The Blue Sequin

Thorndyke stood looking up and down the platform with anxiety that increased as the time drew near for the departure of the train.

"This is very unfortunate," he said, reluctantly stepping into an empty smoking compartment as the guard executed a flourish with his green flag. "I am afraid we have missed our friend." He closed the door, and, as the train began to move, thrust his head out of the window.

"Now I wonder if that will be he," he continued. "If so, he has caught the train by the skin of his teeth, and is now in one of the rear compartments."

The subject of Thorndyke's speculations was Mr. Edward Stopford, of the firm of Stopford and Myers, of Portugal Street, solicitors, and his connection with us at present arose out of a telegram that had reached our chambers on the preceding evening. It was reply-paid, and ran thus:

"CAN YOU COME HERE TO-MORROW TO DIRECT DEFENCE? IMPORTANT CASE. ALL COSTS UNDERTAKEN BY US.--STOPFORD AND MYERS."

Thorndyke's reply had been in the affirmative, and early on this present morning a further telegram--evidently posted overnight--had been delivered: "SHALL LEAVE FOR WOLDHURST BY 8.25 FROM CHARING CROSS. WILL CALL FOR YOU IF POSSIBLE. EDWARD STOPFORD."

He had not called, however, and, since he was unknown personally to us both, we could not judge whether or not he had been among the passengers on the platform.

"It is most unfortunate," Thorndyke repeated, "for it deprives us of that preliminary consideration of the case which is so invaluable." He filled his pipe thoughtfully, and, having made a fruitless inspection of the platform at London Bridge, took up the paper that he had bought at the bookstall, and began to turn over the leaves, running his eye quickly down the columns, unmindful of the journalistic baits in paragraph or article.

"It is a great disadvantage," he observed, while still glancing through the paper, "to come plump into an inquiry without preparation--to be confronted with the details before one has a chance of considering the case in general terms. For instance--"

He paused, leaving the sentence unfinished, and as I looked up inquiringly I saw that he had turned over another page, and was now reading attentively.

"This looks like our case, Jervis," he said presently, handing me the paper and indicating a paragraph at the top of the page. It was quite brief, and was headed "Terrible Murder in Kent," the account being as follows:

"A shocking crime was discovered yesterday morning at the little town of Woldhurst, which lies on the branch line from Halbury Junction. The discovery was made by a porter who was inspecting the carriages of the train which had just come in. On opening the door of a first-class compartment, he was horrified to find the body of a fashionably-dressed woman stretched upon the floor. Medical aid was immediately summoned, and on the arrival of the divisional surgeon, Dr. Morton, it was ascertained that the woman had not been dead more than a few minutes.

"The state of the corpse leaves no doubt that a murder of a most brutal kind has been perpetrated, the cause of death being a penetrating wound of the head, inflicted with some pointed implement, which must have been used with terrible violence, since it has perforated the skull and entered the brain. That robbery was not the motive of the crime is made clear by the fact that an expensively fitted dressing-bag was found on the rack, and that the dead woman's jewellery, including several valuable diamond rings, was untouched. It is rumoured that an arrest has been made by the local police."

"A gruesome affair," I remarked, as I handed back the paper, "but the report does not give us much information."

"It does not," Thorndyke agreed, "and yet it gives us something to consider. Here is a perforating wound of the skull, inflicted with some pointed implement--that is, assuming that it is not a bullet wound. Now, what kind of implement would be capable of inflicting such an injury? How would such an implement be used in the confined space of a railway-carriage, and what sort of person would be in possession of such an implement? These are preliminary questions that are worth considering, and I commend them to you, together with the further problems of the possible motive--excluding robbery--and any circumstances other than murder which might account for the injury."

"The choice of suitable implements is not very great," I observed.

"It is very limited, and most of them, such as a plasterer's pick or a geological hammer, are associated with certain definite occupations. You have a notebook?"

I had, and, accepting the hint, I produced it and pursued my further reflections in silence, while my companion, with his notebook also on his knee, gazed steadily out of the window. And thus he remained, wrapped in thought, jotting down an entry now and again in his book, until the train slowed down at Halbury Junction, where we had to change on to a branch line.

As we stepped out, I noticed a well-dressed man hurrying up the platform from the rear and eagerly scanning the faces of the few passengers who had alighted. Soon he espied us, and, approaching quickly, asked, as he looked from one of us to the other:

"Dr. Thorndyke?"

"Yes," replied my colleague, adding: "And you, I presume, are Mr. Edward Stopford?"

The solicitor bowed. "This is a dreadful affair," he said, in an agitated manner. "I see you have the paper. A most shocking affair. I am immensely relieved to find you here. Nearly missed the train, and feared I should miss you."

"There appears to have been an arrest," Thorndyke began.

"Yes--my brother. Terrible business. Let us walk up the platform; our train won't start for a quarter of an hour yet."

We deposited our joint Gladstone and Thorndyke's travelling-case in an empty first-class compartment, and then, with the solicitor between us, strolled up to the unfrequented end of the platform.

"My brother's position," said Mr. Stopford, "fills me with dismay--but let me give you the facts in order, and you shall judge for yourself. This poor creature who has been murdered so brutally was a Miss Edith Grant. She was formerly an artist's model, and as such was a good deal employed by my brother, who is a painter--Harold Stopford, you know, A.R.A. now--"

"I know his work very well, and charming work it is."

"I think so, too. Well, in those days he was quite a youngster--about twenty--and he became very intimate with Miss Grant, in quite an innocent way, though not very discreet; but she was a nice respectable girl, as most English models are, and no one thought any harm. However, a good many letters passed between them, and some little presents, amongst which was a beaded chain carrying a locket, and in this he was fool enough to put his portrait and the inscription, 'Edith, from Harold.'

"Later on Miss Grant, who had a rather good voice, went on the stage, in the comic opera line, and, in consequence, her habits and associates changed somewhat; and, as Harold had meanwhile become engaged, he was naturally anxious to get his letters back, and especially to exchange the locket for some less compromising gift. The letters she eventually sent him, but refused absolutely to part with the locket.

"Now, for the last month Harold has been staying at Halbury, making sketching excursions into the surrounding country, and yesterday morning he took the train to Shinglehurst, the third station from here, and the one before Woldhurst.

"On the platform here he met Miss Grant, who had come down from London, and was going on to Worthing. They entered the branch train together, having a first-class compartment to themselves. It seems she was wearing his locket at the time, and he made another appeal to her to make an exchange, which she refused, as before. The discussion appears to have become rather heated and angry on both sides, for the guard and a porter at Munsden both noticed that they seemed to be quarrelling; but the upshot of the affair was that the lady snapped the chain, and tossed it together with the locket to my brother, and they parted quite amiably at Shinglehurst, where Harold got out. He was then carrying his full sketching kit, including a large holland umbrella, the lower joint of which is an ash staff fitted with a powerful steel spike for driving into the ground.

"It was about half-past ten when he got out at Shinglehurst; by eleven he had reached his pitch and got to work, and he painted steadily for three hours. Then he packed up his traps, and was just starting on his way back to the station, when he was met by the police and arrested.

"And now, observe the accumulation of circumstantial evidence against him. He was the last person seen in company with the murdered woman--for no one seems to have seen her after they left Munsden; he appeared to be quarrelling with her when she was last seen alive, he had a reason for possibly wishing for her death, he was provided with an implement--a spiked staff--capable of inflicting the injury which caused her death, and, when he was searched, there was found in his possession the locket and broken chain, apparently removed from her person with violence.

"Against all this is, of course, his known character--he is the gentlest and most amiable of men--and his subsequent conduct--imbecile to the last degree if he had been guilty; but, as a lawyer, I can't help seeing that appearances are almost hopelessly against him."

"We won't say 'hopelessly,'" replied Thorndyke, as we took our places in the carriage, "though I expect the police are pretty cocksure. When does the inquest open?"

"To-day at four. I have obtained an order from the coroner for you to examine the body and be present at the post-mortem."

"Do you happen to know the exact position of the wound?"

"Yes; it is a little above and behind the left ear--a horrible round hole, with a ragged cut or tear running from it to the side of the forehead."

"And how was the body lying?"

"Right along the floor, with the feet close to the off-side door."

"Was the wound on the head the only one?"

"No; there was a long cut or bruise on the right cheek--a contused wound the police surgeon called it, which he believes to have been inflicted with a heavy and rather blunt weapon. I have not heard of any other wounds or bruises."

"Did anyone enter the train yesterday at Shinglehurst?" Thorndyke asked.

"No one entered the train after it left Halbury."

Thorndyke considered these statements in silence, and presently fell into a brown study, from which he roused only as the train moved out of Shinglehurst station.

"It would be about here that the murder was committed," said Mr. Stopford; "at least, between here and Woldhurst."

Thorndyke nodded rather abstractedly, being engaged at the moment in observing with great attention the objects that were visible from the windows.

"I notice," he remarked presently, "a number of chips scattered about between the rails, and some of the chair-wedges look new. Have there been any platelayers at work lately?"

"Yes," answered Stopford, "they are on the line now, I believe--at least, I saw a gang working near Woldhurst yesterday, and they are said to have set a rick on fire; I saw it smoking when I came down."

"Indeed; and this middle line of rails is, I suppose, a sort of siding?"

"Yes; they shunt the goods trains and empty trucks on to it. There are the remains of the rick--still smouldering, you see."

Thorndyke gazed absently at the blackened heap until an empty cattle-truck on the middle track hid it from view. This was succeeded by a line of goods-waggons, and these by a passenger coach, one compartment of which--a first-class--was closed up and sealed. The train now began to slow down rather suddenly, and a couple of minutes later we brought up in Woldhurst station.

It was evident that rumours of Thorndyke's advent had preceded us, for the entire staff--two porters, an inspector, and the station-master-- were waiting expectantly on the platform, and the latter came forward, regardless of his dignity, to help us with our luggage.

"Do you think I could see the carriage?" Thorndyke asked the solicitor.

"Not the inside, sir," said the station-master, on being appealed to. "The police have sealed it up. You would have to ask the inspector."

"Well, I can have a look at the outside, I suppose?" said Thorndyke, and to this the station-master readily agreed, and offered to accompany us.

"What other first-class passengers were there?" Thorndyke asked.

"None, sir. There was only one first-class coach, and the deceased was the only person in it. It has given us all a dreadful turn, this affair has," he continued, as we set off up the line. "I was on the platform when the train came in. We were watching a rick that was burning up the line, and a rare blaze it made, too; and I was just saying that we should have to move the cattle-truck that was on the mid-track, because, you see, sir, the smoke and sparks were blowing across, and I thought it would frighten the poor beasts. And Mr. Felton he don't like his beasts handled roughly. He says it spoils the meat."

"No doubt he is right," said Thorndyke. "But now, tell me, do you think it is possible for any person to board or leave the train on the off-side unobserved? Could a man, for instance, enter a compartment on the off-side at one station and drop off as the train was slowing down at the next, without being seen?"

"I doubt it," replied the station-master. "Still, I wouldn't say it is impossible."

"Thank you. Oh, and there's another question. You have a gang of men at work on the line, I see. Now, do those men belong to the district?"

"No, sir; they are strangers, every one, and pretty rough diamonds some of 'em are. But I shouldn't say there was any real harm in 'em. If you was suspecting any of 'em of being mixed up in this--"

"I am not," interrupted Thorndyke rather shortly. "I suspect nobody; but I wish to get all the facts of the case at the outset."

"Naturally, sir," replied the abashed official; and we pursued our way in silence.

"Do you remember, by the way," said Thorndyke, as we approached the empty coach, "whether the off-side door of the compartment was closed and locked when the body was discovered?"

"It was closed, sir, but not locked. Why, sir, did you think -?"

"Nothing, nothing. The sealed compartment is the one, of course?"

Without waiting for a reply, he commenced his survey of the coach, while I gently restrained our two companions from shadowing him, as they were disposed to do. The off-side footboard occupied his attention specially, and when he had scrutinized minutely the part opposite the fatal compartment, he walked slowly from end to end with his eyes but a few inches from its surface, as though he was searching for something.

Near what had been the rear end he stopped, and drew from his pocket a piece of paper; then, with a moistened finger-tip he picked up from the footboard some evidently minute object, which he carefully transferred to the paper, folding the latter and placing it in his pocket-book.

He next mounted the footboard, and, having peered in through the window of the sealed compartment, produced from his pocket a small insufflator or powder-blower, with which he blew a stream of impalpable smoke-like powder on to the edges of the middle window, bestowing the closest attention on the irregular dusty patches in which it settled, and even measuring one on the jamb of the window with a pocket-rule. At length he stepped down, and, having carefully looked over the near-side footboard, announced that he had finished for the present.

As we were returning down the line, we passed a working man, who seemed to be viewing the chairs and sleepers with more than casual interest.

"That, I suppose, is one of the plate-layers?" Thorndyke suggested to the station-master.

"Yes, the foreman of the gang," was the reply.

"I'll just step back and have a word with him, if you will walk on slowly." And my colleague turned back briskly and overtook the man, with whom he remained in conversation for some minutes.

"I think I see the police inspector on the platform," remarked Thorndyke, as we approached the station.

"Yes, there he is," said our guide. "Come down to see what you are after, sir, I expect." Which was doubtless the case, although the officer professed to be there by the merest chance.

"You would like to see the weapon, sir, I suppose?" he remarked, when he had introduced himself.

"The umbrella-spike," Thorndyke corrected. "Yes, if I may. We are going to the mortuary now."

"Then you'll pass the station on the way; so, if you care to look in, I will walk up with you."

This proposition being agreed to, we all proceeded to the police-station, including the station-master, who was on the very tiptoe of curiosity.

"There you are, sir," said the inspector, unlocking his office, and ushering us in. "Don't say we haven't given every facility to the defence. There are all the effects of the accused, including the very weapon the deed was done with."

"Come, come," protested Thorndyke; "we mustn't be premature." He took the stout ash staff from the officer, and, having examined the formidable spike through a lens, drew from his pocket a steel calliper-gauge, with which he carefully measured the diameter of the spike, and the staff to which it was fixed. "And now," he said, when he had made a note of the measurements in his book, "we will look at the colour-box and the sketch. Ha! a very orderly man, your brother. Mr. Stopford. Tubes all in their places, palette-knives wiped clean, palette cleaned off and rubbed bright, brushes wiped--they ought to be washed before they stiffen--all this is very significant." He unstrapped the sketch from the blank canvas to which it was pinned, and, standing it on a chair in a good light, stepped back to look at it.

"And you tell me that that is only three hours' work!" he exclaimed, looking at the lawyer. "It is really a marvellous achievement."

"My brother is a very rapid worker," replied Stopford dejectedly.

"Yes, but this is not only amazingly rapid; it is in his very happiest vein--full of spirit and feeling. But we mustn't stay to look at it longer." He replaced the canvas on its pins, and having glanced at the locket and some other articles that lay in a drawer, thanked the inspector for his courtesy and withdrew.

"That sketch and the colour-box appear very suggestive to me," he remarked, as we walked up the street.

"To me also," said Stopford gloomily, "for they are under lock and key, like their owner, poor old fellow."

He sighed heavily, and we walked on in silence.

The mortuary-keeper had evidently heard of our arrival, for he was waiting at the door with the key in his hand, and, on being shown the coroner's order, unlocked the door, and we entered together; but, after a momentary glance at the ghostly, shrouded figure lying upon the slate table, Stopford turned pale and retreated, saying that he would wait for us outside with the mortuary-keeper.

As soon as the door was closed and locked on the inside, Thorndyke glanced curiously round the bare, whitewashed building. A stream of sunlight poured in through the skylight, and fell upon the silent form that lay so still under its covering-sheet, and one stray beam glanced into a corner by the door, where, on a row of pegs and a deal table, the dead woman's clothing was displayed.

"There is something unspeakably sad in these poor relics, Jervis," said Thorndyke, as we stood before them. "To me they are more tragic, more full of pathetic suggestion, than the corpse itself. See the smart, jaunty hat, and the costly skirts hanging there, so desolate and forlorn; the dainty lingerie on the table, neatly folded--by the mortuary-man's wife, I hope--the little French shoes and open-work silk stockings. How pathetically eloquent they are of harmless, womanly vanity, and the gay, careless life, snapped short in the twinkling of an eye. But we must not give way to sentiment. There is another life threatened, and it is in our keeping."

He lifted the hat from its peg, and turned it over in his hand. It was, I think, what is called a "picture-hat"--a huge, flat, shapeless mass of gauze and ribbon and feather, spangled over freely with dark-blue sequins. In one part of the brim was a ragged hole, and from this the glittering sequins dropped off in little showers when the hat was moved.

"This will have been worn tilted over on the left side," said Thorndyke, "judging by the general shape and the position of the hole."

"Yes," I agreed. "Like that of the Duchess of Devonshire in Gainsborough's portrait."

"Exactly."

He shook a few of the sequins into the palm of his hand, and, replacing the hat on its peg, dropped the little discs into an envelope, on which he wrote, "From the hat," and slipped it into his pocket. Then, stepping over to the table, he drew back the sheet reverently and even tenderly from the dead woman's face, and looked down at it with grave pity. It was a comely face, white as marble, serene and peaceful in expression, with half-closed eyes, and framed with a mass of brassy, yellow hair; but its beauty was marred by a long linear wound, half cut, half bruise, running down the right cheek from the eye to the chin.

"A handsome girl," Thorndyke commented--"a dark-haired blonde. What a sin to have disfigured herself so with that horrible peroxide." He smoothed the hair back from her forehead, and added: "She seems to have applied the stuff last about ten days ago. There is about a quarter of an inch of dark hair at the roots. What do you make of that wound on the cheek?"

"It looks as if she had struck some sharp angle in falling, though, as the seats are padded in first-class carriages, I don't see what she could have struck."

"No. And now let us look at the other wound. Will you note down the description?" He handed me his notebook, and I wrote down as he dictated: "A clean-punched circular hole in skull, an inch behind and above margin of left ear--diameter, an inch and seven-sixteenths; starred fracture of parietal bone; membranes perforated, and brain entered deeply; ragged scalp-wound, extending forward to margin of left orbit; fragments of gauze and sequins in edges of wound. That will do for the present. Dr. Morton will give us further details if we want them."

He pocketed his callipers and rule, drew from the bruised scalp one or two loose hairs, which he placed in the envelope with the sequins, and, having looked over the body for other wounds or bruises (of which there were none), replaced the sheet, and prepared to depart.

As we walked away from the mortuary, Thorndyke was silent and deeply thoughtful, and I gathered that he was piecing together the facts that he had acquired. At length Mr. Stopford, who had several times looked at him curiously, said:

"The post-mortem will take place at three, and it is now only half-past eleven. What would you like to do next?"

Thorndyke, who, in spite of his mental preoccupation, had been looking about him in his usual keen, attentive way, halted suddenly.

"Your reference to the post-mortem," said he, "reminds me that I forgot to put the ox-gall into my case."

"Ox-gall!" I exclaimed, endeavouring vainly to connect this substance with the technique of the pathologist. "What were you going to do with-- "

But here I broke off, remembering my friend's dislike of any discussion of his methods before strangers.

"I suppose," he continued, "there would hardly be an artist's colourman in a place of this size?"

"I should think not," said Stopford. "But couldn't you got the stuff from a butcher? There's a shop just across the road."

"So there is," agreed Thorndyke, who had already observed the shop. "The gall ought, of course, to be prepared, but we can filter it ourselves-- that is, if the butcher has any. We will try him, at any rate."

He crossed the road towards the shop, over which the name "Felton" appeared in gilt lettering, and, addressing himself to the proprietor, who stood at the door, introduced himself and explained his wants.

"Ox-gall?" said the butcher. "No, sir, I haven't any just now; but I am having a beast killed this afternoon, and I can let you have some then. In fact," he added, after a pause, "as the matter is of importance, I can have one killed at once if you wish it."

"That is very kind of you," said Thorndyke, "and it would greatly oblige me. Is the beast perfectly healthy?"

"They're in splendid condition, sir. I picked them out of the herd myself. But you shall see them--ay, and choose the one that you'd like killed."

"You are really very good," said Thorndyke warmly. "I will just run into the chemist's next door, and get a suitable bottle, and then I will avail myself of your exceedingly kind offer."

He hurried into the chemist's shop, from which he presently emerged, carrying a white paper parcel; and we then followed the butcher down a narrow lane by the side of his shop. It led to an enclosure containing a small pen, in which were confined three handsome steers, whose glossy, black coats contrasted in a very striking manner with their long, greyish-white, nearly straight horns.

"These are certainly very fine beasts, Mr. Felton," said Thorndyke, as we drew up beside the pen, "and in excellent condition, too."

He leaned over the pen and examined the beasts critically, especially as to their eyes and horns; then, approaching the nearest one, he raised his stick and bestowed a smart tap on the under-side of the right horn, following it by a similar tap on the left one, a proceeding that the beast viewed with stolid surprise.

"The state of the horns," explained Thorndyke, as he moved on to the next steer, "enables one to judge, to some extent, of the beast's health."

"Lord bless you, sir," laughed Mr. Felton, "they haven't got no feeling in their horns, else what good 'ud their horns be to 'em?"

Apparently he was right, for the second steer was as indifferent to a sounding rap on either horn as the first. Nevertheless, when Thorndyke approached the third steer, I unconsciously drew nearer to watch; and I noticed that, as the stick struck the horn, the beast drew back in evident alarm, and that when the blow was repeated, it became manifestly uneasy.

"He don't seem to like that," said the butcher. "Seems as if--Hullo, that's queer!"

Thorndyke had just brought his stick up against the left horn, and immediately the beast had winced and started back, shaking his head and moaning. There was not, however, room for him to back out of reach, and Thorndyke, by leaning into the pen, was able to inspect the sensitive horn, which he did with the closest attention, while the butcher looked on with obvious perturbation.

"You don't think there's anything wrong with this beast, sir, I hope," said he.

"I can't say without a further examination," replied Thorndyke. "It may be the horn only that is affected. If you will have it sawn off close to the head, and sent up to me at the hotel, I will look at it and tell you. And, by way of preventing any mistakes, I will mark it and cover it up, to protect it from injury in the slaughter-house."

He opened his parcel and produced from it a wide-mouthed bottle labelled "Ox-gall," a sheet of gutta-percha tissue, a roller bandage, and a stick of sealing-wax. Handing the bottle to Mr. Felton, he encased the distal half of the horn in a covering by means of the tissue and the bandage, which he fixed securely with the sealing-wax.

"I'll saw the horn off and bring it up to the hotel myself, with the ox-gall," said Mr. Felton. "You shall have them in half an hour."

He was as good as his word, for in half an hour Thorndyke was seated at a small table by the window of our private sitting-room in the Black Bull Hotel. The table was covered with newspaper, and on it lay the long grey horn and Thorndyke's travelling-case, now open and displaying a small microscope and its accessories. The butcher was seated solidly in an armchair waiting, with a half-suspicious eye on Thorndyke for the report; and I was endeavouring by cheerful talk to keep Mr. Stopford from sinking into utter despondency, though I, too, kept a furtive watch on my colleague's rather mysterious proceedings.

I saw him unwind the bandage and apply the horn to his ear, bending it slightly to and fro. I watched him, as he scanned the surface closely through a lens, and observed him as he scraped some substance from the pointed end on to a glass slide, and, having applied a drop of some reagent, began to tease out the scraping with a pair of mounted needles. Presently he placed the slide under the microscope, and, having observed it attentively for a minute or two, turned round sharply.

"Come and look at this, Jervis," said he.

I wanted no second bidding, being on tenterhooks of curiosity, but came over and applied my eye to the instrument.

"Well, what is it?" he asked.

"A multipolar nerve corpuscle--very shrivelled, but unmistakable."

"And this?"

He moved the slide to a fresh spot.

"Two pyramidal nerve corpuscles and some portions of fibres."

"And what do you say the tissue is?"

"Cortical brain substance, I should say, without a doubt."

"I entirely agree with you. And that being so," he added, turning to Mr. Stopford, "we may say that the case for the defence is practically complete."

"What, in Heaven's name, do you mean?" exclaimed Stopford, starting up.

"I mean that we can now prove when and where and how Miss Grant met her death. Come and sit down here, and I will explain. No, you needn't go away, Mr. Felton. We shall have to subpoena you. Perhaps," he continued, "we had better go over the facts and see what they suggest. And first we note the position of the body, lying with the feet close to the off-side door, showing that, when she fell, the deceased was sitting, or more probably standing, close to that door. Next there is this." He drew from his pocket a folded paper, which he opened, displaying a tiny blue disc. "It is one of the sequins with which her hat was trimmed, and I have in this envelope several more which I took from the hat itself.

"This single sequin I picked up on the rear end of the off side footboard, and its presence there makes it nearly certain that at some time Miss Grant had put her head out of the window on that side.

"The next item of evidence I obtained by dusting the margins of the off-side window with a light powder, which made visible a greasy impression three and a quarter inches long on the sharp corner of the right-hand jamb (right-hand from the inside, I mean).

"And now as to the evidence furnished by the body. The wound in the skull is behind and above the left ear, is roughly circular, and measures one inch and seven-sixteenths at most, and a ragged scalp-wound runs from it towards the left eye. On the right cheek is a linear contused wound three and a quarter inches long. There are no other injuries.

"Our next facts are furnished by this." He took up the horn and tapped it with his finger, while the solicitor and Mr. Felton stared at him in speechless wonder. "You notice it is a left horn, and you remember that it was highly sensitive. If you put your ear to it while I strain it, you will hear the grating of a fracture in the bony core. Now look at the pointed end, and you will see several deep scratches running lengthwise, and where those scratches end the diameter of the horn is, as you see by this calliper-gauge, one inch and seven-sixteenths. Covering the scratches is a dry blood-stain, and at the extreme tip is a small mass of a dried substance which Dr. Jervis and I have examined with the microscope and are satisfied is brain tissue."

"Good God!" exclaimed Stopford eagerly. "Do you mean to say--"

"Let us finish with the facts, Mr. Stopford," Thorndyke interrupted. "Now, if you look closely at that blood-stain, you will see a short piece of hair stuck to the horn, and through this lens you can make out the root-bulb. It is a golden hair, you notice, but near the root it is black, and our calliper-gauge shows us that the black portion is fourteen sixty-fourths of an inch long. Now, in this envelope are some hairs that I removed from the dead woman's head. They also are golden hairs, black at the roots, and when I measure the black portion I find it to be fourteen sixty-fourths of an inch long. Then, finally, there is this."

He turned the horn over, and pointed to a small patch of dried blood. Embedded in it was a blue sequin.

Mr. Stopford and the butcher both gazed at the horn in silent amazement; then the former drew a deep breath and looked up at Thorndyke.

"No doubt," said he, "you can explain this mystery, but for my part I am utterly bewildered, though you are filling me with hope."

"And yet the matter is quite simple," returned Thorndyke, "even with these few facts before us, which are only a selection from the body of evidence in our possession. But I will state my theory, and you shall judge." He rapidly sketched a rough plan on a sheet of paper, and continued: "These were the conditions when the train was approaching Woldhurst: Here was the passenger-coach, here was the burning rick, and here was a cattle-truck. This steer was in that truck. Now my hypothesis is that at that time Miss Grant was standing with her head out of the off-side window, watching the burning rick. Her wide hat, worn on the left side, hid from her view the cattle-truck which she was approaching, and then this is what happened." He sketched another plan to a larger scale. "One of the steers--this one--had thrust its long horn out through the bars. The point of that horn struck the deceased's head, driving her face violently against the corner of the window, and then, in disengaging, ploughed its way through the scalp, and suffered a fracture of its core from the violence of the wrench. This hypothesis is inherently probable, it fits all the facts, and those facts admit of no other explanation."

The solicitor sat for a moment as though dazed; then he rose impulsively and seized Thorndyke's hands. "I don't know what to say to you," he exclaimed huskily, "except that you have saved my brother's life, and for that may God reward you!"

The butcher rose from his chair with a slow grin.

"It seems to me," said he, "as if that ox-gall was what you might call a blind, eh, sir?"

And Thorndyke smiled an inscrutable smile.

When we returned to town on the following day we were a party of four, which included Mr. Harold Stopford. The verdict of "Death by misadventure," promptly returned by the coroner's jury, had been shortly followed by his release from custody, and he now sat with his brother and me, listening with rapt attention to Thorndyke's analysis of the case.

"So, you see," the latter concluded, "I had six possible theories of the cause of death worked out before I reached Halbury, and it only remained to select the one that fitted the facts. And when I had seen the cattle-truck, had picked up that sequin, had heard the description of the steers, and had seen the hat and the wounds, there was nothing left to do but the filling in of details."

"And you never doubted my innocence?" asked Harold Stopford.

Thorndyke smiled at his quondam client.

"Not after I had seen your colour-box and your sketch," said he, "to say nothing of the spike."

The Moabite Cipher

A large and motley crowd lined the pavements of Oxford Street as Thorndyke and I made our way leisurely eastward. Floral decorations and drooping bunting announced one of those functions inaugurated from time to time by a benevolent Government for the entertainment of fashionable loungers and the relief of distressed pickpockets. For a Russian Grand Duke, who had torn himself away, amidst valedictory explosions, from a loving if too demonstrative people, was to pass anon on his way to the Guildhall; and a British Prince, heroically indiscreet, was expected to occupy a seat in the ducal carriage.

Near Rathbone Place Thorndyke halted and drew my attention to a smart-looking man who stood lounging in a doorway, cigarette in hand.

"Our old friend Inspector Badger," said Thorndyke. "He seems mightily interested in that gentleman in the light overcoat. How d'ye do, Badger?" for at this moment the detective caught his eye and bowed. "Who is your friend?"

"That's what I want to know, sir," replied the inspector. "I've been shadowing him for the last half-hour, but I can't make him out, though I believe I've seen him somewhere. He don't look like a foreigner, but he has got something bulky in his pocket, so I must keep him in sight until the Duke is safely past. I wish," he added gloomily, "these beastly Russians would stop at home. They give us no end of trouble."

"Are you expecting any--occurrences, then?" asked Thorndyke.

"Bless you, sir," exclaimed Badger, "the whole route is lined with plain-clothes men. You see, it is known that several desperate characters followed the Duke to England, and there are a good many exiles living here who would like to have a rap at him. Hallo! What's he up to now?"

The man in the light overcoat had suddenly caught the inspector's too inquiring eye, and forthwith dived into the crowd at the edge of the pavement. In his haste he trod heavily on the foot of a big, rough-looking man, by whom he was in a moment hustled out into the road with such violence that he fell sprawling face downwards. It was an unlucky moment. A mounted constable was just then backing in upon the crowd, and before he could gather the meaning of the shout that arose from the bystanders, his horse had set down one hind-hoof firmly on the prostrate man's back.

The inspector signalled to a constable, who forthwith made a way for us through the crowd; but even as we approached the injured man, he rose stiffly and looked round with a pale, vacant face.

"Are you hurt?" Thorndyke asked gently, with an earnest look into the frightened, wondering eyes.

"No, sir," was the reply; "only I feel queer--sinking--just here."

He laid a trembling hand on his chest, and Thorndyke, still eyeing him anxiously, said in a low voice to the inspector: "Cab or ambulance, as quickly as you can."

A cab was led round from Newman Street, and the injured man put into it. Thorndyke, Badger, and I entered, and we drove off up Rathbone Place. As we proceeded, our patient's face grew more and more ashen, drawn, and anxious; his breathing was shallow and uneven, and his teeth chattered slightly. The cab swung round into Goodge Street, and then--suddenly, in the twinkling of an eye--there came a change. The eyelids and jaw relaxed, the eyes became filmy, and the whole form subsided into the corner in a shrunken heap, with the strange gelatinous limpness of a body that is dead as a whole, while its tissues are still alive.

"God save us! The man's dead!" exclaimed the inspector in a shocked voice--for even policemen have their feelings. He sat staring at the corpse, as it nodded gently with the jolting of the cab, until we drew up inside the courtyard of the Middlesex Hospital, when he got out briskly, with suddenly renewed cheerfulness, to help the porter to place the body on the wheeled couch.

"We shall know who he is now, at any rate," said he, as we followed the couch to the casualty-room. Thorndyke nodded unsympathetically. The medical instinct in him was for the moment stronger than the legal.

The house-surgeon leaned over the couch, and made a rapid examination as he listened to our account of the accident. Then he straightened himself up and looked at Thorndyke.

"Internal haemorrhage, I expect," said he. "At any rate, he's dead, poor beggar!--as dead as Nebuchadnezzar. Ah! here comes a bobby; it's his affair now."

A sergeant came into the room, breathing quickly, and looked in surprise from the corpse to the inspector. But the latter, without loss of time, proceeded to turn out the dead man's pockets, commencing with the bulky object that had first attracted his attention; which proved to be a brown-paper parcel tied up with red tape.

"Pork-pie, begad!" he exclaimed with a crestfallen air as he cut the tape and opened the package. "You had better go through his other pockets, sergeant."

The small heap of odds and ends that resulted from this process tended, with a single exception, to throw little light on the man's identity; the exception being a letter, sealed, but not stamped, addressed in an exceedingly illiterate hand to Mr. Adolf Schoenberg, 213, Greek Street, Soho.

"He was going to leave it by hand, I expect," observed the inspector, with a wistful glance at the sealed envelope. "I think I'll take it round myself, and you had better come with me, sergeant."

He slipped the letter into his pocket, and, leaving the sergeant to take possession of the other effects, made his way out of the building.

"I suppose, Doctor," said he, as we crossed into Berners Street, "you are not coming our way! Don't want to see Mr. Schoenberg, h'm?"

Thorndyke reflected for a moment. "Well, it isn't very far, and we may as well see the end of the incident. Yes; let us go together."

No. 213, Greek Street, was one of those houses that irresistibly suggest to the observer the idea of a church organ, either jamb of the doorway being adorned with a row of brass bell-handles corresponding to the stop-knobs.

These the sergeant examined with the air of an expert musician, and having, as it were, gauged the capacity of the instrument, selected the middle knob on the right-hand side and pulled it briskly; whereupon a first-floor window was thrown up and a head protruded. But it afforded us a momentary glimpse only, for, having caught the sergeant's upturned eye, it retired with surprising precipitancy, and before we had time to speculate on the apparition, the street-door was opened and a man emerged. He was about to close the door after him when the inspector interposed.

"Does Mr. Adolf Schoenberg live here?"

The new-comer, a very typical Jew of the red-haired type, surveyed us thoughtfully through his gold-rimmed spectacles as he repeated the name.

"Schoenberg--Schoenberg? Ah, yes! I know. He lives on the third-floor. I saw him go up a short time ago. Third-floor back;" and indicating the open door with a wave of the hand, he raised his hat and passed into the street.

"I suppose we had better go up," said the inspector, with a dubious glance at the row of bell-pulls. He accordingly started up the stairs, and we all followed in his wake.

There were two doors at the back on the third-floor, but as the one was open, displaying an unoccupied bedroom, the inspector rapped smartly on the other. It flew open almost immediately, and a fierce-looking little man confronted us with a hostile stare.

"Well?" said he.

"Mr. Adolf Schoenberg?" inquired the inspector.

"Well? What about him?" snapped our new acquaintance.

"I wished to have a few words with him," said Badger.

"Then what the deuce do you come banging at my door for?" demanded the other.

"Why, doesn't he live here?"

"No. First-floor front," replied our friend, preparing to close the door.

"Pardon me," said Thorndyke, "but what is Mr. Schoenberg like? I mean--"

"Like?" interrupted the resident. "He's like a blooming Sheeny, with a carroty beard and gold gig-lamps!" and, having presented this impressionist sketch, he brought the interview to a definite close by slamming the door and turning the key.

With a wrathful exclamation, the inspector turned towards the stairs, down which the sergeant was already clattering in hot haste, and made his way back to the ground-floor, followed, as before, by Thorndyke and me. On the doorstep we found the sergeant breathlessly interrogating a smartly-dressed youth, whom I had seen alight from a hansom as we entered the house, and who now stood with a notebook tucked under his arm, sharpening a pencil with deliberate care.

"Mr. James saw him come out, sir," said the sergeant. "He turned up towards the Square."

"Did he seem to hurry?" asked the inspector.

"Rather," replied the reporter. "As soon as you were inside, he went off like a lamplighter. You won't catch him now."

"We don't want to catch him," the detective rejoined gruffly; then, backing out of earshot of the eager pressman, he said in a lower tone: "That was Mr. Schoenberg, beyond a doubt, and it is clear that he has some reason for making himself scarce; so I shall consider myself justified in opening that note."

He suited the action to the word, and, having cut the envelope open with official neatness, drew out thc enclosure.

"My hat!" he exclaimed, as his eye fell upon the contents. "What in creation is this? It isn't shorthand, but what the deuce is it?"

He handed the document to Thorndyke, who, having held it up to the light and felt the paper critically, proceeded to examine it with keen interest. It consisted of a single half-sheet of thin notepaper, both sides of which were covered with strange, crabbed characters, written with a brownish-black ink in continuous lines, without any spaces to indicate the divisions into words; and, but for the modern material which bore the writing, it might have been a portion of some ancient manuscript or forgotten codex.

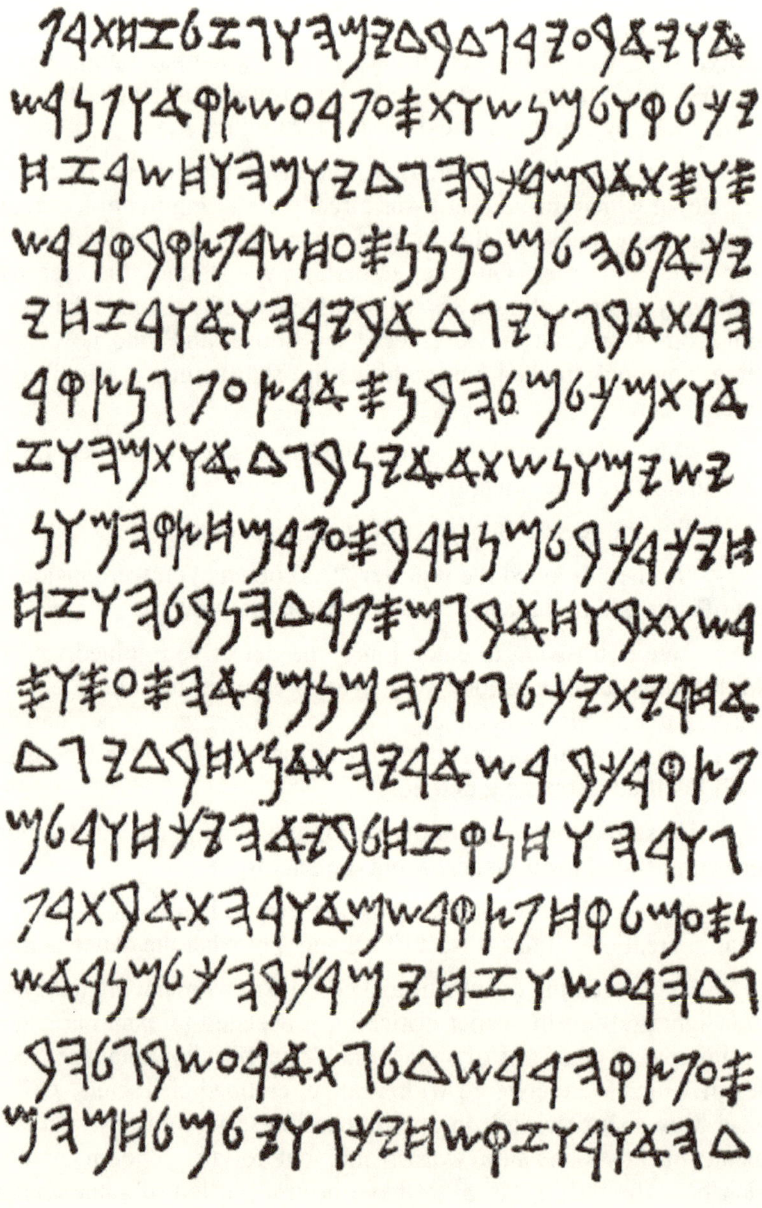

THE CIPHER

"What do you make of it, Doctor?" inquired the inspector anxiously, after a pause, during which Thorndyke had scrutinized the strange writing with knitted brows.

"Not a great deal," replied Thorndyke. "The character is the Moabite or Phoenician--primitive Semitic, in fact--and reads from right to left. The language I take to be Hebrew. At any rate, I can find no Greek words, and I see here a group of letters which may form one of the few Hebrew words that I know--the word badim, 'lies.' But you had better get it deciphered by an expert."

"If it is Hebrew," said Badger, "we can manage it all right. There are plenty of Jews at our disposal."

"You had much better take the paper to the British Museum," said Thorndyke, "and submit it to the keeper of the Phoenician antiquities for decipherment."

Inspector Badger smiled a foxy smile as he deposited the paper in his pocket-book. "We'll see what we can make of it ourselves first," he said; "but many thanks for your advice, all the same, Doctor. No, Mr. James, I can't give you any information just at present; you had better apply at the hospital."

"I suspect," said Thorndyke, as we took our way homewards, "that Mr. James has collected enough material for his purpose already. He must have followed us from the hospital, and I have no doubt that he has his report, with 'full details,' mentally arranged at this moment. And I am not sure that he didn't get a peep at the mysterious paper, in spite of the inspector's precautions."

"By the way," I said, "what do you make of the document?"

"A cipher, most probably," he replied. "It is written in the primitive Semitic alphabet, which, as you know, is practically identical with primitive Greek. It is written from right to left, like the Phoenician, Hebrew, and Moabite, as well as the earliest Greek, inscriptions. The paper is common cream-laid notepaper, and the ink is ordinary indelible Chinese ink, such as is used by draughtsmen. Those are the facts, and without further study of the document itself, they don't carry us very far."

"Why do you think it is a cipher rather than a document in straightforward Hebrew?"

"Because it is obviously a secret message of some kind. Now, every educated Jew knows more or less Hebrew, and, although he is able to read and write only the modern square Hebrew character, it is so easy to transpose one alphabet into another that the mere language would afford no security. Therefore, I expect that, when the experts translate this document, the translation or transliteration will be a mere farrago of unintelligible nonsense. But we shall see, and meanwhile the facts that we have offer several interesting suggestions which are well worth consideration."

"As, for instance -?"

"Now, my dear Jervis," said Thorndyke, shaking an admonitory forefinger at me, "don't, I pray you, give way to mental indolence. You have these few facts that I have mentioned. Consider them separately and collectively, and in their relation to the circumstances. Don't attempt to suck my brain when you have an excellent brain of your own to suck."

On the following morning the papers fully justified my colleague's opinion of Mr. James. All the events which had occurred, as well as a number that had not, were given in the fullest and most vivid detail, a lengthy reference being made to the paper "found on the person of the dead anarchist," and "written in a private shorthand or cryptogram."

The report concluded with the gratifying--though untrue--statement that "in this intricate and important case, the police have wisely secured the assistance of Dr. John Thorndyke, to whose acute intellect and vast experience the portentous cryptogram will doubtless soon deliver up its secret."

"Very flattering," laughed Thorndyke, to whom I read the extract on his return from the hospital, "but a little awkward if it should induce our friends to deposit a few trifling mementoes in the form of nitro-compounds on our main staircase or in the cellars. By the way, I met Superintendent Miller on London Bridge. The 'cryptogram,' as Mr. James calls it, has set Scotland Yard in a mighty ferment."

"Naturally. What have they done in the matter?"

"They adopted my suggestion, after all, finding that they could make nothing of it themselves, and took it to the British Museum. The

Museum people referred them to Professor Poppelbaum, the great palaeographer, to whom they accordingly submitted it."

"Did he express any opinion about it?"

"Yes, provisionally. After a brief examination, he found it to consist of a number of Hebrew words sandwiched between apparently meaningless groups of letters. He furnished the Superintendent off-hand with a translation of the words, and Miller forthwith struck off a number of hectograph copies of it, which he has distributed among the senior officials of his department; so that at present"--here Thorndyke gave vent to a soft chuckle--"Scotland Yard is engaged in a sort of missing word--or, rather, missing sense--competition. Miller invited me to join in the sport, and to that end presented me with one of the hectograph copies on which to exercise my wits, together with a photograph of the document."

"And shall you?" I asked.

"Not I," he replied, laughing. "In the first place, I have not been formally consulted, and consequently am a passive, though interested, spectator. In the second place, I have a theory of my own which I shall test if the occasion arises. But if you would like to take part in the competition, I am authorized to show you the photograph and the translation. I will pass them on to you, and I wish you joy of them."

He handed me the photograph and a sheet of paper that he had just taken from his pocket-book, and watched me with grim amusement as I read out the first few lines.

"Woe, city, lies, robbery, prey, noise, whip, rattling, wheel, horse, chariot, day, darkness, gloominess, clouds, darkness, morning, mountain, people, strong, fire, them, flame."

"It doesn't look very promising at first sight," I remarked. "What is the Professor's theory?"

"His theory--provisionally, of course--is that the words form the message, and the groups of letters represent mere filled-up spaces between the words."

"But surely," I protested, "that would be a very transparent device."

Thorndyke laughed. "There is a childlike simplicity about it," said he, "that is highly attractive--but discouraging. It is much more probable that the words are dummies, and that the letters contain the message. Or, again, the solution may lie in an entirely different direction. But listen! Is that cab coming here?"

It was. It drew up opposite our chambers, and a few moments later a brisk step ascending the stairs heralded a smart rat-tat at our door. Flinging open the latter, I found myself confronted by a well-dressed stranger, who, after a quick glance at me, peered inquisitively over my shoulder into the room.

"I am relieved, Dr. Jervis," said he, "to find you and Dr. Thorndyke at home, as I have come on somewhat urgent professional business. My name," he continued, entering in response to my invitation, "is Barton, but you don't know me, though I know you both by sight. I have come to ask you if one of you--or, better still, both--could come to-night and see my brother."

"That," said Thorndyke, "depends on the circumstances and on the whereabouts of your brother."

"The circumstances," said Mr. Barton, "are, in my opinion, highly suspicious, and I will place them before you--of course, in strict confidence."

Thorndyke nodded and indicated a chair.

"My brother," continued Mr. Barton, taking the proffered seat, "has recently married for the second time. His age is fifty-five, and that of his wife twenty-six, and I may say that the marriage has been--well, by no means a success. Now, within the last fortnight, my brother has been attacked by a mysterious and extremely painful affection of the stomach, to which his doctor seems unable to give a name. It has resisted all treatment hitherto. Day by day the pain and distress increase, and I feel that, unless something decisive is done, the end cannot be far off."

"Is the pain worse after taking food?" inquired Thorndyke.

"That's just it!" exclaimed our visitor. "I see what is in your mind, and it has been in mine, too; so much so that I have tried repeatedly to obtain samples of the food that he is taking. And this morning I succeeded." Here he took from his pocket a wide-mouthed bottle, which, disengaging from its paper wrappings, he laid on the table. "When I called, he was taking his breakfast of arrowroot, which he complained had a gritty taste, supposed by his wife to be due to the sugar. Now I had provided myself with this bottle, and, during the absence of his wife, I managed unobserved to convey a portion of the arrowroot that he had left into it, and I should be greatly obliged if you would examine it and tell me if this arrowroot contains anything that it should not."

He pushed the bottle across to Thorndyke, who carried it to the window, and, extracting a small quantity of the contents with a glass rod, examined the pasty mass with the aid of a lens; then, lifting the bell-glass cover from the microscope, which stood on its table by the window, he smeared a small quantity of the suspected matter on to a glass slip, and placed it on the stage of the instrument.

"I observe a number of crystalline particles in this," he said, after a brief inspection, "which have the appearance of arsenious acid."

"Ah!" ejaculated Mr. Barton, "just what I feared. But are you certain?"

"No," replied Thorndyke; "but the matter is easily tested."

He pressed the button of the bell that communicated with the laboratory, a summons that brought the laboratory assistant from his lair with characteristic promptitude.

"Will you please prepare a Marsh's apparatus, Polton," said Thorndyke.

"I have a couple ready, sir," replied Polton.

"Then pour the acid into one and bring it to me, with a tile."

As his familiar vanished silently, Thorndyke turned to Mr. Barton.

"Supposing we find arsenic in this arrowroot, as we probably shall, what do you want us to do?"

"I want you to come and see my brother," replied our client.

"Why not take a note from me to his doctor?"

"No, no; I want you to come--I should like you both to come--and put a stop at once to this dreadful business. Consider! It's a matter of life and death. You won't refuse! I beg you not to refuse me your help in these terrible circumstances."

"Well," said Thorndyke, as his assistant reappeared, "let us first see what the test has to tell us."

Polton advanced to the table, on which he deposited a small flask, the contents of which were in a state of brisk effervescence, a bottle labelled "calcium hypochlorite," and a white porcelain tile. The flask was fitted with a safety-funnel and a glass tube drawn out to a fine jet, to which Polton cautiously applied a lighted match. Instantly there sprang from the jet a tiny, pale violet flame. Thorndyke now took the tile, and held it in the flame for a few seconds, when the appearance of the surface remained unchanged save for a small circle of condensed moisture. His next proceeding was to thin the arrowroot with distilled water until it was quite fluid, and then pour a small quantity into the funnel. It ran slowly down the tube into the flask, with the bubbling contents of which it became speedily mixed. Almost immediately a change began to appear in the character of the flame, which from a pale violet turned gradually to a sickly blue, while above it hung a faint cloud of white smoke. Once more Thorndyke held the tile above the jet, but this time, no sooner had the pallid flame touched the cold surface of the porcelain, than there appeared on the latter a glistening black stain.

"That is pretty conclusive," observed Thorndyke, lifting the stopper out of the reagent bottle, "but we will apply the final test." He dropped a few drops of the hypochlorite solution on to the tile, and immediately the black stain faded away and vanished. "We can now answer your question, Mr. Barton," said he, replacing the stopper as he turned to our client. "The specimen that you brought us certainly contains arsenic, and in very considerable quantities."

"Then," exclaimed Mr. Barton, starting from his chair, "you will come and help me to rescue my brother from this dreadful peril. Don't refuse me, Dr. Thorndyke, for mercy's sake, don't refuse."

Thorndyke reflected for a moment.

"Before we decide," said he, "we must see what engagements we have."

With a quick, significant glance at me, he walked into the office, whither I followed in some bewilderment, for I knew that we had no engagements for the evening.

"Now, Jervis," said Thorndyke, as he closed the office door, "what are we to do?"

"We must go, I suppose," I replied. "It seems a pretty urgent case."

"It does," he agreed. "Of course, the man may be telling the truth, after all."

"You don't think he is, then?"

"No. It is a plausible tale, but there is too much arsenic in that arrowroot. Still, I think I ought to go. It is an ordinary professional risk. But there is no reason why you should put your head into the noose."

"Thank you," said I, somewhat huffily. "I don't see what risk there is, but if any exists I claim the right to share it."

"Very well," he answered with a smile, "we will both go. I think we can take care of ourselves."

He re-entered the sitting-room, and announced his decision to Mr. Barton, whose relief and gratitude were quite pathetic.

"But," said Thorndyke, "you have not yet told us where your brother lives."

"Rexford," was the reply--"Rexford, in Essex. It is an out-of-the-way place, but if we catch the seven-fifteen train from Liverpool Street, we shall be there in an hour and a half."

"And as to the return? You know the trains, I suppose?"

"Oh yes," replied our client; "I will see that you don't miss your train back."

"Then I will be with you in a minute," said Thorndyke; and, taking the still-bubbling flask, he retired to the laboratory, whence he returned in a few minutes carrying his hat and overcoat.

The cab which had brought our client was still waiting, and we were soon rattling through the streets towards the station, where we arrived in time to furnish ourselves with dinner-baskets and select our compartment at leisure.

During the early part of the journey our companion was in excellent spirits. He despatched the cold fowl from the basket and quaffed the rather indifferent claret with as much relish as if he had not had a single relation in the world, and after dinner he became genial to the verge of hilarity. But, as time went on, there crept into his manner a certain anxious restlessness. He became silent and preoccupied, and several times furtively consulted his watch.

"The train is confoundedly late!" he exclaimed irritably. "Seven minutes behind time already!"

"A few minutes more or less are not of much consequence," said Thorndyke.

"No, of course not; but still--Ah, thank Heaven, here we are!"

He thrust his head out of the off-side window, and gazed eagerly down the line; then, leaping to his feet, he bustled out on to the platform while the train was still moving.

Even as we alighted a warning bell rang furiously on the up-platform, and as Mr. Barton hurried us through the empty booking-office to the outside of the station, the rumble of the approaching train could be heard above the noise made by our own train moving off.

"My carriage doesn't seem to have arrived yet," exclaimed Mr. Barton, looking anxiously up the station approach. "If you will wait here a moment, I will go and make inquiries."

He darted back into the booking-office and through it on to the platform, just as the up-train roared into the station. Thorndyke followed him with quick but stealthy steps, and, peering out of the booking-office door, watched his proceedings; then he turned and beckoned to me.

"There he goes," said he, pointing to an iron footbridge that spanned the line; and, as I looked, I saw, clearly defined against the dim night sky, a flying figure racing towards the "up" side.

It was hardly two-thirds across when the guard's whistle sang out its shrill warning.

"Quick, Jervis," exclaimed Thorndyke; "she's off!"

He leaped down on to the line, whither I followed instantly, and, crossing the rails, we clambered up together on to the foot-board opposite an empty first-class compartment. Thorndyke's magazine knife, containing, among other implements, a railway-key, was already in his hand. The door was speedily unlocked, and, as we entered, Thorndyke ran through and looked out on to the platform.

"Just in time!" he exclaimed. "He is in one of the forward compartments."

He relocked the door, and, seating himself, proceeded to fill his pipe.

"And now," said I, as the train moved out of the station, "perhaps you will explain this little comedy."

"With pleasure," he replied, "if it needs any explanation. But you can hardly have forgotten Mr. James's flattering remarks in his report of the Greek Street incident, clearly giving the impression that the mysterious document was in my possession. When I read that, I knew I must look out for some attempt to recover it, though I hardly expected such promptness. Still, when Mr. Barton called without credentials or appointment, I viewed him with some suspicion. That suspicion deepened when he wanted us both to come. It deepened further when I found an impossible quantity of arsenic in his sample, and it gave place to certainty when, having allowed him to select the trains by which we were to travel, I went up to the laboratory and examined the time-table; for I then found that the last train for London left Rexford ten minutes after we were due to arrive. Obviously this was a plan to get us both safely out of the way while he and some of his friends ransacked our chambers for the missing document."

"I see; and that accounts for his extraordinary anxiety at the lateness of the train. But why did you come, if you knew it was a 'plant'?"

"My dear fellow," said Thorndyke, "I never miss an interesting experience if I can help it. There are possibilities in this, too, don't you see?"

"But supposing his friends have broken into our chambers already?"

"That contingency has been provided for; but I think they will wait for Mr. Barton--and us."

Our train, being the last one up, stopped at every station, and crawled slothfully in the intervals, so that it was past eleven o'clock when we reached Liverpool Street. Here we got out cautiously, and, mingling with the crowd, followed the unconscious Barton up the platform, through the barrier, and out into the street. He seemed in no special hurry, for, after pausing to light a cigar, he set off at an easy pace up New Broad Street.

Thorndyke hailed a hansom, and, motioning me to enter, directed the cabman to drive to Clifford's Inn Passage.

"Sit well back," said he, as we rattled away up New Broad Street. "We shall be passing our gay deceiver presently--in fact, there he is, a living, walking illustration of the folly of underrating the intelligence of one's adversary."

At Clifford's Inn Passage we dismissed the cab, and, retiring into the shadow of the dark, narrow alley, kept an eye on the gate of Inner Temple Lane. In about twenty minutes we observed our friend approaching on the south side of Fleet Street. He halted at the gate, plied the knocker, and after a brief parley with the night-porter vanished through the wicket. We waited yet five minutes more, and then, having given him time to get clear of the entrance, we crossed the road.

The porter looked at us with some surprise.

"There's a gentleman just gone down to your chambers, sir," said he. "He told me you were expecting him."

"Quite right," said Thorndyke, with a dry smile, "I was. Good-night."

We slunk down the lane, past the church, and through the gloomy cloisters, giving a wide berth to all lamps and lighted entries, until, emerging into Paper Buildings, we crossed at the darkest part to King's Bench Walk, where Thorndyke made straight for the chambers of our friend Anstey, which were two doors above our own.

"Why are we coming here?" I asked, as we ascended the stairs.

But the question needed no answer when we reached the landing, for through the open door of our friend's chambers I could see in the darkened room Anstey himself with two uniformed constables and a couple of plain-clothes men.

"There has been no signal yet, sir," said one of the latter, whom I recognized as a detective-sergeant of our division.

"No," said Thorndyke, "but the M.C. has arrived. He came in five minutes before us."

"Then," exclaimed Anstey, "the ball will open shortly, ladies and gents. The boards are waxed, the fiddlers are tuning up, and--"

"Not quite so loud, if you please, sir," said the sergeant. "I think there is somebody coming up Crown Office Row."

The ball had, in fact, opened. As we peered cautiously out of the open window, keeping well back in the darkened room, a stealthy figure crept out of the shadow, crossed the road, and stole noiselessly into the entry of Thorndyke's chambers. It was quickly followed by a second figure, and then by a third, in which I recognized our elusive client.

"Now listen for the signal," said Thorndyke. "They won't waste time. Confound that clock!"

The soft-voiced bell of the Inner Temple clock, mingling with the harsher tones of St. Dunstan's and the Law Courts, slowly told out the hour of midnight; and as the last reverberations were dying away, some metallic object, apparently a coin, dropped with a sharp clink on to the pavement under our window.

At the sound the watchers simultaneously sprang to their feet.

"You two go first," said the sergeant, addressing the uniformed men, who thereupon stole noiselessly, in their rubber-soled boots, down the stone stairs and along the pavement. The rest of us followed, with less attention to silence, and as we ran up to Thorndyke's chambers, we were aware of quick but stealthy footsteps on the stairs above.

"They've been at work, you see," whispered one of the constables, flashing his lantern on to the iron-bound outer door of our sitting-room, on which the marks of a large jemmy were plainly visible.

The sergeant nodded grimly, and, bidding the constables to remain on the landing, led the way upwards.

As we ascended, faint rustlings continued to be audible from above, and on the second-floor landing we met a man descending briskly, but without hurry, from the third. It was Mr. Barton, and I could not but admire the composure with which he passed the two detectives. But suddenly his glance fell on Thorndyke, and his composure vanished. With a wild stare of incredulous horror, he halted as if petrified; then he broke away and raced furiously down the stairs, and a moment later a muffled shout and the sound of a scuffle told us that he had received a check. On the next flight we met two more men, who, more hurried and less self-possessed, endeavoured to push past; but the sergeant barred the way.

"Why, bless me!" exclaimed the latter, "it's Moakey; and isn't that Tom Harris?"

"It's all right, sergeant," said Moakey plaintively, striving to escape from the officer's grip. "We've come to the wrong house, that's all."

The sergeant smiled indulgently. "I know," he replied. "But you're always coming to the wrong house, Moakey; and now you're just coming along with me to the right house."

He slipped his hand inside his captive's coat, and adroitly fished out a large, folding jemmy; whereupon the discomforted burglar abandoned all further protest.

On our return to the first-floor, we found Mr. Barton sulkily awaiting us, handcuffed to one of the constables, and watched by Polton with pensive disapproval.

"I needn't trouble you to-night, Doctor," said the sergeant, as he marshalled his little troop of captors and captives. "You'll hear from us in the morning. Good-night, sir."

The melancholy procession moved off down the stairs, and we retired into our chambers with Anstey to smoke a last pipe.

"A capable man, that Barton," observed Thorndyke--"ready, plausible, and ingenious, but spoilt by prolonged contact with fools. I wonder if the police will perceive the significance of this little affair."

"They will be more acute than I am if they do," said I.

"Naturally," interposed Anstey, who loved to "cheek" his revered senior, "because there isn't any. It's only Thorndyke's bounce. He is really in a deuce of a fog himself."

However this may have been, the police were a good deal puzzled by the incident, for, on the following morning, we received a visit from no less a person than Superintendent Miller, of Scotland Yard.

"This is a queer business," said he, coming to the point at once--"this burglary, I mean. Why should they want to crack your place, right here in the Temple, too? You've got nothing of value here, have you? No 'hard stuff,' as they call it, for instance?"

"Not so much as a silver teaspoon," replied Thorndyke, who had a conscientious objection to plate of all kinds.

"It's odd," said the superintendent, "deuced odd. When we got your note, we thought these anarchist idiots had mixed you up with the case--you saw the papers, I suppose--and wanted to go through your rooms for some reason. We thought we had our hands on the gang, instead of which we find a party of common crooks that we're sick of the sight of. I tell you, sir, it's annoying when you think you've hooked a salmon, to bring up a blooming eel."

"It must be a great disappointment," Thorndyke agreed, suppressing a smile.

"It is," said the detective. "Not but what we're glad enough to get these beggars, especially Halkett, or Barton, as he calls himself--a mighty slippery customer is Halkett, and mischievous, too--but we're not wanting any disappointments just now. There was that big jewel job in Piccadilly, Taplin and Horne's; I don't mind telling you that we've not got the ghost of a clue. Then there's this anarchist affair. We're all in the dark there, too."

"But what about the cipher?" asked Thorndyke.

"Oh, hang the cipher!" exclaimed the detective irritably. "This Professor Poppelbaum may be a very learned man, but he doesn't help us much. He says the document is in Hebrew, and he has translated it into Double Dutch. Just listen to this!" He dragged out of his pocket a bundle of papers, and, dabbing down a photograph of the document before Thorndyke, commenced to read the Professor's report. "'The document is written in the characters of the well-known inscription of Mesha, King of Moab' (who the devil's he? Never heard of him. Well known, indeed!) 'The language is Hebrew, and the words are separated by groups of letters, which are meaningless, and obviously introduced to mislead and confuse the reader. The words themselves are not strictly consecutive, but, by the interpellation of certain other words, a series of intelligible sentences is obtained, the meaning of which is not very clear, but is no doubt allegorical. The method of decipherment is shown in the accompanying tables, and the full rendering suggested on the enclosed sheet. It is to be noted that the writer of this document was apparently quite unacquainted with the Hebrew language, as appears from the absence of any grammatical construction.' That's the Professor's report, Doctor, and here are the tables showing how he worked it out. It makes my head spin to look at 'em."

He handed to Thorndyke a bundle of ruled sheets, which my colleague examined attentively for a while, and then passed on to me.

"This is very systematic and thorough," said he. "But now let us see the final result at which he arrives."

"It may be all very systematic," growled the superintendent, sorting out his papers, "but I tell you, sir, it's all BOSH!" The latter word he jerked out viciously, as he slapped down on the table the final product of the Professor's labours. "There," he continued, "that's what he calls the 'full rendering,' and I reckon it'll make your hair curl. It might be a message from Bedlam."

Thorndyke took up the first sheet, and as he compared the constructed renderings with the literal translation, the ghost of a smile stole across his usually immovable countenance.

"The meaning is certainly a little obscure," he observed, "though the reconstruction is highly ingenious; and, moreover, I think the Professor is probably right. That is to say, the words which he has supplied are probably the omitted parts of the passages from which the words of the cryptogram were taken. What do you think, Jervis?"

	Space	Word	Space	Word	Space	Word
Moabite	[illegible]	[illegible]	[illegible]	[illegible]	[illegible]	[illegible]
Hebrew		בְּדִים		עִיר		אוֹי
Translation		LIES		CITY		WOE
Moabite	[illegible]	[illegible]	[illegible]	[illegible]	[illegible]	[illegible]
Hebrew		קוֹל		טֶרֶף		גָּזֵל
Translation		NOISE		PREY		ROBBERY
Moabite	[illegible]	[illegible]	[illegible]	[illegible]	[illegible]	[illegible]
Hebrew		אוֹפָן		רַעַשׁ		שׁוֹט
Translation		WHEEL		RATTLING		WHIP
Moabite	[illegible]	[illegible]	[illegible]	[illegible]	[illegible]	[illegible]
Hebrew		יוֹם		מֶרְכָּבָה		סוּס
Translation		DAY		CHARIOT		HORSE

THE PROFESSOR'S ANALYSIS.

Handwritten: Analysis of the cipher with translation into modern square Hebrew characters + a translation into English. N.B. The cipher reads from right to left.

He handed me the two papers, of which one gave the actual words of the cryptogram, and the other a suggested reconstruction, with omitted words supplied. The first read:

"Woe city lies robbery prey noise whip rattling wheel horse chariot day darkness gloominess cloud darkness morning mountain people strong fire them flame."

Turning to the second paper, I read out the suggested rendering:

"'Woe *to the bloody* city! *It is full of* lies *and* robbery; *the* prey *departeth not. The* noise *of a* whip, *and the noise of the* rattling *of the* wheel*s*, *and of the prancing* horse*s*, *and of the jumping* chariot*s*.

"'*A* day *of* darkness *and of* gloominess, *a day of* cloud*s*, *and of thick* darkness, *as the* morning *spread upon the* mountain*s*, *a great* people *and a* strong.

"'*A* fire *devoureth before* them, *and behind them a* flame *burneth*.'"

Here the first sheet ended, and, as I laid it down, Thorndyke looked at me inquiringly.

"There is a good deal of reconstruction in proportion to the original matter," I objected. "The Professor has 'supplied' more than three-quarters of the final rendering."

"Exactly," burst in the superintendent; "it's all Professor and no cryptogram."

"Still, I think the reading is correct," said Thorndyke. "As far as it goes, that is."

"Good Lord!" exclaimed the dismayed detective. "Do you mean to tell me, sir, that that balderdash is the real meaning of the thing?"

"I don't say that," replied Thorndyke. "I say it is correct as far as it goes; but I doubt its being the solution of the cryptogram."

"Have you been studying that photograph that I gave you?" demanded Miller, with sudden eagerness.

"I have looked at it," said Thorndyke evasively, "but I should like to examine the original if you have it with you."

"I have," said the detective. "Professor Poppelbaum sent it back with the solution. You can have a look at it, though I can't leave it with you without special authority."

He drew the document from his pocket-book and handed it to Thorndyke, who took it over to the window and scrutinized it closely. From the window he drifted into the adjacent office, closing the door after him; and presently the sound of a faint explosion told me that he had lighted the gas-fire.

"Of course," said Miller, taking up the translation again, "this gibberish is the sort of stuff you might expect from a parcel of crack-brained anarchists; but it doesn't seem to mean anything."

"Not to us," I agreed; "but the phrases may have some pre-arranged significance. And then there are the letters between the words. It is possible that they may really form a cipher."

"I suggested that to the Professor," said Miller, "but he wouldn't hear of it. He is sure they are only dummies."

"I think he is probably mistaken, and so, I fancy, does my colleague. But we shall hear what he has to say presently."

"Oh, I know what he will say," growled Miller. "He will put the thing under the microscope, and tell us who made the paper, and what the ink is composed of, and then we shall be just where we were." The superintendent was evidently deeply depressed.

We sat for some time pondering in silence on the vague sentences of the Professor's translation, until, at length, Thorndyke reappeared, holding the document in his hand. He laid it quietly on the table by the officer, and then inquired: "Is this an official consultation?"

"Certainly," replied Miller. "I was authorized to consult you respecting the translation, but nothing was said about the original. Still, if you want it for further study, I will get it for you."

"No, thank you," said Thorndyke. "I have finished with it. My theory turned out to be correct."

"Your theory!" exclaimed the superintendent, eagerly. "Do you mean to say -?"

"And, as you are consulting me officially, I may as well give you this."

He held out a sheet of paper, which the detective took from him and began to read.

"What is this?" he asked, looking up at Thorndyke with a puzzled frown. "Where did it come from?"

"It is the solution of the cryptogram," replied Thorndyke.

The detective re-read the contents of the paper, and, with the frown of perplexity deepening, once more gazed at my colleague.

"This is a joke, sir; you are fooling me," he said sulkily.

"Nothing of the kind," answered Thorndyke. "That is the genuine solution."

"But it's impossible!" exclaimed Miller. "Just look at it, Dr. Jervis."

I took the paper from his hand, and, as I glanced at it, I had no difficulty in understanding his surprise. It bore a short inscription in printed Roman capitals, thus:

"THE PICKERDILLEY STUF IS UP THE CHIMBLY 416 WARDOUR ST 2ND FLOUR BACK IT WAS HID BECOS OF OLD MOAKEYS JOOD MOAKEY IS A BLITER."

"Then that fellow wasn't an anarchist at all?" I exclaimed.

"No," said Miller. "He was one of Moakey's gang. We suspected Moakey of being mixed up with that job, but we couldn't fix it on him. By Jove!" he added, slapping his thigh, "if this is right, and I can lay my hands on the loot! Can you lend me a bag, doctor? I'm off to Wardour Street this very moment."

We furnished him with an empty suit-case, and, from the window, watched him making for Mitre Court at a smart double.

"I wonder if he will find the booty," said Thorndyke. "It just depends on whether the hiding-place was known to more than one of the gang. Well, it has been a quaint case, and instructive, too. I suspect our friend Barton and the evasive Schoenberg were the collaborators who produced that curiosity of literature."

"May I ask how you deciphered the thing?" I said. "It didn't appear to take long."

"It didn't. It was merely a matter of testing a hypothesis; and you ought not to have to ask that question," he added, with mock severity, "seeing that you had what turn out to have been all the necessary facts, two days ago. But I will prepare a document and demonstrate to you to-morrow morning."

"So Miller was successful in his quest," said Thorndyke, as we smoked our morning pipes after breakfast. "The 'entire swag,' as he calls it, was 'up the chimbly,' undisturbed."

He handed me a note which had been left, with the empty suit-case, by a messenger, shortly before, and I was about to read it when an agitated knock was heard at our door. The visitor, whom I admitted, was a rather haggard and dishevelled elderly gentleman, who, as he entered, peered inquisitively through his concave spectacles from one of us to the other.

"Allow me to introduce myself, gentlemen," said he. "I am Professor Poppelbaum."

Thorndyke bowed and offered a chair.

"I called yesterday afternoon," our visitor continued, "at Scotland Yard, where I heard of your remarkable decipherment and of the convincing proof of its correctness. Thereupon I borrowed the cryptogram, and have spent the entire night in studying it, but I cannot connect your solution with any of the characters. I wonder if you would do me the great favour of enlightening me as to your method of decipherment, and so save me further sleepless nights? You may rely on my discretion."

"Have you the document with you?" asked Thorndyke.

The Professor produced it from his pocket-book, and passed it to my colleague.

"You observe, Professor," said the latter, "that this is a laid paper, and has no water-mark?"

"Yes, I noticed that."

"And that the writing is in indelible Chinese ink?"

"Yes, yes," said the savant impatiently; "but it is the inscription that interests me, not the paper and ink."

"Precisely," said Thorndyke. "Now, it was the ink that interested me when I caught a glimpse of the document three days ago. 'Why,' I asked myself, 'should anyone use this troublesome medium'--for this appears to be stick ink--'when good writing ink is to be had?' What advantages has Chinese ink over writing ink? It has several advantages as a drawing ink, but for writing purposes it has only one: it is quite unaffected by wet. The obvious inference, then, was that this document was, for some reason, likely to be exposed to wet. But this inference instantly suggested another, which I was yesterday able to put to the test--thus."

He filled a tumbler with water, and, rolling up the document, dropped it in. Immediately there began to appear on it a new set of characters of a curious grey colour. In a few seconds Thorndyke lifted out the wet paper, and held it up to the light, and now there was plainly visible an inscription in transparent lettering, like a very distinct water-mark. It was in printed Roman capitals, written across the other writing, and read:

"THE PICKERDILLEY STUF IS UP THE CHIMBLY 416 WARDOUR ST 2ND FLOUR BACK IT WAS HID BECOS OF OLD MOAKEYS JOOD MOAKEY IS A BLITER."

The Professor regarded the inscription with profound disfavour.

"How do you suppose this was done?" he asked gloomily.

"I will show you," said Thorndyke. "I have prepared a piece of paper to demonstrate the process to Dr. Jervis. It is exceedingly simple."

He fetched from the office a small plate of glass, and a photographic dish in which a piece of thin notepaper was soaking in water.

"This paper," said Thorndyke, lifting it out and laying it on the glass, "has been soaking all night, and is now quite pulpy."

He spread a dry sheet of paper over the wet one, and on the former wrote heavily with a hard pencil, "Moakey is a bliter." On lifting the upper sheet, the writing was seen to be transferred in a deep grey to the wet paper, and when the latter was held up to the light the inscription stood out clear and transparent as if written with oil.

"When this dries," said Thorndyke, "the writing will completely disappear, but it will reappear whenever the paper is again wetted."

The Professor nodded.

"Very ingenious," said he--"a sort of artificial palimpsest, in fact. But I do not understand how that illiterate man could have written in the difficult Moabite script."

"He did not," said Thorndyke. "The 'cryptogram' was probably written by one of the leaders of the gang, who, no doubt, supplied copies to the other members to use instead of blank paper for secret communications. The object of the Moabite writing was evidently to divert attention from the paper itself, in case the communication fell into the wrong hands, and I must say it seems to have answered its purpose very well."

The Professor started, stung by the sudden recollection of his labours.

"Yes," he snorted; "but I am a scholar, sir, not a policeman. Every man to his trade."

He snatched up his hat, and with a curt "Good-morning," flung out of the room in dudgeon.

Thorndyke laughed softly.

"Poor Professor!" he murmured. "Our playful friend Barton has much to answer for."

The Mandarin's Pearl

Mr. Brodribb stretched out his toes on the kerb before the blazing fire with the air of a man who is by no means insensible to physical comfort.

"You are really an extraordinarily polite fellow, Thorndyke," said he.

He was an elderly man, rosy-gilled, portly, and convivial, to whom a mass of bushy, white hair, an expansive double chin, and a certain prim sumptuousness of dress imparted an air of old-world distinction. Indeed, as he dipped an amethystine nose into his wine-glass, and gazed thoughtfully at the glowing end of his cigar, he looked the very type of the well-to-do lawyer of an older generation.

"You are really an extraordinarily polite fellow, Thorndyke," said Mr. Brodribb.

"I know," replied Thorndyke. "But why this reference to an admitted fact?"

"The truth has just dawned on me," said the solicitor. "Here am I, dropping in on you, uninvited and unannounced, sitting in your own armchair before your fire, smoking your cigars, drinking your Burgundy-- and deuced good Burgundy, too, let me add--and you have not dropped a single hint of curiosity as to what has brought me here."

"I take the gifts of the gods, you see, and ask no questions," said Thorndyke.

"Devilish handsome of you, Thorndyke--unsociable beggar like you, too," rejoined Mr. Brodribb, a fan of wrinkles spreading out genially from the corners of his eyes; "but the fact is I have come, in a sense, on business--always glad of a pretext to look you up, as you know--but I want to take your opinion on a rather queer case. It is about young Calverley. You remember Horace Calverley? Well, this is his son. Horace and I were schoolmates, you know, and after his death the boy, Fred, hung on to me rather. We're near neighbours down at Weybridge, and very good friends. I like Fred. He's a good fellow, though cranky, like all his people."

"What has happened to Fred Calverley?" Thorndyke asked, as the solicitor paused.

"Why, the fact is," said Mr. Brodribb, "just lately he seems to be going a bit queer--not mad, mind you--at least, I think not--but undoubtedly queer. Now, there is a good deal of property, and a good many highly interested relatives, and, as a natural consequence, there is some talk of getting him certified. They're afraid he may do something involving the estate or develop homicidal tendencies, and they talk of possible suicide--you remember his father's death--but I say that's all bunkum. The fellow is just a bit cranky, and nothing more."

"What are his symptoms?" asked Thorndyke.

"Oh, he thinks he is being followed about and watched, and he has delusions; sees himself in the glass with the wrong face, and that sort of thing, you know."

"You are not highly circumstantial," Thorndyke remarked.

Mr. Brodribb looked at me with a genial smile.

"What a glutton for facts this fellow is, Jervis. But you're right, Thorndyke; I'm vague. However, Fred will be here presently. We travel down together, and I took the liberty of asking him to call for me. We'll get him to tell you about his delusions, if you don't mind. He's not shy about them. And meanwhile I'll give you a few preliminary facts. The trouble began about a year ago. He was in a railway accident, and that knocked him all to pieces. Then he went for a voyage to recruit, and the ship broke her propeller-shaft in a storm and became helpless. That didn't improve the state of his nerves. Then he went down the Mediterranean, and after a month or two, back he came, no better than when he started. But here he is, I expect."

He went over to the door and admitted a tall, frail young man whom Thorndyke welcomed with quiet geniality, and settled in a chair by the fire. I looked curiously at our visitor. He was a typical neurotic-- slender, fragile, eager. Wide-open blue eyes with broad pupils, in which I could plainly see the characteristic "hippus"--that incessant change of size that marks the unstable nervous equilibrium--parted lips, and wandering taper fingers, were as the stigmata of his disorder. He was of the stuff out of which prophets and devotees, martyrs, reformers, and third-rate poets are made.

"I have been telling Dr. Thorndyke about these nervous troubles of yours," said Mr. Brodribb presently. "I hope you don't mind. He is an old friend, you know, and he is very much interested."

"It is very good of him," said Calverley. Then he flushed deeply, and added: "But they are not really nervous, you know. They can't be merely subjective."

"You think they can't be?" said Thorndyke.

"No, I am sure they are not." He flushed again like a girl, and looked earnestly at Thorndyke with his big, dreamy eyes. "But you doctors," he said, "are so dreadfully sceptical of all spiritual phenomena. You are such materialists."

"Yes," said Mr. Brodribb; "the doctors are not hot on the supernatural, and that's the fact."

"Supposing you tell us about your experiences," said Thorndyke persuasively. "Give us a chance to believe, if we can't explain away."

Calverley reflected for a few moments; then, looking earnestly at Thorndyke, he said: "Very well; if it won't bore you, I will. It is a curious story."

"I have told Dr. Thorndyke about your voyage and your trip down the Mediterranean," said Mr. Brodribb.

"Then," said Calverley, "I will begin with the events that are actually connected with these strange visitations. The first of these occurred in Marseilles. I was in a curio-shop there, looking over some Algerian and Moorish tilings, when my attention was attracted by a sort of charm or pendant that hung in a glass case. It was not particularly beautiful, but its appearance was quaint and curious, and took my fancy. It consisted of an oblong block of ebony in which was set a single pear-shaped pearl more than three-quarters of an inch long. The sides of the ebony block were lacquered--probably to conceal a joint--and bore a number of Chinese characters, and at the top was a little gold image with a hole through it, presumably for a string to suspend it by. Excepting for the pearl, the whole thing was uncommonly like one of those ornamental tablets of Chinese ink.

"Now, I had taken a fancy to the thing, and I can afford to indulge my fancies in moderation. The man wanted five pounds for it; he assured me that the pearl was a genuine one of fine quality, and obviously did not believe it himself. To me, however, it looked like a real pearl, and I determined to take the risk; so I paid the money, and he bowed me out with a smile--I may almost say a grin--of satisfaction. He would not have been so well pleased if he had followed me to a jeweller's to whom I took it for an expert opinion; for the jeweller pronounced the pearl to be undoubtedly genuine, and worth anything up to a thousand pounds.

"A day or two later, I happened to show my new purchase to some men whom I knew, who had dropped in at Marseilles in their yacht. They were highly amused at my having bought the thing, and when I told them what I had paid for it, they positively howled with derision.

"'Why, you silly guffin,' said one of them, a man named Halliwell, 'I could have had it ten days ago for half a sovereign, or probably five shillings. I wish now I had bought it; then I could have sold it to you.'

"It seemed that a sailor had been hawking the pendant round the harbour, and had been on board the yacht with it.

"'Deuced anxious the beggar was to get rid of it, too,' said Halliwell, grinning at the recollection. 'Swore it was a genuine pearl of priceless value, and was willing to deprive himself of it for the trifling sum of half a jimmy. But we'd heard that sort of thing before. However, the curio-man seems to have speculated on the chance of meeting with a greenhorn, and he seems to have pulled it off. Lucky curio man!'

"I listened patiently to their gibes, and when they had talked themselves out I told them about the jeweller. They were most frightfully sick; and when we had taken the pendant to a dealer in gems who happened to be staying in the town, and he had offered me five hundred pounds for it, their language wasn't fit for a divinity students' debating club. Naturally the story got noised abroad, and when I left, it was the talk of the place. The general opinion was that the sailor, who was traced to a tea-ship that had put into the harbour, had stolen it from some Chinese passenger; and no less than seventeen different Chinamen came forward to claim it as their stolen property.

"Soon after this I returned to England, and, as my nerves were still in a very shaky state, I came to live with my cousin Alfred, who has a large house at Weybridge. At this time he had a friend staying with him, a certain Captain Raggerton, and the two men appeared to be on very intimate terms. I did not take to Raggerton at all. He was a good-looking man, pleasant in his manners, and remarkably plausible. But the fact is-- I am speaking in strict confidence, of course--he was a bad egg. He had been in the Guards, and I don't quite know why he left; but I do know that he played bridge and baccarat pretty heavily at several clubs, and that he had a reputation for being a rather uncomfortably lucky player. He did a good deal at the race-meetings, too, and was in general such an obvious undesirable that I could never understand my cousin's intimacy with him, though I must say that Alfred's habits had changed somewhat for the worse since I had left England.

"The fame of my purchase seems to have preceded me, for when, one day, I produced the pendant to show them, I found that they knew all about it. Raggerton had heard the story from a naval man, and I gathered vaguely that he had heard something that I had not, and that he did not care to tell me; for when my cousin and he talked about the pearl, which they did pretty often, certain significant looks passed between them, and certain veiled references were made which I could not fail to notice.

"One day I happened to be telling them of a curious incident that occurred on my way home. I had travelled to England on one of Holt's big China boats, not liking the crowd and bustle of the regular passenger-lines. Now, one afternoon, when we had been at sea a couple of days, I took a book down to my berth, intending to have a quiet read till tea-time. Soon, however, I dropped off into a doze, and must have remained asleep for over an hour. I awoke suddenly, and as I opened my eyes, I perceived that the door of the state-room was half-open, and a well-dressed Chinaman, in native costume, was looking in at me. He closed the door immediately, and I remained for a few moments paralyzed by the start that he had given me. Then I leaped from my bunk, opened the door, and looked out. But the alley-way was empty. The Chinaman had vanished as if by magic.

"This little occurrence made me quite nervous for a day or two, which was very foolish of me; but my nerves were all on edge--and I am afraid they are still."

"Yes," said Thorndyke. "There was nothing mysterious about the affair. These boats carry a Chinese crew, and the man you saw was probably a Serang, or whatever they call the gang-captains on these vessels. Or he may have been a native passenger who had strayed into the wrong part of the ship."

"Exactly," agreed our client. "But to return to Raggerton. He listened with quite extraordinary interest as I was telling this story, and when I had finished he looked very queerly at my cousin.

"'A deuced odd thing, this, Calverley,' said he. 'Of course, it may be only a coincidence, but it really does look as if there was something, after all, in that--'

"'Shut up, Raggerton,' said my cousin. 'We don't want any of that rot.'

"'What is he talking about?" I asked.

"'Oh, it's only a rotten, silly yarn that he has picked up somewhere. You're not to tell him, Raggerton.'

"'I don't see why I am not to be told,' I said, rather sulkily. 'I'm not a baby.'

"'No,' said Alfred, 'but you're an invalid. You don't want any horrors.'

"In effect, he refused to go into the matter any further, and I was left on tenterhooks of curiosity.

"However, the very next day I got Raggerton alone in the smoking-room, and had a little talk with him. He had just dropped a hundred pounds on a double event that hadn't come off, and I expected to find him pliable. Nor was I disappointed, for, when we had negotiated a little loan, he was entirely at my service, and willing to tell me everything, on my promising not to give him away to Alfred.

"'Now, you understand,' he said, 'that this yarn about your pearl is nothing but a damn silly fable that's been going the round in Marseilles. I don't know where it came from, or what sort of demented rotter invented it; I had it from a Johnnie in the Mediterranean Squadron, and you can have a copy of his letter if you want it.'

"I said that I did want it. Accordingly, that same evening he handed me a copy of the narrative extracted from his friend's letter, the substance of which was this: "About four months ago there was lying in Canton Harbour a large English barque. Her name is not mentioned, but that is not material to the story. She had got her cargo stowed and her crew signed on, and was only waiting for certain official formalities to be completed before putting to sea on her homeward voyage. Just ahead of her, at the same quay, was a Danish ship that had been in collision outside, and was now laid up pending the decision of the Admiralty Court. She had been unloaded, and her crew paid off, with the exception of one elderly man, who remained on board as ship-keeper. Now, a considerable part of the cargo of the English barque was the property of a certain wealthy mandarin, and this person had been about the vessel a good deal while she was taking in her lading.

"One day, when the mandarin was on board the barque, it happened that three of the seamen were sitting in the galley smoking and chatting with the cook--an elderly Chinaman named Wo-li--and the latter, pointing out the mandarin to the sailors, expatiated on his enormous wealth, assuring them that he was commonly believed to carry on his person articles of sufficient value to buy up the entire lading of a ship.

"Now, unfortunately for the mandarin, it chanced that these three sailors were about the greatest rascals on board; which is saying a good deal when one considers the ordinary moral standard that prevails in the forecastle of a sailing-ship. Nor was Wo-li himself an angel; in fact, he was a consummate villain, and seems to have been the actual originator of the plot which was presently devised to rob the mandarin.

"This plot was as remarkable for its simplicity as for its cold-blooded barbarity. On the evening before the barque sailed, the three seamen, Nilsson, Foucault, and Parratt, proceeded to the Danish ship with a supply of whisky, made the ship-keeper royally drunk, and locked him up in an empty berth. Meanwhile Wo-li made a secret communication to the mandarin to the effect that certain stolen property, believed to be his, had been secreted in the hold of the empty ship. Thereupon the mandarin came down hot-foot to the quay-side, and was received on board by the three seamen, who had got the covers off the after-hatch in readiness. Parratt now ran down the iron ladder to show the way, and the mandarin followed; but when they reached the lower deck, and looked down the hatch into the black darkness of the lower hold, he seems to have taken fright, and begun to climb up again. Meanwhile Nilsson had made a running bowline in the end of a loose halyard that was rove through a block aloft, and had been used for hoisting out the cargo. As the mandarin came up, he leaned over the coaming of the hatch, dropped the noose over the Chinaman's head, jerked it tight, and then he and Foucault hove on the fall of the rope. The unfortunate Chinaman was dragged from the ladder, and, as he swung clear, the two rascals let go the rope, allowing him to drop through the hatches into the lower hold. Then they belayed the rope, and went down below. Parratt had already lighted a slush-lamp, by the glimmer of which they could see the mandarin swinging to and fro like a pendulum within a few feet of the ballast, and still quivering and twitching in his death-throes. They were now joined by Wo-li, who had watched the proceedings from the quay, and the four villains proceeded, without loss of time, to rifle the body as it hung. To their surprise and disgust, they found nothing of value excepting an ebony pendant set with a single large pearl; but Wo-li, though evidently disappointed at the nature of the booty, assured his comrades that this alone was well worth the hazard, pointing out the great size and exceptional beauty of the pearl. As to this, the seamen know nothing about pearls, but the thing was done, and had to be made the best of; so they made the rope fast to the lower deck-beams, cut off the remainder and unrove it from the block, and went back to their ship.

"It was twenty-four hours before the ship-keeper was sufficiently sober to break out of the berth in which he had been locked, by which time the barque was well out to sea; and it was another three days before the body of the mandarin was found. An active search was then made for the murderers, but as they were strangers to the ship-keeper, no clues to their whereabouts could be discovered.

"Meanwhile, the four murderers were a good deal exercised as to the disposal of the booty. Since it could not be divided, it was evident that it must be entrusted to the keeping of one of them. The choice in the first place fell upon Wo-li, in whose chest the pendant was deposited as soon as the party came on board, it being arranged that the Chinaman should produce the jewel for inspection by his confederates whenever called upon.

"For six weeks nothing out of the common occurred; but then a very singular event befell. The four conspirators were sitting outside the galley one evening, when suddenly the cook uttered a cry of amazement and horror. The other three turned to see what it was that had so disturbed their comrade, and then they, too, were struck dumb with consternation; for, standing at the door of the companion-hatch--the barque was a flush-decked vessel--was the mandarin whom they had left for dead. He stood quietly regarding them for fully a minute, while they stared at him transfixed with terror. Then he beckoned to them, and went below.

"So petrified were they with astonishment and mortal fear that they remained for a long time motionless and dumb. At last they plucked up courage, and began to make furtive inquiries among the crew; but no one-- not even the steward--knew anything of any passengers, or, indeed, of any Chinaman, on board the ship, excepting Wo-li.

"At day-break the next morning, when the cook's mate went to the galley to fill the coppers, he found Wo-li hanging from a hook in the ceiling. The cook's body was stiff and cold, and had evidently been hanging several hours. The report of the tragedy quickly spread through the ship, and the three conspirators hurried off to remove the pearl from the dead man's chest before the officers should come to examine it. The cheap lock was easily picked with a bent wire, and the jewel abstracted; but now the question arose as to who should take charge of it. The eagerness to be the actual custodian of the precious bauble, which had been at first displayed, now gave place to equally strong reluctance. But someone had to take charge of it, and after a long and angry discussion Nilsson was prevailed upon to stow it in his chest.

"A fortnight passed. The three conspirators went about their duties soberly, like men burdened with some secret anxiety, and in their leisure moments they would sit and talk with bated breath of the apparition at the companion-hatch, and the mysterious death of their late comrade.

"At last the blow fell.

"It was at the end of the second dog-watch that the hands were gathered on the forecastle, preparing to make sail after a spell of bad weather. Suddenly Nilsson gave a husky shout, and rushed at Parratt, holding out the key of his chest.

"'Here you, Parratt,' he exclaimed, 'go below and take that accursed thing out of my chest.'

"'What for--' demanded Parratt; and then he and Foucault, who was standing close by, looked aft to see what Nilsson was staring at.

"Instantly they both turned white as ghosts, and fell trembling so that they could hardly stand; for there was the mandarin, standing calmly by the companion, returning with a steady, impassive gaze their looks of horror. And even as they looked he beckoned and went below.

"'D'ye hear, Parratt--' gasped Nilsson; 'take my key and do what I say, or else--'

"But at this moment the order was given to go aloft and set all plain sail; the three men went off to their respective posts, Nilsson going up the fore-topmast rigging, and the other two to the main-top. Having finished their work aloft, Foucault and Parratt who were both in the port watch, came down on deck, and then, it being their watch below, they went and turned in.

"When they turned out with their watch at midnight, they looked about for Nilsson, who was in the starboard watch, but he was nowhere to be seen. Thinking he might have slipped below unobserved, they made no remark, though they were very uneasy about him; but when the starboard watch came on deck at four o'clock, and Nilsson did not appear with his mates, the two men became alarmed, and made inquiries about him. It was now discovered that no one had seen him since eight o'clock on the previous evening, and, this being reported to the officer of the watch, the latter ordered all hands to be called. But still Nilsson did not appear. A thorough search was now instituted, both below and aloft, and as there was still no sign of the missing man, it was concluded that he had fallen overboard.

"But at eight o'clock two men were sent aloft to shake out the fore-royal. They reached the yard almost simultaneously, and were just stepping on to the foot-ropes when one of them gave a shout; then the pair came sliding down a backstay, with faces as white as tallow. As soon as they reached the deck, they took the officer of the watch forward, and, standing on the heel of the bowsprit, pointed aloft. Several of the hands, including Foucault and Parratt, had followed, and all looked up; and there they saw the body of Nilsson, hanging on the front of the fore-topgallant sail. He was dangling at the end of a gasket, and bouncing up and down on the taut belly of the sail as the ship rose and fell to the send of the sea.

"The two survivors were now in some doubt about having anything further to do with the pearl. But the great value of the jewel, and the consideration that it was now to be divided between two instead of four, tempted them. They abstracted it from Nilsson's chest, and then, as they could not come to an agreement in any other way, they decided to settle who should take charge of it by tossing a coin. The coin was accordingly spun, and the pearl went to Foucault's chest.

"From this moment Foucault lived in a state of continual apprehension. When on deck, his eyes were for ever wandering towards the companion hatch, and during his watch below, when not asleep, he would sit moodily on his chest, lost in gloomy reflection. But a fortnight passed, then three weeks, and still nothing happened. Land was sighted, the Straits of Gibraltar passed, and the end of the voyage was but a matter of days. And still the dreaded mandarin made no sign.

"At length the ship was within twenty-four hours of Marseilles, to which port a large part of the cargo was consigned. Active preparations were being made for entering the port, and among other things the shore tackle was being overhauled. A share in this latter work fell to Foucault and Parratt, and about the middle of the second dog-watch--seven o'clock in the evening--they were sitting on the deck working an eye-splice in the end of a large rope. Suddenly Foucault, who was facing forward, saw his companion turn pale and stare aft with an expression of terror. He immediately turned and looked over his shoulder to see what Parratt was staring at. It was the mandarin, standing by the companion, gravely watching them; and as Foucault turned and met his gaze, the Chinaman beckoned and went below.

"For the rest of that day Parratt kept close to his terrified comrade, and during their watch below he endeavoured to remain awake, that he might keep his friend in view. Nothing happened through the night, and the following morning, when they came on deck for the forenoon watch, their port was well in sight. The two men now separated for the first time, Parratt going aft to take his trick at the wheel, and Foucault being set to help in getting ready the ground tackle.

"Half an hour later Parratt saw the mate stand on the rail and lean outboard, holding on to the mizzen-shrouds while he stared along the ship's side. Then he jumped on to the deck and shouted angrily:

'Forward, there! What the deuce is that man up to under the starboard cat-head--'

"The men on the forecastle rushed to the side and looked over; two of them leaned over the rail with the bight of a rope between them, and a third came running aft to the mate. 'It's Foucault, sir,' Parratt heard him say. 'He's hanged hisself from the cat-head.'

"As soon as he was off duty, Parratt made his way to his dead comrade's chest, and, opening it with his pick-lock, took out the pearl. It was now his sole property, and, as the ship was within an hour or two of her destination, he thought he had little to fear from its murdered owner. As soon as the vessel was alongside the wharf, he would slip ashore and get rid of the jewel, even if he sold it at a comparatively low price. The thing looked perfectly simple.

"In actual practice, however, it turned out quite otherwise. He began by accosting a well-dressed stranger and offering the pendant for fifty pounds; but the only reply that he got was a knowing smile and a shake of the head. When this experience had been repeated a dozen times or more, and he had been followed up and down the streets for nearly an hour by a suspicious gendarme, he began to grow anxious. He visited quite a number of ships and yachts in the harbour, and at each refusal the price of his treasure came down, until he was eager to sell it for a few francs. But still no one would have it. Everyone took it for granted that the pearl was a sham, and most of the persons whom he accosted assumed that it had been stolen. The position was getting desperate. Evening was approaching--the time of the dreaded dog-watches--and still the pearl was in his possession. Gladly would he now have given it away for nothing, but he dared not try, for this would lay him open to the strongest suspicion.

"At last, in a by-street, he came upon the shop of a curio-dealer. Putting on a careless and cheerful manner, he entered and offered the pendant for ten francs. The dealer looked at it, shook his head, and handed it back.

"'What will you give me for it--' demanded Parratt, breaking out into a cold sweat at the prospect of a final refusal.

"The dealer felt in his pocket, drew out a couple of francs, and held them out.

"'Very well,' said Parratt. He took the money as calmly as he could, and marched out of the shop, with a gasp of relief, leaving the pendant in the dealer's hand.

"The jewel was hung up in a glass case, and nothing more was thought about it until some ten days later, when an English tourist, who came into the shop, noticed it and took a liking to it. Thereupon the dealer offered it to him for five pounds, assuring him that it was a genuine pearl, a statement that, to his amazement, the stranger evidently believed. He was then deeply afflicted at not having asked a higher price, but the bargain had been struck, and the Englishman went off with his purchase.

"This was the story told by Captain Raggerton's friend, and I have given it to you in full detail, having read the manuscript over many times since it was given to me. No doubt you will regard it as a mere traveller's tale, and consider me a superstitious idiot for giving any credence to it."

"It certainly seems more remarkable for picturesqueness than for credibility," Thorndyke agreed. "May I ask," he continued, "whether Captain Raggerton's friend gave any explanation as to how this singular story came to his knowledge, or to that of anybody else?"

"Oh yes," replied Calverley; "I forgot to mention that the seaman, Parratt, very shortly after he had sold the pearl, fell down the hatch into the hold as the ship was unloading, and was very badly injured. He was taken to the hospital, where he died on the following day; and it was while he was lying there in a dying condition that he confessed to the murder, and gave this circumstantial account of it."

"I see," said Thorndyke; "and I understand that you accept the story as literally true?"

"Undoubtedly." Calverley flushed defiantly as he returned Thorndyke's look, and continued: "You see, I am not a man of science: therefore my beliefs are not limited to things that can be weighed and measured. There are things, Dr. Thorndyke, which are outside the range of our puny intellects; things that science, with its arrogant materialism, puts aside and ignores with close-shut eyes. I prefer to believe in things which obviously exist, even though I cannot explain them. It is the humbler and, I think, the wiser attitude."

"But, my dear Fred," protested Mr. Brodribb, "this is a rank fairy-tale."

Calverley turned upon the solicitor. "If you had seen what I have seen, you would not only believe: you would know."

"Tell us what you have seen, then," said Mr. Brodribb.

"I will, if you wish to hear it," said Calverley. "I will continue the strange history of the Mandarin's Pearl."

He lit a fresh cigarette and continued:

"The night I came to Beechhurst--that is my cousin's house, you know--a rather absurd thing happened, which I mention on account of its connection with what has followed. I had gone to my room early, and sat for some time writing letters before getting ready for bed. When I had finished my letters, I started on a tour of inspection of my room. I was then, you must remember, in a very nervous state, and it had become my habit to examine the room in which I was to sleep before undressing, looking under the bed, and in any cupboards and closets that there happened to be. Now, on looking round my new room, I perceived that there was a second door, and I at once proceeded to open it to see where it led to. As soon as I opened the door, I got a terrible start. I found myself looking into a narrow closet or passage, lined with pegs, on which the servant had hung some of my clothes; at the farther end was another door, and, as I stood looking into the closet, I observed, with startled amazement, a man standing holding the door half-open, and silently regarding me. I stood for a moment staring at him, with my heart thumping and my limbs all of a tremble; then I slammed the door and ran off to look for my cousin.

"He was in the billiard-room with Raggerton, and the pair looked up sharply as I entered.

"'Alfred,' I said, 'where does that passage lead to out of my room--'

"'Lead to--' said he. 'Why, it doesn't lead anywhere. It used to open into a cross corridor, but when the house was altered, the corridor was done away with, and this passage closed up. It is only a cupboard now.'

"'Well, there's a man in it--or there was just now.'

"'Nonsense!' he exclaimed; 'impossible! Let us go and look at the place.'

"He and Raggerton rose, and we went together to my room. As we flung open the door of the closet and looked in, we all three burst into a laugh. There were three men now looking at us from the open door at the other end, and the mystery was solved. A large mirror had been placed at the end of the closet to cover the partition which cut it off from the cross corridor.

"This incident naturally exposed me to a good deal of chaff from my cousin and Captain Raggerton; but I often wished that the mirror had not been placed there, for it happened over and over again that, going to the cupboard hurriedly, and not thinking of the mirror, I got quite a bad shock on being confronted by a figure apparently coming straight at me through an open door. In fact, it annoyed me so much, in my nervous state, that I even thought of asking my cousin to give me a different room; but, happening to refer to the matter when talking to Raggerton, I found the Captain so scornful of my cowardice that my pride was touched, and I let the affair drop.

"And now I come to a very strange occurrence, which I shall relate quite frankly, although I know beforehand that you will set me down as a liar or a lunatic. I had been away from home for a fortnight, and as I returned rather late at night, I went straight to my room. Having partly undressed, I took my clothes in one hand and a candle in the other, and opened the cupboard door. I stood for a moment looking nervously at my double, standing, candle in hand, looking at me through the open door at the other end of the passage; then I entered, and, setting the candle on a shelf, proceeded to hang up my clothes. I had hung them up, and had just reached up for the candle, when my eye was caught by something strange in the mirror. It no longer reflected the candle in my hand, but instead of it, a large coloured paper lantern. I stood petrified with astonishment, and gazed into the mirror; and then I saw that my own reflection was changed, too; that, in place of my own figure, was that of an elderly Chinaman, who stood regarding me with stony calm.

"I must have stood for near upon a minute, unable to move and scarce able to breathe, face to face with that awful figure. At length I turned to escape, and, as I turned, he turned also, and I could see him, over my shoulder, hurrying away. As I reached the door, I halted for a moment, looking back with the door in my hand, holding the candle above my head; and even so he halted, looking back at me, with his hand upon the door and his lantern held above his head.

"I was so much upset that I could not go to bed for some hours, but continued to pace the room, in spite of my fatigue. Now and again I was impelled, irresistibly, to peer into the cupboard, but nothing was to be seen in the mirror save my own figure, candle in hand, peeping in at me through the half-open door. And each time that I looked into my own white, horror-stricken face, I shut the door hastily and turned away with a shudder; for the pegs, with the clothes hanging on them, seemed to call to me. I went to bed at last, and before I fell asleep I formed the resolution that, if I was spared until the next day, I would write to the British Consul at Canton, and offer to restore the pearl to the relatives of the murdered mandarin.

"On the following day I wrote and despatched the letter, after which I felt more composed, though I was haunted continually by the recollection of that stony, impassive figure; and from time to time I felt an irresistible impulse to go and look in at the door of the closet, at the mirror and the pegs with the clothes hanging from them. I told my cousin of the visitation that I had received, but he merely laughed, and was frankly incredulous; while the Captain bluntly advised me not to be a superstitious donkey.

"For some days after this I was left in peace, and began to hope that my letter had appeased the spirit of the murdered man; but on the fifth day, about six o'clock in the evening, happening to want some papers that I had left in the pocket of a coat which was hanging in the closet, I went in to get them. I took in no candle, as it was not yet dark, but left the door wide open to light me. The coat that I wanted was near the end of the closet, not more than four paces from the mirror, and as I went towards it I watched my reflection rather nervously as it advanced to meet me. I found my coat, and as I felt for the papers, I still kept a suspicious eye on my double. And, even as I looked, a most strange phenomenon appeared: the mirror seemed for an instant to darken or cloud over, and then, as it cleared again, I saw, standing dark against the light of the open door behind him, the figure of the mandarin. After a single glance, I ran out of the closet, shaking with agitation; but as I turned to shut the door, I noticed that it was my own figure that was reflected in the glass. The Chinaman had vanished in an instant.

"It now became evident that my letter had not served its purpose, and I was plunged in despair; the more so since, on this day, I felt again the dreadful impulse to go and look at the pegs on the walls of the closet. There was no mistaking the meaning of that impulse, and each time that I went, I dragged myself away reluctantly, though shivering with horror. One circumstance, indeed, encouraged me a little; the mandarin had not, on either occasion, beckoned to me as he had done to the sailors, so that perhaps some way of escape yet lay open to me.

"During the next few days I considered very earnestly what measures I could take to avert the doom that seemed to be hanging over me. The simplest plan, that of passing the pearl on to some other person, was out of the question; it would be nothing short of murder. On the other hand, I could not wait for an answer to my letter; for even if I remained alive, I felt that my reason would have given way long before the reply reached me. But while I was debating what I should do, the mandarin appeared to me again; and then, after an interval of only two days, he came to me once more. That was last night. I remained gazing at him, fascinated, with my flesh creeping, as he stood, lantern in hand, looking steadily in my face. At last he held out his hand to me, as if asking me to give him the pearl; then the mirror darkened, and he vanished in a flash; and in the place where he had stood there was my own reflection looking at me out of the glass.

"That last visitation decided me. When I left home this morning the pearl was in my pocket, and as I came over Waterloo Bridge, I leaned over the parapet and flung the thing into the water. After that I felt quite relieved for a time; I had shaken the accursed thing off without involving anyone in the curse that it carried. But presently I began to feel fresh misgivings, and the conviction has been growing upon me all day that I have done the wrong thing. I have only placed it for ever beyond the reach of its owner, whereas I ought to have burnt it, after the Chinese fashion, so that its non-material essence could have joined the spiritual body of him to whom it had belonged when both were clothed with material substance.

"But it can't be altered now. For good or for evil, the thing is done, and God alone knows what the end of it will be."

As he concluded, Calverley uttered a deep sigh, and covered his face with his slender, delicate hands. For a space we were all silent and, I think, deeply moved; for, grotesquely unreal as the whole thing was, there was a pathos, and even a tragedy, in it that we all felt to be very real indeed.

Suddenly Mr. Brodribb started and looked at his watch.

"Good gracious, Calverley, we shall lose our train."

The young man pulled himself together and stood up. "We shall just do it if we go at once," said he. "Good-bye," he added, shaking Thorndyke's hand and mine. "You have been very patient, and I have been rather prosy, I am afraid. Come along, Mr. Brodribb."

Thorndyke and I followed them out on to the landing, and I heard my colleague say to the solicitor in a low tone, but very earnestly: "Get him away from that house, Brodribb, and don't let him out of your sight for a moment."

I did not catch the solicitor's reply, if he made any, but when we were back in our room I noticed that Thorndyke was more agitated than I had ever seen him.

"I ought not to have let them go," he exclaimed. "Confound me! If I had had a grain of wit, I should have made them lose their train."

He lit his pipe and fell to pacing the room with long strides, his eyes bent on the floor with an expression sternly reflective. At last, finding him hopelessly taciturn, I knocked out my pipe and went to bed.

As I was dressing on the following morning, Thorndyke entered my room. His face was grave even to sternness, and he held a telegram in his hand.

"I am going to Weybridge this morning," he said shortly, holding the "flimsy" out to me. "Shall you come?"

I took the paper from him, and read:

"COME, FOR GOD'S SAKE! F.C. IS DEAD. YOU WILL UNDERSTAND.--BRODRIBB."

I handed him back the telegram, too much shocked for a moment to speak. The whole dreadful tragedy summed up in that curt message rose before me in an instant, and a wave of deep pity swept over me at this miserable end to the sad, empty life.

"What an awful thing, Thorndyke!" I exclaimed at length. "To be killed by a mere grotesque delusion."

"Do you think so?" he asked dryly. "Well, we shall see; but you will come?"

"Yes," I replied; and as he retired, I proceeded hurriedly to finish dressing.

Half an hour later, as we rose from a rapid breakfast, Polton came into the room, carrying a small roll-up case of tools and a bunch of skeleton keys.

"Will you have them in a bag, sir?" he asked.

"No," replied Thorndyke; "in my overcoat pocket. Oh, and here is a note, Polton, which I want you to take round to Scotland Yard. It is to the Assistant Commissioner, and you are to make sure that it is in the right hands before you leave. And here is a telegram to Mr. Brodribb."

He dropped the keys and the tool-case into his pocket, and we went down together to the waiting hansom.

At Weybridge Station we found Mr. Brodribb pacing the platform in a state of extreme dejection. He brightened up somewhat when he saw us, and wrung our hands with emotional heartiness.

"It was very good of you both to come at a moment's notice," he said warmly, "and I feel your kindness very much. You understood, of course, Thorndyke?"

"Yes," Thorndyke replied. "I suppose the mandarin beckoned to him."

Mr. Brodribb turned with a look of surprise. "How did you guess that?" he asked; and then, without waiting for a reply, he took from his pocket a note, which he handed to my colleague. "The poor old fellow left this for me," he said. "The servant found it on his dressing-table."

Thorndyke glanced through the note and passed it to me. It consisted of but a few words, hurriedly written in a tremulous hand.

"He has beckoned to me, and I must go. Good-bye, dear old friend."

"How does his cousin take the matter?" asked Thorndyke.

"He doesn't know of it yet," replied the lawyer. "Alfred and Raggerton went out after an early breakfast, to cycle over to Guildford on some business or other, and they have not returned yet. The catastrophe was discovered soon after they left. The maid went to his room with a cup of tea, and was astonished to find that his bed had not been slept in. She ran down in alarm and reported to the butler, who went up at once and searched the room; but he could find no trace of the missing one, except my note, until it occurred to him to look in the cupboard. As he opened the door he got rather a start from his own reflection in the mirror; and then he saw poor Fred hanging from one of the pegs near the end of the closet, close to the glass. It's a melancholy affair--but here is the house, and here is the butler waiting for us. Mr. Alfred is not back yet, then, Stevens?"

"No, sir." The white-faced, frightened-looking man had evidently been waiting at the gate from distaste of the house, and he now walked back with manifest relief at our arrival. When we entered the house, he ushered us without remark up on to the first-floor, and, preceding us along a corridor, halted near the end. "That's the room, sir," said he; and without another word he turned and went down the stairs.

We entered the room, and Mr. Brodribb followed on tiptoe, looking about him fearfully, and casting awe-struck glances at the shrouded form on the bed. To the latter Thorndyke advanced, and gently drew back the sheet.

"You'd better not look, Brodribb," said he, as he bent over the corpse. He felt the limbs and examined the cord, which still remained round the neck, its raggedly-severed end testifying to the terror of the servants who had cut down the body. Then he replaced the sheet and looked at his watch. "It happened at about three o'clock in the morning," said he. "He must have struggled with the impulse for some time, poor fellow! Now let us look at the cupboard."

We went together to a door in the corner of the room, and, as we opened it, we were confronted by three figures, apparently looking in at us through an open door at the other end.

"It is really rather startling," said the lawyer, in a subdued voice, looking almost apprehensively at the three figures that advanced to meet us. "The poor lad ought never to have been here."

It was certainly an eerie place, and I could not but feel, as we walked down the dark, narrow passage, with those other three dimly-seen figures silently coming towards us, and mimicking our every gesture, that it was no place for a nervous, superstitious man like poor Fred Calverley. Close to the end of the long row of pegs was one from which hung an end of stout box-cord, and to this Mr. Brodribb pointed with an awe-struck gesture. But Thorndyke gave it only a brief glance, and then walked up to the mirror, which he proceeded to examine minutely. It was a very large glass, nearly seven feet high, extending the full width of the closet, and reaching to within a foot of the floor; and it seemed to have been let into the partition from behind, for, both above and below, the woodwork was in front of it. While I was making these observations, I watched Thorndyke with no little curiosity. First he rapped his knuckles on the glass; then he lighted a wax match, and, holding it close to the mirror, carefully watched the reflection of the flame. Finally, laying his cheek on the glass, he held the match at arm's length, still close to the mirror, and looked at the reflection along the surface. Then he blew out the match and walked back into the room, shutting the cupboard door as we emerged.

"I think," said he, "that as we shall all undoubtedly be subpoenaed by the coroner, it would be well to put together a few notes of the facts. I see there is a writing-table by the window, and I would propose that you, Brodribb, just jot down a précis of the statement that you heard last night, while Jervis notes down the exact condition of the body. While you are doing this, I will take a look round."

"We might find a more cheerful place to write in," grumbled Mr. Brodribb; "however--"

Without finishing the sentence, he sat down at the table, and, having found some sermon paper, dipped a pen in the ink by way of encouraging his thoughts. At this moment Thorndyke quietly slipped out of the room, and I proceeded to make a detailed examination of the body: in which occupation I was interrupted at intervals by requests from the lawyer that I should refresh his memory.

We had been occupied thus for about a quarter of an hour, when a quick step was heard outside, the door was opened abruptly, and a man burst into the room. Brodribb rose and held out his hand.

"This is a sad home-coming for you, Alfred," said he.

"Yes, my God!" the newcomer exclaimed. "It's awful."

He looked askance at the corpse on the bed, and wiped his forehead with his handkerchief. Alfred Calverley was not extremely prepossessing. Like his cousin, he was obviously neurotic, but there were signs of dissipation in his face, which, just now, was pale and ghastly, and wore an expression of abject fear. Moreover, his entrance was accompanied by that of a perceptible odour of brandy.

He had walked over, without noticing me, to the writing-table, and as he stood there, talking in subdued tones with the lawyer, I suddenly found Thorndyke at my side. He had stolen in noiselessly through the door that Calverley had left open.

"Show him Brodribb's note," he whispered, "and then make him go in and look at the peg."

With this mysterious request, he slipped out of the room as silently as he had come, unperceived either by Calverley or the lawyer.

"Has Captain Raggerton returned with you?" Brodribb was inquiring.

"No, he has gone into the town," was the reply; "but he won't be long. This will be a frightful shock to him."

At this point I stepped forward. "Have you shown Mr. Calverley the extraordinary letter that the deceased left for you?" I asked.

"What letter was that?" demanded Calverley, with a start.

Mr. Brodribb drew forth the note and handed it to him. As he read it through, Calverley turned white to the lips, and the paper trembled in his hand.

"'He has beckoned to me, and I must go,'" he read. Then, with a furtive glance at the lawyer: "Who had beckoned? What did he mean?"

Mr. Brodribb briefly explained the meaning of the allusion, adding: "I thought you knew all about it."

"Yes, yes," said Calverley, with some confusion; "I remember the matter now you mention it. But it's all so dreadful and bewildering."

At this point I again interposed. "There is a question," I said, "that may be of some importance. It refers to the cord with which the poor fellow hanged himself. Can you identify that cord, Mr. Calverley?"

"I!" he exclaimed, staring at me, and wiping the sweat from his white face; "how should I? Where is the cord?"

"Part of it is still hanging from the peg in the closet. Would you mind looking at it?"

"If you would very kindly fetch it--you know I--er--naturally--have a--"

"It must not be disturbed before the inquest," said I; "but surely you are not afraid--"

"I didn't say I was afraid," he retorted angrily. "Why should I be?"

With a strange, tremulous swagger, he strode across to the closet, flung open the door, and plunged in.

A moment later we heard a shout of horror, and he rushed out, livid and gasping.

"What is it, Calverley?" exclaimed Mr. Brodribb, starting up in alarm.

But Calverley was incapable of speech. Dropping limply into a chair, he gazed at us for a while in silent terror; then he fell back uttering a wild shriek of laughter.

Mr. Brodribb looked at him in amazement. "What is it, Calverley?" he asked again.

As no answer was forthcoming, he stepped across to the open door of the closet and entered, peering curiously before him. Then he, too, uttered a startled exclamation, and backed out hurriedly, looking pale and flurried.

"Bless my soul!" he ejaculated. "Is the place bewitched?"

He sat down heavily and stared at Calverley, who was still shaking with hysteric laughter; while I, now consumed with curiosity, walked over to the closet to discover the cause of their singular behaviour. As I flung open the door, which the lawyer had closed, I must confess to being very considerably startled; for though the reflection of the open door was plain enough in the mirror, my own reflection was replaced by that of a Chinaman. After a momentary pause of astonishment, I entered the closet and walked towards the mirror; and simultaneously the figure of the Chinaman entered and walked towards me. I had advanced more than halfway down the closet when suddenly the mirror darkened; there was a whirling flash, the Chinaman vanished in an instant, and, as I reached the glass, my own reflection faced me.

I turned back into the room pretty completely enlightened, and looked at Calverley with a new-born distaste. He still sat facing the bewildered lawyer, one moment sobbing convulsively, the next yelping with hysteric laughter. He was not an agreeable spectacle, and when, a few moments later, Thorndyke entered the room, and halted by the door with a stare of disgust, I was moved to join him. But at this juncture a man pushed past Thorndyke, and, striding up to Calverley, shook him roughly by the arm.

"Stop that row!" he exclaimed furiously. "Do you hear? Stop it!"

"I can't help it, Raggerton," gasped Calverley. "He gave me such a turn-- the mandarin, you know."

"What!" ejaculated Raggerton.

He dashed across to the closet, looked in, and turned upon Calverley with a snarl. Then he walked out of the room.

"Brodribb," said Thorndyke, "I should like to have a word with you and Jervis outside." Then, as we followed him out on to the landing, he continued: "I have something rather interesting to show you. It is in here."

He softly opened an adjoining door, and we looked into a small unfurnished room. A projecting closet occupied one side of it, and at the door of the closet stood Captain Raggerton, with his hand upon the key. He turned upon us fiercely, though with a look of alarm, and demanded:

"What is the meaning of this intrusion? and who the deuce are you? Do you know that this is my private room?"

"I suspected that it was," Thorndyke replied quietly. "Those will be your properties in the closet, then?"

Raggerton turned pale, but continued to bluster. "Do I understand that you have dared to break into my private closet?" he demanded.

"I have inspected it," replied Thorndyke, "and I may remark that it is useless to wrench at that key, because I have hampered the lock."

"The devil you have!" shouted Raggerton.

"Yes; you see, I am expecting a police-officer with a search warrant, so I wished to keep everything intact."

Raggerton turned livid with mingled fear and rage. He stalked up to Thorndyke with a threatening air, but, suddenly altering his mind, exclaimed, "I must see to this!" and flung out of the room.

Thorndyke took a key from his pocket, and, having locked the door, turned to the closet. Having taken out the key to unhamper the lock with a stout wire, he reinserted it and unlocked the door. As we entered, we found ourselves in a narrow closet, similar to the one in the other room, but darker, owing to the absence of a mirror. A few clothes hung from the pegs, and when Thorndyke had lit a candle that stood on a shelf, we could see more of the details.

"Here are some of the properties," said Thorndyke. He pointed to a peg from which hung a long, blue silk gown of Chinese make, a mandarin's cap, with a pigtail attached to it, and a beautifully-made papier-mâché mask. "Observe," said Thorndyke, taking the latter down and exhibiting a label on the inside, marked "Renouard a Paris," "no trouble has been spared."

He took off his coat, slipped on the gown, the mask, and the cap, and was, in a moment, in that dim light, transformed into the perfect semblance of a Chinaman.

"By taking a little more time," he remarked, pointing to a pair of Chinese shoes and a large paper lantern, "the make-up could be rendered more complete; but this seems to have answered for our friend Alfred."

"But," said Mr. Brodribb, as Thorndyke shed the disguise, "still, I don't understand--"

"I will make it clear to you in a moment," said Thorndyke. He walked to the end of the closet, and, tapping the right-hand wall, said: "This is the back of the mirror. You see that it is hung on massive well-oiled hinges, and is supported on this large, rubber-tyred castor, which evidently has ball bearings. You observe three black cords running along the wall, and passing through those pulleys above. Now, when I pull this cord, notice what happens."

He pulled one cord firmly, and immediately the mirror swung noiselessly inwards on its great castor, until it stood diagonally across the closet, where it was stopped by a rubber buffer.

"Bless my soul!" exclaimed Mr. Brodribb. "What an extraordinary thing!"

The effect was certainly very strange, for, the mirror being now exactly diagonal to the two closets they appeared to be a single, continuous passage, with a door at either end. On going up to the mirror, we found that the opening which it had occupied was filled by a sheet of plain glass, evidently placed there as a precaution to prevent any person from walking through from one closet into the other, and so discovering the trick.

"It's all very puzzling," said Mr. Brodribb; "I don't clearly understand it now."

"Let us finish here," replied Thorndyke, "and then I will explain. Notice this black curtain. When I pull the second cord, it slides across the closet and cuts off the light. The mirror now reflects nothing into the other closet; it simply appears dark. And now I pull the third cord."

He did so, and the mirror swung noiselessly back into its place.

"There is only one other thing to observe before we go out," said Thorndyke, "and that is this other mirror standing with its face to the wall. This, of course, is the one that Fred Calverley originally saw at the end of the closet; it has since been removed, and the larger swinging glass put in its place. And now," he continued, when we came out into the room, "let me explain the mechanism in detail. It was obvious to me, when I heard poor Fred Calverley's story, that the mirror was 'faked,' and I drew a diagram of the probable arrangement, which turns out to be correct. Here it is." He took a sheet of paper from his pocket and handed it to the lawyer. "There are two sketches. Sketch 1 shows the mirror in its ordinary position, closing the end of the closet. A person standing at A, of course, sees his reflection facing him at, apparently, A 1. Sketch 2 shows the mirror swung across. Now a person standing at A does not see his own reflection at all; but if some other person is standing in the other closet at B, A sees the reflection of B apparently at B 1-- that is, in the identical position that his own reflection occupied when the mirror was straight across."

"I see now," said Brodribb; "but who set up this apparatus, and why was it done?"

"Let me ask you a question," said Thorndyke. "Is Alfred Calverley the next-of-kin?"

"No; there is Fred's younger brother. But I may say that Fred has made a will quite recently very much in Alfred's favour."

"There is the explanation, then," said Thorndyke. "These two scoundrels have conspired to drive the poor fellow to suicide, and Raggerton was clearly the leading spirit. He was evidently concocting some story with which to work on poor Fred's superstitions when the mention of the Chinaman on the steamer gave him his cue. He then invented the very picturesque story of the murdered mandarin and the stolen pearl. You remember that these 'visitations' did not begin until after that story had been told, and Fred had been absent from the house on a visit. Evidently, during his absence, Raggerton took down the original mirror, and substituted this swinging arrangement; and at the same time procured the Chinaman's dress and mask from the theatrical property dealers. No doubt he reckoned on being able quietly to remove the swinging glass and other properties and replace the original mirror before the inquest."

"By God!" exclaimed Mr. Brodribb, "it's the most infamous, cowardly plot I have ever heard of. They shall go to gaol for it, the villains, as sure as I am alive."

But in this Mr. Brodribb was mistaken; for immediately on finding themselves detected, the two conspirators had left the house, and by nightfall were safely across the Channel; and the only satisfaction that the lawyer obtained was the setting aside of the will on facts disclosed at the inquest.

As to Thorndyke, he has never to this day forgiven himself for having allowed Fred Calverley to go home to his death.

The Aluminium Dagger

The "urgent call"--the instant, peremptory summons to professional duty--is an experience that appertains to the medical rather than the legal practitioner, and I had supposed, when I abandoned the clinical side of my profession in favour of the forensic, that henceforth I should know it no more; that the interrupted meal, the broken leisure, and the jangle of the night-bell, were things of the past; but in practice it was otherwise. The medical jurist is, so to speak, on the borderland of the two professions, and exposed to the vicissitudes of each calling, and so it happened from time to time that the professional services of my colleague or myself were demanded at a moment's notice. And thus it was in the case that I am about to relate.

The sacred rite of the "tub" had been duly performed, and the freshly-dried person of the present narrator was about to be insinuated into the first instalment of clothing, when a hurried step was heard upon the stair, and the voice of our laboratory assistant, Polton, arose at my colleague's door.

"There's a gentleman downstairs, sir, who says he must see you instantly on most urgent business. He seems to be in a rare twitter, sir--"

Polton was proceeding to descriptive particulars, when a second and more hurried step became audible, and a strange voice addressed Thorndyke.

"I have come to beg your immediate assistance, sir; a most dreadful thing has happened. A horrible murder has been committed. Can you come with me now?"

"I will be with you almost immediately," said Thorndyke. "Is the victim quite dead?"

"Quite. Cold and stiff. The police think--"

"Do the police know that you have come for me?" interrupted Thorndyke.

"Yes. Nothing is to be done until you arrive."

"Very well. I will be ready in a few minutes."

"And if you would wait downstairs, sir," Polton added persuasively, "I could help the doctor to get ready."

With this crafty appeal, he lured the intruder back to the sitting-room, and shortly after stole softly up the stairs with a small breakfast tray, the contents of which he deposited firmly in our respective rooms, with a few timely words on the folly of "undertaking murders on an empty stomach." Thorndyke and I had meanwhile clothed ourselves with a celerity known only to medical practitioners and quick-change artists, and in a few minutes descended the stairs together, calling in at the laboratory for a few appliances that Thorndyke usually took with him on a visit of investigation.

As we entered the sitting-room, our visitor, who was feverishly pacing up and down, seized his hat with a gasp of relief. "You are ready to come?" he asked. "My carriage is at the door;" and, without waiting for an answer, he hurried out, and rapidly preceded us down the stairs.

The carriage was a roomy brougham, which fortunately accommodated the three of us, and as soon as we had entered and shut the door, the coachman whipped up his horse and drove off at a smart trot.

"I had better give you some account of the circumstances, as we go," said our agitated friend. "In the first place, my name is Curtis, Henry Curtis; here is my card. Ah! and here is another card, which I should have given you before. My solicitor, Mr. Marchmont, was with me when I made this dreadful discovery, and he sent me to you. He remained in the rooms to see that nothing is disturbed until you arrive."

"That was wise of him," said Thorndyke. "But now tell us exactly what has occurred."

"I will," said Mr. Curtis. "The murdered man was my brother-in-law, Alfred Hartridge, and I am sorry to say he was--well, he was a bad man. It grieves me to speak of him thus--*de mortuis*, you know--but, still, we must deal with the facts, even though they be painful."

"Undoubtedly," agreed Thorndyke.

"I have had a great deal of very unpleasant correspondence with him-- Marchmont will tell you about that--and yesterday I left a note for him, asking for an interview, to settle the business, naming eight o'clock this morning as the hour, because I had to leave town before noon. He replied, in a very singular letter, that he would see me at that hour, and Mr. Marchmont very kindly consented to accompany me. Accordingly, we went to his chambers together this morning, arriving punctually at eight o'clock. We rang the bell several times, and knocked loudly at the door, but as there was no response, we went down and spoke to the hall-porter. This man, it seems, had already noticed, from the courtyard, that the electric lights were full on in Mr. Hartridge's sitting-room, as they had been all night, according to the statement of the night-porter; so now, suspecting that something was wrong, he came up with us, and rang the bell and battered at the door. Then, as there was still no sign of life within, he inserted his duplicate key and tried to open the door-- unsuccessfully, however, as it proved to be bolted on the inside. Thereupon the porter fetched a constable, and, after a consultation, we decided that we were justified in breaking open the door; the porter produced a crowbar, and by our unified efforts the door was eventually burst open. We entered, and--my God! Dr. Thorndyke, what a terrible sight it was that met our eyes! My brother-in-law was lying dead on the floor of the sitting-room. He had been stabbed--stabbed to death; and the dagger had not even been withdrawn. It was still sticking out of his back."

He mopped his face with his handkerchief, and was about to continue his account of the catastrophe when the carriage entered a quiet side-street between Westminster and Victoria, and drew up before a block of tall, new, red-brick buildings. A flurried hall-porter ran out to open the door, and we alighted opposite the main entrance.

"My brother-in-law's chambers are on the second-floor," said Mr. Curtis. "We can go up in the lift."

The porter had hurried before us, and already stood with his hand upon the rope. We entered the lift, and in a few seconds were discharged on to the second floor, the porter, with furtive curiosity, following us down the corridor. At the end of the passage was a half-open door, considerably battered and bruised. Above the door, painted in white lettering, was the inscription, "Mr. Hartridge"; and through the doorway protruded the rather foxy countenance of Inspector Badger.

"I am glad you have come, sir," said he, as he recognized my colleague. "Mr. Marchmont is sitting inside like a watch-dog, and he growls if any of us even walks across the room."

The words formed a complaint, but there was a certain geniality in the speaker's manner which made me suspect that Inspector Badger was already navigating his craft on a lee shore.

We entered a small lobby or hall, and from thence passed into the sitting-room, where we found Mr. Marchmont keeping his vigil, in company with a constable and a uniformed inspector. The three rose softly as we entered, and greeted us in a whisper; and then, with one accord, we all looked towards the other end of the room, and so remained for a time without speaking.

There was, in the entire aspect of the room, something very grim and dreadful. An atmosphere of tragic mystery enveloped the most commonplace objects; and sinister suggestions lurked in the most familiar appearances. Especially impressive was the air of suspense--of ordinary, every-day life suddenly arrested--cut short in the twinkling of an eye. The electric lamps, still burning dim and red, though the summer sunshine streamed in through the windows; the half-emptied tumbler and open book by the empty chair, had each its whispered message of swift and sudden disaster, as had the hushed voices and stealthy movements of the waiting men, and, above all, an awesome shape that was but a few hours since a living man, and that now sprawled, prone and motionless, on the floor.

"This is a mysterious affair," observed Inspector Badger, breaking the silence at length, "though it is clear enough up to a certain point. The body tells its own story."

We stepped across and looked down at the corpse. It was that of a somewhat elderly man, and lay, on an open space of floor before the fireplace, face downwards, with the arms extended. The slender hilt of a dagger projected from the back below the left shoulder, and, with the exception of a trace of blood upon the lips, this was the only indication of the mode of death. A little way from the body a clock-key lay on the carpet, and, glancing up at the clock on the mantelpiece, I perceived that the glass front was open.

"You see," pursued the inspector, noting my glance, "he was standing in front of the fireplace, winding the clock. Then the murderer stole up behind him--the noise of the turning key must have covered his movements--and stabbed him. And you see, from the position of the dagger on the left side of the back, that the murderer must have been left-handed. That is all clear enough. What is not clear is how he got in, and how he got out again."

"The body has not been moved, I suppose," said Thorndyke.

"No. We sent for Dr. Egerton, the police-surgeon, and he certified that the man was dead. He will be back presently to see you and arrange about the post-mortem."

"Then," said Thorndyke, "we will not disturb the body till he comes, except to take the temperature and dust the dagger-hilt."

He took from his bag a long, registering chemical thermometer and an insufflator or powder-blower. The former he introduced under the dead man's clothing against the abdomen, and with the latter blew a stream of fine yellow powder on to the black leather handle of the dagger. Inspector Badger stooped eagerly to examine the handle, as Thorndyke blew away the powder that had settled evenly on the surface.

THE ALUMINIUM DAGGER

"No finger-prints," said he, in a disappointed tone. "He must have worn gloves. But that inscription gives a pretty broad hint."

He pointed, as he spoke, to the metal guard of the dagger, on which was engraved, in clumsy lettering, the single word, "TRADITORE."

"That's the Italian for 'traitor,'" continued the inspector, "and I got some information from the porter that fits in with that suggestion. We'll have him in presently, and you shall hear."

"Meanwhile," said Thorndyke, "as the position of the body may be of importance in the inquiry, I will take one or two photographs and make a rough plan to scale. Nothing has been moved, you say? Who opened the windows?"

"They were open when we came in," said Mr. Marchmont. "Last night was very hot, you remember. Nothing whatever has been moved."

Thorndyke produced from his bag a small folding camera, a telescopic tripod, a surveyor's measuring-tape, a boxwood scale, and a sketch-block. He set up the camera in a corner, and exposed a plate, taking a general view of the room, and including the corpse. Then he moved to the door and made a second exposure.

"Will you stand in front of the clock, Jervis," he said, "and raise your hand as if winding it? Thanks; keep like that while I expose a plate."

I remained thus, in the position that the dead man was assumed to have occupied at the moment of the murder, while the plate was exposed, and then, before I moved, Thorndyke marked the position of my feet with a blackboard chalk. He next set up the tripod over the chalk marks, and took two photographs from that position, and finally photographed the body itself.

The photographic operations being concluded, he next proceeded, with remarkable skill and rapidity, to lay out on the sketch-block a ground-plan of the room, showing the exact position of the various objects, on a scale of a quarter of an inch to the foot--a process that the inspector was inclined to view with some impatience.

"You don't spare trouble, Doctor," he remarked; "nor time either," he added, with a significant glance at his watch.

"No," answered Thorndyke, as he detached the finished sketch from the block; "I try to collect all the facts that may bear on a case. They may prove worthless, or they may turn out of vital importance; one never knows beforehand, so I collect them all. But here, I think, is Dr. Egerton."

The police-surgeon greeted Thorndyke with respectful cordiality, and we proceeded at once to the examination of the body. Drawing out the thermometer, my colleague noted the reading, and passed the instrument to Dr. Egerton.

"Dead about ten hours," remarked the latter, after a glance at it. "This was a very determined and mysterious murder."

"Very," said Thorndyke. "Feel that dagger, Jervis."

I touched the hilt, and felt the characteristic grating of bone.

"It is through the edge of a rib!" I exclaimed.

"Yes; it must have been used with extraordinary force. And you notice that the clothing is screwed up slightly, as if the blade had been rotated as it was driven in. That is a very peculiar feature, especially when taken together with the violence of the blow."

"It is singular, certainly," said Dr. Egerton, "though I don't know that it helps us much. Shall we withdraw the dagger before moving the body?"

"Certainly," replied Thorndyke, "or the movement may produce fresh injuries. But wait." He took a piece of string from his pocket, and, having drawn the dagger out a couple of inches, stretched the string in a line parallel to the flat of the blade. Then, giving me the ends to hold, he drew the weapon out completely. As the blade emerged, the twist in the clothing disappeared. "Observe," said he, "that the string gives the direction of the wound, and that the cut in the clothing no longer coincides with it. There is quite a considerable angle, which is the measure of the rotation of the blade."

"Yes, it is odd," said Dr. Egerton, "though, as I said, I doubt that it helps us."

"At present," Thorndyke rejoined dryly, "we are noting the facts."

"Quite so," agreed the other, reddening slightly; "and perhaps we had better move the body to the bedroom, and make a preliminary inspection of the wound."

We carried the corpse into the bedroom, and, having examined the wound without eliciting anything new, covered the remains with a sheet, and returned to the sitting-room.

"Well, gentlemen," said the inspector, "you have examined the body and the wound, and you have measured the floor and the furniture, and taken photographs, and made a plan, but we don't seem much more forward. Here's a man murdered in his rooms. There is only one entrance to the flat, and that was bolted on the inside at the time of the murder. The windows are some forty feet from the ground; there is no rain-pipe near any of them; they are set flush in the wall, and there isn't a foothold for a fly on any part of that wall. The grates are modern, and there isn't room for a good-sized cat to crawl up any of the chimneys. Now, the question is, How did the murderer get in, and how did he get out again?"

"Still," said Mr. Marchmont, "the fact is that he did get in, and that he is not here now; and therefore he must have got out; and therefore it must have been possible for him to get out. And, further, it must be possible to discover how he got out."

The inspector smiled sourly, but made no reply.

"The circumstances," said Thorndyke, "appear to have been these: The deceased seems to have been alone; there is no trace of a second occupant of the room, and only one half-emptied tumbler on the table. He was sitting reading when apparently he noticed that the clock had stopped-- at ten minutes to twelve; he laid his book, face downwards, on the table, and rose to wind the clock, and as he was winding it he met his death."

"By a stab dealt by a left-handed man, who crept up behind him on tiptoe," added the inspector.

Thorndyke nodded. "That would seem to be so," he said. "But now let us call in the porter, and hear what he has to tell us."

The custodian was not difficult to find, being, in fact, engaged at that moment in a survey of the premises through the slit of the letter-box.

"Do you know what persons visited these rooms last night?" Thorndyke asked him, when he entered looking somewhat sheepish.

"A good many were in and out of the building," was the answer, "but I can't say if any of them came to this flat. I saw Miss Curtis pass in about nine."

"My daughter!" exclaimed Mr. Curtis, with a start. "I didn't know that."

"She left about nine-thirty," the porter added.

"Do you know what she came about?" asked the inspector.

"I can guess," replied Mr. Curtis.

"Then don't say," interrupted Mr. Marchmont. "Answer no questions."

"You're very close, Mr. Marchmont," said the inspector; "we are not suspecting the young lady. We don't ask, for instance, if she is left-handed."

He glanced craftily at Mr. Curtis as he made this remark, and I noticed that our client suddenly turned deathly pale, whereupon the inspector looked away again quickly, as though he had not observed the change.

"Tell us about those Italians again," he said, addressing the porter. "When did the first of them come here?"

"About a week ago," was the reply. "He was a common-looking man--looked like an organ-grinder--and he brought a note to my lodge. It was in a dirty envelope, and was addressed 'Mr. Hartridge, Esq., Brackenhurst Mansions,' in a very bad handwriting. The man gave me the note and asked me to give it to Mr. Hartridge; then he went away, and I took the note up and dropped it into the letter-box."

"What happened next?"

"Why, the very next day an old hag of an Italian woman--one of them fortune-telling swines with a cage of birds on a stand--came and set up just by the main doorway. I soon sent her packing, but, bless you! she was back again in ten minutes, birds and all. I sent her off again--I kept on sending her off, and she kept on coming back, until I was reg'lar wore to a thread."

"You seem to have picked up a bit since then," remarked the inspector with a grin and a glance at the sufferer's very pronounced bow-window.

"Perhaps I have," the custodian replied haughtily. "Well, the next day there was a ice-cream man--a reg'lar waster, he was. Stuck outside as if he was froze to the pavement. Kept giving the errand-boys tasters, and when I tried to move him on, he told me not to obstruct his business. Business, indeed! Well, there them boys stuck, one after the other, wiping their tongues round the bottoms of them glasses, until I was fit to bust with aggravation. And he kept me going all day.

"Then, the day after that there was a barrel-organ, with a mangy-looking monkey on it. He was the worst of all. Profane, too, he was. Kept mixing up sacred tunes and comic songs: 'Rock of Ages,' 'Bill Bailey,' 'Cujus Animal,' and 'Over the Garden Wall.' And when I tried to move him on, that little blighter of a monkey made a run at my leg; and then the man grinned and started playing, 'Wait till the Clouds roll by.' I tell you, it was fair sickening."

He wiped his brow at the recollection, and the inspector smiled appreciatively.

"And that was the last of them?" said the latter; and as the porter nodded sulkily, he asked: "Should you recognize the note that the Italian gave you?"

"I should," answered the porter with frosty dignity.

The inspector bustled out of the room, and returned a minute later with a letter-case in his hand. "This was in his breast-pocket," said he, laying the bulging case on the table, and drawing up a chair. "Now, here are three letters tied together. Ah! this will be the one." He untied the tape, and held out a dirty envelope addressed in a sprawling, illiterate hand to "Mr. Hartridge, Esq." "Is that the note the Italian gave you?"

The porter examined it critically. "Yes," said he; "that is the one."

The inspector drew the letter out of the envelope, and, as he opened it, his eyebrows went up.

"What do you make of that, Doctor?" he said, handing the sheet to Thorndyke.

Thorndyke regarded it for a while in silence, with deep attention. Then he carried it to the window, and, taking his lens from his pocket, examined the paper closely, first with the low power, and then with the highly magnifying Coddington attachment.

"I should have thought you could see that with the naked eye," said the inspector, with a sly grin at me. "It's a pretty bold design."

"Yes," replied Thorndyke; "a very interesting production. What do you say, Mr. Marchmont?"

The solicitor took the note, and I looked over his shoulder. It was certainly a curious production. Written in red ink, on the commonest notepaper, and in the same sprawling hand as the address, was the following message: "You are given six days to do what is just. By the sign above, know what to expect if you fail." The sign referred to was a skull and crossbones, very neatly, but rather unskilfully, drawn at the top of the paper.

"This," said Mr. Marchmont, handing the document to Mr. Curtis, "explains the singular letter that he wrote yesterday. You have it with you, I think?"

"Yes," replied Mr. Curtis; "here it is."

He produced a letter from his pocket, and read aloud: "'Yes: come if you like, though it is an ungodly hour. Your threatening letters have caused me great amusement. They are worthy of Sadler's Wells in its prime.

"'ALFRED HARTRIDGE.'"

"Was Mr. Hartridge ever in Italy?" asked Inspector Badger.

"Oh yes," replied Mr. Curtis. "He stayed at Capri nearly the whole of last year."

"Why, then, that gives us our clue. Look here. Here are these two other letters; E.C. postmark--Saffron Hill is E.C. And just look at that!"

He spread out the last of the mysterious letters, and we saw that, besides the *memento mori*, it contained only three words: "Beware! Remember Capri!"

"If you have finished, Doctor, I'll be off and have a look round Little Italy. Those four Italians oughtn't to be difficult to find, and we've got the porter here to identify them."

"Before you go," said Thorndyke, "there are two little matters that I should like to settle. One is the dagger: it is in your pocket, I think. May I have a look at it?"

The inspector rather reluctantly produced the dagger and handed it to my colleague.

"A very singular weapon, this," said Thorndyke, regarding the dagger thoughtfully, and turning it about to view its different parts. "Singular both in shape and material. I have never seen an aluminium hilt before, and bookbinder's morocco is a little unusual."

"The aluminium was for lightness," explained the inspector, "and it was made narrow to carry up the sleeve, I expect."

"Perhaps so," said Thorndyke.

He continued his examination, and presently, to the inspector's delight, brought forth his pocket lens.

"I never saw such a man!" exclaimed the jocose detective. "His motto ought to be, 'We magnify thee.' I suppose he'll measure it next."

The inspector was not mistaken. Having made a rough sketch of the weapon on his block, Thorndyke produced from his bag a folding rule and a delicate calliper-gauge. With these instruments he proceeded, with extraordinary care and precision, to take the dimensions of the various parts of the dagger, entering each measurement in its place on the sketch, with a few brief, descriptive details.

"The other matter," said he at length, handing the dagger back to the inspector, "refers to the houses opposite."

He walked to the window, and looked out at the backs of a row of tall buildings similar to the one we were in. They were about thirty yards distant, and were separated from us by a piece of ground, planted with shrubs and intersected by gravel paths.

"If any of those rooms were occupied last night," continued Thorndyke, "we might obtain an actual eyewitness of the crime. This room was brilliantly lighted, and all the blinds were up, so that an observer at any of those windows could see right into the room, and very distinctly, too. It might be worth inquiring into."

"Yes, that's true," said the inspector; "though I expect, if any of them have seen anything, they will come forward quick enough when they read the report in the papers. But I must be off now, and I shall have to lock you out of the rooms."

As we went down the stairs, Mr. Marchmont announced his intention of calling on us in the evening, "unless," he added, "you want any information from me now."

"I do," said Thorndyke. "I want to know who is interested in this man's death."

"That," replied Marchmont, "is rather a queer story. Let us take a turn in that garden that we saw from the window. We shall be quite private there."

He beckoned to Mr. Curtis, and, when the inspector had departed with the police-surgeon, we induced the porter to let us into the garden.

"The question that you asked," Mr. Marchmont began, looking up curiously at the tall houses opposite, "is very simply answered. The only person immediately interested in the death of Alfred Hartridge is his executor and sole legatee, a man named Leonard Wolfe. He is no relation of the deceased, merely a friend, but he inherits the entire estate--about twenty thousand pounds. The circumstances are these:

Alfred Hartridge was the elder of two brothers, of whom the younger, Charles, died before his father, leaving a widow and three children. Fifteen years ago the father died, leaving the whole of his property to Alfred, with the understanding that he should support his brother's family and make the children his heirs."

"Was there no will?" asked Thorndyke.

"Under great pressure from the friends of his son's widow, the old man made a will shortly before he died; but he was then very old and rather childish, so the will was contested by Alfred, on the grounds of undue influence, and was ultimately set aside. Since then Alfred Hartridge has not paid a penny towards the support of his brother's family. If it had not been for my client, Mr. Curtis, they might have starved; the whole burden of the support of the widow and the education of the children has fallen upon him.

"Well, just lately the matter has assumed an acute form, for two reasons. The first is that Charles's eldest son, Edmund, has come of age. Mr. Curtis had him articled to a solicitor, and, as he is now fully qualified, and a most advantageous proposal for a partnership has been made, we have been putting pressure on Alfred to supply the necessary capital in accordance with his father's wishes. This he had refused to do, and it was with reference to this matter that we were calling on him this morning. The second reason involves a curious and disgraceful story. There is a certain Leonard Wolfe, who has been an intimate friend of the deceased. He is, I may say, a man of bad character, and their association has been of a kind creditable to neither. There is also a certain woman named Hester Greene, who had certain claims upon the deceased, which we need not go into at present. Now, Leonard Wolfe and the deceased, Alfred Hartridge, entered into an agreement, the terms of which were these: (1) Wolfe was to marry Hester Greene, and in consideration of this service (2) Alfred Hartridge was to assign to Wolfe the whole of his property, absolutely, the actual transfer to take place on the death of Hartridge."

"And has this transaction been completed?" asked Thorndyke.

"Yes, it has, unfortunately. But we wished to see if anything could be done for the widow and the children during Hartridge's lifetime. No doubt, my client's daughter, Miss Curtis, called last night on a similar mission--very indiscreetly, since the matter was in our hands; but, you know, she is engaged to Edmund Hartridge--and I expect the interview was a pretty stormy one."

Thorndyke remained silent for a while, pacing slowly along the gravel path, with his eyes bent on the ground: not abstractedly, however, but with a searching, attentive glance that roved amongst the shrubs and bushes, as though he were looking for something.

"What sort of man," he asked presently, "is this Leonard Wolfe? Obviously he is a low scoundrel, but what is he like in other respects? Is he a fool, for instance?"

"Not at all, I should say," said Mr. Curtis. "He was formerly an engineer, and, I believe, a very capable mechanician. Latterly he has lived on some property that came to him, and has spent both his time and his money in gambling and dissipation. Consequently, I expect he is pretty short of funds at present."

"And in appearance?"

"I only saw him once," replied Mr. Curtis, "and all I can remember of him is that he is rather short, fair, thin, and clean-shaven, and that he has lost the middle finger of his left hand."

"And he lives at?"

"Eltham, in Kent. Morton Grange, Eltham," said Mr. Marchmont. "And now, if you have all the information that you require, I must really be off, and so must Mr. Curtis."

The two men shook our hands and hurried away, leaving Thorndyke gazing meditatively at the dingy flower-beds.

"A strange and interesting case, this, Jervis," said he, stooping to peer under a laurel-bush. "The inspector is on a hot scent--a most palpable red herring on a most obvious string; but that is his business. Ah, here comes the porter, intent, no doubt, on pumping us, whereas--" He smiled genially at the approaching custodian, and asked: "Where did you say those houses fronted?"

"Cotman Street, sir," answered the porter. "They are nearly all offices."

"And the numbers? That open second-floor window, for instance?"

"That is number six; but the house opposite Mr. Hartridge's rooms is number eight."

"Thank you."

Thorndyke was moving away, but suddenly turned again to the porter.

"By the way," said he, "I dropped something out of the window just now-- a small flat piece of metal, like this." He made on the back of his visiting card a neat sketch of a circular disc, with a hexagonal hole through it, and handed the card to the porter. "I can't say where it fell," he continued; "these flat things scale about so; but you might ask the gardener to look for it. I will give him a sovereign if he brings it to my chambers, for, although it is of no value to anyone else, it is of considerable value to me."

The porter touched his hat briskly, and as we turned out at the gate, I looked back and saw him already wading among the shrubs.

The object of the porter's quest gave me considerable mental occupation. I had not seen Thorndyke drop any thing, and it was not his way to finger carelessly any object of value. I was about to question him on the subject, when, turning sharply round into Cotman Street, he drew up at the doorway of number six, and began attentively to read the names of the occupants.

"'Third-floor,'" he read out, "'Mr. Thomas Barlow, Commission Agent.' Hum! I think we will look in on Mr. Barlow."

He stepped quickly up the stone stairs, and I followed, until we arrived, somewhat out of breath, on the third-floor. Outside the Commission Agent's door he paused for a moment, and we both listened curiously to an irregular sound of shuffling feet from within. Then he softly opened the door and looked into the room. After remaining thus for nearly a minute, he looked round at me with a broad smile, and noiselessly set the door wide open. Inside, a lanky youth of fourteen was practising, with no mean skill, the manipulation of an appliance known by the appropriate name of diabolo; and so absorbed was he in his occupation that we entered and shut the door without being observed. At length the shuttle missed the string and flew into a large waste-paper basket; the boy turned and confronted us, and was instantly covered with confusion.

"Allow me," said Thorndyke, rooting rather unnecessarily in the waste-paper basket, and handing the toy to its owner. "I need not ask if Mr. Barlow is in," he added, "nor if he is likely to return shortly."

"He won't be back to-day," said the boy, perspiring with embarrassment; "he left before I came. I was rather late."

"I see," said Thorndyke. "The early bird catches the worm, but the late bird catches the diabolo. How did you know he would not be back?"

"He left a note. Here it is."

He exhibited the document, which was neatly written in red ink. Thorndyke examined it attentively, and then asked:

"Did you break the inkstand yesterday?"

The boy stared at him in amazement. "Yes, I did," he answered. "How did you know?"

"I didn't, or I should not have asked. But I see that he has used his stylo to write this note."

The boy regarded Thorndyke distrustfully, as he continued:

"I really called to see if your Mr. Barlow was a gentleman whom I used to know; but I expect you can tell me. My friend was tall and thin, dark, and clean-shaved."

"This ain't him, then," said the boy. "He's thin, but he ain't tall or dark. He's got a sandy beard, and he wears spectacles and a wig. I know a wig when I see one," he added cunningly, "'cause my father wears one. He puts it on a peg to comb it, and he swears at me when I larf."

"My friend had injured his left hand," pursued Thorndyke.

"I dunno about that," said the youth. "Mr. Barlow nearly always wears gloves; he always wears one on his left hand, anyhow."

"Ah well! I'll just write him a note on the chance, if you will give me a piece of notepaper. Have you any ink?"

"There's some in the bottle. I'll dip the pen in for you."

He produced, from the cupboard, an opened packet of cheap notepaper and a packet of similar envelopes, and, having dipped the pen to the bottom of the ink-bottle, handed it to Thorndyke, who sat down and hastily scribbled a short note. He had folded the paper, and was about to address the envelope, when he appeared suddenly to alter his mind.

"I don't think I will leave it, after all," he said, slipping the folded paper into his pocket. "No. Tell him I called--Mr. Horace Budge--and say I will look in again in a day or two."

The youth watched our exit with an air of perplexity, and he even came out on to the landing, the better to observe us over the balusters; until, unexpectedly catching Thorndyke's eye, he withdrew his head with remarkable suddenness, and retired in disorder.

To tell the truth, I was now little less perplexed than the office-boy by Thorndyke's proceedings; in which I could discover no relevancy to the investigation that I presumed he was engaged upon: and the last straw was laid upon the burden of my curiosity when he stopped at a staircase window, drew the note out of his pocket, examined it with his lens, held it up to the light, and chuckled aloud.

"Luck," he observed, "though no substitute for care and intelligence, is a very pleasant addition. Really, my learned brother, we are doing uncommonly well."

When we reached the hall, Thorndyke stopped at the housekeeper's box, and looked in with a genial nod.

"I have just been up to see Mr. Barlow," said he. "He seems to have left quite early."

"Yes, sir," the man replied. "He went away about half-past eight."

"That was very early; and presumably he came earlier still?"

"I suppose so," the man assented, with a grin; "but I had only just come on when he left."

"Had he any luggage with him?"

"Yes, sir. There was two cases, a square one and a long, narrow one, about five foot long. I helped him to carry them down to the cab."

"Which was a four-wheeler, I suppose?"

"Yes, sir."

"Mr. Barlow hasn't been here very long, has he?" Thorndyke inquired.

"No. He only came in last quarter-day--about six weeks ago."

"Ah well! I must call another day. Good-morning;" and Thorndyke strode out of the building, and made directly for the cab-rank in the adjoining street. Here he stopped for a minute or two to parley with the driver of a four-wheeled cab, whom he finally commissioned to convey us to a shop in New Oxford Street. Having dismissed the cabman with his blessing and a half-sovereign, he vanished into the shop, leaving me to gaze at the lathes, drills, and bars of metal displayed in the window. Presently he emerged with a small parcel, and explained, in answer to my inquiring look: "A strip of tool steel and a block of metal for Polton."

His next purchase was rather more eccentric. We were proceeding along Holborn when his attention was suddenly arrested by the window of a furniture shop, in which was displayed a collection of obsolete French small-arms--relics of the tragedy of 1870--which were being sold for decorative purposes. After a brief inspection, he entered the shop, and shortly reappeared carrying a long sword-bayonet and an old Chassepot rifle.

"What may be the meaning of this martial display?" I asked, as we turned down Fetter Lane.

"House protection," he replied promptly. "You will agree that a discharge of musketry, followed by a bayonet charge, would disconcert the boldest of burglars."

I laughed at the absurd picture thus drawn of the strenuous house-protector, but nevertheless continued to speculate on the meaning of my friend's eccentric proceedings, which I felt sure were in some way related to the murder in Brackenhurst Chambers, though I could not trace the connection.

After a late lunch, I hurried out to transact such of my business as had been interrupted by the stirring events of the morning, leaving Thorndyke busy with a drawing-board, squares, scale, and compasses, making accurate, scaled drawings from his rough sketches; while Polton, with the brown-paper parcel in his hand, looked on at him with an air of anxious expectation.

As I was returning homeward in the evening by way of Mitre Court, I overtook Mr. Marchmont, who was also bound for our chambers, and we walked on together.

"I had a note from Thorndyke," he explained, "asking for a specimen of handwriting, so I thought I would bring it along myself, and hear if he has any news."

When we entered the chambers, we found Thorndyke in earnest consultation with Polton, and on the table before them I observed, to my great surprise, the dagger with which the murder had been committed.

"I have got you the specimen that you asked for," said Marchmont. "I didn't think I should be able to, but, by a lucky chance, Curtis kept the only letter he ever received from the party in question."

He drew the letter from his wallet, and handed it to Thorndyke, who looked at it attentively and with evident satisfaction.

"By the way," said Marchmont, taking up the dagger, "I thought the inspector took this away with him."

"He took the original," replied Thorndyke. "This is a duplicate, which Polton has made, for experimental purposes, from my drawings."

"Really!" exclaimed Marchmont, with a glance of respectful admiration at Polton; "it is a perfect replica--and you have made it so quickly, too."

"It was quite easy to make," said Polton, "to a man accustomed to work in metal."

"Which," added Thorndyke, "is a fact of some evidential value."

At this moment a hansom drew up outside. A moment later flying footsteps were heard on the stairs. There was a furious battering at the door, and, as Polton threw it open, Mr. Curtis burst wildly into the room.

"Here is a frightful thing, Marchmont!" he gasped. "Edith--my daughter-- arrested for the murder. Inspector Badger came to our house and took her. My God! I shall go mad!"

Thorndyke laid his hand on the excited man's shoulder. "Don't distress yourself, Mr. Curtis," said he. "There is no occasion, I assure you. I suppose," he added, "your daughter is left-handed?"

"Yes, she is, by a most disastrous coincidence. But what are we to do? Good God! Dr. Thorndyke, they have taken her to prison--to prison-- think of it! My poor Edith!"

"We'll soon have her out," said Thorndyke. "But listen; there is someone at the door."

A brisk rat-tat confirmed his statement; and when I rose to open the door, I found myself confronted by Inspector Badger. There was a moment of extreme awkwardness, and then both the detective and Mr. Curtis proposed to retire in favour of the other.

"Don't go, inspector," said Thorndyke; "I want to have a word with you. Perhaps Mr. Curtis would look in again, say, in an hour. Will you? We shall have news for you by then, I hope."

Mr. Curtis agreed hastily, and dashed out of the room with his characteristic impetuosity. When he had gone, Thorndyke turned to the detective, and remarked dryly:

"You seem to have been busy, inspector?"

"Yes," replied Badger; "I haven't let the grass grow under my feet; and I've got a pretty strong case against Miss Curtis already. You see, she was the last person seen in the company of the deceased; she had a grievance against him; she is left-handed, and you remember that the murder was committed by a left-handed person."

"Anything else?"

"Yes. I have seen those Italians, and the whole thing was a put-up job. A woman, in a widow's dress and veil, paid them to go and play the fool outside the building, and she gave them the letter that was left with the porter. They haven't identified her yet, but she seems to agree in size with Miss Curtis."

"And how did she get out of the chambers, with the door bolted on the inside?"

"Ah, there you are! That's a mystery at present--unless you can give us an explanation." The inspector made this qualification with a faint grin, and added: "As there was no one in the place when we broke into it, the murderer must have got out somehow. You can't deny that."

"I do deny it, nevertheless," said Thorndyke. "You look surprised," he continued (which was undoubtedly true), "but yet the whole thing is exceedingly obvious. The explanation struck me directly I looked at the body. There was evidently no practicable exit from the flat, and there was certainly no one in it when you entered. Clearly, then, the murderer had never been in the place at all."

"I don't follow you in the least," said the inspector.

"Well," said Thorndyke, "as I have finished with the case, and am handing it over to you, I will put the evidence before you seriatim. Now, I think we are agreed that, at the moment when the blow was struck, the deceased was standing before the fireplace, winding the clock. The dagger entered obliquely from the left, and, if you recall its position, you will remember that its hilt pointed directly towards an open window."

"Which was forty feet from the ground."

"Yes. And now we will consider the very peculiar character of the weapon with which the crime was committed."

He had placed his hand upon the knob of a drawer, when we were interrupted by a knock at the door. I sprang up, and, opening it, admitted no less a person than the porter of Brackenhurst Chambers. The man looked somewhat surprised on recognizing our visitors, but advanced to Thorndyke, drawing a folded paper from his pocket.

"I've found the article you were looking for, sir," said he, "and a rare hunt I had for it. It had stuck in the leaves of one of them shrubs."

Thorndyke opened the packet, and, having glanced inside, laid it on the table.

"Thank you," said he, pushing a sovereign across to the gratified official. "The inspector has your name, I think?"

"He have, sir," replied the porter; and, pocketing his fee, he departed, beaming.

"To return to the dagger," said Thorndyke, opening the drawer. "It was a very peculiar one, as I have said, and as you will see from this model, which is an exact duplicate." Here he exhibited Polton's production to the astonished detective. "You see that it is extraordinarily slender, and free from projections, and of unusual materials. You also see that it was obviously not made by an ordinary dagger-maker; that, in spite of the Italian word scrawled on it, there is plainly written all over it 'British mechanic.' The blade is made from a strip of common three-quarter-inch tool steel; the hilt is turned from an aluminium rod; and there is not a line of engraving on it that could not be produced in a lathe by any engineer's apprentice. Even the boss at the top is mechanical, for it is just like an ordinary hexagon nut. Then, notice the dimensions, as shown on my drawing. The parts A and B, which just project beyond the blade, are exactly similar in diameter--and such exactness could hardly be accidental. They are each parts of a circle having a diameter of 10.9 millimetres--a dimension which happens, by a singular coincidence, to be exactly the calibre of the old Chassepot rifle, specimens of which are now on sale at several shops in London. Here is one, for instance."

He fetched the rifle that he had bought, from the corner in which it was standing, and, lifting the dagger by its point, slipped the hilt into the muzzle. When he let go, the dagger slid quietly down the barrel, until its hilt appeared in the open breech.

"Good God!" exclaimed Marchmont. "You don't suggest that the dagger was shot from a gun?"

"I do, indeed; and you now see the reason for the aluminium hilt--to diminish the weight of the already heavy projectile--and also for this hexagonal boss on the end?"

"No, I do not," said the inspector; "but I say that you are suggesting an impossibility."

"Then," replied Thorndyke, "I must explain and demonstrate. To begin with, this projectile had to travel point foremost; therefore it had to be made to spin--and it certainly was spinning when it entered the body, as the clothing and the wound showed us. Now, to make it spin, it had to be fired from a rifled barrel; but as the hilt would not engage in the rifling, it had to be fitted with something that would. That something was evidently a soft metal washer, which fitted on to this hexagon, and which would be pressed into the grooves of the rifling, and so spin the dagger, but would drop off as soon as the weapon left the barrel. Here is such a washer, which Polton has made for us."

He laid on the table a metal disc, with a hexagonal hole through it.

"This is all very ingenious," said the inspector, "but I say it is impossible and fantastic."

"It certainly sounds rather improbable," Marchmont agreed.

"We will see," said Thorndyke. "Here is a makeshift cartridge of Polton's manufacture, containing an eighth charge of smokeless powder for a 20-bore gun."

He fitted the washer on to the boss of the dagger in the open breech of the rifle, pushed it into the barrel, inserted the cartridge, and closed the breech. Then, opening the office-door, he displayed a target of padded strawboard against the wall.

"The length of the two rooms," said he, "gives us a distance of thirty-two feet. Will you shut the windows, Jervis?"

I complied, and he then pointed the rifle at the target. There was a dull report--much less loud than I had expected--and when we looked at the target, we saw the dagger driven in up to its hilt at the margin of the bull's-eye.

"You see," said Thorndyke, laying down the rifle, "that the thing is practicable. Now for the evidence as to the actual occurrence. First, on the original dagger there are linear scratches which exactly correspond with the grooves of the rifling. Then there is the fact that the dagger was certainly spinning from left to right--in the direction of the rifling, that is--when it entered the body. And then there is this, which, as you heard, the porter found in the garden."

He opened the paper packet. In it lay a metal disc, perforated by a hexagonal hole. Stepping into the office, he picked up from the floor the washer that he had put on the dagger, and laid it on the paper beside the other. The two discs were identical in size, and the margin of each was indented with identical markings, corresponding to the rifling of the barrel.

The inspector gazed at the two discs in silence for a while; then, looking up at Thorndyke, he said:

"I give in, Doctor. You're right, beyond all doubt; but how you came to think of it beats me into fits. The only question now is, Who fired the gun, and why wasn't the report heard?"

"As to the latter," said Thorndyke, "it is probable that he used a compressed-air attachment, not only to diminish the noise, but also to prevent any traces of the explosive from being left on the dagger. As to the former, I think I can give you the murderer's name; but we had better take the evidence in order. You may remember," he continued, "that when Dr. Jervis stood as if winding the clock, I chalked a mark on the floor where he stood. Now, standing on that marked spot, and looking out of the open window, I could see two of the windows of a house nearly opposite. They were the second-and third-floor windows of No. 6, Cotman Street. The second-floor is occupied by a firm of architects; the third-floor by a commission agent named Thomas Barlow. I called on Mr. Barlow, but before describing my visit, I will refer to another matter. You haven't those threatening letters about you, I suppose?"

"Yes, I have," said the inspector; and he drew forth a wallet from his breast-pocket.

"Lot us take the first one, then," said Thorndyke. "You see that the paper and envelope are of the very commonest, and the writing illiterate. But the ink does not agree with this. Illiterate people usually buy their ink in penny bottles. Now, this envelope is addressed with Draper's dichroic ink--a superior office ink, sold only in large bottles--and the red ink in which the note is written is an unfixed, scarlet ink, such as is used by draughtsmen, and has been used, as you can see, in a stylographic pen. But the most interesting thing about this letter is the design drawn at the top. In an artistic sense, the man could not draw, and the anatomical details of the skull are ridiculous. Yet the drawing is very neat. It has the clean, wiry line of a machine drawing, and is done with a steady, practised hand. It is also perfectly symmetrical; the skull, for instance, is exactly in the centre, and, when we examine it through a lens, we see why it is so, for we discover traces of a pencilled centre-line and ruled cross-lines. Moreover, the lens reveals a tiny particle of draughtsman's soft, red, rubber, with which the pencil lines were taken out; and all these facts, taken together, suggest that the drawing was made by someone accustomed to making accurate mechanical drawings. And now we will return to Mr. Barlow. He was out when I called, but I took the liberty of glancing round the office, and this is what I saw. On the mantelshelf was a twelve-inch flat boxwood rule, such as engineers use, a piece of soft, red rubber, and a stone bottle of Draper's dichroic ink. I obtained, by a simple ruse, a specimen of the office notepaper and the ink. We will examine it presently. I found that Mr. Barlow is a new tenant, that he is rather short, wears a wig and spectacles, and always wears a glove on his left hand. He left the office at 8.30 this morning, and no one saw him arrive. He had with him a square case, and a narrow, oblong one about five feet in length; and he took a cab to Victoria, and apparently caught the 8.51 train to Chatham."

"Ah!" exclaimed the inspector.

"But," continued Thorndyke, "now examine those three letters, and compare them with this note that I wrote in Mr. Barlow's office. You see that the paper is of the same make, with the same water-mark, but that is of no great significance. What is of crucial importance is this: You see, in each of these letters, two tiny indentations near the bottom corner. Somebody has used compasses or drawing-pins over the packet of notepaper, and the points have made little indentations, which have marked several of the sheets. Now, notepaper is cut to its size after it is folded, and if you stick a pin into the top sheet of a section, the indentations on all the underlying sheets will be at exactly similar distances from the edges and corners of the sheet. But you see that these little dents are all at the same distance from the edges and the corner." He demonstrated the fact with a pair of compasses. "And now look at this sheet, which I obtained at Mr. Barlow's office. There are two little indentations-- rather faint, but quite visible--near the bottom corner, and when we measure them with the compasses, we find that they are exactly the same distance apart as the others, and the same distance from the edges and the bottom corner. The irresistible conclusion is that these four sheets came from the same packet."

The inspector started up from his chair, and faced Thorndyke. "Who is this Mr. Barlow?" he asked.

"That," replied Thorndyke, "is for you to determine; but I can give you a useful hint. There is only one person who benefits by the death of Alfred Hartridge, but he benefits to the extent of twenty thousand pounds. His name is Leonard Wolfe, and I learn from Mr. Marchmont that he is a man of indifferent character--a gambler and a spendthrift. By profession he is an engineer, and he is a capable mechanician. In appearance he is thin, short, fair, and clean-shaven, and he has lost the middle finger of his left hand. Mr. Barlow is also short, thin, and fair, but wears a wig, a board, and spectacles, and always wears a glove on his left hand. I have seen the handwriting of both these gentlemen, and should say that it would be difficult to distinguish one from the other."

"That's good enough for me," said the inspector. "Give me his address, and I'll have Miss Curtis released at once."

♦ ♦ ♦ ♦ ♦

The same night Leonard Wolfe was arrested at Eltham, in the very act of burying in his garden a large and powerful compressed-air rifle. He was never brought to trial, however, for he had in his pocket a more portable weapon--a large-bore Derringer pistol--with which he managed to terminate an exceedingly ill-spent life.

"And, after all," was Thorndyke's comment, when he heard of the event, "he had his uses. He has relieved society of two very bad men, and he has given us a most instructive case. He has shown us how a clever and ingenious criminal may take endless pains to mislead and delude the police, and yet, by inattention to trivial details, may scatter clues broadcast. We can only say to the criminal class generally, in both respects, 'Go thou and do likewise.'"

A Message from the Deep Sea

The Whitechapel Road, though redeemed by scattered relics of a more picturesque past from the utter desolation of its neighbour the Commercial Road, is hardly a gay thoroughfare. Especially at its eastern end, where its sordid modernity seems to reflect the colourless lives of its inhabitants, does its grey and dreary length depress the spirits of the wayfarer. But the longest and dullest road can be made delightful by sprightly discourse seasoned with wit and wisdom, and so it was that, as I walked westward by the side of my friend John Thorndyke, the long, monotonous road seemed all too short.

We had been to the London Hospital to see a remarkable case of acromegaly, and, as we returned, we discussed this curious affection, and the allied condition of gigantism, in all their bearings, from the origin of the "Gibson chin" to the physique of Og, King of Bashan.

"It would have been interesting," Thorndyke remarked as we passed up Aldgate High Street, "to have put one's finger into His Majesty's pituitary fossa--after his decease, of course. By the way, here is Harrow Alley; you remember Defoe's description of the dead-cart waiting out here, and the ghastly procession coming down the alley." He took my arm and led me up the narrow thoroughfare as far as the sharp turn by the "Star and Still" public-house, where we turned to look back.

"I never pass this place," he said musingly, "but I seem to hear the clang of the bell and the dismal cry of the carter--"

He broke off abruptly. Two figures had suddenly appeared framed in the archway, and now advanced at headlong speed. One, who led, was a stout, middle-aged Jewess, very breathless and dishevelled; the other was a well-dressed young man, hardly less agitated than his companion. As they approached, the young man suddenly recognized my colleague, and accosted him in agitated tones.

"I've just been sent for to a case of murder or suicide. Would you mind looking at it for me, sir? It's my first case, and I feel rather nervous."

Here the woman darted back, and plucked the young doctor by the arm.

"Hurry! hurry!" she exclaimed, "don't stop to talk." Her face was as white as lard, and shiny with sweat; her lips twitched, her hands shook, and she stared with the eyes of a frightened child.

"Of course I will come, Hart," said Thorndyke; and, turning back, we followed the woman as she elbowed her way frantically among the foot-passengers.

"Have you started in practice here?" Thorndyke asked as we hurried along.

"No, sir," replied Dr. Hart; "I am an assistant. My principal is the police-surgeon, but he is out just now. It's very good of you to come with me, sir."

"Tut, tut," rejoined Thorndyke. "I am just coming to see that you do credit to my teaching. That looks like the house."

We had followed our guide into a side street, halfway down which we could see a knot of people clustered round a doorway. They watched us as we approached, and drew aside to let us enter. The woman whom we were following rushed into the passage with the same headlong haste with which she had traversed the streets, and so up the stairs. But as she neared the top of the flight she slowed down suddenly, and began to creep up on tiptoe with noiseless and hesitating steps. On the landing she turned to face us, and pointing a shaking forefinger at the door of the back room, whispered almost inaudibly, "She's in there," and then sank half-fainting on the bottom stair of the next flight.

I laid my hand on the knob of the door, and looked back at Thorndyke. He was coming slowly up the stairs, closely scrutinizing floor, walls, and handrail as he came. When he reached the landing, I turned the handle, and we entered the room together, closing the door after us. The blind was still down, and in the dim, uncertain light nothing out of the common was, at first, to be seen. The shabby little room looked trim and orderly enough, save for a heap of cast-off feminine clothing piled upon a chair. The bed appeared undisturbed except by the half-seen shape of its occupant, and the quiet face, dimly visible in its shadowy corner, might have been that of a sleeper but for its utter stillness and for a dark stain on the pillow by its side.

Dr. Hart stole on tiptoe to the bedside, while Thorndyke drew up the blind; and as the garish daylight poured into the room, the young surgeon fell back with a gasp of horror.

"Good God!" he exclaimed; "poor creature! But this is a frightful thing, sir!"

The light streamed down upon the white face of a handsome girl of twenty-five, a face peaceful, placid, and beautiful with the austere and almost unearthly beauty of the youthful dead. The lips were slightly parted, the eyes half closed and drowsy, shaded with sweeping lashes; and a wealth of dark hair in massive plaits served as a foil to the translucent skin.

Our friend had drawn back the bedclothes a few inches, and now there was revealed, beneath the comely face, so serene and inscrutable, and yet so dreadful in its fixity and waxen pallor, a horrible, yawning wound that almost divided the shapely neck.

Thorndyke looked down with stern pity at the plump white face.

"It was savagely done," said he, "and yet mercifully, by reason of its very savagery. She must have died without waking."

"The brute!" exclaimed Hart, clenching his fists and turning crimson with wrath. "The infernal cowardly beast! He shall hang! By God, he shall hang!" In his fury the young fellow shook his fists in the air, even as the moisture welled up into his eyes.

Thorndyke touched him on the shoulder. "That is what we are here for, Hart," said he. "Get out your notebook;" and with this he bent down over the dead girl.

At the friendly reproof the young surgeon pulled himself together, and, with open notebook, commenced his investigation, while I, at Thorndyke's request, occupied myself in making a plan of the room, with a description of its contents and their arrangements. But this occupation did not prevent me from keeping an eye on Thorndyke's movements, and presently I suspended my labours to watch him as, with his pocket-knife, he scraped together some objects that he had found on the pillow.

"What do you make of this?" he asked, as I stepped over to his side. He pointed with the blade to a tiny heap of what looked like silver sand, and, as I looked more closely, I saw that similar particles were sprinkled on other parts of the pillow.

"Silver sand!" I exclaimed. "I don't understand at all how it can have got there. Do you?"

Thorndyke shook his head. "We will consider the explanation later," was his reply. He had produced from his pocket a small metal box which he always carried, and which contained such requisites as cover-slips, capillary tubes, moulding wax, and other "diagnostic materials." He now took from it a seed-envelope, into which he neatly shovelled the little pinch of sand with his knife. He had closed the envelope, and was writing a pencilled description on the outside, when we were startled by a cry from Hart.

"Good God, sir! Look at this! It was done by a woman!"

He had drawn back the bedclothes, and was staring aghast at the dead girl's left hand. It held a thin tress of long, red hair.

Thorndyke hastily pocketed his specimen, and, stepping round the little bedside table, bent over the hand with knitted brows. It was closed, though not tightly clenched, and when an attempt was made gently to separate the fingers, they were found to be as rigid as the fingers of a wooden hand. Thorndyke stooped yet more closely, and, taking out his lens, scrutinized the wisp of hair throughout its entire length.

"There is more here than meets the eye at the first glance," he remarked. "What say you, Hart?" He held out his lens to his quondam pupil, who was about to take it from him when the door opened, and three men entered. One was a police-inspector, the second appeared to be a plain-clothes officer, while the third was evidently the divisional surgeon.

"Friends of yours, Hart?" inquired the latter, regarding us with some disfavour.

Thorndyke gave a brief explanation of our presence to which the newcomer rejoined:

"Well, sir, your *locus standi* here is a matter for the inspector. My assistant was not authorized to call in outsiders. You needn't wait, Hart."

With this he proceeded to his inspection, while Thorndyke withdrew the pocket-thermometer that he had slipped under the body, and took the reading.

The inspector, however, was not disposed to exercise the prerogative at which the surgeon had hinted; for an expert has his uses.

"How long should you say she'd been dead, sir?" he asked affably.

"About ten hours," replied Thorndyke.

The inspector and the detective simultaneously looked at their watches. "That fixes it at two o'clock this morning," said the former. "What's that, sir?"

The surgeon was pointing to the wisp of hair in the dead girl's hand.

"My word!" exclaimed the inspector. "A woman, eh? She must be a tough customer. This looks like a soft job for you, sergeant."

"Yes," said the detective. "That accounts for that box with the hassock on it at the head of the bed. She had to stand on them to reach over. But she couldn't have been very tall."

"She must have been mighty strong, though," said the inspector; "why, she has nearly cut the poor wench's head off." He moved round to the head of the bed, and, stooping over, peered down at the gaping wound. Suddenly he began to draw his hand over the pillow, and then rub his fingers together. "Why," he exclaimed, "there's sand on the pillow--silver sand! Now, how can that have come there?"

The surgeon and the detective both came round to verify this discovery, and an earnest consultation took place as to its meaning.

"Did you notice it, sir?" the inspector asked Thorndyke.

"Yes," replied the latter; "it's an unaccountable thing, isn't it?"

"I don't know that it is, either," said the detective, he ran over to the washstand, and then uttered a grunt of satisfaction. "It's quite a simple matter, after all, you see," he said, glancing complacently at my colleague. "There's a ball of sand-soap on the washstand, and the basin is full of blood-stained water. You see, she must have washed the blood off her hands, and off the knife, too--a pretty cool customer she must be--and she used the sand-soap. Then, while she was drying her hands, she must have stood over the head of the bed, and let the sand fall on to the pillow. I think that's clear enough."

"Admirably clear," said Thorndyke; "and what do you suppose was the sequence of events?"

The gratified detective glanced round the room. "I take it," said he, "that the deceased read herself to sleep. There is a book on the table by the bed, and a candlestick with nothing in it but a bit of burnt wick at the bottom of the socket. I imagine that the woman came in quietly, lit the gas, put the box and the hassock at the bedhead, stood on them, and cut her victim's throat. Deceased must have waked up and clutched the murderess's hair--though there doesn't seem to have been much of a struggle; but no doubt she died almost at once. Then the murderess washed her hands, cleaned the knife, tidied up the bed a bit, and went away. That's about how things happened, I think, but how she got in without anyone hearing, and how she got out, and where she went to, are the things that we've got to find out."

"Perhaps," said the surgeon, drawing the bedclothes over the corpse, "we had better have the landlady in and make a few inquiries." He glanced significantly at Thorndyke, and the inspector coughed behind his hand. My colleague, however, chose to be obtuse to these hints: opening the door, he turned the key backwards and forwards several times, drew it out, examined it narrowly, and replaced it.

"The landlady is outside on the landing," he remarked, holding the door open.

Thereupon the inspector went out, and we all followed to hear the result of his inquiries.

"Now, Mrs. Goldstein," said the officer, opening his notebook, "I want you to tell us all that you know about this affair, and about the girl herself. What was her name?"

The landlady, who had been joined by a white-faced, tremulous man, wiped her eyes, and replied in a shaky voice: "Her name, poor child, was Minna Adler. She was a German. She came from Bremen about two years ago. She had no friends in England--no relatives, I mean. She was a waitress at a restaurant in Fenchurch Street, and a good, quiet, hard-working girl."

"When did you discover what had happened?"

"About eleven o'clock. I thought she had gone to work as usual, but my husband noticed from the back yard that her blind was still down. So I went up and knocked, and when I got no answer, I opened the door and went in, and then I saw--" Here the poor soul, overcome by the dreadful recollection, burst into hysterical sobs.

"Her door was unlocked, then; did she usually lock it?"

"I think so," sobbed Mrs. Goldstein. "The key was always inside."

"And the street door; was that secure when you came down this morning?"

"It was shut. We don't bolt it because some of the lodgers come home rather late."

"And now tell us, had she any enemies? Was there anyone who had a grudge against her?"

"No, no, poor child! Why should anyone have a grudge against her? No, she had no quarrel--no real quarrel--with anyone; not even with Miriam."

"Miriam!" inquired the inspector. "Who is she?"

"That was nothing," interposed the man hastily. "That was not a quarrel."

"Just a little unpleasantness, I suppose, Mr. Goldstein?" suggested the inspector.

"Just a little foolishness about a young man," said Mr. Goldstein. "That was all. Miriam was a little jealous. But it was nothing."

"No, no. Of course. We all know that young women are apt to--"

A soft footstep had been for some time audible, slowly descending the stair above, and at this moment a turn of the staircase brought the newcomer into view. And at that vision the inspector stopped short as if petrified, and a tense, startled silence fell upon us all. Down the remaining stairs there advanced towards us a young woman, powerful though short, wild-eyed, dishevelled, horror-stricken, and of a ghastly pallor: and her hair was a fiery red.

Stock still and speechless we all stood as this apparition came slowly towards us; but suddenly the detective slipped back into the room, closing the door after him, to reappear a few moments later holding a small paper packet, which, after a quick glance at the inspector, he placed in his breast pocket.

"This is my daughter Miriam that we spoke about, gentlemen," said Mr. Goldstein. "Miriam, those are the doctors and the police."

The girl looked at us from one to the other. "You have seen her, then," she said in a strange, muffled voice, and added: "She isn't dead, is she? Not really dead?" The question was asked in a tone at once coaxing and despairing, such as a distracted mother might use over the corpse of her child. It filled me with vague discomfort, and, unconsciously, I looked round towards Thorndyke.

To my surprise he had vanished.

Noiselessly backing towards the head of the stairs, where I could command a view of the hall, or passage, I looked down, and saw him in the act of reaching up to a shelf behind the street door. He caught my eye, and beckoned, whereupon I crept away unnoticed by the party on the landing. When I reached the hall, he was wrapping up three small objects, each in a separate cigarette-paper; and I noticed that he handled them with more than ordinary tenderness.

"We didn't want to see that poor devil of a girl arrested," said he, as he deposited the three little packets gingerly in his pocket-box. "Let us be off." He opened the door noiselessly, and stood for a moment, turning the latch backwards and forwards, and closely examining its bolt.

I glanced up at the shelf behind the door. On it were two flat china candlesticks, in one of which I had happened to notice, as we came in, a short end of candle lying in the tray, and I now looked to see if that was what Thorndyke had annexed; but it was still there.

I followed my colleague out into the street, and for some time we walked on without speaking. "You guessed what the sergeant had in that paper, of course," said Thorndyke at length.

"Yes. It was the hair from the dead woman's hand; and I thought that he had much better have left it there."

"Undoubtedly. But that is the way in which well-meaning policemen destroy valuable evidence. Not that it matters much in this particular instance; but it might have been a fatal mistake."

"Do you intend to take any active part in this case?" I asked.

"That depends on circumstances. I have collected some evidence, but what it is worth I don't yet know. Neither do I know whether the police have observed the same set of facts; but I need not say that I shall do anything that seems necessary to assist the authorities. That is a matter of common citizenship."

The inroads made upon our time by the morning's adventures made it necessary that we should go each about his respective business without delay; so, after a perfunctory lunch at a tea-shop, we separated, and I did not see my colleague again until the day's work was finished, and I turned into our chambers just before dinner-time.

Here I found Thorndyke seated at the table, and evidently full of business. A microscope stood close by, with a condenser throwing a spot of light on to a pinch of powder that had been sprinkled on to the slide; his collecting-box lay open before him, and he was engaged, rather mysteriously, in squeezing a thick white cement from a tube on to three little pieces of moulding-wax.

"Useful stuff, this Fortafix," he remarked; "it makes excellent casts, and saves the trouble and mess of mixing plaster, which is a consideration for small work like this. By the way, if you want to know what was on that poor girl's pillow, just take a peep through the microscope. It is rather a pretty specimen."

I stepped across, and applied my eye to the instrument. The specimen was, indeed, pretty in more than a technical sense. Mingled with crystalline grains of quartz, glassy spicules, and water-worn fragments of coral, were a number of lovely little shells, some of the texture of fine porcelain, others like blown Venetian glass.

"These are Foraminifera!" I exclaimed.

"Yes."

"Then it is not silver sand, after all?"

"Certainly not."

THE SAND FROM THE MURDERED WOMAN'S PILLOW, MAGNIFIED 25 DIAMETERS.

"But what is it, then?"

Thorndyke smiled. "It is a message to us from the deep sea, Jervis; from the floor of the Eastern Mediterranean."

"And can you read the message?"

"I think I can," he replied, "but I shall know soon, I hope."

I looked down the microscope again, and wondered what message these tiny shells had conveyed to my friend. Deep-sea sand on a dead woman's pillow! What could be more incongruous? What possible connection could there be between this sordid crime in the east of London and the deep bed of the "tideless sea" -

Meanwhile Thorndyke squeezed out more cement on to the three little pieces of moulding-wax (which I suspected to be the objects that I had seen him wrapping up with such care in the hall of the Goldsteins' house); then, laying one of them down on a glass slide, with its cemented side uppermost, he stood the other two upright on either side of it. Finally he squeezed out a fresh load of the thick cement, apparently to bind the three objects together, and carried the slide very carefully to a cupboard, where he deposited it, together with the envelope containing the sand and the slide from the stage of the microscope.

He was just locking the cupboard when a sharp rat-tat on our knocker sent him hurriedly to the door. A messenger-boy, standing on the threshold, held out a dirty envelope.

"Mr. Goldstein kept me a awful long time, sir," said he; "I haven't been a-loitering."

Thorndyke took the envelope over to the gas-light, and, opening it, drew forth a sheet of paper, which he scanned quickly and almost eagerly; and, though his face remained as inscrutable as a mask of stone, I felt a conviction that the paper had told him something that he wished to know.

The boy having been sent on his way rejoicing, Thorndyke turned to the bookshelves, along which he ran his eye thoughtfully until it alighted on a shabbily-bound volume near one end. This he reached down, and as he laid it open on the table, I glanced at it, and was surprised to observe that it was a bi-lingual work, the opposite pages being apparently in Russian and Hebrew.

"The Old Testament in Russian and Yiddish," he remarked, noting my surprise. "I am going to get Polton to photograph a couple of specimen pages--is that the postman or a visitor?"

It turned out to be the postman, and as Thorndyke extracted from the letter-box a blue official envelope, he glanced significantly at me.

"This answers your question, I think, Jervis," said he. "Yes; coroner's subpoena and a very civil letter: 'sorry to trouble you, but I had no choice under the circumstances'--of course he hadn't--'Dr. Davidson has arranged to make the autopsy to-morrow at 4 p.m., and I should be glad if you could be present. The mortuary is in Barker Street, next to the school.' Well, we must go, I suppose, though

Davidson will probably resent it." He took up the Testament, and went off with it to the laboratory.

We lunched at our chambers on the following day, and, after the meal, drew up our chairs to the fire and lit our pipes. Thorndyke was evidently preoccupied, for he laid his open notebook on his knee, and, gazing meditatively into the fire, made occasional entries with his pencil as though he were arranging the points of an argument. Assuming that the Aldgate murder was the subject of his cogitations, I ventured to ask:

"Have you any material evidence to offer the coroner?"

He closed his notebook and put it away. "The evidence that I have," he said, "is material and important; but it is disjointed and rather inconclusive. If I can join it up into a coherent whole, as I hope to do before I reach the court, it will be very important indeed--but here is my invaluable familiar, with the instruments of research." He turned with a smile towards Polton, who had just entered the room, and master and man exchanged a friendly glance of mutual appreciation. The relations of Thorndyke and his assistant were a constant delight to me: on the one side, service, loyal and whole-hearted; on the other, frank and full recognition.

"I should think those will do, sir," said Polton, handing his principal a small cardboard box such as playing-cards are carried in. Thorndyke pulled off the lid, and I then saw that the box was fitted internally with grooves for plates, and contained two mounted photographs. The latter were very singular productions indeed; they were copies each of a page of the Testament, one Russian and the other Yiddish; but the lettering appeared white on a black ground, of which it occupied only quite a small space in the middle, leaving a broad black margin. Each photograph was mounted on a stiff card, and each card had a duplicate photograph pasted on the back.

Thorndyke exhibited them to me with a provoking smile, holding them daintily by their edges, before he slid them back into the grooves of their box.

"We are making a little digression into philology, you see," he remarked, as he pocketed the box. "But we must be off now, or we shall keep Davidson waiting. Thank you, Polton."

The District Railway carried us swiftly eastward, and we emerged from Aldgate Station a full half-hour before we were due.

Nevertheless, Thorndyke stepped out briskly, but instead of making directly for the mortuary, he strayed off unaccountably into Mansell Street, scanning the numbers of the houses as he went. A row of old houses, picturesque but grimy, on our right seemed specially to attract him, and he slowed down as we approached them.

"There is a quaint survival, Jervis," he remarked, pointing to a crudely painted, wooden effigy of an Indian standing on a bracket at the door of a small old-fashioned tobacconist's shop. We halted to look at the little image, and at that moment the side door opened, and a woman came out on to the doorstop, where she stood gazing up and down the street.

Thorndyke immediately crossed the pavement, and addressed her, apparently with some question, for I heard her answer presently: "A quarter-past six is his time, sir, and he is generally punctual to the minute."

"Thank you," said Thorndyke; "I'll bear that in mind;" and, lifting his hat, he walked on briskly, turning presently up a side-street which brought us out into Aldgate. It was now but five minutes to four, so we strode off quickly to keep our tryst at the mortuary; but although we arrived at the gate as the hour was striking, when we entered the building we found Dr. Davidson hanging up his apron and preparing to depart.

"Sorry I couldn't wait for you," he said, with no great show of sincerity, "but a post-mortem is a mere farce in a case like this; you have seen all that there was to see. However, there is the body; Hart hasn't closed it up yet."

With this and a curt "good-afternoon" he departed.

"I must apologize for Dr. Davidson, sir," said Hart, looking up with a vexed face from the desk at which he was writing out his notes.

"You needn't," said Thorndyke; "you didn't supply him with manners; and don't let me disturb you. I only want to verify one or two points."

Accepting the hint, Hart and I remained at the desk, while Thorndyke, removing his hat, advanced to the long slate table, and bent over its burden of pitiful tragedy. For some time he remained motionless, running his eye gravely over the corpse, in search, no doubt, of bruises and indications of a struggle. Then he stooped and narrowly examined the wound, especially at its commencement and end. Suddenly he drew nearer, peering intently as if something had attracted his attention, and having taken out his lens, fetched a small sponge, with which he dried an exposed process of the spine. Holding his lens before the dried spot, he again scrutinized it closely, and then, with a scalpel and forceps, detached some object, which he carefully washed, and then once more examined through his lens as it lay in the palm of his hand. Finally, as I expected, he brought forth his "collecting-box," took from it a seed-envelope, into which he dropped the object--evidently something quite small--closed up the envelope, wrote on the outside of it, and replaced it in the box.

"I think I have seen all that I wanted to see," he said, as he pocketed the box and took up his hat. "We shall meet to-morrow morning at the inquest." He shook hands with Hart, and we went out into the relatively pure air.

On one pretext or another, Thorndyke lingered about the neighbourhood of Aldgate until a church bell struck six, when he bent his steps towards Harrow Alley. Through the narrow, winding passage he walked, slowly and with a thoughtful mien, along Little Somerset Street and out into Mansell Street, until just on the stroke of a quarter-past we found ourselves opposite the little tobacconist's shop.

Thorndyke glanced at his watch and halted, looking keenly up the street. A moment later he hastily took from his pocket the cardboard box, from which he extracted the two mounted photographs which had puzzled me so much. They now seemed to puzzle Thorndyke equally, to judge by his expression, for he held them close to his eyes, scrutinizing them with an anxious frown, and backing by degrees into the doorway at the side of the tobacconist's. At this moment I became aware of a man who, as he approached, seemed to eye my friend with some curiosity and more disfavour; a very short, burly young man, apparently a foreign Jew, whose face, naturally sinister and unprepossessing, was further disfigured by the marks of smallpox.

"Excuse me," he said brusquely, pushing past Thorndyke; "I live here."

"I am sorry," responded Thorndyke. He moved aside, and then suddenly asked: "By the way, I suppose you do not by any chance understand Yiddish?"

"Why do you ask?" the newcomer demanded gruffly.

"Because I have just had these two photographs of lettering given to me. One is in Greek, I think, and one in Yiddish, but I have forgotten which is which." He held out the two cards to the stranger, who took them from him, and looked at them with scowling curiosity.

"This one is Yiddish," said he, raising his right hand, "and this other is Russian, not Greek." He held out the two cards to Thorndyke, who took them from him, holding them carefully by the edges as before.

"I am greatly obliged to you for your kind assistance," said Thorndyke; but before he had time to finish his thanks, the man had entered, by means of his latchkey, and slammed the door.

Thorndyke carefully slid the photographs back into their grooves, replaced the box in his pocket, and made an entry in his notebook.

"That," said he, "finishes my labours, with the exception of a small experiment which I can perform at home. By the way, I picked up a morsel of evidence that Davidson had overlooked. He will be annoyed, and I am not very fond of scoring off a colleague; but he is too uncivil for me to communicate with."

♦ ♦ ♦ ♦ ♦

The coroner's subpoena had named ten o'clock as the hour at which Thorndyke was to attend to give evidence, but a consultation with a well-known solicitor so far interfered with his plans that we were a quarter of an hour late in starting from the Temple. My friend was evidently in excellent spirits, though silent and preoccupied, from which I inferred that he was satisfied with the results of his labours; but, as I sat by his side in the hansom, I forbore to question him, not from mere unselfishness, but rather from the desire to hear his evidence for the first time in conjunction with that of the other witnesses.

The room in which the inquest was held formed part of a school adjoining the mortuary. Its vacant bareness was on this occasion enlivened by a long, baize-covered table, at the head of which sat the coroner, while one side was occupied by the jury; and I was glad to observe that the latter consisted, for the most part, of genuine working men, instead of the stolid-faced, truculent "professional jurymen" who so often grace these tribunals.

A row of chairs accommodated the witnesses, a corner of the table was allotted to the accused woman's solicitor, a smart dapper gentleman in gold pince-nez, a portion of one side to the reporters, and several ranks of benches were occupied by a miscellaneous assembly representing the public.

There were one or two persons present whom I was somewhat surprised to see. There was, for instance, our pock-marked acquaintance of Mansell Street, who greeted us with a stare of hostile surprise; and there was Superintendent Miller of Scotland Yard, in whose manner I seemed to detect some kind of private understanding with Thorndyke. But I had little time to look about me, for when we arrived, the proceedings had already commenced. Mrs. Goldstein, the first witness, was finishing her recital of the circumstances under which the crime was discovered, and, as she retired, weeping hysterically, she was followed by looks of commiseration from the sympathetic jurymen.

The next witness was a young woman named Kate Silver. As she stepped forward to be sworn she flung a glance of hatred and defiance at Miriam Goldstein, who, white-faced and wild of aspect, with her red hair streaming in dishevelled masses on to her shoulders, stood apart in custody of two policemen, staring about her as if in a dream.

"You were intimately acquainted with the deceased, I believe?" said the coroner.

"I was. We worked at the same place for a long time--the Empire Restaurant in Fenchurch Street--and we lived in the same house. She was my most intimate friend."

"Had she, as far as you know, any friends or relations in England?"

"No. She came to England from Bremen about three years ago. It was then that I made her acquaintance. All her relations were in Germany, but she had many friends here, because she was a very lively, amiable girl."

"Had she, as far as you know, any enemies--any persons, I mean, who bore any grudge against her and were likely to do her an injury?"

"Yes. Miriam Goldstein was her enemy. She hated her."

"You say Miriam Goldstein hated the deceased. How do you know that?"

"She made no secret of it. They had had a violent quarrel about a young man named Moses Cohen. He was formerly Miriam's sweetheart, and I think they were very fond of one another until Minna Adler came to lodge at the Goldsteins' house about three months ago. Then Moses took a fancy to Minna, and she encouraged him, although she had a sweetheart of her own, a young man named Paul Petrofsky, who also lodged in the Goldsteins' house. At last Moses broke off with Miriam, and engaged himself to Minna. Then Miriam was furious, and complained to Minna about what she called her perfidious conduct; but Minna only laughed, and told her she could have Petrofsky instead."

"And what did Minna say to that?" asked the coroner.

"She was still more angry, because Moses Cohen is a smart, good-looking young man, while Petrofsky is not much to look at. Besides, Miriam did not like Petrofsky; he had been rude to her, and she had made her father send him away from the house. So they were not friends, and it was just after that that the trouble came."

"The trouble?"

"I mean about Moses Cohen. Miriam is a very passionate girl, and she was furiously jealous of Minna, so when Petrofsky annoyed her by taunting her about Moses Cohen and Minna, she lost her temper, and said dreadful things about both of them."

"As, for instance -?"

"She said that she would kill them both, and that she would like to cut Minna's throat."

"When was this?"

"It was the day before the murder."

"Who heard her say these things besides you?"

"Another lodger named Edith Bryant and Petrofsky. We were all standing in the hall at the time."

"But I thought you said Petrofsky had been turned away from the house."

"So he had, a week before; but he had left a box in his room, and on this day he had come to fetch it. That was what started the trouble. Miriam had taken his room for her bedroom, and turned her old one into a workroom. She said he should not go to her room to fetch his box."

"And did he?"

"I think so. Miriam and Edith and I went out, leaving him in the hall. When we came back the box was gone, and, as Mrs. Goldstein was in the kitchen and there was nobody else in the house, he must have taken it."

"You spoke of Miriam's workroom. What work did she do?"

"She cut stencils for a firm of decorators."

Here the coroner took a peculiarly shaped knife from the table before him, and handed it to the witness.

"Have you ever seen that knife before?" he asked.

"Yes. It belongs to Miriam Goldstein. It is a stencil-knife that she used in her work."

This concluded the evidence of Kate Silver, and when the name of the next witness, Paul Petrofsky, was called, our Mansell Street friend came forward to be sworn. His evidence was quite brief, and merely corroborative of that of Kate Silver, as was that of the next witness, Edith Bryant. When these had been disposed of, the coroner announced:

"Before taking the medical evidence, gentlemen, I propose to hear that of the police-officers, and first we will call Detective-sergeant Alfred Bates."

The sergeant stepped forward briskly, and proceeded to give his evidence with official readiness and precision.

"I was called by Constable Simmonds at eleven-forty-nine, and reached the house at two minutes to twelve in company with Inspector Harris and Divisional Surgeon Davidson. When I arrived Dr. Hart, Dr. Thorndyke, and Dr. Jervis were already in the room. I found the deceased woman, Minna Adler, lying in bed with her throat cut. She was dead and cold. There were no signs of a struggle, and the bed did not appear to have been disturbed. There was a table by the bedside on which was a book and an empty candlestick. The candle had apparently burnt out, for there was only a piece of charred wick at the bottom of the socket. A box had been placed on the floor at the head of the bed and a hassock stood on it. Apparently the murderer had stood on the hassock and leaned over the head of the bed to commit the murder. This was rendered necessary by the position of the table, which could not have been moved without making some noise and perhaps disturbing the deceased. I infer from the presence of the box and hassock that the murderer is a short person."

"Was there anything else that seemed to fix the identity of the murderer?"

"Yes. A tress of a woman's red hair was grasped in the left hand of the deceased."

As the detective uttered this statement, a simultaneous shriek of horror burst from the accused woman and her mother. Mrs. Goldstein sank half-fainting on to a bench, while Miriam, pale as death, stood as one petrified, fixing the detective with a stare of terror, as he drew from his pocket two small paper packets, which he opened and handed to the coroner.

"The hair in the packet marked A," said he, "is that which was found in the hand of the deceased; that in the packet marked B is the hair of Miriam Goldstein."

Here the accused woman's solicitor rose. "Where did you obtain the hair in the packet marked B?" he demanded.

"I took it from a bag of combings that hung on the wall of Miriam Goldstein's bedroom," answered the detective.

"I object to this," said the solicitor. "There is no evidence that the hair from that bag was the hair of Miriam Goldstein at all."

Thorndyke chuckled softly. "The lawyer is as dense as the policeman," he remarked to me in an undertone. "Neither of them seems to see the significance of that bag in the least."

"Did you know about the bag, then?" I asked in surprise.

"No. I thought it was the hair-brush."

I gazed at my colleague in amazement, and was about to ask for some elucidation of this cryptic reply, when he held up his finger and turned again to listen.

"Very well, Mr. Horwitz," the coroner was saying, "I will make a note of your objection, but I shall allow the sergeant to continue his evidence."

The solicitor sat down, and the detective resumed his statement.

"I have examined and compared the two samples of hair, and it is my opinion that they are from the head of the same person. The only other observation that I made in the room was that there was a small quantity of silver sand sprinkled on the pillow around the deceased woman's head."

"Silver sand!" exclaimed the coroner. "Surely that is a very singular material to find on a woman's pillow?"

"I think it is easily explained," replied the sergeant. "The wash-hand basin was full of bloodstained water, showing that the murderer had washed his--or her--hands, and probably the knife, too, after the crime. On the washstand was a ball of sand-soap, and I imagine that the murderer used this to cleanse his--or her--hands, and, while drying them, must have stood over the head of the bed and let the sand sprinkle down on to the pillow."

"A simple but highly ingenious explanation," commented the coroner approvingly, and the jurymen exchanged admiring nods and nudges.

"I searched the rooms occupied by the accused woman, Miriam Goldstein, and found there a knife of the kind used by stencil cutters, but larger than usual. There were stains of blood on it which the accused explained by saying that she cut her finger some days ago. She admitted that the knife was hers."

This concluded the sergeant's evidence, and he was about to sit down when the solicitor rose.

"I should like to ask this witness one or two questions," said he, and the coroner having nodded assent, he proceeded: "Has the finger of the accused been examined since her arrest?"

"I believe not," replied the sergeant. "Not to my knowledge, at any rate."

The solicitor noted the reply, and then asked: "With reference to the silver sand, did you find any at the bottom of the wash-hand basin?"

The sergeant's face reddened. "I did not examine the wash-hand basin," he answered.

"Did anybody examine it?"

"I think not."

"Thank you." Mr. Horwitz sat down, and the triumphant squeak of his quill pen was heard above the muttered disapproval of the jury.

"We shall now take the evidence of the doctors, gentlemen," said the coroner, "and we will begin with that of the divisional surgeon. You saw the deceased, I believe, Doctor," he continued, when Dr. Davidson had been sworn, "soon after the discovery of the murder, and you have since then made an examination of the body?"

"Yes. I found the body of the deceased lying in her bed, which had apparently not been disturbed. She had been dead about ten hours, and rigidity was complete in the limbs but not in the trunk. The cause of death was a deep wound extending right across the throat and dividing all the structures down to the spine. It had been inflicted with a single sweep of a knife while deceased was lying down, and was evidently homicidal. It was not possible for the deceased to have inflicted the wound herself. It was made with a single-edged knife, drawn from left to right; the assailant stood on a hassock placed on a box at the head of the bed and leaned over to strike the blow. The murderer is probably quite a short person, very muscular, and right-handed. There was no sign of a struggle, and, judging by the nature of the injuries, I should say that death was almost instantaneous. In the left hand of the deceased was a small tress of a woman's red hair. I have compared that hair with that of the accused, and am of opinion that it is her hair."

"You were shown a knife belonging to the accused?"

"Yes; a stencil-knife. There were stains of dried blood on it which I have examined and find to be mammalian blood. It is probably human blood, but I cannot say with certainty that it is."

"Could the wound have been inflicted with this knife?"

"Yes, though it is a small knife to produce so deep a wound. Still, it is quite possible."

The coroner glanced at Mr. Horwitz. "Do you wish to ask this witness any questions?" he inquired.

"If you please, sir," was the reply. The solicitor rose, and, having glanced through his notes, commenced: "You have described certain blood-stains on this knife. But we have heard that there was blood-stained water in the wash-hand basin, and it is suggested, most reasonably, that the murderer washed his hands and the knife. But if the knife was washed, how do you account for the bloodstains on it?"

"Apparently the knife was not washed, only the hands."

"But is not that highly improbable?"

"No, I think not."

"You say that there was no struggle, and that death was practically instantaneous, but yet the deceased had torn out a lock of the murderess's hair. Are not those two statements inconsistent with one another?"

"No. The hair was probably grasped convulsively at the moment of death. At any rate, the hair was undoubtedly in the dead woman's hand."

"Is it possible to identify positively the hair of any individual?"

"No. Not with certainty. But this is very peculiar hair."

The solicitor sat down, and, Dr. Hart having been called, and having briefly confirmed the evidence of his principal, the coroner announced: "The next witness, gentleman, is Dr. Thorndyke, who was present almost accidentally, but was actually the first on the scene of the murder. He has since made an examination of the body, and will, no doubt, be able to throw some further light on this horrible crime."

Thorndyke stood up, and, having been sworn, laid on the table a small box with a leather handle. Then, in answer to the coroner's questions, he described himself as the lecturer on Medical Jurisprudence at St. Margaret's Hospital, and briefly explained his connection with the case. At this point the foreman of the jury interrupted to ask that his opinion might be taken on the hair and the knife, as these were matters of contention, and the objects in question were accordingly handed to him.

"Is the hair in the packet marked A in your opinion from the same person as that in the packet marked B?" the coroner asked.

"I have no doubt that they are from the same person," was the reply.

"Will you examine this knife and tell us if the wound on the deceased might have been inflicted with it?"

Thorndyke examined the blade attentively, and then handed the knife back to the coroner.

"The wound might have been inflicted with this knife," said he, "but I am quite sure it was not."

"Can you give us your reasons for that very definite opinion?"

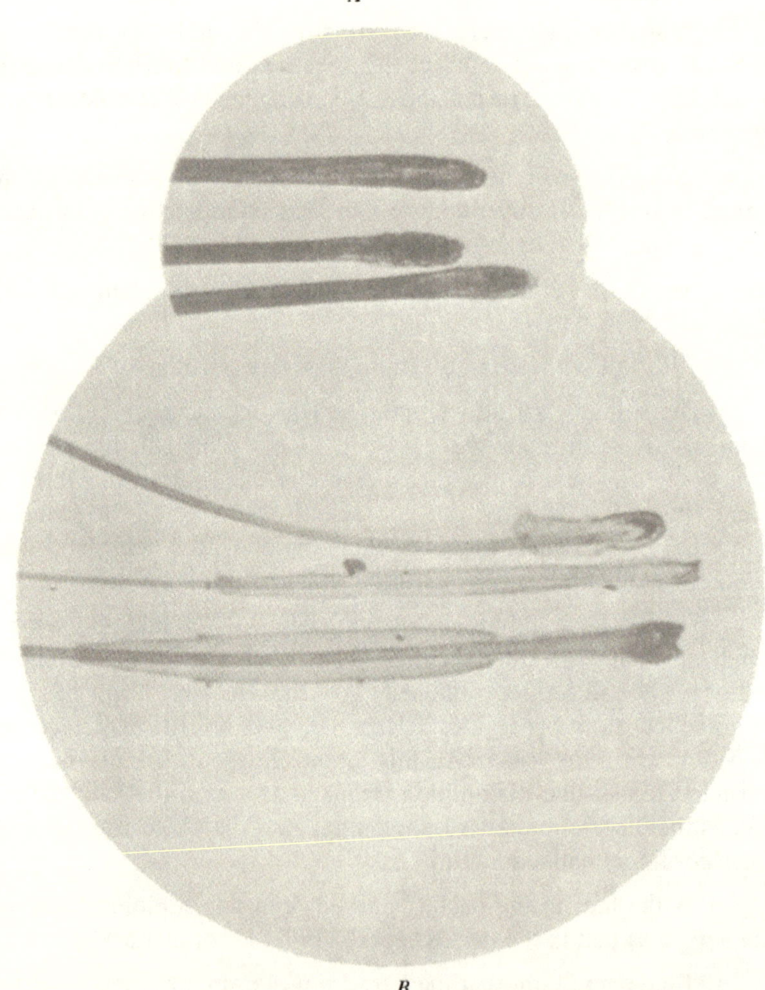

A, SHED HAIRS SHOWING THE NAKED BULB, MAGNIFIED 32 DIAMETERS. B, HAIRS PLUCKED FROM SCALP, SHOWING THE ADHERENT ROOT-SHEATHS, MAGNIFIED 20 DIAMETERS.

"I think," said Thorndyke, "that it will save time if I give you the facts in a connected order." The coroner bowed assent, and he proceeded: "I will not waste your time by reiterating facts already stated. Sergeant Bates has fully described the state of the room, and I have nothing to add on that subject. Dr. Davidson's description of the body covers all the facts: the woman had been dead about ten hours, the wound was unquestionably homicidal, and was inflicted in the manner that he has described. Death was apparently instantaneous, and I should say that the deceased never awakened from her sleep."

"But," objected the coroner, "the deceased held a lock of hair in her hand."

"That hair," replied Thorndyke, "was not the hair of the murderer. It was placed in the hand of the corpse for an obvious purpose; and the fact that the murderer had brought it with him shows that the crime was premeditated, and that it was committed by someone who had had access to the house and was acquainted with its inmates."

As Thorndyke made this statement, coroner, jurymen, and spectators alike gazed at him in open-mouthed amazement. There was an interval of intense silence, broken by a wild, hysteric laugh from Mrs. Goldstein, and then the coroner asked:

"How did you know that the hair in the hand of the corpse was not that of the murderer?"

"The inference was very obvious. At the first glance the peculiar and conspicuous colour of the hair struck me as suspicious. But there were three facts, each of which was in itself sufficient to prove that the hair was probably not that of the murderer.

"In the first place there was the condition of the hand. When a person, at the moment of death, grasps any object firmly, there is set up a condition known as cadaveric spasm. The muscular contraction passes immediately into rigor mortis, or death-stiffening, and the object remains grasped by the dead hand until the rigidity passes off. In this case the hand was perfectly rigid, but it did not grasp the hair at all. The little tress lay in the palm quite loosely and the hand was only partially closed. Obviously the hair had been placed in it after death. The other two facts had reference to the condition of the hair itself. Now, when a lock of hair is torn from the head, it is evident that all the roots will be found at the same end of the lock. But in the present instance this was not the case; the lock of hair which lay in the dead woman's hand had roots at both ends, and so could not have been torn from the head of the murderer. But the third fact that I observed was still more conclusive. The hairs of which that little tress was composed had not been pulled out at all. They had fallen out spontaneously. They were, in fact, shed hairs--probably combings. Let me explain the difference. When a hair is shed naturally, it drops out of the little tube in the skin called the root sheath, having been pushed out by the young hair growing up underneath; the root end of such a shed hair shows nothing but a small bulbous enlargement--the root bulb. But when a hair is forcibly pulled out, its root drags out the root sheath with it, and this can be plainly seen as a glistening mass on the end of the hair. If Miriam Goldstein will pull out a hair and pass it to me, I will show you the great difference between hair which is pulled out and hair which is shed."

The unfortunate Miriam needed no pressing. In a twinkling she had tweaked out a dozen hairs, which a constable handed across to Thorndyke, by whom they were at once fixed in a paper-clip. A second clip being produced from the box, half a dozen hairs taken from the tress which had been found in the dead woman's hand were fixed in it. Then Thorndyke handed the two clips, together with a lens, to the coroner.

"Remarkable!" exclaimed the latter, "and most conclusive." He passed the objects on to the foreman, and there was an interval of silence while the jury examined them with breathless interest and much facial contortion.

"The next question," resumed Thorndyke, "was, Whence did the murderer obtain these hairs? I assumed that they had been taken from Miriam Goldstein's hair-brush; but the sergeant's evidence makes it pretty clear that they were obtained from the very bag of combings from which he took a sample for comparison."

"I think, Doctor," remarked the coroner, "you have disposed of the hair clue pretty completely. May I ask if you found anything that might throw any light on the identity of the murderer?"

"Yes," replied Thorndyke, "I observed certain things which determine the identity of the murderer quite conclusively." He turned a significant glance on Superintendent Miller, who immediately rose, stepped quietly to the door, and then returned, putting something into his pocket. "When I entered the hall," Thorndyke continued, "I noted the following facts: Behind the door was a shelf on which were two china candlesticks. Each was fitted with a candle, and in one was a short candle-end, about an inch long, lying in the tray. On the floor, close to the mat, was a spot of candle-wax and some faint marks of muddy feet. The oil-cloth on the stairs also bore faint footmarks, made by wet galoshes. They were ascending the stairs, and grew fainter towards the top. There were two more spots of candle-wax on the stairs, and one on the handrail; a burnt end of a wax match halfway up the stairs, and another on the landing. There were no descending footmarks, but one of the spots of wax close to the balusters had been trodden on while warm and soft, and bore the mark of the front of the heel of a galosh descending the stairs. The lock of the street door had been recently oiled, as had also that of the bedroom door, and the latter had been unlocked from outside with a bent wire, which had made a mark on the key. Inside the room I made two further observations. One was that the dead woman's pillow was lightly sprinkled with sand, somewhat like silver sand, but greyer and less gritty. I shall return to this presently.

"The other was that the candlestick on the bedside table was empty. It was a peculiar candlestick, having a skeleton socket formed of eight flat strips of metal. The charred wick of a burnt-out candle was at the bottom of the socket, but a little fragment of wax on the top edge showed that another candle had been stuck in it and had been taken out, for otherwise that fragment would have been melted. I at once thought of the candle-end in the hall, and when I went down again I took that end from the tray and examined it. On it I found eight distinct marks corresponding to the eight bars of the candlestick in the bedroom. It had been carried in the right hand of some person, for the warm, soft wax had taken beautifully clear impressions of a right thumb and forefinger. I took three moulds of the candle-end in moulding wax, and from these moulds have made this cement cast, which shows both the fingerprints and the marks of the candlestick." He took from his box a small white object, which he handed to the coroner.

"And what do you gather from these facts?" asked the coroner.

"I gather that at about a quarter to two on the morning of the crime, a man (who had, on the previous day visited the house to obtain the tress of hair and oil the locks) entered the house by means of a latchkey. We can fix the time by the fact that it rained on that morning from half-past one to a quarter to two, this being the only rain that has fallen for a fortnight, and the murder was committed at about two o'clock. The man lit a wax match in the hall and another halfway up the stairs. He found the bedroom door locked, and turned the key from outside with a bent wire. He entered, lit the candle, placed the box and hassock, murdered his victim, washed his hands and knife, took the candle-end from the socket and went downstairs, where he blew out the candle and dropped it into the tray.

"The next clue is furnished by the sand on the pillow. I took a little of it, and examined it under the microscope, when it turned out to be deep-sea sand from the Eastern Mediterranean. It was full of the minute shells called 'Foraminifera,' and as one of these happened to belong to a species which is found only in the Levant, I was able to fix the locality."

"But this is very remarkable," said the coroner. "How on earth could deep-sea sand have got on to this woman's pillow?"

"The explanation," replied Thorndyke, "is really quite simple. Sand of this kind is contained in considerable quantities in Turkey sponges. The warehouses in which the sponges are unpacked are often strewn with it ankle deep; the men who unpack the cases become dusted over with it, their clothes saturated and their pockets filled with it. If such a person, with his clothes and pockets full of sand, had committed this murder, it is pretty certain that in leaning over the head of the bed in a partly inverted position he would have let fall a certain quantity of the sand from his pockets and the interstices of his clothing. Now, as soon as I had examined this sand and ascertained its nature, I sent a message to Mr. Goldstein asking him for a list of the persons who were acquainted with the deceased, with their addresses and occupations. He sent me the list by return, and among the persons mentioned was a man who was engaged as a packer in a wholesale sponge warehouse in the Minories. I further ascertained that the new season's crop of Turkey sponges had arrived a few days before the murder.

"The question that now arose was, whether this sponge-packer was the person whose fingerprints I had found on the candle-end. To settle this point, I prepared two mounted photographs, and having contrived to meet the man at his door on his return from work, I induced him to look at them and compare them. He took them from me, holding each one between a forefinger and thumb. When he returned them to me, I took them home and carefully dusted each on both sides with a certain surgical dusting-powder. The powder adhered to the places where his fingers and thumbs had pressed against the photographs, showing the fingerprints very distinctly. Those of the right hand were identical with the prints on the candle, as you will see if you compare them with the cast." He produced from the box the photograph of the Yiddish lettering, on the black margin of which there now stood out with startling distinctness a yellowish-white print of a thumb.

Thorndyke had just handed the card to the coroner when a very singular disturbance arose. While my friend had been giving the latter part of his evidence, I had observed the man Petrofsky rise from his seat and walk stealthily across to the door. He turned the handle softly and pulled, at first gently, and then with more force. But the door was locked. As he realized this, Petrofsky seized the handle with both hands and tore at it furiously, shaking it to and fro with the violence of a madman, and his shaking limbs, his starting eyes, glaring insanely at the astonished spectators, his ugly face, dead white, running with sweat and hideous with terror, made a picture that was truly shocking.

Suddenly he let go the handle, and with a horrible cry thrust his hand under the skirt of his coat and rushed at Thorndyke. But the superintendent was ready for this. There was a shout and a scuffle, and then Petrofsky was born down, kicking and biting like a maniac, while Miller hung on to his right hand and the formidable knife that it grasped.

"I will ask you to hand that knife to the coroner," said Thorndyke, when Petrofsky had been secured and handcuffed, and the superintendent had readjusted his collar. "Will you kindly examine it, sir," he continued, "and tell me if there is a notch in the edge, near to the point--a triangular notch about an eighth of an inch long?"

The coroner looked at the knife, and then said in a tone of surprise: "Yes, there is. You have seen this knife before, then?"

"No, I have not," replied Thorndyke. "But perhaps I had better continue my statement. There is no need for me to tell you that the fingerprints on the card and on the candle are those of Paul Petrofsky; I will proceed to the evidence furnished by the body.

"In accordance with your order, I went to the mortuary and examined the corpse of the deceased. The wound has been fully and accurately described by Dr. Davidson, but I observed one fact which I presume he had overlooked. Embedded in the bone of the spine--in the left transverse process of the fourth vertebra--I discovered a small particle of steel, which I carefully extracted."

He drew his collecting-box from his pocket, and taking from it a seed-envelope, handed the latter to the coroner. "That fragment of steel is in this envelope," he said, "and it is possible that it may correspond to the notch in the knife-blade."

Amidst an intense silence the coroner opened the little envelope, and let the fragment of steel drop on to a sheet of paper. Laying the knife on the paper, he gently pushed the fragment towards the notch. Then he looked up at Thorndyke.

"It fits exactly," said he.

There was a heavy thud at the other end of the room and we all looked round.

Petrofsky had fallen on to the floor insensible.

♦ ♦ ♦ ♦ ♦

"An instructive case, Jervis," remarked Thorndyke, as we walked homewards--"a case that reiterates the lesson that the authorities still refuse to learn."

"What is that?" I asked.

"It is this. When it is discovered that a murder has been committed, the scene of that murder should instantly become as the Palace of the Sleeping Beauty. Not a grain of dust should be moved, not a soul should be allowed to approach it, until the scientific observer has seen everything in situ and absolutely undisturbed. No tramplings of excited constables, no rummaging by detectives, no scrambling to and fro of bloodhounds. Consider what would have happened in this case if we had arrived a few hours later. The corpse would have been in the mortuary, the hair in the sergeant's pocket, the bed rummaged and the sand scattered abroad, the candle probably removed, and the stairs covered with fresh tracks.

"There would not have been the vestige of a clue."

"And," I added, "the deep sea would have uttered its message in vain."

The Magic Casket

The Magic Casket

It was in the near neighbourhood of King's Road, Chelsea, that chance, aided by Thorndyke's sharp and observant eyes, introduced us to the dramatic story of the Magic Casket. Not that there was anything strikingly dramatic in the opening phase of the affair, nor even in the story of the casket itself. It was Thorndyke who added the dramatic touch, and most of the magic, too; and I record the affair principally as an illustration of his extraordinary capacity for producing odd items of out-of-the-way knowledge and instantly applying them in the most unexpected manner.

Eight o'clock had struck on a misty November night when we turned out of the main road, and, leaving behind the glare of the shop windows, plunged into the maze of dark and narrow streets to the north. The abrupt change impressed us both, and Thorndyke proceeded to moralise on it in his pleasant, reflective fashion.

"London is an inexhaustible place," he mused. "Its variety is infinite. A minute ago we walked in a glare of light, jostled by a multitude. And now look at this little street. It is as dim as a tunnel, and we have got it absolutely to ourselves. Anything might happen in a place like this."

Suddenly he stopped. We were, at the moment, passing a small church or chapel, the west door of which was enclosed in an open porch; and as my observant friend stepped into the latter and stooped, I perceived in the deep shadow against the wall, the object which had evidently caught his eye.

"What is it?" I asked, following him in.

"It is a handbag," he replied; "and the question is, what is it doing here?"

He tried the church door, which was obviously locked, and coming out, looked at the windows.

"There are no lights in the church." said he; "the place is locked up, and there is nobody in sight. Apparently the bag is derelict. Shall we have a look at it?"

Without waiting for an answer, he picked it up and brought it out into the mitigated darkness of the street, where we proceeded to inspect it. But at the first glance it told its own tale; for it had evidently been locked, and it bore unmistakable traces of having been forced open.

"It isn't empty," said Thorndyke. "I think we had better see what is in it. Just catch hold while I get a light."

He handed me the bag while he felt in his pocket for the tiny electric lamp which he made a habit of carrying, and an excellent habit it is. I held the mouth of the bag open while he illuminated the interior, which we then saw to be occupied by several objects neatly wrapped in brown paper. One of these Thorndyke lifted out, and untying the string and removing the paper, displayed a Chinese stoneware jar. Attached to it was a label, bearing the stamp of the Victoria and Albert Museum, on which was written:

"Miss MABEL BONNET,

168 Willow Walk, Fulham Road, W."

"That tells us all that we want to know," said Thorndyke, re-wrapping the jar and tenderly replacing it in the bag. "We can't do wrong in delivering the things to their owner, especially as the bag itself is evidently her property, too," and he pointed to the gilt initials, "M. B.," stamped on the morocco.

It took us but a few minutes to reach the Fulham Road, but we then had to walk nearly a mile along that thoroughfare before we arrived at Willow Walk--to which an obliging shopkeeper had directed us--and, naturally, No. 168 was at the farther end.

As we turned into the quiet street we almost collided with two men, who were walking at a rapid pace, but both looking back over their shoulders. I noticed that they were both Japanese--well-dressed, gentlemanly- looking men--but I gave them little attention, being interested, rather, in what they were looking at. This was a taxicab which was dimly visible by the light of a street lamp at the farther end of the "Walk," and from which four persons had just alighted. Two of these had hurried ahead to knock at a door, while the other two walked very slowly across the pavement and up the steps to the threshold. Almost immediately the door was opened; two of the shadowy figures entered, and the other two returned slowly to the cab and as we came nearer, I could see that these latter were policemen in uniform. I had just time to note this fact when they both got into the cab and were forthwith spirited away.

"Looks like a street accident of some kind," I remarked; and then, as I glanced at the number of the house we were passing, I added: "Now, I wonder if that house happens to be--yes, by Jove! it is. It is 168! Things have been happening, and this bag of ours is one of the dramatis personae."

The response to our knock was by no means prompt. I was, in fact, in the act of raising my hand to the knocker to repeat the summons when the door opened and revealed an elderly servant-maid, who regarded us inquiringly, and, as I thought, with something approaching alarm.

"Does Miss Mabel Bonney live here?" Thorndyke asked.

"Yes, sir," was the reply; "but I am afraid you can't see her just now, unless it is something urgent. She is rather upset, and particularly engaged at present."

"There is no occasion whatever to disturb her," said Thorndyke. "We have merely called to restore this bag, which seemed to have been lost;" and with this he held it out towards her. She grasped it eagerly with a cry of surprise, and as the mouth fell open, she peered into it.

"Why," she exclaimed, "they don't seem to have taken anything, after all, Where did you find it, sir?"

In the porch of a church in Spelton Street," Thorndyke replied, and was turning away when the servant said earnestly: "Would you kindly give me your name and address, sir? Miss Bonney will wish to write and thank you."

"There is really no need," said he; but she interrupted anxiously: "If you would be so kind, sir. Miss Bonney will be so vexed if she is unable to thank you; and besides, she may want to ask you some questions about it."

"That is true," said Thorndyke (who was restrained only by good manners from asking one or two questions, himself). He produced his card-case, and having handed one of his cards to the maid, wished her " good- evening" and retired.

"That bag had evidently been pinched," I remarked, as we walked back towards the Fulham Road.

"Evidently," he agreed, and was about to enlarge on the matter when our attention was attracted to a taxi, which was approaching from the direction of the main road. A man's head was thrust out of the window, and as the vehicle passed a street lamp, I observed that the head appertained to an elderly gentleman with very white hair and a very fresh face.

"Did you see who that was?" Thorndyke asked.

"It looked like old Brodribb," I replied.

"It did; very much. I wonder where he is of to."

He turned and followed, with a speculative eye, the receding taxi, which presently swept alongside the kerb and stopped, apparently opposite the house from we had just come. As the vehicle came to rest, the door flew open and the passenger shot out like an elderly, but agile, Jack-in-the-box, and bounced up the steps.

"That is Brodribb's knock, sure enough," said I, as the old-fashioned flourish reverberated up the quiet street. "I have heard it too often on our own knocker to mistake it. But we had better not let him see us watching him."

As we went once more on our way, I took a sly glance, now and again, at my friend, noting with a certain malicious enjoyment his profoundly cogitative air. I knew quite well what was happening in his mind for his mind reacted to observed facts in an invariable manner. And here was a group of related facts: the bag, stolen, but deposited intact; the museum label; the injured or sick person--probably Miss Bonney, her self-- brought home under police escort; and the arrival, post-haste, of the old lawyer; a significant group of facts. And there was Thorndyke, under my amused and attentive observation, fitting them together in various combinations to see what general conclusion emerged. Apparently my own mental state was equally clear to him, for he remarked, presently, as if response to an unspoken comment: "Well, I expect we shall know all about it before many days have passed if Brodribb sees my card, as he most probably will. Here comes an omnibus that will suit us. Shall we hop on?"

He stood at the kerb and raised his stick; and as the accommodation on the omnibus was such that our seats were separated, there was no opportunity to pursue the subject further, even if there had been anything to discuss.

But Thorndyke's prediction was justified sooner than I had expected. For we had not long finished our supper, and had not yet closed the "oak," when there was heard a mighty flourish on the knocker of our inner door.

"Brodribb, by Jingo!" I exclaimed, and hurried across the room to let him in.

"No, Jervis," he said as I invited him to enter, "I am not coming in. Don't want to disturb you at this time of night. I've just called to make an appointment for to-morrow with a client."

"Is the client's name Bonney?" I asked.

He started and gazed at me in astonishment. "Gad, Jervis!" he exclaimed, "you are getting as bad as Thorndyke. How the deuce did you know that she was my client?"

"Never mind how I know. It is our business to know everything in these chambers. But if your appointment concerns Miss Mabel Bonney, for the Lord's sake come in and give Thorndyke a chance of a night's rest. At present, he is on broken bottles, as Mr. Bumble would express it."

On this persuasion, Mr. Brodribb entered, nothing loath--very much the reverse, in fact--and having bestowed a jovial greeting on Thorndyke, glanced approvingly round the room.

"Ha!" said he, "you look very cosy. If you are really sure I am not--"

I cut him short by propelling him gently towards the fire, beside which I deposited him in an easy chair, while Thorndyke pressed the electric bell which rang up in the laboratory.

"Well," said Brodribb, spreading himself out comfortably before the fire like a handsome old Tom-cat, "if you are going to let me give you a few particulars--but perhaps you would rather that I should not talk shop?"

"Now you know perfectly well, Brodribb," said Thorndyke, "that 'shop' is the breath of life to us all. Let us have those particulars."

Brodribb sighed contentedly and placed his toes on the fender (and at this moment the door opened softly and Polton looked into the room. He took s single, understanding glance at our visitor, and withdrew, shutting the door without a sound).

I am glad," pursued Brodribb, "to have this opportunity of a preliminary chat, because there are certain things that one can say better when the client is not present; and I am deeply interested in Bonney's affairs. The crisis in those affairs which has brought me here is of quite recent date--in fact, it dates from this evening. But I know your partiality for having events related in their proper sequence, so I will leave today's happenings for the moment and tell you the story--the whole of which is material to the case--from the beginning."

Here there was a slight interruption, due to Polton's noiseless entry with a tray on which was a decanter, a biscuit box, and three port glasses. This he deposited, on a small table, which he placed within convenient reach of our guest. Then, with a glance of altruistic satisfaction at our old friend, he stole out like a benevolent ghost.

Dear, dear!" exclaimed Brodribb, beaming on the decanter, "this is really too bad. You ought not to indulge me in this way."

"My dear Brodribb," replied Thorndyke, "you are a benefactor to us. You give us a pretext for taking a glass of port. We can't drink alone, you know."

"I should, if I had a cellar like yours," chuckled Brodribb, sniffing ecstatically at his glass. He took a sip, with his eyes closed, savoured it solemnly, shook his head, and set the glass down on the table.

"To return to our case," he resumed; "Miss Bonney is the daughter of a solicitor, Harold Bonney--you may remember him. He had offices in Bedford Row; and there, one morning, a client came to him and asked him to take care of some property while he, the said client, ran over to Paris, where he had some urgent business. The property in question was a collection of pearls of most unusual size and value, forming a great necklace, which had been unstrung for the sake of portability. It is not clear where they came from, but as the transaction occurred soon after the Russian Revolution, we may make a guess. At any rate, there they were, packed loosely in a leather bag, the string of which was sealed with the owner's seal.

"Bonney seems to have been rather casual about the affair. He gave the client a receipt for the bag, stating the nature of the contents, which he had not seen, and deposited it, in the client's presence, in the safe in his private office. Perhaps he intended to take it to the bank or transfer it to his strong-room, but it is evident that he did neither; for his managing clerk, who kept the second key of the strong-room--without which the room could not be opened--knew nothing of the transaction. When he went home at about seven o'clock, he left Bonney hard at work in his office, and there is no doubt that the pearls were still in the safe.

That night, at about a quarter to nine, it happened that a couple of C.I.D. officers were walking up Bedford Row when they saw three men come out of one of the houses. Two of them turned up towards Theobald's Road, but the third came south, towards them. As he passed them, they both recognised him as a Japanese named Uyenishi, who was believed to be a member of a cosmopolitan gang and whom the police were keeping under observation. Naturally, their suspicions were aroused. The first two men had hurried round the corner and were out of sight; and when they turned to look after Uyenishi, he had mended his pace considerably and was looking back at them. Thereupon one of the officers, named Barker, decided to follow the Jap, while the other, Holt, reconnoitred the premises.

"Now, as soon as Barker turned, the Japanese broke into a run. It was just such a night as this dark and, slightly foggy. In order to keep his man in sight, he had to run, too; and he found that he had a sprinter to deal with. From the bottom of Bedford Row, Uyenishi darted across and shot down Hand Court like a lamp- lighter. Barker followed, but at the Holborn end his man was nowhere to be seen. However, he presently learned from a man at a shop door that the fugitive had run past and turned up Brownlow Street, so off he went again in pursuit. But when he got to the top of the street, back in Bedford Row, he was done. There was no sign of the man, and no one about from whom he could make inquiries. All he could do was to cross the road and walk up Bedford Row to see if Holt had made any discoveries.

"As he was trying to identify the house, his colleague came out on to the doorstep and beckoned him in and this was the story that he told. He had recognised the house by the big lamp-standard; and as the place was all dark, he had gone into the entry and tried the office door. Finding it unlocked, he had entered the clerks' office, lit the gas, and tried the door of the private office, but found it locked. He knocked at it, but getting no answer, had a good look round the clerk's office; and there, presently, on the floor in a dark corner, he found a key. This he tried in the door of the private office, and finding that it fitted, turned it and opened the door. As he did so, the light from the outer office fell on the body of a man lying on the floor just inside.

"A moment's inspection showed that the man had been murdered--first knocked on the head and then finished with a knife. Examination of the pockets showed that the dead man was Harold Bonney, and also that no robbery from the person seemed to have been committed. Nor was there any sign of any other kind of robbery. Nothing seemed to have been disturbed, and the safe had not been broken into, though that was not very conclusive, as the safe key was in the dead man's pocket. However, a murder had been committed, and obviously Uyenishi was either the murderer or an accessory; so Holt had, at once, rung up Scotland Yard on the office telephone, giving all the particulars.

"I may say at once that Uyenishi disappeared completely and at once. He never went to his lodgings at Limehouse, for the police were there before he could have arrived. A lively hue and cry was kept up. Photographs of the wanted man were posted outside every police-station, and a watch was set at all the ports. But he was never found. He must have got away at once on some outward-bound tramp from the Thames. And there we will leave him for the moment.

"At first it was thought that nothing had been stolen, since the managing clerk could not discover that any thing was missing. But a few days later the client returned from Paris, and presenting his receipt, asked for his pearls. But the pearls had vanished. Clearly they had been the object of the crime. The robbers must have known about them and traced them to the office. Of course the safe had been opened with its own key, which was then replaced in the dead man's pocket.

"Now, I was poor Bonney's executor, and in that capacity I denied his liability in respect of the pearls on the ground that he was a gratuitous bailee--there being no evidence that any consideration had been demanded--and that being murdered cannot be construed as negligence. But Miss Mabel, who was practically the sole legatee, insisted on accepting liability. She said that the pearls could have been secured in the bank or the strong-room, and that she was morally, if not legally, liable for their loss; and she insisted on handing to the owner the full amount at which he valued them. It was a wildly foolish proceeding, for he would certainly have accepted half the sum. But still I take my hat off to a person--man or woman--who can accept poverty in preference to a broken covenant"; and here Brodribb, being in fact that sort of person himself, had to be consoled with a replenished glass.

"And mind you," he resumed, "when I speak of poverty, I wish to be taken literally. The estimated value of those pearls was fifty thousand pounds--if you can imagine anyone out of Bedlam giving such a sum for a parcel of trash like that; and when poor Mabel Bonney had paid it, she was left with the prospect of having to spread her butter mighty thin for the rest of her life. As a matter of fact, she has had to sell one after another of her little treasures to pay just her current expenses, and I'm hanged if I can see how she is going to carry on when she has sold the last of them. But there, I mustn't take up your time with her private troubles. Let us return to our muttons.

"First, as to the pearls They were never traced, and it seems probable that they were never disposed of. For, you see, pearls are different from any other kind of gems. You can cut up a big diamond, but you can't cut up a big pearl. And the great value of this necklace was due not only to the size, the perfect shape and 'orient' of the separate pearls, but to the fact that the whole set was perfectly matched. To break up the necklace was to destroy a good part of its value.

"And now as to our friend Uyenishi. He disappeared, as I have said; but he reappeared at Los Angeles, in custody of the police, charged with robbery and murder. He was taken red-handed and was duly convicted and sentenced to death; but for some reason--or more probably, for no reason, as we should think--the sentence was commuted to imprisonment for life. Under these circumstances, the English police naturally took no action, especially as they really had no evidence against him.

"Now Uyenishi was, by trade, a metal-worker; a maker of those pretty trifles that are so dear to the artistic Japanese, and when he was in prison he was allowed to set up a little workshop and practise his trade on a small scale. Among other things that he made was a little casket in the form of a seated figure, which he said he wanted to give to his brother as a keepsake. I don't know whether any permission was granted for him to make this gift, but that is of no consequence; for Uyenishi got influenza and was carried off in a few days by pneumonia; and the prison authorities learned that his brother had been killed, a week or two previously, in a shooting affair at San Francisco. So the casket remained on their hands.

"About this time, Miss Bonney was invited to accompany an American lady on a visit to California, and accepted gratefully. While she was there she paid a visit to the prison to inquire whether Uyenishi had ever made any kind of statement concerning the missing pearls. Here she heard of Uyenishi's recent death; and the governor of the prison, as he could not give her any information, handed over to her the casket as a sort of memento. This transaction came to the knowledge of the press, and--well, you know what the Californian press is like. There were 'some comments,' as they would say, and quite an assortment of Japanese, of shady antecedents, applied to the prison to have the casket 'restored' to them as Uyenishi's heirs. Then Miss Bonney's rooms at the hotel were raided by burglars--but the casket was in the hotel strong-room--and Miss Bonney and her hostess were shadowed by various undesirables in such a disturbing fashion that the two ladies became alarmed and secretly made their way to New York. But there another burglary occurred, with the same unsuccessful result, and the shadowing began again. Finally, Miss Bonney, feeling that her presence was a danger to her friend, decided to return to England, and managed to get on board the ship without letting her departure be known in advance.

"But even in England she has not been left in peace. She has had an uncomfortable feeling of being watched and attended, and has seemed to be constantly meeting Japanese men in the streets, especially in the vicinity of her house. Of course, all the fuss is about this infernal casket; and when she told me what was happening, I promptly popped the thing in my pocket and took it, to my office, where I stowed it in the strong-room. And there, of course, it ought to have remained. but it didn't. One day Miss Bonney told me that she was sending some small things to a loan exhibition of oriental works of art at the South Kensington Museum, and she wished to include the casket. I urged her strongly to do nothing of the kind, but she persisted; and the end of it was that we went to the museum together, with her pottery and stuff in a handbag and the casket in my pocket.

"It was a most imprudent thing to do, for there the beastly casket was, for several months, exposed in a glass case for anyone to see, with her name on the label; and what was worse, full particulars of the origin of the thing. However, nothing happened while it was there--the museum is not an easy place to steal from--and all went well until it was time to remove the things after the close of the exhibition. Now, to-day was the appointed day, and, as on the previous occasion, she and I went to the museum together. But the unfortunate thing is that we didn't come away together. Her other exhibits were all pottery, and these were dealt with first, so that she had her handbag packed and was ready to go before they had begun on the metal work cases. As we were not going the same way, it didn't seem necessary for her to wait; so she went off with her bag and I stayed behind until the casket was released, when I put it in my pocket and went borne, where I locked the thing up again in the strong-room.

"It was about seven when I got borne. A little after eight I heard the telephone ring down in the office, and down I went, cursing the untimely ringer, who turned out to be a policeman at St. George's Hospital. He said he bad found Miss Bonney lying unconscious in the street and had taken her to the hospital, where she had been detained for a while, but she was now recovered and he was taking her home. She would like me, if possible, to go and see her at once. Well, of course, I set off forthwith and got to her house a few minutes after her arrival, and just after you bad left.

"She was a good deal upset, so I didn't worry her with many questions, but she gave me a short account of her misadventure, which amounted to this: She had started to walk home from the museum along the Brompton Road, and she was passing down a quiet street between that and Fulham Road when she heard soft footsteps behind her. The next moment, a scarf or shawl was thrown over her head and drawn tightly round her neck. At the same moment, the bag was snatched from her hand. That is all that she remembers, for she was half and so terrified that she fainted, and knew no more until she found herself in a cab with two policemen who were taking her to the hospital.

"Now it is obvious that her assailants were in search of that damned casket, for the bag had been broken open and searched, but nothing taken or damaged; which suggests the Japanese again, for a British thief would have smashed the crockery. I found your card there, and I put it to Miss Bonney that we had better ask you to help us--I told her all about you-- and she agreed emphatically. So that is why I am here, drinking your port and robbing you of your night's rest."

"And what do you want me to do?" Thorndyke asked.

"Whatever you think best," was the cheerful reply. "In the first place, this nuisance must be put a stop to--this shadowing and hanging about. But apart from that, you must see that there is something queer about this accursed casket. The beastly thing is of no intrinsic value. The museum man turned up his nose at it. But it evidently has some extrinsic value, and no small value either. If it is good enough for these devils to follow it all the way from the States, as they seem to have done, it is good enough for us to try to find out what its value is. That is where you come in. I propose to bring Miss Bonney to see you to-morrow, and I will bring the infernal casket, too. Then you will ask her a few questions, take a look at the casket--through the microscope, if necessary--and tell us all about it in your usual necromantic way."

Thorndyke laughed as he refilled our friend's glass. "If faith will move mountains, Brodribb," said he, "you ought to have been a civil engineer. But it is certainly a rather intriguing problem."

"Ha!" exclaimed the old solicitor; "then it's all right. I've known you a good many years, but I've never known you to be stumped; and you are not going to be stumped now. What time shall I bring her? Afternoon or evening would suit her best."

"Very well," replied Thorndyke; "bring her to tea--say, five o'clock. How will that do?"

"Excellently; and here's good luck to the adventure." He drained his glass, and the decanter being now empty, he rose, shook our hands warmly, and took his departure in high spirits.

It was with a very lively interest that I looked for ward to the prospective visit. Like Thorndyke, I found the case rather intriguing. For it was quite clear, as our shrewd old friend had said, that there was something more than met the eye in the matter of this casket.

Hence, on the following afternoon, when, on the stroke of five, footsteps became audible on our stairs, I awaited the arrival of our new client with keen curiosity, both as to herself and her mysterious property.

To tell the truth, the lady was better worth looking at than the casket. At the first glance, I was strongly prepossessed in her favour, and so, I think, was Thorndyke. Not that she was a beauty, though comely enough. But she was an example of a type that seems to be growing rarer; quiet, gentle, soft-spoken, and a lady to her finger-tips; a little sad-faced and care worn, with a streak or two of white in her prettily- disposed black hair, though she could not have been much over thirty-five. Altogether a very gracious and winning personality.

When we had been presented to her by Brodribb--who treated her as if she had been a royal personage- and had enthroned her in the most comfortable easy- chair, we inquired as to her health, and were duly thanked for the salvage of the bag. Then Polton brought in the tray, with an air that seemed to demand an escort of choristers; the tea was poured out, and the informal proceedings began.

She had not, however, much to tell; for she had not seen her assailants, and the essential facts of the case had been fully presented in Brodribb's excellent summary. After a very few questions, therefore, we came to the next stage; which was introduced by Brodribb's taking from his pocket a small parcel which he proceeded to open.

There," said he, "that is the *fons et origo mali*. Not much to look at, I think you will agree." He set the object down on the table and glared at it malevolently, while Thorndyke and I regarded it with a more impersonal interest. It was not much to look at. Just an ordinary Japanese casket in the form of a squat, shapeless figure with a silly little grinning face, of which the head and shoulders opened on a hinge; a pleasant enough object, with its quiet, warm colouring, but certainly not a masterpiece of art.

Thorndyke picked it up and turned it over slowly for preliminary inspection; then he went on to examine it detail by detail, watched closely, in his turn, by Brodribb and me. Slowly and methodically, his eye--fortified by a watchmaker's eyeglass--travelled over every part of the exterior. Then he opened it, and I having examined the inside of the lid, scrutinised the bottom from within, long and attentively. Finally, he turned the casket upside down and examined the bottom from without, giving to it the longest and most rigorous inspection of all--which puzzled me somewhat, for the bottom was absolutely plain At length, he passed the casket and the eyeglass to me without comment.

"Well," said Brodribb, "what is the verdict?"

"It is of no value as a work of art," replied Thorndyke. "The body and lid are just castings of common white metal--an antimony alloy, I should say. The bronze colour is lacquer."

"So the museum man remarked." said Brodribb.

"But," continued Thorndyke, "there is one very odd thing about it. The only piece of fine metal in it is in the part which matters least. The bottom is a separate plate of the alloy known to the Japanese as Shakudo--an alloy of copper and gold."

"Yes," said Brodribb, "the museum man noted that, too, and couldn't make out why it had been put there."

"Then," Thorndyke continued, "there is another anomalous feature; the inside of the bottom is covered with elaborate decoration--just the place where decoration is most inappropriate, since it would be covered up by the contents of the casket. And, again, this decoration is etched; not engraved or chased. But etching is a very unusual process for this purpose, if it is ever used at all by Japanese metal-workers. My impression is that it is not; for it is most unsuitable for decorative purposes. That is all that I observe, so far."

"And what do you infer from your observations?" Brodribb asked.

I should like to think the matter over," was the reply. "There is an obvious anomaly, which must have some significance. But I won't embark on speculative opinions at this stage. I should like, however, to take one or two photographs of the casket, for reference; but that will occupy some time. You will hardly want to wait so long."

"No," said Brodribb. "But Miss Bonney is coming with me to my office to go over some documents and discuss a little business. When we have finished, I will come back and fetch the confounded thing."

"There is no need for that," replied Thorndyke. "As soon as I have done what is necessary, I will bring it up to your place."

To this arrangement Brodribb agreed readily, and he and his client prepared to depart. I rose, too, and as I happened to have a call to make in Old Square, Lincoln's Inn, I asked permission to walk with them.

As we came out into King's Bench Walk I noticed a smallish, gentlemanly-looking man who had just passed our entry and now turned in at the one next door; and by the light of the lamp in the entry he looked to me like a Japanese. I thought Miss Bonney had observed him, too, but she made no remark, and neither did I. But, passing up Inner Temple Lane, we nearly overtook two other men, who--though I got but a back view of them and the light was feeble enough--aroused my suspicions by their neat, small figures. As we approached, they quickened their pace, and one of them looked back over his shoulder; and then my suspicions were confirmed, for it was an unmistakable Japanese face that looked round at us. Miss Bonney saw that I had observed the men, for she remarked, as they turned sharply at the Cloisters and entered Pump Court: "You see, I am still haunted by Japanese."

"I noticed them," said Brodribb. "They are probably law students. But we may as well be companionable"; and with this, he, too, headed for Pump Court.

We followed our oriental friends across the Lane into Fountain Court, and through that and Devereux Court out to Temple Bar, where we parted from them; they turning westward and we crossing to Bell Yard, up which we walked, entering New Square by the Carey Street gate. At Brodribb's doorway we halted and looked back, but no one was in sight. I accordingly went my way, promising to return anon to hear Thorndyke's report, and the lawyer and his client disappeared through the portal.

My business occupied me longer than I had expected, I but nevertheless, when I arrived at Brodribb's premises--where he lived in chambers over his office--Thorndyke had not yet made his appearance. A quarter of an hour later, however, we heard his brisk step on the stairs, and as Brodribb threw the door open, he entered and produced the casket from his pocket.

"Well," said Brodribb, taking it from him and locking it, for the time being, in a drawer, "has the oracle Spoken; and if so, what did he say?"

"Oracles," replied Thorndyke, "have a way of being more concise than explicit. Before I attempt to interpret the message, I should like to view the scene of the escape; to see if there was any intelligible reason why this man Uyenishi should have returned up Brownlow Street into what must have been the danger zone. I think that is a material question."

"Then," said Brodribb, with evident eagerness, "let us all walk up and have a look at the confounded place. It is quite close by."

We all agreed instantly, two of us, at least, being on the tip-toe of expectation. For Thorndyke, who habitually understated his results, had virtually admitted that the casket had told him something; and as we walked up the Square to the gate in Lincoln's Inn Fields, I watched him furtively, trying to gather from his im passive face a hint as to what the something amounted to, and wondering how the movements of the fugitive bore on the solution of the mystery. Brodribb was similarly occupied, and as we crossed from Great Turnstile and took our way up Brownlow Street, I could see that his excitement was approaching bursting-point.

At the top of the street Thorndyke paused and looked up and down the rather dismal thoroughfare which forms a continuation of Bedford Row and bears its name. Then he crossed to the paved island surrounding the pump which stands in the middle of the road, and from thence surveyed the entrances to Brownlow Street and Hand Court; and then he turned and looked thoughtfully at the pump.

"A quaint old survivor, this," he remarked, tapping the iron shell with his knuckles. "There is a similar one, you may remember, in Queen Square, and another at Aldgate. But that is still in use."

"Yes," Brodribb assented, almost dancing with im patience and inwardly damning the pump, as I could see, "I've noticed it."

I suppose," Thorndyke proceeded, in a reflective tone, "they had to remove the handle. But it was rather a pity."

"Perhaps it was," growled Brodribb, whose complexion was rapidly developing affinities to that of a pickled cabbage, " but what the d--"

Here he broke off short and glared silently at Thorndyke, who had raised his arm and squeezed his hand into the opening once occupied by the handle. He groped in the interior with an expression of placid interest, and presently reported: "The barrel is still there, and so, apparently, is the plunger "--(Here I heard Brodribb mutter huskily, "Damn the barrel and the plunger too!") "but my hand is rather large for the exploration. Would you, Miss Bonney, mind slipping your hand in and telling me if I am right?"

We all gazed at Thorndyke in dismay, but in a moment Miss Bonney recovered from her astonishment, and with a deprecating smile, half shy, half amused, she slipped off her glove, and reaching up--it was rather high for her--inserted her hand into the narrow slit. Brodribb glared at her and gobbled like a turkey-cock, and I watched her with a sudden suspicion that something was going to happen. Nor was I mistaken. For, as I looked, the shy, puzzled smile faded from her face and was succeeded by an expression of incredulous astonishment. Slowly she withdrew her hand, and as it came out of the slit it dragged something after it. I started forward, and by the light of the lamp above the pump I could see that the object was a leather bag secured by a string from which hung a broken seal.

"It can't be!" she gasped as, with trembling fingers, she untied the string. Then, as she peered into the open mouth, she uttered a little cry. "It is! It is! It is the necklace!"

Brodribb was speechless with amazement. So was I; and I was still gazing open-mouthed at the bag in Miss Bonney's hands when I felt Thorndyke touch my arm. I turned quickly and found him offering me an automatic pistol. "Stand by, Jervis," he said quietly, looking towards Gray's Inn.

I looked in the same direction, and then perceived three men stealing round the corner from Jockey' Fields. Brodribb saw them, too, and snatching the bag of pearls from his client's hands, buttoned it into his breast pocket and placed himself before its owner, grasping his stick with a war-like air. The three men filed along the pavement until they were opposite us, when they turned simultaneously and bore down on the pump, each man, as I noticed, holding his right hand behind him. In a moment, Thorndyke's hand, grasping a pistol, flew up--as did mine, also--and he called out sharply: "Stop! If any man moves a hand, I fire."

The challenge brought them up short, evidently unprepared for this kind of reception. What would have happened next it is impossible to guess. But at this moment a police whistle sounded and two constables ran out from Hand Court. The whistle was instantly echoed from the direction of Warwick Court, whence two more constabulary figures appeared through the postern gate of Gray's Inn. Our three attendants hesitated but for an instant. Then, with one accord, they turned tail and flew like the wind round into Jockey's Fields, with the whole posse of constables close on their heels.

"Remarkable coincidence," said Brodribb, "that those policemen should happen to be on the look-out. Or isn't it a coincidence?"

"I telephoned to the station superintendent before I started," replied Thorndyke, "warning him of a possible breach of the peace at this spot."

Brodribb chuckled. "You're a wonderful man, Thorndyke. You think of everything. I wonder if the police will catch those fellows."

"It is no concern of ours," replied Thorndyke. "We've got the pearls, and that finishes the business. There will be no more shadowing, in any case."

Miss Bonney heaved a comfortable little sigh and glanced gratefully at Thorndyke. "You can have no idea what a relief that is!" she exclaimed; " to say nothing of the treasure-trove."

We waited some time, but as neither the fugitives nor the constables reappeared, we presently made our way back down Brownlow Street. And there it was that Brodribb had an inspiration.

"I'll tell you what," said bc. "I will just pop these things in my strong-room--they will be perfectly safe there until the bank opens to-morrow--and then we'll go and have a nice little dinner. I'll pay the piper."

"Indeed you won't!" exclaimed Miss Bonney. "This is my thanksgiving festival, and the benevolent wizard shall be the guest of the evening."

"Very well, my dear," agreed Brodribb. "I will pay and charge it to the estate. But I stipulate that the benevolent wizard shall tell us exactly what the oracle said. That is essential to the preservation of my sanity."

"You shall have his *ipissima verba*," Thorndyke promised; and the resolution was carried, *nem. con.*

An hour and a half later we were seated around a table in a private room of a café to which Mr. Brodribb had conducted us. I may not divulge its whereabouts, though I may, perhaps, hint that we approached it by way of Wardour Street. At any rate, we had dined, even to the fulfilment of Brodribb's ideal, and coffee and liqueurs furnished a sort of gastronomic doxology. Brodribb had lighted a cigar and Thorndyke had produced a vicious-looking little black cheroot, which he regarded fondly and then returned to its abiding-place as unsuited to the present company.

"Now," said Brodribb, watching Thorndyke fill his pipe (as understudy of the cheroot aforesaid), "we are waiting to hear the words of the oracle."

"You shall hear them," Thorndyke replied. "There were only five of them. But first, there are certain introductory matters to be disposed of. The solution of this problem is based on two well-known physical facts, one metallurgical and the other optical."

"Ha!" said Brodribb. "But you must temper the wind to the shorn lamb, you know, Thorndyke. Miss Bonney and I are not scientists."

"I will put the matter quite simply, but you must have the facts. The first relates to the properties of malleable metals--excepting iron and steel--and especially of copper and its alloys. If a plate of such metal or alloy--say, bronze, for instance--is made red-hot and quenched in water, it becomes quite soft and flexible--the reverse of what happens in the case of iron. Now, if such a plate of softened metal be placed on a steel anvil and hammered, it becomes extremely hard and brittle."

"I follow that," said Brodribb.

"Then see what follows. If, instead of hammering the soft plate, you put on it the edge of a blunt chisel and strike on that chisel a sharp blow, you produce an indented line. Now the plate remains soft; but the metal forming the indented line has been hammered and has become hard. There is now a line of hard metal on the soft plate. Is that clear?"

"Perfectly," replied Brodribb; and Thorndyke accordingly continued: "The second fact is this: If a beam of light falls on a polished surface which reflects it, and if that surface is turned through a given angle, the beam of light is deflected through double that angle."

"H'm!" grunted Brodribb. "Yes. No doubt. I hope we are not going to get into any deeper waters, Thorndyke."

"We are not," replied the latter, smiling urbanely. "We are now going to consider the application of these facts. Have you ever seen a Japanese magic mirror?

"Never; nor even heard of such a thing."

"They are bronze mirrors, just like the ancient Greek or Etruscan mirrors--which are probably 'magic' mirrors, too. A typical specimen consists of a circular or oval plate of bronze, highly polished on the face and decorated on the back with chased ornament--commonly a dragon or some such device--and furnished with a handle. The ornament is, as I have said, chased; that is to say, it is executed in indented lines made with chasing tools, which are, in effect, small chisels, more or less blunt, which are struck with a chasing-hammer.

"Now these mirrors have a very singular property. Although the face is perfectly plain, as a mirror should be, yet, if a beam of sunlight is caught on it and reflected, say, on to a white wall, the round or oval patch of light on the wall is not a plain light patch. It shows quite clearly the ornament on the back of the mirror."

"But how extraordinary!" exclaimed Miss Bonney.

"It sounds quite incredible." I said.

"It does," Thorndyke agreed. "And yet the explanation is quite simple. Professor Sylvanus Thompson pointed it out years ago. It is based on the facts which I have just stated to you. The artist who makes one of these mirrors begins, naturally, by annealing the metal until it is quite soft. Then he chases the design on the back, and this design then shows slightly on the face. But he now grinds the face perfectly flat with fine emery and water so that the traces of the design are complete obliterated. Finally, he polishes the face with rouge on a soft buff.

"But now observe that wherever the chasing-tool has made a line, the metal is hardened right through, so that the design is in hard metal on a soft matrix. But the hardened metal resists the wear of the polishing buffer more than the soft metal does. The result is that the act of polishing causes the design to appear in faint relief on the face. Its projection is infinitesimal--less than the hundred-thousandth of an inch--and totally invisible to the eye. But, minute as it is, owing to the optical law which I mentioned--which, in effect, doubles the projection--it is enough to influence the reflection of light. As a consequence, every chased line appears on the patch of light as a dark line with a bright border, and so the whole design is visible. I think that is quite clear."

"Perfectly clear," Miss Bonney and Brodribb agreed.

"But now," pursued Thorndyke, "before we come to the casket, there is a very curious corollary which I must mention. Supposing our artist, having finished the mirror, should proceed with a scraper to erase the design from the back; and on the blank, scraped surface to etch a new design. The process of etching does not harden the metal, so the new design does not appear on the reflection. But the old design would. For although it was invisible on the face and had been erased from the back, it would still exist in the substance of the metal and continue to influence the reflection. The odd result would be that the design which would be visible in the patch of light on the wall would be a different one from that on the back of the mirror.

"No doubt, you see what I am leading up to. But I will take the investigation of the casket as it actually occurred. It was obvious, at once, that the value of the thing was extrinsic. It had no intrinsic value, either in material or workmanship. What could that value be? The clear suggestion was that the casket was the vehicle of some secret message or information. It had been made by Uyenishi, who had almost certainly had possession of the missing pearls, and who had been so closely pursued that be never had an opportunity to communicate with his confederates. It was to be given to a man who was almost certainly one of those confederates; and, since the pearls had never been traced, there was a distinct probability that the (presumed) message referred to some hiding-place in which Uyenishi had concealed them during his flight, and where they were probably still hidden.

"With these considerations in my mind, I examined the casket, and this was what I found. The thing, itself, was a common white-metal casting, made presentable by means of lacquer. But the white metal bottom had been cut out and replaced by a plate of fine bronze--Shakudo. The inside of this was covered with an etched design, which immediately aroused my suspicions. Turning it over, I saw that the outside of the bottom was not only smooth and polished; it was a true mirror. It gave a perfectly undistorted reflection of my face. At once, I suspected that the mirror held the secret; that the message, whatever it was, had been chased on the back, had then been scraped away and an etched design worked on it to hide the traces of the scraper.

"As soon as you were gone, I took the casket up to the laboratory and threw a strong beam of parallel light from a condenser on the bottom, catching the reflection on a sheet of white paper. The result was just what I had expected. On the bright oval patch on the paper could be seen the shadowy, but quite distinct, forms of five words in the Japanese character.

"I was in somewhat of a dilemma, for I have no knowledge of Japanese, whereas the circumstances were such as to make it rather unsafe to employ a translator. However, as I do just know the Japanese characters and possess a Japanese dictionary, I determined to make an attempt to fudge out the words myself. If I failed, I could then look for a discreet translator.

"However, it proved to be easier than I had expected, for the words were detached; they did not form a sentence, and so involved no questions of grammar. I spelt out the first word and then looked it up in the dictionary. The translation was 'pearls.' This looked hopeful, and I went on to the next, of which the translation was 'pump.' The third word floored me. It seemed to be 'jokkis,' or 'jokkish,' but there was no such word in the dictionary; so I turned to the next word, hoping that it would explain its predecessor. And it did. The fourth word was 'fields,' and the last word was evidently 'London.' So the entire group read 'Pearls, Pump, Jokkis, Fields, London.'

"Now, there is no pump, so far as I know, in Jockey Fields, but there is one in Bedford Row close to the corner of the Fields, and exactly opposite the end of Brownlow Street And by Mr. Brodribb's account, Uyenishi, in his flight, ran down Hand Court and re turned up Brownlow Street, as if he were making for the pump. As the latter is disused and the handle-hole is high up, well out of the way of children, it offers quite a good temporary hiding-place, and I had no doubt that the bag of pearls had been poked into it and was probably there still. I was tempted to go at once and explore; but I was anxious that the discovery should be made by Miss Bonney, herself, and I did not dare to make a preliminary exploration for fear of being shadowed. If I had found the treasure I should have had to take it and give it to her; which would have been a flat ending to the adventure. So I had to dissemble and be the occasion of much smothered objurgation on the part of my friend Brodribb. And that is the whole story of my interview with the oracle."

Our mantelpiece is becoming a veritable museum of trophies of victory, the gifts of grateful clients. Among them is a squat, shapeless figure of a Japanese gentleman of the old school, with a silly grinning little face--The Magic Casket. But its possession is no longer a menace. Its sting has been drawn; its magic is exploded; its secret is exposed, and its glory departed.

The Contents of a Mare's Nest

"IT is very unsatisfactory," said Mr. Stalker, of the Griffin' Life Assurance Company, at the close of a consultation on a doubtful claim. "I suppose we shall have to pay up."

"I am sure you will," said Thorndyke. "The death was properly certified, the deceased is buried, and you have not a single fact with which to support an application for further inquiry."

"No," Stalker agreed. "But I am not satisfied. I don't believe that doctor really knew what she died from. I wish cremation were more usual."

"So, I have no doubt, has many a poisoner," Thorndyke remarked dryly.

Stalker laughed, but stuck to his point. "I know you don't agree," said he," but from our point of view it is much more satisfactory to know that the extra precautions have been taken. In a cremation case, you have not to depend on the mere death certificate; you have the cause of death verified by an independent authority, and it is difficult to see how any miscarriage can occur."

Thorndyke shook his head. "It is a delusion, Stalker. You can't provide in advance for unknown contingencies. In practice, your special precautions degenerate into mere formalities. If the circumstances of a death appear normal, the independent authority will certify; if they appear abnormal, you won't get a certificate at all. And if suspicion arises only after the cremation has taken place, it can neither be confirmed nor rebutted."

"My point is," said Stalker, "that the searching examination would lead to discovery of a crime before cremation."

"That is the intention," Thorndyke admitted. "But no examination, short of an exhaustive post-mortem, would make it safe to destroy a body so that no reconsideration of the cause of death would be possible."

Stalker smiled as he picked up his hat. "Well," be said, "to a cobbler there is nothing like leather, and I suppose that to a toxicologist there is nothing like an exhumation," and with this parting shot he took his leave.

We had not seen the last of him, however. In the course of the same week he looked in to consult us on a fresh matter.

"A rather queer case has turned up," said he. "I don't know that we are deeply concerned in it, but we should like to have your opinion as to how we stand. The position is this: Eighteen months ago, a man named Ingle insured with us for fifteen hundred pounds, and he was then accepted as a first-class life. He has recently died--apparently from heart failure, the heart being described as fatty and dilated--and his wife, Sibyl, who is the sole legatee and executrix, has claimed payment.

But just as we were making arrangements to pay, a caveat has been entered by a certain Margaret Ingle, who declares that she is the wife of the deceased and claims the estate as next-of-kin. She states that the alleged wife, Sibyl, is a widow named Huggard who contracted a bigamous marriage with the deceased, knowing that he had a wife living."

"An interesting situation," commented Thorndyke, "but, as you say, it doesn't particularly concern you. It is a matter for the Probate Court."

"Yes," agreed Stalker. "But that is not all. Margaret Ingle not only charges the other woman with bigamy; she accuses her of having made away with the deceased."

"On what grounds?"

"Well, the reasons she gives are rather shadowy. She states that Sibyl's husband, James Huggard, died under suspicious circumstances--there seems to have been some suspicion that he had been poisoned--and she asserts that Ingle was a healthy, sound man and could not have died from the causes alleged."

"There is some reason in that," said Thorndyke, "if he was really a first-class life only eighteen months ago. As to the first husband, Huggard, we should want some particulars: as to whether there was an inquest what was the alleged cause of death, and what grounds there were for suspecting that he had been poisoned. If there really were any suspicious circumstances, it would be advisable to apply to the Home Office for an order to exhume the body of Ingle and verify the cause of death."

Stalker smiled somewhat sheepishly. "Unfortunately," said he, "that is not possible. Ingle was cremated."

"Ah!" said Thorndyke, "that is, as you say, unfortunate. It clearly increases the suspicion of poisoning, but destroys the means of verifying that suspicion."

"I should tell you," said Stalker," that the cremation was in accordance with the provisions of the will."

"That is not very material," replied Thorndyke. "In fact, it rather accentuates the suspicious aspect of the case; for the knowledge that the death of the deceased would be followed by cremation might act as a further inducement to get rid of him by poison. There were two death certificates, of course?"

"Yes. The confirmatory certificate was given by Dr. Halbury, of Wimpole Street. The medical attendant was a Dr. Barber, of Howland Street. The deceased lived in Stock-Orchard Crescent, Holloway."

"A good distance from Howland Street," Thorndyke remarked. "Do you know if Halbury made a post- mortem? I don't suppose he did."

"No, he didn't," replied Stalker.

"Then," said Thorndyke," his certificate is worthless. You can't tell whether a man has died from heart failure by looking at his dead body. He must have just accepted the opinion of the medical attendant. Do I understand that you want me to look into this case?"

"If you will. It is not really our concern whether or not the man was poisoned, though I suppose we should have a claim on the estate of the murderer. But we should like you to investigate the case; though how the deuce you are going to do it I don't quite see."

"Neither do I," said Thorndyke. "However, we must get into touch with the doctors who signed the certificates, and possibly they may be able to clear the whole matter up."

"Of course," said I, "there is the other body--that of Huggard--which might be exhumed--unless he was cremated, too."

"Yes," agreed Thorndyke; "and for the purposes of the criminal law, evidence of poisoning in that case would be sufficient. But it would hardly help the Griffin Company, which is concerned exclusively with Ingle deceased. Can you let us have a précis of the facts relating to this case, Stalker?"

"I have brought one with me," was the reply; "a short statement, giving names, addresses, dates, and other particulars. Here it is"; and he handed Thorndyke a sheet of paper bearing a tabulated statement.

When Stalker had gone Thorndyke glanced rapidly through the précis and then looked at his watch. "If we make our way to Wimpole Street at once," said he, "we ought to catch Halbury. That is obviously the first thing to do. He signed the 'C' certificate, and we shall be able to judge from what he tells us whether there is any possibility of foul play. Shall we start now?"

As I assented, he slipped the précis in his pocket and we set forth. At the top of Middle Temple Lane we chartered a taxi by which we were shortly deposited at Dr. Halbury's door and a few minutes later were ushered into his consulting room, and found him shovelling a pile of letters into the waste-paper basket.

"How d'ye do?" he said briskly, holding out his hand. "I'm up to my eyes in arrears, you see. Just back from my holiday. What can I do for you?"

"We have called," said Thorndyke, "about a man named Ingle."

"Ingle--Ingle," repeated Halbury. "Now, let me see--"

"Stock-Orchard Crescent, Holloway," Thorndyke explained.

"Oh, yes. I remember him. Well, how is he?"

"He's dead," replied Thorndyke.

"Is he really?" exclaimed Halbury. "Now that shows how careful one should be in one's judgments. I half suspected that fellow of malingering. He was supposed to have a dilated heart, but I couldn't make out any appreciable dilatation. There was excited, irregular action. That was all. I had a suspicion that he had been dosing himself with trinitrine. Reminded me of the cases of cordite chewing that I used to meet with in South Africa. So he's dead, after all. Well, it's queer. Do you know what the exact cause of death was?"

"Failure of a dilated heart is the cause stated on the certificates--the body was cremated; and the 'C' Certificate was signed by you."

"By me!" exclaimed the physician. "Nonsense! It's a mistake. I signed a certificate for a Friendly Society. Ingle brought it here for me to sign--but I didn't even know he was dead. Besides, I went away for my holiday a few days after I saw the man and only came back yesterday. What makes you think I signed the death certificate?"

Thorndyke produced Stalker's précis and handed it to Halbury, who read out his own name and address with a puzzled frown. "This is an extraordinary affair," said he. "It will have to be looked into."

"It will, indeed," assented Thorndyke; "especially as a suspicion of poisoning has been raised."

"Ha!" exclaimed Halbury. "Then it was trinitrine, you may depend. But I suspected him unjustly. It was somebody else who was dosing him; perhaps that sly- looking baggage of a wife of his. Is anyone in particular suspected?

"Yes. The accusation, such as it is, is against the wife."

"H'm. Probably a true bill. But she's done us. Artful devil. You can't get much evidence out of an urnful of ashes. Still, somebody has forged my signature. I suppose that is what the hussy wanted that certificate for--to get a specimen of my handwriting. I see the 'B' certificate was signed by a man named Meeking. Who's he? It was Barber who called me in for an opinion."

"I must find out who he is," replied Thorndyke. "Possibly Dr. Barber will know. I shall go and call on him now."

"Yes," said Dr. Halbury, shaking hands as we rose to depart, "you ought to see Barber. He knows the history of the case, at any rate."

From Wimpole Street we steered a course for Howland Street, and here we had the good fortune to arrive just as Dr. Barber's car drew up at the door. Thorndyke introduced himself and me, and then introduced the subject of his visit, but said nothing, at first, about our call on Dr. Halbury.

"Ingle," repeated Dr. Barber. "Oh, yes, I remember him. And you say he is dead. Well, I'm rather surprised. I didn't regard his condition as serious."

"Was his heart dilated?" Thorndyke asked.

"Not appreciably. I found nothing organic; no valvular disease. It was more like a tobacco heart. But it's odd that Meeking didn't mention the matter to me--he was my locum, you know. I handed the case over to him when I went on my holiday. And you say he signed the death certificate?"

"Yes; and the 'B' certificate for cremation, too."

"Very odd," said Dr. Barber. "Just con in and let us have a look at the day book."

We followed him into the consulting room, and there, while he was turning over the leaves of the day book, I ran my eye along the shelf over the writing-table from which he had taken it; on which I observed the usual collection of case books and books of certificates and notification forms, including the book of death certificates.

"Yes;" said Dr. Barber, "here we are; 'Ingle, Mr., Stock-Orchard Crescent." The last visit was on the 4th of September, and Meeking seems to have given some sort of certificate. Wonder if he used a printed form." He took down two of the books and turned over the counterfoils.

"Here we are," he said presently; "Ingle, Jonathan, 4 September. Now recovered and able to resume duties.' That doesn't look like dying, does it? Still, we may as well make sure."

He reached down the book of death certificates and began to glance through the most recent entries.

"No," he said, turning over the leaves, "there doesn't seem to be-- Hullo! What's this? Two blank counterfoils; and about the date, too; between the 2nd and 13th of September. Extraordinary! Meeking is such a careful, reliable man."

He turned back to the day book and read through the fortnight's entries. Then he looked up with an anxious frown.

"I can't make this out," he said. "There is no record of any patient having died in that period."

"Where is Dr. Meeking at present? " I asked.

Somewhere in the South Atlantic," replied Barber. "He left here three weeks ago to take up a post on a Royal Mail Boat. So he couldn't have signed the certificate in any case."

That was all that Dr. Barber had to tell us, and a few minutes later we took our departure.

"This case looks pretty fishy," I remarked, as we turned down Tottenham Court Road.

"Yes," Thorndyke agreed. "There is evidently something radically wrong. And what strikes me especially is the cleverness of the fraud; the knowledge and judgment and foresight that are displayed."

"She took pretty considerable risks," I observed.

"Yes, but only the risks that were unavoidable. Everything that could be foreseen has been provided for. All the formalities have been complied with--in appearance. And you must notice, Jervis, that the scheme did actually succeed. The cremation has taken place. Nothing but the incalculable accident of the appearance of the real Mrs. Ingle, and her vague and apparently groundless suspicions, prevented the success from being final. If she had not come on the scene, no questions would ever have been asked."

"No," I agreed. "The discovery of the plot is a matter of sheer bad luck. But what do you suppose has really happened?"

Thorndyke shook his head.

"It is very difficult to say. The mechanism of the affair is obvious enough, but the motives and purpose are rather incomprehensible. The illness was apparently a sham, the symptoms being produced by nitro-glycerine or some similar heart poison. The doctors were called in, partly for the sake of appearances and partly to get specimens of their handwriting. The fact that both the doctors happened to be away from home and one of them at sea at the time when verbal questions might have been asked--by the undertaker, for instance--suggests that this had been ascertained in advance. The death certificate forms were pretty certainly stolen by the woman when she was left alone in Barber's consulting- room, and, of course, the cremation certificates could be obtained on application to the crematorium authorities. That is all plain sailing. The mystery is, what is it all about? Barber or Meeking would almost certainly have given a death certificate, although the death was un expected, and I don't suppose Halbury would have refused to confirm it. They would have assumed that their diagnosis had been at fault."

"Do you think it could have been suicide, or an in advertent overdose of trinitrine?"

"Hardly. If it was suicide, it was deliberate, for the purpose of getting the insurance money for the woman, unless there was some further motive behind. And the cremation, with all its fuss and formalities, is against suicide; while the careful preparation seems to exclude inadvertent poisoning. Then, what was the motive for the sham illness except as a preparation for an abnormal death?"

"That is true," said I. "But if you reject suicide, isn't it rather remarkable that the victim should have provided for his own cremation?"

"We don't know that he did," replied Thorndyke. "There is a suggestion of a capable forger in this business. It is quite possible that the will itself is a forgery."

"So it is!" I exclaimed. "I hadn't thought of that."

"You see," continued Thorndyke, "the appearances suggest that cremation was a necessary part of the programme; otherwise these extraordinary risks would not have been taken. The woman was sole executrix and could have ignored the cremation clause. But if the cremation was necessary, why was it necessary? The suggestion is that there was something suspicious in the appearance of the body; something that the doctors, would certainly have observed or that would have been discovered if an exhumation had taken place."

"You mean some injury or visible signs of poisoning?"

"I mean something discoverable by examination even after burial."

"But what about the undertaker? Wouldn't he have noticed anything palpably abnormal?"

"An excellent suggestion, Jervis. We must see the undertaker. We have his address: Kentish Town Road--a long way from deceased's house, by the way. We had better get on a bus and go there now."

A yellow omnibus was approaching as he spoke. We hailed it and sprang on, continuing our discussion as we were borne northward.

Mr. Burrell, the undertaker, was a pensive-looking, profoundly civil man who was evidently in a small way, for he combined with his funeral functions general carpentry and cabinet making. He was perfectly willing to give any required information, but he seemed to have very little to give.

"I never really saw the deceased gentleman," he said in reply to Thorndyke's cautious inquiries. "When I took the measurements, the corpse was covered with a sheet; and as Mrs. Ingle was in the room, I made the business as short as possible."

"You didn't put the body in the coffin, then?"

"No. I left the coffin at the house, but Mrs. Ingle said that she and the deceased gentleman's brother would lay the body in it."

"But didn't you see the corpse when you screwed the coffin-lid down?"

"I didn't screw it down. When I got there it was screwed down already. Mrs. Ingle said they had to close up the coffin, and I dare say it was necessary. The weather was rather warm; and I noticed a strong smell of formalin."

"Well," I said, as we walked back down the Kentish Town Road, "we haven't got much more forward."

"I wouldn't say that," replied Thorndyke. "We have a further instance of the extraordinary adroitness with which this scheme was carried out; and we have confirmation of our suspicion that there was something unusual in the appearance of the body. It is evident that this woman did not dare to let even the undertaker see it. But one can hardly help admiring the combination of daring and caution, the boldness with which these risks were taken, and the care and judgment with which they were provided against. And again I point out that the risks were justified by the result. The secret of that man's death appears to have been made secure for all time."

It certainly looked as if the mystery with which we were concerned were beyond the reach of investigation. Of course, the woman could be prosecuted for having forged the death certificates, to say nothing of the charge of bigamy. But that was no concern of ours or Stalker's. Jonathan Ingle was dead, and no one could say how he died.

On our arrival at our chambers we found a telegram that had just arrived, announcing that Stalker would call on us in the evening; and as this seemed to suggest that he had some fresh information we looked forward to his visit with considerable interest. Punctually at six o'clock he made his appearance and at once opened the subject.

"There are some new developments in this Ingle case," said he. "In the first place, the woman, Huggard, has bolted. I went to the house to make a few inquiries and found the police in possession. They had come to arrest her on the bigamy charge, but she had got wind of their intentions and cleared out. They made a search of the premises, but I don't think they found anything of interest except a number of rifle cartridges; and I don't know that they are of much interest either, for she could hardly have shot him with a rifle."

"What kind of cartridges were they?" Thorndyke asked.

Stalker put his hand in his pocket.

"The inspector let me have one to show you," said he; and he laid on the table a military cartridge of the pattern of some twenty years ago. Thorndyke picked it up, and taking from a drawer a pair of pliers drew the bullet out of the case and inserted into the latter a pair of dissecting forceps. When he withdrew the forceps, their points grasped one or two short strings of what looked like cat-gut.

"Cordite!" said I. "So Halbury was probably right, and this is how she got her supply." Then, as Stalker looked at me inquiringly, I gave him a short account of the results of our investigations.

"Ha!" he exclaimed, "the plot thickens. This juggling with the death certificates seems to connect itself with another kind of juggling that I came to tell you about. You know that Ingle was Secretary and Treasurer to a company that bought and sold land for building estates. Well, I called at their office after I left you and had a little talk with the chairman. From him I learned that Ingle had practically complete control of the financial affairs of the company, that he received and paid all moneys and kept the books. Of late, however, some of the directors have had a suspicion that all was not well with the finances, and at last it was decided to have the affairs of the company thoroughly overhauled by a firm of chartered accountants. This decision was communicated to Ingle, and a couple of days later a letter arrived from his wife saying that he had had a severe heart attack and asking that the audit of the books might be postponed until he recovered and was able to attend at the office."

"And was it postponed?" I asked.

"No," replied Stalker. "The accountants were asked to get to work at once, which they did; with the result that they discovered a number of discrepancies in the books and a sum of about three thousand pounds unaccounted for. It isn't quite obvious how the frauds were carried out, but it is suspected that some of the returned cheques are fakes with forged endorsements."

"Did the company communicate with Ingle on the subject?" asked Thorndyke.

"No. They had a further letter from Mrs. Ingle--that is, Huggard-- saying that Ingle's condition was very serious; so they decided to wait until he had recovered. Then, of course, came the announcement of his death, on which the matter was postponed pending the probate of the will. I suppose a claim will be made on the estate, but as the executrix has absconded, the affair has become rather complicated."

"You were saying," said Thorndyke, "that the fraudulent death certificates seem to be connected with these frauds on the company. What kind of connection do you assume?"

"I assume--or at least, suggest," replied Stalker, "that this was a case of suicide. The man, Ingle, saw that his frauds were discovered, or were going to be, and that he was in for a long term of penal servitude, so he just made away with himself. And I think that if the murder charge could be dropped, Mrs. Huggard might be induced to come forward and give evidence as to the suicide."

Thorndyke shook his head.

"The murder charge couldn't be dropped," said he. "if it was suicide, Huggard was certainly an accessory; and in law, an accessory to suicide is an accessory to murder. But, in fact, no official charge of murder has been made, and at present there are no means of sustaining such a charge. The identity of the ashes might be assumed to be that stated in the cremation order, but the difficulty is the cause of death. Ingle was admittedly ill. He was attended for heart disease by three doctors. There is no evidence that he did not die from that illness."

"But the illness was due to cordite poisoning," said I, "That is what we believe. But no one could swear to it. And we certainly could not swear that he died from cordite poisoning."

"Then," said Stalker, "apparently there is no means of finding out whether his death was due to natural causes, suicide, or murder?"

"There is only one chance," replied Thorndyke. "It is just barely possible that the cause of death might be ascertainable by an examination of the ashes."

"That doesn't seem very hopeful," said I. "Cordite poisoning would certainly leave no trace."

"We mustn't assume that he died from cordite poisoning," said Thorndyke. "Probably he did not. That may have masked the action of a less obvious poison, or death might have been produced by some new agent."

"But," 1 objected, "how many poisons are there that could be detected in the ashes? No organic poison would leave any traces, nor would metallic poisons such as mercury, antimony, or arsenic."

"No," Thorndyke agreed. "But there are other metallic poisons which could be easily recovered from the ashes; lead, tin, gold, and silver, for instance. But it is useless to discuss speculative probabilities. The only chance that we have of obtaining any new facts is by an examination of the ashes. It seems infinitely improbable that we shall learn anything from it, but there is the bare possibility and we ought not to leave it untried."

Neither Stalker nor I made any further remark, but I could see that the same thought was in both our minds. It was not often that Thorndyke was "gravelled"; but apparently the resourceful Mrs. Huggard had set him a problem that was beyond even his powers. When an investigator of crime is reduced to the necessity of examining a potful of ashes in the wild hope of ascertaining from them how the deceased met his death, one may assume that he is at the very end of his tether. It is a forlorn hope indeed.

Nevertheless, Thorndyke seemed to view the matter quite cheerfully, his only anxiety being lest the Home Secretary should refuse to make the order authorising the examination. And this anxiety was dispelled a day or two later by the arrival of a letter giving the necessary authority, and informing him that a Dr. Hemming--known to us both as an expert pathologist--had been deputed to be present at the examination and to confer with him as to the necessity for a chemical analysis.

On the appointed day Dr. Hemming called at our chambers and we set forth together for Liverpool Street; and as we drove thither it became evident to me that his view of our mission was very similar to my own. For, though he talked freely enough, and on professional topics, he maintained a most discreet silence on the subject of the forthcoming inspection; indeed, the first reference to the subject was made by Thorndyke himself just as the train was approaching Corfield, where the crematorium was situated.

"I presume," said he, "you have made all necessary arrangements, Hemming?"

"Yes," was the reply. "The superintendent will meet us and will conduct us to the catacombs, and there, in our presence, will take the casket from its niche in the columbarium and have it conveyed to the office, where the examination will be made. I thought it best to use these formalities, though, as the casket is sealed and bears the name of the deceased, there is not much point in them."

"No," said Thorndyke, "but I think you were right. It would be easy to challenge the identity of a mass of ashes if all precautions were not taken, seeing that the ashes themselves are unidentifiable."

"That was what I felt," said Hemming; and then, as the train slowed down, he added: "This is our station, and that gentleman on the platform, I suspect, is the superintendent."

The surmise turned out to be correct; but the cemetery official was not the only one present bearing that title; for as we were mutually introducing ourselves, a familiar tall figure approached up the platform from the rear of the train--our old friend Superintendent Miller of the Criminal Investigation Department.

"I don't wish to intrude," said he, as he joined the group and was presented by Thorndyke to the strangers, "but we were notified by the Home Office that an investigation was to be made, so I thought I would be on the spot to pick up any crumbs of information that you may drop. Of course, I am not asking to be present at the examination."

"You may as well be present as an additional witness to the removal of the urn," said Thorndyke; and Miller accordingly joined the party, which now made its way from the station to the cemetery.

The catacombs were in a long, low arcaded building at the end of the pleasantly-wooded grounds, and on our way thither we passed the crematorium, a smallish, church-like edifice with a perforated chimney-shaft partly concealed by the low spire. Entering the catacombs, we were conducted to the "columbarium," the walls of which were occupied by a multitude of niches or pigeon-holes, each niche accommodating a terra-cotta urn or casket. The superintendent proceeded to near the end of the gallery, where he halted, and opening the register, which he had brought with him, read out a number and the name "Jonathan Ingle," and then led us to a niche bearing that number and name, in which reposed a square casket, on which was inscribed the name and date of death. When we had verified these particulars, the casket was tenderly lifted from its place by two attendants, who carried it to a well-lighted room at the end of the building, where a large table by a window had been covered with white paper. Having placed the casket on the table, the attendants retired, and the superintendent then broke the seals and removed the cover.

For a while we all stood looking in at the contents of the casket without speaking; and I found myself contrasting them with what would have been revealed by the lifting of a coffin-lid. Truly corruption had put on incorruption. The mass of snow-white, coral-like fragments, delicate, fragile, and lace-like in texture, so far from being repulsive in aspect, were almost attractive. I ran my eye, with an anatomist's curiosity, over these dazzling remnants of what had lately been a man, half-unconsciously seeking to identify and give a name to particular fragments, and a little surprised at the difficulty of determining that this or that irregularly-shaped white object was a part of any one of the bones with which I had thought myself so familiar.

Presently Hemming looked up at Thorndyke and asked: "Do you observe anything abnormal in the appearance of these ashes? I don't."

"Perhaps," replied Thorndyke, "we had better turn them out on to the table, so that we can see the whole of them."

This was done very gently, and then Thorndyke proceeded to spread out the heap, touching the fragments with the utmost delicacy--for they were extremely fragile and brittle--until the whole collection was visible.

"Well," said Hemming, when we had once more looked them over critically, "what do you say? I can see no trace of any foreign substance. Can you?"

"No," replied Thorndyke. "And there are some other things that I can't see. For instance, the medical referee reported that the proposer had a good set of sound teeth. Where are they? I have not seen a single fragment of a tooth. Yet teeth are far more resistant to fire than bones, especially the enamel caps."

Hemming ran a searching glance over the mass of fragments and looked up with a perplexed frown.

"I certainly can't see any sign of teeth," he admitted; and it is rather curious, as you say. Does the fact suggest any particular significance to you?"

By way of reply, Thorndyke delicately picked up a flat fragment and silently held it out towards us. I looked at it and said nothing; for a very strange suspicion was beginning to creep into my mind.

"A piece of a rib," said Hemming. "Very odd that it should have broken across so cleanly. It might have been cut with a saw."

Thorndyke laid it down and picked up another, larger fragment, which I had already noticed.

"Here is another example," said he, handing it to our colleague.

"Yes," agreed Hemming. "It is really rather extraordinary. It looks exactly as if it had been sawn across."

"It does," agreed Thorndyke. "What bone should you say it is?"

"That is what I was just asking myself," replied Hemming, looking at the fragment with a sort of half- vexed smile. "It seems ridiculous that a competent anatomist should be in any doubt with as large a portion as this, but really I can't confidently give it a name. The shape seems to me to suggest a tibia, but of course it is much too small. Is it the upper end of the ulna?"

"I should say no," answered Thorndyke. Then he picked out another of the larger fragments, and handing it to Hemming, asked him to name it.

Our friend began to look somewhat worried.

"It is an extraordinary thing, you know," said he, "but I can't tell you what bone it is part of. It is clearly the shaft of a long bone, but I'm hanged if I can say which. It is too big for a metatarsal and too small for any of the main limb bones. It reminds one of a diminutive thigh bone."

"It does," agreed Thorndyke "very strongly." While Hemming had been speaking he had picked out four more large fragments, and these he now laid in a row with the one that had seemed to resemble a tibia in shape. Placed thus together, the five fragments bore an obvious resemblance.

"Now," said he, "look at these. There are five of them. They are parts of limb bones, and the bones of which they are parts were evidently exactly alike, excepting that three were apparently from the left side and two from the right. Now, you know, Hemming, a man has only four limbs and of those only two contain similar bones. Then two of them show distinct traces of what looks like a saw-cut."

Hemming gazed at the row of fragments with a frown of deep cogitation.

"It is very mysterious," he said. "And looking at them in a row they strike me as curiously like tibia in shape; not in size."

"The size," said Thorndyke, " is about that of a sheep's tibia."

"A sheep's?" exclaimed Hemming, staring in amazement, first at the calcined bones and then at my colleague.

"Yes; the upper half, sawn across in the middle of the shank."

Hemming was thunderstruck. "It is an astounding affair!" he exclaimed. "You mean to suggest--"

"I suggest," said Thorndyke, "that there is not a sign of a human bone in the whole collection. But there are very evident traces of at least five legs of mutton."

For a few moments there was a profound silence, broken only by a murmur of astonishment from the cemetery official and a low chuckle from Superintendent Miller, who had been listening with absorbed interest. At length Hemming spoke.

"Then, apparently, there was no corpse in the coffin at all?"

"No," answered Thorndyke. "The weight was made up, and the ashes furnished, by joints of butcher's meat. I dare say, if we go over the ashes carefully, we shall be able to judge what they were. But it is hardly necessary. The presence of five legs of mutton and the absence of a single recognisable fragment of a human skeleton, together with the forged certificates, gives us a pretty I conclusive case. The rest, I think we can leave to Superintendent Miller."

♦ ♦ ♦ ♦ ♦

"I take it, Thorndyke," said I, as the train moved out of the station, "that you came here expecting to find what you did find?"

"Yes," he replied. "It seemed to me the only possibility, having regard to all the known facts."

"When did it first occur to you?"

"It occurred to me as a possibility as soon as we discovered that the cremation certificates had been forged; but it was the undertaker's statement that seemed to clench the matter."

"But he distinctly stated that he measured the body."

"True. But there was nothing to show that it was a dead body. What was perfectly clear was that there was something that must on no account be seen; and when Stalker told us of the embezzlement we had a body of evidence that could point to only one conclusion. Just consider that evidence.

"Here we had a death, preceded by an obviously sham illness and followed by cremation with forged certificates. Now, what was it that had happened? There were four possible hypotheses. Normal death, suicide, murder, and fictitious death. Which of these hypotheses fitted the facts?

"Normal death was apparently excluded by the forged certificates.

"The theory of suicide did not account for the facts. It did not agree with the careful, elaborate preparation. And why the forged certificates? If Ingle had really died, Meeking would have certified the death. And why the cremation? There was no purpose in taking those enormous risks.

"The theory of murder was unthinkable. These certificates were almost certainly forged by Ingle himself, who we know was a practised forger. But the idea of the victim arranging for his own cremation is an absurdity.

"There remained only the theory of fictitious death; and that theory fitted all the facts perfectly. First, as to the motive. Ingle had committed a felony. He had to disappear. But what kind of disappearance could be so effectual as death and cremation? Both the prosecutors and the police would forthwith write him off and forget him. Then there was the bigamy--a criminal offence in itself. But death would not only wipe that off; after 'death' he could marry Huggard regularly under another name, and he would have shaken off his deserted wife for ever. And he stood to gain fifteen hundred pounds from the Insurance Company. Then see how this theory explained the other facts. A fictitious death made necessary a fictitious illness. It necessitated the forged certificates, since there was no corpse. It made cremation highly desirable; for suspicion might easily have arisen, and then the exhumation of a coffin containing a dummy would have exploded the fraud. But successful cremation would cover up the fraud for ever. It explained the concealment of the corpse from the undertaker, and it even explained the smell of formalin which he noticed."

"How did it?" I asked.

"Consider, Jervis," he replied. "The dummy in this coffin had to be a dummy of flesh and bone which would yield the correct kind of ash. Joints of butcher's meat would fulfil the conditions. But the quantity required would be from a hundred and fifty to two hundred pounds. Now Ingle could not go to the butcher and order a whole sheep to be sent the day before the funeral. The joints would have to be bought gradually and stored. But the storage of meat in warm weather calls for some kind of preservative; and formalin is highly effective, as it leaves no trace after burning.

"So you see that the theory of fictitious death agreed with all the known circumstances, whereas the alternative theories presented inexplicable discrepancies and contradictions. Logically, it was the only possible theory, and, as you have seen, experiment proved it to be the true one."

As he concluded, Dr. Hemming took his pipe from his mouth and laughed softly.

"When I came down to-day," said he, "I had all the facts which you had communicated to the Home Office, and I was absolutely convinced that we were coming to examine a mare's nest. And yet, now I have heard your exposition, the whole thing looks perfectly obvious."

"That is usually the case with Thorndyke's conclusions," said I. "They are perfectly obvious--when you have heard the explanation."

Within a week of our expedition, Ingle was in the hands of the police. The apparent success of the cremation adventure had misled him to a sense of such complete security that he had neglected to cover his tracks, and he had accordingly fallen an easy prey to our friend Superintendent Miller. The police were highly gratified, and so were the directors of the Griffin Life Assurance Company.

The Stalking Horse

As Thorndyke and I descended the stairs of the foot bridge at Densford Junction we became aware that something unusual had happened. The platform was nearly deserted save at one point, where a small but dense crowd had collected around the open door of a first-class compartment of the down train; heads were thrust out of the windows of the other coaches, and at intervals doors opened and inquisitive passengers ran along to join the crowd, from which an excited porter detached himself just as we reached the platform.

"You'd better go for Dr. Pooke first," the station-master called after him.

On this, Thorndyke stepped forward.

"My friend and I," said he, "are medical men. Can we be of any service until the local doctor arrives?"

"I'm very much afraid not, sir," was the reply, "but you'll see." He cleared a way for us and we approached the open door.

At the first glance there appeared to be nothing to account for the awe-stricken expression with which the bystanders peered into the carriage and gazed at its solitary occupant. For the motionless figure that sat huddled in the corner seat, chin on breast, might have been a sleeping man. But it was not. The waxen pallor of the face and the strange, image-like immobility forbade the hope of any awakening.

"It looks almost as if he had passed away in his sleep," said the station when we had concluded our brief examination and ascertained certainly that the man was dead. "Do you think it was a heart attack, sir?"

Thorndyke shook his head and touched with his finger a depressed spot on the dead man's waistcoat. When he withdrew his finger it was smeared with blood.

"Good God!" the official gasped, in a horrified whisper. "The man has been murdered!" He stared incredulously at the corpse for a few moments and then turned and sprang out of the compartment, shutting the door behind him, and we heard him giving orders for the coach to be separated and shunted into the siding.

"This is a gruesome affair, Jervis," my colleague, said as he sat down on the seat opposite the dead man and cast a searching glance round the compartment. "I wonder who this poor fellow was and what was the object of the murder? It looks almost too determined, for a common robbery; and, in fact, the body does not appear to have been robbed." Here he stooped suddenly to pick up one or two minute fragments of glass which seemed to have been trodden into the carpet, and which he examined closely in the palm of his hand. I leaned over and looked at the fragments, and we agreed that they were portions of the bulb of an electric torch or flash-lamp.

"The significance of these--if they have any," said Thorndyke, "we can consider later. But if they are recent, it would appear that the metal part of the bulb has been picked up and taken away. That might be an important fact. But, on the other hand, the fragments may have been here some time and have no connection with the tragedy; though you notice that they were lying opposite the body and opposite the seat which the murderer must have occupied when the crime was committed."

As he was speaking, the uncoupled coach began slowly to move towards the siding, and we both stooped to make a further search for the remainder of the lamp-bulb, And then, almost at the same moment, we perceived two objects lying under the opposite seat--the seat occupied by the dead man. One was a small pocket-handkerchief, the other a sheet of notepaper.

"This," said I, as I picked up the former, "accounts for the strong smell of scent in the compartment."

"Possibly," Thorndyke agreed, "though you will notice that the odour does not come principally from the handkerchief, but from the back cushion of the corner seat. But here is something more distinctive--a most incriminating piece of evidence, unless it can be answered by an undeniable alibi." He held out to me a sheet of letter paper, both pages of which were covered with writing in bright blue ink, done with a Hectograph or some similar duplicator. It was evidently a circular letter, for it bore the printed heading, "Women's

Emancipation League, 16 Barnabas Square, S.W.," and the contents appeared to refer to a" militant demonstration" planned for the near future.

"It is dated the day before yesterday," commented Thorndyke, "so that it might have been lying here for twenty-four hours, though that is obviously improbable; and as this is neither the first sheet nor the last, there are--or have been--at least two more sheets. The police will have something to start on, at any rate."

He laid the letter on the seat and explored both of the hat-racks, taking down the dead man's hat, gloves, and umbrella, and noting in the hat the initials "F. B." He had just replaced them when voices became audible outside, and the station-master climbed up on the foot- board and opened the door to admit two men, one of whom I assumed to be a doctor, the other being a police inspector.

"The station-master tells me that this is a case of homicide," said the former, addressing us jointly.

"That is what the appearances suggest," replied Thorndyke. "There is a bullet wound, inflicted apparently at quite short range--the waistcoat is perceptibly singed--and we have found no weapon in the compartment."

The doctor stepped past us and proceeded to make a rapid examination of the body.

"Yes," he said, "I agree with you. The position of the wound and the posture of the body both suggest that death was practically instantaneous. If it had been suicide, the pistol would have been in the hand or on the floor. There is no clue to the identity of the murderer, I suppose?"

"We found these on the floor under the dead man's seat," replied Thorndyke, indicating the letter and the handkerchief; "and there is some glass trodden into the carpet--apparently the remains of an electric flash- lamp."

The inspector pounced on the handkerchief and the letter, and having scrutinised the former vainly in search of name or initials, turned to the letter.

"Why, this is a suffragist's letter!" he exclaimed. "But it can't have anything to do with this affair. They are mischievous beggars, but they don't do this sort of thing." Nevertheless, he carefully bestowed both articles in a massive wallet, and approaching the corpse, remarked: "We may as well see who he is while we are waiting for the stretcher."

With a matter-of-fact air, which seemed somewhat to shock the station-master, he unbuttoned the coat of the passive figure in the corner and thrust his hand into the breast pocket, drawing out a letter-case which he opened, and from which he extracted a visiting card. As he glanced at it, his face suddenly took on an expression of amazement.

"God!" he exclaimed in a startled tone. "Who do you think he is, doctor? He is Mr. Francis Burnham!"

The doctor looked at him with an interrogative frown. "Burnham-- Burnham," he repeated. "Let me see, now--"

"Don't you know? The anti-suffrage man. Surely--"

"Yes, yes," interrupted the doctor. "Of course I remember him. The arch-enemy of the suffrage movement and--yes, of course." The doctor's brisk speech changed abruptly into a hesitating mumble. Like the inspector, he had suddenly "seen a great light"; and again, like the officer, his perception had begotten a sudden reticence.

Thorndyke glanced at his watch. "Our train is a minute overdue," said he. "We ought to get back to the platform." Taking a card from his case, he handed it to the inspector, who looked at it and slightly raised his eyebrows.

"I don't think my evidence will be of much value," said he; "but, of course, I am at your service if you want it." With this and a bow to the doctor and the station-master, he climbed down to the ground; and when I had given the inspector my card, I followed, and we made our way to the platform.

The case was not long in developing. That very evening, as Thorndyke and I were smoking our after-dinner pipes by the fire, a hurried step was heard on the stair and was followed by a peremptory knock on our door. The visitor was a man of about thirty, with a clean-shaved face, an intense and rather neurotic expression, and a restless, excited manner. He introduced himself by the name of Cadmus Bawley, and thereby, in effect, indicated the purpose of his visit.

"You know me by name, I expect," he said, speaking rapidly and with a sharp, emphatic manner, "and probably you can guess what I have come about. You have seen the evening paper, of course?"

"I have not," replied Thorndyke.

"Well," said Mr. Bawley, "you know about the murder of the man Burnham, because I see that you were present at the discovery; and you know that part of a circular letter from our League was found in the compartment. Perhaps you will not be surprised to learn that Miss Isabel Dalby has been arrested and charged with the murder."

"Indeed!" said Thorndyke.

"Yes. It's an infamous affair! A national disgrace!" exclaimed Bawley, banging the table with his fist. "A manifest plot of the enemies of social reform to get rid of a high-minded, noble-hearted lady whose championship of this great Cause they are unable to combat by fair means in the open. And it is a wild absurdity, too. As to the fellow, Burnham, I can't pretend to feel any regret--"

"May I suggest "--Thorndyke interrupted somewhat stiffly--" that the expression of personal sentiments is neither helpful nor discreet? My methods of defence--if that is what you have come about--are based on demonstration rather than rhetoric. Could you give us the plain facts?"

Mr. Cadmus Bawley looked unmistakably sulky, but after a short pause, he began his recital in a somewhat lower key.

"The bald facts," he said, "are these: This after noon, at half-past two, Miss Dalby took the train from King's Cross to Holmwood. This is the train that stops at Densford Junction and is the one in which Burnham travelled. She took a first-class ticket and occupied a compartment for ladies only, of which she was the only occupant. She got out at Holmwood and went straight to the house of our Vice-President, Miss Carleigh--who has been confined to her room for some days--and stayed there about an hour. She came back by the four-fifteen train, and I met her at the station--King's Cross--at a quarter to five. We had tea at a restaurant opposite the station, and over our tea we discussed the plans for the next demonstration, and arranged the rendezvous and the most convenient routes for retreat and dispersal when the police should arrive. This involved the making of sketch plans, and these Miss Dalby drew on a sheet of paper that she took from her pocket, and which happened to be part of the circular letter referring to the raid. After tea we walked together down Gray's Inn Road and parted at Theobald's Road, I going on to the head-quarters and she to her rooms in Queen Square. On her arrival home, she found two detectives waiting outside her house, and then--and then, in short, she was arrested, like a common criminal, and taken to the police station, where she was searched and the remainder of the circular letter found in her pocket. Then she was formally charged with the murder of the man Burnham, and she was graciously permitted to send a telegram to head-quarters. It arrived just after I got there, and, of course, I at once went to the police station. The police refused to accept bail, but they allowed me to see her to make arrangements for the defence."

"Does Miss Dalby offer any suggestion," asked Thorndyke, "as to how a sheet of her letter came to be in the compartment with the murdered man?"

"Oh, yes!" replied Mr. Bawley. "I had forgotten that. It wasn't her letter at all. She destroyed her copy of the letter as soon as she had read it."

"Then," inquired Thorndyke, "how came the letter to be in her pocket?"

"Ah," replied Bawley, "that is the mystery. She thinks someone must have slipped it into her pocket to throw suspicion on her."

"Did she seem surprised to find it in her pocket when you were having tea together?"

"No. She had forgotten having destroyed her copy. She only remembered it when I told her that the sheet had been found in Burnham's carriage."

"Can she produce the fragments of the destroyed letter?"

"No, she can't. Unfortunately she burned it."

"Do these circular letters bear any distinguishing mark? Are they addressed to members by name?"

"Only on the envelopes. The letters are all alike. They are run off a duplicator. Of course, if you don't believe the story--"

"I am not judging the case," interrupted Thorndyke; "I am simply collecting the facts. What do you want me to do?"

"If you feel that you could undertake the defence I should like you to do so. We shall employ the solicitors to the League, Bird & Marshall, but I know they will be willing and glad to act with you."

"Very well," said Thorndyke. "I will investigate the case and consult with your solicitors. By the way, do the police know about the sheet of the letter on which the plans were drawn?"

"No. I thought it best to say nothing about that, and I have told Miss Dalby not to mention it."

"That is just as well," said Thorndyke. "Have you the sheet with the plan on it?"

I haven't it about me," was the reply. "It is in my desk at my chambers."

"You had better let me have it to look at," said Thorndyke.

"You can have it if you want it, of course," said Bawley, "but it won't help you. The letters are all alike, as I have told you."

"I should like to see it, nevertheless," said Thorndyke; "and perhaps you could give me some account of Mr. Burnham. What do you know about him?"

Mr. Bawley shut his lips tightly, and his face took on an expression of vindictiveness verging on malignity.

"All I know about Burnham," he said, "is that he was a fool and a ruffian. He was not only an enemy of the great reform that our League stands for; he was a treacherous enemy--violent, crafty, and indefatigably active. I can only regard his death as a blessing to mankind."

"May I ask," said Thorndyke, "if any members of your League have ever publicly threatened to take personal measures against him?

"Yes," snapped Bawley. "Several of us--including myself--have threatened to give him the hiding that he deserved. But a hiding is a different thing from murder, you know."

"Yes," Thorndyke agreed somewhat dryly; then he asked: "Do you know anything about Mr. Burnham's occupation and habits?"

"He was a sort of manager of the London and Suburban Bank. His job was to supervise the suburban branches, and his habit was to visit them in rotation. He was probably going to the branch at Holmwood when he was killed. That is all I can tell you about him."

"Thank you," said Thorndyke; and as our visitor rose to depart he continued: "Then I will look into the case and arrange with your solicitors to have Miss Dalby properly represented at the inquest; and I shall be glad to have that sheet of the letter as soon as you can send or leave it."

"Very well," said Bawley, "though, as I have told you, it won't be of any use to you. It is only a duplicated circular."

"Possibly," Thorndyke assented. "But the other sheets will be produced in Court, so I may as well have an opportunity of examining it beforehand."

For some minutes after our client had gone Thorndyke remained silent and reflective, copying his rough notes into his pocket-book and apparently amplifying and arranging them. Presently he looked up at me with an unspoken question in his eyes.

"It is a queer case," said I. "The circumstantial evidence seems to be strongly against Miss Dalby, but it is manifestly improbable that she murdered the man."

It seems so," he agreed. "But the case will be decided on the evidence; and the evidence will be considered by a judge, not by a Home Secretary. You notice the importance of Burnham's destination?"

"Yes. He was evidently dead when the train arrived at Holmwood. But it isn't clear how long he had been dead."

"The evidence," said Thorndyke," points strongly to the tunnel between Cawden and Holmwood as the place where the murder was committed. You will remember that the up-express passed our train in the tunnel. If the adjoining compartments were empty, the sound of a pistol shot would be completely drowned by the noise of the express thundering past. Then you will remember the fragments of the electric bulb that we picked up, and that there was no light on in the carriage. That is rather significant. It not only suggests that the crime was committed in the dark, but there is a distinct suggestion of preparation--arrangement and premeditation. It suggests that the murderer knew what the circumstances would be and provided for them."

"Yes; and that is rather a point against our client. But I don't quite see what you expect to get out of that sheet of the letter. It is the presence of the letter, rather than its matter, that constitutes the evidence against Miss Dalby."

"I don't expect to learn anything from it," replied Thorndyke; "but the letter will be the prosecution's trump card, and it is always well to know in advance exactly what cards your opponent holds. It is a mere matter of routine to examine everything, relevant or irrelevant."

The inquest was to be held at Densford on the third day after the discovery of the body. But in the interval certain new facts had come to light. One was that the deceased was conveying to the Holmwood branch of the bank a sum of three thousand pounds, of which one thousand was in gold and the remainder in Bank of England notes, the whole being contained in a leather handbag. This bag had been found, empty, in a ditch by the side of the road which led from the station to the house of Miss Carleigh, the Vice-President of the Women's Emancipation League. It was further stated that the ticket-collector at Holmwood had noticed that Miss Dalby--whom he knew by sight--was carrying a bag of the kind described when she passed the barrier, and that when she returned, about an hour later, she had no bag with her. On the other hand, Miss Carleigh had stated that the bag which Miss Dalby brought to her house was her (Miss Carleigh's) property, and she had produced it for the inspection of the police. So that already there was some conflict of evidence, with a balance distinctly against Miss Dalby.

"There is no denying," said Thorndyke, as we discussed the case at the breakfast table on the morning of the inquest, " that the circumstantial evidence is formidably complete and consistent, while the rebutting evidence is of the feeblest. Miss Dalby's statement that the letter had been put into her pocket by some unknown person will hardly be taken seriously, and even Miss Carleigh's statement with reference to the bag will not carry much weight unless she can furnish corroboration."

"Nevertheless," said I, "the general probabilities are entirely in favour of the accused. It is grossly improbable that a lady like Miss Dalby would commit a robbery with murder of this cold-blooded, deliberate type."

"That may be," Thorndyke retorted, "but a jury has to find in accordance with the evidence."

"By the way," said I, "did Bawley ever send you that sheet of the letter that you asked for?"

"No, confound him! But I have sent Polton round to get it from him, so that I can look it over carefully in the train. Which reminds me that I can't get down in time for the opening of the inquest. You had better travel with the solicitors and see the shorthand writers started. I shall have to come down by a later train."

Half an hour later, just as I was about to start, a familiar step was heard on the stair, and then our laboratory assistant, Polton, let himself in with his key.

"Just caught him, sir, as he was starting for the station," he said, with a satisfied, crinkly smile, laying an envelope on the table, and added, "Lord! how he did swear!"

Thorndyke chuckled, and having thanked his assistant, opened the envelope and handed it to me. It contained a single sheet of letter-paper, exactly similar to the one that we had found in the railway carriage, excepting that the writing filled one side and a quarter only, and, since it concluded with the signature "Letitia Humboe, President," it was evidently the last sheet. There was no water-mark nor anything, so far as I could see, to distinguish it from the dozens of other impressions that had been run off on the duplicator with it, excepting the roughly-pencilled plan on the blank side of the sheet.

"Well," I said as I put on my hat and walked towards the door, "I suspect that Bawley was right. You won't get much help from this to support Miss Dalby's rather improbable statement." And Thorndyke agreed that appearances were not very promising.

The scene in the coffee-room of "The Plough" Inn at Densford was one with which I was familiar enough. The quiet, business-like coroner, the half-embarrassed jurors, the local police and witnesses and the spectators, penned up at one end of the room, were all well-known characters. The unusual feature was the handsome, distinguished-looking young lady who sat on a plain Windsor chair between two inscrutable policemen, watched intently by Mr. Cadmus Bawley. Miss Dalby was pale and obviously agitated, but quiet, resolute, and somewhat defiant in manner. She greeted me with a pleasant smile when I introduced myself, and hoped that I and my colleague would have no difficulty in disposing of" this grotesque and horrible accusation."

I need not describe the proceedings in detail. Evidence of the identity of the deceased having been taken, Dr. Pooke deposed that death was due to a wound of the heart produced by a spherical bullet, apparently fired from a small, smooth-bore pistol at very short range. The wound was in his opinion not self-inflicted. The coroner then produced the sheet of the circular letter found in the carriage, and I was called to testify to the finding of it. The next witness was Superintendent Miller of the Criminal Investigation Department, who produced the two sheets of the letter which were taken from Miss Dalby's pocket when she was arrested. These he handed to the coroner for comparison with the one found in the carriage with the body of deceased.

"There appear," said the coroner, after placing the three sheets together," to be one or more sheets missing. The two you have handed me are sheets one and three, and the one found in the railway carriage is sheet two."

"Yes," the witness agreed, "sheet four is missing, but I have a photograph of it. Here is a set of the complete letter," and he laid four unmounted prints on the table.

The coroner examined them with a puzzled frown. "May I ask," he said, "how you obtained these photographs?"

"They are not photographs of the copy that you have," the witness explained, "but of another copy of the same letter which we intercepted in the post. That letter was addressed to a stationer's shop to be called for. We have considered it necessary to keep ourselves informed of the contents of these circulars, so that we can take the necessary precautions; and as the envelopes are marked with the badge and are invariably addressed in blue ink, it is not difficult to identify them."

"I see," said the coroner, glaring stonily at Mr. Bawley, who had accompanied the superintendent's statement with audible and unfavourable comments. "Is that the whole of your evidence? Thank you. Then, if there is no cross-examination, I will call the next witness. Mr. Bernard Parsons."

Mr. Parsons was the general manager of the London and Suburban Bank, and he deposed that deceased was, on the day when be met his death, travelling to Holmwood to visit and inspect the new local branch of the bank, and that he was taking thither the sum of three thousand pounds, of which one thousand was in gold and the remainder in Bank of England notes--mostly five-pound notes. He carried the notes and specie in a strong leather handbag.

"Can you say if either of these is the bag that he carried?" the coroner asked, indicating two largish, black leather bags that his officer had placed on the table.

Mr. Parsons promptly pointed to the larger of the two, which was smeared externally with mud. The coroner noted the answer and then asked: "Did anyone besides yourself know that deceased was making this visit?"

"Many persons must have known," was the reply. "Deceased visited the various branches in a fixed order. He came to Holmwood on the second Tuesday in the month."

"And would it be known that he had this great sum of money with him?"

"The actual amount would not be generally known, but he usually took with him supplies of specie and notes--sometimes very large sums--and this would be known to many of the bank staff, and probably to a good many persons outside. The Holmwood Branch consumes a good deal of specie, as most of the customers pay in cheques and draw out cash for local use."

This was the substance of Mr. Parsons' evidence, and when he sat down the ticket-collector was called. That official identified Miss Dalby as one of the passengers by the train in which the body of deceased was found. She was carrying a bag when she passed the barrier. He could not identify either of the bags, but both were similar to the one that she was carrying. She returned about an hour later and caught an up-train, and he noticed that she was then not carrying a bag. He could not say whether any of the other passengers was carrying a bag. There were very few first-class passengers by that train, but a large number of third- class--mostly fruit-pickers--and they made a dense crowd at the barrier so that he did not notice individual passengers particularly. He noticed Miss Dalby because he knew her by sight, as she often came to Holmwood with other suffragist ladies. He did not see which carriage Miss Dalby came from, and he did not see any first-class compartment with an open door.

The coroner noted down this evidence with thoughtful deliberation, and I was considering whether there were any questions that it would be advisable to ask the witness when I felt a light touch on my shoulder, and looking up perceived a constable holding out a telegram. Observing that it was addressed to "Dr. Jervis, Plough Inn, Densford," I nodded to the constable, and taking the envelope from him, opened it and unfolded the paper. The telegram was from Thorndyke, in the simple code that he had devised for our private use. I was able to decode it without referring to the key--which each of us always carried in his pocket-- and it then read:

"I AM STARTING FOR FOLKESTONE RE BURNHAM DECEASED. FOLLOW IMMEDIATELY AND BRING MILLER IF YOU CAN FOR POSSIBLE ARREST. MEET ME ON PIER NEAR OSTEND BOAT. THORNDYKE."

Accustomed as I was to my colleague's inveterate habit of acting in the least expected manner, I must confess that I gazed at the decoded message in absolute stupefaction. I had been totally unaware of the faintest clue beyond the obvious evidence to which I had been listening, and behold! here was Thorndyke with an entirely fresh case, apparently cut-and-dried, and the unsuspected criminal in the hollow of his hand. It was astounding.

Unconsciously I raised my eyes--and met those of Superintendent Miller, fixed on me with devouring curiosity. I held up the telegram and beckoned, and immediately he tip-toed across and took a seat by my side. I laid the decoded telegram before him, and when he had glanced through it, I asked in a whisper: "Well, what do you say?"

By way of reply, he whisked out a time-table, conned it eagerly for a few minutes, and then held it towards me with his thumb-nail on the words "Densford Junction."

"There's a fast train up in seven minutes," he whispered hoarsely. "Get the coroner to excuse us and let your solicitors carry on for you."

A brief, and rather vague, explanation secured the assent of the coroner--since we had both given our evidence--and the less willing agreement of my clients. In another minute the superintendent and I were heading for the station, which we reached just as the train swept up alongside the platform.

"This is a queer start," said Miller, as the train moved out of the station; "but, Lord! there is never any calculating Dr. Thorndyke's moves. Did you know that he had anything up his sleeve?"

"No; but then one never does know. He is as close as an oyster. He never shows his hand until he can play a trump card. But it is possible that he has struck a fresh clue since I left."

"Well," rejoined Miller, "we shall know when we get to the other end And I don't mind telling you that it will be a great relief to me if we can drop this charge against Miss Dalby."

From time to time during the journey to London, and from thence to Folkestone, the superintendent reverted to Thorndyke's mysterious proceedings. But it was useless to speculate. We had not a single fact to guide us; and when, at last, the train ran into Folkestone Central Station we were as much in the dark as when we started.

Assuming that Thorndyke would have made any necessary arrangements for assistance from the local police, we chartered a cab and proceeded direct to the end of Rendez-vous Street--a curiously appropriate destination, by the way. Here we alighted in order that we might make our appearance at the meeting-place as inconspicuously as possible, and, walking towards the harbour, perceived Thorndyke waiting on the quay, ostensibly watching the loading of a barge, and putting in their case a pair of prismatic binoculars with which he had apparently observed our arrival.

"I am glad you have come, Miller," he said, shaking the superintendent's hand. "I can't make any promises, but I have no doubt that it is a case for you even if it doesn't turn out all that I hope and expect. The Cornflower is our ship, and we had better go on board separately in case our friends are keeping a look-out. I have arranged matters with the captain, and the local superintendent has got some plain-clothes men on the pier."

With this we separated. Thorndyke went on in advance, and Miller and I followed at a discreet interval.

As I descended the gangway a minute or so after Miller, a steward approached me, and having asked my name requested me to follow him, when he conducted me to the purser's office, in which I found Thorndyke and Miller in conversation with the purser.

The gentlemen you are inquiring for," said the latter, "are in the smoking-room playing cards with another passenger. I have put a tarpaulin over one of the ports, in case you want to have a look at them without being seen."

"Perhaps you had better make a preliminary inspection, Miller," said Thorndyke. "You may know some of them."

To this suggestion the superintendent agreed, and forthwith went off with the purser, leaving me and Thorndyke alone. I at once took the opportunity to demand an explanation. "I take it that you struck some new evidence after I left you?"

"Yes," Thorndyke replied. "And none too soon, as you see. I don't quite know what it will amount to, but I think we have secured the defence, at any rate and that is really all that we are concerned with. The positive aspects of the case are the business of the police. But here comes Miller, looking very pleased with himself, and with the purser."

The superintendent, however, was not only pleased; he was also not a little puzzled.

"Well!" he exclaimed, "this is a quaint affair. We have got two of the leading lights of the suffrage movement in there. One is Jameson, the secretary of the Women's Emancipation League, the other is Pinder, their chief bobbery-monger. Then there are two men named Dorman and Spiller, both of them swell crooks, I am certain, though we have never been able to fix anything on them. The fifth man I don't know."

"Neither do I," said Thorndyke. "My repertoire includes only four. And now we will proceed to sort them out. Could we have a few words with Mr. Thorpe--in here, if you don't mind."

"Certainly," replied the purser "I'll go and fetch him." He bustled away in the direction of the smoking- room, whence he presently reappeared, accompanied by a tall, lean man who wore large bi-focal spectacles of the old-fashioned, split-lens type, and was smoking a cigar. As the newcomer approached down the alley-way, it was evident that he was nervous and uneasy, though he maintained a certain jaunty swagger that accorded ill with a pronounced, habitual stoop. As he entered the cabin, however, and became aware of the portentous group of strangers, the swagger broke down completely; suddenly his face became ashen and haggard, and he peered through his great spectacles from one to the others, with an expression of undisguisable terror.

"Mr. Thorpe?" queried Thorndyke; and the superintendent murmured: "Alias Pinder."

"Yes," was the reply, in a husky undertone. "What can I do for you?"

Thorndyke turned to the superintendent. "I charge this man," said he, "with having murdered Francis Burnham in the train between London and Holmwood."

The superintendent was visibly astonished, but not more so than the accused, on whom Thorndyke's statement produced the most singular effect. In a moment, his terror seemed to drop from him; the colour returned to his face, the haggard expression of which gave place to one of obvious relief.

Miller stood up, and addressing the accused, began "It is my duty to caution you--" but the other interrupted: "Caution your grandmother! You are talking a parcel of dam' nonsense. I was in Birmingham when the murder was committed. I can prove it, easily."

The superintendent was somewhat taken aback, for the accused spoke with a confidence that carried conviction.

"In that case," said Thorndyke, "you can probably explain how a letter belonging to you came to be found in the carriage with the murdered man."

"Belonging to me!" exclaimed Thorpe. "What the deuce do you mean? That letter belonged to Miss Dalby. The rest of it was found in her pocket."

"Precisely," said Thorndyke. "One sheet had been placed in the railway carriage and the remainder in Miss Dalby's pocket to fix suspicion on her. But it was your letter, and the inference is that you disposed of it in that manner for the purpose that I have stated."

"But," persisted Thorpe, with visibly-growing un easiness, "this was a duplicated circular. You couldn't tell one copy from another."

"Mr. Pinder," said Thorndyke, in an impressively quiet tone, "if I tell you that I ascertained from that letter that you had taken a passage on this ship in the name of Thorpe, you will probably understand what I mean."

Apparently he did understand, for, once more, the colour faded from his face and he sat down heavily on a locker, fixing on Thorndyke a look of undisguised dismay. Thus he sat for some moments, motionless and silent, apparently thinking hard.

Suddenly he started up. "My God!" he exclaimed, "I see now what has happened. The infernal scoundrel! First he put it on to Miss Dalby, and now he has put it on to me. Now I understand why he looked so startled when I ran against him."

"What do you mean?" asked Thorndyke.

"I'll tell you," replied Pinder. "As I move about a good deal--and for other reasons--I used to have my suffrage letters sent to a stationer's shop in Barlow Street--"

"I know," interrupted the superintendent; "Bedall's. I used to look them over and take photographs of them." He grinned craftily as he made this statement, and, rather to my surprise, the accused grinned too. A little later I understood that grin.

Well," continued Pinder, "I used to collect these letters pretty regularly. But this last letter was delivered while I was away at Birmingham. Before I came back I met a man who gave me certain--er-- instructions--you know what they were," he added, addressing Thorndyke-- " so I did not need the letter. But, of course, I couldn't leave it there uncollected, so when I got back to London, I called for it. That was two days ago. To my astonishment Miss Bedall declared that I had collected it three days previously. I assured her that I was not in London on that day, but she was positive that I had called. 'I remember clearly,' she said, 'giving you the letter myself.' Well, there was no arguing. Evidently she had given the letter to the wrong person--she is very near-sighted, I should say, judging by the way she holds things against her nose--but how it happened I couldn't understand. But I think I understand now. There is one person only in the world who knew that I had my letters addressed there: a sort of pal of mine named Payne. He happened to be with me one evening when I called to collect my letters. Now, Payne chanced to be a good deal like me--at least he is tall and thin and stoops a bit; but he does not wear spectacles. He tried on my spectacles once for a joke, and then he really looked extremely like me. He looked in a mirror and remarked on the resemblance himself. Now, Payne did not belong to the Women's League, and I suggest that he took advantage of this resemblance to get possession of this letter. He got a pair of spectacles like mine and personated me at the shop."

"Why should he want to get possession of that letter?" Miller demanded.

"To plant it as he has planted it," replied Pinder. "and set the police on a false trail."

"This sounds pretty thin," said Miller. "You are accusing this man of having murdered Mr. Burnham. What grounds have you for this accusation?"

"My grounds," replied Pinder, "are, first, that he stole this letter which has been found, obviously planted; and, second, that he had a grudge against Burnham and knew all about his movements."

"Indeed!" said Miller, with suddenly increased interest. "Then who and what is this man Payne?"

"Why," replied Pinder, "until a month ago, he was assistant cashier at the Streatham branch of the bank. Then Burnham came down and hoofed him out without an hour's notice. I don't know what for, but I can guess."

"Do you happen to know where Payne is at this moment?"

"Yes, I do. He is on this ship, in the smoking-room--only he is Mr. Shenstone now. And mighty sick he was when he found me on board."

The superintendent looked at Thorndyke. "What do you think about it, doctor?" he asked.

"I think," said Thorndyke," that we had better have Mr. Shenstone in here and ask him a few questions. Would you see if you can get him to come here?" he added, addressing the purser, who had been listening with ecstatic enjoyment.

"I'll get him to come along all right," replied the purser, evidently scenting a new act in this enthralling drama; and away he bustled, all agog. In less than a minute we saw him returning down the alley-way, with a tall, thin man, who, at a distance, was certainly a good deal like Pinder, though the resemblance diminished as he approached. He, too, was obviously agitated, and seemed to be plying the purser with questions. But when he came opposite the door of the cabin he stopped dead and seemed disposed to shrink back.

"Is that the man?" Thorndyke demanded sharply and rather loudly, springing to his feet as he spoke.

The effect of the question was electrical. As Thorndyke rose, the new-comer turned, and, violently thrusting the purser aside, raced madly down the alley-way and out on to the deck.

"Stop that man!" roared Miller, darting out in pursuit; and at the shout a couple of loitering deck- hands headed the fugitive off from the gangway. Following, I saw the terrified man swerving this way and that across the littered deck to avoid the seamen, who joined in the pursuit; I saw him make a sudden frantic burst for a baggage-slide springing from a bollard up to the bulwark-rail. Then his foot must have tripped on a lashing, for he staggered for a moment, flung out his arms with a wild shriek, and plunged headlong into the space between the ship's side and the quay wall.

In an instant the whole ship was in an uproar. An officer and two hands sprang to the rail with ropes and a boathook, while others manned the cargo derrick and lowered a rope with a running bowline between the ship and the quay.

"He's gone under," a hoarse voice proclaimed from below; "but I can see him jammed against the side."

There were a couple of minutes of sickening suspense. Then the voice from below was heard again. "Heave up!"

The derrick-engine rattled, the taut rope came up slowly, and at length out of that horrid gulf arose a limp and dripping shape that, as it cleared the bulwark, was swung inboard and let down gently on the deck. Thorndyke and I stooped over him. But it was a dead man's face that we looked into; and a tinge of blood on the lips told the rest of the tale.

"Cover him up," said the superintendent. "He's out of our jurisdiction now. But what's going on there?"

Following his look, I perceived a small scattered crowd of men all running furiously along the quay towards the town. Some of them I judged to be the late inmates of the smoking-room and some plain-clothes men. The only figure that I recognised was that of Mr. Pinder, and he was already growing small in the distance.

"The local police will have to deal with them," said Miller. Then turning to the purser, he asked: "What baggage had this man?"

"Only two cabin trunks," was the reply. "They are both in his state-room."

To the state-room we followed the purser, when Miller had possessed himself of the dead man's keys, and the two trunks were hoisted on to the bunk and opened. Each trunk contained a large cash-box, and each cash-box contained five hundred pounds in gold and a big bundle of notes. The latter Miller examined closely, checking their numbers by a column of entries in his pocket-book.

"Yes," he reported at length; "it's a true bill. These are the notes that were stolen from Mr. Burnham. And now I will have a look at the baggage of those other four sportsmen."

This being no affair of ours, Thorndyke and I went ashore and slowly made our way towards the town. But presently the superintendent overtook us in high glee, with the news that he had discovered what appeared to be the accumulated" swag "of a gang of swell burglars for whom he had been for some months vainly on the look-out.

"How was it done?" repeated Thorndyke in reply to Miller's question, as we sat at a retired table in the "Lord Warden" Hotel. "Well, it was really very simple. I am afraid I shall disappoint you if you expect anything ingenious and recondite. Of course, it was obvious that Miss Dalby had not committed this atrocious murder and robbery; and it was profoundly improbable that this extremely incriminating letter had been dropped accidentally. That being so, it was almost certain that the letter had been 'planted,' as Pinder expressed it. But that was a mere opinion that helped us not at all. The actual solution turned upon a simple chemical fact with which I happened to be acquainted; which is this : that all the basic coal-tar dyes, and especially methylene blue, dye oxycellulose without requiring a mordant, but do not react in this way on cellulose. Now, good paper is practically pure cellulose; and if you dip a sheet of such paper into certain oxidising liquids, such as a solution of potassium chlorate with a slight excess of hydrochloric acid, the paper is converted into oxycellulose. But if instead of immersing the paper, you write on it with a quill or glass pen dipped in the solution, only the part which has been touched by the pen is changed into oxycellulose. No change is visible to the eye: but if a sheet of paper written on with this colourless fluid is dipped in a solution of, say, methylene blue, the invisible writing immediately becomes visible. The oxycellulose takes up the blue dye.

"Now, when I picked up that sheet of the letter in the railway carriage and noted that the ink used appeared to be methylene blue, this fact was recalled to my mind. Then, on looking at it closely, I seemed to detect a certain slight spottiness in the writing. There were points on some of the letters that were a little deeper in colour than the rest; and it occurred to me that it was possible that these circulars might be used to transmit secret messages of a less innocent kind than those that met the unaided eye, just as these political societies might form an excellent cover for the operations of criminal associations. But if the circulars had been so used, it is evident that the secret writing would not be on all the circulars. The prepared sheets would be used only for the circulars that were to be sent to particular persons, and in those cases the secret writing would probably be in the nature of a personal communication, either to a particular individual or to a small group. The possible presence of a secret message thus became of vital evidential importance; for if it could be shown that this letter was addressed to some person other than Miss Dalby, that would dispose of the only evidence connecting her with the crime.

"It happened, most fortunately, that I was able to get possession of the final sheet of this letter--"

"Of course it did," growled Miller, with a sour smile.

It reached me," continued Thorndyke, "only after Dr. Jervis had started for Densford. The greater part of one side was blank, excepting for a rough plan drawn in pencil, and this blank side I laid down on a sheet of glass and wetted the written side with a small wad of cotton-wool dipped in distilled water. Of course, the blue writing began to run and dissolve out; and then, very faintly, some other writing began to show through in reverse. I turned the paper over, and now the new writing, though faint, was quite legible, and became more so when I wiped the blue-stained cotton-wool over it a few times. A solution of methylene blue would have made it still plainer, but I used water only, as I judged that the blue writing was intended to furnish the dye for development. Here is the final result."

He drew from his pocket a letter-case, from which he extracted a folded paper which he opened and laid on the table. It was stained a faint blue, through which the original writing could be seen, dim and blurred, while the secret message, though very pale, was quite sharp and clear. And this was the message:

'...so although we are not actually blown on, the position is getting risky and it's time for us to hop. I have booked passages for the four of us to Ostend by the Cornflower, which sails on Friday evening next (20th). The names of the four illustrious passengers are, Walsh (that's me), Grubb (Dorman), Jenkins (Spiller) and Thorpe (that's you). Get those names well into your canister--better make a note of them--and turn up in good time on Friday."

"Well," said Miller, as he handed back the letter, "we can't know everything--unless we are Dr. Thorndyke. But there's one thing I do know."

"What is that?" I asked.

"I know why that fellow Pinder grinned when I told him that I had photographed his confounded letters."

The Naturalist at Law

A hush had fallen on the court as the coroner concluded his brief introductory statement and the first witness took up his position by the long table. The usual preliminary questions elicited that Simon Moffet, the witness aforesaid, was fifty-eight years of age, that he followed the calling of a shepherd and that he was engaged in supervising the flocks that fed upon the low-lying meadows adjoining the little town of Bantree in Buckinghamshire.

"Tell us how you came to discover the body," said the coroner.

"'Twas on Wednesday morning, about half-past five," Moffet began. "I was getting the sheep through the gate into the big meadow by Reed's farm, when I happened to look down the dyke, and then I noticed a boot sticking up out of the water. Seemed to me as if there was a foot in it by the way it stuck up, so as soon as all the sheep was in, I shut the gate and walked down the dyke to have a look at un. When I got close I see the toe of another boot just alongside. Looks a bit queer, I thinks, but I couldn't see anything more, 'cause the duck-weed is that thick as it looks as if you could walk on it. Hows'ever, I clears away the weed with my stick, and then I see 'twas a dead man. Give me a rare turn, it did. He was a-layin' at the bottom of the ditch with his head near the middle and his feet up close to the bank. Just then young Harry Walker comes along the cart-track on his way to work, so I shows him the body and sends him back to the town for to give notice at the police station."

"And is that all you know about the affair?"

"Ay. Later on I see the sergeant come along with a man wheelin' the stretcher, and 1 showed him where the body was and helped to pull it out and load it on the stretcher. And that's all I know about it."

On this the witness was dismissed and his place taken by a shrewd-looking, business-like police sergeant, who deposed as follows:

"Last Wednesday, the 8th of May, at 6.15 a.m., I received information from Henry Walker that a dead body was lying in the ditch by the cart-track leading from Ponder's Road to Reed's farm. I proceeded there forthwith, accompanied by Police-Constable Ketchum, and taking with us a wheeled stretcher. On the track I was met by the last witness, who conducted me to the place where the body was lying and where I found it in the position that he has described; but we had to clear away the duck-weed before we could see it distinctly. I examined the bank carefully, but could see no trace of footprints, as the grass grows thickly right down to the water's edge. There were no signs of a struggle or any disturbance on the bank. With the aid of Moffet and Ketchum, I drew the body out and placed it on the stretcher. I could not see any injuries or marks of violence on the body or anything unusual about it. I conveyed it to the mortuary, and with Constable Ketchum's assistance removed the clothing and emptied the pockets, putting the contents of each pocket in a separate envelope and writing the description on each. In a letter-case from the coat pocket were some visiting cards bearing the name and address of Mr. Cyrus Pedley, of 21 Hawtrey Mansions, Kensington, and a letter signed Wilfred Pedley, apparently from deceased's brother. Acting on instructions, I communicated with him and served a summons to attend this inquest."

"With regard to the ditch in which you found the body," said the coroner," can you tell us how deep it is?"

"Yes; I measured it with Moffet's crook and a tape measure. In the deepest part, where the body was lying, it is four feet two inches deep. From there it slopes up pretty sharply to the bank."

So far as you can judge, if a grown man fell into the ditch by accident, would he have any difficulty in getting out?"

"None at all, I should say, if he were sober and in ordinary health. A man of medium height, standing in the middle at the deepest part, would have his head and shoulders out of water; and the sides are not too steep to climb up easily, especially with the grass and rushes on the bank to lay hold of."

"You say there were no signs of disturbance on the bank. Were there any in the ditch itself?

"None that I could see. But, of course, signs of disturbance soon disappear in water. The duck-weed drifts about as the wind drives it, and there are creatures moving about on the bottom. I noticed that deceased had some weed grasped in one hand."

This concluded the sergeant's evidence, and as he retired, the name of Dr. Albert Parton was called. The new witness was a young man of grave and professional aspect, who gave his evidence with an extreme regard for clearness and accuracy.

"I have made an examination of the body of the deceased," he began, after the usual preliminaries. "It is that of a healthy man of about forty-five. I first saw it about two hours after it was found. It had then been dead from twelve to fifteen hours. Later I made a complete examination. I found no injuries, marks of violence or any definite bruises, and no signs cf disease."

"Did you ascertain the cause of death?" the coroner asked.

"Yes. The cause of death was drowning."

"You are quite sure of that?"

"Quite sure. The lungs contained a quantity of water and duck-weed, and there was more than a quart of water mixed with duck-weed and water-weed in the stomach. That is a clear proof of death by drowning. The water in the lungs was the immediate cause of death, by making breathing impossible, and as the water and weed in the stomach must have been swallowed, they furnish conclusive evidence that deceased was alive when he fell into the water."

"The water and weed could not have got into the stomach after death?

"No, that is quite impossible. They must have been swallowed when the head of the deceased was just below the surface; and the water must have been drawn into the lungs by spasmodic efforts to breathe when the mouth was under water."

"Did you find any signs indicating that deceased might have been intoxicated?"

"No. I examined the water from the stomach very carefully with that question in view, but there was no trace of alcohol--or, indeed, of anything else. It was simple ditch-water. As the point is

important I have preserved it, and--" here the witness produced a paper parcel which he unfastened, revealing a large glass jar containing about a quart of water plentifully sprinkled with duck-weed. This he presented to the coroner, who waved it away hastily and indicated the jury; to whom it was then offered and summarily rejected with emphatic head-shakes. Finally it came to rest on the table by the place where I was sitting with my colleague, Dr. Thorndyke, and our client, Mr. Wilfred Pedley. I glanced at it with faint interest, noting how the duck-weed plants had risen to the surface and floated, each with its tassel of roots hanging down into the water, and how a couple of tiny, flat shells, like miniature ammonites, had sunk and lay on the bottom of the jar. Thorndyke also glanced at it; indeed, he did more than glance, for he drew the jar towards him and examined its contents in the systematic way in which it was his habit to examine everything. Meanwhile the coroner asked: "Did you find anything abnormal or unusual, or anything that could throw light on how deceased came to be in the water?"

"Nothing whatever," was the reply. "I found simply that deceased met his death by drowning."

Here, as the witness seemed to have finished his evidence, Thorndyke interposed.

"The witness states, sir, there were no definite bruises. Does he mean that there were any marks that might have been bruises?"

The coroner glanced at Dr. Parton, who replied: "There was a faint mark on the outside of the right arm, just above the elbow, which had somewhat the appearance of a bruise, as if the deceased had been struck with a stick. But it was very indistinct. I shouldn't like to swear that it was a bruise at all."

This concluded the doctor's evidence, and when he had retired, the name of our client, Wilfred Pedley, was called. He rose, and having taken the oath and given his name and address, deposed: "I have viewed the body of deceased. It is that of my brother, Cyrus Pedley, who is forty-three years of age. The last time I saw deceased alive was on Tuesday morning, the day before the body was found."

"Did you notice anything unusual in his manner or state of mind?"

The witness hesitated but at length replied: "Yes. He seemed anxious and depressed. He had been in low spirits for some time past, but on this occasion he seemed more so than usual."

"Had you any reason to suspect that he might contemplate taking his life?"

"No," the witness replied, emphatically, "and I do not believe that he would, under any circumstances, have contemplated suicide."

"Have you any special reason for that belief?"

"Yes. Deceased was a highly conscientious man and he was in my debt. He had occasion to borrow two thousand pounds from me, and the debt was secured by an insurance on his life. If he had committed suicide that insurance would be invalidated and the debt would remain unpaid. From my knowledge of him, I feel certain that he would not have done such a thing."

The coroner nodded gravely, and then asked: "What was deceased's occupation?"

"He was employed in some way by the Foreign Office, I don't know in what capacity. I know very little about his affairs."

"Do you know if he had any money worries or any troubles or embarrassments of any kind?"

"I have never heard of any; but deceased was a very reticent man. He lived alone in his flat, taking his meals at his club, and no one knew-- at least, I did not--how he spent his time or what was the state of his finances. He was not married, and I am his only near relative."

"And as to deceased's habits. Was he ever addicted to taking more stimulants than was good for him?

"Never," the witness replied emphatically. "He was a most temperate and abstemious man."

"Was he subject to fits of any kind, or fainting attacks?"

"I have never heard that he was."

"Can you account for his being in this solitary place at this time-- apparently about eight o'clock at night?"

"I cannot. It is a complete mystery to me. I know of no one with whom either of us was acquainted in this district. I had never heard of the place until I got the summons to the inquest."

This was the sum of our client's evidence, and, so far, things did not look very favourable from our point of view--we were retained on the insurance question, to rebut, if possible, the suggestion of suicide. How ever, the coroner was a discreet man, and having regard to the obscurity of the case--and perhaps to the interests involved--summed up in favour of an open verdict; and the jury, taking a similar view, found that deceased met his death by drowning, but under what circumstances there was no evidence to show.

"Well," I said, as the court rose, "that leaves it to the insurance people to make out a case of suicide if they can. I think you are fairly safe, Mr. Pedley. There is no positive evidence."

"No," our client replied. "But it isn't only the money I am thinking of. It would be some consolation to me for the loss of my poor brother if I had some idea how he met with his death, and could feel sure that it was an unavoidable misadventure. And for my own satisfaction--leaving the insurance out of the question--I should like to have definite proof that it was not suicide."

He looked half-questioningly at Thorndyke, who nodded gravely. "Yes," the latter agreed, "the suggestion of suicide ought to be disposed of if possible, both for legal and sentimental reasons. How far away is the mortuary?"

"A couple of minutes' walk," replied Mr. Pedley. "Did you wish to inspect the body?"

"If it is permissible," replied Thorndyke; "and then I propose to have a look at the place where the body was found."

"In that case," our client said, "I will go down to the Station Hotel and wait for you. We may as well travel up to town together, and you can then tell me if you have seen any further light on the mystery."

As soon as he was gone, Dr. Parton advanced, tying the string of the parcel which once more enclosed the jar of ditch-water.

"I heard you say, sir, that you would like to inspect the body," said he. "If you like, I will show you the way to the mortuary. The sergeant will let us in, won't you, sergeant? This gentleman is a doctor as well as a lawyer."

"Bless you, sir," said the sergeant, "I know who Dr. Thorndyke is, and I shall feel it an honour to show him anything he wishes to see."

Accordingly we set forth together, Dr. Parton and Thorndyke leading the way.

"The coroner and the jury didn't seem to appreciate my exhibit," the former remarked with a faint grin, tapping the parcel as he spoke.

"No," Thorndyke agreed; "and it is hardly reason able to expect a layman to share our own matter-of-fact outlook. But you were quite right to produce the specimen. That ditch-water furnishes conclusive evidence on a vitally material question. Further, I would advise you to preserve that jar for the present, well covered and under lock and key."

Parton looked surprised. "Why?" he asked. "The inquest is over and the verdict pronounced."

"Yes, but it was an open verdict, and an open verdict leaves the case in the air. The inquest has thrown no light on the question as to how Cyrus Pedley came by his death."

"There doesn't seem to me much mystery about it," said the doctor. "Here is a man found drowned in a shallow ditch which he could easily have got out of if he had fallen in by accident. He was not drunk. Apparently he was not in a fit of any kind. There are no marks of violence and no signs of a struggle, and the man is known to have been in an extremely depressed state of mind. It looks like a clear case of suicide, though I admit that the jury were quite right, in the absence of direct evidence."

"Well," said Thorndyke, "it will be my duty to contest that view if the insurance company dispute the claim on those grounds."

"I can't think what you will have to offer in answer to the suggestion of suicide," said Parton.

"Neither can I, at present," replied Thorndyke "But the case doesn't look to me quite so simple as it does to you."

"You think it possible that an analysis of the contents of this jar may be called for?"

"That is a possibility," replied Thorndyke. "But I mean that the case is obscure, and that some further inquiry into the circumstances of this man's death is by no means unlikely."

"Then," said Parton, "I will certainly follow your advice and lock up this precious jar. But here we are at the mortuary. Is there anything in particular that you want to see?"

"I want to see all that there is to see," Thorndyke replied. "The evidence has been vague enough so far. Shall we begin with that bruise or mark that you mentioned?"

Dr. Parton advanced to the grim, shrouded figure that lay on the slate-topped table, like some solemn effigy on an altar tomb, and drew back the sheet that covered it. We all approached, stepping softly, and stood beside the table, looking down with a certain awesome curiosity at the still, waxen figure that, but a few hours since, had been a living man like ourselves The body was that of a good-looking, middle-aged man with a refined, intelligent face--slightly disfigured by a scar on the cheek--now set in the calm, reposeful expression that one so usually finds on the faces of the drowned; with drowsy, half-closed eyes and slightly parted lips that revealed a considerable gap in the upper front teeth.

Thorndyke stood awhile looking down on the dead man with a curious questioning expression. Then his eye travelled over the body, from the placid face to the marble-like torso and the hand which, though now relaxed, still lightly grasped a tuft of water-weed. The latter Thorndyke gently disengaged from the limp hand, and, after a glance at the dark green, feathery fronds, laid it down and stooped to examine the right arm at the spot above the elbow that Parton had spoken of.

Yes," he said, "I think I should call it a bruise, though it is very faint. As you say, it might have been produced by a blow with a stick or rod. I notice that there are some teeth missing. Presumably he wore a plate?"

"Yes," replied Parton; "a smallish gold plate with four teeth on it--at least, so his brother told me. Of course, it fell out when he was in the water, but it hasn't been found; in fact, it hasn't been looked for."

Thorndyke nodded and then turned to the sergeant. "Could I see what you found in the pockets?" he asked.

The sergeant complied readily, and my colleague watched his orderly procedure with evident approval. The collection of envelopes was produced from an attaché-case and conveyed to a side table, where the sergeant emptied out the contents of each into a little heap, opposite which he placed the appropriate envelope with its written description. Thorndyke ran his eye over the collection--which was commonplace enough--until he came to the tobacco pouch, from which protruded the corner of a scrap of crumpled paper. This he drew forth and smoothed out the creases, when it was seen to be a railway receipt for an excess fare.

"Seems to have lost his ticket or travelled without one," the sergeant remarked. "But not on this line."

"No," agreed Thorndyke. "It is the Tilbury and Southend line. But you notice the date. It is the 18th; and the body was found on the morning of Wednesday, the 19th. So it would appear that he must have come into this neighbourhood in the evening; and that he must have come either by way of London or by a very complicated cross-country route. I wonder what brought him here."

He produced his notebook and was beginning to copy the receipt when the sergeant said: "You had better take the paper, sir. It is of no use to us now, and it isn't very easy to make out."

Thorndyke thanked the officer, and, handing me the paper, asked: "What do you make of it, Jervis?"

I scrutinised the little crumpled scrap and deciphered with difficulty the hurried scrawl, scribbled with a hard, ill-sharpened pencil.

"It seems to read 'Ldn to C.B'. or 'S.B', 'Hlt'--that is some 'Halt,' I presume. But the amount, 4/9, is clear enough, and that will give us a clue if we want one." I returned the paper to Thorndyke, who bestowed it in his pocket-book and then remarked: "I don't see any keys."

"No, sir," replied the sergeant, "there aren't any. Rather queer, that, for he must have had at least a latch key. They must have fallen out into the water."

"That is possible," said Thorndyke, "but it would be worth while to make sure. Is there anyone who could show us the place where the body was found?"

"I will walk up there with you myself, sir, with pleasure," said the sergeant, hastily repacking the envelopes. "It is only a quarter of an hour's walk from here."

"That is very good of you, sergeant," my colleague responded; "and as we seem to have seen everything here, I propose that we start at once. You are not coming with us, Parton?"

"No," the doctor replied. "I have finished with the case and I have got my work to do." He shook hands with us heartily and watched us--with some curiosity, I think--as we set forth in company with the sergeant.

His curiosity did not seem to me to be unjustified. In fact, I shared it. The presence of the police officer precluded discussion, but as we took our way out of the town I found myself speculating curiously on my colleague's proceedings. To me, suicide was written plainly on every detail of the case. Of course, we did not wish to take that view, but what other was possible? Had Thorndyke some alternative theory? Or was he merely, according to his invariable custom, making an impartial survey of everything, no matter how apparently trivial, in the hope of lighting on some new and informative fact?

The temporary absence of the sergeant, who had stopped to speak to a constable on duty, enabled me to put the question: "Is this expedition intended to clear up anything in particular?"

"No," he replied, "excepting the keys, which ought to be found. But you must see for yourself that this is not a straightforward case. That man did not come all this way merely to drown himself in a ditch. I am quite in the dark at present, so there is nothing for it but to examine everything with our own eyes and see if there is anything that has been overlooked that may throw some light on either the motive or the circumstances. It is always desirable to examine the scene of a crime or a tragedy."

Here the return of the sergeant put a stop to the discussion and we proceeded on our way in silence. Already we had passed out of the town, and we now turned out of the main road into a lane or by-road, bordered by meadows and orchards and enclosed by rather high hedgerows.

"This is Ponder's Road," said the sergeant. "It leads to Renham, a couple of miles farther on, where it joins the Aylesbury Road. The cart track is on the left a little way along."

A few minutes later we came to our turning, a narrow and rather muddy lane, the entrance to which was shaded by a grove of tall elms. Passing through this shady avenue, we came out on a grass-covered track, broken by deep wagon-ruts and bordered on each side by a ditch, beyond which was a wide expanse of marshy meadows.

"This is the place," said the sergeant, halting by the side of the right-hand ditch and indicating a spot where the rushes had been flattened down. "It was just as you see it now, only the feet were just visible sticking out of the duck-weed, which had drifted back after Moffet had disturbed it."

We stood awhile looking at the ditch, with its thick mantle of bright green, spotted with innumerable small dark objects and showing here and there a faint track where a water-vole had swum across.

"Those little dark objects are water-snails, I suppose," said I, by way of making some kind of remark.

"Yes," replied Thorndyke; "the common Amber shell, I think--*Succinea putris*." He reached out his stick and fished up a sample of the duck-weed, on which one or two of the snails were crawling. "Yes," he repeated. "*Succinea putris* it is; a queer little left handed shell, with the spire, as you see, all lop-sided. They have a habit of swarming in this extraordinary way. You notice that the ditch is covered with them."

I had already observed this, but it hardly seemed to be worth commenting on under the present circumstances--which was apparently the sergeant's view also, for he looked at Thorndyke with some surprise, which developed into impatience when my colleague proceeded further to expand on the subject of natural history.

"These water-weeds," he observed, "are very remarkable plants in their various ways. Look at this duck-weed, for instance. Just a little green oval disc with a single root hanging down into the water, like a tiny umbrella with a long handle; and yet it is a complete plant, and a flowering plant, too." He picked a specimen off the end of his stick and held it up by its root to exhibit its umbrella-like form; and as he did so, he looked in my face with an expression that I felt to be somehow significant; but of which I could not extract the meaning.

But there was no difficulty in interpreting the expression on the sergeant's face. He had come here on business and be wanted to "cut the cackle and get to the hosses."

"Well, sergeant," said Thorndyke, "there isn't much to see, but I think we ought to have a look for those keys. He must have had keys of some kind, if only a latchkey; and they must be in this ditch."

The sergeant was not enthusiastic. "I've no doubt you are right, sir," said he; " but I don't see that we should be much forrader if we found them. However, we may as well have a look, only I can't stay more than a few minutes. I've got my work to do at the station."

"Then," said Thorndyke, "let us get to work at once. We had better hook out the weed and look it over; and if the keys are not in that, we must try to expose the bottom where the body was lying. You must tell us if we are working in the right place."

With this he began, with the crooked handle of his stick, to rake up the tangle of weed that covered the bottom of the ditch and drag the detached masses ashore, piling them on the bank and carefully looking them through to see if the keys should chance to be entangled in their meshes. In this work I took my part under the sergeant's direction, raking in load after load of the delicate, stringy weed, on the pale green ribbon-like leaves of which multitudes of the water- snails were creeping; and sorting over each batch in hopeless and fruitless search for the missing keys. In about ten minutes we had removed the entire weedy covering from the bottom of the ditch over an area of from eight to nine feet--the place which, according to the sergeant, the body had occupied; and as the duck- weed had been caught by the tangled masses of water-weed that we had dragged ashore, we now had an uninterrupted view of the cleared space save for the clouds of mud that we had stirred up.

"We must give the mud a few minutes to settle," said Thorndyke.

"Yes," the sergeant agreed, "it will take some time; and as it doesn't really concern me now that the inquest is over, I think I will get back to the station if you will excuse me."

Thorndyke excused him very willingly, I think, though politely and with many thanks for his help. When he had gone I remarked, "I am inclined to agree with the sergeant. If we find the keys we shan't be much forrader."

"We shall know that he had them with him," he replied. "Though, of course, if we don't find them, that will not prove that they are not here. Still, I think we should try to settle the question."

His answer left me quite unconvinced; but the care with which he searched the ditch and sorted out the weed left me in no doubt that, to him, the matter seemed to be of some importance. However, nothing came of the search. If the keys were there they were buried in the mud, and eventually we had to give up the search and make our way back towards the station.

As we passed out of the lane into Ponder's Road, Thorndyke stopped at the entrance, under the trees, by a little triangle of turf which marked the beginning of the lane, and looked down at the muddy ground.

"Here is quite an interesting thing, Jervis," he remarked, "which shows us how standardised objects tend to develop an individual character. These are the tracks of a car, or more probably a tradesman's van, which was fitted with Barlow tyres. Now there must be thousands of vans fitted with these tyres; they are the favourite type for light covered vans, and when new they are all alike and indistinguishable. Yet this tyre--of the off hind wheel--has acquired a character which would enable one to pick it out with certainty from ten thousand others. First,. you see, there is a deep cut in the tyre at an angle of forty-five, then a kidney-shaped 'Blakey' has stuck in the outer tyre without puncturing the inner; and finally some adhesive object--perhaps a lump of pitch from a newly-mended road--has become fixed on just behind the 'Blakey.' Now, if we make a rough sketch of those three marks and indicate their distance apart, thus "--here he made a rapid sketch in his notebook, and wrote in the intervals in inches--" we have the means of swearing to the identity of a vehicle which we have never seen."

"And which," I added, "had for some reason swerved over to the wrong side of the road. Yes, I should say that tyre is certainly unique. But surely most tyres are identifiable when they have been in use for some time."

"Exactly," he replied. "That was my point. The standardised thing is devoid of character only when it is new."

It was not a very subtle point, and as it was fairly obvious I made no comment, but presently reverted to the case of Pedley deceased.

"I don't quite see why you are taking all this trouble. The insurance claim is not likely to be contested. No one can prove that it was a case of suicide, though I should think no one will feel any doubt that it was, at least that is my own feeling."

Thorndyke looked at me with an expression of reproach.

"I am afraid that my learned friend has not been making very good use of his eyes," said he. "He has allowed his attention to be distracted by superficial appearances."

"You don't think that it was suicide, then?" I asked, considerably taken aback.

It isn't a question of thinking," he replied. "It was certainly not suicide. There are the plainest indications of homicide; and, of course, in the particular circumstances, homicide means murder."

I was thunderstruck. In my own mind I had dismissed the case somewhat contemptuously as a mere commonplace suicide. As my friend had truly said, I had accepted the obvious appearances and let them mislead me, whereas Thorndyke had followed his golden rule of accepting nothing and observing everything. But what was it that he had observed? I knew that it was useless to ask, but still I ventured on a tentative question.

"When did you come to the conclusion that it was a case of homicide?"

"As soon as I had had a good look at the place where the body was found," he replied promptly.

This did not help me much, for I had given very little attention to anything but the search for the keys. The absence of those keys was, of course, a suspicious fact, if it was a fact. But we had not proved their absence; we had only failed to find them.

"What do you propose to do next?" I asked.

"Evidently," he answered, "there are two things to be done. One is to test the murder theory--to look for more evidence for or against it; the other is to identify the murderer, if possible. But really the two problems are one, since they involve the questions Who had a motive for killing Cyrus Pedley? and Who had the opportunity and the means?"

Our discussion brought us to the station, where, outside the hotel, we found Mr. Pedley waiting for us.

"I am glad you have come," said he. "I was beginning to fear that we should lose this train. I suppose there is no new light on this mysterious affair?"

"No," Thorndyke replied. "Rather there is a new problem. No keys were found in your brother's pockets, and we have failed to find them in the ditch; though, of course, they may be there."

"They must be," said Pedley. "They must have fallen out of his pocket and got buried in the mud, unless he lost them previously, which is most unlikely. It is a pity, though. We shall have to break open his cabinets and drawers, which he would have hated. He was very fastidious about his furniture."

"You will have to break into his flat, too," said I. "No," he replied, "I shan't have to do that. I have a duplicate of his latchkey. He had a spare bedroom which he let me use if I wanted to stay in town." As be spoke, he produced his key-bunch and exhibited a small Chubb latchkey. "I wish we had the others, though," he added.

Here the up-train was heard approaching and we hurried on to the platform, selecting an empty first- class compartment as it drew up. As soon as the train had started, Thorndyke began his inquiries, to which I listened attentively.

"You said that your brother had been anxious and depressed lately. Was there anything inure than this? Any nervousness or foreboding?"

"Well yes," replied Pedley. "Looking back, I seem to see that the possibility of death was in his mind. A week or two ago he brought his will to me to see if it was quite satisfactory to me as the principal beneficiary and he handed to me his last receipt for the insurance premium. That looks a little suggestive."

"It does," Thorndyke agreed. "And as to his occupation and his associates, what do you know about them? "

"His private friends are mostly my own, but of his official associates I know nothing. He was connected with the Foreign Office; but in what capacity I don't know at all. He was extremely reticent on the subject. I only know that he travelled about a good deal, presumably on official business."

This was not very illuminating, but it was all our client had to tell; and the conversation languished somewhat until the train drew up at Marylebone, when Thorndyke said, as if by an after-thought: "You have your brother's latchkey. How would it be if we just took a glance at the flat? Have you time now?"

"I will make time," was the reply, "if you want to see the flat. I don't see what you could learn from inspecting it; but that is your affair. I am in your hands."

"I should like to look round the rooms," Thorndyke answered; and as our client assented, we approached a taxi-cab and entered while Pedley gave the driver the necessary directions. A quarter of an hour later we drew up opposite a tall block of buildings, and Mr. Pedley, having paid off the cab, led the way to the lift.

The dead man's flat was on the third floor, and, like the others, was distinguished only by the number on the door. Mr. Pedley inserted the key into the latch, and having opened the door, preceded us across the small lobby into the sitting-room.

"Ha!" he exclaimed, as he entered, "this solves your problem." As he spoke, he pointed to the table, on which lay a small bunch of keys, including a latch key similar to the one that he had shown us. "But," he continued, "it is rather extraordinary. It just shows what a very disturbed state his mind must have been in."

"Yes," Thorndyke agreed, looking critically about the room; "and as the latchkey is there, it raises the question whether the keys may have been out of his possession. Do you know what the various locked receptacles contain?"

"I know pretty well what is in the bureau; but as to the cupboard above it, I have never seen it open and don't know what he kept in it. I always assumed that he reserved it for his official papers. I will just see if anything seems to have been disturbed."

He unlocked and opened the flap of the old-fashioned bureau and pulled out the small drawers one after the other, examining the contents of each. Then he opened each of the larger drawers and turned over the various articles in them. As he closed the last one, he reported "Everything seems to be in order--cheque-book, insurance policy, a few share certificates, and so on. Nothing seems to have been touched. Now we will try the cupboard, though I don't suppose its contents would be of much interest to anyone but himself. I wonder which is the key."

He looked at the keyhole and made a selection from the bunch, but it was evidently the wrong key. He tried another and yet another with a like result, until he had exhausted the resources of the bunch.

"It is very remarkable," he said. "None of these keys seems to fit. I wonder if he kept this particular key locked up or hidden. It wasn't in the bureau. Will you try what you can do?"

He handed the bunch to Thorndyke, who tried all the keys in succession with the same result. None of them was the key belonging to the lock. At length, having tried them all, he inserted one and turned it as far as it would go. Then he gave a sharp pull; and immediately the door came open.

"Why, it was unlocked after all!" exclaimed Mr. Pedley. "And there is nothing in it. That is why there was no key on the bunch. Apparently he didn't use the cupboard."

Thorndyke looked critically at the single vacant shelf, drawing his finger along it in two places and inspecting his finger-tips. Then he turned his attention to the lock, which was of the kind that is screwed on the inside of the door, leaving the bolt partly exposed. He took the bolt in his fingers and pushed it out and then in again; and by the way it moved I could see that the spring was broken. On this he made no comment, but remarked "The cupboard has been in use pretty lately. You can see the trace of a largish volume--possibly a box-file--on the shelf. There is hardly any dust there whereas the rest of the shelf is fairly thickly coated However, that does not carry us very far; and the appearance of the rooms is otherwise quite normal."

"Quite," agreed Pedley. "But why shouldn't it be? You didn't suspect--"

"I was merely testing the suggestion offered by the absence of the keys," said Thorndyke. "By the way, have you communicated with the Foreign Office?"

"No," was the reply, "but I suppose I ought to. What had I better say to them?"

"I should merely state the facts in the first instance. But you can, if you like, say that I definitely reject the idea of suicide."

"I am glad to hear you say that," said Pedley. "Can I give any reasons for your opinion?"

"Not in the first place," replied Thorndyke. "I will consider the case and let you have a reasoned report in a day or two, which you can show to the Foreign Office and also to the insurance company."

Mr. Pedley looked as if he would have liked to ask some further questions, but as Thorndyke now made his way to the door, he followed in silence, pocketing the keys as we went out. He accompanied us down to the entry and there we left him, setting forth in the direction of South Kensington Station.

"It looked to me," said I, as soon as we were out of ear-shot, "as if that lock had been forced. What do you think?"

"Well," he answered, "locks get broken in ordinary use, but taking all the facts together, I think you are right. There are too many coincidences for reasonable probability. First, this man leaves his keys, including his latchkey, on the table, which is an. extraordinary thing to do. On that very occasion, he is found dead under inexplicable circumstances. Then, of all the locks in his rooms, the one which happens to be broken is the one of which the key is not on the bunch. That is a very suspicious group of facts."

It is," I agreed. "And if there is, as you say--though I can't imagine on what grounds--evidence of foul play, that makes it still more suspicious. But what is the next move? Have you anything in view?"

"The next move," he replied, "is to clear up the mystery of the dead man's movements on the day of his death. The railway receipt shows that on that day be travelled down somewhere into Essex. From that place, he took a long, cross-country journey of which the destination was a ditch by a lonely meadow in Buckinghamshire. The questions that we have to answer are, What was he doing in Essex? Why did he make that strange journey? Did he make it alone? and, if not, Who accompanied him?

"Now, obviously, the first thing to do is to locate that place in Essex; and when we have done that, to go down there and see if we can pick up any traces of the dead man."

"That sounds like a pretty vague quest," said I; "but if we fail, the police may be able to find out some thing. By the way, we want a new Bradshaw."

"An excellent suggestion, Jervis," said he. "I will get one as we go into the station."

A few minutes later, as we sat on a bench waiting for our train, he passed to me the open copy of Bradshaw, with the crumpled railway receipt.

"You see," said he, "it was apparently ' G.B.Hlt.,' and the fare from London was four and ninepence. Here is Great Buntingfield Halt, the fare to which is four and ninepence. That must be the place. At any rate, we will give it a trial. May I take it that you are coming to lend a hand? I shall start in good time to morrow morning."

I assented emphatically. Never had I been more completely in the dark than I was in this case, and seldom had I known Thorndyke to be more positive and confident. Obviously, he had something up his sleeve; and I was racked with curiosity as to what that some thing was.

On the following morning we made a fairly early start, and half-past ten found us seated in the train, looking out across a dreary waste of marshes, with the estuary of the Thames a mile or so distant. For the first time in my recollection Thorndyke had come unprovided with his inevitable "research case," but I noted that he had furnished himself with a botanist's vasculum--or tin collecting-case--and that his pocket bulged as if he had some other appliances concealed about his person. Also that he carried a walking-stick that was strange to me.

"This will be our destination, I think," he said, as the train slowed down; and sure enough it presently came to rest beside a little makeshift platform on which was displayed the name " Great Buntingfield Halt." We were the only passengers to alight, and the guard, having noted the fact, blew his whistle and dismissed the little station with a contemptuous wave of his flag.

Thorndyke lingered on the platform after the train had gone, taking a general survey of the country. Half a mile away to the north a small village was visible; while to the south the marshes stretched away to the river, their bare expanse unbroken save by a solitary building whose unredeemed hideousness proclaimed it a factory of some kind. Presently the station-master approached deferentially, and as we proffered our tickets, Thorndyke remarked: "You don't seem overburdened with traffic here."

"No, sir. You're right," was the emphatic reply. 'Tis a dead-alive place. Excepting the people at the Golomite Works and one now and then from the village, no one uses the halt. You're the first strangers I've seen for more than a month."

"Indeed," said Thorndyke. "But I think you are forgetting one. An acquaintance of mine came here last Tuesday--and by the same token, he hadn't got a ticket and had to pay his fare."

"Oh, I remember," the station-master replied. "You mean a gentleman with a scar on his cheek. But I don't count him as a stranger. He has been here before; I think he is connected with the works, as he always goes up their road."

"Do you happen to remember what time he came back?" Thorndyke asked.

"He didn't come back at all," was the reply. "I am sure of that, because I work the halt and level crossing by myself. I remember thinking it queer that he didn't come back, because the ticket that he had lost was a return. He must have gone back in the van belonging to the works--that one that you see coming towards the crossing."

As he spoke, he pointed to a van that was approaching down the factory road--a small covered van with the name "Golomite Works" painted, not on the cover, but on a board that was attached to it. The station- master walked towards the crossing to open the gates, and we followed; and when the van had passed, Thorndyke wished our friend "Good morning," and led the way along the road, looking about him with lively interest and rather with the air of one looking for something in particular.

We had covered about two-thirds of the distance to the factory when the road approached a wide ditch; and from the attention with which my friend regarded it, I suspected that this was the something for which he had been looking. It was, however, quite unapproachable, for it was bordered by a wide expanse of soft mud thickly covered with rushes and trodden deeply by cattle. Nevertheless, Thorndyke followed its margin, still looking about him keenly, until, about a couple of hundred yards from the factory, I observed a small decayed wooden staging or quay, apparently the remains of a vanished footbridge. Here Thorndyke halted and unbuttoning his coat, began to empty out his pockets, producing first the vasculum, then a small case containing three wide-mouthed bottles--both of which he deposited on the ground--and finally a sort of miniature landing- net, which he proceeded to screw on to the ferrule of his stick.

"I take it," said I, "that these proceedings are a blind to cover some sort of observations."

"Not at all," he replied. "We are engaged in the study of pond and ditch natural history, and a most fascinating and instructive study it is. The variety of forms is endless. This ditch, you observe, like the one at Bantree, is covered with a dense growth of duck-weed: but whereas that ditch was swarming with *succinea* here there is not a single *succinea* to be seen."

I grunted a sulky assent, and watched suspiciously as he filled the bottles with water from the ditch and then made a preliminary sweep with his net.

"Here is a trial sample," said he, holding the loaded net towards me. "Duck-weed, horn-weed, *Planorbis nautileus*, but no *succinea*. What do you think of it, Jervis?"

I looked distastefully at the repulsive mess, but yet with attention, for I realised that there was a meaning in his question. And then, suddenly, my attention sharpened. I picked out of the net a strand of dark green, plumy weed and examined it. "So this is horn-weed," I said. "Then it was a piece of horn-weed that Cyrus Pedley held grasped in his hand; and now I come to think of it, I don't remember seeing any horn-weed in the ditch at Bantree."

He nodded approvingly. "There wasn't any," said he.

"And these little ammonite-like shells are just like those that I noticed at the bottom of Dr. Parton's jar. But I don't remember seeing any in the Bantree ditch."

"There were none there," said he. "And the duck-weed?"

"Oh, well," I replied," duck-weed is duck-weed, and there's an end of it."

He chuckled aloud at my answer, and quoting: "A primrose by the river's brim A yellow primrose was to him," bestowed a part of the catch in the vasculum, then turned once more to the ditch and began to ply his net vigorously, emptying out each netful on the grass, looking it over quickly and then making a fresh sweep, dragging the net each time through the mud at the bottom. I watched him now with a new and very lively interest; for enlightenment was dawning, mingled with some self- contempt and much speculation as to how Thorndyke had got his start in this case.

But I was not the only interested watcher. At one of the windows of the factory I presently observed a man who seemed to be looking our way. After a few seconds' inspection he disappeared, to reappear almost immediately with a pair of field-glasses, through which he took a long look at us. Then he disappeared again, but in less than a minute I saw him emerge from a side door and advance hurriedly towards us.

"We are going to have a notice of ejectment served on us, I fancy," said I.

Thorndyke glanced quickly at the approaching stranger but continued to ply his net, working, as I noticed, methodically from left to right. When the man came within fifty yards he hailed us with a brusque inquiry as to what our business was. I went forward to meet him and, if possible, to detain him in conversation; but this plan failed, for he ignored me and bore straight down on Thorndyke.

"Now, then," said he, "what's the game? What are you doing here?"

Thorndyke was in the act of raising his net from the water, but he now suddenly let it fall to the bottom of the ditch while he turned to confront the stranger.

"I take it that you have some reason for asking," said he.

"Yes, I have," the other replied angrily and with a slight foreign accent that agreed with his appearance--he looked like a Slav of some sort. "This is private land. It belongs to the factory. I am the manager."

"The land is not enclosed," Thorndyke remarked.

"I tell you the land is private land," the fellow retorted excitedly. "You have no business here. I want to know what you are doing."

"My good sir," said Thorndyke, "there is no need to excite yourself. My friend and I are just collecting botanical and other specimens."

"How do I know that?" the manager demanded. He looked round suspiciously and his eye lighted on the vasculum. "What have you got in that thing?" he asked.

"Let him see what is in it," said Thorndyke, with a significant look at me.

Interpreting this as an instruction to occupy the man's attention for a few moments, I picked up the vasculum and placed myself so that he must turn his back to Thorndyke to look into it. I fumbled awhile with the catch, but at length opened the case and began to pick out the weed strand by strand. As soon as the stranger's back was turned Thorndyke raised his net and quickly picked out of it something which he slipped into his pocket. Then he advanced towards us, sorting out the contents of his net as he came.

"Well," he said, "you see we are just harmless naturalists. By the way, what did you think we were looking for?"

"Never mind what I thought," the other replied fiercely. "This is private land. You have no business here, and you have got to clear out."

"Very well," said Thorndyke. "As you please. There are plenty of other ditches." He took the vasculum and the case of bottles, and having put them in his pocket, unscrewed his net, wished the stranger "Good-morning," and turned back towards the station. The man stood watching us until we were near the level crossing, when he, too, turned back and retired to the factory.

"I saw you take something out of the net," said I. "What was it?"

He glanced back to make sure that the manager was out of sight. Then he put his hand in his pocket, drew it out closed, and suddenly opened it. In his palm lay a small gold dental plate with four teeth on it.

"My word!" I exclaimed; "this clenches the matter with a vengeance. That is certainly Cyrus Pedley's plate. It corresponds exactly to the description."

"Yes," he replied, "it is practically a certainty. Of course, it will have to be identified by the dentist who made it. But it is a foregone conclusion."

I reflected as we walked towards the station on the singular sureness with which Thorndyke had followed what was to me an invisible trail. Presently I said "What is puzzling me is how you got your start in this case. What gave you the first hint that it was homicide and not suicide or misadventure?"

"It was the old story, Jervis," he replied; "just a matter of observing and remembering apparently trivial details. Here, by the way, is a case in point."

He stopped and looked down at a set of tracks in the soft, earth road-- apparently those of the van which we had seen cross the line. I followed the direction of his glance and saw the clear impression of a Blakey's protector, preceded by that of a gash in the tyre and followed by that of a projecting lump.

"But this is astounding!" I exclaimed. "It is almost certainly the same track that we saw in Ponder's Road."

"Yes," he agreed. "I noticed it as we came along." He brought out his spring-tape and notebook, and handing the latter to me, stooped and measured the distances between the three impressions. I wrote them down as he called them out, and then we compared them with the note made in Ponder's Road. The measurements were identical, as were the relative positions of the impressions.

"This is an important piece of evidence," said he. "I wish we were able to take casts, but the notes will be pretty conclusive. And now," he continued as we resumed our progress towards the station, "to return to your question. Parton's evidence at the inquest proved that Cyrus Pedley was drowned in water which contained duck-weed. He produced a specimen and we both saw it. We saw the duck-weed in it and also two *Planorbis* shells. The presence of those two shells proved that the water in which he was drowned must have swarmed with them. We saw the body, and observed that one hand grasped a wisp of horn-weed. Then we went to view the ditch and we examined it. That was when I got, not a mere hint, but a crucial and conclusive fact. The ditch was covered with duck-weed, as we expected. But it was the wrong duck-weed."

"The wrong duck-weed!" I exclaimed. "Why, how many kinds of duck-weed are there?"

"There are four British species," he replied. "The Greater Duck-weed, the Lesser Duck-weed, the Thick Duck-weed, and the

Ivy-leaved Duckweed. Now the specimens in Parton's jar I noticed were the Greater Duck-weed, which is easily distinguished by its roots, which are multiple and form a sort of tassel. But the duck-weed on the Bantree ditch was the Lesser Duck weed, which is smaller than the other, but is especially distinguished by having only a single root. It is impossible to mistake one for the other.

"Here, then, was practically conclusive evidence of murder. Cyrus Pedley had been drowned in a pond or ditch. But not in the ditch in which his body was found. Therefore his dead body had been conveyed from some other place and put into this ditch. Such a proceeding furnishes prima facie evidence of murder. But as soon as the question was raised, there was an abundance of confirmatory evidence. There was no horn-weed or *Planorbis* shells in the ditch, but there were swarms of *succinea*, some of which would inevitably have been swallowed with the water. There was an obscure linear pressure mark on the arm of the dead man, just above the elbow: such a mark as might be made by a cord if a man were pinioned to render him helpless. Then the body would have had to be conveyed to this place in some kind of vehicle; and we found the traces of what appeared to be a motor-van, which had approached the cart-track on the wrong side of the road, as if to pull up there. It was a very conclusive mass of evidence; but it would have been useless but for the extraordinarily lucky chance that poor Pedley had lost his railway ticket and preserved the receipt; by which we were able to ascertain where he was on the day of his death and in what locality the murder was probably committed. But that is not the only way in which Fortune has favoured us. The station-master's information was, and will be, invaluable. Then it was most fortunate for us that there was only one ditch on the factory land; and that that ditch was accessible at only one point, which must have been the place where Pedley was drowned."

"The duck-weed in this ditch is, of course, the Greater Duck-weed?"

"Yes. I have taken some specimens as well as the horn-weed and shells."

He opened the vasculum and picked out one of the tiny plants, exhibiting the characteristic tassel of roots.

"I shall write to Parton and tell him to preserve the jar and the horn-weed if it has not been thrown away. But the duck-weed alone, produced in evidence, would be proof enough that Pedley was not drowned in the Bantree ditch; and the dental plate will show where he was drowned."

"Are you going to pursue the case any farther?" I asked.

"No," he replied. "I shall call at Scotland Yard on my way home and report what I have learned and what I can prove in court. Then I shall have finished with the case. The rest is for the police, and I imagine they won't have much difficulty. The circumstances seem to tell their own story. Pedley was employed by the Foreign Office, probably on some kind of secret service. I imagine that he discovered the existence of a gang of evil-doers--probably foreign revolutionaries, of whom we may assume that our friend the manager of the factory is one; that he contrived to associate himself with them and to visit the factory occasionally to ascertain what was made there besides Golomite--if Golomite is not itself an illicit product. Then I assume that he was discovered to be a spy, that he was lured down here; that he was pinioned and drowned some time on Tuesday night and his body put into the van and conveyed to a place miles away from the scene of his death, where it was deposited in a ditch apparently identical in character with that in which he was drowned. It was an extremely ingenious and well-thought-out plan. It seemed to have provided for every kind of inquiry, and it very narrowly missed being successful."

"Yes," I agreed. "But it didn't provide for Dr. John Thorndyke."

"It didn't provide for a searching examination of all the details," he replied; "and no criminal plan that I have ever met has done so. The completeness of the scheme is limited by the knowledge of the schemers, and, in practice, there is always something overlooked. In this case, the criminals were unlearned in the natural history of ditches."

Thorndyke's theory of the crime turned out to be substantially correct. The Golomite Works proved to be a factory where high explosives were made by a gang of cosmopolitan revolutionaries who were all known to the police. But the work of the latter was simplified by a detailed report which the dead man had deposited at his bank and which was discovered in time to enable the police to raid the factory and secure the whole gang. When once they were under lock and key, further information was forthcoming; for a charge of murder against them jointly soon produced King's Evidence sufficient to procure a conviction of the three actual perpetrators of the murder.

Mr. Ponting's Alibi

Thorndyke looked doubtfully at the pleasant-faced athletic-looking clergyman who had just come in, bearing Mr. Brodribb's card as an explanatory credential.

"I don't quite see," said he, "why Mr. Brodribb sent you to me. It seems to be a purely legal matter which he could have dealt with himself, at least as well as I can."

"He appeared to think otherwise," said the clergyman. (" The Revd. Charles Meade" was written on the card.)

At any rate," he added with a persuasive smile, "here I am, and I hope you are not going to send me away."

"I shouldn't offer that affront to my old friend Brodribb," replied Thorndyke, smiling in return; "so we may as well get to business, which, in the first place, involves the setting out of all the particulars. Let us begin with the lady who is the subject of the threats of which you spoke."

"Her name," said Mr. Meade, "is Miss Millicent Fawcett. She is a person of independent means, which she employs in works of charity. She was formerly a hospital sister, and she does a certain amount of voluntary work in the parish as a sort of district nurse. She has been a very valuable help to me and we have been close friends for several years; and I may add, as a very material fact, that she has consented to marry me in about two months' time. So that, you see, I am properly entitled to act on her behalf."

"Yes," agreed Thorndyke. "You are an interested party. And now, as to the threats. What do they amount to?"

"That," replied Meade," I can't tell you. I gathered quite by chance, from some words that she dropped, that she had been threatened. But she was unwilling to say more on the subject, as she did not take the matter seriously. She is not at all nervous. However, I told her I was taking advice; and I hope you will be able to extract more details from her. For my own part, I am decidedly uneasy."

"And as to the person or persons who have uttered the threats. Who are they? and out of what circumstances have the threats arisen?"

"The person is a certain William Ponting, who is Miss Fawcett's step-brother--if that is the right term. Her father married, as his second wife, a Mrs. Ponting, a widow with one son. This is the son. His mother died before Mr. Fawcett, and the latter, when he died, left his daughter, Millicent, sole heir to his property. That has always been a grievance to Ponting. But now he has another. Miss Fawcett made a will some years ago by which the bulk of her rather considerable property is left to two cousins, Frederick and James Barnett, the sons of her father's sister. A comparatively small amount goes to Ponting. When he heard this he was furious. He demanded a portion at least equal to the others, and has continued to make this demand from time to time. In fact, he has been extremely troublesome, and appears to be getting still more so. I gathered that the threats were due to her refusal to alter the will."

"But," said I, "doesn't he realise that her marriage will render that will null and void?"

"Apparently not," replied Meade; "nor, to tell the truth, did I realise it myself. Will she have to make a new will?"

"Certainly," I replied. "And as that new will may be expected to be still less favourable to him, that will presumably be a further grievance."

"One doesn't understand," said Thorndyke, "why he should excite himself so much about her will. What are their respective ages?"

"Miss Fawcett is thirty-six and Ponting is about forty."

"And what kind of man is he?" Thorndyke asked.

"A very unpleasant kind of man, I am sorry to say. Morose, rude, and violent-tempered. A spendthrift and a cadger. He has had quite a lot of money from Miss Fawcett--loans, which, of course, are never repaid. And he is none too industrious, though he has a regular job on the staff of a weekly paper. But he seems to be always in debt."

"We may as well note his address," said Thorndyke.

"He lives in a small flat in Bloomsbury--alone now, since he quarrelled with the man who used to share it with him. The address is 12 Borneo House, Devonshire Street."“

"What sort of terms is he on with the cousins, his rivals?"

"No sort of terms now," replied Meade. "They used to be great friends. So much so that he took his present flat to be near them--they live in the adjoining flat, number 12 Sumatra House. But since the trouble about the wills he is hardly on speaking terms with them."

"They live together, then?"

"Yes, Frederick and his wife and James, who is unmarried. They are rather a queer lot, too. Frederick is a singer on the variety stage, and James accompanies him on various instruments. But they are both sporting characters of a kind, especially James, who does a bit on the turf and engages in other odd activities. Of course, their musical habits are a grievance to Ponting. He is constantly making complaints of their disturbing him at his work."

Mr. Meade paused and looked wistfully at Thorndyke, who was making full notes of the conversation.

"Well," said the latter, "we seem to have got all the facts excepting the most important--the nature of the threats. What do you want us to do?"

"I want you to see Miss Fawcett--with me, if possible--and induce her to give you such details as would enable you to put a stop to the nuisance. You couldn't come to-night, I suppose? It is a beast of a night, but I would take you there in a taxi--it is only to Tooting Bec. What do you say?" he added eagerly, as Thorndyke made no objection. "We are sure to find her in, because her maid is away on a visit to her home and she is alone in the house."

Thorndyke looked reflectively at his watch.

"Half-past eight," he remarked, "and half an hour to get there. These threats are probably nothing but ill-temper. But we don't know. There may be some thing more serious behind them; and, in law as in medicine, prevention is better than a post-mortem. What do you say, Jervis?"

What could I say? I would much sooner have sat by the fire with a book than turn out into the murk of a November night. But I felt it necessary, especially as Thorndyke had evidently made up his mind.

Accordingly I made a virtue of necessity; and a couple of minutes later we had exchanged the cosy room for the chilly darkness of Inner Temple Lane, up which the gratified parson was speeding ahead to capture a taxi. At the top of the Lane we perceived him giving elaborate instructions to a taxi-driver as he held the door of the cab open; and Thorndyke, having carefully disposed of his research- case--which, to my secret amusement, he had caught up, from mere force of habit, as we started--took his seat, and Meade and I followed.

As the taxi trundled smoothly along the dark streets, Mr. Meade filled in the details of his previous sketch, and, in a simple, manly, unaffected way dilated upon his good fortune and the pleasant future that lay before him. It was not, perhaps, a romantic marriage, he admitted; but Miss Fawcett and he had been faithful friends for years, and faithful friends they would remain till death did them part. So he ran on, now gleefully, now with a note of anxiety, and we listened by no means unsympathetically, until at last the cab drew up at a small, unpretentious house, standing in its own little grounds in a quiet suburban road.

"She is at home, you see," observed Meade, pointing to a lighted ground-floor window. He directed the taxi-driver to wait for the return journey, and striding up the path, delivered a characteristic knock at the door. As this brought no response, he knocked again and rang the bell. But still there was no answer, though twice I thought I heard the sound of a bolt being either drawn or shot softly. Again Mr. Meade plied the knocker more vigorously, and pressed the push of the bell, which we could hear ringing loudly within.

"This is very strange," said Meade, in an anxious tone, keeping his thumb pressed on the bell-push. "She can't have gone out and left the electric light on. What had we better do?"

"We had better enter without more delay," Thorndyke replied. "There were certainly sounds from within. Is there a side gate?"

Meade ran off towards the side of the house, and Thorndyke and I glanced at the lighted window, which was slightly open at the top.

"Looks a bit queer," I remarked, listening at the letter-box.

Thorndyke assented gravely, and at this moment Meade returned, breathing hard.

"The side gate is bolted inside," said he; and at this I recalled the stealthy sound of the bolt that I had heard. "What is to be done?"

Without replying, Thorndyke handed me his research- case, stepped across to the window, sprang up on the sill, drew down the upper sash and disappeared between the curtains into the room. A moment later the street door opened and Meade and I entered the hall. We glanced through the open doorway into the lighted room, and I noticed a heap of needlework thrown hastily on the dining- table. Then Meade switched on the hall light, and Thorndyke walked quickly past him to the half-open door of the next room. Before entering, he reached in and switched on the light; and as he stepped into the room he partly closed the door behind him.

"Don't come in here, Meade!" he called out. But the parson's eye, like my own, had seen something before the door closed: a great, dark stain on the carpet just within the threshold. Regardless of the admonition, he pushed the door open and darted into the room. Following him, I saw him rush forward, fling his arms up wildly, and with a dreadful, strangled cry, sink upon his knees beside a low couch on which a woman was lying.

"Merciful God!" he gasped. "She is dead! Is she dead, doctor? Can nothing be done?"

Thorndyke shook his head. "Nothing," he said in a low voice. "She is dead."

Poor Meade knelt by the couch, his hands clutching at his hair and his eyes riveted on the dead face, the very embodiment of horror and despair.

God Almighty!" he exclaimed in the same strangled undertone. "How frightful! Poor, poor Millie! Dear, sweet friend!" Then suddenly--almost savagely--he turned to Thorndyke. " But it can't be, doctor! It is impossible--unbelievable. That, I mean!" and he pointed to the dead woman's right hand, which held an open razor.

Our poor friend had spoken my own thought. It was incredible that this refined, pious lady should have inflicted those savage wounds, that gaped scarlet beneath the waxen face. There, indeed, was the razor lying in her hand. But what was its testimony worth? My heart rejected it; but yet, unwillingly, I noted that the wounds seemed to support it; for they had been made from left to right, as they would have been if self-inflicted.

"It is hard to believe," said Thorndyke, "but there is only one alternative. Someone should acquaint the police at once."

"I will go," exclaimed Meade, starting up. "I know the way and the cab is there." He looked once more with infinite pity and affection at the dead woman. "Poor, sweet girl!" he murmured. "If we can do no more for you, we can defend your memory from calumny and call upon the God of Justice to right the innocent and punish the guilty."

With these words and a mute farewell to his dead friend, he hurried from the room, and immediately afterwards we heard the street door close.

As he went out, Thorndyke's manner changed abruptly. He had been deeply moved--as who would not have been--by this awful tragedy that had in a moment shattered the happiness of the genial, kindly parson. Now he turned to me with a face set and stern. "This is an abominable affair, Jervis," he said in an ominously quiet voice.

"You reject the suggestion of suicide, then?" said I, with a feeling of relief that surprised me.

"Absolutely," he replied. "Murder shouts at us from everything that meets our eye. Look at this poor woman, in her trim nurse's dress, with her unfinished needlework lying on the table in the next room and that preposterous razor loose in her limp hand. Look at the savage wounds. Four of them, and the first one mortal. The great bloodstain by the door, the great bloodstain on her dress from the neck to the feet. The gashed collar, the cap-string cut right through. Note that the bleeding had practically ceased when she lay down. That is a group of visible facts that is utterly inconsistent with the idea of suicide. But we are wasting time. Let us search the premises thoroughly. The murderer has pretty certainly got away, but as he was in the house when we arrived, any traces will be quite fresh."

As he spoke he took his electric lamp from the research- case and walked to the door.

"We can examine this room later," he said, "but we had better look over the house. If you will stay by the stairs and watch the front and back doors, I will look through the upper rooms."

He ran lightly up the stairs while I kept watch below, but he was absent less than a couple of minutes.

"There is no one there," he reported, "and as there is no basement we will just look at this floor and then examine the grounds."

After a rapid inspection of the ground-floor rooms, including the kitchen, we went out by the back door, which was unbolted, and inspected the grounds. These consisted of a largish garden with a small orchard at the side. In the former we could discover no traces of any kind, but at the end of the path that crossed the orchard we came an a possible clue. The orchard was enclosed by a five-foot fence, the top of which bristled with hooked nails; and at the point opposite to the path, Thorndyke's lantern brought into view one or two wisps of cloth caught on the hooks.

"Someone has been over here," said Thorndyke, but as this is an orchard, there is nothing remarkable in the fact. However, there is no fruit on the trees now, and the cloth looks fairly fresh. There are two kinds, you notice: a dark blue and a black and white mixture of some kind."

"Corresponding, probably, to the coat and trousers," I suggested.

"Possibly," he agreed, taking from his pocket a couple of the little seed-envelopes of which he always carried a supply. Very delicately he picked the tiny wisps of cloth from the hooks and bestowed each kind in a separate envelope. Having pocketed these, he leaned over the fence and threw the light of his lamp along the narrow lane or alley that divided the orchard from the adjoining premises. It was ungravelled and covered with a growth of rank grass, which suggested that it was little frequented. But immediately below was a small patch of bare earth, and on this was a very distinct impression of a foot, covering several less distinct prints.

"Several people have been over here at different times," I remarked.

"Yes," Thorndyke agreed. "But that sharp foot print belongs to the last one over, and he is our concern. We had better not confuse the issues by getting over ourselves. We will mark the spot and explore from the other end." He laid his handkerchief over the top of the fence and we then went back to the house.

"You are going to take a plaster cast, I suppose?" said I; and as he assented, I fetched the research-case from the drawing-room.

Then we fixed the catch of the front-door latch and went out, drawing the door to after us.

We found the entrance to the alley about sixty yards from the gate, and entering it, walked slowly forwards, scanning the ground as we went. But the bright lamplight showed nothing more than the vague marks of trampling feet on the grass until we came to the spot marked by the handkerchief on the fence.

It is a pity," I remarked, "that this footprint has obliterated the others."

"On the other hand," he replied, "this one, which is the one that interests us, is remarkably clear and characteristic: a circular heel and a rubber sole of a recognisable pattern mended with a patch of cement paste. It is a footprint that could be identified beyond a doubt."

As he was speaking, he took from the research-case the water-bottle, plaster-tin, rubber mixing-bowl and spoon, and a piece of canvas with which to "reinforce" the cast. Rapidly, he mixed a bowlful--extra thick, so that it should set quickly and hard--dipped the canvas into it, poured the remainder into the footprint, and laid the canvas on it.

I will get you to stay here, Jervis," said he, "until the plaster has set. I want to examine the body rather more thoroughly before the police arrive, particularly the back."

"Why the back?" I asked.

"Did not the appearance of the body suggest to you the advisability of examining the back?" he asked, and then, without waiting for a reply, he went off, leaving the inspection-lamp with me.

His words gave me matter for profound thought during my short vigil. I recalled the appearance of the dead woman very vividly--indeed, I am not likely ever to forget it--and I strove to connect that appearance with his desire to examine the back of the corpse. But there seemed to be no connection at all. The visible injuries were in front, and I had seen nothing to suggest the existence of any others. From time to time I tested the condition of the plaster, impatient to rejoin my colleague but fearful of cracking the thin cast by raising it prematurely. At length the plaster seemed to be hard enough, and trusting to the strength of the canvas, I prised cautiously at the edge, when, to my relief, the brittle plate came up safely and I lifted it clear. Wrapping it carefully in some spare rag, I packed it in the research-case, and then, taking this and the lantern, made my way back to the house.

When I had let down the catch and closed the front door, I went to the drawing-room, where I found Thorndyke stooping over the dark stain at the threshold and scanning the floor as if in search of something. I re ported the completion of the cast and then asked him what he was looking for.

"I am looking for a button," he replied. "There is one missing from the back; the one to which the collar was fastened."

"Is it of any importance?" I asked.

"It is important to ascertain when and where it became detached," he replied. "Let us have the inspection- lamp."

I gave him the lamp, which he placed on the floor, turning it so that its beam of light travelled along the surface. Stooping to follow the light, I scrutinised the floor minutely but in vain.

"It may not be here at all," said I; but at that moment the bright gleam, penetrating the darkness under a cabinet, struck a small object close to the wall. In a moment I had thrown myself prone on the carpet, and reaching under the cabinet, brought forth a largish mother-of-pearl button.

"You notice," said Thorndyke, as he examined it, "that the cabinet is near the window, at the opposite end of the room to the couch. But we had better see that it is the right button."

He walked slowly towards the couch, still stooping and searching the floor with the light. The corpse, I noticed, had been turned on its side, exposing the back and the displaced collar. Through the strained button-hole of the latter Thorndyke passed the button without difficulty.

"Yes," he said, "that is where it came from. You will notice that there is a similar one in front. By the way," he continued, bringing the lamp close to the surface of the grey serge dress, "I picked off one or two hairs--animal hairs; cat and dog they looked like. Here are one or two more. Will you hold the lamp while I take them off?"

"They are probably from some pets of hers," I remarked, as he picked them off with his forceps and deposited them in one of the invaluable seed-envelopes. "Spinsters are a good deal addicted to pets, especially cats and dogs."

"Possibly," he replied. "But I could see none in front, where you would expect to find them, and there seem to be none on the carpet. Now let us replace the body as we found it and just have a look at our material before the police arrive. I expected them here before this."

We turned the body back into its original position, and taking the research-case and the lamp, went into the dining-room. Here Thorndyke rapidly set up the little travelling microscope, and bringing forth the seed- envelopes, began to prepare slides from the contents of some while I prepared the others. There was time only for a very hasty examination, which Thorndyke made as soon as the specimens were mounted.

"The clothing," he reported, with his eye at the microscope, "is woollen in both cases. Fairly good quality. The one a blue serge, apparently indigo dyed; the other a mixture of black and white, no other colour. Probably a fine tabby or a small shepherd's plaid."

"Serge coat and shepherd's plaid trousers," I suggested. "Now see what the hairs are." I handed him the slide, on which I had roughly mounted the collection in oil of lavender, and he placed it on the stage.

"There are three different kinds of hairs here," he reported, after a rapid inspection. "Some are obviously from a cat--a smoky Persian. Others are long, rather fine tawny hairs from a dog. Probably a Pekinese. But there are two that I can't quite place. They look like monkey's hairs, but they are a very unusual colour. There is a perceptible greenish tint, which is extremely uncommon in mammalian hairs. But I hear the taxi approaching. We need not be expansive to the local police as to what we have observed. This will probably be a case for the C.I.D."

I went out into the hall and opened the door as Meade came up the path, followed by two men; and as the latter came into the light, I was astonished to recognise in one of them our old friend, Detective-Superintendent Miller, the other being, apparently, the station superintendent.

"We have kept Mr. Meade a long time," said Miller, "but we knew you were here, so the time wouldn't be wasted. Thought it best to get a full statement before we inspected the premises. How do, doctor?" he added, shaking hands with Thorndyke. "Glad to see you here. I suppose you have got all the facts. I understood so from Mr. Meade."

"Yes," replied Thorndyke, "we have all the antecedents of the case, and we arrived within a few minutes of the death of the deceased."

"Ha!" exclaimed Miller. "Did you? And I expect you have formed an opinion on the question as to whether the injuries were self-inflicted?"

"I think," said Thorndyke," that it would be best to act on the assumption that they were not--and to act promptly."

"Precisely," Miller agreed emphatically. "You mean that we had better find out at once where a certain person was at--What time did you arrive here?"

"It was two minutes to nine when the taxi stopped," replied Thorndyke; "and, as it is now only twenty-five minutes to ten, we have good time if Mr. Meade can spare us the taxi. I have the address."

"The taxi is waiting for you," said Mr. Meade, "and the man has been paid for both journeys. I shall stay here in case the superintendent wants anything." He shook our hands warmly, and as we bade him farewell and noted the dazed, despairing expression and lines of grief that had already eaten into the face that had been so blithe and hopeful, we both thought bitterly of the few fatal minutes that had made us too late to save the wreckage of his life.

We were just turning away when Thorndyke paused and again faced the clergyman. "Can you tell me," he asked, "whether Miss Fawcett had any pets? Cats, dogs, or other animals?"

Meade looked at him in surprise, and Superintendent Miller seemed to prick up his ears. But the former answered simply: "No. She was not very fond of animals; she reserved her affections for men and women."

Thorndyke nodded gravely, and picking up the research-case walked slowly out of the room, Miller and I following.

As soon as the address had been given to the driver and we had taken our seats in the taxi, the superintendent opened the examination-in-chief.

"I see you have got your box of magic with you, doctor," he said, cocking his eye at the research-case. "Any luck?"

"We have secured a very distinctive footprint," replied Thorndyke, "but it may have no connection with the case."

"I hope it has," said Miller. "A good cast of a footprint which you can let the jury compare with the boot is first-class evidence." He took the cast, which I had produced from the research-case, and turning it over tenderly and gloatingly, exclaimed: "Beautiful! beautiful! Absolutely distinctive! There can't be another exactly like it in the world. It is as good as a fingerprint. For the Lord's sake take care of it. It means a conviction if we can find the boot."

The superintendent's efforts to engage Thorndyke in discussion were not very successful, and the conversational brunt was borne by me. For we both knew my colleague too well to interrupt him if he was disposed to be meditative. And such was now his disposition. Looking at him as he sat in his corner, silent but obviously wrapped in thought, I knew that he was mentally sorting out the data and testing the hypotheses that they yielded.

"Here we are," said Miller, opening the door as the taxi stopped. "Now what are we going to say? Shall I tell him who I am?"

"I expect you will have to," replied Thorndyke, "if you want him to let us in."

"Very well," said Miller. "But I shall let you do the talking, because I don't know what you have got up your sleeve."

Thorndyke's prediction was verified literally. In response to the third knock, with an obbligato accompaniment on the bell, wrathful footsteps-- I had no idea footsteps could be so expressive--advanced rapidly along the lobby, the door was wrenched open--but only for a few inches--and an angry, hairy face appeared in the opening.

"Now then," the hairy person demanded, "what the deuce do you want?"

"Are you Mr. William Pouting?" the superintendent inquired.

"What the devil is that to do with you?" was the genial answer--in the Scottish mode.

"We have business," Miller began persuasively.

"So have I," the presumable Ponting replied, "and mine won't wait."

"But our business is very important," Miller urged.

"So is mine," snapped Ponting, and would have shut the door but for Miller's obstructing foot, at which he kicked viciously, but with unsatisfactory results, as he was shod in light slippers, whereas the superintendent's boots were of constabulary solidity.

"Now, look here," said Miller, dropping his conciliatory manner very completely, "you'd better stop this nonsense. I am a police officer, and I am going to come in"; and with this he inserted a massive shoulder and pushed the door open.

"Police officer, are you?" said Ponting. "And what might your business be with me?"

"That is what I have been waiting to tell you," said Miller. "But we don't want to do our talking here."

"Very well," growled Panting. "Come in. But understand that I am busy. I've been interrupted enough this evening."

He led the way into a rather barely furnished room with a wide bay-window in which was a table fitted with a writing-slope and lighted by an electric standard lamp. A litter of manuscript explained the nature of his business and his unwillingness to receive casual visitors. He sulkily placed three chairs, and then, seating himself, glowered at Thorndyke and me.

"Are they police officers, too?" he demanded.

"No," replied Miller, "they are medical gentlemen. Perhaps you had better explain the matter, doctor," he added, addressing Thorndyke, who thereupon opened the proceedings.

"We have called," said he, "to inform you that Miss Millicent Fawcett died suddenly this evening."

"The devil!" exclaimed Panting. "That's sudden with a vengeance. What time did this happen?"

"About a quarter to nine."

"Extraordinary!" muttered Ponting. "I saw her only the day before yesterday, and she seemed quite well then. What did she die of?"

"The appearances," replied Thorndyke, "suggest suicide."

"Suicide!" gasped Ponting. "Impossible! I can't believe it. Do you mean to tell me she poisoned herself?"

"No," said Thorndyke, "it was not poison. Death was caused by injuries to the throat inflicted with a razor."

"Good God!" exclaimed Ponting. "What a horrible thing! But," he added, after a pause, "I can't believe she did it herself, and I don't. Why should she commit suicide? She was quite happy, and she was just going to be married to that mealy-faced parson. And a razor, too! How do you suppose she came by a razor? Women don't shave. They smoke and drink and swear, but they haven't taken to shaving yet. I don't believe it. Do you?"

He glared ferociously at the superintendent who replied: "I am not sure that I do. There's a good deal in what you've just said, and the same objections bad occurred to us. But you see, if she didn't do it herself, someone else must have done it, and we should like to find out who that someone is. So we begin by ascertaining where any possible persons may have been at a quarter to nine this evening."

Ponting smiled like an infuriated cat. "So you think me a possible person, do you?" said he.

"Everyone is a possible person," Miller replied blandly, "especially when he is known to have uttered threats."

The reply sobered Panting considerably. For a few moments he sat, looking reflectively at the superintendent; then, in comparatively quiet tones, he said: "I have been working here since six o'clock. You can see the stuff for yourself, and I can prove that it has been written since six."

The superintendent nodded, but made no comment, and Ponting gazed at him fixedly, evidently thinking hard. Suddenly he broke into a harsh laugh.

"What is the joke?" Miller inquired stolidly.

"The joke is that I have got another alibi--a very complete one. There are compensations in every evil. I told you I had been interrupted in my work already this evening. It was those fools next door, the Barnetts-- cousins of mine. They are musicians, save the mark! Variety stage, you know. Funny songs and jokes for mental defectives. Well, they practise their infernal ditties in their rooms, and the row comes into mine, and an accursed nuisance it is. However, they have agreed not to practise on Thursdays and Fridays--my busy nights--and usually they don't. But to-night, just as I was in the thick of my writing, I suddenly heard the most unholy din; that idiot, Fred

Barnett, bawling one of his imbecile songs--'When the pigs their wings have folded,' and balderdash of that sort--and the other donkey accompanying him on the clarinet, if you please! I stuck it for a minute or two. Then I rushed round to their flat and raised Cain with the bell and knocker. Mrs. Fred opened the door, and I told her what I thought of it. Of course she was very apologetic, said they had forgotten that it was Thursday and promised that he would make her husband stop. And I suppose she did, for by the time I got back to my rooms the row had ceased. I could have punched the whole lot of them into a jelly, but it was all for the best as it turns out."

"What time was it when you went round there?" asked Miller.

"About five minutes past nine," replied Ponting. The church bell had struck nine when the row began."

"Hm!" grunted Miller, glancing at Thorndyke. Well, that is all we wanted to know, so we need not keep you from your work any longer."

He rose, and being let out with great alacrity, stumped down the stairs, followed by Thorndyke and me. As we came out into the street, he turned to us with a deeply disappointed expression.

Well," he exclaimed, "this is a suck-in. I was in hopes that we had pounced on our quarry before he had got time to clear away the traces. And now we've got it all to do. You can't get round an alibi of that sort."

I glanced at Thorndyke to see how he was taking this unexpected check. He was evidently puzzled, and I could see by the expression of concentration in his face that he was trying over the facts and inferences in new combinations to meet this new position. Probably he had noticed, as I had, that Ponting was wearing a tweed suit, and that therefore the shreds of clothing from the fence could not be his unless he had changed. But the alibi put him definitely out of the picture, and, as Miller had said, we now had nothing to give us a lead.

Suddenly Thorndyke came out of his reverie and addressed the superintendent.

"We had better put this alibi on the basis of ascertained fact. It ought to be verified at once. At present we have only Ponting's unsupported statement."

"It isn't likely that he would risk telling a lie," Miller replied gloomily.

"A man who is under suspicion of murder will risk a good deal," Thorndyke retorted, "especially if he is guilty. I think we ought to see Mrs. Barnett before there is any opportunity of collusion."

"There has been time for collusion already," said Miller. "Still, you are quite right, and I see there is a light in their sitting-room, if that is it, next to Ponting's. Let us go up and settle the matter now. I shall leave you to examine the witness and say what you think it best to say."

We entered the building and ascended the stairs to the Barnetts' flat, where Miller rang the bell and executed a double knock. After a short interval the door was opened and a woman looked out at us inquisitively.

"Are you Mrs. Frederick Barnett?" Thorndyke inquired. The woman admitted her identity in a tone of some surprise, and Thorndyke explained: "We have called to make a few inquiries concerning your neighbour, Mr. Ponting, and also about certain matters relating to your family. I am afraid it is a rather unseasonable hour for a visit, but as the affair is of some importance and time is an object, I hope you will overlook that."

Mrs. Barnett listened to this explanation with a puzzled and rather suspicious air. After a few moments' hesitation, she said: "I think you had better see my husband, if you will wait here a moment I will go and tell him." With this, she pushed the door to, without actually closing it, and we heard her retire along the lobby, presumably to the sitting-room. For, during the short colloquy, I had observed a door at the end of the lobby, partly open, through which I could see the end of a table covered with a red cloth.

The "moment" extended to a full minute, and the superintendent began to show signs of impatience.

"I don't see why you didn't ask her the simple question straight out," he said, and the same question had occurred to me. But at this point footsteps were heard approaching, the door opened, and a man confronted us, holding the door open with his left hand, his right being wrapped in a handkerchief. He looked suspiciously from one to the other of us, and asked stiffly: "What is it that you want to know? And would you mind telling me who you are?"

"My name is Thorndyke," was the reply. "I am the legal adviser of the Reverend Charles Meade, and these two gentlemen are interested parties. I want to know what you can tell me of Mr. Ponting's recent movements-- to-day, for instance. When did you last see him?"

The man appeared to be about to refuse any conversation, but suddenly altered his mind, reflected for a few moments, and then replied: "I saw him from my window at his--they are bay- windows--about half-past eight. But my wife saw him later than that. If you will come in she can tell you the time exactly." He led the way along the lobby with an obviously puzzled air. But he was not more puzzled than I, or than Miller, to judge by the bewildered glance that the superintendent cast at me, as he followed our host along the lobby. I was still meditating on Thorndyke's curiously indirect methods when the sitting- room door was opened; and then I got a minor surprise of another kind. When I had last looked into the room, the table had been covered by a red cloth. It was now bare; and when we entered the room I saw that the red cover had been thrown over a side table, on which was some bulky and angular object. Apparently it had been thought desirable to conceal that object, whatever it was, and as we took our seats beside the bare table, my mind was busy with conjectures as to what that object could be.

Mr. Barnett repeated Thorndyke's question to his wife, adding: "I think it must have been a little after nine when Ponting came round. What do you say?"

"Yes," she replied, "it would be, for I heard it strike nine just before you began your practice, and he came a few minutes after."

"You see," Barnett explained, "I am a singer, and my brother, here, accompanies me on various instruments, and of course we have to practise. But we don't practise on the nights when Ponting is busy--Thursdays and Fridays--as he said that the music disturbed him. To-night, however, we made a little mistake. I happen to have got a new song that I am anxious to get ready--it has an illustrative accompaniment on the clarinet, which my brother will play. We were so much taken up with the new song that we all forgot what day of the week it was, and started to have a good practice. But before we had got through the first verse, Ponting came round, battering at the door like a madman. My wife went out and pacified him, and of course we shut down for the evening."

While Mr. Barnett was giving his explanation, I looked about the room with vague curiosity. Somehow--I cannot tell exactly how--I was sensible of something queer in the atmosphere of this place; of a certain indefinite sense of tension. Mrs. Barnett looked pale and flurried. Her husband, in spite of his volubility, seemed ill at ease, and the brother, who sat huddled in an easy-chair, nursing a dark-coloured Persian cat. stared into the fire, and neither moved nor spoke. And again I looked at the red table-cloth and wondered what it covered.

"By the way," said Barnett, after a brief pause, "what is the point of these inquiries of yours? About Ponting, I mean. What does it matter to you where he was this evening?"

As he spoke, he produced a pipe and tobacco-pouch. and proceeded to fill the former, holding it in his bandaged right hand and filling it with his left. The facility with which he did this suggested that he was left-handed, an inference that was confirmed by the ease with which he struck the match with his left hand, and by the fact that he wore a wrist-watch on his right wrist.

"Your question is a perfectly natural one," said Thorndyke. "The answer to it is that a very terrible thing has happened. Miss Millicent Fawcett, who is, I think, a connection of yours, met her death this evening under circumstances of grave suspicion. She died, either by her own hand or by the hand of a murderer, a few minutes before nine o'clock. Hence it has become I necessary to ascertain the whereabouts at that time of any persons on whom suspicion might reasonably fall."

"Good God!" exclaimed Barnett. "What a shocking thing!"

The exclamation was followed by a deep silence, amidst which I could hear the barking of a dog in an adjacent room, the unmistakable sharp, treble yelp of a Pekinese. And again I seemed to be aware of a strange sense of tension in the occupants of this room. On hearing Thorndyke's answer, Mrs. Barnett had turned deadly pale and let her head fall forward on her hand. Her husband had sunk on to a chair, and he, too, looked pale and deeply shocked, while the brother continued to stare silently into the fire.

At this moment Thorndyke astonished me by an exhibition of what seemed-- under the tragic circumstances--the most outrageous bad manners and bad taste. Rising from his chair with his eyes fixed on a print which hung on the wall above the red-covered table, he said:

"That looks like one of Cameron's etchings," and forthwith stepped across the room to examine it, resting his hand, as he leaned forward, on the object covered by the cloth.

"Mind where you are putting your hand, sir!" Fred Barnett called out, springing to his feet.

Thorndyke looked down at his hand, and deliberately raising a corner of the cloth, looked under. "There is no harm done," he remarked quietly, letting the cloth drop; and with another glance at the print, he went back to his chair.

Once more a deep silence fell upon the room, and I had a vague feeling that the tension had increased. Mrs. Barnett was as white as a ghost and seemed to catch at her breath. Her, husband watched her with a wild, angry expression and smoked furiously, while the superintendent--also conscious of something abnormal in the atmosphere of the room--looked furtively from the woman to the man and from him to Thorndyke.

Yet again in the silence the shrill barking of the Pekinese dog broke out, and somehow that sound connected itself in my mind with the Persian cat that dozed on the knees of the immovable man by the fire. I looked at the cat and at the man, and even as I looked, I was startled by a most extraordinary apparition. Above the man's shoulder, slowly rose a little round head like the head of a diminutive, greenish-brown man. Higher and higher the tiny monkey raised itself, resting on its little hands to peer at the strangers. Then, with sudden coyness, like a shy baby, it popped down out of sight.

I was thunderstruck. The cat and the dog I had noted merely as a curious coincidence. But the monkey--and such an unusual monkey, too--put coincidences out of the question. I stared at the man in positive stupefaction. Somehow that man was connected with that unforgettable figure lying upon the couch miles away. But how? When that deed of horror was doing, he had been here in this very room. Yet, in some way, he had been concerned in it. And suddenly a suspicion dawned upon me that Thorndyke was waiting for the actual perpetrator to arrive.

"It is a most ghastly affair," Barnett repeated presently in a husky voice. Then, after a pause, he asked: "Is there any sort of evidence as to whether she killed herself or was killed by somebody else?"

"I think that my friend, here, Detective-Superintendent Miller, has decided that she was murdered." He looked at the bewildered superintendent, who replied with an inarticulate grunt.

"And is there any clue as to who the--the murderer may be? You spoke of suspected persons just now."

"Yes," replied Thorndyke, "there is an excellent clue, if it can only be followed up. We found a most unmistakable footprint; and what is more, we took a plaster cast of it. Would you like to see the cast?"

Without waiting for a reply, he opened the research- case and took out the cast, which he placed in my hands.

"Just take it round and show it to them," he said.

The superintendent had witnessed Thorndyke's amazing proceedings with an astonishment that left him speechless. But now he sprang to his feet, and, as I walked round the table, he pressed beside me to guard the precious cast from possible injury. I laid it carefully down on the table, and as the light fell on it obliquely, it presented a most striking appearance--that of a snow- white boot-sole on which the unshapely patch, the circular heel, and the marks of wear were clearly visible.

The three spectators gathered round, as near as the superintendent would let them approach, and I observed them closely, assuming that this incomprehensible move of Thorndyke's was a device to catch one or more of them off their guard. Fred Barnett looked at the cast stolidly enough, though his face had gone several shades paler, but Mrs. Barnett stared at it with starting eyeballs and dropped jaw--the very picture of horror and dismay. As to James Barnett, whom I now saw clearly for the first time, he stood behind the woman with a singularly scared and haggard face, and his eyes riveted on the white boot-sole. And now I could see that he wore a suit of blue serge and that the front both of his coat and waistcoat were thickly covered with the shed hairs of his pets.

There was something very uncanny about this group of persons gathered around that accusing footprint, all as still and rigid as statues and none uttering a sound. But something still more uncanny followed. Suddenly the deep silence of the room was shattered by the shrill notes of a clarinet, and a brassy voice burst forth:

"When the pigs their wings have folded

And the cows are in their nest--"

We all spun round in amazement, and at the first glance the mystery of the crime was solved. There stood Thorndyke with the red table-cover at his feet, and at his side, on the small table, a massively-constructed phonograph of the kind used in offices for dictating letters, but fitted with a convoluted metal horn in place of the rubber ear-tubes.

A moment of astonished silence was succeeded by a wild confusion. Mrs. Barnett uttered a piercing shriek and fell back on to a chair, her husband broke away and rushed at Thorndyke, who instantly gripped his wrist and pinioned him, while the superintendent, taking in the situation at a glance, fastened on the unresisting James and forced him down into a chair. I ran round, and having stopped the machine--for the preposterous song was hideously incongruous with the tragedy that was enacting--went to Thorndyke's assistance and helped him to remove his prisoner from the neighbourhood of the instrument.

"Superintendent Miller," said Thorndyke, still maintaining a hold on his squirming captive, " I believe you are a justice of the peace?"

"Yes," was the reply, "ex officio."

"Then," said Thorndyke, "I accuse these three persons of being concerned in the murder of Miss Millicent Fawcett; Frederick Barnett as the principal who actually committed the murder, James Barnett as having aided him by holding the arms of the deceased, and Mrs. Barnett as an accessory before the fact in that she worked this phonograph for the purpose of establishing a false alibi."

"I knew nothing about it!" Mrs. Barnett shrieked hysterically. "They never told me why they wanted me to work the thing."

"We can't go into that now," said Miller. "You will be able to make your defence at the proper time and place. Can one of you go for assistance or must I blow my whistle?"

"You had better go, Jervis," said Thorndyke. "I can hold this man until reinforcements arrive. Send a constable up and then go on to the station. And leave the outer door ajar."

I followed these directions, and having found the police station, presently returned to the flat with four constables and a sergeant in two taxis.

When the prisoners had been removed, together with the three animals-- the latter in charge of a zoophilist constable--we searched the bedrooms. Frederick Barnett had changed his clothing completely, but in a locked drawer--the lock of which Thorndyke picked neatly, to the superintendent's undisguised admiration--we found the discarded garments, including a pair of torn shepherd's plaid trousers, covered with blood stains, and a new, empty razor-case. These things, together with the wax cylinder of the phonograph, Miller made up into a neat parcel and took away with him.

"Of course," said I, as we walked homewards, "the general drift of this case is quite obvious. But it seemed to me that you went to the Barnetts' flat with a definite purpose already formed, and with a definite suspicion in your mind. Now, I don't see how you came to suspect the Barnetts."

I think you will," he replied," if you will recall the incidents in their order from the beginning, including poor Meade's preliminary statement. To begin with the appearances of the body: the suggestion of suicide was transparently false. To say nothing of its incongruity with the character and circumstances of the deceased and the very unlikely weapon used, there were the gashed collar and the cut cap-string. As you know, it is a well-established rule that suicides do not damage their clothing. A man who cuts his own throat doesn't cut his collar. He takes it off. He removes all obstructions. Naturally, for he wishes to complete the act as easily and quickly as possible, and he has time for preparation. But the murderer must take things as he finds them and execute his purpose as best he can.

"But further; the wounds were inflicted near the door, but the body was on the couch at the other end of the room. We saw, from the absence of bleeding, that she was dying--in fact, apparently dead--when she lay down. She must therefore have been carried to the couch after the wounds were inflicted.

"Then there were the blood-stains. They were all in front, and the blood had run down vertically. Then she must have been standing upright while the blood was flowing. Now there were four wounds, and the first one was mortal, it divided the common carotid artery and the great veins. On receiving that wound she would ordinarily have fallen down. But she did not fall, or there would have been a blood-stain across the neck. Why did she not fall? The obvious suggestion was that someone was holding her up. This suggestion was confirmed by the absence of cuts on her hands--which would certainly have been cut if someone bad not been holding them. It was further confirmed by the rough crumpling of the collar at the back: so rough that the button was torn off. And we found that button near the door.

"Further, there were the animal hairs. They were on the back only. There were none on the front--where they would have been if derived from the animals--or anywhere else. And we learned that she kept no animals. All these appearances pointed to the presence of two persons, one of whom stood behind her and held her arms while the other stood in front and committed the murder. The cloth on the fence supported this view, being probably derived from two different pairs of trousers. The character of the wounds made it nearly certain that the murderer was left-handed.

"While we were returning in the cab, I reflected on these facts and considered the case generally. First, what was the motive? There was nothing to suggest robbery, nor was it in the least like a robber's crime. What other motive could there be? Well, here was a comparatively rich woman who had made a will in favour of certain persons, and she was going to be married. On her marriage the will would automatically become void, and she was not likely to make another will so favourable to those persons. Here, then, was a possible motive, and that motive applied to Ponting, who had actually uttered threats and was obviously suspect.

"But, apart from those threats, Ponting was not the principal suspect, for he benefited only slightly under the will. The chief beneficiaries were the Barnetts, and Miss Fawcett's death would benefit them, not only by securing the validity of the will, but by setting the will into immediate operation. And there were two of them. They therefore fitted the circumstances better than Ponting did. And when we came to interview Ponting, he went straight out of the picture. His manuscript would probably have cleared him--with his editor's confirmation. But the other alibi was conclusive.

"What instantly struck me, however, was that Ponting's alibi was also an alibi for the Barnetts. But there was this difference: Ponting had been seen; the Barnetts had only been heard. Now, it has often occurred to me that a very effective false alibi could be worked with a gramophone or a phonograph--especially with one on which one can make one's own records. This idea now recurred to me; and at once it was supported by the appearance of an arranged effect. Ponting was known to be at work. It was practically certain that a blast of 'music' would bring him out. Then he would be available, if necessary, as a witness to prove an alibi. It seemed to be worth while to investigate.

"When we came to the flat we encountered a man with an injured hand--the right, it would have been more striking if it had been his left. But it presently turns out that be is left-handed; which is still more striking as a coincidence. This man is extraordinarily ready to answer questions which most persons would have refused to answer at all. Those answers contain the alibi.

"Then there was the incident of the table--I think you noticed it. That cover was on the large table when we arrived, but it was taken off and thrown over something, evidently to conceal it. But I need not pursue the details. When I had seen the cat, heard the dog, and then seen the monkey, I determined to see what was under the table-cover; and finding that it was a phonograph with the cylinder record still on the drum, I decided to 'go Nap' and chance making a mistake. For until we had tried the record, the alibi remained. If it had failed, I should have advised Miller to hold a boot parade. Fortunately we struck the right record and completed the case."

Mrs. Barnett's defence was accepted by the magistrate and the charge against her was dismissed. The other two were committed for trial, and in due course paid the extreme penalty. "Yet another illustration," was Thorndyke's comment, "of the folly of that kind of criminal who won't let well alone, and who will create false clues. If the Barnetts had not laid down those false tracks, they would probably never have been suspected. It was their clever alibi that led us straight to their door."

Pandora's Box

"I see our friend, S. Chapman, is still a defaulter," said I, as I ran my eye over the "personal" column of The Times.

Thorndyke looked up interrogatively.

"Chapman?" he repeated; "let me see, who is he?"

"The man with the box. I read you the advertisement the other day. Here it is again. 'If the box left in the luggage-room by S. Chapman is not claimed within a week from this date, it will be sold to defray expenses.--Alexander Butt, "Red Lion" Hotel, Stoke Varley, Kent.' That sounds like an ultimatum; but it has been appearing at intervals for the last month. As the first notice expired about three weeks ago, the question is, why doesn't Mr. Butt sell the box and have done with it?"

"He may have some qualms as to the legality of the proceeding," said Thorndyke. "It would be interesting to know what expenses he refers to and what is the value of the box."

The latter question was resolved a day or two later by the appearance in our chambers of an agitated gentleman, who gave his name as George Chapman. After apologising for his unannounced visit he explained: "I have come to you on the advice of my solicitor and on behalf of my brother, Samuel, who has become involved in a most extraordinary and horrible set of complications. At present he is in custody of the police charged with an atrocious murder."

"That is certainly a rather serious complication," Thorndyke observed dryly. "Perhaps you had better give us an account of the circumstances-- the whole set of circumstances, from the beginning."

I will," said Mr. Chapman, "without any reservations. The only question is, which is the beginning? There are the business and the domestic affairs. Perhaps I had better begin with the business concerns. My brother was a sort of travelling agent for a firm of manufacturing jewellers. He held a stock of the goods, which he used as samples for large orders, but in the case of small retailers he actually supplied the goods himself. When travelling, he usually carried his stock in a small Gladstone bag, but he kept the bulk of it in a safe in his house, and he used to go home at week-ends, or oftener, to replenish his travelling stock. Now, about two months ago he left home on a trip, but instead of taking a selection of his goods, he took the entire stock in a largish wooden box, leaving the safe empty. What he meant to do I don't know, and that's the fact. I offer no opinion. The circumstances were peculiar, as you will hear presently, and his proceedings were peculiar; for he went down to Stoke Varley--a village not far from Folkestone--put up at the 'Red Lion,' and deposited his box in the luggage-room that is kept for the use of commercial travellers; and then, after staying there for a few days, came up to London to make some arrangements for selling or letting his house--which, it seems, he had decided to leave. He came up in the evening, and the very next morning the first of his adventures befell, and a very alarming one it was.

"It appears that, as he was walking down a quiet street, he saw a lady's purse lying on the pavement. Naturally he picked it up, and as it contained nothing to show the name or address of the owner, he put it in his pocket, intending to hand it in at a police station. Shortly after this, he got into an omnibus, and a well-dressed woman entered at the same time and sat down next to him. Just as the conductor was coming in to collect the fares, the woman began to search her pocket excitedly, and then, turning to my brother, called on him loudly to return her purse. Of course, he said that he knew nothing about her purse, whereupon she roundly accused him of having picked her pocket, declaring to the conductor that she had felt him take out her purse, and demanding that the omnibus should be stopped and a policeman fetched. At this moment a policeman was seen on the pavement. The conductor stopped the omnibus and hailed the constable, who came, and having examined the floor of the vehicle without finding the missing purse, and taken the conductor's name and number, took my brother into custody and conducted him and the woman to the police station. Here the inspector took down from the woman a description of the stolen purse and its contents, which my brother, to his utter dismay, recognised as that of the purse which he had picked up and which was still in his pocket. Immediately, he gave the inspector an account of the incident and produced the purse; but it is hardly necessary to say that the inspector refused to take his explanation seriously.

"Then my brother did a thing which was natural enough, but which did not help him. Seeing that he was practically certain to be convicted--for there was really no answer to the charge--he gave a false name and refused his address. He was then locked up in a cell for the night, and the next morning was brought before the magistrate, who, having heard the evidence of the woman and the inspector and having listened without comment to my brother's story, committed him for trial at the Central Criminal Court, and refused bail. He was then removed to Brixton, where he was detained for nearly a month, pending the opening of the sessions.

"At length the day of his trial drew near. But it was then found that the woman who had accused him had left her lodgings and could not be traced. As there was no one to prosecute, and as the disappearance of the woman put a rather new light upon my brother's story, the case against him was allowed to drop, and he was released.

"He went home by train, and at the station he bought a copy of The Times to read on the way. Before opening it he chanced to run his eye over the 'personal' column, and there his attention was arrested by his own name in an advertisement--"

"Relating to a box?" said I.

"Precisely. Then you have seen it. Well, considering the value of the contents of that box, he was naturally rather anxious. At once he sent off a telegram saying that he would call on the following day before noon to claim the box and pay what was owing. And he did so. Yesterday morning he took an early train down to Stoke Varley and went straight to the 'Red Lion.' On his arrival he was asked to step into the coffee-room, which he did; and there he found three police officers, who forthwith arrested him on a charge of murder. But before going into the particular that charge I had better give you an account of his domestic affairs on which this incredible and horrible accusation turns.

"My brother, I am sorry to say, was living with a woman who was not his wife. He had originally intended to marry her, but his association with her--which lasted over several years--did not encourage that intention. She was a terrible woman, and she led him a terrible life. Her temper was ungovernable; and when she had taken too much to drink--which was a pretty frequent occurrence--she was not only noisy and quarrelsome, but physically violent as well. Her antecedents were disreputable--she had been connected with the seamy side of the music-hall stage; her associations were disreputable; she brought questionable women to my brother's house; she consorted with men of doubtful character, and her relations with them were equally doubtful. Indeed, with one of them, a man named Gamble, I should say that her relations were not doubtful at all, though I understand he was a married man.

"Well, my brother put up with her for years, living a life that cut him off from all decent society. But at last his patience gave way (and I may add that he made the acquaintance of a very desirable lady, who was willing to condone his past and marry him if he could secure a possible future). After a particularly outrageous scene, he ordered the woman-- Rebecca Mings was her name--out of the house and declared their relationship at an end.

"But she refused to be shaken off. She kept possession of the street-door key, and she returned again and again, and made a public scandal. The last time she created such an uproar when the door was bolted against her that a crowd collected in the street and my brother was forced to let her in. She stayed with him some hours, alone in the house--for the only servant he had was a daily girl who left at three o'clock--and went away quite quietly about ten at night. But, although a good many people saw her go into the house, no one but my brother seems to have seen her leave it; a most disastrous circumstance, for, from the moment when she left the house, no one ever saw her again. She did not go to her lodgings that night. She disappeared utterly--until--but I must go back now to the 'Red Lion ' at Stoke Varley.

"When my brother was arrested on the charge of having murdered Rebecca Mings, certain particulars were given to him; and when I went down there in response to a telegram, I gathered some more. The circumstances are these : About a fortnight after my brother had left to come to London, some of the 'commercials' who used the luggage-room complained of an unpleasant odour in it, which was presently traced to my brother's box. As that box appeared to have been abandoned, the landlord became suspicious, and communicated with the police. They telephoned to the London police, who found my brother's house shut up and his whereabouts unknown. Thereupon the local police broke open the box and found in it a woman's left arm and a quantity of blood-stained clothing. On which they caused the advertisement to be put in The Times, and meanwhile they made certain inquiries. It appeared that my brother had spent part of his time at Stoke Varley fishing in the little river. On learning this, the police proceeded to dredge the river, and presently they brought up a right arm--apparently the fellow of the one found in the box--and a leg divided into three parts, evidently a woman's. Now, as to the arm found in the box, there could be no question about its identity, for it bore a very distinct tattooed inscription consisting of the initials R. M. above a heart transfixed by an arrow, with the initials J. B. underneath. A few inquiries elicited the fact that the woman, Rebecca Mings, who had disappeared, bore such a tattooed mark on her left arm and certain persons who had known her, having been sworn to secrecy, were shown the arm, and recognised the mark without hesitation. Further inquiries showed that Rebecca Mings was last seen alive entering my brother's house, as I have described; and on this information the police broke into the house and searched it."

"Do you know if they found anything?" Thorndyke asked.

"I don't," replied Chapman, "but I infer that they did. The police at Stoke Varley were very courteous and kind, but they declined to give any particulars about the visit to the house. However, we shall hear at the inquest if they made any discoveries."

"And is that all that you have to tell us?" asked Thorndyke.

"Yes," was the reply, "and enough, too. I make no comment on my brother's story, and I won't ask whether you believe it. I don't expect you to. The question is whether you would undertake the defence. I suppose it isn't necessary for a lawyer to be convinced of his client's innocence in order to convince the jury."

"You are thinking of an advocate," said Thorndyke. "I am not an advocate, and I should not defend a man whom I believed to be guilty. The most that I can do is to investigate the case. If the result of the investigation is to confirm the suspicions against your brother, I shall, go no farther in the case. You will have to get an ordinary criminal barrister to defend your brother. If, on the other hand, I find reasonable grounds for believing him innocent, I will undertake the defence. What do you say to that?"

"I've no choice," replied Chapman; "and I suppose if you find all the evidence against him, the defence won't matter much."

"I am afraid that is so," said Thorndyke. "And, now there are one or two questions to be cleared up. First, does your brother offer any explanation of the presence of these remains in his box? "

"He supposes that somebody at the 'Red Lion' must have taken the jewellery out and put the remains in. Anyone could get access to the luggage-room by asking for the key at the office."

"Well," said Thorndyke," that is conceivable. Then, as to the person who might have made this exchange. Is there anyone who had any reason for wishing to make away with deceased?"

"No," replied Chapman. "Plenty of people disliked her, but no one but my brother had any motive for getting rid of her."

"You spoke of a man with whom she was on somewhat intimate terms. There had been no quarrel or breach there, I suppose?"

"The man Gamble, you mean. No, I should say they were the best of friends. Besides, Gamble had no responsibilities in regard to her. He could have dropped her whenever he was tired of her."

"Do you know anything about him?" Thorndyke asked.

"Very little. He has been a rolling stone, and has been in all sorts of jobs, I believe. He was in the New Zealand trade for some time, and dealt in all sorts of things--among others, in smoked human heads; sold them to collectors and museums, I understand. So he would have had some previous experience," Chapman added with a faint grin.

"Not in dismemberment," said Thorndyke. "Those will have been ancient Maori heads--relics of the old head hunters. There are some in the Hunterian Museum. But, as you say, there seems to be no motive in Gamble's case, even if there had been the opportunity; whereas, in your brother's case, there seem to have been both the motive and the opportunity. I suppose your brother never threatened the deceased?"

"I am sorry to say he did," replied Chapman. "On several occasions, and before witnesses, too, he threatened to put her out of the way. Of course he never meant it--he was really the mildest of men. But it was a foolish thing to do and most unfortunate, as things have turned out."

"Well." said Thorndyke, "I will look into the matter and let you know what I think of it. It is unnecessary to remark that appearances are not very encouraging."

"No, I can see that," said Chapman, rising and producing his card-case. "But we must hope for the best." He laid his card on the table, and having shaken hands with us gloomily, took his departure.

It doesn't do to take things at their face value," I remarked, when he had gone; "but I don't think we have "ever had a more hopeless-looking case. All it wants to complete it is the discovery of remains in Chapman's house."

"In that respect," said Thorndyke, "it may already be complete. But it hardly wants that finishing touch. On the evidence that we have, any jury would find a verdict of 'guilty' without leaving the box. The only question for us is whether the face value of the evidence is its real value. If it is, the defence will be a mere formality."

"I suppose," said I, "you will begin the investigation at Stoke Varley?"

"Yes," he replied. "We begin by checking the alleged facts. If they are really as stated, we shall probably need to go no farther. And we had better lose no time, as the remains may be moved into the jurisdiction of a London coroner, and we ought to see everything in situ as far as possible. I suggest that we postpone the rest of to-day's business and start at once, taking Scotland Yard on the way to get authority to inspect the remains and the premises."

In a few minutes we were ready for the expedition. While Thorndyke packed the "research-case" with the necessary instruments, I gave instructions to our laboratory assistant, Polton, as to what was to be done in our absence, and then, when we had consulted the time-table, we set forth by way of the Embankment.

At Scotland Yard, on inquiring for our friend, Superintendent Miller, we received the slightly unwelcome news that he was at Stoke Varley, inquiring into the case. However, the authorisation was given readily enough, and, armed with this, we made our way to Charing Cross Station, arriving there in good time to catch our train.

We had just given up our tickets and turned out into the pleasant station approach of Stoke Varley when Thorndyke gave a soft chuckle. I looked at him inquiringly, and he explained " Miller has had a telegram, and we are going to have facilities, with a little supervision." Following the direction of his glance, I now observed the superintendent strolling towards us, trying to look surprised, but achieving only a somewhat sheepish grin.

"Well, I'm sure, gentlemen!" he exclaimed. "This is an unexpected pleasure. You don't mean to say you are engaged in this treasure-trove case?"

"Why not?" asked Thorndyke.

"Well, I'll tell you why not," replied' Miller. " Because it's no go. You'll only waste your time and injure your reputation. I may as well let you know, in confidence, that we've been through Chapman's house in London. It wasn't very necessary; but still, if there was a vacancy in his coffin for one or two more nails, we've knocked them in."

"What did you find in his house?" Thorndyke asked.

"We found," replied Miller, "in a cupboard in his bedroom, a good-sized bottle of hyoscine tablets, about two-thirds full--one-third missing. No great harm in that; he might have taken 'em himself. But when we went down into the cellar, we noticed that the place smelt--well, a bit graveyardy, so to speak. So we had a look round. It was a stone-floored cellar, not very even, but so far as we could see, none of the flagstones seemed to have been disturbed. We didn't want the job of digging the whole of them up, so I just filled a bucket with water and poured it over the floor. Then I watched.

"In less than a minute one big flagstone near the middle went nearly dry, while the water still stood on all the others. 'What O!' says I. 'Loose earth underneath here.' So we got a crow-bar and prised up that big flag; and sure enough, underneath it we found a good-sized bundle done up in a sheet. I won't go into unpleasant particulars--not that it would upset you, I suppose--but that bundle contained human remains."

"Any bones?" inquired Thorndyke.

"No. Mostly in'ards and some skin from the front of the body. We handed them over to the Home Office experts, and they examined them and made an analysis Their report states that the remains are those of a woman of about thirty-five--that was about Mings' age--and that the various organs contained a large quantity of hyoscine; more than enough to have caused death. So there you are. If you are going to conduct the defence, you won't get much glory from it."

"It is very good of you, Miller," said Thorndyke, "to have given us this private information. It is very helpful, though I have not undertaken the defence. I have merely come down to check the facts and see if there is any material for a defence. And I shall go through the routine, as I am here. Where are the remains?"

"In the mortuary. I'll show you the way, and as I happen to have the key in my pocket, I can let you in."

We passed through the outskirts of the village, gathering a small train of stealthy followers, who dogged us to the door of the mortuary and hungrily watched us as the superintendent let us in and locked the door after us.

"There you are," said Miller, indicating the slate table on which the remains lay, covered by a sheet soaked in an antiseptic. "I've seen all I want to see." And he retired into a corner and lit his pipe.

The remnants of mortality, disclosed by the removal of the sheet, were dreadfully suggestive of crime in its most brutal and horrible form, but they offered little information. The dismemberment had been manifestly rude and unskilful, and the remains were clearly those of a woman of medium size and apparently in the prime of life. The principal interest centred in the left arm, the waxen skin of which bore a very distinct tattoo-mark, consisting of the initials R. M. over a very symmetrical heart, transfixed by an arrow, beneath which were the initials J. B. The letters were Roman capitals about half an inch high, well-formed and finished with serifs, and the heart and arrow quite well drawn. I looked reflectively at the device, standing out in dull blue from its ivory-like background, and speculated vaguely as to who J. B. might have been and how many predecessors and successors he had had. And then my interest waned, and I joined the superintendent in the corner. It was a sordid case, and a conviction being a foregone conclusion, it did not seem to call for further attention.

Thorndyke, however, seemed to think otherwise. But that was his way. When he was engaged in an investigation he put out of his mind everything that he had been told and began from the very beginning. That was what he was doing now. He was inspecting these remains as if they had been the remains of some unidentified person. He made, and noted down, minute measurements of the limbs; he closely examined every square inch of surface; he scrutinised each finger separately, and then with the aid of his portable inking-plate and roller, took a complete set of finger-prints. He measured all the dimensions of the tattoo-marks with a delicate calliper-gauge, and then examined the marks themselves, first with a common lens and then with the high-power Coddington. The principles that he laid down in his lectures at the hospital were: "Accept no statement without verification; observe every fact independently for yourselves; and keep an open mind." And, certainly, no one ever carried out more conscientiously his own precepts.

"Do you know, Dr. Jervis," the superintendent whispered to me as Thorndyke brought his Coddington to bear on the tattoo-marks," I believe this lens business is becoming a habit with the doctor. It's my firm conviction that if somebody were to blow up the Houses of Parliament, he'd go and examine the ruins through a magnifying glass. Just look at him poring over those tattooed letters that you could read plainly twenty feet away!"

Meanwhile, Thorndyke, unconscious of these criticisms, placidly continued his inspection. From the table, with its gruesome burden, he transferred his attention to the box, which had been placed on a bench by the window, examining it minutely inside and out; feeling with his fingers the dark grey paint with which it was coated and the white-painted initials, "S. C.," on the lid, which he also measured carefully. He even copied into his note book the maker's name, which was stamped on a small brass label affixed to the inside of the lid, and the name of the lock-maker, and inspected the screws which had drawn from the wood when it was forced open. At length he put away his notebook, closed the research-case and announced that he had finished, adding the inquiry: "How do you get to the 'Red Lion' from here?"

"It's only a few minutes' walk," said Miller. " I'll show you the way. But you're wasting your time, doctor, you are indeed. You see," he continued, when he had locked up the mortuary and pocketed the key, "that suggestion of Chapman's is ridiculous on the face of it. Just imagine a man bringing a portmanteau full of human remains into the luggage-room of a commercial hotel, opening it and opening another's man's box, and swapping the contents of the one for the other with the chance of one of the commercials coming in at any moment. Supposing one of 'em had, what would he have had to say? 'Hallo!' says the baggy, ' you seem to have got somebody's arm in your box.' 'So I have,' says Chapman. 'I expect it's my wife's. Careless woman! must have dropped it in when she was packing the box.' Bah! It's a fool's explanation. Besides, how could he have got Chapman's box open? We couldn't. It was a first-class lock. We had to break it open, but it hadn't been broken open before. No, sir, that cat won't jump. Still, you needn't take my word for it. Here is the place, and here is Mr. Butt, himself, standing at his own front door looking as pleasant as the flowers in May, like the lump of sugar that you put in a fly-trap to induce 'em to walk in."

The landlord, who had overheard--without difficulty--the concluding passage of Miller's peroration, smiled genially; and when the purpose of the visit had been explained, suggested a "modest quencher" in the private parlour as an aid to conversation.

"I wanted," said Thorndyke, waiving the suggestion of the "quencher," "to ascertain whether Chapman's theory of an exchange of contents could be seriously entertained."

Well, sir," said the landlord, "the fact is that it couldn't. That room is a public room, and people may be popping in there at any time all day. We don't usually keep it locked. It isn't necessary. We know most of our customers, and the contents of the packages that are stowed in the room are principally travellers' samples of no considerable value. The thing would have been impossible in the daytime, and we lock the room up at night."

"Have you had any strangers staying with you in the interval between Chapman's going away and the discovery of the remains? "

"Yes. There was a Mr. Doler; he had two cabin trunks: and a uniform case which went to the luggage-room. And then there was a lady, Mrs. Murchison. She had a lot of stuff in there: a small, flat trunk, a hat- box, and a big dress-basket--one of these great basket pantechnicons that ladies take about with them. And there was another gentleman--I forget his name, but you will see it in the visitors' book--he had a couple of largish portmanteaux in there. Perhaps you would like to see the book?"

"I should," said Thorndyke, and when the book was produced and the names of the guests pointed out, he copied the entries into his notebook, adding the particulars of their luggage.

"And now, sir," said Miller, "I suppose you won't be happy until you've seen the room itself?"

"Your insight is really remarkable, superintendent," my colleague replied. "Yes, I should like to see the room."

There was little enough to see, however, when we arrived there. The key was in the door, and the latter was not only unlocked but stood ajar; and when we pushed it open and entered we saw a small room, empty save for a collection of portmanteaux, trunks, and Gladstone bags. The only noteworthy fact was that it was at the end of a corridor, covered with linoleum, so that anyone inside would have a few seconds' notice of another person's approach. But evidently that would have been of little use in the alleged circumstances. For the hypothetical criminal must have emptied Chapman's box of the jewellery before he could put the incriminating objects into it; so that, apart from the latter, the arrival of an inopportune visitor would have found him apparently in the act of committing a robbery. The suggestion was obviously absurd.

"By the way," said Thorndyke, as we descended the stairs, "where is the central character of this drama--Chapman? He is not here, I suppose?"

"Yes, he is," replied Miller. "He is committed for trial, but we are keeping him here until we know where the inquest is to be held. You would probably like to have a few words with him? Well, I'll take you along to the police station and tell them who you are, and then perhaps you would like to come back here and have some lunch or dinner before you return to town."

I warmly seconded the latter proposal, and the arrangement having been made, we set forth for the police station, which we gathered from Miller was incorporated with a small local prison. Here we were shown into what appeared to be a private office, and presently a sergeant entered, ushering in a man whom we at once recognised from his resemblance to our client, Mr. George Chapman, disguised though it was by his pallor, his unshaven face, and his air of abject misery. The sergeant, having announced him by name, withdrew with the superintendent and locked the door on the outside. As soon as we were alone, Thorndyke rapidly acquainted the prisoner with the circumstances of his brother's visit and then continued: "Now, Mr. Chapman, you want me to undertake your defence. If I do so, I must have all the facts. If there is anything known to you that your brother has not told me, I ask you to tell it to me without reservation."

Chapman shook his head wearily.

"I know nothing more than you know," said he. "The whole affair is a mystery that I can make nothing of. I don't expect you to believe me. Who would, with all this evidence against me? But I swear to God that I know nothing of this abominable crime. When I brought that box down here, it contained my stock of jewellery and nothing else; and after I put it in the luggage-room, I never opened it."

"Do you know of anybody who might have had a motive for getting rid of Rebecca Mings?"

"Not a soul," replied Chapman. "She led me the devil's own life, but she was popular enough with her own friends. And she was an attractive woman in her way: a fine, well-built woman, rather big--she stood five-feet-seven--with a good complexion and very handsome golden hair. Such as her friends were--they were a shady lot--I think they were fond of her, and I don't believe she had any enemies."

"Some hyoscine was found in your house," said Thorndyke. "Do you know anything about it?"

"Yes. I got it when I suffered from neuralgia. But I never took any. My doctor heard about it and sent me to the dentist. The bottle was never opened. It contained a hundred tablets."

"And with regard to the box," said Thorndyke. "Had you had it long?"

"Not very long. I bought it at Fletchers, in Holborn, about six months ago."

"And you have nothing more to tell us?"

"No," he replied. "I wish I had"; and then, after a pause, he asked with a wistful look at Thorndyke: "Are you going to undertake my defence, sir? I can see that there is very little hope, but I should like to be given just a chance."

I glanced at Thorndyke, expecting at the most a cautious and conditional reply. To my astonishment he answered: "There is no need to take such a gloomy view of the case, Mr. Chapman. I shall undertake the defence, and I think you have quite a fair chance of an acquittal."

On this amazing reply I reflected, not without some self-condemnation, during our walk to the hotel and the meal that preceded our departure. For it was evident that I had missed something vital. Thorndyke was a cautious man and little given to making promises or forecasts of results. He must have picked up some evidence of a very conclusive kind; but what that evidence could be, I found it impossible to imagine. The superintendent, too, was puzzled, I could see, for Thorndyke made no secret of his intention to go on with tile case. But Miller's delicate attempts to pump him came to nothing; and when he had escorted us to the station and our train moved off, I could see him standing on the platform, gently scratching the back of his head and gazing speculatively at our retreating carriage.

As soon as we were clear of the station, I opened my attack.

"What on earth," I demanded, "did you mean by giving that poor devil, Chapman, hopes of acquittal? I can't see that he has a dog's chance."

Thorndyke looked at me gravely.

"My impression is, Jervis." he said, "that you have not kept an open mind in this case. You have allowed yourself to fall under the suggestive influence of the obvious; whereas the function of the investigator is to consider the possible alternatives of the obvious inference. And you have not brought your usual keen attention to bear on the facts. If you had considered George Chapman's statement attentively you would have noticed that it contained some very curious and significant suggestions; and if you had examined those dismembered remains critically, you would have seen that they confirmed those suggestions in a very remarkable manner."

"As to George Chapman's statement," said I, "the only suggestive point that I recall is the reference to those Maori heads. But, as you, yourself, pointed out, the dealers in those heads don't do the dismemberment."

Thorndyke shook his head a little impatiently.

Tut, tut, Jervis," said he, "that isn't the point at all. Any fool can cut up a dead body as this one has been cut up. The point is that that statement, carefully considered, yields a definite and consistent alternative to the theory that Samuel Chapman killed this woman and dismembered her body; and that alternative theory is supported by the appearance of these remains. I think you will see the point if you recall Chapman's statement, and reflect on the possible bearing of the various incidents that he described."

In this, however, Thorndyke was unduly optimistic. I recalled the statement completely enough, and reflected on it frequently and profoundly during the next few days; but the more I thought of it the more conclusive did the case against the accused appear.

Meanwhile, my colleague appeared to be taking no steps in the matter, and I assumed that he was waiting for the inquest. It is true that, when, on one occasion, he had accompanied me towards the City, and leaving me in Queen Victoria Street disappeared into the premises of Messrs. Burden Brothers, lock manufacturers, I was inclined to associate his proceedings with his minute examination of the lock at Stoke Varley. And, again, when our laboratory assistant, Polton, was seen to issue forth, top-hatted and armed with an umbrella and an attaché-case, I suspected some sort of "private inquiries," possibly connected with the case. But from Thorndyke I could get no information at all. My tentative "pumpings" elicited one unvarying reply. "You have the facts, Jervis. You heard George Chapman's statement, and you have seen the remains. Give me a reasonable theory and I will discuss it with pleasure." And that was how the matter remained. I had no reasonable theory--other than that of the police--and there was accordingly no discussion.

On a certain evening, a couple of days before the inquest--which had been postponed in the hope that some further remains might be discovered--I observed signs of an expected visitor: a small table placed by the supernumerary arm-chair and furnished with a tray bearing a siphon, a whisky-decanter and a box of cigars. Thorndyke caught my inquiring glance at these luxuries, for which neither of us had any use, and proceeded to explain.

"I have asked Miller to look in this evening--he is due now. I have been working at this Chapman case, and, as it is now complete, I propose to lay my cards on the table."

"Is that safe?" said I. "Supposing the police still go for a conviction and try to forestall your evidence?"

"They won't," he replied. "They couldn't. And it would be most improper to let the case go for trial on a false theory. But here is Miller; and a mighty twitter he is in, I have no doubt."

He was. Without even waiting for the customary cigar, he plumped down into the chair, and dragging a letter from his pocket, fixed a glare of astonishment on my placid colleague.

"This letter of yours, sir," said he, "is perfectly incomprehensible to me. You say that you are prepared to put us in possession of the facts of this Chapman case. But we are in possession of the facts already. We are absolutely certain of a conviction. Let me remind you, sir, of what those facts are. We have got a dead body which has been identified beyond all doubt. Part of that body was found in a box which is the property of Samuel Chapman, which was brought by him and deposited by him at the 'Red Lion 'Hotel. Another part of that body was found in his dwelling-house. A supply of poison--an uncommon poison, too--similar to that which killed the dead person, has also been found in his house; and the dead body is that of a woman with whom Chapman was known to be on terms of enmity and whom he has threatened, in the presence of witnesses, to kill. Now, sir, what have you got to say to those facts?"

Thorndyke regarded the agitated detective with a quiet smile. "My comments, Miller," said he, "can be put in a nut-shell. You have got the wrong man, you have got the wrong box, and you have got the wrong body."

The superintendent was thunderstruck, and no wonder. So was I. As to Miller, he drew himself forward until he was sitting on the extreme edge of the chair, and for some moments stared at my impassive colleague in speechless amazement. At length he burst out: "But, my dear sir! This is sheer nonsense--at least, that's what it sounds like, though I know it can't be. Let's begin with the body. You say it's the wrong one."

"Yes. Rebecca Mings was a biggish woman. Her height was five-feet-seven. This woman was not more than five-feet-four."

"Bah!" exclaimed Miller. "You can't judge to an inch or two from parts of a dismembered body. You are forgetting the tattoo-mark. That clenches the identity beyond any possible doubt."

"It does, indeed," said Thorndyke. "That is the crucial evidence. Rebecca Mings had a certain tattoo mark on her left forearm. This woman had not."

"Had not!" shrieked Miller, coming yet farther forward on his chair. (I expected, every moment, to see him sitting on the floor.) "Why, I saw it; and so did you."

"I am speaking of the woman, not of the body," said Thorndyke. "The mark that you saw was a post-mortem tattoo-mark. It was made after death. But the fact that it was made after death is good evidence, that it was not there during life."

"Moses!" exclaimed the superintendent. "This is a facer. Are you perfectly sure it was done after death?"

"Quite sure. The appearance, through a powerful lens, is unmistakable. Tattoo-marks are made, as you know, of course, by painting Indian ink on the skin and pricking it in with fine needles. In the living skin the needle-wounds heal up at once and disappear, but in the dead skin the needle-holes remain unclosed and can be easily seen with a lens. In this case the skin had been well washed and the surface pressed with some smooth object; but the holes were plainly visible and the ink was still in them."

"Well, I'm sure!" said Miller. "I never heard of tattooing a dead body before."

"Very few people have, I expect," said Thorndyke. "But there is one class of persons who know all about it: the persons who deal in Maori heads."

"Indeed?" queried Miller. "How does it concern them?"

"Those heads are usually elaborately tattooed, and the value of a head depends on the quality of the tattooing. Now, when those heads became objects of trade, the dealers conceived the idea of touching up defective specimens by additional tattooing on the dead head, and from this they proceeded to obtain heads which had no tattoo-marks, and turn them into tattooed heads."

"Well, to be sure," said the superintendent, with a grin, "what wicked men there are in the world, aren't there, Dr. Jervis?"

I murmured a vague assent, but I was principally conscious of a desire to kick myself for having failed to pick this invaluable clue out of George Chapman's statement.

"And now," said Miller," we come to the box. How do you know it is the wrong one? "

"That," replied Thorndyke, "is proved even more conclusively. The original box was made by Fletchers, in Holborn. It was sold to Chapman, and his initials painted on it, on the 9 of last April. I have seen the entry in the day-book. The locks of these boxes are made by Burden Brothers of Queen Victoria Street, and as they are quite high-class locks each is given a registered number, which is stamped on the lock. The number on the box that you have is 5007, and Burden's books show that it was made and sold to Fletchers about the middle of July--the sale was dated the 13th. Therefore this can not be Chapman's box."

"Apparently not," Miller agreed. "But whose box is it? And what has become of Chapman's box?"

"That," replied Thorndyke, "was presumably taken away in Mrs. Murchison's dress-basket."

"Then who the deuce is Mrs. Murchison?" demanded the superintendent.

"I should say," replied Thorndyke, "that she was formerly known as Rebecca Mings."

"The deceased!" exclaimed Miller, falling back in his chair with a guffaw. "My eye! What a lark it is! But she must have some sauce, to walk off with the jewellery and leave her own dismembered remains in exchange! By the way, whose remains are they?"

"We shall come to that presently," Thorndyke answered. "Now we have to consider the man you have in custody."

"Yes," agreed Miller, "we must settle about him. Of course if it isn't his box, and the body isn't Mings' body, that puts him out of it so far. But there are those remains that we dug up in his cellar. What about them?"

"That question," replied Thorndyke, "will, I think, be answered by a general review of the case. But I must, remind you that if the box is not Chapman's, it is some other person's; that is to say, that if Chapman goes out of the case, as to the Stoke Varley incidents, someone else comes in. So, if the body is not Mings' body, it is some other woman's, and that other woman must have disappeared. And now let us review the case as a whole.

"You know about the pocket-picking charge. It was obviously a false charge, deliberately prepared by 'planting' the purse; that is, it was a conspiracy. Now what was the object of this conspiracy? Clearly it was to get Chapman out of the way while the boxes were exchanged at Stoke Varley, and the remains deposited in the river and elsewhere. Then who were the conspirators--other than the agent who planted the purse?

"They--if there were more than one--must have had access to Mings, dead or alive, in order to make the exact copy, or tracing, of her tattoo-mark. They must have had some knowledge of the process of post-mortem tattooing. They must have had access to Chapman's house. And, since they had in their possession the dead body of a woman, they must have been associated with some woman who has disappeared.

"Who is there who answers this description? Well, of course, Mings had access to herself, though she could hardly have taken a tracing from her own arm, and she had access to Chapman's house, since she had possession of the latchkey. Then there is a man named Gamble, with whom Mings was on terms of great intimacy. Now Gamble was formerly a dealer in tattooed Maori heads, so he may be assumed to know something about post-mortem tattooing. And I have ascertained that Gamble's wife has disappeared from her usual places of resort. So here are two persons who, together, agree with the description of the conspirators. And now let us consider the train of events in connection with the dates.

"On July the 29th Chapman came to town from Stoke Varley. On the 30th he was arrested as a pick pocket. On the 31st he was committed for trial. On the 2nd of August Mrs. Gamble went away to the country. No one seems to have seen her go, but that is the date on which she is reported to have gone. On August the 5th Mrs. Murchison deposited at Stoke Varley a box which must have been purchased between the 13th of July and the 4th of August, and which contained a woman's arm. On the 14th of August that box was opened by the police. On the 18th human remains were discovered in Chapman's house. On the 27th Chapman was released from Brixton. On the 28th he was arrested for murder at Stoke Varley. I think, Miller, you will agree that that is a very striking succession of dates."

"Yes," Miller agreed. "It looks like a true bill. If you will give me Mr. Gamble's address, I'll call on him."

"I'm afraid you won't find him at home," said Thorndyke. "He has gone into the country, too; and I gather from his landlord, who holds a returned cheque, that Mr. Gamble's banking account has gone into the country with him."

"Then," said the superintendent "I suppose I must take a trip into the country, too."

"Well, Thorndyke," I said, as I laid down the paper containing the report of the trial of Gamble and Mings for the murder of Theresa Gamble, one morning about four months later, "you ought to be very highly gratified. After sentencing Gamble to death and Mings to fifteen years' penal servitude, the judge took the opportunity to compliment the police on their ingenuity in unravelling this crime, and the Home Office experts on their skill in detecting the counterfeit tattoo-marks. What do you think of that?"

"I think," replied Thorndyke, "that his lordship showed a very proper and appreciative spirit."

The Trail Of Behemoth

Or all the minor dissipations in which temperate men indulge there is none, I think, more alluring than the after-breakfast pipe. I had just lit mine and was standing before the fire with the unopened paper in my hand when my ear caught the sound of hurried footsteps ascending the stair. Now experience has made me somewhat of a connoisseur in footsteps. A good many are heard on our stair, heralding the advent of a great variety of clients, and I have learned to distinguish those which are premonitory of urgent cases. Such I judged the present ones to be, and my judgment was confirmed by a hasty, importunate tattoo on our small brass knocker, Regretfully taking the much-appreciated pipe from my mouth, I crossed the room and threw the door open.

Good morning, Dr. Jervis," said our visitor, a barrister whom I knew slightly. "Is your colleague at home?"

No, Mr. Bidwell," I replied. "I am sorry to say he is out of town. He won't be back until the day after to-morrow."

Mr. Bidwell was visibly disappointed.

"Ha! Pity!" he exclaimed; and then with quick tact he added "But still, you are here. It comes to the same thing."

I don't know about that," said I. "But, at any rate, I am at your service."

"Thank you," said he. "And in that case I will ask you to come round with me at once to Tanfield Court. A most shocking thing has happened. My old friend and neighbour, Giles Herrington has been--well, he is dead--died suddenly, and I think there can be no doubt that he was killed. Can you come now? I will give you the particulars as we go."

I scribbled a hasty note to say where I had gone, and having laid it on the table, got my hat and set forth with Mr. Bidwell.

"It has only just been discovered," said he, as we crossed King's Bench Walk. "The laundress who does his chambers and mine was battering at my door when I arrived--I don't live in the Temple, you know. She was as pale as a ghost and in an awful state of alarm and agitation. It seems that she had gone up to Herrington's chambers to get his breakfast ready as usual; but when she went into the sitting-room she found him lying dead on the floor. Thereupon she rushed down to my chambers--I am usually an early bird--and there I found her, as I said, battering at my door, although she has a key.

"Well, I went up with her to my friend's chambers--they are on the first floor, just over mine--and there, sure enough, was poor old Giles lying on the floor, cold and stiff. Evidently he had been lying there all night."

"Were there any marks of violence on the body?" I asked.

"I didn't notice any," he replied, "but I didn't look very closely. What I did notice was that the place was all in disorder--a chair overturned and things knocked off the table. It was pretty evident that there had been a struggle and that he had not met his death by fair means."

"And what do you want us to do?" I asked.

"Well," he replied, "I was Herrington's friend; about the only friend he had, for he was not an amiable or a sociable man; and I am the executor of his will.

"Appearances suggest very strongly that he has been murdered, and I take it upon myself to see that his murderer is brought to account. Our friendship seems to demand that. Of course, the police will go into the affair, and if it turns out to be all plain sailing, there will be nothing for you to do. But the murderer, if there is one, has got to be secured and convicted, and if the police can't manage it, I want you and Thorndyke to see the case through. This is the place."

He hurried in through the entry and up the stairs to the first-floor landing, where he rapped loudly at the closed "oak" of a set of chambers above which was painted the name of "Mr. Giles Herrington."

After an interval, during which Mr. Bidwell repeated the summons, the massive door opened and a familiar face looked out: the face of Inspector Badger of the Criminal Investigation Department. The expression that it bore was not one of welcome, and my experience of the inspector caused me to brace myself up for the inevitable contest.

"What is your business?" he inquired forbiddingly.

Mr. Bidwell took the question to himself and replied: "I am Mr. Herrington's executor, and in that capacity I have instructed Dr. Jervis and his colleague, Dr. Thorndyke, to watch the case on my behalf. I take it that you are a police officer?"

"I am," replied Badger, "and I can't admit any unauthorised persons to these chambers."

"We are not unauthorised persons," said Mr. Bidwell. "We are here on legitimate business. Do I understand that you refuse admission to the legal representatives of the deceased man?"

In the face of Mr. Bidwell's firm and masterful attitude, Badger began, as usual, to weaken. Eventually, having warned us to convey no information to anybody, he grudgingly opened the door and admitted us.

"I have only just arrived, myself," he said. "I happened to be in the porter's lodge on other business when the laundress came and gave the alarm."

As I stepped into the room and looked round, I saw at a glance the clear indications of a crime. The place was in the utmost disorder. The cloth had been dragged from the table, littering the floor with broken glass, books, a tobacco jar, and various other objects. A chair sprawled on its back, the fender was dislodged from its position, the hearth-rug was all awry; and in the midst of the wreckage, on the space of floor between the table and the fireplace, the body of a man was stretched in a not uneasy posture.

I stooped over him and looked him over searchingly; an elderly man, clean-shaved and slightly bald, with a grim, rather forbidding countenance, which was not, however, distorted or apparently unusual in expression. There were no obvious injuries, but the crumpled state of the collar caused me to look more closely at the throat and neck, and I then saw pretty plainly a number of slightly discoloured marks, such as would be made by fingers tightly grasping the throat. Evidently Badger had already observed them, for he remarked: "There's no need to ask you what he died of, doctor; I can see that for myself."

"The actual cause of death," said I, "is not quite evident. He doesn't appear to have died from suffocation, but those are very unmistakable marks on the throat."

"Uncommonly," agreed Badger; "and they are enough for my purpose without any medical hair-splittings. How long do you think he has been dead?"

"From nine to twelve hours," I replied, "but nearer nine, I should think."

The inspector looked at his watch.

"That makes it between nine o'clock and midnight, but nearer midnight," said he. "Well, we shall hear if the night porter has anything to tell us. I've sent word for him to come over, and the laundress, too. And here is one of 'em."

It was, in fact, both of them, for when the inspector opened the door, they were discovered conversing eagerly in whispers. "One at a time," said Badger. "I'll have the porter in first"; and having admitted the man, he unceremoniously shut tile door on the woman. The night porter saluted me as he came in--we were old acquaintances--and then halted near the door, where he stood stiffly, with his eyes riveted on tile corpse.

Now," said Badger, "I want you to try to remember if you let in any strangers last night, and if so, what their business was."

"I remember quite well," the porter replied. "I let in three strangers while I was on duty. One was going to Mr. Bolter in Fig Tree Court, one was going: to Sir Alfred Blain's chambers, and the third said he had an appointment with Mr. Herrington."

"Ha!" exclaimed Badger, rubbing his hands. "Now, what time did you let him in?"

"It was just after ten-fifteen."

"Can you tell us what he was like and how he was dressed?"

"Yes," was the reply. "He didn't know where Tanfield Court was, and I had to walk down and show him, so I was able to have a good look at him. He was a middle-sized man, rather thin, dark hair, small moustache, no beard, and he had a long, sharp nose with a bump on the bridge. He wore a soft felt hat, a loose light overcoat, and he carried a thickish rough stick."

"What class of man was he? Seem to be a gentleman?"

"He was quite a gentlemanly kind of man, so far as I could judge, but he looked a bit shabby as to his clothes."

"Did you let him out?"

"Yes. He came to the gate a few minutes before eleven."

"And did you notice anything unusual about him then?"

"I did," the porter replied impressively. "I noticed that his collar was all crumpled and his hat was dusty and dented. His face was a bit red, and he looked rather upset, as if he had been having a tussle with somebody. I looked at him particularly and wondered what had been happening, seeing that Mr. Herrington was a quiet, elderly gentleman, though he was certainly a bit peppery at times."

The inspector took down these particulars gleefully in a large notebook and asked: "Is that all you know of the affair?" And when the porter replied that it was, he said: "Then I will ask you to read this statement and sign your name below it."

The porter read through his statement and carefully signed his name at the foot. He was about to depart when Badger said: "Before you go, perhaps you had better help us to move the body into the bedroom. It isn't decent to leave it lying there."

Accordingly the four of us lifted the dead man and carried him into the bedroom, where we laid him on the undisturbed bed and covered him with a rug. Then the porter was dismissed, with instructions to send in Mrs. Runt.

The laundress's statement was substantially a repetition of what Mr. Bidwell had told me. She had let herself into the chambers in the usual way, had come suddenly on the dead body of the tenant, and had forthwith rushed downstairs to give the alarm. When she had concluded the inspector stood for a few moments looking thoughtfully at his notes.

"I suppose," he said presently, "you haven't looked round these chambers this morning? Can't say if there is anything unusual about them, or anything missing?"

The laundress shook her head.

"I was too upset," she said, with another furtive glance at the place where the corpse had lain; "but," she added, letting her eyes roam vaguely round the room, "there doesn't seem to be anything missing, so far as I can see--wait! Yes, there is. There's something gone from that nail on the wall; and it was there yesterday morning, because I remember dusting it."

"Ha!" exclaimed Badger. "Now what was it that was hanging on that nail?"

"Well," Mrs. Runt replied hesitatingly, "I really don't know what it was. Seemed like a sort of sword or dagger, but I never looked at it particularly, and I never took it off its nail. I used to dust it as it hung."

"Still," said Badger, "you can give us some sort of description of it, I suppose?"

"I don't know that I can," she replied. "It had a leather case, and the handle was covered with leather, I think, and it had a sort of loop, and it used to hang on that nail."

"Yes, you said that before," Badger commented sourly. "When you say it had a case, do you mean a sheath?"

"You can call it a sheath if you like," she retorted, evidently ruffled by the inspector's manner, "I call it a case."

"And how big was it? How long, for instance?"

Mrs. Runt held out her hands about a yard apart, looked at them critically, shortened the interval to a foot, extended it to two, and still varying the distance, looked vaguely at the inspector.

"I should say it was about that," she said.

"About what?" snorted Badger. "Do you mean a foot or two feet or a yard? Can't you give us some idea?"

"I can't say no clearer than what I have," she snapped. "I don't go round gentlemen's chambers measuring the things."

It seemed to me that Badger's questions were rather unnecessary, for the wall-paper below the nail gave the required information. A coloured patch on the faded ground furnished a pretty clear silhouette of a broad bladed sword or large dagger, about two feet six inches long, which had apparently hung from the nail by a loop or ring at the end of the handle. But it was not my business to point this out. I turned to Bidwell and asked:

"Can you tell us what the thing was?"

"I am afraid I can't," he replied. "I have very seldom been in these chambers. Herrington and I usually met in mine and went to the club. I have a dim recollection of something hanging on that nail, but I have not the least idea what it was or what it was like. But do you think it really matters? The thing was almost certainly a curio of some kind. It couldn't have been of any appreciable value. It is absurd, on the face of it, to suppose that this man came to Herrington's chambers, apparently by appointment, and murdered him for the sake of getting possession of an antique sword or dagger. Don't you think so?"

I did, and so, apparently, did the inspector, with the qualification that the thing seemed to have disappeared, and its disappearance ought to be accounted for; which was perfectly true, though I did not quite see how the "accounting for" was to be effected. However, as the laundress had told all that she knew, Badger gave her her dismissal and she retired to the landing, where I noticed that the night porter was still lurking. Mr. Bidwell also took his departure, and happening, a few moments later, to glance out of the window, I saw him walking slowly across the court, apparently conferring with the laundress and the porter.

As soon as we were alone, Badger assumed a friendly and confidential manner and proceeded to give advice.

"I gather that Mr. Bidwell wants you to investigate this case, but I don't fancy it is in your line at all. It is just a matter of tracing that stranger and getting hold of him. Then we shall have to find out what property there was on these premises. The laundress says that there is nothing missing, but of course no one supposes that the man came here to take the furniture. It is most probable that the motive was robbery of some kind. There's no sign of anything broken open; but then, there wouldn't be, as the keys were available."

Nevertheless he prowled round the room, examining every receptacle that had a lock and trying the drawers of the writing-table and of what looked like a file cabinet.

"You will have your work cut out," I remarked, "to trace that man. The porter's description was pretty vague."

"Yes," he replied; "there isn't much to go on. That's where you come in," he added with a grin, "with your microscopes and air-pumps and things. Now if Dr. Thorndyke was here he would just sweep a bit of dust from the floor and collect any stray oddments and have a good look at them through his magnifier, and then we should know all about it. Can't you do a bit in that line? There's plenty of dust on the floor. And here's a pin. Wonderful significant thing is a pin. And here's a wax vesta; now, that ought to tell you quite a lot. And here is the end of a leather boot-lace--at least, that is what it looks like. That must have come out of somebody's boot. Have a look at it, doctor, and see if you can tell me what kind of boot it came out of and whose boot it was."

He laid the fragment, and the match, and the pin on the table and grinned at me somewhat offensively. Inwardly I resented his impertinence-- perhaps the more so since I realised that Thorndyke would probably not have been so completely gravelled as I undoubtedly was. But I considered it politic to take his clumsy irony in good part, and even to carry on his elephantine joke. Accordingly, I picked up the three "clues," one after the other, and examined them gravely, noting that the supposed boot-lace appeared to be composed of whalebone or vulcanite.

"Well, inspector," I said. "I can't give you the answer off-hand. There's no microscope here. But I will examine these objects at my leisure and let you have the information in due course."

With that 1 wrapped them with ostentatious care in a piece of note and bestowed them in my pocket, a proceeding which the inspector watched with a sour smile.

"I'm afraid you'll be too late," said he. "Our men will probably pick up the tracks while you are doing the microscope stunt. However, I mustn't stay here any longer. We can't do anything until we know what valuables there were on the premises; and I must have the body removed and examined by the police surgeon."

He moved towards the door, and as I had no further business in the rooms, I followed, and leaving him to lock up, I took my way back to our chambers.

When Thorndyke returned to town a couple of days later, I mentioned the case to him. But what Badger had said appeared to be true. It was a case of ascertaining the identity of the stranger who had visited the dead man on that fatal night, and this seemed to be a matter for the police rather than for us. So the case remained in abeyance until the evening following the inquest, when Mr. Bidwell called on us, accompanied by a Mr. Carston, whom he introduced as an old friend of his and of Herrington's family.

"I have called," he said, "to bring you a full report of the evidence at the inquest. 1 had a shorthand writer there, and this is a typed transcript of his notes. Nothing fresh transpired beyond what Dr. Jervis knows and has probably told you, but I thought you had better have all the information in writing."

"There is no clue as to who the suspicious visitor was, I suppose?" said Thorndyke.

Not the slightest," replied Bidwell. "The porter's description is all they have to go on, and of course it would apply to hundreds of persons. But, in connection with that, there is a question on which I should like to take your opinion. Poor Herrington once mentioned to me that he was subjected to a good deal of annoyance by a certain person who from time to time applied to him for financial help. I gathered that some sort of claim was advanced, and that the demands for money were more or less of the nature of blackmail. Giles didn't say who the person was, but I got the impression that he was a relative. Now, my friend Carston, who attended the inquest with me, noticed that the porter's description of the stranger would apply fairly well to a nephew of Giles's, whom he knows slightly and who is a somewhat shady character; and the question that Carston and I have been debating is whether these facts ought to be communicated to the police. It is a serious matter to put a man under suspicion on such very slender data; and yet--"

"And yet," said Carston, "the facts certainly fit the circumstances. This fellow--his name is Godfrey Herrington--is a typical ne'er-do-well. Nobody knows how he lives. He doesn't appear to do any work. And then there is the personality of the deceased. I didn't know Giles Herrington very well, but I knew his brother, Sir Gilbert, pretty intimately, and if Giles was at all like him, a catastrophe might easily have occurred."

"What was Sir Gilbert's special characteristic?" Thorndyke asked.

"Unamiability," was the reply. "He was a most cantankerous, overbearing man, and violent at times. I knew him when I was at the Colonial Office with him,, and one of his official acts will show the sort of man he was. You may remember it, Bidwell--the Bekwè affair. There was some trouble in Bekwè, which is one of the minor kingdoms bordering on Ashanti, and Sir Gilbert was sent out as a special commissioner to settle it. And settle it he did with a vengeance. He took up an armed force, deposed the king of Bekwè, seized the royal stool, message stick, state sword, drums, and the other insignia of royalty, and brought them away with him. And what made it worse was that he treated these important things as mere loot kept some of them himself and gave away others as presents to his friends.

"It was an intolerably high-handed proceeding, and it caused a rare outcry. Even the Colonial Governor protested, and in the end the Secretary of State directed the Governor to reinstate the king and restore the stolen insignia, as these things went with the royal title and were necessary for the ceremonies of reinstatement or the accession of a new king."

"And were they restored?" asked Bidwell.

"Most of them were. But just about this time Gilbert died, and as the whereabouts of one or two of them were unknown, it was impossible to collect them then. I don't know if they have been found since."

Here Thorndyke led Mr. Carston back to the point from which he had digressed.

"You are suggesting that certain peculiarities of temper and temperament on the part of the deceased might have some bearing on the circumstances of his death."

"Yes," said Carston. "If Giles Herrington was at all like his brother--I don't know whether he was--" here he looked inquiringly at Bidwell, who nodded emphatically.

"I should say he was, undoubtedly," said he. "He was my friend, and I was greatly attached to him; but to others, I must admit, he must have appeared a decidedly morose, cantankerous, and irascible man."

"Very well," resumed Carston. "If you imagine this cadging, blackmailing wastrel calling on him and trying to squeeze him, and then you imagine Herrington refusing to be squeezed and becoming abusive and even violent, you have a fair set of antecedents for--for what, in fact, did happen."

"By the way," said Thorndyke, "what exactly did happen, according to the evidence?"

The medical evidence," replied Bidwell, "showed that the immediate cause of death was heart failure. There were marks of fingers on the throat, as you know, and various other bruises. It was evident that deceased had been violently assaulted, but death was not directly due to the injuries."

"And the finding of the jury?" asked Thorndyke.

"Wilful murder, committed by some person unknown."

It doesn't appear to me," said I, that Mr. Carston's suggestion has much present bearing on the case. It is really a point for the defence. But we are concerned with the identity of the unknown man."

"I am inclined to agree with Dr. Jervis," said Bidwell., " We have got to catch the hare before we go into culinary details."

My point is," said Carston, "that Herrington's peculiar temper suggests a set of circumstances that would render it probable that his visitor was his nephew Godfrey."

"There is some truth in that," Thorndyke agreed. It is highly speculative, but a reasonable speculation cannot be disregarded when the known facts are so few. My feeling is that the police ought to be informed of the existence of this man and his possible relations with the deceased. As to whether he is or is not the suspected stranger, that could be settled at once if he were confronted with the night porter."

Yes, that is true," said Bidwell "I think Carston and I had better call at Scotland Yard and give the Assistant Commissioner a hint on the subject. It will have to be a very guarded hint, of course."

Was the question of motive raised?" Thorndyke asked. "As to robbery, for instance."

"There is no evidence of robbery," replied Bidwell. "I have been through all the receptacles in the chambers, and everything seems intact. The keys were in poor Giles's pocket and nothing seems to have been disturbed; indeed, it doesn't appear that there was any portable property of value on the premises."

"Well," said Thorndyke, "the first thing that has to be done is to establish the identity of the nocturnal visitor. That is the business of the police. And if you call and tell them what you have told us, they will, at least, have something to investigate. They should have no difficulty in proving either that he is or is not the man whom the porter let in at the gate; and until they have settled that question, there is no need for us to take any action."

"Exactly," said Bidwell, rising and taking up his hat. "If the police can complete the case, there is nothing for us to do. However, I will leave you the report of the inquest to look over at your leisure, and will keep you informed as to how the case progresses."

When our two friends had gone, Thorndyke sat for some time turning over the sheets of the report and glancing through the depositions of the witnesses. Presently he remarked: "If it turns out that this man, Godfrey Herrington, is not the man whom the porter let in, the police will be left in the air. Apart from Bidwell's purely speculative suggestion, there seems to be no clue whatever to the visitor's identity."

"Badger would like to hear you say that," said I. "He was very sarcastic respecting our methods of research," and here I gave him an account of my interview with the inspector, including the "clues" with which he had presented me.

"It was like his impudence," Thorndyke commented smilingly, "to pull the leg of my learned junior. Still, there was a germ of sense in what he said. A collection of dust from the floor of that room, in which two men had engaged in a violent struggle, would certainly yield traces of both of them."

"Mixed up with the traces of a good many others," I remarked.

"True," he admitted. "But that would not affect the value of a positive trace of a particular individual. Supposing, for instance, that Godfrey Herrington were known to have dyed hair; and suppose that one or more dyed male hairs were found in the dust from the floor of the room. That would establish a probability that he had been in that room, and also that he was the person who had struggled with the deceased."

"Yes, I see that," said I. " Perhaps I ought to have collected some of the dust. But it isn't too late now, as Bidwell has locked up the chambers, Meanwhile, let me present you with Badger's clues. They came off the floor."

I searched in my pocket and produced the paper packet, the existence of which I had forgotten, and having opened it, offered it to him with an ironical bow. He looked gravely at the little collection, and, disregarding the pin and the match, picked out the third object and examined it curiously.

"That is the alleged boot-lace end," he remarked. "It doesn't do much credit to Badger's powers of observation. It is as unlike leather as it could well be."

"Yes," I agreed, "it is obviously whalebone or vulcanite."

"It isn't vulcanite," said he, looking closely at the broken end and getting out his pocket lens for a more minute inspection.

"What do you suppose it is?" I asked, my curiosity stimulated by the evident interest with which he was examining the object.

"We needn't suppose," he replied. "I fancy that if we get Polton to make a cross section of it, the micro- scope will tell us what it is. I will take it up to him." As he went out and I heard him ascending to the laboratory where our assistant, Polton, was at work, I was conscious of a feeling of vexation and a sense of failure. It was always thus. I had treated this fragment with the same levity as had the inspector, just dropping it into my pocket and forgetting it. Probably the thing was of no interest or importance; but whether it was or not, Thorndyke would not be satisfied until he knew for certain what it was. And that habit of examining everything, of letting nothing pass without the closest scrutiny, was one of the great secrets of his success as an investigator.

When he came down again I reopened the subject. It has occurred to me," I said, "that it might be as well for us to have a look at that room. My inspection was rather perfunctory, as Badger was there."

"I have just been thinking the same," he replied. "If Godfrey is not the man, and the police are left stranded, Bidwell will look to us to take up the inquiry, and by that time the room may have been disturbed. I think we will get the key from Bidwell to-morrow morning and make a thorough examination. And we may as well adopt Badger's excellent suggestion respecting the dust. I will instruct

Polton to come over with us and bring a full-sized vacuum-cleaner, and we can go over what he collects at our leisure."

Agreeably to this arrangement, we presented ourselves on the following morning at Mr. Bidwell's chambers, accompanied by Polton, who, however, being acutely conscious of the vacuum-cleaner, which was thinly disguised in brown paper, sneaked up the stairs and got out of sight. Bidwell opened the door himself, and Thorndyke explained our intentions to him.

"Of course you can have the key," he said, "but I don't know that it is worth your while to go into the matter. There have been developments since I saw you last night. When Carston and I called at Scotland Yard we found that we were too late. Godfrey Herrington had come forward and made a voluntary statement."

"That was wise of him," said Thorndyke, "but he would have been wiser still to have notified the porter of what had happened and sent for a doctor. He claims that the death was a misadventure, of course?"

"Not at all," replied Bidwell. "He states that when be left, Giles was perfectly well; so well that he was able to kick him--Godfrey--down the stairs and pitch him out on to the pavement. It seems, according to his account, that he called to try to get some financial help from his uncle. He admits that he was rather importunate and persisted after Giles had definitely refused. Then Giles got suddenly into a rage, thrust him out of the chambers, ran him down the stairs, and threw him out into Tanfield Court. It is a perfectly coherent story, and quite probable up to a certain point, but it doesn't account for the bruises on Giles's body or the finger-marks on his throat."

"No," agreed Thorndyke; "either he is lying, or he is the victim of some very inexplicable circumstances. But I gather that you have no further interest in the case?"

Bidwell reflected.

"Well," he said, "I don't know about that. Of course I don't believe him, but it is just possible that he is telling the truth. My feeling is that, if he is guilty, I want him convicted; but if by any chance he is innocent--well, he is Giles's nephew, and I suppose it is my duty to see that he has a fair chance. Yes, I think I would like you to watch the case independently--with a perfectly open mind, neither for nor against. But I don't see that there is much that you can do."

"Neither do I," said Thorndyke. "But one can observe and note the visible facts, if there are any. Has anything been done to the rooms?"

"Nothing whatever," was the reply. "They are just as Dr. Jervis and I found them the morning after the catastrophe."

With this he handed Thorndyke the key and we ascended to the landing, where we found Polton on guard with the vacuum-cleaner, like a sentry armed with some new and unorthodox weapon.

The appearance of the room was unchanged. The half-dislodged table-cloth, the litter of broken glass on the floor, even the displaced fender and hearth-rug, were just as I had last seen them. Thorndyke looked about him critically and remarked "The appearances hardly support Godfrey's statement. There was clearly a prolonged and violent struggle, not a mere ejectment. And look at the table cloth. The uncovered part of the table is that nearest the door, and most of the things have fallen off at the end nearest the fireplace. Obviously, the body that dislodged the cloth was moving away from the door, not towards it, which again suggests something more than an unresisted ejectment."

He again looked round, and his glance fell on the nail and the coloured silhouette on the wall-paper.

"That, I presume," said he, "is where the mysterious sword or dagger hung. It is rather large for a dagger and somewhat wide for a sword, though barbaric swords are of all shapes and sizes."

He produced his spring tape and carefully measured the phantom shape on the wall. "Thirty-one inches long," he reported, "including the loop at the end of the handle, by which it hung; seven and a half inches at the top of the scabbard, tapering rather irregularly to three inches at the tip. A curious shape. I don't remember ever having seen a sword quite like it."

Meanwhile Polton, having picked up the broken glass and other objects, had uncovered the vacuum-cleaner and now started the motor--which was driven by an attached dry battery--and proceeded very systematically to trundle the machine along the floor. At every two or three sweeps he paused to empty the receiver, placing the grey, felt-like mass on a sheet of paper, with a pencilled note of the part of the room from whence it came. The size of these masses of felted dust, and the astonishing change in the colour of the carpet that marked the trail of the cleaner, suggested that Mrs. Runt's activities had been of a somewhat perfunctory character. Polton's dredgings apparently represented the accumulations of years.

"Wonderful lot of hairs in this old dust," Polton remarked as he deposited a fresh consignment on the paper, "especially in this lot. It came from under that looking-glass on the wall. Perhaps that clothes brush that hangs under the glass accounts for it."

"Yes," I agreed, "they will be hairs brushed off Mr. Herrington's collar and shoulders. But," I added, taking the brush from its nail and examining it, "Mrs. Runt seems to have used the glass, too. There are three long hairs still sticking to the brush."

As Thorndyke was still occupied in browsing inquisitively round the room, I proceeded to make a preliminary inspection of the heaps of dust, picking out the hairs and other recognisable objects with my pocket forceps, and putting them on a separate sheet of paper. Of the former, the bulk were pretty obviously those of the late tenant--white or dull black male hairs--but Mrs. Runt had contributed quite liberally, for I picked out of the various heaps over a dozen long hairs, the mousy brown colour of which seemed to identify them as hers. The remainder were mostly ordinary male hairs of various colours, eyebrow hairs and eyelashes, of no special interest, with one exception. This was a black hair which lay flat on the paper in a Close coil, like a tiny watch-spring.

"I wonder who this negro was," said I, inspecting it through my lens.

"Probably some African or West Indian Law student," Thorndyke suggested. "There are always a good many about the Inns of Court."

He came round to examine my collection, and while he was viewing the negro hair with the aid of my lens, I renewed my investigation of the little dust-heaps. Presently I made a new discovery.

"Why," I exclaimed, "here is another of Badger's boot-laces--another piece of the same one, I think. By the way, did you ascertain what that boot-lace really was?"

"Yes," he replied. "Polton made a section of it and mounted it; and furthermore, he made a magnified photograph of it. I have the photograph in my pocket, so you can answer your own question."

He produced from his letter-case a half-plate print which he handed to me and which I examined curiously.

It is a singular object," said I, "but I don't quite make it out. It looks rather like a bundle of hairs embedded in some transparent substance."

That, in effect," he replied, "is what it is. It is an elephant's hair, probably from the tail. But, as you see, it is a compound hair; virtually a group of hairs agglutinated into a single stem. Most very large hairs are compound. A tiger's whiskers, for instance, are large, stiff hairs which, if cut across, are seen to be formed of several largish hairs fused together; and the colossal hair which grows on the nose of the rhinoceros--the so-called nasal horn--is made up of thousands of subordinate hairs."

"It is a remarkable-looking thing," I said, handing back the photograph; "very distinctive--if you happen to know what it is. But the mystery is how on earth it came here. There are no elephants in the Temple."

I certainly haven't noticed any," he replied; "and, as you say, the presence of an elephant's hair in a room in the middle of London is a rather remarkable circumstance. And yet, perhaps, if we consider all the other circumstances, it may not be impossible to form a conjecture as to how it came here. I recommend the problem to my learned friend for consideration at his leisure and now, as we have seen all that there is to see--which is mighty little--we may as well leave Polton to finish the collection of data from the floor. We can take your little selection with us."

He folded the paper containing the hairs that I had picked out into a neat packet, which he slipped into his pocket; then, having handed the key of the outer door to Polton, for return to Mr. Bidwell, he went out and I followed. We descended the stairs slowly, both of us deeply reflective. As to the subject of his meditations I could form no opinion, but my own were occupied by the problem which he had suggested; and the more I reflected on it, the less capable of solution did it appear.

We had nearly reached the ground floor when I became aware of quick footsteps descending the stairs behind us. Near the entry our follower overtook us, and as we stood aside to let him pass, I had a brief vision of a shortish, dapper, smartly-dressed coloured man--apparently an African or West Indian--who carried a small suit-case and a set of golf-clubs.

"Now," said I, in a low tone, "I wonder if that gentleman is the late owner of that negro hair that I picked up. It seems intrinsically probable as he appears to live in this building, and would be a near neighbour of Herrington's." I halted at the entry and read out the only name painted on the door-post as appertaining to the second floor--Mr. Kwaku Essien, which, I decided, seemed to fit a gentleman of colour.

But Thorndyke was not listening His long legs were already carrying him, with a deceptively leisurely air, across Tanfield Court in the wake of Mr. Essien, and at about the same pace. I put on a spurt and over took him, a little mystified by his sudden air of purpose and by the fact that he was not walking in the direction of our chambers. Still more mystified was I when it became clear that Thorndyke was following the African and keeping at a constant distance in rear of him; but I made no comment until, having pursued our quarry to the top of Middle Temple Lane, we saw him hail a taxi and drive off. Then I demanded an explanation.

"I wanted to see him fairly out of the precincts," was the reply. "because I have a particular desire to see what his chambers are like. I only hope his door has a practicable latch."

I stared at him in dismay.

"You surely don't contemplate breaking into his chambers!" I exclaimed.

"Certainly not," he replied. "if the latch Won't yield to gentle persuasion I shall give it up. But don't let me involve you, Jervis. I admit that it is a slightly irregular proceeding."

"Irregular!" I repeated. "It is house-breaking, pure and simple I can only hope that you won't be able to get in."

The hope turned out to be a vain one, as I had secretly feared. When we had reconnoitred the stairs and established the encouraging fact that the third floor was untenanted, we inspected the door above which our victim's name was painted; and a glance at the yawning key of an old-fashioned draw-latch told me that the deed was as good as done.

"Now, Jervis," said Thorndyke, producing from his pocket the curious instrument that he described as a "smoker's companion"--it was an undeniable pick- lock, made by Polton under his direction--"you had better clear out and wait for me at our chambers."

"I shall do nothing of the kind," I replied. "I am an accessory before the fact already, so I may as well stay and see the crime committed."

"Then in that case," said he, "you had better keep a look-out from the landing window and call me if any one comes to the house. That will make us perfectly safe."

I accordingly took my station at the window, and Thorndyke, having knocked several times at the "oak" without eliciting any response, set to work with the smoker's companion. In less than a minute the latch clicked, the outer door opened, and Thorndyke, pushing the inner door open, entered, leaving both doors ajar. I was devoured by curiosity as to what his purpose was. Obviously it must be a very definite one to justify this most extraordinary proceeding. But I dared not leave my post for a moment, seeing that we were really engaged in a very serious breach of the law and it was of vital importance that we should not be surprised in the act. I was therefore unable to observe my colleague's proceedings, and I waited impatiently to see if anything came of this unlawful entry.

I had waited thus some ten minutes, keeping a close watch on the pavement below, when I heard Thorndyke quickly cross the room and approach the door. A moment later he came out on the landing, bearing in his hand an object which, while it enlightened me as to the purpose of the raid, added to my mystification.

"That looks like the missing sword from Herrington's room!" I exclaimed, gazing at it in amazement.

"Yes," he replied. "I found it in a drawer in the bedroom. Only it isn't a sword."

"Then, what the deuce is it? " I demanded, for the thing looked like a broad-bladed sword in a soft leather scabbard of somewhat rude native workman ship.

By way of reply he slowly drew the object from its sheath, and as it came into sight, I uttered an exclamation of astonishment. To the inexpert eye it appeared an elongated body about nine inches in length covered with coarse, black leather, from either side of which sprang a multitude of what looked like thick, black wires. Above, it was furnished with a leather handle which was surmounted by a suspension loop of plaited leather.

I take it," said I, "that this is an elephant's tail."

"Yes," he replied, "and a rather remarkable specimen. The hairs are of unusual length. Some of them, you see, are nearly eighteen inches long."

"And what are you going to do now?" I asked.

"I am going to put it back where I found it. Then I shall run down to Scotland Yard and advise Miller to get a search warrant. He is too discreet to ask inconvenient questions."

I must admit that it was a great relief to me when, a minute later, Thorndyke came out and shut the door; but I could not deny that the raid had been justified by the results. What had, presumably, been a mere surmise had been converted into a definite fact on which action could confidently be taken.

I suppose," said I, as we walked down towards the Embankment en route for Scotland Yard, "I ought to have spotted this case."

"You had the means," Thorndyke replied. "At your first visit you learned that an object of some kind had disappeared from the wall. It seemed to be a trivial object of no value, and not likely to be connected with the crime. So you disregarded it. But it had disappeared. Its disappearance was not accounted for, and that disappearance seemed to coincide in time with the death of Herrington. It undoubtedly called for investigation. Then you found on the floor an object the nature of which was unknown to you. Obviously, you ought to have ascertained what it was."

"Yes, I ought," I admitted, "though I am not sure that I should have been much forrader even then. In fact, I am not so very much forrader even now. I don't see how you spotted this man Essien, and I don't understand why he took all this trouble and risk and even committed a murder to get possession of this trumpery curio. Of course I can make a vague guess. But I should like to hear how you ran the man and the thing to earth."

"Very well," said Thorndyke. "Let me retrace the train of discoveries and inferences in their order. First I learned that an object, supposed to be a barbaric sword of some kind, had disappeared about the time of the murder--if it was a murder. Then we heard from Carston that Sir Gilbert Herrington had appropriated the insignia and ceremonial objects belonging to the king of Bekwè; that some had subsequently been restored, but others had been given to friends as curios. As I listened to that story, the possibility occurred to me that this curio which had disappeared might be one of the missing ceremonial objects. It was not only possible: it was quite probable. For Giles Herrington was a very likely person to have received one of these gifts, and his morose temper made it unlikely that he would restore it. And then, since such an object would be of great value to somebody, and since it was actually stolen property, there would be good reasons why some interested person should take forcible possession of it. This, of course, was mere hypothesis of a rather shadowy kind. But when you produced an object which I at once suspected, and then proved, to be an elephant's hair, the hypothesis became a reasonable working theory. For, among the ceremonial objects which form what we may call the regalia of a West African king is the elephant's tail which is carried before him by a special officer as a symbol of his power and strength. An elephant's tail had pretty certainly been stolen from the king, and Carston said nothing about its having been restored.

"Well, when we went to Herrington's chambers just now, it was clear to me that the thing which had disappeared was certainly not a sword. The phantom shape. on the wall did not show much, but it did show plainly that the object had hung from the nail by a large loop at the end of the handle. But the suspension loop of a sword or dagger is always on the scabbard, never on the hilt. But if the thing was not a sword, what was it? The elephant's hair that you found on the floor seemed to answer the question.

"Now, as we came in, I had noticed on the doorpost the West African name, Kwaku Essien. A man whose name is Kwaku is pretty certainly a negro. But if this was an elephant's tail, its lawful owner was a negro, and that owner wanted to recover it and was morally entitled to take possession of it. Here was another striking agreement.

The chambers over Herrington's were occupied by a negro. Finally, you found among the floor dust a negro's hair. Then a negro had actually been in this room. But from what we know of Herrington, that negro was not there as an invited visitor. All the probabilities pointed to Mr. Essien. But the probabilities were not enough to act on. Then we had a stroke of sheer luck. We got the chance to explore Essien's chambers and seek the crucial fact. But here we are at Scotland Yard."

That night, at about eight o'clock, a familiar tattoo on our knocker announced the arrival of Mr. Superintendent Miller, not entirely unexpected as I guessed.

"Well," he said, as I let him in, "the coloured nobleman has come home. I've just had a message from the man who was detailed to watch the premises."

"Are you going to make the arrest now?" asked Thorndyke.

"Yes, and I should be glad if you could come across with me. You know more about the case than I do."

Thorndyke assented at once, and we set forth together. As we entered Tanfield Court we passed a man who was lurking in the shadow of an entry, and who silently indicated the lighted windows of the chambers for which we were bound. Ascending the stairs up which I had lately climbed with unlawful intent, we halted at Mr. Essien's door, on which the superintendent executed an elaborate flourish with his stick, there being no knocker. After a short interval we heard a bolt with drawn, the door opened a short distance, and in the interval a black race appeared looking out at us suspiciously.

"Who are you, and what do you want?" the owner of the face demanded gruffly.

"You are Mr. Kwaku Essien, I think?" said Miller, unostentatiously insinuating his foot into the door opening.

"Yes," was the reply. "But I don't know you. What is your business?"

"I am a police officer," Miller replied, edging his foot in a little farther, "and I hold a warrant to arrest you on the charge of having murdered Mr. Giles Herrington."

Before the superintendent had fairly finished his sentence, the dusky face vanished and the door slammed violently--on to the superintendent's massive foot. That foot was instantly reinforced by a shoulder and for a few moments there was a contest of forces, opposite but not equal. Suddenly the door flew open and the superintendent charged into the room. I had a momentary vision of a flying figure, closely pursued, darting through into an inner room, of the slamming of a second door--once more on an intercepting foot. And then--it all seemed to have happened in a few seconds--a dejected figure, sitting on the edge of a bed, clasping a pair of manacled hands and watching Miller as he drew the elephant's tail out of a drawer in the dressing-chest.

"This--er--article," said Miller, "belonged to Mr. Herrington, and was stolen from his premises on the night of the murder."

Essien shook his head emphatically.

"No," he replied. "You are wrong. I stole no thing, and I did not murder Mr. Herrington. Listen to me and I will tell you all about it."

Miller administered the usual caution and the prisoner continued: "This elephant-brush is one of many things stolen, years ago, from the king of Bekwè. Some of those things--most of them--have been restored, but this could not be traced for a long time. At last it became known to me that Mr. Herrington had it, and I wrote to him asking him to give it up and telling him who I was--I am the eldest living son of the king's sister, and there fore, according to our law, the heir to the kingdom. But he would not give it up or even sell it. Then, as I am a student of the Inn, I took these chambers above his, intending, when I had an opportunity, to go in and take possession of my uncle's property. The opportunity came that night that you have spoken of. I was coming up the stairs to my chambers when, as I passed his door, I heard loud voices inside as of people quarrelling. I had just reached my own door and opened it when I heard his door open, and then a great uproar and the sound of a struggle. I ran down a little way and looked over the banisters, and then I saw him thrusting a man across the landing and down the lower stairs. As they disappeared, I ran down, and finding his door ajar, I went in to recover my property. It took me a little time to find it, and I had just taken it from the nail and was going out with it when, at the door, I met Mr. Herrington coming in. He was very excited already, and when he saw me he seemed to go mad. I tried to get past him, but he seized me and dragged me back into the room, wrenching the thing out of my hand. He was very violent. I thought he wanted to kill me, and I had to struggle for my life. Suddenly he let go his hold of me, staggered back a few paces, and then fell on the floor. I stooped over him, thinking that he was taken ill, and wondering what I had better do. But soon I saw that he was not ill; he was dead. Then I was very frightened. I picked up the elephant brush and put it back into its case, and I went out very quietly, shut the door, and ran up to my rooms. That is what happened. There was no robbery and murder."

"Well," said Miller, as the prisoner and his escort disappeared towards the gate, "I suppose, in a technical sense, it is murder, but they are hardly likely to press the charge."

"I don't think it is even technically," said Thorndyke. "My feeling is that he will be acquitted if he is sent for trial. Meanwhile, I take it that my client, Godfrey Herrington, will be released from custody at once."

Yes, doctor," replied Miller, "I will see to that now. He has had better luck than he deserved, I suspect, in having his case looked after by you. I don't fancy he would have got an acquittal if he had gone for trial."

Thorndyke's forecast was nearly correct, but there was no acquittal, since there was no trial. The case against Kwaku Essien never got farther than the Grand Jury.

The Pathologist to the Rescue

"I hope," said I, as I looked anxiously out of our window up King's Bench Walk, "that our friend, Foxley, will turn up to time, or I shall lose the chance of hearing his story. I must be in court by half-past eleven. The telegram said that he was a parson, didn't it?"

"Yes," replied Thorndyke. "The Reverend Arthur Foxley."

"Then perhaps this may be he. There is a parson crossing from the Row in this direction, only he has a girl with him. He didn't say anything about a girl, did he?"

"No. He merely asked for the appointment. How ever," he added, as he joined me at the window and watched the couple approaching with their eyes apparently fixed on the number above our portico, "this is evidently our client, and punctual to the minute."

In response to the old-fashioned flourish on our little knocker, he opened the inner door and invited the clergyman and his companion to enter; and while the mutual introductions were in progress, I looked critically at our new clients. Mr. Foxley was a typical and favour able specimen of his class: a handsome, refined, elderly gentleman, prim as to his speech, suave and courteous in bearing, with a certain engaging simplicity of manner which impressed me very favourably. His companion I judged to be a parishioner for she was what ladies are apt to describe as "not quite"; that is to say, her social level appeared to appertain to the lower strata of the middle-class. But she was a fine, strapping girl, very sweet-faced and winsome, quiet and gentle in manner and obviously in deep trouble, for her clear grey eyes--fixed earnestly, almost devouringly, on Thorndyke--were reddened and swimming with unshed tears.

"We have sought your aid, Dr. Thorndyke," the clergyman began, "on the advice of my friend, Mr. Brodribb, who happened to call on me on some business. He assured me that you would be able to solve our difficulties if it were humanly possible, so I have come to lay those difficulties before you. I pray to God that you may be able to help us, for my poor young friend here, Miss Markham, is in a most terrible position, as you will understand when I tell you that her future husband, a most admirable young man named Robert Fletcher, is in the custody of the police, charged with robbery and murder."

Thorndyke nodded gravely, and the clergyman continued: "I had better tell you exactly what has happened. The dead man is one Joseph Riggs, a maternal uncle of Fletcher's, a strange, eccentric man, solitary, miserly, and of a violent, implacable temper. He was quite well-to-do, though penurious and haunted constantly by an absurd fear of poverty. His nephew, Robert, was apparently his only known relative, and, under his will, was his sole heir. Recently, however, Robert has become engaged to my friend, Miss Lilian, and this engagement was violently opposed by his uncle, who had repeatedly urged him to make what he called a profitable marriage. For Miss Lilian is a dowerless maiden--dowerless save for those endowments with which God has been pleased to enrich her, and which her future husband has properly prized above mere material wealth. However, Riggs declared, in his brutal way, that he was not going to leave his property to the husband of a shop-woman, and that Robert might look out for a wife with money or be struck out of his will.

"The climax was reached yesterday when Robert, in response to a peremptory summons, went to see his uncle. Mr. Riggs was in a very intractable mood. He demanded that Robert should break off his engagement unconditionally and at once, and when Robert bluntly insisted on his right to choose his own wife the old man worked himself up into a furious rage, shouting, cursing, using the most offensive language and even uttering threats of personal violence. Finally, he drew his gold watch from his pocket and laid it with its chain on the table then, opening a drawer, he took out a bundle of bearer bonds and threw them down by the watch.

"'There, my friend,' said he, that is your inheritance. That is all you will get from me, living or dead. Take it and go, and don't let me ever set eyes on you again.'

"At first Robert refused to accept the gift, but his uncle became so violent that eventually, for peace's sake, he took the watch and the bonds, intending to return them later, and went away. He left at half-past five, leaving his uncle alone in the house."

"How was that?" Thorndyke asked. "Was there no servant?"

"Mr. Riggs kept no resident servant. The young woman who did his housework came at half-past eight in the morning and left at half-past four. Yesterday she waited until five to get tea ready, but then, as the uproar in the sitting-room was still unabated, she thought it best to go. She was afraid to go in to lay the tea-things.

"This morning, when she arrived at the house, she found the front door unlocked, as it always was during the day. On entering, her attention was at once attracted by two or three little pools of blood on the floor of the hall, or passage. Somewhat alarmed by this, she looked into the sitting-room, and finding no one there, and being impressed by the silence in the house, she went along the passage to a back room--a sort of study or office, which was usually kept locked when Mr. Riggs was not in. Now, however, it was unlocked and the door was ajar; so having first knocked and receiving no answer, she pushed open the door and looked in; and there, to her horror, she saw her employer lying on the floor, apparently dead, with a wound on the side of his head and a pistol on the floor by his side.

"Instantly she turned and rushed out of the house, and she was running up the street in search of a police man when she encountered me at a corner and burst out with her dreadful tidings. I walked with her to the police station, and as we went she told me what had happened on the previous afternoon. Naturally, I was profoundly shocked and also alarmed, for I saw that--rightly or wrongly--suspicion must immediately fail on Robert Fletcher. The servant, Rose Turnmill, took it for granted that he had murdered her master; and when we found the station inspector, and Rose had repeated her statement to him, it was evident that he took the same view.

"With him and a sergeant, we went back to the house; but on the way we met Mr. Brodribb, who was staying at the 'White Lion' and had just come out for a walk. I told him, rapidly, what had occurred and begged him to come with us, which, with the inspector's consent, he did; and as we walked I explained to him the awful position that Robert Fletcher might be placed in, and asked him to advise me what to do. But, of course, there was nothing to be said or done until we had seen the body and knew whether any suspicion rested on Robert.

"We found the man Riggs lying as Rose had said. He was quite dead, cold and stiff. There was a pistol wound on the right temple, and a pistol lay on the floor at his right side. A little blood--but not much--had trickled from the wound and lay in a small pool on the oilcloth. The door of an iron safe was open and a bunch of keys hung from the lock; and on a desk one or two share certificates were spread out. On searching the dead man's pockets it was found that the gold watch which the servant told us he usually carried was missing, and when Rose went to the bedroom to see if it was there, it was nowhere to be found.

"Apart from the watch, however, the appearances suggested that the man had taken his own life. But against this view was the blood on the hall floor. The dead man appeared to have fallen at once from the effects of the shot, and there had been very little bleeding. Then how came the blood in the hall? The inspector decided that it could not have been the blood of the deceased; and when we examined it and saw that there were several little pools and that they seemed to form a track towards the street door, he was convinced that the blood had fallen from some person who had been wounded and was escaping from the house. And, under the circumstances, he was bound to assume that that person was Robert Fletcher; and on that assumption, he dispatched the sergeant forthwith to arrest Robert.

"On this I held a consultation with Mr. Brodribb, who pointed out that the case turned principally on the blood in the hall. If it was the blood of deceased, and the absence of the watch could be explained, a verdict of suicide could be accepted. But if it was the blood of some other person, that fact would point to murder. The question, he said, would have to be settled, if possible, and his advice to me, if I believed Robert to be innocent--which, from my knowledge of him, I certainly did--was this: Get a couple of small, clean, labelled bottles from a chemist and--with the inspector's consent--put in one a little of the blood from the hall and in the other some of the blood of the deceased. Seal them both in the inspector's presence and mine and take them up to Dr. Thorndyke. If it is possible to answer the question, Are they or are they not from the same person? he will answer it.

"Well, the inspector made no objection, so I did what he advised. And here are the specimens. I trust they may tell us what we want to know."

Here Mr. Foxley took from his attaché-case a small cardboard box, and opening it, displayed two little wide-mouthed bottles carefully packed in cotton wool. Lifting them out tenderly, he placed them on the table before Thorndyke. They were both neatly corked, sealed--with Brodribb's seal, as I noticed--and labelled; the one inscribed "Blood of Joseph Riggs," and the other "Blood of unknown origin," and both signed "Arthur Foxley" and dated. At the bottom of each was a small mass of gelatinous blood-clot.

Thorndyke looked a little dubiously at the two bottles, and addressing the clergyman, said: "I am afraid Mr. Brodribb has rather over-estimated our resources. There is no known method by which the blood of one person can be distinguished with certainty from that of another."

"Dear, dear!" exclaimed Mr. Foxley. "How disappointing! Then these specimens are useless, after all?"

"I won't say that; but it is in the highest degree improbable that they will yield any information. You must build no expectations on them."

"But you will examine them and see if anything is to be gleaned," the parson urged, persuasively.

"Yes, I will examine them. But you realise that if they should yield any evidence, that evidence might be unfavourable?"

"Yes; Mr. Brodribb pointed that out, but we are willing to take the risk, and so, I may say, is Robert Fletcher, to whom I put the question."

"Then you have seen Mr. Fletcher since the discovery?"

"Yes, I saw him at the police station after his arrest. It was then that he gave me--and also the police--the particulars that I have repeated to you. He had to make a statement, as the dead man's watch and the bonds were found in his possession."

"With regard to the pistol. Has it been identified?"

"No. It is an old-fashioned derringer which no one has ever seen before, so there is no evidence as to whose property it was."

"And as to those share certificates which you spoke of as lying on the desk. Do you happen to remember what they were?"

"Yes, they were West African mining shares; Abu sum Pa-pa was the name, I think."

"Then," said Thorndyke," Mr. Riggs had been losing money. The Abusum Pa-pa Company has just gone into liquidation. Do you know if anything had been taken from the safe?"

it is impossible to say, but apparently not, as there was a good deal of money in the cash-box, which we unlocked and inspected. But we shall hear more to-morrow at the inquest, and I trust we shall hear something there from you. But in any case I hope you will attend to watch the proceedings on behalf of poor Fletcher. And if possible, to be present at the autopsy at eleven o'clock. Can you manage that?"

"Yes. And I shall come down early enough to make an inspection of the premises if the police will give the necessary facilities."

Mr. Foxley thanked him effusively, and when the details as to the trains had been arranged, our clients rose to depart. Thorndyke shook their hands cordially, and as he bade farewell to Miss Markham he murmured a few words of encouragement. She looked up at him gratefully and appealingly as she naïvely held his hand.

"You will try to help us, Dr. Thorndyke, won't you?" she urged. "And you will examine that blood very, very carefully. Promise that you will. Remember that poor Robert's life may hang upon what you can tell about it."

I realise that, Miss Markham," he replied gently, "and I promise you that the specimens shall be most thoroughly examined; and further, that no stone shall be left unturned in my endeavours to bring the truth to light."

At his answer, spoken with infinite kindliness and sympathy, her eyes filled and she turned away with a few broken words of thanks, and the good clergyman--himself not unmoved by the little episode--took her arm and led her to the door.

"Well," I remarked as their retreating footsteps died away, "old Brodribb's enthusiasm seems to have let you in for a queer sort of task; and I notice that you appear to have accepted Fletcher's statement."

"Without prejudice," he replied. "I don't know Fletcher, but the balance of probabilities is in his favour. Still, that blood-track in the hall is a curious feature. It certainly requires explanation."

"It does, indeed!" I exclaimed, "and you have got to find the explanation! Well, I wish you joy of the job. I suppose you will carry out the farce to the bitter end as you have promised? "

Certainly," he replied. "But it is hardly a farce. I should have looked the specimens over in any case. One never knows what illuminating fact a chance observation may bring into view."

I smiled sceptically.

"The fact that you are asked to ascertain is that these two samples of blood came from the same person. If there are any means of proving that, they are unknown to me. I should have said it was an impossibility."

"Of course," he rejoined, "you are quite right, speaking academically and in general terms. No method of identifying the blood of individual persons has hitherto been discovered. But yet I can imagine the possibility, in particular and exceptional cases, of an actual, personal identification by means of blood. What does my learned friend think?"

"He thinks that his imagination is not equal to the required effort," I answered; and with that I picked up my brief-bag and went forth to my duties at the courts.

That Thorndyke would keep his promise to poor Lilian Markham was a foregone conclusion, preposterous as the examination seemed. But even my long experience of my colleague's scrupulous conscientiousness had not prepared me for the spectacle which met my eyes when I returned to our chambers. On the table stood the microscope, flanked by three slide-boxes. Each box held six trays, and each tray held six slides--a hundred and eight slides in all!

But why three boxes? I opened one. The slides--carefully mounted blood-films--were labelled "Joseph Riggs." Those in the second box were labelled," Blood from hall floor." But when I opened the third box, I beheld a collection of empty slides labelled "Robert Fletcher"!

I chuckled aloud. Prodigious! Thorndyke was going even one better than his promise. He was not only going to examine--probably had examined-- the two samples produced; he was actually going to collect a third sample for himself!

I picked out one of Mr. Riggs's slides and laid it on the stage of the microscope. Thorndyke seemed to have been using a low-power objective-- the inch-and-a-half. After a glance through this, I swung round the nose- piece to the high power. And then I got a further surprise. The brightly-coloured "white" corpuscles showed that Thorndyke had actually been to the trouble of staining the films with eosin! Again I murmured, "Prodigious!" and put the slide back in its box. For, of course, it showed just what one expected: blood--or rather, broken-up blood-clot. From its appearance I could not even have sworn that it was human blood.

I had just closed the box when Thorndyke entered the room. His quick eye at once noted the changed objective and he remarked: "I see you have been having a look at the specimens."

"A specimen." I corrected. "Enough is as good as a feast."

"Blessed are they who are easily satisfied," be retorted; and then he added: "I have altered my arrangements, though I needn't interfere with yours. I shall go down to Southaven to-night; in fact, I am starting in a few minutes."

"Why?" I asked.

"For several reasons. I want to make sure of the post-mortem tomorrow morning, I want to pick up any further facts that are available, and finally, I want to prepare a set of blood-films from Robert Fletcher. We may as well make the series complete," he added with a smile, to which I replied by a broad grin.

"Really, Thorndyke," I protested. "I'm surprised at you, at your age, too. She is a nice girl, but she isn't so beautiful as to justify a hundred and eight blood- films."

I accompanied him to the taxi, followed by Polton, who carried his modest luggage, and then returned to speculate on his probable plan of campaign. For, of course, he had one. His purposive, resolute manner told me that he had seen farther into this case than I had. I accepted that as natural and inevitable. Indeed, I may admit that my disrespectful badinage covered a belief in his powers hardly second even to old Brodribb's. I was, in fact, almost prepared to discover that those preposterous blood-films had, after all, yielded some "illuminating fact" which had sent him hurrying down to Southaven in search of corroboration.

When I alighted from the train on the following day at a little past noon, I found him waiting on the platform, ready to conduct me to his hotel for an early lunch.

"All goes well, so far," he reported. "I attended the post-mortem, and examined the wound thoroughly. The pistol was held in the right hand not more than two inches from the head; probably quite close, for the skin is scorched and heavily tattooed with black powder grains. I find that Riggs was right-handed. So the prima facie probabilities are in favour of suicide; and the recent loss of money suggests a reasonable motive."

"But what about that blood in the hall?"

"Oh, we have disposed of that. I completed the blood- film series last night."

I looked at him quickly to see if he was serious or only playing a facetious return-shot. But his face was as a face of wood.

"You are an exasperating old devil, Thorndyke!" I exclaimed with conviction. Then, knowing that cross- examination would be futile, I asked: "What are we going to do after lunch?"

"The inspector is going to show us over 'the scene of the tragedy,' as the newspapers would express it."

I noted gratefully that he had reserved this item for me, and dismissed professional topics for the time being, concentrating my attention on the old-world, amphibious streets through which we were walking. There is always something interesting in the aspect of a sea-port town, even if it is only a small one like Southaven.

The inspector arrived with such punctuality that he found us still at the table and was easily induced to join us with a cup of coffee and to accept a cigar--administered by Thorndyke, as I suspected, with the object of hindering conversation. I could see that his interest in my colleague was intense and not unmingled with awe, a fact which, in conjunction with the cigar, restrained him from any undue manifestations of curiosity, but not from continuous, though furtive, observation of my friend. Indeed, when we arrived at the late Mr. Riggs's house, I was secretly amused by the close watch that he kept on Thorndyke's movements, unsensational as the inspector turned out to be.

The house, itself, presented very little of interest excepting its picturesque old-world exterior, which fronted on a quiet by-street and was furnished with a deep bay which, as Thorndyke ascertained, commanded a clear view of the street from end to end. It was a rather shabby, neglected little house, as might have been expected, and our examination of it yielded, so far as I could see, only a single fact of any significance: which was that there appeared to be no connection what ever between the blood-stain on the study floor and the train of large spots from the middle of the hall to the street door. And on this piece of evidence--definitely unfavourable from our point of view--Thorndyke concentrated his attention when he had made a preliminary survey.

Closely followed by the watchful inspector, he browsed round the little room, studying every inch of the floor between the blood-stain and the door. The latter he examined minutely from top to bottom, especially as to the handle, the jambs, and the lintel. Then he went out into the hall, scrutinising the floor inch by inch, poring over the walls, and even looking behind the framed prints that hung on them. A reflector lamp suspended by a nail on the wall received minute and prolonged attention, as did also a massive lamp-hook screwed into one of the beams of the low ceiling, of which Thorndyke remarked as he stooped to pass under it, that it must have been fixed there by a dwarf.

"Yes," the inspector agreed, "and a fool. A swinging lamp hung on that hook would have blocked the whole fairway. There isn't too much room as it is. What a pity we weren't a bit more careful about footprints in this place. There are plenty of tracks of wet feet here on this oil-cloth; faint, but you could have made them out all right if they hadn't been all on top of one another. There's Mr. Foxley's, the girl's, mine, and the men who carried out the body, but I'm hanged if I can tell which is which. It's a regular mix up."

"Yes," I agreed, "it is all very confused. But I notice one rather odd thing. There are several faint traces of a large right foot, but I can't see any sign of the corresponding left foot. Can you?"

"Perhaps this is it," said Thorndyke, pointing to a large, vague oval mark. "I have noticed that it seems to occur in some sort of connection with the big right foot; but I must admit that it is not a very obvious foot-print."

"I shouldn't have taken it for a foot-print at all, or at any rate, not a human foot-print. It is more like the spoor of some big animal."

"It is," Thorndyke agreed; "but whatever it is, it seems to have been here before any of the others arrived. You notice that wherever it occurs, it seems to have been trodden on by some of the others."

"Yes, I had noticed that, and the same is true of the big right foot, so it seems probable that they are connected, as you say. But I am hanged if I can make anything of it. Can you, inspector?"

The inspector shook his head. He could not recognise the mark as a foot-print, but he could see very plainly that he had been a fool not to have taken more care to protect the floor.

When the examination of the hall was finished, Thorndyke opened the door and looked at the big, flat doorstep. "What was the weather like here on Wednesday evening?" he asked.

"Showery," the inspector replied; "and there were one or two heavy showers during the night. You were noticing that there are no blood-tracks on the doorstep. But there wouldn't be in any case; for if a man had come out of this door dropping blood, the blood would have dropped on wet stone and got washed away at once."

Thorndyke admitted the truth of this; and so another item of favourable evidence was extinguished. The probability that the blood in the hall was that of some person other than the deceased remained undisturbed; and I could not see that a single fact had been elicited by our inspection of the house that was in any way helpful to our client. Indeed, it appeared to me that there was absolutely no case for the defence, and I even asked myself whether we were not, in fact, merely trying to fudge up a defence for an obviously guilty man. It was not like Thorndyke to do that. But how did the case stand? There was a suggestion of suicide, but a clear possibility of homicide. There was strong evidence that a second person had been in the house, and that person appeared to have received a wound. But a wound suggested a struggle; and the servant's evidence was to the effect that when she left the house a violent altercation was in progress. The deceased was never again seen alive; and the other party to the quarrel bad been found with property of the dead man in his possession. Moreover, there was a clear motive for the crime, stupid as that crime was. For the dead man had threatened to revoke his will but as he had presumably not done so, his death left the will still operative. In short, everything pointed to the guilt of our client, Robert Fletcher.

I had just reached this not very gratifying conclusion when a statement of Thorndyke's shattered my elaborate summing up into impalpable fragments.

"I suppose, sir," said the inspector, "there isn't anything that you would care to tell us, as you are for the defence. But we are not hostile to Fletcher. In fact, he hasn't been charged. He is only being detained in custody until we have heard what turns up at the inquest. I know you have examined that blood that Mr. Foxley took, and Fletcher's blood, too, and you've seen the premises. We have given all the facilities that we could, and if you could give us any sort of hint that might be useful, I should be very much obliged."

Thorndyke reflected for a few moments. Then he replied: "There is no reason for secrecy in regard to you, inspector, who have been so helpful and friendly, so I will be quite frank. I have examined both samples of blood and Fletcher's, and I have inspected the premises; and what I am able to say definitely is this: the blood in the hall is not the blood of the deceased--"

"Ah!" exclaimed the inspector, " I was afraid it wasn't."

"And it is not the blood of Robert Fletcher."

"Isn't it now! Well, I am glad to hear that."

"Moreover," continued Thorndyke, "it was shed well after nine o'clock at night, probably not earlier than midnight."

"There, now!" the inspector exclaimed, with an admiring glance at Thorndyke, "just think of that. See what it is to be a man of science! I suppose, sir, you couldn't give us any sort of description of the person who dropped that blood in the hall?"

Staggered as I had been by Thorndyke's astonishing statements, I could not repress a grin at the inspector's artless question. But the grin faded rather abruptly as Thorndyke replied in matter-of-fact tones: "A detailed description is, of course, impossible. I can only sketch out the probabilities. But if you should happen to meet with a negro--a tall negro with a bandaged head or a contused wound of the scalp and a swollen leg--you had better keep your eye on him. The leg which is swollen is probably the left."

The inspector was thrilled; and so was I, for that matter. The thing was incredible; but yet I knew that Thorndyke's amazing deductions were the products of perfectly orthodox scientific methods. Only I could form no sort of guess as to how they had been arrived at. A negro's blood is no different from any other person's, and certainly affords no clue to his height or the condition of his legs. I could make nothing of it: and as the dialogue and the inspector's note-takings brought us to the little town hall in which the inquest was to be held, I dismissed the puzzle until such time as Thorndyke chose to solve it.

When we entered the town hall we found everything in readiness for the opening of the proceedings. The jury were already in their places and the coroner was just about to take his seat at the head of the long table. We accordingly slipped on to the two chairs that were found for us by the inspector, and the latter took his place behind the jury and facing us. Near to him Mr. Foxley and Miss Markham were seated, and evidently hailed our arrival with profound relief, each of them smiling us a silent greeting. A professional-looking man sitting next to Thorndyke I assumed to be the medical witness, and a rather good young man who sat apart with a police constable I identified as Robert Fletcher.

The evidence of the "common" witnesses, who deposed to the general facts, told us nothing that we did not already know, excepting that it was made clear that Fletcher had left his uncle's house not later than seven o'clock and that thereafter until the following morning his whereabouts were known. The medical witness was cautious, and kept an uneasy eye on Thorndyke. The wound which caused the death of deceased might have been inflicted by himself or by some other person. He had originally given the probable time of death as six or seven o'clock on Wednesday evening. He now admitted reply to a question from Thorndyke that he had not taken the temperature of the body, and that the rigidity and other conditions were not absolutely inconsistent with a considerable later time of death. Death might even have occurred after midnight.

In spite of this admission, however, the sum of the evidence tended strongly to implicate Fletcher, and one or two questions from jurymen suggested a growing belief in his guilt. I had no doubt whatever that if the case had been put to the jury at this stage, a unanimous verdict of "wilful murder" would have been the result. But, as the medical witness returned to his seat, the coroner fixed an inquisitive eye on Thorndyke.

"You have not been summoned as a witness, Dr. Thorndyke," said he, "but I understand that you have made certain investigations in this case. Are you able to throw any fresh light on the circumstances of the death of the deceased, Joseph Riggs?

"Yes," Thorndyke replied. "I am in a position to give important and material evidence."

Thereupon he was sworn, and the coroner, still watching him curiously, said: "I am informed that you have examined samples of the blood of deceased and the blood which was found in the hall of deceased's house. Did you examine them, and if so, what was the object of the examination?"

"I examined both samples and also samples of the blood of Robert Fletcher. The object was to ascertain whether the blood on the hall floor was the blood of the deceased or of Robert Fletcher."

The coroner glanced at the medical witness, and a faint smile appeared on the face of each.

"And did you," the former asked in a slightly ironical tone, "form any opinion on the subject?"

"I ascertained definitely that the blood in the hall was neither that of the deceased nor that of Robert Fletcher."

The coroner's eyebrows went up, and once more he glanced significantly at the doctor.

"But," he demanded incredulously, "is it possible to distinguish the blood of one person from that of another?"

"Usually it is not, but in certain exceptional cases it is. This happened to be an exceptional case."

"In what respect?"

"It happened," Thorndyke replied, "that the person whose blood was found in the hall suffered from the parasitic disease known as filariasis. His blood was infested with swarms of a minute worm named *Filaria nocturna*. I have here," he continued, taking out of his research-case the two bottles and the three boxes, "thirty-six mounted specimens of this blood, and in every one of them one or more of the parasites is to be seen. I have also thirty-six mounted specimens each of the blood of the deceased and. the blood of Robert Fletcher. In not one of these specimens is a single parasite to be found. Moreover, I have examined Robert Fletcher and the body of the deceased, and can testify that no sign of filarial disease was to be discovered in either. Hence it is certain, that the blood found in the halt was not the blood of either of these two persons."

The ironic smile had faded from the coroner's face. He was evidently deeply impressed, and his manner was quite deferential as he asked: "Do these very remarkable observations of yours lead to any further inferences?"

"Yes," replied Thorndyke. "They render it certain that this blood was shed no earlier than nine o'clock and probably nearer midnight."

"Really!" the astonished coroner exclaimed. "Now, how is it possible to fix the time in that exact manner?"

"By inference from the habits of the parasite," Thorndyke explained. "This particular *filaria* is distributed by the mosquito, and its habits are adapted to the habits of the mosquito. During the day, the worms are not found in the blood; they remain hidden in the tissues of the body. But about nine o'clock at night they begin to migrate from the tissues into the blood, and remain in the blood during the hours when the mosquitoes are active. Then about six o'clock in the morning, they leave the blood and migrate back into the tissues.

"There is another very similar species--*Filaria diurna*--which has exactly opposite habits, adapted to day-flying suctorial insects. It appears in the blood about eleven in the forenoon and goes back into the tissues at about six o'clock in the evening."

"Astonishing!" exclaimed the coroner. "Wonderful! By the way, the parasites that you found could not, I suppose, have been *Filaria diurna*?"

"No," Thorndyke replied. "The time excludes that possibility. The blood was certainly shed after six. They were undoubtedly nocturna, and the large numbers found suggest a late hour. The parasites come out of the tissues very gradually, and it is only about midnight that they appear in the blood in really large numbers."

"That is very important," said the coroner. "But does this disease affect any particular class of persons?"

"Yes," Thorndyke replied. "As the disease is con fined to tropical countries, the sufferers are naturally residents of the tropics, and nearly always natives. In West Africa, for instance, it is common among the negroes but practically unknown among the white residents."

"Should you say that there is a distinct probability that this unknown person was a negro?"

"Yes. But apart from the *filaria* there is direct evidence that he was. Searching for some cause of the bleeding, I noticed a lamp-hook screwed into the ceiling, and low enough to strike a tall man's head. I examined it closely, and observed on it a dark, shiny mark, like a blood-smear, and one or two short coiled hairs which I recognised as the scalp-hairs of a negro. I have no doubt that the unknown man is a negro, and that he has a wound of the scalp."

"Does filarial disease produce any effects that can be recognised?

"Frequently it does. One of the commonest effects produced by *Filaria nocturna*, especially among negroes, is the condition known as elephantiasis. This consists of an enormous swelling of the extremities, most usually of one leg, including the foot; whence the name. The leg and foot look like those of an elephant. As a matter of fact, the negro who was in the hall suffered from elephantiasis of the left leg. I observed prints of the characteristically deformed foot on the oil-cloth covering the floor."

Thorndyke's evidence was listened to with intense interest by everyone present, including myself. Indeed, so spell-bound was his audience that one could have heard a pin drop; and the breathless silence continued for some seconds after he had ceased speaking. Then, in the midst of the stillness, I heard the door creak softly behind me.

There was nothing particularly significant in the sound. But its effects were amazing. Glancing at the inspector, who faced the door, I saw his eyes open and his jaw drop until his face was a very mask of astonishment. And as this expression was reflected on the faces of the jurymen, the coroner and everyone present, excepting Thorndyke, whose back was towards the door, I turned to see what had happened. And then I was as astonished as the others.

The door had been pushed open a few inches and a head thrust in--a negro's head, covered with a soiled and blood rag forming a rough bandage. As I gazed at the black, shiny, inquisitive face, the man pushed the door farther open and shuffled into the room; and instantly there arose on all sides a soft rustle and an inarticulate murmur followed by breathless silence, while every eye was riveted on the man's left leg.

It certainly was a strange, repulsive--looking member, its monstrous bulk exposed to view through the slit trouser and its great shapeless foot--shoeless, since no shoe could have contained it--rough and horny like the foot of an elephant. But it was tragic and pitiable, too for the man, apart from this horrible excrescence, was a fine, big, athletic-looking fellow.

The coroner was the first to recover. Addressing Thorndyke, but keeping an eye on the negro, he said: "Your evidence, then, amounts to this: On the night of Joseph Riggs' death, there was a stranger in the house. That stranger was a negro, who seems to have wounded his head and who, you say, had a swelled left leg."

"Yes," Thorndyke admitted, "that is the substance of my evidence."

Once more a hush fell on the room. The negro stood near the door, rolling his eyes to and fro over the assembly as if uneasily conscious that everyone was looking at him. Suddenly, he shuffled up to the foot of the table and addressed the coroner in deep, buzzing, resonant tones. "You tink I kill dat ole man! I no kill um. He kill himself. I look um."

Having made this statement, he rolled his eyes defiantly round the court, and then turned his face expectantly towards the coroner, who said: "You say you know that Mr. Riggs killed himself?"

"Yas. I look um. He shoot himself. You tink I shoot urn. I tell you I no shoot um. Why I fit kill this man? I no sabby um."

"Then," said the coroner, "if you know that he killed himself, you must tell us all that you know; and you must swear to tell us the truth."

"Yas," the negro agreed, "I tell you eberyting one time. I tell you de troof. Dat ole man kill himself."

When the coroner had explained to him that he was not bound to make any statement that would incriminate him, as he still elected to give evidence, he was sworn and proceeded to make his statement with curious fluency and self-possession.

"My name Robert Bruce. Dat my English name. My country name Kwaku Mensab. I live for Winnebah on de Gold Coast. Dis time I cook's mate for dat steamer Leckie. On Wednesday night I lay in my bunk. I no fit sleep. My leg he chook me. I look out of de porthole. Plenty moon live. In my country when de moon big, peoples walk about. So I get up. I go ashore to walk about de town. Den de rain come. Plenty rain. Rain no good for my sickness. So I try for open house doors. No fit. All doors locked. Den I come to dis ole man's house. I turn de handle. De door open. I go in. I look in one room. All dark. Nobody live. Den I look annudder room. De door open a little. Light live inside. I no like dat I tink, spose somebody come out and see me, be link I come for teef someting. So I tink I go away.

"Den someting make 'Ping!' same like gun. I hear someting fail down in dat room. I go to de door and I sing out, 'Who live in dere?' Nobody say nutting. So I open de door and look in. De room full ob smoke. I look dat ale man on de floor. I look dat pistol. I sabby dat ole man kill himself. Den I frighten too much. I run out. D place all dark. Someting knock my head. He make blood come plenty. I go back for ship. I no say nutting to nobody. Dis day I hear peoples talk 'bout dis inquess to find out who kill dat ole man. So I come to hear what peoples say. I hear dat gentleman say I kill dat ole man. So I tell you eberyting. I tell you de troof. Finish."

"Do you know what time it was when you came ashore?" the coroner asked.

"Yas. When I come down de ladder I hear eight bells ring. I get back to de ship jus' before dey ring two bells in de middle watch."

"Then you came ashore at midnight and got back just before one o'clock?"

"Yas. Dat is what I say."

A few more questions put by the coroner having elicited nothing fresh, the case was put briefly to the jury.

"You have heard the evidence, gentlemen, and most remarkable evidence it was. Like myself, you must have been deeply impressed by the amazing skill with which Dr. Thorndyke reconstructed the personality of the unknown visitor to that house, and even indicated correctly the very time of the visit, from an examination of a mere chance blood-stain. As to the statement of Kwaku Mensab, I can only say that I see no reason to doubt its truth. You will note that it is in complete agreement with Dr. Thorndyke's evidence, and it presents no inconsistencies or improbabilities. Possibly the police may wish to make some further inquiries, but for our purposes it is the evidence of an eyewitness, and as such must be given full weight. With these remarks, I leave you to consider your verdict."

The jury took but a minute or two to deliberate. Indeed, only one verdict was possible if the evidence was to be accepted, and that was agreed on unanimously--suicide whilst temporarily insane. As soon as it was announced, the inspector, formally and with congratulations, released Fletcher from custody, and presently retired in company with the negro to make a few inquiries on board the ship.

The rising of the court was the signal for a wild demonstration of enthusiasm and gratitude to Thorndyke. To play his part efficiently in that scene he would have needed to be furnished, like certain repulsive Indian deities, with an unlimited outfit of arms. For everyone wanted to shake his hand, and two of them--Mr. Foxley and Miss Markham--did so with such pertinacity as entirely to exclude the other candidates.

"I can never thank you enough," Miss Markham exclaimed, with swimming eyes, "if I should live to be a hundred. But I shall think of you with gratitude every day of my life. Whenever I look at Robert, I shall remember that his liberty, and even his life, are your gifts."

Here she was so overcome by grateful emotion that she again seized and pressed his hand. I think she was within an ace of kissing him; but being, perhaps, doubtful how he would take it, compromised by kissing Robert instead. And, no doubt, it was just as well.

Gleanings from the Wreckage

There was a time, and not so very long ago, when even the main streets of London, after midnight, were as silent as--not the grave; that is an unpleasant simile. Besides, who has any experience of conditions in the grave? But they were nearly as silent as the streets of a village. Then the nocturnal pedestrian could go his way encompassed and soothed by quiet, which was hardly disturbed by the rumble of a country wagon wending to market or the musical tinkle of the little bells on the collar of the hansom-cab horse sedately drawing some late reveller homeward.

Very different is the state of those streets nowadays. Long after the hour when the electric trams have ceased from troubling and the motor omnibuses are at rest, the heavy road transport from the country thunders through the streets; the air is rent by the howls of the electric hooter, and belated motor-cyclists fly past, stuttering explosively like perambulant Lewis guns with an in exhaustible charge.

"Let us get into the by-streets," said Thorndyke, as a car sped past us uttering sounds suggestive of a dyspeptic dinosaur. "We don't want our conversation seasoned with mechanical objurgations. In the back-streets it is still possible to hear oneself speak and forget the march of progress."

We turned into a narrow by-way with the confidence of the born and bred Londoner in the impossibility of losing our direction, and began to thread the intricate web of streets in the neighbourhood of a canal.

"It is a remarkable thing," Thorndyke resumed anon, "that every new application of science seems to be designed to render the environment of civilised man more and more disagreeable. If the process goes much farther, as it undoubtedly will, we shall presently find ourselves looking back wistfully at the Stone-age as the golden age of human comfort."

At this point his moralising was cut short by a loud, sharp explosion. We both stopped and looked about from the parapet of the bridge that we were crossing.

"Quite like old times," Thorndyke remarked. "Carries one back to 1915, when friend Fritz used to call on us. Ah! There is the place; the top story of that tail building across the canal." He pointed as he spoke to a factory- like structure, from the upper windows of which a lurid light shone and rapidly grew brighter.

"It must be down the next turning," said I, quickening my pace.

But he restrained me, remarking: "There is no hurry. That was the sound of high explosive, and those flames suggest nitro compounds burning. Festina lente. There may be some other packets of high explosives."

He had hardly finished speaking when a flash of dazzling violet light burst from the burning building. The windows flew out bodily, the roof opened in places, and almost at the same moment the clang of a violent explosion shook the ground under our feet, a puff of wind stirred our hair, and then came a clatter of falling glass and slates.

We made our way at a leisurely pace towards the scene of the explosion, through streets lighted up by the ruddy glare from the burning factory. But others were less cautious. In a few minutes the street was filled by one of those crowds which, in London, seem mysteriously to spring up in an instant where but a moment before not a person was to be seen. Before we had reached the building, a fire-engine had rumbled past us, and already a sprinkling of policemen had appeared as if, like the traditional frogs, they had dropped from the clouds.

In spite of the ferocity of its outbreak, the fire seemed to be no great matter, for even as we looked and before the fire-hose was fully run out, the flames began to die down. Evidently, they had been dealt with by means of extinguishers within the building, and the services of the engine would not be required after all. Noting this flat ending to what had seemed so promising a start, we were about to move off and resume our homeward journey when I observed a uniformed inspector who was known to us, and who, observing us at the same instant, made his way towards us through the crowd.

"You remind me, sir," said be, when he had wished us good-evening," of the stories of the vultures that make their a in the sky from nowhere when a camel drops dead in the desert. I don't mean anything uncomplimentary," he hastened to add. "I was only thinking of the wonderful instinct that has brought you to this very spot at this identical moment, as if you had smelt a case afar off."

"Then your imagination has misled you," said Thorndyke, "for I haven't smelt a case, and I don't smell one now. Fires are not in my province."

"No, sir," replied the inspector, "but bodies are, and the fireman tells me that there is a dead man up there--or at least the remains of one. I am going up to inspect. Do you care to come up with me?"

Thorndyke considered for a. moment, but I knew what his answer would be, and I was not mistaken.

"As a matter of professional interest, I should," he replied, "but I don't want to be summoned as a witness at the inquest."

"Of course you don't, sir," the inspector agreed, "and I will see that you are not summoned, unless an expert witness is wanted. I need not mention that you have been here; but I should be glad of your opinion for my own guidance in investigating the case."

He led us through the crowd to the door of the building, where we were joined by a fireman--whose helmet I should have liked to borrow--by whom we were piloted up the stairs. Half up we met the night-watchman, carrying an exhausted extinguisher and a big electric lantern, and he joined our procession, giving us the news as we ascended.

"It's all safe up above," said he, "excepting the roof; and that isn't so very much damaged. The big windows saved it. They blew out and let off the force of the explosion. The floor isn't damaged at all. It's girder and concrete. But poor Mr. Manford caught it properly. He was fairly blown to bits."

"Do you know how it happened?" the inspector asked.

"I don't," was the reply. "When I came on duty Mr. Manford was up there in his private laboratory. Soon afterwards a friend of his--

a foreign gentleman of the name of Bilsky--came to see him. I took him up, and then Mr. Manford said he had some business to do, and after that he had got a longish job to do and would be working late. So he said I might turn in and he would let me know when he had finished. And he did let me know with a vengeance, poor chap I lay down in my clothes, and I hadn't been asleep above a couple of hours when some noise woke me up. Then there came a most almighty bang. I rushed for an extinguisher and ran upstairs, and there I found the big laboratory all ablaze, the windows blown out and the ceiling down. But it wasn't so bad as it looked. There wasn't very much stuff up there; only the experimental stuff, and that burned out almost at once. I got the rest of the fire out in a few minutes."

"What stuff is it that you are speaking of?" the inspector asked.

"Celluloid, mostly, I think," replied the watchman. "They make films and other celluloid goods in the works. But Mr. Manford used to do experiments in the material up in his laboratory. This time he was working with alloys, melting them on the gas furnace. Dangerous thing to do with all that inflammable stuff about. I don't know what there was up there, exactly. Some of it was celluloid, I could see by the way it burned, but the Lord knows what it was that exploded. Some of the raw stuff, perhaps."

At this point we reached the top floor, where a door blown off its hinges and a litter of charred wood fragments filled the landing. Passing through thc yawning doorway, we entered the laboratory and looked on a hideous scene of devastation. The windows were mere holes, the ceiling a gaping space fringed with black and ragged lathing, through which the damaged roof was visible by the light of the watchman's powerful lantern. The floor was covered with the fallen plaster and fragments of blackened woodwork, but its own boards were only slightly burnt in places, owing, no doubt, to their being fastened directly to the concrete which formed the actual floor.

"You spoke of some human remains," said the inspector.

"Ah!" said the watchman, "you may well say 'remains'. Just come here." He led the way over the rubbish to a corner of the laboratory, where he halted and threw the light of his lantern down on a brownish, dusty, globular object that lay on the floor half buried in plaster. "That's all that's left of poor Mr. Manford; that and a few other odd pieces. I saw a hand over the other side."

Thorndyke picked up the head and placed it on the blackened remnant of a bench, where, with the aid of the watchman's lantern and the inspection lamp which I produced from our research-case, he examined it curiously. It was extremely, but unequally, scorched. One ear was completely shrivelled, and most of the face was charred to the bone. But the other ear was almost intact; and though most of the hair was burned away to the scalp, a tuft above the less damaged ear was only singed, so that it was possible to see that the hair had been black, with here and there a stray white hair.

Thorndyke made no comments, but I noticed that he examined the gruesome object minutely, taking nothing for granted. The inspector noticed this, too; and when the examination was finished, looked at him inquiringly.

"Anything abnormal, sir?" he asked.

"No," replied Thorndyke; "nothing that is not accounted for by fire and the explosion. I see he had no natural teeth, so he must have worn a complete set of false teeth. That should help in the formal identification, if the plates are not completely destroyed."

"There isn't much need for identification," said the watchman, "seeing that there was nobody in the building but him and me. His friend went away about half-past twelve. I heard Mr. Manford let him out."

"The doctor means at the inquest," the inspector explained. "Somebody has got to recognise the body if possible."

He took the watchman's lantern, and throwing its light on the floor, began to search among the rubbish. Very soon he disinterred from under a heap of plaster the headless trunk. Both legs were attached, though the right was charred below the knee and the foot blown off, and one complete arm. The other arm--the right--was intact only to the elbow. Here, again, the burning was very unequal. In some parts the clothing had been burnt off or blown away completely; in others, enough was left to enable the watchman to recognise it with certainty. One leg was much more burnt than the other; and whereas the complete arm was only scorched, the dismembered one was charred almost to the bone. When the trunk had been carried to the bench and laid there beside the head, the lights were turned on it for Thorndyke to make his inspection.

"It almost seems," said the police officer, as the hand was being examined, "as if one could guess how he was standing when the explosion occurred. I think I can make out finger-marks--pretty dirty ones, too-- on the back of the hand, as if he had been standing with his hands clasped together behind him while he watched something that he was experimenting with." The inspector glanced for confirmation at Thorndyke, who nodded approvingly.

"Yes," he said, "I think you are right. They are very indistinct, but the marks are grouped like fingers. The small mark near the wrist suggests a little finger and the separate one near the knuckle looks like a fore-finger, while the remaining two marks are close together." He turned the band over and continued "And there, in the palm, just between the roots of the third and fourth fingers, seems to be the trace of a thumb. But they are all very faint. You have a quick eye, inspector."

The gratified officer, thus encouraged, resumed his explorations among the debris in company with the watchman--the fireman had retired after a professional look round--leaving Thorndyke to continue his examination of the mutilated corpse, at which I looked on unsympathetically. For we had had a long day and I was tired and longing to get home. At length I drew out my watch, and with a portentous yawn, entered a mild protest.

"It is nearly two o'clock," said I. "Don't you think we had better be getting on? This really isn't any concern of ours, and there doesn't seem to bc anything in it, from our point of view."

"Only that we are keeping our intellectual joints supple," Thorndyke replied with a smile. "But it is getting late. Perhaps we had better adjourn the inquiry."

At this moment, however, the inspector discovered the missing forearm-- completely charred--with the fingerless remains of the hand, and almost immediately afterwards the watchman picked up a dental plate of some white metal, which seemed to be practically uninjured. But our brief inspection of these objects elicited nothing of interest, and having glanced at them, we took our departure, avoiding on the stairs an eager reporter, all agog for "copy."

A few days later we received a visit, by appointment, from a Mr. Herdman, a solicitor who was unknown to us and who was accompanied by the widow of Mr. James Manford, the victim of the explosion. In the interval the inquest had been opened but had been adjourned for further examination of the premises and the remains. No mention had been made of our visit to the building, and so far as I knew nothing had been said to anybody on the subject.

Mr. Herdman came to the point with business directness.

"I have called," he said, "to secure your services, if possible, in regard to the matter of which I spoke in my letter. You have probably seen an account of the disaster in the papers?"

"Yes," replied Thorndyke. "I read the report of the inquest."

"Then you know the principal facts. The inquest, as you know, was adjourned for three weeks. When it is resumed; I should like to retain you to attend on behalf of Mrs. Manford."

"To watch the case on her behalf?" Thorndyke suggested.

"Well, not exactly," replied Herdman. "I should ask you to inspect the premises and the remains of poor Mr. Manford, so that, at the adjourned inquest, you could give evidence to the effect that the explosion and the death of Mr. Manford were entirely due to accident."

"Does anyone say that they were not?" Thorndyke asked.

"No, certainly not," Mr. Herdman replied hastily. "Not at all. But I happened, quite by chance, to see the manager of the 'Pilot' Insurance Society, on another matter, and I mentioned the case of Mr. Manford. He then let drop a remark which made me slightly uneasy. He observed that there was a suicide clause in the policy, and that the possibility of suicide would have to be ruled out before the claim could be settled. Which suggested a possible intention to contest the claim."

"But," said Thorndyke, "I need not point out to you that if he sets up the theory of suicide, it is for him to prove it, not for you to disprove it. Has anything transpired which would lend colour to such a suggestion?"

"Nothing material," was the reply. "But we should feel more happy if you could be present and give positive evidence that the death was accidental."

"That," said Thorndyke, "would be hardly possible. But my feeling is that the suicide question is negligible. There is nothing to suggest it, so far as I know. Is there anything known to you?"

The solicitor glanced at his client and replied somewhat evasively: "We are anxious to secure ourselves. Mrs. Manford is left very badly off, unless there is some personal property that we don't know about. If the insurance is not paid, she will be absolutely ruined. There isn't enough to pay the debts. And I think the suicide question might be raised--even successfully--on several points. Manford had been rather queer lately: jumpy and rather worried. Then, he was under notice to terminate his engagement at the works. His finances were in a confused state; goodness knows why, for he had a liberal salary. And then there was some domestic trouble. Mrs. Manford had actually consulted me about getting a separation. Some other woman, you know."

"I should like to forget that," said Mrs. Manford; "and it wasn't that which worried him. Quite the contrary. Since it began he had been quite changed. So smart in his dress and so particular in his appearance. He even took to dyeing his hair. I remember that he opened a fresh bottle of dye the very morning before his death and took no end of trouble putting it on. It wasn't that entanglement that made him jumpy. It was his money affairs. He had too many irons in the fire."

Thorndyke listened with patient attention to these rather irrelevant details and inquired: "What sort of irons?"

"I will tell 'you," said Herdman. " About three months ago he had need for two thousand pounds; for what purpose, I can't say, but Mrs. Manford thinks it was to invest in certain valuables that he used to purchase from time to time from a Russian dealer named Bilsky. At any rate, he got this sum on short loan from a Mr. Clines, but meanwhile arranged for a longer loan with a Mr. Elliott on a note of hand and an agreement to insure his life for the amount.

"As a matter of fact, the policy was made out in Elliott's name, he having proved an insurable interest. So if the insurance is paid, Elliott is settled with. Otherwise the debt falls on the estate, which would be disastrous; and to make it worse, the day before his death, he drew out five hundred pounds--nearly the whole balance--as he was expecting to see Mr. Bilsky, who liked to be paid in bank-notes. He did see him, in fact, at the laboratory, but they couldn't have done any business, as no jewels were found."

"And the bank-notes?"

"Burned with the body, presumably. He must have had them with him."

"You mentioned," said Thorndyke, "that he occasionally bought jewels from this Russian. What became of them?"

"Ah!" replied Herdman, "there is a gleam of hope there. He had a safe deposit somewhere. We haven't located it yet, but we shall. There may be quite a nice little nest-egg in it. But meanwhile there is the debt to Elliott. He wrote to Manford about it a day or two ago. Von have the letter, I think," he added, addressing Mrs. Manford, who thereupon produced two envelopes from her handbag and laid them on the table.

"This is Mr. Elliott's letter," she said. "Merely a friendly reminder, you see, telling him that he is just off to the Continent and that he has given his wife a power of attorney to act in his absence."

Thorndyke glanced through the letter and made a few notes of its contents. Then he looked inquiringly at the other envelope.

"That," said Mrs. Manford, "'is a photograph of my husband. I thought it might help you if you were going to examine the body."

As Thorndyke drew the portrait out and regarded it thoughtfully, I recalled the shapeless, blackened fragments of its subject; and when he passed it to me, I inspected it with a certain grim interest, and mentally compared it with those grisly remains. It was a commonplace face, rather unsymmetrical--the nose was deflected markedly to the left, and the left eye had a pronounced divergent squint. The bald head, with an abundant black fringe and an irregular scar on the side of the forehead, sought compensation in a full beard and moustache, both apparently jet-black. It was not an attractive countenance, and it was not improved by a rather odd-shaped ear--long, lobeless, and pointed above, like the ear of a satyr.

"I realise your position," said Thorndyke, "but I don't quite see what you want of me. If," he continued, addressing the solicitor," you had thought of my giving ex parte evidence, dismiss the idea. I am not a witness-advocate. All I can undertake to do is to investigate the case and try to discover what really happened. But in that case, whatever I may discover I shall disclose to the coroner. Would that suit you?"

The lawyer looked doubtful and rather glum, but Mrs. Manford interposed, firmly: "Why not? We are not proposing any deception, but I am certain that he did not commit suicide. I agree unreservedly to what you propose."

With this understanding--which the lawyer was disposed to boggle at-- our visitors took their leave. As soon as they were gone, I gave utterance to the surprise with which I had listened to Thorndyke's proposal.

"I am astonished at your undertaking this case. Of course, you have given them fair warning, but still, it will be unpleasant if you have to give evidence unfavourable to your client."

"Very," he agreed. "But what makes you think I may have to?"

"Well, you seem to reject the probability of suicide, but have you forgotten the evidence at the inquest?"

"Perhaps I have," he replied blandly. "Let us go over it again."

I fetched the report from the office, and spreading it out on the table began to read it aloud. Passing over the evidence of the inspector and the fireman, I came to that of the night-watchman.

"Shortly after I came on duty at ten o'clock, a foreign, gentleman named Bilsky called to see Mr. Manford. I knew him by sight, because he had called once or twice before at about the same time. I took him up to the laboratory, where Mr. Manford was doing something with a big crucible on the gas furnace. He told me that he had some business to transact with Mr. Bilsky and when he had finished he would let him out. Then he was going to do some experiments in making alloys, and as they would probably take up most of the night he said I might as well turn in. He said he would call me when he was ready to go. So I told him to be careful with the furnace and not set the place on fire and burn me in my bed, and then I went downstairs. I had a look round to see that everything was in order, and then I took off my boots and laid down. About half- past twelve I heard Mr. Manford and Bilsky come down. I recognised Mr. Bilsky by a peculiar cough that he had and by the sound of his stick and his limping tread--he had something the matter with his right foot and walked quite lame."

"You say that the deceased came down with him," said the coroner. "Are you quite sure of that?"

'Well, I suppose Mr. Manford came down with him, but I can't say I actually heard him."

"You did not hear him go up again?"

"No, I didn't. But I was rather sleepy and I wasn't listening very particular. Well, then I went to sleep and slept till about half-past one, when some noise woke me. I was just getting up to see what it was when I heard a tremendous bang, right overhead. I ran down and turned the gas off at the main and then I got a fire extinguisher and ran up to the laboratory. The place seemed to be all in a blaze, but it wasn't much of a fire after all, for by the time the fire engines arrived I had got it practically out."

The witness then described the state of the laboratory and the finding of the body, but as this was already known to us, I passed on to the evidence of the next witness, the superintendent of the fire brigade, who had made a preliminary inspection of the premises. It was a cautious statement and subject to the results of a further examination; but clearly the officer was not satisfied as to the cause of the outbreak. There seemed to have been two separate explosions, one near a cupboard and another--apparently the second--in the cupboard itself; and there seemed to be a burned track connecting the two spots. This might have been accidental or it might have been arranged. Witness did not think that the explosive was celluloid. It seemed to be a high explosive of some kind. But further investigations were being made.

The superintendent was followed by Mrs. Manford, whose evidence was substantially similar to what she and Mr. Herdman had told us, and by the police surgeon, whose description of the remains conveyed nothing new to us. Finally, the inquest was adjourned for three weeks to allow of further examination of the premises and the remains.

"Now," I said, as I folded up the report, "I don't see how you are able to exclude suicide. If the explosion was arranged to occur when Manford was in the laboratory, what object, other than suicide, can be imagined?"

Thorndyke looked at me with an expression that I knew only too well. "Is it impossible," he asked, "to imagine that the object might have been homicide?"

"But," I objected, "there was no one there but Manford--after Bilsky left."

"Exactly," he agreed, dryly; "after Bilsky left. But up to that time there were two persons there."

I must confess that I was startled, but as I rapidly reviewed the circumstances I perceived the cogency of Thorndyke's suggestion. Bilsky had been present when Manford dismissed the night-watchman. He knew that there would be no interruption. The inflammable and explosive materials were there, ready to his hand. Then Bilsky had gone down to the door alone instead of being conducted down and let out; a very striking circumstance, this. Again, no jewels had been found though the meeting had been ostensibly for the purpose of a deal; and the bank-notes had vanished utterly. This was very remarkable. In view of the large sum, it was nearly certain that the notes would be in a close bundle, and we all know how difficult it is to burn tightly-folded paper. Yet they had vanished without leaving a trace. Finally, there was Bilsky himself. Who was he? Apparently a dealer in stolen property--a hawker of the products of robbery and murder committed during the revolution.

Yes," I admitted, "the theory of homicide is certainly tenable, But unless some new facts can be produced, it must remain a matter of speculation."

"I think, Jervis," he rejoined, "you must be overlooking the facts that are known to us. We were there. We saw the place within a few minutes of the explosion and we examined the body. What we saw established a clear presumption of homicide, and what we have heard this, morning confirms it. I may say that I communicated my suspicions the very next day to the coroner and to Superintendent Miller."

"Then you must have seen more than I did," I began. But he shook his head and cut short my protestations.

"You saw what I saw, Jervis, but you did not interpret its meaning. However, it is not too late. Try to recall the details of our adventure and what our visitors have told us. I don't think you will then entertain the idea of suicide."

I was about to put one or two leading questions, but at this moment footsteps became audible ascending our stairs. The knock which followed informed me that our visitor was Superintendent Miller, and I rose to admit him.

"Just looked in to report progress," he announced as he subsided into an arm-chair. "Not much to report, but what there is supports your view of the case. Bilsky has made a clean bolt. Never went home to his hotel. Evidently meant to skedaddle, as he has left nothing of any value behind. But it was a stupid move, for it would have raised suspicion in any case. The notes were a consecutive batch. All the numbers are known, but, of course, none of them have turned up yet. We have made inquiries about Bilsky, and gather that he is a shady character; practically a fence who deals in the jewellery stolen from those unfortunate Russian aristocrats. But we shall have him all right. His description has been circulated at all the seaports and he is an easy man to spot with his lame foot and his stick and a finger missing from his right hand."

Thorndyke nodded, and seemed to reflect for a moment. Then he asked: "Have you made any other inquiries?"

"No; there is nothing more to find out until we get hold of our man, and when we do, we shall look to you to secure the conviction. I suppose you are quite certain as to your facts?"

Thorndyke shook his head with a smile.

"I am never certain until after the event. We can only act on probabilities."

I understand," said the superintendent, casting a sly look at me; "but your probabilities are good enough for me."

With this, he picked up his hat and departed, leaving us to return to the occupations that our visitors had interrupted.

I heard no more of the Manford case for about a week, and assumed that Thorndyke's interest in it had ceased. But I was mistaken, as I discovered when he remarked casually one evening: "No news of Bilsky, so far; and time is running on. I am proposing to make a tentative move in a new direction." I looked at him inquiringly, and he continued : "It appears, 'from information received,' that Elliott had some dealings with him, so I propose to call at his house to-morrow and see if we can glean any news of the lost sheep."

"But Elliott is abroad," I objected.

"True; but his wife isn't; and she evidently knows all about his affairs. I have invited Miller to come with me in case he would like to put any questions; and you may as well come, too, if you are free."

It did not sound like a very thrilling adventure, but one never knew with Thorndyke. I decided to go with him, and at that the matter dropped, though I speculated a little curiously on the source of the information. So, apparently, had the superintendent, for when he arrived on the following morning he proceeded to throw out a few cautious feelers, but got nothing for his pains beyond vague generalities.

"It is a purely tentative proceeding," said Thorndyke, "and you mustn't be disappointed if nothing comes of it."

"I shall be, all the same," replied Miller, with a sly glance at my senior, and with this we set forth on our quest.

The Elliotts' house was, as I knew, in some part of Wimbledon, and thither we made our way by train. From the station we started along a wide, straight main street from which numbers of smaller streets branched off. At the corner of one of these I noticed a man standing, apparently watching our approach; and something in his appearance seemed to me familiar. Suddenly he took off his hat, looked curiously into its interior, and put it on again. Then he turned about and walked quickly down the side street. I looked at his retreating figure as we crossed the street, wondering who he could be. And then it flashed upon me that the resemblance was to a certain ex-sergeant Barber whom Thorndyke occasionally employed for observation duties. Just as I reached this conclusion, Thorndyke halted and looked about him doubtfully.

I am afraid we have come too far," said he. "I fancy we ought to have gone down that last turning." We accordingly faced about and walked back to the corner, where Thorndyke read out the name, Mendoza Avenue.

"Yes," he said, "this is the way," and we thereupon turned down the Avenue, following it to the bottom, where it ended in a cross-road, the name of which, Berners Park, I recognised as that which I had seen on Elliott's letter.

"Sixty-four is the number," said Thorndyke, "so as this corner house is forty-six and the next is forty-eight, it will be a little way along on this side, just about where you can see that smoke--which, by the way, seems to be coming out of a window."

"Yes, by Jove!" I exclaimed. "The staircase window, apparently. Not our house, I hope!"

But it was. We read the number and the name, 'Green Bushes', on the gate as we came up to it, and we hurried up the short path to the door. There was no knocker, but when Miller fixed his thumb on the bell-push, we heard a loud ringing within. But there was no response; and meanwhile the smoke poured more and more densely out of the open window above.

"Rum!" exclaimed Miller, sticking to the bell-push like a limpet. "House seems to be empty."

"I don't think it is." Thorndyke replied calmly.

The superintendent looked at him with quick suspicion, and then glanced at the ground-floor window.

"That window is unfastened," said he, "and here comes a constable."

Sure enough, a policeman was approaching quickly, looking up at the houses. Suddenly he perceived the smoke and quickened his pace, arriving just as Thorndyke had pulled down the upper window-sash and was preparing to climb over into the room. The, constable hailed him sternly, but a brief explanation from Miller reduced the officer to a state of respectful subservience, and we all followed Thorndyke through the open window, from which smoke now began to filter.

"Send the constable upstairs to give the alarm," Thorndyke instructed Miller in a low tone. The order was given without question, and the next moment the officer was bounding up the stairs, roaring like a whole fire brigade., Meanwhile, the superintendent browsed along the hall through the dense smoke, sniffing inquisitively, and at length approached the street door. Suddenly, from the heart of the reek, his voice issued in tones of amazement.

"Well, I'm hanged! It's a plumber's smoke-rocket. Some fool has stuck it through into the letter-cage!"

In the silence which followed this announcement I heard an angry voice from above demand: "What is all this infernal row about? And what are you doing here?"

"Can't you see that the house is on fire?" was the constable's, stern rejoinder. "You'd better come down and help to put it out."

The command was followed by the sound of descending footsteps, on which Thorndyke ran quickly up the stairs, followed by the superintendent and me. We met the descending party on the landing, opposite a window, and here we all stopped, gazing at one another with mutual curiosity. The man who accompanied the constable looked distinctly alarmed--as well he might--and somewhat hostile.

"Who put that smoke in the hall?" Miller demanded fiercely. "And why didn't you come down when you heard us ringing the bell?"

"I don't know what you a talking about." the man replied sulkily, "or what business this is of yours. Who are you? And what are you doing in my house?"

"In your house?" repeated Thorndyke. "Then you will be Mr. Elliott?"

The man turned a startled glance on him and replied angrily: "Never you mind who I am. Get out of this house."

"But I do mind who you are," Thorndyke rejoined mildly. "I came here to see Mr. Elliott. Are you Mr. Elliott?

"No, I am not. Mr. Elliott is abroad. if you like to send a letter here for him, I will forward it when I get his address."

While this conversation had been going on, I had been examining the stranger, not without curiosity. For his appearance was somewhat unusual. In the first place, he wore an unmistakable wig, and his shaven face bore an abundance of cuts and scratches, suggesting a recently and unskilfully mown beard. His spectacles did not disguise a pronounced divergent squint of the left eye; but what specially caught my attention was the ear-- large ear, lobeless and pointed at the tip like the ear of a satyr. As I looked at this, and at the scraped face, the squint and the wig, a strange suspicion flashed into my mind; and then, as I noted that the nose was markedly deflected to the left, I turned to glance at Thorndyke.

"Would you mind telling us your name?" the latter asked blandly.

"My name is--is--Johnson; Frederick Johnson."

"Ah," said Thorndyke. "I thought it was Manford--James Manford--and I think so still. I suggest that you have a scar on the right side of your forehead, just under the wig. May we see?"

As Thorndyke spoke the name, the man turned a horrible livid grey and started back as if to retreat up the stairs. But the constable blocked the way; and as the man was struggling to push past, Miller adroitly snatched off the wig; and there, on the forehead, was the tell-tale scar.

For an appreciable time we all stood stock-still like the figures of a tableau. Then Thorndyke turned to the superintendent.

"I charge this man, James Manford, with the murder of Stephan Bilsky."

Again there was a brief interval of intolerable silence. In the midst of it, we heard the street door open and shut, and a woman's voice called up the stairs: " Whatever is all this smoke? Are you up there, Jim?

I pass over the harrowing details of the double arrest. I am not a policeman, and to me such scenes are intensely repugnant. But we must needs stay until two taxis and four constables had conveyed the prisoners away from the still reeking house to the caravanserai of the law. Then, at last, we went forth with relief into the fresh air and bent our steps towards the station.

"I take it," Miller said reflectively, "that you never suspected Bilsky?"

"I did at first. But when Mrs. Manford and the solicitor told their tale I realised that he was the victim and that Manford must be the murderer."

"Let us have the argument," said I. "It is obvious that I have been a blockhead, but I don't mind our old friend here knowing it."

"Not a blockhead, Jervis," he corrected. "You were half asleep that night and wholly uninterested. If you had been attending to the matter, you would have observed several curious and anomalous appearances. For instance, you would have noticed that the body was, in parts, completely charred, and brittle. Now we saw the outbreak of the fire and we found it extinguished when we reached the building. Its duration was a matter of minutes; quite insufficient to reduce a body to that state. For, as you know, a human body is an extremely incombustible thing. The appearance suggested the destruction of a body which had been already burnt; and this suggestion was emphasised by the curiously unequal distribution of the charring. The right hand was burnt to a cinder and blown to pieces. The left hand was only scorched. The right foot was utterly destroyed, but the left foot was nearly intact. The face was burned away completely, and yet there were parts of the head where the hair was only singed.

"Naturally, with these facts in mind, I scrutinised those remains narrowly. And presently something much more definite and sinister came to light. On the left hand, there was a faint impression of another hand-- very indistinct and blurred, but still unmistakably a hand."

"I remember," said I, "the inspector pointed it out as evidence that the deceased had been standing with his hands clasped before or behind him; and I must admit that it seemed a reasonable inference."

"So it did, because you were both assuming that the man had been alone and that it must therefore have been the impression of his own hand. For that reason, neither of you looked at it critically. If you had, you would have seen at once that it was the impression of a left hand."

"You are quite right," I confessed ruefully. "As the man was stated to have been alone, the hand impression did not interest inc. And it was a mere group of smudges, after all. You are sure that it was a left hand?"

"Quite," be replied. "Blurred as the smudges were, one could make out the relative lengths of the fingers. And there was the thumb mark at the distal end of the palm, but pointing to the outer side of the hand. Try how you may, you can't get a right hand into that position.

"Well, then, here was a crucial fact. The mark of a left hand on a left hand proved the presence of a second person, and at once raised a strong presumption of homicide, especially when considered in conjunction with the unaccountable state of the body. During the evening, a visitor had come and gone, and on him--Bilsky--the suspicion naturally fell. But Mrs. Manford unwittingly threw an entirely new light on the case. You remember she told us that her husband had opened a new bottle of hair dye on the very morning before the explosion and had applied it with unusual care. Then his hair was dyed. But the hair of the corpse was not dyed. Therefore the corpse was not the corpse of Manford. Further, the presumption of murder applied now to Manford, and the body almost certainly was that of Bilsky."

"How did you deduce that the hair of the corpse was not dyed?" I asked.

"I didn't deduce it at all. I observed it. You remember a little patch of hair above the right ear, very much singed but still recognisable as hair? Well, in that patch I made out distinctly two or three white hairs. Naturally, when Mrs. Manford spoke of the dye, I recalled those white hairs, for though you may find silver hairs among the gold, you don't find them among the dyed. So the corpse could not be Manford's and was presumably that of Bilsky.

"But the instant that this presumption was made, a quantity of fresh evidence arose to support it. The destruction of the body was now understandable. Its purpose was to prevent identification. The parts destroyed were the parts that had to be destroyed for that purpose: the face was totally unrecognisable, and the right hand and right foot were burnt and shattered to fragments. But these were Bilsky's personal marks. His right hand was mutilated and his right foot deformed. And the fact that the false teeth found were undoubtedly Manford's was conclusive evidence of the intended deception.

"Then there were those very queer financial transactions, of which my interpretation was this: Manford borrowed two thousand pounds from Clines. With this he opened an account in the name of Elliott. As Elliott, he lent himself two thousand pounds which he repaid Clines-- subject to an insurance of his life for that amount, taken out in Elliott's name."

"Then he would have gained nothing," I objected.

"On the contrary, he would have stood to gain two thousand pounds on proof of his own death. That, I assumed, was his scheme : to murder Bilsky, to arrange for Bilsky's corpse to personate his own, and then, when the insurance was paid, to abscond the company of some woman this sum, with the valuables that he had taken from Bilsky, and the five hundred pounds that he had withdrawn from the bank.

"But this was only theory. It had to be tested; and as we had Elliott's address, I did the only thing that was possible. I employed our friend, ex-Sergeant Barber, to watch the house. He took lodgings in a house nearly opposite and kept up continuous observation, which soon convinced him that there was someone on the premises besides Mrs. Elliott. Then, late one night, he saw a man come out and walk away quickly. He followed the man for some distance, until the stranger turned back and began to retrace his steps. Then Barber accosted him, asking for a direction, and carefully inspecting him. The man's appearance tallied exactly with the description that I had given--I had assumed that he would probably shave off his beard--and with the photograph; so Barber, having seen him home, reported to me. And that is the whole story."

"Not quite the whole," said Miller, with a sly grin. "There is that smoke-rocket. If it hadn't been for the practical joker who slipped that through the letter-slit, we could never have got into that house. I call it a most remarkable coincidence."

"So do I," Thorndyke agreed, without moving a muscle; " but there is a special providence that watches over medical jurists."

We were silent for a few moments. Then I remarked: "This will come as a terrible shock to Mrs. Manford."

"I am afraid it will," Thorndyke agreed. "But it will be better for her than if Manford had absconded with this woman, taking practically every penny that he possessed with him. She stood to lose a worthless husband in either event. At least we have saved her from poverty. And, knowing the facts, we were morally and legally bound to further the execution of justice."

"A very proper sentiment," said the superintendent, "though I am not quite clear as to the legal aspects of that smoke-rocket."

The Puzzle Lock

The Puzzle Lock

I do not remember what was the occasion of my dining with Thorndyke at Giamborini's on the particular evening that is now in my mind. Doubtless, some piece of work completed had seemed to justify the modest festival. At any rate, there we were, seated at a somewhat retired table, selected by Thorndyke, with our backs to the large window through which the late June sunlight streamed. We had made our preliminary arrangements, including a bottle of Barsac, and were inspecting dubiously a collection of semi- edible hors d'oeuvres, when a man entered and took possession of a table just in front of ours, which had apparently been reserved for him, since he walked directly to it and drew away the single chair that had been set aslant against it.

I watched with amused interest his methodical procedure, for he was clearly a man who took his dinner seriously. A regular customer, too, I judged by the waiter's manner and the reserved table with its single chair. But the man himself interested me. He was out of the common and there was a suggestion of character, with perhaps a spice of oddity, in his appearance. He appeared to be about sixty years of age, small and spare, with a much-wrinkled, mobile and rather whimsical face, surmounted by a crop of white, upstanding hair. From his waistcoat pocket protruded the ends of a fountain-pen, a pencil and a miniature electric torch such as surgeons use; a silver-mounted Coddington lens hung from his watch-guard and the middle finger of his left hand bore the largest seal ring that I have ever seen.

"Well," said Thorndyke, who had been following my glance, "what do you make of him?"

"I don't quite know," I replied. "The Coddington suggests a naturalist or a scientist of some kind, but that blatant ring doesn't. Perhaps he is an antiquary or a numismatist or even a philatelist. He deals with small objects of some kind."

At this moment a man who had just entered strode up to our friend's table and held out his hand, which the other shook, with no great enthusiasm, as I thought. Then the newcomer fetched a chair, and setting it by the table, seated himself and picked up the menu card, while the other observed him with a shade of disapproval. I judged that he would rather have dined alone, and that the personality of the new arrival--a flashy, bustling, obtrusive type of man--did not commend him.

From this couple my eye was attracted to a tall man who had halted near the door and stood looking about the room as if seeking someone. Suddenly he spied an empty, single table, and, bearing down on it, seated himself and began anxiously to study the menu under the supervision of a waiter. I glanced at him with slight disfavour. One makes allowances for the exuberance of youth, but when a middle-aged man presents the combination of heavily-greased heir parted in the middle, a waxed moustache of a suspiciously intense black, a pointed imperial and a single eye-glass, evidently ornamental in function, one views him with less tolerance. However, his get-up was not my concern, whereas my dinner was, and I had given this my undivided attention for some minutes when I heard Thorndyke emit a soft chuckle.

"Not bad," he remarked, setting down his glass.

"Not at all," I agreed, "for a restaurant wine."

"I was not alluding to the wine," said he "but to our friend Badger."

"The inspector!" I exclaimed. "He isn't here, is he? I don't see him."

"I am glad to hear you say that, Jervis," said he. "It is a better effort than I thought. Still, he might manage his properties a little better. That is the second time his eye-glass has been in the soup."

Following, the direction of his glance, I observed the man with the waxed moustache furtively wiping his eye-glass; and the temporary absence of the monocular grimace enabled me to note a resemblance to the familiar features of the detective officer.

"If you say that is Badger, I suppose it is," said I. "He is certainly a little like our friend. But I shouldn't have recognised him."

"I don't know that I should," said Thorndyke, "but for the little unconscious tricks of movement. You know the habit he has of stroking the back of his head, and of opening his mouth and scratching the side of his chin. I saw him do it just now. He had forgotten his imperial until he touched it, and then the sudden arrest of movement was very striking. It doesn't do to forget a false beard."

"I wonder what his game is," said I. "The disguise suggests that he is on the look-out for somebody who might know him; but apparently that somebody has not turned up yet. At any rate, he doesn't seem to be watching anybody in particular."

"No," said Thorndyke. "But there is somebody whom he seems rather to avoid watching. Those two men at the table in front of ours are in his direct line of vision, but he hasn't looked at them once since he sat down, though I noticed that he gave them one quick glance before he selected his table. I wonder if he has observed us. Probably not, as we have the strong light of the window behind us and his attention is otherwise occupied."

I looked at the two men and from them to the detective, and I judged that my friend was right. On the inspector's table was a good-sized fern in an ornamental pot, and this he had moved so that it was directly between him and the two strangers, to whom he must have been practically invisible; and now I could see that he did, in fact, steal an occasional glance at them over the edge of the menu card. Moreover, as their meal drew to an end, he hastily finished his own and beckoned to the waiter to bring the bill.

"We may as well wait and see them off," said Thorndyke, who had already settled our account. "Badger always interests me. He is so ingenious and he has such shockingly bad luck."

We had not long to wait. The two men rose from the table and walked slowly to the door, where they paused to light their cigars before going out. Then Badger rose, with his back towards them and his eyes on the mirror opposite; and as they went out, he snatched up his hat and stick and followed. Thorndyke looked at me inquiringly.

"Do we indulge in the pleasures of the chase?" he asked, and as I replied in the affirmative, we, too, made our way out and started in the wake of the inspector.

As we followed Badger at a discreet distance, we caught an occasional glimpse of the quarry ahead, whose proceedings evidently caused the inspector some embarrassment, for they had a way of stopping suddenly to elaborate some point that they were discussing, whereby it became necessary for the detective to drop farther in the rear than was quite safe, in view of the rather crowded state of the pavement. On one of these occasions, when the older man was apparently delivering himself of some excruciating joke, they both turned suddenly and looked back, the joker pointing to some object on the opposite side of the road. Several people turned to see what was being pointed at, and, of course, the inspector had to turn, too, to avoid being recognised. At this moment the two men popped into an entry, and when the inspector once more turned they were gone.

As soon as he missed them, Badger started forward almost at a run, and presently halted at the large entry of the Celestial Bank Chambers, into which he peered eagerly. Then, apparently sighting his quarry, he darted in, and we quickened our pace and followed. Half-way down the long hall we saw him standing at the door of a lift, frantically pressing the call-button.

"Poor Badger!" chuckled Thorndyke, as we walked past him unobserved. "His usual luck! He will hardly run them to earth now in this enormous building. We may as well go through to the Blenheim Street entrance."

We pursued our way along the winding corridor and were close to the entrance when I noticed two men coming down the staircase that led to the ball.

"By Jingo I Here they are!" I exclaimed. "Shall we run back and give Badger the tip?"

Thorndyke hesitated. But it was too late. A taxi had just driven up and was discharging its fare. The younger man, catching the driver's eye, ran out and seized the door-handle; and when his companion had entered the cab, he gave an address to the driver, and, stepping in quickly, slammed the door. As the cab moved off, Thorndyke pulled out his notebook and pencil and jotted down the number of the vehicle. Then we turned and retraced our steps; but when we reached the lift-door, the inspector had disappeared. Presumably, like the incomparable Tom Bowling, he had gone aloft.

"We must give it up, Jervis," said Thorndyke. "I will send him anonymously the number of the cab, and that is all we can do. But I am sorry for Badger."

With this we dismissed the incident from our minds--at least, I did; assuming that I had seen the last of the two strangers. Little did I suspect how soon and under what strange and tragic circumstances I should meet with them again!

It was about a week later that we received a visit from our old friend, Superintendent Miller of the Criminal Investigation Department. The passing years had put us on a footing of mutual trust and esteem, and the capable, straightforward detective officer was always a welcome visitor.

I've just dropped in," said Miller, cutting off the end of the inevitable cigar, "to tell you about a rather queer case that we've got in hand. I know you are always interested in queer cases."

Thorndyke smiled blandly. He had heard that kind of preamble before, and he knew, as did I, that when Miller became communicative we could safely infer that the Millerian bark was in shoal water.

"It is a case," the superintendent continued, "of a very special brand of crook. Actually there is a gang, but it is the managing director that we have particularly got our eye on."

"Is he a regular 'habitual,' then?" asked Thorndyke.

Well," replied Miller, "as to that, I can't positively say. The fact is that we haven't actually seen the man to be sure of him."

"I see," said Thorndyke, with a grim smile. "You mean to say that you have got your eye on the place where he isn't."

"At the present moment," Miller admitted, "that is the literal fact. We have lost sight of the man we suspected, but we hope to pick him up again presently. We want him badly, and his pals too. It is probably quite a small gang, but they are mighty fly; a lot too smart to be at large. And they'll take some catching, for there is someone running the concern with a good deal more brains than crooks usually have."

"What is their lay?" I asked.

"Burglary," he replied. "Jewels and plate, but principally jewels; and the special feature of their work is that the swag disappears completely every time. None of the stuff has ever been traced. That is what drew our attention to them. After each robbery we made a round of all the fences, but there was not a sign. The stuff seemed to have vanished into smoke. Now that is very awkward. If you never see the men and you can't trace the stuff, where are you? You've got nothing to go on."

"But you seem to have got a clue of some kind." I said.

"Yes. There isn't a lot in it; but it seemed worth following up. One of our men happened to travel down to Colchester with a certain man, and when he came back two days later, he noticed this same man on the platform at Colchester and saw him get out at Liverpool Street. In the interval there had been a jewel robbery at Colchester. Then there was a robbery at Southampton, and our man went at once to Waterloo and saw all the trains in. On the second day, behold! the Colchester sportsman turns up at the barrier, so our man, who had a special taxi waiting, managed to track him home and afterwards got some particulars about him. He is a chap named Shemmonds; belongs to a firm of outside brokers. But nobody seems to know much about him and he doesn't put in much time at the office.

"Well, then, Badger took him over and shadowed him for a day or two, but just as things were looking interesting, he slipped off the hook. Badger followed him to a restaurant, and, through the glass door, saw him go up to an elderly man at a table and shake hands with him. Then he took a chair at the table himself, so Badger popped in and took a seat near them where he could keep them in view. They went out together and Badger followed them, but he lost them in the Celestial Bank Chambers. They went up in the lift just before he could get to the door and that was the last he saw of them. But we have ascertained that they left the building in a taxi and that the taxi set them down at Great Turnstile."

"It was rather smart of you to trace the cab," Thorndyke remarked.

"You've got to keep your eyes skinned in our line of business," said Miller. "But now we come to the real twister. From the time those two men went down Great Turnstile, nobody has set eyes on either of them. They seem to have vanished into thin air."

"You found out who the other man was, then?" said I.

"Yes. The restaurant manager knew him; an old chap named Luttrell. And we knew him, too, because he has a thumping burglary insurance, and when he goes out of town he notifies his company, and they make arrangements with us to have the premises watched."

"What is Luttrell?" I asked.

"Well, he is a bit of a mug, I should say, at least that's his character in the trade. Goes in for being a dealer in jewels and antiques, but he'll buy anything--furniture, pictures, plate, any blooming thing. Does it for a hobby, the regular dealers say. Likes the sport of bidding at the sales. But the knock-out men hate him; never know what he's going to do. Must have private means, for though he doesn't often drop money, he can't make much. He's no salesman. It is the buying that he seems to like. But he is a regular character, full of cranks and oddities. His rooms in Thavies Inn look like the British Museum gone mad. He has got electric alarms from all the doors up to his bedroom and the strong-room in his office is fitted with a puzzle lock instead of keys."

"That doesn't seem very safe," I remarked.

"It is," said Miller. "This one has fifteen alphabets. One of our men has calculated that it has about forty billion changes. No one is going to work that out, and there are no keys to get lost. But it is that strong- room that is worrying us, as well as the old joker himself. The Lord knows how much valuable stuff there is in it. What we are afraid of is that Shemmonds may have made away with the old chap and be lying low, waiting to swoop down on that strong-room."

"But you said that Luttrell goes away sometimes," said I.

"Yes; but then he always notifies his insurance company and he seals up his strong-room with a tape round the door-handle and a great seal on the door-post. This time he hasn't notified the company and the door isn't sealed. There's a seal on the door-post--left from last time, I expect-- but only the cut ends of tape. I got the caretaker to let me see the place this morning; and, by the way, doctor, I have taken a leaf out of your book. I always carry a bit of squeezing wax in my pocket now and a little box of French chalk. Very handy they are, too. As I had 'em with me this morning, I took a squeeze of the seal. May want it presently for identification."

He brought out of his pocket a small tin box from which he carefully extracted an object wrapped in tissue paper. When the paper had been tenderly removed there was revealed a lump of moulding wax, one side of which was flattened and bore a sunk design.

"It's quite a good squeeze," said Miller, handing it to Thorndyke. "I dusted the seal with French chalk so that the wax shouldn't stick to it."

My colleague examined the "squeeze" through his lens, and passing it and the lens to me, asked: "Has this been photographed, Miller?"

"No," was the reply, "but it ought to be before it gets damaged."

"It ought, certainly," said Thorndyke, "if you value it. Shall I get Polton to do it now?"

The superintendent accepted the offer gratefully and Thorndyke accordingly took the squeeze up to the laboratory, where he left it for our assistant to deal with. When he returned, Miller remarked: "It is a baffling case, this. Now that Shemmonds has dropped out of sight, there is nothing to go on and nothing to do but wait for something else to happen; another burglary or an attempt on the strong-room."

"Is it clear that the strong-room has not been opened?" asked Thorndyke.

No, it isn't," replied Miller. "That's part of the trouble. Luttrell has disappeared and he may be dead. If he is, Shemmonds will probably have been through his pockets. Of course there is no strong-room key. That is one of the advantages of a puzzle lock. But it is quite possible that Luttrell may have kept a note of the combination and carried it about him. It would have been risky to trust entirely to memory. And he would have had the keys of the office about him. Any one who had those could have slipped in during business hours without much difficulty. Luttrell's premises are empty, but there are people in and out all day going to the other offices. Our man can't follow them all in. I suppose you can't make any suggestion, doctor?"

"I am afraid I can't," answered Thorndyke. "The case is so very much in the air. There is nothing against Shemmonds but bare suspicion. He has disappeared only in the sense that you have lost sight of him, and the same is true of Luttrell--though there is an abnormal element in his case. Still, you could hardly get a search-warrant on the facts that are known at present."

"No," Miller agreed, "they certainly would not authorise us to break open the strong-room, and nothing short of that would be much use."

Here Polton made his appearance with the wax squeeze in a neat little box such as jewellers use.

"I've got two enlarged negatives," said he; "nice clear ones. How many prints shall I make for Mr. Miller?"

"Oh, one will do, Mr. Polton," said the superintendent. "If I want any more I'll ask you." He took up the little box, and, slipping it in his pocket, rose to depart. "I'll let you know, doctor, how the case goes on, and perhaps you wouldn't mind turning it over a bit in the interval. Something might occur to you."

Thorndyke promised to think over the case, and when we had seen the superintendent launched down the stairs, we followed Polton up to the laboratory, where we each picked up one of the negatives and examined it against the light. I had already identified the seal by its shape--a *vesica piscis* or boat-shape--with the one that I had seen on Mr. Luttrell's finger. Now, in the photograph, enlarged three diameters, I could clearly make out the details. The design was distinctive and curious rather than elegant. The two triangular spaces at the ends were occupied respectively by a *memento mori* and a winged hour-glass and the central portion was filled by a long inscription in Roman capitals, of which I could at first make nothing.

"Do you suppose this is some kind of cryptogram?" I asked.

"No," Thorndyke replied. "I imagine the words were run together merely to economise space. This is what I make of it."

He held the negative in his left hand, and with his right wrote down in pencil on a slip of paper the following four lines of doggerel verse

EHEU ALAS HOW FAST THE DAM FUGACES
LABUNTUR ANNI ESPECIALLY IN THE CASES
OF POOR OLD BLOKES LIKE YOU AND ME POSTHUMUS
WHO ONLY WAIT FOR VERMES TO CONSUME US."

"Well," I exclaimed, "it is a choice specimen; one of old Luttrell's merry conceited jests, I take it. But the joke was hardly worth the labour of engraving on a seal."

"It is certainly a rather mild jest," Thorndyke admitted. "But there may be something more in it than meets the eye."

He looked at the inscription reflectively and appeared to read it through once or twice. Then he replaced the negative in the drying rack, and, picking up the paper, slipped it into his pocket-book.

"I don't quite see," said I, "why Miller brought this case to us or what he wants you to think over. In fact, I don't see that there is a case at all."

"It is a very shadowy case," Thorndyke admitted. "Miller has done a good deal of guessing, and so has Badger; and it may easily turn out that they have found a mare's nest. Nevertheless there is something to think about."

"As, for instance--?"

"Well, Jervis, you saw the men; you saw how they behaved; you have heard Miller's story and you have seen Mr. Luttrell's seal. Put all those data together and you have the material for some very interesting speculation, to say the least. You might even carry it beyond speculation."

I did not pursue the subject, for I knew that when Thorndyke used the word "speculation," nothing would induce him to commit himself to an opinion. But later, bearing in mind the attention that he had seemed to bestow on Mr. Luttrell's schoolboy verses, I got a print from the negative and studied the foolish in exhaustively. But if it had any hidden meaning--and I could imagine no reason for supposing that it had--that meaning remained hidden; and the only conclusion at which I could arrive was that a man of Luttrell's age might have known better than to write such nonsense.

The superintendent did not leave the matter long in suspense. Three days later he paid us another visit. and half-apologetically reopened the subject.

"I am ashamed to come badgering you like this," he said, "but I can't get this case out of my head. I've a feeling that we ought to, get a move of some kind on. And, by the way--though that is nothing to do with it-- I've copied out the stuff on that seal and I can't make any sense of it. What the deuce are fugaces? I suppose 'vermes' are worms, though I don't see why he spelt it that way."

"The verses," said Thorndyke, "are apparently a travesty of a Latin poem; one of the odes of Horace which begins:

```
Eheu fugaces, Postume, Postume, Labuntur anni,'
```

which means, in effect, 'Alas! Postume, the flying years slip by.'

"Well," said Miller, "any fool knows that--any middle-aged fool, at any rate. No need to put it into Latin. However, it's of no consequence. To return to this case; I've got an authority to look over Luttrell's premises--not to pull anything about, you know, just to look round. I called in on my way here to let the caretaker know that I should be coming in later. I thought that perhaps you might like to come with me. I wish you would, doctor. You've got such a knack of spotting things that other people overlook."

He looked wistfully at Thorndyke, and as the latter was considering the proposal, he added: "The caretaker mentioned a rather odd circumstance. It seems that he keeps an eye on the electric meters in the building and that he has noticed a leakage of current in Mr. Luttrell's. It is only a small leak; about thirty watts an hour. But he can't account for it in any way. He has been right through the premises to see if any lamp has been left on in any of the rooms. But all the switches are off everywhere, and it can't be a short circuit. Funny, isn't it?

It was certainly odd, but there seemed to me nothing in it to account for the expression of suddenly awakened interest that I detected in Thorndyke's face. However, it evidently had some special significance for him, for he asked almost eagerly "When are you making your inspection?"

"I am going there now," replied Miller, and he added coaxingly, "Couldn't you manage to run round with me?"

Thorndyke stood up. "Very well," said he. "Let us go together. You may as well come, too, Jervis, if you can spare an hour."

I agreed readily, for my colleague's hardly disguised interest in the inspection suggested a definite problem in his mind; and we at once issued forth and made our way by Mitre Court and Fetter Lane to the abode of the missing dealer, an old-fashioned house near the end of Thavies Inn.

"I've been over the premises once," said Miller, as the caretaker appeared with the keys, "and I think we had better begin the regular inspection with the offices. We can examine the stores and living-rooms afterwards."

We accordingly entered the outer office, and as this was little more than a waiting-room, we passed through into the private office, which had the appearance of having been used also as a sitting-room or study. It was furnished with an easy-chair, a range of book-shelves and a handsome bureau book-case, while in the end wall was the massive iron door of the strong-room. On this, as the chief object of interest, we all bore down, and the superintendent expounded its peculiarities.

It is quite a good idea," said he, "this letter-lock. There's no keyhole--though a safe-lock is pretty hopeless to pick even if there was a keyhole--and no keys to get lost. As to guessing what the 'open sesame' may be--well, just look at it. You could spend a life time on it and be no forrader."

The puzzle lock was contained in the solid iron door post, through a slot in which a row of fifteen A's seemed to grin defiance on the would-be safe-robber. I put my finger on the milled edges of one or two of the letters and rotated the discs, noticing how easily and smoothly they turned.

"Well," said Miller, "it's no use fumbling with that. I'm just going to have a look through his ledger and see who his customers were. The book-case is unlocked. I tried it last time. And we'd better leave this as we found it."

He put back the letters that I had moved, and turned away to explore the book-case; and as the letter-lock appeared to present nothing but an insoluble riddle, I followed him, leaving Thorndyke earnestly gazing at the meaningless row of letters.

The superintendent glanced back at him with an indulgent smile.

"The doctor is going to work out the combination," he chuckled. "Well, well. There are only forty billion changes and he's a young man for his age."

With this encouraging comment, he opened the glass door of the book-case, and reaching down the ledger, laid it on the desk-like slope of the bureau.

"It is a poor chance," said he, opening the ledger at the index, "but some of these people may be able to give us a hint where to look for Mr. Luttrell, and it is worth while to know what sort of business he did."

He ran his finger down the list of names and had just turned to the account of one of the customers when we were startled by a loud click from the direction of the strong-room. We both turned sharply and beheld Thorndyke grasping the handle of the strong-room door, and I saw with amazement that the door was now slightly ajar.

"God!" exclaimed Miller, shutting the ledger and starting forward, "he's got it open!" He strode over to the door, and directing an eager look at the indicator of the lock, burst into a laugh. "Well, I'm hanged!" he exclaimed. "Why, it was unlocked all the time! To think that none of us had the sense to tug the handle! But isn't it just like old Luttrell to have a fool's answer like that to the blessed puzzle!"

I looked at the indicator, not a little astonished to observe the row of fifteen A's, which apparently formed the key combination. It may have been a very amusing joke on Mr. Luttrell's part, but it did not look very secure. Thorndyke regarded us with an inscrutable glance and still grasped the handle, holding the door a bare half-inch open.

"There is something pushing against the door," said he. "Shall I open it?

"May as well have a look at the inside," replied Miller. Thereupon Thorndyke released the handle and quickly stepped aside. The door swung slowly open and the dead body of a man fell out into the room and rolled over on to its back.

"Mercy on us!" gasped Miller, springing back hastily and staring with horror and amazement at the grim apparition. "That is not Luttrell." Then, suddenly starting forward and stooping over the dead man, be exclaimed "Why, it is Shemmonds. So that is where be disappeared to. I wonder what became of Luttrell?"

"There is somebody else in the strong-room," said Thorndyke; and now, peering in through the doorway, I perceived a dim light, which seemed to come from a hidden recess, and by which I could see a pair of feet projecting round the corner. In a moment Miller had sprung in, and I followed. The strong-room was L shaped in plan, the arm of the L formed by a narrow passage at right angles to the main room. At the end of this a single small electric bulb was burning, the light of which showed the body of an elderly man stretched on the floor of the passage. I recognised him instantly in spite of the dimness of the light and the disfigurement caused by a ragged wound on the forehead.

"We had better get him out of this," said Miller, speaking in a flurried tone, partly due to the shock of the horrible discovery and partly to the accompanying physical unpleasantness, "and then we will have a look round, This wasn't just a mere robbery. We are going to find things out."

With my help he lifted Luttrell's corpse and together we carried it out, laying it on the floor of the room at the farther end, to which we also dragged the body of Shemmonds.

"There is no mystery as to how it happened," I said, after a brief inspection of the two corpses. "Shemmonds evidently shot the old man from behind with the pistol close to the back of the head. The hair is all scorched round the wound of entry and the bullet came out at the forehead."

"Yes," agreed Miller, "that is all clear enough. But the mystery is why on earth Shemmonds didn't let himself out. He must have known that the door was unlocked. Yet instead of turning the handle, he must have stood there like a fool, battering at the door with his fists. Just look at his hands."

"The further mystery," said Thorndyke who, all this time, had been making a minute examination of the lock both front without and within, "is how the door came to be shut. That is quite a curious problem."

"Quite," agreed Miller. "But it will keep. And there is a still more curious problem inside there. There is nearly all the swag from that Colchester robbery. Looks as if Luttrell was in it."

Half reluctantly he re-entered the strong-room and Thorndyke and I followed. Near the angle of the passage he stooped to pick up an automatic pistol and a small, leather book, which he opened and looked into by the light of the lamp. At the first glance he uttered an exclamation and shut the book with a snap.

"Do you know what this is?" he asked, holding it out to us. "It is the nominal roll, address book and journal of the gang. We've got them in the hollow of our hand; and it is dawning upon me that old

Luttrell was the managing director whom I have been looking for so long. Just run your eyes along those shelves. That's loot; every bit of it. I can identify the articles from the lists that I made out."

He stood looking gloatingly along the shelves with their burden of jewellery, plate and other valuables. Then his eye lighted on a drawer in the end wall just under the lamp; an iron drawer with a disproportionately large handle and bearing a very legible label inscribed "unmounted stones."

"We'll have a look at his stock of unmounted gems," said Miller; and with that he bore down on the drawer, and seizing the handle, gave a vigorous pull. "Funny," said he. "It isn't locked, but something seems to be holding it back."

He planted his foot on the wall and took a fresh purchase on the handle. "Wait a moment, Miller," said Thorndyke; but even as he spoke, the superintendent gave a mighty heave; the drawer came out a full two feet; there was a loud click, and a moment later the strong-room door slammed.

"Good God!" exclaimed Miller, letting go the drawer, which immediately slid in with another click. "What was that?"

"That was the door shutting," replied Thorndyke. "Quite a clever arrangement; like the mechanism of a repeater watch. Pulling out the drawer wound up and released a spring that shut the door. Very ingenious."

"But," gasped Miller, turning an ashen face to my colleague, "we're shut in."

"You are forgetting," said I--a little nervously, I must admit--"that the lock is as we left it."

The superintendent laughed, somewhat hysterically. "What a fool I am!" said he. "As bad as Shemmonds. Still we may as well--" Here he started along the passage and I heard him groping his way to the door, and later heard the handle turn. Suddenly the deep silence of the tomb-like chamber was rent by a yell of terror.

"The door won't move! It's locked fast!"

On this I rushed along the passage with a sickening fear at my heart. And even as I ran, there rose before my eyes the horrible vision of the corpse with the battered hands that had fallen out when we opened the door of this awful trap. He had been caught as we were caught. How soon might it not be that some stranger would be looking in on our corpses.

In the dim twilight by the door I found Miller clutching the handle and shaking it like a madman. His self-possession was completely shattered. Nor was my own condition much better. I flung my whole weight on the door in the faint hope that the lock was not really closed, but the massive iron structure was as immovable as a stone wall. I was nevertheless, gathering myself up for a second charge when I heard Thorndyke's voice close behind me.

"That is no use, Jervis. The door is locked. But there is nothing to worry about."

As he spoke, there suddenly appeared a bright circle of light from the little electric lamp that he always carried in his pocket. Within the circle, and now clearly visible, was a second indicator of the puzzle lock on the inside of the door-post. Its appearance was vaguely reassuring, especially in conjunction with Thorndyke's calm voice; and it evidently appeared so to Miller, for he remarked, almost in his natural tones:

"But it seems to be unlocked still. There is the same AAAAAA that it showed when we came in."

It was perfectly true. The slot of the letter-lock still showed the range of fifteen A's, just as it had when the door was open. Could it be that the lock was a dummy and that there was some other means of opening the door? I was about to put this question to Thorndyke when he put the lamp into my hand, and, gently pushing me aside, stepped up to the indicator.

"Keep the light steady, Jervis," said he, and forth with he began to manipulate the milled edges of the letter discs, beginnings as I noticed, at the right or reverse end of the slot and working backwards. I watched him with feverish interest and curiosity, as also did Miller, looking to see some word of fifteen letters develop in the slot. Instead of which, I saw, to my amazement and bewilderment my colleague's finger transforming the row of A's into a succession of M's, which, however, were presently followed by an L and some X's. When the row was completed it looked like some remote, antediluvian date set down in Roman numerals.

"Try the handle now, Miller," said Thorndyke.

The superintendent needed no second bidding. Snatching at the handle, he turned it and bore heavily on the door. Almost instantly a thin line of light appeared at the edge; there was a sharp click, and the door swung right open. We fell out immediately--at least the superintendent and I did--thankful to find ourselves outside and alive. But, as we emerged, we both became aware of a man, white-faced and horror-stricken of aspect, stooping over the two corpses at the other end of the room. Our appearance was so sudden and unexpected--for the massive solidity of the safe-door had rendered our movements inaudible outside--that, for a moment or two, he stood immovable, staring at us, wild-eyed and open-mouthed. Then, suddenly, he sprang up erect, and, darting to the door, opened it and rushed out with Miller close on his heels.

He did not get very far. Following the superintendent, I saw the fugitive wriggling in the embrace of a tall man on the pavement, who, with Miller's assistance, soon had a pair of handcuffs snapped on the man's wrists and then departed with his captive in search of a cab.

"That's one of 'em, I expect," said Miller, as we returned to the office; then, as his glance fell on the open strong-room door, he mopped his face with his handkerchief. "That door gives me the creeps to look at it," said he. "Lord I what a shake-up that was! I've never had such a scare in my life. When I heard that door shut and I remembered how that poor devil, Shemmonds, came tumbling out--phoo!" He wiped his brow again, and, walking towards the strong-room door, asked: "By the way, what was the magic word after all?" He stepped up to the indicator, and, after a quick glance, looked round at me in surprise. "Why!" he exclaimed, "blow me if it isn't AAAA still! But the doctor altered it, didn't he?"

At this moment Thorndyke appeared from the strong- room, where he had apparently been conducting some explorations, and to him the superintendent turned for an explanation.

"It is an ingenious device," said he; "in fact, the whole strong-room is a monument of ingenuity, somewhat misapplied, but perfectly effective, as Mr. Shemmonds's corpse testifies. The key-combination is a number expressed in Roman numerals, but the lock has a fly-back mechanism which acts as soon as the door begins to open. That was how Shemmonds was caught. He, no doubt purposely, avoided watching Luttrell set the lock-- or else Luttrell didn't let him--but as he went in with his intended victim, he looked at the indicator and saw the row of A's, which he naturally assumed to be the key. Then, when he tried to let himself out, of course, the lock wouldn't open."

"It is rather odd that he didn't try some other combinations," said I.

"He probably did," replied Thorndyke "but when they failed he would naturally come back to the A's, which be had seen when the door was open. This is how it works."

He shut the door, and then, closely watched by the superintendent and me, turned the milled rims of the letter-discs until the indicator showed a row of numerals thus: MMMMMMMCCCLXXXV. Grasping the handle, he turned it and gave a gentle pull, when the door began to open. But the instant it started from its bed, there was a loud click and all the letters of the indicator flew back to A.

"Well, I'm jiggered!" exclaimed Miller. "It must have been an awful suck-in for that poor blighter, Shemmonds. Took me in, too. I saw those A's and the door open, and I thought I knew all about it. But what beats me, doctor, is how you managed to work it out. I can't see what you had to go on. Would it be allowable to ask how it was done?"

"Certainly," replied Thorndyke "but we had better defer the explanation. You have got those two bodies to dispose of and some other matters, and we must get back to our chambers. I will write down the key-combination, in case you want it, and then you must come and see us and let us know what luck you have had."

He wrote the numerals on a slip of paper, and when he had handed it to the superintendent, we took our leave.

"I find myself," said I, as we walked home, "in much the same position as Miller. I don't see what you had to go on. It is clear to me that you not only worked out the lock-combination--from the seal inscription, as I assume--but that you identified Luttrell as the director of the gang. I don't, in the least, understand how you did it."

"And yet, Jervis," said he, "it was an essentially simple case. If you review it and cast up the items of evidence, you will see that we really had all the facts. The problem was merely to co-ordinate them and extract their significance. Take first the character of Luttrell. We saw the man in company with another, evidently a fairly intimate acquaintance. They were being shadowed by a detective, and it is pretty clear that they detected the sleuth, for they shook him off quite neatly. Later, we learn from Miller that one of these men is suspected to be a member of a firm of swell burglars and that the other is a well-to-do, rather eccentric and very miscellaneous dealer, who has a strong-room fitted with a puzzle lock. I am astonished that the usually acute Miller did not notice how well Luttrell fitted the part of the managing director whom he was looking for. Here was a dealer who bought and sold all sorts of queer but valuable things, who must have had unlimited facilities for getting rid of stones, bullion and silver, and who used a puzzle lock. Now, who uses a puzzle lock? No one, certainly, who can conveniently use a key. But to the manager of a gang of thieves it would be a valuable safeguard, for he might at any moment be robbed of his keys, and perhaps made away with. But he could not be robbed of the secret passwords and his possession of it would be a security against murder. So you see that the simple probabilities pointed to Luttrell as the head of the gang.

"And now consider the problem of the lock. First, we saw that Luttrell wore on his left hand a huge, cumbrous seal ring, that he carried a Coddington lens on his watch-guard, and a small electric lamp in his pocket. That told us very, little. But when Miller told us about the lock and showed us the squeeze of the seal, and when we saw that the seal bore a long inscription in minute lettering, a connection began to appear. As Miller justly observed, no man--especially no elderly man--could trust the key combination exclusively to his memory. He would carry about him some record to which he could refer in case his memory failed him. But that record would hardly be one that anybody could read, or the secrecy and safety of the lock would be gone. It would probably be some kind of cryptogram; and when we saw this inscription and considered it in conjunction with the lens and the lamp, it seemed highly probable that the key-combination was contained in the inscription; and that probability was further increased when we saw the nonsensical doggerel of which the inscription was made up. The suggestion was that the verses bad been made for some purpose independent of their sense. Accordingly I gave the inscription very careful consideration.

Now we learned from Miller that the puzzle lock had fifteen letters. The key might be one long word, such as 'superlativeness', a number of short words, or some chemical or other formula. Or it was possible that it might be of the nature of a chronogram. I have never heard of chronograms being used for secret records or messages, but it has often occurred to me that they would be extremely suitable. And this was an exceptionally suitable case."

"Chronogram," said I. "Isn't that something connected with medals?"

"They have often been used on medals," he replied. "In effect, a chronogram is an inscription some of the letters of which form a date connected with the subject of the inscription. Usually the date letters are or cut larger than the others for convenience in reading, but, of course, this is not essential. The principle of a chronogram is this. The letters of the Roman alphabet are of two kinds: those that are simply letters and nothing else, and those that are numerals as well as letters. The numeral letters are M = a thousand, D = five hundred, C = one hundred, L = fifty, X = ten, V = five, and I = one. Now, in deciphering a chronogram, you pick out all the numeral letters and add them up without regard to their order. The total gives you the date.

"Well, as I said, it occurred to me that this might be of the nature of a chronogram; but as the lock had letters and not figures, the number, if there was one, would have to be expressed in Roman numerals, and it would have to form a number of fifteen numeral letters. As it was thus quite easy to put my hypothesis to the test, I proceeded to treat the inscription as a chronogram and decipher it; and behold! it yielded a number of fifteen letters, which, of course, was as near certainty as was possible, short of actual experiment."

"Let us see how you did the decipherment," I said, as we entered our chambers and shut the door. I procured a large note-block and pencil, and, laying them on the table, drew up two chairs.

"Now," said I, "fire away."

"Very well," he said. "We will begin by writing the inscription in proper chronogram form with the numeral letters double size and treating the U's as V's and the W's as double V's according to the rules."

Here he wrote out the inscription in Roman capitals thus:

"eheV aLas hoVV fast the DaM fVgaCes LabVntVr annI espeCIaLLy In the Cases of poor oLD bLokes LIke yoV anD Me posthVMVs VVho onLy VVaIt for VerMes to ConsVMe Vs."

"Now," said he, "let us make a column of each line and add them up, thus:

1. V=5, L=50, VV=10, D=500, M=1000, V=5, C=100--Total 1670

2. L=50, V=5, V=5, I=1, C=100, I=1, L=50, L=50, I=1, C=100--Total 363

3. L=50, D=500, L=50, L=50, I=1, V=5, D=500, M=1000, V=5, M=1000, V=5--Total 3166

4. VV=10, L=50, VV=10, I=1, V=5, M=1000, C=100, V=5, M=1000, V=5--Total 2186

"Now," he continued "we take the four totals and add them together, thus:

1670+363+3166+2186 = 7385

and we get the grand total of seven thousand three hundred and eighty-five and this, expressed in Roman numerals, is MMMMMMMCCCLXXXV. Here, then, is a number consisting of fifteen letters, the exact number of spaces in the indicator of the puzzle lock; and I repeat that this striking coincidence, added to, or rather multiplied into, the other probabilities, made it practically certain that this was the key-combination. It remained only to test it by actual experiment."

"By the way," said I," I noticed that you perked up rather suddenly when Miller mentioned the electric meter."

"Naturally," he replied. "It seemed that there must be a small lamp switched on somewhere in the building, and the only place that had not been examined was the strong-room. But if there was a lamp alight there, someone had been in the strong-room. And, as, the only person who was known to be able to get in was missing, it seemed probable that he was in there still. But if he was, he was pretty certainly dead; and there was quite a considerable probability that some one else was in there with him, since his companion was missing, too, and both had disappeared at the same time. But I must confess that that spring drawer was beyond my expectations, though I suspected it as soon as I saw Miller pulling at it. Luttrell was an ingenious old rascal; he almost deserved a better fate. However, I expect his death will have delivered the gang into the hands of the police."

Events fell out as Thorndyke surmised. Mr. Luttrell's little journal, in conjunction with the confession of the spy who had been captured on the premises, enabled the police to swoop down on the disconcerted gang before any breath of suspicion had reached them; with the result that they are now secured in strong-rooms of another kind whereof the doors are fitted with appliances as effective as, though less ingenious than, Mr. Luttrell's puzzle lock.

The Green Check Jacket

The visits of our old friend, Mr. Brodribb, even when strictly professional, usually took the outward form of a friendly call. On the present occasion there was no such pretence. The old solicitor entered our chambers carrying a small suit-case (the stamped initials on which, "R.M.," I noticed, instantly attracted an inquisitive glance from Thorndyke, being obviously not Mr. Brodribb's own) which he placed on the table and then shook hands with an evident air of business.

"I have come, Thorndyke," he said, with unusual directness, "to ask your advice on a matter which is causing me some uneasiness. Do you know Reginald Merrill?"

"Slightly," was the reply. "I meet him occasionally in court; and, of course, I know him as the author of that interesting book on Prehistoric Flint-mines."

"Well," said Brodribb, "he has disappeared. He is missing. I don't like to use the expression; but when a responsible man is absent from his usual places of resort, when he apparently had no expectation of being so absent, and when he has made no provision for such absence, I think we may regard him as having disappeared in a legal sense. His absence calls for active inquiry."

"Undoubtedly," agreed Thorndyke; "and I take it that you are the person on whom the duty devolves?"

I think so. I am his solicitor and the executor of his will--at least I believe so; and the only near relative of his whom I know is his nephew and heir, Ethelbert Crick, his sister's son. But Crick seems to have disappeared, too; and about the same time as Merrill. It is an extraordinary affair."

"You say that you believe you are Merrill's executor. Haven't you seen the will?"

"I have seen a will. I have it in my safe. But Merrill said he was going to draw up another, and he may have done so. But if he has, he will almost certainly have appointed me his executor, and I shall assume that he has and act accordingly."

""“Was there any special reason for making a new will?" Thorndyke asked.

"Yes," replied Brodribb. "He has just come into quite a considerable fortune, and he was pretty well off before. Under the old will, practically the whole of his property went to Crick. There was a small bequest to a man named Samuel Horder, his cousin's son; and Horder was the alternative legatee if Crick should die before Merrill. Now, I understood Merrill to say that, in view of this extra fortune, he wished to do rather more for Horder, and I gathered that he proposed to divide the estate more or less equally between the two men. The whole estate was more than he thought necessary for Crick. And now, as we have cleared up the preliminaries, I will give you the circum stances of the disappearance.

"Last Wednesday, the 5th, I had a note from him saying that he would have some reports ready for me on the following day, but that he would be away from his office from 10.30 a.m. to about 6.30, and suggesting that I should send round in the evening if I wanted the papers particularly. Now it happened that my clerk, Page, had to go to a place near London Bridge on Thursday morning, and, oddly enough, he saw Mr. Merrill come out of Edginton's, the ship-fitters, with a man who was carrying a largish hand-bag. There was nothing in it, of course, but Page is an observant man and he noticed Merrill's companion so far as to observe that he was wearing a Norfolk jacket of a greenish shepherd's plaid and a grey tweed hat. He also noted the time by the big clock in the street near to Edginton's--11.46--and that Merrill looked up at it, and that the two men then walked off rather quickly in the direction of the station. Well, in the evening, I sent Page round to Merrill's chambers in Fig-tree Court to get the papers. He arrived there just after 6.30, but he found the oak shut, and though he rapped at the door on the chance that Merrill might have come in--he lives in the chambers adjoining the office--there was no answer. So he went for a walk round the Temple, deciding to return a little later.

"Well, he had gone as far as the cloisters and was loitering there to look in the window of the wig shop when he saw a man in a greenish shepherd's plaid jacket and a tweed hat coming up Pump

Court. As the man approached Page thought he recognised him; in fact, he felt so sure that he stopped him and asked him if he knew what time Mr. Merrill would be home. But the man looked at him in astonishment. 'Merrill?' said he. 'I don't know anyone of that name.' Thereupon Page apologised and explained how be bad been misled by the pattern and colour of the jacket.

"After walking about for nearly half an hour, Page went back to Merrill's chambers; but the oak was shut and he could get no answer by rapping with his stick, so he scribbled a note and dropped it into the letter- box and came away. The next morning I sent him round again, but the chambers were still shut up, and they have been shut up ever since; and nothing what ever has been seen or heard of Merrill.

"On Saturday, thinking it possible that Crick might be able to give me some news of his uncle, I called at his lodgings; and then, to my astonishment, I learned that he also was missing. He had gone away early on Thursday morning, saying that he had to go on business to Rochester, and that he might not be home to dinner. But he never came home at all. I called again on Sunday evening, and, as he had still not returned, I decided to take more active measures.

"This afternoon, immediately after lunch, I called at the Porter's Lodge, and, having briefly explained the circumstances and who I was, asked the porter to bring the duplicate key--which he had for the laundress--and accompany me to Mr. Merrill's chambers to see if, by chance, the tenant might be lying in them dead or insensible. He assured me that this could not be the case, since he had given the key every morning to the laundress, who had, in fact, returned it to him only a couple of hours previously. Nevertheless, he took the key and looked up the laundress, who had rooms near the lodge, who was fortunately at home and who turned out to be a most respectable and intelligent elderly woman; and we went together to Merrill's chambers. The porter admitted us, and when we had been right I through the set and ascertained definitely that Merrill was not there, he handed the key to the laundress, Mrs. Butler, and went away.

"When he was gone, I had a talk with Mrs. Butler, from which some rather startling facts transpired. It seemed that on Thursday, as Merrill was going to be out all day, she took the opportunity to have a grand clean-up of the chambers, to tidy up the lobby, and to look over the chests of drawers and the wardrobe and shake out and brush the clothes and see that no moths had got in. 'When I had finished,' she said, 'the place was like the inside of a band-box; just as he liked to see it.'

"'And, after all, Mrs. Butler,' said I, 'he never did see it.'

"'Oh, yes, he did,' says she. 'I don't know when he came in, but when I let myself in the next morning, I could see that he had been in since I left.'

"'How did you know that?' I asked.

"'Well,' says she,' I left the carpet-sweeper standing against the wardrobe door. I remembered it after I left and would have gone back and moved it, but I had already handed the key in at the Porter's Lodge. But when I went in next morning it wasn't there. It had been moved into the corner by the fireplace. Then the looking-glass had been moved. I could see that, because, before I went away, I had tidied my hair by it, and being short, I had to tilt it to see my face in it. Now it was tilted to suit a tall person and I could not see myself in it. Then I saw that the shaving had been moved, and when I put it back in its place, I found it was damp. It wouldn't have kept damp for twenty-four hours at this time of year.' That was perfectly true, you know, Thorndyke."

"Perfectly," agreed Thorndyke, "that woman is an excellent observer."

"Well," continued Brodribb, "on this she examined the shaving soap and the sponge and found them both perceptibly damp. It appeared practically certain that Merrill had been in on the preceding evening and had shaved; but by way of confirmation, I suggested that she should look over his clothes and see whether he had changed any of his garments. She did so, beginning with those that were hanging in the wardrobe, which she took down one at a time. Suddenly she gave a cry of surprise, and I got a bit of a start myself when she handed out a greenish shepherd's plaid Norfolk jacket.

'That,' she said, 'was not here when I brushed these clothes,' and it was obvious from its dusty condition that it could not have been; 'and,' she added,' I have never seen it before to my knowledge, and I think I should have remembered it.' I asked her if there was any coat missing and she answered that she had brushed a grey tweed jacket that seemed to have disappeared.

"Well, it was a queer affair. The first thing to be done was to ascertain, if possible whether that jacket was or was not Merrill's.

That, I thought, you would be able to judge better than I; so I borrowed his suit-case and popped the jacket into it, together with another jacket that was undoubtedly his, for comparison. Here is the suit-case and the two jackets are inside."

"It is really a question that could be better decided by a tailor," said Thorndyke. "The differences of measurement can't be great if they could both be worn by the same person. But we shall see." He rose, and having spread some sheets of newspaper over the table, opened the suit-case and took out the two jackets, which ho laid out side by side. Then, with his spring-tape, he proceeded systematically to measure the two garments, entering each pair of measurements on a slip of paper divided into two columns. Mr. Brodribb and I watched him expectantly and compared the two sets of figures as they were written down; and very soon it became evident that they were, at least, not identical. At length Thorndyke laid down the tape, and picking up the paper, studied it closely.

"I think," he said, "we may conclude that these two jackets were not made for the same person. The differences are not great, but they are consistent. The elbow creases, for instance, agree with the total length of the sleeves. The owner of the green jacket has longer arms and a bigger span than Merrill, but his chest measurement is nearly two inches greater and he has much more sloping shoulders. He could hardly have buttoned Merrill's jacket."

"Then," said Brodribb, "the next question is, did Merrill come home in some other man's coat or did some other man enter his chambers? From what Page has told us it seems pretty evident that a stranger must have got into those chambers. But if that is so, the questions arise : What the deuce was the fellow's object in changing into Merrill's clothes and shaving? How did he get into Merrill's chambers? What was he doing there? What has become of Merrill? And what is the meaning of the whole affair?"

"To some of those questions," said Thorndyke, "the answers are fairly obvious. If we assume, as I do, that the owner of the green jacket is the man whom Page saw at London Bridge and afterwards in the cloisters, the reason for the change of garments becomes plain enough. Page told the man that he had identified him by this very distinctive jacket as the person with whom Merrill was last seen alive. Evidently that man's safety demanded hat he should get rid of the incriminating jacket without delay. Then, as to his having shaved: did Page give you any description of the man?"

"Yes; he was a tallish man, about thirty-five, with a large dark moustache and a torpedo beard."

"Very well," said Thorndyke; "then we may say that the man who went into Merrill's chambers was a moustached bearded man in a green jacket and that he man who came out was a clean-shaved man in a grey jacket, whom Page himself would probably have passed without a second glance. That is clear enough. And as to how he got into the chambers, evidently he let himself in with Merrill's key; and if he did, I am afraid we can make a pretty shrewd guess as to what has become of Merrill, and only hope that we are guessing wrong. As to what this man was doing in those chambers and what is the meaning of the whole affair, that is a more difficult question. If the man had Merrill's latchkey, we may assume that he had the rest of Merrill's keys; that he had, in fact, free access to any locked receptacles in those chambers. The circumstances suggest that he entered the chambers for the purpose of getting possession of some valuable objects contained in them. Do you happen to know whether Merrill had any property of considerable value on the premises?"

"I don't," replied Brodribb. "He had a safe, but I don't know what he kept in it. Principally documents, I should think. Certainly not money, in any considerable amounts. The only thing of value that I actually know of is the new will; and that would only be valuable in certain circumstancces."

The abrupt and rather ambiguous conclusion of Mr. Brodribb's statement was not lost either on Thorndyke or on me. Apparently the cautious old lawyer had suddenly realised, as I had, that if anything had happened to Merrill, those "certain circumstances" had already come into being. From what he had told us it appeared that, under the new will, Crick stood to inherit a half of Mr. Merrill's fortune, whereas under the old will he stood to inherit nearly the whole. And it was a great fortune. The loss or destruction of the new will would be worth a good many thousand pounds to Mr. Crick.

"Well," said Brodribb, after a pause, "what is to be done? I suppose I ought to communicate with the police."

"You will have to, sooner or later," said Thorndyke; "but meanwhile, leave these two jackets--or, at least, the green one--with me for the present and let me see if I can extract any further information from it."

"You won't find anything in the pockets but dirt. I've tried them."

"I hope you left the dirt," said Thorndyke.

I did," replied Brodribb, "excepting what came out on my fingers. Very well; I'll leave the coats with you for to-day, and I will see if I can get any further news of Crick from his landlady."

With this the old solicitor shook hands and went off with such an evident air of purpose that I remarked: "Brodribb is off to find out whether Mr. Crick was the proprietor of a green plaid Norfolk jacket."

Thorndyke smiled. "It was rather quaint," said he, "to see the sudden way in which he drew in his horns when the inwardness of the affair dawned on him. But we mustn't start with a preconceived theory. Our business is to get hold of some more facts. There is little enough to go on at present. Let us begin by having a good look at this green jacket."

He picked it up and carried it to the window, where we both looked it over critically.

"It is rather dusty," I remarked, "especially on the front, and there is a white mark on the middle button."

"Yes. Chalk, apparently; and if you look closely, there are white traces on the other buttons and on the front of the coat. The back is much less dusty."

As he spoke, Thorndyke turned the garment round, and then, from the side of the skirt, picked a small, hair-like object which he felt between his finger and thumb, looked at closely and handed to me.

"A bit of barley beard," said I, "and there are two more on the other side. He must have walked along a narrow path through a barley field-- the state of the front of his coat almost suggests that he had crawled."

"Yes; it is earthy dust; but Polton's extractor will give us more information about that. We had better hand it over to him; but first we will go through the pockets in spite of Brodribb's discouragement."

"By Jove!" I exclaimed, as I thrust my hand into one of the side pockets, "he was right about the dirt. Look at this." I drew out my hand with a quite considerable pinch of dry earth and one or two little fragments of chalk. "It looks as if he had been crawling in loose earth."

"It does," Thorndyke agreed, inspecting his own "catch"--a pinch of reddish earth and a fragment of chalk of the size of a large pea. "The earth is very characteristic, this red-brown loam that you find overlying the chalk. All his outside pockets seem to have caught more or less of it. However, we can leave Polton to collect it and prepare it for examination. I'll take the coat up to him now, and while he is working at it I think I will walk round to Edginton's and see if I can pick up any further particulars."

He went up to the laboratory floor, where our assistant, Polton, carried on his curious and varied activities, and when he returned we sallied forth together. In Fleet Street we picked up a disengaged taxicab, by which we were whisked across Blackfriars Bridge and a few minutes later set down at the corner of Tooley Street. We made our way to the ship-chandler's shop, where Thorndyke proceeded to put a few discreet questions to the manager, who listened politely and with sympathetic interest.

"The difficulty is," said he, "that there were a good many gentlemen in here last Thursday. You say they came about I I.45. If you could tell me what they bought, we could look at the bill-duplicate book and that might help us."

"I don't actually know what they bought," said Thorndyke. "It might have been a length of rope; a rope, perhaps, say twelve or fourteen fathoms or perhaps more. But I may be wrong."

I stared at Thorndyke in amazement. Long as I known him, this extraordinary faculty of instantaneous induction always came on me as a fresh surprise. I had supposed that in this case we had absolutely nothing to go on; and yet here he was with at least a tentative suggestion before the inquiry appeared to have begun. And that suggestion was clear evidence that he had already arrived at a hypothetical solution of the mystery. I was still pondering on this astonishing fact when the manager approached with an open book and accompanied by an assistant.

"I see," said he, "that there is an entry, apparently about mid-day on Thursday, of the sale of a fifteen-fathom length of deep-sea lead-line, and my friend, here, remembers selling it."

"Yes," the assistant confirmed, "I remember it because he wanted to get it into his hand-bag, and it took the three of us to stuff it in. Thick lead-line is pretty stiff when it's new."

"Do you remember what these gentlemen were like and how they were dressed?"

"One was a rather elderly gentleman, clean-shaved, I think. The other I remember better because he had rather queer-looking eyes--very pale grey. He had a pointed beard and he wore a greenish check coat and a cloth hat. That's all I remember about him."

"It is more than most people would have remembered," said Thorndyke. "I am very much obliged to you; and I think I will ask you to let me have a fifteen-fathom length of that same lead-line."

By this time my capacity for astonishment was exhausted. What on earth could my colleague want with a deep-sea lead-line? But, after all, why not? If he had then and there purchased a Trotman's anchor, a shark-hook and a set of International code signals, I should have been prepared to accept the proceeding with out comment. Thorndyke was a law unto himself.

Nevertheless, as I walked homeward by his side, carrying the coil of rope, I continued to speculate on this singular case. Thorndyke had arrived at a hypothetical solution of Mr. Brodribb's problem; and it was evidently correct, so far, as the entry in the bill-book proved. But what was the connection between a dusty jacket and a length of thin rope? And why this particular length? I could make nothing of it. But I determined, as soon as we got home, to see what new facts Polton's activities had brought to light.

The results were disappointing. Polton's dust extractor had been busy, and the products in the form of tiny heaps of dust, were methodically set out on a sheet of white paper, each little heap covered with a watch-glass and accompanied by its written particulars as to the part of the garment from which it had come. I examined a few samples under the microscope, but though curious and interesting, as all dust is, they showed nothing very distinctive. The dust might have come from anyone's coat. There was, of course, a good deal of yellowish sandy loam, a few particles of chalk, a quantity of fine ash, clinker and particles of coal--railway dust from a locomotive--ordinary town and house dust and some oddments such as pollen grains, including those of the sow-thistle, mallow, poppy and valerian, and in one sample I found two scales from the wing of the common blue butterfly. That was all; and it told me nothing but that the owner of the coat had recently been in a chalk district and that he had taken a railway journey.

While I was working with the microscope, Polton was busy with an occupation that I did not understand. He had cemented the little pieces of chalk that we had found in the pockets to a plate of glass by means of pitch, and he was now brushing them under water with a soft brush and from time to time decanting the milky water into a tall sediment glass. Now, as most people know, chalk is largely composed of microscopic shells--foraminifera--which can be detached by gently brushing the chalk under water. But what was the object? There was no doubt that the material was chalk, and we knew that foraminifera were there. Why trouble to prove what is common knowledge? I questioned Polton, but he knew nothing of the purpose of the investigation. He merely beamed on me like a crinkly old graven image and went on brushing. I dipped up a sample of the white sediment and examined it under the microscope. Of course there were foraminifera, and very beautiful they were. But what about it? The whole proceeding looked purposeless. And yet I knew that it was not. Thorndyke was the last man in the world to expend his energies in flogging a dead horse.

Presently he came up to the laboratory, and, when he had looked at the dust specimens and confirmed my opinion of them, he fell to work on the chalk sediment. Having prepared a number of slides, he sat down at the microscope with a sharp pencil and a block of smooth paper with the apparent purpose of cataloguing and making drawings of the foraminifera. And at this task I left him while I went forth to collect some books that I had ordered from a bookseller in the Charing Cross Road.

When I returned with my purchases about an hour later I found him putting back in a press a portfolio of large-scale Ordnance maps of Kent which he had apparently been consulting, and I noticed on the table his sheet of drawings and a monograph of the fossil foraminifera.

"Well, Thorndyke," I said cheerfully," I suppose this time, you know exactly what has become of Merrill."

"I can guess," he replied, "and so can you. But the actual data are distressingly vague. We have certain indications, as you will have noticed. The trouble will be to bring them to a focus. It is a case for constructive imagination on the one hand and the method of exclusion on the other. I shall make a preliminary circle-round tomorrow."

"Meaning by that?"

"I have a hypothesis. It is probably wrong. If it is, we must try another, and yet another. Every time we fail we shall narrow the field of inquiry until by eliminating one possibility after another, we may hope to arrive at the solution. My first essay will take me down into Kent."

"You are not going into those wild regions alone, Thorndyke," said I. "You will need my protection and support to say nothing of my invaluable advice. I presume you realise that?"

"Undoubtedly." he replied gravely. "I was reckoning on a two-man expedition. Besides, you are as much interested in the case as I am. And now, let us go forth and dine and fortify ourselves for the perils of tomorrow."

In the course of dinner I led the conversation to the products of Polton's labours and remarked upon their very indefinite significance; but Thorndyke was more indefinite still, as he usually was in cases of a highly speculative character.

"You are expecting too much from Polton," he said with a smile. "This is not a matter of foraminifera or pollen or butterfly-scales; they are only items of circumstantial evidence. What we have to do is to consider the whole body of facts in our possession; what Brodribb has told us, what we know for ourselves and what we have ascertained by investigation. The case is still very much in the air, but it is not so vague as you seem to imply."

This was all I could get out of him; and as the "whole body of facts" yielded no suggestion at all to me, I could only possess my soul in patience and hope for some enlightenment on the morrow.

About a quarter to eleven on the following morning, while Thorndyke was giving final instructions to Polton and I was speculating on the contents of the suit-case that was going to accompany us, footsteps became audible on our stairs. Their crescendo terminated in a flourish on our little brass knocker which I recognised as Brodribb's knock. I accordingly opened the door, and in walked our old friend. His keen blue eye took in at once our informal raiment and the suit-case and lighted up with something like curiosity.

"Off on an expedition?" he asked.

"Yes," replied Thorndyke. "A little trip down into Kent. Gravesend, in fact."

"Gravesend," repeated Brodribb with further awakened interest. "That was rather a favourite resort of poor Merrill's. By the way, your expedition is not connected with his disappearance, I suppose?"

"As a matter of fact it is," replied Thorndyke. "Just a tentative exploration, you know."

"I know," said Brodribb, all agog now, "and I'm coming with you. I've got a clear day and I'm not going to take a refusal."

"No refusal was contemplated," rejoined Thorndyke. "You'll probably waste a day, but we shall benefit by your society. Polton will let your clerk know that you haven't absconded, or you can look in at the office yourself. We have plenty of time."

Brodribb chose the latter plan, which enabled him to exchange his tall hat and morning coat for a soft hat and jacket, and we accordingly made our way to Charing Cross via Lincoln's Inn, where Brodribb's office was situated. I noticed that Brodribb, with his customary discretion, asked no questions, though he must have observed, as I had, the striking fact that Thorndyke had in some way connected Merrill with Gravesend; and in fact with the exception of Brodribb's account of his failure to get any news of Mr. Crick, no reference was made to the nature of our expedition until we alighted at our destination.

On emerging from the station, Thorndyke turned to the left and led the way out of the approach into a street, on the opposite side of which a rather grimy statue of Queen Victoria greeted us with a supercilious stare. Here we turned to the south along a prosperous thoroughfare, and presently crossing a main road, followed its rather sordid continuation until the urban squalor began to be tempered by traces of rusticity, and the suburb became a village. Passing a pleasant looking inn and a smithy, which seemed to have an out-patient department for invalid carts, we came into a quiet lane offering a leafy vista with glimpses of thatched and tiled cottages whose gardens were gay with summer flowers. Opposite these, some rough stone steps led up to a stile by the side of an open gate which gave access to a wide cart-track. Here Thorndyke halted, and producing his pocket map-case, com pared the surroundings with the map. At length he pocketed the case, and turning towards the cart-track, said: "This is our way, for better or worse. In a few minutes we shall probably know whether we have found a clue or a mare's nest."

We followed the track up a rise until, reaching the crest of the hill, we saw stretching away below us a wide, fertile valley with wooded heights beyond, over the brow of which peeped the square tower of some village church.

"Well," said Brodribb, taking off his hat to enjoy the light breeze, "clue or no clue, this is perfectly delightful and well worth the journey. Just look at those charming little blue butterflies fluttering round that mallow. What a magnificent prospect And where, but in Kent, will you see such a barley field as that?"

It was, indeed, a beautiful landscape. But as my eye travelled over the enormous barley field, its tawny surface rippling, in golden waves before the summer breeze, it was not the beauty of the scene that occupied my mind. I was thinking of those three ends of barley beard that we had picked from the skirts of the green jacket. The cart-track had now contracted to a foot path; but it was a broader path than I should have looked for, running straight across the great field to a far-away stile; and half way along it on the left hand side I could see, rising above the barley, the top of a rough fence around a small, square enclosure that looked like a pound--though it was in an unlikely situation.

We pursued the broad path across the field until we were nearly abreast of the pound, and I was about to draw Thorndyke's attention to it, when I perceived a narrow lane through the barley--hardly a path, but rather a track, trodden through the crop by some persons who had gone to the enclosure. Into this track Thorndyke turned as if he had been looking for it, and walked towards the enclosure, closely scrutinising the ground as he went. Brodribb and I, of course, followed in single file, brushing through the barley as we went; and as we drew nearer we could see that there was an opening in the enclosing fence and that inside was a deep hollow the edges of which were fringed with clumps of pink valerian. At the opening of the fence Thorndyke halted and looked back.

"Well," said Brodribb, "is it going to be a mare's nest? "

"No," replied Thorndyke. "It is a clue, and something more!"

As he spoke, he pointed to the foot of one of the principal posts of the fence, to which was secured a short length of rope, the frayed ends of which suggested that it had broken under a heavy strain. And now I could see what the enclosure was. Inside it was a deep pit, and at the bottom of the pit, to one side, was a circular hole, black as night, and apparently leading down into the bowels of the earth.

"That must be a dene hole," said I, looking at the yawning cavity.

"It is," Thorndyke replied.

"Ha," said Brodribb, "so that is a dene hole, is it? Damned unpleasant looking place. Dene holes were one of poor Merrill's hobbies. He used to go down to explore them. I hope you are not suggesting that he went down this one."

"I am afraid that is what has happened, Brodribb," was the reply. "That end of rope looks like his. It is deep-sea lead-line. I have a length of it here, bought at the same place as he bought his, and probably cut from the same sample." He opened the suit-case, and taking out the coil of line that we had bought, flung it down by the foot of the post. Obviously it was identical with the broken end. "However," he added," we shall see."

"We are going down, are we?" asked Brodribb.

"We?" repeated Thorndyke. "I am going down if it is practicable. Not otherwise. If it is an ordinary seventy-foot shaft with perpendicular sides, we shall have to get proper appliances. But you had better stay above, in any case."

"Nonsense!" exclaimed Brodribb. "I am not such a back number as you think. I have been a mountain-climber in my time and I'm not a bit nervous. I can get down all right if there is any foothold, and I've got a rope to hang on to. And you can see for yourself that somebody has been down with a rope only."

"Yes," replied Thorndyke, "but I don't see that that somebody has come up again."

"No," Brodribb admitted; "that's true. The rope seems to have broken; and you say your rope is the same stuff?

Thorndyke looked at me inquiringly as I stooped and examined the frayed end of the strange rope.

"What do you say, Jervis?" he asked.

"That rope didn't break," I replied. "It has been, chafed or sawn through. It is quite different in appearance from a broken end."

"That was what I decided as soon as I saw it," said Thorndyke. "Besides, a new rope of this size and quality couldn't possibly break under the weight of a man."

Brodribb gazed at the frayed end with an expression of horror.

"What a diabolical thing!" he exclaimed. "You mean that some wretch deliberately cut the rope and let another man drop down the shaft! But it can't be. I really think you must be mistaken. It must have been a defective rope."

"Well, that is what it looks like," replied Thorndyke. He made a 'running bowline" at the end of our rope and slipped the loop over his shoulders, drawing it tight under his arms. Then he turned towards the pit. "You had better take a couple of turns round the foot of the post, Jervis," said he, "and pay out just enough to keep the rope taut."

He took an electric inspection-lamp from the suit case, slipped the battery in his pocket and hooked the bull's-eye to a button-hole, and when all was ready, he climbed down into the pit, crossed the sloping floor, and crouching down, peered into the forbidding hole, throwing down it a beam of light from his bull's-eye. Then he stood up and grasped the rope.

"It is quite practicable," said he; "only about twenty feet deep, and good foothold all the way." With this he crouched once more, backed into the hole and disappeared from view. He evidently descended pretty quickly, to judge by the rate at which I had to pay out the rope, and in quite a short time I felt the tension slacken and began to haul up the line. As the loop came out of the hole, Mr. Brodribb took possession of it, and regardless of my protests, proceeded to secure it under his arms.

"But how the deuce am I going to get down?" I demanded.

"That's all right, Jervis," he replied persuasively. "I'll just have a look round and then come up and let you down."

It being obviously useless to argue, I adjusted the rope and made ready to pay out. He climbed down into the pit with astonishing agility, backed into the hole and disappeared; and the tension of the rope informed me that he was making quite a rapid descent. He had nearly reached the bottom when there were borne to my ears the hollow reverberations of what sounded like a cry of alarm. But all was apparently well, for the rope continued to draw out steadily, and when at last its tension relaxed, I felt an unmistakable signal shake, and at once drew it up.

As my curiosity made me unwilling to remain passively waiting for Brodribb's return, I secured the end of the rope to the post with a "fisherman's bend" and let myself down into the pit. Advancing to the hole, I lay down and put my head over the edge. A dim light from Thorndyke's lamp came up the shaft and showed me that we were by no means the first explorers, for there were foot-holes cut in the chalk all the way down, apparently of some considerable age. With the aid of these and the rope, it appeared quite easy to descend and I decided to go down forthwith. Accordingly I backed towards the shaft, found the first of the foot-holes, and grasping the rope with one hand and using the other to hang on to the upper cavities, easily let myself down the well-like shaft. As I neared the bottom the light of the lamp was thrown full on the shaft-wall; a pair of hands grasped me and I heard Thorndyke's voice saying: "Look where you are treading, Jervis"; on which I looked down and saw immediately below me a man lying on his face by an irregular coil of rope.

I stepped down carefully on to the chalk floor and looked round. We were in a small chamber in one side of which was the black opening of a low tunnel. Thorndyke and Brodribb were standing at the feet of the prostrate figure examining a revolver which the solicitor held.

"It has certainly been fired," said the latter. "One chamber is empty and the barrel is foul."

"That may be," replied Thorndyke; "but there is no bullet wound. This man died from a knife wound in the chest." He threw the light of his lamp on the corpse and as I turned it partly over to verify his statement, he added: "This is poor Mr. Merrill. We found the revolver lying by his side."

"The cause of death is clear enough," said I, "and it certainly wasn't suicide. The question is--" At this moment Thorndyke stooped and threw a beam of light down the tunnel, and Brodribb and I simultaneously uttered an exclamation. At the extreme end, about forty feet away, the body of another man lay. Instantly Brodribb started forward, and stooping to clear the low roof--it was about four feet six inches high--hurried along the tunnel. Thorndyke and I followed close behind. As we reached the body, which was lying supine with a small electric torch by its side, and the light of Thorndyke's lamp fell on the upturned face, Brodribb gasped: " God save us! it's Crick! And here is the knife." He was about to pick up the weapon when Thorndyke put out his hand.

"That knife," said he, "must be touched by no hand but the one that dealt the blow. It may be crucial evidence."

"Evidence of what?" demanded Brodribb. "There is Merrill with a knife wound in his chest and a pistol by his side. Here is Crick with a bullet wound in his breast, a knife by his side and the empty sheath secured round his waist. What more evidence do you want?"

"That depends on what you seek to prove," said Thorndyke. "What is your interpretation of the facts that you have stated?

"Why, it is as plain as daylight," answered Brodribb, "incredible as the affair seems, having regard to the characters of the two men. Crick stabbed Merrill and Merrill shot him dead. Then Merrill tried to escape, but the rope broke, he was trapped and he bled to death at the foot of the shaft."

"And who do you say died first?" Thorndyke asked.

It was a curious question and it caused me to look inquisitively at my colleague. But Brodribb answered promptly: "Why, Crick, of course. Here he lies where he fell. There is a track of blood along the floor of the tunnel, as you can see, and there is Merrill at the entrance, dead in the act of trying to escape."

Thorndyke nodded in a rather mysterious way and there was a brief silence. Then I ventured to remark: "You seem to be losing sight of the man with the green jacket."

Brodribb started and looked at me with a frown of surprise.

Bless my soul!" he exclaimed, "so I am. I had clean forgotten him in these horrors. But what is your point? Is there any evidence that he has been here?"

"I don't know," said I. "He bought the rope and he was seen with Merrill apparently going towards London Bridge Station. And I gather that it was the green jacket that piloted Thorndyke to this place."

In a sense," Thorndyke admitted, "that is so. But we will talk about that later. Meanwhile there are one or two facts that I will draw your attention to. First as to the wounds; they are almost identical in position. Each is on the left side, just below the nipple; a vital spot, which would be fully exposed by a man who was climbing down holding on to a rope. Then, if you look along the floor where I am throwing the light, you can see a distinct trace of something having been dragged along, although there seems to have been an effort to obliterate it; and the blood marks are more in the nature of smears than drops." He gently turned the body over and pointed to the back, which was thickly covered with chalk. "This corpse has obviously been dragged along the floor," he continued. "It wouldn't have been marked in that way by merely falling. Further, the rope, when last seen, was being stuffed into a hand-bag. The rope is here, but where is the hand-bag? Finally, the rope was cut by some one outside, and evidently after the murders had been committed."

As he concluded, he spread his handkerchief over the knife, and wrapping it up carefully without touching it with his fingers, placed it in his outside breast-pocket. Then we went back towards the shaft, where Thorndyke knelt down by the body of Merrill and systematically emptied the pockets.

"What are you searching for?" asked Brodribb.

"Keys," was the reply; "and there aren't any, It is a vital point, seeing that the man with the green jacket evidently let himself into Merrill's chambers that same day."

"Yes," Brodribb agreed with a reflective frown; "it is. But tell us, Thorndyke, how you reconstruct this horrible crime."

"My theory," said Thorndyke "is that the three men came here together. They made the rope fast to the post. The stranger in the green jacket came down first and waited at the foot of the shaft. Merrill came down next, and the stranger stabbed him just as he reached the bottom, while his arms were still up hanging on to the rope. Crick followed and was shot in the same place and the same manner. Then the stranger dragged Crick's body along the tunnel, swept away the marks as well as he could, put the knife and the lamp by the body, dropped the revolver by Merrill's corpse, took the keys and went up, sawed through the rope--probably with a pocket saw--and threw the end down the shaft. Then he took the next train to London and went straight to Merrill's chambers, where he opened the safe or other receptacles and took possession of what he wanted."

Brodribb nodded. "It was a diabolically clever scheme," said he.

"The scheme was ingenious enough," Thorndyke agreed, "but the execution was contemptible. He has left traces at every turn. Otherwise we shouldn't be here. He has acted on the assumption that the world contains no one but fools. But that is a fool's assumption."

When we had ascended, in the reverse order of our descent, Thorndyke detached our rope and also the frayed end, which we took with us, and we then took our way back towards the town; and I noted that as we stood by the dene hole, there was not a human creature in sight; nor did we meet a single person until we were close to the village. It was an ideal spot for a murder.

"I suppose you will notify the police?" said Brodribb.

"Yes," replied Thorndyke. "I shall call on the Chief Constable and give him the facts and advise him to keep some of them to himself for the present, and also to arrange for an adjournment of the inquest. Our friend with the green jacket must be made to think that he has played a trump card."

Apparently the Chief Constable was a man who knew all the moves of criminal investigation, for at the inquest the discovery was attributed to the local police acting on information received from somebody who had "noticed the broken rope."

None of us was summoned to give evidence nor were our names mentioned, but the inquest was adjourned for three weeks, for further inquiries.

But in those three weeks there were some singular developments, of which the scene was the clerks' office at Mr. Brodribb's premises in Lincoln's Inn. There late on a certain forenoon, Thorndyke and I arrived, each provided with a bag and a sheaf of documents, and were duly admitted by Mr. Page.

"Now," said Thorndyke, "are you quite confident, Mr. Page, that you would recognise this man, even if he had shaved off his beard and moustache?"

"Quite confident," replied Page. "I should know him by his eyes. Very queer eyes they were; light, greenish grey. And I should know his voice, too."

"Good," said Thorndyke; and as Page disappeared into the private office, we sat down and examined our documents, eyed furtively by the junior clerk. Some ten minutes later the door opened and a man entered; and the first glance at him brought my nerves to concert pitch. He was a thick-set, muscular man, clean-shaved and rather dark. But my attention was instantly arrested by his eyes--singularly pale eyes which gave an almost unhuman character to his face. He reminded me of a certain species of lemur that I once saw.

"I have got an appointment with Mr. Brodribb," he said, addressing the clerk. "My name is Horder."

The clerk slipped off his stool and moved towards the door of the private office, but at that moment Page came out. As his eyes met Horder's, he stopped dead; and instantly the two men seemed to stiffen like a couple of dogs that have suddenly met at a street corner. I watched Horder narrowly. He had been rather pale when he came in. Now he was ghastly, and his whole aspect indicated extreme nervous tension.

"Did you wish to see Mr. Brodribb?" asked Page, still gazing intently at the other.

"Yes," was the irritable reply; "I have given my name once--Horder."

Mr. Page turned and re-entered the private office, leaving the door ajar.

Mr. Horder to see you, sir," I heard him say. He came out and shut the door. "If you will sit down, Mr. Brodribb will see you in a minute or two," he said, offering a chair; he then took his hat from a peg, glanced at his watch and went out.

A couple of minutes passed. Once, I thought I heard stealthy footsteps out in the entry; but no one came in or knocked. Presently the door of the private office opened and a tall gentleman came out. And then, once more, my nerves sprang to attention. The tall gentleman was Detective-Superintendent Miller.

The superintendent walked across the office, opened the door, looked out, and then, leaving it ajar, came back to where Horder was sitting.

"You are Mr. Samuel Horder, I think," said he.

"Yes, I am," was the reply. "What about it?"

"I am a police officer, and I arrest you on a charge of having unlawfully entered the premises of the late Reginald Merrill; and it is my duty to caution you--"

Here Horder, who had risen to his feet, and slipped his right hand under the skirt of his coat, made a sudden spring at the officer. But in that instant Thorndyke had gripped his right arm at the elbow and wrist and swung him round; the superintendent seized his left arm while I pounced upon the revolver in his right hand and kept its muzzle pointed to the floor. But it was an uncomfortable affair. Our prisoner was a strong man and he fought like a wild beast; and he had his finger hooked round the trigger of the revolver. The four of us, locked together, gyrated round the office, knocking over chairs and bumping against the walls, the junior clerk skipped round the room with his eyes glued on the pistol and old Brodribb charged out of his sanctum, flourishing a long ruler. However, it did not last long. In the midst of the uproar, two massive constables stole in and joined the fray. There was a yell from the prisoner, the revolver rattled to the floor and then I heard two successive metallic clicks.

"He'll be all right now," murmured the constable who had fixed on the handcuffs, with the manner of one who has administered a soothing remedy.

"I notice," said Thorndyke, when the prisoner had been removed, "that you charged him only with unlawful entry."

"Yes," replied Miller, "until we have taken his finger-prints. Mr. Singleton has developed up three fingers and a thumb, beautifully clear, on that knife that you gave us. If they prove to be Horder's finger prints, of course, it is a true bill for the murder."

The finger-prints on the knife proved undoubtedly to be Horder's. But the case did not rest on them alone. When his rooms were searched, there were found not only Mr. Merrill's keys but also Mr. Merrill's second will, which had been missed from the safe when it was opened by the maker's locksmith; thus illustrating afresh the perverse stupidity of the criminal mind.

"A satisfactory case," remarked Thorndyke, "in respect of the result; but there was too much luck for us to take much credit from it. On Brodribb's opening statement, it was pretty clear that a crime had been committed. Merrill was missing and some one had possession of his keys and had entered his premises. It also appeared nearly certain that the thing stolen must be the second will, since there was nothing else of value to steal; and the will was of very great value to two persons, Crick and Horder, to each of whom its destruction was worth many thousands of pounds. To both of them its value was conditional on the immediate death of Merrill, before another will could be made; and to Horder it was further conditional on the death of Crick and that he should die before Merrill--for otherwise the estate would go to Crick's heirs or next of kin. The prima facie suspicion therefore fell on these two men. But Crick was missing; and the question was, had he absconded or was he dead?

"And now as to the investigation. The green jacket showed earthy dust and chalk on the front and chalk-marks on the buttons. The indication was that the wearer had either crawled on chalky ground or climbed up a chalky face. But the marks on the buttons suggested climbing; for a horizontal surface is usually covered by soil, whereas on a vertical surface the chalk is exposed. But the time factor showed us that this man could not have travelled far from London. He was seen going towards London Bridge Station about the time when a train was due to go down to Kent. That train went to Maidstone and Gillingham, calling at Gravesend, Strood, Snodland, Rochester, Chatham and other places abounding in chalk and connected with the cement industry. In that district there were no true cliffs, but there were numerous chalk-pits, railway embankments and other excavations. The evidence pointed to one of these excavations. Then Crick was known to have gone to Rochester--earlier in the day--which further suggested the district, though Rochester is the least chalky part of it.

"The question was, what kind of excavation had been climbed into? And for what purpose had the climbing been performed? But here the personality of the missing man gave us a hint. Merrill had written a book to prove that dene holes were simply prehistoric flint-mines. He had explored a number of dene holes and described them in his book. Now the district through which this train had passed was peculiarly rich in dene holes; and then there was the suggestive fact that Merrill had been last seen coming out of a rope- seller's shop. This latter fact was so important that I followed it up at once by calling at Edginton's. There I ascertained that Merrill or his companion had bought a fifteen-fathom length of deep-sea lead-line. Now this was profoundly significant. The maximum depth of a dene hole is about seventy feet. Fifteen fathoms--ninety feet--is therefore the exact length required, allowing for loops and fastenings. This new fact converted the dene-hole hypothesis into what was virtually a certainty, especially when one considered how readily these dangerous pits lent themselves either to fatal accidents or to murder. I accordingly adopted the dene-hole suggestion as a working hypothesis.

"The next question was, 'Where was this dene-hole?' And an uncommonly difficult question it was. I began to fear that the inquiry would fail from the impossibility of solving it. But at this point I got some help from a new quarter. I had given the coat to Polton to extract the dust and I had told him to wash the little lumps of chalk for foraminifera."

"What are foraminifera?" asked Brodribb.

"They are minute sea shells. Chalk is largely composed of them; and although chalk is in no sense a local rock, there is nevertheless a good deal of variation in the species of foraminifera found in different localities. So I had the chalk washed out as a matter of routine. Well, the dust was confirmatory but not illuminating. There was railway dust, of the South Eastern type--I expect you know it--chalk, loam dust, pollen-grains of the mallow and valerian (which grows in chalk-pits and railway cuttings) and some wing scales of the common blue butterfly, which haunts the chalk--I expect he had touched a dead butterfly. But all this would have answered for a good part of Kent. Then I examined the foraminifera and identified the species by the plates in Warnford's Monograph. The result was most encouraging. There were nine species in all, and of these five were marked as 'found in the Gravesend chalk,' two more 'from the Kentish chalk' and the other two 'from the English chalk.' This was a very striking result. More than half the contained foraminifera were from the Gravesend chalk.

"The problem now was to determine the geologic meaning of the term Gravesend. I ruled out Rochester, as I had heard of no dene holes in that neighbourhood, and I consulted Merrill's book and the large-scale Ordnance map. Merrill had worked in the Gravesend district and the adjacent part of Essex and he gave a list of the dene holes that he had explored, including the Clapper Napper Hole in Swanscombe Wood. But, checking his list by the Ordnance map, I found that there was one dene hole marked on the map which was not in his list. As it was evidently necessary to search all the dene holes in the district, I determined to begin with the one that he seemed to have missed. And there luck favoured us. It turned out to be the right one."

"I don't see that there was much luck in it," said Brodribb. "You calculated the probabilities and adopted the greatest."

"At any rate," said Thorndyke, "there was Merrill and there was Crick; and as soon as I saw them I knew that Horder was the murderer. For the whole tableau had obviously been arranged to demonstrate that Crick died before Merrill and establish Horder as Merrill's heir."

"A diabolical plot," commented Brodribb. "Horribly ingenious, too. By the way--which of them did die first in your opinion?"

"Merrill, I should say, undoubtedly," replied Thorndyke.

"That will be good hearing for Crick's next of kin," said Brodribb. "And you haven't done with this case yet, Thorndyke. I shall retain you on the question of survivorship."

The Seal of Nebuchadnezzar

"I suppose, Thorndyke," said I, "footprints yield quite a lot of information if you think about them enough?"

The question was called forth by the circumstance of my friend halting and stooping to examine the little pit made in the loamy soil of the path by the walking stick of some unknown wayfarer. Ever since we had entered this path--to which we had been directed by the station-master of Pinwell Junction as a short cut to our destination--I had noticed my friend scanning its surface, marked with numerous footprints, as if he were mentally reconstructing the personalities of the various travellers who had trodden it before us. This I knew to be a habit of his, almost unconsciously pursued; and the present conditions certainly favoured it, for here, as the path traversed a small wood, the slightly moist, plastic surface took impressions with the sharpness of moulding wax.

"Yes," he answered, "but you must do more than think. You need to train your eyes to observe in conspicuous characteristics."

"Such as these, for instance," said. I, with a grin, pointing to a blatant print of a Cox's "Invicta" rubber sole with its prancing-horse trade-mark.

Thorndyke smiled. "A man," said he, "who wears a sole like that is a mere advertising agent. He who runs may read those characteristics, but as there are thousands of persons wearing 'Invicta' soles, the observation merely identifies the wearer as a member of a large genus. It has to be carried a good deal further to identify him as an individual; otherwise, a standardised sole is apt to be rather misleading than helpful, Its gross distinctiveness tends to divert the novice's attention from the more specific characteristics which he would seek in a plain footprint like that of this man's companion."

"Why companion?" I asked. "The two men were walking the same way, but what evidence is there that they were companions?"

"A good deal, if you follow the series of tracks, as I have been doing. In the first place, there is the stride. Both men were rather tall, as shown by the size of their feet, but both have a distinctly short stride. Now the leather-soled man's short stride is accounted for by the way in which he put down his stick. He held it stiffly, leaning upon it to some extent and helping himself with it. There is one impression of the stick to every two paces; every impression of his left foot has a stick impression opposite to it. The suggestion is that he was old, weak or infirm. But the rubber-soled man walked with his stick in the ordinary way--one stick impression to every four paces. His abnormally short stride is not to be accounted for excepting by the assumption that he stepped short to keep pace with the other man.

"Then the two sets of footprints are usually separate. Neither man has trodden nor set his stick on the other man's tracks, excepting in those places where the path is too narrow for them to walk abreast, and there, in the one case I noticed the rubber soles treading on the prints of the leather soles, whereas at this spot the prints of the leather soles are imposed on those of the rubber soles. That, of course, is conclusive evidence that the two men were here at the same time."

"Yes," I agreed, "that settles the question without troubling about the stride. But after all, Thorndyke, this is a matter of reasoning, as I said; of thinking about the footprints and their meaning. No special acuteness of observation or training of vision comes into it. The mere facts are obvious enough; it is their interpretation that yields the knowledge."

"That is true so far," said he, "but we haven't exhausted our material. Look carefully at the impressions of the two sticks and tell me if you see any thing remarkable in either of them?"

I stooped and examined the little pits that the two sticks had made in the path, and, to tell the truth, found them extremely unilluminating.

"They seem very much alike," I said. "The rubber-soled man's stick is rather larger than the other and the leather-soled man's stick has made deeper holes--probably because it was smaller and he was leaning on it more heavily."

Thorndyke shook his head. “You’ve missed the point, Anstey, and you’ve missed it because you have failed to observe the visible facts. It is quite a neat point, too, and might in certain circumstances be a very important one.”

“Indeed,” said I. “What is the point?”

“That,” said he, “I shall leave you to infer from the visible facts, which are these: first, the impressions of the smaller stick are on the right-hand side of the man who made them, and second, that each impression is shallowest towards the front and the right-hand side.”

I examined the impressions carefully and verified Thorndyke’s statement.

Well,” I said, “what about it? What does it prove?”

Thorndyke smiled in his exasperating fashion. “The proof,” said he, “is arrived at by reasoning from the facts. My learned friend has the facts. If he will consider them, the conclusion will emerge.”

“But,” said I, “I don’t see your drift. The impression is shallower on one side, I suppose, because the ferrule of the stick was worn away on that side. But I repeat, what about it? Do you expect me to infer why the fool that it belonged to wore his stick away all at one side?”

“Now, don’t get irritable, Anstey,” said he. “Preserve a philosophic calm. I assure you that this is quite an interesting problem.”

So it may be,” I replied. “But I’m hanged if I can imagine why he wore his stick down in that way. However, it doesn’t really matter. It isn’t my stick--and by Jingo, here is old Brodribb--caught us in the act of wasting our time on academic chin-wags and delaying his business. The debate is adjourned.”

Our discussion had brought us to the opening of the wood, which now framed the figure of the solicitor. As he caught sight of us, he hurried forward, holding out his hand.

“Good men and true!” he exclaimed. “I thought you would probably come this way, and it is very good of you to have come at all, especially as it is a mere formality.”

“What is?” asked Thorndyke. “Your telegram spoke of an ‘alleged suicide.’ I take it that there is some ground for inquiry?”

"I don't know that there is," replied Brodribb. "But the deceased was insured for three thousand pounds, which will be lost to the estate if the suicide is confirmed. So I put it to my fellow that it was worth an expert's fee to make sure whether or not things are what they seem. A verdict of death by misadventure will save us three thousand pounds. Verbum sap." As he concluded, the old lawyer winked with exaggerated cunning and stuck his elbow into my ribs.

Thorndyke ignored the facetious suggestion of bribery and corruption and inquired dryly: "What are the circumstances of the case?"

"I'd better give you a sketch of them before we get to the house," replied Brodribb. "The dead man is Martin Rowlands, the brother of my neighbour in New Square, Tom Rowlands. Poor old Tom found the telegram waiting when he got to his office this morning and immediately rushed into my office with it and begged me to come down here with him. So I came. Couldn't refuse a brother solicitor. He's waiting at the house now.

"The circumstances are these. Last evening, when he bad finished dinner, Rowlands went out for a walk. That is his usual habit in the summer months--it is light until nearly half-past nine nowadays. Well, that is the last time he was seen alive by the servants. No one saw him come in. But there was nothing unusual in that, for he had a private entrance to the annexe in which his library, museum and workrooms were situated, and when he returned from his walk, he usually entered the house that way and went straight to his study or workroom and spent the evening there. So the servants very seldom saw him after dinner.

"Last night he evidently followed his usual custom. But, this morning, when the housemaid went to his bedroom with his morning tea, she was astonished to find the room empty and the bed undisturbed. She at once reported to the housekeeper, and the pair made their way to the annexe. There they found the study door locked, and as there was no answer after repeated knockings, they went out into the grounds to reconnoitre. The study window was closed and fastened, but the workroom window was unbolted, so that they were able to open it from outside. Then the housemaid climbed in and went to the side door, which she opened and admitted the housekeeper. The two went to the workroom, and as the door which communicated with the study was open, they were able to enter the latter, and there they found Martin Rowlands, sitting in an arm-chair by the table, stone-dead, cold and stiff. On the table were a whisky decanter, a siphon of soda water, a box of cigars, an ash-bowl with the stump of a cigar in it, and a bottle of photographic tabloids of cyanide of potassium.

"The housekeeper immediately sent off for a doctor and dispatched a telegram to Tom Rowlands at his office. The doctor arrived about nine and decided that the deceased had been dead about twelve hours. The cause of death was apparently cyanide poisoning, but, of course, that will be ascertained or disproved by the post-mortem. Those are all the known facts at present. The doctor helped the servants to place the body on a sofa, but as it is as stiff as a frozen sheep, they might as well have left it where it was."

"Have the police been communicated with?" I asked.

"No," replied Brodribb. "There were no suspicious circumstances, so far as any of us could see, and I don't know that I should have felt justified in sending for you--though I always like to have Thorndyke's opinion in a case of sudden death--if it had not been for the insurance."

Thorndyke nodded. "It looks like a straightforward case of suicide," said he. "As to the state of deceased's affairs, his brother will be able to give us any necessary information, I suppose?

"Yes," replied Brodribb. "As a matter of fact, I think Martin has been a bit worried just lately; but Tom will tell you about that. This is the place."

We turned in at a gateway that opened into the grounds of a substantial though unpretentious house, and as we approached the front door, it was opened by a fresh-coloured, white-haired man whom we both knew pretty well in our professional capacities. He greeted us cordially, and though he was evidently deeply shocked by the tragedy, struggled to maintain a calm, business-like manner.

"It is good of you to come down," said he; "but I am afraid we have troubled you rather unnecessarily. Still, Brodribb thought it best--*ex abundantia cautelce*, you know--to have the circumstances reviewed by a competent authority. There is nothing abnormal in the affair excepting its having happened. My poor brother was the sanest of men, I should say, and we are not a suicidal family. I suppose you had better see the body first?"

As Thorndyke assented, he conducted us to the end of the hall and into the annexe, where we entered the study, the door of which was now open, though the key was still in the lock. The table still bore the things that Brodribb had described, but the chair was empty, and its late occupant lay on a sofa, covered with a large table-cloth. Thorndyke advanced to the sofa and gently drew away the cloth, revealing the body of a man, fully dressed, lying stiffly and awkwardly on its back with the feet raised and the stiffened limbs extended. There was something strangely and horribly artificial in the aspect of the corpse, for, though it was lying down, it had the posture of a seated figure, and thus bore the semblance of a hideously realistic effigy which had been picked up from a chair and laid down. I stood looking at it from a little distance with a layman's distaste for the presence of a dead body, but still regarding it with attention and some curiosity. Presently my glance fell on the soles of the shoes--which were, indeed, exhibited plainly enough--and I noted, as an odd coincidence that they were "Invicta" rubber soles, like those which we had just been discussing in the wood; that it was even possible that those very footprints had been made by the feet of this grisly lay figure.

"I expect, Thorndyke," Brodribb said tactfully, "you would rather make your inspection alone. If you should want us, you will find us in the dining room," and with this he retired, taking Mr. Rowlands with him.

As soon as they were gone I drew Thorndyke's attention to the rubber soles.

"It is a queer thing," said I, "but we may have actually been discussing this poor fellow's own prints."

"As a matter of fact, we were," he replied, pointing to a drawing-pin that had been trodden on and had stuck into one of the rubber heels. "I noticed this at the time, and apparently you did not, which illustrates what I was saying about the tendency of these very distinctive types of sole to distract attention from those individual peculiarities which are the ones that really matter."

"Then," said I, "if they were his footprints, the man with the remarkable stick was with him. I wonder who he was. Some neighbour who was walking home from the station with him, I expect."

"Probably," said Thorndyke, "and as the prints were quite recent--they might even have been made last night--that person may be wanted as a witness at the inquest as the last person who saw deceased alive. That depends on the time the prints were made."

He walked back to the sofa and inspected the corpse very methodically, giving close attention to the mouth and hands. Then he made a general inspection of the room, examined the objects on the table and the floor under it, strayed into the adjoining workshop, where he peered into the deep laboratory sink, took an empty tumbler from a shelf, held it up to the light and inspected the shelf--where a damp ring showed that the tumbler had been put there to drain--and from the workshop wandered into a little lobby and from thence out at the side door, down the flagged path to the side gate and back again.

"It is all very negative," he remarked discontentedly, as we returned to the study, "except that bottle of tabloids, which is pretty positive evidence of premeditation. That looks like a fresh box of cigars. Two missing. One stump in the ash-tray and more ash than one cigar would account for. However, let us go into the dining and hear what Rowlands has to tell us," and with this he walked out and crossed the hall and I followed him.

As we entered the dining the two men looked at us and Brodribb asked: "Well, what is the verdict?"

"At present," Thorndyke replied, "it is an open verdict. Nothing has come to light that disagrees with the obvious appearances. But I should like to hear more of the antecedents of the tragedy. You were saying that deceased had been somewhat worried lately. What does that amount to?"

It amounts to nothing," said Rowlands "at least, I should have thought so, in the case of a level-headed man like my brother. Still as it is all there is, so far as I know, to account for what has happened, I had better give you the story, It seems trivial enough.

"Some short time ago, a Major Cohen, who h just come home from Mesopotamia, sold to dealer named Lyon a small gold cylinder seal that he had picked up in the neighbourhood of Baghdad. The Lord knows how he came by it, but he had it and he showed it to Lyon, who bought it of him for a matter of twenty pounds. Cohen, of course, knew nothing about the thing, and Lyon didn't know much more, for although he is a dealer, he is no expert. But he is a very clever faker--or rather, I should say, restorer, for he does quite a legitimate trade. He was a jeweller and watch-jobber originally, a most ingenious workman, and his line is to buy up damaged antiques and restore them. Then he sells them to minor collectors, though quite honestly as restorations, so I oughtn't to call him a faker. But, as I said, he has no real knowledge of antiques, and all he saw in Cohen's seal was a gold cylinder seal, apparently ancient and genuine, and on that he bought it for about twice the value of the gold and thought no more about it.

"About a fortnight later, my brother Martin went to his shop in Petty France, Westminster, to get some repairs done, and Lyon, knowing that my brother was a collector of Babylonian antiquities, showed him the seal; and Martin, seeing at once that it was genuine and a thing of some interest and value, bought it straight-way for forty pounds without examining it at all minutely, as it was obviously worth that much in any case. But when he got home and took a rolled impression of it on moulding wax, he made a most astonishing discovery. The impression showed a mass of minute cuneiformic characters, and on deciphering these he learned with amazement and delight that this was none other than the seal of Nebuchadnezzar.

"Hardly able to believe in his good fortune, he hurried off to the British Museum and showed his treasure to the Keeper of the Babylonian Antiquities, who fully confirmed the identity of the seal and was naturally eager to acquire it for the Museum. Of course, Martin wouldn't sell it, but he allowed the keeper to take a record of its weight and measurements and to make an impression on clay to exhibit in the case of seal-rollings.

"Meanwhile, it seems that Cohen, before disposing of the seal, had amused himself by making a number of rolled impressions on clay. Some of these he took to Lyon, who bought them for a few shillings and put one of them in his shop window as a curio. There it was seen and recognised by an American Assyriologist, who went in and bought it and then began to question Lyon closely as to whence he had obtained it. The dealer made no secret of the matter, but gave Cohen's name and address, saying nothing, however, about the seal. In fact, he was unaware of the connection between the seal and the rollings as Cohen had sold him the latter as genuine clay tablets which he said he had found in Mesopotamia. But, of course, the expert saw that it was a recent rolling and that some one must have the seal.

"Accordingly, off he went to Cohen and questioned him closely, whereupon Cohen began to smell a rat. He admitted that he had had the seal, but refused to say what had become of it until the expert told him what it was and how much it was worth. This the expert did, very reluctantly and in strict confidence, and when Cohen learned that it was the seal of Nebuchadnezzar and that it was worth anything up to ten thousand pounds, he nearly fainted; and then he and the expert together bustled off to Lyon's shop.

"But now Lyon smelt a rat, too. He refused absolutely to disclose the whereabouts of the seal; and having, by now, guessed that the seal-rollings were those of the seal, he took one of them to the British Museum, and then, of course, the murder was out. And further to complicate the matter, the Assyriologist, Professor Bateman, seems to have talked freely to his American friends at his hotel, with the result that Lyon's shop was besieged by wealthy American collectors, all. roaring for the seal and all perfectly regardless of cost. Finally, as they could get no change out of Lyon, they went to the British Museum, where they learned that my brother had the seal and got his address--or rather mine, for he had, fortunately for himself, given my office as his address. Then they proceeded to bombard him with letters, as also did Cohen and Lyon.

"It was an uncomfortable situation. Cohen was like a madman. He swore that Lyon had swindled him and he demanded to have the seal returned or the proper price paid. Lyon, for his part, went about like a roaring lion of Judah, making a similar demand; and the millionaire collectors offered wild sums for the seal. Poor Martin was very much worried about it. He was particularly unhappy about Cohen, who had actually found the seal and who was a disabled soldier--he had been wounded in both legs and was permanently lame. As to Lyon, he had no grievance, for he was a dealer and it was his business to know the value of his own stock; but still it was hard luck even on him. And then there were the collectors, pestering him daily with entreaties and extravagant offers. It was very worrying for him. They would probably have come down here to see him, but he kept his private address a close secret.

"I don't know what he meant to do about it. What he did was to arrange with me for the loan of my private office and have a field day, interviewing the whole lot of them--Lyon, the Professor and the assorted millionaires. That was three days ago, and the whole boiling of them turned up; and by the same token one of them was the kind of pestilent fool that walks off with the wrong hat or umbrella."

"Did he walk off with your hat?" asked Brodribb.

"No, but he took my stick; a nice old stick that belonged to my father."

"What sort of stick did he leave in its place?" Thorndyke asked.

"Well," replied Rowlands, "I must admit that there was some excuse, for the stick that he left was almost a facsimile of my own. I don't think I should have noticed it but for the feel. When I began to walk with it, I was aware of something unusual in the feel of it."

"Perhaps it was not quite the same length as yours," Thorndyke suggested.

"No, it wasn't that," said Rowlands. "The length was all right, but there was some more subtle difference. Possibly, as I am left-handed and carry my stick on the left side, it may in the course of years have acquired a left-handed bias, if such a thing is possible. I'll go and get the stick for you to see."

He went out of the room and returned in a few moments with an old-fashioned Malacca cane, the ivory handle of which was secured by a broad silver band. Thorndyke took it from him and looked it over with a degree of interest and attention that rather surprised me. For the loss of Rowlands' stick was a trivial incident and no concern of ours. Nevertheless, my colleague inspected it most methodically, handle, silver band and ferrule; especially the ferrule, which he examined as if it were quite a rare and curious object.

"You needn't worry about your stick, Tom," said Brodribb with a mischievous smile. "Thorndyke will get it back if you ask him nicely."

"It oughtn't to be very difficult," said Thorndyke, handing back the stick," if you have a list of the visitors who called that day."

"Their names will be in the appointments book," said Rowlands. "I must look them up. Some of them I remember--Cohen, Lyon, Bateman and two or three of the collectors. But to return to our history. I don't know what passed at the interviews or what Martin intended to do, but I have no doubt he made some notes on the subject. I must search for them, for, of course, we shall have to dispose of the seal."

"By the way," said Thorndyke, "where is the seal?"

"Why, it is here in the safe," replied Rowlands; "and it oughtn't to be. It should have been taken to the bank."

"I suppose there is no doubt that it is in the safe?" said Thorndyke.

"No," replied Rowlands; "at least--" He stood up suddenly. "I haven't seen it," he said. "Perhaps we had better make sure."

He led the way quickly to the study, where he halted and stood looking at the shrouded corpse. "The key will be in his pocket," he said, almost in a whisper. Then, slowly and reluctantly, he approached the sofa, and gently drawing away the cover from the body, began to search the dead man's pockets.

"Here it is," he said at length, producing a bunch of keys and separating one, which he apparently knew. He crossed to the safe, and inserting the key, threw open the door.

"Ha!" he exclaimed with evident relief, "it is all right.. Your question gave me quite a start. Is it necessary to open the packet?"

He held out a little sealed parcel on which was written "The Seal of Nebuchadnezzar," and looked inquiringly at Thorndyke.

"You spoke of making sure," the latter replied with a faint smile.

"Yes, I suppose it would be best," said Rowlands; and with that, he cut the thread with which it was fastened, broke the seal and opened the package, disclosing a small cardboard box in which lay a cylindrical abject rolled up in a slip of paper.

Rowlands picked it out, and removing the paper, displayed a little cylinder of gold pitted all over with minute cuneiform characters. It was about an inch and a quarter long by half an inch thick and had a hole bored through its axis from end to end.

"This paper, I see," said Rowlands, "contains a copy of the keeper's description of the seal--its weight, dimensions and so on. We may as well take care of that."

He handed the little cylinder to Thorndyke, who held it delicately in his fingers and looked at it with a gravely reflective air. Indeed, small as it was, there was some thing very impressive in its appearance and in the thought that it had been handled by and probably worn on the person of the great king in those remote, almost mythical times, so familiar and yet so immeasurably far away. So I reflected as I watched Thorndyke inspecting the venerable little object in his queer, exact, scientific way, examining the minute characters through his lens, scrutinising the ends and even peering through the central hole.

"I notice," he said, glancing at the paper which Rowlands held, "that the keeper has given only one transverse diameter, apparently assuming that it is a true cylinder. But it isn't. The diameter varies. It is not quite circular in section and the sides are not perfectly parallel."

He produced his pocket calliper-gauge, and, closing the jaws on the cylinder, took the reading of the vernier. Then he turned the cylinder, on which the gauge became visibly out of contact.

"There is a difference of nearly two millimetres," he said when he had again closed the gauge and taken the reading.

"Ah, Thorndyke," said Brodribb," that keeper hadn't got your mathematically exact eye; and, in fact, the precise measurements don't seem to matter much."

"On the other hand," retorted Thorndyke, "inexact measurements are of no use at all."

When we had all handled and inspected the seal, Rowlands repacked it and returned it to the safe, and we went back to the dining-room.

"Well, Thorndyke," said Brodribb, "how does the insurance question stand? What is our position?"

"I think," Thorndyke replied, "that we will leave the question open until the inquest has been held. You must insist on an expert analysis, and perhaps that may throw fresh light on the matter. And now we must be off to the station. I expect you have plenty to do."

"We have," said Brodribb, "so I won't offer to walk with you. You know the way."

Politely but firmly declining Rowlands' offer of material hospitality, Thorndyke took up his research-case, and having shaken hands with our hosts, we followed them to the door and took our departure.

"Not a very satisfactory case," I remarked as we set forth along the road, "but you can't make a bull's-eye every time."

"No," he agreed; "you can only observe and note the facts. Which reminds me that we have some data to collect in the wood. I shall take casts of those foot prints in case they should turn out to be of importance. It is always a useful precaution, seeing that footprints are fugitive."

It seemed to me an excessive precaution, but I made no comment; and when we arrived at the footpath through the wood and he had selected the sharpest foot prints, I watched him take out from his case the plaster-tin, water-bottle, spoon and little rubber bowl, and wondered what was in his mind. The "Invicta" footprints were obviously those of the dead man. But what if they were? And of what use were the casts of the other man's feet? The man was unknown, and as far as I could see, there was nothing suspicious in his presence here. But when Thorndyke had poured the liquid plaster into the two pairs of footprints, he went on to a still more incomprehensible proceeding. Mixing some fresh plaster, he filled up with it two adjoining impressions of the strange man's stick. Then, taking a reel of thread from the case, he cut off about two yards, and stretching it taut, held it exactly across the middle of the two holes, until the plaster set and fixed it in position. After waiting for the plaster to set hard, and having, meanwhile, taken up and packed the casts of the footprints, he gently raised, first the one and then the other cast; each of which was a snowy white facsimile of the tip of the stick which had made the impression the two casts, being joined by a length of thread which gave the exact distance apart of the two impressions.

"I suppose," said I, as he made a pencil mark on one of the casts, "the thread is to show the length of the stride?"

"No," he answered. "It is to show the exact direction in which the man was walking and to mark the front and back of the stick."

I could make nothing of this. It was highly ingenious, but what on earth was the use of it? What could it possibly prove?

I put a few tentative questions, but could get no explanation beyond the obvious truth that it was of no use to postpone the collection of evidence until after the event. What event he was referring to, I did not gather; nor was I any further enlightened when, on arriving at Victoria, he hailed a taxicab and directed the driver to set him down at Scotland Yard.

"You had better not wait," he said, as he got out. I have some business to talk over with Miller or the Assistant Commissioner and may be detained some time. But I shall be at home all the evening."

Taking this as an invitation to drop in at his chambers, I did so after dinner and made another ineffectual attempt to pump him.

I am sorry to be so evasive," said he, "but this case is so extremely speculative that I cannot come to any definite conclusion until I have more data. I may have been theorising in the air. But I am going forth tomorrow morning at half-past eight in the hope of putting some of my inferences to the test. If my learned friend would care to lend his distinguished support to the expedition, his society would be appreciated. But it will be a case of passive observation and quite possibly nothing will happen."

"Well, I will come and look on," said I. "Passive observation is my speciality"; and with this I took my departure, rather more mystified than ever.

Punctually, next morning at half-past eight, I arrived at the entry of Thorndyke's chambers. A taxicab was already waiting at the kerb, and, as I stepped on the threshold, my colleague appeared on the stairs. Together we entered the cab which at once moved off, and proceeding down Middle Temple Lane to the Embankment, headed westward. Our first stopping place was New Scotland Yard, but there Thorndyke remained only a minute or two. Our further progress was in the direction of Westminster, and in a few minutes we drew up at the corner of Petty France, where we alighted and paid off the taxi. Sauntering slowly westward and passing a large, covered car that was drawn up by the pavement, we presently encountered no less a person than Mr. Superintendent Miller, dressed in the height of fashion and smoking a cigar. The meeting was not, apparently, unexpected, for Miller began, without preamble: "It's all right, so far, doctor, unless we are too late. It will be an awful suck-in if we are. Two plain-clothes men have been here ever since you called yesterday evening, and nothing has happened yet."

"You mustn't treat it as a certainty, Miller," said Thorndyke. "We are only acting on reasonable probabilities. But it may be a false shot, after all."

Miller smiled indulgently. "I know, sir. I've heard you say that sort of thing before. At any rate, he's there at present; I saw him just now through the shop window--and, by gum! here he is!"

I followed the superintendent's glance and saw a tallish, elderly man advancing on the opposite side of the street. He walked stiffly with the aid of a stick and with a pronounced stoop as if suffering from some weakness of the back, and he carried in his free hand a small wooden case suspended by a rug-strap. But what instantly attracted my attention was his walking-stick, which appeared, so far as I could remember, to be an exact replica of the one that Tom Rowlands had shown us.

We continued to walk westward, allowing Mr. Lyon--as I assumed him to be--to pass us. Then we turned back and followed at a little distance; and I noticed that two tall, military-looking men whom we had met kept close behind us. At the corner of Petty France Mr. Lyon hailed a taxicab; and Miller quickened his pace and bore down on the big covered car.

"Jump in," he said, opening the door as Lyon entered the cab. "We mustn't lose sight of him," and with this he fairly shoved Thorndyke and me into the car, and having spoken a word to the driver, stepped in himself and was followed by the two plain-clothes men. The car started forward, and having made a spurt which brought it within a few yards of the taxi, slowed down to the pace of the latter and followed it through the increasing traffic until we turned into Whitehall, where our driver allowed the taxi to draw ahead somewhat. At Charing Cross, however, we closed up and kept immediately behind our quarry in the dense traffic of the Strand; and when it turned to cross opposite the Acropolis Hotel, we still followed and swept past it in the hotel courtyard so that we reached the main entrance first. By the time that Mr. Lyon had paid his fare we had already entered and were waiting in the hall of the hotel.

As he followed us in, he paused and looked about him until his glance fell on a stoutish, clean-shaved man who was sitting in a wicker chair, who, on catching his eye, rose and advanced towards him. At this moment Superintendent Miller touched him on the shoulder, causing him to spin round with an expression of very distinct alarm.

"Mr. Maurice Lyon, I think," said Miller. "I am a detective officer." He paused and looked hard at the dealer, who had turned deathly pale. Then he continued: "You are carrying a walking-stick which I believe is not your property."

Lyon gave a gasp of relief. "You are quite right," said he. "But I don't know whose property it is. If you do, I shall be pleased to return it in exchange for my own, which I left by mistake."

He held it out in an irresolute fashion, and Miller took it from him and handed it to Thorndyke.

"Is that the stick?" he asked.

Thorndyke looked the stick over quickly, and then, inverting it, made a minute examination of the ferrule, finishing up by taking its dimensions in two diameters and comparing the results with some written notes.

Mr. Lyon fidgeted impatiently. "There's no need for all this fuss," said he. "I have told you that the stick is not mine."

"Quite so," said Miller, "but we must have a few words privately about that stick."

Here he turned to an hotel official, who had just arrived under the guidance of one of the plain-clothes men, and who suggested rather anxiously that our business would be better transacted in a private room at the back of the building than in the public hall. He was just moving off to show us the way when the clean-shaved stranger edged up to Lyon and extended his hand towards the wooden case.

"Shall I take this?" he asked suavely.

"Not just now, sir," said Miller, firmly fending him off. "Mr. Lyon will talk to you presently."

"But that case is my property," the other objected truculently; "and who are you, anyway?"

"I am a police officer," replied Miller. "But if that is your property, you had better come with us and keep an eye on it."

I have never seen a man look more uncomfortable than did the owner of that case--with the exception of Mr. Lyon; whose complexion had once more taken on a tallowy whiteness. But as the manager led the way to the back of the hall the two men followed silently, shepherded by the superintendent and the rest of our party, until we reached a small, marble-floored lobby or ante-room, when our conductor shut us in and retired.

"Now," said Miller, "I want to know what is in that case."

"I can tell you," said the stranger. "It is a piece of sculpture, and it belongs to me."

Miller nodded. "Let us have a look at it," said he.

There being no table, Lyon sat down on a chair, and resting the case on his knees, unfastened the straps with trembling fingers on which a drop of sweat fell now and again from his forehead. When the case was free, he opened the lid and displayed the head of a small plaster bust, a miniature copy of Donatello's "St. Cecilia," the shoulders of which were wedged in with balls of paper. These Lyon picked out clumsily, and when he had removed the last of them, he lifted out the bust with infinite care and held it out for Miller's inspection. The officer took it from him tenderly--after an eager glance into the empty case--and holding it with both hands, looked at it rather blankly.

"Feels rather damp," he remarked with a some what nonplussed air; and then he cast an obviously inquiring glance at Thorndyke, who took the bust from him, and holding it poised in the palm of his hand, appeared to be estimating its weight. Glancing past him at Lyon, I noticed with astonishment that the dealer was watching him with a ghastly stare of manifest terror, while the stranger was hardly less disturbed.

"For God's sake, man, be careful!" the latter exclaimed, starting forward. "You'll drop it!"

The prediction was hardly uttered before it was verified. Drop it he did; and in a perfectly deliberate, purposeful manner, so that the bust fell on its back on the marble floor and was instantly shattered into a hundred fragments. It was an amazing affair. But what followed was still more amazing. For, as the snowy fragments scattered to right and left, from one of them a little yellow metal cylinder detached itself and rolled slowly along the floor. The stranger darted forward and stooped to seize it; but Miller stooped, too, and I judged that the superintendent's cranium was the harder, for he rose, rubbing his head with one hand and with the other holding out the cylinder to Thorndyke.

"Can you tell us what this is, doctor?" he asked.

"Yes," was the reply. "It is the seal of Nebuchadnezzar, and it is the property of the executors of the late Martin Rowlands, who was murdered the night before last."

As he finished speaking, Lyon slithered from his chair and lay upon the floor insensible, while the stranger made a sudden burst for the door, where he was instantly folded in the embrace of a massive plain-clothes man, who held him immovable while his colleague clicked on the handcuffs.

"So," I remarked, as we walked home, "your casts of the stick and the footprints were not wanted after all."

"On the contrary," he replied," they are wanted very much. If the seal should fail to hang Mr. Lyon, the casts will assuredly fit the rope round his neck." (This, by the way, actually happened. The defence that Lyon received the seal from some unknown person was countered by the unexpected production in court of the casts of Lyon's feet and the stick, which proved that the prisoner had been at Pinwell, and in the company of the deceased at or about the date of the murder, and secured his conviction.)

"By the way," said I," how did you fix this crime on Lyon? It began, I think, with those stick impressions in the wood. What was there peculiar about those impressions?"

"Their peculiarity was that they were the impressions of a stick which apparently did not belong to the person who was carrying it."

"Good Lord, Thorndyke!" I exclaimed, "is that possible? How could an impression on the ground suggest ownership?

"It is a curious point," he replied, "though essentially simple, which turns on the way in which the ferrule of a stick becomes worn. In a plain, symmetrical stick with out a handle, the ferrule wears evenly all round; but in a stick with a crook or other definite handle, which is grasped in a particular way and always put down in the same position, the ferrule becomes worn on one side--the side opposite the handle, or the front of the stick. But the important point is that the bevel of wear is not exactly opposite the handle. It is slightly to one side, for this reason. A man puts his stick down with the handle fore and aft; but as he steps forward, his hand swings away from his body, rotating the stick slightly outward. Consequently, the wear on the ferrule is slightly inward. That is to say, that in a right-handed man's stick the wear is slightly to the left and in a left-handed man's stick the wear is slightly to the right. But if a right-handed man walks with a left-handed stick, the impression on the ground will show the bevel of wear on the right side--which is the wrong side; and the right-handed rotation will throw it still farther to the right. Now in this case, the impressions showed a shallow part, corresponding to the bevel of wear, on the right side. Therefore it was a left-handed stick. But it was being carried in the right hand. Therefore it--apparently--did not belong to the person who was carrying it.

"Of course, as the person was unknown, the point was merely curious and did not concern us. But see how quickly circumstantial evidence mounts up. When we saw the feet of deceased, we knew that the footprints in the wood were his. Consequently the man with the stick was in his company; and that man at once came into the picture. Then Tom Rowlands told us that he had lost his stick and that he was left-handed; arid he showed us the stick that he had got in exchange, and behold! that is a right-handed stick, as I ascertained by examining the ferrule. Here, then, is a left-handed man who has lost a stick and got a right-handed one in exchange; and there, in the wood, was a right-handed man who was carrying a left-handed stick and who was in company with the deceased. It was a striking coincidence. But further, the suggestion was that this unknown man was one of those who had called at Tom's office, and therefore one who wanted to get possession of the seal. This instantly suggested the question, Did he succeed in getting possession of the seal? We went to the safe and at once it became obvious that he did."

"The seal in the safe was a forgery, of course?"

"Yes; and a bad forgery, though skilfully done. It was an electrotype ; it was unsymmetrical ; it did not agree with the keeper's measurements; and the perforation, though soiled at the ends, was bright in the middle from the boring tool."

"But how did you know that Lyon had made it?"

"I didn't. But he was by far the most probable person. He had a seal-rolling, from which an electro could be made, and he had the great skill that was necessary to turn a flat electro into a cylinder. He was an experienced faker of antiques, and he was a dealer who would have facilities for getting rid of the stolen seal. But it was only a probability, though, as time pressed, we had to act on it. Of course, when we saw him with the stick in his hand, it became virtually a certainty."

"And how did you guess that the seal was in the bust?"

"I had expected to find it enclosed in some plaster object, that being the safest way to hide it and smuggle it out of this country and into the United States. When I saw the bust, it was obvious. It was a hastily-made copy of one of Brucciani's busts. The plaster was damp--Brucciani's bake theirs dry--and had evidently been made only a few hours. So I broke it. If I had been mistaken 1 could have replaced it for five shillings, but the whole circumstances made it practically a certainty."

"Have you any idea as to how Lyon administered the poison?"

"We can only surmise," he replied. "Probably he took with him some solution of cyanide--if that was what was used--and poured it into Rowlands' whisky when his attention was otherwise occupied. It would be quite easy; and a single gulp of a quick-acting poison like that would finish the business in a minute or two. But we are not likely ever to know the details."

The evidence at the inquest showed that Thorndyke was probably right, and his evidence at the trial clenched the case against Lyon. As to the other man--who proved to be an American dealer well known to the New York Customs officials--the case against him broke down from lack of evidence that he was privy either to the murder or the theft. And so ended the case of Nebuchadnezzar's seal: a case that left Mr. Brodribb more than ever convinced that Thorndyke was either gifted with a sixth sense which enabled him to smell out evidence or was in league with some familiar demon who did it for him.

Phyllis Annesley's Peril

"One is sometimes disposed to regret," said Thorndyke, as we sat waiting for the arrival of Mr. Mayfield, the solicitor, "that our practice is so largely concerned with the sordid and the unpleasant."

"Yes," I agreed. "Medical Jurisprudence is not always a particularly delicate subject. But it is our line of practice and we have got to take it as we find it."

"A philosophic conclusion, Jervis," he rejoined," and worthy of my learned friend. It happens that the most intimate contact of Law and Medicine is in crimes against the person and consequently the proper study of the Medical Jurist is crime of that type. It is a regrettable fact, but we must accept it."

"At the same time," said I, "there don't seem to be any Medico-legal issues in this Bland case. The woman was obviously murdered. The only question is, who murdered her? And the answer to that question seems pretty obvious."

"It does," said Thorndyke. "But we shall be better able to judge when we have heard what Mayfield has to tell us. And I think I hear him coming up the stairs now."

I rose to open the door for our visitor, and, as he entered, I looked at him curiously. Mr. Mayfield was quite a young man, and the mixture of deference and nervousness in his manner as he entered the room suggested no great professional experience.

"I am afraid, sir," said he, taking the easy-chair that Thorndyke offered him, "that I ought to have come to you sooner, for the inquest, or, at least, the police court proceedings."

"You reserved your defence, I think?" said Thorndyke.

"Yes," replied the solicitor, with a wry smile. "I had to. There seemed to be nothing to say. So I put in a plea of Not Guilty and reserved the defence in the hope that something might turn up. But I am gravelled completely. It looks a perfectly hopeless case. I don't know how it strikes you, sir."

"I have seen only the newspaper reports," said Thorndyke. "They are certainly not encouraging. But let us disregard them. I suggest that you recite the facts of the case and I can ask any questions that are necessary to elucidate it further."

"Very well, sir," said Mayfield. "Then I will begin with the disappearance of Mrs. Lucy Bland. That occurred about the eighteenth of last May. At that time she was living, apart from her husband, at Wimbledon, in furnished lodgings. After lunch on the eighteenth she went out, saying that she should not be home until night. She was seen by someone who knew her at Wimbledon Station on the down side about three o'clock. At shortly after six probably on the same day, she went to the Post Office at Lower Ditton to buy some stamps. The postmistress, who knew her by sight, is certain that she called there, but cannot swear to the exact date. At any rate, she did not go home that night and was never seen alive again. Her landlady communicated with her husband and he at once applied to the police. But all the inquiries that were made led to nothing. She had disappeared without leaving a trace.

"The discovery was made four months later, on the sixteenth of September. On that day some workmen went to 'The Larches,' a smallish, old-fashioned, river side house just outside Lower Ditton, to examine the electric wiring. The house was let to a new tenant, and as the meter had shown an unaccountable leakage of current during the previous quarter, they went to see what was wrong.

"To get at the main, they had to take up part of the floor of the dining-room; and when they got the boards up, they were horrified to discover a pair of feet--evidently a woman's feet--projecting from under the next board. They immediately went to the police station and reported what they had seen, whereupon the inspector and a sergeant accompanied them back to the house and directed them to take up several more boards--which they did; and there, jammed in between the joists, was the body of a woman who was subsequently identified as Mrs. Lucy Bland. The corpse appeared to be perfectly fresh and only quite recently dead; but at the post mortem it was discovered that it had been embalmed or preserved by injecting a solution of formaldehyde and might have been dead three or four months. The cause of death was given at the inquest as suffocation, probably preceded by the forcible administration of chloroform."

"The house, I understand," said Thorndyke," belongs to one of the accused?"

"Yes. Miss Phyllis Annesley. It is her freehold, and she lived in it until recently. Last autumn, however, she took to travelling about and then partly dismantle the house and stored most of the furniture; but she kept two bedrooms furnished and the kitchen and dining, room in just usable condition, and she used to put up there for a day or two in the intervals of her journeys, either alone or with her maid."

"And as to Miss Annesley's relations with the Blands?"

"She had known them both for some years. With Leonard Bland she was admittedly on affectionate terms, though there is no suggestion of improper relations between them. But Bland used to visit her when she lived there and they used to go for picnics on the river in the boat belonging to the house. Mrs. Bland also occasionally visited Miss Annesley, and they seem to have been on quite civil terms. Of course, she knew about her husband's affection for the lady, but she doesn't seem to have had any strong feeling about it."

"And what were the relations of the husband and wife?" asked Thorndyke.

"Rather queer. They didn't suit one another, so they simply agreed to go their own ways. But they don't seem to have been unfriendly, and Mr. Bland was most scrupulous in regard to his financial obligations to his wife. He not only allowed her liberal maintenance but went out of his way to make provision for her. I will give you an instance, which impressed me very much.

"An old acquaintance of his, a Mr. Julius Wicks, who had been working for some years in the film studio at Los Angeles, came to England about a year ago and proposed to Bland that they should start one or two picture theatres in the provinces, Bland to find the money--which he was able to do--and Wicks to provide the technical knowledge and do the actual management. Bland agreed, and a partnership was arranged on the basis of two-thirds of the profits to Bland and one-third to Wicks; with the proviso that if Bland should die, all his rights as partner should be vested in his wife."

"And supposing Wicks should die?"

"Well, Wicks was not married, though he was engaged to a film actress. On his death, his share would go to Bland, and similarly, on Bland's death, if he should die after his wife, his share would go to his partner."

"Bland seems to have been a fairly good business man," said I.

"Yes," Mayfield agreed. "The arrangement was all in his favour. But he was the capitalist, you see. However, the point is that Bland was quite mindful of his wife's interests. There was nothing like enmity."

"Then," said Thorndyke, "one motive is excluded. Was the question of divorce ever raised?"

It couldn't be," said Mayfield. "There were no grounds on either side. But it seems to have been recognised and admitted that if Bland had been free he would have married Miss Annesley. They were greatly attached to one another."

"That seems a fairly solid motive," said I.

"It appears to be," Mayfield admitted. "But to me, who have known these people for years and have always had the highest opinion of them, it seems--Well, I can't associate this atrocious crime with them at all. However, that is not to the point. I must get on with the facts.

"Very soon after the discovery at 'The Larches,' the police learned that there had been rumours in Lower Ditton for some time past of strange happenings at the house and that two labourers named Brodie and Stanton knew something definite. They accordingly looked up these two men and examined them separately, when both men made substantially identical statements, which were to this effect:

"About the middle of May--neither of them was able to give an exact date--between nine and ten in the evening, they were walking together along the lane in which 'The Larches' is situated when they saw a man lurking in the front garden of the house. As they were passing, he came to the gate and beckoned to them, and when they approached he whispered: 'I say, mates, there's something rummy going on in this house.'

"'How do you know?' asked Brodie.

"'I've been looking in through a hole in the shutter,' the man replied. 'They seem to be hiding something under the floor. Come and have a look.'

"The two men followed him up the garden to the back of the house, where he took them to one of the windows of a ground-floor room and pointed to two holes in the outside shutters.

"'Just take a peep in through them,' said he.

"Each of the men put an eye to one of the holes and looked in; and this is what they both saw :--There were two rooms, communicating, with a wide arch between them. Through the arch and at the far end of the second room were two persons, a man and a woman. They were on their hands and knees, apparently doing something to the floor. Presently the man, who had on a painter's white blouse, rose and picked up a board which he stood on end against the wall. Then he stooped again and seemed to lay hold of something that lay on the floor--something that looked like a large bundle or a roll of carpet. At this moment something passed across in front of the holes and shut out the view--so that there must have been a third person in the room. When the obstructing body moved away again, the man was kneeling on the floor looking down at the bundle and the woman had come forward and was standing just in the arch with a pair of pincers in her hand. She was dressed in a spotted pinafore with a white sailor collar, and both the men recognised her at once as Miss Annesley."

"They knew her by sight, then?" said Thorndyke.

"Yes. They were Ditton men. It is a small place and everybody in it must have known Miss Annesley and Bland, too, for that matter. Well, they saw her standing in the archway quite distinctly. Neither of the men has the least doubt as to her identity. They watched her for perhaps half a minute. Then the invisible person inside moved in front of the peepholes and shut out the scene.

"When the obstruction moved away, the woman was back in the farther room, kneeling on the floor. The bundle had disappeared and the man was in the act of taking the board, which he had rested against the wall, and laying it in its place in the floor. After this, the obstruction kept coming and going, so that the watchers only got occasional glimpses of what was going on. They saw the man apparently hammering nails into the floor and they heard faint sounds of knocking. On one occasion, towards the end of the proceedings, they saw the man standing in the archway with his face towards them, apparently looking at something in his hand. They couldn't see what the thing was, but they clearly recognised the man as Mr. Bland, whom they both knew well by sight. Then the view was shut out again, and when they next saw Mr. Bland, he was standing by Miss Annesley in the farther room, looking down at the floor and taking off his blouse. As it seemed that the business was over and that Bland and Miss Annesley would probably be coming out, the men thought it best to clear off, lest they should be seen.

"As they walked up the lane, they discussed the mysterious proceedings that they had witnessed, but could make nothing of them. The stranger suggested that perhaps Miss Annesley was hiding her plate or valuables to keep them safe while she was travelling, and hinted that it might be worth someone's while to take the floor up later on and see what was there. But this suggestion Brodie and Stanton, who are most respectable men, condemned strongly, and they agreed that, as the affair was no concern of theirs, they had better say nothing about it. But they evidently must have talked to some extent, for the affair got to be spoken about in the village, and, of course, when the body was discovered under the floor, the gossip soon reached the ears of the police."

"Has the third man come forward to give evidence?" Thorndyke asked.

"No, he has not been found yet. He was a stranger to both the men; apparently a labourer or farm-hand on tramp. But nothing is known about him. So that is the case; and it is about as hopeless as it is possible to be. Of course, there is the known character of the accused; but against that is a perfectly intelligible motive and the evidence of two eye-witnesses. Do you think you would be disposed to undertake the defence, sir? I realise that it is asking a great deal of you."

"I should like to think the matter over," said Thorndyke, "and make a few preliminary inquiries. And I should want to read over the depositions in full detail. Can you let me have them?"

"I have a verbatim report of the police court proceedings and of the inquest. I will leave them with you now. And when may I hope to have your decision? "

"By the day after to-morrow at the latest," was the reply, on which the young solicitor produced a bundle of papers from his bag, and having laid them on the table, thanked us both and took his leave.

"Well, Thorndyke," I said when Mayfield had gone, "I am fairly mystified. I know you would not undertake a merely formal defence, but what else you could do is, I must confess, beyond my imagination. It seems to me that the prosecution have only to call the witnesses and the verdict of ' Guilty ' follows automatically."

"That is how it appears to me," said Thorndyke. "And if it still appears so when I have read the reports and made my preliminary investigations, I shall decline the brief. But appearances are sometimes misleading."

With this he took the reports and the notebook, in which he had made a few brief memoranda of Mayfield's summary of the case, and drawing a chair to the table, proceeded, with quiet concentration, to read through and make notes on the evidence. When he had finished, he passed the reports to me and rose, pocketing his note book and glancing at his watch.

"Read the evidence through carefully, Jervis," said he," and tell me if you see any possible way out. I have one or two calls to make, but I shall not be more than an hour. When I come back, I should like to hear your views on the case."

During his absence I read the reports through with the closest attention. Something in Thorndyke's tone had seemed to hint at a possible flaw in the case for the prosecution. But I could find no escape from the conviction that these two persons were guilty. The reports merely amplified what Mayfield had told us; and the added detail, especially in the case of the eye witnesses, only made the evidence more conclusive. I could not see the material for even a formal defence.

In less than an hour my colleague re-entered the room, and I was about to give him my impressions of the evidence when he said "It is rather early, Jervis, but I think we had better go and get some lunch. I have arranged to go down to Ditton this afternoon and have a look at the house. Mayfield has given me a note to the police sergeant, who has the key and is virtually in possession."

"I don't see what you will gain by looking at the house," said I.

"Neither do I," he replied. "But it is a good rule always to inspect the scene of a crime and o the evidence as far as possible."

"Well," I said, "it is a forlorn hope. I have read through the evidence and it seems to me that the accused are as good as convicted. I can see no line of defence at all. Can you?"

"At present I cannot," he replied. "But there are one or two points that I should like to clear up before I decide whether or not to undertake the defence. And I have a great belief in first-hand observation."

We consumed a simplified lunch at one of our regular haunts in Fleet Street and from thence were conveyed by a taxi to Waterloo, where we caught the selected train to Lower Ditton. I had put the reports in my pocket, and during our journey I read them over again, to see if I could discover any point that would be cleared up by an inspection of the premises.

For, in spite of the rather vague purpose implied by Thorndyke's explanation, something in my colleague's manner, coupled with long experience of his method made me suspect that he had some definite object in L view. But nothing was said by either of us during the journey, nor did we discuss the case; indeed, so far as 1 could see, there was nothing to discuss.

Our reception at the Lower Ditton Police Station was something more than cordial. The sergeant recognised Thorndyke instantly--it appeared that he was an enthusiastic admirer of my colleague--and after a brief glance at Mayfield's note, took a key from his desk and put on his helmet.

"Lord bless you, sir," said he, "I don't need to be told who you are. I've seen you in court, and heard you. I'll come along with you to the house myself."

I suspected that Thorndyke would have gladly dispensed with this attention, but he accepted it with genial courtesy, and we went forth through the village and along the quiet lane in which the ill-omened house was situated. And as we went, the sergeant commented on the case with curiously unofficial freedom.

"You've got your work cut out, sir, if you are going to conduct the defence. But I wish you luck. I've known Miss Annesley for some years-- she was well known in the village here--and a nicer, gentler, more pleasant lady you wouldn't wish to meet. To think of her in connection with a murder--and such a murder, too--such a brutal, callous affair! Well, it's beyond me. And yet there it is, unless those two men are lying."

"Is there any reason to suppose that they are?" I asked.

"Well, no; there isn't. They are good, sober, decent men. And it would be such an atrociously wicked lie. And they both knew the prisoners, and liked them. Everybody liked Mr. Bland and Miss Annesley, though their friendship for one another may not have been quite in order. But I can tell you, sir, these two men are frightfully cut up at having to give evidence. This is the house!"

He opened a gate and we entered the garden, beyond which was a smallish, old-fashioned house, of which the ground-floor windows were protected by outside shutters. We walked round to the back of the house, where was another garden with a lawn and a path leading down to the river.

"Is that a boat-house?" Thorndyke asked, pointing to a small gable that appeared above a clump of lilac bushes.

"Yes, replied the sergeant. "And there is a boat in it; a good, beamy, comfortable tub that Miss Annesley and her friend used to go out picnicking in. This is the window that the men peeped in at, but you can't see much now because the room is all dark."

I looked at the two French windows, which opened on to the lawn, and reflected on this new instance of the folly of wrong-doers. Each window was fitted with a pair of strong shutters, which bolted on the inside, and each shutter was pierced, about five feet from the sill, by a circular hole a little over an inch in diameter. It seemed incredible that two sane persons, engaged in the concealment of a murdered body, should have left those four holes uncovered for any chance eavesdropper to spy on their doings.

But my astonishment at this lack of precaution was still greater when the sergeant admitted us and we stood inside the room, for both the windows, as well as the pair in the farther room, were furnished with heavy curtains.

"Yes," said the sergeant, in answer to my comment "it's a queer thing how people overlook matters of vital importance. You see, they drew the drawing-room curtains all right, but they forgot these. Is there anything in particular that you want to see, sir?"

"I should like to see where the body was hidden,' said Thorndyke, "but I will just look round the rooms first."

He walked slowly to and fro, looking about him and evidently fixing the appearance of the rooms on his memory. Not that there was much to see or remember. The two nearly square rooms communicated through a wide arch, once closed by curtains, as shown by the brass curtain-rod. The back room had been completely dismantled with the exception of the window curtains, but the front room, although the floor and the walls, were bare, was not entirely unfurnished. The sideboard was still in position and bore at each end a tall electric light standard, as did also the mantelpiece. There were three dining chairs and a good-sized gate-leg table stood closed against the wall.

"I see you have not had the floor-boards nailed down," said Thorndyke.

"No, sir; not yet. So we can see where the body was hidden and where the electric main is. The electricians took up the wrong board at first-- that is how they came to discover the body. And one of them said that the boards over the main had been raised recently, and he thought that the-- er--the accused had meant to hide the body there, but when they got the floor up they struck the main and had to choose a fresh place."

He stooped, and lifting the loose boards, which he stood on end against the mantelpiece, exposed the joists and the earth floor about a foot below them. In one of the spaces the electric main ran and in the adjoining one the apparently disused gas main.

"This is where we found poor Mrs. Bland," said the sergeant, pointing to an empty space. "It was an awful sight. Gave me quite a turn. The poor lady was lying on her side jammed down between the joists and her nose flattened up against one of the timbers. They must have been brutes that did it, and I can't--I really can't believe that Miss Annesley was one of them."

"It looks a narrow place for a body to lie in," said I.

"The joists are sixteen inches apart," said Thorndyke, laying his pocket rule across the space, "and two and a half inches thick. Heavy timber and wide spaces."

He stood up, and turning round, looked towards the windows of the back room. I followed his glance and noted, almost with a start, the two holes in the shutter of the left-hand window (the right-hand window, of course, from outside) glaring into the darkened room like a pair of inquisitive, accusing eyes. The holes in the other window were hardly visible, and the reason for the difference was obvious. The one window had small panes and thick muntins, or sash-bars, whereas the other was glazed, with large sheets of plate glass and had no muntins.

"Of course it would be dark at the time," I said in response to his unspoken comment, "and this room would be lighted up, more or less."

"Not so very dark in May," he replied. "There is a furnished bedroom, isn't there, sergeant?"

"Two, sir," was the reply; and the sergeant forthwith opened the door and led the way across the hall and up the stairs.

"This is Miss Annesley's room," he said, opening a door gingerly and peering in.

We entered the room and looked about us with vague curiosity. It was a simply-furnished room, but dainty and tasteful, with its small four-post bedstead, light easy-chair and little, ladylike writing-table.

"That's Mr. Bland," said the sergeant, pointing to a double photograph-frame on the table, "and the lady is Miss Annesley herself."

I took up the frame and looked curio at the two portraits. For a pair of murderers they were certainly uncommonly prepossessing. The man, who looked about thirty-five, was a typical good-looking, middle- class Englishman, while the woman was distinctly handsome, with a thoughtful, refined and gentle cast of face.

"She has something of a Japanese air," said I, "with that coil on the top of the head and the big ivory hairpin stuck through it."

I passed the frame to Thorndyke, who regarded each portrait attentively, and then, taking both photograph out of the frame, closely examined each in turn, back and front, before replacing them.

"The other bedroom," said the sergeant as Thorndyke laid down the frame, "is the spare room. There's nothing to see in it."

Nevertheless he conducted us into it, and when we I had verified his statement we returned downstairs.

"Before we go," said Thorndyke, "I will just see what is opposite those holes."

He walked to the window and was just looking out through one of the holes when the sergeant, who had followed him closely, suddenly slid along the floor and nearly fell.

"Well, I never!" he exclaimed, recovering himself and stooping to pick up some small object. "There's a dangerous thing to leave lying about the floor. Bit of slate pencil--at least, that is what it looks like."

He handed it to Thorndyke, who glanced at it and remarked "Yes, things that roll under the foot are apt to produce broken bones; but I think you had better take care of it. I may have to ask you something about it at the trial."

We bade the sergeant farewell at the bottom of the lane, and as we turned into the footpath to the station I said: "We don't seem to have picked up very much more than Mayfield told us--excepting that bit of slate pencil. By the way, why did you tell the sergeant to keep it?"

"On the broad principle of keeping everything, relevant or irrelevant. But it wasn't slate pencil; it was a fragment of a small carbon rod."

"Presumably dropped by the electricians who had been working in the room," said I, and then asked "Have you come to any decision about this case?"

"Yes; I shall undertake the defence."

"Well," I said, "I can't imagine what line you will take. Strong suspicion would have fallen on these two persons even if there had been no witnesses; but the evidence of those two eye-witnesses seems to clench the matter."

"Precisely," said Thorndyke. "That is my position. I rest my case on the evidence of those two men--as I hope it will appear under cross-examination."

This statement of Thorndyke's gave me much food or reflection during the days that followed. But it was not very nourishing food, for the case still remained perfectly incomprehensible. To be sure, if the evidence of the two eye-witnesses could be shown to be false, the ease against the prisoners would break down, since it would bring another suspected person into view. But their evidence was clearly not false. They were men of known respectability and no one doubted the truth of their statements.

Nor was the obscurity of the case lightened in any way by Thorndyke's proceedings. We called together on the two prisoners, but from neither did we elicit any fresh facts. Neither could establish a clear alibi or suggest any explanation of the eye-witnesses' statements. They gave a simple denial of having been in the house at that time or of having ever taken up the floor.

Both prisoners, however, impressed me favourably. Bland, whom we interviewed at Brixton, seemed a pleasant, manly fellow, frank and straightforward though quite shrewd and business-like; while Miss Annesley, whom we saw at Holloway, was a really charming young lady-- sweet-faced, dignified and very gracious and gentle in manner. In one respect, indeed, I found her disappointing. The picturesque coil had disappeared from the top of her head and her hair had been shortened ("bobbed" is, I believe, the correct term) into a mere fringe. Thorndyke also noticed the change, and in fact commented on it.

"Yes," she admitted, "it is a disimprovement in my case. It doesn't suit me. But I really had no choice. When I was in Paris in the spring I had an accident. I was having my hair cleaned with petrol when it caught fire. It was most alarming. The hairdresser had the presence of mind to throw a damp towel over my head, and that saved my life. But my hair was nearly all burnt. There was nothing for it but to have it trimmed as evenly as possible. But it looked horrid at first. I had my photograph taken by Barton soon after I came home, just as a record, you know, and it looks awfully odd. I look like a Bluecoat boy."

"By the way," said Thorndyke, "when did you return?"

"I landed in England about the middle of April and went straight to my little flat at Paddington, where I have been living ever since."

"You don't remember where you were on the eighteenth of May?

"I was living at my flat, but I can't remember what I did on that day. You don't, as a rule, unless you keep a diary, which I do not."

This was not very promising. As we came away from the prison, I felt, on the one hand, a conviction that this sweet, gracious lady could have had no hand in this horrible crime, and on the other an utter despair of extricating her from the web of circumstances in which she had become enmeshed.

From Thorndyke I could gather nothing, except that he was going on with his investigations--a significant fact, in his case. To my artfully disguised questions he had one invariable reply: "My dear Jervis, you have read the evidence, you have seen the house, you have all the facts. Think the case over and consider the possibilities of cross-examination." And that was all I could get out of him.

He was certainly very busy, but his activities only increased my bewilderment. He sent a well-known architect down to make a scale-plan of the house and grounds; and he dispatched Polton to take photographs of the place from every possible point of view. The latter, indeed, was up to his eyes in work, and enjoying himself amazingly, but as secret as an oyster. As he went about, beaming with happiness and crinkling with self-complacency, he exasperated me to that extent that I could have banged his little head against the wall. In short, though I had watched the development of the case from the beginning, I was still without a glimmer of understanding of it even when I took my seat in court on the morning of the trial.

It was a memorable occasion, and every incident in it is still vivid in my memory. Particularly do I remember looking with a sort of horrified fascination at the female prisoner, standing by her friend in the dock, pale but composed and looking the very type and picture of womanly beauty and dignity; and reflecting with a shudder that the graceful neck-- looking longer and more slender from the shortness of the hair--might very probably be, within a matter of days, encircled by the hangman's rope. These lugubrious reflections were interrupted by the entrance of two persons, a man and a woman, who were apparently connected with the case, since as they took their seats they both looked towards the dock and exchanged silent greetings with the prisoners.

"Do you know who those people are, Mayfield?" I asked.

"That is Mr. Julius Wicks, Mr. Bland's partner, and his fiancée, Miss Eugenia Kropp, the film actress," he replied.

I was about to ask him if they were here to give evidence when, the preliminaries having come to an end, the counsel for the Crown, Sir John Turville, rose and began his opening speech.

It was a good speech and eminently correct; but its very moderation made it the more damaging. It began with an outline of the facts, almost identical with Mayfield's summary, and a statement of the evidence which would presently be given by the principal witnesses.

"And now," said Sir John, when he had finished his recital, "let us bring these facts to a focus. Considered as a related group, this is what they show us. On the sixteenth of September there is found, concealed under the floor of a certain room in a certain house, the body of a woman who has evidently been murdered. That woman is the separated wife of a man who is on affectionate terms with another woman whom he would admittedly wish to marry and who would be willing to marry him. This murdered woman is, in short, the obstacle to the marriage desired by these two persons. Now the house in which the corpse is concealed is the property of one of those two persons, and both of them have access to it; and no other person has access to it. Here, then, to begin with, is a set of profoundly suspicious circumstances.

"But there are others far more significant. That unfortunate lady, the unwanted wife of the prisoner, Bland, disappeared mysteriously on the eighteenth of last May; and witnesses will prove that the body was deposited under the floor on or about that date. Now, on or about that same date, in that same house, in that same room, in the same part of that room, those two persons, the prisoners at the bar, were seen by two eminently respectable witnesses in the act of concealing some large object under the floor. What could that object have been? The floor of the room has been taken up and nothing whatever but the corpse of this poor murdered lady has been found under it. The irresistible conclusion is that those two persons were then and there engaged in concealing that corpse.

"To sum up, then, the reasons or believing that the prisoners are guilty of the crime with which they are charged are threefold. They had an intelligible and strong motive to commit that crime; they had the opportunity to commit it; and we have evidence from two eye-witnesses which makes it practically an observed fact that the prisoners did actually commit that crime."

As the Crown counsel sat down, pending the swearing of the first witness, I turned to Thorndyke and said anxiously: "I can't imagine what you are going to reply to that."

"My reply," he answered quietly, "will be largely governed by what I am able to elicit in cross-examination." Here the first witness was called-- the electrician who discovered the body--and gave his evidence, but Thorndyke made no cross-examination. He was followed by the sergeant, who described the discovery in more detail. As the Crown counsel sat down, Thorndyke rose, and I pricked up my ears.

"Have you mentioned everything that you saw or found in this room?" he asked.

"Yes, at that time. Later--on the second of October--I found a small piece of a carbon pencil on the floor of the front room near the window."

He produced from his pocket an envelope from which he extracted the fragment of the alleged "slate pencil" and passed it to Thorndyke, who, having passed to the judge with the intimation that he wished it to be put in evidence, sat down. The judge inspected the fragment curiously and then cast an inquisitive glance at Thorndyke--as he had done once or twice before. For my colleague's appearance in the role of counsel was a rare event, and one usually productive of surprises.

To the long succession of witnesses who followed Thorndyke listened attentively but did not cross-examine, I saw the judge look at him curiously from time to time and my own curiosity grew more and more intense. Evidently he was saving himself up for the crucial witnesses. At length the name of James Brodie was called, and a serious-looking elderly workman entered the box. He gave his evidence clearly and confidently, though with manifest reluctance, and I could see that his vivid description of that sinister scene made a great impression on the jury. When the examination in chief was finished, Thorndyke rose, and the judge settled himself to listen with an air of close attention.

"Have you ever been inside 'The Larches'?" Thorndyke asked.

"No, sir. I've passed the house twice every day for years, but I've never been inside it."

"When you looked in through the shutter, was the room well lighted?"

"No, 'twas very dim. I could only just see what the people were doing."

"Yet you recognised Miss Annesley quite clearly?"

"Not at first, I didn't. Not until she came and stood in the archway. The light seemed quite good there."

"Did you see her come out of the front room and walk to the arch?"

"No. I saw her in the front room and then something must have stopped up the hole, for 'twas all dark. Then the hole got clear again and I saw her standing in the arch. But I only saw her for a moment or two. Then the hole got stopped again and when it opened she was back in the front room."

"How did you know that the woman in the front room was Miss Annesley? Could you see her face in that dim light?"

"No, but I could tell her by her dress. She wore a striped pinafore with a big, white sailor-collar. Besides, there wasn't nobody else there."

"And with regard to Mr. Bland. Did you see him walk out of the front room and up to the arch?"

"No. 'Twas the same as with Miss Annesley. Something kept passing across the hole. I see him in the front room; then I see him in the arch and then I see him in the front room again."

"When they were in the archway, were they moving or standing still?"

"They both seemed to be standing quite still."

"Was Miss Annesley looking straight towards you?"

"No. Her face was turned away a little."

"I want you to look at these photographs and tell us if any of them shows the head in the position in which you saw it."

He handed a bundle of photographs to the witness, who looked at them, one after another, and at length picked out one.

"That is exactly how she looked," said he. "She might have been standing for this very picture."

He passed the photograph to Thorndyke, who noted the number written on it and passed it to the judge, who also noted the number and laid it on his desk. Thorndyke then resumed: "You say the light was very dim in the front room, Were the electric lamps alight?"

"None that I could see were alight."

"How many electric lamps could you see?"

"Well, there was three hanging from the ceiling and there was two standards on the mantelpiece and one on the sideboard. None of them was alight."

"Was there only one standard on the sideboard?"

"There may have been more, but I couldn't see 'em because I could only see just one corner of the sideboard."

"Could you see the whole of the mantelpiece?"

"Yes. There was a standard lamp at each end."

"Could you see anything on the near side of the mantelpiece?"

"There was a table there: a folding table with twisted legs. But I could only see part of that. The side of the arch cut it off."

"You have said that you could see Miss Annesley quite clearly and could see how she was dressed. Could you see how her hair was arranged?"

"Yes. 'Twas done up on the top of her head in what they calls a bun and there was a sort of a skewer stuck through it."

As the witness gave this answer, a light broke on me. Not a very clear light, for the mystery was still unsolved. But I could see that Thorndyke had a very definite strategic plan. And, glancing at the dock, I was immediately aware that the prisoners had seen the light, too.

"You have described what looked like a hole in the floor," Thorndyke resumed, "where some boards had been raised, near the middle of the room. Was that hole nearer the sideboard or nearer the mantel piece?"

"It was nearer the mantelpiece," the witness replied; on which Thorndyke sat down, the witness left the box, and both the judge and the counsel for the prosecution rapidly turned over their notes with evident surprise.

The next witness was Albert Stanton and his evidence was virtually a repetition of Brodie's; and when, in cross Thorndyke put over again the same series of questions, he elicited precisely the same answers even to the recognition of the same photograph. And again I began to see a glimmer of light. But only a glimmer.

Stanton being the last of the witnesses for the Crown, his brief re-examination by Sir John Turville completed the case for the prosecution. Thereupon Thorndyke rose and announced that he called witnesses, and forth with the first of them appeared in the box. This was Frederick Stokes, A.R.I.B.A., architect, and he deposed that he had made a careful survey of the house called "The Larches" at Lower Ditton and prepared a plan on the scale of half an inch to a foot. He swore that the plan--of which he produced the original and a number of lithographed duplicates--was true and exact in every respect. Thorndyke took the plans from him and passing them to the judge asked that the original should be put in evidence and the duplicates handed to the jury.

The next witness was Joseph Barton of Kensington, photographer. He deposed to having taken photographs of Miss Annesley on various occasions, the last being on the twenty-third of last April. He produced copies of them all with the date written on each. He swore that the dates written were the correct dates. The photographs were handed up to the judge, who looked them over, one by one. Suddenly he seemed, as it were, to stiffen and turned quickly from the photographs to his notes; and I knew that he had struck the last portrait--the one with the short hair.

As the photographer left the box, his place was taken by no less a person than our ingenious laboratory assistant; who, having taken his place, beamed on the judge, the jury and the court in general, with a face wreathed in crinkly smiles. Nathaniel Polton, being sworn, deposed that, on the fifteenth of October, he proceeded to "The Larches" at Lower Ditton and took three photographs of the ground-floor rooms. The first was taken through the right-hand hole of the shutter marked A in the plan; the second through the left-hand hole, and the third from a point inside the back room between the windows and nearer to the window marked B. He produced those photographs with the particulars written on each. He had also made some composite photographs showing the two prisoners dressed as the witnesses, Brodie and Stanton, had described them. The bodies in those photographs were the bodies of Miss Winifred Blake and Mr. Robert Anstey, K.C., respectively. On these bodies the heads of the prisoners had been printed; and here Polton described the method of substitution in detail. The purpose of the photographs was to show that a photograph could be produced with the head of one person and the body of another. He also deposed to having seen and taken possession of two photographs, one of each of the two prisoners, which he found in the bedroom and which he now produced and passed to the judge. And this completed his evidence.

Thorndyke now called the prisoner, Bland, and having elicited from him a sworn denial of the charge, proceeded to examine him respecting the profits from his three picture theatres; which, it appeared, amount to over six thousand pounds per annum.

"In the event of your death, what becomes of this valuable property?"

"If my wife had been alive it would have gone to her, but as she is dead, it goes to my partner and manager, Mr. Julius Wicks."

"In whose custody was the house at Ditton while Miss Annesley was in France?"

"In mine. The keys were in my possession."

"Were the keys ever out of your possession?"

Only for one day. My partner, Mr. Wicks, asked to be allowed to use the boat for a trip on the river and to take a meal in the house. So lent him the keys, which he returned the next day."

After a short cross-examination, Bland returned to the dock and was succeeded by Miss Annesley, who, having given a sworn denial of the charge, described her movements in France and in London about the period of the crime. She also described, in answer to a question, the circumstances under which she had lost her hair.

"Can you remember the date on which this accident happened?" Thorndyke asked.

"Yes. It was on the thirtieth of March. I made a note of the date, so that I could see how long my hair took to grow."

As Thorndyke sat down, the counsel for the prosecution rose and made a somewhat searching cross-examination, but without in any way shaking the prisoner's evidence. When this was concluded and

Miss Annesley had returned to the dock, Thorndyke rose to address the court for the defence.

"I shall not occupy your time, gentlemen," he began, "by examining the whole mass of evidence nor by arguing the question of motive. The guilt or innocence of the prisoners turns on the accuracy or inaccuracy of the evidence of the two witnesses, Brodie and Stanton; and to the examination of that evidence I shall confine myself.

"Now that evidence, as you may have noticed, presents some remarkable discrepancies. In the first place, both witnesses describe what they saw in identical terms. They saw exactly the same things in exactly the same relative positions. But this is a physical impossibility, if they were really looking into a room; for they were looking in from different points of view; through different holes, which were two feet six inches apart. But there is another much more striking discrepancy. Both these men have described, most intelligently, fully and clearly, a number of objects in that room which were totally invisible to both of them; and they have described as only partly visible other objects which were in full view. Both witnesses, for instance, have described the mantelpiece with its two standard lamps and a table with twisted legs on the near side of it; and both saw one corner only of the sideboard. But if you look at the architect's plan and test it with a straight-edge, you will see that neither the mantelpiece nor the table could possibly be seen by either. The whole of that side of the room was hidden from them by the jamb of the arch. While as to the sideboard, the whole of it, with its two standards, was visible to Brodie, and to Stanton the whole of it excepting a small portion of the near side. But further, if you lay the straight-edge on the point marked C and test it against the sides of the arch, you will see that a person standing at that spot would get the exact view described by both the witnesses. I pass round duplicate plans with pencil lines ruled on them; but in case you find any difficulty in following the plans, I have put in the photographs of the room taken by Polton. The first photograph was taken through the hole used by Brodie, and shows exactly what he would have seen on looking through that hole; and you see that it agrees completely with the plan but disagrees totally with his description. The second photograph shows what was visible to Stanton; and the third photograph, taken from the point marked C, shows exactly the view described by both the witnesses, but which neither of them could possibly have seen under the circumstances stated.

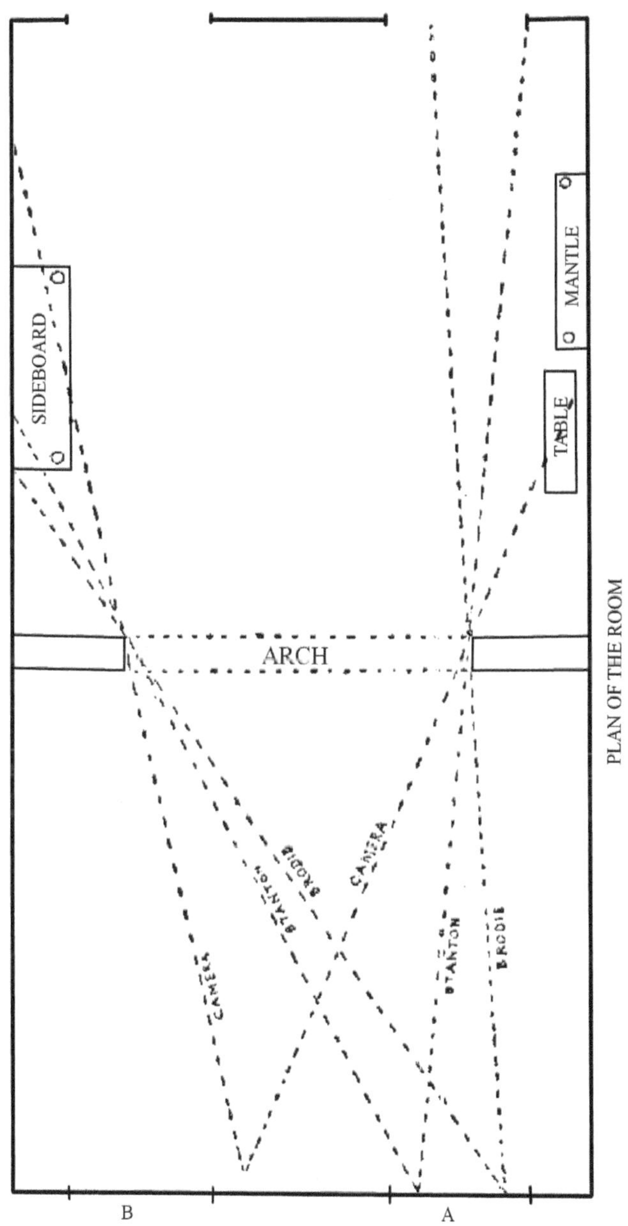

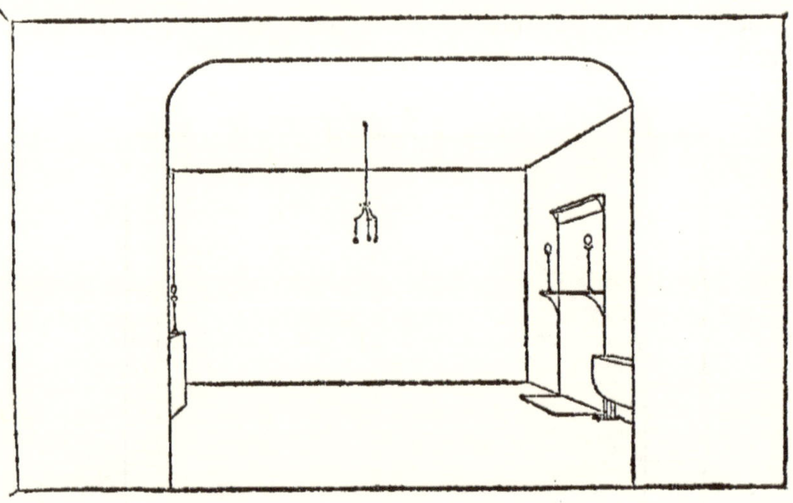

THE ROOM AS DESCRIBED BY BRODIE.

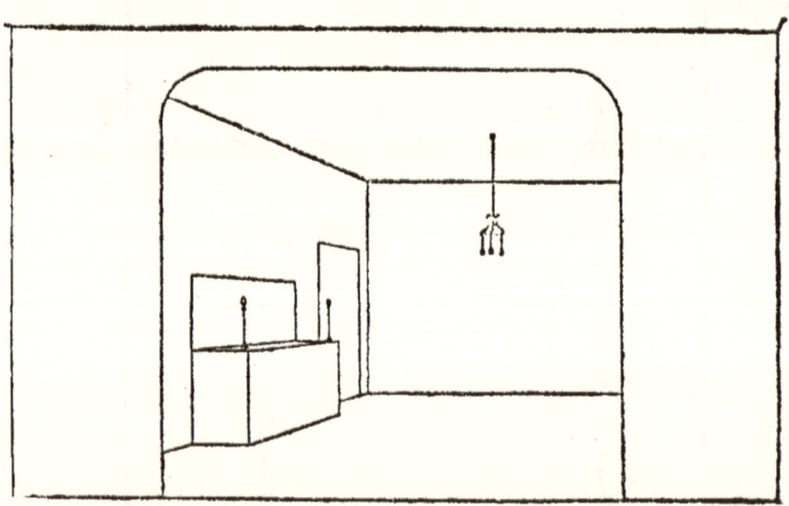

THE ROOM AS SEEN FROM BRODIE'S SPYHOLE.

"Now what is the explanation of these extraordinary discrepancies? No one, I suppose, doubts the honesty of, these witnesses. I certainly do not. I have no doubt whatever that they were telling the truth to the best of their belief. Yet they have stated that they saw things which it is physically impossible that they could have seen. How can these amazing contradictions be reconciled?"

He paused, and in the breathless silence, I noticed that the judge was gazing at him with an expression of intense expectancy; an expression that was reflected on the jury and indeed on every person present.

"Well, gentlemen," he resumed, "there is one explanation which completely reconciles these contradictions; and that explanation also reconciles all the other strange contradictions and discrepancies which you may have noticed. If we assume that these two men, instead of looking through an arch into a room, as they believed, were really looking at a moving picture thrown on a screen stretched across the arch, all the contradictions vanish. Everything becomes perfectly plain, consistent and understandable.

"Thus both men, from two different points of view, saw exactly the same scene; naturally, if they were both looking at the same picture, but otherwise quite impossible. Again, both men, from the point A, saw a view which was visible only from the point C. Perfectly natural if they were both looking at a picture taken from the point C ; for a picture is the same picture from whatever point of view it is seen. But otherwise a physical impossibility.

"You may object that these men would have seen the difference between a picture and a real room. Per haps they would, even in that dim light--if they had looked at the scene with both eyes. But each man was looking with only one eye--through a small hole. Now it requires the use of both eyes to distinguish between a solid object and a flat picture. To a one-eyed man there is no difference--which is probably the reason that one-eyed artists are such accurate draughtsmen--they see the world around them as a flat picture, just as they draw it, whereas a two-eyed artist has to turn the solid into the flat. For the same reason, if you look at a picture with one eye shut it tends to look solid, really because the frame and the solid objects around it have gone flat. So that, if this picture was coloured, as it must have been, it would have been indistinguishable, to these one-eyed observers, from the solid reality.

"Then, let us see how the other contradictions disappear. There is the appearance of the prisoner Annesley. She was seen--on or after the eighteenth of May--with her long hair coiled on the top of her head. But at that date her hair was quite short. You have heard the evidence and you have the photograph taken on the twenty-third of April showing her with short hair, like a man's. Here is a contradiction which vanishes at once if you realise that these men were not looking at Miss Annesley at all, but at a photograph of her taken more than a year previously.

"And everything agrees with this assumption. The appearance of Miss Annesley has been declared by the witnesses to be identical with that photograph--a copy of which was in the house and could have been copied by anyone who had access to the house. Her figure was perfectly stationary. She appeared suddenly in the arch and then disappeared; she was not seen to come or to go. And the light kept coming and going, with intervals of darkness which are inexplicable, but that exactly fitted these appearances and disappearances. Then the figure was well lighted, though the room was nearly dark. Of course it was well lighted. It had to be recognised. And of course the rest of the room was dimly lighted, because the film-actors in the background had to be unrecognised.

"Then there is the extraordinary dress; the striped pinafore with the great white collar and the painter's blouse worn by Bland. Why this ridiculous masquerade? Its purpose is obvious. It was to make these observers believe that the portraits in the arch--which they mistook for real people--were the same persons as the film-actors in the background, whose features they could not distinguish. And Mr. Polton has shown us how the clothing of the portraits was managed.

"Then there is the lighting of the room. How was it lighted? None of the electric lamps was alight. But--a piece of a carbon pencil from an arc lamp, such as kinematographers use, has been found near the point C, from which spot the picture would have been taken and exhibited ; and the electric light meter showed, about this date, an unaccountable leakage of current such as would be explained by the use of an arc lamp.

"Then the evidence of the witnesses shows the hole in the floor in the wrong place. Of course it could not have been a real hole, for the gas and electric mains were just underneath. It was probably an oblong of black paper. But why was it in the wrong place? The explanation, I suggest, is that the picture was taken before the murder (and probably shown before the murder, too); that the spot shown was the one in which it was intended to bury the body, but that when the floor was taken up after the murder, the mains were found underneath and a new spot had to be chosen.

"Finally--as to the discrepancies--what has become of the third spectator? The mysterious man who came to the gate and called in these two men from the lane--along which they were known to pass every day at about the same time? Who is this mysterious individual? And where is he? Can we give him a name? Can we say that he is at this moment in this court, sitting amongst the spectators, listening to the pleadings in defence of his innocent victims, the prisoners who stand at the bar on their deliverance? I affirm, gentlemen, that we can. And more than that it is not permitted to me to say."

He paused, and a strange, impressive hush fell on the court. Men and women furtively looked about them; the jury stared openly into the body of the court, and the judge, looking up from his notes, cast a searching glance among the spectators. Suddenly my eye lighted on Mr. Wicks and his fiancée. The man was wiping away the sweat that streamed down his ashen, ghastly face; the woman had rested her head in her hands, and was trembling as if in an ague-fit.

I was not the only observer. One after another--spectators, ushers, jurymen, counsel, judge--noticed the terror-stricken pair, until every eye in the court was turned on them. And the silence that fell on the place was like the silence of the grave.

It was a dramatic moment. The air was electric; the crowded court tense with emotion. And Thorndyke, looking, with his commanding figure and severe impassive face, like a personification of Fate and Justices stood awhile motionless and silent, letting emotion set the coping-stone on reason.

At length he resumed his address. "Before concluding," he began, "I have to say a few words on another aspect of the case. The learned counsel for the prosecution, referring to the motive for this crime, has suggested a desire on the part of the prisoners to remove the obstacle to their marriage. But it has been given in evidence that there are other persons who had a yet stronger and more definite motive for getting rid of the deceased Lucy Bland. You have heard that in the event of Bland's death, his partner, Julius Wicks, stood to inherit property of the value of six thousand pounds per annum, provided that Bland's wife was already dead. Now, the murder of Lucy Bland has fulfilled one of the conditions for the devolution of this property; and if you should convict and his lordship should sentence the prisoner,

Bland, then his death on the gallows would fulfil the other condition and this great property would pass to his partner, Julius Wicks--This is a material point; as is also the fact that Wicks is, as you have heard, an expert film-producer and kinema operator; that he has been proved to have had access to the house at Ditton, and that he is engaged to a film-actress.

"In conclusion, I submit that the evidence of Brodie and Stanton makes it certain that they were looking at a moving picture, and that all the other evidence confirms that certainty. But the evidence of this moving picture is the evidence of a conspiracy to throw suspicion on the prisoners. But a conspiracy implies conspirators. And there can be no doubt that those conspirators were the actual murderers of Lucy Bland. But if this be so, and I affirm that there can be no possible doubt that it is so, then it follows that the prisoners are innocent of the crime with which they are charged, and I accordingly ask you for a verdict of' Not Guilty.'"

As Thorndyke sat down a faint hum arose in the court; but still all eyes were turned towards Wicks and Eugenia Kropp. A moment later the pair rose and walked unsteadily towards the door. But here, I noticed, Superintendent Miller had suddenly appeared and stood at the portal with a uniformed constable. As Wicks and Miss Kropp reached the door, I saw the constable shake his head. With, or without authority, he was refusing to let them leave the court. There was a brief pause. Suddenly there broke out a confused uproar; a scuffle, a loud shriek, the report of a pistol and the shattering of glass; and then I saw Miller grasping the man's wrists and pinning him to the wall, while the shrieking woman struggled with the constable to get to the door.

After the removal of the disturbers--in custody--events moved swiftly. The Crown counsel's reply was brief and colourless, practically abandoning the charge, while the judge's summing-up was a mere précis of Thorndyke's argument with a plain direction for an acquittal. But nothing more was needed; for the jury had so clearly made up their minds that the clerk had hardly uttered his challenge when the foreman replied with the verdict of "Not Guilty." A minute later, when the applause had subsided and after brief congratulations by the judge, the prisoners came down from the dock, into the court, moist-eyed but smiling, to wring Thorndyke's hands and thank him for this wonderful deliverance.

"Yes," agreed Mayfield--himself disposed furtively to wipe his eyes-- "that is the word. It was wonderful And yet it was all so obvious--when you knew."

A Sower of Pestilence

The affectionate relations that existed between Thorndyke and his devoted follower, Polton, were probably due, at least in part, to certain similarities in their characters. Polton was an accomplished and versatile craftsman, a man who could do anything, and do it well; and Thorndyke has often said that if he had not been a man of science, he would, by choice, have; been a skilled craftsman. Even as things were, he was a masterly manipulator of all instruments of research, and a good enough workman to devise new appliances and processes and to collaborate with his assistant ix carrying them out.

Such a collaboration was taking place when the present case opened. It had occurred to Thorndyke that lithography might be usefully applied to medico-legal research, and on this particular morning he and Polton were experimenting in the art of printing from the stone. In the midst of their labours the bell from our chambers below was heard to ring, and Polton, reluctantly laying down the inking roller and wiping his hands on the southern aspect of his trousers, departed to open the door.

"It's a Mr. Rabbage," he reported on his return. "Says he has an appointment with you, sir."

"So he has," said Thorndyke. "And, as I under stand that he is going to offer us a profound mystery for solution, you had better come down with me, Jervis, and hear what be has to say."

Mr. Rabbage turned out to be a elderly gentleman who, as we entered, peered at us through a pair of deep, concave spectacles and greeted us "with a smile that was child like and bland." Thorndyke looked him over and adroitly brought him to the point.

"Yes," said Mr. Rabbage, "it is really a most mysterious affair that has brought me here. I have already laid it before a very talented detective officer whom I know slightly--a Mr. Badger; but he frankly admitted that it was beyond him and strongly advised me to consult you."

"Inspector Badger was kind enough to pay me a very handsome compliment," said Thorndyke.

"Yes. He said that you would certainly be able to solve this mystery without any difficulty. So here I am. And perhaps I had better explain who I am, in case you don't happen to know my name. I am the director of the St. Francis Home of Rest for aged, invalid and destitute cats: an institution where these deserving animals are enabled to convert the autumn of their troubled lives into a sort of Indian summer of comfort and repose. The home is, I may say, my own venture. I support it out of my own means. But I am open to receive contributions; and to that end there is secured to the garden railings a large box with a wide slit and an inscription inviting donations of money, of articles of value, or of food or delicacies for the inmates."

"And do you get much?" I asked.

Of money," he replied, "very little. Of articles of value, none at all. As to gifts of food, they are numerous, but they often display a strange ignorance of the habits of the domestic cat. Such things, for instance, as pickles and banana-skins, though doubtless kindly meant, are quite unsuitable as diet. But the most singular donation that I have ever received was that which I found in the box the day before yesterday. There were a number of articles, but all apparently from the same donor ; and their character was so mysterious that I showed them to Mr. Badger, as I have told you, who was as puzzled as I was and referred me to you. The collection comprised three ladies' purses, a morocco-leather wallet and a small aluminium case. I have brought them with me to show you."

"What did the purses contain? "Thorndyke asked.

"Nothing," replied Mr. Rabbage, gazing at us with wide-open eyes. "They were perfectly empty. That is the astonishing circumstance."

"And the leather wallet? "

"Empty, too, excepting for a few odd papers."

"And the aluminium case?"

"Ah!" exclaimed Mr. Rabbage, "that was the most amazing of all. It contained a number of glass tubes! and those tubes contained--

now, what do you suppose?" He paused impressively, and then, as neither of us offered a suggestion, be answered his own question. "Fleas and lice! Yes, actually! Fleas and lice! Isn't that an extraordinary donation?"

"It is certainly," Thorndyke agreed. "Anyone might have known that, with a houseful of cats, you could produce your own fleas."

"Exactly," said Mr. Rabbage. "That is what instantly occurred to me, and also, I may say, to Mr. Badger. But let me show you the things."

He produced from a hand-bag and spread out on the table a collection of articles which were, evidently, the "husks" of the gleanings of some facetious pickpocket, to whom Mr. Rabbage's donation-box must have appeared as a perfect God-send. Thorndyke picked up the purses, one after the other, and having glanced at their empty interiors, put them aside. The letter-wallet he looked through more attentively, but without disturbing its contents, and then he took up and opened the aluminium case. This certainly was a rather mysterious affair. It opened like a cigarette case. One side was fitted with six glass specimen-tubes, each provided with a well-fitting parchment cap, perforated with a number of needle-holes; and of the six tubes, four contained fleas--about a dozen in each tube--some of which were dead, but others still alive, and the remaining two lice, all of which were dead. In the opposite side of the case, secured with a catch, was a thin celluloid note-tablet on which some numbers had been written in pencil.

"Well," said Mr. Rabbage, when the examination was finished, "can you offer any solution of the mystery?"

Thorndyke shook his head gravely. "Not offhand," he replied. "This is a matter which will require careful consideration. Leave these things with me for further examination and I will let you know, in the course of a few days, what conclusion we arrive at."

"Thank you," said Mr. Rabbage, rising and holding out his hand. "You have my address, I think."

He glanced at his watch, snatched up his hand-bag and darted to the door; and a moment later we heard him bustling down the stairs in the hurried, strenuous manner that is characteristic of persons who spend most of their lives doing nothing.

"I'm surprised at you, Thorndyke," I said when he had gone, "encouraging that ass, Badger, in his silly practical jokes. Why didn't you tell this old nincompoop that he had just got a pick-pocket's leavings and have done with it?"

"For the reason, my learned brother, that I haven't done with it. I am a little curious as to whose pocket has been picked, and what that person was doing with a collection of fleas and lice."

I don't see that it is any business of yours," said I. "And as to the vermin, I should suggest that the owner of the case is an entomologist who specialises in *epizoa*. Probably he is collecting varieties and races."

"And how," asked Thorndyke, opening the case and handing it to me, "does my learned friend account for the faint scent of aniseed that exhales from this collection?

"I don't account for it at all," said I. "It is a nasty smell. I noticed it when you first opened the case. I can only suppose that the flea-merchant likes it, or thinks that the fleas do."

"The latter seems the more probable," said Thorndyke, "for you notice that the odour seems to principally from the parchment caps of the four tubes that contain fleas. The caps of the louse tubes don't seem to be scented. And now let us have a little closer look at the letter-wallet."

He opened the wallet and took out its contents, which were unilluminating enough. Apparently it had been gutted by the pickpocket and only the manifestly valueless articles left. One or two bills, recording purchases at shops, a time-table, a brief letter in French, without its envelope and bearing neither address, date, nor signature, and a set of small maps mounted on thin card: this was the whole collection, and not one of the articles appeared to furnish the slightest clue to the identity of the owner.

Thorndyke looked at the letter curiously and read it aloud.

It is just a little singular," he remarked, "that this note should be addressed to nobody by name, should bear neither address, date, nor signature, and should have had its envelope removed. There is almost an appearance of avoiding the means of identification. Yet the matter is simple and innocent enough: just an appointment to meet at the Mile End Picture Palace. But these maps are more interesting; in fact, they are quite curious."

He took them out of the wallet--lifting them carefully by the edges, I noticed--and laid them out on the table. There were seven cards, and each had a map, or rather a section, pasted on both sides. The sections had been cut out of a three map of London, and as each card was three inches by four and a half, each section represented an area of one mile by a mile and a half. They had been very carefully prepared neatly stuck on the cards and varnished, and every section bore a distinguishing letter. But the most curious feature was a number of small circles drawn in pencil on various parts of the maps, each circle enclosing a number.

"What do you make of those circles, Thorndyke?" I asked.

"One can only make a speculative hypothesis," be replied. "I am disposed to associate them with the fleas and lice. You notice that the maps all represent the most squalid parts of East London--Spitalfields, Bethnal Green, Whitechapel, and so forth, where the material would be plentiful; and you also notice that the celluloid tablet in the insect case bears a number of pencilled jottings that might refer to these maps. Here, for instance, is a note, 'B 21 a + b--,' and you observe that each entry has an a and a b with either a plus or a minus sign. Now, if we assume that a means fleas and b lice, or vice versa, the maps and the notes together might form a record of collections or experiments with a geographical basis."

"They might," I agreed, "but there isn't a particle of evidence that they do. It is a most fantastic hypothesis. We don't know, and we have no reason to suppose, that the insect-case and the wallet were the property of the same person. And we have no means of finding out whether they were or were not."

"There I think you do us an injustice, Jervis," said he. "Are we not lithographers?"

"I don't see where the lithography comes in," said I.

"Then you ought to. This is a test case. These maps are varnished, and are thus virtually lithographic transfer paper; and the celluloid tablet also has a non-absorbent surface. Now, if you handle transfer paper carelessly when drawing on it, you are apt to find, when you have transferred to the stone, that your finger prints ink up, as well as the drawing. So it is possible that if we put these maps and the note-tablet on the stone, we may be able to ink up the prints of the fingers that have handled them and so prove whether they were or were not the same fingers."

"That would be interesting as an experiment," said I," though I don't see that it matters two straws whether they were the same or not."

"Probably it doesn't," he replied, "though it may. But we have a new method and we may as well try it."

We took the things up to the laboratory and explained the problem to Polton, who entered into the inquiry with enthusiasm. Producing from a cupboard a fresh stone, he picked the maps out of the wallet one by one (with a pair of watchmaker's tweezers) and fell to work forthwith on the task of transferring the invisible--and possibly non-existent-- fingerprints from the maps and the note-tablet to the stone. I watched him go through the various processes in his neat, careful, dexterous fashion and hoped that all his trouble would not be in vain. Nor was it; for when he began cautiously ink up the stone, it was evident that something was there, though it was not so evident what that something was. Presently, however, the vague markings took more definite shape, and now could be recognised eight rather confused masses of finger-prints, badly smeared, some incomplete, and all mixed up and superimposed so as to make the identification of any one print almost an impossibility.

Thorndyke looked them over dubiously. "It is a dreadful muddle," said he, "but I think we can pick out the prints well enough for identification if that should be necessary. Which of these is the notes tablet, Polton?"

"The one in the right-hand top corner, sir," was the reply.

"Ah!" said Thorndyke, "then that answers our question. Confused as the impressions are, you can see quite plainly that the left thumb is the same thumb as that on the maps."

"Yes," I agreed after making the comparison, "there is not much doubt that they are the same. And now the question is, what about it?"

"Yes," said Thorndyke; "that is the question." And with this we retired from the laboratory, leaving Polton joyfully pulling off proofs.

During the next few days I had a vague impression that my colleague was working at this case, though with what object I could not imagine. Mr. Rabbage's problem was too absurd to take seriously, and Thorndyke was beyond working out cases, as he used to at one time, for the sake of mere experience. However, a day or two later, a genuine case turned up and occupied our attention to some purpose.

It was about six in the evening when Mr. Nicholas Balcombe called on us by appointment, and proceeded, in a business-like fashion, to state his case.

"I was advised by my friend Stalker, of the Griffin Life Assurance Office, to consult you," said he. "Stalker tells me that you have got him out of endless difficulties, and I am hoping that you will be able to help me out of mine, though they are not so clearly within your province as Stalker's. But you will know about that better than I do.

"I am the manager of Rutherford's Bank--the Cornhill Branch--and I have just had a very alarming experience. The day before yesterday, about three in the afternoon, a deed-box was handed in with a note from one of our customers--Mr. Pilcher, the solicitor, of Pilcher, Markham and Sudburys--asking us to deposit it in our strong-room and give the bearer a receipt for it. Of course this was done, in the ordinary way of business; but there was one exceptional circumstance that turns out to have been, as it would appear, providential. Owing to the increase of business our strong-room had become insufficient for our needs, and we have lately had a second one built on the most modern lines and perfectly fire-proof. This had not been taken into use when Pilcher's deed-box arrived, but as the old room was very full, I opened the new room and saw the deed-box deposited in it.

"Well, nothing happened up to the time that I left the bank, but about two o'clock in the morning the night watchman noticed a smell of burning, and on investigating, located the smell as apparently proceeding from the door of the new strong-room. He at once reported to the senior clerk, whose turn it was to sleep on the premises, and the latter at once telephoned to the police station. In a few minutes a police officer arrived with a couple of firemen and a hand-extinguisher. The clerk took them down to the strong-room and unlocked the door. As soon as it was opened, a volume of smoke and fumes burst out, and then they saw the deed-box--or rather the distorted remains of it--lying on the floor. The police took possession of what was left, but a very cursory examination on the spot showed that the box was, in effect, an incendiary bomb, with a slow time fuse or some similar arrangement."

"Was any damage done?" Thorndyke asked.

"Mercifully, no," replied Mr. Balcombe. "But just think of what might have happened! If I had put the box in the old strong-room it is certain that thousands of pounds' worth of valuable property would have been destroyed. Or again, if instead of an incendiary bomb the box had contained a high explosive, the whole building would probably have been blown to pieces."

"What explanation does Pilcher give?"

"A very simple one. He knows nothing about it. The note was a forgery; and on the firm's headed paper, or a perfect imitation of it. And mind you," Mr. Balcombe continued, "my experience is not a solitary one. I have made private inquiries of other bank managers, and I find that several of them have been subjected to similar outrages, some with serious results. And probably there are more. They don't talk about these things, you know. Then there are those fires: the great timber fire at Stepney, and those big warehouse fires near the London Docks; there is something queer about them. It looks as if some gang was at work for purposes of pure mischief and destruction."

"You have consulted the police, of course?"

"Yes. And they know something, I feel sure. But they are extremely reticent; so I suppose they don't know enough. At any rate, I should like you to investigate the case independently and so would my directors. The position is most alarming."

"Could you let me see Pilcher's letter?" Thorndyke asked.

"I have brought it with me," said Balcombe. "Thought you would probably want to examine it. I will leave it with you; and if we can give you any other information or assistance, we shall be only too glad."

"Was the box brought by hand?" inquired Thorndyke.

"Yes," replied Balcombe, "but I didn't see the bearer. I can get you a description from the man who received the package, if that would be any use."

"We may as well have it," said Thorndyke, "and the name and address of the person giving it, in case he is wanted as a witness."

"You shall have it," said Balcombe, rising and picking up his hat. "I will see to it myself. And you will let me know, in due course, if any information comes to hand?"

Thorndyke gave the required promise and our client took his leave.

"Well," I said with a laugh, as the brisk footsteps died away on the stairs, "you have had a very handsome compliment paid you. Our friend seems to think that you are one of those master craftsmen who can make bricks, not only without straw, but without clay. There's absolutely nothing to go on."

"It is certainly rather in the air," Thorndyke agreed. "There is this letter and the description of the man who left the packet, when we get it, and neither of them is likely to help us much."

He looked over the letter and its envelope, held the former up to the light and then handed them to me.

"We ought to find out whether this is Pilcher's own paper or an imitation," said I, when I had examined the letter and envelope without finding anything in the least degree distinctive or characteristic; "because, if it is their paper, the unknown man must have had some sort of connection with their establishment or staff."

"There must have been some sort of connection in any case," said Thorndyke. "Even an imitation implies possession of an original. But you are quite right. It is a line of inquiry, and practically the only one that offers."

The inquiry was made on the following day, and the fact clearly established that the paper was Pitcher's paper, but the ink was not their ink. The handwriting appeared to be disguised, and no one connected with the firm was able to recognise it. The staff, even to the caretaker, were all eminently respectable and beyond suspicion of being implicated in an affair of the kind.

"But after all," said Mr. Pitcher, "there are a hundred ways in which a sheet of paper may go astray if anyone wants it : at the printer's, the stationer's, or even in this office--for the paper is always in the letter-rack on the table."

Thus our only clue--if so it could be called--came to an end, and I waited with some curiosity to see what Thorndyke would do next. But so far as I could see, he did nothing, nor did he make any reference to this obscure case during the next few days. We had a good deal of other work on hand, and I assumed that this fully occupied his attention.

One evening, about a week later, he made the first reference to the case and a very mysterious communication it seemed to me.

"I have projected a little expedition for to-morrow," said he. "I am proposing to spend the day, or part of it, in the pastoral region of Bethnal Green."

"In connection with any of our cases?" I asked.

"Yes," he replied. "Balcombe's. I have been making some cautious inquiries with Polton's assistance, principally among hawkers and coffee-shop keepers, and I think I have struck a promising track."

"What kind of inquiries have you been making?" said I.

"I have been looking for a man, or men, engaged in giving street entertainments. That is what our data seemed to suggest, among other possibilities."

"Our data!" I exclaimed. "I didn't know we had any."

"We had Balcombe's account of the attempt to burn the bank. That gave us some hint as to the kind of man to look for. And there were certain other data, which my learned friend may recall."

"I don't recall anything suggesting a street entertainer," said I.

"Not directly," he replied. "It was one of several hypotheses, but it is probably the correct one, as I have heard of such a person as I had assumed, and have ascertained where he is likely to be found on certain days. To-morrow I propose to go over his beat in the hope of getting a glimpse of him. If you think of coming with me, I may remind you that it is not a dressy neighbourhood."

On the following morning we set forth about ten o'clock, and as raiment which is inconspicuous at Bethnal Green may be rather noticeable in the Temple, we slipped out by the Tudor Street gate and made our way to Blackfriars Station. In place of the usual "research-case," I noticed that Thorndyke was carrying a somewhat shabby wood-fibre attaché case, and that he had no walking-stick. We got out at Aldgate and presently struck up Vallance Street in the direction of Bethnal Green; and by the brisk pace and the direct route adopted, I judged that Thorndyke had a definite objective. However, when we entered the maze of small streets adjoining the Bethnal Green Road, our pace was reduced to a saunter, and at corners and crossroads Thorndyke halted from time to time to look along the streets; and occasionally he referred to a card which he produced from his pocket, on which were written the names of streets and days of the week.

A couple of hours passed in this apparently aimless perambulation of the back streets.

"It doesn't look as if you were going to have much luck," I remarked, suppressing a yawn. "And I am not sure that we are not, in our turn, being 'spotted'. I have noted a man--a small, shabby-looking fellow, apparently keeping us in view from a distance, though I don't see him at the moment."

"It is quite likely," said Thorndyke. "This is a shady neighbourhood, and any native could see that we don't belong to it. Good morning! Taking a little fresh air?"

The latter question was addressed to a man who was standing at the door of a small coffee-shop, having apparently come to the surface for a "breather."

"Dunno about fresh," was the reply, "but it's the best there is. By the by, I saw one of them blokes what I was a-tellin' you about go by just now. Foreigner with the rats. If you want to see him give a show, I expect you'll find him in that bit of waste ground off Bolter's Rents."

"Bolter's Rents?" Thorndyke repeated. "Is that a turning out of Salcombe Street?"

"Quite right," was the reply. "Half-way up on the right-hand side."

Thanking our informant, Thorndyke strode off up the street, and as we turned the next corner I glanced back. At the moment, the small man whom I had noticed before stepped out of a doorway and came after us at a pace suggesting anxiety not to lose sight of us.

Bolter's Rents turned out to be a wide paved alley, one side of which opened into a patch of waste ground where a number of old houses had been demolished. This space had an unspeakably squalid appearance; for not only had the debris of the demolished houses been left in unsavoury heaps, but the place had evidently been adopted by the neighbourhood as a general dumping-ground for household refuse. The earth was strewn with vegetable, and even animal, leavings; flies and bluebottles hummed around and settled in hundreds on the garbage, and the air was pervaded by an odour like that of an old-fashioned brick dust-bin.

But in spite of these trifling disadvantages, a consider able crowd had collected, mainly composed of women and children; and at the centre of the crowd a man was giving an entertainment with a troupe of performing rats. We had sauntered slowly up the "Rents" and now halted to look on. At the moment, a white rat was climbing a pole at the top of which a little flag was stuck in a socket. We watched him rapidly climb the pole, seize the flagstaff in his teeth, lift it out of the socket, climb down the pole and deliver the flag to his master. Then a little carriage was produced and the rat harnessed into it, another white rat being dressed in a cloak and placed in the seat, and the latter--introduced to the audience as Lady Murphy--was taken for a drive round the stage.

While the entertainment was proceeding I inspected the establishment and its owner. The stage was composed of light hinged boards opened out on a small four-wheeled hand-cart, apparently home-made. At one end was a largish cage, divided by a wire partition into two parts, one of which contained a number of white and piebald rats, while the inmates of the other compartment were all wild rats; but not, I noted, the common brown or Norway rat, but the old-fashioned British black rat. I remarked upon the circumstance to Thorndyke.

"Yes," he said, "they were probably caught locally. The sewers here will be inhabited by brown rats, but the houses, in an old neighbourhood like this, will be infested principally by the black rat. What do you make of the exhibitor?"

I had already noticed him, and now unobtrusively examined him again. He was a medium-sized man with a sallow complexion, dark, restless eyes-- which frequently wandered in our direction--a crop of stiff, bushy, upstanding hair--he wore no hat--and a ragged beard.

"A Slav of some kind, I should think," was my reply; "a Russian, or perhaps a Lett. But that beard is not perfectly convincing."

"No," Thorndyke agreed, "but it is a good makes up. Perhaps we had better move on flow; we have a deputy, you observe."

As he spoke, the small man whom I had observed following us strolled up the Rents; and as he drew nearer, revealed to my astonished gaze no less a person than our ingenious laboratory assistant, Polton. Strangely altered, indeed, was our usually neat and spruce artificer with his seedy clothing and grubby hands; but as he sauntered up, profoundly unaware of our existence, a faint reminiscence of the familiar crinkly smile stole across his face.

We were just moving off when a chorus of shrieks mingled with laughter arose from the spectators, who hastily scattered right and left, and I had a momentary glimpse of a big black rat bounding across the space, to disappear into one of the many heaps of debris. It seemed that the exhibitor had just opened the cage to take out a black rat when one of the waiting performers--presumably a new recruit--had seized the opportunity to spring out and escape.

"Well," a grinning woman remarked to me, genially, "there's plenty more where that one came from. You should see this place on a moonlight night! Fair alive with 'em it is."

We sauntered up the Rents and along the cross street at the top; and as we went, I reflected on the very singular inquiry in which Thorndyke seemed to be engaged. The rat-tamer's appearance was suspicious. He didn't quite look the part, and his beard was almost certainly a make-up--and a skilful one, too, for it was no mere "property" beard ; and the restless, furtive eyes, and a certain suppressed excitement in his bearing, hinted at something more than met the eye. But if this was Mr. Balcombe's incendiary, how had Thorndyke arrived at his identity, and, above all, by what process of reasoning had he contrived to associate the bank outrage with performing rats,? That he had done so, his systematic procedure made quite clear. But how? It had seemed to me that we had not a single fact on which to start an investigation.

We had walked the length of the cross street, and had halted before turning, when a troop of children emerged from the Rents. Then came the exhibitor, towing his cart, with the cage shrouded in a cloth, then more children, and finally, at a little distance, Polton, slouching along idly but keeping the cart in view.

"I think," said Thorndyke, "it would be instructive, as a study in urban sanitation, to have a look round the scene of the late exhibition."

We retraced our steps down Bolter's Rents, now practically deserted, and wandered around the patch of waste land and in among the piles of bricks and rotting timber where the houses had been pulled down.

"Your lady friend was right," said Thorndyke. "This is a perfect Paradise for rats. Convenient residences among the ruins and unlimited provisions to be had for the mere picking up."

"Apparently you were right, too," said I, "as to the species inhabiting these eligible premises. That seems to be a black rat," and I pointed to a deceased specimen that lay near the entrance to a burrow.

Thorndyke stooped over the little corpse, and after a brief inspection, drew a glove on his right hand.

"Yes," he said, "this is a typical specimen of *Mus rattus*, though it is unusually light in colour. I think it will be worth taking away to examine at our leisure."

Glancing round to see that we were unobserved, he opened his attaché case and took from it a largish tin canister and removed the lid--which, I noted, was anointed at the joint with vaseline. Stooping, he picked up the dead rat by the tail with his gloved fingers dropped it into the canister, clapped on the lid, and replaced it in the attaché case. Then he pulled off the glove and threw it on a rubbish heap.

"You are mighty particular," said I.

"A dead rat is a dirty thing," said he, "and it was only an old glove."

On our way home I made various cautious attempt to extract from Thorndyke some hint as to the purpose of his investigation and his mode of procedure. But I could extract nothing from him beyond certain generalities.

"When a man," said he, "introduces an incendiary bomb into the strong-room of a bank, we may reasonably inquire as to his motives. And when we have reached the fairly obvious conclusion as to what those motives must be, we may ask ourselves what kind of conduct such motives will probably generate; that is, what sort of activities will be likely to be associated with such motives and with the appropriate state of mind. And when we have decided on that, too, we may look for a person engaged in those activities; and if we find such a person we may consider that we have a prima facie case. The rest is a matter of verification."

"That is all very well, Thorndyke," I objected, "but if I find a man trying to set fire to a bank, I don't immediately infer that his customary occupation is exhibiting performing rats in a back street of Bethnal Green."

Thorndyke laughed quietly. "My learned friend's observation is perfectly just. It is not a universal rule. But we are dealing with a specific case in which certain other facts are known to us. Still, the connection, if there is one, has yet to be established. This exhibitor may turn out not to be Balcombe's man after all."

"And if he is not?"

"I think we shall want him all the same; but I shall know better in a couple of hours' time."

What transpired during those two hours I did not discover at the time, for I had an engagement to dine with some legal friends and must needs hurry away as soon as I had purified myself from the effects of our travel in the unclean East. When I returned to our chambers, about half-past ten, I found Thorndyke seated in his easy chair immersed in a treatise on old musical instruments. Apparently he had finished with the case.

"How did Polton get on?" I asked.

"Admirably," replied Thorndyke. "He shadowed our entertaining friend from Bethnal Green to a by street in Ratcliff, where he apparently resides. But he did more than that. We had made up a little book of a dozen leaves of transfer paper in which I wrote in French some infallible rules for taming rats. Just as the man was going into his house, Polton accosted him and asked him for an expert opinion on these directions. The foreign gentleman was at first impatient and huffy, but when he had glanced at the book, he became interested, and a good deal amused, and finally read the whole set of rules through attentively. Then he handed the book back to Polton and recommended him to follow the rules carefully, offering to supply him with a few rats to experiment on, an offer which Polton asked him to hold over for a day or two.

"As soon as he got home, Polton dismembered the book and put the leaves down on the stone, with this result."

He took from his pocket-book a number of small pieces of paper, each of which was marked more or less distinctly with lithographed reproductions of fingerprints, and laid them on the table. I looked through them attentively, and with a faint sense of familiarity.

"Isn't that left thumb," said I, "rather similar to the print on the maps from Mr. Rabbage's letter wallet?"

"It is identical," he replied. "Here are the proofs of the map-prints and the note-tablet. If you compare them you can see that not only the left thumb but the other prints are the same in all."

Careful comparison showed that this was so.

"But," I exclaimed, "I don't understand this at all. These are the finger-prints of Mr. Rabbage's mysterious entomologist. I thought you were looking for Balcombe's man."

"My impression," he replied "is that they are t same person, though the evidence is far from conclusive. But we shall soon know. I have sworn an information against the foreign gent, and Miller has arranged to raid the house at Ratcliff early to-morrow and as it promises to be a highly interesting event, I propose to be present. Shall I have the pleasure of my learned friend's company? "

"Most undoubtedly," I replied, "though I am absolutely in the dark as to the meaning of the whole affair."

"Then," said Thorndyke, "I recommend you to go over the history of both cases systematically in the interval."

Six o'clock on the following morning found us in an empty house in Old Gravel Lane, Ratcliff, in company with Superintendent Miller and three stalwart plain clothes men, awaiting the report of a patrol. We were all dressed in engineers' overalls, reeking with naphthalin. Our trousers were tucked into our socks, and socks and boots were thickly smeared with vaseline, as were our wrists, around which our sleeves were bound closely with tape. These preparations, together with an automatic pistol served out to each of us, gave me some faint inkling of the nature of the case, though it was still very confused in my mind.

About a quarter-past six a messenger arrived and reported that the house which was to be raided was open. Thereupon Miller and one of his men set forth, and the rest of us followed at short intervals. On arriving at the house, which was but a short distance from our rendezvous, we found a stolid plain-clothes man guarding the open door and a frowsy-looking woman, who carried a jug of milk, angrily demanding in very imperfect English to be allowed to pass into her house. Pushing past the protesting housekeeper, we entered the grimy passage, where Miller was just emerging from a ground-floor room.

"That is the woman's quarters," said he, "and the kitchen seems to be a sort of rat-menagerie. We'd better try the first-floor."

He led the way up the stairs, and when he reached the landing he tried the handle of the front room. Finding the door locked or bolted, he passed on to the back room and tried the door of that, with the same result. Then, holding up a warning finger, he proceeded to whistle a popular air in a fine, penetrating tone, and to perform a double shuffle on the bare floor. Almost immediately an angry voice was heard in the front room, and slippered feet padded quickly across the floor. Then a bolt was drawn noisily, the door flew open, and for an instant I had a view of the rat-show man, clothed in a suit of very soiled pyjamas. But it was only for an instant. Even as our eyes met, he tried to slam the door to, and failing--in consequence of an intruding constabulary foot-- he sprang back, leaped over a bed and darted through a communicating doorway into the back room and shut and bolted the door.

"That's unfortunate," said Miller. "Now we're going to have trouble."

The superintendent was right. On the first attempt to force the door, a pistol-shot from within blew a hole in the top panel and made a notch in the ear of the would-be invader. The latter replied through the hole, and there followed a sort of snarl and the sound of a shattered bottle. Then, as the constable stood aside and shot after shot came from within, the door became studded with ragged holes. Meanwhile Miller, Thorndyke and I tiptoed out on the landing, and taking as long a run as was possible, flung ourselves, simultaneously on the back-room door. The weight of three large men was too much for the crazy woodwork. As we fell on it together, there was a bursting crash, the hinges tore away, the door flew inwards, and we staggered into the room.

It was a narrow shave for some of us. Before we could recover our footing, the showman had turned with his pistol pointing straight at Miller's head. A bare instant before it exploded, Thorndyke, whose momentum had carried him half-way across the room, caught it with an upward snatch, and its report was followed by a harmless shower of plaster from the ceiling. Immediately our quarry changed his tactics.

Leaving the pistol in Thorndyke's grasp, he darted across the room towards a work-bench on which stood a row of upright, cylindrical tins. He was in the act of reaching out for one of these when Thorndyke grasped his pyjamas between the shoulders and dragged him back, while Miller rushed forward and seized him. For a few moments there was a frantic and furious struggle, for the fellow fought with hands and feet and teeth with the ferocity of a wild cat, and, overpowered as he was, still strove to drag his captors towards the bench. Suddenly, once more, a pistol-shot rang out, and then all was still. By accident or design the struggling man had got hold of the pistol that Thorndyke still grasped and pressed the trigger, and the bullet had entered his own head just above the ear.

"Pooh!" exclaimed Miller, rising and wiping his forehead, "that was a near one. If you hadn't stopped him, doctor, we'd all have gone up like rockets."

"You think those things are bombs, then?" said I.

"Think!" he repeated. "I removed two exactly like them from the General Post Office, and they turned out to be charged with T.N.T. And those square ones on the shelf are twin brothers of the one that went off in Rutherford's Bank."

As we were speaking, I happened to glance round at the doorway, and there, to my surprise, was the woman whom we had seen below, still holding the jug of milk and staring in with an expression of horror at the dead revolutionary. Thorndyke also observed her, and stepping across to where she stood, asked: "Can you tell me if there has been, or is now, anyone sick in this house?

"Yes," the woman replied, without removing her eyes from the dead man. "Dere is a chentleman sick upstairs. I haf not seen him. He used to look after him," and she nodded to the dead body of the showman.

"I think we will go up and have a look at this sick gentleman," said Thorndyke. "You had better not come, Miller."

We started together up the stairs, and as we went I asked: "Do you suppose this is a case of plague?"

"No," he replied. "I fancy the plague department is in the kitchen; but we shall see."

He looked round the landing which we had now reached and then opened the door of the front room, Immediately I was aware of a strange, intensely fetid odour, and glancing into the room, I perceived a man lying, apparently in a state of stupor, in a bed covered with indescribably filthy bed-clothes. Thorndyke entered and approached the bed, and I followed. The light was rather dim, and it was not until we were quite close that I suddenly recognised the disease.

"Good God!" I exclaimed, "it is typhus!"

"Yes," said Thorndyke; "and look at the bed clothes, and look at the poor devil's neck. We can see now how that villain collected his specimens."

I stooped over the poor, muttering, unconscious wretch and was filled with horror. Bed-clothes, pillow and patient were all alike crawling with vermin.

♦ ♦ ♦ ♦ ♦

"Of course," I said as we walked homewards, "I see the general drift of this case, but what I can't under stand is how you connected up the facts."

"Well," replied Thorndyke, "let us set out the argument and trace the connections. The starting--point was the aluminium case that Mr. Rabbage brought us. Those tubes of fleas and lice were clearly an abnormal phenomenon. They might, as you suggested, have belonged to a scientific collector; but that was not probable. The fleas were alive, and were meant to remain alive, as the perforated caps of the tubes proved,' And the lice had merely died, as lice quickly do if they are not fed. They did not appear to have been killed, But against your view there were two very striking facts, one of which I fancy you did not observe. The fleas were not the common human flea; they were Asiatic rat-fleas."

"You are quite right," I admitted. "I did not notice that."

"Then," he continued, "there was the aniseed with which the parchment caps of the tubes were scented. Now aniseed is irresistible to rats. It is an infallible bait. But it is not specially attractive to fleas. What then was the purpose of the scent? The answer, fantastic as it was, had to be provisionally accepted because it was the only one that suggested itself. If one of these tubes had been exposed to rats--dropped down a rat-hole, for instance--it is certain that the rats would have gnawed off the parchment cap. Then the fleas would have been liberated, and as they were rat-fleas, they would have immediately fastened upon the rats. The tubes, therefore, appeared to be an apparatus for disseminating rat-fleas.

"But why should anyone want to disseminate rat- fleas? That question at once brought into view another striking fact, Here, in these tubes, were rat-fleas and body-lice: both carriers of deadly disease. The rat-flea is a carrier of plague; the body-louse is a carrier of typhus. It was an impressive coincidence. It suggested that the dissemination of rat-fleas might be really the dissemination of plague; and if the lice were distributed, too, that might mean the distribution of typhus.

"And now consider the maps. The circles on them all marked old slum-areas tenanted by low-class aliens. But old slums abound in rats; and low-class aliens abound in body-lice. Here was another coincidence. Then there was the note-tablet bearing numbers associated with the letters a and b and plus and minus signs. The letters a and b might mean rat and louse or plague and typhus, and the plus and minus might mean a success or a failure to produce an outbreak of disease. That was merely speculative, but it was quite consistent.

"So far we were dealing with a hypothesis based on simple observation. But that hypothesis could be proved or disproved. The question was: Were these insects infected insects, or were they not? To settle this I took one flea from each of the four tubes and 'sowed' it on agar, with the result that from each flea I got a typical culture of plague bacillus, which I verified with Haffkine's 'Stalactite test.' I also examined one louse from each of the two tubes, and in each case got a definite typhus reaction. So the insects were infected and the hypothesis was confirmed.

"The next thing was to find the owner of the tubes, Now the circles on the maps indicated some sort of activity, presumably connected with rats and carried on in these areas.

I visited those areas and got into conversation with the inhabitants on the subject of rats, rat-catchers, rat pits, sewermen, and everything bearing on rats; and at length I heard of an exhibitor of performing rats. You know the rest. We found the man, we observe that all his rats, excepting the tame white ones, were I black rats--the special plague-carrying species--and we found on this spot a dead rat, which I ascertained on examining the body, had died of plague. Finally there was Polton's little book giving us the finger prints of the owner of the aluminium case. That completed the identification; and inquiries at the Local Government Board showed that cases of plague and typhus had occurred in the marked areas."

"Had not the authorities taken any steps in the matter?" I asked.

Oh, yes," he replied. "They had carried out an energetic rat campaign in the London Docks, the likeliest source of infection. Naturally, they would not think of a criminal lunatic industriously sowing plague broad cast."

"Then how did you connect this man with the bank outrage?"

"I never did, very conclusively," he replied. "It was mostly a matter of inference. You see, the two crimes were essentially similar. They were varieties of the same type. Both were cases of idiotic destructiveness, and the agent in each was evidently a moral imbecile who was a professed enemy of society. Such persons are rare in this country, and when they occur are usually foreigners, most commonly Russians, or East Europeans of some kind. The only actual clue was the date on Pilcher's letter, the rather peculiar figures of which were extraordinarily like those on the maps and the note-tablet. Still, it was little more than a guess, though it happens to have turned out correct."

"And how do you suppose this fellow avoided getting plague and typhus himself?"

"It was quite likely that he had had both. But he could easily avoid the typhus by keeping himself clean and his clothing disinfected; and as to the plague, he could have used Haffkine's plague-prophylactic and given it to the woman. Clearly it would not have suited him to have a case of plague in the house and have the health officer inspecting the premises."

That was the end of the case, unless I should include in the history a very handsome fee sent to my colleague by the President of the Local Government Board.

"I think we have earned it," said Thorndyke; "and yet I am not sure that Mr. Rabbage is not entitled to a share."

And in fact, when that benevolent person called a few days later to receive a slightly ambiguous report and tender his fee, he departed beaming, bearing a donation wherewith to endow an additional bed, cot, or basket, in the St. Francis Home of Rest.

Rex v. Burnaby

IT is a normal incident in general medical practice that the family doctor soon drifts into the position of a family friend. The Burnabys had been among my earliest patients, and mutual sympathies had quickly brought about the more intimate relationship. It was a pleasant household, pervaded by a quiet geniality and a particularly attractive homely, unaffected culture. It was an interesting household, too, for the disparity in age between the husband and wife made the domestic conditions a little unusual and invited speculative observation. And there were other matters, to be referred to presently.

Frank Burnaby was a somewhat delicate man of about fifty: quiet, rather shy, gentle, kindly, and singularly innocent and trustful. He held a post at the Records Office, and was full of quaint and curious lore derive from the ancient documents on which he worked: selections from which he would retail in the family circle with a picturesque imagination and a fund of quiet, dry humour that made them delightful to listen to. I have never met a more attractive man, or one whom 1 liked better or respected more.

Equally attractive, in an entirely different way, was his wife: an extremely charming and really beautiful woman of under thirty--little more than a girl, in fact: amiable, high-spirited and full of fun and frolic, but nevertheless an accomplished, cultivated woman with a strong interest in her husband's pursuits. They appeared to me an exceedingly happy and united couple deeply attached to one another and in perfect sympathy. There were four children--three boys and a girl--of Burnaby's by his first wife; and their devotion to their young stepmother spoke volumes for her care of them.

But there was a fly in the domestic ointment: at least, that was what I felt. There was another family friend, a youngish man named Cyril Parker. Not that I had anything against him, personally, but I was not quite happy about the relationship. He was a markedly good-looking man, pleasant, witty, and extremely well informed; for he was a partner in a publishing house and acted as reader for the firm; whence it happened that he, like Mr. Burnaby, gathered stores of interesting matter from his professional reading. But I could not disguise from myself that his admiration and affection for Mrs. Burnaby were definitely inside the danger zone, and that the intimacy--on his side, at any rate--was growing rather ominously. On her side there seemed nothing more than frank, though very pronounced, friendship. But I looked at the relationship askance. She was a woman whom any man might have fallen in love with, and I did not like the expression that I sometimes detected in Parker's eyes when he was looking at her. Still, there was nothing in the conduct of either to which the slightest exception could have been taken or which in any way foreshadowed the terrible disaster which was so shortly to befall.

The starting-point of the tragedy was a comparatively trivial event. By much poring over crabbed manuscripts, Mr. Burnaby developed symptoms of eye-strain which caused me to send him to an oculist for an opinion and a prescription for suitable spectacles. On the evening of the day on which he had consulted the oculist, I received an urgent summons from Mrs. Burnaby, and, on arriving at the house, found her husband somewhat seriously ill. His symptoms were rather puzzling, for they corresponded to no known disease. His face was flushed, his temperature slightly raised, his pulse rapid, though the breathing was slow, his throat was excessively dry, and his pupils widely dilated. It was an extraordinary condition, resembling nothing within my knowledge excepting atropine poisoning.

"Has he been taking medicine of any kind?" I asked.

Mrs. Burnaby shook her head. "He never takes any drugs or medicine but what you prescribe; and it couldn't be anything that he has taken, because the attack came on quite soon after he came home, before he had either food or drink."

It was very mysterious and the patient himself could throw no light on the origin of the attack. While I was reflecting on the matter, I happened to glance at the mantelpiece, on which I noticed a drop labelled "The Eye Drops" and a prescription envelope. Opening the latter I found the oculist's prescription for the drops--a very weak solution of atropine sulphate.

"Has he had any of these drops?" I asked.

"Yes," replied Mrs. Burnaby. "I dropped some into his eyes as soon as he came in; two drops in each eye, according to the directions."

It was very odd. The amount of atropine in those four drops was less than a hundredth of a grain; an impossibly small dose to produce the symptoms. Yet he had all the appearance of having taken a poisonous dose, which he obviously had not, since the drop-bottle was nearly full. I could make nothing of it. However, I treated it as a case of atropine poisoning; and as the treatment produced marked improvement, I went home, more mystified than ever.

When I called on the following morning, I learned that he was practically well, and had gone to his office. But that evening I had another urgent message, and on hurrying round to Burnaby's house, found him suffering from an attack similar to, but even more severe than, the one on the previous day. I immediately administered an injection of pilocarpine and other appropriate remedies, and had the satisfaction of seeing a rapid improvement in his condition. But whereas the efficacy of the treatment proved that the symptoms were really due to atropine, no atropine appeared to have been taken excepting the minute quantity contained in the eye-drops.

It was very mysterious. The most exhaustive inquiries failed to suggest any possible source of the poison excepting the drops; and as each attack had occurred a short time after the use of them, it was impossible to ignore the apparent connection, in spite of the absurdly minute dose.

"I can only suppose," said I, addressing Mrs. Burnaby and Mr. Parker, who had called to make inquiries, "that Burnaby is the subject of an idiosyncrasy--that he is abnormally sensitive to this drug."

"Is that a known condition?" asked Parker.

"Oh, yes," I replied. "People vary enormously in the way in which they react to drugs. Some are so intolerant of particular drugs--iodine, for instance--that ordinary medicinal doses produce poisonous effects, while others have the most extraordinary tolerance. Christisori, in his Treatise on Poisons, gives a case of a man, unaccustomed to opium, who took nearly an ounce of laudanum without any effect--a dose that would have killed an ordinary man. These drugs are terrible pitfalls for the doctor who doesn't know his patient. Just think what might have happened to Burnaby if someone had given him a full medicinal dose of belladonna."

"Does belladonna have the same effect as atropine?" asked Mrs. Burnaby.

"It is the same," I replied. "Atropine is the active principle of belladonna."

"What a mercy," she exclaimed, "that we discovered this idiosyncrasy in time. I suppose he had better discontinue the drops?"

"Yes," I answered, "most emphatically; and I will write to Mr. Haines and let him know that the atropine is impracticable."

I accordingly wrote to the oculist, who was politely sceptical as to the connection between the drops and the attacks. However, Burnaby settled the matter by refusing point-blank to have any further dealings with atropine; and his decision was so far justified that, for the time being, the attacks did not recur.

A couple of months passed. The incident had, to a great extent, faded from my mind. But then it was revived in a way that not only filled me with astonishment but caused me very grave anxiety. I was just about to set out on my morning round when Burnaby's housemaid met me at my door, breathing quickly and carrying a note. It was from Mrs. Burnaby, begging me to call at once and telling me that her husband had been seized by an attack similar to the previous ones. I ran back for my emergency bag and then hurried round to the house, where I found Burnaby lying on a sofa, very flushed, rather alarmed, and exhibiting well-marked symptoms of atropine poisoning. The attack, however, was not a very severe one, and the application of the appropriate remedies soon produced a change for the better.

"Now, Burnaby," I said, as he sat up with a sigh of relief. "what have you been up to? Haven't been tinkering with those drops again?"

"No," he replied. "Why should I? Haines has finished with my eyes."

"Well, you've been taking something with atropine in it."

"I suppose I have, but I can't imagine what. I have had no medicine of any kind."

"No pills, lozenges, liniment, plaster, or ointment?"

"Nothing medicinal of any sort," he replied. "In fact, I have swallowed nothing to-day but my breakfast; and the attack came on directly after, though it was a simple enough meal, goodness knows--just a couple of pigeon's eggs and some toast and tea."

"Pigeon's eggs," said I, with a grin, "why not sparrow's?"

"Cyril sent them--as a joke, I think," Mrs. Burnaby explained (Cyril, of course, was Mr. Parker), "but I must say Frank enjoyed them. You see, Cyril has taken lately to keeping pigeons and rabbits and other edible beasts, and I think he has done it principally for Frank's sake, as you have ordered him a special diet. We are constantly getting things from Cyril now--pigeons and rabbits especially; and much younger than we can buy them at the shops."

"Yes," said Burnaby, "he is most generous. I should think he supplies more than half my diet. I hardly like to accept so much from him.'

"It gives him pleasure to send these gifts," said Mrs. Burnaby; "but I wish it gave him pleasure to slaughter the creatures first. He always brings or sends them alive, and the cook hates killing them. As to me, I couldn't do it, though I deal with the corpses afterwards. I prepare nearly all Frank's food myself."

"Yes," said Burnaby, with a glance of deep affection at his wife, "Margaret is an artist in kickshaws and I consume the works of art. I can tell you, doctor, I live like a fighting cock."

This was all very well, but it was beside the question; which was, where did the atropine come from? If Burnaby had swallowed nothing but his breakfast, it would seem that the atropine must have been in that. I pointed this out.

"But you know, doctor," said Burnaby," that isn't possible. We can write the eggs off. You can't get poison into an egg without making a hole in the shell, and these eggs were intact. And as to the bread and butter, and the tea, we all had the same, and none of the others seem any the worse."

That isn't very conclusive," said I. "A dose of atropine that would be poisonous to you would probably have no appreciable effect on the others. But, of course, the real mystery is how on earth atropine could have got into any of the food."

It couldn't," said Burnaby and that really was my own conviction. But it was an unsatisfactory conclusion, for it left the mystery unexplained; and when a length I took my leave, to continue my rounds of visits, it was with the uncomfortable feeling that I had failed to trace the origin of the danger or to secure my patient against its recurrence.

Nor was my uneasiness unjustified. Little more than a week had passed when a fresh summons brought me to Burnaby's house, full of bewilderment and apprehension. And indeed there was good cause for apprehension; for when I arrived, to find Burnaby lying speechless and sightless his blue eyes turned to blank discs of black, glittering with the unnatural "belladonna sparkle,"--when I felt his racing pulse and watched his vain efforts to swallow a sip of water,--I began to ask myself whether he was not beyond recall. The same question was asked mutely by the terrified eyes of his wife, who rose like a ghost from his bedside as I entered the room. But once more he responded to the remedies, though more slowly this time, and at the end of an hour I was relieved to see that the urgent danger was past, although he still remained very ill.

Meanwhile, inquiries failed utterly to elicit any explanation of the attack. The symptoms had set in shortly after dinner; a simple meal, consisting of a pigeon cooked en casserole by Mrs. Burnaby herself, vegetables and a light pudding which had been shared by the rest of the family, and a little Chablis from a bottle that I been unsealed and opened in the dining-room. Nothing else had been taken and no medicaments of any kind used. On the other hand, any doubts as to the nature of the attack were set at rest by a chemical test made by me and confirmed by the Clinical Research Association, Atropine was demonstrably present, though the amount was comparatively small. But its source remained an impenetrable mystery.

It was a profoundly disturbing state of affairs. The last attack had narrowly missed a fatal termination and the poison was still untraced. From the same unknown source a fresh charge might be delivered at any moment, and who could say what the result would be? Poor Burnaby was in a state of chronic terror and his wife began to look haggard and worn with constant anxiety and apprehension. Nor was I in much better case myself, for, whatever should befall, the responsibility was mine. I racked my brains for some possible explanation, but could think of none, though there were times when a horrible thought would creep into my mind, only to be indignantly cast out.

One evening a few days after the last attack, I received a visit from Burnaby's brother, a pathologist attached to one of the London hospitals, but not in practice. Very different was Dr. Burnaby from his gentle, amiable brother; a strong, resolute, energetic man and none too suave in manner. We were already acquainted, so no introductions were necessary, and he came to the point with characteristic directness.

"You can guess what I have come about, Jardine--this atropine business. What is being done in the matter?"

"I don't know that anything is being done," I answered lamely. "I can make nothing of it."

"Waiting for the next attack and the inquest, h'm? Well, that won't do, you know. This affair has got to be stopped before it is too late. If you don't know where the poison comes from, somebody does. H'm! And it is time to find out who that somebody is. There aren't many to choose from. I am going there now to have a look round and make a few inquiries. You'd better come with me."

"Are they expecting you?" I asked.

"No," he answered gruffly; "but I'm not a stranger and neither are you."

I decided to go round with him, though I didn't much like his manner. This was evidently meant to be a surprise visit, and I had no great difficulty in guessing at what was in his mind. On the other hand, I was not sorry to share the responsibility with a man of his position and a relative of the patient. Accordingly, I set forth with him willingly enough; and it is significant of my state of mind at this time, that I took my emergency bag with me.

When we arrived Burnaby and his wife were just sitting down to dinner-- the children took their evening meal by themselves--and they welcomed us with the ready hospitality that made this such a pleasant household. Dr. Burnaby's place was laid opposite mine, and I was faintly amused to note his eye furtively travelling over the table, evidently assessing each article of food as a possible vehicle of atropine. "If you had only let us know you were coming, Jim," said Mrs. Burnaby when the joint made its appearance, "we would have had something better than saddle of mutton. As it is, you must take pot-luck."

"Saddle of mutton is good enough for me," replied Dr. Burnaby. "But what on earth is that stuff that Frank has got?" he added, as Burnaby lifted the lid from a little casserole.

"That," she answered, "is a fricassee of rabbit. Such a tiny creature it was; a mere infant. Cook nearly wept at having to kill it."

"Kill it!" exclaimed the doctor; "do you buy your rabbits alive?"

"We didn't buy this one," she replied. "It was brought by Cyril--Mr. Parker, you know," she added hastily and with a slight flush, as she caught a grim glance of interrogation. "He sends quite a lot of poultry and rabbits and things for Frank from his little farm."

"Ha!" said the doctor with a reflective eye on the casserole. "H'm! Breeds them himself, hey? Whereabouts is his farm?"

"At Eltham. But it isn't really a farm. He just keeps rabbits and fowls and pigeons in a place at the back of his garden."

"Is your cook English?" Dr. Burnaby asked, glancing again at the casserole. "That affair of Frank's has rather a French look."

"Bless you, Jim," said Burnaby, "I am not dependent on mere cooks. I am a pampered gourmet. Margaret prepares most of my food with her own sacred hands. Cooks can't do this sort of thing"; and he helped himself afresh from the casserole.

Dr. Burnaby seemed to reflect profoundly upon this explanation. Then he abruptly changed the subject from cookery to the Lindisfarne Gospels and thereby set his brother's chin wagging to a new tune. For Burnaby's affections as a scholar were set on seventh- and eighth-century manuscripts and his knowledge of them was as great as his enthusiasm.

"Oh, get on with your dinner, Frank, you old windbag," exclaimed Mrs. Burnaby. "You are letting everything get cold."

So I am, dear," he admitted, "but--I won't be a minute. I just want Jim to see those collotypes of the Durham Book. Excuse me."

He sprang up from the table and darted into the adjoining library, whence he returned almost immediately carrying a small portfolio.

"These are the plates," he said, handing the portfolio to his brother. "Have a look at them while I dispose of the arrears."

He took up his knife and fork and made as if to resume his meal. Then he laid them down and leaned back in his chair. "I don't think I want any more, after all," he said.

The tone in which he spoke caused me to look at him critically; for my talk with his brother had made me a little nervous and apprehensive of further trouble. What I now saw was by no means reassuring. A slight flush and a trace of anxiety in his expression made me ask, with outward composure but inward alarm: "You are feeling quite fit, I hope, Burnaby?"

"Well, not so very," he replied. "My eyes are going a bit misty and my throat--" Here he worked his lips and swallowed as if with some effort.

I rose hastily, and, catching a terrified glance from his wife, went to him and looked into his eyes. And thereupon my heart sank. For already his pupils were twice their natural size and the darkened eyes exhibited the too-familiar sparkle. I was sensible of a thrill of terror, and, as I looked into Burnaby's now distinctly alarmed face, his brother's ominous words echoed in my ears. Had I waited "for the next attack and the inquest"?

The symptoms, once started, developed apace. From moment to moment he grew worse, and the rapid enlargement of the pupils gave an alarming hint as to the intensity of the poisoning. I darted out into the hail for my bag, and as I re-entered, I saw him rise, groping blindly with his hands, until his wife, ashen-faced and trembling, took his arm and led him to the door.

"I had better give him a dose of pilocarpine at once," I said, getting out my hypodermic syringe and glancing at Dr. Burnaby, who watched me with stony composure.

"Yes," he agreed, "and a little morphine, too! and he will probably need some stimulant. I won't come up; only be in the way."

I followed the patient up to the bedroom and administered the antidotes forthwith. Then, while he was getting partially undressed with his wife's help, I went downstairs in search of brandy and hot water, I was about to enter the dining-room when, through the partly-open door, I saw Dr. Burnaby standing by the fireplace with his open hand-bag--which he had fetched in from the hall--on the table before him, and in his hand a little Bohemian glass jar from the mantel piece. Involuntarily, I halted for a moment; and as I did so, he carefully deposited the little ornament in the bag and closed the latter, locking it with a small key which he then put in his pocket.

It was an excessively odd proceeding, but, of course, it was no concern of mine. Nevertheless, instead of entering the dining-room, I stole softly towards the kitchen and fetched the hot water myself. When I returned, the bag was back on the hall table and I found Dr. Burnaby grimly pacing up and down the dining room. He asked me a few questions while I was looking for the brandy, and then, somewhat to my surprise, proposed to come up and lend a hand with the patient.

On entering the bedroom, we found poor Burnaby lying half-undressed on the bed and in a very pitiable state; terrified, physically distressed and inclined to ramble mentally. His wife knelt by the bed, white-faced, red-eyed and evidently panic-stricken, though she was quite quiet and self-restrained. As we entered, she rose to make way for us, and while we were examining the patient's pulse and listening to his racing heart, she silently busied herself with the preparations for administering the stimulants.

"You don't think he is going to die, do you?" she whispered, as Dr. Burnaby handed me back my stethoscope.

"It is no use thinking," he replied dryly--and I thought rather callously--"we shall see" ; and with this he turned his back to her and looked at his brother with a gloomy frown.

For more than an hour that question was an open one. From moment to moment I expected to feel the wildly-racing pulse flicker out; to hear the troubled breathing die away in an expiring rattle. From time to time we cautiously increased the antidotes and administered restoratives, but I must confess that I had little hope. Dr. Burnaby was undisguisedly pessimistic. And as the weary minutes dragged on, and I looked momentarily for the arrival of the dread messenger, there would keep stealing into my mind a question that I hardly dared to entertain. What was the meaning of it all? Whence had the poison come? And why, in this household, had it found its way to Burnaby alone--the one inmate to whom it was specially deadly?

At last--at long last--there came a change; hardly perceptible at first, and viewed with little confidence. But after a time it became more pronounced; and then, quite rapidly, the symptoms began to clear up. The patient swallowed with ease, and great relish, a cup of coffee; the heart slowed down, the breathing became natural, and presently, as the morphine began to take effect, he sank into a doze which passed by degrees into a quiet sleep.

"I think he will do now," said Dr. Burnaby, "so I won't stay any longer. But it was a near thing, Jardine; most uncomfortably near."

He walked to the door, where, as he went out, he turned and bowed stiffly to his sister-in-law. I followed him down the stairs, rather expecting him to revert to the subject of his visit to me. But he made no reference to it, nor, indeed, did he say anything until he stood on the doorstep with his bag in his hand. Then he made a somewhat cryptic remark: "Well, Jardine," he said, "the Durham Book saved him. But for those collotypes, he would be a dead man."; and with that he walked away, leaving me to interpret as best I could this decidedly obscure remark.

A quarter of an hour later, as Burnaby was peacefully asleep and apparently out of all danger, I took my own departure, and as soon as I was outside the house, I proceeded to put into execution a plan that had been forming in my mind during the last hour. There was some mystery in this case that was evidently beyond my powers to solve. But solved it had to be, if Burnaby's life was to be saved, to say nothing of my own reputation; so I had decided to put the facts before my friend and former teacher, Dr. Thorndyke, and seek his advice, and if necessary, his assistance.

It was now past ten o'clock, but I determined to take my chance of finding him at his chambers, and accordingly, having found a taxi, I directed the driver to set me down at the gate of Inner Temple Lane. My former experience of Thorndyke's habits led me to be hopeful, and my hopes were not unjustified on this occasion, for when I had mounted to the first pair landing of No. 5A King's Bench Walk, and assaulted the knocker of the inner door, I was relieved to find him not only at home, but alone and disengaged. "It's a deuce of a time to come knocking you up," I said, as he shook my hand, "but I am in rather a hole, and the matter is urgent, so--"

"So you paid me the compliment of treating me as a friend," said he. "Very proper of you. What is the nature of your difficulty?"

"Why, I've got a case of recurrent atropine poisoning and I can make absolutely nothing of it."

Here I began to give a brief outline sketch of the facts, but after a minute or two he stopped me.

"It is of no use being sketchy, Jardine," said he. "The night is young. Let us have a complete history of the case, with particulars of all the persons concerned and their mutual relations. And don't spare detail."

He seated himself with a notebook on his knee, and when he had lighted his pipe, I plunged into the narrative of the case, beginning with the eye-drop incident and finishing with the alarming events of the present evening.

He listened with close attention, refraining from interrupting me excepting occasionally to ask for a date, which he jotted down with a few other notes. When I had finished, he laid aside his notebook, and, as he knocked out his pipe, observed: "A very remarkable case, Jardine, and interesting by reason of the unusual nature of the poison."

"Oh, hang the interest!" I exclaimed. "I am not a toxicologist. I am a general practitioner; and I want to know what the deuce I ought to do."

I think," said he, "that your duty is perfectly obvious. You ought to communicate with the police, either alone or in conjunction with some member of the family."

I looked at him in dismay. "But," I faltered, "what have I got to tell the police?"

"What you have told me," he replied; "which, put in a nutshell, amounts to this: Frank Burnaby has had three attacks of atropine poisoning, disregarding the eye-drops. Each attack has appeared to be associated with some article of food prepared by Mrs. Burnaby and supplied by Mr. Cyril Parker."

"But, good God!" I exclaimed, "you don't suspect Mrs. Burnaby?"

"I suspect nobody," he replied. "It may not be criminal poisoning at all. But Mr. Burnaby has to be protected, and the case certainly needs investigation."

"You don't think I could make a few inquiries myself first? " I suggested.

He shook his head. "The risk is too great," he replied. "The man might die before you reached a conclusion; whereas a few inquiries made by the police would probably put a stop to the affair, unless the poisoning is in some inconceivable way inadvertent."

That was what his advice amounted to, and I felt that he was right. But it put on me a horribly unpleasant duty; and as I wended homewards I tried to devise some means of mitigating its unpleasantness Finally I decided to try to persuade Mrs. Burnaby to make a joint communication with me.

But the necessity never arose. When I made my morning visit, I found a taxicab drawn up opposite the door and the housemaid who admitted me looked as if she had seen a ghost.

"Why, what is the matter, Mabel?" I asked, as she ushered me funereally into the drawing-room.

She shook her head. "I don't know, sir. Something awful, I'm afraid. I'll tell them you are here." With this she shut the door and departed.

The housemaid's manner and the unusually formal reception filled me with vague forebodings. But even as I was wondering what could have happened, the question was answered by the entry of a tall man who looked like a guardsman in mufti.

"Dr. Jardine?" he asked; and as I nodded, he explained, presenting his card, "I am Detective Lane. I have been instructed to make some inquiries in respect of certain information which we have received. It is stated that Mr. Frank Burnaby is suffering from the effects of poison. So far as you know, is that true?"

"I hope he is recovered now," I replied, "but he was suffering last night from what appeared to be atropine poisoning."

"Have there been any previous attacks of the same kind?" the sergeant asked.

"Yes," I answered. "This was the fifth attack; but the first two were evidently due to some eye-drops that he had used."

"And in the case of the other three; have you any idea as to how the poison came to be taken? Whether it was in the food, for instance?"

"I have no idea, sergeant. I know nothing more than what I have told you; and, of course, I am not going to make any guesses. Is it admissible to ask who gave the information?"

"I am afraid not, sir," he replied. "But you will soon know. There is a definite charge against Mrs. Burnaby--I have just made the arrest--and we shall want your evidence for the prosecution."

I stared at him in utter consternation. "Do you mean," I gasped, "that you have arrested Mrs. Burnaby?"

"Yes," he replied; "on a charge of having administered poison to her husband."

I was absolutely thunderstruck. And yet, when I remembered Thorndyke's words and recalled my own dim and hastily-dismissed surmises, there was nothing so very surprising in this shocking turn of events.

"Could I have a few words with Mrs. Burnaby?" I asked.

"Not alone," he replied, "and better not at all. Still, if you have any business--"

"I have," said I; whereupon he led the way to the dining-room, where I found Mrs. Burnaby seated rigidly in a chair, pale as death, but quite calm though rather dazed. Opposite her a military-looking man sat stiffly by the table with an air of being unconscious of her presence, and he took no notice as I walked over to his prisoner and silently pressed her hand.

"I've come, Mrs. Burnaby," said I, "to ask if there is anything that you want me to do. Does Burnaby know about this horrible affair?

No," she answered. "You will have to tell him if he is fit to hear it; and if not, I want you to let my father know as soon as you can. That is all; and you had better go now, as we mustn't detain these gentlemen. Good-bye."

She shook my hand unemotionally, and when I had faltered a few words of vague encouragement and sympathy, I went out of the room, but waited in the hall to see the last of her.

The police officers were most polite and considerate. When she came out, they attended her in quite a deferential manner. As the sergeant was in the act of opening the street door, the bell rang; and when the door opened it disclosed Mr. Parker standing on threshold. He was about to address Mrs. Burnaby but she passed him with a slight bow, and descended the steps, preceded by the sergeant and followed by the detective. The former held the door of the cab open while she entered, when he entered also and shut the door. The detective took his seat beside the driver and the cab moved off.

"What is in the wind, Jardine?" Parker asked looking at me with a distinctly alarmed expression. "Those fellows look like plain-clothes policemen."

"They are," said I. "They have just arrest Mrs. Burnaby on a charge of having attempted to poison her husband."

I thought Parker would have fallen. As it was, he staggered to a hall chair and dropped on it in a state of collapse. "Good God!" he gasped. "What a frightful thing! But there can't possibly be any evidence--any real grounds for suspecting her. It must be just a wild guess. I wonder who started it."

On this subject I had pretty strong suspicions, but I did not mention them; and when I had seen Parker into the dining-room and explained matters a little further I went upstairs, bracing myself for my very disagreeable task.

Burnaby was quite recovered, though rather torpid from the effects of the morphine. But my news roused him most effectually. In a moment he was out of bed, hurriedly preparing to dress; and though his pale, set face told how deeply the catastrophe had shocked him, he was quite collected and had all his wits about him.

"It's of no use letting our emotions loose, doctor," said he, in reply to my expressions of sympathy. "Margaret is in a very dangerous position. You have only to consider what she is--a young, beautiful woman--and what I am, to realise that. We must act promptly. I shall go and see her father; he is a very capable lawyer; and we must get a first-class counsel."

This seemed to be an opportunity for mentioning Thorndyke's peculiar qualifications in a case of this kind, and I did so. Burnaby listened attentively, apparently not unimpressed; but he replied cautiously: "We shall have to leave the choice of the counsel to Harratt; but if you care, meanwhile, to consult with Dr. Thorndyke, you have my authority. I will tell Harratt."

On this I took my departure, not a little relieved at the way he had taken the evil tidings; and as soon as I had disposed of the more urgent part of my work, I betook myself to Thorndyke's chambers, just in time to catch him on his return from the Courts.

"Well, Jardine," he said, when I had brought the history up to date, "what is it that you want me to do?"

"I want you to do what you can to establish Mrs. Burnaby's innocence," I replied.

He looked at me reflectively for a few moments; then he said, quietly but rather significantly: "It is not my practice to give ex parte evidence. An expert witness cannot act as an advocate. If I investigate the evidence in this case, it will have to be at your risk, as representing the accused, since any fact, no matter how damaging, which is in the possession of the witness must be disclosed in accordance with the terms of the oath, to say nothing of the obvious duty of every person to further the ends of justice. Speaking as a lawyer, and taking the known facts at their face value, I do not advise you to employ me to investigate the case at large. You might find that you had merely strengthened the hand of the prosecution.

"But I will make a suggestion. There seems to me to be in this case a very curious and interesting possibility. Let me investigate that independently. If my inquiries yield a positive result, I will let you know and you can call me as a witness. If they yield a negative result, you had better leave me out of the case."

To this suggestion I necessarily agreed; but when I took my leave of Thorndyke I went away with a sense of discouragement and failure. His reference to "the face value of the known facts" clearly implied that those facts were adverse to the accused; while the " curious possibility" suggested nothing but a forlorn hope from which he had no great expectations.

I need not follow the weary business in detail. At the first hearing before the magistrate the police merely stated the charge and gave evidence of arrest, both they and the defence asking for a remand and neither apparently desiring to show their hand. Accordingly the case was adjourned for seven days, and as bail was refused, the prisoner was detained in custody.

During those seven dreary days I spent as much time as I could with Burnaby, and though I was filled with admiration of his fortitude and self his drawn and pallid face wrung my heart. In those few days he seemed to have changed into an old man. At his house I also met Mr. Harratt, Mrs. Burnaby's father, a fine, dignified man and a typical old lawyer; and it was unspeakably pathetic to see the father and the husband of the accused woman each trying to support the courage of the other while both were torn with anxiety and apprehension. On one occasion Mr. Parker was present and looked more haggard and depressed than either. But Mr. Harratt's manner towards him was so frigid and forbidding that he did not repeat his visit. At these meetings we discussed the case freely, which was a further affliction to me. For even I could not fail to see that any evidence that I could give directly supported the case for the prosecution.

So six of the seven days ran out, and all the time there was no word from Thorndyke. But on the evening of the sixth day I received a letter from him, curt and dry, but still giving out a ray of hope. This was the brief message:

"I have gone into the question of which I spoke to you and consider that the point is worth raising. I have accordingly written to Mr. Harratt advising him to that effect."

It was a somewhat colourless communication. But I knew Thorndyke well enough to realise that his promises usually understated his intentions. And when, on the following morning, I met Mr. Harratt and Burnaby at the court, something in their manner--a new vivacity and expectancy – suggested that Thorndyke had been more explicit in his communication to the lawyer. But, all the same, their anxiety, for all their outward courage, was enough to have touched a heart of stone.

The spectacle that that court presented when the case was called forms a tableau that is painted on my memory in indelible colours. The mingling of squalor and tragedy, of frivolity and dread solemnity--the grave magistrate on the bench, the stolid policemen, the busy, preoccupied lawyers, and the gibbering crowd of spectators, greedy for sensation, with eager eyes riveted on the figure in the dock--offered such a medley of contrasts as I hope never to look upon again.

As to the prisoner herself, her appearance brought my heart into my mouth. Rigid as a marble statue and nearly as void of colour, she stood in the dock, guarded by two constables, looking with stony bewilderment on the motley scene, outwardly calm, but with the calm of one who looks death in the face; and when the prosecuting counsel rose to open the case for the police, she looked at him as a victim on the scaffold might look upon the executioner.

As I listened to the brief opening address, my heart sank, though the counsel, Sir Harold Layton, K.C., presented his case with that scrupulous fairness to the accused that makes an English court of justice a thing without parallel in the world. But the mere facts, baldly stated without comment, were appalling. No persuasive rhetoric was needed to show that they led direct to the damning conclusion.

Frank Burnaby, an elderly man, married to a young and beautiful woman, had on three separate occasions had administered to him a certain deadly poison, to wit, atropine. It would be proved that he had suffered from the effects of that poison; that the symptoms followed the taking of certain articles of food of which he alone had partaken; that the said food did actually contain the said poison; and that the food which contained the poison was specially prepared for his sole consumption by his wife, the accused, with her own hands. No evidence was at present available as to how the accused obtained the poison or that she had any such poison in her possession, nor would any suggestion be offered as to the motive of the crime. But, on the evidence of the actual administration of the poison, he would ask that the prisoner be committed for trial. He then proceeded to call the witnesses, of whom I was naturally the first. When I had been sworn and given my description, the counsel asked a few questions which elicited the history of the case and which I need not repeat. He then continued:

"Have you any doubt as to the cause of Mr. Burnaby's symptoms?"

"No. They were certainly due to atropine poisoning."

"Has Mr. Burnaby any constitutional peculiarity in respect of atropine?"

"Yes. He is abnormally susceptible to the effects of atropine."

"Was this peculiar susceptibility known to the accused?"

"Yes. It was communicated to her by me."

"Was it known, so far as you are aware, to any other persons?"

"Mr. Parker was present when I told her, and Mr. Burnaby and his brother, Dr. Burnaby, were also informed."

"Is there any way, so far as you know, in which the accused could have obtained possession of atropine?"

"Only by having the oculist's prescription for the eye-drops made up."

"Do you know of any medium, other than the food, by which atropine might have been taken by Mr. Burnaby?"

"I do not," I replied; and this concluded my evidence. But as I stepped out of the witness-box, I reflected gloomily that every word that I had spoken was a rivet in the fetters of the silent figure in the dock.

The next witness was the cook. She testified that she had killed and skinned the rabbit and had then handed it to the accused, who made it into a fricassee and prepared it for the table. Witness took no part in the preparation and she was absent from the kitchen on one occasion for several minutes, leaving the accused there alone.

When the cook had concluded her evidence, the name of James Burnaby was called, and the doctor entered the witness-box, looking distinctly uncomfortable, but grim and resolute. The first few questions elicited the circumstances of his visit to his brother's house and of the sudden attack of illness. That illness he had at once recognised as acute atropine poisoning, and had assumed that the poison was in the specially prepared food.

"Did you take any measures to verify this opinion?" counsel asked.

"Yes. As soon as I was alone, I took part of the remainder of the rabbit and put it in a glass jar which I found on the mantelpiece and which I first rinsed out with water. Later, I carried the sample of food to Professor Berry, who analysed it in my presence and found it to contain atropine. He obtained from it a thirtieth of a grain of atropine sulphate."

"Is that a poisonous dose?"

"Not to an ordinary person, though it is considerably beyond the medicinal dose. But it would have been a poisonous dose to Frank Burnaby. If he had swallowed this, in addition to what he had already taken, I feel no doubt that it would have killed him."

This concluded the case for the prosecution, and a black case it undoubtedly looked. There was no cross-examination; and as Thorndyke had arrived some time previously and conferred with Mr. Harratt and his counsel, I concluded that the defence would take the form of a counter-attack by the raising of a fresh issue. And so it turned out. When Thorndyke entered the witness-box and had disposed of the preliminaries, the counsel for the defence "gave him his head."

"You have made certain investigations in regard to this case, I believe?" Thorndyke assented, and the counsel continued: "I will not ask you specific questions, but will request you to describe your investigations and their result, and tell us what caused you to make them."

"This case," Thorndyke began, "was brought to my notice by Dr. Jardine, who gave me all the facts known to him. These facts were very remarkable, and, taken together, they suggested a possible explanation of the poisoning. There were four striking points in the case. First, there was the very unusual nature of the poison. Second, the abnormal susceptibility of Mr. Burnaby to this particular poison. Third, the fact that all the food in which the poison appeared to have been conveyed came from the same source: it was sent by Mr. Cyril Parker. Fourth, that food consisted of pigeon's eggs, pigeon's flesh, and rabbit's flesh."

"What is there remarkable about that?" the counsel asked.

"The remarkable point is that the pigeon and the rabbit have an extraordinary immunity to atropine. Most vegetable-feeding birds and animals are more or less immune to vegetable poisons. Many birds and animals are largely immune to atropine; but among birds the pigeon is exceptionally immune, while the rabbit is the most extreme instance among animals. A single rabbit can take without the slightest harm more than a hundred times the quantity of atropine that would kill a man; and rabbits habitually feed freely on the leaves and berries of the belladonna or deadly nightshade."

"Does the deadly nightshade contain atropine?" the counsel asked.

"Yes. Atropine is the active principle of the belladonna plant and gives to it its poisonous properties."

"And if an animal, such as a rabbit, were to feed on the nightshade plant, would its flesh be poisonous?"

"Yes. Cases of belladonna poisoning from eating rabbit have been recorded--by Firth and Bentley, for instance."

"And you suspected that the poison in this case had been contained in the pigeon and the rabbit themselves?"

"Yes. It was a striking coincidence that the poisoning should follow the consumption of these two specially immune animals. But there was a further reason for connecting them. The symptoms were strictly proportionate to the probable amount of poison in each case. Thus the symptoms were only slight after eating the pigeon's eggs. But the eggs of a poisoned pigeon could contain only a minute quantity of the poison. After eating the pigeon the symptoms were much more severe, and the body of a pigeon which had fed on belladonna would contain much more atropine than could be contained in an egg. Finally, after eating the rabbit, the symptoms were extremely violent; but a rabbit has the greatest immunity and is the most likely to have eaten large quantities of belladonna leaves."

"Did you take any measures to put your theory to the test? "

"Yes. Last Monday I went to Eltham, where I had ascertained that Mr. Cyril Parker lives, and inspected his premises from the outside. At the end of his garden is a small paddock enclosed by a wall. Approaching this across a meadow and looking over the wall, I saw that the enclosure was provided with small fowl-houses, pigeon-cotes, and rabbit hutches. All these were open and their inmates were roaming about the paddock. On one side of the enclosure, by the wall was a dense mass of deadly nightshade plants, extending the whole length of the wall and about a couple of yards in width. At one part of this was a ring fence of wire netting, and inside it were five half-grown rabbits, There was a basket containing a small quantity of cabbage leaves and other green stuff, but as I watched, I saw the young rabbits browsing freely on the nightshade plants in preference to the food provided for them.

"On the following day I went to Eltham again taking with me an assistant who carried a young rabbit in a small hamper. We watched the paddock until the coast was clear. Then my assistant got over the wall and abstracted a young rabbit from inside the ring fence and handed it to me. He then took the rabbit from the hamper and dropped it inside the fence. As soon as we were clear of the meadow, we killed the captured rabbit-- to prevent any possible elimination of any poison that it might have swallowed. On arriving in London, I at once took the dead rabbit to St. Margaret's Hospital, where, in the chemical laboratory, and in the presence of Dr. Woodford, the Professor of

Chemistry, I skinned it and prepared it as if for cooking by removing the viscera. I then separated the flesh from the bones and handed the former to Dr. Woodford, who, in my presence, carried out an exhaustive chemical test for atropine. The result was that atropine was found to be present in all the muscles; and, on making a quantitative test, the muscles alone yielded no less than .93 grain."

"Is that a poisonous dose?" the counsel asked.

"Yes; it is a poisonous dose for a normal man. In the case of an abnormally susceptible person like Mr. Burnaby it would certainly be a fatal dose."

This completed Thorndyke's evidence. There was no cross and the magistrate put no questions. When Dr. Woodford had been called and had given confirmatory evidence, Mrs. Burnaby's counsel proceeded to address the bench. But the magistrate cut him short.

"There is really no case to argue," said he. "The evidence of the expert witnesses makes it perfectly clear that the poison was already in the food when it came into the hands of the accused. Consequently the charge against her of introducing the poison falls to the ground and the case must be dismissed. I am sure everyone will sympathise with the unfortunate lady who has been the victim of these extraordinary circumstances, and will rejoice, as I do, at the clearing up of the mystery. The prisoner is discharged."

It was a dramatic moment when, amidst the applause of the spectators, Mrs. Burnaby stepped down from the dock and clasped her husband's outstretched hand But, overwhelmed as they both were by the sudden relief, I thought it best not to linger, but, after congratulations, to take myself off with Thorndyke, But one pleasant incident I witnessed before I went Dr. Burnaby had been standing apart, evidently some what embarrassed, when suddenly Mrs. Burnaby ran to him and held out her hand.

"I suppose, Margaret," he said gruffly, "you think I'm an old beast?"

"Indeed I don't," she replied. "You acted quite properly, and I respect you for having the moral courage to do it. And don't forget, Jim, that you action has saved Frank's life. But for you, there would have been no Dr. Thorndyke; and but for Dr. Thorndyke, there would have been another poisoned rabbit."

"What do you make of this case?" I asked, as Thorndyke and I walked away from the court. "Do you suppose the poisoning was accidental?

He shook his head. "No, Jardine," he replied. "There are too many coincidences. You notice that the poisoned animals did not appear until after Mr Parker had learned from you that Burnaby was abnormally sensitive to atropine and could consequently be poisoned by an ordinary medicinal dose. Then the sending of the animals alive looks like a precaution divert suspicion from himself and confuse the issue Again, that ring fence among the belladonna plans has a fishy look, and the plants themselves were not only abnormally numerous but many of them very young and looked as if they had been planted. Further, I happen to know that Parker's firm published, only last year, a book on toxicology in which the immunity of pigeons and rabbits was mentioned and which Parker probably read."

"Then do you believe that he intended to let Mrs. Burnaby--the woman with whom he was in love--bear the brunt of his crime? It seems incredibly villainous and cowardly."

"I do not," he replied. "I imagine that the rabbit that I captured, or one of the others, would have been sent to Burnaby in a few days' time. The cook would probably have prepared it for him and it would almost certainly have killed him; and his death would have been proof of Mrs. Burnaby's innocence. Suspicion would have been transferred to the cook. But I don't suppose any action will be taken against him, for it is practically certain that no jury would convict him on my evidence."

Thorndyke was right in his opinion. No proceedings were taken against Parker. But the house of the Burnabys knew him no more.

A Mystery of the Sand-Hills

I have occasionally wondered how often Mystery and Romance present themselves to us ordinary men of affairs only to be passed by without recognition. More often, I suspect than most of us imagine. The uncanny tendency of my talented friend John Thorndyke to become involved in strange, mysterious and abnormal circumstances has almost become a joke against him. But yet, on reflection, I am disposed to think that his experiences have not differed essentially from those of other men, but that his extraordinary powers of observation and rapid inference have enabled him to detect abnormal elements in what, to ordinary men, appeared to be quite commonplace occurrences. Certainly this was so in the singular Roscoff case, in which, if I had been alone, I should assuredly have seen nothing to merit more than a passing attention.

It happened that on a certain summer morning--it was the fourteenth of August, to be exact--we were discussing this very subject as we walked across the golf-links from Sandwich towards the sea. I was spending a holiday in the old town with my wife, in order that she might paint the ancient streets, and we had induced Thorndyke to come down and stay with us for a few days. This was his last morning, and we had come forth betimes to stroll across the sand-hills to Shellness.

It was a solitary place in those days. When we came off the sand-hills on to the smooth, sandy beach, there was not a soul in sight, and our own footprints were the first to mark the firm strip of sand between high-water mark and the edge of the quiet surf.

We had walked a hundred yards or so when Thorndyke stopped and looked down at the dry sand above tide-marks and then along the wet beach.

"Would that be a shrimper?" he cogitated, referring to some impressions of bare feet in the sand. "If so, he couldn't have come from Pegwell, for the River Stour bars the way. But he came out of the sea and seems to have made straight for the sand-hills."

"Then he probably was a shrimper," said I, not deeply interested.

"Yet," said Thorndyke, "it was an odd time for a shrimper to be at work."

"What was an odd time?" I demanded. "When was he at work?"

"He came out of the sea at this place," Thorndyke replied, glancing at his watch, "at about half-past eleven last night, or from that to twelve."

"Good Lord, Thorndyke!" I exclaimed, "how on earth do you know that?"

"But it is obvious, Anstey," he replied. "It is now half-past nine, and it will be high-water at eleven, as we ascertained before we came out. Now, if you look at those footprints on the sand, you see that they stop short--or rather begin--about two-thirds of the distance from high-water mark to the edge of the surf. Since they are visible and distinct, they must have been made after last high-water. But since they do not extend to the water's edge, they must have been made when the tide was going out; and the place where they begin is the place where the edge of the surf was when the footprints were made. But the place is, as we see, about an hour below the high-water mark, Therefore, when the man came out of the sea, the tide had been going down for an hour, roughly. As it is high-water at eleven this morning, it was high-water at about ten-forty last night; and as the man came out of the sea about an hour after high-water, he must have come out at, or about, eleven-forty. Isn't that obvious?"

"Perfectly," I replied, laughing. "It is as simple as sucking eggs when you think it out. But how the deuce do you manage always to spot these obvious things at a glance? Most men would have just glanced at those footprints and passed them without a second thought."

"That", he replied, "is a mere matter of habit; the habit of trying to extract the significance of simple appearances. It has become almost automatic with me."

During our discussion we had been walking forward slowly, straying on to the edge of the sand-hills. Suddenly, in a hollow between the hills, my eye lighted upon a heap of clothes, apparently, to judge by their orderly disposal, those of a bather. Thorndyke also had observed them and we approached together and looked down on them curiously.

"Here is another problem for you," said I. "Find the bather. I don't see him anywhere."

"You won't find him here," said Thorndyke. "These clothes have been out all night. Do you see the little spider's web on the boots with a few dewdrops still clinging to it? There has been no dew forming for a good many hours. Let us have a look at the beach."

We strode out through the loose sand and stiff, reedy grass to the smooth beach, and here we could plainly see a line of prints of naked feet leading straight down to the sea, but ending abruptly about two-thirds of the way to the water's edge.

"This looks like our nocturnal shrimper," said I. "He seems to have gone into the sea here and come out at the other place. But if they are the same footprints, he must have forgotten to dress before he went home. It is a quaint affair."

"It is a most remarkable affair," Thorndyke agreed; "and if the footprints are not the same it will be still more inexplicable."

He produced from his pocket a small spring tape-measure with which he carefully took the lengths of two of the most distinct footprints and the length of the stride. Then we walked back along the beach to the other set of tracks, two of which he measured in the same manner.

"Apparently they are the same," he said, putting away his tape; "indeed, they could hardly be otherwise. But the mystery is, what has become of the man? He couldn't have gone away without his clothes, unless he is a lunatic, which his proceedings rather suggest. There is just the possibility that he went into the sea again and was drowned. Shall we walk along towards Shellness and see if we can find any further traces?"

We walked nearly half a mile along the beach, but the smooth surface of the sand was everywhere unbroken. At length we turned to retrace our steps; and at this moment I observed two men advancing across the sand-hills. By the time we had reached the mysterious heap of garments they were quite near, and, attracted no doubt by the intentness with which we were regarding the clothes, they altered their course to see what we were looking at. As they approached, I recognized one of them as a barrister named Hallet, a neighbour of mine in the Temple, whom I had already met in the town, and we exchanged greetings.

"What is the excitement?" he asked, looking at the heap of clothes and then glancing along the deserted beach; "and where is the owner of the togs? I don't see him anywhere."

"That is the problem," said I. "He seems to have disappeared."

"Gad!" exclaimed Hallett, "if he has gone home without his clothes, He'll create a sensation in the town! What?"

Here the other man, who carried a set of golf clubs, stooped over the clothes with a look of keen interest.

"I believe I recognize these things, Hallett; in fact, I am sure I do. That waistcoat, for instance. You must have noticed that waistcoat. I saw you playing with the chap a couple of days ago. Tall, clean-shaven, dark fellow. Temporary member, you know. What was his name? Popoff, or something like that?"

"Roscoff," said Hallett. "Yes, by Jove, I believe you are right. And now I come to think of it, he mentioned to me that he sometimes came up here for a swim. He said he particularly liked a paddle by moonlight, and I told him he was a fool to run the risk of bathing in a lonely place like this, especially at night."

"Well, that is what he seems to have done," said Thorndyke, "for these clothes have certainly been here all night, as you can see by that spider's web."

"Then he has come to grief, poor beggar!" said Hallett; "probably got carried away by the current. There is a devil of a tide here on the flood."

He started to walk towards the beach, and the other man, dropping his clubs, followed.

"Yes," said Hallett, "that is what has happened. You can see his footprints plainly enough going down to the sea; but there are no tracks coming back."

"There are some tracks of bare feet coming out of the sea farther up the beach," said I, "which seem to be his."

Hallett shook his head. "They can't be his," he said, "for it is obvious that he never did come back. Probably they are the tracks of some shrimper. The question is, what are we to do! Better take his things to the dormy-house and then let the police know what has happened."

We went back and began to gather up the clothes, each of us taking one or two articles.

"You were right, Morris," said Hallett, as he picked up the shirt. "Here's his name, "P. Roscoff", and I see it is on the vest and the shorts, too. And I recognize the stick now not that that matters, as the clothes are marked."

On our way across the links to the dormy-house mutual introductions took place. Morris was a London solicitor, and both he and Hallett knew Thorndyke by name.

"The coroner will have an expert witness," Hallett remarked as we entered the house. "Rather a waste in a simple case like this. We had better put the things in here."

He opened the door of a small room furnished with a good-sized table and a set of lockers, into one of which he inserted a key.

"Before we lock them up," said Thorndyke, "I suggest that we make and sign a list of them and of the contents of the pockets to put with them."

"Very well," agreed Hallett. "You know the ropes in these cases. I'll write down the descriptions, if you will call them out."

Thorndyke looked over the collection and first enumerated the articles: a tweed jacket and trousers, light, knitted wool waistcoat, black and yellow stripes, blue cotton shirt, net vest and shorts, marked in ink "P. Roscoff", brown merino socks, brown shoes, tweed cap, and a walking-stick--a mottled Malacca cane with a horn crooked handle. When Hallett had written down this list, Thorndyke laid the clothes on the table and began to empty the pockets, one at a time, dictating the descriptions of the articles to Hallett while Morris took them from him and laid them on a sheet of newspaper. In the jacket pockets were a handkerchief, marked "P.R."; a letter-case containing a few stamps, one or two hotel bills and local tradesmen's receipts, and some visiting cards inscribed "Mr. Peter Roscoff, Bell Hotel, Sandwich"; a leather cigarette-case, a 3B pencil fitted with a point-protector, and a fragment of what Thorndyke decided to be vine charcoal.

"That lot is not very illuminating," remarked Morris, peering into the pockets of the letter-case. "No letter or anything indicating his permanent address. However, that isn't our concern." He laid aside the letter-case, and picking up a pocket-knife that Thorndyke had just taken from the trousers pocket, examined it curiously. "Queer knife, that," he remarked. 'steel blade--mighty sharp, too--nail file and an ivory blade. Silly arrangement, it seems. A paperknife is more convenient carried loose, and you don't want a handle to it."

"Perhaps it was meant for a fruit-knife," suggested Hallett, adding it to the list and glancing at a little heap of silver coins that Thorndyke had just laid down. "I wonder", he added, "what has made that money turn so black. Looks! as if he had been taking some medicine containing sulphur. What do you think, doctor?"

"It is quite a probable explanation," replied Thorndyke, "though we haven't the means of testing it. But you notice that this vesta-box from the other pocket is quite bright, which is rather against your theory."

He held out a little silver box bearing the engraved monogram "P.R.", the burnished surface of which contrasted strongly with the dull brownish-black of the coins. Hallett looked at it with an affirmative grunt, and having entered it in his list and added a bunch of keys and a watch from the waistcoat pocket, laid down his pen.

"That's the lot, is it?" said he, rising and beginning to gather up the clothes. "My word! Look at the sand on the table! Isn't it astonishing how saturated with sand one's clothes become after a day on the links here? When I undress at night, the bathroom floor is like the bottom of a bird-cage. Shall I put the things in the locker now?"

"I think", said Thorndyke, "that, as I may have to give evidence, I should like to look them over before you put them away."

Hallett grinned. "There's going to be some expert evidence after all," he said. "Well, fire away, and let me know when you have finished. I am going to smoke a cigarette outside."

With this, he and Morris sauntered out, and I thought it best to go with them, though I was a little curious as to my colleague's object in examining these derelicts. However, my curiosity was not entirely baulked, for my friends went no farther than the little garden that surrounded the house, and from the place where we stood I was able to look in through the window and observe Thorndyke's proceedings.

Very methodical they were. First he laid on the table a sheet of newspaper and on this deposited the jacket, which he examined carefully all over, picking some small object off the inside near the front, and giving special attention to a thick smear of paint which I had noticed on the left cuff. Then, with his spring tape he measured the sleeves and other principal dimensions. Finally, holding the jacket upside down, he beat it gently with his stick, causing a shower of sand to fall on the paper. He then laid the jacket aside, and, taking from his pocket one or two seed envelopes (which I believe he always carried), very carefully shot the sand from the paper into one of them and wrote a few words on it--presumably the source of the sand--and similarly disposing of the small object that he had picked off the surface.

This rather odd procedure was repeated with the other garments--a fresh sheet of newspaper being used for each and with the socks, shoes, and cap. The latter he examined minutely, especially as to the inside, from which he picked out two or three small objects, which I could not see, but assumed to be hairs. Even the walking-stick was inspected and measured, and the articles from the pockets scrutinized afresh, particularly the curious pocket-knife, the ivory blade of which he examined on both sides through his lens.

Hallett and Morris glanced in at him from time to time with indulgent smiles, and the former remarked:

"I like the hopeful enthusiasm of the real pukka expert, and the way he refuses to admit the existence of the ordinary and commonplace. I wonder what he has found out from those things. But here he is. Well, doctor, what's the verdict? Was it temporary insanity or misadventure?"

Thorndyke shook his head. "The inquiry is adjourned pending the production of fresh evidence," he replied, adding: "I have folded the clothes up and put all the effects together in a paper parcel, excepting the stick."

When Hallett had deposited the derelicts in the locker, he came out and looked across the links with an air of indecision.

"I suppose," said he, "we ought to notify the police. I'll do that. When do you think the body is likely to wash up, and where?"

"It is impossible to say," replied Thorndyke. "The set of the current is towards the Thames, but the body might wash up anywhere along the coast. A case is recorded of a bather drowned off Brighton whose body came up six weeks later at Walton-on-the-Naze. But that was quite exceptional. I shall send the coroner and the Chief Constable a note with my address, and I should think you had better do the same. And that is all that we can do, until we get the summons for the inquest, if there ever is one."

To this we all agreed; and as the morning was now spent we walked back together across the links to the town, where we encountered my wife returning homeward with her sketching kit. This Thorndyke and I took possession of and having parted from Hallett and Morris opposite the Barbican, we made our way to our lodgings in quest of lunch. Naturally, the events of the morning were related to my wife and discussed by us all, but I noted that Thorndyke made no reference to his inspection of the clothes, and accordingly I said nothing about the matter before my wife; and no opportunity of opening the subject occurred until the evening, when I accompanied him to the station. Then, as we paced the platform while waiting for his train, I put my question:

"By the way, did you extract any information from those garments? I saw you going through them very thoroughly."

"I got a suggestion from them," he replied, "but it is such an odd one that I hardly like to mention it. Taking the appearances at their face value, the suggestion was that the clothes were not all those of the same man. There seemed to be traces of two men, one of whom appeared to belong to this district, while the other would seem to have been associated with the eastern coast of Thanet between Ramsgate and Margate, and by preference, on the scale of probabilities, to Dumpton or Broadstairs."

"How on earth did you arrive at the localities?" I asked.

"Principally," he replied, "by the peculiarities of the sand which fell from the garments and which was not the same in all of them. You see, Anstey," he continued, 'sand is analogous to dust. Both consist of minute fragments detached from larger masses; and just as, by examining microscopically the dust of a room, you can ascertain the colour and material of the carpets, curtains, furniture coverings, and other textiles, detached particles of which form the dust of that room, so, by examining sand, you can judge of the character of the cliffs, rocks, and other large masses that occur in the locality, fragments of which become ground off by the surf and incorporated in the sand of the beach. Some of the sand from these clothes is very characteristic and will probably be still more so when I examine it under the microscope."

"But", I objected, "isn't there a fallacy in that line of reasoning? Might not one man have worn the different garments at different times and in different places?"

"That is certainly a possibility that has to be borne in mind," he replied. "But here comes my train. We shall have to adjourn this discussion until you come back to the mill."

As a matter of fact, the discussion was never resumed, for, by the time that I came back to "the mill", the affair had faded from my mind, and the accumulations of grist monopolized my attention; and it is probable that it would have passed into complete oblivion but for the circumstance of its being revived in a very singular manner, which was as follows.

One afternoon about the middle of October my old friend, Mr. Brodribb, a well-known solicitor, called to give me some verbal instructions. When he had finished our business, he said:

"I've got a client waiting outside, whom I am taking up to introduce to Thorndyke. You'd better come along with us."

"What is the nature of your client's case?" I asked.

"Hanged if I know," chuckled Brodribb. "He won't say. That's why I am taking him to our friend. I've never seen Thorndyke stumped yet, but I think this case will put the lid on him. Are you coming?"

"I am, most emphatically," said I, "if your client doesn't object."

"He's not going to be asked," said Brodribb. "He'll think you are part of the show. Here he is."

In my outer office we found a gentlemanly, middle-aged man to whom Brodribb introduced me, and whom he hustled down the stairs and up King's Bench Walk to Thorndyke's chambers. There we found my colleague earnestly studying a will with the aid of a watchmaker's eye-glass, and Brodribb opened the proceedings without ceremony.

"I've brought a client of mine, Mr. Capes, to see you, Thorndyke. He has a little problem that he wants you to solve."

Thorndyke bowed to the client and then asked:

"What is the nature of the problem?"

"Ah!" said Brodribb, with a mischievous twinkle, "that's what you've got to find out. Mr. Capes is a somewhat reticent gentleman."

Thorndyke cast a quick look at the client and from him to the solicitor. It was not the first time that old Brodribb's high spirits had overflowed in the form of a "leg-pull", though Thorndyke had no more whole-hearted admirer than the shrewd, facetious old lawyer.

Mr. Capes smiled a deprecating smile. "It isn't quite so bad as that," he said. "But I really can't give you much information. It isn't mine to give. I am afraid of telling someone else's secrets, if I say very much."

"Of course you mustn't do that," said Thorndyke. "But, I suppose you can indicate in general terms the nature of your difficulty and the kind of help you want from us."

"I think I can," Mr. Capes replied. "At any rate, I will try. My difficulty is that a certain person with whom I wish to communicate has disappeared in what appears to me to be a rather remarkable manner. When I last heard from him, he was staying at a certain seaside resort and he stated in his letter that he was returning on the following day to his rooms in London. A few days later, I called at his rooms and found that he had not yet returned. But his luggage, which he had sent on independently, had arrived on the day which he had mentioned. So it is evident that he must have left his seaside lodgings. But from that day to this I have had no communication from him, and he has never returned to his rooms nor written to his landlady."

"About how long ago was this?" Thorndyke asked.

"It is just about two months since I heard from him."

"You don't wish to give the name of the seaside resort where he was staying."

"I think I had better not," answered Mr. Capes. "There are circumstances--they don't concern me, but they do concern him very much--which seem to make it necessary for me to say as little as possible."

"And there is nothing further that you can tell us?"

"I am afraid not, excepting that, if I could get into communication with him, I could tell him of something very much to his advantage and which might prevent him from doing something which it would be much better that he should not do."

Thorndyke cogitated profoundly while Brodribb watched him with undisguised enjoyment. Presently my colleague looked up and addressed our secretive client.

"Did you ever play the game of "Clump", Mr. Capes? It is a somewhat legal form of game in which one player asks questions of the others, who are required to answer "yes" or "no" in the proper witness-box style."

"I know the game," said Capes, looking a little puzzled, "but—"

"Shall we try a round or two?" asked Thorndyke, with an unmoved countenance. "You don't wish to make any statements, but if I ask you certain specific questions, will you answer "yes or no"?"

Mr. Capes reflected awhile. At length he said: "I am afraid I can't commit myself to a promise. Still, if you like to ask a question or two, I will answer them if I can."

"Very well," said Thorndyke, "then, as a start, supposing I suggest that the date of the letter that you received was the thirteenth of August? What do you say? Yes or no?"

Mr. Capes sat bolt upright and stared at Thorndyke open-mouthed.

"How on earth did you guess that?" he exclaimed in an astonished tone. "It's most extraordinary! But you are right. It was dated the thirteenth."

"Then," said Thorndyke, "as we have fixed the time we will have a try at the place. What do you say if I suggest that the seaside resort was in the neighbourhood of Broadstairs?"

Mr. Capes was positively thunderstruck. As he sat gazing at Thorndyke he looked like amazement personified.

"But," he exclaimed, "you can't be guessing! You know! You know that he was at Broadstairs. And yet, how could you? I haven't even hinted at who he is."

"I have a certain man in my mind," said Thorndyke, "who may have disappeared from Broadstairs. Shall I suggest a few personal characteristics?"

Mr. Capes nodded eagerly and Thorndyke continued:

"If I suggest, for instance, that he was an artist--a painter in oil"-- Capes nodded again--"that he was somewhat fastidious as to his pigments?"

"Yes," said Capes. "Unnecessarily so in my opinion, and I am an artist myself. What else?"

"That he worked with his palette in his right hand and held his brush with his left?"

"Yes, yes," exclaimed Capes, half-rising from his chair; "and what was he like?"

"By gum," murmured Brodribb, "we haven't stumped him after all."

Evidently we had not, for he proceeded:

"As to his physical characteristics, I suggest that he was a shortish man--about five feet seven--rather stout, fair hair, slightly bald and wearing a rather large and ragged moustache."

Mr. Capes was astounded--and so was I, for that matter--and for some moments there was a silence, broken only by old Brodribb, who sat chuckling softly and rubbing his hands. At length Mr. Capes said:

"You have described him exactly, but I needn't tell you that. What I do not understand at all is how you knew that I was referring to this particular man, seeing that I mentioned no name. By the way, sir, may I ask when you saw him last?"

"I have no reason to suppose," replied Thorndyke, "that I have ever seen him at all"; an answer that reduced Mr. Capes to a state of stupefaction and brought our old friend Brodribb to the verge of apoplexy. "This man," Thorndyke continued, "is a purely hypothetical individual whom I have described from certain traces left by him. I have reason to believe that he left Broadstairs on the fourteenth of August and I have certain opinions as to what became of him thereafter. But a few more details would be useful, and I shall continue my interrogation. Now this man sent his luggage on separately. That suggests a possible intention of breaking his journey to London. What do you say?"

"I don't know," replied Capes, "but I think it probable."

"I suggest that he broke his journey for the purpose of holding an interview with some other person."

"I cannot say," answered Capes, "but if he did break his journey it would probably be for that purpose."

"And supposing that interview to have taken place, would it be likely to be an amicable interview?"

"I am afraid not. I suspect that my--er--acquaintance might have made certain proposals which would have been unacceptable, but which he might have been able to enforce. However, that is only surmise," Capes added hastily. "I really know nothing more than I have told you, except the missing man's name, and that I would rather not mention."

"It is not material," said Thorndyke, "at least, not at present. If it should become essential, I will let you know."

"M—yes," said Mr. Capes. "But you were saying that you had certain opinions as to what has become of this person."

"Yes," Thorndyke replied; 'speculative opinions. But they will have to be verified. If they turn out to be correct--or incorrect either--I will let you know in the course of a few days. Has Mr. Brodribb your address?"

"He has; but you had better have it, too."

He produced his card, and, after an ineffectual effort to extract a statement from Thorndyke, took his departure.

The third act of this singular drama opened in the same setting as the first, for the following Sunday morning found my colleague and me following the path from Sandwich to the sea. But we were not alone this time. At our side marched Major Robertson, the eminent dog trainer, and behind him trotted one of his superlatively educated fox-hounds.

We came out on the shore at the same point as on the former occasion, and turning towards Shellness, walked along the smooth sand with a careful eye on the not very distinctive landmarks. At length Thorndyke halted.

"This is the place," said he. "I fixed it in my mind by that distant tree, which coincides with the chimney of that cottage on the marshes. The clothes lay in that hollow between the two big sand-hills."

We advanced to the spot, but, as a hollow is useless as a landmark, Thorndyke ascended the nearest sand-hill and stuck his stick in the summit and tied his handkerchief to the handle.

"That," he said, "will serve as a centre which we can keep in sight, and if we describe a series of gradually widening concentric circles round it, we shall cover the whole ground completely."

"How far do you propose to go?" asked the major.

We must be guided by the appearance of the ground," replied Thorndyke. "But the circumstances suggest that if there is anything buried, it can't be very far from where the clothes were laid. And it is pretty certain to be in a hollow."

The major nodded; and when he had attached a long leash to the dog's collar, we started, at first skirting the base of the sand-hill, and then, guided by our own footmarks in the loose sand, gradually increasing the distance from the high mound, above which Thorndyke's handkerchief fluttered in the light breeze. Thus we continued, walking slowly, keeping close to the previously made circle of footprints and watching the dog; who certainly did a vast amount of sniffing, but appeared to let his mind run unduly on the subject of rabbits.

In this way half an hour was consumed, and I was beginning to wonder whether we were going after all to draw a blank, when the dog's demeanour underwent a sudden change. At the moment we were crossing a range of high sand-hills, covered with stiff, reedy grass and stunted gorse, and before us lay a deep hollow, naked of vegetation and presenting a bare, smooth surface of the characteristic greyish-yellow sand. On the side of the hill the dog checked, and, with upraised muzzle, began to sniff the air with a curiously suspicious expression, clearly unconnected with the rabbit question. On this, the major unfastened the leash, and the dog, left to his own devices, put his nose to the ground and began rapidly to cast to and fro, zig-zagging down the side of the hill and growing every moment more excited. In the same sinuous manner he proceeded across the hollow until he reached a spot near the middle; and here he came to a sudden stop and began to scratch up the sand with furious eagerness.

"It's a find, sure enough!" exclaimed the major, nearly as excited as his pupil; and, as he spoke, he ran down the hillside, followed by me and Thorndyke, who, as he reached the bottom, drew from his "poacher's pocket" a large fern-trowel in a leather sheath. It was not a very efficient digging implement, but it threw up the loose sand faster than the scratchings of the dog.

It was easy ground to excavate. Working at the spot that the dog had located, Thorndyke had soon hollowed out a small cavity some eighteen inches deep. Into the bottom of this he thrust the pointed blade of the big trowel. Then he paused and looked round at the major and me, who were craning eagerly over the little pit.

"There is something there," said he. "Feel the handle of the trowel."

I grasped the wooden handle, and, working it gently up and down, was aware of a definite but somewhat soft resistance. The major verified my observation, and then Thorndyke resumed his digging, widening the pit and working with increased caution. Ten minutes" more careful excavation brought into view a recognizable shape--a shoulder and upper arm; and following the lines of this, further diggings disclosed the form of a head and shoulders plainly discernable though still shrouded in sand. Finally, with the point of the trowel and a borrowed handkerchief--mine--the adhering sand was cleared away; and then, from the bottom of the deep, funnel-shaped hole, there looked up at us, with a most weird and horrible effect, the discoloured face of a man.

In that face, the passing weeks had wrought inevitable changes, on which I need not dwell. But the features were easily recognizable, and I could see at once that the man corresponded completely with Thorndyke's description. The cheeks were full; the hair on the temples was of a pale, yellowish brown; a straggling, fair moustache covered the mouth; and, when the sand had been sufficiently cleared away, I could see a small, tonsure-like bald patch near the back of the crown. But I could see something more than this. On the left temple, just behind the eyebrow, was a ragged, shapeless wound such as might have been made by a hammer.

"That turns into certainty what we have already surmised," said Thorndyke, gently pressing the scalp around the wound. "It must have killed him instantly. The skull is smashed in like an egg-shell. And this is undoubtedly the weapon," he added, drawing out of the sand beside the body a big, hexagon-headed screw-bolt, "very prudently buried with the body. And that is all that really concerns us. We can leave the police to finish the disinterment; but you notice, Anstey, that the corpse is nude with the exception of the vest and probably the pants. The shirt has disappeared. Which is exactly what we should have expected."

Slowly, but with the feeling of something accomplished, we took our way back to the town, having collected Thorndyke's stick on the way. Presently, the major left us, to look up a friend at the club house on the links. As soon as we were alone, I put in a demand for an elucidation.

"I see the general trend of your investigations," said I "but I can't imagine how they yielded so much detail; as to the personal appearance of this man, for instance."

"The evidence in this case," he replied, "was analogous to circumstantial evidence. It depended on the cumulative effect of a number of facts, each separately inconclusive, but all pointing to the same conclusion. Shall I run over the data in their order and in accordance with their connections?"

I gave an emphatic affirmative, and he continued:

"We begin, naturally, with the first fact, which is, of course, the most interesting and important; the fact which arrests attention, which shows that something has to be explained and possibly suggests a line of inquiry. You remember that I measured the footprints in the sand for comparison with the other footprints. Then I had the dimensions of the feet of the presumed bather. But as soon as I looked at the shoes which purported to be those of that bather, I felt a conviction that his feet would never go into them.

"Now, that was a very striking fact--if it really was a fact--and it came on top of another fact hardly less striking, The bather had gone into the sea; and at a considerable distance he had unquestionably come out again. Then, could be no possible doubt. In foot-measurement an, length of stride the two sets of tracks were indentical; and there were no other tracks. That man had come ashore and he had remained ashore. But yet he had not put on his clothes. He couldn't have gone away naked; but obviously he was not there. As a criminal lawyer, you must admit that there was prima fade evidence of something very abnormal and probably criminal.

On our way to the dormy-house, I carried the stick in the same hand as my own and noted that it was very little shorter. Therefore it was a tall man's stick. Apparently, then, the stick did not belong to the shoes, but to the man who had made the footprints. Then, when we came to the dormy-house, another striking fact presented itself. You remember that Hallett commented on the quantity of sand that fell from the clothes on to the table. I am astonished that he did not notice the very peculiar character of that sand. It was perfectly unlike the sand which would fall from his own clothes. The sand on the sand-hills is dune sand-- wind-borne sand, or, as the legal term has it, æolian sand; and it is perfectly characteristic. As it has been carried by the wind, it is necessarily fine. The grains are small; and as the action of the wind sorts them out, they are extremely uniform in size. Moreover, by being continually blown about and rubbed together, they become rounded by mutual attrition. And then dune sand is nearly pure sand, composed of grains of silica unmixed with other substances.

"Beach sand is quite different. Much of it is half-formed, freshly broken down silica and is often very coarse; and, as I pointed out at the time, it is mixed with all sorts of foreign substances derived from masses in the neighbourhood. This particular sand was loaded with black and white particles, of which the white were mostly chalk, and the black particles of coal. Now there is very little chalk in the Shellness sand, as there are no cliffs quite near, and chalk rapidly disappears from sand by reason of its softness; and there is no coal."

"Where does the coal come from?" I asked.

"Principally from the Goodwins," he replied. "It is derived from the cargoes of colliers whose wrecks are embedded in those sands, and from the bunkers of wrecked steamers. This coal sinks down through the seventy odd feet of sand and at last works out at the bottom, where it drifts slowly across the floor of the sea in a north-westerly direction until some easterly gale throws it up on the Thanet shore between Ramsgate and Foreness Point. Most of it comes up at Dumpton and Broadstairs, there you may see the poor people, in the winter, gathering coal pebbles to feed their fires.

"This sand, then, almost certainly came from the Thanet coast; but the missing man, Roscoff, had been staying in Sandwich, playing golf on the sand-hills. This was another striking discrepancy, and it made me decide to examine the clothes exhaustively, garment by garment. I did so; and this is what I found.

"The jacket, trousers, socks and shoes were those of a shortish, rather stout man, as shown by measurements, and the cap was his, since it was made of the same cloth as the jacket and trousers.

"The waistcoat, shirt, underclothes and stick were those of a tall man.

"The garments, socks and shoes of the short man were charged with Thanet beach sand, and contained no dune sand, excepting the cap, which might have fallen off on the sand-hills.

"The waistcoat was saturated with dune sand and contained no beach sand, and a little dune sand was obtained from the shirt and under-garments. That is to say, that the short man's clothes contained beach sand only, while the tall man's clothes contained only dune sand.

"The short man's clothes were all unmarked; the tall man's clothes were either marked or conspicuously recognizable, as the waistcoat and also the stick.

"The garments of the short man which had been left were those that could not have been worn by a tall man without attracting instant attention and the shoes could not have been put on at all; whereas the garments of the short man which had disappeared--the waistcoat, shirt and underclothes-- were those that could have been worn by a tall man without attracting attention. The obvious suggestion was that the tall man had gone off in the short man's shirt and waistcoat but otherwise in his own clothes.

"And now as to the personal characteristics of the short man. From the cap I obtained five hairs. They were all blond, and two of them were of the peculiar, atrophic, "point of exclamation" type that grow at the margin of a bald area. Therefore he was a fair man and partially bald. On the inside of the jacket, clinging to the rough tweed, I found a single long, thin, fair moustache hair, which suggested a long, soft moustache. The edge of the left cuff was thickly marked with oil-paint-not a single smear, but an accumulation such as a painter picks up when he reaches with his brush hand across a loaded palette. The suggestion--not very conclusive--was that he was an oil-painter and left-handed. But there was strong confirmation. There was an artist's pencil--3B--and a stump of vine charcoal such as an oil-painter might carry. The silver coins in his pocket were blackened with sulphide as they would be if a piece of artist's soft, vulcanized rubber has been in the pocket with them. And there was the pocket-knife. It contained a sharp steel pencil-blade, a charcoal file and an ivory palette-blade; and that palette-blade had been used by a left-handed man."

"How did you arrive at that?" I asked.

"By the bevels worn at the edges," he replied. "An old palette-knife used by a right-handed man shows a bevel of wear on the under side of the left-hand edge and the upper side of the right-hand edge; in the case of a left handed man the wear shows on the under side of the right hand edge and the upper side of the left-hand edge. This being an ivory blade, showed the wear very distinctly and proved conclusively that the user was left-handed; and as an ivory palette-knife is used only by fastidiously careful painters for such pigments as the cadmiums, which might be discoloured by a steel blade, one was justified in assuming that he was somewhat fastidious as to his pigments."

As I listened to Thorndyke's exposition I was profoundly impressed. His conclusions, which had sounded like mere speculative guesses, were, I now realized, based upon an analysis of the evidence as careful and as impartial as the summing up of a judge. And these conclusions he had drawn instantaneously from the appearances of things that had been before my eyes all the time and from which I had learned nothing.

"What do you suppose is the meaning of the affair?" I asked presently. "What was the motive of the murder?"

"We can only guess," he replied. "But, interpreting Capes" hints, I should suspect that our artist friend was a blackmailer; that he had come over here to squeeze Roscoff--perhaps not for the first time--and that his victim lured him out on the sand-hills for a private talk and then took the only effective means of ridding himself of his persecutor. That is my view of the case; but, of course, it is only surmise."

Surmise as it was, however, it turned out to be literally correct. At the inquest Capes had to tell all that he knew, which was uncommonly little, though no one was able to add to it. The murdered man, Joseph Bertrand, had fastened on Roscoff and made a regular income by blackmailing him. That much Capes knew; and he knew that the victim had been in prison and that that was the secret. But who Roscoff was and what was his real name--for Roscoff was apparently a nom de guerre--he had no idea. So he could not help the police. The murderer had got clear away and there was no hint as to where to look for him; and so far as I know, nothing has ever been heard of him since.

The Apparition of Burling Court

Thorndyke seldom took a formal holiday. He did not seem to need one. As he himself put it, "A holiday implies the exchange of a less pleasurable occupation for one more pleasurable. But there is no occupation more pleasurable than the practice of Medical Jurisprudence." Moreover, his work was less affected by terms and vacations than that of an ordinary barrister, and the Long Vacation often found him with his hands full. Even when he did appear to take a holiday the appearance tended to be misleading, and it was apt to turn out that his disappearance from his usual haunts was associated with a case of unusual interest at a distance.

Thus it was on the occasion when our old friend, Mr. Brodribb, of Lincoln's Inn, beguiled him into a fortnight's change at St. David's-at-Cliffe, a seaside hamlet on the Kentish coast. There was a case in the background, and a very curious case it turned out to be, though at first it appeared to me quite a commonplace affair; and the manner of its introduction was as follows.

One hot afternoon in the early part of the Long Vacation the old solicitor dropped in for a cup of tea and a chat. That, at least, was how he explained his visit; but my experience of Mr. Brodribb led me to suspect some ulterior purpose in the call, and as he sat by the open window, teacup in hand, looking, with his fine pink complexion, his silky white hair and his faultless "turn out," the very type of the courtly, old-fashioned lawyer, I waited expectantly for the matter of his visit to transpire. And, presently, out it came.

"I am going to take a little holiday down at St. David's," said he. "Just a quiet spell by the sea, you know. Delightful place. So quiet and restful and so breezy and fresh. Ever been there?"

"No," replied Thorndyke. "I only just know the name."

"Well, why shouldn't you come down for a week or so? Both of you. I shall stay at Burling Court, the Lumleys' place. I can't invite you there as I'm only a guest, but I know of some comfortable rooms in the village that I could get for you. I wish you would come down, Thorndyke," he added after a pause. "I'm rather unhappy about young Lumley--I'm the family lawyer, you know, and so was my father and my grandfather, so I feel almost as if the Lumleys were my own kin--and I should like to have your advice and help."

"Why not have it now?" suggested Thorndyke.

"I will," he replied; "but I should like your help on the spot too. I'd like you to see Lumley have a talk with him and tell me what you think of him."

"What is amiss with him?" Thorndyke asked.

"Well," answered Brodribb, "it looks uncomfortably like insanity. He has delusions--sees apparitions and that sort of thing. And there is some insanity in the family. But I had better give you the facts in their natural order.

"About four months ago Giles Lumley of Burling Court died; and as he was a widower without issue, the estate passed to his nearest male relative, my present client, Frank Lumley, who was also the principal beneficiary under the will. At the time of Giles' death Frank was abroad, but a cousin of his, Lewis Price, was staying at the house with his wife as a more or less permanent guest; and as Price's circumstances were not very flourishing, and as he is the next heir to the estate, Frank--who is a bachelor--wrote to him at once telling him to look upon Burling Court as his home for as long as he pleased."

That was extremely generous of him," I remarked

"Yes," Brodribb agreed; "Frank is a good fellow; a very high-minded gentleman and a very sweet man but a little queer--very queer just now. Well, Frank came back from abroad and took up his abode at the house; and for a time all went well. Then, one day, Price called on me and gave me some very unpleasant news. It seemed that Frank, who had always been rather neurotic and imaginative, had been interesting himself a good deal in psychical research and--and balderdash of that kind, you know. Well, there was no great harm in that, perhaps. But just lately he had taken to seeing visions and--what was worse--talking about them; so much so that Price got uneasy and privately invited a mental specialist down to lunch ; and the specialist, having had a longish talk with Frank, Price confidentially that he (Frank) was obviously suffering from insane delusions. Thereupon Price called me and begged me to see Frank myself and what ought to be done; so I made an occasion for him to come and see me at the office."

"And what did you think of him?" asked Thorndyke.

I was horrified--horrified," said Mr. Brodribb. "I assure you, Thorndyke, that that poor young man sat in my office and talked like a stark lunatic. Quite quietly, you know. No excitement, though he was evidently anxious and unhappy. But there he sat gravely talking the damnedest nonsense you ever heard."

"As, for instance--?"

"Well, his infernal visions. Luminous birds flying about in the dark, and a human head suspended in mid air--upside down, too. But I had better give you his story as he told it. I made full shorthand notes as he was talking, and I've brought them with me, though I hardly need them.

"His trouble seems to have begun soon after he took up his quarters at Burling Court. Being a bookish sort of fellow, he started to go through his library systematically; and presently he came across a small manuscript book, which turned out to be a soft of family history, or rather a collection of episodes. It was rather a lurid little book, for it apparently dwelt chiefly on the family crime, the family spectre and the family madness."

"Did you know about these heirlooms?" Thorndyke asked.

"No; it was the first I'd heard of "em. Price knew there was some soft of family superstition, but he didn't know what it was; and Giles knew about it--so Price tells me--but didn't care to talk about it. He never mentioned it to me."

"What is the nature of the tradition? " inquired Thorndyke.

"I'll tell you," said Brodribb, taking out his notes. "I've got it all down, and poor Frank reeled the stuff off as if he had learned it by heart. The book, which is dated 1819, was apparently written by a Walter Lumley and the story of the crime and the spook runs thus:

"About 1720 the property passed to a Gilbert Lumley, a naval officer, who then gave up the sea, married and settled down at Burling Court. A year or two later some trouble arose about his wife and a man named Glynn, a neighbouring squire. With or without cause, Lumley became violently jealous, and the end of it was that he lured Glynn to a large cavern in the cliffs and there murdered him. It was a most ferocious and vindictive crime. The cavern, which was then used by smugglers, had a beam across the roof bearing a tackle for hoisting out boat cargoes, and this tackle Lumley fastened to Glynn's ankles--having first pinioned him--and hoisted him up so that he hung head downwards a foot or so clear of the floor of the cave. And there he left him hanging until the rising tide flowed into the cave and drowned him.

"The very next day the murder was discovered, and as Lumley was the nearest justice of the peace, the discoverers reported to him and took him to the cave to the body. When he entered the cave the corpse was stilt hanging as he had left the living man, and a bat was flittering round and round the dead man's head. He had the body taken down and carried to Glynn's house and took the necessary measures for the inquest. Of course, everyone suspected him of the murder, but there was no evidence against him. The verdict was murder by some person unknown, and as Gilbert Lumley was not sensitive, everything seemed to have gone quite satisfactorily.

"But it hadn't. One night, exactly a month after murder, Gilbert retired to his bedroom in the dark. He was in the act of feeling along the mantelpiece for the tinder-box, when he became aware of a dim light moving about the room. He turned round quickly and then s that it was a bat--a most uncanny and abnormal bat that seemed to give out a greenish ghostly light--flitting round and round his bed. On this, remembering the bat in the cavern, he rushed out of the room in the very devil of a fright. Presently he returned with one of the servants and a couple of candles; but the bat had disappeared.

"From that time onward, the luminous bat haunted Gilbert, appearing in dark rooms, on staircases and passages and corridors, until his nerves were all on end and he did not dare to move about the house at night without a candle or a lantern. But that was not the worst. Exactly two months after the murder the next stage of the haunting began. He had retired to his bedroom and was just about to get into bed when he remembered that he had left his watch in the little dressing-room that adjoined his chamber. With a candle in his hand he went to the dressing-room and flung open the door. And then he stopped dead and stood as if turned into stone; for, within a couple of yards of him, suspended in mid-air, was a man's head hanging upside down.

"For some seconds he stood rooted to the spot, unable to move. Then he uttered a cry of horror and rushed back to his room and down to the hall. There was no doubt whose head it was, strange and horrible as it looked in that unnatural, inverted position; for he had seen it twice before in that very position hanging in the cavern. Evidently he had not got rid of Glynn.

"That night, and every night henceforward, he slept in his wife's room. And all through the night he was conscious of a strange and dreadful impulse to rise and go down to the shore; to steal into the cavern and wait for the flowing tide. He lay awake, fighting against the invisible power that seemed to be drawing him to destruction, and by the morning the horrid impulse began to weaken. But he went about in terror, not daring to go near the shore and afraid to trust himself alone.

"A month passed. The effect of the apparition grew daily weaker and an abundance of lights in the house protected him from the visitation of the bat. Then, exactly three months after the murder, he saw the head again. This time it was in the library, where he had gone to fetch a book. He was standing by the book shelves and had just taken out a volume, when, as he turned away, there the hideous thing was, hanging in hat awful, grotesque posture, chin upwards and the scanty hair dropping down like wet fringe. Gilbert dropped the book that he was holding and fled from the room with a shriek; and all that night invisible hands seemed to be plucking at him to draw him away to where he voices of the waves were reverberating in the cavern.

"This second visitation affected him profoundly. He could not shake off that sinister impulse to steal away to the shore. He was a broken man, the victim of an abiding terror, clinging for protection to the very servants, creeping abroad with shaking limbs and an apprehensive eye towards the sea. And ever in his ears was the murmur of the surf and the hollow echoes of the cavern.

Already he had sought forgetfulness in drink; and sought it in vain. Now he took refuge in opiates. Every night, before retiring to the dreaded bed, he mingled laudanum with the brandy that brought him stupor if not repose. And brandy and opium began to leave their traces in the tremulous hand, the sallow cheek and the bloodshot eye. And so another month passed.

"As the day approached that would mark the fourth month, his terror of the visitation that he now anticipated reduced him to a state of utter prostration. Sleep--even drugged sleep--appeared that night to be out of the question, and he decided to sit up with his family, hoping by that means to escape the dreaded visitor. But it was a vain hope. Hour after hour he sat in his elbow chair by the fire, while his wife dozed in her chair opposite, until the clock in the hall struck twelve. He listened and counted the strokes of the bell, leaning back with his eyes closed. Half the weary night was gone. As the last stroke sounded and a deep silence fell on the house, he opened his eyes--and looked into the face of Glynn within a few inches of his own.

"For some moments he sat with dropped jaw and dilated eyes staring in silent horror at this awful thing; then with an agonised screech he slid from his chair into a heap on the floor.

"At noon on the following day he was missed from the house. A search was made in the grounds and in the neighbourhood, but he was nowhere to be found. At last some one thought of the cavern, of which he had spoken in his wild mutterings and a party of searchers made their way thither. And there they found him when the tide went out, lying on the wet sand with the brown sea-tangle wreathed about his limbs and the laudanum bottle-- now full of sea water--by his side.

"With the death of Gilbert Lumley it seemed that the murdered man's spirit was appeased. During the life- lime of Gilbert's son, Thomas, the departed Glynn made no sign. But on his death and the succession of his son Arthur--then a middle-aged man--the visitations began again, and in the same order. At the end of the first month the luminous bat appeared; at the end of the second, the inverted head made its entry, and again at the third and the fourth months; and within twenty-four hours of the last visitation, the body of Arthur Lumley was found in the cavern. And so it has been from that time onward. One generation escapes untouched by the curse; but in the next, Glynn and the sea claim their own."

"Is that true, so far as you know?" asked Thorndyke.

"I can't say," answered Brodribb. "I am now only quoting Walter Lumley's infernal little book. But I remember that, in fact, Giles' father was drowned. I understood that his boat capsized, but that may have been only a story to cover the suicide.

"Well now, I have given you the gruesome history from this book that poor Frank had the misfortune to find. You see that had had it all off by heart and had evidently read it again and again. Now I come to his own story, which he told me very quietly but with intense conviction and very evident forebodings.

"He found this damned book a few days after his arrival at Burling Court, and it was clear to him that, if the story was true, he was the next victim, since his predecessor, Giles, had been left in peace. And so it turned out. Exactly a month after his arrival, going up to his bedroom in the dark--no doubt expecting this apparition--as soon as he opened the door he saw a thing like a big glow-worm or firefly flitting round the room. It is evident that he was a good deal upset, for he rushed downstairs in a state of great agitation and fetched Price up to see it. But the strange thing was--though perhaps not so very strange, after all--that, although the thing was still there, flitting about the room, Price could see nothing. However, he pulled up the blind--the window was wide open--and the bat flopped out and disappeared.

"During the next month the bat reappeared several times, in the bedroom, in corridors and once in a garret, when it flew out as Frank opened the door."

"What was he doing in the garret?" asked Thorndyke.

"He went up to fetch an ancient coffin-stool that Mrs. Price had seen there and was telling him about. Well, this went on until the end of the second month. And then came the second act. It seems that by some infernal stupidity, he was occupying the bedroom that had been used by Gilbert. Now on this night, as soon as he had gone up, he must needs pay a visit to the little dressing-room, which is now known as" Gilbert's cabin"--so he tells me, for I was not aware of it--and where Gilbert's cutlass, telescope, quadrant and the old navigator's watch are kept."

"Did he take a light with him?" inquired Thorndyke.

"I think not. There is a gas jet in the corridor and presumably he lit that. Then he opened the door of the cabin; and immediately he saw, a few feet in front of him, a man's head, upside down, apparently hanging in mid-air. It gave him a fearful shock--the more so, perhaps, because he half expected it--and, as before, he ran downstairs, all of a tremble. Price had gone to bed but Mrs. Price came up with him, and he showed hr the horrible thing which was still hanging in the middle of the dark room.

"But Mrs. Price could see nothing. She assured him that it was all his imagination; and in proof of it, she walked into the room, right through the head, as it seemed, and when she had found the matches, she lit the gas. Of course, there was nothing whatever in the room.

"Another month passed. The bat appeared at intervals and kept poor Frank's nerves in a state of constant tension. On the night of the appointed day, as you will anticipate, Frank went again to Gilbert's cabin, drawn there by an attraction that one can quite understand. And there, of course, was the confounded head as before. That was a fortnight ago. So, you see, the affair is getting urgent. Either there is some truth in this weird story--which I don't believe for a moment--or poor old Frank is ripe for the asylum. But in any case something will have to be done."

"You spoke just now," said Thorndyke, "of some insanity in the family. What does it amount to, leaving these apparitions out of the question?"

"Well, a cousin of Frank's committed suicide in an asylum."

"And Frank's parents?

"They were quite sane. The cousin was the son of Frank's mother's sister; and she was all right, too. But the boy's father had to be put away."

"Then," said Thorndyke, "the insanity doesn't seem to be in Frank's family at all, in a medical sense. Legal inheritance and physiological inheritance do not follow the same lines. If his mother's sister married a lunatic, he might inherit that lunatic's property, but he could not inherit his insanity. There was no blood relationship."

"No, that's true," Brodribb admitted, "though Frank certainly seems as mad as a hatter. But now, to come back to the holiday question, what do you say to a week or so at St. David's?"

Thorndyke looked at me interrogatively. "What says my learned friend?" he asked.

"I say: Let us put up the shutters and leave Polton in charge," I replied; and Thorndyke assented without a murmur.

Less than a week later, we were installed in the very comfortable rooms that Mr. Brodribb had found for us in the hamlet of

St. David's, within five minutes' walk of the steep gap-way that led down to the beach. Thorndyke entered into the holiday with an enthusiasm that would have astonished the denizens of King Bench Walk. He explored the village, he examined the church, inside and out, he sampled all the footpaths with the aid of the Ordnance map, he foregathered with the fishermen on the beach and renewed his acquaintance with boat-craft, and he made a pilgrimage to the historic cavern--it was less than a mile along the shore--arid inspected its dark and chilly interior with the most lively curiosity.

We had not been at St. David's twenty-four hours before we made the acquaintance of Frank Lumley. Mr. Brodribb saw to that. For the old solicitor was profoundly anxious about his client--he took his responsibilities very seriously, did Mr. Brodribb. His "family" clients were to him as his own kin, and their interests his own interests--and his confidence in Thorndyke's wisdom was unbounded. We were very favourably impressed by the quiet, gentle, rather frail young man, and for my part, I found him, for a certifiable lunatic, a singularly reasonable and intelligent person. Indeed, apart from his delusions--or rather hallucinations--he seemed perfectly sane; for a somewhat eager interest in psychical and supernormal phenomena (of which he made no secret) is hardly enough to create a suspicion of a man's sanity.

But he was clearly uneasy about his own mental condition. He realised that the apparitions might be the products of a disordered brain, though that not his own view of them; and he discussed them us in the most open and ingenuous manner.

"You don't think," Thorndyke suggested, "that these apparitions may possibly be natural appearances which you have misinterpreted or exaggerated in consequence of having read that very circumstantial story?"

Lumley shook his head emphatically. "It is impossible," said he. "How could I? Take the case of the bat. I have seen it on several occasions quite distinctly. It was obviously a bat; but yet it seemed full of a ghostly, greenish light like that of a glow-worm. If it was not what it appeared, what was it? And then the head. There it was, perfectly clear and solid and real, hanging in mid-air within three or four feet of me. I could have touched it if I had dared."

"What size did it appear?" asked Thorndyke.

Lumley reflected. "It was not quite life-size. I should say about two-thirds the size of an ordinary head."

"Should you recognise the face if you saw it again?

"I can't say," replied Lumley. "You see, it was upside down. I haven't a very clear picture of it--I mean as to what the face would have been like the right way up."

"Was the room quite dark on both occasions?" Thorndyke asked.

"Yes, quite. The gas jet in the corridor is just above the door and does not any light into the room."

"And what is there opposite the door?"

"There is a small window, but that is usually kept shuttered nowadays. Under the window is a small folding dressing-table that belonged to Gilbert Lumley. He had it made when he came home from sea."

Thus Lumley was quite lucid and coherent in his answers. His manner was perfectly sane; it was only the matter that was abnormal. Of the reality of the apparitions he had not the slightest doubt, and he never varied in the smallest degree in his description of their appearance. The fact that they had been invisible both to Mr. Price and his wife he explained by pointing out that the curse applied only to the direct descendants of Gilbert Lumley, and to those only in alternate generations.

After one of our conversations, Thorndyke expressed a wish to see the little manuscript book that had been the cause of all the trouble--or at least had been the forerunner; and Lumley promised to bring it to our rooms on the following afternoon. But then came an interruption to our holiday, not entirely unexpected; an urgent telegram from one of our solicitor friends asking consultation on an important and intricate case that had just been put into his hands, and making it necessary for us to go up to town by an early train on the following morning.

We sent a note to Brodribb, telling him that we should be away from St. David's for perhaps a day or two, and on our way to the station he overtook us.

"I am sorry you have had to break your holiday," he said; " but I hope you will be back before Thursday."

"Why Thursday, in particular?" inquired Thorndyke.

"Because Thursday is the day on which that damned head is due to make its third appearance. It will be an anxious time. Frank hasn't said anything, but I know his nerves are strung up to concert pitch."

"You must watch him," said Thorndyke. "Don't let him out of your sight if you can help it."

"That's all very well," said Brodribb, "but he isn't a child, and I am not his keeper. He is the master of the house and I am just his guest. I can't follow him about if he wants to be alone."

"You mustn't stand on politeness, Brodribb," rejoined Thorndyke. "It will be a critical time and you must keep him in sight."

"I shall do my best," Brodribb said anxiously, "but I do hope you will be back by then."

He accompanied us dejectedly to the platform and stayed with us until our train came in. Suddenly, just as we were entering our carriage, he thrust his hand into his pocket.

"God bless me!" he exclaimed, "I had nearly forgotten this book. Frank asked me to give it to you." As he spoke, he drew out a little rusty calf-bound volume and handed it to Thorndyke. "You can look through it at your leisure," said he, "and if you think it best to chuck the infernal thing out of the window, do so. I suspect poor Frank is none the better for conning it over perpetually as he does."

I thought there was a good deal of reason in Brodribb's opinion. If Lumley's illusions were, as I suspected, the result of suggestion produced by reading the narrative, that suggestion would certainly tend to be reinforced by conning it over and over again. But the old lawyer's proposal was hardly practicable.

As soon as the train had fairly started, Thorndyke proceeded to inspect the little volume; and his manner of doing so was highly characteristic. An ordinary person would have opened the book and looked through the contents, probably seeking out at once the sinister history of Gilbert Lumley.

Not so Thorndyke. His inspection began at the very beginning and proceeded systematically to deal with every fact that the book had to disclose. First he made an exhaustive examination of the cover; scrutinised the corners; inspected the bottom edges and compared them with the top edges; and compared the top and bottom head-caps. Then he brought out his lens and examined the tooling, which was simple in character and worked in "blind"--i.e. not gilt. He also inspected the head-bands through the glass, and then he turned his attention to the interior. He looked carefully at both end-papers, he opened the sections and examined the sewing-thread, he held the leaves up to the light and tested the paper by eye and by touch and he viewed the writing in several places through his lens. Finally he handed the book and the lens to me without remark.

It was a quaint little volume, with a curiously antique air, though it was but a century old. The cover was of rusty calf, a good deal rubbed, but not in bad condition; for the joints were perfectly sound; but then it had probably had comparatively little use. The paper--a laid paper with very distinct wire-lines but no watermark--had turned with age to a pale, creamy buff; the writing had faded to a warm brown, but was easily legible and very clearly and carefully written. Having noted these points, I turned over the leaves until I came to the story of Gilbert Lumley and the ill-fated Glynn, which I read through attentively, observing that Mr. Brodribb's notes had given the whole substance of the narrative with singular completeness.

"This story," I said, as I handed the book back to Thorndyke, "strikes me as rather unreal and unconvincing. One doesn't see how Walter Lumley got his information."

"No," agreed Thorndyke. "It is on the plane of fiction. The narrator speaks in the manner of a novelist with complete knowledge of events and actions which were apparently known only to the actors."

"Do you think it possible that Walter Lumley was simply romancing?"

"I think it quite possible, and in fact very probable that the whole narrative is fictitious," he replied. "We shall have to go into that question later on. For the present, I suppose, we had better give our attention to the case that we have in hand at the moment."

The little volume was accordingly put away, and for the rest of the journey our conversation was occupied with the matter of the consultation that formed our immediate business. As this, however, had no connection with the present history, I need make no further reference to it beyond stating that it kept us both busy for three days and that we finished with it on the evening of the third.

"Do you propose to go down to St. David's to-night or to-morrow?" I asked, as we let ourselves into our chambers.

"To-night," replied Thorndyke. "This is Thursday, you know, and Brodribb was anxious that we should be back some time to-day. I have sent him a telegram saying that we shall go down by the train that arrives about ten o'clock. So if he wants us, he can meet us it the station or send a message."

"I wonder," said I, "if the apparition of Glynn's head will make its expected visitation to-night."

"It probably will if there is an opportunity," Thorndyke replied. "But I hope that Brodribb will manage to prevent the opportunity from occurring. And, talking of Lumley, as we have an hour to spare, we may as well finish our inspection of his book. I snipped off a corner of one of the leaves and gave it to Polton to boil up in weak caustic soda. It will be ready for examination by now."

"You don't suspect that the book has been faked, do you?" said I.

"I view that book with the deepest suspicion," he replied, opening a drawer and producing the little volume. "Just look at it, Jervis. Look at the cover, for instance."

"Well," I said, turning the book over in my hand, "the cover looks ancient enough to me; typical old, rusty calf with a century's wear on it."

"Oh, there's no doubt that it is old calf," said he; "just the sort of leather that you could skin off the cover of an old quarto or folio. But don't you see that the signs of wear are all in the wrong places? How does a book wear in use? Well, first there are the bottom edges, which rub on the shelf. Then the corners, which are the thinnest leather and the most exposed. Then the top head-cap, which the finger hooks into in pulling the book from the shelf. Then the joint or hinge, which wears through from frequent opening and shutting. The sides get the least wear of all. But in this book, the bottom edges, the corners, the top head-cap and the joints are perfectly sound. They are not more worn than the sides; and the tooling is modern in character. It looks quite fresh and the tool-marks are impressed on the marks of wear instead of being themselves worn. The appearances suggest to me a new binding with old leather.

"Then look at the paper. It professes to be discoloured by age. But the discoloration of the leaves of an old book occurs principally at the edges, where the paper has become oxidised by exposure to the air. The leaves of this book are equally discoloured all over. To me they suggest a bath of weak tea rather than old age.

"Again, there is the writing. Its appearance is that of faded writing done with the old-fashioned writing ink--made with iron sulphate and oak-galls. But it doesn't look quite the right colour. However, we can easily test that. If it is old iron-gall ink, a drop of ammonium sulphide will turn it black. Let us take the book up to the laboratory and try it--and we had better have a "control" to compare it with."

He ran his eye along the book-shelves and took down a rusty-looking volume of Humphry Clinker, the end- paper of which bore several brown and faded signatures.

Here is a signature dated 1803," said he. "That will be near enough"; and with the two books in his hand he led the way upstairs to the laboratory. Here he took down the ammonium sulphide bottle, and dipping up a little of the liquid in a fine glass tube, opened the cover of Humphry Clinker and carefully deposited a tiny drop on the figure 3 in the date. Almost immediately the. ghostly brown began to darken until it at length became jet black. Then, in the same way, he opened Walter Lumley's manuscript book and on the 9 of the date, 1819, he deposited a drop of the solution. But this time there was no darkening of the pale brown writing; on the contrary, it faded rapidly to a faint and muddy violet.

"It is not an iron ink," said Thorndyke, and it looks suspiciously like an aniline brown. But let us see what the paper is made of. Have you boiled up that fragment, Polton?"

"Yes, sir," answered our laboratory assistant, "and I've washed the soda out of it, so it's all ready."

He produced a labelled test-tube containing a tiny corner of paper floating in water, which he carefully emptied into a large watch-glass. From this Thorndyke transferred the little pulpy fragment to a microscope slide and, with a pair of mounted needles, broke it up into its constituent fibres. Then he dropped on it a drop of aniline stain, removed the surplus with blotting- paper, added a drop of glycerine and put on it a large cover-slip.

"There, Jervis," said he, handing me the slide, "let us have your opinion on Walter Lumley's paper."

I placed the slide on the stage of the microscope and proceeded to inspect the specimen. But no exhaustive examination was necessary. The first glance settled the matter.

"It is nearly all wood," I said. "Mechanical wood fibre, with some esparto, a little cotton and a few linen fibres."

"Then," said Thorndyke, "it is a modern paper. Mechanical wood-pulp-- prepared by Keller's process--was first used in paper-making in 1840. 'Chemical wood-pulp' came in later; and esparto was not used until 1860. So we can say with confidence that this paper was not made until more than twenty years after the date that is written on it. Probably it is of quite recent manufacture."

"In that case," said I, "this book is a counterfeit--presumably fraudulent."

"Yes. In effect it is a forgery."

"But that seems to suggest a conspiracy."

It does," Thorndyke agreed; "especially if it is considered in conjunction with the apparitions. The suggestion is that this book was prepared for the purpose of inducing a state of mind favourable to the acceptance of supernatural appearances. The obvious inference is that the apparitions themselves were an imposture produced for fraudulent purposes. But it is time for us to go."

We shook hands with Polton, and, having collected our suit-cases from the sitting-room, set forth for the station.

During the journey down I reflected on the new turn that Frank Lumley's affairs had taken. Apparently, Brodribb had done his client an injustice. Lumley was not so mad as the old lawyer had supposed. He was merely credulous and highly suggestible. The "hallucinations" were real phenomena which he had simply misinterpreted. But who was behind these sham illusions? And what was it all about? I tried to open the question with Thorndyke; but though he was willing to discuss the sham manuscript book and the technique of its production, he would commit himself to nothing further.

On our arrival at St. David's, Thorndyke looked up and down the platform and again up the station approach. "No sign of Brodribb or any messenger," he remark 'so we may assume that all is well at Burling Court up to the present. Let us hope that Brodribb's presence has had an inhibitory effect on the apparitions."

Nevertheless, it was evident that he was not quite easy in his mind. During supper he appeared watchful and preoccupied, and when, after the meal, he proposed a stroll down to the beach, he left word with our landlady as to where he was to be found if he should be wanted.

It was about a quarter to eleven when we arrived at the shore, and the tide was beginning to run out. The beach was deserted with the exception of a couple of fishermen who had apparently come in with the tide and who were making their boat secure for the before going home. Thorndyke approached them, addressing the older fisherman, remarked: "That is a big, powerful boat. Pretty fast, too, isn't she?"

"Ay, sir," was the reply; "fast and weatherly, she is. What we calls a galley-punt. Built at Deal for the hovelling trade--salvage, you know, sir--but there ain't no hovelling nowadays, not to speak of."

"Are you going out to-morrow?" asked Thorndyke.

"Not as I knows of, sir. Was you thinking of a bit of fishing?"

"If you are free," said Thorndyke, "I should like to charter the boat for to-morrow. I don't know what time I shall be able to start, but if you will stand by ready to put off at once when I come down we can count the waiting as sailing."

"Very well, sir," said the fisherman; "the boat's yours for the day to-morrow. Any time after six, or earlier, if you like, if you come down here you'll find me and my mate standing by with a stock of bait and the boat ready to push off."

"That will do admirably," said Thorndyke; and the morrow's programme being thus settled, we wished the fishermen good-night and walked slowly back to our lodgings, where, after a final pipe, we turned in.

On the following morning, just as we were finishing a rather leisurely breakfast, we saw from our window our friend Mr. Brodribb hurrying down the street towards our house. I ran out and opened the door, and as he entered I conducted him into our sitting-room. From his anxious and flustered manner it was obvious that something had gone wrong, and his first words con firmed the sinister impression.

"I'm afraid we're in for trouble, Thorndyke," said he. "Frank is missing."

"Since when?" asked Thorndyke.

"Since about eight o'clock this morning. He is nowhere about the house and he hasn't had any breakfast."

"When was he last seen?" Thorndyke asked. "And where?"

"About eight o'clock, in the breakfast-room. Apparently he went in there to say "good-bye" to the Prices--they have gone on a visit for the day to Folkestone and were having an early breakfast so as to catch the eight-thirty train. But he didn't have breakfast with them. He just went in and wished them a pleasant journey and then it appears that he went out for a stroll in the grounds. When I came down to breakfast at half-past eight, the Prices had gone and Frank hadn't come in. The maid sounded the gong, and as Frank still did not appear, she went out into the grounds to look for him; and presently I went out myself. But he wasn't there and he wasn't anywhere in the house. I don't like the look of it at all. He is usually very regular and punctual at meals. What do you think we had better do, Thorndyke?"

My colleague looked at his watch and rang the bell.

I think, Brodribb," said he, "that we must act on the obvious probabilities and provide against the one great danger that is known to us. Mrs. Robinson," he added, addressing the landlady, who, had answered the bell in person, " can you let us have a jug of strong coffee at once?"

Mrs. Robinson could, and bustled away to prepare it, while Thorndyke produced from a cupboard a large vacuum flask.

I don't quite follow you, Thorndyke," said Mr. Brodribb. "What probabilities and what danger do you mean?"

"I mean that, up to the present, Frank Lumley has exactly reproduced in his experiences and his actions the experiences and actions of Gilbert Lumley as set forth in Walter Lumley's narrative. The overwhelming probability is that he will continue to reproduce the story of Gilbert to the end. He probably saw the apparition for the third time last night, and is even now preparing for the final act."

"Good God!" gasped Brodribb. "What a fool I am! You mean the cave? But we can never get there now. It will be high water in an hour and the beach at St. David's Head will be covered already. Unless we can get a boat," he added despairingly.

"We have got a boat," said Thorndyke. "I chartered one last night."

"Thank the Lord!" exclaimed Brodribb. "But you always think of everything--though I don't know what you want that coffee for."

"We may not want it at all," said Thorndyke, as he poured the coffee, which the landlady had just brought, into the vacuum flask," but on the other hand we may."

He deposited the flask in a hand-bag, in which I observed a small emergency-case, and then turned to Brodribb.

"We had better get down to the beach now," said he.

As we emerged from the bottom of the gap-way we saw our friends of the previous night laying a double line of planks across the beach from the boat to the margin of the surf; for the long galley-punt, with her load of ballast, was too heavy, over the shingle. They had just got the last plank laid as we reached the boat, and as they observed us they came running back with half a dozen of their mates.

"Jump aboard, gentlemen," said our skipper, with a slightly dubious eye on Mr. Brodribb--for the boat's gunwale was a good four feet above the beach. "We'll have her afloat in a jiffy."

We climbed in and hauled Mr. Brodribb in after us. The tall mast was already stepped--against the middle thwart in the odd fashion of galley-punts--and the great sail was hooked to the traveller and the tack-hook ready for hoisting. The party of boatmen gathered round and each took a tenacious hold of gunwale or thole. The skipper gave time with a jovial "Yo-ho!" his mates joined in with a responsive howl and heaved as one man. The great boat moved forward, and gathering way, slid swiftly along the greased planks towards the edge of the surf. Then her nose splashed into the sea; the skipper and his mate sprang in over the transom; the tall lug-sail soared up the mast and filled and the skipper let the rudder slide down its pintles and grasped the tiller.

"Did you want to go anywheres in particklar?" he inquired.

"We want to make for the big cave round St. David's Head," said Thorndyke, " and we want to get there well before high water."

"We'll do that easy enough, sir," said the skipper "with this breeze. "Tis but about a mile and we've got three-quarters of an hour to do it in."

He took a pull at the main sheet and, putting the helm down, brought the boat on a course parallel to the coast. Quietly but swiftly the water slipped past, one after another fresh headlands opened out till, in about a quarter of an hour, we were abreast of St. David's Head with the sinister black shape of the cavern in full view over the port bow. Shortly afterwards the sail was lowered and our crew, reinforced by Thorndyke and me, took to the oars, pulling straight towards the shore with the cavern directly ahead.

As the boat grounded on the beach Thorndyke Brodribb and I sprang out and hurried across the sand and shingle to the gloomy and forbidding hole in white cliff. At first, coming out of the bright sunlight we seemed to be plunged in absolute darkness, and groped our way insecurely over the heaps of slippery sea-tangle that littered the floor. Presently our eyes grew accustomed to the dim light, and we could trace faintly the narrow, tunnel-like passage with its slimy green and the jagged roof nearly black with age. At the farther end it grew higher; and here I could see the small, dark bodies of bats hanging from the roof and clinging to the walls, and one or two fluttering blindly and noiselessly like large moths in the hollows of the vault above. But it was not the bats that engrossed my attention. Far away, at the extreme end, I could dimly discern the prostrate figure of a man lying motionless on a patch of smooth sand; a dreadful shape that seemed to sound the final note of tragedy to which the darkness, the clammy chill of the cavern and the ghostly forms of he bats had been a fitting prelude.

"My God!" gasped Brodribb, "we're too late!" He broke into a shambling run and Thorndyke and I darted on ahead. The man was Frank Lumley, of course, and a glance at him gave us at least a ray of hope. He was lying in an easy posture with closed eyes and was still breathing, though his respiration was shallow and slow. Beside him on the sand lay a little bottle and near it a cork. I picked up the former and read on the label "Laudanum: Poison" and a local druggist's name and address. But it was empty save for a few drops, the appearance and smell of which confirmed the label.

Thorndyke, who had been examining the unconscious man's eyes with a little electric lamp, glanced at the bottle.

"Well," said he, "we know the worst. That is a two-drachm phial, so if he took the lot his condition is not hopeless."

As he spoke he opened the hand-bag, and taking out the emergency-case, produced from it a hypodermic syringe and a tiny bottle of atropine solution. I drew up Lumley's sleeve while the syringe was filled and Thorndyke then administered the injection.

"It is opium poisoning, I suppose?" said I.

"Yes," was the answer. "His pupils are like pin points; but his pulse is not so bad. I think we can safely move him down to the boat."

Thereupon we lifted him, and with Brodribb supporting his feet, we moved in melancholy procession down the cave. Already the waves were lapping the beach at the entrance and even trickling in amongst the seaweed; and the boat, following the rising tide, had her bows within the cavern. The two fishermen, who were steadying the boat with their oars, greeted our appearance, carrying the body, with exclamations of astonishment. But they asked no questions, simply taking the unconscious man from us and laying him gently on the grating in the stern-sheets.

"Why, 'tis Mr. Lumley!" exclaimed the skipper.

"Yes," said Thorndyke; and having given them a few words of explanation, he added: "I look to you to keep this affair to yourselves."

To this the two men agreed heartily, and the boat having been pushed off and the sail hoisted, the skipper asked: "Do we sail straight back, sir?"

"Yes," replied Thorndyke, "but we won't land yet. Stand on and off opposite the gap-way."

Already, as a result of the movement, the patient stupor appeared less profound. And now Thorndyke took definite measures to rouse him, shaking him gently and constantly changing his position. Presently Lumley drew a deep sighing breath, and opened his eyes for a moment. Then Thorndyke sat him up, and producing the vacuum-flask, made him swallow a few teaspoonful of coffee. This procedure was continued for over an hour while the boat cruised up and down opposite the landing-place half a mile or so from the shore. Constantly our patient relapsed into stuporous sleep, only to be roused again and given a sip of coffee.

At length he recovered so far as to be able to sit up--lurching from side to side as the boat rolled--and drowsily answer questions spoken loudly in his ears. A quarter of an hour later, as he still continued to improve, Thorndyke ordered the skipper to bring the boat to the landing-place.

"I think he could walk now," said he, "and the exercise will rouse him more completely."

The boat was accordingly beached and Lumley assisted to climb out; and though at first he staggered as if he would fall, after a few paces he was able to walk fairly steadily, supported on either side by me and Thorndyke. The effort of ascending the steep gap-way revived him further; and by the time we reached the gate of Burling Court--half a mile across the fields--he was almost able to stand alone.

But even when he had arrived home he was not allowed to rest, earnestly as he begged to be left in peace. First Thorndyke insisted on his taking a light meal, and then proceeded to question him as to the events of the previous night.

"I presume, Lumley," said he, "that you saw the apparition of Glynn's head?"

"Yes. After Mr. Brodribb had seen me to bed, I got up and went to Gilbert's cabin. Something seemed to draw me to it. And as soon as I opened the door, there was the head hanging in the air within three feet of me. Then I knew that Glynn was calling me, and--well, you know the rest."

"I understand," said Thorndyke. "But now I want you to come to Gilbert's cabin with me and show me exactly where you were and where the head was."

Lumley was profoundly reluctant and tried to postpone the demonstration. But Thorndyke would listen to no refusal, and at last Lumley rose wearily and conducted his tormentor up the stairs, followed by Brodribb and me.

We went first to Lumley's bedroom and from that into a corridor, into which some other bedrooms opened. The corridor was dimly lighted by a single window, and when Thorndyke had drawn the thick curtain over this, the place was almost completely dark. At one end of the corridor was the small, narrow door of the "cabin," over which was a gas bracket. Thorndyke lighted the gas and opened the door and we then saw that the room was in total darkness, its only window being closely shuttered and the curtains drawn. Thorndyke struck a match and lit the gas and we then looked curiously about the little room.

It was a quaint little apartment, to which its antique furniture and contents gave an old-world air. An ancient hanger, quadrant and spy-glass hung on the wall, a large, dropsical-looking watch, inscribed "Thomas Tompion, Londini fecit," reposed on a little velvet cushion in the middle of a small, black mahogany table by the window, and a couple of Cromwellian chairs stood against the wall. Thorndyke looked curiously at the table, which was raised on wooden blocks, and Lumley explained: "That was Gilbert's dressing-table. He had it made for his cabin on board ship."

"Indeed," said Thorndyke. "Then Gilbert was a rather up-to-date gentleman. There wasn't much mahogany furniture before 1720. Let us have a look I at the interior arrangements."

He lifted the watch, and having placed it on a chair, raised the lid of the table, disclosing a small wash basin, a little squat ewer and other toilet appliances. The table lid, which was held upright by a brass strut, held a rather large dressing-mirror enclosed in a projecting case.

"I wonder," said I, "why the table was stood on those blocks."

"Apparently," said Thorndyke, "for the purpose of bringing the mirror to the eye-level of a person standing up."

The answer gave Brodribb an idea. "I suppose, Frank," said he, "it was not your own reflection in the mirror that you saw?"

"How could it be?" demanded Lumley. "The head was upside down, and besides, it was quite near to me."

No, that's true," said Brodribb; and turning away from the table he picked up the old navigator's watch "A queer old timepiece, this," he remarked.

"Yes," said Lumley; "but it's beautifully made. Let me show you the inside."

He took off the outer case and opened the inner one, exhibiting the delicate workmanship of the interior to Brodribb and me, while Thorndyke continued to pore over the inner fittings of the table. Suddenly my colleague said: "Just go outside, you three, and shut the door. I want to try an experiment."

Obediently we all filed out and closed the door, waiting expectantly in the corridor. In a couple of minutes Thorndyke came out and before he shut the door I noticed that the little room was now in darkness. He walked us a short distance down the corridor and then, halting, said

"Now, Lumley, I want you to go into the cabin and tell us what you see."

Lumley appeared a little reluctant to go in alone, but eventually he walked towards the cabin and opened the door. Instantly he uttered a cry of horror, and closing the door, ran back to us, trembling, agitated, wild-eyed.

"It is there now!" he exclaimed. "I saw it distinctly."

"Very well," said Thorndyke. "Now you go and look, Brodribb."

Mr. Brodribb showed no eagerness. With very obvious trepidation he advanced to the door and threw it open with a jerk. Then, with a sharp exclamation, he slammed it to, and came hurrying back, his usually pink complexion paled down to a delicate mauve.

"Horrible! Horrible!" he exclaimed. "What the devil is it, Thorndyke?"

A sudden suspicion flashed into my mind. I strode forward, and turning the handle of the door, pulled it open. And then I was not surprised that Brodribb had been startled. Within a yard of my face, clear, distinct and solid, was an inverted head, floating in mid-air in the pitch-dark room. Of course, being prepared for it, I saw at a glance what it was; recognised my own features, strangely and horribly altered as they were by their inverted position. But even now that I knew what it was, the thing had a most appalling, uncanny aspect.

"Now," said Thorndyke, "let us go in and explode the mystery. Just stand outside the door, Jervis, while I demonstrate."

He produced a sheet of white paper from his pocket, and smoothing it out, let our two friends into the room. First," said he, holding the paper out flat at the eye-level, "you see on this paper a picture of Dr. Jervis's head upside down."

So there is," said Brodribb; "like a magic-lantern picture."

"Exactly like," agreed Thorndyke; "and of exactly the same nature. Now let us see how it is produced."

He struck a match and lit the gas; and instantly all our eyes turned towards the open dressing-table.

"But that is not the same mirror that we saw just now," said Brodribb.

"No," replied Thorndyke. "The frame is reversible on a sliding hinge and I have turned it round. On one side is the ordinary flat looking-glass which you saw before ; on the other is this concave shaving-mirror. You observe that, if you stand close to it, you see your face the right way up and magnified; if you go back to the door, you see your head upside down and smaller."

"But," objected Lumley, "the head looked quite solid and seemed to be right out in the room."

So it was, and is still. But the effect of reality is destroyed by the fact that you can now see the frame of the mirror enclosing the image, so that the head appears to be in the mirror. But in the dark, you could only see the image. The mirror was invisible."

Brodribb reflected on this explanation. Presently he said: "I don't think I quite understand it now."

Thorndyke took a pencil from his pocket and began to draw a diagram on the sheet of paper that he still held.

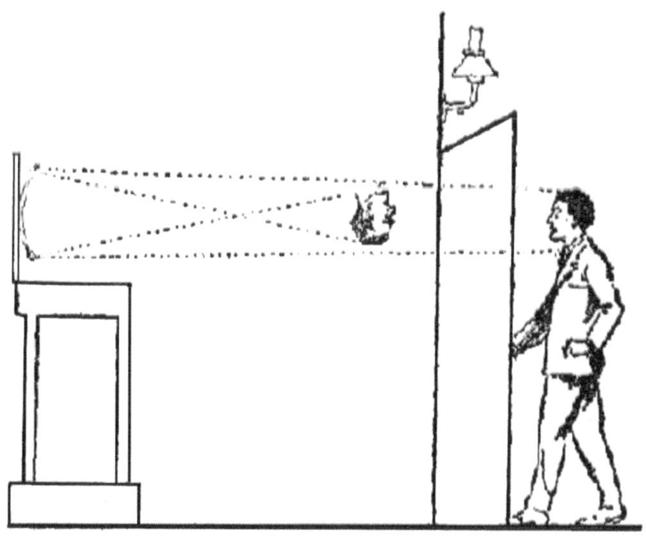

"The figure that you see in an ordinary flat looking glass," he explained," is what is called a "virtual image." It appears to be behind the mirror, but of course it is not there. It is an optical illusion. But the image from a concave mirror is in front of the mirror and is a real image like that of a magic-lantern or a camera, and, like them, inverted. This diagram will explain matters. Here is Lumley standing at the open door of the room. His figure is well lighted by the gas over the door (which, however, throws no light into the room) and is clearly reflected by the mirror, which throws forward a bright inverted image. But, as the room is dark and the mirror invisible, he sees only the image, which looks like--and in fact is--a real object standing in mid-air."

"But why did I see only the head?" asked Lumley.

"Because the head occupied the whole of the mirror. If the mirror had been large enough you would have seen the full-length figure."

Lumley reflected for a moment. "It almost looks if this had been arranged," he said at length.

"Of course it has been arranged," said Thorndyke "and very cleverly arranged, too. And now let us go and see if anything else has been arranged. Which is Mr. Price's room?"

"He has three rooms, which open out of this corridor," said Lumley; and he conducted us to a door at the farther end, which Thorndyke tried and found locked.

"It is a case for the smoker's companion," said he, producing from his pocket an instrument that went by that name, but which looked suspiciously like a lock-pick. At any rate, after one or two trials-- which Mr Brodribb watched with an appreciative smile--the bolt shot back and the door opened.

We entered what was evidently the bedroom, around which Thorndyke cast a rapid glance and then asked: "What are the other rooms?"

I think he uses them to tinker in," said Lumley, "but I don't quite know what he does in them. All three rooms communicate."

We advanced to the door of communication and, finding it unlocked, passed through into the next room. Here, on a large table by the window, was a litter of various tools and appliances.

"What is that thing with the wooden screws? " Brodribb asked.

"A bookbinder's sewing-press," replied Thorndyke. "And here are some boxes of finishing tools. Let us look over them."

He took up the boxes one after the other and inspected the ends of the tools--brass stamps for impressing the ornaments on book covers. Presently he lifted out two, a leaf and a flower. Then he produced from his coat pocket the little manuscript book, and laying it on the table, picked up from the floor a little fragment of leather. Placing this also on the table, he pressed two of the tools on it, leaving a clear impression of a leaf and a flower. Finally he laid the scrap of leather on the book, when it was obvious that the leaf and flower were identical replicas of the leaves and flowers which formed the decoration of the book cover.

"This is very curious," said Lumley. "They seem to be exactly alike."

"They are exactly alike," said Thorndyke. "I affirm that the tooling on that book was done with these tools, and the leaves sewn on that press."

"But the book is a hundred years old," objected Lumley.

Thorndyke shook his head. "The leather is old," said he, "but the book is new. We have tested the paper and found it to be of recent manufacture. But now let us see what is in that little cupboard. There seem to be some bottles there."

He ran his eye along the shelves, crowded with bottles and jars of varnish, glair, oil, cement and other material.

"Here," he said, taking down a small bottle of dark- coloured powder, "is some aniline brown. That probably produced the ancient and faded writing. But this is more illuminating--in more senses than one." He picked out a little, wide-mouthed bottle labelled "Radium Paint for the hands and figures of luminous watches."

"Ha!" exclaimed Brodribb; "a very illuminating discovery, as you say."

"And that," said Thorndyke, looking keenly round the room," seems to be all there is here. Shall we take a glance at the third room?"

We passed through the communicating doorway and found ourselves in a small apartment practically unfurnished and littered with trunks, bags and various lumber. As we stood looking about us, Thorndyke sniffed suspiciously.

"I seem to detect a sort of mousy odour," said he, glancing round inquisitively. "Do you notice it, Jervis?"

I did; and with the obvious idea in my mind began I to prowl round the room in search of the source, Suddenly my eye lighted on a smallish box, in the top of which a number of gimlet-holes had been bored. I raised the lid and peered in. The interior was covered with filth and on the bottom lay a dead bat.

We all stood for a few seconds looking in silence at the little corpse. Then Thorndyke closed the box and tucked it under his arm.

"This completes the case, I think," said he. "What time does Price return?"

He is expected home about seven o'clock," said Lumley. Then he added with a troubled expression: "I don't understand all this. What does it mean?"

It is very simple," replied Thorndyke. "You have a sham ancient book containing an evidently fabulous story of supernatural events; and you have a series of appliances and arrangements for producing illusions which seem to repeat those events. The book was planted where it was certain to be found and read, and the illusions began after it was known that it actually had been read. It is a conspiracy."

"But why?" demanded Lumley. "What was the object?"

"My dear Frank," said Brodribb, "you seem forget that Price is the next of kin and the heir to your estate on your death."

Lumley's eyes filled. He seemed overcome with grief and disgust. "It is incredible," he murmured huskily. "Thu baseness of it is beyond belief."

Price and his wife arrived home at about seven o'clock, A meal had been prepared for them, and when they had finished, a servant was sent in to ask Mr. Price to speak with Mr. Brodribb in the study. There we all awaited him, Lumley being present by his own wish; and on the table were deposited the little book, the scrap of leather, the two finishing tools, the pot of radium paint and the box containing the dead bat. Presently Price entered, accompanied by his wife; and at the sight of the objects on the table they both turned deathly pale. Mr. Brodribb placed chairs for them, and when they were seated he began in a dry, stern voice:

"I have sent for you, Mr. Price, to give you certain information. These two gentlemen, Dr. Thorndyke and Dr. Jervis, are eminent criminal lawyers whom I have commissioned to make investigations and to advise me in this matter. Their investigations have discloser the existence of a forged manuscript, a dead bat, a pot of luminous paint and a concave mirror. I need not enlarge on those discoveries. My intention is to prosecute you and your wife for conspiracy to procure the suicide of Mr. Frank Lumley. But, at Mr. Lumley's request, I have consented to delay the proceedings for forty-eight hours. During that period you will be at liberty to act as you think best."

For some seconds there was a tense silence. The two crestfallen conspirators sat with their eyes fixed on the floor, and Mrs. Price choked down a half-hysterical sob. Then they rose; and Price, without looking at any of us, said in a low voice: "Very well. Then I suppose we had better clear out."

"And the best thing, too," remarked Brodribb, when they had gone; "for I doubt if we could have carried our bluff into court."

On the wall of our sitting-room in the Temple there hang, to this day, two keys. One is that of the postern gate of Burling Court, and the other belongs to the suite of rooms that were once occupied by Mr. Lewis Price; and they hang there, by Frank Lumley's wish, as a token that Burling Court is a country home to which we have access at all hours and seasons as tenants in virtue of an inalienable right.

The Mysterious Visitor

"So," said Thorndyke, looking at me reflectively, "you are a full-blown medical practitioner with a practice of your own. How the years slip by! It seems but the other day that you were a student, gaping at me from the front bench of the lecture theatre."

"Did I gape?" I asked incredulously.

"I use the word metaphorically," said he, " to denote ostentatious attention. You always took my lecture very seriously. May I ask if you have ever found them of use in your practice?"

"I can't say that I have ever had any very thrilling medico-legal experiences since that extraordinary cremation case that you investigated--the case of Septimus Maddock, you know. But that reminds me that there is a little matter that I meant to speak to you about. It is of no interest, but I just wanted your advice, though it even my business, strictly speaking. It concerns a patient of mine, a man named Crofton, who has disappeared rather unaccountably."

"And do you call that a case of no medico-legal interest?" demanded Thorndyke.

"Oh, there's nothing in it. He just went away for a holiday and he hasn't communicated with his friends very recently. That is all. What makes me a little uneasy is that there is a departure from his usual habits--he is generally a fairly regular correspondent--that seems a little significant in view of his personality. He is markedly neurotic and his family history is by means what one would wish."

"That is an admirable thumb-nail sketch, Jardine," said Thorndyke "but it lacks detail. Let us have a full-size picture."

"Very well," said I, "but you mustn't let me bore you. To begin with Crofton: he is a nervous, anxious, worrying sort of fellow, everlastingly fussing about money affairs, and latterly this tendency has been getting worse. He fairly got the jumps about his financial position; felt that he was steadily drifting into bankruptcy and couldn't get that out of his mind. It was all bunkum. I am more or less a friend of the family, and I know that there was nothing to worry about. Mrs. Crofton assured me that, although they were a trifle hard up, they could rub along quite safely.

"As he seemed to be getting the hump worse and worse, I advised him to go away for a change and stay in a boarding-house where he would see some fresh faces. Instead of that, he elected to go down to a bungalow that he has at Seasalter, near Whitstable, and lets out in the season. He proposed to stay by himself and spend his time in sea-bathing and country walks. I wasn't very keen on this, for solitude was the last thing that he wanted. There was a strong family history of melancholia and some unpleasant rumours of suicide. I didn't like his being alone at all. However, another friend of the family, Mrs. Crofton's brother in fact, a chap named Ambrose, offered to go down and spend a week-end with him to give him a start, and afterwards to run down for an afternoon whenever he was able. So off he went with Ambrose on Friday, the sixteenth of June, and for a time all went well. He seemed to be improving in health and spirits and wrote to his wife regularly two or three times a week. Ambrose went down as often as he could to cheer him up, and the last time brought back the news that Crofton thought of moving on to Margate for a further change. So, of course, he didn't go down to the bungalow again.

"Well, in due course, a letter came from Margate; it had been written at the bungalow, but the postmark was Margate and bore the same date--the sixteenth of July--as the letter itself. I have it with me. Mrs. Crofton sent it for me to see and I haven't returned it yet. But there is nothing of interest in it beyond the statement that he was going on to Margate by the next train and would write again when he had found rooms there. That was the last that was heard of him. He never wrote and nothing is known of his movements excepting that he left Seasalter and arrived at Margate. This is the letter."

I handed it to Thorndyke, who glanced at the mark and then laid it on the table for examination later. "Have any inquiries been made?" he asked.

"Yes. His photograph has been sent to the Margate police, but, of course--well, you know what Margate like in July. Thousands of strangers coming and gong every day. It is hopeless to look for him in that crowd and it is quite possible that he isn't there now. But his disappearance is most inopportune, for a big legacy hats just fallen in, and, naturally, Mrs. Crofton is frantically anxious to let him know. It is a matter of about thirty thousand pounds."

"Was this legacy expected?" asked Thorndyke.

"No. The Croftons knew nothing about it. They didn't know that the old lady--Miss Shuler--had made a will or that she had very much to leave; and they didn't know that she was likely to die, or even that she was ill. Which is rather odd; for she was ill for a month or two and, as she suffered from a malignant abdominal tumour, it was known that she couldn't recover."

"When did she die?"

"On the thirteenth of July."

Thorndyke raised his eyebrows. "Just three days before the date of this letter," he remarked; "so that if he should never reappear, this letter will be the sole evidence that he survived her. It is an important document. It may come to represent a value of f thousand pounds."

"It isn't so important as it looks," said I. " Miss Shuler's will provides that if Crofton should die before the estatrix, the legacy should go to his wife. So whether he is alive or not, the legacy is quite safe. But we must hope that he is alive, though I must confess to some little anxiety on his account."

Thorndyke reflected a while on this statement. Presently he asked: "Do you know if Crofton has made a will?"

"Yes, he has," I replied; "quite recently. I was one of the witnesses and I read it through at Crofton's request. It was full of the usual legal verbiage, but it might have been stated in a dozen words. He leaves practically everything to his wife, but instead of saying so it enumerates the property item by item."

"It was drafted, I suppose, by the solicitor?"

"Yes; another friend of the family named Jobson, and he is the executor and residuary legatee."

Thorndyke nodded and again became deeply reflective. Still meditating, he took up the letter, and as he inspected it, I watched him curiously and not without a certain secret amusement. First he looked over the envelope, back and front. Then he took from his pocket powerful Coddington lens and with this examined the flap and the postmark. Next, he drew out the letter, held ii up to the light, then read it through and finally examined various parts of the writing through his lens. "Well," I asked, with an irreverent grin, "I should think you have extracted the last grain of meaning from it."

He smiled as he put away his lens and handed the letter back to me.

"As this may have to be produced in proof of survival," said he," it had better be put in a place of safety. I notice that he speaks of returning later to the bungalow. I take it that it has been ascertained that he did not return there?"

"I don't think so. You see, they have been waiting for him to write. You think that some one ought--"

I paused; for it began to be borne in on me that Thorndyke was taking a somewhat gloomy view of the case.

"My dear Jardine," said he, "I am merely following your own suggestion. Here is a man with an inherited tendency to melancholia and suicide who has suddenly disappeared. He went away from an empty house and announced his intention of returning to it later. As that house is the only known locality in which he could be sought, it is obvious that it ought to have been examined. And even if he never came back there, the house might contain some clues to his present whereabouts."

This last sentence put an idea into my mind which I was a little shy of broaching. What was a clue to Thorndyke might be perfectly meaningless to an ordinary person. I recalled his amazing interpretations of most commonplace facts in the mysterious Maddock case and the idea took fuller possession. At length I said tentatively: "I would go down myself if I felt competent. To morrow is Saturday, and I could get a colleague to look after my practice; there isn't much doing just now. But when you speak of clues, and when I remember what duffer I was last time--I wish it were possible for you to have a look at the place."

To my surprise, he assented almost with enthusiasm.

"Why not?" said he. "It is a week-end. We can put up at the bungalow, I suppose, and have a little gipsy holiday. And there are undoubtedly points of interest in the case. Let us go down to-morrow. We can lunch in the train and have the afternoon before us. You had better get a key from Mrs. Crofton, or, if she hasn't got one, an authority to visit the house. We may want that if we have to enter without a key. And we go alone, of course."

I assented joyfully. Not that I had any expectations as to what we might learn from our inspection. But something in Thorndyke's manner gave me the impression that he had extracted from my account of the case some significance that was not apparent to me.

The bungalow stood on a space of rough ground a little way behind the sea-wall, along which we walked towards it from Whitstable, passing on our way a ship-builder's yard and a slipway, on which a collier brigantine was hauled up for repairs. There were one or two other bungalows adjacent, but a considerable distance apart, and we looked at them as we approached to make out the names painted on the gates.

"That will probably be the one," said Thorndyke, indicating a small building enclosed within a wooden fence and provided, like the others, with a bathing hut just above high-water mark. Its solitary, deserted aspect and lowered blinds supported his opinion, and when we reached the gate, the name "Middlewick" painted on it settled the matter.

"The next question is," said I, "how the deuce we are going to get in? The gate is locked, and there is no bell. Is it worth while to hammer at the fence?"

"I wouldn't do that," replied Thorndyke. "The place is pretty certainly empty or the gate wouldn't be locked. We shall have to climb over unless there is a back gate unlocked, so the less noise we make the better."

We walked round the enclosure, but there was no other gate, nor was there any tree or other cover to disguise our rather suspicious proceedings.

"There's no help for it, Jardine," said Thorndyke, "so here goes."

He put his green canvas suit-case on the ground, grasped the top of the fence with both hands and went over like a harlequin. I picked up the case and handed it over to him, and, having taken a quick glance round, followed my leader.

"Well," I said," here we are. And now, how are we to get into the house?"

"We shall have to pick a lock if there is no door open, or else go in by a window. Let us take a look round."--We walked round the house to the back door, but found it not only locked, but bolted top and bottom, as Thorndyke ascertained with his knifeblade. The windows were all casements and all fastened with their catches.

"The front door will be the best," said Thorndyke. "It can't be bolted unless he got out by the chimney and I think my 'smoker's companion' will be able to cope with an ordinary door-lock. It looked like a common builder's fitting."

As he spoke, we returned to the front of the house and he produced the 'smoker's companion' from his pocket (I don't know what kind of smoker it was designed to accompany). The lock was apparently a simple affair, for the second trial with the 'companion' shot back the bolt, and when I turned the handle, the door opened. As a precaution, I called out to inquire if there was anybody within, and then, as there was no answer, we entered, walking straight into the living-room, as there was no hall or lobby.

A couple of paces from the threshold we halted to look round the room, and on me the aspect of the place produced a vague sense of discomfort. Though it was early in a bright afternoon, the room was almost completely dark, for not only were the blinds lowered, but the curtains were drawn as well.

"It looks," said I, peering about the dim and gloomy apartment with sun-dazzled eyes, "as if he had gone away at night. He wouldn't have drawn the curtains in the daytime."

"One would think not," Thorndyke agreed; "but it doesn't follow."

He stepped to the front window and drawing back the curtains pulled up the blind, revealing a half-curtain of green serge over the lower part of the window. As the bright daylight flooded the room, he stood with his back to the window looking about with deep attention, letting his eyes travel slowly over the walls, the furniture, and especially the floor. Presently he stooped to pick up a short match-end which lay just under the table opposite the door, and as he looked at it thoughtfully, he pointed to a couple of spots of candle grease on the linoleum near the table. Then he glanced at the mantelpiece and from that to an ash-bowl on the table.

These are only trifling discrepancies," said he, "but they are worth noting. You see," he continued in response to my look of inquiry, "that this room is severely trim and orderly. Everything seems to be in place. The match-box, for instance, has its fixed receptacle above the mantelpiece, and there is a bowl for the burnt matches, regularly used, as its contents show. Yet there is a burnt match thrown on the floor, although the bowl is on the table quite handy. And the match, you notice, is not of the same kind as those in the box over the mantelpiece, which is a large Bryant and May, or as the burnt matches in the bowl which have evidently come from it. But if you look in the bowl," he continued, picking it up, "you will see two burnt matches of this same kind-- apparently the small size Bryant and May--one burnt quite short and one only half burnt. The suggestion is fairly obvious, but, as I say, there is a slight discrepancy."

I don't know," said I, "that either the suggestion or the discrepancy is very obvious to me."

He walked over to the mantelpiece and took the match box from its case.

"You see," said he, opening it, "that this box is nearly full. It has an appointed place and it was in that place. We find a small match, burnt right out, under the table opposite the door, and two more in the bowl under the hanging lamp. A reasonable inference is that some one came in in the dark and struck a match as he entered. That match must have come from a box that he brought with him in his pocket. It burned out and he struck another, which also burned out while he was raising the chimney of the lamp, and he struck a third to light the lamp. But if that person was Crofton, why did he need to strike a match to light the room when the match-box was in its usual place ; and why did he throw the match-end on the floor?"

"You mean that the suggestion is that the person was not Crofton ; and I think you are right. Crofton doesn't carry matches in his pocket. He uses wax vestas and carries them in a silver case."

"It might possibly have been Ambrose," Thorndyke suggested.

"I don't think so," said I. "Ambrose uses a petrol lighter."

Thorndyke nodded. "There may be nothing in it," said he, "but it offers a suggestion. Shall we look over the rest of the premises? "

He paused for a moment to glance at a small key board on the wall on which one or two keys were hanging, each distinguished by a little ivory label and by the name written underneath the peg; then he opened a door in the corner of the room. As this led into the kitchen, I closed it and opened an adjoining one which gave access to a bedroom.

"This is probably the extra bedroom," he remarked as we entered. "The blinds have not been drawn down, and there is a general air of trimness that suggests the tidy up of an unoccupied room. And the bed looks if it had been out of use."

After an attentive look round, he returned to the living room and crossed to the remaining door. As he opened it, we looked into a nearly dark room, both the windows being covered by thick serge curtains.

"Well," he observed, when he had drawn back the curtains and raised the blinds, "there is nothing painfully tidy here. That is a very roughly-made bed, and the blanket is outside the counterpane."

He looked critically about the room and especially the bedside table.

"Here are some more discrepancies," said he. "There are two candlesticks, in one of which the candle has burned itself right out, leaving a fragment of wick. There are five burnt matches in it, two large ones from the box by its side and three small ones, of which two are mere stumps. The second candle is very much guttered, and I think "--he lifted it out of the socket--" yes, it has been used out of the candlestick. You see that the grease has run down right to the bottom and there is a distinct impression of a thumb--apparently a left thumb--made while the grease was warm. Then you notice the mark on the table of a tumbler which had contained some liquid that was not water, but there is no tumbler. However, it may be an old mark, though it looks fresh."

It is hardly like Crofton to leave an old mark on the table," said I. "He is a regular old maid. We had better see if the tumbler is in the kitchen."

"Yes," agreed Thorndyke. "But I wonder what he was doing with that candle. Apparently he took it out-of-doors, as there is a spot on the floor of the living-room ; and you see that there are one or two spots on the floor here." He walked over to a chest of drawers near the door and was looking into a drawer which he had pulled out, and which I could see was full of clothes, when I observed a faint smile spreading over his face. "Come round here, Jardine," he said in a low voice, "and take a peep through the crack of the door."

I walked round, and, applying my eye to the crack, looked across the living-room at the end window. Above the half-curtain I could distinguish the unmistakable top of a constabulary helmet.

"Listen," said Thorndyke. "They are in force."

As he spoke, there came from the neighbourhood of the kitchen a furtive scraping sound, suggestive of a pocket knife persuading a window-catch. It was followed by the sound of an opening window and then of a stealthy entry. Finally, the kitchen door opened softly, some one tip-toed across the living-room and a burly police-sergeant appeared, framed in the bedroom doorway.

"Good afternoon, sergeant," said Thorndyke, with a genial smile.

"Yes, that's all very well," was the response, "but the question is, who might you be, and what might you be doing in this house?"

Thorndyke briefly explained our business, and, when, we had presented our cards and Mrs. Crofton's written authority, the sergeant's professional stiffness vanished like magic.

"It's all right, Tomkins," he sang out to an invisible myrmidon. "You had better shut the window and go out by the front door. You must excuse me, gentlemen," he added; "but the tenant of the next bungalow cycled down and gave us the tip. He watched you through his glasses and saw you pick the front-door lock. It did look a bit queer, you must admit."

Thorndyke admitted it freely with a faint chuckle, and we walked across the living-room to the kitchen. Here, the sergeant's presence seemed to inhibit comments, but I noticed that my colleague cast a significant glance at a frying-pan that rested on a Primus stove. The congealed fat in it presented another "discrepancy"; for I could hardly imagine the fastidious Crofton going away and leaving it in that condition.

Noting that there was no unwashed tumbler in evidence, I followed my friend back to the living-room, where he paused with his eye on the key-board.

"Well," remarked the sergeant, "if he ever did come back here, it's pretty clear that he isn't here now. You've been all over the premises, I think?"

"All excepting the bathing-hut," replied Thorndyke; and, as he spoke, he lifted the key so labelled from its hook.

The sergeant laughed softly. "He's not very likely to have taken up quarters there," said he. "Still, there nothing like being thorough. But you notice that the key of the front door and that of the gate have both been taken away, so we can assume that he has taken himself away too."

"That is a reasonable inference," Thorndyke admitted; "but we may as well make our survey complete."

With this he led the way out into the garden and to the gate, where he unblushingly produced the 'smoker's companion' and insinuated its prongs into the keyhole.

"Well, I'm sure!" exclaimed the sergeant as the lock clicked and the gate opened. "That's a funny sort of tool; and you seem quite handy with it, too. Might I have a look at it?"

He looked at it so very long and attentively, when Thorndyke handed it to him, that I suspected him of an intention to infringe the patent. By the time he had finished his inspection we were at the bottom of the bank below the sea-wall and Thorndyke had inserted the key into the lock of the bathing-hut. As the sergeant returned the 'companion' Thorndyke took it and pocketed it then he turned the key and pushed the door open; and the officer started back with a shout of amazement.

It was certainly a grim spectacle that we looked in on. The hut was a small building about six feet square, devoid of any furniture or fittings, excepting one or two pegs high up the wall. The single, unglazed window was closely shuttered, and on the bare floor in the farther corner a man was sitting, leaning back into the corner, with his head dropped forward on his breast. The man was undoubtedly Arthur Crofton. That much I could say with certainty, notwithstanding the horrible changes wrought by death and the lapse of time. "But," I added when I had identified the body, "I should have said that he had been dead more than a fortnight. He must have come straight back from Margate and done this. And that will probably be the missing tumbler," I concluded, pointing to one that stood on the floor close to the right hand of the corpse.

"No doubt," replied Thorndyke, somewhat abstractedly. He had been looking critically about the interior of the hut, and now remarked: "I wonder why he did not shoot the bolt instead of locking himself in; and what has become of the key? He must have taken it out of the lock and put it in his pocket."

He looked interrogatively at the sergeant, who having no option but to take the hint, advanced with an expression of horrified disgust and proceeded very gingerly to explore the dead man's clothing.

"Ah!" he exclaimed at length, "here we are." He drew from the waistcoat pocket a key with a small ivory label attached to it. "Yes, this is the one. You see, it is marked " Bathing-hut."

He handed it to Thorndyke, who looked at it attentively, and even with an appearance of surprise, and then, producing an indelible pencil from his pocket, wrote on the label, "Found on body."

The first thing," said he, "is to ascertain it fits the lock."

"Why, it must," said the sergeant, "if he locked himself in with it."

"Undoubtedly," Thorndyke agreed, "but that is the point. It doesn't look quite similar to the other one."

He drew out the key which we had brought from the house and gave it to me to hold. Then he tried the key from the dead man's pocket; but it not only did not fit, it would not even enter the keyhole.

The sceptical indifference faded suddenly from the sergeant's face. He took the key from Thorndyke, having tried it with the same result, stood up and stared, round-eyed, at my colleague.

"Well!" he exclaimed. "This is a facer! It's the wrong key!"

"There may be another key on the body," said Thorndyke. "It isn't likely, but, you had better make sure."

The sergeant showed no reluctance this time. He searched the dead man's pockets thoroughly and produced a bunch of keys. But they were all quite small keys, none of them in the least resembling that of the hut door. Nor, I noticed, did they include those of the bungalow door or the garden gate. Once more the officer drew himself up and stared at Thorndyke.

"There's something rather fishy about this affair," said he.

"There is," Thorndyke agreed. "The door was certainly locked; and as it was not locked from within, it must have been locked from without. Then that key--the wrong key--was presumably placed in the dead man's pocket by some other person. And there are some other suspicious facts. A tumbler has disappeared from the bedside table, and there is a tumbler here. You notice one or two spots of candle-grease on the floor here, and it looks as if a candle had been stood in that corner near the door. There is no candle here now; but in the bedroom there is a candle which has been carried without a candle stick and which, by the way, bears an excellent impression of a thumb. The first thing to do will be to take the deceased's finger-prints. Would you mind fetching my case from the bedroom, Jardine?"

I ran back to the house (not unobserved by the gentleman in the next bungalow) and, catching up the case, carried it down to the hut. When I arrived there I found Thorndyke holding the tumbler delicately in his gloved left hand while he examined it against the light with the aid of his lens. He handed the latter to me and observed.

"If you look at this carefully, Jardine, you will see a very interesting thing. There are the prints of two different thumbs--both left hands, and therefore of different persons. You will remember that the tumbler stood by the right hand of the body and that the table, which bore the mark of a tumbler, was at the left-hand side of the bed."

When I had examined the thumb-prints he placed the tumbler carefully on the floor and opened his "research- case," which was fitted as a sort of portable laboratory. From this he took a little brass box containing an ink- tube, a tiny roller and some small cards, and, using the box-lid as an inking plate, he proceeded methodically to take the dead man's finger-prints, writing the particulars on each card.

"I don't quite see what you want with Crofton's finger-prints," said I. "The other man's would be more to the point."

"Undoubtedly," Thorndyke replied. "But we have to prove that they are another man's--that they are not Crofton's. And there is that print on the candle. That is a very important point to settle; and as we have finished here, we had better go and settle it at once."

He closed his case, and, taking up the tumbler with his gloved hand, led the way back to the house, the sergeant following when he had locked the door. We proceeded directly to the bedroom, where Thorndyke took the candle from its socket and, with the aid of his lens, compared it carefully with the two thumb-prints on the card, and then with the tumbler.

"It is perfectly clear," said he. "This is a mark of a left thumb. It is totally unlike Crofton's and it appears to be identical with the strange thumb-print on the tumbler. From which it seems to follow that the stranger took the candle from this room to the hut and brought it back. But he probably blew it out before leaving the house and lit it again in the hut."

The sergeant and I examined the cards, the candle and the tumbler, and then the former asked: "I suppose you have no idea whose thumb-print that might be? You don't know, for instance, of anyone who might have had any motive for making away with Mr. Crofton?

"That," replied Thorndyke, "is rather a question for the coroner's jury."

"So it is," the sergeant agreed. "But there won't be much question about their verdict. It is a pretty clear case of wilful murder."

To this Thorndyke made no reply excepting to give some directions as to the safe-keeping of the candle and tumbler; and our proposed "gipsy holiday" being now evidently impossible, we took our leave of the sergeant--who already had our cards--and wended back to the station.

"I suppose," said I, "we shall have to break the news to Mrs. Crofton."

That is hardly our business," he replied. "We can leave that to the solicitor or to Ambrose. If you know the lawyer's address, you might send him a telegram, arranging a meeting at eight o'clock to-night. Give no particulars. Just say "Crofton found," but mark the telegram "urgent" so that he will keep the appointment."

On reaching the station, I sent off the telegram, and very soon afterwards the London train was signalled. It turned out to be a slow train, which gave us ample time to discuss the case and me ample time for reflection. And, in fact, I reflected a good deal; for there was a rather uncomfortable question in my mind--the very question that the sergeant had raised and that Thorndyke had obviously evaded. Was there anyone who might have had a motive for making away with Crofton? It was an awkward question when one remembered the great legacy that had just fallen in and the terms of Miss Shuler's will; which expressly provided that, if Crofton died before his wife, the legacy should go to her. Now, Ambrose was the wife's brother; and Ambrose had been in the bungalow alone with Crofton, and nobody else was known to have been there at all. I meditated on these facts uncomfortably and would have liked to put the case to Thorndyke; but his reticence, his evasion of the sergeant's question and his decision to communicate with the solicitor rather than with the family showed pretty clearly what was in his mind and that he did not wish to discuss the matter.

Promptly at eight o'clock, having dined at a restaurant, we presented ourselves at the solicitor's house and were shown into the study, where we found Mr. Jobson seated at a writing-table. He looked at Thorndyke with some surprise, and when the introductions had been made, said somewhat dryly: "We may take it that Dr. Thorndyke is in some way connected with our rather confidential business?"

"Certainly," I replied. "That is why he is here."

Jobson nodded. "And how is Crofton?" he asked, "and where did you dig him up?"

"I am sorry to say," I replied, "that he is dead. It is a dreadful affair. We found his body locked in the bathing-hut. He was sitting in a corner with a tumbler on the floor by his side."

"Horrible ! horrible!" exclaimed the solicitor. "He ought never to have gone there alone. I said so at the time. And it is most unfortunate on account of the insurance, though that is not a large amount. Still the suicide clause, you know--"

"I doubt whether the insurance will be affected," said Thorndyke. "The coroner's finding will almost certainly be wilful murder."

Jobson was thunderstruck. In a moment his face grew livid and he gazed at Thorndyke with an expression of horrified amazement.

"Murder!" he repeated incredulously. "But you said he was locked in the hut. Surely that is clear proof of suicide."

"He hadn't locked himself in, you know. There was no key inside."

"Ah!" The solicitor spoke almost in a tone relief. "But, perhaps--did you examine his pockets?"

"Yes; and we found a key labelled 'Bathing hut.' But it was the wrong key. It wouldn't go into the lock. There is no doubt whatever that the door was locked from the outside."

"Good God!" exclaimed Jobson, in a faint voice. "It does look suspicious. But still, I can't believe--It seems quite incredible."

"That may be," said Thorndyke, "but it is all perfectly clear. There is evidence that a stranger entered the bungalow at night and that the affair took place in the bedroom. From thence the stranger carried the body down to the hut and he also took a tumbler and a candle from the bedside table. By the light of the candle--which was stood on the floor of the hut in a corner--he arranged the body, having put into its pocket a key from the board in the living-room. Then he locked the hut, went back to the house, put the key on its peg and the candle in its candlestick. Then he locked up the house and the garden gate and took the keys away with him."

The solicitor listened to this recital in speechless amazement. At length he asked: "How long ago do you suppose this happened?"

"Apparently on the night of the fifteenth of this month," was the reply.

"But," objected Jobson, "he wrote home on the sixteenth."

"He wrote," said Thorndyke," on the sixth. Somebody put a one in front of the six and posted the letter at Margate on the sixteenth. I shall give evidence to that effect at the inquest."

I was becoming somewhat mystified. Thorndyke's dry, stern manner--so different from his usual suavity--and the solicitor's uncalled-for agitation, seemed to hint at something more than met the eye. I watched Jobson as he lit a cigarette--with a small Bryant and May match, which he threw on the floor--and listened expectantly for his next question. At length he asked: "Was there any sort of--er--clue as to who this stranger might be?"

"The man who will be charged with the murder? Oh, yes. The police have the means of identifying him with absolute certainty."

"That is, if they can find him," said Jobson.

"Naturally. But when all the very remarkable facts have transpired at the inquest, that individual will probably come pretty clearly into view."

Jobson continued to smoke furiously with his eyes fixed on the floor, as if he were thinking hard. Presently he asked, without looking up: "Supposing they do find this man. What then? What evidence is there that he murdered Crofton?"

"You mean direct evidence?" said Thorndyke. "I can't say, as I did not examine the body; but the circumstantial evidence that I have given you would be enough to convict unless there were some convincing explanation other than murder. And I may say," he added, "that if the suspected person has a plausible explanation to offer, he would be well advised to produce it before he is charged. A voluntary statement has a good deal more weight than the same statement made by a prisoner in answer to a charge."

There was an interval of silence, in which I looked bewilderment from Thorndyke's stern visage to the pale face of the solicitor. At length the latter rose abruptly and, after one or two quick strides up and down the room, halted by the fireplace, and, still avoiding Thorndyke's eye, said, somewhat brusquely, though in a low, husky voice: "I will tell you how it happened. I went down to Seasalter, as you said, on the night of the fifteenth, on the chance of finding Crofton at the bungalow. I wanted to tell him of Miss Shuler's death and of the provisions her will."

"You had some private information on that subject, I presume?" said Thorndyke.

"Yes. My cousin was her solicitor and he kept me informed about the will."

"And about the state of her health?"

"Yes. Well, when I arrived at the bungalow, it was in darkness. The gate and the front door were unlocked, so I entered, calling out Crofton's name. As no one answered, I struck a match and lit the lamp. Then I went into the bedroom and struck a match there; and by its light I could see Crofton lying on the bed, quite still. I spoke to him, but he did not answer or move. Then I lighted a candle on his table; and now I could see what I had already guessed, that he was dead, and that he had been dead some time--probably more than a week.

"It was an awful shock to find a dead man in this solitary house, and my first impulse was to rush out and give the alarm. But when I went into the living-room, I happened to see a letter lying on writing-table and noticed that it was in his own hand and addressed to his wife. Unfortunately, I had the curiosity to take it out of the unsealed envelope and read it. It was dated the sixth and stated his intention of going to Margate for a time and then coming back to the bungalow.

"Now, the reading of that letter exposed me to an enormous temptation. By simply putting a one in front of the six and thus altering the date from the sixth to the sixteenth and posting the letter at Margate, I stood to gain thirty thousand pounds. I saw that at a glance. But I did not decide immediately to do it. I pulled down the blinds, drew the curtains and locked up the house while I thought it over. There seemed to be practically no risk, unless someone should come to the bungalow and notice that the state of the body did not agree with the altered date on the letter. I went back and looked at the dead man. There was a burnt-out candle by his side and a tumbler containing the dried-up remains of some brown liquid. He had evidently poisoned himself. Then it occurred to me that, if I put the body and the tumbler in some place where they were not likely to be found for some time, the discrepancy between the condition of the body and the date of the letter would not be noticed.

"For some time I could think of no suitable place, but at last I remembered the bathing-hut. No one would look there for him. If they came to the bungalow and didn't find him there, they would merely conclude that he had not come back from Margate. I took the candle and the key from the key-board and went down to the hut; but there was a key in the door already, so I brought the other key back and put it in Crofton's pocket, never dreaming that it might not be the duplicate. Of course, I ought to have tried it in the door.

"Well, you know the rest. I took the body down about two in the morning, locked up the hut, brought away the key and hung it on the board, took the counterpane off the bed, as it had some marks on it, and re-made the bed with the blanket outside. In the morning I took the train to Margate, posted the letter, after altering the date, and threw the gate-key and that of the front door into the sea.

"That is what really happened. You may not believe me; but I think you will as you have seen the body and will realise that I had no motive for killing Crofton before the fifteenth, whereas Crofton evidently died before that date."

"I would not say 'evidently,' said Thorndyke; "but, as the date of his death is the vital point in your defence, you would be wise to notify the coroner of the importance of the issue."

♦ ♦ ♦ ♦ ♦

"I don't understand this case," I said, as we walked homewards (I was spending the evening with Thorndyke). "You seemed to smell a rat from the very first. And I don't see how you spotted Jobson. It is a mystery to me."

It wouldn't be if you were a lawyer," he replied. "The case against Jobson was contained in what you told me at our first interview. You yourself commented on the peculiarity of the will that he drafted for Crofton. The intention of the latter was to leave all his property to his wife. But instead of saying so, the will specified each item of property, and appointed a residuary legatee, which was Jobson himself. This might have appeared like mere legal verbiage; but when Miss Shuler's legacy was announced, the transaction took on a rather different aspect. For this legacy was not among the items specified in the will. Therefore it did not go to Mrs. Crofton. It would be included in the residue of the estate and would go to the residuary legatee."

"The deuce it would!" I exclaimed.

"Certainly; until Crofton revoked his will or made a fresh one. This was rather suspicious. It suggested that Jobson had private information as to Miss Shuler's will and had drafted Crofton's will in accordance with it; and as she died of malignant disease, her doctor must have known for some time that she was dying and it looked as if jobson had information on that point, too. Now the position of affairs that you described to me was this:

"Crofton, a possible suicide, had disappeared, and had made no fresh will.

"Miss Shuler died on the thirteenth, leaving thirty thousand pounds to Crofton, if he survived her, or if he did not, then to Mrs. Crofton. The important question then was whether Crofton was alive or dead; and if he was dead, whether he had died before or after the thirteenth. For if he died before the thirteenth the legacy went to Mrs. Crofton, but if he died after that date the legacy went to Jobson.

"Then you showed me that extraordinarily opportune letter dated the sixteenth. Now, seeing that that date was worth thirty thousand pounds to Jobson, I naturally scrutinised it narrowly. The letter was written with ordinary blue-black ink. But this ink, even in the open, takes about a fortnight to blacken completely. In a closed envelope it takes considerably longer. On examining this date through a lens, the one was very perceptibly bluer than the six. It had therefore been added later. But for what reason? And by whom?

"The only possible reason was that Crofton was dead and had died before the thirteenth. The only person who had any motive for making the alteration was Jobson. Therefore, when we started for Seasalter I already felt sure that Crofton was dead and that the letter had been posted at Margate by Jobson. I had further no doubt that Crofton's body was concealed somewhere on the premises of the bungalow. All that I had to do was to verify those conclusions."

"Then you believe that Jobson has told us the truth?"

"Yes. But I suspect that he went down there with the deliberate intention of making away with Crofton before he could make a fresh will. The finding of Crofton's body must have been a fearful disappointment, but I must admit that he showed considerable resource in dealing with the situation; and he failed only by the merest chance. I think his defence against the murder charge will be admitted; but, of course, it will involve plea of guilty to the charge of fraud in connection with the legacy."

Thorndyke's forecast turned out to be correct. Jobson was acquitted of the murder of Arthur Crofton, but is at present "doing time" in respect of the forged letter and the rest of his too-ingenious scheme.

Dr. Thorndyke's Case Book

The Case of the White Footprints

"Well," said my friend Foxton, pursuing a familiar and apparently inexhaustible topic, "I'd sooner have your job than my own."

"I've no doubt you would," was my unsympathetic reply. "I never met a man who wouldn't. We all tend to consider other men's jobs in terms of their advantages and our own in terms of their drawbacks. It is human nature."

"Oh, it's all very well for you to be so beastly philosophical," retorted Foxton. "You wouldn't be if you were in my place. Here, in Margate, it's measles, chicken-pox and scarlatina all the summer, and bronchitis, colds and rheumatism an the winter. A deadly monotony. Whereas you and Thorndyke sit there in your chambers and let your clients feed you up with the raw material of romance. Why, your life is a sort of everlasting Adelphi drama."

"You exaggerate, Foxton," said I. "We, like you, have our routine work, only it is never heard of outside the Law Courts; and you, like every other doctor, must run up against mystery and romance from time to time."

Foxton shook his head as he held out his hand for my cup. "I don't," said be. "My practice yields nothing but an endless round of dull routine."

And then, as if in commentary on this last statement, the housemaid burst into the room and, with hardly dissembled agitation, exclaimed:

"If you please, sir, the page from Beddingfield's Boarding-house says that a lady has been found dead in her bed and would you go round there immediately."

"Very well, Jane," said Foxton, and as the maid retired, he deliberately helped himself to another fried egg and, looking across the table at me, exclaimed: "Isn't that always the way? Come immediately--now--this very instant, although the patient may have been considering for a day or two whether he'll send for you or not. But directly he decides you must spring out of bed, or jump up from your breakfast, and run."

"That's quite true," I agreed; "but this really does seem to be an urgent case."

"What's the urgency?" demanded Foxton. "The woman is already dead. Anyone would think she was in imminent danger of coming to life again and that my instant arrival the only thing that could prevent such a catastrophe."

"You've only a third-hand statement that she is dead," said I. "It is just possible that she isn't; and even if she is, as you will have to give evidence at the inquest, you do want the police to get there first and turn out the room before you've made your inspection."

"Gad!" exclaimed Foxton. "I hadn't thought of that. Yes. You're right. I'll hop round at once."

He swallowed the remainder of the egg at a single gulp rose from the table. Then he paused and stood for a few moments looking down at me irresolutely.

"I wonder, Jervis," he said, "if you would mind coming round with me. You know all the medico-legal ropes, and I don't. What do you say?"

I agreed instantly, having, in fact, been restrained only by delicacy from making the suggestion myself; and when I had fetched from my room my pocket camera and telescopic tripod, we set forth together without further delay.

Beddingfield's Boarding-house was but a few minutes walk from Foxton's residence being situated near the middle of Ethelred Road, Cliftonville, a quiet, suburban street which abounded in similar establishments, many of which, I noticed, were undergoing a spring-cleaning and renovation to prepare them for the approaching season.

"That's the house," said Foxton, "where that woman is standing at the front door. Look at the boarders, collected at the dining-room window. There's a rare commotion in that house, I'll warrant."

Here, arriving at the house, he ran up the steps and accosted in sympathetic tones the elderly woman who stood by the open street door.

"What a dreadful thing this is, Mrs. Beddingfield! Terrible! Most distressing for you!"

"Ah, you're right, Dr. Foxton," she replied. "It's an awful affair. Shocking. So bad for business, too. I do hope, and trust there won't be any scandal."

"I'm sure I hope not," said Foxton. "There shan't be I can help it. And as my friend Dr. Jervis, who is staying with me for a few days, is a lawyer as well as a doctor, we shall have the best advice. When was the affair discovered?"

"Just before I sent for you, Dr. Foxton. The maid, noticed that Mrs. Toussaint--that is the poor creature's name--had not taken in her hot water, so she knocked at the door. As she couldn't get any answer, she tried the door and found it bolted on the inside, and then she came and told me. I went up and knocked loudly, and then, as I couldn't get any reply, I told our boy, James, to force the door open with a case-opener, which he did quite easily as the bolt was only a small one. Then I went in, all of a tremble, for I had a presentiment that there was something wrong; and there she was lying stone dead, with a most 'orrible stare on her face and an empty bottle in her hand."

"A bottle, eh!" said Foxton.

"Yes. She'd made away with herself, poor thing; and all on account of some silly love affair--and it was hardly even that."

"Ah," said Foxton. "The usual thing. You must tell us about that later. Now we'd better go up and see the patient--at least the--er--perhaps you'll show us the room, Mrs. Beddingfield."

The landlady turned and preceded us up the stairs to the first-floor back, where she paused, and softly opening a door, peered nervously into the room. As we stepped past her and entered, she seemed inclined to follow, but, at a significant glance from me, Foxton persuasively ejected her and closed the door. Then we stood silent for a while and looked about us.

In the aspect of the room there was something strangely incongruous with the tragedy that had been enacted within its walls; a mingling of the commonplace and the terrible that almost amounted to anticlimax. Through the wide-open window the bright spring sunshine streamed in on the garish wallpaper and cheap furniture; from the street below, the periodic shouts of a man selling 'sole and mack-ro!" broke into the brisk staccato of a barrel-organ and both sounds mingled with a raucous voice close at hand, cheerfully trolling a popular song, and accounted for by a linen-clad elbow that bobbed in front of the window and evidently appertained to a house-painter on an adjacent ladder.

It was all very commonplace and familiar and discordantly out of character with the stark figure that lay on the bed like a waxen effigy symbolic of tragedy. Here was none of that gracious somnolence in which death often presents itself with a suggestion of eternal repose. This woman was dead; horribly, aggressively dead. The thin, sallow face was rigid as stone, the dark eyes stared into infinite space with a horrid fixity that was quite disturbing to look on. And yet the posture of the corpse was not uneasy, being, in fact, rather curiously symmetrical, with both arms outside the bedclothes and both hands closed, the right grasping, as Mrs. Beddingfield had said, an empty bottle.

"Well," said Foxton, as he stood looking down on the dead woman, "it seems a pretty clear case. She appears to have laid herself out and kept hold of the bottle so that there should be no mistake. How long do you suppose this woman has been dead, Jervis?"

I felt the rigid limbs and tested the temperature of the body surface.

"Not less than six hours," I replied. "Probably more. I should say that she died about two o'clock this morning."

"And that is about all we can say," said Foxton, "until the post-mortem has been made. Everything looks quite straightforward. No signs of a struggle or marks of violence. That blood on the mouth is probably due to her biting her lip when she drank from the bottle. Yes; here's a little cut on the inside of the lip, corresponding to the upper incisors. By the way, I wonder if there is anything left in the bottle."

As he spoke, he drew the small, unlabelled, green glass phial from the closed hand--out of which it slipped quite easily--and held it up to the light.

"Yes," he exclaimed, "there's more than a drachm left; quite enough for an analysis. But I don't recognize the smell. Do you?"

I sniffed at the bottle and was aware of a faint unfamiliar vegetable odour.

"No," I answered. "It appears to be a watery solution of some kind, but I can't give it a name. Where is the cork?"

"I haven't seen it," he replied. "Probably it is on the floor somewhere."

We both stooped to look for the missing cork and presently found it in the shadow, under the little bedside table. But, in the course of that brief search, I found something else, which had indeed been lying in full view all the time--a wax match. Now a wax match is a perfectly innocent and very commonplace object, but yet the presence of this one gave me pause. In the first place, women do not, as a rule, use wax matches, though there was not much in that. What was more to the point was that the candlestick by the bedside contained a box of safety matches, and that, as the burnt remains of one lay in the tray, it appeared to have been used to light the candle. Then why the wax match?

While I was turning over this problem Foxton had corked the bottle, wrapped it carefully in a piece of paper which he took from the dressing-table and bestowed it in his pocket.

"Well, Jervis," said he, "I think we've seen everything. The analysis and the post-mortem will complete the case. Shall we go down and hear what Mrs. Beddingfield has to say?"

But that wax match, slight as was its significance, taken alone, had presented itself to me as the last of a succession of phenomena each of which was susceptible of a sinister interpretation; and the cumulative effect of these slight suggestions began to impress me somewhat strongly.

"One moment, Foxton," said I. "Don't let us take anything for granted. We are here to collect evidence, and we must go warily. There is such a thing as homicidal poisoning, you know."

"Yes, of course," he replied, "but there is nothing to suggest it in this case; at least, I see nothing. Do you?"

"Nothing very positive," said I; "but there are some facts that seem to call for consideration. Let us go over what we have seen. In the first place, there is a distinct discrepancy in the appearance of the body. The general easy, symmetrical posture, like that of a figure on a tomb, suggests the effect of a slow, painless poison. But look at the face. There is nothing reposeful about that. It is very strongly suggestive of pain or terror or both."

"Yes," said Foxton, "that is so. But you can't draw any satisfactory conclusions from the facial expression of dead bodies. Why, men who have been hanged, or even, stabbed, often look as peaceful as babes."

"Still," I urged "it is a fact to be noted. Then there is that cut on the lip. It may have been produced in the way you suggest; but it may equally well be the result of pressure on the mouth."

Foxton made no comment on this beyond a slight shrug of the shoulders, and I continued: "Then there is the state of the hand. It was closed, but, it did not really grasp the object it contained. You drew the bottle out without any resistance. It simply lay in the closed hand. But that is not a normal state of affairs. As you know, when a person dies grasping any object, either the hand relaxes and lets it drop, or the muscular action passes into cadaveric spasm and grasps the object firmly. And lastly, there is this wax match. Where did it come from? The dead woman apparently lit her candle with a safety match from the box. It is a small matter, but it wants explaining."

Foxton raised his eyebrows protestingly. "You're like all specialists, Jervis," said he. "You see your speciality in everything. And while you are straining these flimsy suggestions to turn a simple suicide into murder, you ignore the really conclusive fact that the door was bolted and had to be broken open before anyone could get in."

"You are not forgetting, I suppose," said I, "that the window was wide open and that there were house-painters about and possibly a ladder left standing against the house."

"As to the ladder," said Foxton, "that is a pure assumption; but we can easily settle the question by asking that fellow out there if it was or was not left standing last night."

Simultaneously we moved towards the window; but halfway we both stopped short. For the question of the ladder had in a moment became negligible. Staring up at us from the dull red linoleum which covered the floor were the impressions of a pair of bare feet, imprinted in white paint with the distinctness of a woodcut. There was no need to ask if they had been made by the dead woman: they were unmistakably the feet of a man, and large feet at that. Nor could there be any doubt as to whence those feet had come. Beginning with startling distinctness under the window, the tracks shed rapidly in intensity until they reached the carpeted portion of the room, where they vanished abruptly; and only by the closest scrutiny was it possible to detect the faint traces of the retiring tracks.

Foxton and I stood for some moments gazing in, silence at the sinister white shapes; then we looked at one another.

"You've saved me from a most horrible blunder, Jervis," said Foxton. "Ladder or no ladder, that fellow came in at the window; and he came in last night, for I saw them painting these window-sills yesterday afternoon. Which side did he come from, I wonder?"

We moved to the window and looked out on the sill. A set of distinct, though smeared impressions on the new paint gave unneeded confirmation and showed that the intruder had approached from the left side, close to which was a cast-iron stack-pipe, now covered with fresh green paint.

"So," said Foxton, "the presence or absence of the ladder is of no significance. The man got into the window somehow, and that's all that matters."

"On the contrary," said I, "the point may be of considerable importance in identification. It isn't everyone who could climb up a stack-pipe, whereas most people could make shift to climb a ladder, even if it were guarded by a plank. But the fact that the man took off his boots and socks suggests that he came up by the pipe. If he had merely aimed at silencing his footfalls, he would probably have removed his boots only."

From the window we turned to examine more closely the footprints on the floor, and while I took a series of measurements with my spring tape Foxton entered them in my notebook.

"Doesn't it strike you as rather odd, Jervis," said he, "that neither of the little toes has made any mark?"

"It does indeed," I replied. "The appearances suggest that the little toes were absent, but I have never met with such a condition. Have you?"

"Never. Of course one is acquainted with the supernumerary toe deformity, but I have never heard of congenitally deficient little toes."

Once more we scrutinized the footprints, and even examined those on the window-sill, obscurely marked on the fresh paint; but, exquisitely distinct as were those on the linoleum, showing every wrinkle and minute skin-marking, not the faintest hint of a little toe was to be seen on either foot.

"It's very extraordinary," said Foxton. "He has certainly lost his little toes, if he ever had any. They couldn't have failed to make some mark. But it's a queer affair. Quite a windfall for the police, by the way; I mean for purposes of identification."

"Yes," I agreed, "and having regard to the importance of the footprints, I think it would be wise to get a photograph of them."

"Oh, the police will see to that," said Foxton. "Besides, we haven't got a camera, unless you thought of using that little toy snapshotter of yours."

As Foxton was no photographer I did not trouble to explain that my camera, though small, had been specially made for scientific purposes.

"Any photograph is better than none," I said, and with this I opened the tripod and set it over one of the most distinct of the footprints, screwed the camera to the goose-neck, carefully framed the footprint in the finder and adjusted the focus, finally making the exposure by means of an Antinous release. This process I repeated four times, twice on a right footprint and twice on a left.

"Well," Foxton remarked, "with all those photographs the police ought to be able to pick up the scent."

"Yes, they've got something to go on; but they'll have to catch their hare before they can cook him. He won't be walking about barefooted, you know."

"No. It's a poor clue in that respect. And now we may as well be off as we've seen all there is to see. I think we won't have much to say to Mrs. Beddingfield. This is a police case, and the less I'm mixed up in it the better it will be for my practice."

I was faintly amused at Foxton's caution when considered by the light of his utterances at the breakfast-table. Apparently his appetite for mystery and romance was easily satisfied. But that was no affair of mine. I waited on the doorstep while he said a few--probably evasive--words to the landlady and then, as we started off together in the direction of the police station, I began to turn over in my mind the salient features of the case. For some time we walked on in silence, and must have been pursuing a parallel train of thought for, when he at length spoke, he almost put my reflections into words.

"You know, Jervis," said he, "there ought to be a clue in those footprints. I realize that you can't tell how many toes a man has by looking at his booted feet. But those unusual footprints ought to give an expert a hint as to what sort of man to look for. Don't they convey any hint to you?"

I felt that Foxton was right; that if my brilliant colleague, Thorndyke, had been in my place he would have extracted from those footprints some leading fact that would have given the police a start along some definite line of inquiry; and that belief, coupled with Foxton's challenge, put me on my mettle.

"They offer no particular suggestions to me at this moment," said I, "but I think that, if we consider them systematically, we may be able to draw some useful deductions."

"Very well," said Foxton, "then let us consider them systematically. Fire away. I should like to hear how you work these things out."

Foxton's frankly spectatorial attitude was a little disconcerting, especially as it seemed to commit me to a result that I was by no means confident of attaining. I therefore began a little diffidently.

"We are assuming that both the feet that made those prints were from some cause devoid of little toes. That assumption--which is almost certainly correct--we treat as a fact, and, taking it as our starting point, the first step in the inquiry is to find some explanation of it. Now there are three possibilities, and only three: deformity, injury, and disease. The toes may have been absent from birth, they may have been lost as a result of mechanical injury, or they may have been lost by disease. Let us take those possibilities in order.

"Deformity we exclude since such a malformation is unknown to us.

"Mechanical injury seems to be excluded by the fact that the two little toes are on opposite sides of the body and could not conceivably be affected by any violence which left the intervening feet uninjured. This seems to narrow the possibilities down to disease; and the question that arises is, What diseases are there which might result in the loss of both little toes?"

I looked inquiringly at Foxton, but he merely nodded encouragingly. His rôle was that of listener.

"Well," I pursued, "the loss of both toes seems to exclude local disease, just as it excluded local injury; and as to general diseases, I can think only of three which might produce this condition--Raynaud's disease, ergotism, and frost-bite."

"You don't call frost-bite a general disease, do you?" objected Foxton.

"For our present purpose, I do. The effects are local, but the cause-- low external temperature--affects the whole body and is a general cause. Well, now, taking the diseases in order. I think we can exclude Raynaud's disease. It does, it is true, occasionally cause the fingers or toes to die and drop off, and the little toes would be especially liable to be affected as being most remote from the heart. But in such a severe case the other toes would be affected. They would be shrivelled and tapered, whereas, if you remember, the toes of these feet were quite plump and full, to judge by the large impressions they made. So I think we may safely reject Raynaud's disease. There remain ergotism and frost-bite; and the choice between them is just a question of relative frequency. Frost-bite is more common; therefore frost-bite is more probable."

"Do they tend equally to affect the little toes?" asked Foxton.

"As a matter of probability, yes. The poison of ergot acting from within, and intense cold acting from without, contract the small blood-vessels and arrest, the circulation. The feet, being the most distant parts of the body from the heart, are the first to feel the effects; and the little toes, which are the most distant parts of the feet, are the most susceptible of all."

Foxton reflected awhile, and then remarked:

"This is all very well, Jervis, but I don't see that you are much forrarder. This man has lost both his little toes and on your showing, the probabilities are that the loss was due either to chronic ergot poisoning or to frost-bite, with a balance of probability in favour of frost-bite. That's all. No proof, no verification, just the law of probability applied to a particular case, which is always unsatisfactory. He may have lost his toes in some totally different way. But even if the probabilities work out correctly, I don't see what use your conclusions would be to the police. They wouldn't tell them what sort of man to look for."

There was a good deal of truth in Foxton's objection. A man who has suffered from ergotism or frost-bite is not externally different from any other man. Still, we had not exhausted the case, as I ventured to point out.

"Don't be premature, Foxton," said I. "Let us pursue our argument a little farther. We have established a probability that this unknown man has suffered either from ergotism or frost-bite. That, as you say, is of no use by itself; but supposing we can show that these conditions tend to affect a particular class of persons, we shall have established a fact that will indicate a line of investigation. And I think we can. Let us take the case of ergotism first.

"Now how is chronic ergot poisoning caused? Not by the medicinal use of the drug, but, by the consumption of the diseased rye in which ergot occurs. It is therefore peculiar to countries in which rye is used extensively as food. Those countries, broadly speaking, are the countries of North-Eastern Europe, and especially Russia and Poland.

"Then take the case of frost-bite. Obviously, the most likely person to get frost-bitten is the inhabitant of a country with a cold climate. The most rigorous climates inhabited by white people are North America and North-Eastern Europe, especially Russia and Poland. So you see, the areas associated with ergotism and frost-bite overlap to some extent. In fact they do more than overlap; for a person even slightly affected by ergot would be specially liable to frost-bite, owing to the impaired circulation. The conclusion is that, racially, in both ergotism and frost-bite, the balance of probability is in favour of a Russian, a Pole, or a Scandinavian.

"Then in the case of frost-bite there is the occupation factor. What class of men tend most to become frost-bitten? Well, beyond all doubt, the greatest sufferers from frost-bite are sailors, especially those on sailing ships, and, naturally, on ships trading to Arctic and sub-Arctic countries. But the bulk of such sailing ships are those engaged in the Baltic and Archangel trade; and the crews of those ships are almost exclusively Scandinavians, Finns, Russians and Poles. So that, again, the probabilities point to a native of North-Eastern Europe, and, taken as a whole, by the over-lapping of factors, to a Russian, a Pole, or a Scandinavian."

Foxton smiled sardonically. "Very ingenious, Jervis," said he. "Most ingenious. As an academic statement of probabilities, quite excellent. But for practical purposes absolutely useless. However, here we are at the police-station. I'll just run in and give them the facts and then go on to the coroner's office."

"I suppose I'd better not come in with you?" I said.

"Well, no," he replied. "You see, you have no official connection with the case, and they mightn't like it. You'd better go and amuse yourself while I get the morning's visits done. We can talk things over at lunch."

With this he disappeared into the police-station, and I turned away with a smile of grim amusement. Experience is apt to make us a trifle uncharitable, and experience had taught me that those who are the most scornful of academic reasoning are often not above retailing it with some reticence as to its original authorship. I had a shrewd suspicion that Foxton was at this very moment disgorging my despised "academic statement of probabilities" to an admiring police-inspector.

My way towards the sea lay through Ethelred Road, and I had traversed about half its length and was approaching the house of the tragedy when I observed Mrs. Beddingfield at the bay window. Evidently she recognized me, for a few moments later she appeared in outdoor clothes on the doorstep and advanced to meet me.

"Have you seen the police?" she asked, as we met.

I replied that Dr. Foxton was even now at the police-station.

"Ah!" she said, "it's a dreadful affair; most unfortunate, too, just at the beginning of the season. A scandal is absolute ruin to a boarding-house. What do you think of the case? Will it be possible to hush it up? Dr. Foxton said you were a lawyer, I think, Dr. Jervis?"

"Yes, I am a lawyer, but really I know nothing of the circumstances of this case. Did I understand that there had been something in the nature of a love affair?"

"Yes--at least--well, perhaps I oughtn't to have said that. But hadn't I better tell you the whole story?--that is, if I am not taking up too much of your time."

"I should be interested to hear what led to the disaster," said I.

"Then," she said, "I will tell you all about it. Will you come indoors, or shall I walk a little way with you?"

As I suspected that the police were at that moment on their way to the house, I chose the latter alternative and led her away seawards at a pretty brisk pace.

"Was this poor lady a widow?" I asked, as we started up the street.

"No, she wasn't," replied Mrs. Beddingfield, "and that was the trouble. Her husband was abroad--at least, he had been, and he was just coming home. A pretty home-coming it will be for him, poor man. He is an officer in the Civil Police at Sierra Leone, but he hasn't been there long. He went there for his health."

"What! To Sierra Leone!" I exclaimed, for the "White Man's Grave" seemed a queer health resort.

"Yes. You see, Mr. Toussaint is a French Canadian, and it seems that he has always been somewhat of a rolling stone. For some time he was in the Klondyke, but he suffered so much from the cold that he had to come away. It injured his health very severely; I don't quite know in what way, but I do know that he was quite a cripple for a time. When he got better he looked out for a post in a warm climate and eventually obtained the appointment of Inspector of Civil Police at Sierra Leone. That was about ten months ago, and when he sailed for Africa his wife came to stay with me, and has been here ever since."

"And this love affair that you spoke of?"

"Yes, but I oughtn't to have called it that. Let me explain what happened. About three months ago a Swedish gentleman--a Mr.

Bergson-- came to stay here, and he seemed to be very much smitten with Mrs. Toussaint."

"And she?"

"Oh, she liked him well enough. He is a tall, good-looking man--though for that matter he is no taller than her husband, nor any better-looking. Both men are over six feet. But there was no harm so far as she was concerned, excepting that she didn't see the position quite soon enough. She wasn't very discreet, in fact I thought it necessary to give her a little advice. However, Mr. Bergson left here and went to live at Ramsgate to superintend the unloading of the iceships (he came from Sweden in one), and I thought the trouble was at an end. But it wasn't, for he took to coming over to see Mrs. Toussaint, and of course I couldn't have that. So at last I had to tell him that he mustn't come to the house again. It was very unfortunate, for on that occasion I think he had been "tasting", as they say in Scotland. He wasn't drunk, but he was excitable and noisy, and when I told him he mustn't come again he made such a disturbance that two of the gentlemen boarders--Mr. Wardale and Mr. Macauley--had to interfere. And then he was most insulting to them, especially to Mr. Macauley, who is a coloured gentleman; called him a "buck nigger" and all sorts of offensive names."

"And how did the coloured gentleman take it?"

"Not very well, I am sorry to say, considering that he is a gentleman--a law student with chambers in the Temple. In fact, his language was so objectionable that Mr. Wardale insisted on my giving him notice on the spot. But I managed to get him taken in next door but one; you see, Mr. Wardale had been a Commissioner at, Sierra Leone--it was through him that Mr. Toussaint got his appointment--so I suppose he was rather on his dignity with coloured people."

"And was that the last you heard of Mr. Bergson?"

"He never came here again, but he wrote several times to Mrs. Toussaint, asking her to meet him. At last, only a few days ago, she wrote to him and told him that the acquaintance must cease."

"And has it ceased?"

"As far as I know, it has."

"Then, Mrs. Beddingfield," said I, "what makes you connect the affair with--with what has happened?"

"Well, you see," she explained, "there is the husband. He was coming home, and is probably in England already."

"Indeed!" said I.

"Yes," she continued. "He went up into the bush to arrest some natives belonging to one of these gangs of murderers--Leopard Societies, I think they are called--and he got seriously wounded. He wrote to his wife from hospital saying that he would be sent home as soon as he was fit to travel, and about ten days ago she got a letter from him saying that he was coming by the next ship.

"I noticed that she seemed very nervous and upset when she got the letters from hospital, and still more so when the last letter came. Of course, I don't know what he said to her in those letters. It may be that he had heard something about Mr. Bergson, and threatened to take some action. Of course, I can't say. I only know that she was very nervous and restless, and when we saw in the paper four days ago that the ship he would be coming by had arrived in Liverpool she seemed dreadfully upset. And she got worse and worse until--well, until last night."

"Has anything been heard of the husband since the ship arrived?" I asked.

"Nothing whatever," replied Mrs. Beddingfield, with a meaning look at me which I had no difficulty in interpreting. "No letter, no telegram, not a word. And you see, if he hadn't come by that ship he would almost certainly have sent a letter to her. He must have arrived in England, but why hasn't he turned up, or at least sent a wire? What is he doing? Why is be staying away? Can he have heard something? And what does he mean to do? That's what kept the poor thing on wires, and that, I feel certain, is what drove her to make away with herself."

It was not my business to contest Mrs. Beddingfield's erroneous deductions. I was seeking information--it seemed that I had nearly exhausted the present source. But one point required amplifying.

"To return to Mr. Bergson, Mrs. Beddingfield," said I "Do I understand that he is a seafaring man?"

"He was," she replied. "At present he is settled at Ramsgate as manager of a company in the ice trade, but formerly he was a sailor. I have heard him say that he was one, of the crew of an exploring ship that went in search of the North Pole and that he was locked up in the ice for months and months. I should have thought he would have had enough of ice after that."

With this view I expressed warm agreement, and having now obtained all the information that appeared to be available I proceeded to bring the interview to an end.

"Well, Mrs. Beddingfield," I said, "it is a rather mysterious affair. Perhaps more light may be thrown on it at the inquest. Meanwhile, I should think that it will be wise of you to keep your own counsel as far as outsiders are concerned."

The remainder of the morning I spent pacing the smooth stretch of sand that lies to the east of the jetty, and reflecting on the evidence that I had acquired in respect of this singular crime. Evidently there was no lack of clues in this case. On the contrary, there were two quite obvious lines of inquiry, for both the Swede and the missing husband presented the characters of the hypothetical murderer. Both had been exposed to the conditions which tend to produce frost-bite; one of them had probably been a consumer of rye meal, and both might be said to have a motive-- though, to be sure, it was a very insufficient one--for committing the crime. Still in both cases the evidence was merely speculative; it suggested a line of investigation but it did nothing more.

When I met Foxton at lunch I was sensible of a curious change in his manner. His previous expansiveness had given place to marked reticence and a certain official secretiveness.

"I don't think, you know, Jervis," he said, when I opened the subject "that we had better discuss this affair. You see, I am the principal witness, and while the case is *sub judice*--well, in fact the police don't want the case talked about."

"But surely I am a witness, too, and in expert witness, moreover--"

"That isn't the view of the police. They look on you as more or less of an amateur, and as you have no official connection with the case, I don't think they propose to subpœna you. Superintendent Platt, who is in charge of the case, wasn't very pleased at my having taken you to the house. Said it was quite irregular. Oh, and by the way, he says you must hand over those photographs."

"But isn't Platt going to have the footprints photographed on his own account?" I objected.

"Of course he is. He is going to have a set of proper photographs taken by an expert photographer--he was mightily amused when he heard about your little snapshot affair. Oh, you can trust Platt. He is a great man. He has had a course of instruction at the Fingerprint Department in London."

"I don't see how that is going to help him, as there aren't any fingerprints in this case."

This was a mere fly-cast on my part, but Foxton rose at once at the rather clumsy bait.

"Oh, aren't there?" he exclaimed. "You didn't happen to spot them, but they were there. Platt has got the prints of a complete right hand. This is in strict confidence, you know," he added, with somewhat belated caution.

Foxton's sudden reticence restrained me from uttering the obvious comment on the superintendent's achievement. I returned to the subject of the photographs.

"Supposing I decline to hand over my film?" said I.

"But I hope you won't--and in fact you mustn't. I am officially connected with the case, and I've got to live with these people. As the police-surgeon, I am responsible for the medical evidence, and Platt expects me to get those photographs from you. Obviously you can't keep them. It would be most irregular."

It was useless to argue. Evidently the police did not want me to be introduced into the case, and after all the superintendent was within his rights, if he chose to regard me, as a private individual and to demand the surrender of the film.

Nevertheless I was loath to give up the photographs, at least until I had carefully studied them. The case was within my own speciality of practice, and was a strange and interesting one. Moreover, it appeared to be in unskilful hands, judging from the fingerprint episode, and then experience had taught me to treasure up small scraps of chance evidence, since one never knew when one might be drawn into a case in a professional capacity. In effect, I decided not to give up the photographs, though that decision committed me to a ruse that I was not very willing to adopt. I would rather have acted quite straightforwardly.

"Well if you insist, Foxton," I said, "I will hand over the film or, if you like, I will destroy it in your presence."

"I think Platt would rather have the film uninjured," said Foxton. "Then he'll know, you know," he added, with a sly grin.

In my heart, I thanked Foxton for that grin. It made my own guileful proceedings so much easier; for a suspicious man invites you to get the better of him if you can.

After lunch I went up to my room, locked the door and took the little camera from my pocket. Having fully wound up the film, I extracted it, wrapped it up carefully and bestowed it in my inside breast-pocket. Then I inserted a fresh film, and going to the open window, took four successive snapshots of the sky. This done, I closed the camera, slipped it into my pocket and went downstairs. Foxton was in the hall, brushing his hat, as I descended, and at once renewed his demand.

"About those photographs, Jervis," said he; "I shall be looking in at the police-station presently, so if you wouldn't mind--"

"To be sure," said I. "I will give you the film now if you like."

Taking the camera from my pocket, I solemnly wound up the remainder of the film, extracted it, stuck down the loose end with ostentatious care, and handed it to him.

"Better not expose it to the light," I said, going the whole hog of deception, "or you may fog the exposures."

Foxton took the spool from me as if it were hot--he was not a photographer--and thrust it into his handbag. He was still thanking me the quite profusely when the front-door bell rang.

The visitor who stood revealed when Foxton opened the door was a small, spare gentleman with a complexion of peculiar brown-papery quality that suggests long residence the tropics. He stepped in briskly and introduced himself and his business without preamble.

"My name is Wardale--boarder at Beddingfield's. I called with reference to the tragic event which--"

Here Foxton interposed in his frostiest official tone. "I am afraid, Mr. Wardale, I can't give you any information about the case at present."

"I saw you two gentlemen at the house this morning--" Mr. Wardale continued, but Foxton again cut him short.

"You did. We were there--or at least, I was--as representative of the Law, and while the case is *sub judice*--"

"It isn't yet," interrupted Wardale.

"Well, I can't enter into any discussion of it--"

"I am not asking you to," said Wardale a little impatiently. "But I understand that one of you is Dr. Jervis."

"I am," said I.

"I must really warn you---—" Foxton began again; but Mr. Wardale interrupted testily:

"My dear sir, I am a lawyer and a magistrate and understand perfectly well what is and what is not permissible. I have come simply to make a professional engagement with Dr. Jervis."

"In what way can I be of service to you?" I asked.

"I will tell you," said Mr. Wardale. "This poor lady, whose death has occurred in so mysterious a manner, was the wife of a man who was, like myself a servant of the Government of Sierra Leone. I was the friend of both of them, and in the absence of the husband I should like to have the inquiry into the circumstances of this lady's death watched by a competent lawyer with the necessary special knowledge of medical evidence. Will you or your colleague, Dr. Thorndyke, undertake to watch the case for me?"

Of course I was willing to undertake the case and said so.

"Then," said Mr. Wardale, "I will instruct my solicitor to write to you and formally retain you in the case. Here is my card. You will find my name in the Colonial Office List, and you know my address here."

He handed me his card, wished us both good afternoon, and then, with a stiff little bow, turned and took his departure.

"I think I had better run up to town and confer with Thorndyke," said I. "How do the trains run?"

"There is a good train in about three-quarters of an hour," replied Foxton.

"Then I will go by it, but I shall come down again to-morrow or the next day, and probably Thorndyke will come down with me."

"Very well," said Foxton. "Bring him in to lunch or dinner, but I can't put him up, I am afraid."

"It would be better not," said I. "Your friend Platt wouldn't like it. He won't want Thorndyke--or me either for that matter. And what about those photographs? Thorndyke will want them, you know."

"He can't have them," said Foxton doggedly, "unless Platt is willing to hand them back; which I don't suppose he will be."

I had private reasons for thinking otherwise, but I kept them to myself; and as Foxton went forth on his afternoon round, I returned upstairs to pack my suitcase and write the telegram to Thorndyke informing him of my movements.

It was only a quarter past five when I let myself into our chambers in King's Bench Walk. To my relief I found my colleague at home and our laboratory assistant, Polton, in the act of laying tea, for two.

"I gather," said Thorndyke, as we shook hands, "that my learned brother brings grist to the mill?"

"Yes," I replied. "Nominally a watching brief, but I think you will agree with me that it is a case for independent investigation."

"Will there be anything in my line, sir?" inquired Polton, who was always agog at the word 'investigation'.

"There is a film to be developed. Four exposures of white footprints on a dark ground."

"Ah!" said Polton, "you'll want good strong negatives, and they ought to be enlarged if they are, from the little camera. Can you give me the dimensions?"

I wrote out the measurements from my notebook and handed him the paper together with the spool of film, with which he retired gleefully to the laboratory.

"And now, Jervis," said Thorndyke, "while Polton is operating on the film and we are discussing our tea, let us have a sketch of the case."

I gave him more than a sketch, for the events were recent and I had carefully sorted out the facts during my journey to town, making rough notes, which I now consulted. To my rather lengthy recital he listened in his usual attentive manner, without any comment, excepting in regard to my manœuvre to retain possession of the exposed film.

"It's almost a pity you didn't refuse." said he. "They could hardly have enforced their demand, and my feeling is that it is more convenient as well as more dignified to avoid direct deception unless one is driven to it. But perhaps you considered that you were."

As a matter of fact I had at the time, but I had since come to Thorndyke's opinion. My little manœuvre was going to be a source of inconvenience presently.

"Well," said Thorndyke, when I had finished my recital, "I think we may take it that the police theory is, in the main, your own theory derived from Foxton."

"I think so, excepting that I learned from Foxton that Superintendent Platt has obtained the complete fingerprints of a right hand."

Thorndyke raised his eyebrows. "Fingerprints!" he exclaimed. "Why, the fellow must be a mere simpleton. But there," he added, "everybody-- police, lawyers, judges, even Galton himself--seems to lose every vestige of common sense as soon as the subject of fingerprints is raised. But it would be interesting to know how he got them and what they are like. We must try to find that out. However, to return to your case, since your theory and the police theory are probably the same, we may as well consider the value of your inferences.

"At present we are dealing with the case in the abstract. Our data are largely assumptions, and our inferences are largely derived from an application of the mathematical laws of probability. Thus we assume that a murder has been committed, whereas it may turn out to have been suicide. We assume the murder to have been committed by the person, who made the footprints, and we assume that that person has no little toes, whereas he may have retracted little toes which do not touch the ground and so leave no impression. Assuming the little toes to be absent, we account for their absence by considering known causes in the order of their probability. Excluding--quite properly, I think--Raynaud's disease, we arrive at frost-bite and ergotism.

"But two persons, both of whom are of a stature corresponding to the size of the footprints, may have had a motive--though a very inadequate one-- for committing the crime, and both have been exposed to the conditions which tend to produce frost-bite, while one of them has, probably, been exposed to the conditions which tend to produce ergotism. The laws of probability point to both of these two men; and the chances in favour of the Swede being the murderer rather than the Canadian would be represented by the common factor--frost-bite--multiplied by the additional factor, ergotism. But this is purely speculative at present. There is no evidence that either man has ever been frost-bitten or has ever eaten spurred rye. Nevertheless, it is a perfectly sound method at this stage. It indicates a line of investigation. If it should transpire that either man has suffered from frost-bite or ergotism, a definite advance would have been made. But here is Polton with a couple of finished prints. How on earth did you manage it in the time, Polton?"

"Why, you see, sir, I just dried the film with spirit," replied Polton. "It saved a lot of time. I will let you have a pair of enlargements in about a quarter of an hour."

Handing us the two wet prints, each stuck on a glass plate, he retired to the laboratory, and Thorndyke and I proceeded to scrutinize the photographs with the aid of our pocket lenses. The promised enlargements were really hardly necessary excepting for the purpose of comparative measurements, for the image of the white footprint, fully two inches long, was so microscopically sharp that, with the assistance of the lens, the minutest detail could be clearly seen.

"There is certainly not a vestige of little toe," remarked Thorndyke, "and the plump appearance of the other toes supports your rejection of Raynaud's disease. Does the character of the footprint convey any other suggestion to you, Jervis?"

"It gives me the impression that the man had been accustomed to go bare-footed in early life and had only taken to boots comparatively recently. The position of the great toe suggests this, and the presence of a number of small scars on the toes and ball of the foot seems to confirm it. A person walking bare-foot would sustain innumerable small wounds from treading on small, sharp objects."

Thorndyke looked dissatisfied. "I agree with you," he said, "as to the suggestion offered by the undeformed state of the great toes; but those little pits do not convey to me the impression of scars produced as you suggest. Still, you may be right."

Here our conversation was interrupted by a knock on the outer oak. Thorndyke stepped out through the lobby and I heard him open the door. A moment or two later he re-entered, accompanied by a short, brown-faced gentleman whom I instantly recognized as Mr. Wardale.

"I must have come up by the same train as you," he remarked, as we shook hands, "and to a certain extent, I suspect, on the same errand. I thought I would like to put our arrangement on a business footing, as I am a stranger to both of you."

"What do you want us to do?" asked Thorndyke.

"I want you to watch the case, and, if necessary, to look into the facts independently."

"Can you give us any information that may help us?"

Mr. Wardale reflected. "I don't think I can," he said at length. "I have no facts that you have not, and any surmises of mine might be misleading. I had rather you kept an open mind. But perhaps we might go into the question of costs."

This, of course, was somewhat difficult, but Thorndyke contrived to indicate the probable liabilities involved, to Mr. Wardale's satisfaction.

"There is one other little matter," said Wardale, as he rose to depart. "I have got a suitcase here which Mrs. Beddingfield lent me to bring some things up to town. It is one that Mr. Macauley left behind when he went away from the boarding-house. Mrs. Beddingfield suggested that I might leave it at his chambers when I had finished with it; but I don't know his address, excepting that it is somewhere in the Temple, and I don't want to meet the fellow if he should happen to have come up to town."

"Is it empty?" asked Thorndyke.

"Excepting for a suit of pyjamas and a pair of shocking old slippers." He opened the suitcase as he spoke and exhibited its contents with a grin.

"Characteristic of a negro, isn't it? Pink silk pyjamas and slippers about three sizes too small."

"Very well," said Thorndyke. "I will get my man to find out the address and leave it there."

As Mr. Wardale went out, Polton entered with the enlarged photographs, which showed the footprints the natural size. Thorndyke handed them to me, and as I sat down to examine them he followed his assistant to the laboratory. He returned in a few minutes, and after a brief inspection of the photographs, remarked:

"They show us nothing more than we have seen, though they may be useful later. So your stock of facts is all we have to go on at present. Are you going home to-night?"

"Yes, I shall go back to Margate to-morrow."

"Then, as I have to call at Scotland Yard, we may as well walk to Charing Cross together."

As we walked down the Strand we gossiped on general topics, but before we separated at Charing Cross, Thorndyke reverted to the case.

"Let me know the date of the inquest," said he, "and try to find out what the poison was--if it was really a poison."

"The liquid that was left in the bottle seemed to be a watery solution of some kind," said I, "as I think I mentioned."

"Yes," said Thorndyke. "Possibly a watery infusion of strophanthus."

"Why strophanthus?" I asked.

"Why not?" demanded Thorndyke. And with this and an inscrutable smile, he turned and walked down Whitehall.

Three days later I found myself at Margate--sitting beside Thorndyke in a room adjoining the Town Hall, in which the inquest on the death of Mrs. Toussaint was to be held. Already the coroner was in his chair, the jury were in their seats and the witnesses assembled in a group of chairs apart. These included Foxton, a stranger who sat by him--presumably the other medical witness--Mrs. Beddingfield, Mr. Wardale, the police superintendent and a well-dressed coloured man, whom I correctly assumed to be Mr. Macauley.

As I sat by my-rather sphinx-like colleague my mind recurred for the hundredth time to his extraordinary powers of mental synthesis. That parting remark of his as to the possible nature of the poison had brought home to me in a flash the fact that he already had a definite theory of this crime, and that his theory was not mine nor that of the police. True, the poison might not be strophanthus, after all, but that would not alter the position. He had a theory of the crime, but yet he was in possession of no facts excepting those with which I had supplied him. Therefore those facts contained the material for a theory, whereas I had deduced from them nothing but the bald, ambiguous mathematical probabilities.

The first witness called was naturally Dr. Foxton, who described the circumstances already known to me. He further stated that he bad been present at the autopsy, that he had found on the throat and limbs of the deceased bruises that suggested a struggle and violent restraint. The immediate cause of death was heart failure, but whether that failure was due to shock, terror, or the action of a poison he could not positively say.

The next witness was a Dr. Prescott, an expert pathologist and toxicologist. He had made the autopsy and agreed with Dr. Foxton as to the cause of death. He had examined the liquid contained in the bottle taken from the hand of the deceased and found it to be a watery infusion or decoction of strophanthus seeds. He had analysed the fluid contained in the stomach and found it to consist largely of the same infusion.

"Is infusion of strophanthus seeds used in medicine?" the coroner asked.

"No," was the reply. "The tincture is the form in which strophanthus is administered unless it is given in the form of strophanthine."

"Do you consider that the strophanthus caused or contributed to death?"

"It is difficult to say," replied Dr. Prescott. "Strophanthus is a heart poison, and there was a very large poisonous dose. But very little had been absorbed, and the appearances were not inconsistent with death from shock."

"Could death have been self-produced by the voluntary taking of the poison?" asked the coroner.

"I should say, decidedly not. Dr. Foxton's evidence shows that the bottle was almost certainly placed in the hands of the deceased after death, and this is in complete agreement with the enormous dose and small absorption."

"Would you say that appearances point to suicidal or homicidal poisoning?"

"I should say that they point to homicidal poisoning, but that death was probably due mainly to shock."

This concluded the expert's evidence. It was followed by that of Mrs. Beddingfield, which brought out nothing new to me but the fact that a trunk had been broken open and a small attaché-case belonging to the deceased abstracted and taken away.

"Do you know what the deceased kept in that case?" the coroner asked.

"I have seen her put her husband's letters into it. She had quite a number of them. I don't know what else she kept in it except, of course, her cheque-book."

"Had she any considerable balance at the bank?"

"I believe she had. Her husband used to send most of his pay home and she used to pay it in and leave it with the bank. She might have two or three hundred pounds to her credit."

As Mrs. Beddingfield concluded Mr. Wardale was called, and he was followed by Mr. Macauley. The evidence of both was quite brief and concerned entirely with the disturbance made by Bergson, whose absence from the court I had already noted.

The last witness was the police superintendent, and he, as I had expected, was decidedly reticent. He did refer to the footprints, but, like Foxton--who presumably had his instructions--he abstained from describing their peculiarities. Nor did he say anything about fingerprints. As to the identity of the criminal, that had to be further inquired into. Suspicion had at first fastened upon Bergson, but it had since transpired that the Swede sailed from Ramsgate on an ice-ship two days before the occurrence of the tragedy. Then suspicion had pointed to the husband, who was known to have landed at Liverpool four days before the death of his wife and who had mysteriously disappeared. But he (the superintendent) had only that morning received a telegram from the Liverpool police informing him that the body of Toussaint had been found floating in the Mersey, and that it bore a number of wounds of an apparently homicidal character. Apparently he had been murdered and his corpse thrown into the river.

"This is very terrible," said the coroner. "Does this second murder throw any light on the case which we are investigating?"

"I think it does," replied the officer, without any great conviction, however; "but it is not advisable to go into details."

"Quite so," agreed the coroner. "Most inexpedient. But are we to understand that you have a clue to the perpetrator of this crime--assuming a crime to have been committed?"

"Yes," replied Platt. "We have several important clues."

"And do they point to any particular individual?"

The superintendent hesitated. "Well . . ." he began with some embarrassment, but the coroner interrupted him:

"Perhaps the question is indiscreet. We mustn't hamper the police, gentlemen, and the point is not really material to our inquiry. You would rather we waived that question, Superintendent?"

"If you please, sir," was the emphatic reply.

"Have any cheques from the deceased woman's cheque book been presented at the bank?"

"Not since her death. I inquired at the bank only this morning."

This concluded the evidence, and after a brief but capable summing-up by the coroner, the jury returned a verdict of "Wilful murder against some person unknown".

As the proceedings terminated, Thorndyke rose and turned round, and then to my surprise I perceived Superintendent Miller, of the Criminal Investigation Department, who had come in unperceived by me and was sitting immediately behind us.

"I have followed your instructions, sir," said he, addressing Thorndyke, "but before we take any definite action I should like to have a few words with you."

He led the way to an adjoining room and, as we entered we were followed by Superintendent Platt and Dr. Foxton.

"Now, Doctor," said Miller, carefully closing the door, "I have carried out your suggestions. Mr. Macauley is being detained, but before we commit ourselves to an arrest we must have something to go upon. I shall want you to make out a prima facie case."

"Very well," said Thorndyke, laying upon the table the small green suitcase that was his almost invariable companion.

"I've seen that prima facie case before," Miller remarked with a grin, as Thorndyke unlocked it and drew out a large envelope. "Now, what have you got there?"

As Thorndyke extracted from the envelope Polton's enlargements of my small photographs, Platt's eyes appeared to bulge, while Foxton gave me a quick glance of reproach.

"These," said Thorndyke "are the full-sized photographs of the footprints of the suspected murderer. Superintendent Platt can probably verify them."

Rather reluctantly Platt produced from his pocket a pair of whole-plate photographs, which he laid beside the enlargements.

"Yes," said Miller, after comparing them, "they are the same footprints. But you say, Doctor, that they are Macauley's footprints. Now, what evidence have you?"

Thorndyke again had recourse to the green case, from which he produced two copper plates mounted on wood and coated with printing ink.

"I propose," said he, lifting the plates out of their protecting frame, "that we take prints of Macauley's feet and compare them with the photographs."

"Yes," said Platt. "And then there are the fingerprints that we've got. We can test those, too."

"You don't want fingerprints if you've got a set of toeprints," objected Miller.

"With regard to those fingerprints," said Thorndyke. "May I ask if they were obtained from the bottle?"

"They were," Platt admitted.

"And were there any other fingerprints?"

"No," replied Platt. "These were the only ones."

As he spoke he laid on the table a photograph showing the prints of the thumb and fingers of a right hand.

Thorndyke glanced at the photograph and, turning to Miller, said:

"I suggest that those are Dr. Foxton's fingerprints."

"Impossible!" exclaimed Platt, and then suddenly fell silent.

"We can soon see," said Thorndyke, producing from the case a pad of white paper. "If Dr. Foxton will lay the finger-tips of his right hand first on this inked plate and then on the paper, we can compare the prints with the photograph."

Foxton placed his fingers on the blackened plate and then pressed them on the paper pad, leaving on the latter four beautifully clear, black fingerprints. These Superintendent Platt scrutinized eagerly, and as his glance travelled from the prints to the photographs he broke into a sheepish grin.

"Sold again!" he muttered. "They are the same prints."

"Well," said Miller, in a tone of disgust, "you must have been a mug not to have thought of that when you knew that Dr. Foxton had handled the bottle."

"The fact, however, is important," said Thorndyke. "The absence of any fingerprints but Dr. Foxton's not only suggests that the murderer took the precaution to wear gloves, but especially it proves that the bottle was not handled by the deceased during life. A suicide's hands will usually be pretty moist and would leave conspicuous, if not very clear, impressions."

"Yes," agreed Miller, "that is quite true. But with regard to these footprints. We can't compel this man to let us examine his feet without arresting him. Don't think, Dr. Thorndyke, that I suspect you of guessing. I've known you too long for that. You've got your facts all right, I don't doubt, but you must let us have enough to justify our arrest."

Thorndyke's answer was to plunge once more into the inexhaustible green case, from which he now produced two objects wrapped in tissue-paper. The paper being removed, there was revealed what looked like a model of an excessively shabby pair of brown shoes.

"These," said Thorndyke, exhibiting the "models" to Superintendent Miller--who viewed them with an undisguised grin--"are plaster casts of the interiors of a pair of slippers--very old and much too tight--belonging to Mr. Macauley. His name was written inside them. The casts have been waxed and painted with raw umber, which has been lightly rubbed off, thus accentuating the prominences and depressions. You will notice that the impressions of the toes on the soles and of the "knuckles" on the uppers appear as prominences; in fact we have in these casts a sketchy reproduction of the actual feet.

"Now, first as to dimensions. Dr. Jervis's measurements of the footprints give us ten inches and three-quarters as, the extreme length and four inches and five-eighths as the extreme width at the heads of the metatarsus. On these casts, as you see, the extreme length is ten inches and five-eighths--the loss of one-eighth being accounted for by the curve of the sole--and the extreme width is four inches and a quarter-- three-eighths being accounted for by the lateral compression of a tight slipper. The agreement of the dimensions is remarkable, considering the unusual size. And now as to the peculiarities of the feet.

"You notice that each toe has made a perfectly distinct impression on the sole, excepting the little toe; of which there is no trace in either cast. And, turning to the uppers, you notice that the knuckles of the toes appear quite distinct and prominent--again excepting the little toes, which have made no impression at all. Thus it is not a case of retracted little toes, for they would appear as an extra prominence. Then, looking at the feet as a whole, it is evident that the little toes are absent; there is a distinct hollow, where there should be a prominence."

"M'yes," said Miller dubiously, "it's all very neat. But isn't it just a bit speculative?"

"Oh, come, Miller," protested Thorndyke; "just consider the facts. Here is a suspected murderer known to have feet of an unusual size and presenting a very rare deformity; and they are the feet of a man who had actually lived in the same house as the murdered woman and who, at the date of the crime, was living only two doors away. What more would you have?"

"Well, there is the question of motive," objected Miller.

"That hardly belongs to a prima facie case," said Thorndyke, "But even if it did, is there not ample matter for suspicion? Remember who the murdered woman was, what her husband was, and who this Sierra Leone gentleman is."

"Yes, yes; that's true," said Miller somewhat hastily, either perceiving the drift of Thorndyke's argument (which I did not), or being unwilling to admit that he was still in the dark. "Yes, we'll have the fellow in and get his actual footprints."

He went to the door and, putting his head out, made some sign, which was almost immediately followed by a trampling of feet, and Macauley entered the room, followed by two large plain-clothes policemen. The negro was evidently alarmed, for he looked about him with the wild expression of a hunted animal. But his manner was aggressive and truculent.

"Why am I being interfered with in this impertinent manner?" he demanded in the deep buzzing voice characteristic of the male negro.

"We want to have a look at your feet, Mr. Macauley," said Miller. "Will you kindly take off your shoes and socks?"

"No," roared Macauley. "I'll see you damned first!"

"Then," said Miller, "I arrest you on a charge of having murdered--"

The rest of the sentence was drowned in a sudden uproar. The tall, powerful negro, bellowing like an angry bull, had whipped out a large, strangely-shaped knife and charged furiously at the Superintendent. But the two plain-clothes men had been watching him from behind and now sprang upon him, each seizing an arm. Two sharp, metallic clicks in quick succession, a thunderous crash and an ear-splitting yell, and the formidable barbarian lay prostrate on the floor with one massive constable sitting astride his chest and the other seated on his knees.

"Now's your chance, Doctor," said Miller. "I'll get his shoes and socks off."

As Thorndyke re-inked his plates, Miller and the local superintendent expertly removed the smart patent shoes and the green silk socks from the feet of the writhing, bellowing negro. Then Thorndyke rapidly and skilfully applied the inked plates to the soles of the feet--which I steadied for the purpose--and followed up with a dexterous pressure of the paper pad, first to one foot and then--having torn off the printed sheet-to the other. In spite of the difficulties occasioned by Macauley's struggles, each sheet presented a perfectly clear and sharp print of the sole of the foot, even the ridge-patterns of the toes and ball of the foot being quite distinct. Thorndyke laid each of the new prints on the table beside the corresponding large photograph, and invited the two superintendents to compare them.

"Yes," said Miller--and Superintendent Platt nodded his acquiescence-- "there can't be a shadow of a doubt. The ink-prints and the photographs are identical, to every line and skin-marking. You've made out your case, Doctor, as you always do."

"So you see," said Thorndyke, as we smoked our evening pipes on the old stone pier, "your method was a perfectly sound one, only you didn't apply it properly. Like too many mathematicians, you started on your calculations before you had secured your data. If you had applied the simple laws of probability to the real data, they would have pointed straight to Macauley."

"How do you suppose he lost his little toes?" I asked.

"I don't suppose at all. Obviously it was a clear case of double ainhum."

"Ainhum!" I exclaimed with a sudden flash of recollection.

"Yes; that was what you overlooked, you compared the probabilities of three diseases either of which only very rarely causes the loss of even one little toe and infinitely rarely causes the loss of both, and none of which conditions is confined to any definite class of persons; and you ignored ainhum, a disease which attacks almost exclusively the little toe, causing it to drop off, and quite commonly destroys both little toes--a disease, moreover, which is confined to the black-skinned races. In European practice ainhum is unknown, but in Africa, and to a less extent in India, it is quite common.

"If you were to assemble all the men in the world who have lost both little toes more than nine-tenths of them would be suffering from ainhum; so that, by the laws of probability, your footprints were, by nine chances to one, those of a man who had suffered from ainhum, and therefore a black-skinned man. But as soon as you had established a black man as the probable criminal, you opened up a new field of corroborative evidence. There was a black man on the spot. That man was a native of Sierra Leone and almost certainly a man of importance there. But the victim's husband had deadly enemies in the native secret societies of Sierra Leone. The letters of the husband to the wife probably contained matter incriminating certain natives of Sierra Leone. The evidence became cumulative, you see. Taken as a whole, it pointed plainly to Macauley, apart from the new fact of the murder of Toussaint in Liverpool, a city with a considerable floating population of West Africans."

"And I gather from your reference to the African poison, strophanthus, that you fixed on Macauley at once when I gave you my sketch of the case?"

"Yes; especially when I saw your photographs of the footprints with the absent little toes and those characteristic chigger-scars on the toes that remained. But it was sheer luck that enabled me to fit the keystone into its place and turn mere probability into virtual certainty. I could have embraced the magician Wardale when he brought us the magic slippers. Still, it isn't an absolute certainty, even now, though I expect it will be by to-morrow."

And Thorndyke was right. That very evening the police entered Macauley's chambers in Tanfield Court, where they discovered the dead woman's attaché-case. It still contained Toussaint's letters to his wife, and one of those letters mentioned by name, as members of a dangerous secret society, several prominent Sierra Leone men, including the accused, David Macauley.

The Blue Scarab

Medico-legal practice is largely concerned with crimes against the person, the details of which are often sordid, gruesome and unpleasant. Hence the curious and romantic case of the Blue Scarab (though really outside our speciality) came as somewhat of a relief. But to me it is of interest principally as illustrating two of the remarkable gifts which made my friend, Thorn unique as an investigator: his uncanny power of picking out the one essential fact at a glance, and his capacity to produce, when required, inexhaustible stores of unexpected knowledge of the most out-of-the-way subjects.

It was late in the afternoon when Mr. James Blowgrave arrived, by appointment, at our chambers, accompanied by his daughter, a rather strikingly pretty girl of about twenty-two; and when we had mutually introduced ourselves, the consultation began without preamble.

"I didn't give any details in my letter to you," said Mr. Blowgrave. "I thought it better not to, for fear you might decline the case. It is really a matter of a robbery, but not quite an ordinary robbery. There are some unusual and rather mysterious features in the case. And as the police hold out very little hope, I have come to ask if you will give me your opinion on the case and perhaps look into it for me. But first I had better tell you how the affair happened.

"The robbery occurred just a fortnight ago, about half-past nine o'clock in the evening. I was sitting in my study with my daughter, looking over some things that I had taken from a small deed-box, when a servant rushed in to tell us that one of the outbuildings was on fire. Now, my study opens by a French window on the garden at the back, and, as the outbuilding was in a meadow at the side of the garden, I went out that way, leaving the French window open; but before going I hastily put the things back in the deed-box and locked it.

"The building--which I used partly as a lumber store and partly as a workshop--was well alight and the whole household was already on the spot, the boy working the pump and the two maids carrying the buckets and throwing water on the fire. My daughter and I joined the party and helped to carry the buckets and take out what goods we could reach from the burning building. But it was nearly half an hour before we got the fire completely extinguished, and then my daughter and I went to our rooms to wash and tidy ourselves up. We returned to the study together, and when I had shut the French window my daughter proposed that we should resume our interrupted occupation. Thereupon I took out of my pocket the key of the deed-box and turned to the cabinet on which the box always stood.

"But there was no deed-box there.

"For a moment I thought I must have moved it, and cast my eyes round the room in search of it. But it was nowhere to be seen, and a moment's reflection reminded me that I had left it in its usual place. The only possible conclusion was that during our absence at the fire, somebody must have come in by the window and taken it. And it looked as if that somebody had deliberately set fire to the outbuilding for the express purpose of luring us all out of the house."

"That is what the appearances suggest," Thorndyke agreed. "Is the study window furnished with a blind, or curtains?"

"Curtains," replied Mr. Blowgrave. "But they were not drawn. Anyone in the garden could have seen into the room; and the garden is easily accessible to an active person who could climb over a low wall."

"So far, then," said Thorndyke, "the robbery might be the work of a casual prowler who had got into the garden and watched you through the window, and assuming that the things you had taken from the box were of value, seized an easy opportunity to make off with them. Were the things of any considerable value?"

"To a thief they were of no value at all. There were a number of share certificates, a lease, one or two agreements, some family photographs and a small box containing an old letter and a scarab. Nothing worth stealing, you see, for the certificates were made out in my name and were therefore unnegotiable."

"And the scarab?"

"That may have been lapis lazuli, but more probably it was a blue glass imitation. In any case it was of no considerable value. It was about an inch and a half long. But before you come to any conclusion, I had better finish the story. The robbery was on Tuesday, the 7th of June. I gave information to the police, with a description of the missing property, but nothing happened until Wednesday, the 15th, when I received a registered parcel bearing, the Southampton postmark. On opening it I found, to my astonishment, the entire contents of the deed-box, with the exception of the scarab, and this rather mysterious communication."

He took from his pocket and handed to Thorndyke an ordinary envelope addressed in typewritten characters, and sealed with a large, elliptical seal, the face of which was covered with minute hieroglyphics.

"This," said Thorndyke," I take to be an impression of the scarab; and an excellent impression it is."

"Yes," replied Mr. Blowgrave," I have no doubt that it is the scarab. It is about the same size."

Thorndyke looked quickly at our client with an expression of surprise. "But," he asked, "don't you recognise the hieroglyphics on it?"

Mr. Blowgrave smiled deprecatingly. "The fact is," said he, "I don't know anything about hieroglyphics, but I should say, as far as I can judge, these look the same. What do you think, Nellie?"

Miss Blowgrave looked at the seal vaguely and replied, "I am in the same position. Hieroglyphics are to me just funny things that don't mean anything. But these look the same to me as those on our scarab, though I expect any other hieroglyphics would, for that matter."

Thorndyke made no comment on this statement, but examined the seal attentively through his lens. Then he drew out the contents of the envelope, consisting of two letters, one typewritten and the other in a faded brown handwriting. The former he read through and then inspected the paper closely, holding it up to the light to observe the watermark.

"The paper appears to be of Belgian manufacture," he remarked, passing it to me. I confirmed this observation and then read the letter, which was headed " Southampton" and ran thus:

DEAR OLD PAL,

I am sending you back some trifles removed in error. The ancient document is enclosed with this, but the curio is at present in the custody of my respected uncle. Hope its temporary loss will not inconvenience you, and that I may be able to return it to you later. Meanwhile, believe me,

Your ever affectionate,
RUDOLPHO.

"Who is Rudolpho?" I asked.

"The Lord knows," replied Mr. Blowgrave. "A pseudonym of our absent friend, I presume. He seems to be a facetious sort of person."

"He does," agreed Thorndyke. "This letter and the seal appear to be what the schoolboys would call a leg-pull. But still, this is all quite normal. He has returned you the worthless things and has kept the one thing that has any sort of negotiable value. Are you quite clear that the scarab is not more valuable than you have assumed?"

"Well," said Mr. Blowgrave, "I have had an expert's opinion on it. I showed it to M. Fouquet, the Egyptologist, when he was over here from Brussels a few months ago, and his opinion was that it was a worthless imitation. Not only was it not a genuine scarab, but the inscription was a sham, too; just a collection of hieroglyphic characters jumbled together without sense or meaning."

"Then," said Thorndyke, taking another look at the seal through his lens, "it would seem that Rudolpho, or Rudolpho's uncle, has got a bad bargain. Which doesn't throw much light on the affair."

At this point Miss Blowgrave intervened. "I think, father," said she, "you have not given Dr. Thorndyke quite all the facts about the scarab. He ought to be told about its connection with Uncle Reuben."

As the girl spoke Thorndyke looked at her with curious expression of suddenly awakened interest. Later I understood the meaning of that look, but at the time there seemed to me nothing particularly arresting in her words.

"It is just a family tradition," Mr. Blowgrave said deprecatingly. "probably it is all nonsense."

"Well, let us have it, at any rate," said Thorndyke. "We may get some light from it."

Thus urged, Mr. Blowgrave hemmed a little shyly and began:

"The story concerns my great-grandfather Silas Blowgrave, and his doings during the war with France. It seems that he commanded a privateer of which he and his brother Reuben were the joint owners, and that in the course of their last cruise they acquired a very remarkable and valuable collection of jewels. Goodness knows how they got them; not very honestly, I suspect, for they appear to have been a pair of precious rascals. Something has been said about the loot from a South American church or cathedral, but there is really nothing known about the affair. There are no documents. It is mere oral tradition and very vague and sketchy. The story goes that when they had sold off the ship, they came down to live at Shawstead in Hertfordshire, Silas occupying the manor house--in which I live at present--and Reuben a farm adjoining. The bulk of the loot they shared out at the end of the cruise, but the jewels were kept apart to be dealt with later--perhaps when the circumstances under which they had been acquired had been forgotten. However, both men were inveterate gamblers and it seems--according to the testimony of a servant of Reuben's who overheard them--that on a certain night when they had been playing heavily, they decided to finish up by playing for the whole collection of jewels as a single stake. Silas, who had the jewels in his custody, was seen to go to the manor house and return to Reuben's house carrying a small, iron chest.

"Apparently they played late into the night, after everyone else but the servant had gone to bed, and the luck was with Reuben, though it seems probable that he gave luck some assistance. At any rate, when the play was finished and the chest handed over, Silas roundly accused him of cheating, and we may assume that a pretty serious quarrel took place. Exactly what happened is not clear, for when the quarrel began Reuben dismissed the servant, who retired to her bedroom in distant part of the house. But in the morning it was discovered that Reuben and the chest of jewels had both disappeared, and there were distinct traces of blood in the room in which the two men had been playing. Silas professed to know nothing about the disappearance; but a strong--and probably just-- suspicion arose that he had murdered his brother and made away with the jewels. The result was that Silas also disappeared, and for a long time his whereabouts was not known even by his wife.

"Later it transpired that he had taken up his abode under an assumed name, in Egypt, and that he had developed an enthusiastic interest in the then new science of Egyptology--the Rosetta Stone had been deciphered only a few years previously. After a time he resumed communication with his wife, but never made any statement as to the mystery of his brother's disappearance. A few months before his death he visited his home in disguise and he then handed to his wife a little sealed packet which was to be delivered to his only son, William, on his attaining the age of twenty-one. That packet contained the scarab and the letter which you have taken from the envelope."

"Am I to read it?" asked Thorndyke.

"Certainly, if you think it worth while," was the reply. Thorndyke opened the yellow sheet of paper and, glancing through the brown and faded writing, read aloud:

CAIRO, 4 March, 1833.
MY DEAR SON,

I am sending you, as my last gift, a valuable scarab and a few words of counsel on which I would bid you meditate. Believe me, there is much wisdom in the lore of Old Egypt. Make it your own. Treasure the scarab as a precious inheritance. Handle it often but show it to none. Give your Uncle Reuben Christian burial. It is your duty, and you will have your reward. He robbed your father, but he shall make restitution.

Farewell!

Your affectionate father,
SILAS BLOWGRAVE.

As Thorndyke laid down the letter he looked inquiringly at our client.

"Well," he said, "here are some plain instructions. How have they been carried out?

"They haven't been carried out at all," replied Mr. Blowgrave. "As to his son William, my grandfather, he was not disposed to meddle in the matter. This seemed to be a frank admission that Silas killed his brother and concealed the body, and William didn't choose to reopen the scandal. Besides, the instructions are not so very plain. It is all very well to say, 'Give your Uncle Reuben Christian burial,' but where the deuce is Uncle Reuben?"

"It is plainly hinted," said Thorndyke," that whoever gives the body Christian burial will stand to benefit, and the word 'restitution' seems to suggest a clue to the whereabouts of the jewels. Has no one thought it worth while to find out where the body is deposited?"

"But how could they?" demanded Blowgrave. "He doesn't give the faintest clue. He talks as if his son knew where the body was. And then, you know, even supposing Silas did not take the jewels with him, there was the question, whose property were they? To begin with, they were pretty certainly stolen property, though no one knows where they came from. Then Reuben apparently got them from Silas by fraud, and Silas got them back by robbery and murder. If William had discovered them he would have had to give them up to Reuben's sons, and yet they weren't strictly Reuben's property. No one had an undeniable claim to them, even if they could have found them."

"But that is not the case now," said Miss Blowgrave.

"No," said Mr. Blowgrave, in answer to Thorndyke's look of inquiry. "The position is quite clear now. Reuben's grandson, my cousin Arthur, has died recently, and as he had no children, he has dispersed his property. The old farm-house and the bulk of his estate he has left to a nephew, but he made a small bequest to my daughter and named her as the residuary legatee. So that what ever rights Reuben had to the jewels are now vested in her, and on my death she will be Silas's heir, too. As a matter of fact," Mr. Blowgrave continued, "we were discussing this very question on the night of the robbery. I may as well tell you that my girl will be left pretty poorly off when I go, for there is a heavy mortgage on our property and mighty little capital. Uncle Reuben's jewels would have made the old home secure for her if we could have laid our hands on them. However, I mustn't take up your time with our domestic affairs."

"Your domestic affairs are not entirely irrelevant," said Thorndyke. "But what is it that you want me to do in the matter?"

"Well," said Blowgrave, "my house has been robbed and my premises set fire to. The police can apparently do nothing. They say there is no clue at all unless the robbery was committed by somebody in the house, which is absurd, seeing that the servants were all engaged in putting out the fire. But I want the robber traced punished, and I want to get the scarab back. It may be intrinsically valueless, as M. Fouquet said, but Silas's testamentary letter seems to indicate that it had some value. At any rate, it is an heirloom, and I am loath to lose it. It seems a presumptuous thing to ask you to investigate a trumpery robbery, but I should take it as a great kindness if you would look into the matter."

"Cases of robbery pure and simple," replied Thorndyke, "are rather alien to my ordinary practice, but in this one there are certain curious features that seem to make an investigation worth while. Yes, Mr. Blowgrave, I will look into the case, and I have some hope that we may be able to lay our hands on the robber, in spite of the apparent absence of clues. I will ask you to leave both these letters for me to examine more minutely, and I shall probably want to make an inspection of the premises--perhaps to-morrow."

"Whenever you like," said Blowgrave. "I am delighted that you are willing to undertake the inquiry. I have heard so much about you from my friend Stalker, of the Griffin Life Assurance Company, for whom you have acted on several occasions."

"Before you go," said Thorndyke," there is one point that we must clear up. Who is there besides yourselves that knows of the existence of the scarab and this letter and the history attaching to them?"

"I really can't say," replied Blowgrave. "No one has seen them but my cousin Arthur. I once showed them to him, and he may have talked about them in the family. I didn't treat the matter as a secret."

When our visitors had gone we discussed the bearings of the case.

"It is quite a romantic story," said I, "and the robbery has its points of interest, but I am rather inclined to agree with the police--there is mighty little to go on."

"There would have been less," said Thorndyke, "if our sporting friend hadn't been so pleased with himself. That typewritten letter was a piece of gratuitous impudence. Our gentleman overrated his security and crowed too loud."

"I don't see that there is much to be gleaned from the letter, all the same," said I.

"I am sorry to hear you say that, Jervis," he exclaimed, "because I was proposing to hand the letter over to you to examine and report on."

"I was only referring to the superficial appearances," I said hastily. "No doubt a detailed examination will bring something more distinctive into view."

"I have no doubt it will," he said, "and as there are reasons for pushing on the investigation as quickly as possible, I suggest that you get to work at once. I will occupy myself with the old letter and the envelope."

On this I began my examination without delay, and as a preliminary I proceeded to take a facsimile photograph of the letter by putting it in a large printing frame with a sensitive plate and a plate of clear glass. The resulting negative showed not only the typewritten lettering, but also the watermark and wire lines of the paper, and a faint grease spot. Next I turned my attention to the lettering itself, and here I soon began to accumulate quite a number of identifiable peculiarities. The machine was apparently a Corona, fitted with the, small "Elite" type, and the alignment was markedly defective. The "lower case"--or small--"a" was well below the line, although the capital "A" appeared to be correctly placed ; the "u" was slightly above the line, and the small "m" was partly clogged with dirt.

Up to this point I had been careful to manipulate the letter with forceps (although it had been handled by at least three persons, to my knowledge), and I now proceeded to examine it for finger-prints. As I could detect none by mere inspection, I dusted the back of the paper with finely powdered fuchsin, and distributed the powder by tapping the paper lightly. This brought into view quite a number of finger-prints, especially round the edges of the letter, and though most of them were very faint and shadowy, it was possible to make out the ridge pattern well enough for our purpose. Having blown off the excess of powder, I took the letter to the room where the large copying camera was set up, to photograph it before developing the finger-prints on the front. But here I found our laboratory assistant, Polton, in possession, with the sealed envelope fixed to the copying easel. "I shan't be a minute, sir," said he. "The doctor wants an enlarged photograph of this seal. I've got the plate in."

I waited while he made his exposure and then proceeded to take the photograph of the letter, or rather of the finger-prints on the back of it. When I had developed the negative I powdered the front of the letter and brought out several more finger-prints--thumbs this time. They were a little difficult to see where they were imposed on the lettering, but, as the latter was bright blue and the fuchsin powder was red, this confusion disappeared in the photograph, in which the lettering was almost invisible while the finger-prints were more distinct than they had appeared to the eye. This completed my examination, and when I had verified the make of typewriter by reference to our album of specimens of typewriting, I left the negatives for Polton to dry and print and went down to the sitting-room to draw up my little report. I had just finished this and was speculating on what had become of Thorndyke, when I heard his quick step on the stair and a few moments later he entered with a roll of paper in his hand. This he unrolled on the table, fixing it open with one or two lead paper-weights, and I came round to inspect it, when I found it to be a sheet of the Ordnance map on the scale of twenty-five inches to the mile.

"Here is the Blowgraves' place," said Thorndyke, "nearly in the middle of the sheet. This is his house--Shawstead Manor--and that will probably be the out-building that was on fire. I take it that the house marked Dingle Farm is the one that Uncle Reuben occupied."

"Probably," I agreed. "But I don't see why you wanted this map if you are going down to the place itself tomorrow."

"The advantage of a map," said Thorndyke, "is that you can see all over it at once and get the lie of the land well into your mind; and you can measure all distances accurately and quickly with a scale and a pair of dividers. When we go down to-morrow, we shall know our way about as well as Blowgrave himself."

"And what use will that be?" I asked. "Where does the topography come into the case?

"Well, Jervis," he replied, "there is the robber, for instance; he came from somewhere and he went somewhere. A study of the map may give us a hint as to his movements. But here comes Polton 'with the documents,' as poor Miss Flite would say. What have you got for us, Polton?

"They aren't quite dry, sir," said Polton, laying four large bromide prints on the table. "There's the enlargement of the seal--ten by eight, mounted--and three unmounted prints of Dr. Jervis's."

Thorndyke looked at my photographs critically. "They're excellent, Jervis," said he. "The finger prints are perfectly legible, though faint. I only hope some of them are the right ones. That is my left thumb. I don't see yours. The small one is presumably Miss Blowgrave's. We must take her finger-prints to-morrow, and her father's, too. Then we shall know if we have got any of the robber's." He ran his eye over my report and nodded approvingly. "There is plenty there to enable us to identify the typewriter if we can get hold of it, and the paper is very distinctive. What do you think of the seal?" he added, laying the enlarged photograph before me.

It is magnificent," I replied, with a grin. "Perfectly monumental."

"What are you grinning at?" he demanded.

"I was thinking that you seem to be counting your chickens in pretty good time," said I. "You are making elaborate preparations to identify the scarab, but you are rather disregarding the classical advice of the prudent Mrs. Glasse."

"I have a presentiment that we shall get that scarab," said he. "At any rate we ought to be in a position to 926 identify it instantly and certainly if we are able to get a sight of it."

"We are not likely to," said I. "Still, there is no harm in providing for the improbable."

This was evidently Thorndyke's view, and he certainly made ample provision for this most improbable contingency; for, having furnished himself with a drawing- board and a sheet of tracing-paper, he pinned the latter over the photograph on the board and proceeded, with a fine pen and hectograph ink, to make a careful and minute tracing of the intricate and bewildering hieroglyphic inscription on the seal. When he had finished it he transferred it to a clay duplicator and took off half-a-dozen copies, one of which he handed to me. I looked at it dubiously and remarked : "You have said that the medical jurist must make all knowledge his province. Has he got to be an Egyptologist, too?"

"He will be the better medical jurist if he is," was the reply, of which I made a mental note for my future guidance. But meanwhile Thorndyke's proceedings were, to me, perfectly incomprehensible. What was his object in making this minute tracing? The seal itself was sufficient for identification. I lingered, awhile hoping that some fresh development might throw a light on the mystery. But his next proceeding was like to have reduced me to stupefaction. I saw him go to the book-shelves and take down a book. As he laid it on the table I glanced at the title, and when I saw that it was Raper's Navigation Tables I stole softly out into the lobby, put on my hat and went for a walk.

When I returned the investigation was apparently concluded, for Thorndyke was seated in his easy chair, placidly reading The Compleat Angler. On the table lay a large circular protractor, a straight-edge, an architect's scale and a sheet of tracing-paper on which was a tracing in hectograph ink of Shawstead Manor.

"Why did you make this tracing?" I asked. "Why not take the map itself? "

"We don't want the whole of it," he replied, "and I dislike cutting up maps."

By taking an informal lunch in the train, we arrived at Shawstead Manor by half-past two. Our approach up the drive had evidently been observed, for Blowgrave and his daughter were waiting at the porch to receive us. The former came forward with outstretched hand, but a distinctly woebegone expression, and exclaimed:

"It is most kind of you to come down; but alas! you are too late."

"Too late for what?" demanded Thorndyke.

"I will show you," replied Blowgrave, and seizing my colleague by the arm, he strode off excitedly to a little wicket at the side of the house, and, passing through it, hurried along a narrow alley that skirted the garden wall and ended in a large meadow, at one end of which stood a dilapidated windmill. Across this meadow he bustled, dragging my colleague with him, until he reached a heap of freshly-turned earth, where he halted and pointed tragically to a spot where the turf had evidently been raised and untidily replaced.

"There!" he exclaimed, stooping to pull up the loose turfs and thereby exposing what was evidently a large hole, recently and hastily filled in. "That was done last night or early this morning, for I walked over this meadow only yesterday evening and there was no sign of disturbed ground then."

Thorndyke stood looking down at the hole with a faint smile. "And what do you infer from that?" he asked.

"Infer!" shrieked Blowgrave. "Why, I infer that whoever dug this hole was searching for Uncle Reuben and the lost jewels!"

"I am inclined to agree with you," Thorndyke said calmly. "He happened to search in the wrong place, but that is his affair."

"The wrong place!" Blowgrave and his daughter exclaimed in unison. "How do you know it is the wrong place?"

"Because," replied Thorndyke, "I believe I know the right place, and this is not it. But we can put the matter to the test, and we had better do so. Can you get a couple of men with picks and shovels? Or shall we handle the tools ourselves?"

"I think that would be better," said Blowgrave, who was quivering with excitement. "We don't want to take anyone into our confidence if we can help it."

"No," Thorndyke agreed. "Then I suggest that you fetch the tools while I locate the spot."

Blowgrave assented eagerly and went off at a brisk trot, while the young lady remained with us and watched Thorndyke with intense curiosity.

"I mustn't interrupt you with questions," said she "but I can't imagine how you found out where Uncle Reuben was buried."

"We will go into that later," he replied; "but first we have got to find Uncle Reuben." He laid his research case down on the ground, and opening it, took out three sheets of paper, each bearing a duplicate of his tracing of the map; and on each was marked a spot on this meadow from which a number of lines radiated like the spokes of a wheel.

"You see, Jervis," he said, exhibiting them to me "the advantage of a map. I have been able to rule off these sets of bearings regardless of obstructions, such as those young trees, which have arisen since Silas's day, and mark the spot in its correct place. If the recent obstructions prevent us from taking the bearings, we can still find the spot by measurements with the land- chain or tape."

"Why have you got three plans?" I asked.

"Because there are three imaginable places. No. 1 is the most likely; No. 2 less likely, but possible; No. 3 is impossible. That is the one that our friend tried last night. No. 1 is among those young trees, and we will now see if we can pick up the bearings in spite of them."

We moved on to the clump of young trees, where Thorndyke took from the research-case a tall, folding camera-tripod and a large prisma compass with an aluminium dial. With the latter he one or two trial bearings and then, setting up the tripod, fixed the compass on it. For some minutes Miss Blowgrave and I watched him as he shifted the tripod from spot to spot, peering through the sight-vane of the compass and glancing occasionally at the map. At length he turned to us and said: "We are in luck. None of these trees interferes with our bearings." He took from the research-case a surveyor's arrow, and sticking it in the ground under the tripod, added: "That is the spot. But we may have to dig a good way round it, for a compass is only a rough instrument."

At this moment Mr. Blowgrave staggered up, breathing hard, and flung down on the ground three picks, two shovels and a spade. "I won't hinder you, doctor, by asking for explanations," said he, "but I am utterly mystified. You must tell us what it all means when we have finished our work."

This Thorndyke promised to do, but meanwhile he took off his coat, and rolling up his shirt sleeves, seized the spade and began cutting out a large square of turf. As the soil was uncovered, Blowgrave and I attacked it with picks and Miss Blowgrave shovelled away the loose earth.

"Do you know how far down we have to go?" I asked.

"The body lies six feet below the surface," Thorndyke replied; and as he spoke he laid down his spade, and taking a telescope from the research-case, swept it round the margin of the meadow and finally pointed it at a farm house some six hundred yards distant, of which he made a somewhat prolonged inspection, after which he took the remaining pick and fell to work on the opposite corner of the exposed square of earth.

For nearly half-an-hour we worked on steadily, gradually eating our way downwards, plying pick and shovel alternately, while Miss Blowgrave cleared the loose earth away from the edges of the deepening pit. Then a halt was called and we came to the surface, wiping our faces.

"I think, Nellie," said Blowgrave, divesting himself of his waistcoat, "a jug of lemonade and four tumblers would be useful, unless our visitors would prefer beer."

We both gave our votes for lemonade, and Miss Nellie tripped away towards the house, while Thorndyke, taking up his telescope, once more inspected the farm house.

"You seem greatly interested in that house," I remarked.

"I am," he replied, handing me the telescope "Just take a look at the window in the right-hand gable, but keep under the tree."

I pointed the telescope at the gable and there observed an open window at which a man was seated. He held a binocular glass to his eyes and the instrument appeared to be directed at us.

"We are being spied on, I fancy," said I, passing the telescope to Blowgrave, "but I suppose it doesn't matter. This is your land, isn't it?"

"Yes," replied Blowgrave, "but still, we didn't want any spectators. That is Harold Bowker," he added steadying the telescope against a tree, "my cousin Arthur's nephew, whom I told you about as having inherited the farm-house. He seems mighty interested in us; but small things interest one in the country."

Here the appearance of Miss Nellie, advancing across the meadow with an inviting-looking basket, diverted our attention from our inquisitive watcher. Six thirsty eyes were riveted on that basket until it drew near and presently disgorged a great glass jug and four tumblers, when we each took off a long and delicious draught and then jumped down into the pit to resume our labours.

Another half-hour passed. We had excavated in some places to nearly the full depth and were just discussing the advisability of another short rest when Blowgrave, who was working in one corner, uttered a loud cry and stood up suddenly, holding something in his fingers. A glance at the object showed it to be a bone, brown and earth-stained, but evidently a bone. Evidently, too, a human bone, as Thorndyke decided when Blowgrave handed it to him triumphantly.

"We have been very fortunate," said he, "to get so near at the first trial. This is from the right great toe, so we may assume that the skeleton lies just outside this pit, but we had better excavate carefully in your corner and see exactly how the bones lie." This he proceeded to do himself, probing cautiously with the spade and clearing the earth away from the corner. Very soon the remaining bones of the right foot came into view and then the ends of the two leg-bones and a portion of the left foot.

"We can see now," said he, "how the skeleton lies, and all we have to do is to extend the excavation in that direction. But there is only room for one to work down here. I think you and Mr. Blowgrave had better dig down from the surface."

On this, I climbed out of the pit, followed reluctantly by Blowgrave, who still held the little brown bone in his hand and was in a state of wild excitement and exultation that somewhat scandalised his daughter.

"It seems rather ghoulish," she remarked, "to be gloating over poor Uncle Reuben's body in this way."

"I know," said Blowgrave, "it isn't reverent. But I didn't kill Uncle Reuben, you know, whereas--well it was a long time ago." With this rather inconsequent conclusion he took a draught of lemonade, seized his pick and fell to work with a will. I, too, indulged in a draught and passed a full tumbler down to Thorndyke. But before resuming my labours I picked up the telescope and once more inspected the farm-house. The window was still open, but the watcher had apparently become bored with the not very thrilling spectacle. At any rate he had disappeared.

From this time onward every few minutes brought some discovery. First, a pair of deeply rusted steel shoe buckles; then one or two buttons, and presently a fine gold watch with a fob-chain and a bunch of seals, looking uncannily new and fresh and seeming more fraught with tragedy than even the bones themselves In his cautious digging, Thorndyke was careful not to disturb the skeleton; and looking down into the narrow trench that was growing from the corner of the pit, I could see both legs, with only the right foot missing, projecting from the miniature cliff. Meanwhile our of the trench was deepening rapidly, so that Thorndyke presently warned us to stop digging and bade us come down and shovel away the earth as he disengaged it.

At length the whole skeleton, excepting the head, was uncovered, though it lay undisturbed as it might have lain in its coffin. And now, as Thorndyke picked away the earth around the head, we could see that the skull was propped forward as if it rested on a high pillow. A little more careful probing with the pick-point served to explain this appearance. For as the earth fell away and disclosed the grinning skull, there came into view the edge and ironbound corners of a small chest.

It was an impressive spectacle; weird, solemn and rather dreadful. There for over a century the ill-fated gambler had lain, his mouldering head pillowed on the booty of unrecorded villainy, booty that had been won by fraud, retrieved by violence, and hidden at last by the final winner with the witness of his crime.

"Here is a fine text for a moralist who would preach on the vanity of riches," said Thorndyke.

We all stood silent for a while, gazing, not without awe, at the stark figure that lay guarding the ill-gotten treasure. Miss Blowgrave--who had been helped down when we descended--crept closer to her father and murmured that it was "rather awful"; while Blowgrave himself displayed a queer mixture of exultation and shuddering distaste.

Suddenly the silence was broken by a voice from above, and we all looked up with a start. A youngish man was standing on the brink of the pit, looking down on us with very evident disapproval.

"It seems that I have come just in the nick of time," observed the new-comer. "I shall have to take pos session of that chest, you know, and of the remains, too, I suppose. That is my ancestor, Reuben Blowgrave."

"Well, Harold," said Blowgrave, "you can have Uncle Reuben if you want him. But the chest belongs to Nellie."

Here Mr. Harold Bowker--I recognised him now as the watcher from the window--dropped down into the pit and advanced with something of a swagger.

"I am Reuben's heir," said he, "through my Uncle Arthur, and I take possession of this property and the remains."

"Pardon me, Harold," said Blowgrave, "but Nellie is Arthur's residuary legatee, and this is the residue of the estate."

"Rubbish!" exclaimed Bowker. "By the way, how did you find out where he was buried?"

Oh, that was quite simple," replied Thorndyke with unexpected geniality. "I'll show you the plan." He climbed up to the surface and returned in a few moments with the three tracings and his letter-case. "This is how we located the spot." He handed the plan numbered 3 to Bowker, who took it from him and stood looking at it with a puzzled frown.

"But this isn't the place," he said at length.

"Isn't it?" queried Thorndyke. "No, of course; I've given you the wrong one. This is the plan." He handed Bowker the plan marked No. 1, and took the other from him, laying it down on a heap of earth. Then, as Bowker pored gloomily over No. 1, he took a knife and a pencil from his pocket, and with his back to our visitor; scraped the lead of the pencil, letting the black powder fall on the plan that he had just laid down. I watched him with some curiosity; and when I observed that the black scrapings fell on two spots near the edges of the paper, a sudden suspicion flashed into my mind, which j was confirmed when I saw him tap the paper lightly with his pencil, gently blow away the powder, and quickly producing my photograph of the typewritten letter from his case, hold it for a moment beside the plan.

"This is all very well," said Bowker, looking up from the plan, "but how did you find out about these bearings?"

Thorndyke swiftly replaced the letter in his case, and turning round, replied, "I am afraid I can't give you any further information."

"Can't you, indeed!" Bowker exclaimed insolently. "Perhaps I shall compel you to. But, at any rate, I forbid any of you to lay hands on my property."

Thorndyke looked at him steadily and said in an ominously quiet tone: "Now, listen to me, Mr. Bowker. Let us have an end of this nonsense. You have played a risky game and you have lost. How much you have lost I can't say until I know whether Mr. Blowgrave intends to prosecute."

"To prosecute!" shouted Bowker. "What the deuce do you mean by prosecute?"

"I mean," said Thorndyke, "that on the 7th of June, after nine o'clock at night, you entered the dwelling-house of Mr. Blowgrave and stole and carried away certain of his goods and chattels. A part of them you have restored, but you are still in possession of some of the stolen property, to wit, a scarab and a deed-box."

As Thorndyke made this statement in his calm, level tones, Bowker's face blanched to a tallowy white, and he stood staring at my colleague, the very picture of astonishment and dismay. But he fired a last shot.

"This is sheer midsummer madness," he exclaimed huskily; "and you know it."

Thorndyke turned to our host. "It is for you to settle, Mr. Blowgrave," said he. "I hold conclusive evidence that Mr. Bowker stole your deed-box. If you decide to prosecute I shall produce that evidence in court and he will certainly be convicted."

Blowgrave and his daughter looked at the accused man with an embarrassment almost equal to his own.

I am astounded," the former said at length; "but I don't want to be vindictive. Look here, Harold, hand over the scarab and we'll say no more about it."

"You can't do that," said Thorndyke. "The law doesn't allow you to compound a robbery. He can return the property if he pleases and you can do as you think best about prosecuting. But you can't make conditions."

There was silence for some seconds; then, without another word, the crestfallen adventurer turned, and scrambling up out of the pit, took a hasty departure.

It was nearly a couple of hours later that, after a leisurely wash and a hasty, nondescript meal, we carried the little chest from the dining-room to the study. Here, when he had closed the French window and drawn the curtains, Mr. Blowgrave produced a set of tools and we fell to work on the iron fastenings of the chest. It was no light task, though a century's rust had thinned the stout bands, but at length the lid yielded to the thrust of a long case-opener and rose with a protesting creak. The chest was lined with a double thickness of canvas, apparently part of a sail, and contained a number of small leathern bags, which, as we lifted them out, one by one, felt as if they were filled with pebbles. But when we untied the thongs of one and emptied its contents into a wooden bowl, Blowgrave heaved a sigh of ecstasy and Miss Nellie uttered a little scream of delight. They were all cut stones, and most of them of exceptional size; rubies, emeralds, sapphires and a few diamonds. As to their value, we could form but the vaguest guess; but Thorndyke, who was a fair, judge of gem-stones, gave it as his opinion that they were fine specimens of their kind, though roughly cut, and that they had probably formed the enrichment of some shrine.

"The question is," said Blowgrave, gazing gloatingly on the bowl of sparkling gems, "what are we to do with them?"

"I suggest," said Thorndyke, "that Dr. Jervis stay here to-night to help you to guard them and that in the morning you take them up to London and deposit them, at your bank."

Blowgrave fell in eagerly with this suggestion, which I seconded. "But," said he, "that chest is a queer-looking package to be carrying abroad. Now, if we only had that confounded deed-box--"

"There's a deed-box on the cabinet behind you," said Thorndyke.

Blowgrave turned round sharply. "God bless us!" he exclaimed. "It has come back the way it went. Harold must have slipped in at the window while we were at tea. Well, I'm glad he has made restitution. When I look at that bowl and think what he must have narrowly missed, I don't feel inclined to be hard on him. I suppose the scarab is inside--not that it matters much now."

The scarab was inside in an envelope; and as Thorndyke turned it over in his hand and examined the hieroglyphics on it through his lens, Miss Blowgrave asked: "Is it of any value, Dr. Thorndyke? It can't have any connection with the secret of the hiding-place, because you found the jewels without it."

"By the way, doctor, I don't know whether it is permissible for me to ask, but how on earth did you find out where the jewels were hidden? To me it looks like black magic."

Thorndyke laughed in a quiet, inward fashion. "There is nothing magical about it," said he. "It was a perfectly simple, straightforward problem. But Miss Nellie is wrong. We had the scarab;

that is to say we had the wax impression of it, which is the same thing. And the scarab was the key to the riddle. You see," he continued, "Silas's letter and the scarab formed together a sort of intelligence test."

"Did they?" said Blowgrave. "Then he drew a blank every time."

Thorndyke chuckled. "His descendants were certainly a little lacking in enterprise," he admitted. "Silas's instructions were perfectly plain and explicit. Whoever would find the treasure must first acquire some knowledge of Egyptian lore and must study the scarab attentively. It was the broadest of hints, but no one--excepting Harold Bowker, who must have heard about the scarab from his Uncle Arthur--seems to have paid any attention to it.

"Now it happens that I have just enough elementary knowledge of the hieroglyphic characters to enable me to spell them out when they are used alphabetically; and as soon as I saw the seal, I could see that these hieroglyphics formed English words. My attention was first attracted by the second group of signs, which spelled the word 'Reuben,' and then I saw that the first group spelled 'Uncle.' Of course, the instant I heard Miss Nellie speak of the connection between the scarab and Uncle Reuben, the murder was out. I saw at a glance that the scarab contained all the required information. Last night I made a careful tracing of the hieroglyphics and then rendered them into our own alphabet. This is the result."

Thorndyke's tracing of the impression of the scarab.

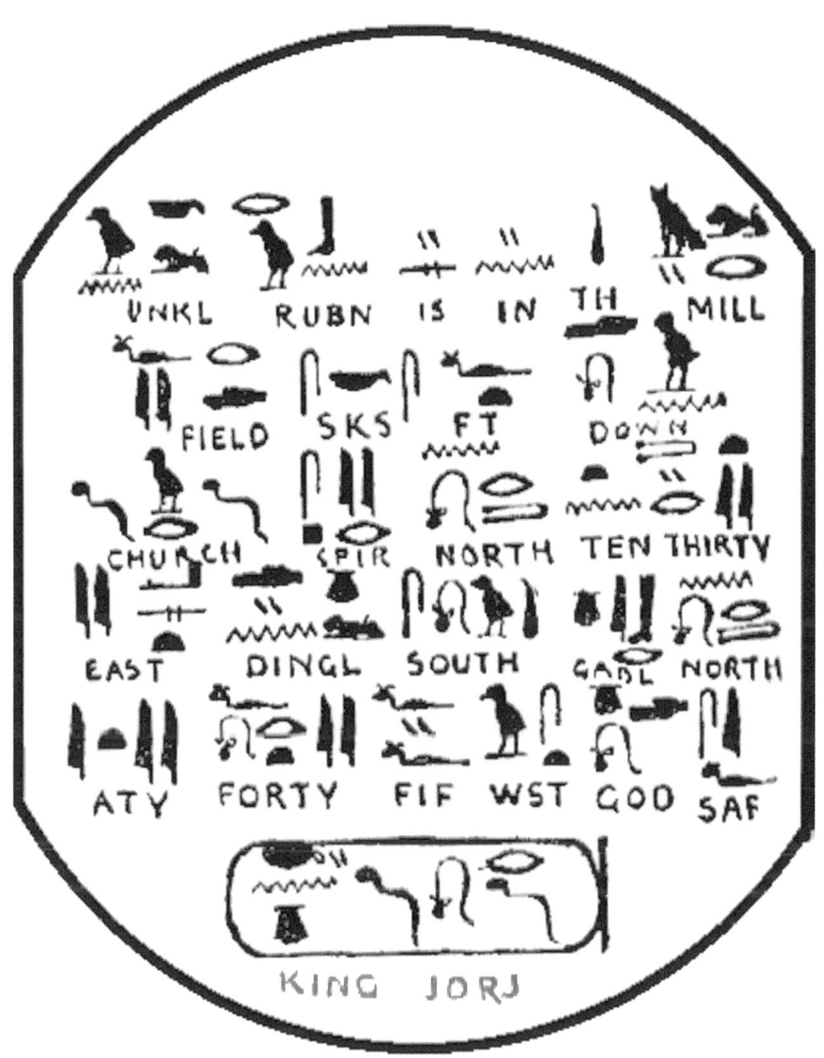

The transliteration of the hieroglyphics.

He took from his letter-case and spread out on the table a duplicate of the tracing which I had seen him make, and of which he had given me a copy. But since I had last seen it, it had received an addition; under each group of signs the equivalents in modern Roman lettering had been written, and these made the following words:

"UNKL RUBN IS IN TH MILL FIELD SKS FT DOWN CHURCH SPIR NORTH TEN THIRTY EAST DINGL SOUTH GABL NORTH ATY FORTY FIF WEST GOD SAF KING JORJ."

Our two friends gazed at Thorndyke's transliteration in blank astonishment. At length Blowgrave remarked: "But this translation must have demanded a very profound knowledge of the Egyptian writing."

"Not at all," replied Thorndyke. "Any intelligent person could master the Egyptian alphabet in an hour. The language, of course, is quite another matter. The spelling of this is a little crude, but it is quite intelligible and does Silas great credit, considering how little was known in his time."

"How do you suppose M. Fouquet came to overlook this?" Blowgrave asked.

"Naturally enough," was the reply. "He was looking for an Egyptian inscription. But this is not an Egyptian inscription. Does he speak English?"

"Very little. Practically not at all."

"Then, as the words are English words and imperfectly spelt, the hieroglyphics must have appeared to him mere nonsense. And he was right as to the scarab being an imitation."

"There is another point," said Blowgrave. "How was it that Harold made that extraordinary mistake about the place? The directions are clear enough. All you had to do was to go out there with a compass and take the bearings just as they were given."

"But," said Thorndyke," that is exactly what he did, and hence the mistake. He was apparently unaware of the phenomenon known as the Secular Variation of the Compass. As you know, the compass does not--usually-- point to true north, hut to the Magnetic North; and the Magnetic North is continually changing its position. When Reuben was buried---about 1810-- it was twenty-four degrees, twenty-six minutes west of true north; at the present time it is fourteen degrees, forty-eight minutes west of true north. So Harold's bearings would be no less than ten degrees out, which of course, gave him a totally wrong position. But Silas was a ship-master, a navigator, and of course knew all about the vagaries of the compass; and, as his directions were intended for use at some date unknown to him, I assumed that the bearings that he gave were true bearings--that when he said 'north' he meant true north, which is always the same; and this turned out to be the case. But I also prepared a plan with magnetic bearings corrected up to date. Here are the three plans: No. 1--the one we used--showing true bearings; No. 2, showing corrected magnetic bearings which might have given us the correct spot; and No. 3, with uncorrected magnetic bearings, giving us the spot where Harold dug, and which could not possibly have been the right spot."

On the following morning I escorted the deed-box, filled with the booty and tied up and sealed with the scarab, to Mr. Blowgrave's bank. And that ended our connection with the case; excepting that, a month or two later, we attended by request the unveiling in Shawstead churchyard of a fine monument to Reuben Blowgrave. This took the slightly inappropriate form of an obelisk, on which were cut the name and approximate dates, with the added inscription: "Cast thy bread upon the waters and it shall return after many days"; concerning which Thorndyke remarked dryly that he supposed the exhortation applied equally even if the bread happened to belong to someone else.

The New Jersey Sphinx

"A rather curious neighbourhood this, Jervis," my friend Thorndyke remarked as we turned into Upper Bedford Place; "a sort of aviary for cosmopolitan birds of passage, especially those of the Oriental variety. The Asiatic and African faces that one sees at the windows of these Bloomsbury boarding houses almost suggest an overflow from the ethnographical galleries of the adjacent British Museum."

"Yes," I agreed," there must be quite a considerable population of Africans, Japanese and Hindus in Bloomsbury; particularly Hindus."

As I spoke, and as if in illustration of my statement, a dark-skinned man rushed out of one of the houses farther down the street and began to advance towards us in a rapid, bewildered fashion, stopping to look at each street door as he came to it. His hatless condition--though he was exceedingly well dressed--and his agitated manner immediately attracted my attention, and Thorndyke's too, for the latter remarked, " Our friend seems to be in trouble. An accident, perhaps, or a case of sudden illness."

Here the stranger, observing our approach, ran for ward to meet us and asked in an agitated tone, "Can you tell me, please, where I can find a doctor?"

"I am a medical man," replied Thorndyke, "and so is my friend."

Our acquaintance grasped Thorndyke's sleeve and exclaimed eagerly, "Come with me, then, quickly, if you please. A most dreadful thing has happened."

He hurried us along at something between a trot and a quick walk, and as we proceeded he continued excitedly, "I am quite confused and terrified; it is all so strange and sudden and terrible."

"Try," said Thorndyke, "to calm yourself a little and tell us what has happened."

"I will," was the agitated reply. "It is my cousin, Dinanath Byramji-- his surname is the same as mine. Just now I went to his room and was horrified to find him lying on the floor, staring at the ceiling and blowing--like this," and he puffed out his cheeks with a soft blowing noise. "I spoke to him and shook his hand, but he was like a dead man. This is the house."

He darted up the steps to an open door at which a rather scared page-boy was on guard, and running along the hall, rapidly ascended the stairs. Following him closely, we reached a rather dark first-floor landing where, at a half-open door, a servant-maid stood listening with an expression of awe to a rhythmical snoring sound that issued from the room.

The unconscious man lay as Mr. Byramji had said staring fixedly at the ceiling with wide-open, glazy eyes, puffing out his cheeks slightly at each breath. But the breathing was shallow and slow, and it grew perceptibly slower, with lengthening pauses. And even as I was timing it with my watch while Thorndyke examined the pupils with the aid of a wax match, it stopped. I laid my finger on the wrist and caught one or two slow, flickering beats. Then the pulse stopped too.

"He is gone, said I. "He must have burst one of the large arteries."

"Apparently," said Thorndyke, "though one would not have expected it at his age. But wait! What is this?"

He pointed to the right ear, in the hollow of which a few drops of blood had collected, and as he spoke he drew his hand gently over the dead man's head and moved it slightly from side to side.

"There is a fracture of the base of the skull," said he, "and quite distinct signs of contusion of the scalp." He turned to Mr. Byramji, who stood wringing his hand and gazing incredulously at the dead man, and asked: "Can you throw any light on this?"

The Indian looked at him vacantly. The sudden tragedy seemed to have paralysed his brain. "I don't understand," said he. "What does it mean?"

"It means," replied Thorndyke, "that he has received a heavy blow on the head."

For a few moments Mr. Byramji continued to stare vacantly at my colleague. Then he seemed suddenly to realise the import of Thorndyke's remark, for he started up excitedly and turned to the door, outside which the two servants were hovering.

"Where is the person gone who came in with my cousin?" he demanded.

"You saw him go out, Albert," said the maid. "Tell Mr. Byramji where he went to."

The page tiptoed into the room with a fearful eye fixed on the corpse, and replied falteringly, "I only see the back of him as he went out, and all I know is that he turned to the left. P'raps he's gone for a doctor."

"Can you give us any description of him?" asked Thorndyke.

"I only see the back of him," repeated the page. "He was a shortish gentleman and he had on a dark suit of clothes and a hard felt hat. That's all I know."

"Thank you," said Thorndyke. "We may want to ask you some more questions presently." and having conducted the page to the door, he shut it and turned to Mr. Byramji.

"Have you any idea who it was that was with your cousin?" he asked.

"None at all," was the reply. "I was sitting in my room opposite, writing, when I heard my cousin come up the stairs with another person, to whom he was talking. I could not hear what he was saying. They went into his room--this room--and I could occasionally catch the sound of their voices. In about a quarter of an hour I heard the door open and shut, and then someone went downstairs, softly and rather quickly. I finished the letter that I was writing, and when I had addressed it I came in here to ask my cousin who the visitor was. I thought it might be someone who had come to negotiate for the ruby."

"The ruby!" exclaimed Thorndyke. "What ruby do you refer to?"

"The great ruby," replied Byramji. "But of course you have not--" He broke off suddenly and stood for a few moments staring at Thorndyke with parted lips and wide-open eyes; then abruptly he turned, and kneeling beside the dead man he began, in a curious, caressing, half-apologetic manner, first to pass his hands gently over the body at the waist and then to unfasten the clothes. This brought into view a handsome, soft leather belt, evidently of native workmanship, worn next to the skin and furnished with three pockets. Mr. Byramji unbuttoned and explored them in quick succession, and it was evident that they were all empty.

"It is gone!" he exclaimed in low, intense tones, "Gone! Ah! But how little would it signify! But thou, dear Dinanath, my brother, my friend, thou art gone, too!"

He lifted the dead man's hand and pressed it to his cheek, murmuring endearments in his own tongue. Presently he laid it down reverently, and sprang up, and I was startled at the change in his aspect. The delicate, gentle, refined face had suddenly become the face of a Fury--fierce, sinister, vindictive.

"This wretch must die!" he exclaimed huskily. "This sordid brute who, without compunction, has crushed out a precious life as one would carelessly crush a fly, for the sake of a paltry crystal--he must die, if I have to follow him and strangle him with my own hands!"

Thorndyke laid his hand on Byramji's shoulder. "I sympathise with you most cordially," said he. "If it is as you think, and appearances suggest, that your cousin has been murdered as a mere incident of robbery, the murderer's life is forfeit, and Justice cries aloud for retribution. The fact of murder will be determined, for or against, by a proper inquiry. Meanwhile we have to ascertain who this unknown man is and what happened while he was with your cousin."

Byramji made a gesture of despair. "But the man has disappeared, and nobody has seen him! What can we do?"

"Let us look around us," plied Thorndyke, "and see if we can judge what has happened in this room. What, for instance, is this?"

He picked up from a corner near the door a small leather object, which he handed to Mr. Byramji. The Indian seized it eagerly, exclaiming: "Ah! It is the little bag in which my cousin used to carry the ruby. So he had taken it from his belt."

"It hasn't been dropped, by any chance?" I suggested.

In an instant Mr. Byramji was down on his knees, peering and groping about the floor, and Thorndyke and I joined in the search. But, as might have been expected there was no sign of the ruby, nor, indeed, of anything else, excepting a hat which I picked up from under the table.

"No," said Mr. Byramji, rising with a dejected air. "It is gone--of course it is gone, and the murderous villain--"

Here his glance fell on the hat, which I had laid on the table, and he bent forward to look at it.

"Whose hat is this?" he demanded, glancing at the chair on which Thorndyke's hat and mine had been placed.

"Is it not your cousin's?" asked Thorndyke. "No, certainly not. His hat was like mine--we bought them both together. It had a white silk lining with his initials, D. B., in gold. This has no lining and is a much older hat. It must be the murderer's hat."

"If it is," said Thorndyke, "that is a most important fact--important in two respects. Could you let us see your hat?"

"Certainly," replied Byramji, walking quickly, but with a soft tread, to the door. As he went out, shutting the door silently behind him, Thorndyke picked up the derelict hat and swiftly tried it on the head of the dead man. As far as I could judge, it appeared to fit, and this Thorndyke confirmed as he replaced it on the table.

"As you see," said he, "it is at least a practical fit, which is a fact of some significance."

Here Mr. Byramji returned with his own hat, which he placed on the table by the side of the other, and thus placed, crown uppermost, the two hats were closely similar. Both were black, hard felts of the prevalent "bowler" shape, and of good quality, and the difference in their age and state of preservation was not striking; but when Byramji turned them over and exhibited their interiors it was seen that whereas the strange hat was unlined save for the leather head-band, Byramji's had a white silk lining and bore the owner's initials in embossed gilt letters.

"What happened," said Thorndyke, when he had carefully compared the two hats, "seems fairly obvious, The two men, on entering, placed their hats crown upwards on the table. In some way--perhaps during a struggle--the visitor's hat was knocked down and rolled under the table. Then the stranger, on leaving, picked up the only visible hat--almost identically similar to his own--and put it on."

"Is it not rather singular," I asked, "that he should not have noticed the different feel of a strange hat?"

"I think not," Thorndyke replied. "If he noticed anything unusual he would probably assume that he had put it on the wrong way round. Remember that he would be extremely hurried and agitated. And when once he had left the house he would not dare to take the risk of returning, though he would doubtless realise the gravity of the mistake. And now," he continued, "would you mind giving us a few particulars? You have spoken of a great ruby, which your cousin had, and which seems to be missing."

"Yes. You shall come to my room and I will tell you about it; but first let us lay my poor cousin decently on his bed."

"I think," said Thorndyke, "the body ought not to be moved until the police have seen it."

"Perhaps you are right," Byramji agreed reluctantly, "though it seems callous to leave him lying there." With a sigh he turned to the door, and Thorndyke followed, carrying the two hats.

"My cousin and I," said our host, when we were seated in his own large bed-sitting-room, "were both interested in gem-stones. I deal in all kinds of stones that are found in the East, but Dinanath dealt almost exclusively in rubies. He was a very fine judge of those beautiful gems, and he used to make periodical tours in Burma in search of uncut rubies of unusual size or quality. About four months ago he acquired at Mogok, in Upper Burma, a magnificent specimen over twenty- eight carats in weight, perfectly flawless and of the most gorgeous colour. It had been roughly cut, but my cousin was intending to have it recut unless he should receive an advantageous offer for it in the meantime."

"What would be the value of such a stone?" I asked.

"It is impossible to say. A really fine large ruby of perfect colour is far, far more valuable than the finest diamond of the same size. It is the most precious of all gems, with the possible exception of the emerald. A fine ruby of five carats is worth about three thousand pounds, but of course, the value rises out of all proportion with increasing size. Fifty thousand pounds would be a moderate price for Dinanath's ruby."

During this recital I noticed that Thorndyke, while listening attentively, was turning the stranger's hat over in his hands, narrowly scrutinising it both inside and outside. As Byramji concluded, he remarked:

"We shall have to let the police know what has happened, but, as my friend and I will be called as witnesses, I should like to examine this hat a little more closely before you hand it over to them. Could you let me have a small, hard brush? A dry nail-brush would do." Our host complied readily--in fact eagerly. Thorndyke's authoritative, purposeful manner had clearly impressed him, for he said as he handed my colleague a new nail-brush: "I thank you for your help and value it. We must not depend on the police only."

Accustomed as I was to Thorndyke's methods, his procedure was not unexpected, but Mr. Byramji watched him with breathless interest and no little surprise as, laying a sheet of notepaper on the table, he brought the hat close to it and brushed firmly but slowly, so that the dust dislodged should fall on it. As it was not a very well-kept hat, the yield was considerable, especially when the brush was drawn under the curl of the brim, and very soon the paper held quite a little heap. Then Thorndyke folded the paper into a small packet and having written "outside" on it, put it in his pocket book.

"Why do you do that? "Mr. Byramji asked. "What will the dust tell you?"

"Probably nothing," Thorndyke replied. "But this hat is our only direct clue to the identity of the man who was with your cousin, and we must make the most of it. Dust, you know, is only a mass of fragments detached from surrounding objects. If the objects are unusual the dust may be quite distinctive. You could easily identify the hat of a miller or a cement worker." As he was speaking he reversed the hat and turned down the leather head-lining, whereupon a number of strips of folded paper fell down into the crown.

"Ah!" exclaimed Byramji, "perhaps we shall learn something now."

He picked out the folded slips and began eagerly to open them out, and we examined them systematically- one by one. But they were singularly disappointing and uninforming. Mostly they consisted of strips of newspaper, with one or two circulars, a leaf from a price list of gas stoves, a portion of a large envelope on which were the remains of an address which read "--n--don, W.C.," and a piece of paper evidently cut down vertically and bearing the right-hand half of some kind of list. This read:

"--el 3 oz. 5 dwts.

--eep 9½ oz."

"Can you make anything of this?" I asked, handing the paper to Thorndyke.

He looked at it reflectively, and answered, as he copied it into his notebook : "It has, at least, some character. If we consider it with the other data we should get some sort of hint from it. But these scraps of paper don't tell us much. Perhaps their most suggestive feature is their quantity and the way in which, as you have no doubt noticed, they were arranged at the sides of the hat. We had better replace them as we found them for the benefit of the police."

The nature of the suggestion to which he referred was not very obvious to me, but the presence of Mr. Byramji rendered discussion inadvisable; nor was there any opportunity, for we had hardly reconstituted the hat when we became aware of a number of persons ascending the stairs, and then we heard the sound of rather peremptory rapping at the door of the dead man's room.

Mr. Byramji opened the door and went out on to the landing, where several persons had collected, including the two servants and a constable.

"I understand," said the policeman, "that there is something wrong here. Is that so?"

"A very terrible thing has happened," replied Byramji. "But the doctors can tell you better than I can." Here he looked appealingly at Thorndyke, and we both went out and joined him.

"A gentleman--Mr. Dinanath Byramji--has met with his death under somewhat suspicious circumstances," said Thorndyke, and, glancing at the knot of naturally curious persons on the landing, he continued: "If you will come into the room where the death occurred, I will give you the facts so far as they are known to us."

With this he opened the door and entered the room with Mr. Byramji, the constable, and me. As the door opened, the bystanders craned forward and a middle- aged woman uttered a cry of horror and followed us into the room.

"This is dreadful!" she exclaimed, with a shuddering glance at the corpse. "The servants told me about it when I came in just now and I sent Albert for the police at once. But what does it mean? You don't think poor Mr. Dinanath has been murdered?"

"We had better get the facts, ma'am," said the constable, drawing out a large black notebook and laying his helmet on the table. He turned to Mr. Byramji, who had sunk into a chair and sat, the picture of grief, gazing at his dead cousin. "Would you kindly tell me what you know about how it happened?"

Byramji repeated the substance of what he had told us, and when the constable had taken down his statement, Thorndyke and I gave the few medical particulars that we could furnish and handed the constable our cards. Then, having helped to lay the corpse on the bed and cover it with a sheet, we turned to take our leave.

"You have been very kind," Mr. Byramji said as he shook our hands warmly. "I am more than grateful. Perhaps I may be permitted to call on you and hear if--if you have learned anything fresh," he concluded discreetly.

"We shall be pleased to see you," Thorndyke replied, "and to give you any help that we can"; and with this we took our departure, watched inquisitively down the stairs by the boarders and the servants who still lurked in the vicinity of the chamber of death.

"If the police have no more information than we have," I remarked as we walked homeward, "they won't have much to go on."

"No," said Thorndyke. "But you must remember that this crime--as we are justified in assuming it to be--is not an isolated one. It is the fourth of practically the same kind within the last six months. I understand that the police have some kind of information respecting the presumed criminal, though it can't be worth much, seeing that no arrest has been made. But there is some new evidence this time. The exchange of hats may help the police considerably."

"In what way? What evidence does it furnish?"

"In the first place it suggests a hurried departure, which seems to connect the missing man with the crime. Then, he is wearing the dead man's hat, and though he is not likely to continue wearing it, it may be seen and furnish a clue. We know that that hat fits him fairly well and we know its size, so that we know the size of his head. Finally, we have the man's own hat."

"I don't fancy the police will get much information from that," said I.

"Probably not," he agreed. "Yet it offered one or two interesting suggestions, as you probably observed."

"It made no suggestions whatever to me," said I.

"Then," said Thorndyke, "I can only recommend you to recall our simple inspection and consider the significance of what we found."

This I had to accept as closing the discussion for the time being, and as I had to make a call at my bookseller's concerning some reports that I had left to be bound, I parted from Thorndyke at the corner of Chichester Rents and left him to pursue his way alone. My business with the bookseller took me longer than I had expected, for I had to wait while the lettering on the backs was completed, and when I arrived at our chambers in King's Bench Walk, I found Thorndyke apparently at the final stage of some experiment evidently connected with our late adventure. The microscope stood on the table with one slide on the stage and a second one beside it; but Thorndyke had apparently finished his microscopical researches, for as I entered he held in his hand a test-tube filled with a smoky-coloured fluid.

"I see that you have been examining the dust from the hat," said I. "Does it throw any fresh light on the case?"

"Very little," he replied. "It is just common dust--assorted fibres and miscellaneous organic and mineral particles. But there are a couple of hairs from the in side of the hat--both lightish brown, and one of the atrophic, note-of-exclamation type that one finds at the margin of bald patches; and the outside dust shows minute traces of lead, apparently in the form of oxide. What do you make of that?"

"Perhaps the man is a plumber or a painter," I suggested.

"Either is possible and worth considering," he replied ; but his tone made clear to me that this was not his own inference; and a row of five consecutive Post Office Directories, which I had already noticed ranged along the end of the table, told me that he had not only formed a hypothesis on the subject, but had probably either confirmed or disproved it. For the Post Office Directory was one of Thorndyke's favourite books of reference; and the amount of curious and recondite information that he succeeded in extracting from its matter-of-fact pages would have surprised no one more than it would the compilers of the work.

At this moment the sound of footsteps ascending our stairs became audible. It was late for business callers, but we were not unaccustomed to late visitors; and a familiar rat-tat of our little brass knocker seemed to explain the untimely visit.

"That sounds like Superintendent Miller's knock," said Thorndyke, as he strode across the room to open the door. And the superintendent it turned out to be. But not alone.

As the door opened the officer entered with two gentlemen, both natives of India, and one of whom was our friend Mr. Byramji.

"Perhaps," said Miller," I had better look in a little later."

"Not on my account," said Byramji. "I have only a few words to say and there is nothing secret about my business. May I introduce my kinsman, Mr. Khambata, a student of the Inner Temple?"

Byramji's companion bowed ceremoniously. "Byramji came to my chambers just now," he explained, "to consult me about this dreadful affair, and he chanced to show me your card. He had not heard of you, but supposed you to be an ordinary medical practitioner. He did not realise that he had entertained an angel unawares. But I, who knew of your great reputation, advised him to put his affairs in your hands--without prejudice to the official investigations," Mr. Khambata added hastily, bowing to the superintendent.

"And I," said Mr. Byramji, "instantly decided to act on my kinsman's advice. I have come to beg you to leave no stone unturned to secure the punishment of my cousin's murderer. Spare no expense. I am a rich man and my poor cousin's property will come to me. As to the ruby, recover it if you can, but it is of no consequence. Vengeance--justice is what I seek. Deliver the wretch into my hands, or into the hands of justice, and I give you the ruby or its value, freely--gladly."

"There is no need," said Thorndyke, "of such extraordinary inducement. If you wish me to investigate this case, I will do so and will use every means at my disposal, without prejudice, as your friend says, to the proper claims of the officers of the law. But you under stand that I can make no promises. I cannot guarantee success."

"We understand that," said Mr. Khambata. "But we know that if you undertake the case, everything that is possible will be done. And now we must leave you to your consultation."

As soon as our clients had gone, Miller rose from his chair with his hand in his breast pocket. "I dare say, doctor," said he, "you can guess what I have come about. I was sent for to look into this Byramji case and I heard from Mr. Byramji that you had been there and that you had made a minute examination of the missing man's hat. So have I; and I don't mind telling you that I could learn nothing from it."

"I haven't learnt much myself," said Thorndyke.

"But you've picked up something," urged Miller, "if it is only a hint; and we have just a little clue. There is very small doubt that this is the same man--'The New Jersey Sphinx,' as the papers call him--that committed those other robberies; and a very difficult type of criminal he is to get hold of. He is bold, he is wary, he plays a lone hand, and he sticks at nothing. He has no confederates, and he kills every time. The American police never got near him but once; and that once gives us the only clues we have."

"Finger-prints?" inquired Thorndyke.

"Yes, and very poor ones, too. So rough that you can hardly make out the pattern. And even those are not absolutely guaranteed to be his; but in any case, finger-prints are not much use until you've got the man. And there is a photograph of the fellow himself, But it is only a snapshot, and a poor one at that. All it shows is that he has a mop of hair and a pointed beard--or at least he had when the photograph was taken. But for identification purposes it is practically worthless. Still, there it is; and what I propose is this: we want this man and so do you; we've worked together before and can trust one another. I am going to lay my cards on the table and ask you to do the same."

"But, my dear Miller," said Thorndyke, "I haven't any cards. I haven't a single solid fact."

The detective was visibly disappointed. Nevertheless, he laid two photographs on the table and pushed them towards Thorndyke, who inspected them through his lens and passed them to me.

"The pattern is very indistinct and broken up," he remarked.

"Yes," said Miller; "the prints must have been made on a very rough surface, though you get prints something like those from fitters or other men who use files and handle rough metal. And now, doctor, can't you give us a lead of any kind?"

Thorndyke reflected a few moments. "I really have not a single real fact," said he, "and I am unwilling to make merely speculative suggestions."

"Oh, that's all right," Miller replied cheerfully. "Give us a start. I shan't complain if it comes to nothing."

"Well," Thorndyke said reluctantly, "I was thinking of getting a few particulars as to the various tenants of No. 51 Clifford's Inn. Perhaps you could do it more easily and it might be worth your while."

"Good!" Miller exclaimed gleefully. "He 'gives to airy nothing a local habitation and a name.'"

"It is probably the wrong name," Thorndyke reminded him.

"I don't care," said Miller. "But why shouldn't we go together? It's too late to-night, and I can't manage to-morrow morning. But say to-morrow after noon. Two heads are better than one, you know, especially when the second one is yours. Or perhaps," he added, with a glance at me, "three would be better still."

Thorndyke considered for a moment or two and then looked at me.

"What do you say, Jervis?" he asked.

As my afternoon was unoccupied, I agreed with enthusiasm, being as curious as the superintendent to know how Thorndyke had connected this particular locality with the vanished criminal, and Miller departed in high spirits with an appointment for the morrow three o'clock in the afternoon.

For some time after the superintendent's depart I sat wrapped in profound meditation. In some mysterious way the address, 51 Clifford's Inn, had emerged from the formless data yielded by the derelict hat. But what had been the connection? Apparently the fragment of the addressed envelope had furnished the clue. But how had Thorndyke extended "--n" into "51, Clifford's Inn"? It was to me a complete mystery.

Meanwhile, Thorndyke had seated himself at writing-table, and I noticed that of the two letters which he wrote, one was written on our headed paper and other on ordinary plain notepaper. I was speculating on the reason for this when he rose, and as he stuck on the stamps, said to me, "I am just going out to post these two letters. Do you care for a short stroll through the leafy shades of Fleet Street? The evening is still young."

"The rural solitudes of Fleet Street attract me I all hours," I replied, fetching my hat from the adjoining office, and we accordingly sallied forth together, strolling up King's Bench Walk and emerging into Fleet Street by way of Mitre Court. When Thorndyke had dropped his letters into the post office box he stood awhile gazing up at the tower of St. Dunstan's Church."

"Have you ever been in Clifford's Inn, Jervis?" he inquired.

"Never," I replied (we passed through it together on an average a dozen times a week), "but it is not too late for an exploratory visit."

We crossed the road, and entering Clifford's Inn Passage, passed through the still half-open gate, crossed the outer court and threaded the tunnel-like entry by the hall to the inner court, in the middle of which Thorndyke halted, and looking up at one of the ancient houses, remarked, "No. 51."

"So that is where our friend hangs out his flag," said I.

"Oh come, Jervis," he protested, "I am surprised at you; you are as bad as Miller. I have merely suggested a possible connection between these premises and the hat that was left at Bedford Place. As to the nature of that connection I have no idea, and there may be no connection at all. I assure you, Jervis, that I am on the thinnest possible ice. I am working on a hypo thesis which is in the highest degree speculative, and I should not have given Miller a hint but that he was so eager and so willing to help--and also that I wanted his finger-prints. But we are really only at the beginning, and may never get any farther."

I looked up at the old house. It was all in darkness excepting the top floor, where a couple of lighted windows showed the shadow of a man moving rapidly about the room. We crossed to the entry and inspected the names painted on the door-posts. The ground floor was occupied by a firm of photo-engravers, the first floor by a Mr. Carrington, whose name stood out conspicuously on its oblong of comparatively fresh white paint, while the tenants of the second floor--old residents, to judge by the faded and discoloured paint in which their names were announced--were Messrs. Burt & Highley, metallurgists.

"Burt has departed," said Thorndyke, as I read out the names; and he pointed to two red lines of erasure which I had not noticed in the dim light, "so the active gentleman above is presumably Mr. Highley, and we may take it that he has residential as well as business premises. I wonder who and what Mr. Carrington is--but I dare say we shall find out to-morrow."

With this he dismissed the professional aspects of Clifford's Inn, and, changing the subject to its history and associations, chatted in his inimitable, picturesque manner until our leisurely perambulations brought us at length to the Inner Temple Gate.

On the following morning we bustled through our work in order to leave the afternoon free, making several joint visits to solicitors from whom we were taking instructions. Returning from the last of these--a City lawyer--Thorndyke turned into St. Helen's Place and halted at a doorway bearing the brass plate of a firm of assayists and refiners. I followed him into the outer office, where, on his mentioning his name, an elderly man came to the counter.

"Mr. Grayson has put out some specimens for you, sir," said he. "They are about thirty grains to the ton--you said that the content was of no importance--I am to tell you that you need not return them. They are not worth treating." He went to a large safe from which he took a canvas bag, and returning to the counter, turned out on it the contents of the bag, consisting , about a dozen good-sized lumps of quartz and a glittering yellow fragment, which Thorndyke picked out and dropped in his pocket.

"Will that collection do?" our friend inquired.

"It will answer my purpose perfectly," Thorndyke replied, and when the specimens had been replaced the bag, and the latter deposited in Thorndyke's hand-bag, my colleague thanked the assistant and we went on our way.

"We extend our activities into the domain of mineralogy," I remarked.

Thorndyke smiled an inscrutable smile. "We also employ the suction pump as an instrument of research," he observed. "However, the strategic uses of chunks of quartz--otherwise than as missiles--will develop themselves in due course, and the interval may be used for reflection."

It was. But my reflection brought no solution. I noticed, however, that when at three o'clock we set forth in company with the superintendent, the bag went with us; and having offered to carry it and having had my offer accepted with a sly twinkle, its weight assured me that the quartz was still inside.

"Chambers and Offices to let," Thorndyke read aloud as we approached the porter's lodge. "That lets us in, I think. And the porter knows Dr. Jervis and me by sight, so he will talk more freely."

"He doesn't know me," said the superintendent, "but I'll keep in the background, all the same."

A pull at the bell brought out a clerical-looking man in a tall hat and a frock coat, who regarded Thorndyke and me through his spectacles with an amiable air of recognition.

"Good afternoon, Mr. Larkin," said Thorndyke. "I am asked to get particulars of vacant chambers. What have you got to let?

Mr. Larkin reflected. "Let me see. There's a ground floor at No. 5 – rather dark--and a small second- pair set at No. 12. And then there is-- oh, yes, there is a good first-floor set at No. 51. They wouldn't have been vacant until Michaelmas, but Mr. Carrington, the tenant, has had to go abroad suddenly. I had a letter from him this morning, enclosing the key. Funny letter, too." He dived into his pocket, and hauling out a bundle of letters, selected one and handed it to Thorndyke with a broad smile.

Thorndyke glanced at the postmark ("London, E."), and having taken out the key, extracted the letter, which he opened and held so that Miller and I could see it. The paper bore the printed heading, "Baltic Shipping Company, Wapping," and the further written heading, "S.S. Gothenburg," and the letter was brief and to the point:

DEAR SIR,

I am giving up my chambers at No. 51, as I have been suddenly called abroad. I enclose the key, but am not troubling you with the rent. The sale of my costly furniture will more than cover it, and the surplus can be expended on painting the garden railings,

Yours sincerely,

A. CARRINGTON.

Thorndyke smilingly replaced the letter and the key in the envelope and asked: "What is the furniture like?"

"You'll see," chuckled the porter, "if you care to look at the rooms. And I think they might suit, They're a good set."

"Quiet?"

""“Yes, pretty quiet. There's a metallurgist overhead--Highley--used to be Burt & Highley, but Burt has gone to the City, and I don't think Highley does much business now."

"Let me see," said Thorndyke, "I think I used to meet Highley sometimes-- a tall, dark man, isn't he?"

"No, that would be Burt. Highley is a little, fairish man, rather bald, with a pretty rich complexion"--here Mr. Larkin tapped his nose knowingly and raised his little finger--"which may account for the falling off of business."

"Hadn't we better have a look at the rooms?" Miller interrupted a little impatiently.

"Can we see them, Mr. Larkin?" asked Thorndyke.

"Certainly," was the reply. "You've got the key. Let me have it when you've seen the rooms; and whatever ever you do," he added with a broad grin, "be careful of the furniture."

"It looks," the superintendent remarked as we crossed the inner court, "as if Mr. Carrington had done a mizzle. That's hopeful. And I see," he continued, glancing at the fresh paint on the door-post as we passed through the entry, "that he hasn't been here long. That's hopeful, too."

We ascended to the first floor, and as Thorndyke unlocked and threw open the door, Miller laughed aloud. The "costly furniture" consisted of a small kitchen table, a Windsor chair and a dilapidated deck- chair. The kitchen contained a gas ring, a small saucepan and a frying-pan, and the bedroom was furnished with a camp-bed devoid of bed-clothes, a wash-hand basin on a packing-case, and a water can.

"Hallo!" exclaimed the superintendent. "He's left a hat behind. Quite a good hat, too." He took it down from the peg, glanced at its exterior and then, turning it over, looked inside. And then his mouth opened with a jerk.

"Great Solomon Eagle!" he gasped. "Do you see, doctor? It's THE hat."

He held it out to us, and sure enough on the white silk lining of the crown were the embossed, gilt letters, D.B., just as Mr. Byramji had described them.

"Yes," Thorndyke agreed, as the superintendent snatched up a greengrocer's paper bag from the kitchen floor and persuaded the hat into it, "it is undoubtedly the missing link. But what are you going to do now?"

"Do!" exclaimed Miller. "Why, I am going to collar the man. These Baltic boats put in at Hull and Newcastle--perhaps he didn't know that--and they are pretty slow boats, too. I shall wire to Newcastle to have the ship detained and take Inspector Badger down to make the arrest. I'll leave you to explain to the porter, and I owe you a thousand thanks for your valuable tip."

With this he bustled away, clasping the precious hat and from the window we saw him hurry across the court and dart out through the postern into Fetter Lane.

"I think Miller was rather precipitate," said Thorndyke. "He should have got a description of the man and some further particulars."

"Yes," said I. "Miller had much better have waited until you had finished with Mr. Larkin. But you can get some more particulars when we take back the key."

"We shall get more information from the gentleman who lives on the floor above, and I think we will go up and interview him now. I wrote to him last night and made a metallurgical appointment, signing myself W. Polton. Your name, if he should ask, is Stevenson."

As we ascended the stairs to the next floor, I meditated on the rather tortuous proceedings of my usually straightforward colleague. The use of the lumps of quartz was now obvious; but why these mysterious tactics? And why, before knocking at the door, did Thorndyke carefully take the reading of the gas meter on the landing?

The door was opened in response to our knock--a shortish, alert-looking, clean-shaved man in a white overall, who looked at us keenly and rather forbiddingly. But Thorndyke was geniality personified.

"How do you do, Mr. Highley?" said he, holding out his hand, which the metallurgist shook coolly. "You got my letter, I suppose?"

"Yes. But I am not Mr. Highley. He's away and I am carrying on. I think of taking over his business if there is any to take over. My name is Sherwood. Have you got the samples?"

Thorndyke produced the canvas bag, which Mr. Sherwood took from him and emptied out on a bench, picking up the lumps of quartz one by one and examining them closely. Meanwhile Thorndyke took a rapid survey of the premises. Against the wall were two cupel furnaces and a third larger furnace like a small pottery kiln. On a set of narrow shelves were several rows of bone-ash cupels, looking like little white flower-pots, and near them was the cupel-press--an appliance into which powdered bone-ash was fed and compressed by a plunger to form the cupels--while by the side of the press was a tub of bone-ash--a good deal coarser, I noticed, than the usual fine powder. This coarseness was also observed by Thorndyke, who edged up to the tub and dipped his hand into the ash and then wiped his fingers on his handkerchief.

"This stuff doesn't seem to contain much gold," said Mr. Sherwood. "But we shall see when we make the assay."

"What do you think of this?" asked Thorndyke, taking from his pocket the small lump of glittering, golden-looking mineral that he had picked out at the assayist's. Mr. Sherwood took it from him and examined it closely. "This looks more hopeful," said he; "rather rich, in fact."

Thorndyke received this statement with an unmoved countenance; but as for me, I stared at Mr. Sherwood in amazement. For this lump of glittering mineral was simply a fragment of common iron pyrites! It would not have deceived a schoolboy, much less a metallurgist.

Still holding the specimen, and taking a watchmaker's lens from a shelf, Mr. Sherwood moved over to the window. Simultaneously, Thorndyke stepped softly to the cupel shelves and quickly ran his eye along the rows of cupels. Presently he paused at one, examined it more closely, and then, taking it from the shelf, began to pick at it with his finger-nail.

At this moment Mr. Sherwood turned and observed him; and instantly there flashed into the metallurgist's face an expression of mingled anger and alarm.

"Put that down!" he commanded peremptorily, and then, as Thorndyke continued to scrape with his finger nail, he shouted furiously, "Do you hear? Drop it!"

Thorndyke took him literally at his word and let the cupel fall on the floor, when it shattered into innumerable fragments, of which one of the largest separated itself from the rest. Thorndyke pounced upon it, and in an instantaneous glance, as he picked it up, I recognised it as a calcined tooth.

Then followed a few moments of weird, dramatic silence. Thorndyke, holding the tooth between his finger and thumb, looked steadily into the eyes of the metallurgist; and the latter, pallid as a corpse, glared at Thorndyke and furtively unbuttoned his overall.

Suddenly the silence broke into a tumult as bewildering as the crash of a railway collision. Sherwood's right hand darted under his overall. Instantly, Thorndyke snatched up another cupel and hurled it with such truth of aim that it shattered on the metallurgist's forehead. And as he flung the missile, he sprang forward, and delivered a swift upper-cut. There was a thunderous crash, a cloud of white dust, and an automatic pistol clattered along the floor.

I snatched up the pistol and rushed to my friend's assistance. But there was no need. With his great strength and his uncanny skill--to say nothing of the effects of the knock-out blow--Thorndyke had the man pinned down immovably.

"See if you can find some cord, Jervis," he said a calm, quiet tone that seemed almost ridiculously out of character with the circumstances.

There was no difficulty about this, for several corded boxes stood in a corner of the laboratory. I cut off two lengths, with one of which I secured the prostrate man's arms. and with the other fastened his knees and ankles.

"Now," said Thorndyke, "if you will take charge of his hands, we will make a preliminary inspection. Let us first see if he wears a belt."

Unbuttoning the man's waistcoat, he drew up the shirt, disclosing a broad, webbing belt furnished with several leather pockets, the buttoned flaps of which he felt carefully, regardless of the stream of threats and imprecations that poured from our victim's swollen lips. From the front pockets he proceeded to the back, passing an exploratory hand under the writhing body.

"Ah!" he exclaimed suddenly, "just turn him over, and look out for his heels."

We rolled our captive over, and as Thorndyke "skinned the rabbit," a central pocket came into view, into which, when he had unbuttoned it, he inserted his fingers. "Yes," he continued, "I think this is what we are looking for." He withdrew his fingers, between which he held a small packet of Japanese paper, and with feverish excitement I watched him open out layer after layer of the soft wrapping. As he turned back the last fold a wonderful crimson sparkle told me that the "great ruby" was found.

"There, Jervis," said Thorndyke, holding the magnificent gem towards me in the palm of his hand, "look on this beautiful, sinister thing, charged with untold potentialities of evil--and thank the gods that it is not yours."

He wrapped it up again carefully and, having bestowed it in an inner pocket, said, "And now give me the pistol and run down to the telegraph office and see if you can stop Miller. I should like him to have the credit for this."

I handed him the pistol and made my way out into Fetter Lane and so down to Fleet Street, where at the post office my urgent message was sent off to Scotland Yard immediately. In a few minutes the reply came that Superintendent Miller had not yet left and that he was starting immediately for Clifford's Inn. A quarter of an hour later he drove up in a hansom to the Fetters Lane gate and I conducted him up to the second floor, where Thorndyke introduced him to his prisoner and witnessed the official arrest.

"You don't see how I arrived at it," said Thorndyke as we walked homeward after returning the key. "Well, I am not surprised. The initial evidence was of the weakest; it acquired significance only by cumulative effect. Let us reconstruct it as it developed.

"The derelict hat was, of course, the starting-point. Now, the first thing one noticed was that it appeared to have had more than one owner. No man would buy a new hat that fitted so badly as to need all that packing; and the arrangement of the packing suggested a long-headed man wearing a hat that had belonged to a man with a short head. Then there were the suggestions offered by the slips of paper. The fragmentary address referred to a place the name of which ended in ' n' and the remainder was evidently 'London, W.C.' Now what West Central place names end in 'n'? It was not a street, a square or a court, and Barbican is not in the W.C. district. It was almost certainly one of the half- dozen surviving Inns of Court or Chancery. But, of course, it was not necessarily the address of the owner of the hat.

"The other slip of paper bore the end of a word ending in 'el,' and another word ending in 'eep,' and connected with these were quantities stated in ounces and pennyweights troy weight. But the only persons who I troy weight are those who deal in precious metals. I inferred therefore that the 'el' was part of 'lemel,' and that the 'eep ' was part of 'floor-sweep,' an inference that was supported by the respective quantities, three ounces five pennyweights of lemel and nine and a half ounces of floor-sweep."

"What is lemel?" I asked.

"It is the trade name for the gold or silver filings that collect in the 'skin' of a jeweller's bench. Floor-sweep is, of course, the dust swept up on the floor of a jeweller's or goldsmith's workshop. The lemel is actual metal, though not of uniform fineness, but the sweep is a mixture of dirt and metal. Both are saved and sent to the refiners to have the gold and silver extracted.

"This paper, then, was connected either with a gold smith or a gold refiner--who might call himself an assayist or a metallurgist. The connection was supported by the leaf of a price list of gas stoves. A metallurgist would be kept well supplied with lists of gas stoves and furnaces. The traces of lead in the dust from the hat gave us another straw blowing the same direction, for gold assayed by the dry process is fused in the cupel furnace with lead; and as the lead oxidises and the oxide is volatile, traces of lead would tend to appear in the dust deposited in the laboratory.

"The next thing to do was to consult the directory; and when I did so, I found that there were no goldsmiths in any of the Inns and only one assayist--Mr. Highley, of Clifford's Inn. The probabilities therefore, slender as they were, pointed to some connection between this stray hat and Mr. Highley. And this was positively all the information that we had when we came out this afternoon.

"As soon as we got to Clifford's Inn, however, the evidence began to grow like a rolling snowball. First there was Larkin's contribution; and then there was the discovery of the missing hat. Now, as soon as I saw that hat my suspicions fell upon the man upstairs. I felt a conviction that the hat had been left there purposely and that the letter to Larkin was just a red herring to create a false trail. Nevertheless, the presence of that hat completely confirmed the other evidence. It showed that the apparent connection was a real connection."

"But," I asked, "what made you suspect the man upstairs?"

"My dear Jervis!" he exclaimed, "consider the facts. That hat was enough to hang the man who left it there. Can you imagine this astute, wary villain making such an idiot's mistake--going away and leaving the means of his conviction for anyone to find? But you are forgetting that whereas the missing hat was found on the first floor, the murderer's hat was connected with the second floor. The evidence suggested that it was Highley's hat. And now, before we go on to the next stage, let me remind you of those finger-prints. Miller thought that their rough appearance was due to the surface on which they had been made, But it was not. They were the prints of a person who was suffering from ichthyosis, palmar psoriasis or sonic dry dermatitis.

"There is one other point. The man we were looking for was a murderer. His life was already forfeit. To such a man another murder more or less is of no consequence. If this man, having laid the false trail, had determined to take sanctuary in Highley's rooms, it was probable that he had already got rid of Highley. And remember that a metallurgist has unrivalled means disposing of a body; for not only is each of his muffle furnaces a miniature crematorium, but the very residue of a cremated body--bone-ash--is one of the materials of his trade.

"When we went upstairs, I first took the reading of the gas meter and ascertained that a large amount of gas had been used recently. Then, when we entered I took the opportunity to shake hands with Mr. Sherwood, and immediately I became aware that he suffered from a rather extreme form of ichthyosis. That was the first point of verification. Then we discovered that he actually could not distinguish between iron pyrites and auriferous quartz. He was not a metallurgist at all. He was a masquerader. Then the bone-ash in the tub was mixed with fragments of calcined bone, and the cupels all showed similar fragments. In one of them I could see part of the crown of a tooth. That was pure luck. But observe that by that time I had enough evidence to justify an arrest. The tooth served only to bring the affair to a crisis; and his response to my unspoken accusation saved us the trouble of further search for confirmatory evidence."

"What is not quite clear to me," said I, "is when and why he made away with Highley. As the body has been completely reduced to bone-ash, Highley must have been dead at least some days."

"Undoubtedly," Thorndyke agreed. "I take it that the course of events was like this: The police have been searching eagerly for this man, and every new crime must have made his position more unsafe--for a criminal can never be sure that he has not dropped some clue. It began to be necessary for him to make some arrangements for leaving the country and mean while to have a retreat in case his whereabouts should chance to be discovered. Highley's chambers were admirable for both purposes. Here was a solitary man who seldom had a visitor, and who would probably not be missed for some considerable time; and in those chambers were the means of rapidly and completely disposing of the body. The mere murder would be a negligible detail to this ruffian.

"I imagine that Highley was done to death at least a week ago, and that the murderer did not take up his new tenancy until the body was reduced to ash. With that large furnace in addition to the small ones, this would not take long. When the new premises were ready, he could make a sham disappearance to cover his actual flight later; and you must see how perfectly misleading that sham disappearance was. If the police had discovered that hat in the empty room only a week later, they would have been certain that he had escaped to one of the Baltic ports; and while they were following his supposed tracks, he could have gone off comfortably via Folkestone or Southampton."

"Then you think he had only just moved into Highley's rooms?"

"I should say he moved in last night. The murder of Byramji was probably planned on some information that the murderer had picked up, and as soon as it was accomplished he began forthwith to lay down the false tracks. When he reached his rooms yesterday afternoon, he must have written the letter to Larkin and gone off at once to the East End to post it. Then he probably had his bushy hair cut short and shaved off his beard and moustache--which would render him quite unrecognisable by Larkin--and moved into Highley's chambers, from which he would have quietly sallied forth in a few days' time to take his passage to the Continent. It was quite a good plan, and but for the accident of taking the wrong hat, would almost certainly have succeeded."

Once every year, on the second of August, there is delivered with unfailing regularity at No. 5A King's Bench Walk a large box of carved sandal-wood filled with the choicest Trichinopoly cheroots and accompanied by an affectionate letter from our late client, Mr. Byramji. For the second of August is the anniversary of the death (in the execution shed at Newgate) of Cornelius Barnett, otherwise known as the "New Jersey Sphinx."

The Touchstone

It happened not uncommonly that the exigencies of practice committed my friend Thorndyke to investigations that lay more properly within the province of the police. For problems that had arisen as secondary consequences of a criminal act could usually not be solved until the circumstances of that act were fully elucidated and, incidentally, the identity of the actor established. Such a problem was that of the disappearance of James Harewood's will, a problem that was propounded to us by our old friend, Mr. Marchmont, when he called on us, by appointment, with the client of whom he had spoken in his note.

It was just four o'clock when the solicitor arrived at our chambers, and as I admitted him he ushered in a gentlemanly-looking man of about thirty-five, whom he introduced as Mr. William Crowhurst.

"I will just stay," said he with an approving glance at the tea-service on the table, "and have a cup of tea with you, and give you an outline of the case. Then I must run away and leave Mr. Crowhurst to fill in the details."

He seated himself in an easy chair within comfortable reach of the table, and as Thorndyke poured out the tea, he glanced over a few notes scribbled on a sheet of paper.

"I may say," he began, stirring his tea thoughtfully, "that this is a forlorn hope. I have brought the case to you, but I have not the slightest expectation that you will be able to help us."

"A very wholesome frame of mind," Thorndyke commented with a smile. "I hope it is that of your client also."

It is indeed," said Mr. Crowhurst; " in fact, it seems to me a waste of your time to go into the matter. Probably you will think so too, when you have heard the particulars."

"Well, let us hear the particulars," said Thorndyke. "A forlorn hope has, at least, the stimulating quality of difficulty. Let us have your outline sketch, Marchmont."

The solicitor, having emptied his cup and pushed it towards the tray for replenishment, glanced at his notes and began: "The simplest way in which to present the problem is to give a brief recital of the events that have given rise to it, which are these: The day before yesterday--that is last Monday--at a quarter to two in the afternoon, Mr. James Harewood executed a will at his house at Merbridge, which is about two miles from Welsbury. There were present four persons: two of his servants, who signed as witnesses, and the two principal beneficiaries--Mr. Arthur Baxfield, a nephew of the testator, and our friend here, Mr. William Crowhurst. The will was a holograph written on the two pages of a sheet of letter-paper. When the witnesses signed, the will was covered by another sheet of paper so that only the space for the signatures was exposed. Neither of the witnesses read the will, nor did either of the beneficiaries; and so far as I am aware, no one but the testator knew what were its actual provisions, though, after the servants had left the room, Mr. Harewood explained its general purport to the beneficiaries."

"And what was its general purport?" Thorndyke asked.

"Broadly speaking," replied Marchmont, "it divided the estate in two very unequal portions between Mr. Baxfield and Mr. Crowhurst. There were certain small legacies of which neither the amounts nor the names of the legatees are known. Then, to Baxfield was given a thousand pounds to enable him either to buy a partnership or to start a small factory--he is a felt hat manufacturer by trade--and the remainder to Crowhurst, who was made executor and residuary legatee. But, of course, the residue of the estate is an unknown quantity, since we don't know either the number or the amounts of the legacies.

"Shortly after the signing of the will, the parties separated. Mr. Harewood folded up the will and put it in a leather wallet which he slipped into his pocket, stating his intention of taking the will forthwith to deposit with his lawyer at Welsbury. A few minutes after his guests had departed, he was seen by one of the servants to leave the house, and afterwards was seen by a neighbour walking along a footpath which, after passing through a small wood, joins the main road about a mile and a quarter from Welsbury. From that time, he was never again seen alive. He never visited the lawyer, nor did anyone see him at or near Welsbury or elsewhere else.

"As he did not return home that night, his housekeeper (he was a widower and childless) became extremely alarmed, and in the morning she communicated with the police. A search-party was organised, and, following the path on which he was last seen, explored the wood--which is known as Gilbert's Copse--and here, at the bottom of an old chalk-pit, they found him lying dead with a fractured skull and a dislocated neck. How he came by these injuries is not at present known; but as the body had been robbed of all valuables, including his watch, purse, diamond ring and the wallet containing the will, there is naturally a strong suspicion that he has been murdered. That, however, is not our immediate concern--at least not mine. I am concerned with the will, which, as you see, has disappeared, and as it has presumably been carried away by a thief who is under suspicion of murder, it is not likely to be returned."

"It is almost certainly destroyed by this time," said Mr. Crowhurst.

"That certainly seems probable," Thorndyke agreed. "But what do you want me to do? You haven't come for counsel's opinion?"

"No," replied Marchmont. "I am pretty clear about the legal position. I shall claim, as the will has presumably been destroyed, to have the testator's wishes carried out in so far as they are known. But I am doubtful as to the view the court may take. It may decide that the testator's wishes are not known, that the provisions of the will are too uncertain to admit of administration."

"And what would be the effect of that decision?" asked Thorndyke.

"In that case," said Marchmont, "the entire estate would go to Baxfield, as he is the next of kin and there was no previous will."

"And what is it that you want me to do?"

Marchmont chuckled deprecatingly. "You have to pay the penalty of being a prodigy, Thorndyke. We are asking you to do an impossibility--but we don't really expect you to bring it off. We ask you to help us to recover the will."

"If the will has been completely destroyed, it can't be recovered," said Thorndyke. "But we don't know that it has been destroyed. The matter is, at least, worth investigating; and if you wish me to look into it, I will."

The solicitor rose with an air of evident relief.

"Thank you, Thorndyke," said he. "I expect nothing--at least, I tell myself that I do--but I can now feel that everything that is possible will be done. And now I must be off. Crowhurst can give you any details that you want."

When Marchmont had gone, Thorndyke turned to our client and asked, "What do you suppose Baxfield will do, if the will is irretrievably lost? Will he press his claim as next of kin?"

"I should say yes," replied Crowhurst. "He is a business man and his natural claims are greater than mine. He is not likely to refuse what the law assigns to him as his right. As a matter of fact, I think he felt that his uncle had treated him unfairly in alienating the property."

"Was there any reason for this diversion of the estate?"

"Well," replied Crowhurst, "Harewood and I have been very good friends and he was under some obligations to me; and then Baxfield had not made himself very acceptable to his uncle. But the principal factor, I think, was a strong tendency of Baxfield's to gamble. He had lost quite a lot of money by backing horses, and a careful, thrifty man like James Harewood doesn't care to leave his savings to a gambler. The thousand pounds that he did leave to Baxfield was expressly for the purpose of investment in a business."

"Is Baxfield in business now?"

"Not on his own account. He is a sort of foreman or shop-manager in a factory just outside Welsbury, and I believe he is a good worker and knows his trade thoroughly."

"And now," said Thorndyke, "with regard to Mr Harewood's death. The injuries might, apparently, have been either accidental or homicidal. What are the probabilities of accident--disregarding the robbery?

"Very considerable, I should say. It is a most dangerous place. The footpath runs close beside the edge of a disused chalk-pit with perpendicular or over hanging sides, and the edge is masked by bushes and brambles. A careless walker might easily fall over--or be pushed over, for that matter."

"Do you know when the inquest is to take place?"

"Yes. The day after to-morrow. I had the subpoena this morning for Friday afternoon at 2.30, at the Welsbury Town Hall."

At this moment footsteps were heard hurriedly ascending the stairs and then came a loud and peremptory rat-tat at our door. I sprang across to see who our visitor was, and as I flung open the door, Mr. Marchmont rushed in, breathing heavily and flourishing a newspaper.

"Here is a new development," he exclaimed. "It doesn't seem to help us much, but I thought you had better know about it at once." He sat down, and putting on his spectacles, read aloud as follows: "A new and curious light has been thrown on the mystery of the death of Mr. James Harewood, whose body was found yesterday in a disused chalk-pit near Merbridge. It appears that on Monday--the day on which Mr. Harewood almost certainly was killed--a passenger alighting from a train at Barwood Junction before it had stopped, slipped and fell between the train and the platform. He was quickly extricated, and as he had evidently sustained internal injuries, he was taken to the local hospital, where he was found to be suffering from a fractured pelvis. He gave his name as Thomas Fletcher, but refused to give any address, saying that he had no relatives. This morning he died, and on his clothes being searched for an address, a parcel, formed of two handkerchiefs tied up with string, was found in his pocket. When it was opened it was found to contain five watches, three watch-chains, a tie-pin and a number of bank-notes. Other pockets contained a quantity of loose money--gold and silver mixed--and a card of the Welsbury Races, which were held on Monday. Of the five watches, one has been identified as the one taken from Mr. Harewood; and the bank-notes have been identified as a batch handed to him by the cashier, of his bank at Welsbury last Thursday and presumably carried in the leather wallet which was stolen from his pocket. This wallet, by the way, has also been found. It was picked up--empty--last night on the railway embankment just outside Welsbury Station. Appearances thus suggest that the man, Fletcher, when on his way to the races, encountered Mr. Harewood in the lonely copse, and murdered and robbed him; or perhaps found him dead in the chalk-pit and robbed the body--a question that is now never likely to be solved."

As Marchmont finished reading, he looked up at Thorndyke. "It doesn't help us much, does it?" said he. "As the wallet was found empty, it is pretty certain that the will has been destroyed."

"Or perhaps merely thrown away," said Thorndyke. "In which case an advertisement offering a substantial reward may bring it to light."

The solicitor shrugged his shoulders sceptically, but agreed to publish the advertisement. Then, once more he turned to go; and as Mr. Crowhurst had no further information to give, he departed with his lawyer.

For some time after they had gone, Thorndyke sat with his brief notes before him, silent and deeply reflective. I, too, maintained a discreet silence, for I knew from long experience that the motionless pose and quiet, impassive face were the outward signs of a mind in swift and strenuous action. Instinctively, I gathered that this apparently chaotic case was being quietly sorted out and arranged in a logical order; that Thorndyke, like a skilful chess-player, was "trying over the moves" before he should lay his hand upon the pieces.

Presently he looked up. "Well?" he asked. "What do you think, Jervis? Is it worth while?"

"That," I replied," depends on whether the will is or is not in existence. If it has been destroyed, an investigation would be a waste of our time and our client's money."

"Yes," he agreed. "But there is quite a good chance that it has not been destroyed. It was probably dropped loose into the wallet, and then might have been picked out and thrown away before the wallet was examined. But we mustn't concentrate too much on the will. If we take up the case-- which I am inclined to do--we must ascertain the actual sequence of events. We have one clear day before the inquest. If we run down to Merbridge to-morrow and go thoroughly over the ground, and then go on to Barwood and find out all we can about the man Fletcher, we may get some new light from the evidence at the inquest."

I agreed readily to Thorndyke's proposal, not that I could see any way into the case, but I felt a conviction that my colleague had isolated some leading fact and had a definite line of research in his mind. And this conviction deepened when, later in the evening, he laid his research-case on the table, and rearranged its contents with evident purpose. I watched curiously the apparatus that he was packing in it and tried--not very successfully--to infer the nature of the proposed investigation. The box of powdered paraffin wax and the spirit blowpipe were obvious enough; but the "dust-aspirator"--a sort of miniature vacuum cleaner--the portable microscope, the coil of Manila line, with an eye spliced into one end, and especially the abundance of blank-labelled microscope slides, all of which I saw him pack in the case with deliberate care, defeated me utterly.

About ten o'clock on the following morning we stepped from the train in Welsbury Station, and having recovered our bicycles from the luggage van, wheeled them through the barrier and mounted. During the train journey we had both studied the one-inch Ordnance map to such purpose that we were virtually in familiar surroundings and immune from the necessity of seeking directions from the natives. As we cleared the town we glanced up the broad by-road to the left which led to the race-course; then we rode on briskly for a mile, which brought us to the spot where the footpath to Merbridge joined the road. Here we dismounted and, lifting our bicycles over the stile, followed the path towards a small wood which we could see ahead, crowning a low hill.

"For such a good path," Thorndyke remarked as we approached the wood, "it is singularly unfrequented. I haven't seen a soul since we left the road." He glanced at the map as the path entered the wood, and when we had walked on a couple of hundred yards, he halted and stood his bicycle against a tree. "The chalk-pit should be about here," said he, "though it is impossible to see. He grasped a stem of one of the small bushes that crowded on to the path and pulled it aside. Then he uttered an exclamation.

"Just look at that, Jervis. It is a positive scandal that a public path should be left in this condition."

Certainly Mr. Crowhurst had not exaggerated. It was a most dangerous place. The parted branches revealed a chasm some thirty feet deep, the brink of which, masked by the bushes, was but a matter of inches from the edge of the path.

"We had better go back," said Thorndyke," and find the entrance to the pit, which seems to be to the right. The first thing is to ascertain exactly where Harewood fell. Then we can come back and examine the place from above."

We turned back, and presently found a faint track which we followed until, descending steeply, it brought us out into the middle of the pit. It was evidently an ancient pit, for the sides were blackened by age, and the floor was occupied by a trees, some of considerable size. Against one of these we leaned our bicycles and then walked slowly round at the foot of the frowning cliff.

"This seems to be below the path," said Thorndyke, glancing up at the grey wall which jutted out above in stages like an inverted flight of steps. "Somewhere hereabouts we should find some traces of the tragedy."

Even as he spoke my eye caught a spot of white on a block of chalk, and on the freshly fractured surface a significant brownish-red stain. The block lay opposite the mouth of an artificial cave--an old wagon-shelter but now empty and immediately under a markedly overhanging part of the cliff.

"This is undoubtedly the place where he fell," said Thorndyke. "You can see where the stretcher was placed--an old-pattern stretcher with wheel-runners--and there is a little spot of broken soil at the top where he came over. Well, apart from the robbery, a clear fall of over thirty feet is enough to account for a fractured skull. Will you stay here, Jervis, while I run up and look at the path?"

He went off towards the entrance, and presently I heard him above, pulling aside the bushes, and after one or two trials, he appeared directly overhead.

"There are plenty of footprints on the path," said he, "but nothing abnormal. No trampling or signs of a struggle. I am going on a little farther."

He withdrew behind the bushes, and I proceeded to inspect the interior of the cave, noting the smoke-blackened roof and the remains of a recent fire, which, with a number of rabbit bones and a discarded tea of the kind used by the professional tramp, seemed not without a possible bearing on our investigation. I was thus engaged when I heard Thorndyke hail me from above and coming out of the cave, I saw his head thrust between the branches. He seemed to be lying down, for his face was nearly on a level with the top of the cliff.

"I want to take an impression," he called out. "Will you bring up the paraffin and the blower? And you might bring the coil of line, too."

I hurried away to the place where our bicycles were standing, and opening the research-case, took out the coil of line, the tin of paraffin wax and the spirit blowpipe, and having ascertained that the container of the latter was full, I ran up the incline and made my way along the path. Some distance along, I found my colleague nearly hidden in the bushes, lying prone, with his head over the edge of the cliff.

"You see, Jervis," he said, as I crawled alongside and looked over, "this is a possible way down, and someone has used it quite recently. He climbed down with his face to the cliff--you can see the clear impression of the toe of a boot in the loam of that projection, and you can even make out the shape of an iron toe-tip. Now the problem is how to get down to take the impression without, dislodging the earth above it. I think I will secure myself with the line."

"It is hardly worth the risk of a broken neck," said I. "Probably the print is that of some schoolboy."

"It is a man's foot," he replied. "Most likely it has no connection with our case. But it may have, and as a shower of rain would obliterate it we ought to secure it." As he spoke, he passed the end of the cord through eye and slipped the loop over his shoulders, drawing tight under his arms. Then, having made the line fast to the butt of a small tree, he cautiously lowered himself over the edge and climbed down to the projection. A soon as he had a secure footing, I passed the spare cord through the ring on the lid of the wax tin and lowered it to him, and when he had unfastened it, I drew up the cord and in the same way let down the blowpipe. Then I watched his neat, methodical procedure. First he took out a spoonful of the powdered, or grated, wax and very delicately sprinkled it on the toe-print until the latter was evenly but very thinly covered. Next he lit the blowlamp, and as soon as the blue flame began to roar from the pipe, he directed it on to the toe-print. Almost instantly the powder melted, glazing the impression like a coat of varnish. The flame was removed and the film of wax at once solidified and became dull and opaque. A second, heavier, sprinkling with the powder, followed by another application of the flame, thickened the film of wax, and this process, repeated four or five times, eventually produced a solid cake. Then Thorndyke extinguished the blowlamp, and securing it and the tin to the cord, directed me to pull them up. "And you might send me down the field-glasses," he added. "There is something farther down that I can't quite make out."

I slipped the glasses from my shoulder, and opening the case, tied the cord to the leather sling and lowered it down the cliff; and then I watched with some curiosity as Thorndyke stood on his insecure perch steadily gazing through the glasses (they were Zeiss 8-prismatics) at a clump of wallflowers that grew from a boss of chalk about half-way down. Presently he lowered the glasses and, slinging them round his neck by their lanyard, turned his attention to the cake of wax. It was by this time quite solid, and when he had tested it, he lifted it carefully, and placed it in the empty binocular case, when I drew it up.

"I want you, Jervis," Thorndyke called up, "to steady the line. I am going down to that wallflower clump."

It looked extremely unsafe, but I knew it was useless to protest, so I hitched the line around a massive stump and took a firm grip of the "fall."

"Ready," I sang out; and forthwith Thorndyke began to creep across the face of the cliff with feet and hands clinging to almost invisible projections. Fortunately, there was at this part no overhang, and though my heart was in my mouth as I watched, I saw him cross the perilous space in safety. Arrived at the clump, he drew an envelope from his pocket, stooped and picked up some small object, which he placed in the envelope, returning the latter to his pocket. Then he gave me another bad five minutes while he recrossed the nearly vertical surface to his starting-point; but at length this, too, was safely accomplished, and when he finally climbed up over the edge and stood beside me on solid earth, I drew a deep breath and turned to revile him.

"Well?" I demanded sarcastically, "what have you gathered at the risk of your neck? Is it samphire or edelweiss?"

He drew the envelope from his pocket, and dipping into it, produced a cigarette-holder--a cheap bone affair, black and clammy with long service and still holding the butt of a hand-made cigarette--and handed it to me. I turned it over, smelled it and hastily handed it back. "For my part," said I, "I wouldn't have risked the cervical vertebra of a yellow cat for it. What do you expect to learn from it?"

"Of course, I expect nothing. We are just collecting facts on the chance that they may turn out to be relevant. Here, for instance, we find that a man has descended, within a few yards of where Harewood fell, by this very inconvenient route, instead of going round to the entrance to the pit. He must have had some reason for adopting this undesirable mode of descent. Possibly he was in a hurry, and probably he belonged to the district, since a stranger would not know of the existence of this short cut. Then it seems likely that this was his cigarette tube. If you look over, you will see by those vertical scrapes on the chalk that he slipped and must have nearly fallen. At that moment he probably dropped the tube, for you notice that the wallflower clump is directly under the marks of his toes."

"Why do you suppose he did not recover the tube?"

"Because the descent slopes away from the position of the clump, and he had no trusty Jervis with a stout cord to help him to cross the space. And if he went down this way because he was hurried, he would not have time to search for the tube. But if the tube was not his, still it belonged to somebody who has been here recently."

"Is there anything that leads you to connect this man with the crime?"

"Nothing but time and place," he replied. "The man has been down into the pit close to where Harewood was robbed and possibly murdered, and as the traces are quite recent, he must have been there near about the time of the robbery. That is all. I am considering the traces of this man in particular because there are no traces of any other. But we may as well have a look at the path, which, as you see, yields good impressions."

We walked slowly along the path towards Merbridge, keeping at the edges and scrutinising the surface closely. In the shady hollows, the soft loam bore prints of many feet, and among them we could distinguish one with an iron toe-tip, but it was nearly obliterated by another studded with hob-nails.

"We shan't get much information here," said Thorndyke as he turned about. "The search-party have trodden out the important prints. Let us see if we can find out where the man with the toe-tips went to."

We searched the path on the Welsbury side of the chalk- pit, but found no trace of him. Then we went into the pit, and having located the place where he descended, sought for some other exit than the track leading to the path. Presently, half-way up the slope, we found a second track, bearing away in the direction of Merbridge. Following this for some distance, we came to a small hollow at the bottom of which was a muddy space. And here we both halted abruptly, for in the damp ground were the clear imprints of a pair of boots which we could sec had, in addition to the toe-tips, half-tips to the heels.

"We had better have wax casts of these," said Thorndyke, "to compare with the boots of the man Fletcher. I will do them while you go back for the bicycles."

By the time that I returned with the machines two of the footprints were covered with a cake each of wax, and Thorndyke had left the track, and was peering among the bushes. I inquired what he was looking for.

"It is a forlorn hope, as Marchmont would say," he replied, "but I am looking to see if the will has been thrown away here. It was quite probably jettisoned at once, and this is the most probable route for the robber to have taken, if he knew of it. You see by the map that it must lead nearly directly to the race-course, and it avoids both the path and the main road. While the wax is setting we might as well look round."

It seemed a hopeless enough proceeding and I agreed to it without enthusiasm. Leaving the track on the opposite side to that which Thorndyke was searching, I wandered among the bushes and the little open spaces, peering about me and reminding myself of that "aged, aged man" who

"Sometimes searched the grassy knolls,

For wheels of hansom cabs."

I had worked my way nearly back to where I could see Thorndyke, also returning, when my glance fell on a small, brown object caught among the branches of a bush. It was a man's pigskin purse; and as I picked it out of the bush I saw that it was open and empty.

With my prize in my hand, I hastened to the spot where Thorndyke was lifting the wax casts. He looked up and asked, "No luck, I suppose?"

I held out the purse, on which he pounced eagerly. "But this is most important, Jervis," he exclaimed. "It is almost certainly Harewood's purse. You see the initials, 'J. H.,' stamped on the flap. Then we were right as to the direction that the robber took. And it would pay to search this place exhaustively for the will, though we can't do that now, as we have to go to Barwood, I wrote to say we were coming. We had better get back to the path now and make for the road. Barwood is only half-an-hour's run."

We packed the casts in the research-case (which was strapped to Thorndyke's bicycle), and turning back, made our way to the path. As it was still deserted, we ventured to mount, and soon reached the road, along which we started at a good pace toward Barwood.

Half-an-hour's ride brought us into the main Street of the little town, and when we dismounted at the police station we found the Chief Constable himself waiting to receive us, courteously eager to assist us, but possessed by a devouring curiosity which was somewhat inconvenient.

"I have done as you asked me in your letter, sir," he said. "Fletcher's body is, of course, in the mortuary, but I have had all his clothes and effects brought here; and I have had them put in my private office, so that you can look them over in comfort."

"It is exceedingly good of you," said Thorndyke, "and most helpful." He unstrapped the research-case, and following the officer into his sanctum, looked round with deep approval. A large table had been cleared for the examination, and the dead pickpocket's clothes and effects neatly arranged at one end.

Thorndyke's first proceeding was to pick up the dead man's boots--a smart but flimsy pair of light brown leather, rather down at heel and in need of re-soling. Neither toes nor heels bore any tips or even nails excepting the small fastening brads. Having exhibited them to me without remark, Thorndyke placed them on a sheet of white paper and made a careful tracing of the soles, a proceeding that seemed to surprise the Chief Constable, for he remarked, "I should hardly have thought that the question of footprints would arise in this case. You can't charge a dead man."

Thorndyke agreed that this seemed to be true; and then he proceeded to an operation that fairly made the officer's eyes bulge. Opening the research-case--into which the officer cast an inquisitive glance--he took out the dust-aspirator, the nozzle of which he inserted into one after another of the dead thief's pockets while I worked the pump. When he had gone through them all, he opened the receiver and extracted quite a considerable ball of dusty fluff. Placing this on a glass slide, he tore it in halves with a pair of mounted needles and passing one half to me, when we both fell to work "teasing", it out into an open mesh, portions of which we separated and laid--each in a tiny pool of glycerine--on blank labelled glass slides, applying to each slide its cover-glass and writing on the label, "Dust from Fletcher's pockets."

When the series was complete, Thorndyke brought out the microscope, and fitting on a one-inch objective, quickly examined the slides, one after another, and then pushed the microscope to me. So far as I could see, the dust was just ordinary dust--principally made up of broken cotton fibres with a few fibres of wool, linen, wood, jute, and others that I could not name and some undistinguishable mineral particles. But I made no comment, and resigning the microscope to the Chief Constable--who glared through it, breathing hard, and remarked that the dust was "rummy-looking stuff "--watched Thorndyke's further proceedings. And very odd proceedings they were.

First he laid the five stolen watches in a row, and with a Coddington lens minutely examined the dial of each, Then he opened the back of each in turn and copied into his notebook the watch-repairers' scratched inscriptions. Next he produced from the case a number of little vulcanite rods, and laying out five labelled slides, dropped a tiny drop of glycerine on each, covering it at once with a watch-glass to protect it from falling dust. Then he stuck a little label on each watch, wrote a number on it and similarly numbered the five slides. His next proceeding was to take out the glass of watch No. 1 and pick up one of the vulcanite rods, which he rubbed briskly on a silk handkerchief and passed across and around the dial of the watch, after which he held the rod close to the glycerine on slide No. 1 and tapped it sharply with the blade of his pocket-knife. Then he dropped a cover- glass on to the glycerine and made a rapid inspection of the specimen through the microscope.

This operation he repeated on the other four watches, using a fresh rod for each, and when he had finished he turned to the open-mouthed officer. "I take it," said he, "that the watch which has the chain attached to it is Mr. Harewood's watch?"

"Yes, sir. That helped us to identify it." Thorndyke looked at the watch reflectively. Attached to the bow by a short length of green tape was a small, rather elaborate key. This my friend picked up, and taking a fresh mounted needle, inserted it into the barrel of the key, from which he then withdrew it with a tiny ball of fluff on its point. I hastily prepared a slide and handed it to him, when, with a pair of dissecting scissors, he cut off a piece of the fluff and let it fall into the glycerine. He repeated this manoeuvre with two more slides and then labelled the three " Key, outside," "middle" and "inside," and in that order examined them under the microscope.

My own examination of the specimens yielded very little. They all seemed to be common dust, though that from the face of watch No. 3 contained a few broken fragments of what looked like animal hairs--possibly cat's-- as also did the key-fluff marked "outside." But if this had any significance, I could not guess what it was. As to the Chief Constable, he clearly looked on the whole proceeding as a sort of legerdemain with no obvious purpose, for he remarked, as we were packing up to go, " I am glad I've seen how you do it, sir. But all the same, I think you are flogging a dead horse. We know who committed the crime and we know he's beyond the reach of the law."

"Well," said Thorndyke, "one must earn one's fee, you know. I shall put Fletcher's boots and the five watches in evidence at the inquest to-morrow, and I will ask you to leave the labels on the watches." With renewed thanks and a hearty handshake he bade the courteous officer adieu, and we rode off to catch the train to London.

That evening, after dinner, we brought out the specimens and went over them at our leisure; and Thorndyke added a further specimen by drawing a knotted piece of twine through the cigarette-holder that he had salved from the chalk-pit, and teasing out the unsavoury, black substance that came out on the string in glycerine on a slide. When he had examined it, he passed it to me, The dark, tarry liquid somewhat obscured the detail, but I could make out fragments of the same animal hairs that I had noted in the other specimens, only here they were much more numerous. I mentioned my observation to Thorndyke. "They are certainly parts of mammalian hairs," I said, "and they look like the hairs of a cat. Are they from a cat?"

"Rabbit," Thorndyke replied curtly; and even then, I am ashamed to admit, I did not perceive the drift of the investigation.

The room in the Welsbury Town Hall had filled up some minutes before the time fixed for the opening of the inquest, and in the interval, when the jury had retired to view the body in the adjacent mortuary, I looked round the assembly. Mr. Marchmont and Mr. Crowhurst were present, and a youngish, horsey-looking man in cord breeches and leggings, whom I correctly guessed to be Arthur Baxfield. Our friend the Chief Constable of Barwood was also there, and with him Thorndyke exchanged a few words in a retired corner. The rest of the company were strangers.

As soon as the coroner and the jury had taken their places the medical witness was called. The cause of death, he stated, was dislocation of the neck, accompanied by a depressed fracture of the skull. The fracture have been produced by a blow with a heavy weapon, or by the deceased falling on his head. The witness adopted the latter view, as the dislocation showed that deceased had fallen in that manner.

The next witness was Mr. Crowhurst, who repeated to the court what he had told us, and further stated that on leaving deceased's house he went straight home, as he had an appointment with a friend. He was followed by Baxfield, who gave evidence to the same effect, and stated that on leaving the house of the deceased he went to his place of business at Welsbury. He was about to retire when Thorndyke rose to cross-examine.

"At what time did you reach your place of business?" he asked.

The witness hesitated for a few moments and then replied, "Half-past four."

"And what time did you leave deceased's house?"

"Two o'clock," was the reply.

"What is the distance?"

"In a direct line, about two miles. But I didn't go direct. I took a round in the country by Lenfield."

"That would take you near the race-course on the way back. Did you go to the races?

"No. The races were just over when I returned."

There was a slight pause and then Thorndyke asked, "Do you smoke much, Mr. Baxfield?"

The witness looked surprised, and so did the jury, but the former replied, "A fair amount. About fifteen cigarettes a day."

"What brand of cigarettes do you smoke, and what kind of tobacco is it?"

"I make my own cigarettes. I make them of shag."

Here protesting murmurs arose from the jury, and the coroner remarked stiffly, "These questions do not appear to have much connection with the subject of this inquiry."

"You may take it, sir," replied Thorndyke, "that they have a very direct bearing on it." Then, turning to the witness he asked, "Do you use a cigarette-tube?

"Sometimes I do," was the reply.

"Have you lost a cigarette-tube lately?"

The witness directed a startled glance at Thorndyke and replied after some hesitation, "I believe I mislaid one a little time ago."

"When and where did you lose that tube?" Thorndyke asked.

"I--I really couldn't say," replied Baxfield, turning perceptibly pale.

Thorndyke opened his dispatch-box, and taking out the tube that he had salved at so much risk, handed it to the witness. "Is that the tube that you lost?" he asked.

At this question Baxfield turned pale as death, and the hand in which he received the tube shook as if with a palsy. "It may be," he faltered. "I wouldn't swear to it. It is like the one I lost."

Thorndyke took it from him and passed it to the coroner. "I am putting this tube in evidence, sir," said he. Then addressing the witness, he said, "You stated that you did not go to the races. Did you go on the course or inside the grounds at all?"

Baxfield moistened his lips and replied, "I just went in for a minute or two, but I didn't stay. The races were over, and there was a very rough crowd."

"While you were in that crowd, Mr Baxfield, did you have your pocket picked?"

There was an expectant silence in the court as Baxfield replied in a low voice: "Yes. I lost my watch."

Again Thorndyke opened the dispatch-box, and taking out a watch (it was the one that had been labelled 3), handed it to the witness. "Is that the watch that you lost?" he asked.

Baxfield held the watch in his trembling hand and replied hesitatingly, "I believe it is, but I won't swear to it."

There was a pause. Then, in grave, impressive tones, Thorndyke said," Now, Mr. Baxfield, I am going to ask you a question which you need not answer if you consider that by doing so you would prejudice your position in any way. That question is, When your pocket was picked, were any articles besides this watch taken from your person? Don't hurry. Consider your answer carefully."

For some moments Baxfield remained silent, regarding Thorndyke with a wild, affrighted stare. At length he began falteringly, "I don't remember missing any thing--" and then stopped.

"Could the witness be allowed to sit down, sir?" Thorndyke asked. And when the permission had been given and a chair placed, Baxfield sat down heavily and cast a bewildered glance round the court. "I think," he said, addressing Thorndyke, "I had better tell you exactly what happened and take my chance of the consequences. When I left my uncle's house on Monday, I took a circuit through the fields and then entered Gilbert's Copse to wait for my uncle and tell him what I thought of his conduct in leaving the bulk of his property to a stranger. I struck the path that I knew my uncle would take and walked along it slowly to meet him. I did meet him--on the path, just above where he was found--and I began to say what was in my mind. But he wouldn't listen. He flew into a rage, and as I was standing in the middle of the path, he tried to push past me. In doing so he caught his foot in a bramble and staggered back, then he disappeared through the bushes and a few seconds after I heard a thud down below. I pulled the bushes aside and looked down into the chalk-pit, and there I saw him lying with his head all on one side. Now, I happened to know of a short cut down into the pit. It was rather a dangerous climb, but I took it to get down as quickly as possible. It was there that I dropped the cigarette-tube. When I got to my uncle I could see that he was dead. His skull was battered and his neck was broken. Then the devil put into my head the idea of making away with the will. But I knew that if I took the will only, suspicion would fall on me. So I took most of his valuables--the wallet, his watch and chain, his purse and his ring. The purse I emptied and threw away, and flung the ring after it. I took the will out of the wallet--it had just been dropped in loose--and put it in an inner pocket. Then I dropped the wallet and the watch and chain into my outside coat pocket.

"I struck across country, intending to make for the race-course and drop the things among the crowd, so that they might be picked up and safely carried away. But when I got there a gang of pickpockets saved me the trouble; they mobbed and hustled me and cleared my pockets of everything but my keys and the will."

"And what has become of the will?" asked Thorndyke.

"I have it here." He dipped into his breast pocket and produced a folded paper, which he handed to Thorndyke, who opened it, and having glanced at it, passed it to the coroner.

That was practically the end of the inquest. The jury decided to accept Baxfield's statement and recorded a verdict of "Death by Misadventure," leaving Baxfield to be dealt with by the proper authorities.

"An interesting and eminently satisfactory case," remarked Thorndyke, as we sat over a rather late dinner. "Essentially simple, too. The elucidation turned, as you probably noticed, on a single illuminating fact."

"I judged that it was so," said I, "though the illumination of that fact has not yet reached me."

"Well," said Thorndyke, "let us first take the general aspect of the case as it was presented by Marchmont. The first thing, of course, that struck one was that the loss of the will might easily have converted Baxfield from a minor beneficiary to the sole heir. But even if the court agreed to recognise the will, it would have to be guided by the statements of the only two men to whom its provisions were even approximately known, and Baxfield could have made any statement he pleased. It was impossible to ignore the fact that the loss of the will was very greatly to Baxfield's advantage.

"When the stolen property was discovered in Fletcher's possession it looked, at the first glance, as if the mystery of the crime were solved. But there were several serious inconsistencies. First, how came Fletcher to be in this solitary wood, remote from any railway or even road? He appeared to be a London pickpocket. When he was killed he was travelling to London by train. It seemed probable that he had come from London by train to ply his trade at the races. Then, as you know, criminological experience shows that the habitual criminal is a rigid specialist. The burglar, the coiner, the pickpocket, each keeps strictly to his own special line Now, Fletcher was a pickpocket, and had evidently be picking pockets on the race-course. The probabilities were against his being the original robber and in favour of his having picked the pocket of the person who robbed Harewood. But if this were so, who was that person? Once more the probabilities suggested Baxfield. There was the motive, as I have said, and further, the pocket-picking had apparently taken place on the race-course, and Baxfield was known to be a frequenter of race-courses. But again, if Baxfield were the person robbed by Fletcher, then one of the five watches was probably Baxfield's watch. Whether it was so or not might have been very difficult to prove, but here came in the single illuminating fact that I have spoken of.

"You remember that when Marchmont opened the case he mentioned that Baxfield was a manufacturer of felt hats, and Crowhurst told us that he was a sort of foreman or manager of the factory."

"Yes, I remember, now you speak of it. But what is the bearing of the fact?"

"My dear Jervis!" exclaimed Thorndyke. "Don't you see that it gave us a touchstone? Consider, now. What is a felt hat? It is just a mass of agglutinated rabbits' hair. The process of manufacture consists in blowing a jet of the more or less disintegrated hair on to a revolving steel cone which is moistened by a spray of an alcoholic solution of shellac. But, of course, a quantity of the finer and more minute particles of the broken hairs miss the cone and float about in the air. The air of the factory is thus charged with the dust of broken rabbit hairs; and this dust settles on and penetrates the clothing of the workers. But when clothing becomes charged with dust, that dust tends to accumulate in the pockets and find its way into the hollows and interstices of any object carried in those pockets. Thus, if one of the five watches was Baxfield's it would almost certainly show traces where this characteristic dust had crept under the bezel and settled on the dial. And so it turned out to be. When I inspected those five watches through the Coddington lens, on the dial of No. 3 I saw a quantity of dust of this character. The electrified vulcanite rod picked it all up neatly and transferred it to the slide, and under the microscope its nature was obvious. The owner of this watch was therefore, almost certainly, employed in a felt hat factory. But, of course, it was necessary to show not only the presence of rabbit hair in this watch but its absence in the others and in Fletcher's pockets; which I did.

"Then with regard to Harewood's watch. There was no rabbit hair on the dial, but there was a small quantity on the fluff from the key barrel. Now, if that rabbit hair had come from Harewood's pocket it would have been uniformly distributed through the fluff. But it was not. It was confined exclusively to the part of the fluff that was exposed. Thus it had come from some pocket other than Harewood's and the owner of that pocket was almost certainly employed in a felt hat factory, and was most probably the owner of watch No. 3. Then there was the cigarette-tube. Its bore was loaded with rabbit hair. But its owner had unquestionably been at the scene of the crime. There was a clear suggestion that his was the pocket in which the stolen watch had been carried and that he was the owner of watch No. 3. The problem was to piece this evidence together and prove definitely who this person was. And that I was able to do by means of a fresh item of evidence, which I acquired when I saw Baxfield at the inquest. I suppose you noticed his boots?"

"I am afraid I didn't," I had to admit.

"Well, I did. I watched his feet constantly, and when he crossed his legs I could see that he had iron toe-tips on his boots. That was what gave me confidence to push the cross-examination."

"It was certainly a rather daring cross-examination and rather irregular, too," said I.

It was extremely irregular," Thorndyke agreed. "The coroner ought not to have permitted it. But it was all for the best. If the coroner had disallowed my questions we should have had to take criminal proceedings against Baxfield, whereas now that we have recovered the will, it is possible that no one will trouble to prosecute him."

Which, I subsequently ascertained, is what actually happened.

A Fisher of Men

"The man," observed Thorndyke, "who would successfully practise the scientific detection of crime must take all knowledge for his province. There is no single fact which may not, in particular circumstances, acquire a high degree of evidential value; and in such circumstances success or failure is determined by the possession or non-possession of the knowledge wherewith to interpret the significance of that fact."

This obiter dictum was thrown off apropos of our investigation of the case rather magniloquently referred to in the press as "The Blue Diamond Mystery"; and more particularly of an incident which occurred in the office of our old friend, Superintendent Miller, at Scotland Yard. Thorndyke had called to verify the few facts which had been communicated to him, and having put away his notebook and picked up his green canvas- covered research-case, had risen to take his leave, when his glance fell on a couple of objects on a side-table--a leather handbag and a walking-stick, lashed together with string, to which was attached a descriptive label.

He regarded them for a few moments reflectively and then glanced at the superintendent.

"Derelicts?" he inquired, "or jetsam?"

"Jetsam," the superintendent replied, "literally jetsam--thrown overboard to lighten the ship."

Here Inspector Badger, who had been a party to the conference, looked up eagerly.

"Yes," he broke in. "Perhaps the doctor wouldn't mind having a look at them. It's quite a nice little problem, doctor, and entirely in your line."

"What is the problem?" asked Thorndyke.

"It's just this," said Badger. "Here is a bag. Now the question is, whose bag is it? What sort of person is the owner? Where did he come from and where has he gone to?"

Thorndyke chuckled. "That seems quite simple," said he. "A cursory inspection ought to dispose of trivial details like those. But how did you come by the bag?"

"The history of the derelicts," said Miller, "is this: About four o'clock this morning, a constable on duty in King's Road, Chelsea, saw a man walking on the opposite side of the road, carrying a handbag. There was nothing particularly suspicious in this, but still the constable thought he would cross and have a closer look at him. As he did so the man quickened his pace and, of course, the constable quickened his. Then the man broke into a run, and so did the constable, and a fine, stern chase started. Suddenly the man shot down a by-street, and as the constable turned the corner he saw his quarry turn into a sort of alley. Following him into this, and gaining on him perceptibly, he saw that the alley ended in a rather high wall. When the fugitive reached the wall he dropped his bag and stick and went over like a harlequin. The constable went over after him, but not like a harlequin--he wasn't dressed for the part. By the time he got over, into a large garden with a lot of fruit trees in it, my nabs had disappeared. He traced him by his footprints across the garden to another wall, and when he climbed over that he found himself in by-street. But there was no sign of our agile friend. The constable ran up and down the street to the next crossings, blowing his whistle, but of course it was no go. So he went back across the garden and secured the bag and stick, which were at once sent here for examination."

"And no arrest has been made?"

"Well," replied Miller with a faint grin, "a constable in Oakley Street who had heard the whistle arrested a man who was carrying a suspicious-looking object. But he turned out to be a cornet player coming home from the theatre."

"Good," said Thorndyke. "And now let us have a look at the bag, which I take it has already been examined?"

"Yes, we've been through it," replied Miller, "but everything has been put back as we found it."

Thorndyke picked up the bag and proceeded to make a systematic inspection of its exterior.

"A good bag," he commented; "quite an expensive one originally, though it has seen a good deal of service. You noticed the muddy marks on the bottom?"

"Yes," said Miller. "Those were probably made when he dropped the bag to jump over the wall."

"Possibly," said Thorndyke, "though they don't look like street mud. But we shall probably get more information from the contents." He opened the bag, and after a glance at its interior, spread out on the table a couple of sheets of foolscap from the stationery rack, on which he began methodically to deposit the contents of the bag, accompanying the process with a sort of running commentary on their obvious characteristics.

"Item one: a small leather dressing-wallet. Rather shabby, but originally of excellent quality. It contains two Swedish razors, a little Washita hone, a diminutive strop, a folding shaving-brush, which is slightly damp to the fingers and has a scent similar to that of the stick of shaving soap. You notice that the hone is distinctly concave in the middle and that the inscription on the razors, 'Arensburg, Eskilstuna, Sweden,' is partly ground away. Then there is a box containing a very dry cake of soap, a little manicure set, a well-worn toothbrush, a nailbrush, dental-brush, button-hook, corn-razor, a small clothesbrush and a pair of small hairbrushes. It seems to me, Badger, that this wallet suggests-- mind, I only say 'suggests'--a pretty complete answer to one of your questions."

"I don't see how," said the inspector. "Tell u what it suggests to you."

"It suggests to me," replied Thorndyke, laying down the lens through which he had been inspecting the hair- brushes, "a middle-aged or elderly man with a shaven upper lip and a beard; a well-preserved, healthy man, neat, orderly, provident and careful as to his appearance; a man long habituated to travelling, and--though I don't insist on this, but the appearances suggest that he had been living for some time in a particular households and that at the time when he lost the bag, he was changing his residence."

"He was that," cackled the inspector, "if the constable's account of the way he went over that wall is to be trusted. But still, I don't see how you have arrived at all those facts."

"Not facts, Badger," Thorndyke corrected. "I said suggestions. And those suggestions may be quite misleading. There may be some factor, such as change of ownership of the wallet, which we have not allowed for. But, taking the appearances at their face value, that is what they suggest. There is the wallet itself, for instance--strong, durable, but shabby with years of wear. And observe that it is a travelling-wallet and would be subjected to wear only during travel. Then further, as to the time factor, there are the hone and the razors. It takes a good many years to wear a Washita hone hollow or to wear away the blade of a Swedish razor until the maker's mark is encroached on. The state of health, and to some extent the age, are suggested by the tooth brush and the dental-brush. He has lost sóme teeth, since he wears a plate, but not many; and he is free from pyorrhoea and alveolar absorption. You don't wear a toothbrush down like this on half a dozen rickety survivors. But a man whose teeth will bear hard brushing is probably well-preserved and healthy."

"You say that he shaves his upper lip but wears a beard," said the inspector. "How do you arrive at that?"

"It is fairly obvious," replied Thorndyke. "We see that he has razors and uses them, and we also see that he has a beard."

"Do we?" exclaimed Badger. "How do we?"

Thorndyke delicately picked a hair from one of the hairbrushes and held it up. "That is not a scalp hair," said he. "I should say that it came from the side of the chin."

Badger regarded the hair with evident disfavour. "Looks to me," he remarked," as if a small tooth-comb might have been useful."

It does," Thorndyke agreed, "but the appearance is deceptive. This is what is called a moniliform hair--like a string of beads. But the bead-like swellings are really parts of the hair. It is a diseased, or perhaps we should say an abnormal, condition." He handed me the hair together with his lens, through which I examined it and easily recognised the characteristic swellings.

"Yes," said I, "it is an early case of *tricliorrexis nodosa*."

"Good Lord!" murmured the inspector. "Sounds like a Russian nobleman. Is it a common complaint?

"It is not a rare disease--if you can call it a disease," I replied," but it is a rare condition, taking the population as a whole."

It is rather a remarkable coincidence that it should happen to occur in this particular case," the superintendent observed.

"My dear Miller," exclaimed Thorndyke, "surely your experience must have impressed on you the astonishing frequency of the unusual and the utter failure of the mathematical laws of probability in practice. Believe me, Miller, the bread-and-butterfly was right. It is the exceptional that always happens."

Having discharged this paradox, he once more dived into the bag, and this time handed out a singular and rather unsavoury-looking parcel, the outer investment of which was formed by what looked like an excessively dirty towel, but which, as Thorndyke delicately unrolled it, was seen to be only half a towel which was supplemented by a still dirtier and excessively ragged coloured handkerchief. This, too, being opened out, disclosed an extremely soiled and rather frayed collar (which, like the other articles, bore no name or mark), and a mass of grass, evidently used as packing material.

The inspector picked up the collar and quoted reflectively, "He is a man, neat, orderly and careful as to his appearance," after which he dropped the collar and ostentatiously wiped his fingers.

Thorndyke smiled grimly but refrained from repartee as he carefully separated the grass from the contained objects, which turned out to be a small telescopic jemmy, a jointed auger, a screwdriver and a bunch of skeleton keys.

"One understands his unwillingness to encounter the constable with these rather significant objects in his possession," Thorndyke remarked. "They would have been difficult to explain away." He took up the heap of grass between his hands and gently compressed it to test its freshness. As he did so a tiny, cigar-shaped object dropped on the paper.

"What is that?" asked the superintendent. "It looks like a chrysalis."

It isn't," said Thorndyke. "It is a shell, a species of Clausilia, I think." He picked up the little shell and closely examined its mouth through his lens. "Yes," he continued, "it is a Clausilia. Do you study our British mollusca, Badger?"

"No, I don't," the inspector replied with emphasis.

"Pity," murmured Thorndyke. "If you did, you would be interested to learn that the name of this little shell is *Clausilia biplicata*."

"I don't care what its beastly name is," said Badger. "I want to know whose bag this is; what the owner is like; and where he came from and where he has gone to. Can you tell us that?"

Thorndyke regarded the inspector with wooden gravity. "It is all very obvious," said he, "very obvious. But still, I think I should like to fill in a few details before making a definite statement. Yes, I think I will reserve my judgment until I have considered the matter a little further."

The inspector received this statement with a dubious grin. He was in somewhat of a dilemma. My colleague was addicted to a certain dry facetiousness, and was probably pulling the inspector's leg. But, on the other hand, I knew, and so did both the detectives, that it was perfectly conceivable that he had actually solved Badger's problem, impossible as it seemed, and was holding back his knowledge until he had seen whither it led.

"Shall we take a glance at the stick?" said he, picking it up as he spoke and running his eye over its not very distinctive features. It was a common ash stick, with a crooked handle polished and darkened by prolonged contact with an apparently ungloved hand, and it was smeared for about three inches from the tip with a yellowish mud. The iron shoe of the ferrule was completely worn away and the deficiency had been made good by driving a steel boot-stud into the exposed end.

"A thrifty gentleman, this," Thorndyke remarked, pointing to the stud as he measured the diameter of the ferrule with his pocket calliper-gauge. "Twenty-three thirty-seconds is the diameter," he added, looking gravely at the inspector. "You had better make a note of that, Badger."

The inspector smiled sourly as Thorndyke laid down the stick, and once more picking up the little green canvas case that contained his research outfit, prepared to depart.

"You will hear from us, Miller," he said, "if we pick up anything that will be useful to you. And now, Jervis, we must really take ourselves off."

As the tinkling hansom bore us down Whitehall towards Waterloo, I remarked, "Badger half suspects you of having withheld from him some valuable information in respect of that bag."

"He does," Thorndyke agreed with a mischievous smile; "and he doesn't in the least suspect me of having given him a most illuminating hint."

"But did you?" I asked, rapidly reviewing the conversation and deciding that the facts elicited from the dressing-wallet could hardly be described as hints.

"My learned friend," he replied, "is pleased to counterfeit obtuseness. It won't do, Jervis. I've known you too long."

I grinned with vexation. Evidently I had missed the point of a subtle demonstration, and I knew that it was useless to ask further questions; and for the remainder of our journey, in the cab I struggled vainly to recover the "illuminating hint" that the detectives--and I--had failed to note. Indeed, so preoccupied was I with this problem that I rather overlooked the fact that the jettisoned bag was really no concern of ours, and that we were actually engaged in the investigation of a crime of which, at present, I knew practically nothing. It was not until we had secured an empty compartment and the train had begun to move that this suddenly dawned on me; whereupon I dismissed the bag problem and applied to Thorndyke for details of the "Brentford Train Mystery."

To call it a mystery," said he, "is a misuse of words. It appears to be a simple train robbery. The identity of the robber is unknown, but there is nothing very mysterious in that; and the crime otherwise is quite commonplace. The circumstances are these:

"Some time ago, Mr. Lionel Montague, of the firm, Lyons, Montague & Salaman, art dealers, bought from a Russian nobleman a very valuable diamond necklace and pendant. The peculiarity of this necklace was that the stones were all of a pale blue colour and pretty accurately matched, so that in addition to the aggregate value of the stones--which were all of large size and some very large--was the value of the piece as a whole due to this uniformity of colour. Mr. Montague gave £70,000 for it, and considered that he had made an excellent bargain. I should mention that Montague was the chief buyer for the firm, and that he spent most of his time travelling about the Continent in search of works of art and other objects suitable for the purposes of his firm, and that, naturally, he was an excellent judge of such things. Now, it seems that he was not satisfied with the settings of this necklace, and as soon as he had purchased it he handed it over to Messrs. Binks, of Old Bond Street, to have the settings replaced by others of better design. Yesterday morning he was notified by Binks that the resetting was completed, and in the afternoon he called to inspect the work and take the necklace away if it was satisfactory. The interview between Binks and Montague took place in a room behind the shop, but it appears that Montague came out into the shop to get a better light for his inspection and Mr. Binks states that as his customer stood facing the door, examining the new settings, he, Binks, noticed a man standing by the doorway furtively watching Mr. Montague."

"There is nothing very remarkable in that," said I. "If a man stands at a shop door with a necklace of blue diamonds in his hand, he is rather likely to attract attention."

"Yes," Thorndyke agreed. "But the significance of an antecedent is apt to be more appreciated after the consequences have developed. Binks is now very emphatic about the furtive watcher. However, to continue: Mr. Montague, being satisfied with the new settings, replaced the necklace in its case, put the latter into his bag--which he had brought with him from the inner room--and a minute or so later left the shop. That was about 5 p.m.; and he seems to have gone direct to the flat of his partner, Mr. Salaman, with whom he had been staying for a fortnight, at Queen's Gate. There he remained until about half-past eight, when he came out accompanied by Mr. Salaman. The latter carried a small suit-case, while Montague carried a handbag in which was the necklace. It is not known whether it contained anything else.

"From Queen's Gate the two men proceeded to Waterloo, walking part of the way and covering the remainder by omnibus."

"By omnibus!" I exclaimed, "with seventy thousand pounds of diamonds about them!"

"Yes, it sounds odd. But people who habitually handle portable property of great value seem to resemble those who habitually handle explosives. They gradually become unconscious of the risks. At any rate, that is how they went, and they arrived safely at Waterloo in time to catch the 9.15 train for Isleworth. Mr. Salaman saw his partner established in an empty first-class compartment and stayed with him, chatting, until the train started.

"Mr. Montague's destination was Isleworth, in which rather unlikely neighbourhood Mr. Jacob Lowenstein, late of Chicago, and now of Berkeley Square, has a sort of river-side villa with a motor boat-house attached. Lowenstein had secured the option of purchasing the blue diamond necklace, and Montague was taking it down to exhibit it and carry out the deal. He was proposing to stay a few days with Lowenstein, and then he was proceeding to Brussels on one of his periodic tours. But he never reached Isleworth. When the train stopped at Brentford, a porter noticed a suit-case on the luggage-rack of an apparently empty first-class compartment. He immediately entered to take possession of it, and was in the act of reaching up to the rack when his foot came in contact with something soft under the seat. Considerably startled, he stooped and peered under, when, to his horror, he perceived the body of a man, quite motionless and apparently dead. Instantly he darted out and rushed up the platform in a state of wild panic until he, fortunately, ran against the station master, with whom and another porter he returned to the compartment. When they drew the body out from under the seat it was found to be still breathing, and they proceeded at once to apply such restoratives as cold water and fresh air, pending the arrival of the police and the doctor, who had been sent for.

"In a few minutes the police arrived accompanied by the police surgeon, and the latter, after a brief examination, decided that the unconscious man was suffering from the effects of a large dose of chloroform, violently and unskilfully administered, and ordered him to be carefully removed to a local nursing home. Mean while, the police had been able, by inspecting the contents of his pockets, to identify him as Mr. Lionel Montague."

"The diamonds had vanished, of course?" said I.

"Yes. The handbag was not in the compartment, and later an empty handbag was picked up on the permanent way between Barnes and Chiswick, which seems to indicate the locality where the robbery took place."

"And what is our present objective?"

"We are going, on instructions from Mr. Salaman, to the nursing home to see what information we can pick up. If Montague has recovered sufficiently to give an account of the robbery, the police will have a description of the robber, and there may not be much for us to do. But you will have noticed that they do not seem to have any information at Scotland Yard at present, beyond what I have given you. So there is a chance yet that we may earn our fees."

Thorndyke's narrative of this somewhat commonplace crime, with the discussion which followed it, occupied us until the train stopped at Brentford Station. A few minutes later we halted in one of the quiet by-streets of this old-world town, at a soberly painted door on which was a brass plate inscribed "St. Agnes Nursing Home." Our arrival had apparently been observed, for the door was opened by a middle-aged lady in a nurse's uniform.

"Dr. Thorndyke?" she inquired; and as my colleague bowed assent she continued: "Mr. Salaman told me you would probably call. I am afraid I haven't very good news for you. The patient is still quite unconscious."

"That is rather remarkable," said Thorndyke.

"It is. Dr. Kingston, who is in charge of the case, is somewhat puzzled by this prolonged stupor. He is inclined to suspect a narcotic--possibly a large dose of morphine--in addition to the effects of the chloroform and the shock."

"He is probably right," said I; "and the marvel is that the man is alive at all after such outrageous treatment."

"Yes," Thorndyke agreed. "He must be pretty tough. Shall we be able to see him?"

"Oh, yes," the matron replied. "I am instructed to give you every assistance. Dr. Kingston would like to have your opinion on the case."

With this she conducted us to a pleasant room on the first floor, where, in a bed placed opposite a large window--left uncurtained--with the strong light falling full on his face, a man lay with closed eyes, breathing quietly and showing no sign of consciousness when we somewhat noisily entered the room. For some time Thorndyke stood by the bedside, looking down at the unconscious man, listening to the breathing and noting its frequency by his watch. Then he felt the pulse, and raising both eyelids, compared the two pupils.

"His condition doesn't appear alarming," was his conclusion. "The breathing is rather shallow, but it is quite regular, and the pulse is not bad though slow. The contracted pupils strongly suggest opium, or more probably morphine. But that could easily be settled by a chemical test. Do you notice the state of the face, Jervis?"

"You mean the chloroform burns? Yes, the handkerchief or pad must have been saturated. But I was also noticing that he corresponds quite remarkably with the description you were giving Badger of the owner of the dressing-wallet. He is about the age you mentioned--roughly about fifty--and he has the same old- fashioned treatment of the beard, the shaven upper lip and the monkey-fringe under the chin. It is rather an odd coincidence."

Thorndyke looked at me keenly. "The coincidence is closer than that, Jervis. Look at the beard itself."

He handed me his lens, and, stooping down, I brought it to bear on the patient's beard. And then I started back in astonishment; for by the bright light I could see plainly that a considerable proportion of the hairs were distinctly moniliform. This man's beard, too, was affected by an early stage of *trichorrexis nodosa*!

"Well!" I exclaimed, "this is really an amazing coincidence. I wonder if it is anything more."

"I wonder," said Thorndyke. "Are those Mr. Montague's things, Matron?"

"Yes," she replied, turning to the side table on which the patient's effects were neatly arranged. "Those are his clothes and the things which were taken from his pockets, and that is his bag. It was found on the line and sent on here a couple of hours ago. There is nothing in it."

Thorndyke looked over the various objects--keys, card-case, pocket-book, etc.--that had been turned out of the patient's pockets, and then picked up the bag, which he turned over curiously and then opened to inspect the interior. There was nothing distinctive about it. It was just a plain, imitation leather bag, fairly new, though rather the worse for its late vicissitudes, lined with coarse linen to which two large, wash-leather pockets had been roughly stitched. As he laid the bag down and picked up his own canvas case, he asked: "What time did Mr. Salaman come to see the patient? "

"He came here about ten o'clock this morning, and he was not able to stay more than half an hour as he had an appointment. But he said he would look in again this evening. You can't stay to see him, I suppose?"

"I'm afraid not," Thorndyke replied; "in fact we must be off now, for both Dr. Jervis and I have some other matters to attend to."

"Are you going straight back to the chambers, Jervis?" Thorndyke asked, as we walked down the main street towards the station.

"Yes," I replied in some surprise. "Aren't you?"

"No. I have a little expedition in view."

"Oh, have you?" I exclaimed, and as I spoke it began to dawn on me that I had overestimated the importance of my other business.

"Yes," said Thorndyke "the fact is that--ha! excuse me one moment, Jervis." He had halted abruptly outside a fishing-tackle shop and now, after a brief glance in through the window, entered with an air of business. I immediately bolted in after him, and was just in time to hear him demand a fishing-rod of a light and inexpensive character. When this had been supplied he asked for a line and one or two hooks; and I was a little surprised--and the vendor was positively scandalised--at his indifference to the quality or character of these appliances. I believe he would have accepted cod-line and a shark-hook if they had been offered.

"And now I want a float," said he.

The shopkeeper produced a tray containing a varied assortment of floats over which Thorndyke ran a critical eye, and finally reduced the shopman to stupefaction by selecting a gigantic, pot-bellied scarlet-and-green atrocity that looked like a juvenile telegraph buoy.

I could not let this outrage pass without comment. "You must excuse me, Thorndyke," I said, "if I venture to point out that the Greenland whale no longer frequents the upper reaches of the Thames."

"You mind your own business," he retorted, stolidly pocketing the telegraph buoy when he had paid for his purchases. "I like a float that you can see."

Here the shopman, recovering somewhat from the shock of surprise, remarked deferentially that it was a long time since a really large pike had been caught in the neighbourhood; whereupon Thorndyke finished him off by replying: "Yes, I've no doubt. They don't use the right sort of floats, you know. Now, when the pike see my float, they will just come tumbling over one another to get on the hook." With this he tucked the rod under his arm and strolled out, leaving the shopman breathing hard and staring harder.

"But what on earth," I asked, as we walked down the street (watched by the shopman who had come out on the pavement to see the last of us), "do you want with such an enormous float? Why, it will be visible a quarter of a mile away."

"Exactly," said Thorndyke. "And what more could a fisher of men require?"

This rejoinder gave me pause. Evidently Thorndyke had something in hand of more than common interest; and again it occurred to me that my own business engagements were of no special urgency. I was about to mention this fact when Thorndyke again halted--at an oilshop this time.

"I think I will step in here and get a little burnt umber," said he.

I followed him into the shop, and while the powder- colour was being weighed and made up into a little packet I reflected profoundly. Fishing-tackle and burnt umber had no obvious associations. I began to be mystified and correspondingly inquisitive.

"What do you want the burnt umber for?" I asked as soon as we were outside.

"To mix with plaster," he replied readily.

"But why do you want to colour the plaster? And what are you going to do with it?"

"Now, Jervis," he admonished with mock severity, "you are not doing yourself justice. An investigator of your experience shouldn't ask for explanations of the obvious."

"And why," I continued, "did you want to know if I was going straight back to the chambers?

"Because I may want some assistance later. Probably Polton will be able to do all that I want, but I wished to know that you would both be within reach of a telegram."

"But," I exclaimed, "what nonsense it is to talk of sending a telegram to me when I'm here!"

"But I may not want any assistance, after all."

"Well," I said doggedly, "you are going to have it whether you want it or not. You've got something on and I'm going to be in it."

"I like your enthusiasm, Jervis," he chuckled; "but it is quite possible that I shall merely find a mare's nest."

"Very well," said I. "Then I'll help you to find it. I've had plenty of experience in that line, to say nothing of my natural gifts. So lead on."

He led on, with a resigned smile, to the station, where we were fortunate enough to find a train just ready to start. But our journey was not a long one, for at Chiswick Thorndyke got out of the train, and on leaving the station struck out eastward with a very evident air of business. As we entered the outskirts of Hammersmith he turned into a by-street which presently brought us out into Bridge Road. Here he turned sharply to the right and, at the same brisk pace, crossed Hammersmith Bridge and made his way to the towing path. As he now slowed down perceptibly, I ventured to inquire whether this was the spot on which he proposed to exhibit his super-float.

"This, I think, will be our fishing-ground," he replied; " but we will look over it carefully and select a suitable pitch."

He continued to advance at an easy pace, and I noticed that, according to his constant habit, he was studying the peculiarities of the various feet that had trodden the path within the last day or two, keeping, for this purpose on the right-hand side, where the shade of a few pollard willows overhanging an indistinct dry ditch had kept the ground soft. We had walked on for nearly half a mile when he halted and looked round.

"I think we had better turn back a little way," said he. "We seem to have overshot our mark."

I made no comment on this rather mysterious observation, and we retraced our steps for a couple of hundred yards, Thorndyke still walking on the side farthest from the river and still keeping his eyes fixed on the ground. Presently he again halted, and looking up and down the path, of which we were at the moment the only occupants, placed the canvas case on the ground and unfastened its clasps.

"This, I think, will be our pitch," said he.

"What are you going to do?" I asked.

"I am going to make one or two casts. And mean while you had better get the fishing-rod fixed together so as to divert the attention of any passers-by."

I proceeded to make ready the fishing-tackle, but at the same time kept a close watch on my colleague's proceedings. And very curious proceedings they were. First he dipped up a little water from the river in the rubber mixing bowl with which he mixed a bowlful of plaster, and into this he stirred a few pinches of burnt umber, whereby its dazzling white was changed to a muddy buff. Then, having looked up and down the path, he stooped and carefully poured the plaster into a couple of impressions of a walking-stick that were visible at the edge of the path and finished up by filling a deep impression of the same stick, at the margin of the ditch, where it had apparently been stuck in the soft, clayey ground.

As I watched this operation, a sudden suspicion flashed into my mind. Dropping the fishing-rod, I walked quickly along the path until I was able to pick up another impression of the stick. A very brief examination of it confirmed my suspicion. At the centre of the little shallow pit was a semicircular impression--clearly that of a half-worn boot-stud.

"Why!" I exclaimed, "this is the stick that we saw at Scotland Yard!"

"I should expect it to be and I believe it is," said Thorndyke. "But we shall be better able to judge from the casts. Pick up your rod. There are two men coming down the path."

He closed his "research-case" and drawing the fishing- line from his pocket, began meditatively to unwind it.

"I could wish," said I, "that our appearance was more in character with the part of the rustic angler; and for the Lord's sake keep float out of sight, or we shall collect a crowd."

Thorndyke laughed softly. "The float," said he, "was intended for Polton. He would have loved it. And the crowd would have been rather an advantage--as you will appreciate when you come to use it."

The two men--builder's labourers, apparently--now passed us with a glance of faint interest at the fishing- tackle; and as they strolled by I appreciated the value of the burnt umber. If the casts bad been made of the snow-white plaster they would have stared conspicuously from the ground and these men would almost certainly have stopped to examine them and see what we were doing. But the tinted plaster was practically invisible.

"You are a wonderful man, Thorndyke," I said, as I announced my discovery. "You foresee everything."

He bowed his acknowledgments, and having tenderly felt one of the casts and ascertained that the plaster had set hard, he lifted it with infinite care, exhibiting a perfect facsimile of the end of the stick, on which the worn boot-stud was plainly visible, even to the remains of the pattern. Any doubt that might have remained as to the identity of the stick was removed when Thorndyke produced his calliper-gauge.

"Twenty-three thirty-seconds was the diameter, I think," said he as he opened the jaws of the gauge and consulted his notes. He placed the cast between the jaws, and as they were gently slid into contact, the index marked twenty-three thirty-seconds.

"Good," said Thorndyke, picking up the other two casts and establishing their identity with the one which we had examined. "This completes the first act." Dropping one cast into his case and throwing the other two into the river, he continued: "Now we proceed to the next and hope for a like success. You notice that he stuck his stick into the ground. Why do you suppose he did that?"

"Presumably to leave his hands free."

"Yes. And now let us sit down here and consider why he wanted his hands free. Just look around and tell me what you see."

I gazed rather hopelessly at the very indistinctive surroundings and began a bald catalogue. "I see a shabby-looking pollard willow, an assortment of suburban vegetation, an obsolete tin saucepan--unserviceable--and a bald spot where somebody seems to have pulled up a small patch of turf."

"Yes," said Thorndyke. "You will also notice a certain amount of dry, powdered earth distributed rather evenly over the bottom of the ditch. And your patch of turf was cut round with a large knife before it was pulled up. Why do you suppose it was pulled up?"

I shook my head. "It's of no use making mere guesses."

"Perhaps not," said he, "though the suggestion is fairly obvious when considered with the other appearances. Between the roots of the willow you notice a patch of grass that looks denser than one would expect from its position. I wonder--"

As he spoke, he reached forward with his stick and prised vigorously at the edge of the patch, with the result that the clump of grass lifted bodily; and when I picked it up and tried it on the bald spot, the nicety with which it fitted left no doubt as to its origin.

"Ha!" I exclaimed, looking at the obviously disturbed earth between the roots of the willow, which the little patch of turf had covered; "the plot thickens. Something seems to have been either buried or dug up there; more probably buried."

"I hope and believe that my learned friend is correct," said Thorndyke, opening his case to abstract a large, powerful spatula.

"What do you expect to find there?" I asked.

"I have a faint hope of finding something wrapped in the half of a very dirty towel," was the reply.

"Then you had better find it quickly," said I, "for there is a man coming along the path from the Putney direction."

He looked round at the distant figure, and driving the spatula into the loose earth stirred it up vigorously.

"I can feel something," he said, digging away with powerful thrusts and scooping the earth out with his hands. Once more he looked round at the approaching stranger--who seemed now to have quickened his pace but was still four or five hundred yards distant. Then, thrusting his hands into the hole, he gave a smart pull. Slowly there came forth a package, about ten inches by six, enveloped in a portion of a peculiarly filthy towel and loosely secured with string. Thorndyke rapidly cast off the string and opened out the towel, disclosing a handsome morocco case with an engraved gold plate.

I pounced on the case and, pressing the catch, raised the lid; and though I had expected no less, it was with something like a shock of surprise that I looked on the glittering row and the dazzling cluster of steely-blue diamonds.

As I closed the casket and deposited it in the green canvas case, Thorndyke, after a single glance at the treasure and another along the path, crammed the towel into the hole and began to sweep the loose earth in on top of it. The approaching stranger was for the moment hidden from us by a bend of the path and a near clump of bushes, and Thorndyke was evidently working to hide all traces before he should appear. Having filled the hole, he carefully replaced the sod of turf and then, moving over to the little bare patch from whence the turf had been removed, he began swiftly to dig it up.

"There," said he, flinging on the path a worm which he had just disinterred, "that will explain our activities. You had better continue the excavation with your pocket knife, and then proceed to the capture of the leviathans. I must run up to the police station and you must keep possession of this pitch. Don't move away from here on any account until I come back or send somebody to relieve you. I will hand you over the float; you'll want that." With a malicious smile he dropped the gaudy monstrosity on the path, and having wiped the spatula and replaced it in the case, picked up the latter and moved away towards Putney.

At this moment the stranger reappeared, walking as if for a wager, and I began to peck up the earth with my pocket-knife.

As the man approached he slowed down by degrees until he came up at something like a saunter. He was followed at a little distance by Thorndyke, who had turned as if he had changed his mind, and now passed me with the remark that "Perhaps Hammersmith would be better." The stranger cast a suspicious glance at him and then turned his attention to me.

"Lookin' for worms?" he inquired, halting and surveying me inquisitively.

I replied by picking one up (with secret distaste) and holding it aloft, and he continued, looking wistfully at Thorndyke's retreating figure: "Your pal seems to have had enough."

"He hadn't got a rod," said I; "but he'll be back presently."

"Ah!" said he, looking steadily over my shoulder in the direction of the willow. "Well, you won't do any good here. The place where they rises is a quarter of a mile farther down--just round the bend there. That's a prime pitch. You just come along with me and I'll show you."

"I must stay here until my friend comes back," said I. "But I'll tell him what you say."

With this I seated myself stolidly on the bank and, having flung the baited hook into the stream, sat and glared fixedly at the preposterous float. My acquaintance fidgeted about me uneasily, endeavouring from time to time to lure me away to the "prime pitch" round the bend. And so the time dragged on until three-quarters of an hour had passed.

Suddenly I observed two taxicabs crossing the bridge, followed by three cyclists. A minute or two later Thorndyke reappeared, accompanied by two other men, and then the cyclists came into view, approaching at a rapid pace.

"Seems to be a regular procession," my friend remarked, viewing the new arrivals with evident uneasiness. As he spoke, one of the cyclists halted and dismounted to examine his tyre, while the other two approached and shot past us. Then they, too, halted and dismounted, and having deposited their machines in the ditch, they came back towards us. By this time I was able--with a good deal of surprise--to identify Thorndyke's two companions as Inspector Badger and Superintendent Miller. Perhaps my acquaintance also recognised them, or possibly the proceedings of the third cyclist--who had also laid down his machine and was approaching on foot--disturbed him. At any rate he glanced quickly from the one group to the other and, selecting the smaller one, sprang suddenly between the two cyclists and sped away along the path like a hare.

In a moment there was a wild stampede. The three cyclists, remounting their machines, pedalled furiously after the fugitive, followed by Badger and Miller on foot. Then the fugitive, the cyclists, and finally the two officers disappeared round the bend of the path.

"How did you know that he was the man?" I asked, when my colleague and I were left alone.

"I didn't, though I had pretty strong grounds for suspicion. But I merely brought the police to set a watch on the place and arrange an ambush. Their encircling movement was just an experimental bluff; they might have been chary of arresting the fellow if he hadn't taken fright and bolted. We have been fortunate all round, for, by a lucky chance, Badger and Miller were at Chiswick making inquiries and I was able to telephone to them to meet me at the bridge."

At this moment the procession reappeared, advancing briskly; and my late adviser marched at the centre securely handcuffed. As he was conducted past me he glared savagely and made some impolite references to a "blooming nark."

"You can take him in one of the taxis," said Miller, "and put your bicycles on top." Then, as the procession moved on towards the bridge he turned to Thorndyke. "I suppose he's the right man, doctor, but he hasn't got any of the stuff on him."

"Of course he hasn't," said Thorndyke.

"Well, do you know where it is?"

Thorndyke opened his case and taking out the casket, handed it to the superintendent. "I shall want a receipt for it," said he.

Miller opened the casket, and at the sight of the glittering jewels both the detectives uttered an exclamation of amazement, and the superintendent demanded: "Where did you get this, sir?

"I dug it up at the foot of that willow."

"But how did you know it was there?"

"I didn't," replied Thorndyke; "but I thought I might as well look, you know," and he bestowed a smile of exasperating blandness on the astonished officer.

The two detectives gazed at Thorndyke, then they looked at one another and then they looked at me; and Badger observed, with profound conviction, that it was a "knock-out." "I believe the doctor keeps a tame clairvoyant," he added.

"And may I take it, sir," said Miller, "that you can establish a prima facie case against this man, so that we can get a remand until Mr. Montague is well enough to identify him?"

"You may," Thorndyke replied. "Let me know when and where he is to be charged and I will attend and give evidence."

On this Miller wrote out a receipt for the jewels and the two officers hurried off to their taxicab, leaving us, as Badger put it, "to our fishing."

As soon as they were out of sight, Thorndyke opened his case and mixed another bowlful of plaster. "We want two more casts," said he; "one of the right foot of the man who buried the jewels and one of the right foot of the prisoner. They are obviously identical, as you can see by the arrangement of the nails and the shape of the new patch on the sole. I shall put the casts in evidence and compare them with the prisoner's right boot."

I understood now why Thorndyke had walked away towards Putney and then returned in rear of the stranger. He had suspected the man and had wanted to get a look at his footprints. But there was a good deal in this case that I did not understand at all.

♦ ♦ ♦ ♦ ♦

"There," said Thorndyke, as he deposited the casts, each with its pencilled identification, in his canvas case, "that is the end of the Blue Diamond Mystery."

"I beg your pardon," said I, "but it isn't. I want a full explanation. It is evident that from the house at Brentford you made a bee line to that willow. You knew then pretty exactly where the necklace was hidden. For all I know, you may have had that knowledge when we left Scotland Yard."

"As a matter of fact, I had," he replied. "I went to Brentford principally to verify the ownership of the wallet and the bag."

"But what was it that directed you with such certainty to the Hammersmith towing-path?"

It was then that he made the observation that I have quoted at the beginning of this narrative.

"In this case," he continued, "a curious fact, well known to naturalists, acquired vital evidential importance. It associated a bag, found in one locality, with another apparently unrelated locality. It was the link that joined up the two ends of a broken chain. I offered that fact to Inspector Badger, who, lacking the knowledge wherewith to interpret it, rejected it with scorn."

"I remember that you gave him the name of that little shell that dropped out of the handful of grass."

"Exactly," said Thorndyke. "That was the crucial fact. It told us where the handful of grass had been gathered."

"I can't imagine how," said I. "Surely you find shells all over the country?"

"That is, in general, quite true," he replied, " but *Clausilia biplicata* is one of the rare exceptions. There are four British species of these queer little univalves (which are so named from the little spring door with which the entrance of the shell is furnished): *Clausilia laminata, rolphii, rugosa* and *biplicata.* The first three species have what we may call a normal distribution, whereas the distribution of *biplicata* is abnormal. This seems to be a dying species. It is in process of becoming extinct in this island. But when a species of animal or plant becomes extinct, it does not fade away evenly over the whole of its habitat, but it disappears in patches, which gradually extend, leaving, as it were, islands of survival. This is what has happened to Clausilia *biplicata.* It has disappeared from this country with the exception of two localities; one of these is in Wiltshire, and the other is the right bank of the Thames at Hammersmith. And this latter locality is extraordinarily restricted. Walk down a few hundred yards towards Putney, and you have walked out of its domain; walk up a few hundred yards towards the bridge, and again you have walked out of its territory. Yet within that little area it is fairly plentiful. If you know where to look--it lives on the bark or at the roots of willow trees--you can usually find one or two specimens. Thus, you see, the presence of that shell associated the handful of grass with a certain willow tree, and that willow was either in Wiltshire or by the Hammersmith towing-path. But there was nothing otherwise to connect it with Wiltshire, whereas there was something to connect it with Hammersmith. Let us for a moment dismiss the shell and consider the other suggestions offered by the bag and stick.

"The bag, as you saw, contained traces of two very different persons. One was a middle-class man, probably middle-aged or elderly, cleanly, careful as to his appearance and of orderly habits; the other, uncleanly, slovenly and apparently a professional criminal. The bag itself seemed to appertain to the former person. It was an expensive bag and showed signs of years of careful use. This, and the circumstances in which it was found, led us to suspect that it was a stolen bag. Now, we knew that the contents of a bag had been stolen. We knew that an empty bag had been picked up on the line between Barnes and Chiswick, and it was probable that the thief had left the train at the latter station. The empty bag had been assumed to be Mr. Montague's, whereas the probabilities--as for instance, the fact of its having been thrown out on the line--suggested that it was the thief's bag, and that Mr. Montague's had been taken away with its contents.

"The point, then, that we had to settle when we left Scotland Yard was whether this apparently stolen bag had any connection with the train robbery. But as soon as we saw Mr. Montague it was evident that he corresponded exactly with the owner of the dressing- wallet; and when we saw the bag that had been found on the line--a shoddy, imitation leather bag--it was practically certain that it was not his, while the roughly- stitched leather pockets, exactly suited to the dimensions of house-breaking tools, strongly suggested that it was a burglar's bag. But if this were so, then Mr. Montague's bag had been stolen, and the robber's effects stuffed into it.

"With this working hypothesis we were now able to take up the case from the other end. The Scotland Yard bag was Montague's bag. It had been taken from Chiswick to the Hammersmith towpath, where--judging from the clay smears on the bottom--it had been laid on the ground, presumably close to a willow tree. The use of the grass as packing suggested that something had been removed from the bag at this place--something that had wedged the tools together and prevented them from rattling; and there appeared to be half a towel missing. Clearly, the towpath was our next field of exploration.

"But, small as this area was geographically, it would have taken a long time to examine in detail. Here, however, the stick gave us invaluable aid. It had a perfectly distinctive tip, and it showed traces of having been stuck about three inches into earth similar to that on the bag. What we had thus to look for was a hole in the ground about three inches deep, and having at the bottom the impression of a half-worn boot-stud. This hole would probably be close to a willow.

"The search turned out even easier than I had hoped. Directly we reached the towpath I picked up the track of the stick, and not one track only, but a double track, showing that our friend had returned to the bridge. All that remained was to follow the track until it came to an end and there we were pretty certain to find the hole in the ground, as, in fact, we did."

"And why," I asked, "do you suppose he buried the stuff?"

"Probably as a precaution, in case he had been seen and described. This morning's papers will have told him that he had not been. Probably, also, he wanted to make arrangements with a fence and didn't want to have the booty about him."

There is little more to tell. When the case was heard on the following morning, Thorndyke's uncannily precise and detailed description of the course of events, coupled with the production of the stolen property, so unnerved the prisoner that he pleaded guilty forthwith.

As to Mr. Montague, he recovered completely in a few days, and a handsome pair of Georgian silver candlesticks may even to this day be seen on our mantelpiece testifying to his gratitude and appreciation of Thorndyke's brilliant conduct of the case.

The Stolen Ingots

"In medico-legal practice," Thorndyke remarked, "one must be constantly on one's guard against the effects of suggestion, whether intentional or unconscious. When the facts of a case are set forth by an informant, they are nearly always presented, consciously or unconsciously, in terms of inference. Certain facts, which appear to the narrator to be the leading facts, are given with emphasis and in detail, while other facts, which appear to be subordinate or trivial, are partially suppressed. But this assessment of evidential value must never be accepted. The whole case must be considered and each fact weighed separately, and then it will commonly happen that the leading fact turns out to be the one that had been passed over as negligible."

The remark was made apropos of a case, the facts of which had just been stated to us by Mr. Halethorpe, of the Sphinx Assurance Company. I did not quite perceive its bearing at the time, but looking back when the case was concluded, I realised that I had fallen into the very error against which Thorndyke's warning should have guarded me.

"I trust," said Mr. Halethorpe, "that I have not come at an inconvenient time. You are so tolerant of unusual hours--"

"My practice," interrupted Thorndyke, "is my recreation, and I welcome you as one who comes to furnish entertainment. Draw your chair up to the fire, light a cigar and tell us your story."

Mr. Halethorpe laughed, but adopted the procedure suggested, and having settled his toes upon the kerb and selected a cigar from the box, he opened the subject of his call.

"I don't quite know what you can do for us," he began, "as it is hardly your business to trace lost property, but I thought I would come and let you know about our difficulty. The fact is that our company looks like dropping some four thousand pounds, which the directors won't like. What has happened is this:

"About two months ago the London House of the Akropong Gold Fields Company applied to us to insure a parcel of gold bars that were to be consigned to Minton and Borwell, the big manufacturing jewellers. The bars were to be shipped at Accra and landed at Bellhaven, which is the nearest port to Minton and Borwell's works. Well, we agreed to underwrite the risk--we have done business with the Akropong people before--and the matter was settled. The bars were put on board the Labadi at Accra, and in due course were landed at Belhaven, where they were delivered to Minton's agents. So far, so good. Then came the catastrophe. The case of bars was put on the train at Belhaven, consigned to Anchester, where Minton's have their factory. But the line doesn't go to Anchester direct. The junction is at Garbridge, a small country station close to the river Crouch, and here the case was put out and locked up in the station-master's office to wait for the Anchester train. It seems that the station-master was called away and detained longer than he had expected, and when the train was signalled he hurried back in a mighty twitter. However, the case was there all right, and he personally superintended its removal to the guard's van and put it in the guard's charge. All went well for the rest of the journey. A member of the firm was waiting at Anchester station with a closed van. The case was put into it and taken direct to the factory, where it was opened in the private office--and found to be full of lead pipe."

"I presume," said Thorndyke, "that it was not the original case."

"No," replied Halethorpe, "but it was a very fair imitation. The label and the marks were correct, but the seals were just plain wax. Evidently the exchange had been made in the station office, and it transpires that although the door was securely locked there was an unfastened window which opened on to the garden, and there were plain marks of feet on the flower-bed outside."

"What time did this happen?" asked Thorndyke.

"The Anchester train came in at a quarter past seven, by which time, of course, it was quite dark."

"And when did it happen?"

"The day before yesterday. We heard of it yesterday morning."

"Are you contesting the claim?"

"We don't want to. Of course, we could plead negligence, but in that case I think we should make a claim on the railway company. But, naturally, we should much rather recover the property. After all, it can't be so very far away."

"I wouldn't say that," said Thorndyke. "This was no impromptu theft. The dummy case was prepared in advance, and evidently by somebody who knew what the real case was like, and how and when it was to be despatched from Belhaven. We must assume that the disposal of the stolen case has been provided for with similar completeness. How far is Garbridge from the river?"

Less than half a mile across the marshes. The detective-inspector – Badger, I think you know him--asked the same question."

"Naturally," said Thorndyke. "A heavy object like this case is much more easily and inconspicuously conveyed by water than on land. And then, see what facilities for concealment a navigable river offers. The case could be easily stowed away on a small craft, or even in a boat; or the bars could be taken out and stowed amongst the ballast, or even, at a pinch, dropped over board at a marked spot and left until the hue and cry was over."

"You are not very encouraging," Halethorpe remarked gloomily. "I take it that you don't much expect that we shall recover those bars."

"We needn't despair," was the reply, "but I want you to understand the difficulties. The thieves have got away with the booty, and that booty is an imperishable material which retains its value even if broken up into unrecognisable fragments. Melted down into small ingots, it would be impossible to identify."

"Well," said Halethorpe, "the police have the matter in hand--Inspector Badger, of the C.I.D., is in charge of the case--but our directors would be more satisfied if you would look into it. Of course we would give you any help we could. What do you say?"

"I am willing to look into the case," said Thorndyke, "though I don't hold out much hope. Could you give me a note to the shipping company and another to the consignees, Minton and Borwell?"

"Of course I will. I'll write them now. I have some of our stationery in my attaché case. But, if you will pardon my saying so, you seem to be starting your inquiry just where there is nothing to be learned. The case was stolen after it left the ship and before it reached the consignees-- although their agent had received it from the ship."

"The point is," said Thorndyke, "that this was a preconcerted robbery, and that the thieves possessed special information. That information must have come either from the ship or from the factory. So, while we must try to pick up the track of the case itself, we must seek the beginning of the clue at the two ends--the ship and the factory one of which it must have started."

"Yes, that's true," said Halethorpe. "Well, I'll write those two notes and then I must run away; and we'll hope for the best."

He wrote the two letters asking for facilities from the respective parties, and then took his departure in a somewhat chastened frame of mind.

"Quite an interesting little problem," Thorndyke remarked, as Halethorpe footsteps died away on the stairs, "but not much in our line. It is really a police case--a case for patient and intelligent inquiry. And that is what we shall have to do--make some careful inquiries on the spot."

"Where do you propose to begin?" I asked.

"At the beginning," he replied. "Belhaven. I propose that we go down there to-morrow morning and pick up the thread at that end."

"What thread?" I demanded. "We know that the package started from there. What else do you expect to learn?"

"There are several curious possibilities in this case, as you must have noticed," he replied "The question is, whether any of them are probabilities. That is what I want to settle before we begin a detailed investigation."

"For my part," said I," I should have supposed that the investigation would start from the scene of the robbery. But I presume that you have seen some possibilities that I have overlooked."

Which eventually turned out to be the case.

♦ ♦ ♦ ♦ ♦

"I think," said Thorndyke as we alighted at Belhaven on the following morning, "we had better go first to the Customs and make quite certain, if we can, that the bars were really in the case when it was delivered to the consignees' agents. It won't do to take it for granted that the substitution took place at Garbridge, although that is by far the most probable theory." Accordingly we made our way to the harbour, where an obliging mariner directed us to our destination.

At the Custom House we were received by a genial officer, who, when Thorndyke had explained his connection with the robbery, entered into the matter with complete sympathy and a quick grasp of the situation.

"I see," said he. "You want clear evidence that the bars were in the case when it left here. Well, I think we can satisfy you on that point. Bullion is not a customable commodity, but it has to be examined and reported. If it is consigned to the Bank of England or the Mint, the case is passed through with the seals unbroken, but as this was a private consignment, the seals will have been broken and the contents of the case examined. Jeffson, show these gentlemen the report on the case of gold bars from the Labadi."

"Would it be possible," Thorndyke asked, "for us to have a few words with the officer who opened the case? You know the legal partiality for personal testimony."

"Of course it would. Jeffson, when these gentlemen have seen the report, find the officer who signed it and let them have a talk with him."

We followed Mr. Jeffson into an adjoining office, where he produced the report and handed it to Thorndyke. The particulars that it gave were in effect those that would be furnished by the ship's manifest and the bill of lading. The case was thirteen inches long by twelve wide and nine inches deep, outside measurement; and its gross weight was one hundred and seventeen pounds three ounces, and it contained four bars of the aggregate weight of one hundred and thirteen pounds two ounces.

"Thank you," said Thorndyke, handing back the report. "And now can we see the officer--Mr. Byrne, I think--just to fill in the details?"

"If you will come with me," replied Mr. Jeffson, "I'll find him for you. I expect he is on the wharf."

We followed our conductor out on to the quay among a litter of cases, crates and barrels, and eventually, amidst a battalion of Madeira wine casks, found the officer deep in problems of "content and ullage," and other customs mysteries. As Jeffson introduced us, and then discreetly retired, Mr. Byrne confronted us, with a mahogany face and truculent blue eye.

"With reference to this bullion," said Thorndyke," I understand that you weighed the bars separately from the case?"

"Oi did," replied Mr. Byrne.

"Did you weigh each bar separately?"

"Oi did not," was the concise reply.

"What was the appearance of the bars--I mean as to shape and size? Were they of the usual type?

"Oi've not had a great deal to do with bullion," said Mr. Byrne, "but Oi should say that they were just ordinary gold bars, about nine inches long by four wide and about two inches deep."

"Was there much packing material in the case?"

"Very little. The bars were wrapped in thick canvas and jammed into the case. There wouldn't be more than about half an inch clearance all round to allow for the canvas. The case was inch and half stuff strengthened with iron bands."

"Did you seal the case after you had closed it up?"

"Oi did. 'Twas all shipshape when it was passed back to the mate. And Oi saw him hand it over to the consignees' agent; so 'twas all in order when it left the wharf."

"That was what I wanted to make sure of," said Thorndyke; and, having pocketed his notebook and thanked the officer, he turned away among the wilderness of merchandise.

So much for the Customs," said he. "I am glad we went there first. As you have no doubt observed, we have picked up some useful information."

"We have ascertained," I replied, "that the case was intact when it was handed over to the consignees' agents, so that our investigations at Garbridge will start from a solid basis. And that, I take it, is all you wanted to know."

"Not quite all," he rejoined. "There are one or two little details that I should like to fill in. I think we will look in on the shipping agents and present Halethorpe's note. We may as well learn all we can before we make our start from the scene of the robbery."

"Well," I said, "I don't see what more there is to learn here. But apparently you do. That seems to be the office, past those sheds."

The manager of the shipping agent's office looked us up and down as he sat at his littered desk with Halethorpe's letter in his hand.

"You've come about that bullion that was stolen," he said brusquely. "Well, it wasn't stolen here. Hadn't you better inquire at Garbridge, where it was?"

"Undoubtedly," replied Thorndyke. "But I am making certain preliminary inquiries. Now, first, as to the bill of lading, who has that--the original, I mean?

"The captain has it at present, but I have a copy."

"Could I see it?" Thorndyke asked.

The manager raised his eyebrows protestingly, but produced the document from a file and handed it to Thorndyke, watching him inquisitively as he copied the particulars of the package into his notebook.

"I suppose," said Thorndyke as he returned the document, "you have a copy of the ship's manifest?"

"Yes," replied the manager, "but the entry in the manifest is merely a copy of the particulars given in the bill of lading."

"I should like to see the manifest, if it is not troubling you too much."

"But," the other protested impatiently," the manifest contains no information respecting this parcel of bullion excepting the one entry, which, as I have told you, has been copied from the bill of lading."

"I realise that," said Thorndyke; "but I should like to look over it, all the same."

Our friend bounced into an inner office and presently returned with a voluminous document, which he slapped down on a side-table.

"There, sir," he said. "That is the manifest. This is the entry relating to the bullion that you are inquiring about. The rest of the document is concerned with the cargo, in which I presume you are not interested."

In this, however, he was mistaken; for Thorndyke, having verified the bullion entry, turned the leaves over and began systematically, though rapidly, to run his eye over the long list from the beginning, a proceeding that the manager viewed with frenzied impatience.

"If you are going to read it right through, sir," the latter observed, "I shall ask you to excuse me. Art is long but life is short," he added with a sour smile.

Nevertheless he hovered about uneasily, and when Thorndyke proceeded to copy some of the entries into his notebook, he craned over and read them without the least disguise, though not without comment.

"Good God, sir!" he exclaimed. "What possible bearing on this robbery can that parcel of scrivelloes have? And do you realise that they are still in the ship's hold?"

"I inferred that they were, as they are consigned to London," Thorndyke replied, drawing his finger down the "description" column and rapidly scanning the entries in it. The manager watched that finger, and as it stopped successively at a bag of gum copal, a case of quartz specimens, a case of six-inch brass screw-bolts, a bag of beni-seed and a package of kola nuts, he breathed hard and muttered like an angry parrot. But Thorndyke was quite unmoved. With calm deliberation he copied out each entry, conscientiously noting the marks, descriptions of packages and contents, gross and net weights, dimensions, names of consignors and consignees, ports of shipment and discharge, and, in fact, the entire particulars. It was certainly an amazing proceeding, and I could make no more of it than could our impatient friend.

At last Thorndyke closed and pocketed his notebook, and the manager heaved a slightly obtrusive sigh. "Is there nothing more, sir?" he asked. "You don't want to examine the ship, for instance? "

The next moment, I think, he regretted his sarcasm, for Thorndyke inquired, with evident interest: "Is the ship still here?

"Yes," was the unwilling admission. "She finishes unloading here at midday to-day and will probably haul into the London Docks to-morrow morning."

"I don't think I need go on board," said Thorndyke, "but you might give me a card in case I find that I want to."

The card was somewhat grudgingly produced, and when Thorndyke had thanked our entertainer for his help, we took our leave and made our way towards the station.

"Well," I said, "you have collected a vast amount of curious information, but I am hanged if I can see that any of it has the slightest bearing on our inquiry."

Thorndyke cast on me a look of deep reproach. "Jervis!" he exclaimed, "you astonish me; you do, indeed. Why, my dear fellow, it stares you in the face!"

"When you say 'it,'" I said a little irritably, "you mean--?"

"I mean the leading fact from which we may deduce the modus operandi of this robbery. You shall look over my notes in the train and sort out the data that we have collected. I think you will find them extremely illuminating."

"I doubt it," said I. "But, meanwhile, aren't we wasting a good deal of time? Halethorpe wants to get the gold back; he doesn't want to know how the thieves contrived to steal it."

"That is a very just remark," answered Thorndyke. My learned friend displays his customary robust common sense. Nevertheless, I think that a clear understanding of the mechanism of this robbery will prove very helpful to us, though I agree with you that we have spent enough time on securing our preliminary data. The important thing now is to pick up a trail from Garbridge. But I see our train is signalled. We had better hurry."

As the train rumbled into station, we looked out for an empty smoking compartment, and having been fortunate enough to secure one, we settled ourselves in opposite corners and lighted our pipes. Then Thorndyke handed me his notebook and as I studied, with wrinkled brows, the apparently disconnected entries, he sat and observed me thoughtfully and with the faintest suspicion of a smile. Again and again I read through those notes with ever-dwindling hopes of extracting the meaning that "stared me in the face." Vainly did I endeavour to connect gum copal, scrivelloes or beni-seed with the methods of the unknown robbers. The entries in the notebook persisted obstinately in remaining totally disconnected and hopelessly irrelevant. At last I shut the book with a savage snap and handed it back to its owner.

"It's no use, Thorndyke," I said. "I can't see the faintest glimmer of light."

"Well," said he," it isn't of much consequence. The practical part of our task is before us, and it may turn out a pretty difficult part. But we have got to recover those bars if it is humanly possible. And here we are at our jumping-off place. This is Garbridge Station--and I see an old acquaintance of ours on the platform."

I looked out, as the train slowed down, and there, sure enough, was no less a person than Inspector Badger of the Criminal Investigation Department.

"We could have done very well without Badger," I remarked.

"Yes," Thorndyke agreed, "but we shall have to take him into partnership, I expect. After all, we are on his territory and on the same errand. How do you do, inspector?" he continued, as the officer, having observed our descent from the carriage, hurried forward with unwonted cordiality.

"I rather expected to see you here, sir," said he. "We heard that Mr. Halethorpe had consulted you. But this isn't the London train."

"No," said Thorndyke. "We've been to Belhaven, just to make sure that the bullion was in the case when it started."

"I could have told you that two days ago," said Badger. "We got on to the Customs people at once. That was all plain sailing; but the rest of it isn't."

"No clue as to how the case was taken away?"

"Oh, yes; that is pretty clear. It was hoisted out, and the dummy hoisted in, through the window of the Station-master's office. And the same night, two men were seen carrying a heavy package, about the size of the bullion-case, towards the marshes. But there the clue ends. The stuff seems to have vanished into thin air. Of course our people are on the look-out for it in various likely directions, but I am staying here with a couple of plain-clothes men. I've a conviction that it is still somewhere in this neighbourhood, and I mean to stick here in the hope that I may spot somebody trying to move it."

As the inspector was speaking we had been walking slowly from the station towards the village, which was on the opposite side of the river. On the bridge Thorndyke halted and looked down the river and over the wide expanse of marshy country.

"This is an ideal place for a bullion robbery," he remarked. "A tidal river near to the sea and a network of creeks, in any one of which one could hide a boat or sink the booty below tide-marks. Have you heard of any strange craft having put in here?"

"Yes. There's a little ramshackle bawley from Leigh--but her crew of two ragamuffins are not Leigh men. And they've made a mess of their visit-- got their craft on the mud on the top of the spring tide. There here she'll be till next spring tide. But I've been over her carefully and I'll swear the stuff isn't aboard her. I bad all the ballast out and emptied the lazarette and the chain locker."

"And what about the barge?"

"She's a regular trader here. Her crew--the skipper and his son--are quite respectable men and they belong here. There they go in that boat; I expect they are off on this tide. But they seem to be making for the bawley."

As he spoke the inspector produced a pair of glasses, through which he watched the movement of the barge's jolly, and a couple of elderly fishermen, who were crossing the bridge, halted to look on. The barge's boat ran alongside the stranded bawley, and one of the rowers hailed; whereupon two men tumbled up from the cabin and dropped into the boat, which immediately pushed off and headed for the barge.

"Them bawley blokes seems to be taking a passage along of old Bill Somers," one of the fishermen remarked, levelling a small telescope at the barge as the boat drew alongside and the four men climbed on board. "Going to work their passage, too," he added as the two passengers proceeded immediately to man the windlass while the crew let go the brails and hooked the main block to the traveller.

"Rum go," commented Badger, glaring at the barge through his glasses; "but they haven't taken anything aboard with them. I could see that."

"You have overhauled the barge, I suppose?" said Thorndyke.

"Yes. Went right through her. Nothing there. She's light. There was no place aboard her where you could hide a split-pea."

"Did you get her anchor up?"

"No," replied Badger. "I didn't. I suppose I ought to have done so. However, they're getting it up themselves now." As he spoke, the rapid clink of a windlass-pawl was borne across the water, and through my prismatic glasses I could see the two passengers working for all they were worth at the cranks. Presently the clink of the pawl began to slow down somewhat and the two bargemen, having got the sails set, joined the toilers at the windlass, but even then there was no great increase of speed.

"Anchor seems to come up uncommon heavy," one of the fishermen remarked.

"Aye," the other agreed. "Got foul of an old mooring, maybe."

"Look out for the anchor, Badger," Thorndyke said in a low voice, gazing steadily through his binocular. "It is out of the ground. The cable is up and down and the barge is drifting off on the tide."

Even as he spoke the ring and stock of the anchor rose slowly out of the water, and now I could see that a second chain was shackled loosely to the cable, down which it had slid until it was stopped by the ring of the anchor. Badger had evidently seen it too, for he ejaculated, "Hallo !" and added a few verbal flourishes which I need not repeat. A few more turns of the windlass brought the flukes of the anchor clear of the water, and dangling against them was an undeniable wooden case, securely slung with lashings of stout chain. Badger cursed volubly, and, turning to the fishermen, exclaimed in a rather offensively peremptory tone:

"I want a boat. Now. This instant."

The elder piscator regarded him doggedly and replied "All right. I ain't got no objection."

"Where can I get a boat?" the inspector demanded, nearly purple with excitement and anxiety.

"Where do you think?" the mariner responded, evidently nettled by the inspector's masterful tone. "Pastrycook's? Or livery stables?"

"Look here," said Badger. "I'm a police officer and I want to board that barge, and I am prepared to pay handsomely. Now where can I get a boat?"

"We'll put you aboard of her," replied the fisherman, "that is, if we can catch her. But I doubt it. She's off, that's what she is. And there's something queer a-going on aboard of her," he added in a somewhat different tone.

There was. I had been observing it. The case had been, with some difficulty, hoisted on board, and then suddenly there had broken out an altercation between the two bargees and their passengers, and this had now developed into what look like a free fight. It was difficult to see exactly what was happening, for the barge was drifting rapidly down the river, and her sails, blowing out first on one side and then on the other, rather obscured the view. Presently, however, the sails filled and a man appeared at the wheel; then the barge jibed round, and with a strong ebb tide and a fresh breeze, very soon began to grow small in the distance.

Meanwhile the fishermen had bustled off in search of a boat, and the inspector had raced to the bridge-head, where he stood gesticulating frantically and blowing his whistle, while Thorndyke continued placidly to watch the receding barge through his binocular.

"What are we going to do?" I asked, a little surprised at my colleague's inaction.

"What can we do?" he asked in reply. "Badger will follow the barge. He probably won't overtake her, but he will prevent her from making a landing until they get out into the estuary, and then he may possibly get assistance. The chase is in his hands."

"Are we going with him?"

"I am not. This looks like being an all-night expedition, and I must be at our chambers to-morrow morning. Besides, the chase is not our affair. But if you would like to join Badger there is no reason why you shouldn't. I can look after the practice."

Well," I said, "I think I should rather like to be in at the death, if it won't inconvenience you. But it is possible that they may get away with the booty."

"Quite," he agreed; "and then it would be useful to know exactly how and where it disappears. Yes, go with them, by all means, and keep a sharp look-out."

At this moment Badger returned with the two plain clothes men whom his whistle had called from their posts, and simultaneously a boat was seen approaching the steps by the bridge, rowed by the two fishermen. The inspector looked at us inquiringly. "Are you coming to see the sport?" he asked.

"Doctor Jervis would like to come with you," Thorndyke replied. "I have to get back to London But you will be a fair boat-load without me."

This appeared to be also the view of the two fishermen, as they brought up at the steps and observed the four passengers; but they made no demur beyond inquiring if there were not any more; and when we had taken our places in the stern sheets, they pushed off and pulled through the bridge and away down stream. Gradually, the village receded and the houses and the bridge grew small and more distant, though they remained visible for a long time over the marshy levels; and still, as I looked back through my glasses, I could see Thorndyke on the bridge, watching the pursuit with his binocular to his eyes.

Meanwhile the fugitive barge, having got some two miles start, seemed to be drawing ahead. But it was only at intervals that we could see her, for the tide was falling fast and we were mostly hemmed in by the high, muddy banks. Only when we entered a straight reach of the river could we see her sails over the land; and every time that she came into view, she appeared perceptibly smaller.

When the river grew wider, the mast was stepped and a good-sized lug-sail hoisted, though one of the fishermen continued to ply his oar on the weather side, while the other took the tiller. This improved our pace appreciably; but still, whenever we caught a glimpse of the barge, it was evident that she was still gaining.

On one of these occasions the man at the tiller, standing up to get a better view, surveyed our quarry intently for nearly a minute and then addressed the inspector.

"She's a-going to give us the go-by, mister," he observed with conviction.

"Still gaining?" asked Badger.

"Aye. She's a-going to slip across the tail of Foulness Sand into the deep channel. And that's the last we shall see of her."

"But can't we get into the channel the same way?" demanded Badger.

"Well, d'ye see," replied the fisherman, "'tis like this. Tide's a-running out, but there'll be enough for her. It'll just carry her out through the Whitaker Channel and across the spit. Then it'll turn, and up she'll go, London way, on the flood. But we shall catch the flood-tide in the Whitaker Channel, and a rare old job we'll have to get out; and when we do get out, that barge'll be miles away."

The inspector swore long and earnestly. He even alluded to himself as a "blithering idiot." But that helped matters not at all. The fisherman's dismal prophecy was fulfilled in every horrid detail. When we were approaching the Whitaker Channel the barge was just crossing the spit, and the last of the ebb-tide was trickling out. By the time we were fairly in the Channel the tide had turned and was already flowing in with a speed that increased every minute; while over the sand we could see the barge, already out in the open estuary, heading to the west on the flood-tide at a good six knots.

Poor Badger was frantic. With yearning eyes fixed on the dwindling barge, he cursed, entreated, encouraged and made extravagant offers. He even took an oar and pulled with such desperate energy that he caught a crab and turned a neat back somersault into the fisherman's lap. The two mariners pulled until their oars bent like canes; but still the sandy banks crept by, inch by inch, and ever the turbid water seemed to pour up the channel more and yet more swiftly. It was a fearful struggle and seemed to last for hours; and when, at last, the boat crawled out across the spit and the exhausted rowers rested on their oars, the sun was just setting and the barge had disappeared into the west.

I was really sorry for Badger. His oversight in respect of the anchor was a very natural one or a landsman, and he had evidently taken infinite pains over the case and shown excellent judgment in keeping a close watch on the neighbourhood of Garbridge; and now, after all his care, it looked as if both the robbers and their booty had slipped through his fingers. It was desperately bad luck.

"Well," said the elder fisherman, "they've give us a run for our money; but they've got clear away. What's to be done now, mister?"

Badger had nothing to suggest excepting that we should pull or sail up the river in the hope of getting some assistance on the way. He was in the lowest depths of despair and dejection. But now, when Fortune seemed to have deserted us utterly, and failure appeared to be an accomplished fact, Providence intervened.

A small steam vessel that had been approaching from the direction of the East Swin suddenly altered her course and bore down as if to speak us. The fisherman who had last spoken looked at her attentively for a few moments and then slapped his thigh. "Saved by gum!" he exclaimed. "This'll do your trick, mister. Here comes a Customs cruiser."

Instantly the two fishermen bent to their oars to meet the oncoming craft, and in a few minutes we were alongside, Badger hailing like a bull of Bashan. A brief explanation to the officer in charge secured a highly sympathetic promise of help. We all scrambled up on deck; the boat was dropped astern at the scope of her painter; the engine-room bell jangled merrily, and the smart, yacht-like vessel began to forge ahead.

"Now then," said the officer, as his craft gathered way, "give us a description of this barge. What is she like?

She's a small stumpy," the senior fisherman explained, "flying light; wants paint badly; steers with a wheel; green transom with Bluebell, Maldon, cut in and gilded. Seemed to be keeping along the north shore."

With these particulars in his mind, the officer explored the western horizon with a pair of night-glasses, although it was still broad daylight. Presently he reported: "There's a stumpy in a line with the Blacktail Spit buoy. Just take a look at her." He handed his glasses to the fisherman, who, after a careful inspection of the stranger, gave it as his opinion that she was our quarry. "Probably makin' for Southend or Leigh," said he, and added: "I'll bet she's bound for Benfleet Creek. Nice quiet place, that, to land the stuff."

Our recent painful experience was now reversed, for as our swift little vessel devoured the miles of water, the barge, which we were all watching eagerly, loomed up larger every minute. By the time we were abreast of the Mouse Lightship, she was but a few hundred yards ahead, and even through my glasses, the name Bluebell was clearly legible. Badger nearly wept with delight; the officer in charge smiled an anticipatory smile; the deck-hands girded up their loins for the coming capture and the plain-clothes men each furtively polished a pair of handcuffs.

At length the little cruiser came fairly abreast of the barge--not unobserved by the two men on her deck. Then she sheered in suddenly and swept alongside. One hand neatly hooked a shroud with a grappling iron and made fast while a couple of preventive officers, the plain men and the inspector jumped down simultaneously on to the barge's deck. For a moment, the two bawley men were inclined to show fight; but the odds were too great. After a perfunctory scuffle they both submitted to be handcuffed and were at once hauled up on board the cruiser and lodged in the fore- peak under guard. Then the chief officer, the two fishermen and I jumped on board the barge and followed Badger down the companion hatch to the cabin.

It was a curious scene that was revealed in that little cupboard-like apartment by the light of Badger's electric torch. On each of the two lockers was stretched man, securely lashed with lead-line and having drawn over his face a knitted stocking cap, while on the little triangular fixed table rested an iron-bound box which I instantly identified by my recollection of the description of the bullion-case in the ship's manifest. It was but the work of a minute to liberate the skipper and his son and send them up, wrathful but substantially uninjured, to refresh on the cruiser; and then the ponderous treasure-chest was borne in triumph by two muscular deck-hands, up the narrow steps, to be hoisted to the Government vessel.

"Well, well," said the inspector, mopping his face with his handkerchief, "all's well that ends well, but I thought I had lost the men and the stuff that time. What are you going to do? I shall stay on board as this boat is going right up to the Custom House in London; but if you want to get home sooner, I dare say the chief officer will put you ashore at Southend."

I decided to adopt this course, and I was accordingly landed at Southend Pier with a telegram from Badger to his head-quarters; and at Southend I was fortunate enough to catch an express train which brought me to Fenchurch Street while the night was still young.

When I reached our chambers, I found Thorndyke seated by the fire, serenely studying a brief. He stood up as I entered and, laying aside the brief, remarked: "You are back sooner than I expected. How sped the chase? Did you catch the barge?"

"Yes. We've got the men and we've got the bullion. But we very nearly lost both"; and here I gave him an account of the pursuit and the capture, to which he listened with the liveliest interest. "That Customs cruiser was a piece of sheer luck," said he, when I had concluded. "I am delighted. This capture simplifies the case for us enormously."

It seems to me to dispose of the case altogether," said L "The property is recovered and the thieves are in custody. But I think most of the credit belongs to Badger."

Thorndyke smiled enigmatically. "I should let him have it all, Jervis," he said; and then, after a reflective pause, he continued: "We will go round to Scotland Yard in the morning to verify the capture. If the package agrees with the description in the bill of lading, the case, as you say, is disposed of."

"It is hardly necessary," said I. "The marks were all correct and the Customs seals were unbroken--but still, I know you won't be satisfied until you have verified everything for yourself. And I suppose you are right."

It was past eleven in the following forenoon when we invaded Superintendent Miller's office at Scotland Yard. That genial officer looked up from his desk as we entered and laughed joyously. "I told you so, Badger," he chuckled, turning to the inspector, who had also looked up and was regarding us with a foxy smile. "I knew the doctor wouldn't be satisfied until he had seen it with his own eyes. I suppose that is what you have come for, sir?"

"Yes," was the reply. "It is a mere formality, of course, but, if you don't mind--"

"Not in the least," replied Miller. "Come along, Badger, and show the doctor your prize."

The two officers conducted us to a room, which the superintendent unlocked, and which contained a small table, a measuring standard, a weighing machine, a set of Snellen's test-types, and the now historic case of bullion. The latter Thorndyke inspected closely, checking the marks and dimensions by his notes.

"I see you haven't opened it," he remarked.

"No," replied Miller. "Why should we? The Customs seals are intact."

"I thought you might like to know what was inside," Thorndyke explained.

The two officers looked at him quickly and the inspector exclaimed: " But we do know. It was opened and checked at the Customs."

"What do you suppose is inside?" Thorndyke asked.

"I don't suppose," Badger replied testily. "I know. There are four bars of gold inside."

"Well," said Thorndyke, "as the representative of the Insurance Company, I should like to see the contents of that case."

The two officers stared at him in amazement, as also, I must admit, did I. The implied doubt seemed utterly contrary to reason.

"This is scepticism with a vengeance!" said Miller. "How on earth is it possible--but there, I suppose if you are not satisfied, we should be justified--"

He glanced at his subordinate, who snorted impatiently: "Oh, open it and let him see the bars. And then, I suppose, he will want us to make an assay of the metal."

The superintendent retired with wrinkled brows and presently returned with a screwdriver, a hammer and a case-opener. Very deftly he broke the seals, extracted the screws and prised up the lid of the case, inside which were one or two folds of thick canvas. Lifting these with something of a flourish, he displayed the upper pair of dull, yellow bars.

"Are you satisfied now, sir?" demanded Badger. "Or do you want to see the other two?"

Thorndyke looked reflectively at the two bars, and the two officers looked inquiringly at him (but one might as profitably have watched the expression on the face of a ship's figure). Then he took from his pocket a folding foot-rule and quickly measured the three dimensions of one of the bars.

"Is that weighing machine reliable?" he asked.

"It is correct to an ounce," the superintendent replied, gazing at my colleague with a slightly uneasy expression. "Why?"

By way of reply Thorndyke lifted out the bar that he had measured and carrying it across to the machine, laid it on the platform and carefully adjusted the weights.

"Well?" the superintendent queried anxiously, as Thorndyke took the reading from the scale.

"Twenty-nine pounds, three ounces," replied Thorndyke.

"Well?" repeated the superintendent. "What about it?"

Thorndyke looked at him impassively for a moment, and then, in the same quiet tone, answered: "Lead."

"What!" the two officers shrieked in unison, darting across to the scale and glaring at the bar of metal. Then Badger recovered himself and expostulated, not without temper, "Nonsense, sir. Look at it. Can't you see that it is gold?"

"I can see that it is gilded," replied Thorndyke.

"But," protested Miller, "the thing is impossible! What makes you think it is lead?"

"It is just a question of specific gravity," was the reply. "This bar contains seventy-two cubic inches of metal and it weighs twenty pounds, three ounces. Therefore it is a bar of lead. But if you are still doubtful, it is quite easy to settle the matter. May I cut a small piece off the bar?"

The superintendent gasped and looked at his subordinate. "I suppose," said he, "under the circumstances, eh, Badger? Yes. Very well, doctor."

Thorndyke produced a strong pocket-knife and, having lifted the bar to the table, applied the knife to one corner and tapped it smartly with the hammer. The blade passed easily through the soft metal, and as the detached piece fell to the floor, the two officers and I craned forward eagerly. And then all possible doubts were set at rest. There was no mistaking the white, silvery lustre of the freshly-cut surface.

"Snakes!" exclaimed the superintendent. "This is a fair knock-out! Why, the blighters have got away with the stuff, after all! Unless," he added, with a quizzical look at Thorndyke, "you know where it is, doctor. I expect you do."

"I believe I do," said Thorndyke, "and if you care to come down with me to the London Docks, I think I can hand it over to you."

The superintendent's face brightened appreciably. Not so Badger's. That afflicted officer flung down the chip of metal that he had been examining, and turning to Thorndyke, demanded sourly: "Why didn't you tell us this before, sir? You let me go off chivvying that damn barge, and you knew all the time that the stuff wasn't on board."

"My dear Badger," Thorndyke expostulated, "don't you see that these lead bars are essential to our case? They prove that the gold bars were never landed and that they are consequently still on the ship. Which empowers us to detain any gold that we may find on her."

"There, now, Badger," said the superintendent, "it's no use for you to argue with the doctor. He's like a giraffe. He can see all round him at once. Let us get on to the Docks."

Having locked the room, we all sallied forth, and, taking a train at Charing Cross Station, made our way by Mark Lane and Fenchurch Street to Wapping, where, following Thorndyke, we entered the Docks and proceeded straight to a wharf near the Wapping entrance. Here Thorndyke exchanged a few words with a Customs official, who hurried away and presently returned, accompanied by an officer of higher rank. The latter, having saluted Thorndyke and cast a slightly amused glance at our little party, said: "They've landed that package that you spoke about. I've had it put in my office for the present. Will you come and have a look at it?"

We followed him to his office behind a long row of sheds, where, on a table, was a strong wooden case, somewhat larger than the " bullion"-case, while on the desk a large, many-leaved document lay open.

"This is your case, I think," said the official; "but you had better check it by the manifest. Here is the entry: 'One case containing seventeen and three-quarter dozen brass six-inch by three-eighths screw-bolts with nuts. Dimensions, sixteen inches by thirteen by nine. Gross weight a hundred and nineteen pounds; net weight a hundred and thirteen pounds.' Consigned to 'Jackson and Walker, 593 Great Alie Street, London, E.' Is that the one?"

"That is the one," Thorndyke replied.

"Then," said our friend," we'll get it open and have a look at those brass screw-bolts."

With a dexterity surprising in an official of such high degree, he had the screws out in a twinkling, and prising up the lid, displayed a fold of coarse canvas. As he lifted this the two police officers peered eagerly into the case; and suddenly the eager expression on Badger's face changed to one of bitter disappointment.

"You've missed fire this time, sir," he snapped. "This is just a case of brass bolts."

"Gold bolts, inspector," Thorndyke corrected, placidly. He picked out one and handed it to the astonished detective. "Did you ever feel a brass bolt of that weight?" he asked.

"Well, it certainly is devilish heavy," the inspector admitted, weighing it in his hand and passing it on to Miller.

"Its weight, as stated on the manifest," said Thorndyke, "works out at well over eight and a half ounces, but we may as well check it." He produced from his pocket a little spring balance, to which he slung the bolt. "You see," he said, "it weighs eight ounces and two- thirds. But a brass bolt of the same size would weigh only three ounces and four-fifths. There is not the least doubt that these bolts are gold; and as you see that their aggregate weight is a hundred and thirteen while the weight of the four missing bars is a hundred and thirteen pounds, two ounces, it is a reasonable inference that these bolts represent those bars; and an uncommonly good job they made of the melting to lose only two ounces. Has the consignee's agent turned up yet?

"He is waiting outside," replied the officer, with a pleased smile, "hopping about like a pea in a frying-pan. I'll call him in."

He did so, and a small, seedy man of strongly Semitic aspect approached the door with nervous caution and a rather pale face. But when his beady eye fell on the open case and the portentous assembly in the office, he turned about and fled along the wharf as if the hosts of the Philistines were at his heels.

"Of course it is all perfectly simple, as you say," I replied to Thorndyke as we strolled back up Nightingale Lane, "but I don't see where you got your start. What made you think that the stolen case was a dummy?"

"At first," Thorndyke replied, "it was just a matter of alternative hypotheses. It was purely speculative. The robbery described by Halethorpe was a very crude affair. It was planned in quite the wrong way. Noting this, I naturally asked myself: What is the right way to steal a case of gold ingots? Now, the outstanding difficulty in such a robbery arises from the ponderous nature of the thing stolen, and the way to overcome that difficulty is to get away with the booty at leisure before the robbery is discovered--the longer the better. It is also obvious that if you can delude someone into stealing your dummy you will have covered up your tracks most completely; for if that someone is caught, the issues are extremely confused, and if he is not caught, all the tracks lead away from you. Of course, he will discover the fraud when he tries to dispose of the swag, but his lips are sealed by the fact that he has, himself, committed a felony. So that is the proper strategical plan and, though it was wildly improbable, and there was nothing whatever to suggest it, still, the possibility that this crude robbery might cover a more subtle one had to be borne in mind. It was necessary to make absolutely certain that the gold bars were really in the case when it left Belhaven. I had practically no doubt that they were. Our visit to the Custom House was little more than a formality, just to give us an undeniable datum from which to make our start. We had to find somebody who had actually seen the case open and verified the contents, and when we found that man--Mr. Byrne--it instantly became obvious that the wildly improbable thing had really happened. The gold bars had already disappeared. I had calculated the approximate size of the real bars. They would contain forty-two cubic inches, and would be about seven inches by three by two. The dimensions given by Byrne--evidently correct, as shown by those of the case, which the bars fitted pretty closely--were impossible. If those bars had been gold, they would have weighed two hundred pounds, instead of the hundred and thirteen pounds shown on his report. The astonishing thing is that Byrne did not observe the discrepancy. There are not many Customs officers who would have let it pass."

"Isn't it rather odd," I asked, "that the thieves should have gambled on such a remote chance?"

"It is pretty certain," he replied, "that they were unaware of the risk they were taking. Probably they assumed--as most persons would have done--that a case of bullion would be merely inspected and passed. Few persons realise the rigorous methods of the Customs officers. But to resume: It was obvious that the 'gold' bars that Byrne had examined were dummies. The next question was, where were the real bars? Had they been made away with, or were they still on the ship? To settle this question I decided to go through the manifest and especially through the column of net weights. And there, presently, I came upon a package the net weight of which was within two ounces of the weight of stolen bars. And that package was a parcel of brass screw-bolts--on a homeward-bound ship! But who on earth sends brass bolts from Africa to London? The anomaly was so striking that I examined the entry more closely, and then I found--by dividing the net weight by the number of bolts--that each of these little bolts weighed over half a pound. But, if this were so, those bolts could be of no other metal than gold or platinum, and were almost certainly gold. Also, their aggregate weight was exactly that of the stolen bars, less two ounces, which probably represented loss in melting."

"And the scrivelloes," said I, "and the gum copal and the kola nuts; what was their bearing on the inquiry? I can't, even now, trace any connection."

Thorndyke cast an astonished glance at me, and then replied with a quiet chuckle: "There wasn't any. Those notes were for the benefit of the shipping gentleman. As he would look over my shoulder, I had to give him something to read and think about. If I had noted only the brass bolts, I should have virtually informed him of the nature of my suspicions."

"Then, really, you had the case complete when we left Belhaven?"

"Theoretically, yes. But we had to recover the stolen case, for without those lead ingots we could not prove that the gold bolts were stolen property, any more than one could prove a murder without evidence of the death of the victim."

"And how do you suppose the robbery was carried out? How was the gold got out of the ship's strong- room?"

"I should say it was never there. The robbers, I suspect, are the ship's mate, the chief engineer and possibly the purser. The mate controls the stowage of cargo, and the chief engineer controls the repair shop and has the necessary skill and knowledge to deal with the metal. On receiving the advice of the bullion consignment, I imagine they prepared the dummy case in agreement with the description. When the bullion arrived, the dummy case would be concealed on deck and the exchange made as soon as the bullion was put on board. The dummy would be sent to the strong-room and the real case carried to a prepared hiding place. Then the engineer would cut up the bars, melt them piecemeal and cast them into bolts in an ordinary casting flask, using an iron bolt as a model, and touching up the screw-threads with a die. The mate could enter the case on the manifest when he pleased, and send the bill of lading by post to the nominal consignee. That is what I imagine to have been the procedure."

Thorndyke's solution turned out to be literally correct. The consignee, pursued by Inspector Badger along the quay, was arrested at the dock gates and immediately volunteered King's evidence. Thereupon the mate, the chief engineer and the purser of the steamship Labadi were arrested and brought to trial; when they severally entered a plea of guilty and described the method of the robbery almost in Thorndyke's words.

The Funeral Pyre

Thorndyke did not often indulge in an evening paper, and was even disposed to view that modern institution with some disfavour; whence it happened that when I entered our chambers shortly before dinner time with a copy of the Evening Gazette in my hand, he fixed upon the folded news-sheet an inquiring and slightly disapproving eye.

"'Orrible discovery near Dartford," I announced, quoting the juvenile vendor.

The disapproval faded from his face, but the inquiring expression remained.

"What is it?" he asked.

"I don't know," I replied; "but it seems t be something in our line."

"My learned friend does us an injustice," he rejoined, with his eye riveted on the paper. "Still, if you are going to make my flesh creep, I will try to endure it."

Thus invited, I opened the paper and read out as follows:

"A shocking tragedy has come to light in a meadow about a mile from Dartford. About two o'clock this morning, a rural constable observed a rick on fire out on the marshes near the creek. By the time he reached it the upper half of the rick was burning fiercely in the strong wind, and as he could do nothing alone, he rent to the adjacent farm-house and gave the alarm. The farmer and two of his sons accompanied the constable to the scene of the conflagration, but the rick was now a blazing mass, roaring in the wind and giving out an intense heat. As it was obviously impossible to save any part of it, and as there were no other ricks near, the farmer decided to abandon it to its fate and went home.

"At eight o'clock he returned to the spot and found the rick still burning, though reduced to a heap of glowing cinders and ashes, and approaching it, he was horrified to perceive a human skull grinning out from the cindery mass. Closer examination showed other bones--all calcined white and chalky--and close to the skull a stumpy clay pipe. The explanation of this dreadful occurrence seems quite simple. The rick was not quite finished, and when the farm hands knocked off work they left the ladder in position. It is assumed that some tramp, in search of a night's lodging, observed the ladder, and climbing up it, made himself comfortable in the loose hay at the top of the rick, where he fell asleep with his lighted pipe in his mouth. This ignited the hay and the man must have been suffocated by the fumes without awakening from his sleep."

"A reasonable explanation," was Thorndyke's comment, "and quite probable; but of course it is pure hypothesis. As a matter of fact, any one of the three conceivable causes of violent death is possible in this case-- accident, suicide or homicide."

"I should have supposed," said I, "that we could almost exclude suicide. It is difficult to imagine a man electing to roast himself to death."

"I cannot agree with my learned friend," Thorndyke rejoined. "I can imagine a case--and one of great medico-legal interest--that would exactly fit the present circumstances. Let us suppose a man, hopelessly insolvent, desperate and disgusted with life, who decides to provide for his family by investing the few pounds that he has left in insuring his life heavily and then making away with himself. How would he proceed? If he should commit suicide by any of the orthodox methods he would simply invalidate his policy. But now, suppose he knows of a likely rick; that he provides himself with some rapidly-acting poison, such as potassium cyanide--he could even use prussic acid if he carried it in a rubber or celluloid bottle, which would be consumed in the fire; that he climbs on to the rick; sets fire to it, and as soon as it is fairly alight, takes his dose of poison and falls back dead among the hay. Who is to contest his family's claim? The fire will have destroyed all traces of the poison, even if they should be sought for. But it is practically certain that the question would never be raised. The claim would be paid without demur."

I could not help smiling at this calm exposition of a practicable crime. "It is a mercy, Thorndyke," I remarked, "that you are an honest man. If you were not--"

"I think," he retorted, "that I should find some better means of livelihood than suicide. But with regard to this case: it will be worth watching. The tramp hypothesis is certainly the most probable; but its very probability makes an alternative hypothesis at least possible. No one is likely to suspect fraudulent suicide; but that immunity from suspicion is a factor that increases the probability of fraudulent suicide. And so, to a less extent, with homicide. We must watch the case and see if there are any further developments."

Further developments were not very long in appearing. The report in the morning paper disposed effectually of the tramp theory without offering any other. "The tragedy of the burning rick," it said, "is taking a some what mysterious turn. It is now clear that the unknown man, who was assumed to have been a tramp, must have been a person of some social position, for careful examination of the ashes by the police have brought to light various articles which would have been carried only by a man of fair means. The clay pipe was evidently one of a pair--of which the second one has been recovered--probably silver-mounted and carried in a case, the steel frame of which has been found. Both pipes are of the 'Burns Cutty" pattern and have neatly scratched on the bowls the initials 'R. R.' The following articles have also been found :--Remains of a watch, probably gold, and a rather singular watch-chain, having alternate links of platinum and gold. The gold links have partly disappeared, but numerous beads of gold have been found, derived apparently from the watch and chain. The platinum links are intact and are fashioned of twisted square wire. A bunch of keys, partly fused; a rock crystal seal, apparently from a ring; a little porcelain mascot figure, with a hole for suspension--possibly from the watch-chain--and a number of artificial teeth. In connection with the latter, a puzzling and slightly sinister aspect has been given to the case by the finding of an upper dental plate by a ditch some two hundred yards from the rick. The plate has two gaps and, on comparison with the skull of the unknown man, these have been found by the police surgeon to correspond with two groups of remaining teeth. Moreover, the artificial teeth found in the ashes all seem to belong to a lower plate. The presence of this plate, so far from the scene of the man's death, is extremely difficult to account for."

As Thorndyke finished reading the extract he looked at me as if inviting some comment.

"It is a most remarkable and mysterious affair," said I, "and naturally recalls to my mind the hypothetical case that you suggested yesterday. If that case was possible then, it is actually probable now. It fits these new facts perfectly not only in respect of the abundant means of identification but even to this dental plate--if we assume that he took the poison as he was approaching the rick, and that the poison was of an acrid or irritating character which caused him to cough or retch. And I can think of no other plausible explanation."

"There are other possibilities," said Thorndyke, but fraudulent suicide is certainly the most probable theory on the known facts. But we shall see. As you say, the body can hardly fail to be identified at a pretty early date."

As a matter of fact it was identified in the course of that same day. Both Thorndyke and I were busily engaged until evening in the courts and elsewhere and had not had time to give this curious case any consideration. But as we walked home together, we encountered Mr. Stalker of the Griffin Life Assurance Company pacing up and down King's Bench Walk near the entry of our chambers.

"Ha!" he exclaimed, striding forward to meet us near the Mitre Court gateway, "you are just the very men I wanted to see. There is a little matter that I want to consult you about. I shan't detain you long."

"It won't matter much if you do," said Thorndyke. "We have finished our routine work for the day and our time is now our own." He led the way up to our chambers, where, having given the fire a stir, he drew up three arm-chairs.

"Now, Stalker," said he. "Warm your toes and tell us your troubles."

Mr. Stalker spread out his hands to the blaze began reflectively: "It will be enough, I think, if I give you the facts--and most of them you probably know already. You have heard about this man whose remains were found in the ashes of a burnt rick? Well, it turns out that he was a certain Mr. Reginald Reed, an outside broker, as I understand; but what is of more interest to us is that he was a client of ours. We have issued a policy on his life for three thousand pounds. I thought I remembered the name when I saw it in the paper this afternoon, so I looked up our b and there it was, sure enough."

"When was the policy issued?" Thorndyke asked.

"Ah!" exclaimed Stalker. "That's the exasperating feature of the case. The policy was issued less than a year ago. He has only paid a single premium. So we stand to drop practically the whole three thousand. Of course, we have to take the fat with the lean, but we don't like to take it in such precious large lumps."

"Of course you don't," agreed Thorndyke. "But now you have come to consult me--about what?"

"Well," replied Stalker, "I put it to you: isn't there something obviously fishy about the case? Are the circumstances normal? For instance, how the devil came a respectable city gentleman to be smoking his pipe in a haystack out in a lonely meadow at two o'clock in the morning, or thereabouts?

"I agree," said Thorndyke, "that the circumstances are highly abnormal. But there is no doubt that the man is dead. Extremely dead, If I may use the expression. What is the point that you wish to raise?"

"I am not raising any point," replied Stalker. "We should like you to attend the inquest and watch the case for us. Of course, in our policies, as you know, suicide is expressly ruled out; and if this should turn out to have been a case of suicide--"

"What is there to suggest that it was?" asked Thorndyke.

"What is there to suggest that it wasn't?" retorted Stalker.

"Nothing," rejoined Thorndyke. "But a negative plea is of no use to you. You will have to furnish positive proof of suicide, or else pay the claim."

"Yes, I realise that," said Stalker, "and I am not suggesting-- But there, it is of no use discussing the matter while we know so little. I leave the case in your hands. Can you attend the inquest?"

"I shall make it my business to do so," replied Thorndyke.

"Very well," said Stalker, rising and putting on his gloves, "then we will leave it at that; and we couldn't leave it in better case."

When our visitor had gone I remarked to Thorndyke: "Stalker seems to have conceived the same idea as my learned senior--fraudulent suicide."

It is not surprising," he replied. "Stalker is a shrewd man and he perceives that when an abnormal thing has happened we may look for an abnormal explanation. Fraudulent suicide was a speculative possibility yesterday: to-day, in the light of these new facts, it is the most probable theory. But mere probabilities won't help Stalker. If there is no direct evidence of suicide--and there is not likely to be any--the verdict will be Death by Misadventure, and the Griffin Company will have to pay."

"I suppose you won't do anything until you have heard what transpires at the inquest?"

"Yes," he replied. "I think we should do well to go down and just go over the ground. At present we have the facts at third hand, and we don't know what may have been overlooked. As to-morrow is fairly free I propose that we make an early start and see the place ourselves."

"Is there any particular point that you want to clear up?"

"No; I have nothing definite in view. The circumstances are compatible with either accident, suicide or homicide, with an undoubted leaning towards suicide. But, at present, I have a completely open mind. I am, in fact, going down to Dartford in the hope of getting a lead in some definite direction."

When we alighted at Dartford Station on the following morning, Thorndyke looked inquiringly up and down the platform until he espied an inspector, when he approached the official and asked for a direction to the site of the burnt rick.

The official glanced at Thorndyke's canvas-covered research-case and at my binocular and camera as he replied with a smile: "You are not the first, by a long way, that has asked that question. There has been a regular procession of Press gentlemen that way this morning. The place is about a mile from here. You take the foot-path to Joyce Green and turn off towards the creek opposite Temple Farm. This is about where the rick stood," he added, as Thorndyke produced his one-inch Ordnance map and a pencil, "a few yards from that dyke."

With this direction and the open map we set forth from the station, and taking our way along the unfrequented path soon left the town behind. As we crossed the second stile, where the path rejoined the road, Thorndyke paused to survey the prospect.

"Stalker's question," he remarked, "was not unreasonable. This road leads nowhere but to the river, and one does rather wonder what a city man can have been doing out on these marshes in the small hours of the morning. I think that will be our objective, where you see those men at work by the shepherd's hut, or whatever it is."

We struck off across the level meadows, out of which arose the red sails of a couple of barges, creeping down the invisible creek; and as we approached our objective the shepherd's hut resolved itself into a contractor's office van, and the men were seen to be working with shovels and sieves on the ashes of the rick. A police inspector was superintending the operations, and when we drew near he accosted us with a civil inquiry as to our business.

Thorndyke presented his card and explained that he was watching the case in the interests of the Griffin Insurance Company. "I suppose," he added, "I shall be given the necessary facilities?"

"Certainly," replied the officer, glancing at my colleague with an odd mixture of respect and suspicion "and if you can spot anything that we've overlooked, you are very welcome. It's all for the public good. Is there anything in particular that you want to see?"

"I should like to see everything that has been recovered so far. The remains of the body have been removed, I suppose?"

"Yes, sir. To the mortuary. But I have got all the effects here."

He led the way to the office--a wooden hut on low wheels--and unlocking the door, invited us to enter. "Here are the things that we have salved," he said, indicating a table covered with white paper on which the various articles were neatly set out, "and I think it's about the lot. We haven't come on anything fresh for the last hour or so."

Thorndyke looked over the collection thoughtfully; picked up and examined successively the two clay pipes--each with the initials "R. R." neatly incised on the bowl--the absurd little mascot figure, so incongruous with its grim surroundings and the tragic circumstances, the distorted keys, the platinum chain-links to several of which shapeless blobs of gold adhered, and the crystal seal; and then, collecting the artificial teeth, arranged them in what appeared to be their correct order and compared them with the dental plate.

"I think," said he, holding the latter in his fingers, "that as the body is not here, I should like to secure the means of comparison of these teeth with the skull. There will be no objection to that, I presume?"

"What did you wish to do?" the inspector asked.

"I should like to take a cast of the plate and a wax impression of the loose teeth. No damage will be done to the originals, of course."

The inspector hesitated, his natural, official tendency to refuse permission apparently contending with a desire to see with his own eyes how the famous expert carried out his mysterious methods of research. In the end the latter prevailed and the official sanction was given, subject to a proviso. "You won't mind my looking on while you do it?"

"Of course not," replied Thorndyke. "Why should I?"

"I thought that perhaps your methods were a sort of trade secret."

Thorndyke laughed softly as he opened the research case. "My dear inspector," said he, "the people who have trade secrets are those who make a profound mystery of simple processes that any schoolboy could carry out with once showing. That is the necessity for the secrecy."

As he was speaking he half-filled a tiny aluminium saucepan with water, and having dropped into it a couple of cakes of dentist's moulding composition, put it to heat over a spirit-lamp. While it was heating he greased the dental plate and the loose teeth, and prepared the little rubber basin and the other appliances for mixing the plaster.

The inspector was deeply interested. With almost ravenous attention he followed these proceedings, and eagerly watched Thorndyke roll the softened composition into the semblance of a small sausage and press it firmly on the teeth of the plate; peered into the plaster tin, and when the liquid plaster was mixed and applied, first to the top and then to the lower surface of the plate, not only observed the process closely but put a number of very pertinent questions.

While the plaster and composition were setting Thorndyke renewed his inspection of the salvage from the rick, picking out a number of iron boot protectors which he placed apart in a little heap.

Then he proceeded to roll out two flat strips of softened composition, into one of which he pressed the loose teeth in what appeared to be their proper order, and into the other the boot protectors--eight in number-- after first dusting the surface with powdered French chalk. By this time the plaster had set hard enough to allow of the mould being opened and the dental plate taken out. Then Thorndyke, having painted the surfaces of the plaster pieces with knotting, put the mould together again and tied it firmly with string, mixed a fresh bowl of plaster and poured it into the mould.

While this was setting Thorndyke made a careful inventory, with my assistance, of the articles found in the ashes and put a few discreet questions to the inspector. But the latter knew very little about the case. His duty was merely to examine and report on the rick for the information of the coroner. The investigation of the case was evidently being conducted from headquarters. There being no information to be gleaned from the officer, we went out and inspected the site of the rick. But here, also, there was nothing to be learned; the surface of the ground was now laid bare and the men who were working with the sieves reported no further discoveries. We accordingly returned to the hut, and as the plaster had now set hard Thorndyke proceeded with infinite care to open the mould. The operation was a complete success, and as my colleague extracted the cast--a perfect replica, in plaster, of the dental plate-- the inspector's admiration was unbounded. "Why," he exclaimed, "excepting for the colour you couldn't tell one from the other; but all the same, I don't quite see what you want it for."

"I want it to compare with the skull," replied Thorndyke, "if I have time to call at the mortuary. As I can't take the original plate with me, I shall need this copy to make the comparison. Obviously, it is important to make sure that this is Reed's plate and not that of some other person. By the way, can you show us the spot where the plate was picked up?"

"Yes," replied the inspector. "You can see the place from here. It was just by that gate at the crossing of the ditch."

"Thank you, inspector," said Thorndyke. "I think we will walk down and have a look at the place." He wrapped the new cast in a soft cloth, and having repacked his research--case, shook hands with the officer and prepared to depart.

"You will notice, Jervis," he remarked as we walked towards the gate, "that this denture was picked up at a spot beyond the rick--farther from the town, I mean. Consequently, if the plate is Reed's, he must have dropped it while he was approaching the rick from the direction of the river. It will be worthwhile to see if we can find out whence he came."

"Yes," I agreed. "But the dropping of the plate is a rather mysterious affair. It must have happened when he took the poison--assuming that he really did poison himself; but one would have expected that he would wait until he got to the rick to take his dose."

"We had better not make too many assumptions while we have so few facts," said Thorndyke. He put down his case beside the gate, which guarded a bridge across a broad ditch, or drainage dyke, and opened his map.

"The question is," said he, "did he come through this gate or was he only passing it? This dyke, you see, opens into the creek about three-quarters of a mile farther down. The probability is, therefore, that if he came up from the river across the marshes he would be on this side of the ditch and would pass the gate. But we had better try both sides. Let us leave our things by the gate and explore the ground for a few hundred yards, one on either side of the ditch. Which side will you take?"

I elected to take the side nearer the creek, and, having put my camera down by the research-case, climbed over the padlocked gate and began to walk slowly along by the side of the ditch, scanning the ground for foot prints showing the impression of boot-protectors. At first the surface was far from favourable for imprints of any kind, being, like that immediately around the gate, covered with thick turf. About a hundred and fifty yards down, however, I came upon a heap of worm-casts on which was plainly visible the print of a heel with a clear impression of a kidney-shaped protector such as I had seen in the hut. Thereupon I hailed Thorndyke and, having stuck my stick in the ground beside the heel-print, went back to meet him at the gate.

"This is rather interesting, Jervis," he remarked, when I had described my find. "The inference seems to be that he came from the creek--unless there is another gate farther down. We had better have our compo impressions handy for comparison." He opened his case and taking from it the strip of composition--now as hard as bone--on which were the impressions of the boot-protectors, slipped it into his outer pocket. We then took up the case and the camera and proceeded to the spot marked by my stick.

"Well," said Thorndyke, "it is not very conclusive, seeing that so many people use boot-protectors, but it is probably Reed's foot-print. Let us hope that we shall find something more distinctive farther on."

We resumed our march, keeping a few yards apart and examining the ground closely as we went. For a full quarter of a mile we went on without detecting any trace of a foot-print on the thick turf. Suddenly we perceived ahead of us a stretch of yellow mud occupying a slight hollow, across which the creek had apparently overflowed at the last spring tide. When we reached it we found that the mud was nearly dry, but still soft enough to take an impression; and the surface was covered with a maze of foot-prints.

We halted at the edge of the patch and surveyed the complicated pattern; and then it became evident that the whole group of prints had been produced by two pairs of feet, with the addition of a row of sheep-tracks.

"This seems to raise an entirely new issue," I re marked.

"It does," Thorndyke agreed. "I think we now begin to see a definite light on the case. But we must go cautiously. Here are two sets of foot-prints of which one is apparently Reed's--to judge by the boot-protectors--while the other prints have been made by a man, whom we will call X, who wore boots or shoes with rubber soles and heels. We had better begin by verifying Reed's." He produced the composition strip from his pocket, and, stooping over one pair of footprints, continued: "I think we may assume that these are Reed's feet. We have on the compo strip impressions of eight protectors from the rick, and on each foot-print there are four protectors. Moreover, the individual protectors are the same on the compo and on the foot-prints. Thus the compo shows two pairs of half-protectors, two single edge-pieces, and two kidney-shaped protectors; while each foot-print shows a pair of half-protectors on the outside of the sole, a single one on the inside and a kidney-shaped piece on the heel. Furthermore, in both cases the protectors are nearly new and show no appreciable signs of wear. The agreement is complete."

"Don't you think," said I, "that we ought to take plaster records of them?"

"I do," he replied, "seeing that a heavy shower or a high tide would obliterate them. If you will make the casts I will, meanwhile, make a careful drawing of the whole group to show the order of imposition."

We fell to work forthwith upon our respective tasks, and by the time I had filled four of the clearest of the foot-prints with plaster,

Thorndyke had completed his drawing with the aid of a set of coloured pencils from the research-case. While the plaster was setting he exhibited and explained the drawing.

"You see, Jervis, that there are four lines of prints and a set of sheep-tracks. The first in order of time are these prints of X, drawn in blue. Then come the sheep, which trod on X's foot-prints. Next comes Reed, alone and after some interval, for he has trodden both on the sheep-tracks and on the tracks of X. Both men were going towards the river. Then we have the tracks of the two men coming back. This time they were together, for their tracks are parallel and neither treads into the prints of the other. Both tracks are rather sinuous as if the men were walking unsteadily, and both have trodden on the sheep-tracks and on the preceding tracks. Next, we have the tracks of X going alone towards the river and treading on all the others excepting number four, which is the tracks of X coming from the river and turning off towards that gate, which opens on to the road. The sequence of events is therefore pretty clear.

"First, X came along here alone to some destination which we have yet to discover. Later--how much later we cannot judge--came Reed, alone. The two men seem to have met, and later returned together, apparently the worse for drink. That is the last we see of Reed. Next comes X, walking back--quite steadily, you notice--towards the river. Later, be returns; but this time, for some reason--perhaps to avoid the neighbourhood of the rick--he crosses the ditch at that gate, apparently to get on the road, though you see by the map that the road is much the longer route to the town. And now we had better get on and see if we can discover the rendezvous to and from which these two men went and came."

As the plaster had now set quite hard I picked up the casts, and when I had carefully packed them in the case we resumed our progress riverwards. I had already noticed, some distance ahead, the mast of what looked like a small cutter yacht standing up above the marshes, and I now drew Thorndyke's attention to it. But he had already observed it and, like me, had marked it as the probable rendezvous of the two men. In a few minutes the probability became a certainty, for a bend in the creek showed us the little vessel--with the name Moonbeam newly painted on the bow--made fast along side a small wooden staging; and when we reached this the bare earth opposite the gangway was seen to be covered with the foot-prints of both men.

"I wonder," said I, "which of them was the owner of the yacht."

"It is pretty obvious, I think," said Thorndyke, "that X was the owner if either of them was. He came to the yacht alone, and he wore rubber-soled shoes such as yachtsmen favour; whereas Reed came when the other man was there, and he wore iron boot-protectors, which no yacht owner would do if he had any respect for his deck-planks. But they may have had a joint interest; appearances suggest that they were painting the woodwork when they were here together, as some of the paint is fresh and some of it old and shabby." He gazed at the yacht reflectively for some time and then remarked: "It would be interesting--and perhaps instructive--to have a look at the inside."

"It would be a flagrant trespass, to put it mildly," said I.

"It would be more than trespass if that padlock is locked," he replied. "But we need not take a pedantic view of the legal position. My learned friend has a serviceable pair of glasses and commands an unobstructed view of a mile or so; and if he maintains an observant attitude while I make an inspection of the premises any trifling irregularity will be of no consequence." As he spoke he felt in his pocket and produced the instrument which our laboratory assistant, Polton, had made from a few pieces of stiff steel wire, and which was euphemistically known as a smoker's companion. With this appliance in his hand he dropped down on to the yacht's deck, and after a quick look round, tried the padlock. Finding it locked he proceeded to operate on it with the smoker's companion, and in a few moments it fell open, when he pushed back the sliding hatch and stepped down into the little cabin.

His exploration did not take long. In a few minutes he reappeared and climbed the short ladder to the staging. "There isn't much to see," he reported, "but what there is is highly suggestive. If you slip down and have a look round, I think you will have no difficulty in forming a plausible reconstruction of the recent events. You had better take the camera. There is light enough for a time exposure."

I handed him the glasses, and dropping on to the deck, stepped down through the open hatch into the cabin. It was an absurd little cave, barely four feet high from the floor to the coach-roof, open to the fore- peak and lighted by a little skylight and two portholes. Of the two sleeping berths, one had evidently been used as a seat, while the other appeared to have been slept in, to judge by the indented pillow arid the tumbled blankets, left just as the occupant had crawled out of them. But the whole interior was in a stale of squalid disorder. Paint-pots and unwashed brushes lay about the floor, in company with a couple of whisky-bottles--one empty and one half-full--two tumblers, a pair of empty siphons and a litter of playing cards scattered broadcast and evidently derived from two packs. It was, as Thorndyke had said, easy to reconstruct the scene of sordid debauchery that the light of the two candles--each in its congealed pool of grease--must have displayed on that night of horror whose dreadful secret had been disclosed by the ashes of the rick. But I could see nothing that would enable me to give a name to the dead man's mysterious companion.

When I had completed my inspection and taken a photograph of the interior, I rejoined Thorndyke, who then descended and replaced the padlock on the closed hatch, relocking it with the invaluable smoker's companion.

"Well, Jervis," said he, as we turned our faces to wards the town, "it seems as if we had accomplished our task, so far as Stalker is concerned. It is still possible that this was a case of suicide, but it is no longer probable. All the appearances point to homicide. I think my learned friend will agree with me in that."

"Undoubtedly," I replied. "And to me there is a strong suggestion of premeditation. I take it that X, the owner of the yacht, enticed Reed out here, possibly to prepare for a cruise; that the two men worked at the repainting while the daylight lasted and then spent the evening drinking and gambling. The fact that they used several packs of cards suggests that they played for pretty heavy stakes. Then, I think, Reed became drunk and X offered to see him safely off the marshes. It is evident that X was not drunk, because, although both tracks appear unsteady when the men were walking together, the tracks of X returning to the yacht are quite steady and straight. I should say that the actual murder took place just after they had got over the gate; that Reed's false teeth fell out while his body was being dragged to the rick, and that this was unnoticed by X owing to the darkness. Then X dragged the body up the ladder and laid it in the middle of the rick at the top, set fire to the rick-- probably on the lee side-and at once made off back to the yacht. There he passed the night, and in the morning he returned to the town along the road, giving the neighbourhood of the rick a wide berth. That is my reading of the evidence."

"Yes," said Thorndyke, "that seems to be the interpretation of the facts. And now all that remains is to give a name to the mysterious X, and I should think that will present no difficulties."

"Are you proposing to inspect the remains at the mortuary?" I asked.

No," he replied. "It would be interesting, but it is not necessary. We have all the available data for identification, and our concern is now not with Reed but with X. We had better get back to London."

On our arrival at the station, we found the bookstall keeper in the act of sticking up a placard of the evening paper on which was the legend: "Rick tragedy; Sensational development."

We immediately provided ourselves each with a copy of the paper, and sitting down on a seat, proceeded to read the heavily-leaded report.

"A new and startling aspect has been given to the rick tragedy by some further inquiries that the police have made. It seems that the dead man, Reed, was a member of the firm of Reed and Jarman, outside brokers, and it now transpires that his partner, Walter Jarman, is also missing. There has been no one at the office this week, but the caretaker states that on Monday evening at about eight o'clock, he saw Mr. Jarman let himself into the office with his key (the rick was first seen to be on fire at two o'clock on Monday morning). It appears that three cheques, payable to the firm and endorsed by Jarman, were paid into the bank--Patmore's--by the first post on Tuesday morning, and that, also on Tuesday morning, Jarman purchased a parcel of diamonds of just over a thousand pounds in value from a diamond merchant in Hatton Garden, who accepted a cheque in payment after telephoning to the bank. It further appears that on the previous Saturday morning, Reed and Jarman visited the bank together and drew out in cash practically their whole balance, leaving only thirty-two pounds. The diamond merchant's cheque was met by the cheques that had just been paid in. It is premature to make any comments, but we may expect some strange disclosures at the inquest, which will be held at Dartford the day after to-morrow."

"I assume," said I, "that the identity of X is no longer a mystery. It looks as if these two men had agreed to realise their assets and abscond, and had then spent the night gambling for the swag, and, oddly enough, Reed appears to have been the winner, for otherwise there would have been no need to murder him."

"That is so," Thorndyke agreed, "assuming that X is Jarman, which is probable, though not certain. But we mustn't go beyond our facts, and we mustn't construct theories from newspaper reports. I think we had better call at Scotland Yard on our way home and verify those particulars."

The report and our own observations occupied us during the journey to London, though our discussion produced no further conclusions. As soon as we arrived at Charing Cross, Thorndyke sprang out of the train, and emerging from the station, walked swiftly towards Whitehall.

Our visit was fortunately timed, for as we approached the entrance to the head-quarters, our old friend, Superintendent Miller, came out. He smiled as he saw us and halted to utter the laconic query "Rick Case?"

"Yes," replied Thorndyke. "We have come to verify the particulars given in the evening paper. Have you seen the report?"

"Yes; and you may take it as correct. Anything else?"

"I should have liked to look over a series of the cheques drawn by the firm. The last two, I suppose, are inaccessible?"

"Yes. They will be at the bank, and we couldn't inspect them without an order of the court. But, as to the others, if they are at the office, I think you could see them. I'll come along with you now if you like, and have a look round myself. Our people are in possession."

We at once closed with the superintendent's offer and proceeded with him by the Underground Railway to the Mansion House, from whence we made our way to Queen Victoria Street, where Reed and Jarman had their offices. A sergeant was in charge at the moment, and to him the superintendent addressed himself.

"Have you found any returned cheques?"

Yes, sir," replied the sergeant; "lots of 'em. We've been through them all."

As he spoke he produced several bundles of cheques and laid them on a desk, the drawers of which all stood open.

"Well," said Miller, "there they are, doctor. I don't know what you want to find out, but I expect you do." He placed a chair by the desk, and as Thorndyke sat down and proceeded to turn the cheques over, he watched him with politely-suppressed curiosity.

It appears," said Thorndyke, "as if these two men had mixed up their private affairs with the business account. Here, for instance, is a cheque drawn by Reed for the Picardy Wine Company. But that company could hardly have been a client. And this one of Jarman's for the Secretary of the St. John's Nursing Home must be a private cheque, and so I should say are these two for F. Waller, Esq., F.R.C.S., and for Andrew Darton, Esq., L.D.S. They are drawn for professional men and both are--like the Nursing Home cheque--stated in even amounts of guineas, whereas the business cheques are in uneven amounts of pounds, shillings and pence."

"I think you are right, sir," said Miller. "The business seems to have been conducted in a very casual manner. And just look at those signatures! Never twice alike. The banks hate that sort of thing, naturally. When a customer signs in the signature book he has given a specimen for reference and he ought to keep to it strictly. A man who varies his signature is asking for trouble."

He is," Thorndyke agreed, as he rapidly entered a few particulars of the cheques in his notebook; "particularly in the case of a firm with a staff of clerks."

He stood up, and having pocketed his notebook, held out his hand.

"I am very much obliged to you, superintendent," he said.

Seen all that you wanted to see?" Miller asked.

"Thank you, yes," Thorndyke replied.

"I should very much like to know what you have seen," Miller rejoined; to which my colleague replied by waving his hand towards the cheques, as he turned to go.

I don't quite see the bearing of those cheques on our inquiry," I said, as we took our way homeward along Cheapside.

"It is not very direct," Thorndyke replied;" but the cheques help us to understand the characters of these two men and their relations with one another; which may be very necessary when we come to the inquest."

During the following day I saw very little of Thorndyke, for our excursion to Dartford had put our work somewhat in arrear and we had to secure a free day for the inquest on the morrow. We met at dinner after the day's work, but, beyond settling the programme for the next day nothing of importance passed with reference to the "Rick Case."

The opening phases of the inquest, though of thrilling interest to the numerous spectators and Press men, did not particularly concern us. The evidence of the rural constable, the farmer and the police inspector-- with whom Thorndyke had a little confidential talk and apparently surprised the officer considerably--merely amplified what we knew already. Of more interest was that of a local dentist who testified to having examined the dental plate and to having compared it with the skull of the dead man. "The plate and the jaw of deceased," he said, "agree completely. The jaw contains five natural teeth in two groups, and the plate has two spaces which exactly correspond to those two groups of teeth. I have tried the plate on the jaw and have no doubt whatever that it belonged to deceased."

"That is a very important fact," Thorndyke remarked to me as the witness retired. "It is the indispensable link in the chain."

"But surely it was obvious?" said I.

"No doubt," he replied. "But now it is proved and in evidence."

I was somewhat puzzled by Thorndyke's remark, but the appearance of a new witness forbade discussion. Mr. Arthur Gerrard was an alert-looking, rather tall man, with bushy, Mephistophelian eyebrows and a small, dark moustache, who wore a pair of large bifocal spectacles, and to whom a small mole at the corner of the mouth imparted the effect of a permanent one-sided smile.

It was on your information," said the coroner," that the identity of the deceased was established."

"Yes," replied the witness, who spoke with a slight, but perceptible, Irish accent. "I saw the description in the papers of the things that had been found in the rick and at once recognised them as Reed's. I knew deceased intimately and had often noticed his peculiar watch-chain and the little china mascot and seen him smoking the clay pipe with his initials scratched on it; and I knew that he wore false teeth."

"Did you meet him frequently?"

"Oh, yes. For more than a year he was my partner in business, and we remained friends after I had dissolved the partnership."

"Why did you dissolve the partnership?"

"I had to. Reed was impossible in a business sense. He gambled incessantly in stocks and I had to pay his losses. I lent him, for this purpose, at one time and another, over two thousand pounds. He gave me bills for the loans, but he was never able to meet them, and in the end, when we dissolved, I got him to insure his life for three thousand pounds and to draw up a document making his debt to me the first charge on his estate in the event of his death."

"Had you ever any reason to suppose that he contemplated suicide?

"None whatever. After he left me, he entered into partnership with a Mr. Walter Jarman, and whenever I met him, he seemed to be quite happy and contented, though I gathered that he was still gambling a good deal. I saw him a week ago to-day and he then told me that he proposed to take a short yachting holiday with his partner, who owned a small cutter. That was the last time that I saw him alive."

As the witness was about to retire, Thorndyke rose, and having obtained the coroner's permission to cross- examine, asked: "You have spoken of a yacht. Do you know what her name is and where she has been kept lately? "

"Her name is the Moonbeam, and I believe Jarman kept her somewhere in the Thames, but I don't know where."

"And as to Jarman himself: what do you know about him, as to his character, for instance?"

"I knew him very slightly. He appeared to be rather a dissipated man. Drank a good deal, I should say, and I think he was a bit of a gambler."

"Do you know if he was a heavy smoker?"

"He didn't smoke at all, but he was an inveterate snuff-taker."

At this point the foreman of the jury interposed with the audible remark that "he didn't see what this had to do with the inquiry," and the coroner looked dubiously at Thorndyke; but as my colleague sat down, the objection was not pursued.

The next witness was the caretaker of the building in which Reed and Jarman's office was situated. His evidence was to the effect that on the previous Monday evening at about eight o'clock, he saw Mr. Jarman let himself into the office with his key. "I don't know how long he stayed there," he continued, in reply to the coroner's question. "I had finished my work and was going up to my rooms at the top of the building. I didn't see him again."

"Did you notice anything unusual in his appearance?" asked Thorndyke, rising to cross-examine. "Was his face at all flushed, for instance?"

"I couldn't say. I was going up the stairs and I just looked back over my shoulder when I heard him. His face was turned away from me."

"But you had no difficult in recognising him?"

"No: I should have known him a mile off. He had his overcoat on, and it is a very peculiar overcoat--light brown with a sort of greenish check. You couldn't possibly mistake it."

"What should you say was Mr. Jarman's height?"

"About five feet nine or ten, I should say."

Here the foreman of the jury again interposed. "Aren't we wasting time, sir?" he inquired impatiently. "These details about Jarman may be very important to the police, but they don't concern us. We are inquiring into the death of Mr. Reginald Reed."

The coroner looked deprecatingly at Thorndyke and remarked "There is some truth in what the foreman says."

"I submit, sir," replied Thorndyke," that there is no truth in it at all. We are not inquiring into the death of Reginald Reed, but into that of a man whose remains were found in a burned rick."

"But the body has been identified as that of Reginald Reed."

"Then," said Thorndyke," I submit that it has been wrongly identified. I suggest that the body is that of Walter Jarman and I am prepared to produce witnesses who will prove that it is."

"But," exclaimed the coroner, "we have just heard the evidence of a witness who states that he saw Jarman alive eighteen hours after the rick was fired."

"I beg your pardon, sir," said Thorndyke. "We have heard the witness say that he saw Jarman's overcoat. He expressly stated that he did not see the man's face."

The coroner hastily conferred with the jury--who openly scoffed at Thorndyke's suggestion--and then said: "I find what you say perfectly incredible and so do the jury. It is utterly irreconcilable with the facts. You had better call your witnesses and let us dispose of this extraordinary suggestion."

Thorndyke bowed to the coroner and called Mr. Andrew Darton; whereupon a middle-aged man of markedly professional aspect came forward and, having been sworn, gave evidence as follows: "I am a dental surgeon. A little over two years ago, Mr. Walter Jarman was under my care. I extracted some loose teeth from both jaws and made him two plates--an upper and a lower."

"Could you identify those plates?"

"Yes. I have with me the plaster model on which those plates were made." He opened a bag and produced a plaster cast of a pair of jaws fitted with a brass hinge so that the jaws could be opened and shut. On the upper jaw were two groups of teeth separated by a space of bare gums, while the lower jaw bore a single group of four front teeth.

"This model," the witness explained, "is an exact replica of the patient's jaws, and the two plates were actually moulded on it." He picked up the dental plate from the table and, amidst a hush of breathless expectancy, opened the mouth of the model and applied the plate to the upper jaw. At a glance, it was obvious that it fitted perfectly. The two groups of the plaster teeth slipped exactly into the spaces on the plate, making a complete row of teeth. Then the witness covered the lower gums with strips of plastic wax, and taking the loose teeth from the table, attached them to the wax; and again the correspondence was evident. The teeth thus applied exactly filled the vacant spaces.

"Can you now identify that plate?" Thorndyke asked.

"Yes," was the reply. "I am quite certain that this is the plate I made for Mr. Jarman and that those loose teeth are from his lower plate."

Thorndyke looked at the coroner, who nodded emphatically. "This evidence seems perfectly conclusive," he admitted. "What do you say, gentlemen?" he added, turning to the jury.

There was no doubt as to their sentiments. With one voice they declared their complete conviction. Had they not seen the demonstration with their own eyes?

"And now, sir," said the coroner," as you appear to know more than anyone else about this case, and as it is perfectly incomprehensible to me, and probably also to the jury, I suggest that you give us an explanation. And you had better make it a sworn statement, so that it can go into the depositions."

"Yes," Thorndyke agreed," especially as I have some evidence to give." He was accordingly sworn and then proceeded to make the following statement:

The first thing that struck me on reading the report of this case was the very remarkable character of the objects found in the ashes of the rick. They included objects composed of platinum, of pipe-clay, of iron and of porcelain--all substances practically indestructible by fire. And these imperishable objects were all highly distinctive and easily identifiable, and two of them actually bore the initials of their owner. There was almost a suggestion of the body having been prepared for identification after burning. This mere suggestion, however, gave place to definite suspicion when I saw the dental plate. That plate presented a most striking discrepancy. Here it is, sir, and you see that it is a clean polished plate of red vulcanite, with not a trace of stain or discoloration. But associated with that plate were two clay pipes. Now, the man who smokes a clay pipe is not only--as a rule--a heavy smoker, but he smokes strong and dark-coloured tobacco. And if he wears a dental plate, that plate becomes encrusted with a black deposit which is very difficult to remove. There is, as you see, no trace of any such deposit, or of any tobacco stain in the interstices of the teeth. It appeared to be almost certainly the plate of a non-smoker. But if that were so, it could not be Reed's. But it had been ascertained by the police surgeon that it fitted the jaw of the skull and undoubtedly belonged to the burned body. Consequently if the plate was not Reed's plate, the skull was not Reed's skull, and the body was not Reed's body. But the watch-chain was Reed's, the pipes were his and the mascot was his. That is to say that the very identifiable and fire-proof property of Reed was associated with the burned body of some other person; that, in other words, the body of some unknown person had been deliberately prepared to counterfeit the body of Reed. This offered a further suggestion and raised a question. The suggestion was that the unknown person had been murdered--presumably somewhere near the spot where the dental plate was found. The question was--What was the object of causing the body to counterfeit that of Reed?

"Now, I knew, from the insurance company, that Reed had insured his life for three thousand pounds. Therefore, somebody stood to gain three thousand pounds by his death. The question was--Who was that somebody? I proceeded to make certain investigations on the spot;"--and here Thorndyke gave a summary of our discoveries on the marsh and on the yacht. "It thus appeared," he continued, "that there were two men on the marshes that night, going towards the rick. One of them was the person whose body was found in the ashes; the other, who went back alone to the yacht, was presumably the person who stood to gain three thousand pounds by Reed's death."

"Have you formed any opinion as to who that person was?" the coroner asked.

"Yes," replied Thorndyke. "I have very little doubt that he was Reginald Reed."

"But," exclaimed the coroner, "we have heard in evidence that it was Mr. Arthur Gerrard who stood to gain the three thousand pounds!"

"Precisely," said Thorndyke; and for a while he and the coroner looked at one another without speaking.

Suddenly the latter cast a searching look around the court. "Where is Mr. Gerrard?" he demanded.

"He left the court about ten minutes ago," said Thorndyke; "and a police inspector left immediately afterwards. I had advised him not to lose sight of Mr. Gerrard."

"Then I take it that you suspect Gerrard of being in collusion with Reed?"

"I suspect that Arthur Gerrard and Reginald Reed are one and the same person."

As Thorndyke made this statement, a murmur of astonishment arose from the jurymen and the spectators. The coroner, after a few moments' puzzled reflection, remarked: "You are not forgetting that Reed's caretaker was present while Gerrard was giving his evidence?" Then, turning to the caretaker, he asked: "What do you say? Was that Mr. Reed who gave evidence under the name of Gerrard?"

The caretaker, who had evidently been thinking furiously, was by no means confident. "I should say not," he replied, "unless he was made up a good deal. He was certainly about the same height and build and colour; but he had a moustache, whereas Mr. Reed was clean-shaved; he had a mole on his face, which Mr. Reed hadn't; he had bushy eyebrows, whereas Mr. Reed had hardly any eyebrows to speak of; and he wore spectacles, which Mr. Reed didn't, and he spoke like an Irishman, whereas Mr. Reed was English. Still it is possible--"

Before he could finish, the door rattled to a heavy concussion. Then it flew open, and Mr. Gerrard staggered into the room, thrust forward by the police inspector. His appearance was marvellously changed, for he had lost his spectacles, and one of his eyebrows had disappeared, as had also the mole and a portion of the built-up moustache. The caretaker started up with an exclamation, but at this moment Gerrard, with a violent effort, wrenched himself free. The inspector sprang forward to recapture him. But he was too late. The prisoner's hand flew upwards; there was a ringing report; and Arthur Gerrard--or Reginald Reed--fell back across a bench with a trickle of blood on his temple and a pistol still clutched in his hand.

"And so," said Stalker, when he called on us the next day for details, "it was a suicide after all. Very lucky, too, seeing that there was no provision in the policy for death by judicial hanging."

Another book you may enjoy from Oxford City Press...

This is the sixth of Josephine Tey's 'Inspector Grant' novels from the golden age of British detective fiction. Grant meets a celebrity photographer, Leslie Searle, briefly at a party in London. He is later astonished to hear that he has vanished in the sleepy village of Salcott St. Mary and sets off to investigate.

Hardcover 2010, Oxford City Press
ISBN-10: **1849025991**, ISBN-13: **978-1-84902-599-7**